SELECTED WRITINGS OF

ROBERT LOUIS

STEVENSON

>>>

EDITED, WITH AN INTRODUCTION, BY

SAXE COMMINS

>>>

THE MODERN LIBRARY

NEW YORK

THE MODERN LIBRARY

IS PUBLISHED BY

RANDOM HOUSE, INC.

BENNETT A. CERF · DONALD S. KLOPFER · ROBERT K. HAAS

Manufactured in the United States of America
By H. Wolff

CONTENTS

33917

Introduction

During the later of the forty-four years of his lifetime, Robert Louis Stevenson became a world legend. Now, more than a half century after his death, he has been made a victim of his own myth. Shorn of the romantic attitudes assumed by and for him, he still retains a generous share of his reputation. The role of posturer, moralizer, courageous invalid, bohemian, wanderer and sentimentalist is forgotten. That myth died in pathos. The reality, however, revives itself year after year and decade after decade in a vibrant body of writing that keeps its glowing youth.

If his survival depended on the picturesque legend alone, Stevenson would have long since faded from memory with the sad futility of his own brief gestures as a dissenter from Calvinism, as a vagrant aesthete, as a casual Tolstoyan and at the end as a feudal chieftain in Samoa. That such bravura antics caught the fancy of the world is indeed a tribute to his vivid personality; that they obscured for his annoyed critics the positive merits of his novels, essays, tales, poetry and records of his travels is a commentary on the unwillingness to distinguish between mannerism and matter.

From Edinburgh to Vailima, on the long journey beset with illness, he was always on display. The tall, gaunt figure crowned with long black hair, the lustrous eyes, the loose, unconventional clothes, the quick, nervous movements of the hands and the animation of the wasting body compelled attention. He crossed the stage of his life with an actor's concern for effect.

His illness itself was endured bravely in an ever-changing dramatic setting. The tubercular's hopefulness kept him constantly on the road of what became a world tour. If epilepsy is the disease of ecstasy, with its sudden clairvoyant flashes, tuberculosis frequently has been considered the malady of optimism. Its fevers induce quick excitement and restlessness. The familiar hectic flush might well pervade the mind, too, and activate it beyond its ordinary tempo. Febrility could account, perhaps, for the first full rush of ideas, the initial high pitch of enthusiasm and the subsequent early exhaustion.

Such a generalization on the emotional pattern of the consumptive is at best misleading, but it applies with a peculiar aptness to Stevenson, who from his childhood suffered from the consuming affliction. The easy optimism of his essays, the tense excitement of his shorter tales, the brilliant beginnings of his adventure novels and the fatigue at their end help to support this non-medical observation about a particular victim of the disease.

In any case, this disability was a dominant factor in his life. The always contrary-minded Gilbert K. Chesterton, however, minimizes its influence and blandly overlooks the poses and preachments as well. He attributes Stevenson's style and spirit to a pasteboard toy theatre and the *Penny Plain and Two-Pence Colored* given to him in his childhood. These, Chesterton insists, shaped the writer's mind and set his imagination free. The peep show was the Scots lad's first window on the world and the cut-outs were the first of a whole lifetime's attempts to tear himself loose from his firm Covenanter's cord.

The Puritan heritage was continuous from the seventeenth century and was handed down from son to son with the family profession of engineering. The long line of Stevensons came into its first national notice with the writer's grandfather, Robert Stevenson, builder of many harbors and docks and designer of eighteen lighthouses at dangerous coastal points of Scotland. The most famous of these beacons was the Bell Rock Lighthouse, which Sir Walter Scott memorialized in his Introduction to *The Pirate,* after a visit under the guidance of its designer. Of Robert Stevenson's thirteen children, five survived, and of these, the three sons followed in their father's footsteps.

On the maternal side there were clerics of stubborn Scots orthodoxy. The Balfours were pious and prolific, and, not to be outdone by the Stevensons, also had thirteen children. The youngest daughter, Margaret Isabella Balfour, was courted and won by Thomas Stevenson, "a stern and unbending Tory," according to his son's subsequent description. That only son was christened, after his birth in 1850, Robert Lewis Balfour Stevenson. Because there flourished in Edinburgh at the time a Liberal by the name of Lewis who publicly supported Gladstone, the indignant father insisted upon a change of the middle name to Louis, and in that form it

became world famous. The "Balfour" was dropped without prejudice or any angry conviction.

In New Town, in the northern quarter of Edinburgh, the
Stevensons brought up their only son in an atmosphere of rigid
conformity through more than the usual infantile illnesses. The
prevailing spirit at 17 Heriot Row, an address adverted to frequently by the always reminiscent writer, was dour and grim with
moral responsibility. The mother, delicate in health but tenacious
enough to survive her offspring, needed help for the upbringing of
her boy, and providentially Alison Cunningham was employed
as a servant. She became Robert's nurse, teacher and, in a very real
sense, his literary godmother.

Herself a militant Covenanter, she had, however, enough imagination and feeling for the drama in the lore of her own people to
forget occasionally the high barriers of a Scotch conscience. The
woman to whom *A Child's Garden of Verses* is dedicated "from
her boy" opened the mind of her frail charge. For him she did
far more than read the Bible, *Pilgrim's Progress* and the romantic
ballads and tales of Scotland's heroes; she dramatized her own and
others' inventions and brought them, living, to the lad's bedside.
Ghosts and witches, Biblical patriarchs and sinners, Highland
adventurers and sea-roving buccaneers came to life for the boy
who was seldom allowed to venture beyond the door of his nursery.
There, wrapped in blankets against the cold Edinburgh winter,
the young prisoner absorbed the fear of hell and damnation and
the first intimations that story-telling could be an art.

The industry by which Stevenson made himself a writer was first
manifested when he was six years old with *A History of Moses*.
The virus was already in his blood. "From that time forward it
was the desire of my heart to be an author," is a confession made
many years later. The childhood resolution was kept with fierce
and unwavering determination for the rest of his life. Certainly
the confinement and coddling of the invalid child helped feed the
egotism of the incipient author. When he was not the general
leading his armies of toy soldiers in grandiose maneuvers, he was
historian, dramatist, editor and pulpiteer within the walls of his
own home. There were only brief interludes of formal schooling.
The search for better health took him on his first travels, to London when he was twelve and to the continent when thirteen.

To achieve commercial publication at sixteen is a feat that may give pleasure to parents but usually brings chagrin to an author. Almost the entire edition of *The Pentland Uprising: A Page of History, 1666,* bearing the imprint of Andrew Elliot, was bought by a proud father. He must have approved of its solemn Covenanter quotations. Robert Louis Stevenson had made an early and respectable debut.

An indifferent student at Edinburgh University, the young man was marked for the oddity of his appearance and the irregularity of his attendance. The influence of his teachers was negligible, but in Fleeming Jenkin, the versatile classicist, critic, linguist and Professor of Engineering, he found a congenial friend whose affectionate biography he wrote twenty years later under the title of *Memoir of Fleeming Jenkin.*

Impelled by the Scots love for debate and doctrine, the undergraduate joined the Conservative Club and the Speculative Society. In the one he could make speeches denouncing liberalism and in the other he could hold forth on such grave matters as "Two Questions on the Relation Between Christ's Teaching and Modern Christianity" and "Law and Free Will." As one of the founders of the *Edinburgh University Magazine* he saw it through four issues and, at least, acquired some practice in essay writing. Then, as before and later, the determination to make an author of himself was paramount. His engineering studies were never allowed to interfere with his writing exercises as he played "the sedulous ape" to Montaigne, Hazlitt, Lamb and other masters of the essay form.

Before long it became apparent to Thomas Stevenson that a break in the family tradition was imminent. To neglect engineering for literature was only a little less objectionable in God's eyes than heresy. Hope that the son had not strayed too far rose with the winning of the Royal Society of Arts medal for a paper on "A New Form of Intermittent Light for Lighthouses." For the father that was a mere reprieve. Both light and hope flickered and went out altogether when the wayward student announced his intention to end his hardly begun engineering career without further ceremony. There was a violent scene. For an only son to break the continuous family line and brush aside a lucrative profession built up through generations was foolhardy, and morally and economically sinful. The younger will prevailed, however, and the revolt ended in compromise. Engineering's loss might be the law's gain. At any rate, the law had acquired a half-hearted apprentice.

Even more villainous in the eyes of the father were the evidences of the son's defections from religious orthodoxy. Skepticis. was like a new revelation to be proclaimed with dramatic flourishes. Before he could realize what he was saying, the garrulous youth heard himself announcing that he was an agnostic. Shortly afterward, carried away by his own eloquence, the boy's avowal of atheism staggered his father. The scandal might have killed him if he had not then taken so much pleasure out of threatening to disinherit this devil's advocate.

Under the shadow of his father's excommunication, the self-conscious rebel tried to find a little solace in the company of less reputable citizens. It is this lonely and perhaps even dissolute period of Stevenson's life that his worshipful biographers prefer to pass over in religious silence. The more candid commentators, proud of a minor revelation, trumpet their discovery that the young man, consorting for the first time with the unregenerate in Edinburgh's unsanctified quarters, might have tasted some of the fruits of pleasure and found them good. In any case, there was Kate Drummond, a Highland girl who had wandered into the lower depths of Edinburgh. The "Claire" of the long-suppressed, youthful poems, must have brought assuagement and a little contrast into the life of the passionate young man of twenty-two.

For two years the law offices of Skene, Edwards and Bilton in Edinburgh housed a reader who pored over more literary than legal volumes. There were frequent interruptions for travel on the continent, on Thomas Stevenson's funds, and more for the restoration of failing health. It was during this period that the unenthusiastic lawyer's clerk met Mrs. Sitwell, who later became the wife of Sidney Colvin. For the "young Heine with the Scotch accent" she had the fillip of encouragement he needed so desperately at the time. He began an article on Walt Whitman and completed an essay, "Ordered South," which saw publication, thanks to Sidney Colvin, in *Macmillan's Magazine.*

Guided by his cousin, R. A. M. Stevenson, the painter, he was introduced to French bohemian life on one of his visits to Paris and found it immensely to his liking. Back again in Edinburgh, with a patched-up understanding with his father and a slight increase in his allowance, Stevenson made desultory attempts to complete his legal training, and, to his own surprise, actually attained admission to the Scottish Bar. At twenty-five he was an advocate waiting for clients at 17 Heriot Row, practicing doggedly so that some day he might become a writer. The exercises at the moment were "Victor Hugo's Romances" and "John Knox and His Relations to Women."

The closest and most consequential friendship of Stevenson's life began on a high note of literary and personal companionship in this period and ended many years later in bitter recrimination. In the endless conjectures about the causes of the breach between these friends, Stevenson's side has been given the most favorable emphasis by his biographers. Certainly the poet, W. E. Henley, brought to the faltering novice the stimulus of his exuberant mind and the good sense of his hard experience. The author of the poem which provided several generations with a bold slogan against Fate no doubt helped to clarify the groping tyro's literary confusions. In and out of season Henley preached the necessity of coming to grips with reality by "keeping his eye on the object."

That object was manifestly not the law. Running away from it to the colony of artists established in Fontainebleau helped to quiet Stevenson's feverish restlessness and satisfied his need for bohemian companionship. There he could strut in fantastic clothes and find listeners for his fanciful and often irresponsible ideas. There he could work as capriciously as he liked on the first part of "Virginibus Puerisque" and lazily plan the canoeing trip he was soon to take with Sir Walter Simpson, recorded in *An Inland Voyage*.

At Grez he met a forceful woman, an American, eleven years older than he, married at the moment and mother of two children. Fanny Van de Grift Osbourne at first captivated and stirred him violently, then protected and dominated him, nursed and policed him, shared and sacrificed for him, won and antagonized his friends and even after his death fought during the twenty years she survived him to control with desperate possessiveness every word that was written about him and every memory of him the world tried to preserve.

The quixotic Scotsman fell in love. The wooing of a lady with a legal husband made the course of his suit far from smooth. Thomas Stevenson might somehow become reconciled to the professional and religious vagaries of his son, but amorous deviations, and with an undivorced woman, could only bring utter ruin. For the present, anyhow, what the father did not know could not possibly hurt his conscience. Sufficient for the day was the final abandonment of the law.

Magazines like *Cornhill* and *London* were beginning to display the writings of Robert Louis Stevenson, and the anguish of the parents was slightly alleviated. "Virginibus Puerisque" made no great stir and "Will o' the Mill" attracted no more attention than it deserved. Goaded by Henley, then editor of *London, The New Arabian Nights* was wrung out of the author and published as a serial. It did neither the magazine, editor nor author much good, since it was received with cold indifference and was generally considered the cause for the discontinuance of the monthly.

Even more disheartening was another physical collapse. The writer was again obliged to leave the dank atmosphere of his Scottish home and go back to France. There Mrs. Osbourne was preparing to return to California, with her son, Lloyd, to arrange for her divorce. Left alone again and without work to engage his pathological energies, Stevenson bought a donkey and started on a journey under summer skies which he set down, when back in bleak Edinburgh, as *Travels with a Donkey in the Cevennes*. Here and there it was welcomed with praise, but the modest first edition was too large for the meager public demand.

Torn by the deception he had to continue with his parents about Mrs. Osbourne, in an actual fever of illness and uncertainty, Stevenson wandered back and forth between England and Scotland. That he should choose just then to write a holier-than-thou essay, "Some Aspects of Robert Burns," is hard to reconcile. To denounce the Scottish bard for his amorous strayings, declaiming against hypocrisy while keeping his own tangled love affair secret, was not so much a paradox as it was flagrant self-deception.

In California Mrs. Osbourne had begun divorce proceedings. Word came that she had fallen ill. Stevenson had to make a quick decision without taking his parents into his confidence. Just before he sailed for New York he found the courage to write his father about his last and worst outrage against Puritan orthodoxy. This *was* the last straw.

All the way across the Atlantic, the erring son tried to obliterate pictures of the dismay at 17 Heriot Row by making notes for *The Amateur Emigrant*. When he landed in America, his health was again at low ebb. Determinedly, but to no avail, he went the rounds of New York's editorial offices. Ill and discouraged, he took the trip across the American continent to San Francisco and Mrs. Osbourne.

Stevenson staggered from San Francisco to Monterey and collapsed at his journey's end. Rest and care brought back a little of his strength. Then he was foolhardy enough to venture alone into the mountains. Again he collapsed, but this time with no one near to help him. After two days of semi-consciousness he was discovered in the hills and rescued by passing ranchmen. Whether he liked it or not, he would have to submit hereafter to the strict regimen of the tubercular.

During his convalescence he became a contributor, at $2.00 a week, to the *Monterey Californian* and completed "The Pavilion on the Links." Files of his journalistic pieces were not preserved. Between December of 1879 and the time when Mrs. Osbourne received her divorce decree and they could be married on May 19, 1880, Stevenson lived in San Francisco in direst straits. He had rented a room in a lodging house at 608 Bush Street and there tried to earn his living, sick and disheartened, without any aid from 17 Heriot Row.

The Amateur Emigrant met with no favor, and even Henley could work up no enthusiasm for "The Story of a Lie." *Prince Otto* was begun and attempts were made to find a job as a correspondent. The San Francisco newspapers needed none. The outlook could not be drearier, especially when his hollow cough racked his body and the doctors shook their heads ominously. Stevenson's little fund had shriveled and he was on the verge of destitution. Mrs. Osbourne, awaiting her divorce, nursed him, and when news of his straits reached Edinburgh, Thomas Stevenson relented enough to create an allowance of two hundred and fifty pounds for his prodigal son. Louis' health and spirits revived instantly. In May, Mrs. Osbourne's divorce was granted, and, soon to be a grandmother, she was married in San Francisco to the sick but always hopeful author.

Their honeymoon was a battle against death. Frequent hemorrhages spurted from Stevenson's lungs and left him drained and helpless. The new Mrs. Stevenson, as determined and managerial a wife as any author ever had, committed herself unsparingly to a task of nursing that was to last for fourteen years, from California to Europe and to the South Seas. She took the invalid and his stepson to Calistoga, north of San Francisco, and thence to Silverado.

There the bridegroom's health was partially restored and he was able to make notes for *The Silverado Squatters.* Later, when this travel record appeared in *Century Magazine,* it was Stevenson's introduction to the American public. Nowhere else did he enjoy such popularity in his lifetime.

It soon became apparent to the bride that nothing short of complete reconciliation with her father-in-law could help to mend her husband's declining health and spirit. She began with a campaign of letters and continued, on her arrival in Scotland one year to the day after Stevenson had sailed for America, with all the personal charm and force at her command to win the esteem of obdurate but generous Thomas Stevenson. She succeeded, as was her habit, in having her way, and Louis was taken back into the bosom of his family. She succeeded equally in alienating some of the writer's best friends, notably Henley.

A trip to the Highlands provided little succor after another set-back, and, in a state of collapse, Stevenson was bundled off to Davos Platz in Switzerland. Here he had the privilege of meeting John Addington Symonds, also tubercular, and a friendship developed after a first antagonism.

The chart of Stevenson's malady fluctuated violently, and in the summer of 1881, he was back in the Highlands, this time in Perthshire. Here, as if he tore it out of the crags of Scotland, he wrote "Thrawn Janet," as shuddering a tale of terror as the literature of the short story can boast, "The Body-Snatcher," a ghoulish piece, and "The Merry Men." Here, too, he began his studies for a projected history of the Highlands, which in itself came to nothing, but was the groundwork for *Kidnapped* and its sequel, *David Balfour,* called at first and even now in England *Catriona.* Worried about his livelihood even more than he was about his health, he made himself a candidate for the Chair of Constitutional Law and History at Edinburgh University, with a stipend of two hundred and fifty pounds a year. The trustees were deaf to his appeals.

Then Thomas Stevenson took a small house for his son and the ingratiating wife at Castleton, Braemar, where idleness begot boredom and boredom restlessness. To amuse his stepson, the reluctant convalescent drew a rough map of an island and scrawled across it "Treasure Island." And so, casually, was begun the story that was to change Stevenson's fortunes completely, if slowly. With the map as his only notes, he began to write feverishly one chapter each day for a fortnight. Then his energy gave out.

Through the intercession of Dr. Alexander Japp, these chapters of the unfinished tale were taken not to a book publisher, but to a boys' paper, *Young Folks,* which ran serials with special emphasis on high adventure and gallantry. When Dr. Japp persuaded the editors to accept the novel, it was given scant announcement and buried in the back columns. The by-line read "Captain George North," and Stevenson was paid the minimum rate. *Treasure Island* failed miserably as a serial. When it had run half its course, its author had become too exhausted to finish it at once. By lashing himself to the task, he managed to bring it through its final install-ment, happy that the ordeal was over and wanting to forget it entirely. In book form, published in 1883, it caught the imagina-tion of the young in spirit everywhere.

At Braemar, too, came the impulse to set down some of the imitative verse he always could dash off with so much facility. The idea for a book of poems that would recapture the enchantment of childhood obsessed him and he began what he then called *Penny Whistle,* only to set it aside in fatigue for a later time when he could complete and publish it as *A Child's Garden of Verses* in 1885.

As might have been foreseen, misty Braemar was found wanting as a health resort. Husband, wife and stepson journeyed back to Edinburgh and again to Davos Platz. There discouraging reports about the reception of *Treasure Island* by readers of *Young Folks* did not deter him from planning new projects. Hope sprang eter-nal in his hollow chest. A life of Hazlitt was outlined and a most uncommercial printing and publishing company was launched, owners, writers, editors, typesetters and pressmen: Robert Louis Stevenson and Lloyd Osbourne. The publications of the Davos Press are rare items today, sought as treasures by collectors and bibliophiles. The junior partner in this business venture was then fourteen years old and the senior thirty-one.

A sick nomad, Stevenson abandoned Davos Platz and tried the curative possibilities of Marseilles and Nice, to little avail. Es-tablished in Hyères in 1883, the bed-ridden but indomitable patient continued to work on *A Child's Garden of Verses* and *Underwoods. The Black Arrow,* his romantic tale of the Roses, was written here on a still undiminished note of optimism. It, too, ran serially in *Young Folks*, but commanded no excited following.

Henley, too exacting an editor to let a wife's antagonism or a popular verdict override his judgment, urged Cassell and Company to publish *Treasure Island* in book form and managed to extract from them one hundred guineas for Stevenson. The payment of "a hundred jingling, tingling, gold-minted quid" proved to be a turning point. The book brought national recognition and words of praise from such oracles as Prime Minister Gladstone, critic Andrew Lang and other celebrities of the kind who still give their benedictions on dust wrappers. After a modest beginning in sales, *Treasure Island* gained momentum and became, as everyone knows, one of the world's most widely read and loved books.

The stimulus of success was no tonic. Stevenson suffered a violent hemorrhage at La Solitude in Hyères and almost bled his life away. Nursed by his invincible wife to sufficient strength to undertake the journey to England, he found a haven in Bournemouth and lived there three years, still hopeful enough to expect to earn many "gold-minted quid" as a playwright. In collaboration with Henley he wrote *Beau Austin*, produced with dismal results by Beerbohm Tree, *Admiral Guinea*, an inconspicuous trifle, and, finally, *Macaire*, the third failure. Even Stevenson was convinced after three futile attempts that the drama was not his metier and the theatre no treasure chest. Henley, however, was not so easily dissuaded from the quest and insisted on more and more collaborations. Mrs. Stevenson, never even dutifully enthusiastic about their joint expedition into the theatre, here interposed with all the strength of her will. She brought the curtain down on their partnership, and their friendship as well.

Stevenson, slightly better in health and now living comfortably in Skerryvore, the house bought for him by his father, went back to writing serials. Resumption of *Prince Otto*, re-written and re-written countless times for stylistic effect and with the substance written right out of it, and *More New Arabian Nights* were the first results of his return to grace and his own natural gifts.

The need for money after his unsuccessful foray into the theatre actually haunted Stevenson's dreams. Now that his father was approaching the end of his life, still guided by his gloomy morality, the son felt the precariousness of his position financially. He wanted to find a "shilling shocker" and earn his complete independence. How the answer to his wish came in his sleep is another of the many legends that cling to Stevenson. *Strange Case of Dr. Jekyll and Mr. Hyde* may well have been the metaphor which psychoanalysts speak of as the remembered cloak of a dream. In Stevenson's perpetual fever, it may have been a kind of a hallucination grown out of a Puritan's long perplexity about the differences between good and evil. Dream or not, the restlessness of his body and mind forced him to set the parable down on paper in a frenzy of words. Apparently Mrs. Stevenson did not share this first flush of excitement, declaring it no improvement on an earlier story, "Markheim." Her criticisms were so icy that the feverish author lost control and angrily burned the manuscript. Whether it was a quarrel grown out of incompatibility or perceptive criticism, the outburst in the end did no damage. Stevenson re-wrote the tale in six days and it was published in January of 1886.

After the reviewers had caught their breaths from shouting superlatives, the clergy took up the cry from their pulpits, underscoring the story's moral significance and proclaiming it as the gospel of the triumph of virtue over vice, the noble over the base, heaven over hell and the angel over the demon. Nothing could more certainly assure the success of the book. If *Treasure Island* was the turning point, *Strange Case of Dr. Jekyll and Mr. Hyde* was the high road Stevenson had been seeking with so much industry and against such outrageous physical odds since his infancy.

The duality of his own nature was never quite so extreme as the polarities in Dr. Jekyll and Mr. Hyde. Yet it could embrace Calvinism and Tolstoyism and renounce both with sudden capriciousness. Toward the end of the Skerryvore period, Stevenson declared himself a disciple of Leo Tolstoy and expatiated with a new convert's conviction on passive resistance, "areas of suffering," Christianity without Christ and a simple solution of the problem of the poor which demanded that the rich merely get off their backs. Starvation and persecution in Ireland aroused him particularly. He was resolved to go there and put himself and his family in the path of bullets from the guns of the British tyrants and exploiters. By the death of a distinguished literary man, and his family, he would focus attention on the plight of the oppressed and bring the world's "odium on these miscreants."

The passion for martyrdom cooled quickly. Ireland was farther from his heart than his own Scotland, and now, drawing upon his notes for the history of the Highlands, he became absorbed in the adventure of writing *Kidnapped* and completed the *Memoir of Fleeming Jenkin*. Meetings with Henry James and discussion of their work established an intimacy which gave the American writer a more penetrating evaluation of the Scotsman's work than Stevenson could have of his. A few sessions with John Singer Sargent for the well-known portrait, visits with Thomas Hardy and Sir Sidney Colvin were infrequent interruptions in the guarded way of life he was allowed. Even when his father died, Stevenson was too ill to attend the funeral. That sad chapter came to an end with genuine remorse and finally with gentle but contrite amends in an essay in *Memories and Portraits*.

When hemorrhages again robbed him of more of the little fund of his strength, his doctors were called in consultation. They decided he would have to leave England for a drier, sunnier climate. First suggested was Colorado, in the vicinity of Denver possibly, or somewhere in the higher altitudes of India. Finally a sanitarium just established in the Adirondack Mountains by Dr. Edward Livingston Trudeau was selected. Stevenson, with an entourage consisting of his mother, wife, stepson and Valentine Roche, a maid, left Europe for the last time.

After a nineteen-day passage in a cattle-boat, the author of *Strange Case of Dr. Jekyll and Mr. Hyde* was met in New York as if he were a conquering hero. In the below-zero winter of Saranac his active symptoms were arrested. Wrapped in buffalo robes against the cold, he took the Spartan treatment with unabated optimism. Soon he was able to work again and complete a series of essays for *Scribner's Magazine* at unprecedented fees. A good start was made on *The Master of Ballantrae* and *The Wrong Box,* the latter a collaboration with Lloyd Osbourne.

The intense cold of Saranac made Stevenson long for tropical warmth, and the dream of owning a yacht on which he could cruise in southern waters beguiled him. While she was on a visit to California, the dauntless Mrs. Stevenson found one. It was the *Casco,* a sailing vessel of seventy-four tons register built for the pleasure of an American of considerable wealth.

Before he left for San Francisco, however, the final rupture with Henley occurred. According to John A. Steuart, one of the more critical biographers, the cumulative quarrels burst into one last

explosion. Mrs. Katharine de Mattos, distantly related to Stevenson and to whom *Dr. Jekyll and Mr. Hyde* is dedicated, wrote a
fairy story which interested Henley as an editor. He had discussed
this tale with the Stevensons while they were still in England and
had tried, unsuccessfully, to sell it. Because magazines one after
the other had rejected it, Mrs. de Mattos lost interest in her story
and decided to withdraw it. The idea of this fairy tale appealed
to Mrs. Stevenson, who wrote and sold a new version based on it.
When it appeared in print, Henley wrote to Saranac, asking why
the story did not bear a double signature. In a fury Stevenson came
to the defense of his wife and demanded a retraction. None came
from England. The friendship was ended.

The *Casco* sailed on the 28th of June, 1888, through the Golden
Gate of San Francisco. A year ago Stevenson had left Europe, never
to return; this was to be his final farewell to America. For seven
months the *Casco* sailed an erratic course with shore intervals on
such islands as Anaho, Taiohae, Tahiti in Papeete. At Taravao
there was another relapse and he was taken, with great difficulty,
to Tautira. Again he was nursed back to a semblance of strength
by the utterly devoted Mrs. Stevenson.

The turn of the new year of 1889 found them established in
Honolulu, with the author committed to the task of feeding copy
for a serial which had begun a few months earlier in *Scribner's
Magazine* and which now lacked its final installments. *The Master
of Ballantrae* had to be finished against a deadline. It had been
started with all the vigor of his imagination and had been carried
forward in a cascade of power and inventiveness. When fatigue set
in and under the compulsion of providing the last chapters with
presses waiting, the portions written in Tahiti and Honolulu were
forced and somewhat less than convincing. Yet the most captious
of Stevenson's critics give it the highest place, next to *Weir of
Hermiston,* among all his novels.

Before leaving on his newly acquired vessel, *Equator,* for a
haphazard cruise in the South Pacific, Stevenson paid a visit of a
week to the leper colony on the island of Molokai. What he observed of the work of Father Pierre Damien, the Belgian priest
whose sacrifices had ended in death only a month or so earlier, provided background for the aroused pamphlet he wrote shortly
afterward. Indignant over a letter published by a Dr. Hyde, a
missionary who assailed Father Damien's character, and indifferent

to libel laws, Stevenson rushed headlong into the fray. His outburst was composed at white heat in a single morning, and he would tolerate no suggested changes. In his anger he entirely forgot the charm his readers had come to expect of him and, for once, wrote a searing piece of invective, harsh, careless of consequences, agitated—and gallant. The storm blew over without damages for libel. The essay remains one of the few written by Stevenson with a lasting glow of passion.

The *Equator* came into Apia Harbor in Samoa. It proved to be port for the wanderer. Here Stevenson bought a piece of land and here he lived, a feudal lord, for three and a half years. A visit to Sydney, Australia, brought on another hemorrhage, and Mrs. Stevenson did her utmost to procure passage so that there could be a last glimpse of Scotland. She succeeded in getting space on the *Janet Nichol,* which did no more than carry them in a wide circle on the Pacific back to Sydney. There, sick and more anxious than ever about money, the restless invalid worked on his *Ballads* and *In the South Seas.* In September of 1890, he moved into temporary quarters built on a cleared piece of land six hundred feet above the sea on the side of Mount Vaea in the forest of Upolu on the island of Samoa. Three miles away was the port town of Apia.

Vailima, the name he gave to the house, became familiar the world over. In Samoan it meant Five Waters, from the confluence of as many streams near by. Piece by piece the parts of his house were carried up the hill by natives and assembled under the supervision of Stevenson and his wife. Gradually the structure grew to imposing proportions, with a main hall large enough for a minor monarch and his retainers. Furniture was brought all the way from Skerryvore and 17 Heriot Row.

In this setting Stevenson participated with dead earnestness in Samoan politics, tootled on his flageolet and worried about money. Celebrated visitors, among them Henry Adams, paid courtesy calls at his far-away protectorate and watched him play Richelieu on a miniature scale.

In a letter written on October 17, 1890, Henry Adams offered this description of Stevenson:

A figure came out that I cannot do justice to. Imagine a man so thin and emaciated that he looked like a bundle of sticks in a bag, with a head and eyes morbidly intelligent and restless. He was costumed in a dirty striped cotton pyjamas, the baggy legs tucked into coarse knit woollen stockings, one of which was bright brown in color, the other a purplish dark tone. . . . When conversation fairly began, though I could not forget the dirt and discomfort, I found Stevenson extremely entertaining. He has the nervous restlessness of his disease, and, although he said he was unusually well, I half expected to see him drop with a hemorrhage at any moment, for he cannot be quiet, but sits down, jumps up, darts off and flies back, at every sentence he utters, and his eyes and features gleam with a hectic glow. He seems weak, and complains that the ride of an hour up to his place costs him a day's work; but, as he describes his travels and life in the South Seas, he has been through what would have broken me into a miserable rag.

Two native chieftains had developed a feud into open warfare for the control of the kingdom. Malietoa Laupepa, aided by distant German influence, had the popular Mataafa as rival for the shabby throne. Stevenson entered the struggle on Mataafa's side and used his pen as if it were a lance in his behalf. He wrote *A Footnote to History: Eight Years of Trouble in Samoa* to win sympathy for Mataafa's cause. Germany resented his intrusion and the partisans of Malietoa made no secret of their antagonism. When Mataafa actually fought a small German landing force and defeated it, his doom was sealed. A mission was sent from Germany, and this only incensed Stevenson the more. Rebellion broke out and the natives went on the warpath. British and German warships intervened; Mataafa was defeated and banished. After punishments and reprisals, a truce was patched up and Malietoa and Stevenson came to terms. The empire-maker went back to the making of books.

Stevenson's driving energy and the need for more and more money kept him to the treadmill of writing. *The Wrecker,* in collaboration with Lloyd Osbourne, *Across the Plains,* "The Beach of Falesa," "The Bottle Imp," verses, essays, letters, sermons and many stories, completed and still-born, some of them so promising in their beginnings and so feeble in their development that they had to be destroyed, kept the pot boiling. "Tusitala," the Samoan natives called him, the Teller of Tales. The tribute was sincere and accurate, as far as it went, but it was a half title. Actually his daemon was a fever, real enough to be recorded alarmingly on a thermometer and abstract enough to drive him inevitably to the fulfillment of the whole, sad pattern of his destiny.

"The Great White Chief" became the symbol of opulence and power to the natives. He entertained his subordinates and the hierarchy of their followers on a lavish scale, and these conspicuous displays required money. His income, now about 5,000 pounds annually, was funneled into Vailima. Only popular novels would keep the golden stream flowing. Rapidly and carelessly he wrote to balance the exchequer of his kingdom.

It was seven years since he had written *Kidnapped* and he still had enough material left over from his history of the Highlands to provide a generous sequel. Alan Breck's companion in swashbuckling adventure, David Balfour, could round out the saga of Scotland's Appin Stewarts. Stevenson was once again back in his element and he wrote joyously and with easy invention. *Catriona,* or *David Balfour* as it is known in America, was published in 1893, and it was the last book Stevenson could finish. One, *St. Ives,* was completed by a hand quite as skillful as his own and in a style that made the first and last parts merge with perfect unity. The writer who brought this unfinished romance to a successful conclusion was the critic and scholar, Sir Arthur Quiller-Couch. *The Ebb-Tide,* the second, was a collaboration with Lloyd Osbourne, and the last and greatest novel of all, even in its truncated form, was *Weir of Hermiston,* on which Stevenson was working on the day of his death.

The former bohemian, now patron and chieftain, held court with almost regal protocol. There were great feasts at which he made speeches and improvised prayers and sermons with a piety that would have made dour Thomas Stevenson smile with pleasure and triumph. Stevenson's mother had come from Europe and could listen approvingly to the tributes paid her only son and to his pronouncements. He was a success in Samoa and in the wide world. Thanks to the efforts of his lifelong friend, Charles Baxter, the Edinburgh Edition of his collected works was in preparation. Honors came in abundance, and not the least touching of these was the gift of a road built by the natives from the main highway up Mount Vaea to his door and called with tender sentiment "The Road of the Loving Heart."

Stevenson's birthday on November 13, 1894, his forty-fourth, was celebrated with pomp. Again on November 29th, the American

Thanksgiving Day, visitors from the United States were his guests. He looked forward to Christmas and more festivities. His kingdom was at peace.

On the evening of December 3, 1894, after a good day's dictation which brought *Weir of Hermiston* almost to 60,000 words, he volunteered to help his wife prepare a salad. Suddenly and without warning he screamed, "My head! My head!" and groped for the main stairway. He fell and lay unconscious, unable to utter another word. Doctors were summoned from Apia, but they could do nothing. Robert Louis Stevenson died of a cerebral hemorrhage—not of tuberculosis.

Native volunteers built a road to the top of Mount Vaea by the afternoon of the next day. The slow ascent to its crest, where a grave had been dug, was made by the family and Tusitala's people. There, wrapped in a Union Jack, he was buried. The fever was gone at last.

» »« «

From the time he scrawled the two-word inscription on the map which charted the course of *Treasure Island* until the last day of his life when he dictated "A wilful convulsion of brute nature" as the final phrase of the unfinished *Weir of Hermiston,* Stevenson's progress as a novelist was uneven. In twelve years he wrote as many novels, four of which were collaborations, if that scheherazade of stories, *The Dynamiter,* which he contrived with the aid of his wife, can be counted as one of the novels.

That he began and ended his work in this field with two books which mark his greatest achievements—and for entirely different reasons—is certainly not a sign of gradual development but of almost erratic mutation. Between 1882 and 1894 his novels represented an alternation of soaring to the zenith and descent to the nadir of his gifts. That *Treasure Island,* with its simplicity, its natural inventions, its accelerating tempo, and its sustained, joyous spirit of adventure and swift action, should be followed by *Prince Otto,* polished so thin that it is transparent, is hardly progression. The one came from the youthful imagination of a writer at play and the other from a practising hand at work.

Taken in the order of their composition, there was an almost regular fluctuation of first- and second-rate novels. The bloodless *Prince Otto* was succeeded by the throbbing excitement and verve of *Kidnapped*. A tired writer lapses, in *The Black Arrow*, into the commonplace devices guaranteed to surprise readers of boys' magazines with a climax for each installment and rebounds in a high leap of the imagination by creating the archetype of the picturesque Byronic villain with a twisted streak of nobility, James Durie of Durisdeer, in *The Master of Ballantrae*.

Two collaborations with Lloyd Osbourne, *The Wrong Box* and *The Wrecker*, the first an elaborate farce that becomes entangled in its own complications and the second by Stevenson's own admission more of a "panorama" than a novel, come next in this chronology of alternating strength and weakness. They suggest a deep gap between the peaks.

Rising again from mere manipulation of plot and the piling of episode upon episode, *David Balfour* offers evidence of a revival of the powers of the novelist with a zest for the hazards of fortune. The buoyancy of Alan Breck and the loyalty and eagerness of his companion in adventure, David, account for the continuing popularity of this sequel to the best of Stevenson's historical romances.

The Ebb-Tide, a collaboration, and *St. Ives*, a fragment, and both cloak-and-dagger concoctions, are down once more on a lower plateau as if in preparation for the final effort to attack the heights. *Weir of Hermiston* took Stevenson to the summit. Here the contriver of devices and the seeker of popular success in need of money no longer depends on the reliable formulas and stock of situations available to the practitioner of his craft; mannerism and moralizings are dropped; the tempting inventions and ingenuities of the virtuoso are scorned. The novelist has at last attained his fullest maturity.

It is impossible to venture a guess whether Stevenson could have sustained the story of the hanging judge and his non-conformist son to a convincing conclusion. The pattern of his previous novels, with their magnificent beginnings in a fever of enthusiasm and their fatigued endings, might well have recurred. The likelihood of such passion spent, however, would be less in *Weir of Hermiston*, for here, at least, he brought to life more forceful central characters, a more convincing theme and a greater certainty in juxtaposing his dramatic incidents than ever he had done before.

Here, for the first time in all his longer writings, are living women. The older and younger Kirsties have reality and credibility; they are alive with their differences and their qualities, which are universal. The younger Kirstie Elliott is a warm, unpredict-able, but always responsive woman, and her aunt, the elder Kirstie, clings to the reader's memory as a figure out of Highland folklore.

But nowhere in the gallery of Stevenson's portraits is there so commanding a personality as the Lord Justice Clerk, the unswerv-able hanging judge, drunk with port and his own convictions. Adam Weir can pronounce the death sentence on a cowering pris-oner with ribald witticisms and with learned legal citations. He adds insult to injury with erudite meanness. He is majestic and ter-rible in his brutal devotion to duty and his reverence of authority. He is the embodiment of stern Calvinism. He looks upon himself as the Lord's own appointee, with the Law as his fortress and his office as his sword. He is answerable only to the last Court where God sits in final jurisdiction.

By the consensus of Stevenson's most bitter critics, Adam Weir is incontestably the most compelling character in all the novels from *Treasure Island* to *Weir of Hermiston*. Those critics had succeeded about thirty years ago in making it a fashion to look with disdain upon the romantic form and content of his works of fiction. Dis-liking him personally, they pilloried him as a posturer and irre-pressible purveyor of charm. Discovering unevenness in some of his novels, they condemned them all as improvisations, lacking in vi-tality, substance and importance. Most savage of the dissenters and certainly the most outspoken was Mr. Frank Swinnerton who, in a book first published in 1914 and revised and re-issued ten years later, insists that Stevenson was grossly overrated as a novelist. He accuses him of having corrupted romance, of having made it senti-mental and incredible. He attributes to the novelist no more than a knack for putting phrases and episodes together in a patchwork that at best is only plausible but is never convincing. Swinnerton, as the spokesman for the minority opinion on Stevenson, represents the extreme of the reaction that occurred at about the time of the First World War and for a decade thereafter. Since then there has been a swing of the pendulum in Stevenson's favor, and now his novels are being read for their own sake and with very little con-cern for the aura that had accumulated around the author.

» »« «

Even at the extreme point on the arc of reaction against Steven-son there was little stinting of praise for his short stories. The grudging Mr. Frank Swinnerton acknowledged, with only slight qualification, that "Stevenson wrote some exceedingly fine short stories, fit to be considered, in their own line, with any that have been written in English."

The more compact medium was ideal for Stevenson's febrile mind. Whether it is generally true or not, his remark that "compression is the mark of a really sovereign style" was peculiarly applicable to his own briefly sustained flights. By compression he achieved intensity and few failures of fatigue. In the short tale, concentration upon character and event, upon quick and vivid perception, upon convincing emotion and a sense of life, was for him a means of expressing in a single, short effort of creation all his restlessness and sick impatience.

Not more than thirty stories were considered worthy of preservation in the Collected Works. They range from the "bogle" tale, "Thrawn Janet," through the extravaganza, "The Suicide Club," to the fairy tale, "The Bottle Imp," and all the way to an anticipation of a Somerset Maugham South Seas tale, "The Beach of Falesà." These stories stand comparison with the best of their kind.

If there were occasional lapses in the quality of his stories, they were far fewer than in the novels or essays. Some of these tales could leave the saccharine aftertaste of "Will o' the Mill," or go lifeless with the synthetic manufacture of "The Misadventures of John Nicholson," or get lost in the ambiguity of intention of "Olalla," but for almost all of the others there are promise and fulfillment in generous measure.

The art that Stevenson acquired at Alison Cunningham's knee found its most colorful flowering in his short stories. Their variety is quite remarkable in an output relatively limited in comparison, let us say, to the more than three hundred stories written by his contemporary, Guy de Maupassant, within ten years. Maupassant, like Stevenson, was born in 1850, and lived forty-three years; Stevenson died in his forty-fourth year. But there the resemblance to the French master of the short story ends.

Never the observer of society who embodied the chronicles of a class in his tales, Stevenson wrote his own from the imagination, usually Scotch in origin, locale and mood, but often also continental or tropical in setting and atmosphere. Never an ironist who impaled his characters on his pen, Stevenson was the story-teller in the tradition of Alison Cunningham, however much he wanted to be considered the successor to Sir Walter Scott. What he learned from his nurse was a lesson never forgotten: story-telling in itself was the art to frighten, teach, amuse, arouse and hold spellbound the listener, now only slightly transformed into the reader and multiplied fabulously in numbers.

» »« «

In the writing of his essays, Stevenson was in effect setting down his autobiography. They concerned themselves a little too frequently with his antecedents, his father, his home, his childhood and adolescence, his school and university days, his problems as a writer and his views on mortality. For the most part they are personal revelations uttered with disarming candor and with the charm he could endlessly summon. They are essays written by a young man, and they have an air of youthful finality. They often contain homilies attractively decorated with picturesque figurines of language. Their sentiment is noble and almost constantly optimistic with the will to make the best of things.

There are, of course, splashes of vivid color, but only now and then do the essays take fire. When Stevenson burned with anger, he wrote "Father Damien." When he felt called upon to defend his own position as a novelist, irked by Henry James's reference to a little book about a quest for hidden treasure, he could write "A Humble Remonstrance" with heat, declaring that "passion is the be-all and the end-all, the plot and the solution, the protagonist and the *deus ex machina* in one."

Calmer and in a more serene mood he wrote the much earlier "Virginibus Puerisque" which offers pretty advice to the lovelorn. It states without much fear of contradiction that marriage is no bed of roses, that falling in love is an illogical adventure, that jealousy is one of the consequences of this ineradicable habit and that truth in the tender emotion makes love possible and mankind happy. In spite of these nicely adorned platitudes, the essay deserves the favor it has enjoyed. It is, apart from its complacency, persuasive in its gentleness and its soft lyricism. It has grace and delicacy.

In an entirely different vein, "Talk and Talkers" is a closely reasoned, provocative and distinguished essay on a subject that is original in conception and adroit in treatment. There are several light pieces carried off jauntily, like "An Apology for Idlers," weightier

ones laden with moral strictures and didactic lectures which announce old axioms as newly discovered truths. Hope shines brightly
through them and they radiate good will. There are essays on the
obvious and the obscure. Never lacking in variety or finesse, always
picturesque and appealing, Stevenson's essays allay more than they
arouse and charm more than they incite.

» »« «

Stevenson's seven books of travel take his readers to near and
remote parts of the world. The first, *Essays of Travel,* begins the
journey at his birthplace, Edinburgh, and proceeds to Cockermouth and Kiswick in England, to Carrick and Galway in Ireland
and across the Channel to France to the mountain town of Le Monastier, and thence to the Alps. *An Inland Voyage* is a chronicle of
a canoe trip on the Scheldt, beginning at Antwerp, continuing to
Brussels and then by way of the Oise to the Seine. Perched on
Modestine, the amiable donkey, the wandering author rambled in
the Cevennes. *The Amateur Emigrant* spans the Atlantic to New
York and *Across the Plains* the American continent. California of
the 1880's is the next port of call in *The Silverado Squatters,* and
the far places of the Pacific bring this world tour to a close with
In the South Seas.

There can be little dispute that *Travels with a Donkey in the
Cevennes* is the best of his travel books. For lightness of mood, for
sharp but seemingly casual observation, for sheer delight in aimless
wandering, it is Stevenson in his easiest and most ingratiating manner. Next in preference is *The Silverado Squatters* because of its
spontaneous response to a California which was just past its frontier days. An exile, sick and lonely and desperate, Stevenson could
understand and portray a Western American scene with a glowing
and avid spirit. The account of his voyage across the Atlantic in
The Amateur Emigrant is a reportage of his impressions of his fel-
low-passengers and their concerns for what they left behind and
what faced them in their search for fortune in the new world. Its
sympathy is praiseworthy; in general effect it is blurred. *Across the
Plains* is a continuation of the log of his trans-Atlantic passage, but
now aboard a train on the journey westward.

Most earnest of the travel books is *In the South Seas,* wherein he
tries to do far more than record the unusual. The natives he describes are not curiosities, but men with problems. Stevenson tries

to be not the observer only, but the participant, and his concern for the plight of the islanders is genuine. His understanding of the involved politics of the Pacific is notable and entirely creditable to him.

Thus the seven books of travel represent a wide variety of place and interest. Not the least picturesque element in these accounts of his wanderings is the wanderer himself.

» »« «

The memory of his childhood under the guidance of Alison Cunningham was vivid enough between his thirty-first and thirty-fifth years for Stevenson to set down in full enchantment *A Child's Garden of Verses*. Not by any means the best poems he wrote, they are enshrined by familiarity as the most beloved. The narrative poems, particularly "Ticonderoga," "The Song of Rahéro" and "Heather Ale," carry themes of deeper poetic feeling and certainly have firm enough a story foundation to sustain their ballad structure.

A Child's Garden of Verses is, however, unique of its kind and beyond comparison with any poetry other than nursery rhymes which are handed down from generation to generation. It has proven to be, by the test of repetition, a half-century-old folklore.

A repository for his miscellanies in verse, including those in Scotch dialect and his songs of travel, *Underwoods* contains many of Stevenson's most popular and most abused poetry. "Requiem," "The Celestial Surgeon," "The Sick Child," "The Spaewife," "The Vagabond," "Wandering Willie," and others have been favorites on many planes of taste. Like his novels, stories, essays, books of travel, and, above all, his life, they do not lack for variety. For Robert Louis Stevenson the world was always full of a number of things.

» »« «

This selection of Stevenson's writings attempts to be both comprehensive and representative. Even in so large a volume, certain exclusions were unavoidable. Manifestly it is impossible to compress thirty volumes into one. The best compromise, then, is to choose the most characteristic works in each field. Such a choice involves personal predilection and a desire to offer as great a variety as the limitations of space will allow.

Thus, as the introductory novel of its section, *Treasure Island* was selected over *Kidnapped* for two reasons. One was a matter of preference and the other that *Kidnapped,* separated from its sequel, *David Balfour,* would be incomplete. *The Master of Ballantrae* is included on its own merits, and *Weir of Hermiston,* though a large fragment, stands incontestably as Stevenson's masterpiece. Collaborations were not considered at all.

To offer one-third of Stevenson's short stories and nine of his essays is, we believe, a generous portion. They were selected on the basis of their importance, variety and interest.

Every item in this collection, with one exception, is complete in itself. That exception is a single chapter, "The Royal Sport Nautique," from *An Inland Voyage,* given here to suggest the flavor of the whole. *Travels with a Donkey in the Cevennes* and *The Silverado Squatters* are printed in their entirety. *A Child's Garden of Verses,* five ballads and nine poems indicate the compass of Stevenson's metrical gifts.

The sections into which this book is divided are: Novels, Short Stories, Essays, Books of Travel and Poems. A sixth category, Letters, was deliberately omitted. A fair representation of the wide range of Stevenson's correspondence, comprising four volumes in his Collected Works, would have been impossible here. The limits of a single volume have been reached and passed. Within the covers of this book are to be found, we hope, those works by which the writer rather than the legend will be known.

SAXE COMMINS

NOVELS

✳ *Treasure Island* ✳

✳

To the Hesitating Purchaser

IF sailor tales to sailor tunes,
    Storm and adventure, heat and cold,
If schooners, islands, and maroons
    And Buccaneers and buried Gold,
And all the old romance, retold
    Exactly in the ancient way,
Can please, as me they pleased of old,
    The wiser youngsters of to-day:

—So be it, and fall on! If not,
    If studious youth no longer crave,
His ancient appetites forgot,
    Kingston, or Ballantyne the brave,
Or Cooper of the wood and wave:
    So be it also! And may I
And all my pirates share the grave
    Where these and their creations lie!

To

S. L. O.

an American Gentleman,
in Accordance with Whose Classic Taste
the Following Narrative Has Been Designed,
It Is Now, in Return for Numerous Delightful Hours,
and with the Kindest Wishes,
dedicated
by His Affectionate Friend,

THE AUTHOR

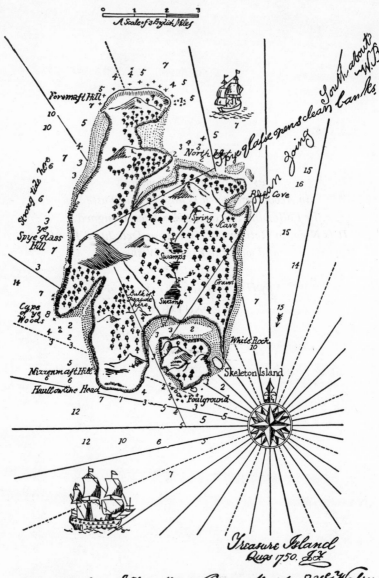

Contents

<hr>

I. THE OLD BUCCANEER

II. THE SEA COOK

III. MY SHORE ADVENTURE

IV. THE STOCKADE

V. MY SEA ADVENTURE

VI. CAPTAIN SILVER

PART ONE

THE OLD BUCCANEER

✳

1. *The Old Sea Dog at the Admiral Benbow*

SQUIRE TRELAWNEY, DR. LIVESEY, AND THE REST OF THESE GENTLE-men having asked me to write down the whole particulars about Treasure Island, from the beginning to the end, keeping nothing back but the bearings of the island, and that only because there is still treasure not yet lifted, I take up my pen in the year of grace 17——, and go back to the time when my father kept the Admiral Benbow inn, and the brown old seaman, with the sabre cut, first took up his lodging under our roof.

I remember him as if it were yesterday, as he came plodding to the inn door, his sea-chest following behind him in a hand-barrow; a tall, strong, heavy, nut-brown man; his tarry pigtail falling over the shoulders of his soiled blue coat; his hands ragged and scarred, with black, broken nails; and the sabre cut across one cheek, a dirty, livid white. I remember him looking round the cove and whistling to himself as he did so, and then breaking out in that old sea-song that he sang so often afterwards:—

"Fifteen men on The Dead Man's Chest—
Yo-ho-ho, and a bottle of rum!"

in the high, old tottering voice that seemed to have been tuned and broken at the capstan bars. Then he rapped on the door with a bit of stick like a handspike that he carried, and when my father appeared, called roughly for a glass of rum. This, when it was brought to him, he drank slowly, like a connoisseur, lingering on the taste, and still looking about him at the cliffs and up at our signboard.

"This is a handy cove," says he at length; "and a pleasant sit-tyated grog-shop. Much company, mate?"

My father told him no, very little company, the more was the pity.

"Well, then," said he, "this is the berth for me. Here you, matey," he cried to the man who trundled the barrow; "bring up along-side and help up my chest. I'll stay here a bit," he continued. "I'm a plain man; rum and bacon and eggs is what I want, and that head up there for to watch ships off. What you mought call me? You mought call me captain. Oh, I see what you're at—there"—and he threw down three or four gold pieces on the threshold. "You can tell me when I've worked through that," says he, looking as fierce as a commander.

And, indeed, bad as his clothes were, and coarsely as he spoke, he had none of the appearance of a man who sailed before the mast; but seemed like a mate or skipper, accustomed to be obeyed or to strike. The man who came with the barrow told us the mail had set him down the morning before at the Royal George; that he had inquired what inns there were along the coast, and hearing ours well spoken of, I suppose, and described as lonely, had chosen it from the others for his place of residence. And that was all we could learn of our guest.

He was a very silent man by custom. All day he hung round the cove, or upon the cliffs, with a brass telescope; all evening he sat in a corner of the parlour next the fire, and drank rum and water very strong. Mostly he would not speak when spoken to; only look up sudden and fierce, and blow through his nose like a fog-horn; and we and the people who came about our house soon learned to let him be. Every day, when he came back from his stroll, he would ask if any seafaring men had gone by along the road. At first we thought it was the want of company of his own kind that made him ask this question; but at last we began to see he was de-sirous to avoid them. When a seaman put up at the Admiral Ben-bow (as now and then some did, making by the coast road for Bristol), he would look in at him through the curtained door be-fore he entered the parlour; and he was always sure to be as silent as a mouse when any such was present. For me, at least, there was no secret about the matter; for I was, in a way, a sharer in his alarms. He had taken me aside one day, and promised me a silver four-penny on the first of every month if I would only keep my "weather-eye open for a seafaring man with one leg," and let him know the moment he appeared. Often enough, when the first of the month came round, and I applied to him for my wage, he would only blow through his nose at me, and stare me down; but before the week was out he was sure to think better of it, bring me my fourpenny piece, and repeat his orders to look out for "the seafaring man with one leg."

How that personage haunted my dreams, I need scarcely tell you. On stormy nights, when the wind shook the four corners of the house, and the surf roared along the cove and up the cliffs, I would see him in a thousand forms, and with a thousand diabolical expressions. Now the leg would be cut off at the knee, now at the hip; now he was a monstrous kind of a creature who had never had but the one leg, and that in the middle of his body. To see him leap and run and pursue me over hedge and ditch was the worst of nightmares. And altogether I paid pretty dear for my monthly fourpenny piece, in the shape of these abominable fancies.

But though I was so terrified by the idea of the seafaring man with one leg, I was far less afraid of the captain himself than anybody else who knew him. There were nights when he took a deal more rum and water than his head would carry; and then he would sometimes sit and sing his wicked, old wild sea-songs, minding nobody; but sometimes he would call for glasses round, and force all the trembling company to listen to his stories or bear a chorus to his singing. Often I have heard the house shaking with "Yo-ho-ho, and a bottle of rum"; all the neighbours joining in for dear life, with the fear of death upon them, and each singing louder than the other, to avoid remark. For in these fits he was the most over-riding companion ever known; he would slap his hand on the table for silence all round; he would fly up in a passion of anger at a question, or sometimes because none was put, and so he judged the company was not following his story. Nor would he allow any one to leave the inn till he had drunk himself sleepy and reeled off to bed.

His stories were what frightened people worst of all. Dreadful stories they were; about hanging, and walking the plank, and storms at sea, and the Dry Tortugas, and wild deeds and places on the Spanish Main. By his own account he must have lived his life among some of the wickedest men that God ever allowed upon the sea; and the language in which he told these stories shocked our plain country people almost as much as the crimes that he described. My father was always saying the inn would be ruined, for people would soon cease coming there to be tyrannised over and put down, and sent shivering to their beds; but I really believe his presence did us good. People were frightened at the time, but on looking back they rather liked it; it was a fine excitement in a quiet country life; and there was even a party of the younger men who pretended to admire him, calling him a "true sea-dog," and a "real old salt," and such like names, and saying there was the sort of man that made England terrible at sea.

In one way, indeed, he bade fair to ruin us; for he kept on staying week after week, and at last month after month, so that all the money had been long exhausted, and still my father never plucked up the heart to insist on having more. If ever he mentioned it, the captain blew through his nose so loudly that you might say he roared, and stared my poor father out of the room. I have seen him wringing his hands after such a rebuff, and I am sure the annoyance and the terror he lived in must have greatly hastened his early and unhappy death.

All the time he lived with us the captain made no change whatever in his dress but to buy some stockings from a hawker. One of the cocks of his hat having fallen down, he let it hang from that day forth, though it was a great annoyance when it blew. I remember the appearance of his coat, which he patched himself upstairs in his room, and which, before the end, was nothing but patches. He never wrote or received a letter, and he never spoke with any but the neighbours, and with these, for the most part, only when drunk on rum. The great sea-chest none of us had ever seen open.

He was only once crossed, and that was towards the end, when my poor father was far gone in a decline that took him off. Dr. Livesey came late one afternoon to see the patient, took a bit of dinner from my mother, and went into the parlour to smoke a pipe until his horse should come down from the hamlet, for we had no stabling at the old Benbow. I followed him in, and I remember observing the contrast the neat, bright doctor, with his powder as white as snow, and his bright, black eyes and pleasant manners, made with the coltish country folk, and above all, with that filthy, heavy, bleared scarecrow of a pirate of ours, sitting far gone in rum, with his arms on the table. Suddenly he—the captain, that is—began to pipe up his eternal song:—

> "Fifteen men on The Dead Man's Chest—
> Yo-ho-ho, and a bottle of rum!
> Drink and the devil had done for the rest—
> Yo-ho-ho, and a bottle of rum!"

At first I had supposed "the dead man's chest" to be that identical big box of his upstairs in the front room, and the thought had been mingled in my nightmares with that of the one-legged sea-faring man. But by this time we had all long ceased to pay any particular notice to the song; it was new, that night, to nobody but Dr. Livesey, and on him I observed it did not produce an agreeable effect, for he looked up for a moment quite angrily before he went on with his talk to old Taylor, the gardener, on a new cure for the rheumatics. In the meantime, the captain gradually brightened up at his own music, and at last flapped his hand upon the table before him in a way we all knew to mean—silence. The voices stopped at once, all but Dr. Livesey's; he went on as before, speaking clear and kind, and drawing briskly at his pipe between every word or two. The captain glared at him for a while, flapped his hand again, glared still harder, and at last broke out with a villainous low oath: "Silence, there, between decks!"

"Were you addressing me, sir?" says the doctor; and when the ruffian had told him, with another oath, that this was so, "I have only one thing to say to you, sir," replies the doctor, "that if you keep on drinking rum, the world will soon be quit of a very dirty scoundrel!"

The old fellow's fury was awful. He sprang to his feet, drew and opened a sailor's claspknife, and, balancing it open on the palm of his hand, threatened to pin the doctor to the wall.

The doctor never so much as moved. He spoke to him, as before, over his shoulder, and in the same tone of voice; rather high, so that all the room might hear, but perfectly calm and steady:—

"If you do not put that knife this instant in your pocket, I promise, upon my honour, you shall hang at next assizes."

Then followed a battle of looks between them; but the captain soon knuckled under, put up his weapon, and resumed his seat, grumbling like a beaten dog.

"And now, sir," continued the doctor, "since I now know there's such a fellow in my district, you may count I'll have an eye upon you day and night. I'm not a doctor only; I'm a magistrate; and if I catch a breath of complaint against you, if it's only for a piece of incivility like to-night's, I'll take effectual means to have you hunted down and routed out of this. Let that suffice."

Soon after Dr. Livesey's horse came to the door, and he rode away; but the captain held his peace that evening, and for many evenings to come.

2.   Black Dog Appears and Disappears

I T WAS NOT VERY LONG AFTER THIS THAT THERE OCCURRED THE FIRST of the mysterious events that rid us at last of the captain, though not, as you will see, of his affairs. It was a bitter cold winter, with long, hard frosts and heavy gales; and it was plain from the first that my poor father was little likely to see the spring. He sank daily, and my mother and I had all the inn upon our hands; and were kept busy enough, without paying much regard to our unpleasant guest.

It was one January morning, very early—a pinching, frosty morning—the cove all gray with hoar-frost, the ripple lapping softly on the stones, the sun still low and only touching the hill-tops and shining far to seaward. The captain had risen earlier than usual, and set out down the beach, his cutlass swinging under the broad skirts of the old blue coat, his brass telescope under his arm, his hat tilted back upon his head. I remember his breath hanging like smoke in his wake as he strode off, and the last sound I heard of him, as he turned the big rock, was a loud snort of indignation, as though his mind was still running upon Dr. Livesey.

Well, mother was upstairs with father; and I was laying the breakfast table against the captain's return, when the parlour door opened, and a man stepped in on whom I had never set my eyes before. He was a pale, tallowy creature, wanting two fingers of the left hand; and, though he wore a cutlass, he did not look much like a fighter. I had always my eye open for seafaring men, with one leg or two, and I remember this one puzzled me. He was not sailorly, and yet he had a smack of the sea about him too.

I asked him what was for his service, and he said he would take rum; but as I was going out of the room to fetch it he sat down upon a table and motioned me to draw near. I paused where I was with my napkin in my hand.

"Come here, sonny," says he. "Come nearer here."

I took a step nearer.

"Is this here table for my mate Bill?" he asked, with a kind of leer.

I told him I did not know his mate Bill; and this was for a person who stayed in our house, whom we called the captain.

"Well," said he, "my mate Bill would be called the captain, as like as not. He has a cut on one cheek, and a mighty pleasant way with him, particularly in drink, has my mate Bill. We'll put it, for argument like, that your captain has a cut on one cheek—and we'll put it, if you like, that that cheek's the right one. Ah, well! I told you. Now, is my mate Bill in this here house?"

I told him he was out walking.

"Which way, sonny? Which way is he gone?"

And when I had pointed out the rock and told him how the captain was likely to return, and how soon, and answered a few other questions, "Ah," said he, "this'll be as good as drink to my mate Bill."

The expression on his face as he said these words was not at all pleasant, and I had my own reasons for thinking that the stranger was mistaken, even supposing he meant what he said. But it was no affair of mine, I thought; and, besides, it was difficult to know what to do. The stranger kept hanging about just inside the inn door, peering round the corner like a cat waiting for a mouse. Once I stepped out myself into the road, but he immediately called me back, and, as I did not obey quick enough for his fancy, a most horrible change came over his tallowy face, and he ordered me in, with an oath that made me jump. As soon as I was back again he returned to his former manner, half fawning, half sneering, patted me on the shoulder, told me I was a good boy, and he had taken quite a fancy to me. "I have a son of my own," said he, "as like you as two blocks, and he's all the pride of my 'art. But the great thing for boys is discipline, sonny—discipline. Now, if you had sailed along of Bill, you wouldn't have stood there to be spoke to twice—not you. That was never Bill's way, nor the way of sich as sailed with him. And here, sure enough, is my mate Bill, with a spy-glass under his arm, bless his old 'art to be sure. You and me'll just go back into the parlour, sonny, and get behind the door, and we'll give Bill a little surprise—bless his 'art, I say again."

So saying, the stranger backed along with me into the parlour, and put me behind him in the corner, so that we were both hidden by the open door. I was very uneasy and alarmed, as you may fancy, and it rather added to my fears to observe that the stranger was certainly frightened himself. He cleared the hilt of his cutlass and loosened the blade in the sheath; and all the time we were waiting there he kept swallowing as if he felt what we used to call a lump in the throat.

At last in strode the captain, slammed the door behind him, without looking to the right or left, and marched straight across the room to where his breakfast awaited him.

"Bill," said the stranger in a voice that I thought he had tried to make bold and big.

The captain spun round on his heel and fronted us; all the brown had gone out of his face, and even his nose was blue; he had the look of a man who sees a ghost, or the evil one, or something worse, if anything can be; and, upon my word, I felt sorry to see him, all in a moment, turn so old and sick.

"Come, Bill, you know me; you know an old shipmate, Bill, surely," said the stranger.

The captain made a sort of gasp.

"Black Dog!" said he.

"And who else?" returned the other, getting more at his ease. "Black Dog as ever was, come for to see his old shipmate Billy, at the Admiral Benbow inn. Ah, Bill, Bill, we have seen a sight of times, us two, since I lost them two talons," holding up his mutilated hand.

"Now, look here," said the captain; "you've run me down; here I am; well, then, speak up: what is it?"

"That's you, Bill," returned Black Dog, "you're in the right of it, Billy. I'll have a glass of rum from this dear child here, as I've took such a liking to; and we'll sit down, if you please, and talk square like old shipmates."

When I returned with the rum, they were already seated on either side of the captain's breakfast table—Black Dog next to the door, and sitting sideways, so as to have one eye on his old shipmate, and one, as I thought, on his retreat.

He bade me go, and leave the door wide open. "None of your

keyholes for me, sonny," he said; and I left them together, and retired into the bar.

For a long time, though I certainly did my best to listen, I could
hear nothing but a low gabbling; but at last the voices began to
grow higher, and I could pick up a word or two, mostly oaths,
from the captain.

"No, no, no, no; and an end of it!" he cried once. And again, "If
it comes to swinging, swing all, say I."

Then all of a sudden there was a tremendous explosion of oaths
and other noises—the chair and table went over in a lump, a clash
of steel followed, and then a cry of pain, and the next instant I
saw Black Dog in full flight, and the captain hotly pursuing, both
with drawn cutlasses, and the former streaming blood from the left
shoulder. Just at the door, the captain aimed at the fugitive one
last tremendous cut, which would certainly have split him to the
chine had it not been intercepted by our big signboard of Admiral
Benbow. You may see the notch on the lower side of the frame to
this day.

The blow was the last of the battle. Once out upon the road,
Black Dog, in spite of his wound, showed a wonderful clean pair of
heels, and disappeared over the edge of the hill in half a minute.
The captain, for his part, stood staring at the signboard like a bewildered man. Then he passed his hand over his eyes several times,
and at last turned back into the house.

"Jim," says he, "rum"; and as he spoke, he reeled a little, and
caught himself with one hand against the wall.

"Are you hurt?" cried I.

"Rum," he repeated. "I must get away from here. Rum! rum!"

I ran to fetch it; but I was quite unsteadied by all that had fallen
out, and I broke one glass and fouled the tap, and while I was still
getting in my own way, I heard a loud fall in the parlour, and, running in, beheld the captain lying full length upon the floor. At the
same instant, my mother, alarmed by the cries and fighting, came
running downstairs to help me. Between us we raised his head. He
was breathing very loud and hard; but his eyes were closed, and his
face a horrible colour.

"Dear, deary me," cried my mother, "what a disgrace upon the
house! And your poor father sick!"

In the meantime, we had no idea what to do to help the captain,
nor any other thought but that he had got his death-hurt in the

scuffle with the stranger. I got the rum, to be sure, and tried to put it down his throat; but his teeth were tightly shut, and his jaws as strong as iron. It was a happy relief for us when the door opened and Doctor Livesey came in, on his visit to my father.

"Oh, doctor," we cried, "what shall we do? Where is he wounded?"

"Wounded? A fiddle-stick's end!" said the doctor. "No more wounded than you or I. The man has had a stroke, as I warned him. Now, Mrs. Hawkins, just you run upstairs to your husband, and tell him, if possible, nothing about it. For my part, I must do my best to save this fellow's trebly worthless life; and Jim here will get me a basin."

When I got back with the basin, the doctor had already ripped up the captain's sleeve, and exposed his great sinewy arm. It was tattooed in several places. "Here's luck," "A fair wind," and "Billy Bones his fancy," were very neatly and clearly executed on the forearm; and up near the shoulder there was a sketch of a gallows and a man hanging from it—done, as I thought, with great spirit.

"Prophetic," said the doctor, touching this picture with his finger. "And now, Master Billy Bones, if that be your name, we'll have a look at the colour of your blood. Jim," he said, "are you afraid of blood?"

"No, sir," said I.

"Well, then," said he, "you hold the basin," and with that he took his lancet and opened a vein.

A great deal of blood was taken before the captain opened his eyes and looked mistily about him. First he recognised the doctor with an unmistakable frown; then his glance fell upon me, and he looked relieved. But suddenly his colour changed, and he tried to raise himself, crying:—

"Where's Black Dog?"

"There is no Black Dog here," said the doctor, "except what you have on your own back. You have been drinking rum; you have had a stroke, precisely as I told you; and I have just, very much against my own will, dragged you head-foremost out of the grave. Now, Mr. Bones——"

"That's not my name," he interrupted.

"Much I care," returned the doctor. "It's the name of a buc-caneer of my acquaintance; and I call you by it for the sake of shortness, and what I have to say to you is this: one glass of rum won't kill you, but if you take one you'll take another and another, and I stake my wig if you don't break off short, you'll die—do you understand that?—die, and go to your own place, like the man in the Bible. Come, now, make an effort. I'll help you to your bed for once."

Between us, with much trouble, we managed to hoist him upstairs, and laid him on his bed, where his head fell back on the pillow, as if he were almost fainting.

"Now, mind you," said the doctor, "I clear my conscience—the name of rum for you is death."

And with that we went off to see my father, taking me with him by the arm.

"This is nothing," he said, as soon as he had closed the door. "I have drawn blood enough to keep him quiet a while; he should lie for a week where he is—that is the best thing for him and you; but another stroke would settle him."

3. *The Black Spot*

ABOUT NOON I STOPPED AT THE CAPTAIN'S DOOR WITH SOME COOLing drinks and medicines. He was lying very much as we had left him, only a little higher, and he seemed both weak and excited.

"Jim," he said, "you're the only one here that's worth anything; and you know I've been always good to you. Never a month but I've given you a silver fourpenny for yourself. And now you see, mate, I'm pretty low, and deserted by all; and Jim, you'll bring me one noggin of rum, now, won't you, matey?"

"The doctor——" I began.

But he broke in cursing the doctor, in a feeble voice, but heartily. "Doctors is all swabs," he said; "and that doctor there, why, what do he know about seafaring men? I been in places hot as pitch, and mates dropping round with Yellow Jack, and the blessed land a-heaving like the sea with earthquakes—what do the doctor know of lands like that?—and I lived on rum, I tell you. It's been meat and drink, and man and wife, to me; and if I'm not to have my rum now I'm a poor old hulk on a lee shore, my blood'll be on you, Jim, and that doctor swab;" and he ran on again for a while with curses. "Look, Jim, how my fingers fidget," he continued, in the pleading tone. "I can't keep 'em still, not I. I haven't had a drop this blessed day. That doctor's a fool, I tell you. If I don't have a drain o' rum, Jim, I'll have the horrors; I seen some on 'em already. I seen old Flint there in the corner, behind you; as plain as print, I seen him; and if I get the horrors, I'm a man that has lived rough, and I'll raise Cain. Your doctor hisself said one glass wouldn't hurt me. I'll give you a golden guinea for a noggin, Jim."

He was growing more and more excited, and this alarmed me for my father, who was very low that day, and needed quiet; besides, I was reassured by the doctor's words, now quoted to me, and rather offended by the offer of a bribe.

"I want none of your money," said I, "but what you owe my father. I'll get you one glass, and no more."

When I brought it to him, he seized it greedily, and drank it out.

"Ay, ay," said he, "that's some better, sure enough. And now, matey, did that doctor say how long I was to lie here in this old berth?"

"A week at least," said I.

"Thunder!" he cried. "A week! I can't do that: they'd have the black spot on me by then. The lubbers is going about to get the wind of me this blessed moment; lubbers as couldn't keep what they got, and want to nail what is another's. Is that seamanly behaviour, now, I want to know? But I'm a saving soul. I never wasted good money of mine, nor lost it neither; and I'll trick 'em again. I'm not afraid on 'em. I'll shake out another reef, matey, and daddle 'em again."

As he was thus speaking, he had risen from bed with great difficulty, holding to my shoulder with a grip that almost made me cry out, and moving his legs like so much dead weight. His words, spirited as they were in meaning, contrasted sadly with the weakness of the voice in which they were uttered. He paused when he had got into a sitting position on the edge.

"That doctor's done me," he murmured. "My ears is singing. Lay me back."

Before I could do much to help him he had fallen back again to his former place, where he lay for a while silent.

"Jim," he said at length, "you saw that seafaring man to-day?"

"Black Dog?" I asked.

"Ah! Black Dog," says he. *"He's* a bad 'un; but there's worse that put him on. Now, if I can't get away nohow, and they tip me the black spot, mind you, it's my old sea-chest they're after; you get on a horse—you can, can't you? Well, then, you get on a horse, and go to—well, yes, I will!—to that eternal doctor swab, and tell him to pipe all hands—magistrates and sich—and he'll lay 'em aboard at the Admiral Benbow,—all old Flint's crew, man and boy, all on 'em that's left. I was first mate, I was, old Flint's first mate, and I'm the on'y one as knows the place. He gave it me to Savannah, when he lay a-dying, like as if I was to now, you see. But you won't peach unless they get the black spot on me, or unless you see that Black Dog again, or a seafaring man with one leg, Jim —him above all."

"But what is the black spot, captain?" I asked.

"That's a summons, mate. I'll tell you if they get that. But you keep your weather-eye open, Jim, and I'll share with you equals, upon my honour."

He wandered a little longer, his voice growing weaker; but soon after I had given him his medicine, which he took like a child, with the remark, "If ever a seaman wanted drugs, it's me," he fell at last into a heavy, swoon-like sleep, in which I left him. What I should have done had all gone well I do not know. Probably I should have told the whole story to the doctor; for I was in mortal fear lest the captain should repent of his confessions and make an end of me. But as things fell out, my poor father died quite suddenly that evening; which put all other matters on one side. Our natural distress, the visits of the neighbours, the arranging of the funeral, and all the work of the inn to be carried on in the meanwhile, kept me so busy that I had scarcely time to think of the captain, far less to be afraid of him.

He got downstairs next morning, to be sure, and had his meals as usual, though he ate little, and had more, I am afraid, than his usual supply of rum, for he helped himself out of the bar, scowling and blowing through his nose, and no one dared to cross him. On the night before the funeral he was as drunk as ever; and it was shocking, in that house of mourning, to hear him singing away at his ugly old sea-song; but, weak as he was, we were all in the fear of death for him, and the doctor was suddenly taken up with a case many miles away, and was never near the house after my father's death. I have said the captain was weak; and indeed he seemed rather to grow weaker than regain his strength. He clambered up and down stairs, and went from the parlour to the bar and back again, and sometimes put his nose out of doors to smell the sea, holding on to the walls as he went for support, and breathing hard and fast like a man on a steep mountain. He never particularly addressed me, and it is my belief he had as good as forgotten his confidences; but his temper was more flighty, and, allowing for his bodily weakness, more violent than ever. He had an alarming way now when he was drunk of drawing his cutlass and laying it bare before him on the table. But with all that, he minded people less, and seemed shut up in his own thoughts and rather wandering. Once, for instance, to our extreme wonder, he piped up to a different air, a kind of country love-song, that he must have learned in his youth before he had begun to follow the sea.

So things passed until, the day after the funeral, and about three o'clock of a bitter, foggy, frosty afternoon, I was standing at the door for a moment, full of sad thoughts about my father, when I saw some one drawing slowly near along the road. He was plainly blind, for he tapped before him with a stick, and wore a great green shade over his eyes and nose; and he was hunched, as if with age or weakness, and wore a huge old tattered sea-cloak with a hood, that made him appear positively deformed. I never saw in my life a more dreadful-looking figure. He stopped a little from the inn, and, raising his voice in an odd sing-song, addressed the air in front of him:—

"Will any kind friend inform a poor blind man, who has lost the precious sight of his eyes in the gracious defence of his native country, England, and God bless King George!—where or in what part of this country he may now be?"

"You are at the Admiral Benbow, Black Hill Cove, my good man," said I.

"I hear a voice," said he—"a young voice. Will you give me your hand, my kind young friend, and lead me in?"

I held out my hand, and the horrible, soft-spoken, eyeless creature gripped it in a moment like a vice. I was so much startled that I struggled to withdraw; but the blind man pulled me close up to him with a single action of his arm.

"Now, boy," he said, "take me in to the captain."

"Sir," said I, "upon my word I dare not."

"Oh," he sneered, "that's it! Take me in straight, or I'll break your arm."

And he gave it, as he spoke, a wrench that made me cry out.

"Sir," I said, "it is for yourself I mean. The captain is not what he used to be. He sits with a drawn cutlass. Another gentleman——"

"Come, now, march," interrupted he; and I never heard a voice so cruel, and cold, and ugly as that blind man's. It cowed me more than the pain; and I began to obey him at once, walking straight in at the door and towards the parlour, where our sick old buccaneer was sitting, dazed with rum. The blind man clung close to me, holding me in one iron fist, and leaning almost more of his weight on me than I could carry. "Lead me straight up to him, and when I'm in view, cry out, 'Here's a friend for you, Bill.' If you don't, I'll do this"—and with that he gave me a twitch that I thought would have made me faint. Between this and that, I was so utterly terrified of the blind beggar that I forgot my terror of the captain, and as I opened the parlour door, cried out the words he had ordered in a trembling voice.

The poor captain raised his eyes, and at one look the rum went out of him, and left him staring sober. The expression of his face was not so much of terror as of mortal sickness. He made a movement to rise, but I do not believe he had enough force left in his body.

"Now, Bill, sit where you are," said the beggar. "If I can't see, I can hear a finger stirring. Business is business. Hold out your right hand. Boy, take his right hand by the wrist and bring it near to my right."

We both obeyed him to the letter, and I saw him pass something from the hollow of the hand that held his stick into the palm of the captain's, which closed upon it instantly.

"And now that's done," said the blind man; and at the words he suddenly left hold of me, and, with incredible accuracy and nimbleness, skipped out of the parlour and into the road, where, as I still stood motionless, I could hear his stick go tap-tap-tapping into the distance.

It was some time before either I or the captain seemed to gather our senses; but at length, and about at the same moment, I released his wrist, which I was still holding, and he drew in his hand and looked sharply into the palm.

"Ten o'clock!" he cried. "Six hours. We'll do them yet," and he sprang to his feet.

Even as he did so, he reeled, put his hand to his throat, stood swaying for a moment, and then, with a peculiar sound, fell from his whole height face foremost to the floor.

I ran to him at once, calling to my mother. But haste was all in vain. The captain had been struck dead by thundering apoplexy. It is a curious thing to understand, for I had certainly never liked the man, though of late I had begun to pity him, but as soon as I saw that he was dead, I burst into a flood of tears. It was the second death I had known, and the sorrow of the first was still fresh in my heart.

4.　*The Sea Chest*

I LOST NO TIME, OF COURSE, IN TELLING MY MOTHER ALL THAT I knew, and perhaps should have told her long before, and we saw ourselves at once in a difficult and dangerous position. Some of the man's money—if he had any—was certainly due to us; but it was not likely that our captain's shipmates, above all the two specimens seen by me, Black Dog and the blind beggar, would be inclined to give up their booty in payment of the dead man's debts. The captain's order to mount at once and ride for Doctor Livesey would have left my mother alone and unprotected, which was not to be thought of. Indeed, it seemed impossible for either of us to remain much longer in the house: the fall of coals in the kitchen grate, the very ticking of the clock, filled us with alarms. The neighbourhood, to our ears, seemed haunted by approaching footsteps; and what between the dead body of the captain on the parlour floor, and the thought of that detestable blind beggar hovering near at hand, and ready to return, there were moments when, as the saying goes, I jumped in my skin for terror. Something must speedily be resolved upon; and it occurred to us at last to go forth together and seek help in the neighbouring hamlet. No sooner said than done. Bare-headed as we were, we ran out at once in the gathering evening and the frosty fog.

The hamlet lay not many hundred yards away though out of view, on the other side of the next cove; and what greatly encouraged me, it was in an opposite direction from that whence the blind man had made his appearance, and whither he had presumably returned. We were not many minutes on the road, though we sometimes stopped to lay hold of each other and hearken. But there was no unusual sound—nothing but the low wash of the ripple and the croaking of the crows in the wood.

It was already candle-light when we reached the hamlet, and I shall never forget how much I was cheered to see the yellow shine in doors and windows; but that, as it proved, was the best of the help we were likely to get in that quarter. For—you would have thought men would have been ashamed of themselves—no soul would consent to return with us to the Admiral Benbow. The more we told of our troubles, the more—man, woman, and child —they clung to the shelter of their houses. The name of Captain Flint, though it was strange to me, was well enough known to some there, and carried a great weight of terror. Some of the men who had been to field-work on the far side of the Admiral Benbow remembered, besides, to have seen several strangers on the road, and, taking them to be smugglers, to have bolted away; and one at least had seen a little lugger in what we called Kitt's Hole. For that matter, any one who was a comrade of the captain's was enough to frighten them to death. And the short and the long of the matter was, that while we could get several who were willing enough to ride to Dr. Livesey's, which lay in another direction, not one would help us to defend the inn.

They say cowardice is infectious; but then argument is, on the other hand, a great emboldener; and so when each had said his say, my mother made them a speech. She would not, she declared, lose money that belonged to her fatherless boy; "If none of the rest of you dare," she said, "Jim and I dare. Back we will go, the way we came, and small thanks to you big, hulking, chicken-hearted men. We'll have that chest open, if we die for it. And I'll thank you for that bag, Mrs. Crossley, to bring back our lawful money in."

Of course, I said I would go with my mother; and of course they all cried out at our foolhardiness; but even then not a man would go along with us. All they would do was to give me a loaded pistol, lest we were attacked; and to promise to have horses ready saddled, in case we were pursued on our return; while one lad was to ride forward to the doctor's in search of armed assistance.

My heart was beating finely when we two set forth in the cold night upon this dangerous venture. A full moon was beginning to rise and peered redly through the upper edges of the fog, and this increased our haste, for it was plain, before we came forth again, that all would be as bright as day, and our departure exposed to the eyes of any watchers. We slipped along the hedges, noiseless and swift, nor did we see or hear anything to increase our terrors, till, to our huge relief, the door of the Admiral Benbow had closed behind us.

I slipped the bolt at once, and we stood and panted for a moment in the dark, alone in the house with the dead captain's body. Then my mother got a candle in the bar, and, holding each other's hands, we advanced into the parlour. He lay as we had left him, on his back, with his eyes open, and one arm stretched out.

"Draw down the blind, Jim," whispered my mother; "they might come and watch outside. And now," said she, when I had done so, "we have to get the key off *that;* and who's to touch it, I should like to know!" and she gave a kind of sob as she said the words.

I went down on my knees at once. On the floor close to his hand there was a little round of paper, blackened on the one side. I could not doubt that this was the *black spot;* and taking it up, I found written on the other side, in a very good, clear hand, this short message: "You have till ten to-night."

"He had till ten, mother," said I; and just as I said it, our old clock began striking. This sudden noise startled us shockingly; but the news was good, for it was only six.

"Now Jim," she said, "that key."

I felt in his pockets, one after another. A few small coins, a thimble, and some thread and big needles, a piece of pigtail tobacco bitten away at the end, his gully with a crooked handle, a pocket compass, and a tinder box, were all that they contained, and I began to despair.

"Perhaps it's round his neck," suggested my mother.

Overcoming a strong repugnance, I tore open his shirt at the neck, and there, sure enough, hanging to a bit of tarry string, which I cut with his own gully, we found the key. At this triumph we were filled with hope, and hurried upstairs, without delay, to the little room where he had slept so long, and where his box had stood since the day of his arrival.

It was like any other seaman's chest on the outside, the initial "B" burned on the top of it with a hot iron, and the corners somewhat smashed and broken as by long, rough usage.

"Give me the key," said my mother; and though the lock was very stiff, she had turned it and thrown back the lid in a twinkling.

A strong smell of tobacco and tar rose from the interior, but nothing was to be seen on the top except a suit of very good clothes, carefully brushed and folded. They had never been worn, my mother said. Under that, the miscellany began—a quadrant, a tin canikin, several sticks of tobacco, two brace of very handsome pistols, a piece of bar silver, an old Spanish watch and some other trinkets of little value and mostly of foreign make, a pair of compasses mounted with brass, and five or six curious West Indian shells. It has often set me thinking since that he should have carried about these shells with him in his wandering, guilty, and hunted life.

In the meantime, we had found nothing of any value but the silver and the trinkets, and neither of these were in our way. Underneath there was an old boat-cloak, whitened with sea-salt on many a harbour-bar. My mother pulled it up with impatience, and there lay before us, the last things in the chest, a bundle tied up in oilcloth, and looking like papers, and a canvas bag, that gave forth, at a touch, the jingle of gold.

"I'll show these rogues that I'm an honest woman," said my mother. "I'll have my dues, and not a farthing over. Hold Mrs. Crossley's bag." And she began to count over the amount of the captain's score from the sailor's bag into the one that I was holding.

It was a long, difficult business, for the coins were of all countries and sizes—doubloons, and louis-d'ors, and guineas, and pieces of eight, and I know not what besides, all shaken together at random. The guineas, too, were about the scarcest, and it was with these only that my mother knew how to make her count.

When we were about half-way through, I suddenly put my hand upon her arm; for I had heard in the silent, frosty air, a sound that brought my heart into my mouth—the tap-tapping of the blind man's stick upon the frozen road. It drew nearer and nearer, while we sat holding our breath. Then it struck sharp on the inn door, and then we could hear the handle being turned, and the bolt rattling as the wretched being tried to enter; and then there was a long time of silence both within and without. At last the tapping recommenced, and, to our indescribable joy and gratitude, died slowly away again until it ceased to be heard.

"Mother," said I, "take the whole and let's be going," for I was sure the bolted door must have seemed suspicious, and would bring the whole hornet's nest about our ears; though how thankful I was that I had bolted it, none could tell who had never met that terrible blind man.

But my mother, frightened as she was, would not consent to take a fraction more than was due to her, and was obstinately unwilling to be content with less. It was not yet seven, she said, by a long way; she knew her rights and she would have them; and she was still arguing with me, when a little low whistle sounded a good way off upon the hill. That was enough, and more than enough for both of us.

"I'll take what I have," she said, jumping to her feet.

"And I'll take this to square the count," said I, picking up the oilskin packet.

Next moment we were both groping downstairs, leaving the candle by the empty chest; and the next we had opened the door and were in full retreat. We had not started a moment too soon. The fog was rapidly dispersing; already the moon shone quite clear on the high ground on either side; and it was only in the exact bottom of the dell and round the tavern door that a thin veil still hung unbroken to conceal the first steps of our escape. Far less than half-way to the hamlet, very little beyond the bottom of the hill, we must come forth into the moonlight. Nor was this all; for the sound of several footsteps running came already to our ears, and as we looked back in their direction, a light tossing to and fro and still rapidly advancing, showed that one of the newcomers carried a lantern.

"My dear," said my mother suddenly, "take the money and run on. I am going to faint."

This was certainly the end for both of us, I thought. How I cursed the cowardice of the neighbours; how I blamed my poor mother for her honesty and her greed, for her past foolhardiness and present weakness! We were just at the little bridge, by good fortune; and I helped her, tottering as she was, to the edge of the bank, where, sure enough, she gave a sigh and fell on my shoulder. I do not know how I found the strength to do it at all, and I am afraid it was roughly done, but I managed to drag her down the bank and a little way under the arch. Farther I could not move her, for the bridge was too low to let me do more than crawl below it. So there we had to stay—my mother almost entirely exposed, and both of us within earshot of the inn.

5.   *The Last of the Blind Man*

M Y CURIOSITY, IN A SENSE, WAS STRONGER THAN MY FEAR; FOR I could not remain where I was, but crept back to the bank again, whence, sheltering my head behind a bush of broom, I might command the road before our door. I was scarcely in position ere my enemies began to arrive, seven or eight of them, running hard, their feet beating out of time along the road, and the man with the lantern some paces in front. Three men ran together, hand in hand; and I made out, even through the mist, that the middle man of this trio was the blind beggar. The next moment his voice showed me that I was right.

"Down with the door!" he cried.

"Ay, ay, sir!" answered two or three; and a rush was made upon the Admiral Benbow, the lantern-bearer following; and then I could see them pause, and hear speeches passed in a lower key, as if they were surprised to find the door open. But the pause was brief, for the blind man again issued his commands. His voice sounded louder and higher, as if he were afire with eagerness and rage.

"In, in, in!" he shouted, and cursed them for their delay.

Four or five of them obeyed at once, two remaining on the road with the formidable beggar. There was a pause, then a cry of surprise, and then a voice shouting from the house:—

"Bill's dead!"

But the blind man swore at them again for their delay.

"Search him, some of you shirking lubbers, and the rest of you aloft and get the chest," he cried.

I could hear their feet rattling up our old stairs, so that the house must have shook with it. Promptly afterwards, fresh sounds of astonishment arose; the window of the captain's room was thrown open with a slam and a jingle of broken glass; and a man leaned out into the moonlight, head and shoulders, and addressed the blind beggar on the road below him.

"Pew," he cried, "they've been before us. Some one's turned the chest out alow and aloft."

"Is it there?" roared Pew.

"The money's there."

The blind man cursed the money.

"Flint's fist, I mean," he cried.

"We don't see it here nohow," returned the man.

"Here, you below there, is it on Bill?" cried the blind man again.

At that, another fellow, probably he who had remained below to search the captain's body, came to the door of the inn. "Bill's been overhauled a'ready," said he, "nothin' left."

"It's these people of the inn—it's that boy. I wish I had put his eyes out!" cried the blind man Pew. "They were here no time ago—they had the door bolted when I tried it. Scatter, lads, and find 'em."

"Sure enough, they left their glim here," said the fellow from the window.

"Scatter and find 'em! Rout the house out!" reiterated Pew, striking with his stick upon the road.

Then there followed a great to-do through all our old inn, heavy feet pounding to and fro, furniture thrown over, doors kicked in, until the very rocks re-echoed, and the men came out again, one after another, on the road, and declared that we were nowhere to be found. And just then the same whistle that had alarmed my mother and myself over the dead captain's money was once more clearly audible through the night, but this time twice repeated. I had thought it to be the blind man's trumpet, so to speak, summoning his crew to the assault; but I now found that it was a signal from the hillside towards the hamlet, and, from its effect upon the buccaneers, a signal to warn them of approaching danger.

"There's Dirk again," said one. "Twice. We'll have to budge, mates."

"Budge, you skulk!" cried Pew. "Dirk was a fool and a coward from the first—you wouldn't mind him. They must be close by; they can't be far; you have your hands on it. Scatter and look for them, dogs! Oh, shiver my soul," he cried, "if I had eyes!"

This appeal seemed to produce some effect, for two of the fellows began to look here and there among the lumber, but half-heartedly, I thought, and with half an eye to their own danger all the time, while the rest stood irresolute on the road.

"You have your hands on thousands, you fools, and you hang a leg! You'd be as rich as kings if you could find it, and you know it's here, and you stand there malingering. There wasn't one of

you dared face Bill, and I did it—a blind man! And I'm to lose
my chance through you! I'm to be a poor, crawling beggar, spong-
ing for rum, when I might be rolling in a coach! If you had the
pluck of a weevil in a biscuit you would catch them still."

"Hang it, Pew, we've got the doubloons!" grumbled one.

"They might have hid the blessed thing," said another. "Take
the Georges, Pew, and don't stand here squalling."

Squalling was the word for it, Pew's anger rose so high at these
objections; till at last, his passion completely taking the upper
hand, he struck at them right and left in his blindness, and his stick
sounded heavily on more than one.

These, in their turn, cursed back at the blind miscreant, threatened him in horrid terms, and tried in vain to catch the stick and
wrest it from his grasp.

This quarrel was the saving of us; for while it was still raging
another sound came from the top of the hill on the side of the
hamlet—the tramp of horses galloping. Almost at the same time a
pistol-shot, flash and report, came from the hedge-side. And that
was plainly the last signal of danger; for the buccaneers turned at
once and ran, separating in every direction, one seaward along
the cove, one slant across the hill, and so on, so that in half a
minute not a sign of them remained but Pew. Him they had deserted, whether in sheer panic or out of revenge for his ill words
and blows, I know not; but there he remained behind, tapping up
and down the road in a frenzy, and groping and calling for his
comrades. Finally he took the wrong turn, and ran a few steps past
me, towards the hamlet, crying:—

"Johnny, Black Dog, Dirk," and other names, "you won't leave
old Pew, mates—not old Pew!"

Just then the noise of horses topped the rise, and four or five
riders came in sight in the moonlight, and swept at full gallop
down the slope.

At this Pew saw his error, turned with a scream, and ran straight
for the ditch, into which he rolled. But he was on his feet again
in a second, and made another dash, now utterly bewildered, right
under the nearest of the coming horses.

The rider tried to save him, but in vain. Down went Pew with a
cry that rang high into the night; and the four hoofs trampled and
spurned him and passed by. He fell on his side, then gently collapsed upon his face, and moved no more.

I leapt to my feet and hailed the riders. They were pulling up, at any rate, horrified at the accident; and I soon saw what they were. One, tailing out behind the rest, was a lad that had gone from the hamlet to Dr. Livesey's; the rest were revenue officers, whom he had met by the way, and with whom he had had the intelligence to return at once. Some news of the lugger in Kitt's Hole had found its way to Supervisor Dance, and set him forth that night in our direction, and to that circumstance my mother and I owed our preservation from death.

Pew was dead, stone dead. As for my mother, when we had carried her up to the hamlet, a little cold water and salts and that soon brought her back again, and she was none the worse for her terror, though she still continued to deplore the balance of the money. In the meantime the supervisor rode on, as fast as he could, to Kitt's Hole; but his men had to dismount and grope down the dingle, leading, and sometimes supporting, their horses, and in continual fear of ambushes; so it was no great matter for surprise that when they got down to the Hole the lugger was already under way, though still close in. He hailed her. A voice replied, telling him to keep out of the moonlight, or he would get some lead in him, and at the same time a bullet whistled close by his arm. Soon after, the lugger doubled the point and disappeared. Mr. Dance stood there, as he said, "like a fish out of water," and all he could do was to despatch a man to B—— to warn the cutter. "And that," said he, "is just about as good as nothing. They've got off clean, and there's an end. Only," he added, "I'm glad I trod on Master Pew's corns"; for by this time he had heard my story.

I went back with him to the Admiral Benbow, and you cannot imagine a house in such a state of smash; the very clock had been thrown down by these fellows in their furious hunt after my mother and myself; and though nothing had actually been taken away except the captain's money-bag and a little silver from the till, I could see at once that we were ruined. Mr. Dance could make nothing of the scene.

"They got the money, you say? Well, then, Hawkins, what in fortune were they after? More money, I suppose?"

"No, sir; not money, I think," replied I. "In fact, sir, I believe I have the thing in my breast-pocket; and, to tell you the truth, I should like to get it put in safety."

"To be sure, boy; quite right," said he. "I'll take it, if you like."

"I thought, perhaps, Dr. Livesey——" I began.

"Perfectly right," he interrupted, very cheerily, "perfectly right—a gentleman and a magistrate. And, now I come to think of it, I might as well ride round there myself and report to him or squire. Master Pew's dead, when all's done; not that I regret it, but he's dead, you see, and people will make it out against an officer of his Majesty's revenue, if make it out they can. Now, I tell you, Hawkins: if you like, I'll take you along."

I thanked him heartily for the offer, and we walked back to the hamlet where the horses were. By the time I had told mother of my purpose they were all in the saddle.

"Dogger," said Mr. Dance, "you have a good horse; take up this lad behind you."

As soon as I was mounted, holding on to Dogger's belt, the supervisor gave the word, and the party struck out at a bouncing trot on to the road to Dr. Livesey's house.

6. *The Captain's Papers*

WE RODE HARD ALL THE WAY, TILL WE DREW UP BEFORE DR. LIVE-sey's door. The house was all dark to the front.

Mr. Dance told me to jump down and knock, and Dogger gave me a stirrup to descend by. The door was opened almost at once by the maid.

"Is Dr. Livesey in?" I asked.

No, she said; he had come home in the afternoon, but had gone up to the Hall to dine and pass the evening with the squire.

"So there we go, boys," said Mr. Dance.

This time, as the distance was short, I did not mount, but ran with Dogger's stirrup-leather to the lodge gates, and up the long, leafless, moonlit avenue to where the white line of the Hall buildings looked on either hand on great old gardens. Here Mr. Dance dismounted, and, taking me along with him, was admitted at a word into the house.

The servant led us down a matted passage, and showed us at the end into a great library, all lined with bookcases and busts upon the top of them, where the squire and Dr. Livesey sat, pipe in hand, on either side of a bright fire.

I had never seen the squire so near at hand. He was a tall man, over six feet high, and broad in proportion, and he had a bluff, rough-and-ready face, all roughened and reddened and lined in his long travels. His eyebrows were very black, and moved readily, and this gave him a look of some temper, not bad, you would say, but quick and high.

"Come in, Mr. Dance," says he, very stately and condescending.

"Good-evening, Dance," says the doctor, with a nod. "And good-evening to you, friend Jim. What good wind brings you here?"

The supervisor stood up straight and stiff, and told his story like a lesson: and you should have seen how the two gentlemen leaned forward and looked at each other, and forgot to smoke in their surprise and interest. When they heard how my mother went back to the inn, Dr. Livesey fairly slapped his thigh, and the squire cried "Bravo!" and broke his long pipe against the grate. Long before it was done, Mr. Trelawney (that, you will remember, was the squire's name), had got up from his seat, and was striding about the room, and the doctor, as if to hear the better, had taken off his powdered wig, and sat there, looking very strange indeed with his own close-cropped black poll.

At last Mr. Dance finished the story.

"Mr. Dance," said the squire, "you are a very noble fellow. And as for riding down that black, atrocious miscreant, I regard it as an act of virtue, sir, like stamping on a cockroach. This lad Hawkins is a trump, I perceive. Hawkins, will you ring that bell? Mr. Dance must have some ale."

"And so, Jim," said the doctor, "you have the thing that they were after, have you?"

"Here it is, sir," said I, and gave him the oilskin packet.

The doctor looked it all over, as if his fingers were itching to open it; but, instead of doing that, he put it quietly in the pocket of his coat.

"Squire," said he, "when Dance has had his ale, he must, of course, be off on his Majesty's service; but I mean to keep Jim Hawkins here to sleep at my house, and, with your permission, I propose we should have up the cold pie, and let him sup."

"As you will, Livesey," said the squire; "Hawkins has earned better than cold pie."

So a big pigeon pie was brought in and put on a side-table, and I made a hearty supper, for I was as hungry as a hawk, while Mr. Dance was further complimented, and at last dismissed.

"And now, squire," said the doctor.

"And now, Livesey," said the squire in the same breath.

"One at a time, one at a time," laughed Dr. Livesey. "You have heard of this Flint, I suppose?"

"Heard of him!" cried the squire. "Heard of him, you say! He was the bloodthirstiest buccaneer that sailed. Blackbeard was a child to Flint. The Spaniards were so prodigiously afraid of him, that, I tell you, sir, I was sometimes proud he was an Englishman. I've seen his top-sails with these eyes, off Trinidad, and the cowardly son of a rum-puncheon that I sailed with put back—put back, sir, into Port of Spain."

"Well, I've heard of him myself, in England," said the doctor. "But the point is, had he money?"

"Money!" cried the squire. "Have you heard the story? What were these villains after but money? What do they care for but money? For what would they risk their rascal carcasses but money?"

"That we shall soon know," replied the doctor. "But you are so confoundedly hot-headed and exclamatory that I cannot get a word in. What I want to know is this: Supposing that I have here in my pocket some clue to where Flint buried his treasure, will that treasure amount to much?"

"Amount, sir!" cried the squire. "It will amount to this; if we have the clue you talk about, I fit out a ship in Bristol dock, and take you and Hawkins here along, and I'll have that treasure if I search a year."

"Very well," said the doctor. "Now, then, if Jim is agreeable, we'll open the packet," and he laid it before him on the table.

The bundle was sewn together, and the doctor had to get out his instrument-case, and cut the stitches with his medical scissors. It contained two things—a book and a sealed paper.

"First of all we'll try the book," observed the doctor.

The squire and I were both peering over his shoulder as he opened it, for Dr. Livesey had kindly motioned me to come round from the side-table, where I had been eating, to enjoy the sport of the search. On the first page there were only some scraps of writing, such as a man with a pen in his hand might make for idleness or practice. One was the same as the tattoo mark, "Billy Bones his fancy"; then there was "Mr. W. Bones, mate." "No more rum." "Off Palm Key he got itt"; and some other snatches, mostly single words and unintelligible. I could not help wondering who it was that had "got itt," and what "itt" was that he got. A knife in his back as like as not.

"Not much instruction there," said Dr. Livesey, as he passed on.

The next ten or twelve pages were filled with a curious series of entries. There was a date at one end of the line and at the other a sum of money, as in common account-books; but instead of explanatory writing, only a varying number of crosses between the two. On the 12th of June, 1745, for instance, a sum of seventy pounds had plainly become due to some one, and there was nothing but six crosses to explain the cause. In a few cases, to be sure, the name of a place would be added, as "Offe Caraccas"; or a mere entry of latitude and longitude, as "62° 17′ 20″, 19° 2′ 40″."

The record lasted over nearly twenty years, the amount of the separate entries growing larger as time went on, and at the end a grand total had been made out after five or six wrong additions, and these words appended, "Bones, his pile."

"I can't make head or tail of this," said Dr. Livesey.

"The thing is as clear as noonday," cried the squire. "This is the black-hearted hound's account-book. These crosses stand for the names of ships or towns that they sank or plundered. The sums are the scoundrel's share, and where he feared an ambiguity, you see he added something clearer. 'Offe Caraccas,' now; you see, here was some unhappy vessel boarded off that coast. God help the poor souls that manned her—coral long ago."

"Right!" said the doctor. "See what it is to be a traveller. Right! And the amounts increase, you see, as he rose in rank."

There was little else in the volume but a few bearings of places noted in the blank leaves towards the end, and a table for reducing French, English, and Spanish moneys to a common value.

"Thrifty man!" cried the doctor. "He wasn't the one to be cheated."

"And now," said the squire, "for the other."

The paper had been sealed in several places with a thimble by way of seal; the very thimble, perhaps, that I had found in the captain's pocket. The doctor opened the seals with great care, and there fell out the map of an island, with latitude and longitude, soundings, names of hills, and bays, and inlets, and every particular that would be needed to bring a ship to a safe anchorage upon its shores. It was about nine miles long and five across, shaped, you might say, like a fat dragon standing up, and had two fine land-locked harbours, and a hill in the centre part marked "The Spy-glass." There were several additions of a later date; but, above all, three crosses of red ink—two on the north part of the island, one in the south-west, and, beside this last, in the same red ink, and in a small, neat hand, very different from the captain's tottery charac-ters, these words: "Bulk of treasure here."

Over on the back the same hand had written this further in-formation:—

"Tall tree, Spy-glass shoulder, bearing a point to the N. of N.N.E.

"Skeleton Island E.S.E. and by E.

"Ten feet.

"The bar silver is in the north cache; you can find it by the trend of the east hummock, ten fathoms south of the black crag with the face on it.

"The arms are easy found, in the sand hill, N. point of north inlet cape, bearing E. and a quarter N.

"J. F."

That was all; but brief as it was, and, to me, incomprehensible, it filled the squire and Dr. Livesey with delight.

"Livesey," said the squire, "you will give up this wretched prac-tice at once. To-morrow I start for Bristol. In three weeks' time—three weeks!—two weeks—ten days—we'll have the best ship, sir, and the choicest crew in England. Hawkins shall come as cabin-boy. You'll make a famous cabin-boy, Hawkins. You, Livesey, are ship's doctor; I am admiral. We'll take Redruth, Joyce, and Hunter. We'll have favourable winds, a quick passage, and not the least difficulty in finding the spot, and money to eat—to roll in—to play duck and drake with ever after."

"Trelawney," said the doctor, "I'll go with you; and, I'll go bail for it, so will Jim, and be a credit to the undertaking. There's only one man I'm afraid of."

"And who's that?" cried the squire. "Name the dog, sir!"

"You," replied the doctor; "for you cannot hold your tongue. We are not the only men who know of this paper. These fellows who attacked the inn to-night—bold, desperate blades, for sure—and the rest who stayed aboard that lugger, and more, I dare say, not far off, are, one and all, through thick and thin, bound that they'll get that money. We must none of us go alone till we get to sea. Jim and I shall stick together in the meanwhile; you'll take Joyce and Hunter when you ride to Bristol, and, from first to last, not one of us must breathe a word of what we've found."

"Livesey," returned the squire, "you are always in the right of it. I'll be as silent as the grave."

PART TWO

THE SEA COOK

★

7. *I Go to Bristol*

IT WAS LONGER THAN THE SQUIRE IMAGINED ERE WE WERE READY for the sea, and none of our first plans—not even Dr. Livesey's, of keeping me beside him—could be carried out as we intended. The doctor had to go to London for a physician to take charge of his practice; the squire was hard at work at Bristol; and I lived on at the Hall under the charge of old Redruth, the gamekeeper, almost a prisoner, but full of sea-dreams and the most charming anticipations of strange islands and adventures. I brooded by the hour together over the map, all the details of which I well remembered. Sitting by the fire in the housekeeper's room, I approached that island in my fancy, from every possible direction; I explored every acre of its surface; I climbed a thousand times to that tall hill they call the Spy-glass, and from the top enjoyed the most wonderful and changing prospects. Sometimes the isle was thick with savages, with whom we fought; sometimes full of dangerous animals that hunted us; but in all my fancies nothing occurred to me so strange and tragic as our actual adventures.

So the weeks passed on, till one fine day there came a letter addressed to Dr. Livesey, with this addition, "To be opened, in the case of his absence, by Tom Redruth, or young Hawkins." Obeying this order, we found, or rather I found—for the gamekeeper was a poor hand at reading anything but print—the following important news:—

> "Old Anchor Inn, Bristol,
> "March 1, 17—.

"Dear Livesey,—As I do not know whether you are at the Hall or still in London, I send this in double to both places.

"The ship is bought and fitted. She lies at anchor, ready for sea. You never imagined a sweeter schooner—a child might sail her—two hundred tons; name *Hispaniola.*

"I got her through my old friend, Blandly, who has proved himself throughout the most surprising trump. The admirable fellow literally slaved in my interest, and so, I may say, did every one in Bristol, as soon as they got wind of what port we sailed for—treasure, I mean."

"Redruth," said I, interrupting the letter, "Doctor Livesey will not like that. The squire has been talking, after all."

"Well, who's a better right?" growled the gamekeeper. "A pretty rum go if squire ain't to talk for Doctor Livesey, I should think."

At that I gave up all attempt at commentary, and read straight on:—

"Blandly himself found the *Hispaniola,* and by the most admirable management got her for the merest trifle. There is a class of men in Bristol monstrously prejudiced against Blandly. They go the length of declaring that this honest creature would do anything for money, that the *Hispaniola* belonged to him, and that he sold it me absurdly high—the most transparent calumnies. None of them dare, however, to deny the merits of the ship.

"So far there was not a hitch. The workpeople, to be sure—riggers and what not—were most annoyingly slow; but time cured that. It was the crew that troubled me.

"I wished a round score of men—in case of natives, buccaneers, or the odious French—and I had the worry of the deuce itself to find so much as half a dozen, till the most remarkable stroke of fortune brought me the very man that I required.

"I was standing on the dock, when, by the merest accident, I fell in talk with him. I found he was an old sailor, kept a public-house, knew all the seafaring men in Bristol, had lost his health ashore, and wanted a good berth as cook to get to sea again. He had hobbled down there that morning, he said, to get a smell of the salt.

"I was monstrously touched—so would you have been—and, out of pure pity, I engaged him on the spot to be ship's cook. Long John Silver, he is called, and has lost a leg; but that I regarded as a recommendation, since he lost it in his country's service under the immortal Hawke. He has no pension, Livesey. Imagine the abominable age we live in!

"Well, sir, I thought I had only found a cook, but it was a crew I had discovered. Between Silver and myself we got together in a few days a company of the toughest old salts imaginable—not pretty to look at, but fellows by their faces, of the most indomitable spirit. I declare we could fight a frigate.

"Long John even got rid of two out of the six or seven I had already engaged. He showed me in a moment that they were just the sort of fresh-water swabs we had to fear in an adventure of importance.

"I am in the most magnificent health and spirits, eating like a bull, sleeping like a tree, yet I shall not enjoy a moment till I hear my old tarpaulins tramping round the capstan. Seaward ho! Hang the treasure! It's the glory of the sea that has turned my head. So now, Livesey, come post; do not lose an hour, if you respect me.

"Let young Hawkins go at once to see his mother, with Redruth for a guard; and then both come full speed to Bristol.
"*John Trelawney.*"

"*Postscript.*—I did not tell you that Blandly, who, by the way, is to send a consort after us if we don't turn up by the end of August, had found an admirable fellow for sailing master—a stiff man, which I regret, but, in all other respects, a treasure. Long John Silver unearthed a very competent man for a mate, a man named Arrow. I have a boatswain who pipes, Livesey; so things shall go man-o'-war fashion on board the good ship *Hispaniola.*

"I forgot to tell you that Silver is a man of substance; I know of my own knowledge that he has a banker's account, which has never been overdrawn. He leaves his wife to manage the inn; and as she is a woman of colour, a pair of old bachelors like you and I may be excused for guessing that it is the wife, quite as much as the health, that send him back to roving.
"*J. T.*

"P.P.S.—Hawkins may stay one night with his mother.
"*J. T.*"

You can fancy the excitement into which that letter put me. was half beside myself with glee; and if ever I despised a man, it was old Tom Redruth, who could do nothing but grumble and lament. Any of the under gamekeepers would gladly have changed places with him; but such was not the squire's pleasure, and the squire's pleasure was like law among them all. Nobody but old Redruth would have dared so much as even to grumble.

The next morning he and I set out on foot for the Admiral Benbow, and there I found my mother in good health and spirits. The captain, who had so long been a cause of so much discomfort, was gone where the wicked cease from troubling. The squire had had everything repaired, and the public rooms and the sign repainted, and had added some furniture—above all, a beautiful arm-chair for mother in the bar. He had found her a boy as an apprentice also, so that she should not want help while I was gone.

It was on seeing that boy that I understood, for the first time, my situation. I had thought up to that moment of the adventures before me, not at all of the home I was leaving; and now at the sight of this clumsy stranger, who was to stay here in my place beside my mother, I had my first attack of tears. I am afraid I led that boy a dog's life; for as he was new to the work, I had a hundred opportunities of setting him right and putting him down, and I was not slow to profit by them.

The night passed, and the next day, after dinner, Redruth and I were afoot again, and on the road. I said good-bye to mother and the cove where I had lived since I was born, and the dear old Admiral Benbow—since he was repainted, no longer quite so dear. One of my last thoughts was of the captain, who had so often strode along the beach with his cocked hat, his sabre-cut cheek, and his old brass telescope. Next moment we had turned the corner, and my home was out of sight.

The mail picked us up about dusk at the Royal George on the heath. I was wedged in between Redruth and a stout old gentleman, and in spite of the swift motion and the cold night air, I must have dozed a great deal from the very first, and then slept like a log up hill and down dale through stage after stage; for when I was awakened at last, it was by a punch in the ribs, and I opened my eyes to find that we were standing still before a large building in a city street, and that the day had already broken a long time.

"Where are we?" I asked.

"Bristol," said Tom. "Get down."

Mr. Trelawney had taken up his residence at an inn far down the docks, to superintend the work upon the schooner. Thither we had now to walk, and our way, to my great delight, lay along the quays and beside the great multitude of ships of all sizes and rigs and nations. In one, sailors were singing at their work; in another, there were men aloft, high over my head, hanging to threads that seemed no thicker than a spider's. Though I had lived by the shore all my life, I seemed never to have been near the sea till then. The smell of tar and salt was something new. I saw the most wonderful figureheads, that had all been far over the ocean. I saw, besides, many old sailors, with rings in their ears, and whiskers curled in ringlets, and tarry pigtails, and their swaggering, clumsy sea-walk; and if I had seen as many kings or archbishops I could not have been more delighted.

And I was going to sea myself; to sea in a schooner, with a piping boatswain, and pig-tailed singing seamen; to sea, bound for an unknown island, and to seek for buried treasures!

While I was still in this delightful dream, we came suddenly in front of a large inn, and met Squire Trelawney, all dressed out like a sea-officer, in stout blue cloth, coming out of the door with a smile on his face, and a capital imitation of a sailor's walk.

"Here you are," he cried, "and the doctor came last night from London. Bravo! the ship's company complete!"

"Oh, sir," cried I, "when do we sail?"

"Sail!" says he. "We sail to-morrow!"

8. *At the Sign of the Spy-glass*

W HEN I HAD DONE BREAKFASTING THE SQUIRE GAVE ME A NOTE addressed to John Silver, at the sign of the Spy-glass, and told me I should easily find the place by following the line of the docks, and keeping a bright look-out for a little tavern with a large brass telescope for sign. I set off, overjoyed at this opportunity to see some more of the ships and seamen, and picked my way among a great crowd of people and carts and bales, for the dock was now at its busiest, until I found the tavern in question.

It was a bright enough little place of entertainment. The sign was newly painted; the windows had neat red curtains; the floor was cleanly sanded. There was a street on either side. and an open door on both, which made the large, low room pretty clear to see in, in spite of clouds of tobacco smoke.

The customers were mostly seafaring men; and they talked so loudly that I hung at the door, almost afraid to enter.

As I was waiting, a man came out of a side room, and, at a glance, I was sure he must be Long John. His left leg was cut off close by the hip, and under the left shoulder he carried a crutch, which he managed with wonderful dexterity, hopping about upon it like a bird. He was very tall and strong, with a face as big as a ham—plain and pale, but intelligent and smiling. Indeed, he seemed in the most cheerful spirits, whistling as he moved about among the tables, with a merry word or a slap on the shoulder for the more favoured of his guests.

Now, to tell you the truth, from the very first mention of Long John in Squire Trelawney's letter, I had taken a fear in my mind that he might prove to be the very one-legged sailor whom I had watched for so long at the old Benbow. But one look at the man before me was enough. I had seen the captain, and Black Dog, and the blind man Pew, and I thought I knew what a buccaneer was like—a very different creature, according to me, from this clean and pleasant-tempered landlord.

I plucked up courage at once, crossed the threshold, and walked right up to the man where he stood, propped on his crutch, talking to a customer.

"Mr. Silver, sir?" I asked, holding out the note.

"Yes, my lad," said he; "such is my name, to be sure. And who may you be?" And then as he saw the squire's letter, he seemed to me to give something almost like a start.

"Oh!" said he, quite loud, and offering his hand, "I see. You are our new cabin-boy; pleased I am to see you."

And he took my hand in his large firm grasp.

Just then one of the customers at the far side rose suddenly and made for the door. It was close by him, and he was out in the street in a moment. But his hurry had attracted my notice, and I recognised him at a glance. It was the tallow-faced man, wanting two fingers, who had come first to the Admiral Benbow.

"Oh," I cried, "stop him! It's Black Dog!"

"I don't care two coppers who he is," cried Silver. "But he hasn't paid his score. Harry, run and catch him."

One of the others who was nearest the door leaped up, and started in pursuit.

'If he were Admiral Hawke he shall pay his score," cried Silver; and then, relinquishing my hand—"Who did you say he was?" he asked. "Black what?"

"Dog, sir," said I. "Has Mr. Trelawney not told you of the buccaneers? He was one of them."

"So?" cried Silver. "In my house! Ben, run and help Harry. One of those swabs, was he? Was that you drinking with him, Morgan? Step up here."

The man whom he called Morgan—an old, gray-haired, mahogany-faced sailor—came forward pretty sheepishly, rolling his quid.

"Now, Morgan," said Long John, very sternly, "you never clapped your eyes on that Black—Black Dog before, did you, now?"

"Not I, sir," said Morgan, with a salute.

"You didn't know his name, did you?"

"No, sir."

"By the powers, Tom Morgan, it's as good for you!" exclaimed the landlord. "If you had been mixed up with the like of that, you would never have put another foot in my house, you may lay to that. And what was he saying to you?"

"I don't rightly know, sir," answered Morgan.

"Do you call that a head on your shoulders, or a blessed dead eye?" cried Long John. "Don't rightly know, don't you! Perhaps you don't happen to rightly know who you was speaking to, perhaps? Come, now, what was he jawing—v'yages, cap'ns, ships? Pipe up! What was it?"

"We was a-talkin' of keel-hauling," answered Morgan.

"Keel-hauling, was you? And a mighty suitable thing, too, and you may lay to that. Get back to your place for a lubber, Tom."

And then, as Morgan rolled back to his seat, Silver added to me, in a confidential whisper, that was very flattering, as I thought:—

"He's quite an honest man, Tom Morgan; on'y stupid. And now," he ran on again aloud, "let's see—Black Dog? No, I don't know the name, not I. Yet I kind of think I've—yes, I've seen the swab. He used to come here with a blind beggar, he used."

"That he did, you may be sure," said I. "I knew that blind man, too. His name was Pew."

"It was!" cried Silver, now quite excited. "Pew! That were his name for certain. Ah, he looked a shark, he did. If we run down this Black Dog, now, there'll be news for Cap'n Trelawney! Ben's a good runner; few seamen run better than Ben. He should run him down, hand over hand, by the powers! He talked o' keel-hauling, did he? *I'll* keel-haul him!"

All the time he was jerking out these phrases he was stumping up and down the tavern on his crutch, slapping tables with his hand, and giving such a show of excitement as would have convinced an Old Bailey judge or a Bow Street runner. My suspicions had been thoroughly reawakened on finding Black Dog at the Spyglass, and I watched the cook narrowly. But he was too deep, and too ready, and too clever for me, and by the time the two men had come back out of breath, and confessed that they had lost the track in a crowd, and been scolded like thieves, I would have gone bail for the innocence of Long John Silver.

"See here, now, Hawkins," said he, "here's a blessed hard thing on a man like me, now, ain't it? There's Cap'n Trelawney—what's he to think? Here I have this confounded son of a Dutchman sitting in my own house, drinking of my own rum! Here you comes and tells me of it plain; and here I let him give us all the slip before my blessed dead-lights! Now, Hawkins, you do me justice with the cap'n. You're a lad, you are, but you're as smart as paint. I see that when you first came in. Now, here it is: What could I do, with this old timber I hobble on? When I was an A.B. master mariner I'd have come up alongside of him, hand over hand, and broached him to in a brace of old shakes, I would; but now——"

And then, all of a sudden, he stopped, and his jaw dropped as though he had remembered something.

"The score!" he burst out. "Three goes o' rum! Why, shiver my timbers, if I hadn't forgotten my score!"

And, falling on a bench, he laughed until the tears ran down his cheeks. I could not help joining; and we laughed together, peal after peal, until the tavern rang again.

"Why, what a precious old sea-calf I am!" he said at last, wiping his cheeks. "You and me should get on well, Hawkins, for I'll take my davy I should be rated ship's boy. But, come now, stand by to go about. This won't do. Dooty is dooty, messmates. I'll put on my old cocked hat, and step along of you to Cap'n Trelawney, and report this here affair. For, mind you, it's serious, young Hawkins; and neither you nor me's come out of it with what I should make so bold as to call credit. Nor you neither, says you; not smart—none of the pair of us smart. But dash my buttons! that was a good 'un about my score."

And he began to laugh again, and that so heartily, that, though I did not see the joke as he did, I was again obliged to join him in his mirth.

On our little walk along the quays, he made himself the most interesting companion, telling me about the different ships that we passed by, their rig, tonnage, and nationality, explaining the work that was going forward—how one was discharging, another taking in cargo, and a third making ready for sea; and every now and then telling me some little anecdote of ships or seamen, or repeating a nautical phrase till I had learned it perfectly. I began to see that here was one of the best of possible shipmates.

When we got to the inn, the squire and Dr. Livesey were seated together, finishing a quart of ale with a toast in it, before they should go aboard the schooner on a visit of inspection.

Long John told the story from first to last with a great deal of spirit and the most perfect truth. "That was how it were, now, weren't it, Hawkins?" he would say, now and again, and I could always bear him entirely out.

The two gentlemen regretted that Black Dog had got away; but we all agreed there was nothing to be done, and after he had been complimented, Long John took up his crutch and departed.

"All hands aboard by four this afternoon," shouted the squire after him.

"Ay, ay, sir," cried the cook, in the passage.

"Well, squire," said Dr. Livesey, "I don't put much faith in your discoveries, as a general thing; but I will say this, John Silver suits me."

"The man's a perfect trump," declared the squire.

"And now," added the doctor, "Jim may come on board with us, may he not?"

"To be sure he may," says squire. "Take your hat, Hawkins, and we'll see the ship."

9.   *Powder and Arms*

T HE HISPANIOLA LAY SOME WAY OUT, AND WE WENT UNDER THE figureheads and round the sterns of many other ships, and their cables sometimes grated underneath our keel, and sometimes swung above us. At last, however, we got alongside, and were met and saluted as we stepped aboard by the mate, Mr. Arrow, a brown old sailor, with earrings in his ears and a squint. He and the squire were very thick and friendly, but I soon observed that things were not the same between Mr. Trelawney and the captain.

This last was a sharp-looking man, who seemed angry with everybody on board, and was soon to tell us why, for we had hardly got down into the cabin when a sailor followed us.

"Captain Smollett, sir, axing to speak with you," said he.

"I am always at the captain's order. Show him in," said the squire.

The captain, who was close behind his messenger, entered at once and shut the door behind him.

"Well, Captain Smollett, what have you to say? All well, I hope; all shipshape and seaworthy."

"Well, sir," said the captain, "better speak plain, I believe, even at the risk of offence. I don't like this cruise; I don't like the men; and I don't like my officer. That's short and sweet."

"Perhaps, sir, you don't like the ship?" inquired the squire, very angry, as I could see.

"I can't speak as to that, sir, not having seen her tried," said the captain. "She seems a clever craft; more I can't say."

"Possibly, sir, you may not like your employer either?" says the squire.

But here Dr. Livesey cut in.

"Stay a bit," said he, "stay a bit. No use of such questions as that but to produce ill-feeling. The captain has said too much, or he has said too little, and I'm bound to say that I require an explanation of his words. You don't, you say, like this cruise. Now, why?"

"I was engaged, sir, on what we call sealed orders, to sail this ship for that gentleman where he should bid me," said the captain. "So far so good. But now I find that every man before the mast knows more than I do. I don't call that fair, now, do you?"

"No," said Dr. Livesey, "I don't."

"Next," said the captain, "I learn we are going after treasure—hear it from my own hands, mind you. Now, treasure is ticklish work; I don't like treasure voyages on any account; and I don't like them, above all, when they are secret, and when (begging your pardon, Mr. Trelawney) the secret has been told to the parrot."

"Silver's parrot?" asked the squire.

"It's a way of speaking," said the captain. "Blabbed, I mean. It's my belief neither of you gentlemen know what you are about; but I'll tell you my way of it—life or death, and a close run."

"That is all clear, and, I dare say, true enough," replied Dr. Livesey. "We take the risk; but we are not so ignorant as you believe us. Next, you say you don't like the crew. Are they not good seamen?"

"I don't like them, sir," returned Captain Smollett. "And I think I should have had the choosing of my own hands, if you go to that."

"Perhaps you should," replied the doctor. "My friend should, perhaps, have taken you along with him; but the slight, if there be one, was unintentional. And you don't like Mr. Arrow?"

"I don't, sir. I believe he's a good seaman; but he's too free with the crew to be a good officer. A mate should keep himself to himself—shouldn't drink with the men before the mast!"

"Do you mean he drinks?" cried the squire.

"No, sir," replied the captain; "only that he's too familiar."

"Well, now, and the short and long of it, captain?" asked the doctor. "Tell us what you want."

"Well, gentlemen, are you determined to go on this cruise?"

"Like iron," answered the squire.

"Very good," said the captain. "Then, as you've heard me very patiently, saying things that I could not prove, hear me a few words more. They are putting the powder and the arms in the fore hold. Now, you have a good place under the cabin; why not put them there?—first point. Then you are bringing four of your own people with you, and they tell me some of them are to be berthed forward. Why not give them the berths here beside the cabin?—second point."

"Any more?" asked Mr. Trelawney.

"One more," said the captain. "There's been too much blabbing already."

"Far too much," agreed the doctor.

"I'll tell you what I've heard myself," continued Captain Smollett: "that you have a map of an island; that there's crosses on

the map to show where treasure is; and that the island lies——"
And then he named the latitude and longitude exactly.

"I never told that," cried the squire, "to a soul!"

"The hands know it, sir," returned the captain.

"Livesey, that must have been you or Hawkins," cried the squire.

"It doesn't much matter who it was," replied the doctor. And I could see that neither he nor the captain paid much regard to Mr. Trelawney's protestations. Neither did I, to be sure, he was so loose a talker; yet in this case I believe he was really right, and that nobody had told the situation of the island.

"Well, gentlemen," continued the captain, "I don't know who has this map; but I make it a point, it shall be kept secret even from me and Mr. Arrow. Otherwise I would ask you to let me resign."

"I see," said the doctor. "You wish us to keep this matter dark, and to make a garrison of the stern part of the ship, manned with my friend's own people, and provided with all the arms and powder on board. In other words, you fear a mutiny."

"Sir," said Captain Smollett, "with no intention to take offence, I deny your right to put words into my mouth. No captain, sir, would be justified in going to sea at all if he had ground enough to say that. As for Mr. Arrow. I believe him thoroughly honest; some of the men are the same; all may be, for what I know. But I am responsible for the ship's safety and the life of every man Jack aboard of her. I see things going, as I think, not quite right. And I ask you to take certain precautions, or let me resign my berth. And that's all."

"Captain Smollett," began the doctor, with a smile, "did ever you hear the fable of the mountain and the mouse? You'll excuse me, I dare say, but you remind me of that fable. When you came in here I'll stake my wig you meant more than this."

"Doctor," said the captain, "you are smart. When I came in here I meant to get discharged. I had no thought that Mr. Trelawney would hear a word."

"No more I would," cried the squire. "Had Livesey not been here I should have seen you to the deuce. As it is, I have heard you. I will do as you desire; but I think the worse of you."

"That's as you please, sir," said the captain. "You'll find I do my duty."

And with that he took his leave.

"Trelawney," said the doctor, "contrary to all my notions, I believe you have managed to get two honest men on board with you —that man and John Silver."

"Silver, if you like," cried the squire; "but as for that intolerable humbug, I declare I think his conduct unmanly, unsailorly, and downright un-English."

"Well," says the doctor, "we shall see."

When we came on deck, the men had begun already to take out the arms and powder, yo-ho-ing at their work, while the captain and Mr. Arrow stood by superintending.

The new arrangement was quite to my liking. The whole schooner had been overhauled; six berths had been made astern, out of what had been the after-part of the main hold; and this set of cabins was only joined to the galley and forecastle by a sparred passage on the port side. It had been originally meant that the captain, Mr. Arrow, Hunter, Joyce, the doctor, and the squire, were to occupy these six berths. Now, Redruth and I were to get two of them, and Mr. Arrow and the captain were to sleep on deck in the companion, which had been enlarged on each side till you might almost have called it a round-house. Very low it was still, of course; but there was room to swing two hammocks, and even the mate seemed pleased with the arrangement. Even he, perhaps, had been doubtful as to the crew, but that is only guess; for, as you shall hear, we had not long the benefit of his opinion.

We were all hard at work, changing the powder and the berths, when the last man or two, and Long John along with them, came off in a shoreboat.

The cook came up the side like a monkey for cleverness, and, as soon as he saw what was doing, "So ho, mates!" says he, "what's this?"

"We're a-changing of the powder, Jack," answers one.

"Why, by the powers," cried Long John, "if we do, we'll miss the morning tide!"

"My orders!" said the captain shortly. "You may go below, my man. Hands will want supper."

"Ay, ay, sir," answered the cook; and, touching his forelock, he disappeared at once in the direction of his galley.

"That's a good man, captain," said the doctor.

"Very likely, sir," replied Captain Smollett. "Easy with that, men—easy," he ran on, to the fellows who were shifting the powder; and then suddenly observing me examining the swivel we carried amidships, a long brass nine—"Here, you ship's boy," he cried, "out o' that! Off with you to the cook and get some work."

And then, as I was hurrying off, I heard him say, quite loudly, to the doctor:—

"I'll have no favourites on my ship."

I assure you I was quite of the squire's way of thinking, and hated the captain deeply.

10.   *The Voyage*

ALL THAT NIGHT WE WERE IN A GREAT BUSTLE GETTING THINGS stowed in their place, and boatfuls of the squire's friends, Mr. Blandly and the like, coming off to wish him a good voyage and a safe return. We never had a night at the Admiral Benbow when I had half the work; and I was dog-tired when, a little before dawn, the boatswain sounded his pipe, and the crew began to man the capstan-bars. I might have been twice as weary, yet I would not have left the deck; all was so new and interesting to me—the brief commands, the shrill note of the whistle, the men bustling to their places in the glimmer of the ship's lanterns.

"Now, Barbecue, tip us a stave," cried one voice.

"The old one," cried another.

"Ay, ay, mates," said Long John, who was standing by, with his crutch under his arm, and at once broke out in the air and words I knew so well:—

"Fifteen men on The Dead Man's Chest—"

And then the whole crew bore chorus:—

"Yo-ho-ho, and a bottle of rum!"

And at the third "ho!" drove the bars before them with a will.

Even at that exciting moment it carried me back to the old Admiral Benbow in a second; and I seemed to hear the voice of the captain piping in the chorus. But soon the anchor was short up; soon it was hanging dripping at the bows; soon the sails began to draw, and the land and shipping to flit by on either side; and before I could lie down to snatch an hour of slumber the *Hispaniola* had begun her voyage to the Isle of Treasure.

I am not going to relate that voyage in detail. It was fairly prosperous. The ship proved to be a good ship, the crew were capable seamen, and the captain thoroughly understood his business. But before we came the length of Treasure Island, two or three things had happened which require to be known.

Mr. Arrow, first of all, turned out even worse than the captain had feared. He had no command among the men, and people did what they pleased with him. But that was by no means the worst of it; for after a day or two at sea he began to appear on deck with hazy eye, red cheeks, stuttering tongue, and other marks of drunkenness. Time after time he was ordered below in disgrace. Sometimes he fell and cut himself; sometimes he lay all day long in his little bunk at one side of the companion; sometimes for a day or two he would be almost sober and attend to his work at least passably.

In the meantime, we could never make out where he got the drink. That was the ship's mystery. Watch him as we pleased, we could do nothing to solve it; and when we asked him to his face, he would only laugh, if he were drunk, and if he were sober, deny solemnly that he ever tasted anything but water.

He was not only useless as an officer, and a bad influence amongst the men, but it was plain that at this rate he must soon kill himself outright; so nobody was much surprised, nor very sorry, when one dark night, with a head sea, he disappeared entirely and was seen no more.

"Overboard!" said the captain. "Well, gentlemen, that saves the trouble of putting him in irons."

But there we were, without a mate; and it was necessary, of course, to advance one of the men. The boatswain, Job Anderson, was the likeliest man aboard, and, though he kept his old title, he served in a way as mate. Mr. Trelawney had followed the sea, and his knowledge made him very useful, for he often took a watch himself in easy weather. And the coxswain, Israel Hands, was a careful, wily, old experienced seaman, who could be trusted at a pinch with almost anything.

He was a great confidant of Long John Silver, and so the mention of his name leads me on to speak of our ship's cook, Barbecue, as the men called him.

Aboard ship he carried his crutch by a lanyard round his neck, to have both hands as free as possible. It was something to see him wedge the foot of the crutch against a bulkhead, and, propped against it, yielding to every movement of the ship, get on with his cooking like some one safe ashore. Still more strange was it to see him in the heaviest of weather cross the deck. He had a line or two rigged up to help him across the widest spaces—Long John's earrings, they were called; and he would hand himself from one place to another, now using the crutch, now trailing it alongside by the lanyard, as quickly as another man could walk. Yet some of the men who had sailed with him before expressed their pity to see him so reduced.

"He's no common man, Barbecue," said the coxswain to me. "He had good schooling in his young days, and can speak like a book when so minded; and brave—a lion's nothing alongside of Long John! I seen him grapple four, and knock their heads together—him unarmed."

All the crew respected and even obeyed him. He had a way of talking to each, and doing everybody some particular service. To me he was unweariedly kind; and always glad to see me in the galley, which he kept as clean as a new pin; the dishes hanging up burnished, and his parrot in a cage in one corner.

"Come away, Hawkins," he would say; "come and have a yarn with John. Nobody more welcome than yourself, my son. Sit you down and hear the news. Here's Cap'n Flint—I calls my parrot Cap'n Flint, after the famous buccaneer—here's Cap'n Flint predicting success to our v'yage. Wasn't you, cap'n?"

And the parrot would say, with great rapidity, "Pieces of eight! pieces of eight! pieces of eight!" till you wondered that it was not out of breath, or till John threw his handkerchief over the cage.

"Now, that bird," he would say, "is, may be, two hundred years old, Hawkins—they lives for ever mostly; and if anybody's seen more wickedness, it must be the devil himself. She's sailed with England, the great Cap'n England, the pirate. She's been at Madagascar, and at Malabar, and Surinam, and Providence, and Portobello. She was at the fishing up of the wrecked plate ships. It's there she learned 'Pieces of eight,' and little wonder; three hundred and fifty thousand of 'em, Hawkins! She was at the boarding of the Viceroy of the Indies out of Goa, she was; and to look at her you would think she was a babby. But you smelt powder—didn't you, cap'n?"

"Stand by to go about," the parrot would scream.

"Ah, she's a handsome craft, she is," the cook would say, and give her sugar from his pocket, and then the bird would peck at the bars and swear straight on, passing belief for wickedness. "There," John would add, "you can't touch pitch and not be mucked, lad. Here's this poor old innocent bird o' mine swearing blue fire, and none the wiser, you may lay to that. She would swear the same, in a manner of speaking, before chaplain." And John would touch his forelock with a solemn way he had, that made me think he was the best of men.

In the meantime, squire and Captain Smollett were still on pretty distant terms with one another. The squire made no bones about the matter; he despised the captain. The captain, on his part, never spoke but when he was spoken to, and then sharp and short and dry, and not a word wasted. He owned, when driven into a corner, that he seemed to have been wrong about the crew, that some of them were as brisk as he wanted to see, and all had behaved fairly well. As for the ship, he had taken a downright fancy to her. "She'll lie a point nearer the wind than a man has a right to expect of his own married wife, sir. But," he would add, "all I say is we're not home again, and I don't like the cruise."

The squire, at this, would turn away and march up and down the deck, chin in air.

"A trifle more of that man," he would say, "and I should explode."

We had some heavy weather, which only proved the qualities of the *Hispaniola*. Every man on board seemed well content, and they must have been hard to please if they had been otherwise; for it is my belief there was never a ship's company so spoiled since Noah put to sea. Double grog was going on the least excuse; there was duff on odd days, as, for instance, if the squire heard it was any man's birthday; and always a barrel of apples standing broached in the waist, for any one to help himself that had a fancy.

"Never knew good come of it yet," the captain said to Dr. Livesey. "Spoil foc's'le hands, make devils. That's my belief."

But good did come of the apple barrel, as you shall hear: for if it had not been for that, we should have had no note of warning, and might all have perished by the hand of treachery.

This was how it came about.

We had run up the trades to get the wind of the island we were after—I am not allowed to be more plain—and now we were running down for it with a bright look-out day and night. It was about the last day of our outward voyage, by the largest computation; some time that night, or, at latest, before noon on the morrow, we should sight the Treasure Island. We were heading S.S.W., and had a steady breeze abeam and a quiet sea. The *Hispaniola* rolled steadily, dipping her bowsprit now and then with a whiff of spray. All was drawing alow and aloft; every one was in the bravest spirits, because we were now so near an end of the first part of our adventure.

Now, just after sundown, when all my work was over, and I was on my way to my berth, it occurred to me that I should like an apple. I ran on deck. The watch was all forward looking out for the island. The man at the helm was watching the luff of the sail, and whistling away gently to himself; and that was the only sound excepting the swish of the sea against the bows and around the sides of the ship.

In I got bodily into the apple barrel, and found there was scarce an apple left; but, sitting down there in the dark, what with the sound of the waters and the rocking movement of the ship, I had either fallen asleep, or was on the point of doing so, when a heavy man sat down with rather a clash close by. The barrel shook as he leaned his shoulders against it, and I was just about to jump up when the man began to speak. It was Silver's voice, and, before I had heard a dozen words, I would not have shown myself for all the world, but lay there, trembling and listening, in the extreme of fear and curiosity; for from these dozen words I understood that the lives of all the honest men aboard depended upon me alone.

11. *What I Heard in the Apple Barrel*

NO, NOT I," SAID SILVER. "FLINT WAS CAP'N; I WAS QUARTER-master, along of my timber leg. The same broadside I lost my leg, old Pew lost his deadlights. It was a master surgeon, him that ampytated me—out of college and all—Latin by the bucket, and what not; but he was hanged like a dog, and sun-dried like the rest, at Corso Castle. That was Roberts's men, that was, and comed of changing names to their ships—*Royal Fortune,* and so on. Now, what a ship was christened, so let her stay, I says. So it was with the *Cassandra,* as brought us all safe home from Malabar, after England took the Viceroy of the Indies; so it was with the old *Walrus,* Flint's old ship, as I've seen a-muck with the red blood and fit to sink with gold."

"Ah!" cried another voice, that of the youngest hand on board, and evidently full of admiration, "he was the flower of the flock, was Flint!"

"Davis was a man, too, by all accounts," said Silver. "I never sailed along of him; first with England, then with Flint, that's my story; and now here on my own account, in a manner of speaking. I laid by nine hundred safe, from England, and two thousand after Flint. That ain't bad for a man before the mast—all safe in bank. 'Tain't earning now, it's saving does it, you may lay to that. Where's all England's men now? I dunno. Where's Flint's? Why, most of 'em aboard here, and glad to get the duff—been begging before that, some on 'em. Old Pew, as had lost his sight, and might have thought shame, spends twelve hundred pound in a year, like a lord in Parliament. Where is he now? Well, he's dead now and under hatches; but for two year before that, shiver my timbers! the man was starving. He begged, and he stole, and he cut throats, and starved at that, by the powers!"

"Well, it ain't much use, after all," said the young seaman.

"'Tain't much use for fools, you may lay to it—that, nor nothing," cried Silver. "But now, you look here: you're young, you are, but you're as smart as paint. I see that when I set my eyes on you, and I'll talk to you like a man."

You may imagine how I felt when I heard this abominable old rogue addressing another in the very same words of flattery as he had used to myself. I think, if I had been able, that I would have killed him through the barrel. Meantime, he ran on, little supposing he was overheard.

"Here it is about gentlemen of fortune. They lives rough, and they risk swinging, but they eat and drink like fighting-cocks, and when a cruise is done, why it's hundreds of pounds instead of hundreds of farthings in their pockets. Now, the most goes for rum and a good fling, and to sea again in their shirts. But that's not the course I lay. I puts it all away, some here, some there, and none too much anywheres, by reason of suspicion. I'm fifty, mark you; once back from this cruise, I set up gentleman in earnest. Time enough, too, says you. Ah, but I've lived easy in the meantime; never denied myself o' nothing heart desires, and slep' soft and ate dainty all my days, but when at sea. And how did I begin? Before the mast, like you!"

"Well," said the other, "but all the other money's gone now, ain't it? You daren't show face in Bristol after this."

"Why, where might you suppose it was?" asked Silver, derisively.

"At Bristol, in banks and places," answered his companion.

"It were," said the cook; "it were when we weighed anchor. But my old missis has it all by now. And the Spy-glass is sold, lease and goodwill and rigging; and the old girl's off to meet me. I would tell you where, for I trust you; but it 'ud make jealousy among the mates."

"And can you trust your missis?" asked the other.

"Gentlemen of fortune," returned the cook, "usually trusts little among themselves, and right they are, you may lay to it. But I have a way with me, I have. When a mate brings a slip on his cable— one as knows me, I mean—it won't be in the same world with old John. There was some that was feared of Pew, and some that was feared of Flint; but Flint his own self was feared of me. Feared he was, and proud. They was the roughest crew afloat, was Flint's; the devil himself would have been feared to go to sea with them. Well, now, I tell you, I'm not a boasting man, and you seen yourself how easy I keep company; but when I was quartermaster, *lambs* wasn't the word for Flint's old buccaneers. Ah, you may be sure of yourself in old John's ship."

"Well, I tell you now," replied the lad, "I didn't half a quarter like the job till I had this talk with you, John; but there's my hand on it now."

"And a brave lad you were, and smart, too," answered Silver, shaking hands so heartily that all the barrel shook, "and a finer figurehead for a gentleman of fortune I never clapped my eyes on."

By this time I had begun to understand the meaning of their terms. By a "gentleman of fortune" they plainly meant neither more nor less than a common pirate, and the little scene that I had overheard was the last act in the corruption of one of the honest hands—perhaps of the last one left aboard. But on this point I was soon to be relieved, for Silver giving a little whistle, a third man strolled up and sat down by the party.

"Dick's square," said Silver.

"Oh, I know'd Dick was square," returned the voice of the coxswain, Israel Hands. "He's no fool, is Dick." And he turned his quid and spat. "But, look here," he went on, "here's what I want to know, Barbecue: how long are we a-going to stand off and on like a blessed bumboat? I've had a'most enough o' Cap'n Smollett; he's hazed me long enough, by thunder! I want to go into thar cabin, I do. I want their pickles and wines, and that."

"Israel," said Silver, "your head ain't much account, nor ever was. But you're able to hear, I reckon; leastways, your ears is big enough. Now, here's what I say: you'll berth forward, and you'll live hard, and you'll speak soft, and you'll keep sober, till I give the word; and you may lay to that, my son."

"Well, I don't say no, do I?" growled the coxswain. "What I say is, when? That's what I say."

"When! by the powers!" cried Silver. "Well, now, if you want to know I'll tell you when. The last moment I can manage; and that's when. Here's a first-rate seaman, Cap'n Smollett, sails the blessed ship for us. Here's this squire and doctor with a map and such—I don't know where it is, do I? No more do you, says you. Well, then, I mean this squire and doctor shall find the stuff and help us to get it aboard, by the powers. Then we'll see. If I was sure of you all, sons of double Dutchmen, I'd have Cap'n Smollett navigate us half-way back again before I struck."

"Why, we're all seamen aboard here, I should think," said the lad Dick.

"We're all foc's'le hands, you mean," snapped Silver. "We can steer a course, but who's to set one? That's what all you gentlemen split on, first and last. If I had my way, I'd have Cap'n Smollett work us back into the trades at least; then we'd have no blessed miscalculations and a spoonful of water a day. But I know the sort you are. I'll finish with 'em at the island, as soon's the blunt's on board, and a pity it is. But you're never happy till you're drunk. Split my sides, I've a sick heart to sail with the likes of you!"

"Easy all, Long John," cried Israel. "Who's a-crossin' of you?"

"Why, how many tall ships, think ye, now, have I seen laid

aboard? and how many brisk lads drying in the sun at Execution Dock?" cried Silver. "And all for this same hurry and hurry and hurry. You hear me? I seen a thing or two at sea, I have. If you would on'y lay your course, and a p'nt to windward, you would ride in carriages, you would. But not you! I know you. You'll have your mouthful of rum to-morrow, and go hang."

"Everybody know'd you was a kind of a chapling, John; but there's others as could hand and steer as well as you," said Israel. "They liked a bit o' fun, they did. They wasn't so high and dry, nohow, but took their fling, like jolly companions every one."

"So?" says Silver. "Well, and where are they now? Pew was that sort, and he died a beggar-man. Flint was, and he died of rum at Savannah. Ah, they was a sweet crew, they was! on'y, where are they?"

"But," asked Dick, "when we do lay 'em athwart, what are we to do with 'em, anyhow?"

"There's the man for me!" cried the cook admiringly. "That's what I call business. Well, what would you think? Put 'em ashore like maroons? That would have been England's way. Or cut 'em down like that much pork? That would have been Flint's or Billy Bones's."

"Billy was the man for that," said Israel. " 'Dead men don't bite,' says he. Well, he's dead now hisself; he knows the long and short on it now; and if ever a rough hand come to port, it was Billy."

"Right you are," said Silver, "rough and ready. But mark you here: I'm an easy man—I'm quite the gentleman, says you; but this time it's serious. Dooty is dooty, mates. I give my vote—death. When I'm in Parlyment, and riding in my coach, I don't want none of these sea-lawyers in the cabin a-coming home, un-looked for, like the devil at prayers. Wait is what I say; but when the time comes, why, let her rip!"

"John," cried the coxswain, "you're a man!"

"You'll say so, Israel, when you see," said Silver. "Only one thing I claim—I claim Trelawney. I'll wring his calf's head off his body with these hands. Dick!" he added, breaking off, "you just jump up, like a sweet lad, and get me an apple, to wet my pipe like."

You may fancy the terror I was in! I should have leaped out

and run for it, if I had found the strength; but my limbs and heart alike misgave me. I heard Dick begin to rise, and then some one seemingly stopped him, and the voice of Hands exclaimed:—

"Oh, stow that! Don't you get sucking of that bilge, John. Let's have a go of the rum."

"Dick," said Silver, "I trust you. I've a gauge on the keg, mind. There's the key; you fill a pannikin and bring it up."

Terrified as I was, I could not help thinking to myself that this must have been how Mr. Arrow got the strong waters that destroyed him.

Dick was gone but a little while, and during his absence Israel spoke straight on in the cook's ear. It was but a word or two that I could catch, and yet I gathered some important news; for, besides other scraps that tended to the same purpose, this whole clause was audible: "Not another man of them'll jine." Hence there were still faithful men on board.

When Dick returned, one after another the trio took the pannikin and drank—one "To luck"; another with a "Here's to old Flint"; and Silver himself saying, in a kind of song, "Here's to ourselves, and hold your luff, plenty of prizes and plenty of duff."

Just then a sort of brightness fell upon me in the barrel, and, looking up, I found the moon had risen, and was silvering the mizzen-top and shining white on the luff of the fore-sail; and almost at the same time the voice of the look-out shouted "Land-ho!"

12.   *Council of War*

THERE WAS A GREAT RUSH OF FEET ACROSS THE DECK. I COULD hear people tumbling up from the cabin and the foc's'le; and, slipping in an instant outside my barrel, I dived behind the fore-sail, made a double towards the stern, and came out upon the open deck in time to join Hunter and Dr. Livesey in the rush for the weather bow.

There all hands were already congregated. A belt of fog had lifted almost simultaneously with the appearance of the moon. Away to the southwest of us we saw two low hills, about a couple of miles apart, and rising behind one of them a third and higher hill, whose peak was still buried in the fog. All three seemed sharp and conical in figure.

So much I saw, almost in a dream, for I had not yet recovered from my horrid fear of a minute or two before. And then I heard the voice of Captain Smollett issuing orders. The *Hispaniola* was laid a couple of points nearer the wind, and now sailed a course that would just clear the island on the east.

"And now, men," said the captain, when all was sheeted home, "has any one of you ever seen that land ahead?"

"I have, sir," said Silver. "I've watered there with a trader I was cook in."

"The anchorage is on the south, behind an islet, I fancy?" asked the captain.

"Yes, sir; Skeleton Island they calls it. It were a main place for pirates once, and a hand we had on board knowed all their names for it. That hill to the nor'ard they calls the Fore-mast Hill; there are three hills in a row running southard—fore, main, and mizzen, sir. But the main—that's the big 'un with the cloud on it—they usually calls the Spy-glass, by reason of a look-out they kept when they was in the anchorage cleaning; for it's there they cleaned their ships, sir, asking your pardon."

"I have a chart here," says Captain Smollett. "See if that's the place."

Long John's eyes burned in his head as he took the chart; but, by the fresh look of the paper, I knew he was doomed to disappointment. This was not the map we found in Billy Bones's chest, but an accurate copy, complete in all things—names and heights and soundings—with the single exception of the red crosses and the written notes. Sharp as must have been this annoyance, Silver had the strength of mind to hide it.

"Yes, sir," said he, "this is the spot to be sure; and very prettily drawed out. Who might have done that, I wonder. The pirates were too ignorant, I reckon. Ay, here it is: 'Capt. Kidd's Anchorage'—just the name my shipmate called it. There's a strong current runs along the south, and then away nor'ard up the west coast. Right you was, sir," says he, "to haul your wind and keep the weather of the island. Leastways, if such was your intention as to enter and careen, and there ain't no better place for that in these waters."

"Thank you, my man," says Captain Smollett. "I'll ask you, later on, to give us a help. You may go."

I was surprised at the coolness with which John avowed his knowledge of the island; and I own I was half frightened when I saw him drawing nearer to myself. He did not know, to be sure, that I had overheard his council from the apple barrel, and yet I had, by this time, taken such a horror of his cruelty, duplicity, and power, that I could scarce conceal a shudder when he laid his hand upon my arm.

"Ah," says he, "this here is a sweet spot, this island—a sweet spot for a lad to get ashore on. You'll bathe, and you'll climb trees, and you'll hunt goats, you will—and you'll get aloft on them hills like a goat yourself. Why, it makes me young again. It was going to forget my timber leg, I was. It's a pleasant thing to be young, and have ten toes, and you may lay to that. When you want to go a bit of exploring, you just ask old John, and he'll put up a snack for you to take along."

And clapping me in the friendliest way upon the shoulder, he hobbled off forward and went below.

Captain Smollett, the squire, and Dr. Livesey were talking together on the quarter-deck, and, anxious as I was to tell them my story, I durst not interrupt them openly. While I was still casting about in my thoughts to find some probable excuse, Dr. Livesey called me to his side. He had left his pipe below, and being a slave to tobacco, had meant that I should fetch it; but as soon as I was near enough to speak and not to be overheard, I broke out immediately: "Doctor, let me speak. Get the captain and squire down to the cabin, and then make some pretence to send for me. I have terrible news."

The doctor changed countenance a little, but next moment he was master of himself.

"Thank you, Jim," said he, quite loudly, "that was all I wanted to know," as if he had asked me a question.

And with that he turned on his heel and rejoined the other two. They spoke together for a little, and though none of them started, or raised his voice, or so much as whistled, it was plain enough that Dr. Livesey had communicated my request; for the next thing that I heard was the captain giving an order to Job Anderson, and all hands were piped on deck.

"My lads," said Captain Smollett, "I've a word to say to you.

This land that we have sighted is the place we have been sailing to. Mr. Trelawney, being a very open-handed gentleman, as we all know, has just asked me a word or two, and as I was able to tell him that every man on board had done his duty, alow and aloft, as I never ask to see it done better, why, he and I and the doctor are going below to the cabin to drink *your* health and luck, and you'll have grog served out for you to drink *our* health and luck. I'll tell you what I think of this: I think it handsome. And if you think as I do, you'll give a good sea cheer for the gentleman that does it."

The cheer followed—that was a matter of course; but it rang out so full and hearty, that I confess I could hardly believe these same men were plotting for our blood.

"One more cheer for Cap'n Smollett," cried Long John, when the first had subsided.

And this also was given with a will.

On the top of that the three gentlemen went below, and not long after, word was sent forward that Jim Hawkins was wanted in the cabin.

I found them all three seated round the table, a bottle of Spanish wine and some raisins before them, and the doctor smoking away, with his wig on his lap, and that, I knew, was a sign that he was agitated. The stern window was open, for it was a warm night, and you could see the moon shining behind on the ship's wake.

"Now, Hawkins," said the squire, "you have something to say. Speak up."

I did as I was bid, and, as short as I could make it, told the whole details of Silver's conversation. Nobody interrupted me till I was done, nor did any one of the three of them make so much as a movement, but they kept their eyes upon my face from first to last.

"Jim," said Dr. Livesey, "take a seat."

And they made me sit down at table beside them, poured me out a glass of wine, filled my hands with raisins, and all three, one after the other, and each with a bow, drank my good health, and their service to me, for my luck and courage.

"Now, captain," said the squire, "you were right, and I was wrong. I own myself an ass, and I await your orders."

"No more an ass than I, sir," returned the captain. "I never heard of a crew that meant to mutiny but what showed signs before, for any man that had an eye in his head to see the mischief and take steps according. But this crew," he added, "beats me."

"Captain," said the doctor, "with your permission, that's Silver. A very remarkable man."

"He'd look remarkably well from a yard-arm, sir," returned the captain. "But this is talk; this don't lead to anything. I see three or four points, and with Mr. Trelawney's permission, I'll name them."

"You, sir, are the captain. It is for you to speak," says Mr. Trelawney grandly.

"First point," began Mr. Smollett. "We must go on, because we can't turn back. If I gave the word to go about, they would rise at once. Second point, we have time before us—at least, until this treasure's found. Third point, there are faithful hands. Now, sir, it's got to come to blows sooner or later; and what I propose is, to take time by the forelock, as the saying is, and come to blows some fine day when they least expect it. We can count, I take it, on your own home servants, Mr. Trelawney?"

"As upon myself," declared the squire.

"Three," reckoned the captain, "ourselves make seven, counting Hawkins here. Now, about the honest hands?"

"Most likely Trelawney's own men," said the doctor; "those he had picked up for himself, before he lit on Silver."

"Nay," replied the squire, "Hands was one of mine."

"I did think I could have trusted Hands," added the captain.

"And to think that they're all Englishmen!" broke out the squire. "Sir, I could find it in my heart to blow the ship up."

"Well, gentlemen," said the captain, "the best that I can say is not much. We must lay to, if you please, and keep a bright look-out. It's trying on a man, I know. It would be pleasanter to come to blows. But there's no help for it till we know our men. Lay to, and whistle for a wind, that's my view."

"Jim here," said the doctor, "can help us more than any one. The men are not shy with him, and Jim is a noticing lad."

"Hawkins, I put prodigious faith in you," added the squire.

I began to feel pretty desperate at this, for I felt altogether helpless; and yet, by an odd train of circumstances, it was indeed through me that safety came. In the meantime, talk as we pleased, there were only seven out of the twenty-six on whom we knew we could rely; and out of these seven one was a boy, so that the grown men on our side were six to their nineteen.

PART THREE

MY SHORE ADVENTURE

══════ ✶ ══════

13. *How I Began My Shore Adventure*

THE APPEARANCE OF THE ISLAND WHEN I CAME ON DECK NEXT morning was altogether changed. Although the breeze had now utterly failed, we had made a great deal of way during the night, and were now lying becalmed about half a mile to the south-east of the low eastern coast. Gray-coloured woods covered a large part of the surface. This even tint was indeed broken up by streaks of yellow sandbreak in the lower lands, and by many tall trees of the pine family, out-topping the others—some singly, some in clumps; but the general colouring was uniform and sad. The hills ran up clear above the vegetation in spires of naked rock. All were strangely shaped, and the Spy-glass, which was by three or four hundred feet the tallest on the island, was likewise the strangest in configuration, running up sheer from almost every side, and then suddenly cut off at the top like a pedestal to put a statue on.

The *Hispaniola* was rolling scuppers under in the ocean swell. The booms were tearing at the blocks, the rudder was banging to and fro, and the whole ship creaking, groaning, and jumping like a manufactory. I had to cling tight to the backstay, and the world turned giddily before my eyes; for though I was a good enough sailor when there was way on, this standing still and being rolled about like a bottle was a thing I never learned to stand without a qualm or so, above all in the morning, on an empty stomach.

Perhaps it was this—perhaps it was the look of the island, with its gray, melancholy woods, and wild stone spires, and the surf that

66

we could both see and hear foaming and thundering on the steep beach—at least, although the sun shone bright and hot, and the shore birds were fishing and crying all around us, and you would have thought any one would have been glad to get to land after being so long at sea, my heart sank, as the saying is, into my boots; and from that first look onward, I hated the very thought of Treasure Island.

We had a dreary morning's work before us, for there was no sign of any wind, and the boats had to be got out and manned, and the ship warped three or four miles round the corner of the island, and up the narrow passage to the haven behind Skeleton Island. I volunteered for one of the boats, where I had, of course, no business. The heat was sweltering, and the men grumbled fiercely over their work. Anderson was in command of my boat, and instead of keeping the crew in order, he grumbled as loud as the worst.

"Well," he said, with an oath, "it's not for ever."

I thought this was a very bad sign; for, up to that day, the men had gone briskly and willingly about their business; but the very sight of the island had relaxed the cords of discipline.

All the way in, Long John stood by the steersman and conned the ship. He knew the passage like the palm of his hand; and though the man in the chains got everywhere more water than was down in the chart, John never hesitated once.

"There's a strong scour with the ebb," he said, "and this here passage has been dug out, in a manner of speaking, with a spade."

We brought up just where the anchor was in the chart, about a third of a mile from either shore, the mainland on one side, and Skeleton Island on the other. The bottom was clean sand. The plunge of our anchor sent up clouds of birds wheeling and crying over the woods; but in less than a minute they were down again, and all was once more silent.

The place was entirely land-locked, buried in woods, the trees coming right down to high-water mark, the shores mostly flat, and the hill-tops standing round at a distance in a sort of amphitheatre, one here, one there. Two little rivers, or, rather, two swamps, emptied out into this pond, as you might call it; and the foliage round that part of the shore had a kind of poisonous brightness. From the ship, we could see nothing of the house or stockade, for they were quite buried among trees; and if it had not been for the chart on the companion, we might have been the first that had ever anchored there since the island arose out of the seas.

There was not a breath of air moving, nor a sound but that of the surf booming half a mile away along the beaches and against the rocks outside. A peculiar stagnant smell hung over the anchorage—a smell of sodden leaves and rotted tree trunks. I observed the doctor sniffing and sniffing, like some one tasting a bad egg.

"I don't know about treasure," he said, "but I'll stake my wig there's fever here."

If the conduct of the men had been alarming in the boat, it became truly threatening when they had come aboard. They lay about the deck growling together in talk. The slightest order was received with a black look, and grudgingly and carelessly obeyed. Even the honest hands must have caught the infection, for there was not one man aboard to mend another. Mutiny, it was plain, hung over us like a thunder-cloud.

And it was not only we of the cabin party who perceived the danger. Long John was hard at work going from group to group, spending himself in good advice, and as for example no man could have shown a better. He fairly outstripped himself in willingness and civility; he was all smiles to every one. If an order were given, John would be on his crutch in an instant, with the cheeriest "Ay, ay, sir!" in the world; and when there was nothing else to do, he kept up one song after another, as if to conceal the discontent of the rest.

Of all the gloomy features of that gloomy afternoon, this obvious anxiety on the part of Long John appeared the worst.

We held a council in the cabin.

"Sir," said the captain, "if I risk another order, the whole ship'll come about our ears by the run. You see, sir, here it is. I get a rough answer, do I not? Well, if I speak back, pikes will be going in two shakes; if I don't, Silver will see there's something under that, and the game's up. Now, we've only one man to rely on."

"And who is that?" asked the squire.

"Silver, sir," returned the captain; "he's as anxious as you and I to smother things up. This is a tiff; he'd soon talk 'em out of it if he had the chance, and what I propose to do is to give him the chance. Let's allow the men an afternoon ashore. If they all go, why, we'll fight the ship. If they none of them go, well, then, we hold the cabin, and God defend the right. If some go, you mark my words, sir, Silver'll bring 'em aboard again as mild as lambs."

It was so decided; loaded pistols were served out to all the sure men; Hunter, Joyce, and Redruth were taken into our confidence, and received the news with less surprise and a better spirit than we had looked for, and then the captain went on deck and addressed the crew.

"My lads," said he, "we've had a hot day, and are all tired and out of sorts. A turn ashore'll hurt nobody—the boats are still in the water; you can take the gigs, and as many as please can go ashore for the afternoon. I'll fire a gun half an hour before sundown."

I believe the silly fellows must have thought they would break their shins over treasure as soon as they were landed; for they all came out of their sulks in a moment, and gave a cheer that started the echo in a far-away hill, and sent the birds once more flying and squalling round the anchorage.

The captain was too bright to be in the way. He whipped out of sight in a moment, leaving Silver to arrange the party; and I fancy it was as well he did so. Had he been on deck he could no longer so much as have pretended not to understand the situation. It was as plain as day. Silver was the captain and a mighty rebellious crew he had of it. The honest hands—and I was soon to see it proved that there were such on board—must have been very stupid fellows. Or, rather, I suppose the truth was this, that all hands were disaffected by the example of the ringleaders—only some more, some less; and a few, being good fellows in the main, could neither be led nor driven any further. It is one thing to be idle and skulk, and quite another to take a ship and murder a number of innocent men.

At last, however, the party was made up. Six fellows were to stay on board, and the remaining thirteen, including Silver, began to embark.

Then it was that there came into my head the first of the mad notions that contributed so much to save our lives. If six men were left by Silver, it was plain our party could not take and fight the ship; and since only six were left, it was equally plain that the cabin party had no present need of my assistance. It occurred to me at once to go ashore. In a jiffy I had slipped over the side, and curled up in the fore-sheets of the nearest boat, and almost at the same moment she shoved off.

No one took notice of me, only the bow oar saying, "Is that you, Jim? Keep your head down." But Silver, from the other boat, looked sharply over and called out to know if that were me; and from that moment I began to regret what I had done.

The crews raced for the beach; but the boat I was in, having some start, and being at once the lighter and the better manned, shot far ahead of her consort, and the bow had struck among the shoreside trees, and I had caught a branch and swung myself out, and plunged into the nearest thicket, while Silver and the rest were still a hundred yards behind.

"Jim, Jim!" I heard him shouting.

But you may suppose I paid no heed; jumping, ducking, and breaking through, I ran straight before my nose, till I could run no longer.

14. *The First Blow*

I WAS SO PLEASED AT HAVING GIVEN THE SLIP TO LONG JOHN, THAT I began to enjoy myself and look around me with some interest on the strange land that I was in.

I had crossed a marshy tract full of willows, bulrushes, and odd, outlandish, swampy trees; and I had now come out upon the skirts of an open piece of undulating, sandy country, about a mile long, dotted with a few pines, and a great number of contorted trees, not unlike the oak in growth, but pale in the foliage, like willows. On the far side of the open stood one of the hills, with two quaint, craggy peaks, shining vividly in the sun.

I now felt for the first time the joy of exploration. The isle was uninhabited; my shipmates I had left behind, and nothing lived in front of me but dumb brutes and fowls. I turned hither and thither among the trees. Here and there were flowering plants, unknown to me; here and there I saw snakes, and one raised his head from a ledge of rock and hissed at me with a noise not unlike the spinning of a top. Little did I suppose that he was a deadly enemy, and that the noise was the famous rattle.

Then I came to a long thicket of these oak-like trees—live, or evergreen, oaks, I heard afterwards, they should be called—which grew low along the sand like brambles, the boughs curiously twisted, the foliage compact, like thatch. The thicket stretched down from the top of one of the sandy knolls, spreading and growing taller as it went, until it reached the margin of the broad, reedy fen, through which the nearest of the little rivers soaked its way into the anchorage. The marsh was steaming in the strong sun, and the outline of the Spy-glass trembled through the haze.

All at once there began to go a sort of bustle among the bulrushes; a wild duck flew up with a quack, another followed, and soon over the whole surface of the marsh a great cloud of birds hung screaming and circling in the air. I judged at once that some of my shipmates must be drawing near along the borders of the fen. Nor was I deceived; for soon I heard the very distant and low tones of a human voice, which, as I continued to give ear, grew steadily louder and nearer.

This put me in a great fear, and I crawled under cover of the nearest live-oak, and squatted there, hearkening, as silent as a mouse.

Another voice answered; and then the first voice, which I now recognised to be Silver's, once more took up the story, and ran on for a long while in a stream, only now and again interrupted by the other. By the sound they must have been talking earnestly, and almost fiercely; but no distinct word came to my hearing.

At last the speakers seemed to have paused, and perhaps to have sat down; for not only did they cease to draw any nearer, but the birds themselves began to grow more quiet, and to settle again to their places in the swamp.

And now I began to feel that I was neglecting my business; that since I had been so foolhardy as to come ashore with these desperadoes, the least I could do was to overhear them at their councils; and that my plain and obvious duty was to draw as close as I could manage, under the favourable ambush of the crouching trees.

I could tell the direction of the speakers pretty exactly, not only by the sound of their voices, but by the behaviour of the few birds that still hung in alarm above the heads of the intruders.

Crawling on all-fours, I made steadily but slowly towards them; till at last, raising my head to an aperture among the leaves, I could see clear down into a little green dell beside the marsh, and closely set about with trees, where Long John Silver and another of the crew stood face to face in conversation.

The sun beat full upon them. Silver had thrown his hat beside him on the ground, and his great, smooth, blond face, all shining with heat, was lifted to the other man's in a kind of appeal.

"Mate," he was saying, "it's because I thinks gold dust of you—gold dust, and you may lay to that! If I hadn't took to you like pitch, do you think I'd have been here a-warning of you? All's up—you can't make nor mend; it's to save your neck that I'm a-speaking, and if one of the wild 'uns knew it, where 'ud I be, Tom—now, tell me, where 'ud I be?"

"Silver," said the other man—and I observed he was not only red in the face, but spoke as hoarse as a crow, and his voice shook, too, like a taut rope—"Silver," says he, "you're old, and you're honest, or has the name for it; and you've money, too, which lots of poor sailors hasn't; and you're brave, or I'm mistook. And will you tell me you'll let yourself be led away with that kind of a mess of swabs? Not you! As sure as God sees me, I'd sooner lose my hand. If I turn agin my dooty——"

And then all of a sudden he was interrupted by a noise. I had found one of the honest hands—well, here, at that same moment, came news of another. Far away out in the marsh there arose, all of a sudden, a sound like the cry of anger, then another on the back of it; and then one horrid, long-drawn scream. The rocks of the Spy-glass re-echoed it a score of times; the whole troop of marsh-birds rose again, darkening heaven, with a simultaneous whirr; and long after that death yell was still ringing in my brain, silence had re-established its empire, and only the rustle of the redescending birds and the boom of the distant surges disturbed the languor of the afternoon.

Tom had leaped at the sound, like a horse at the spur; but Silver had not winked an eye. He stood where he was, resting lightly on his crutch, watching his companion like a snake about to spring.

"John!" said the sailor, stretching out his hand.

"Hands off!" cried Silver, leaping back a yard, as it seemed to me, with the speed and security of a trained gymnast.

"Hands off, if you like, John Silver," said the other. "It's a black conscience that can make you feared of me. But, in heaven's name, tell me what was that?"

"That?" returned Silver, smiling away, but warier than ever, his eye a mere pin-point in his big face, but gleaming like a crumb of glass. "That? Oh, I reckon that'll be Alan."

At this poor Tom flashed out like a hero.

"Alan!" he cried. "Then rest his soul for a true seaman! And as for you, John Silver, long you've been a mate of mine, but you're mate of mine no more. If I die like a dog, I'll die in my dooty. You've killed Alan, have you? Kill me, too, if you can. But I defies you."

And with that, this brave fellow turned his back directly on the cook, and set off walking for the beach. But he was not destined to go far. With a cry, John seized the branch of a tree, whipped the crutch out of his armpit, and sent that uncouth missile hurtling through the air. It struck poor Tom, point foremost, and with stunning violence, right between the shoulders in the middle of his back. His hands flew up, he gave a sort of gasp, and fell.

Whether he were injured much or little, none could ever tell. Like enough, to judge from the sound, his back was broken on the spot. But he had no time given him to recover. Silver, agile as a monkey, even without leg or crutch, was on the top of him next moment, and had twice buried his knife up to the hilt in that defenceless body. From my place of ambush, I could hear him pant aloud as he struck the blows.

I do not know what it rightly is to faint, but I do know that for the next little while the whole world swam away from before me in a whirling mist; Silver and the birds, and the tall Spy-glass hill-top, going round and round and topsy-turvy before my eyes, and all manner of bells ringing and distant voices shouting in my ear.

When I came again to myself, the monster had pulled himself together, his crutch under his arm, his hat upon his head. Just before him Tom lay motionless upon the sward; but the murderer minded him not a whit, cleansing his blood-stained knife the while upon a wisp of grass. Everything else was unchanged, the sun still shining mercilessly on the steaming marsh and the tall pinnacle of the mountain, and I could scarce persuade myself that murder had been actually done, and a human life cruelly cut short a moment since, before my eyes.

But now John put his hand into his pocket, brought out a whistle, and blew upon it several modulated blasts, that rang far across the heated air. I could not tell, of course, the meaning of the signal; but it instantly awoke my fears. More men would be coming. I might be discovered. They had already slain two of the honest people; after Tom and Alan, might not I came next?

Instantly I began to extricate myself and crawl back again, with what speed and silence I could manage, to the more open portion of the wood. As I did so, I could hear hails coming and going between the old buccaneer and his comrades, and this sound of danger lent me wings. As soon as I was clear of the thicket, I ran as I never ran before, scarce minding the direction of my flight, so long as it led me from the murderers; and as I ran, fear grew and grew upon me, until it turned into a kind of frenzy.

Indeed, could any one be more entirely lost than I? When the gun fired, how should I dare to go down to the boats amongst those fiends, still smoking from their crime? Would not the first of them who saw me wring my neck like a snipe's? Would not my absence itself be an evidence to them of my alarm, and therefore of my fatal knowledge? It was all over, I thought. Good-bye to the *Hispaniola;* good-bye to the squire, the doctor, the captain! There was nothing left for me but death by starvation, or death by the hands of the mutineers.

All this while, as I say, I was still running, and, without taking any notice, I had drawn near to the foot of the little hill with the two peaks, and had got into a part of the island where the live-oaks grew more widely apart, and seemed more like forest trees in their bearing and dimensions. Mingled with these were a few scattered pines, some fifty, some nearer seventy, feet high. The air, too, smelt more freshly than down beside the marsh.

And here a fresh alarm brought me to a standstill with a thumping heart.

15. *The Man of the Island*

FROM THE SIDE OF THE HILL, WHICH WAS HERE STEEP AND STONY, a spout of gravel was dislodged, and fell rattling and bounding through the trees. My eyes turned instinctively in that direction, and I saw a figure leap with great rapidity behind the trunk of a pine. What it was, whether bear or man or monkey, I could in no wise tell. It seemed dark and shaggy; more I knew not. But the terror of this new apparition brought me to a stand.

I was now, it seemed, cut off upon both sides; behind me the murderers, before me this lurking nondescript. And immediately I began to prefer the dangers that I knew to those I knew not. Silver himself appeared less terrible in contrast with this creature of the woods, and I turned on my heel, and, looking sharply behind me over my shoulder, began to retrace my steps in the direction of the boats.

Instantly the figure reappeared, and, making a wide circuit, began to head me off. I was tired, at any rate; but had I been as fresh as when I rose, I could see it was in vain for me to contend in speed with such an adversary. From trunk to trunk the creature flitted like a deer, running manlike on two legs, but unlike any man that I had ever seen, stooping almost double as it ran. Yet a man it was, I could no longer be in doubt about that.

I began to recall what I had heard of cannibals. I was within an ace of calling for help. But the mere fact that he was a man, however wild, had somewhat reassured me, and my fear of Silver began to revive in proportion. I stood still, therefore, and cast about for some method of escape; and as I was so thinking, the recollection of my pistol flashed into my mind. As soon as I remembered I was not defenceless, courage glowed again in my heart; and I set my face resolutely for this man of the island, and walked briskly towards him.

He was concealed by this time behind another tree trunk; but he must have been watching me closely, for as soon as I began to move in his direction he reappeared and took a step to meet me. Then he hesitated, drew back, came forward again, and as last, to my wonder and confusion, threw himself on his knees and held out his clasped hands in supplication.

At that I once more stopped.

"Who are you?" I asked.

"Ben Gunn," he answered, and his voice sounded hoarse and awkward, like a rusty lock. "I'm poor Ben Gunn, I am; and I haven't spoke with a Christian these three years."

I could now see that he was a white man like myself, and that his features were even pleasing. His skin, wherever it was exposed, was burnt by the sun; even his lips were black; and his fair eyes looked quite startling in so dark a face. Of all the beggar-men that I had seen or fancied, he was the chief for raggedness. He was clothed with tatters of old ship's canvas and old sea cloth; and this

extraordinary patchwork was all held together by a system of the
most various and incongruous fastenings, brass buttons, bits of
stick, and loops of tarry gaskin. About his waist he wore an old
brass-buckled leather belt, which was the one thing solid in his
whole accoutrement.

"Three years!" I cried. "Were you shipwrecked?"

"Nay, mate," said he—"marooned."

I had heard the word, and I knew it stood for a horrible kind of
punishment common enough among the buccaneers, in which the
offender is put ashore with a little powder and shot, and left
behind on some desolate and distant island.

"Marooned three years agone," he continued, "and lived on
goats since then, and berries, and oysters. Wherever a man is, says
I, a man can do for himself. But, mate, my heart is sore for
Christian diet. You mightn't happen to have a piece of cheese
about you, now? No? Well, many's the long night I've dreamed
of cheese—toasted, mostly—and woke up again, and here I
were."

"If ever I can get on board again," said I, "you shall have cheese
by the stone."

All this time he had been feeling the stuff of my jacket, smooth-
ing my hands, looking at my boots, and generally, in the intervals
of his speech, showing a childish pleasure in the presence of a
fellow-creature. But at my last words he perked up into a kind of
startled slyness.

"If ever you can get aboard again, says you?" he repeated. "Why,
now, who's to hinder you?"

"Not you, I know," was my reply.

"And right you was," he cried. "Now you—what do you call
yourself, mate?"

"Jim," I told him.

"Jim, Jim," says he, quite pleased apparently. "Well, now, Jim,
I've lived that rough as you'd be ashamed to hear of. Now, for
instance, you wouldn't think I had a pious mother—to look at
me?" he asked.

"Why, no, not in particular," I answered.

"Ah, well," said he, "but I had—*re*markable pious. And I was
a civil, pious boy, and could rattle off my catechism that fast, as
you couldn't tell one word from another. And here's what it come
to, Jim, and it begun with chuck-farthen on the blessed grave-

stones! That's what it begun with, but it went further'n that; and
so my mother told me, and predicked the whole, she did, the pious
woman! But it were Providence that put me here. I've thought it
all out in this here lonely island, and I'm back on piety. You don't
catch me tasting rum so much; but just a thimbleful for luck, of
course, the first chance I have. I'm bound I'll be good, and I see
the way to. And, Jim"—looking all round him, and lowering his
voice to a whisper—"I'm rich."

I now felt sure that the poor fellow had gone crazy in his solitude, and I suppose I must have shown the feeling in my face, for
he repeated the statement hotly:—

"Rich! rich! I says. And I'll tell you what: I'll make a man of
you, Jim. Ah, Jim, you'll bless your stars, you will, you was the
first that found me!"

And at this there came suddenly a lowering shadow over his face,
and he tightened his grasp upon my hand, and raised a forefinger
threateningly before my eyes.

"Now, Jim, you tell me true: that ain't Flint's ship?" he asked.

At this I had a happy inspiration. I began to believe that I had
found an ally, and I answered him at once.

"It's not Flint's ship, and Flint is dead; but I'll tell you true,
as you ask me—there are some of Flint's hands aboard; worse luck
for the rest of us."

"Not a man—with one—leg?" he gasped.

"Silver?" I asked.

"Ah, Silver!" says he; "that were his name."

"He's the cook; and the ringleader, too."

He was still holding me by the wrist, and at that he gave it quite
a wring.

"If you was sent by Long John," he said, "I'm as good as pork,
and I know it. But where was you, do you suppose?"

I had made my mind up in a moment, and by way of answer
told him the whole story of our voyage, and the predicament in
which we found ourselves. He heard me with the keenest interest,
and when I had done he patted me on the head.

"You're a good lad, Jim," he said; "and you're all in a clove
hitch, ain't you? Well, you just put your trust in Ben Gunn—Ben
Gunn's the man to do it. Would you think it likely, now, that your
squire would prove a liberal-minded one in case of help—him being in a clove hitch, as you remark?"

I told him the squire was the most liberal of men.

"Ay, but you see," returned Ben Gunn, "I didn't mean giving me a gate to keep, and a shuit of livery clothes, and such; that's not my mark, Jim. What I mean is, would he be likely to come down to the toon of, say, one thousand pounds out of money that's as good as a man's own already?"

"I am sure he would," said I. "As it was, all hands were to share."

"*And* a passage home?" he added, with a look of great shrewdness.

"Why," I cried, "the squire's a gentleman. And besides, if we got rid of the others, we should want you to help work the vessel home."

"Ah," said he, "so you would." And he seemed very much relieved.

"Now, I'll tell you what," he went on. "So much I'll tell you and no more. I were in Flint's ship when he buried the treasure; he and six along—six strong seamen. They were ashore nigh on a week, and us standing off and on in the old *Walrus*. One fine day up went the signal, and here come Flint by himself in a little boat, and his head done up in a blue scarf. The sun was getting up, and mortal white he looked about the cut-water. But, there he was, you mind, and the six all dead—dead and buried. How he done it, not a man aboard us could make out. It was battle, murder, and sudden death, leastways—him against six. Billy Bones was the mate; Long John he was quartermaster; and they asked him where the treasure was. 'Ah,' says he, 'you can go ashore, if you like, and stay,' he says; 'but as for the ship, she'll beat up for more, by thunder!' That's what he said.

"Well, I was in another ship three years back, and we sighted this island. 'Boys,' said I, 'here's Flint's treasure; let's land and find it.' The cap'n was displeased at that; but my messmates were all of a mind, and landed. Twelve days they looked for it, and every day they had the worse word for me, until one fine morning all hands went aboard. 'As for you, Benjamin Gunn,' says they, 'here's a musket,' they says, 'and a spade, and pick-axe. You can stay here, and find Flint's money for yourself,' they says.

"Well, Jim, three years have I been here, and not a bite of Christian diet from that day to this. But now, you look here; look at me.

Do I look like a man before the mast? No, says you. Nor I weren't, neither, I says."

With that he winked and pinched me hard.

"Just you mention them words to your squire, Jim"—he went on: "Nor he weren't, neither—that's the words. Three years he were the man of this island, light and dark, fair and rain; and sometimes he would, maybe, think upon a prayer (says you), and sometimes he would, maybe, think of his old mother, so be as she's alive (you'll say); but the most part of Gunn's time (this is what you'll say)—the most part of his time was took up with another matter. And then you'll give him a nip, like I do."

And he pinched me again in the most confidential manner.

"Then," he continued—"then you'll up, and you'll say this: Gunn is a good man (you'll say), and he puts a precious sight more confidence—a precious sight, mind that—in a gen'leman born than in these gen'lemen of fortune having been one hisself."

"Well," I said, "I don't understand one word that you've been saying. But that's neither here nor there; for how am I to get on board?"

"Ah," said he, "that's the hitch, for sure. Well, there's my boat, that I made with my two hands. I keep her under the white rock. If the worst comes to the worst, we might try that after dark. Hi!" he broke out, "what's that?"

For just then, although the sun had still an hour or two to run, all the echoes of the island awoke and bellowed to the thunder of a cannon.

"They have begun to fight!" I cried. "Follow me."

And I began to run towards the anchorage, my terrors all forgotten; while, close at my side, the marooned man in his goatskins trotted easily and lightly.

"Left, left," says he; "keep to your left hand, mate Jim! Under the trees with you! Theer's where I killed my first goat. They don't come down here now; they're all mast-headed on them mountings for the fear of Benjamin Gunn. Ah! and there's the cetemery"—cemetery, he must have meant. "You see the mounds? I come here and prayed, nows and thens, when I thought maybe a Sunday would be about doo. It weren't quite a chapel, but it seemed more solemn like; and then, says you, Ben Gunn was short-handed—no chapling, nor so much as a Bible and a flag, you says."

So he kept talking as I ran, neither expecting nor receiving any answer.

The cannon-shot was followed, after a considerable interval, by a volley of small arms.

Another pause, and then, not a quarter of a mile in front of me, I beheld the Union Jack flutter in the air above a wood.

THE STOCKADE

★

16. NARRATIVE CONTINUED BY THE DOCTOR: *How the Ship Was Abandoned*

IT WAS ABOUT HALF-PAST ONE—THREE BELLS IN THE SEA PHRASE— that the two boats went ashore from the *Hispaniola*. The captain, the squire, and I were talking matters over in the cabin. Had there been a breath of wind we should have fallen on the six mutineers who were left aboard with us, slipped our cable, and away to sea. But the wind was wanting; and, to complete our helplessness, down came Hunter with the news that Jim Hawkins had slipped into a boat and was gone ashore with the rest.

It never occurred to us to doubt Jim Hawkins; but we were alarmed for his safety. With the men in the temper they were in, it seemed an even chance if we should see the lad again. We ran on deck. The pitch was bubbling in the seams; the nasty stench of the place turned me sick; if ever man smelt fever and dysentery, it was in that abominable anchorage. The six scoundrels were sitting grumbling under a sail in the forecastle; ashore we could see the gigs made fast, and a man sitting in each, hard by where the river runs in. One of them was whistling "Lillibullero."

Waiting was a strain; and it was decided that Hunter and I should go ashore with the jollyboat, in quest of information. The gigs had leaned to their right; but Hunter and I pulled straight in, in the direction of the stockade upon the chart. The two who were left guarding their boats seemed in a bustle at our appearance; "Lillibullero" stopped off, and I could see the pair discussing what they ought to do. Had they gone and told Silver, all might have turned out differently; but they had their orders, I suppose, and decided to sit quietly where they were and hark back again to "Lillibullero."

There was a slight bend in the coast, and I steered so as to put it between us; even before we landed we had thus lost sight of the gigs. I jumped out, and came as near running as I durst, with a big silk handkerchief under my hat for coolness' sake, and a brace of pistols ready primed for safety.

I had not gone a hundred yards when I came on the stockade.

This was how it was: a spring of clear water rose almost at the top of a knoll. Well, on the knoll, and enclosing the spring, they had clapped a stout log-house, fit to hold two score people on a pinch, and loop-holed for musketry on every side. All round this they had cleared a wide space, and then the thing was completed by a paling six feet high, without door or opening, too strong to pull down without time and labour, and too open to shelter the be-siegers. The people in the log-house had them in every way; they stood quiet in shelter and shot the others like partridges. All they wanted was a good watch and food; for, short of a complete sur-prise, they might have held the place against a regiment.

What particularly took my fancy was the spring. For, though we had a good enough place of it in the cabin of the *Hispaniola*, with plenty of arms and ammunition, and things to eat, and excellent wines, there had been one thing overlooked—we had no water. I was thinking this over, when there came ringing over the island the cry of a man at the point of death. I was not new to violent death—I have served his Royal Highness the Duke of Cumber-land, and got a wound myself at Fontenoy—but I know my pulse went dot and carry one. "Jim Hawkins is gone" was my first thought.

It is something to have been an old soldier, but more still to have been a doctor. There is no time to dilly-dally in our work. And so now I made up my mind instantly, and with no time lost returned to the shore, and jumped on board the jolly-boat.

By good fortune Hunter pulled a good oar. We made the water fly; and the boat was soon alongside, and I aboard the schooner.

I found them all shaken, as was natural. The squire was sitting down, as white as a sheet, thinking of the harm he had led us to, the good soul! and one of the six forecastle hands was little better.

"There's a man," says Captain Smollett, nodding towards him, "new to this work. He came nigh-hand fainting, doctor, when he heard the cry. Another touch of the rudder and that man would join us."

I told my plan to the captain, and between us we settled on the details of its accomplishment.

We put old Redruth in the gallery between the cabin and the forecastle, with three or four loaded muskets and a mattress for protection. Hunter brought the boat round under the stern-port, and Joyce and I set to work loading her with powder tins, muskets, bags of biscuits, kegs of pork, a cask of cognac, and my invaluable medicine chest.

In the meantime, the squire and the captain stayed on deck, and the latter hailed the coxswain, who was the principal man aboard.

"Mr. Hands," he said, "here are two of us with a brace of pistols each. If any one of you six make a signal of any description, that man's dead."

They were a good deal taken aback; and after a little consultation, one and all tumbled down the fore companion, thinking, no doubt, to take us on the rear. But when they saw Redruth waiting for them in the sparred gallery, they went about ship at once, and a head popped out again on deck.

"Down, dog!" cries the captain.

And the head popped back again; and we heard no more, for a time, of these six very faint-hearted seamen.

By this time, tumbling things in as they came, we had the jolly-boat loaded as much as we dared. Joyce and I got through the stern-port, and we made for shore again, as fast as oars could take us.

This second trip fairly aroused the watchers along shore. "Lilli-bullero" was dropped again; and just before we lost sight of them behind the little point, one of them whipped ashore and disappeared. I had half a mind to change my plan and destroy their boats, but I feared that Silver and the others might be close at hand, and all might very well be lost by trying for too much.

We had soon touched land in the same place as before, and set to provision the block house. All three made the first journey, heavily laden, and tossed our stores over the palisade. Then, leaving Joyce to guard them—one man, to be sure, but with half a dozen muskets —Hunter and I returned to the jolly-boat, and loaded ourselves once more. So we proceeded without pausing to take breath, till the whole cargo was bestowed when the two servants took up their position in the block house, and I, with all my power, sculled back to the *Hispaniola*.

That we should have risked a second boat load seems more daring than it really was. They had the advantage of numbers, of course, but we had the advantage of arms. Not one of the men ashore had a musket, and before they could get within range for pistol shooting, we flattered ourselves we should be able to give a good account of a half-dozen at least.

The squire was waiting for me at the stern window, all his faintness gone from him. He caught the painter and made it fast, and we fell to loading the boat for our very lives. Pork, powder, and biscuit was the cargo, with only a musket and a cutlass apiece for squire and me and Redruth and the captain. The rest of the arms and powder we dropped overboard in two fathoms and a half of water, so that we could see the bright steel shining far below us in the sun, on the clean, sandy bottom.

By this time the tide was beginning to ebb, and the ship was swinging round to her anchor. Voices were heard faintly halloaing in the direction of the two gigs; and though this reassured us for Joyce and Hunter, who were well to the eastward, it warned our party to be off.

Redruth retreated from his place in the gallery, and dropped into the boat, which we then brought round to the ship's counter, to be handier for Captain Smollett.

"Now, men," said he, "do you hear me?"

There was no answer from the forecastle.

"It's to you, Abraham Gray—it's to you I am speaking."

Still no reply.

"Gray," resumed Mr. Smollett, a little louder, "I am leaving this ship, and I order you to follow your captain. I know you are a good man at bottom, and I dare say not one of the lot of you's as bad as he makes out. I have my watch here in my hand; I give you thirty seconds to join me in."

There was a pause.

"Come, my fine fellow," continued the captain, "don't hang so long in stays. I'm risking my life, and the lives of these good gentlemen every second."

There was a sudden scuffle, a sound of blows, and out burst Abraham Gray with a knife-cut on the side of the cheek, and came running to the captain, like a dog to the whistle.

"I'm with you, sir," said he.

And the next moment he and the captain had dropped aboard of us, and we had shoved off and given way.

We were clear out of the ship; but not yet ashore in our stockade.

17. NARRATIVE CONTINUED BY THE DOCTOR:
The Jolly-Boat's Last Trip

THIS FIFTH TRIP WAS QUITE DIFFERENT FROM ANY OF THE OTHERS. In the first place, the little gallipot of a boat that we were in was gravely overloaded. Five grown men, and three of them—Trelawney, Redruth, and the captain—over six feet high, was already more than she was meant to carry. Add to that the powder, pork, and bread-bags. The gunwale was lipping astern. Several times we shipped a little water, and my breeches and the tails of my coat were all soaking wet before we had gone a hundred yards.

The captain made us trim the boat, and we got her to lie a little more evenly. All the same, we were afraid to breathe.

In the second place, the ebb was now making—a strong rippling current running westward through the basin, and then south'ard and seaward down the straits by which we had entered in the morning. Even the ripples were a danger to our overloaded craft; but the worst of it was that we were swept out of our true course, and away from our proper landing-place behind the point. If we let the current have its way we should come ashore beside the gigs, where the pirates might appear at any moment.

"I cannot keep her head for the stockade, sir," said I to the captain. I was steering, while he and Redruth, two fresh men, were at the oars. "The tide keeps washing her down. Could you pull a little stronger?"

"Not without swamping the boat," said he. "You must bear up, sir, if you please—bear up until you see you're gaining."

I tried, and found by experiment that the tide kept sweeping us westward until I had laid her head due east, or just about right angles to the way we ought to go.

"We'll never get ashore at this rate," said I.

"If it's the only course that we can lie, sir, we must even lie it," returned the captain. "We must keep up-stream. You see, sir," he went on, "if once we dropped to leeward of the landing-place, it's hard to say where we should get ashore, besides the chance of being boarded by the gigs; whereas, the way we go the current must slacken, and then we can dodge back along the shore."

"The current's less a'ready, sir," said the man Gray, who was sitting in the fore-sheets; "you can ease her off a bit."

"Thank you, my man," said I, quite as if nothing had happened; for we had all quietly made up our minds to treat him like one of ourselves.

Suddenly the captain spoke up again, and I thought his voice was a little changed.

"The gun!" said he.

"I have thought of that," said I, for I made sure he was thinking of a bombardment of the fort. "They could never get the gun ashore, and if they did, they could never haul it through the woods."

"Look astern, doctor," replied the captain. We had entirely forgotten the long nine; and there, to our horror, were the five rogues busy about her, getting off her jacket, as they called the stout tarpaulin cover under which she sailed. Not only that, but it flashed into my mind at the same moment that the round-shot and the powder for the gun had been left behind, and a stroke with an axe would put it all into the possession of the evil ones aboard.

"Israel was Flint's gunner," said Gray hoarsely.

At any risk, we put the boat's head direct for the landing-place. By this time we had got so far out of the run of the current that we kept steerage way even at our necessarily gentle rate of rowing, and I could keep her steady for the goal. But the worst of it was, that with the course I now held, we turned our broadside instead of our stern to the *Hispaniola,* and offered a target like a barn door.

I could hear, as well as see, that brandy-faced rascal, Israel Hands, plumping down a round-shot on the deck.

"Who's the best shot?" asked the captain.

"Mr. Trelawney, out and away," said I.

"Mr. Trelawney, will you please pick me off one of these men, sir? Hands, if possible," said the captain.

Trelawney was as cool as steel. He looked to the priming of his gun.

"Now," cried the captain, "easy with that gun, sir, or you'll swamp the boat. All hands stand by to trim her when he aims."

The squire raised his gun, the rowing ceased, and we leaned over to the other side to keep the balance, and all was so nicely contrived that we did not ship a drop.

They had the gun, by this time, slewed round upon the swivel, and Hands, who was at the muzzle with the rammer, was, in consequence, the most exposed. However, we had no luck; for just as Trelawney fired, down he stooped, the ball whistled over him, and it was one of the other four who fell.

The cry he gave was echoed, not only by his companions on board, but by a great number of voices from the shore, and looking in that direction I saw the other pirates trooping out from among the trees and tumbling into their places in the boats.

"Here come the gigs, sir," said I.

"Give way, then," cried the captain. "We mustn't mind if we swamp her now. If we can't get ashore, all's up."

"Only one of the gigs is being manned, sir," I added, "the crew of the other most likely going round by shore to cut us off."

"They'll have a hot run, sir," returned the captain. "Jack's ashore, you know. It's not them I mind; it's the round-shot. Carpet-bowls! My lady's maid couldn't miss. Tell us, squire, when you see the match, and we'll hold water."

In the meanwhile we had been making headway at a good pace for a boat so overloaded, and we had shipped but little water in the process. We were now close in; thirty or forty strokes and we should beach her; for the ebb had already disclosed a narrow belt of sand below the clustering trees. The gig was no longer to be feared; the little point had already concealed it from our eyes. The ebb-tide, which had so cruelly delayed us, was now making reparation, and delaying our assailants. The one source of danger was the gun.

"If I durst," said the captain, "I'd stop and pick off another man."

But it was plain that they meant nothing should delay their shot. They had never so much as looked at their fallen comrade though he was not dead, and I could see him trying to crawl away.

"Ready!" cried the squire.

"Hold!" cried the captain, quick as an echo.

And he and Redruth backed with a great heave that sent her stern bodily under water. The report fell in at the same instant of time. This was the first that Jim heard, the sound of the squire's shot not having reached him. Where the ball passed not one of us precisely knew; but I fancy it must have been over our heads, and that the wind of it may have contributed to our disaster.

At any rate, the boat sank by the stern, quite gently, in three feet of water, leaving the captain and myself, facing each other, on our feet. The other three took complete headers, and came up again, drenched and bubbling.

So far there was no great harm. No lives were lost, and we could wade ashore in safety. But there were all our stores at the bottom, and, to make things worse, only two guns out of five remained in a state for service. Mine I had snatched from my knees and held over my head, by a sort of instinct. As for the captain, he had carried his over his shoulder by a bandoleer, and, like a wise man, lock uppermost. The other three had gone down with the boat.

To add to our concern we heard voices already drawing near us in the woods along shore; and we had not only the danger of being cut off from the stockade in our half-crippled state, but the fear before us whether, if Hunter and Joyce were attacked by half a dozen, they would have the sense and conduct to stand firm. Hunter was steady, that we knew; Joyce was a doubtful case—a pleasant, polite man for a valet, and to brush one's clothes, but not entirely fitted for a man of war.

With all this in our minds, we waded ashore as fast as we could, leaving behind us the poor jolly-boat, and a good half of all our powder and provisions.

18. NARRATIVE CONTINUED BY THE DOCTOR: *End of the First Day's Fighting*

WE MADE OUR BEST SPEED ACROSS THE STRIP OF WOOD THAT NOW divided us from the stockade; and at every step we took the voices of the buccaneers rang nearer. Soon we could hear their footfalls as they ran, and the cracking of the branches as they breasted across a bit of thicket.

I began to see we should have a brush for it in earnest, and looked to my priming.

"Captain," said I, "Trelawney is the dead shot. Give him your gun; his own is useless."

They exchanged guns, and Trelawney, silent and cool as he had been since the beginning of the bustle, hung a moment on his heel to see that all was fit for service. At the same time, observing Gray to be unarmed, I handed him my cutlass. It did all our hearts good to see him spit in his hand, knit his brows, and make the blade sing through the air. It was plain from every line of his body that our new hand was worth his salt.

Forty paces farther we came to the edge of the wood and saw the stockade in front of us. We struck the enclosure about the middle of the south side, and, almost at the same time, seven mutineers—Job Anderson, the boatswain, at their head, appeared in full cry at the south-western corner.

They paused, as if taken aback; and before they recovered, not only the squire and I, but Hunter and Joyce from the block house, had time to fire. The four shots came in rather a scattering volley; but they did the business; one of the enemy actually fell, and the rest, without hesitation, turned and plunged into the trees.

After reloading, we walked down the outside of the palisade to see the fallen enemy. He was stone dead—shot through the heart.

We began to rejoice over our good success, when just at that moment a pistol cracked in the bush, a ball whistled close past my ear, and poor Tom Redruth stumbled and fell his length on the ground. Both the squire and I returned the shot; but as we had nothing to aim at, it is probable we only wasted powder. Then we reloaded, and turned our attention to poor Tom.

The captain and Gray were already examining him; and I saw with half an eye that all was over.

I believe the readiness of our return volley had scattered the mutineers once more, for we were suffered without further molestation to get the poor old gamekeeper hoisted over the stockade, and carried, groaning and bleeding, into the log-house.

Poor old fellow, he had not uttered one word of surprise, complaint, fear, or even acquiescence, from the very beginning of our troubles till now, when we had laid him down in the log-house to die. He had lain like a Trojan behind his mattress in the gallery; he had followed every order silently, doggedly, and well; he was the oldest of our party by a score of years; and now, sullen, old, serviceable servant, it was he that was to die.

The squire dropped down beside him on his knees and kissed his hand, crying like a child.

"Be I going, doctor?" he asked.

"Tom, my man," said I, "you're going home."

"I wish I had had a lick at them with the gun first," he replied.

"Tom," said the squire, "say you forgive me, won't you?"

"Would that be respectful like, from me to you, squire?" was the answer. "Howsoever, so be it, amen!"

After a little while of silence, he said he thought somebody might read a prayer. "It's the custom, sir," he added, apologetically. And not long after, without another word, he passed away.

In the meantime the captain, whom I had observed to be wonderfully swollen about the chest and pockets, had turned out a great many various stores—the British colours, a Bible, a coil of stoutish rope, pen, ink, the log-book, and pounds of tobacco. He had found a longish fir-tree lying felled and cleared in the enclosure, and with the help of Hunter, he had set it up at the corner of the log-house where the trunks crossed and made an angle. Then, climbing on the roof, he had with his own hand bent and run up the colours.

This seemed mightily to relieve him. He re-entered the log-house and set about counting up the stores, as if nothing else existed. But he had an eye on Tom's passage for all that; and as soon as all was over, came forward with another flag, and reverently spread it on the body.

"Don't you take on, sir," he said, shaking the squire's hand. "All's well with him; no fear for a hand that's been shot down in his duty to captain and owner. It mayn't be good divinity, but it's a fact."

Then he pulled me aside.

"Dr. Livesey," he said, "in how many weeks do you and squire expect the consort?"

I told him it was a question, not of weeks, but of months; that if we were not back by the end of August, Blandly was to send to find us; but neither sooner nor later. "You can calculate for yourself," I said.

"Why, yes," returned the captain, scratching his head, "and making a large allowance, sir, for all the gifts of Providence, I should say we were pretty close hauled."

"How do you mean?" I asked.

"It's a pity, sir, we lost that second load. That's what I mean," replied the captain. "As for powder and shot, we'll do. But the ra-

tions are short, very short—so short, Dr. Livesey, that we're perhaps as well without that extra mouth."

And he pointed to the dead body under the flag.

Just then, with a roar and a whistle, a round-shot passed high
above the roof of the log-house and plumped far beyond us in the
wood.

"Oho!" said the captain. "Blaze away! You've little enough
powder already, my lads."

At the second trial, the aim was better, and the ball descended
inside the stockade, scattering a cloud of sand, but doing no
further damage.

"Captain," said the squire, "the house is quite invisible from
the ship. It must be the flag they are aiming at. Would it not be
wiser to take it in?"

"Strike my colours!" cried the captain. "No, sir, not I"; and, as
soon as he had said the words, I think we all agreed with him. For
it was not only a piece of stout, seamanly, good feeling; it was good
policy besides, and showed our enemies that we despised their cannonade.

All through the evening they kept thundering away. Ball after
ball flew over or fell short, or kicked up the sand in the enclosure;
but they had to fire so high that the shot fell dead and buried
itself in the soft sand. We had no ricochet to fear; and though one
popped in through the roof of the log-house and out again through
the floor, we soon got used to that sort of horse-play, and minded
it no more than cricket.

"There is one thing good about all this," observed the captain:
"the wood in front of us is likely clear. The ebb has made a good
while; our stores should be uncovered. Volunteers to go and bring
in pork."

Gray and Hunter were the first to come forward. Well armed,
they stole out of the stockade; but it proved a useless mission. The
mutineers were bolder than we fancied, or they put more trust in
Israel's gunnery. For four or five of them were busy carrying off
our stores, and wading out with them to one of the gigs that lay
close by, pulling an oar or so to hold her steady against the current.

Silver was in the stern sheets in command; and every man of
them was now provided with a musket from some secret magazine
of their own.

The captain sat down to his log, and here is the beginning of the entry:—

"Alexander Smollett, master; David Livesey, ship's doctor; Abraham Gray, carpenter's mate; John Trelawney, owner; John Hunter and Richard Joyce, owner's servants, landsmen—being all that is left faithful of the ship's company—with stores for ten days at short rations, came ashore this day, and flew British colours on the log-house in Treasure Island. Thomas Redruth, owner's servant, landsman, shot by the mutineers; James Hawkins, cabin-boy——"

And at the same time I was wondering over poor Jim Hawkins's fate.

A hail on the land side.

"Somebody hailing us," said Hunter, who was on guard.

"Doctor! squire! captain! Hallo, Hunter, is that you?" came the cries.

And I ran to the door in time to see Jim Hawkins, safe and sound, come climbing over the stockade.

19. NARRATIVE RESUMED BY JIM HAWKINS:
The Garrison in the Stockade

As SOON AS BEN GUNN SAW THE COLOURS HE CAME TO A HALT, stopped me by the arm, and sat down.

"Now," said he, "there's your friends, sure enough."

"Far more likely it's the mutineers," I answered.

"That!" he cried. "Why, in a place like this, where nobody puts in but gen'lemen of fortune, Silver would fly the Jolly Roger, you don't make no doubt of that. No; that's your friends. There's been blows, too, and I reckon your friends has had the best of it; and here they are ashore in the old stockade, as was made years and years ago by Flint. Ah, he was the man to have a headpiece, was Flint! Barring rum, his match were never seen. He was afraid of none, not he; only Silver—Silver was that genteel."

"Well," said I, "that may be so, and so be it; all the more reason that I should hurry on and join my friends."

"Nay, mate," returned Ben, "not you. You're a good boy, or I'm mistook; but you're only a boy, all told. Now, Ben Gunn is fly. Rum wouldn't bring me there, where you're going—not rum wouldn't, till I see your born gen'leman, and gets it on his word of honour. And you won't forget my words! 'A precious sight (that's what you'll say), a precious sight more confidence'—and then nips him."

And he pinched me the third time with the same air of cleverness.

"And when Ben Gunn is wanted, you know where to find him, Jim. Just wheer you found him to-day. And him that comes is to have a white thing in his hand: and he's to come alone. Oh! and you'll say this: 'Ben Gunn,' says you, 'has reasons of his own.' "

"Well," said I, "I believe I understand. You have something to propose, and you wish to see the squire or the doctor; and you're to be found where I found you. Is that all?"

"And when? says you," he added. "Why, from about noon observation to about six bells."

"Good," said I, "and now may I go?"

"You won't forget?" he inquired anxiously. "Precious sight, and reasons of his own, says you. Reasons of his own; that's the mainstay; as between man and man. Well, then"—still holding me—"I reckon you can go, Jim. And, Jim, if you was to see Silver, you wouldn't go for to sell Ben Gunn? Wild horses wouldn't draw it from you? No, says you. And if them pirates camp ashore, Jim, what would you say but there'd be widders in the morning?"

Here he was interrupted by a loud report, and a cannon ball came tearing through the trees and pitched in the sand, not a hundred yards from where we two were talking. The next moment each of us had taken to his heels in a different direction.

For a good hour to come frequent reports shook the island, and balls kept crashing through the woods. I moved from hiding-place to hiding-place, always pursued, or so it seemed to me, by these terrifying missiles. But towards the end of the bombardment, though still I durst not venture in the direction of the stockade, where the balls fell oftenest, I had begun, in a manner, to pluck up my heart again; and after a long detour to the east, crept down among the shore-side trees.

The sun had just set, the sea breeze was rustling and tumbling in the woods, and ruffling the gray surface of the anchorage; the tide, too, was far out, and great tracts of sand lay uncovered; the air, after the heat of the day, chilled me through my jacket.

The *Hispaniola* still lay where she had anchored; but, sure enough, there was the Jolly Roger, the black flag of piracy, flying from her peak. Even as I looked, there came another red flash and another report, that sent the echoes clattering, and one more round-shot whistled through the air. It was the last of the cannonade.

I lay for some time, watching the bustle which succeeded the attack. Men were demolishing something with axes on the beach near the stockade; the poor jolly-boat, I afterwards discovered. Away, near the mouth of the river, a great fire was glowing among the trees, and between that point and the ship one of the gigs kept coming and going, the men, whom I had seen so gloomy, shouting at the oars like children. But there was a sound in their voices which suggested rum.

At length I thought I might return towards the stockade. I was pretty far down on the low, sandy spit that encloses the anchorage to the east, and is joined at half-water to Skeleton Island; and now, as I rose to my feet, I saw, some distance farther down the spit, and rising from among low bushes, an isolated rock, pretty high, and peculiarly white in colour. It occurred to me that this might be the white rock of which Ben Gunn had spoken, and that some day or other a boat might be wanted, and I should know where to look for one.

Then I skirted among the woods until I had regained the rear, or shoreward side, of the stockade, and was soon warmly welcomed by the faithful party.

I had soon told my story, and began to look about me. The loghouse was made of unsquared trunks of pine—roof, walls, and floor. The latter stood in several places as much as a foot or a foot and a half above the surface of the sand. There was a porch at the door, and under this porch the little spring welled up into an artificial basin of a rather odd kind—no other than a great ship's kettle of iron, with the bottom knocked out, and sunk "to her bearings," as the captain said, among the sand.

Little had been left beside the framework of the house; but in one corner there was a stone slab laid down by way of hearth and an old rusty iron basket to contain the fire.

The slopes of the knoll and all the inside of the stockade had been cleared of timber to build the house, and we could see by the stumps what a fine and lofty grove had been destroyed. Most of the soil had been washed away or buried in drift after the removal of the trees; only where the streamlet ran down from the kettle a thick bed of moss and some ferns and little creeping bushes were still green among the sand. Very close around the stockade—too close for defence, they said—the wood still flourished high and dense, all of fir on the land side, but towards the sea with a large admixture of live-oaks.

The cold evening breeze, of which I have spoken, whistled through every chink of the rude building, and sprinkled the floor with a continual rain of fine sand. There was sand in our eyes, sand in our teeth, sand in our suppers, sand dancing in the spring at the bottom of the kettle, for all the world like porridge beginning to boil. Our chimney was a square hole in the roof: it was but a little part of the smoke that found its way out, and the rest eddied about the house, and kept us coughing and piping the eye.

Add to this that Gray, the new man, had his face tied up in a bandage for a cut he had got in breaking away from the mutineers; and that poor old Tom Redruth, still unburied, lay along the wall, stiff and stark, under the Union Jack.

If we had been allowed to sit idle, we should all have fallen into the blues, but Captain Smollett was never the man for that. All hands were called up before him, and he divided us into watches. The doctor, and Gray, and I, for one; the squire, Hunter, and Joyce upon the other. Tired as we all were, two were sent out for firewood; two more were set to dig a grave for Redruth; the doctor was named cook; I was put sentry at the door; and the captain himself went from one to another, keeping up our spirits, and lending a hand wherever it was wanted.

From time to time the doctor came to the door for a little air and to rest his eyes, which were almost smoked out of his head; and whenever he did so, he had a word for me.

"That man Smollett," he said once, "is a better man than I am. And when I say that it means a deal, Jim."

Another time he came and was silent for a while. Then he put his head on one side, and looked at me.

"Is this Ben Gunn a man?" he asked.

"I do not know, sir," said I. "I am not very sure whether he's sane."

"If there's any doubt about the matter, he is," returned the doctor. "A man who has been three years biting his nails on a desert island, Jim, can't expect to appear as sane as you or me. It doesn't lie in human nature. Was it cheese you said he had a fancy for?"

"Yes, sir, cheese," I answered.

"Well, Jim," says he, "just see the good that comes of being dainty in your food. You've seen my snuff-box, haven't you? And you never saw me take snuff; the reason being that in my snuff-box I carry a piece of Parmesan cheese—a cheese made in Italy, very nutritious. Well, that's for Ben Gunn!"

Before supper was eaten we buried old Tom in the sand, and stood round him for a while bareheaded in the breeze. A good deal of firewood had been got in, but not enough for the captain's fancy; and he shook his head over it, and told us we "must get back to this to-morrow rather livelier." Then, when we had eaten our pork, and each had a good stiff glass of brandy grog, the three chiefs got together in a corner to discuss our prospects.

It appears they were at their wits' end what to do, the stores being so low that we must have been starved into surrender long before help came. But our best hope, it was decided, was to kill off the buccaneers until they either hauled down their flag or ran away with the *Hispaniola*. From nineteen they were already reduced to fifteen, two others were wounded, and one, at least—the man shot beside the gun—severely wounded, if he were not dead. Every time we had a crack at them, we were to take it, saving our own lives, with the extremest care. And, besides that, we had two able allies—rum and the climate.

As for the first, though we were about half a mile away, we could hear them roaring and singing late into the night; and as for the second, the doctor staked his wig that, camped where they were in the marsh and unprovided with remedies, the half of them would be on their backs before a week.

"So," he added, "if we are not all shot down first, they'll be glad to be packing in the schooner. It's always a ship, and they can get to buccaneering again, I suppose."

"First ship that ever I lost," said Captain Smollett.

I was dead tired, as you may fancy; and when I got to sleep, which was not till after a great deal of tossing, I slept like a log of wood.

The rest had long been up, and had already breakfasted and increased the pile of firewood by about half as much again, when I was awakened by a bustle and the sound of voices.

"Flag of truce!" I heard some one say; and then, immediately after, with a cry of surprise, "Silver himself!"

And, at that, up I jumped, and, rubbing my eyes, ran to a loop hole in the wall.

20. *Silver's Embassy*

SURE ENOUGH, THERE WERE TWO MEN JUST OUTSIDE THE STOCKADE, one of them waving a white cloth; the other, no less a person than Silver himself, standing placidly by.

It was still quite early, and the coldest morning that I think I ever was abroad in; a chill that pierced into the marrow. The sky was bright and cloudless overhead, and the tops of the trees shone rosily in the sun. But where Silver stood with his lieutenant all was still in shadow, and they waded knee deep in a low, white vapour, that had crawled during the night out of the morass. The chill and the vapour taken together told a poor tale of the island. It was plainly a damp, feverish, unhealthy spot.

"Keep indoors, men," said the captain. "Ten to one this is a trick."

Then he hailed the buccaneer.

"Who goes? Stand, or we fire."

"Flag of truce," cried Silver.

The captain was in the porch, keeping himself carefully out of the way of a treacherous shot should any be intended. He turned and spoke to us:—

"Doctor's watch on the look-out. Dr. Livesey, take the north side, if you please; Jim, the east; Gray, west. The watch below, all hands to load muskets. Lively, men, and careful."

And then he turned again to the mutineers.

"And what do you want with your flag of truce?" he cried.

This time it was the other man who replied.

"Cap'n Silver, sir, to come on board and make terms," he shouted.

"Cap'n Silver! Don't know him. Who's he?" cries the captain. And we could hear him adding to himself: "Cap'n, is it? My heart, and here's promotion!"

Long John answered for himself.

"Me, sir. These poor lads have chosen me cap'n, after your desertion, sir"—laying a particular emphasis upon the word "desertion." "We're willing to submit, if we can come to terms, and no bones about it. All I ask is your word, Cap'n Smollett, to let me safe and sound out of this here stockade, and one minute to get out o' shot before a gun is fired."

"My man," said Captain Smollett, "I have not the slightest desire to talk to you. If you wish to talk to me, you can come, that's all. If there's any treachery, it'll be on your side, and the Lord help you."

"That's enough, cap'n," shouted Long John cheerily. "A word from you's enough. I know a gentleman, and you may lay to that."

We could see the man who carried the flag of truce attempting to hold Silver back. Nor was that wonderful, seeing how cavalier had been the captain's answer. But Silver laughed at him aloud, and slapped him on the back, as if the idea of alarm had been absurd. Then he advanced to the stockade, threw over his crutch, got a leg up, and with great vigour and skill succeeded in surmounting the fence and dropping safely to the other side.

I will confess that I was far too much taken up with what was going on to be of the slightest use as sentry; indeed, I had already deserted my eastern loophole, and crept up behind the captain, who had now seated himself on the threshold, with his elbows on his knees, his head in his hands, and his eyes fixed on the water, as it bubbled out of the old iron kettle in the sand. He was whistling to himself, "Come, Lassies and Lads."

Silver had terrible hard work getting up the knoll. What with the steepness of the incline, the thick tree stumps, and the soft sand, he and his crutch were as helpless as a ship in stays. But he stuck to it like a man in silence, and at last arrived before the captain, whom he saluted in the handsomest style. He was tricked out in his best; an immense blue coat, thick with brass buttons, hung as low as to his knees, and a fine laced hat was set on the back of his head.

"Here you are, my man," said the captain, raising his head. "You had better sit down."

"You ain't a-going to let me inside, cap'n?" complained Long John. "It's a main cold morning, to be sure, sir, to sit outside upon the sand."

"Why, Silver," said the captain, "if you had pleased to be an honest man, you might have been sitting in your galley. It's your own doing. You're either my ship's cook—and then you were treated handsome—or Cap'n Silver, a common mutineer and pirate, and then you can go hang!"

"Well, well, cap'n," returned the sea cook, sitting down as he was bidden on the sand, "you'll have to give me a hand up again, that's all. A sweet pretty place you have of it here. Ah, there's Jim! The top of the morning to you, Jim. Doctor, here's my service. Why, there you all are together like a happy family, in a manner of speaking."

"If you have anything to say, my man, better say it," said the captain.

"Right you were, Cap'n Smollett," replied Silver. "Dooty is dooty, to be sure. Well, now, you look here, that was a good lay of yours last night. I don't deny it was a good lay. Some of you pretty handy with a handspike-end. And I'll not deny neither but what some of my people was shook—maybe all was shook; maybe I was shook myself; maybe that's why I'm here for terms. But you mark me, cap'n, it won't do twice, by thunder! We'll have to do sentry-go, and ease off a point or so on the rum. Maybe you think we were all a sheet in the wind's eye. But I'll tell you I was sober; I was on'y dog tired; and if I'd a awoke a second sooner I'd a caught you at the act, I would. He wasn't dead when I got round to him, not he."

"Well?" says Captain Smollett, as cool as can be.

All that Silver said was a riddle to him, but you would never have guessed it from his tone. As for me, I began to have an inkling. Ben Gunn's last words came back to my mind. I began to suppose that he had paid the buccaneers a visit while they all lay drunk together round their fire, and I reckoned up with glee that we had only fourteen enemies to deal with.

"Well, here it is," said Silver. "We want that treasure, and we'll have it—that's our point! You would just as soon save your lives, I reckon; and that's yours. You have a chart, haven't you?"

"That's as may be," replied the captain.

"Oh, well, you have, I know that," returned Long John. "You needn't be so husky with a man; there ain't a particle of service in that, and you may lay to it. What I mean is, we want your chart. Now, I never meant you no harm, myself."

"That won't do with me, my man," interrupted the captain.

"We know exactly what you meant to do, and we don't care; for now, you see, you can't do it."

And the captain looked at him calmly, and proceeded to fill a pipe.

"If Abe Gray——" Silver broke out.

"Avast there!" cried Mr. Smollett. "Gray told me nothing, and I asked him nothing; and what's more, I would see you and him and this whole island blown clean out of the water into blazes first. So there's my mind for you, my man, on that."

This little whiff of temper seemed to cool Silver down. He had been growing nettled before, but now he pulled himself together.

"Like enough," said he. "I would set no limits to what gentlemen might consider shipshape, or might not, as the case were. And seein' as how you are about to take a pipe, cap'n, I'll make so free as do likewise."

And he filled a pipe and lighted it; and the two men sat silently smoking for quite a while, now looking each other in the face, now stopping their tobacco, now leaning forward to spit. It was as good as the play to see them.

"Now," resumed Silver, "here it is. You give us the chart to get the treasure by, and drop shooting poor seamen, and stoving of their heads in while asleep. You do that, and we'll offer you a choice. Either you come aboard along of us, once the treasure's shipped, and then I'll give you my affy-davy, upon my word of honour, to clap you somewhere safe ashore. Or, if that ain't to your fancy, some of my hands being rough, and having old scores, on account of hazing, then you can stay here, you can. We'll divide stores with you, man for man; and I'll give my affy-davy, as before, to speak the first ship I sight, and send 'em here to pick you up. Now you'll own that's talking. Handsomer you couldn't look to get, not you. And I hope"—raising his voice—"that all hands in this here block-house will overhaul my words, for what is spoke to one is spoke to all."

Captain Smollett rose from his seat, and knocked the ashes of his pipe in the palm of his left hand.

"Is that all?" he asked.

"Every last word, by thunder!" answered John. "Refuse that, and you've seen the last of me but musket-balls."

"Very good," said the captain. "Now you'll hear me. If you'll come up one by one, unarmed, I'll engage to clap you all in irons, and take you home to a fair trial in England. If you won't, my name is Alexander Smollett, I've flown my sovereign's colours, and I'll see you all to Davy Jones. You can't find the treasure. You can't sail the ship—there's not a man among you fit to sail the ship. You can't fight us—Gray, there, got away from five of you. Your ship's in irons, Master Silver; you're on a lee shore, and so you'll find. I stand here and tell you so; and they're the last good words you'll get from me; for, in the name of heaven, I'll put a bullet in your back when next I meet you. Tramp, my lad. Bundle out of this, please, hand over hand, and double quick."

Silver's face was a picture; his eyes started in his head with wrath. He shook the fire out of his pipe.

"Give me a hand up!" he cried.

"Not I," returned the captain.

"Who'll give me a hand up?" he roared.

Not a man among us moved. Growling the foulest imprecations, he crawled along the sand till he got hold of the porch and could hoist himself again upon his crutch. Then he spat into the spring.

"There!" he cried, "that's what I think of ye. Before an hour's out, I'll stove in your old block-house like a rum puncheon. Laugh, by thunder, laugh! Before an hour's out ye'll laugh upon the other side. Them that die'll be the lucky ones."

And with a dreadful oath he stumbled off, ploughed down the sand, was helped across the stockade, after four or five failures, by the man with the flag of truce, and disappeared in an instant afterwards among the trees.

21. *The Attack*

As SOON AS SILVER DISAPPEARED, THE CAPTAIN, WHO HAD BEEN closely watching him, turned towards the interior of the house, and found not a man of us at his post but Gray. It was the first time we had ever seen him angry.

"Quarters!" he roared. And then, as we all slunk back to our places, "Gray," he said, "I'll put your name in the log; you've stood by your duty like a seaman. Mr. Trelawney, I'm surprised at you, sir. Doctor, I thought you had worn the king's coat! If that was how you served at Fontenoy, sir, you'd have been better in your berth."

The doctor's watch were all back at their loop-holes, the rest were busy loading the spare muskets, and every one with a red face, you may be certain, and a flea in his ear, as the saying is.

The captain looked on for a while in silence. Then he spoke.

"My lads," said he, "I've given Silver a broadside. I pitched it in red-hot on purpose; and before the hour's out, as he said, we shall be boarded. We're outnumbered, I needn't tell you that, but we fight in shelter; and, a minute ago, I should have said we fought with discipline, I've no manner of doubt that we can drub them, if you choose."

Then he went the rounds, and saw, as he said, that all was clear.

On the two short sides of the house, east and west, there were only two loopholes; on the south side where the porch was, two again; and on the north side, five. There was a round score of muskets for the seven of us; the firewood had been built into four piles—tables, you might say—one about the middle of each side, and on each of these tables some ammunition and four loaded muskets were laid ready to the hand of the defenders. In the middle, the cutlasses lay ranged.

"Toss out the fire," said the captain; "the chill is past, and we mustn't have smoke in our eyes."

The iron fire basket was carried bodily out by Mr. Trelawney, and the embers smothered among sand.

"Hawkins hasn't had his breakfast. Hawkins, help yourself, and back to your post to eat it," continued Captain Smollett. "Lively, now, my lad; you'll want it before you've done. Hunter, serve out a round of brandy to all hands."

And while this was going on, the captain completed, in his own mind, the plan of the defence.

"Doctor, you will take the door," he resumed. "See and don't expose yourself; keep within, and fire through the porch. Hunter, take the east side, there. Joyce, you stand by the west, my man. Mr. Trelawney, you are the best shot, you and Gray will take this long north side, with the five loopholes; it's there the danger is. If they can get up to it, and fire in upon us through our own ports, things would begin to look dirty. Hawkins, neither you nor I are much account at the shooting; we'll stand by to load and bear a hand."

As the captain had said, the chill was past. As soon as the sun had climbed above our girdle of trees, it fell with all its force upon the clearing, and drank up the vapours at a draught. Soon the sand was baking, and the resin melting in the logs of the block-house. Jackets and coats were flung aside; shirts thrown open at the neck, and rolled up to the shoulders; and we stood there, each at his post, in a fever of heat and anxiety.

An hour passed away.

"Hang them!" said the captain. "This is as dull as the doldrums. Gray, whistle for a wind."

And just at that moment came the first news of the attack.

"If you please, sir," said Joyce, "if I see any one, am I to fire?"

"I told you so!" cried the captain.

"Thank you, sir," returned Joyce, with the same quiet civility.

Nothing followed for a time; but the remark had set us all on the alert, straining ears and eyes—the musketeers with their pieces balanced in their hands, the captain out in the middle of the blockhouse, with his mouth very tight and a frown on his face.

So some seconds passed, till suddenly Joyce whipped up his musket and fired. The report had scarcely died away ere it was re-peated and repeated from without in a scattering volley, shot be-hind shot, like a string of geese, from every side of the enclosure. Several bullets struck the log-house, but not one entered; and, as the smoke cleared away and vanished, the stockade and the woods around it looked as quiet and empty as before. Not a bough waved, not the gleam of a musket-barrel betrayed the presence of our foes.

"Did you hit your man?" asked the captain.

"No, sir," replied Joyce. "I believe not, sir."

"Next best thing to tell the truth," muttered Captain Smollett. "Load his gun, Hawkins. How many should you say there were on your side, doctor?"

"I know precisely," said Dr. Livesey. "Three shots were fired on this side. I saw the three flashes—two close together—one farther to the west."

"Three!" repeated the captain. "And how many on yours, Mr. Trelawney?"

But this was not so easily answered. There had come many from the north—seven, by the squire's computation; eight or nine, ac-cording to Gray. From the east and west only a single shot had been fired. It was plain, therefore, that the attack would be de-veloped from the north, and that on the other three sides we were only to be annoyed by a show of hostilities. But Captain Smollett made no change in his arrangements. If the mutineers succeeded in crossing the stockade, he argued, they would take possession of any unprotected loophole, and shoot us down like rats in our own stronghold.

Nor had we much time left to us for thought. Suddenly, with a loud huzza, a little cloud of pirates leaped from the woods on the north side, and ran straight on the stockade. At the same moment, the fire was once more opened from the woods, and a rifle ball sang through the doorway, and knocked the doctor's musket into bits.

The boarders swarmed over the fence like monkeys. Squire and Gray fired again and yet again; three men fell, one forwards into the enclosure, two back on the outside. But of these, one was evidently more frightened than hurt, for he was on his feet again in a crack, and instantly disappeared among the trees.

Two had bit the dust, one had fled, four had made good their footing inside our defences; while from the shelter of the woods seven or eight men, each evidently supplied with several muskets, kept up a hot though useless fire on the log-house.

The four who had boarded made straight before them for the building, shouting as they ran, and the men among the trees shouted back to encourage them. Several shots were fired; but, such was the hurry of the marksmen, that not one appears to have taken effect. In a moment, the four pirates had swarmed up the mound and were upon us.

The head of Job Anderson, the boatswain, appeared at the middle loop-hole.

"At 'em, all hands—all hands!" he roared, in a voice of thunder.

At the same moment, another pirate grasped Hunter's musket by the muzzle, wrenched it from his hands, plucked it through the loophole, and, with one stunning blow, laid the poor fellow senseless on the floor. Meanwhile a third, running unharmed all round the house, appeared suddenly in the doorway, and fell with his cutlass on the doctor.

Our position was utterly reversed. A moment since we were firing, under cover, at an exposed enemy; now it was we who lay uncovered, and could not return a blow.

The log-house was full of smoke, to which we owed our comparative safety. Cries and confusion, the flashes and reports of pistol shots, and one loud groan, rang in my ears.

"Out, lads, out, and fight 'em in the open! Cutlasses!" cried the captain.

I snatched a cutlass from the pile, and some one, at the same time snatching another, gave me a cut across the knuckles which I hardly felt. I dashed out of the door into the clear sunlight. Some one was close behind, I knew not whom. Right in front, the doctor was pursuing his assailant down the hill, and, just as my eyes fell upon, beat down his guard, and set him sprawling on his back, with a great slash across the face.

"Round the house, lads! round the house!" cried the captain; and even in the hurly-burly I perceived a change in his voice.

Mechanically I obeyed, turned eastwards, and with my cutlass raised, ran round the corner of the house. Next moment I was face to face with Anderson. He roared aloud, and his hanger went up above his head, flashing in the sunlight. I had not time to be afraid, but, as the blow still hung impending, leaped in a trice upon one side, and missing my foot in the soft sand, rolled head-long down the slope.

When I had first sallied from the door, the other mutineers had been already swarming up the palisade to make an end of us. One man, in a red night-cap, with his cutlass in his mouth, had even got upon the top and thrown a leg across. Well, so short had been the interval, that when I found my feet again all was in the same posture, the fellow with the red night-cap still half-way over, another still just showing his head above the top of the stockade. And yet, in this breath of time, the fight was over, and the victory was ours.

Gray, following close behind me, had cut down the big boat-swain ere he had time to recover from his lost blow. Another had been shot at a loophole in the very act of firing into the house, and now lay in agony, the pistol still smoking in his hand. A third, as I had seen, the doctor had disposed of at a blow. Of the four who had scaled the palisade, one only remained unaccounted for, and he, having left his cutlass on the field, was now clambering out again with the fear of death upon him.

"Fire—fire from the house!" cried the doctor. "And you, lads, back into cover."

But his words were unheeded, no shot was fired, and the last boarder made good his escape, and disappeared with the rest into the wood. In three seconds nothing remained of the attacking party but the five who had fallen, four on the inside, and one on the outside, of the palisade.

The doctor and Gray and I ran full speed for shelter. The survivors would soon be back where they had left their muskets, and at any moment the fire might recommence.

The house was by this time somewhat cleared of smoke, and we saw at a glance the price we had paid for victory. Hunter lay beside his loop-hole, stunned; Joyce by his, shot through the head, never to move again; while right in the centre, the squire was supporting the captain, one as pale as the other.

"The captain's wounded," said Mr. Trelawney.

"Have they run?" asked Mr. Smollett.

"All that could, you may be bound," returned the doctor; "but there's five of them will never run again."

"Five!" cried the captain. "Come, that's better. Five against three leaves us four to nine. That's better odds than we had at starting. We were seven to nineteen then, or thought we were, and that's as bad to bear." *

* The mutineers were soon only eight in number, for the man shot by Mr. Trelawney on board the schooner died that same evening of his wound. But this was, of course, not known till after by the faithful party.

PART FIVE

MY SEA ADVENTURE

✶

22. *How I Began My Sea Adventure*

THERE WAS NO RETURN OF THE MUTINEERS—NOT SO MUCH AS AN-
other shot out of the woods. They had "got their rations for
that day," as the captain put it, and we had the place to ourselves
and a quiet time to overhaul the wounded and get dinner. Squire
and I cooked outside in spite of the danger, and even outside
we could hardly tell what we were at, for horror of the loud groans
that reached us from the doctor's patients.

Out of the eight men who had fallen in the action, only three
still breathed—that one of the pirates who had been shot at the
loophole, Hunter, and Captain Smollett; and of these the first
two were as good as dead; the mutineer, indeed, died under the
doctor's knife, and Hunter, do what we could, never recovered
consciousness in this world. He lingered all day, breathing loudly
like the old buccaneer at home in his apoplectic fit; but the bones
of his chest had been crushed by the blow and his skull fractured
in falling, and some time in the following night, without sign or
sound, he went to his Maker.

As for the captain, his wounds were grievous indeed, but not
dangerous. No organ was fatally injured. Anderson's ball—for it
was Job that shot him first—had broken his shoulder-blade and
touched the lung, not badly; the second had only torn and displaced some muscles in the calf. He was sure to recover, the doctor
said, but, in the meantime and for weeks to come, he must not
walk nor move his arm, nor so much as speak when he could
help it.

My own accidental cut across the knuckles was a flea-bite. Dr.

Livesey patched it up with plaster, and pulled my ears for me into the bargain.

After dinner the squire and the doctor sat by the captain's side a while in consultation; and when they had talked to their heart's content, it being then a little past noon, the doctor took up his hat and pistols, girt on a cutlass, put the chart in his pocket, and with a musket on his shoulder, crossed the palisade on the north side, and set off briskly through the trees.

Gray and I were sitting together at the far end of the block-house, to be out of earshot of our officers consulting; and Gray took his pipe out of his mouth and fairly forgot to put it back again, so thunderstruck he was at this occurrence.

"Why, in the name of Davy Jones," said he, "is Dr. Livesey mad?"

"Why, no," says I. "He's about the last of this crew for that, I take it."

"Well, shipmate," said Gray, "mad he may not be; but if *he's* not, you mark my words, *I* am."

"I take it," replied I, "the doctor has his idea; and if I am right, he's going now to see Ben Gunn."

I was right, as appeared later; but in the meantime, the house being stifling hot, and the little patch of sand inside the palisade ablaze with midday sun, I began to get another thought into my head, which was not by any means so right. What I began to do was to envy the doctor, walking in the cool shadow of the woods, with the birds about him, and the pleasant smell of the pines, while I sat grilling, with my clothes stuck to the hot resin, and so much blood about me, and so many poor dead bodies lying all around, that I took a disgust of the place that was almost as strong as fear.

All the time I was washing out the blockhouse, and then washing up the things from dinner, this disgust and envy kept growing stronger and stronger, till at last, being near a bread-bag, and no one then observing me, I took the first step towards my escapade, and filled both pockets of my coat with biscuit.

I was a fool, if you like, and certainly I was going to do a foolish, over-bold act; but I was determined to do it with all the precautions in my power. These biscuits, should anything befall me, would keep me, at least, from starving till far on in the next day.

The next thing I laid hold of was a brace of pistols, and as I already had a powder-horn and bullets, I felt myself well supplied with arms.

As for the scheme I had in my head, it was not a bad one in itself. I was to go down the sandy spit that divides the anchorage on the east from the open sea, find the white rock I had observed last evening, and ascertain whether it was there or not that Ben Gunn had hidden his boat; a thing quite worth doing, as I still believe. But as I was certain I should not be allowed to leave the enclosure, my only plan was to take French leave, and slip out when nobody was watching; and that was so bad a way of doing it as made the thing itself wrong. But I was only a boy, and I had made my mind up.

Well, as things at last fell out, I found an admirable opportunity. The squire and Gray were busy helping the captain with his bandages; the coast was clear; I made a bolt for it over the stockade and into the thicket of the trees, and before my absence was observed I was out of cry of my companions.

This was my second folly, far worse than the first, as I left but two sound men to guard the house; but like the first, it was a help towards saving all of us.

I took my way straight for the east coast of the island, for I was determined to go down the sea side of the spit to avoid all chance of observation from the anchorage. It was already late in the afternoon, although still warm and sunny. As I continued to thread the tall woods I could hear from far before me not only the continuous thunder of the surf, but a certain tossing of foliage and grinding of boughs which showed me the sea breeze had set in higher than usual. Soon cool draughts of air began to reach me; and a few steps farther I came forth into the open borders of the grove, and saw the sea lying blue and sunny to the horizon, and the surf tumbling and tossing its foam along the beach.

I have never seen the sea quiet round Treasure Island. The sun might blaze overhead, the air be without a breath, the surface smooth and blue, but still these great rollers would be running along all the external coast, thundering and thundering by day and night; and I scarce believe there is one spot in the island where a man would be out of earshot of their noise.

I walked along beside the surf with great enjoyment, till, thinking I was now got far enough to the south, I took the cover of some thick bushes, and crept warily up to the ridge of the spit.

Behind me was the sea, in front the anchorage. The sea breeze, as though it had the sooner blown itself out by its unusual violence, was already at an end; it had been succeeded by light, variable airs from the south and south-east, carrying great banks of fog; and the anchorage, under lee of Skeleton Island, lay still and leaden as when first we entered it. The *Hispaniola*, in that unbroken mirror, was exactly portrayed from the truck to the water line, the Jolly Roger hanging from her peak.

Alongside lay one of the gigs, Silver in the sternsheets—him I could always recognise—while a couple of men were leaning over the stern bulwarks, one of them with a red cap—the very rogue that I had seen some hours before stride-legs upon the palisade. Apparently they were talking and laughing, though at that distance— upwards of a mile—I could, of course, hear no word of what was said. All at once, there began the most horrid, unearthly screaming, which at first startled me badly, though I soon remembered the voice of Captain Flint, and even thought I could make out the bird by her bright plumage as she sat perched upon her master's wrist.

Soon after the jolly-boat shoved off and pulled for shore, and the man with the red cap and his comrade went below by the cabin companion.

Just about the same time the sun had gone down behind the Spy-glass, and as the fog was collecting rapidly, it began to grow dark in earnest. I saw I must lose no time if I were to find the boat that evening.

The white rock, visible enough above the brush, was still some eighth of a mile farther down the spit, and it took me a goodish while to get up with it, crawling, often on all-fours, among the scrub. Night had almost come when I laid my hand on its rough sides. Right below it there was an exceedingly small hollow of green turf, hidden by banks and a thick underwood about knee-deep, that grew there very plentifully; and in the centre of the dell, sure enough, a little tent of goat-skins, like what the gipsies carry about with them in England.

I dropped into the hollow, lifted the side of the tent, and there was Ben Gunn's boat—home-made if ever anything was home-made; a rude, lop-sided framework of tough wood, and stretched upon that a covering of goatskin, with the hair inside. The thing was extremely small, even for me, and I can hardly imagine that it could have floated with a full-sized man. There was one thwart set as low as possible, a kind of stretcher in the bows, and a double paddle for propulsion.

I had not then seen a coracle, such as the ancient Britons made, but I have seen one since, and I can give you no fairer idea of Ben Gunn's boat than by saying it was like the first and the worst coracle ever made by man. But the great advantage of the coracle it certainly possessed, for it was exceedingly light and portable.

Well, now that I had found the boat, you would have thought I had had enough of truantry for once; but, in the meantime, I had taken another notion, and became so obstinately fond of it, that I would have carried it out, I believe, in the teeth of Captain Smollett himself. This was to slip out under cover of the night, cut the *Hispaniola* adrift, and let her go ashore where she fancied. I had quite made up my mind that the mutineers, after their repulse of the morning, had nothing nearer their hearts than to up anchor and away to sea; this, I thought, it would be a fine thing to prevent; and now that I had seen how they left their watchmen unprovided with a boat, I thought it might be done with little risk.

Down I sat to wait for darkness, and made a hearty meal of biscuit. It was a night out of ten thousand for my purpose. The fog had now buried all heaven. As the last rays of daylight dwindled and disappeared, absolute blackness settled down on Treasure Island. And when, at last, I shouldered the coracle, and groped my way stumblingly out of the hollow where I had supped, there were but two points visible on the whole anchorage.

One was the great fire on shore, by which the defeated pirates lay carousing in the swamp. The other, a mere blur of light upon the darkness, indicated the position of the anchored ship. She had swung round to the ebb—her bow was now towards me—the only lights on board were in the cabin; and what I saw was merely a reflection on the fog of the strong rays that flowed from the stern window.

The ebb had already run some time, and I had to wade through a long belt of swampy sand, where I sank several times above the ankle, before I came to the edge of the retreating water, and wading a little way in, with some strength and dexterity, set my coracle, keel downwards, on the surface.

23.　*The Ebb-Tide Turns*

THE CORACLE—AS I HAD AMPLE REASON TO KNOW BEFORE I WAS done with her—was a very safe boat for a person of my height and weight, both buoyant and clever in a seaway; but she was the most cross-grained, lop-sided craft to manage. Do as you please, she always made more leeway than anything else, and turning round and round was the manœuvre she was best at. Even Ben Gunn himself has admitted that she was "queer to handle till you knew her way."

Certainly I did not know her way. She turned in every direction but the one I was bound to go; the most part of the time we were broadside on, and I am very sure I never should have made the ship at all but for the tide. By good fortune, paddle as I pleased, the tide was still sweeping me down; and there lay the *Hispaniola* right in the fairway, hardly to be missed.

First she loomed before me like a blot of something yet blacker than darkness, then her spars and hull began to take shape, and the next moment, as it seemed (for the further I went, the brisker grew the current of the ebb), I was alongside of her hawser, and had laid hold.

The hawser was as taut as a bowstring—so strong she pulled upon her anchor. All round the hull, in the blackness, the rippling current bubbled and chattered like a little mountain stream. One cut with my sea-gully, and the *Hispaniola* would go humming down the tide.

So far so good; but it next occurred to my recollection that a taut hawser, suddenly cut, is a thing as dangerous as a kicking horse. Ten to one, if I were so foolhardy as to cut the *Hispaniola* from her anchor, I and the coracle would be knocked clean out of the water.

This brought me to a full stop, and if fortune had not again particularly favoured me, I should have had to abandon my design. But the light airs which had begun blowing from the south-east and south had hauled round after nightfall into the south-west.

Just while I was meditating, a puff came, caught the *Hispaniola*, and forced her up into the current; and, to my great joy, I felt the hawser slacken in my grasp, and the hand by which I held it dip for a second under water.

With that I made my mind up, took out my gully, opened it with my teeth, and cut one strand after another, till the vessel only swung by two. Then I lay quiet, waiting to sever these last when the strain should be once more lightened by a breath of wind.

All this time I had heard the sound of loud voices from the cabin; but, to say truth, my mind had been so entirely taken up with other thoughts that I had scarcely given ear. Now, however, when I had nothing else to do, I began to pay more heed.

One I recognised for the coxswain's, Israel Hands, that had been Flint's gunner in former days. The other was, of course, my friend of the red night-cap. Both men were plainly the worse of drink, and they were still drinking; for, even while I was listening, one of them, with a drunken cry, opened the stern window and threw out something, which I divined to be an empty bottle. But they were not only tipsy; it was plain that they were furiously angry. Oaths flew like hailstones, and every now and then there came forth such an explosion as I thought was sure to end in blows. But each time the quarrel passed off, and the voices grumbled lower for a while, until the next crisis came, and, in its turn, passed away without result.

On shore, I could see the glow of the great camp fire burning warmly through the shore-side trees. Some one was singing, a dull, old droning sailor's song, with a droop and a quaver at the end of every verse, and seemingly no end to it at all but the patience of the singer. I had heard it on the voyage more than once, and remembered these words:—

"But one man of her crew alive,
What put to sea with seventy-five."

And I thought it was a ditty rather too dolefully appropriate for a company that had met such cruel losses in the morning. But, indeed, from what I saw, all these buccaneers were as callous as the sea they sailed on.

At last the breeze came; the schooner sidled and drew nearer in the dark; I felt the hawser slacked once more, and with a good, tough effort, cut the last fibres through.

The breeze had but little action on the coracle, and I was almost instantly swept against the bows of the *Hispaniola*. At the same time the schooner began to turn upon her heel, spinning slowly, end for end, across the current.

I wrought like a fiend, for I expected every moment to be swamped; and since I found I could not push the coracle directly off, I now shoved straight astern. At length I was clear of my dangerous neighbour; and just as I gave the last impulsion, my hands came across a light cord that was trailing overboard across the stern bulwarks. Instantly I grasped it.

Why I should have done so I can hardly say. It was at first mere instinct; but once I had it in my hands and found it fast, curiosity began to get the upper hand, and I determined I should have one look through the cabin window.

I pulled in hand over hand on the cord, and, when I judged myself near enough, rose at infinite risk to about half my height, and thus commanded the roof and a slice of the interior of the cabin.

By this time the schooner and her little consort were gliding pretty swiftly through the water; indeed, we had already fetched up level with the camp fire. The ship was talking, as sailors say, loudly, treading the innumerable ripples with an incessant weltering splash; and until I got my eye above the window-sill I could not comprehend why the watchmen had taken no alarm. One glance, however, was sufficient; and it was only one glance that I durst take from that unsteady skiff. It showed me Hands and his companion locked together in deadly wrestle, each with a hand upon the other's throat.

I dropped upon the thwart again, none too soon, for I was near overboard. I could see nothing for the moment but these two furious, encrimsoned faces, swaying together under the smoky lamp; and I shut my eyes to let them grow once more familiar with the darkness.

The endless ballad had come to an end at last, and the whole diminished company about the camp fire had broken into the chorus I had heard so often:—

"Fifteen men on The Dead Man's Chest—
Yo-ho-ho, and a bottle of rum!

Drink and the devil had done for the rest—
Yo-ho-ho, and a bottle of rum!"

I was just thinking how busy drink and the devil were at that very moment in the cabin of the *Hispaniola,* when I was surprised by a sudden lurch of the coracle. At the same moment she yawed sharply and seemed to change her course. The speed in the meantime had greatly increased.

I opened my eyes at once. All round me were little ripples, combing over with a sharp, bristling sound and slightly phosphorescent. The *Hispaniola* herself, a few yards in whose wake I was still being whirled along, seemed to stagger in her course, and I saw her spars toss a little against the blackness of the night; nay, as I looked longer, I made sure she also was wheeling to the southward.

I glanced over my shoulder, and my heart jumped against my ribs. There, right behind me, was the glow of the camp fire. The current had turned at right angles, sweeping round along with it the tall schooner and the little dancing coracle; ever quickening, ever bubbling higher, ever muttering louder, it went spinning through the narrows for the open sea.

Suddenly the schooner in front of me gave a violent yaw, turning, perhaps, through twenty degrees; and almost at the same moment one shout followed another from on board; I could hear feet pounding on the companion ladder; and I knew that the two drunkards had at last been interrupted in their quarrel and awakened to a sense of their disaster.

I lay down flat in the bottom of that wretched skiff, and devoutly recommended my spirit to its Maker. At the end of the straits, I made sure we must fall into some bar of raging breakers, where all my troubles would be ended speedily; and though I could, perhaps, bear to die, I could not bear to look upon my fate as it approached.

So I must have lain for hours, continually beaten to and fro upon the billows, now and again wetted with flying sprays, and never ceasing to expect death at the next plunge. Gradually weariness grew upon me; a numbness, an occasional stupor, fell upon my mind even in the midst of my terrors; until sleep at last supervened, and in my sea-tossed coracle I lay and dreamed of home and the old Admiral Benbow.

24.   *The Cruise of the Coracle*

I T WAS BROAD DAY WHEN I AWOKE, AND FOUND MYSELF TOSSING AT
the south-west end of Treasure Island. The sun was up, but
was still hid from me behind the great bulk of the Spy-glass, which
on this side descended almost to the sea in formidable cliffs.

Haulbowline Head and Mizzen-mast Hill were at my elbow; the
hill bare and dark, the head bound with cliffs forty or fifty feet
high, and fringed with great masses of fallen rock. I was scarce a
quarter of a mile to seaward, and it was my first thought to paddle
in and land.

That notion was soon given over. Among the fallen rocks the
breakers spouted and bellowed; loud reverberations, heavy sprays
flying and falling, succeeded one another from second to second;
and I saw myself, if I ventured nearer, dashed to death upon the
rough shore, or spending my strength in vain to scale the beetling
crags.

Nor was that all; for crawling together on flat tables of rock,
or letting themselves drop into the sea with loud reports, I beheld huge slimy monsters—soft snails, as it were, of incredible
bigness—two or three score of them together, making the rocks to
echo with their barkings.

I have understood since that they were sea-lions, and entirely
harmless. But the look of them, added to the difficulty of the shore
and the high running of the surf, was more than enough to disgust me of that landing-place. I felt willing rather to starve at sea
than to confront such perils.

In the meantime I had a better chance, as I supposed, before
me. North of Haulbowline Head, the land runs in a long way, leaving, at low tide, a long stretch of yellow sand. To the north of
that, again, there comes another cape—Cape of the Woods, as it
was marked upon the chart—buried in tall green pines, which descended to the margin of the sea.

I remembered what Silver had said about the current that sets
northward along the whole west coast of Treasure Island; and
seeing from my position that I was already under its influence, I
preferred to leave Haulbowline Head behind me, and reserve my
strength for an attempt to land upon the kindlier-looking Cape of
the Woods.

There was a great, smooth swell upon the sea. The wind blowing steady and gentle from the south, there was no contrariety between that and the current, and the billows rose and fell unbroken.

Had it been otherwise, I must long ago have perished; but as it was, it is surprising how easily and securely my little and light boat could ride. Often, as I still lay at the bottom, and kept no more than an eye above the gunwale, I would see a big blue summit heaving close above me; yet the coracle would but bounce a little, dance as if on springs, and subside on the other side into the trough as lightly as a bird.

I began after a little to grow very bold, and sat up to try my skill at paddling. But even a small change in the disposition of the weight will produce violent changes in the behaviour of a coracle. And I had hardly moved before the boat, giving up at once her gentle dancing movement, ran straight down a slope of water so steep that it made me giddy, and struck her nose with a spout of spray, deep into the side of the next wave.

I was drenched and terrified, and fell instantly back into my old position, whereupon the coracle seemed to find her head again, and led me as softly as before among the billows. It was plain she was not to be interfered with, and at that rate, since I could in no way influence her course, what hope had I left of reaching land?

I began to be horribly frightened, but I kept my head, for all that. First, moving with all care, I gradually baled out the coracle with my sea-cap; then getting my eye once more above the gunwale, I set myself to study how it was she managed to slip so quietly through the rollers.

I found each wave, instead of the big, smooth, glossy mountain it looks from shore, or from a vessel's deck, was for all the world like any range of hills on the dry land, full of peaks and smooth places and valleys. The coracle, left to herself, turning from side to side, threaded, so to speak, her way through these lower parts, and avoided the steep slopes and higher, toppling summits of the wave.

"Well, now," thought I to myself, "it is plain I must lie where I am, and not disturb the balance; but it is plain, also, that I can put the paddle over the side, and from time to time, in smooth places, give her a shove or two towards land." No sooner thought upon than done. There I lay on my elbows, in the most trying attitude, and every now and again gave a weak stroke or two to turn her head to shore.

It was very tiring, and slow work, yet I did visibly gain ground; and, as we drew near the Cape of the Woods, though I saw I must infallibly miss that point, I had still made some hundred yards of easting. I was, indeed, close in. I could see the cool, green tree-tops swaying together in the breeze, and I felt sure I should make the next promontory without fail.

It was high time, for I now began to be tortured with thirst. The glow of the sun from above, its thousandfold reflection from the waves, the sea-water that fell and dried upon me, caking my very lips with salt, combined to make my throat burn and my brain ache. The sight of the trees so near at hand had almost made me sick with longing; but the current had soon carried me past the point; and, as the next reach of sea opened out, I beheld a sight that changed the nature of my thoughts.

Right in front of me, not half a mile away, I beheld the *Hispaniola* under sail. I made sure, of course, that I should be taken; but I was so distressed for want of water, that I scarce knew whether to be glad or sorry at the thought; and, long before I had come to a conclusion, surprise had taken entire possession of my mind, and I could do nothing but stare and wonder.

The *Hispaniola* was under her main-sail and two jibs, and the beautiful white canvas shone in the sun like snow or silver. When I first sighted her, all her sails were drawing; she was lying a course about north-west; and I presumed the men on board were going round the island on their way back to the anchorage. Presently she began to fetch more and more to the westward, so that I thought they had sighted me and were going about in chase. At last, however, she fell right into the wind's eye, was taken dead aback, and stood there a while helpless, with her sails shivering.

"Clumsy fellows," said I; "they must still be drunk as owls." And I thought how Captain Smollett would have set them skipping.

Meanwhile, the schooner gradually fell off, and filled again upon another tack, sailed swiftly for a minute or so, and brought up once more dead in the wind's eye. Again and again was this repeated. To and fro, up and down, north, south, east, and west, the *Hispaniola* sailed by swoops and dashes, and at each repetition ended as she had begun, with idly-flapping canvas. It became plain to me that nobody was steering. And, if so, where were the men? Either they were dead drunk, or had deserted her, I thought, and perhaps if I could get on board, I might return the vessel to her captain.

The current was bearing coracle and schooner southward at an equal rate. As for the latter's sailing, it was so wild and intermittent, and she hung each time so long in irons, that she certainly gained nothing, if she did not even lose. If only I dared to sit up and paddle, I made sure that I could overhaul her. The scheme had an air of adventure that inspired me, and the thought of the water breaker beside the fore companion doubled my growing courage.

Up I got, was welcomed almost instantly by another cloud of spray, but this time stuck to my purpose; and set myself, with all my strength and caution, to paddle after the unsteered *Hispaniola*. Once I shipped a sea so heavy that I had to stop and bale, with my heart fluttering like a bird; but gradually I got into the way of the thing, and guided my coracle among the waves, with only now and then a blow upon her bows and a dash of foam in my face.

I was now gaining rapidly on the schooner; I could see the brass glisten on the tiller as it banged about; and still no soul appeared upon her decks. I could not choose but suppose she was deserted. If not, the men were lying drunk below, where I might batten them down, perhaps, and do what I chose with the ship.

For some time she had been doing the worst thing possible for me—standing still. She headed nearly due south, yawing, of course, all the time. Each time she fell off her sails partly filled, and these brought her, in a moment, right to the wind again. I have said this was the worst thing possible for me; for helpless as she looked in this situation, with the canvas cracking like cannon, and the blocks trundling and banging on the deck, she still continued to run away from me, not only with the speed of the current, but by the whole amount of her leeway, which was naturally great.

But now, at last, I had my chance. The breeze fell, for some seconds, very low, and the current gradually turning her, the *Hispaniola* revolved slowly round her centre, and at last presented me her stern, with the cabin window still gaping open, and the lamp over the table still burning on into the day. The main-sail hung drooped like a banner. She was stock-still, but for the current.

For the last little while I had even lost; but now redoubling my efforts, I began once more to overhaul the chase.

I was not a hundred yards from her when the wind came again in a clap; she filled on the port tack, and was off again, stooping and skimming like a swallow.

My first impulse was one of despair, but my second was towards joy. Round she came, till she was broadside on to me—round still till she had covered a half, and then two-thirds, and then three-quarters of the distance that separated us. I could see the waves boiling white under her forefoot. Immensely tall she looked to me from my low station in the coracle.

And then, of a sudden, I began to comprehend. I had scarce time to think—scare time to act and save myself. I was on the summit of one swell when the schooner came swooping over the next. The bowsprit was over my head. I sprang to my feet, and leaped, stamping the coracle under water. With one hand I caught the jib-boom, while my foot was lodged between the stay and the brace; and as I still clung there panting, a dull blow told me that the schooner had charged down upon and struck the coracle, and that I was left without retreat on the *Hispaniola*.

25. I Strike the Jolly Roger

I HAD SCARCE GAINED A POSITION ON THE BOWSPRIT, WHEN THE flying jib flapped and filled upon the other tack, with a report like a gun. The schooner trembled to her keel under the reverse; but next moment, the other sails still drawing, the jib flapped back again, and hung idle.

This had nearly tossed me off into the sea; and now I lost no time, crawled back along the bowsprit, and tumbled head foremost on the deck.

I was on the lee-side of the forecastle, and the mainsail, which was still drawing, concealed from me a certain portion of the after-deck. Not a soul was to be seen. The planks, which had not been swabbed since the mutiny, bore the print of many feet; and an empty bottle, broken by the neck, tumbled to and fro like a live thing in the scuppers.

Suddenly the *Hispaniola* came right into the wind. The jibs behind me cracked aloud; the rudder slammed to; the whole ship gave a sickening heave and shudder, and at the same moment the main-boom swung inboard, the sheet groaning in the blocks, and showed me the lee afterdeck.

There were the two watchmen, sure enough: red-cap on his back, as stiff as a handspike, with his arms stretched out like those of a crucifix, and his teeth showing through his open lips; Israel Hands propped against the bulwarks, his chin on his chest, his hands lying open before him on the deck, his face as white, under its tan, as a tallow candle.

For a while the ship kept bucking and sidling like a vicious horse, the sails filling, now on one tack, now on another, and the boom swinging to and fro till the mast groaned aloud under the strain. Now and again, too, there would come a cloud of light sprays over the bulwark, and a heavy blow of the ship's bows against the swell; so much heavier weather was made of it by this great rigged ship than by my home made, lop-sided coracle, now gone to the bottom of the sea.

At every jump of the schooner, red-cap slipped to and fro; but— what was ghastly to behold—neither his attitude nor his fixed teeth-disclosing grin was anyway disturbed by this rough usage. At every jump, too, Hands appeared still more to sink into himself and settle down upon the deck, his feet sliding ever the farther out, and the whole body canting towards the stern, so that his face became, little by little, hid from me; and at last I could see nothing beyond his ear and the frayed ringlet of one whisker.

And at the same time, I observed around both of them, splashes of dark blood upon the planks, and began to feel sure that they had killed each other in their drunken wrath.

While I was thus looking and wondering, in a calm moment, when the ship was still, Israel Hands turned partly round, and, with a low moan, writhed himself back to the position in which I had seen him first. The moan, which told of pain and deadly weakness, and the way in which his jaw hung open, went right to my heart. But when I remembered the talk I had overheard from the apple barrel, all pity left me.

I walked aft until I reached the mainmast.

"Come aboard, Mr. Hands," I said ironically. He rolled his eyes round heavily; but he was too far gone to express surprise. All he could do was to utter one word, "Brandy."

It occurred to me there was no time to lose; and, dodging the boom as it once more lurched across the deck, I slipped aft, and down the companion-stairs into the cabin.

It was such a scene of confusion as you can hardly fancy. All the lock-fast places had been broken open in quest of the chart. The floor was thick with mud, where ruffians had sat down to drink or consult after wading in the marshes round their camp. The bulkheads, all painted in clear white, and beaded round with gilt, bore a pattern of dirty hands. Dozens of empty bottles clinked together in corners to the rolling of the ship. One of the doctor's medical books lay open on the table, half of the leaves gutted out, I suppose, for pipelights. In the midst of all this the lamp still cast a smoky glow, obscure and brown as umber.

I went into the cellar; all the barrels were gone, and of the bottles a most surprising number had been drunk out and thrown away. Certainly, since the mutiny began, not a man of them could ever have been sober.

Foraging about, I found a bottle with some brandy left, for Hands; and for myself I routed out some biscuit, some pickled fruits, a great bunch of raisins, and a piece of cheese. With these I came on deck, put down my own stock behind the rudder-head, and well out of the coxswain's reach, went forward to the water-breaker, and had a good, deep drink of water, and then, and not till then, gave Hands the brandy.

He must have drunk a gill before he took the bottle from his mouth.

"Ay," said he, "by thunder, but I wanted some o' that!"

I had sat down already in my own corner and begun to eat. "Much hurt?" I asked him.

He grunted, or rather I might say, he barked.

"If that doctor was aboard," he said, "I'd be right enough in a couple of turns; but I don't have no manner of luck, you see, and that's what's the matter with me. As for that swab, he's good as dead, he is," he added, indicating the man with the red cap. "He warn't no seaman, anyhow. And where mought you have come from?"

"Well," said I, "I've come aboard to take possession of this ship, Mr. Hands; and you'll please regard me as your captain until further notice."

He looked at me sourly enough, but said nothing. Some of the colour had come back into his cheeks, though he still looked very sick, and still continued to slip out and settle down as the ship banged about.

"By the bye," I continued, "I can't have these colours, Mr. Hands; and, by your leave, I'll strike 'em. Better none than these."

And, again dodging the boom, I ran to the colour lines, handed down their cursed black flag, and chucked it overboard.

"God save the king!" said I, waving my cap; "and there's an end to Captain Silver!"

He watched me keenly and slyly, his chin all the while on his breast.

"I reckon," he said at last—"I reckon Cap'n Hawkins, you'll kind of want to get ashore, now. S'pose we talks."

"Why, yes," said I, "with all my heart, Mr. Hands. Say on." And I went back to my meal with a good appetite.

"This man," he began, nodding feebly at the corpse—"O'Brien were his name—a rank Irelander—this man and me got the canvas on her, meaning for to sail her back. Well, *he's* dead now, he is— as dead as bilge; and who's to sail this ship, I don't see. Without I gives you a hint, you ain't that man, as far's I can tell. Now, look here, you give me food and drink, and a old scarf or ankecher to tie my wound up, you do; and I'll tell you how to sail her; and that's about square all round, I take it."

"I'll tell you one thing," says I: "I'm not going back to Captain Kidd's anchorage. I mean to get into North Inlet, and beach her quietly there."

"To be sure you did," he cried. "Why, I ain't sich an internal lubber, after all. I can see, can't I? I've tried my fling, I have, and I've lost, and it's you has the wind of me. North Inlet? Why, I haven't no ch'ice, not I! I'd help you sail her up to Execution Dock, by thunder! so I would."

Well, as it seemed to me, there was some sense in this. We struck our bargain on the spot. In three minutes I had the *Hispaniola* sailing easily before the wind along the coast of Treasure Island, with good hopes of turning the northern point ere noon, and beating down again as far as North Inlet before high water, when we might beach her safely, and wait till the subsiding tide permitted us to land.

Then I lashed the tiller and went below to my own chest, where

I got a soft silk handkerchief of my mother's. With this, and with my aid, Hands bound up the great bleeding stab he had received in the thigh, and after he had eaten a little, and had a swallow or two more of the brandy, he began to pick up visibly, sat straighter up, spoke louder and clearer, and looked in every way another man.

The breeze served us admirably. We skimmed before it like a bird, the coast of the island flashing by, and the view changing every minute. Soon we were past the high lands and bowling beside low, sandy country, sparsely dotted with dwarf pines, and soon we were beyond that again, and had turned the corner of the rocky hill that ends the island on the north.

I was greatly elated with my new command, and pleased with the bright, sunshiny weather and these different prospects of the coast. I had now plenty of water and good things to eat, and my conscience, which had smitten me hard for my desertion, was quieted by the great conquest I had made. I should, I think, have had nothing left me to desire but for the eyes of the coxswain as they followed me derisively about the deck, and the odd smile that appeared continually on his face. It was a smile that had in it something both of pain and weakness—a haggard, old man's smile; but there was, besides that, a grain of derision, a shadow of treachery, in his expression as he craftily watched, and watched, and watched me at my work.

26. *Israel Hands*

THE WIND, SERVING US TO A DESIRE, NOW HAULED INTO THE WEST. We could run so much the easier from the north-east corner of the island to the mouth of the North Inlet. Only, as we had no power to anchor, and dared not beach her till the tide had flowed a good deal farther, time hung on our hands. The coxswain told me how to lay the ship to; after a good many trials I succeeded, and we both sat in silence, over another meal.

"Cap'n," said he at length, with that same uncomfortable smile, "here's my old shipmate, O'Brien; s'pose you was to heave him overboard. I ain't partic'lar as a rule, and I don't take no blame for settling his hash; but I don't reckon him ornamental now, do you?"

"I'm not strong enough, and I don't like the job; and there he lies, for me," said I.

"This here's an unlucky ship—this *Hispaniola*, Jim," he went on, blinking. "There's a power of men been killed in this *Hispaniola*—a sight o' poor seamen dead and gone since you and me took ship to Bristol. I never seen sich dirty luck, not I. There was this here O'Brien, now—he's dead, ain't he? Well, now, I'm no scholar, and you're a lad as can read and figure; and to put it straight, do you take it as a dead man is dead for good, or do he come alive again?"

"You can kill the body, Mr. Hands, but not the spirit; you must know that already," I replied. "O'Brien there is in another world, and maybe watching us."

"Ah!" says he. "Well, that's unfort'nate—appears as if killing parties was a waste of time. Howsomever, sperrits don't reckon for much, by what I've seen. I'll chance it with the sperrits, Jim. And now, you've spoke up free, and I'll take it kind if you'd step down into that there cabin and get me a—well, a—shiver my timbers! I can't hit the name on't; well, you get me a bottle of wine, Jim—this here brandy's too strong for my head."

Now, the coxswain's hesitation seemed to be unnatural; and as for the notion of his preferring wine to brandy, I entirely disbelieved it. The whole story was a pretext. He wanted me to leave the deck—so much was plain; but with what purpose I could in no way imagine. His eyes never met mine; they kept wandering to and fro, up and down, now with a look to the sky, now with a flitting glance upon the dead O'Brien. All the time he kept smiling, and putting his tongue out in the most guilty, embarrassed manner, so that a child could have told that he was bent on some deception. I was prompt with my answer, however, for I saw where my advantage lay; and that with a fellow so densely stupid I could easily conceal my suspicions to the end.

"Some wine?" I said. "Far better. Will you have white or red?"

"Well, I reckon it's about the blessed same to me, shipmate," he replied; "so it's strong, and plenty of it, what's the odds?"

"All right," I answered. "I'll bring you port, Mr. Hands. But I'll have to dig for it."

With that I scuttled down the companion with all the noise I could, slipped off my shoes, ran quietly along the sparred gallery, mounted the forecastle ladder, and popped my head out of the fore companion. I knew he would not expect to see me there; yet I took every precaution possible; and certainly the worst of my suspicions proved too true.

He had risen from his position to his hands and knees; and, though his leg obviously hurt him pretty sharply when he moved —for I could hear him stifle a groan—yet it was at a good, rattling rate that he trailed himself across the deck. In half a minute he had reached the port scuppers, and picked, out of a coil of rope, a long knife, or rather a short dirk, discoloured to the hilt with blood. He looked upon it for a moment, thrusting forth his under jaw, tried the point upon his hand, and then, hastily concealing it in the bosom of his jacket, trundled back again into his old place against the bulwark.

That was all that I required to know. Israel could move about; he was now armed; and if he had been at so much trouble to get rid of me, it was plain that I was meant to be the victim. What he would do afterwards—whether he would try to crawl right across the island from North Inlet to the camp among the swamps, or whether he would fire Long Tom, trusting that his own comrades might come first to help him, was, of course, more than I could say.

Yet I felt sure that I could trust him in one point, since in that our interests jumped together, and that was in the disposition of the schooner. We both desired to have her stranded safe enough, in a sheltered place, and so that, when the time came, she could be got off again with as little labour and danger as might be; and until that was done I considered that my life would certainly be spared.

While I was thus turning the business over in my mind, I had not been idle with my body. I had stolen back to the cabin, slipped once more into my shoes, and laid my hand at random on a bottle of wine, and now, with this for an excuse, I made my reappearance on the deck.

Hands lay as I had left him, all fallen together in a bundle, and with his eyelids lowered, as though he were too weak to bear the light. He looked up, however, at my coming, knocked the neck off the bottle, like a man who had done the same thing often, and took a good swig, with his favourite toast of "Here's luck!" Then he lay quiet for a little, and then, pulling out a stick of tobacco, begged me to cut him a quid.

"Cut me a junk o' that," says he, "for I haven't no knife, and hardly strength enough, so be as I had. Ah, Jim, Jim, I reckon I've missed stays! Cut me a quid, as'll likely be the last, lad; for I'm for my long home, and no mistake."

"Well," said I, "I'll cut you some tobacco; but if I was you and thought myself so badly, I would go to my prayers, like a Christian man."

"Why?" said he. "Now, you tell me why."

"Why?" I cried. "You were asking me just now about the dead. You've broken your trust; you've lived in sin and lies and blood; there's a man you killed lying at your feet this moment; and you ask me why! For God's mercy, Mr. Hands, that's why."

I spoke with a little heat, thinking of the bloody dirk he had hidden in his pocket, and designed, in his ill thoughts, to end me with. He, for his part, took a great draught of the wine, and spoke with the most unusual solemnity.

"For thirty years," he said, "I've sailed the seas, and seen good and bad, better and worse, fair weather and foul, provisions running out, knives going, and what not. Well, now, I tell you, I never seen good come o' goodness yet. Him as strikes first is my fancy; dead men don't bite; them's my views—amen, so be it. And now, you look here," he added, suddenly changing his tone, "we've had about enough of this foolery. The tide's made good enough by now. You just take my orders, Cap'n Hawkins, and we'll sail slap in and be done with it."

All told, we had scarce two miles to run; but the navigation was delicate, the entrance to this northern anchorage was not only narrow and shoal, but lay east and west, so that the schooner must be nicely handled to be got in. I think I was a good, prompt subaltern, and I am very sure that Hands was an excellent pilot; for we went about and about, and dodged in, shaving the banks, with a certainty and a neatness that were a pleasure to behold.

Scarcely had we passed the heads before the land closed around us. The shores of North Inlet were as thickly wooded as those of the southern anchorage; but the space was longer and narrower, and more like, what in truth it was, the estuary of a river. Right before us, at the southern end we saw the wreck of a ship in the last stages of dilapidation. It had been a great vessel of three masts, but had lain so long exposed to the injuries of the weather, that it was hung about with great webs of dripping seaweed, and on the deck of it shore bushes had taken root, and now flourished thick with flowers. It was a sad sight, but it showed us that the anchorage was calm.

"Now," said Hands, "look there; there's a pet bit for to beach a ship in. Fine flat sand, never a catspaw, trees all around of it, and flowers a-blooming like a garding on that old ship."

"And once beached," I inquired, "how shall we get her off again?"

"Why, so," he replied; "you take a line ashore there on the other side at low water: take a turn about one o' them big pines; bring it back, take a turn around the capstan, and lie-to for the tide. Come high water, all hands take a pull upon the line, and off she comes as sweet as natur'. And now, boy, you stand by. We're near the bit now, and she's too much way on her. Starboard a little—so—steady—starboard—larboard a little—steady—steady!"

So he issued his commands, which I breathlessly obeyed; till, all of a sudden, he cried, "Now, my hearty, luff!" And I put the helm hard up, and the *Hispaniola* swung round rapidly, and ran stem on for the low wooded shore.

The excitement of these last manœuvres had somewhat interfered with the watch I had kept hitherto, sharply enough, upon the coxswain. Even then I was still so much interested, waiting for the ship to touch, that I had quite forgot the peril that hung over my head, and stood craning over the starboard bulwarks and watching the ripples spreading wide before the bows. I might have fallen without a struggle for my life, had not a sudden disquietude seized upon me, and made me turn my head. Perhaps I had heard a creak, or seen his shadow moving with the tail of my eye; perhaps it was an instinct like a cat's; but, sure enough, when I looked round, there was Hands, already half-way towards me, with the dirk in his right hand.

We must both have cried out aloud when our eyes met; but while mine was the shrill cry of terror, his was a roar of fury like a charging bull's. At the same instant he threw himself forward, and I leapt sideways towards the bows. As I did so, I left hold of the tiller, which sprang sharp to leeward; and I think this saved my life, for it struck Hands across the chest, and stopped him, for the moment, dead.

Before he could recover, I was safe out of the corner where he had me trapped, with all the deck to dodge about. Just forward of the mainmast I stopped, drew a pistol from my pocket, took a cool aim, though he had already turned and was once more coming directly after me, and drew the trigger. The hammer fell, but there followed neither flash nor sound; the priming was useless with sea water. I cursed myself for my neglect. Why had not I, long before, reprimed and reloaded my only weapons? Then I should not have been, as now, a mere fleeing sheep before this butcher.

Wounded as he was, it was wonderful how fast he could move, his grizzled hair tumbling over his face, and his face itself as red as a red ensign with his haste and fury. I had no time to try my other pistol, nor, indeed, much inclination, for I was sure it would be useless. One thing I saw plainly; I must not simply retreat before him, or he would speedily hold me boxed into the bows, as a moment since he had so nearly boxed me in the stern. Once so caught, and nine or ten inches of the blood-stained dirk would be my last experience on this side of eternity. I placed my palms against the mainmast, which was of a goodish bigness, and waited, every nerve upon the stretch.

Seeing that I meant to dodge, he also paused; and a moment or two passed in feints on his part, and corresponding movements upon mine. It was such a game as I had often played at home about the rocks of Black Hill Cove; but never before, you may be sure, with such a wildly beating heart as now. Still, as I say, it was a boy's game, and I thought I could hold my own at it, against an elderly seaman with a wounded thigh. Indeed, my courage had begun to rise so high, that I allowed myself a few darting thoughts on what would be the end of the affair; and while I saw certainly that I could spin it out for long, I saw no hope of any ultimate escape.

Well, while things stood thus, suddenly the *Hispaniola* struck, staggered, ground for an instant in the sand, and then, swift as a blow, canted over to the port side, till the deck stood at an angle of forty-five degrees, and about a puncheon of water splashed into the scupper holes, and lay, in a pool, between the deck and bulwark.

We were both of us capsized in a second, and both of us rolled, almost together, into the scuppers; the dead red-cap, with his arms still spread out, tumbling stiffly after us. So near were we, indeed, that my head came against the coxswain's foot with a crack that made my teeth rattle. Blow and all, I was the first afoot again; for Hands had got involved with the dead body. The sudden canting of the ship had made the deck no place for running on; I had to find some new way of escape, and that upon the instant, for my foe was almost touching me. Quick as thought I sprang into the mizzen shrouds, rattled up hand over hand, and did not draw a breath till I was seated on the cross-trees.

I had been saved by being prompt; the dirk had struck not half a foot below me, as I pursued my upward flight; and there stood Israel Hands, with his mouth open and his face upturned to mine, a perfect statue of surprise and disappointment.

Now that I had a moment to myself, I lost no time in changing the priming of my pistol, and then, having one ready for service, and to make assurance doubly sure, I proceeded to draw the load of the other, and recharge it afresh from the beginning.

My new employment struck Hands all of a heap; he began to see the dice going against him; and after an obvious hesitation, he also hauled himself heavily into the shrouds, and, with the dirk in his teeth, began slowly and painfully to mount. It cost him no end of time and groans to haul his wounded leg behind him; and I had quietly finished my arrangements before he was much more than a third of the way up. Then, with a pistol in either hand, I addressed him.

"One more step, Mr. Hands," said I, "and I'll blow your brains out! Dead men don't bite, you know," I added, with a chuckle.

He stopped instantly. I could see by the working of his face that he was trying to think, and the process was so slow and laborious that, in my new-found security, I laughed aloud. At last, with a swallow or two, he spoke, his face still wearing the same expression of extreme perplexity. In order to speak he had to take the dagger from his mouth, but, in all else, he remained unmoved.

"Jim," says he, "I reckon we're fouled, you and me, and we'll have to sign articles. I'd have had you but for that there lurch; but I don't have no luck, not I; and I reckon I'll have to strike, which comes hard, you see, for a master mariner to a ship's younker like you, Jim."

I was drinking in his words and smiling away, as conceited as a cock upon a wall, when, all in a breath, back went his right hand, over his shoulder. Something sang like an arrow through the air: I felt a blow and then a sharp pang, and there I was pinned by the shoulder to the mast. In the horrid pain and surprise of the moment—I scarce can say it was by my own volition, and I am sure it was without a conscious aim—both my pistols went off, and both escaped out of my hands. They did not fall alone; with a choked cry, the coxswain loosed his grasp upon the shrouds, and plunged head first into the water.

27.   *"Pieces of Eight"*

O WING TO THE CANT OF THE VESSEL, THE MASTS HUNG FAR OUT over the water, and from my perch on the cross-trees I had nothing below me but the surface of the bay. Hands, who was not so far up, was, in consequence, nearer to the ship, and fell between me and the bulwarks. He rose once to the surface in a lather of foam and blood, and then sank again for good. As the water settled I could see him lying huddled together on the clean, bright sand in the shadow of the vessel's sides. A fish or two whipped past his body. Sometimes, by the quivering of the water, he appeared to move a little, as if he were trying to rise. But he was dead enough, for all that, being both shot and drowned, and was food for fish in the very place where he had designed my slaughter.

I was no sooner certain of this than I began to feel sick, faint, and terrified. The hot blood was running over my back and chest. The dirk, where it had pinned my shoulder to the mast, seemed to burn like a hot iron; yet it was not so much these real sufferings that distressed me, for these, it seemed to me, I could bear without a murmur; it was the horror I had upon my mind of falling from the cross-trees into that still green water, beside the body of the coxswain.

I clung with both hands till my nails ached, and I shut my eyes as if to cover up the peril. Gradually my mind came back again, my pulses quieted down to a more natural time, and I was once more in possession of myself.

It was my first thought to pluck forth the dirk; but either it stuck too hard or my nerve failed me; and I desisted with a violent shudder. Oddly enough, that very shudder did the business. The knife, in fact, had come the nearest in the world to missing me altogether; it held me by a mere pinch of skin. and this the shudder tore away. The blood ran down the faster, to be sure; but I was my own master again, and only tacked to the mast by my coat and shirt.

These last I broke through with a sudden jerk, and then regained the deck by the starboard shrouds. For nothing in the world would I have again ventured, shaken as I was, upon the overhanging port shrouds, from which Israel had so lately fallen

I went below, and did what I could for my wound; it pained me a good deal, and still bled freely; but it was neither deep nor dangerous, nor did it greatly gall me when I used my arm. Then I looked around me, and as the ship was now, in a sense, my own, I began to think of clearing it from its last passenger—the dead man O'Brien.

He had pitched, as I have said, against the bulwarks, where he lay like some horrible, ungainly sort of puppet; life-sized, indeed, but how different from life's colour or life's comeliness! In that position, I could easily have my way with him; and as the habit of tragical adventures had worn off almost all my terror for the dead, I took him by the waist as if he had been a sack of bran, and, with one good heave, tumbled him overboard. He went in with a sounding plunge; the red cap came off, and remained floating on the surface; and as soon as the splash subsided, I could see him and Israel lying side by side, both wavering with the tremulous movement of the water. O'Brien, though still quite a young man, was very bald. There he lay, with that bald head across the knees of the man who had killed him, and the quick fishes steering to and fro over both.

I was now alone upon the ship; the tide had just turned. The sun was within so few degrees of setting that already the shadow of the pines upon the western shore began to reach right across the anchorage, and fall in patterns on the deck. The evening breeze had sprung up, and though it was well warded off by the hill with the two peaks upon the east, the cordage had begun to sing a little softly to itself and the idle sails to rattle to and fro.

I began to see a danger to the ship. The jibs I speedily doused and brought tumbling to the deck; but the mainsail was a harder matter. Of course, when the schooner canted over, the boom had swung out-board, and the cap of it and a foot or two of sail hung even under water. I thought this made it still more dangerous; yet the strain was so heavy that I half feared to meddle. At last,

I got my knife and cut the halyards. The peak dropped instantly, a great belly of loose canvas floated broad upon the water; and since, pull as I liked, I could not budge the downhaul, that was the extent of what I could accomplish. For the rest, the *Hispaniola* must trust to luck, like myself.

By this time the whole anchorage had fallen into shadow—the last rays, I remember, falling through a glade of the wood, and shining bright as jewels, on the flowery mantle of the wreck. It began to be chill; the tide was rapidly fleeting seaward, the schooner settling more and more on her beam-ends.

I scrambled forward and looked over. It seemed shallow enough, and holding the cut hawser in both hands for a last security, I let myself drop softly overboard. The water scarcely reached my waist; the sand was firm and covered with ripple marks, and I waded ashore in great spirits, leaving the *Hispaniola* on her side, with her mainsail trailing wide upon the surface of the bay. About the same time the sun went fairly down, and the breeze whistled low in the dusk among the tossing pines.

At least, and at last, I was off the sea, nor had I returned thence empty-handed. There lay the schooner, clear at last from bucca-neers and ready for our own men to board and get to sea again. I had nothing nearer my fancy than to get home to the stockade and boast of my achievements. Possibly I might be blamed a bit for my truantry, but the recapture of the *Hispaniola* was a clench-ing answer, and I hoped that even Captain Smollett would confess I had not lost my time.

So thinking, and in famous spirits, I began to set my face home-ward for the blockhouse and my companions. I remembered that the most easterly of the rivers which drain into Captain Kidd's anchorage ran from the two-peaked hill upon my left; and I bent my course in that direction that I might pass the stream while it was small. The wood was pretty open, and keeping along the lower spurs, I had soon turned the corner of that hill, and not long after waded to the mid-calf across the water-course.

This brought me near to where I had encountered Ben Gunn, the maroon; and I walked more circumspectly, keeping an eye on every side. The dusk had come nigh hand completely, and, as I opened out the cleft between the two peaks, I became aware of a wavering glow against the sky, where, as I judged, the man of the island was cooking his supper before a roaring fire. And yet I wondered, in my heart, that he should show himself so careless. For if I could see this radiance, might it not reach the eyes of Silver himself where he camped upon the shore among the marshes?

Gradually the night fell blacker; it was all I could do to guide myself even roughly towards my destination; the double hill behind me and the Spy-glass on my right hand loomed faint and fainter; the stars were few and pale; and in the low ground where I wandered I kept tripping among bushes and rolling into sandy pits.

Suddenly a kind of brightness fell about me. I looked up; a pale glimmer of moonbeams had alighted on the summit of the Spy-glass, and soon after I saw something broad and silvery moving low down behind the trees, and knew the moon had risen.

With this to help me, I passed rapidly over what remained to me of my journey; and, sometimes walking, sometimes running, impatiently drew near to the stockade. Yet, as I began to thread the grove that lies before it, I was not so thoughtless but that I slacked my pace and went a trifle warily. It would have been a poor end of my adventures to get shot down by my own party in mistake.

The moon was climbing higher and higher; its light began to fall here and there in masses through the more open districts of the wood; and right in front of me a glow of a different colour appeared among the trees. It was red and hot, and now and again it was a little darkened—as if were the embers of a bonfire smouldering.

For the life of me, I could not think what it might be.

At last I came right down upon the borders of the clearing. The western end was already steeped in moonshine; the rest, and the block-house itself, still lay in a black shadow, chequered with long, silvery streaks of light. On the other side of the house an immense fire had burned itself into clear embers and shed a steady, red reverberation, contrasted strongly with the mellow paleness of the moon. There was not a soul stirring, nor a sound besides the noises of the breeze.

I stopped, with much wonder in my heart, and perhaps a little terror also. It had not been our way to build great fires; we were, indeed, by the captain's orders, somewhat niggardly of firewood;

and I began to fear that something had gone wrong while I was absent.

I stole round by the eastern end, keeping close in shadow, and at a convenient place, where the darkness was thickest, crossed the palisade.

To make assurance surer, I got upon my hands and knees, and crawled, without a sound, towards the corner of the house. As I drew nearer, my heart was suddenly and greatly lightened. It is not a pleasant noise in itself, and I have often complained of it at other times; but just then it was like music to hear my friends snoring together so loud and peaceful in their sleep. The sea cry of the watch, that beautiful "All's well," never fell more reassuringly on my ear.

In the meantime, there was no doubt of one thing; they kept an infamous bad watch. If it had been Silver and his lads that were now creeping in on them, not a soul would have seen daybreak. That was what it was, thought I, to have the captain wounded; and again I blamed myself sharply for leaving them in that danger with so few to mount guard.

By this time I had got to the door and stood up. All was dark within, so that I could distinguish nothing by the eye. As for sounds, there was the steady drone of the snorers, and a small occasional noise, a flickering or pecking that I could in no way account for.

With my arms before me I walked steadily in. I should lie down in my own place (I thought, with a silent chuckle) and enjoy their faces when they found me in the morning.

My foot struck something yielding—it was a sleeper's leg; and he turned and groaned, but without awaking.

And then, all of a sudden, a shrill voice broke forth out of the darkness:—

"Pieces of eight! pieces of eight! pieces of eight! pieces of eight! pieces of eight!" and so forth, without pause or change, like the clacking of a tiny mill.

Silver's green parrot, Captain Flint! It was she whom I had heard pecking at a piece of bark; it was she, keeping better watch than any human being, who thus announced my arrival with her wearisome refrain.

I had no time left me to recover. At the sharp, clipping tone of the parrot, the sleepers awoke and sprang up; and with a mighty oath, the voice of Silver cried:—

"Who goes?"

I turned to run, struck violently against one person, recoiled, and ran full into the arms of a second, who, for his part, closed upon and held me tight.

"Bring a torch, Dick," said Silver, when my capture was thus assured.

And one of the men left the log-house and presently returned with a lighted brand.

PART SIX

CAPTAIN SILVER

✳

28. *In the Enemy's Camp*

THE RED GLARE OF THE TORCH, LIGHTING UP THE INTERIOR OF THE blockhouse, showed me the worst of my apprehensions real-ised. The pirates were in possession of the house and stores; there was the cask of cognac, there were the pork and bread, as before; and, what tenfold increased my horror, not a sign of any prisoner. I could only judge that all had perished, and my heart smote me sorely that I had not been there to perish with them.

There were six of the buccaneers, all told; not another man was left alive. Five of them were on their feet, flushed and swollen, suddenly called out of the first sleep of drunkenness. The sixth had only risen upon his elbow: he was deadly pale, and the blood-stained bandage round his head told that he had recently been wounded, and still more recently dressed. I remembered the man who had been shot and had run back among the woods in the great attack, and doubted not that this was he.

The parrot sat, preening her plumage, on Long John's shoulder. He himself, I thought, looked somewhat paler and more stern than I was used to. He still wore the fine broadcloth suit in which he had fulfilled his mission, but it was bitterly the worse for wear, daubed with clay and torn with the sharp briers of the wood.

"So," said he, "here's Jim Hawkins, shiver my timbers! dropped in, like, eh? Well, come, I take that friendly."

And thereupon he sat down across the brandy cask, and began to fill a pipe.

"Give me a loan of the link, Dick," said he; and then, when he had a good light, "that'll do, lad," he added; "stick the glim in the wood heap; and you, gentlemen, bring yourselves to!—you needn't stand up for Mr. Hawkins; *he'll* excuse you, you may lay to that. And so, Jim"—stopping the tobacco—"here you were, and quite a pleasant surprise for poor old John. I see you were smart when first I set my eyes on you; but this here gets away from me clean, it do."

To all this, as may be well supposed, I made no answer. They had set me with my back against the wall; and I stood there, looking Silver in the face, pluckily enough, I hope, to all outward appearance, but with black despair in my heart.

Silver took a whiff or two of his pipe with great composure, and then ran on again.

"Now, you see, Jim, so be as you *are* here," says he, "I'll give you a piece of my mind. I've always liked you, I have, for a lad of spirit, and the picter of my own self when I was young and handsome. I always wanted you to jine and take your share, and die a gentleman, and now, my cock, you've got to. Cap'n Smollett's a fine seaman, as I'll own up to any day, but stiff on discipline. 'Dooty is dooty,' says he, and right he is. Just you keep clear of the cap'n. The doctor himself is gone dead again you—'ungrateful scamp' was what he said; and the short and the long of the whole story is about here: you can't go back to your own lot, for they won't have you; and, without you start a third ship's company all by yourself, which might be lonely, you'll have to jine with Captain Silver."

So far so good. My friends, then, were still alive, and though I partly believed the truth of Silver's statement, that the cabin party were incensed at me for my desertion, I was more relieved than distressed by what I heard.

"I don't say nothing as to your being in our hands," continued Silver, "though there you are, and you may lay to it. I'm all for argyment; I never seen good come out o' threatening. If you like the service, well, you'll jine; and if you don't, Jim, why, you're free to answer no—free and welcome, shipmate; and if fairer can be said by mortal seaman, shiver my sides!"

"Am I to answer, then?" I asked, with a very tremulous voice. Through all this sneering talk, I was made to feel the threat of death that overhung me, and my cheeks burned and my heart beat painfully in my breast.

"Lad," said Silver, "no one's a-pressing of you. Take your bearings. None of us won't hurry you, mate; time goes so pleasant in your company, you see."

"Well," says I, growing a bit bolder, "if I'm to choose, I declare I have a right to know what's what, and why you're here, and where my friends are."

"Wot's wot?" repeated one of the buccaneers, in a deep growl. "Ah, he'd be a lucky one as knowed that!"

"You'll, perhaps, batten down your hatches till you're spoke, my friend," cried Silver truculently to this speaker. And then, in his first gracious tones, he replied to me: "Yesterday morning, Mr. Hawkins," said he, "in the dogwatch, down came Doctor Livesey with a flag of truce. Says he, 'Cap'n Silver, you're sold out. Ship's gone.' Well, maybe we'd been taking a glass, and a song to help it round. I won't say no. Leastways none of us had looked out. We looked out, and, by thunder! the old ship was gone. I never seen a pack o' fools look fishier; and you may lay to that, if I tells you that looked the fishiest. 'Well,' says the doctor, 'let's bargain.' We bargained, him and I, and here we are: stores, brandy, blockhouse, the firewood you was thoughtful enough to cut, and, in a manner of speaking, the whole blessed boat, from cross-trees to keelson. As for them, they've tramped; I don't know where's they are."

He again drew quietly at his pipe.

"And lest you should take it into that head of yours," he went on, "that you was included in the treaty, here's the last word that was said: 'How many are you,' says I, 'to leave?' 'Four,' says he— 'four, and one of us wounded. As for that boy, I don't know where he is, confound him,' says he, 'nor I don't much care. We're about sick of him.' These was his words."

"Is that all?" I asked.

"Well, it's all that you're to hear, my son," returned Silver.

"And now I am to choose?"

"And now you are to choose, and you may lay to that," said Silver.

"Well," said I, "I am not such a fool but I know pretty well what I have to look for. Let the worst come to the worst, it's little I care. I've seen too many die since I fell in with you. But there's a thing or two I have to tell you," I said, and by this time I was quite excited; "and the first is this: here you are, in a bad way: ship lost, treasure lost, men lost; your whole business gone to wreck; and if you want to know who did it—it was I! I was in the apple barrel the night we sighted land, and I heard you, John, and you, Dick Johnson, and Hands, who is now at the bottom of the sea, and told every word you said before the hour was out. And as for the schooner, it was I who cut her cable, and it was I that killed the men you had aboard of her, and it was I who brought her where you'll never see her more, not one of you. The laugh's on my side; I've had the top of this business from the first; I no more fear you than I fear a fly. Kill me, if you please, or spare me. But one thing I'll say, and no more; if you spare me, bygones are bygones, and when you fellows are in court for piracy, I'll save you all I can. It is for you to choose. Kill another and do your-selves no good, or spare me and keep a witness to save you from the gallows."

I stopped, for, I tell you, I was out of breath, and, to my wonder, not a man of them moved, but all sat staring at me like as many sheep. And while they were still staring, I broke out again:—

"And now, Mr. Silver," I said, "I believe you're the best man here, and if things go the worst, I'll take it kind of you to let the doctor know the way I took it."

"I'll bear it in mind," said Silver, with an accent so curious that I could not, for the life of me, decide whether he were laughing at my request, or had been favourably affected by my couarge.

"I'll put one to that," cried the old mahogany-faced seaman—Morgan by name—whom I had seen in Long John's public-house upon the quays of Bristol. "It was him that knowed Black Dog."

"Well, and see here," added the sea-cook, "I'll put another again to that, by thunder! for it was this same boy that faked the chart from Billy Bones. First and last, we've split upon Jim Hawkins!"

"Then here goes!" said Morgan, with an oath. And he sprang up, drawing his knife as if he had been twenty.

"Avast there!" cried Silver. "Who are you, Tom Morgan? Maybe you thought you was cap'n here, perhaps. By the powers, but I'll teach you better! Cross me, and you'll go where many a good man's gone before you, first and last, these thirty year back—some to the yardarm, shiver my sides! and some by the board, and all to feed the fishes. There's never a man looked me between the eyes and seen a good day a'terwards. Tom Morgan, you may lay to that."

Morgan paused; but a hoarse murmur rose from the others.

"Tom's right," said one.

"I stood hazing long enough from one," added another. "I'll be hanged if I'll be hazed by you, John Silver."

"Did any of you gentlemen want to have it out with *me?*" roared Silver, bending far forward from his position on the keg, with his pipe still glowing in his right hand. "Put a name on what you're at; you ain't dumb, I reckon. Him that wants shall get it. Have I lived this many years, and a son of a rum puncheon cock his hat athwart my hawse at the latter end of it? You know the way; you're all gentlemen o' fortune, by your account. Well, I'm ready. Take a cutlass, him that dares, and I'll see the colour of his inside, crutch and all, before that pipe's empty."

Not a man stirred; not a man answered.

"That's your sort, is it?" he added, returning his pipe to his mouth. "Well, you're a gay lot to look at, anyway. Not much worth to fight, you ain't. P'r'aps you can understand King George's English. I'm cap'n here by 'lection. I'm cap'n here because I'm the best man by a long sea-mile. You won't fight as gentlemen o' fortune should; then, by thunder, you'll obey, and you may lay to it! I like that boy, now; I never seen a better boy than that. He's more a man than any pair of rats of you in this here house, and what I say is this: let me see him that'll lay a hand on him— that's what I say, and you may lay to it."

There was a long pause after this. I stood straight up against the wall, my heart still going like a sledge-hammer, but with a ray of hope now shining in my bosom. Silver leant back against the wall, his arms crossed, his pipe in the corner of his mouth, as calm as though he had been in church; yet his eye kept wandering furtively, and he kept the tail of it on his unruly followers. They, on their part, drew gradually together towards the far end of the blockhouse, and the low hiss of their whispering sounded in my ear continuously like a stream. One after another they would look up, and the red light of the torch would fall for a second on their nervous faces; but it was not towards me, it was towards Silver that they turned their eyes.

"You seem to have a lot to say," remarked Silver, spitting far into the air. "Pipe up and let me hear it, or lay to."

"Ax your pardon, sir," returned one of the men, "you're pretty free with some of the rules; maybe you'll kindly keep an eye upon the rest. This crew's dissatisfied; this crew don't vally bullying a marlin-spike; this crew has its rights like other crews, I'll make so free as that; and by your own rules, I take it we can talk together. I ax your pardon, sir, acknowledging you to be capting at this present; but I claim my right, and steps outside for a council."

And with an elaborate sea-salute, this fellow, a long, ill-looking, yellow-eyed man of five-and-thirty, stepped coolly towards the door and disappeared out of the house. One after another, the rest followed his example; each making a salute as he passed; each adding some apology. "According to rules," said one. "Fo'c'sle council," said Morgan. And so with one remark or another, all marched out, and left Silver and me alone with the torch.

The sea-cook instantly removed his pipe.

"Now, look you here, Jim Hawkins," he said, in a steady whisper, that was no more than audible, "you're within half a plank of death, and, what's a long sight worse, of torture. They're going to throw me off. But, you mark, I stand by you through thick and thin. I didn't mean to; no, not till you spoke up. I was about desperate to lose that much blunt, and be hanged into the bargain. But I see you was the right sort. I says to myself: "You stand by Hawkins, John, and Hawkins'll stand by you. You're his last card, and, by the living thunder, John, he's yours! Back to back, says I. You save your witness, and he'll save your neck!"

I began dimly to understand.

"You mean all's lost?" I asked.

"Ay, by gum, I do!" he answered. "Ship gone, neck gone—that's the size of it. Once I looked into that bay, Jim Hawkins, and seen no schooner—well, I'm tough, but I gave out. As for that lot and their council, mark me, they're outright fools and cowards. I'll save your life—if so be as I can—from them. But, see here, Jim— tit for tat—you save Long John from swinging."

I was bewildered; it seemed a thing so hopeless he was asking— he, the old buccaneer, the ringleader throughout.

"What I can do, that I'll do," I said.

"It's a bargain!" cried Long John. "You speak up plucky, and, by thunder! I've a chance."

He hobbled to the torch, where it stood propped among the firewood, and took a fresh light to his pipe.

"Understand me, Jim," he said, returning. "I've a head on my shoulders, I have. I'm on squire's side now. I know you've got that ship safe somewheres. How you done it, I don't know, but safe it is. I guess Hands and O'Brien turned soft. I never much believed in neither of *them*. Now, you mark me. I ask no questions, nor I won't let others. I know when a game's up, I do; and I know a lad that's staunch. Ah, you that's young—you and me might have done a power of good together!"

He drew some cognac from the cask into a tin cannikin.

"Will you taste, messmate?" he asked; and when I had refused: "Well, I'll take a drain myself, Jim," said he. "I need a caulker, for there's trouble on hand. And, talking o' trouble, why did that doctor give me the chart, Jim?"

My face expressed a wonder so unaffected that he saw the needlessness of further questions.

"Ah, well, he did, though," said he. "And there's something under that, no doubt—something surely, under that, Jim—bad or good."

And he took another swallow of the brandy, shaking his great fair head like a man who looks forward to the worst.

29. *The Black Spot Again*

THE COUNCIL OF THE BUCCANEERS HAD LASTED SOME TIME WHEN one of them re-entered the house, and with a repetition of the same salute, which had in my eyes an ironical air, begged for a moment's loan of the torch. Silver briefly agreed; and this emissary retired again, leaving us together in the dark.

"There's a breeze coming, Jim," said Silver, who had, by this time, adopted quite a friendly and familiar tone.

I turned to the loophole nearest me and looked out. The embers of the great fire had so far burned themselves out, and now glowed so low and duskily, that I understood why these conspirators desired a torch. About half-way down the slope to the stockade, they were collected in a group; one held the light; another was on his knees in their midst, and I saw the blade of an open knife shine in his hand with varying colours, in the moon and torch-light. The rest were all somewhat stooping, as though watching the manœuvres of this last. I could just make out that he had a book as well as a knife in his hand; and was still wondering how any-

shook the house. "Why, I give you my word, I'm sick to speak to you. You've neither sense nor memory, and I leave it to fancy where your mothers was that let you come to sea. Sea! Gentlemen o' fortune! I reckon tailors is your trade."

"Go on, John," said Morgan. "Speak up to the others."

"Ah, the others!" returned John. "They're a nice lot, ain't they? You say this cruise is bungled. Ah! by gum, if you could understand how bad it's bungled, you would see! We're that near the gibbet that my neck's stiff with thinking on it. You've seen 'em, maybe, hanged in chains, birds about 'em, seamen p'inting 'em out as they go down with the tide. 'Who's that?' says one. 'That! Why, that's John Silver. I knowed him well,' says another. And you can hear the chains a-jangle as you go about and reach for the other buoy. Now, that's about where we are, every mother's son of us, thanks to him, and Hands, and Anderson, and other ruination fools of you. And if you want to know about number four, and that boy, why, shiver my timbers! isn't he a hostage? Are we a-going to waste a hostage? No, not us; he might be our last chance, and I shouldn't wonder. Kill that boy? not me, mates! And number three? Ah, well, there's a deal to say to number three. Maybe you don't count it nothing to have a real college doctor come to see you every day—you, John, with your head broke—or you, George Merry, that had the ague shakes upon you not six hours agone, and has your eyes the colour of lemon peel to this same moment on the clock? And maybe, perhaps, you didn't know there was a consort coming, either? But there is; and not so long till then; and we'll see who'll be glad to have a hostage when it comes to that. And as for number two, and why I made a bargain—well, you came crawling on your knees to me to make it—on your knees you came, you was that downhearted—and you'd have starved, too, if I hadn't—but that's a trifle! you look there—that's why!"

And he cast down upon the floor a paper that I instantly recognised—none other than the chart on yellow paper, with the three red crosses, that I had found in the oilcloth at the bottom of the captain's chest. Why the doctor had given it to him was more than I could fancy.

But if it were inexplicable to me, the appearance of the chart was incredible to the surviving mutineers. They leaped upon it like cats upon a mouse. It went from hand to hand, one tearing it from another; and by the oaths and the cries and the childish laughter with which they accompanied their examination, you would have thought, not only they were fingering the very gold, but were at sea with it, besides, in safety.

"Yes," said one, "that's Flint sure enough. J. F., and a score below, with a clove hitch to it; so he done ever."

"Mighty pretty," said George. "But how are we to get away with it, and us no ship?"

Silver suddenly sprang up, and supporting himself with a hand against the wall: "Now I give you warning, George," he cried. "One more word of your sauce, and I'll call you down and fight you. How? Why, how do I know? You had ought to tell me that—you and the rest, that lost me my schooner, with your interference, burn you! But not you, you can't; you hain't got the invention of a cockroach. But civil you can speak, and shall, George Merry, you may lay to that."

"That's fair enow," said the old man Morgan.

"Fair! I reckon so," said the sea-cook. "You lost the ship; I found the treasure. Who's the better man at that? And now I resign, by thunder! Elect whom you please to be your cap'n now; I'm done with it."

"Silver!" they cried. "Barbecue for ever! Barbecue for cap'n!"

"So that's the toon, is it?" cried the cook. "George, I reckon you'll have to wait another turn, friend; and lucky for you as I'm not a revengeful man. But that was never my way. And now, ship-mates, this black spot? 'Tain't much good now, is it? Dick's crossed his luck and spoiled his Bible, and that's about all."

"It'll do to kiss the book on still, won't it?" growled Dick, who was evidently uneasy at the curse he had brought upon himself.

"A Bible with a bit cut out!" returned Silver derisively. "Not it. It don't bind no more'n a ballad-book."

"Don't it, though?" cried Dick, with a sort of joy. "Well, I reckon that's worth having, too."

"Here, Jim—here's a cur'osity for you," said Silver; and he tossed me the paper.

It was a round about the size of a crown piece. One side was blank, for it had been the last leaf; the other contained a verse or two of Revelation—these words among the rest, which struck sharply home upon my mind: "Without are dogs and murderers." The printed side had been blackened with wood ash, which already began to come off and soil my fingers; on the blank side had been written with the same material the one word "Depposed." I have that curiosity beside me at this moment; but not a trace of writing now remains beyond a single scratch, such as a man might make with his thumb-nail.

That was the end of the night's business. Soon after, with a drink all round, we lay down to sleep, and the outside of Silver's vengeance was to put George Merry up for sentinel, and threaten him with death if he should prove unfaithful.

It was long ere I could close an eye, and Heaven knows I had matter enough for thought in the man whom I had slain that afternoon, in my own most perilous position, and, above all, in the remarkable game that I saw Silver now engaged upon—keeping the mutineers together with one hand, and grasping, with the other, after every means, possible and impossible, to make his peace and save his miserable life. He himself slept peacefully, and snored aloud; yet my heart was sore for him, wicked as he was, to think on the dark perils that environed, and the shameful gibbet that awaited him.

30. *On Parole*

I WAS WAKENED—INDEED, WE WERE ALL WAKENED, FOR I COULD see even the sentinel shake himself together from where he had fallen against the door-post—by a clear, hearty voice hailing us from the margin of the wood:—

"Blockhouse, ahoy!" it cried. "Here's the doctor."

And the doctor it was. Although I was glad to hear the sound, yet my gladness was not without admixture. I remembered with confusion my insubordinate and stealthy conduct; and when I saw where it had brought me—among what companions and surrounded by what dangers—I felt ashamed to look him in the face.

He must have risen in the dark, for the day had hardly come; and when I ran to a loophole and looked out, I saw him standing, like Silver once before, up to the mid-leg in creeping vapour.

"You, doctor! Top o' the morning to you, sir!" cried Silver, broad awake and beaming with good-nature in a moment. "Bright and early, to be sure; and it's the early bird, as the saying goes, that gets the rations. George, shake up your timbers, son, and help Dr.

Livesey over the ship's side. All a-doin' well, your patients was—all well and merry."

So he pattered on, standing on the hill-top, with his crutch under his elbow, and one hand upon the side of the log-house—quite the old John in voice, manner, and expression.

"We've quite a surprise for you, too, sir," he continued. "We've a little stranger here—he! he! A noo boarder and lodger, sir, and looking fit and taut as a fiddle; slep' like a supercargo, he did, right alongside of John—stem to stem we was, all night."

Dr. Livesey was by this time across the stockade and pretty near the cook; and I could hear the alteration in his voice as he said,—

"Not Jim?"

"The very same Jim as ever was," says Silver.

The doctor stopped outright, although he did not speak, and it was some seconds before he seemed able to move on.

"Well, well," he said at last, "duty first and pleasure afterwards, as you might have said yourself, Silver. Let us overhaul these patients of yours."

A moment afterwards he had entered the block-house, and, with one grim nod to me, proceeded with his work among the sick. He seemed under no apprehension, though he must have known that his life, among these treacherous demons, depended on a hair; and he rattled on to his patients as if he were paying an ordinary professional visit in a quiet English family. His manner, I suppose, reacted on the men; for they behaved to him as if nothing had occurred—as if he were still ship's doctor, and they still faithful hands before the mast.

"You're doing well, my friend," he said to the fellow with the bandaged head; "and if ever any person had a close shave, it was you; your head must be as hard as iron. Well, George, how goes it? You're a pretty colour, certainly; why, your liver, man, is upside down. Did you take that medicine? Did he take that medicine, men?"

"Ay, ay, sir; he took it, sure enough," returned Morgan.

"Because, you see, since I am mutineers' doctor, or prison doctor, as I prefer to call it," says Dr. Livesey, in his pleasantest way, "I make it a point of honour not to lose a man for King George (God bless him!) and the gallows."

The rogues looked at each other, but swallowed the home-thrust in silence.

"Dick don't feel well, sir," said one.

"Don't he?" replied the doctor. "Well, step up here, Dick, and let me see your tongue. No, I should be surprised if he did! The man's tongue is fit to frighten the French. Another fever."

"Ah, there," said Morgan, "that comed of spi'ling Bibles."

"That comed—as you call it—of being arrant asses," retorted the doctor, "and not having sense enough to know honest air from poison, and the dry land from a vile, pestiferous slough. I think it most probable—though, of course, it's only an opinion—that you'll all have the deuce to pay before you get that malaria out of your systems. Camp in a bog, would you? Silver, I'm surprised at you. You're less of a fool than many, take you all round; but you don't appear to me to have the rudiments of a notion of the rules of health.

"Well," he added, after he had dosed them round, and they had taken his prescriptions, with really laughable humility, more like charity school-children than blood-guilty mutineers and pirates— "well, that's done for to-day. And now I should wish to have a talk with that boy, please."

And he nodded his head in my direction carelessly.

George Merry was at the door, spitting and spluttering over some bad-tasted medicine; but at the first word of the doctor's proposal he swung round with a deep flush, and cried "No!" and swore.

Silver struck the barrel with his open hand.

"Si-lence!" he roared, and looked about him positively like a lion. "Doctor," he went on, in his usual tones, "I was a-thinking of that, knowing as how you had a fancy for the boy. We're all humbly grateful for your kindness, and, as you see, puts faith in you, and takes the drugs down like that much grog. And I take it, I've found a way as'll suit all. Hawkins, will you give me your word of honour as a young gentleman—for a young gentleman you are, although poor born—your word of honour not to slip your cable?"

I readily gave the pledge required.

"Then, doctor," said Silver, "you just step outside o' that stockade, and once you're there, I'll bring the boy down on the inside, and I reckon you can yarn through the spars. Good-day to you, sir, and all our dooties to the squire and Cap'n Smollett."

The explosion of disapproval, which nothing but Silver's black looks had restrained, broke out immediately the doctor had left the house. Silver was roundly accused of playing double—of trying to make a separate peace for himself—of sacrificing the interests of his accomplices and victims; and, in one word, of the identical, exact thing that he was doing. It seemed to me so obvious, in this case, that I could not imagine how he was to turn their anger. But he was twice the man the rest were; and his last night's victory had given him a huge preponderance on their minds. He called them all the fools and dolts you can imagine, said it was necessary I should talk to the doctor, fluttered the chart in their faces, asked them if they could afford to break the treaty the very day they were bound a treasure-hunting.

"No, by thunder!" he cried, "it's us must break the treaty when the time comes; and till then I'll gammon that doctor, if I have to ile his boots with brandy."

And then he bade them get the fire lit, and stalked out upon his crutch, with his hand on my shoulder, leaving them in a disarray, and silenced by his volubility rather than convinced.

"Slow, lad, slow," he said. "They might round upon us in a twinkle of an eye, if we was seen to hurry."

Very deliberately, then, did we advance across the sand to where the doctor awaited us on the other side of the stockade, and as soon as we were within easy speaking distance, Silver stopped.

"You'll make a note of this here also, doctor," says he, "and the boy'll tell you how I saved his life, and were deposed for it, too, and you may lay to that. Doctor, when a man's steering as near the wind as me—playing chuck-farthing with the last breath in his body, like—you wouldn't think it too much, mayhap, to give him one good word? You'll please bear in mind it's not my life only now—it's that boy's into the bargain; and you'll speak me fair, doctor, and give me a bit o' hope to go on, for the sake of mercy."

Silver was a changed man, once he was out there and had his back to his friends and the block-house; his cheeks seemed to have fallen in, his voice trembled; never was a soul more dead in earnest.

"Why, John, you're not afraid?" asked Dr. Livesey.

"Doctor, I'm no coward! no, not I—not *so* much!" and he snapped his fingers. "If I was I wouldn't say it. But I'll own up fairly, I've the shakes upon me for the gallows. You're a good man and a true; I never seen a better man! And you'll not forget what I done good, not any more than you'll forget the bad, I know. And I step aside—see here—and leave you and Jim alone. And you'll put that down for me, too, for it's a long stretch, is that!"

So saying, he stepped back a little way, till he was out of earshot, and there sat down upon a tree-stump and began to whistle; spinning round now and again upon his seat so as to command a sight, sometimes of me and the doctor, and sometimes of his unruly ruffians as they went to and fro in the sand, between the fire —which they were busy rekindling—and the house, from which they brought forth pork and bread to make the breakfast.

"So, Jim," said the doctor sadly, "here you are. As you have brewed, so shall you drink, my boy. Heaven knows, I cannot find it in my heart to blame you; but this much I will say, be it kind or unkind: when Captain Smollett was well, you dared not have gone off; and when he was ill, and couldn't help it, by George, it was downright cowardly!"

I will own that here I began to weep. "Doctor," I said, "you might spare me. I have blamed myself enough; my life's forfeit anyway, and I should have been dead by now, if Silver hadn't stood for me; and doctor, believe this, I can die—and I dare say I deserve it—but what I fear is torture. If they come to torture me——"

"Jim," the doctor interrupted, and his voice was quite changed, "Jim, I can't have this. Whip over, and we'll run for it."

"Doctor," said I, "I passed my word."

"I know, I know," he cried. "We can't help that, Jim, now. I'll take it on my shoulders, holus bolus, blame and shame, my boy; but stay here, I cannot let you. Jump! One jump, and you're out, and we'll run for it like antelopes."

"No," I replied, "you know right well you wouldn't do the thing yourself; neither you, nor squire, nor captain; and no more will I. Silver trusted me; I passed my word, and back I go. But, doctor, you did not let me finish. If they come to torture me, I might slip a word of where the ship is; for I got the ship, part by luck and part by risking, and she lies in North Inlet, on the southern beach, and just below highwater. At half tide she must be high and dry."

"The ship!" exclaimed the doctor.

Rapidly I described to him my adventures, and he heard me out in silence.

"There is a kind of fate in this," he observed, when I had done. "Every step, it's you that saves our lives; and do you suppose by any chance that we are going to let you lose yours? That would be a poor return, my boy. You found out the plot; you found Ben Gunn—the best deed that ever you did, or will do, though you live to ninety. Oh, by Jupiter, and talking of Ben Gunn! why, this is the mischief in person. Silver!" he cried, "Silver!—I'll give you a piece of advice," he continued, as the cook drew near again; "don't you be in any great hurry after that treasure."

"Why, sir, I do my possible, which that ain't," said Silver. "I can only, asking your pardon, save my life and the boy's by seeking for that treasure; and you may lay to that."

"Well, Silver," replied the doctor, "if that is so, I'll go one step farther: look out for squalls when you find it."

"Sir," said Silver, "as between man and man, that's too much and too little. What you're after, why you left the blockhouse, why you've given me that there chart, I don't know, now, do I? and yet I done your bidding with my eyes shut and never a word of hope! But, no, this here's too much. If you won't tell me what you mean plain out, just say so, and I'll leave the helm."

"No," said the doctor musingly, "I've no right to say more; it's not my secret, you see, Silver, or, I give you my word, I'd tell it you. But I'll go as far with you as I dare go, and a step beyond; for I'll have my wig sorted by the captain or I'm mistaken! And, first, I'll give you a bit of hope: Silver, if we both get alive out of this wolf-trap, I'll do my best to save you, short of perjury."

Silver's face was radiant. "You couldn't say more, I'm sure, sir, not if you was my mother," he cried.

"Well, that's my first concession," added the doctor. "My second is a piece of advice: Keep the boy close beside you, and when you need help, halloo. I'm off to seek it for you, and that itself will show you if I speak at random. Good-bye, Jim."

And Dr. Livesey shook hands with me through the stockade, nodded to Silver, and set off at a brisk pace into the wood.

31.　*The Treasure Hunt—Flint's Pointer*

J IM," SAID SILVER, WHEN WE WERE ALONE, "IF I SAVED YOUR LIFE, you saved mine; and I'll not forget it. I seen the doctor waving you to run for it—with the tail of my eye, I did; and I seen you say no, as plain as hearing. Jim, that's one to you. This is the first glint of hope I had since the attack failed, and I owe it you. And now, Jim, we're to go in for this here treasure-hunting, with sealed orders, too, and I don't like it; and you and me must stick close, back to back like, and we'll save our necks in spite o' fate and fortune."

Just then a man hailed us from the fire that breakfast was ready, and we were soon seated here and there about the sand over biscuit and fried junk. They had lit a fire fit to roast an ox; and it was now grown so hot that they could only approach it from the windward, and even there not without precaution. In the same wasteful spirit they had cooked, I suppose, three times more than we could eat; and one of them, with an empty laugh, threw what was left into the fire, which blazed and roared again over this unusual fuel. I never in my life saw men so careless of the morrow; hand to mouth is the only word that can describe their way of doing; and what with wasted food and sleeping sentries, though they were bold enough for a brush and be done with it, I could see their entire unfitness for anything like a prolonged campaign.

Even Silver, eating away, with Captain Flint upon his shoulder, had not a word of blame for their recklessness. And this the more surprised me, for I thought he had never shown himself so cunning as he did then.

"Ay, mates," said he, "it's lucky you have Barbecue to think for you with this here head. I got what I wanted, I did. Sure enough, they have the ship. Where they have it, I don't know yet; but once we hit the treasure, we'll have to jump about and find out. And then, mates, us that has the boats, I reckon, has the upper hand."

Thus he kept running on, with his mouth full of the hot bacon: thus he restored their hope and confidence, and, I more than suspect, repaired his own at the same time.

"As for hostage," he continued, "that's his last talk, I guess, with them he loves so dear. I've got my piece o' news, and thanky to him for that; but it's over and done. I'll take him in a line when we go treasure-hunting, for we'll keep him like so much gold, in case of accidents, you mark, and in the meantime. Once we got the ship and treasure both, and off to sea like jolly companions, why, then, we'll talk Mr. Hawkins over, we will, and we'll give him his share, to be sure, for all his kindness."

It was no wonder the men were in a good humour now. For my part, I was horribly cast down. Should the scheme he had now sketched prove feasible, Silver, already doubly a traitor, would not hesitate to adopt it. He had still a foot in either camp, and there was no doubt he would prefer wealth and freedom with the pirates to a bare escape from hanging, which was the best he had to hope on our side.

Nay, and even if things so fell out that he was forced to keep his faith with Dr. Livesey, even then what danger lay before us! What a moment that would be when the suspicions of his followers turned to certainty, and he and I should have to fight for dear life —he, a cripple, and I, a boy—against five strong and active seamen!

Add to this double apprehension, the mystery that still hung over the behaviour of my friends; their unexplained desertion of the stockade; their inexplicable cession of the chart; or, harder still to understand, the doctor's last warning to Silver, "Look out for squalls when you find it"; and you will readily believe how little taste I found in my breakfast, and with how uneasy a heart I set forth behind my captors on the quest for treasure.

We made a curious figure, had any one been there to see us; all in soiled sailor clothes, and all but me armed to the teeth. Silver had two guns slung about him—one before and one behind—besides the great cutlass at his waist, and a pistol in each pocket of his square-tailed coat. To complete his strange appearance, Captain Flint sat perched upon his shoulder and gabbled odds and ends of purposeless sea-talk. I had a line about my waist, and followed obediently after the sea-cook, who held the loose end of the rope, now in his free hand, now between his powerful teeth. For all the world, I was led like a dancing bear.

The other men were variously burthened; some carrying picks and shovels—for that had been the very first necessary they brought ashore from the *Hispaniola*—others laden with pork, bread, and brandy for the midday meal. All the stores, I observed, came from our stock; and I could see the truth of Silver's words the night before. Had he not struck a bargain with the doctor, he and his mutineers, deserted by the ship, must have been driven to subsist on clear water and the proceeds of their hunting. Water would have been little to their taste; a sailor is not usually a good shot; and besides all that, when they were so short of eatables, it was not likely they would be very flush of powder.

Well, thus equipped, we all set out—even the fellow with the broken head, who should certainly have kept in shadow—and straggled, one after another, to the beach, where the two gigs awaited us. Even these bore traces of the drunken folly of the pirates, one in a broken thwart, and both in their muddied and unbaled condition. Both were to be carried along with us, for the sake of safety; and so, with our numbers divided between them, we set forth upon the bosom of the anchorage.

As we pulled over, there was some discussion on the chart. The red cross was, of course, far too large to be a guide; and the terms of the note on the back, as you will hear, admitted of some ambiguity. They ran, the reader may remember, thus:—

"Tall tree, Spy-glass Shoulder, bearing a point to the N. of N.N.E.
"Skeleton Island E.S.E. and by E.
"Ten feet."

A tall tree was thus the principal mark. Now, right before us, the anchorage was bounded by a plateau from two to three hundred feet high, adjoining on the north the sloping southern shoulder of the Spy-glass, and rising again towards the south into the rough cliffy eminence called the Mizzen-mast Hill. The top of the plateau was dotted thickly with pine trees of varying height. Every here and there, one of a different species rose forty or fifty feet clear above its neighbours, and which of these was the particular "tall tree" of Captain Flint could only be decided on the spot, and by the readings of the compass.

Yet, although that was the case, every man on board the boats had picked a favourite of his own ere we were half-way over, Long John alone shrugging his shoulders and bidding them wait till they were there.

We pulled easily, by Silver's directions, not to weary the hands prematurely; and, after quite a long passage, landed at the mouth of the second river—that which runs down a woody cleft of the

Spy-glass. Thence, bending to our left, we began to ascend the slope towards the plateau.

At the first outset, heavy, miry ground and a matted, marish vegetation, greatly delayed our progress; but by little and little the hill began to steepen and become stony under foot, and the wood to change its character and to grow in a more open order. It was, indeed, a most pleasant portion of the island that we were now approaching. A heavy-scented broom and many flowering shrubs had almost taken the place of grass. Thickets of green nutmeg trees were dotted here and there with the red columns and the broad shadow of the pines; and the first mingled their spice with the aroma of the others. The air, besides, was fresh and stirring, and this, under the sheer sunbeams, was a wonderful refreshment to our senses.

The party spread itself abroad, in a fan shape, shouting and leaping to and fro. About the centre, and a good way behind the rest, Silver and I followed—I tethered by my rope, he ploughing, with deep pants, among the sliding gravel. From time to time, indeed, I had to lend him a hand, or he must have missed his footing and fallen backward down the hill.

We had thus proceeded for about half a mile, and were approaching the brow of the plateau, when the man upon the farthest left began to cry aloud, as if in terror. Shout after shout came from him, and the others began to run in his direction.

"He can't 'a' found the treasure," said old Morgan, hurrying past us from the right, "for that's clean a-top."

Indeed, as we found when we also reached the spot, it was something very different. At the foot of a pretty big pine, and involved in a green creeper, which had even partly lifted some of the smaller bones, a human skeleton lay, with a few shreds of clothing, on the ground. I believe a chill struck for a moment to every heart.

"He was a seaman," said George Merry, who, bolder than the rest, had gone up close, and was examining the rags of clothing. "Leastways, this is good sea-cloth."

"Ay, ay," said Silver, "like enough; you wouldn't look to find a bishop here, I reckon. But what sort of a way is that for bones to lie? 'Tain't in natur'."

Indeed, on a second glance, it seemed impossible to fancy that the body was in a natural position. But for some disarray (the work, perhaps, of the birds that had fed upon him, or of the slow-growing creeper that had gradually enveloped his remains) the man lay perfectly straight—his feet pointing in one direction, his hands, raised above his head like a diver's, pointing directly in the opposite.

"I've taken a notion into my old numskull," observed Silver. "Here's the compass; there's the tip-top p'int o' Skeleton Island, stickin' out like a tooth. Just take a bearing, will you, along the line of them bones."

It was done. The body pointed straight in the direction of the island, and the compass read duly E.S.E. and by E.

"I thought so," cried the cook; "this here is a p'inter. Right up there is our line for the Pole Star and the jolly dollars. But, by thunder! if it don't make me cold inside to think of Flint. This is one of *his* jokes, and no mistake. Him and these six was alone here; he killed 'em, every man; and this one he hauled here and laid down by compass, shiver my timbers! They're long bones, and the hair's been yellow. Ay, that would be Allardyce. You mind Allardyce, Tom Morgan?"

"Ay, ay," returned Morgan, "I mind him; he owed me money, he did, and took my knife ashore with him."

"Speaking of knives," said another, "why don't we find his'n lying round? Flint warn't the man to pick a seaman's pocket; and the birds, I guess, would leave it be."

"By the Powers, and that's true!" cried Silver.

"There ain't a thing left here," said Merry, still feeling round among the bones, "not a copper doit nor a baccy box. It don't look nat'ral to me."

"No, by gum, it don't," agreed Silver; "not nat'ral, nor not nice, says you. Great guns! messmates, but if Flint was living, this would be a hot spot for you and me. Six they were, and six are we; and bones is what they are now."

"I saw him dead with these here deadlights," said Morgan. "Billy took me in. There he laid, with penny-pieces on his eyes."

"Dead—ay, sure enough he's dead and gone below," said the fellow with the bandage; "but if ever sperrit walked, it would be Flint's. Dear heart, but he died bad, did Flint!"

"Ay, that he did," observed another; "now he raged, and now he hollered for the rum, and now he sang. 'Fifteen Men' were his only song, mates; and I tell you true, I never rightly liked to hear it since. It was main hot, and the windy was open, and I hear that old song comin' out as clear as clear—and the death-haul on the man a'ready."

"Come, come," said Silver, "stow this talk. He's dead, and he don't walk, that I know; leastways, he won't walk by day, and you may lay to that. Care killed a cat. Fetch ahead for the doubloons."

We started, certainly; but in spite of the hot sun and the staring daylight, the pirates no longer ran separate and shouting through the wood, but kept side by side and spoke with bated breath. The terror of the dead buccaneer had fallen on their spirits.

32. *The Treasure Hunt—The Voice Among the Trees*

PARTLY FROM THE DAMPING INFLUENCE OF THIS ALARM, PARTLY to rest silver and the sick folk, the whole party sat down as soon as they had gained the brow of the ascent.

The plateau being somewhat tilted towards the west, this spot on which we had paused commanded a wide prospect on either hand. Before us, over the tree-tops, we beheld the Cape of the Woods fringed with surf; behind, we not only looked down upon the anchorage and Skeleton Island, but saw—clear across the spit and the eastern lowlands—a great field of open sea upon the east. Sheer above us rose the Spy-glass, here dotted with single pines, there black with precipices. There was no sound but that of the distant breakers, mounting from all round, and the chirp of countless insects in the brush. Not a man, not a sail upon the sea; the very largeness of the view increased the sense of solitude.

Silver, as he sat, took certain bearings with his compass.

"There are three 'tall trees,'" said he, "about in the right line from Skeleton Island. 'Spy-glass Shoulder,' I take it, means that lower p'int there. It's child's play to find the stuff now. I've half a mind to dine first."

"I don't feel sharp," growled Morgan. "Thinkin' o' Flint—I think it were—as done me."

"Ah, well, my son, you praise your stars he's dead," said Silver.

"He were an ugly devil," cried a third pirate with a shudder; "that blue in the face, too!"

"That was how the rum took him," added Merry. "Blue! well, I reckon he was blue. That's a true word."

Ever since they had found the skeleton and got upon this train of thought, they had spoken lower and lower, and they had almost got to whispering by now, so that the sound of their talk hardly interrupted the silence of the wood. All of a sudden, out of the middle of the trees in front of us, a thin, high, trembling voice struck up the well-known air and words:—

> "Fifteen men on The Dead Man's Chest—
> Yo-ho-ho, and a bottle of rum!"

I never have seen men more dreadfully affected than the pirates. The colour went from their six faces like enchantment; some leaped to their feet, some clawed hold of others; Morgan grovelled on the ground.

"It's Flint, by——!" cried Merry.

The song had stopped as suddenly as it began—broken off, you would have said, in the middle of a note, as though some one had laid his hand upon the singer's mouth. Coming so far through the clear, sunny atmosphere among the green tree-tops, I thought it had sounded airily and sweetly; and the effect on my companions was the stranger.

"Come," said Silver, struggling with his ashen lips to get the word out, "this won't do. Stand by to go about. This is a rum start, and I can't name the voice: but it's some one skylarking— some one that's flesh and blood, and you may lay to that."

His courage had come back as he spoke, and some of the colour to his face along with it. Already the others had begun to lend an ear to this encouragement, and were coming a little to themselves, when the same voice broke out again—not this time singing, but in a faint distant hail, that echoed yet fainter among the clefts of the Spy-glass.

"Darby M'Graw," it wailed—for that is the word that best describes the sound—"Darby M'Graw! Darby M'Graw!" again and again and again; and then rising a little higher, and with an oath that I leave out, "Fetch aft the rum, Darby!"

The buccaneers remained rooted to the ground, their eyes starting from their heads. Long after the voice had died away they still stared in silence, dreadfully, before them.

"That fixes it!" gasped one. "Let's go."

"They was his last words," moaned Morgan, "his last words above board."

Dick had his Bible out, and was praying volubly. He had been well brought up, had Dick, before he came to sea and fell among bad companions.

Still, Silver was unconquered. I could hear his teeth rattle in his head; but he had not yet surrendered.

"Nobody in this here island ever heard of Darby," he muttered; "not one but us that's here." And then, making a great effort, "Shipmates," he cried, "I'm here to get that stuff, and I'll not be beat by man nor devil. I never was feared of Flint in his life, and, by the Powers, I'll face him dead. There's seven hundred thousand pound not a quarter of a mile from here. When did ever a gentleman o' fortune show his stern to that much dollars, for a boosy old seaman with a blue mug—and him dead, too?"

But there was no sign of re-awakening courage in his followers; rather, indeed, of growing terror at the irreverence of his words.

"Belay there, John!" said Merry. "Don't you cross a sperrit."

And the rest were all too terrified to reply. They would have run away severally had they dared; but fear kept them together, and kept them close by John, as if his daring helped them. He, on his part, had pretty well fought his weakness down.

"Sperrit? Well, maybe," he said. "But there's one thing not clear to me. There was an echo. Now, no man ever seen a sperrit with a shadow; well, then, what's he doing with an echo to him, I should like to know? That ain't in natur', surely?"

This argument seemed weak enough to me. But you can never tell what will affect the superstitious, and, to my wonder, George Merry was greatly relieved.

"Well, that's so," he said. "You've a head upon your shoulders, John, and no mistake. 'Bout ship, mates! this here crew is on a wrong tack, I do believe. And come to think on it, it was like Flint's voice, I grant you, but not just so clear-away like it, after all. It was liker somebody else's voice now—it was liker——"

"By the Powers, Ben Gunn!" roared Silver.

"Ay, and so it were," cried Morgan, springing on his knees. "Ben Gunn it were!"

"It don't make much odds, do it, now?" asked Dick. "Ben Gunn's not here in the body, any more'n Flint."

But the older hands greeted this remark with scorn.

"Why, nobody minds Ben Gunn," cried Merry; "dead or alive, nobody minds him."

It was extraordinary how their spirits had returned, and how the natural colour had revived in their faces. Soon they were chatting together, with intervals of listening; and not long after, hearing no further sound, they shouldered the tools and set forth again, Merry walking first with Silver's compass to keep them on the right line with Skeleton Island. He had said the truth: dead or alive, nobody minded Ben Gunn.

Dick alone still held his Bible, and looked around him as he went, with fearful glances; but he found no sympathy, and Silver even joked him on his precautions.

"I told you," said he—"I told you, you had sp'iled your Bible. If it ain't no good to swear by, what do you suppose a sperrit would give for it? Not that!" and he snapped his big fingers, halting a moment on his crutch.

But Dick was not to be comforted; indeed it was soon plain to me that the lad was falling sick; hastened by heat, exhaustion, and the shock of his alarm, the fever predicted by Doctor Livesey was evidently growing swiftly higher.

It was fine open walking here, upon the summit; our way lay a little downhill, for, as I have said, the plateau tilted towards the west. The pines, great and small, grew wide apart: and even between the clumps of nutmeg and azalea, wide open spaces baked in the hot sunshine. Striking, as we did, pretty near north-west across the island, we drew, on the one hand, even nearer under the shoulders of the Spy-glass, and on the other, looked ever wider over that western bay where I had once tossed and trembled in the coracle.

The first of the tall trees was reached, and by the bearing, proved the wrong one. So with the second. The third rose nearly two hundred feet in the air above a clump of underwood; a giant of a vegetable, with a red column as big as a cottage, and a wide shadow around in which a company could have manœuvred. It was conspicuous far to sea both on the east and west, and might have been entered as a sailing mark upon the chart.

But it was not its size that now impressed my companions; it was the knowledge that seven hundred thousand pounds in gold lay somewhere buried beneath its spreading shadow. The thought of the money, as they drew nearer, swallowed up their previous terrors. Their eyes burned in their heads; their feet grew speedier and lighter; their whole soul was bound up in that fortune, that whole lifetime of extravagance and pleasure, that lay waiting there for each of them.

Silver hobbled, grunting, on his crutch; his nostrils stood out and quivered; he cursed like a madman when the flies settled on his hot and shiny countenance; he plucked furiously at the line that held me to him, and, from time to time, turned his eyes upon me with a deadly look. Certainly he took no pains to hide his thoughts; and certainly I read them like print. In the immediate nearness of the gold, all else had been forgotten; his promise and the doctor's warning were both things of the past; and I could not doubt that he hoped to seize upon the treasure, find and board the *Hispaniola* under cover of night, cut every honest throat about that island, and sail away as he had at first intended, laden with crimes and riches.

Shaken as I was with these alarms, it was hard for me to keep up with the rapid pace of the treasure-hunters. Now and again I stumbled; and it was then that Silver plucked so roughly at the rope and launched at me his murderous glances. Dick, who had dropped behind us, and now brought up the rear, was babbling to himself both prayers and curses, as his fever kept rising. This also added to my wretchedness, and, to crown all, I was haunted by the thought of the tragedy that had once been acted on that plateau, when that ungodly buccaneer with the blue face—he who died at Savannah, singing and shouting for drink—had there, with his own hand, cut down his six accomplices. This grove, that was now so peaceful, must then have rung with cries, I thought; and even with the thought I could believe I heard it ringing still.

We were now at the margin of the thicket.

"Huzza, mates, all together!" shouted Merry; and the foremost broke into a run.

And suddenly, not ten yards farther, we beheld them stop. A low cry arose. Silver doubled his pace, digging away with the foot of his crutch like one possessed; and next moment he and I had come also to a dead halt.

Before us was a great excavation, not very recent, for the sides had fallen in and grass had sprouted on the bottom. In this were the shaft of a pick broken in two and the boards of several packing-cases strewn around. On one of these boards I saw, branded with a hot iron, the name *Walrus*—the name of Flint's ship.

All was clear to probation. The *cache* had been found and rifled; the seven hundred thousand pounds were gone!

33. *The Fall of a Chieftain*

THERE NEVER WAS SUCH AN OVERTURN IN THIS WORLD. EACH OF these six men was as though he had been struck. But with Silver the blow passed almost instantly. Every thought of his soul had been set full-stretch, like a racer, on that money; well, he was brought up in a single second, dead; and he kept his head, found his temper, and changed his plan before the others had had time to realise the disappointment.

"Jim," he whispered, "take that, and stand by for trouble."

And he passed me a double-barrelled pistol.

At the same time he began quietly moving northward, and in a few steps had put the hollow between us two and the other five. Then he looked at me and nodded, as much as to say, "Here is a narrow corner," as, indeed, I thought it was. His looks were now quite friendly; and I was so revolted at these constant changes, that I could not forbear whispering, "So you've changed sides again."

There was no time left for him to answer in. The buccaneers, with oaths and cries, began to leap, one after another, into the pit, and to dig with their fingers, throwing the boards aside as they did so. Morgan found a piece of gold. He held it up with a perfect spout of oaths. It was a two-guinea piece, and it went from hand to hand among them for a quarter of a minute.

"Two guineas!" roared Merry, shaking it at Silver. "That's your seven hundred thousand pounds, is it? You're the man for bargains, ain't you? You're him that never bungled nothing, you wooden-headed lubber!"

"Dig away, boys," said Silver, with the coolest insolence; "you'll find some pig-nuts and I shouldn't wonder."

"Pig-nuts!" repeated Merry, in a scream. "Mates, do you hear that? I tell you, now, that man there knew it all along. Look in the face of him, and you'll see it wrote there."

"Ah, Merry," remarked Silver, "standing for cap'n again? You're a pushing lad, to be sure."

But this time every one was entirely in Merry's favour. They began to scramble out of the excavation, darting furious glances behind them. One thing I observed, which looked well for us: they all got out upon the opposite side from Silver.

Well, there we stood, two on one side, five on the other, the pit between us, and nobody screwed up high enough to offer the first blow. Silver never moved; he watched them, very upright on his crutch, and looked as cool as ever I saw him. He was brave, and no mistake.

At last, Merry seemed to think a speech might help matters.

"Mates," says he, "there's two of them alone there; one's the old cripple that brought us all here and blundered us down to this; the other's that cub that I mean to have the heart of. Now, mates——"

He was raising his arm and his voice, and plainly meant to lead a charge. But just then—crack! crack! crack!—three musket-shots flashed out of the thicket. Merry tumbled head foremost into the excavation; the man with the bandage spun round like a teetotum, and fell all his length upon his side, where he lay dead, but still twitching; and the other three turned and ran for it with all their might.

Before you could wink, Long John had fired two barrels of a pistol into the struggling Merry; and as the man rolled up his eyes at him in the last agony, "George," said he, "I reckon I settled you."

At the same moment the doctor, Gray, and Ben Gunn joined us, with smoking muskets, from among the nutmeg trees.

"Forward!" cried the doctor. "Double quick, my lads. We must head 'em off the boats."

And we set off, at a great pace, sometimes plunging through the bushes to the chest.

I tell you, but Silver was anxious to keep up with us. The work that man went through, leaping on his crutch till the muscles of his chest were fit to burst, was work no sound man ever equalled; and so thinks the doctor. As it was, he was already thirty yards behind us, and on the verge of strangling, when we reached the brow of the slope.

"Doctor," he hailed, "see there! no hurry!"

Sure enough there was no hurry. In a more open part of the

plateau, we could see the three survivors still running in the same direction as they had started, right for Mizzen-mast Hill. We were already between them and the boats; and so we four sat down to breathe, while Long John, mopping his face, came slowly up with us.

"Thank ye kindly, doctor," says he. "You came in in about the nick, I guess, for me and Hawkins. And so it's you, Ben Gunn!" he added. "Well, you're a nice one, to be sure."

"I'm Ben Gunn, I am," replied the maroon, wriggling like an eel in his embarrassment. "And," he added, after a long pause, "how do, Mr. Silver. Pretty well, I thank ye, says you."

"Ben, Ben," murmured Silver, "to think as you've done me!"

The doctor sent back Gray for one of the pickaxes, deserted, in their flight, by the mutineers; and then as we proceeded leisurely downhill to where the boats were lying, related, in a few words, what had taken place. It was a story that profoundly interested Silver; and Ben Gunn, the half-idiot maroon, was the hero from beginning to end.

Ben, in his long, lonely wanderings about the island, had found the skeleton—it was he that had rifled it; he had found the treasure; he had dug it up (it was the haft of his pickaxe that lay broken in the excavation); he had carried it on his back, in many weary journeys, from the foot of a tall pine to a cave he had on the two-pointed hill at the north-east angle of the island, and there it had lain stored in safety since two months before the arrival of the *Hispaniola*.

When the doctor had wormed his secret from him, on the afternoon of the attack, and when next morning he saw the anchorage deserted, he had gone to Silver, given him the chart, which was now useless—given him the stores, for Ben Gunn's cave was well supplied with goats' meat salted by himself—given anything and everything to get a chance of moving in safety from the stockade to the two-pointed hill, there to be clear of malaria and keep a guard upon the money.

"As for you, Jim," he said, "it went against my heart, but I did what I thought best for those who had stood by their duty; and if you were not one of these, whose fault was it?"

That morning, finding that I was to be involved in the horrid disappointment he had prepared for the mutineers, he had run all the way to the cave, and. leaving squire to guard the captain, had taken Gray and the maroon, and started, making the diagonal across the island, to be at hand beside the pine. Soon, however, he saw that our party had the start of him; and Ben Gunn, being fleet of foot, had been despatched in front to do his best alone. Then it had occurred to him to work upon the superstitions of his former shipmates; and he was so far successful that Gray and the doctor had come up and were already ambushed before the arrival of the treasure-hunters.

"Ah," said Silver, "it were fortunate for me that I had Hawkins here. You could have let old John be cut to bits, and never given it a thought, doctor."

"Not a thought," replied Doctor Livesey cheerily.

And by this time we had reached the gigs. The doctor, with the pickaxe, demolished one of them, and then we all got aboard the other and set out to go round by sea for North Inlet.

This was a run of eight or nine miles. Silver, though he was almost killed already with fatigue, was set to an oar, like the rest of us, and we were soon skimming swiftly over a smooth sea. Soon we passed out of the straits and doubled the south-east corner of the island, round which, four days ago, we had towed the *Hispaniola*.

As we passed the two-pointed hill, we could see the black mouth of Ben Gunn's cave, and a figure standing by it, leaning on a musket. It was the squire; and we waved a handkerchief and gave him three cheers, in which the voice of Silver joined as heartily as any.

Three miles farther, just inside the mouth of North Inlet, what should we meet but the *Hispaniola,* cruising by herself! The last flood had lifted her; and had there been much wind, or a strong tide current, as in the southern anchorage, we should never had found her more, or found her stranded beyond help. As it was, there was little amiss, beyond the wreck of the mainsail. Another anchor was got ready, and dropped in a fathom and a half of water. We all pulled round again to Rum Cove, the nearest point for Ben Gunn's treasure-house; and then Gray, single-handed, returned with the gig to the *Hispaniola,* where he was to pass the night on guard.

A gentle slope ran up from the beach to the entrance of the cave.

At the top, the squire met us. To me he was cordial and kind, saying nothing of my escapade, either in the way of blame or praise. At Silver's polite salute he somewhat flushed.

"John Silver," he said, "you're a prodigious villain and impostor—a monstrous impostor, sir. I am told I am not to prosecute you. Well, then, I will not. But the dead men, sir, hang about your neck like millstones."

"Thank you kindly, sir," replied Long John, again saluting.

"I dare you to thank me!" cried the squire. "It is a gross dereliction of my duty. Stand back."

And thereupon we all entered the cave. It was a large, airy place, with a little spring and a pool of clear water, overhung with ferns. The floor was sand. Before a big fire lay Captain Smollett: and in a far corner, only duskily flickered over by the blaze, I beheld great heaps of coin and quadrilaterals built of bars of gold. That was Flint's treasure that we had come so far to seek, and that had cost already the lives of seventeen men from the *Hispaniola*. How many it had cost in the amassing, what blood and sorrow, what good ships scuttled on the deep, what brave men walking the plank blindfold, what shot of cannon, what shame and lies and cruelty, perhaps no man alive could tell. Yet there were still three upon that island—Silver, and old Morgan, and Ben Gunn—who had each taken his share in these crimes, as each had hoped in vain to share in the reward.

"Come in, Jim," said the captain. "You're a good boy in your line, Jim; but I don't think you and me'll go to sea again. You're too much of the born favourite for me. Is that you, John Silver? What brings you here, man?"

"Come back to my dooty, sir," returned Silver.

"Ah!" said the captain; and that was all he said.

What a supper I had of it that night, with all my friends around me; and what a meal it was, with Ben Gunn's salted goat, and some delicacies and a bottle of old wine from the *Hispaniola!* Never, I am sure, were people gayer or happier. And there was Silver, sitting back almost out of the firelight, but eating heartily, prompt to spring forward when anything was wanted, even joining quietly in our laughter—the same bland, polite, obsequious seaman of the voyage out.

34. *And Last*

THE NEXT MORNING WE FELL EARLY TO WORK, FOR THE TRANS-
portation of this great mass of gold near a mile by land to the
beach, and thence three miles by boat to the *Hispaniola,* was a considerable task for so small a number of workmen. The three fellows still abroad upon the island did not greatly trouble us; a
single sentry on the shoulder of the hill was sufficient to ensure us
against any sudden onslaught, and we thought, besides, they had
had more than enough of fighting.

Therefore the work was pushed on briskly. Gray and Ben Gunn
came and went with the boat, while the rest, during their absences, piled treasure on the beach. Two of the bars, slung in a
rope's end, made a good load for a grown man—one that he was
glad to walk slowly with. For my part, as I was not much use at
carrying, I was kept busy all day in the cave, packing the minted
money into bread-bags.

It was a strange collection, like Billy Bones's hoard for the diversity of coinage, but so much larger and so much more varied
that I think I never had more pleasure than in sorting them.
English, French, Spanish, Portuguese, Georges, and Louises, doubloons and double guineas and moidores and sequins, the pictures
of all the kings of Europe for the last hundred years, strange Oriental pieces stamped with what looked like wisps of string or bits of
spider's web, round pieces and square pieces, and pieces bored
through the middle, as if to wear them round your neck—nearly
every variety of money in the world must, I think, have found a
place in that collection; and for number, I am sure they were like
autumn leaves, so that my back ached with stooping and my
fingers with sorting them out.

Day after day this work went on; by every evening a fortune
had been stowed aboard, but there was another fortune waiting
for the morrow; and all this time we heard nothing of the three
surviving mutineers.

At last—I think it was on the third night—the doctor and I
were strolling on the shoulder of the hill where it overlooks the
lowlands of the isle, when, from out the thick darkness below, the
wind brought us a noise between shrieking and singing. It was
only a snatch that reached our ears, followed by the former silence.

"Heaven forgive them," said the doctor; " 'tis the mutineers!"

"All drunk, sir," struck in the voice of Silver from behind us.

Silver, I should say, was allowed his entire liberty, and, in spite of daily rebuffs, seemed to regard himself once more as quite a privileged and friendly dependant. Indeed, it was remarkable how well he bore these slights, and with what unwearying politeness he kept on trying to ingratiate himself with all. Yet, I think, none treated him better than a dog; unless it was Ben Gunn, who was still terribly afraid of his old quartermaster, or myself, who had really something to thank him for; although for that matter, I suppose, I had reason to think even worse of him than anybody else, for I had seen him meditating a fresh treachery upon the plateau. Accordingly, it was pretty gruffly that the doctor answered him.

"Drunk or raving," said he.

"Right you were, sir," replied Silver; "and precious little odds which, to you and me."

"I suppose you would hardly ask me to call you a humane man," returned the doctor with a sneer, "and so my feelings may surprise you, Master Silver. But if I were sure they were raving—as I am morally certain one, at least, of them is down with fever—I should leave this camp, and, at whatever risk to my own carcass, take them the assistance of my skill."

"Ask your pardon, sir, you would be very wrong," quoth Silver. "You would lose your precious life, and you may lay to that. I'm on your side now, hand and glove; and I shouldn't wish for to see the party weakened, let alone yourself, seeing as I know what I owes you. But these men down there, they couldn't keep their word—no, not supposing they wished to; and what's more, they couldn't believe as you could."

"No," said the doctor. "You're the man to keep your word, we know that."

Well, that was about the last news we had of the three pirates. Only once we heard a gunshot a great way off, and supposed them to be hunting. A council was held, and it was decided that we must desert them on the island—to the huge glee, I must say, of Ben Gunn, and with the strong approval of Gray. We left a good stock of powder and shot, the bulk of the salt goat, a few medicines, and some other necessaries, tools, clothing, a spare sail, a fathom or two of rope, and, by the particular desire of the doctor, a hand-some present of tobacco.

That was about our last doing on the island. Before that, we had got the treasure stowed, and had shipped enough water and the remainder of the goat meat, in case of any distress; and at last, one fine morning, we weighed anchor, which was about all that we could manage, and stood out of North Inlet, the same colours flying that the captain had flown and fought under at the palisade.

The three fellows must have been watching us closer than we thought for, as we soon had proved. For, coming through the narrows, we had to lie very near the southern point, and there we saw all three of them kneeling together on a spit of sand, with their arms raised in supplication. It went to all our hearts, I think, to leave them in that wretched state; but we could not risk another mutiny; and to take them home for the gibbet would have been a cruel sort of kindness. The doctor hailed them and told them of the stores we had left, and where they were to find them. But they continued to call us by name, and appeal to us, for God's sake, to be merciful, and not leave them to die in such a place.

At last, seeing the ship still bore on her course, and was now swiftly drawing out of earshot, one of them—I know not which it was—leapt to his feet with a hoarse cry, whipped his musket to his shoulder, and sent a shot whistling over Silver's head and through the main-sail.

After that, we kept under cover of the bulwarks, and when next I looked out they had disappeared from the spit, and the spit itself had almost melted out of sight in the growing distance. That was, at least, the end of that; and before noon, to my inexpressible joy, the highest rock of Treasure Island had sunk into the blue round of sea.

We were so short of men that every one on board had to bear a hand—only the captain lying on a mattress in the stern and giving his orders; for, though greatly recovered, he was still in want of quiet. We laid her head for the nearest port in Spanish America, for we could not risk the voyage home without fresh hands; and as it was, what with baffling winds and a couple of fresh gales, we were all worn out before we reached it.

It was just at sundown when we cast anchor in a most beautiful land-locked gulf, and were immediately surrounded by shore boats full of Negroes, and Mexican Indians, and half-bloods, selling fruits and vegetables, and offering to dive for bits of money. The sight of so many good-humoured faces (especially the blacks), the taste of the tropical fruits, and, above all, the lights that began to shine in the town, made a most charming contrast to our dark and bloody sojourn on the island; and the doctor and the squire, taking me along with them, went ashore to pass the early part of the night. Here they met the captain of an English man-of-war, fell in talk with him, went on board his ship, and, in short, had so agreeable a time, that day was breaking when we came alongside the *Hispaniola*.

Ben Gunn was on deck alone, and, as soon as we came on board, he began, with wonderful contortions, to make us a confession. Silver was gone. The maroon had connived at his escape in a shore boat some hours ago, and he now assured us he had only done so to preserve our lives, which would certainly have been forfeit if "that man with the one leg had stayed aboard." But this was not all. The sea-cook had not gone empty handed. He had cut through a bulkhead unobserved, and had removed one of the sacks of coin, worth, perhaps, three or four hundred guineas, to help him on his further wanderings.

I think we were all pleased to be so cheaply quit of him.

Well, to make a long story short, we got a few hands on board, made a good cruise home, and the *Hispaniola* reached Bristol just as Mr. Blandly was beginning to think of fitting out her consort. Five men only of those who had sailed returned with her. "Drink and the devil had done for the rest," with a vengeance; although, to be sure, we were not quite in so bad a case as that other ship they sang about:—

> "With one man of her crew alive,
> What put to sea with seventy-five."

All of us had an ample share of the treasure, and used it wisely or foolishly, according to our natures. Captain Smollett is now retired from the sea. Gray not only saved his money, but, being suddenly smit with the desire to rise, also studied his profession; and he is now mate and part owner of a fine full-rigged ship; married besides, and father of a family. As for Ben Gunn, he got a thousand pounds, which he spent or lost in three weeks, or, to be more exact, in nineteen days. for he was back begging on the twentieth. Then he was given a lodge to keep, exactly as he had feared upon the island; and he still lives, a great favourite, though something of a butt, with the country boys, and a notable singer in church on Sundays and saints' days.

Of Silver we have heard no more. That formidable seafaring man with one leg has at last gone clean out of my life; but I dare say he met his old Negress, and perhaps still lives in comfort with her and Captain Flint. It is to be hoped so, I suppose, for his chances of comfort in another world are very small.

The bar silver and the arms still lie, for all that I know, where Flint buried them; and certainly they shall lie there for me. Oxen and wain-ropes would not bring me back again to that accursed island; and the worst dreams that ever I have are when I hear the surf booming about its coasts, or start upright in bed, with the sharp voice of Captain Flint still ringing in my ears: "Pieces of eight! pieces of eight!"

The Master of Ballantrae

A WINTER'S TALE

✳

To Sir Percy Florence and Lady Shelley

. There is a tale which extends over many years and travels into many countries. By a peculiar fitness of circumstances the writer began, continued it, and concluded it among distant and diverse scenes. Above all, he was much upon the sea. The character and fortune of the fraternal enemies, the hall and shrubbery of Durrisdeer, the problem of Mackellar's homespun and how to shape it for superior flights; these were his company on deck in many star-reflecting harbours, ran often in his mind at sea to the tune of slatting canvas, and were dismissed (something of the suddenest) on the approach of squalls. It is my hope that these surroundings of its manufacture may to some degree find favour for my story with seafarers and sealovers like yourselves.

And at least here is a dedication from a great way off; written by the loud shores of a subtropical island near upon ten thousand miles from Boscombe Chine and Manor: scenes which rise before me as I write, along with the faces and voices of my friends.

Well, I am for the sea once more; no doubt Sir Percy also. Let us make the signal B. R. D. !
Waikiki, May 17, 1889.

R. L. S.

Contents

Summary of Events During the Master's Wanderings

THE FULL TRUTH OF THIS ODD MATTER IS WHAT THE WORLD HAS long been looking for and public curiosity is sure to welcome. It so befell that I was intimately mingled with the last years and history of the house; and there does not live one man so able as myself to make these matters plain, or so desirous to narrate them faithfully. I knew the Master; on many secret steps of his career, I have an authentic memoir in my hand; I sailed with him on his last voyage almost alone; I made one upon that winter's journey of which so many tales have gone abroad; and I was there at the man's death. As for my late Lord Durrisdeer, I served him and loved him near twenty years; and thought more of him the more I knew of him. Altogether, I think it not fit that so much evidence should perish; the truth is a debt I owe my lord's memory; and I think my old years will flow more smoothly and my white hair lie quieter on the pillow when the debt is paid.

The Duries of Durrisdeer and Ballantrae were a strong family in the south-west from the days of David First. A rhyme still current in the country-side—

> Kittle folk are the Durrisdeers,
> They ride wi' ower mony spears—

bears the mark of its antiquity; and the name appears in another, which common report attributes to Thomas of Ercildoune himself—I cannot say how truly, and which some have applied—I dare not say with how much justice—to the events of this narration:

> Twa Duries in Durrisdeer,
> Ane to tie and ane to ride,
> An ill day for the groom
> And a waur day for the bride.

Authentic history besides is filled with their exploits which (to our modern eyes) seem not very commendable; and the family suffered its full share of those ups and downs to which the great houses of Scotland have been ever liable. But all these I pass over, to come to that memorable year 1745, when the foundations of this tragedy were laid.

At that time there dwelt a family of four persons in the house of Durrisdeer, near St. Bride's, on the Solway shore; a chief hold of their race since the reformation. My old lord, eighth of the name, was not old in years, but he suffered prematurely from the disabilities of age; his place was at the chimney-side; there he sat reading, in a lined gown, with few words for any man, and wry words for none: the model of an old retired housekeeper; and yet his mind very well nourished with study, and reputed in the country to be more cunning than he seemed. The Master of Ballantrae, James in baptism, took from his father the love of serious reading; some of his tact perhaps as well, but that which was only policy in the father became black dissimulation in the son. The face of his behaviour was merely popular and wild: he sat late at wine, later at the cards; had the name in the country of "an unco man for the lasses"; and was ever in the front of broils. But for all he was the first to go in, yet it was observed he was invariably the best to come off; and his partners in mischief were usually alone to pay the piper. This luck or dexterity got him several ill-wishers, but with the rest of the country, enhanced his reputation; so that great things were looked for in his future, when he should have gained more gravity. One very black mark he had to his name; but the matter was hushed up at the time, and so defaced by legends before I came into those parts, that I scruple to set it down. If it was true, it was a horrid fact in one so young; and if false, it was a horrid calumny. I think it notable that he had always vaunted himself quite implacable, and was taken at his word; so that he had the addition among his neighbours of "an ill man to cross." Here was altogether a young nobleman (not yet twenty-four in the year '45) who had made a figure in the country beyond his time of life. The less marvel if there were little heard of the second son, Mr. Henry (my late Lord Durrisdeer), who was neither very bad nor yet very able, but an honest, solid sort of lad like many of his neighbours. Little heard, I say; but indeed it was a case of little spoken. He was known among the salmon fishers in the firth, for that was a sport that he assiduously followed; he was an excellent good horse-doctor besides; and took a chief hand, almost from a boy, in the management of the estates. How hard a part that was, in the situation of that family, none knows better than myself; nor yet with how little colour of justice a man may there acquire the reputation of a tyrant and a miser. The fourth person in the house was Miss Alison Graeme, a near kinswoman, an orphan, and the heir to a considerable fortune which her father had acquired in trade. This money was loudly called for by my lord's necessities; indeed the land was deeply mortgaged; and Miss Alison was designed accordingly to be the Master's wife, gladly enough on her side; with how much goodwill on his, is another matter. She was a comely girl and in those days very spirited and self-willed; for the old lord having no daughter of his own, and my lady being long dead, she had grown up as best she might.

To these four, came the news of Prince Charlie's landing, and set them presently by the ears. My lord, like the chimney-keeper that he was, was all for temporising. Miss Alison held the other side, because it appeared romantical; and the Master (though I have heard they did not agree often) was for this once of her opinion. The adventure tempted him, as I conceive; he was tempted by the opportunity to raise the fortunes of the house, and not less by the hope of paying off his private liabilities, which were heavy beyond all opinion. As for Mr. Henry, it appears he said little enough at first; his part came later on. It took the three a whole day's disputation, before they agreed to steer a middle course, one son going forth to strike a blow for King James, my lord and the other staying at home to keep in favour with King George. Doubtless this was my lord's decision; and as is well known, it was the part played by many considerable families. But the one dispute settled, another opened. For my lord, Miss Alison and Mr. Henry all held the one view: that it was the cadet's part to go out; and the Master, what with restlessness and vanity, would at no rate consent to stay at home. My lord pleaded, Miss Alison wept, Mr. Henry was very plain spoken: all was of no avail.

"It is the direct heir of Durrisdeer that should ride by his King's bridle," says the Master.

"If we were playing a manly part," says Mr. Henry, "there might be sense in such talk. But what are we doing? Cheating at cards!"

"We are saving the house of Durrisdeer, Henry," his father said.

"And see, James," said Mr. Henry, "if I go, and the Prince has the upper-hand, it will be easy to make your peace with King James. But if you go, and the expedition fails, we divide the right and the title. And what shall I be then?"

"You will be Lord Durrisdeer," said the Master. "I put all I have upon the table."

"I play at no such game," cries Mr. Henry. "I shall be left in such a situation as no man of sense and honour could endure. I shall be neither fish nor flesh!" he cried. And a little after, he had another expression, plainer perhaps than he intended. "It is your duty to be here with my father," said he. "You know well enough you are the favourite."

"Ay?" said the Master. "And there spoke Envy! Would you trip up my heels—Jacob?" said he, and dwelled upon the name maliciously.

Mr. Henry went and walked at the low end of the hall without reply; for he had an excellent gift of silence. Presently he came back.

"I am the cadet and I *should* go," said he. "And my lord here is the master, and he says I *shall* go. What say ye to that, my brother?"

"I say this, Harry," returned the Master, "that when very obstinate folk are met, there are only two ways out: Blows—and I think none of us could care to go so far; or the arbitrament of chance—and here is a guinea piece. Will you stand by the toss of the coin?"

"I will stand and fall by it," said Mr. Henry. "Heads, I go; shield, I stay."

The coin was spun and it fell shield. "So there is a lesson for Jacob," says the Master.

"We shall live to repent of this," says Mr. Henry, and flung out of the hall.

As for Miss Alison, she caught up that piece of gold which had just sent her lover to the wars, and flung it clean through the family shield in the great painted window.

"If you loved me as well as I love you, you would have stayed," cried she.

" 'I could not love you, dear, so well, loved I not honour more,' " sang the Master.

"O!" she cried, "you have no heart—I hope you may be killed!" and she ran from the room, and in tears to her own chamber.

It seems the Master turned to my lord with his most comical manner, and says he, "This looks like a devil of a wife."

"I think you are a devil of a son to me," cried his father, "you that have always been the favourite, to my shame be it spoken. Never a good hour have I gotten of you, since you were born; no, never one good hour," and repeated it again the third time.

Whether it was the Master's levity, or his insubordination, or Mr.
Henry's word about the favourite son, that had so much disturbed
my lord, I do not know; but I incline to think it was the last, for I
have it by all accounts that Mr. Henry was more made up to from
that hour.

Altogether it was in pretty ill blood with his family that the
Master rode to the north; which was the more sorrowful for others
to remember when it seemed too late. By fear and favour, he had
scraped together near upon a dozen men, principally tenants'
sons; they were all pretty full when they set forth, and rode up
the hill by the old abbey, roaring and singing, the white cockade
in every hat. It was a desperate venture for so small a company to
cross the most of Scotland unsupported; and (what made folk
think so the more) even as that poor dozen was clattering up the
hill, a great ship of the king's navy, that could have brought them
under with a single boat, lay with her broad ensign streaming
in the bay. The next afternoon, having given the Master a fair
start, it was Mr. Henry's turn; and he rode off, all by himself, to
offer his sword and carry letters from his father to King George's
government. Miss Alison was shut in her room and did little but
weep, till both were gone; only she stitched the cockade upon the
Master's hat and (as John Paul told me) it was wetted with tears
when he carried it down to him.

In all that followed, Mr. Henry and my old lord were true to
their bargain. That ever they accomplished anything is more
than I could learn; and that they were anyway strong on the
King's side, more than I believe. But they kept the letter of loyalty,
corresponded with my Lord President, sat still at home, and had
little or no commerce with the Master while that business lasted.
Nor was he, on his side, more communicative. Miss Alison, indeed,
was always sending him expresses, but I do not know if she had
many answers. Macconochie rode for her once, and found the
Highlanders before Carlisle, and the Master riding by the Prince's
side in high favour; he took the letter (so Macconochie tells),
opened it, glanced it through with a mouth like a man whistling,
and stuck it in his belt, whence, on his horse passaging, it fell
unregarded to the ground. It was Macconochie who picked it up;
and he still kept it, and indeed I have seen it in his hands. News
came to Durrisdeer of course, by the common report, as it goes
travelling through a country, a thing always wonderful to me. By

that means the family learned more of the Master's favour with
the Prince, and the ground it was said to stand on: for by a
strange condescension in a man so proud—only that he was a
man still more ambitious—he was said to have crept into nota-
bility by truckling to the Irish. Sir Thomas Sullivan, Colonel
Burke and the rest were his daily comrades, by which course he
withdrew himself from his own countryfolk. All the small in-
trigues, he had a hand in fomenting; thwarted my Lord George
upon a thousand points; was always for the advice that seemed
palatable to the Prince, no matter if it was good or bad; and seems
upon the whole (like the gambler he was all through life) to have
had less regard to the chances of the campaign than to the greatness of favour he might aspire to, if (by any luck) it should succeed. For the rest, he did very well in the field; no one questioned
that; for he was no coward.

The next was the news of Culloden, which was brought to Durrisdeer by one of the tenants' sons, the only survivor, he declared,
of all those that had gone singing up the hill. By an unfortunate
chance, John Paul and Macconochie had that very morning found
the guinea piece (which was the root of all the evil) sticking in a
holly bush; they had been "up the gait," as the servants say at
Durrisdeer, to the change-house; and if they had little left of the
guinea, they had less of their wits. What must John Paul do, but
burst into the hall where the family sat at dinner, and cry the
news to them that "Tam Macmorland was but new lichtit at the
door, and—wirra, wirra—there were nane to come behind him"?

They took the word in silence like folk condemned; only Mr.
Henry carrying his palm to his face, and Miss Alison laying her
head outright upon her hands. As for my lord, he was like ashes.

"I have still one son," says he. "And, Henry, I will do you this
justice, it is the kinder that is left."

It was a strange thing to say in such a moment: but my lord had
never forgotten Mr. Henry's speech, and he had years of injustice
on his conscience. Still it was a strange thing; and more than Miss
Alison could let pass. She broke out and blamed my lord for his
unnatural words, and Mr. Henry because he was sitting there in
safety when his brother lay dead, and herself because she had given
her sweetheart ill words at his departure; calling him the flower
of the flock, wringing her hands, protesting her love, and crying
on him by his name; so that the servants stood astonished.

Mr. Henry got to his feet and stood holding his chair; it was he that was like ashes now.

"O," he burst out suddenly, "I know you loved him!"

"The world knows that, glory be to God!" cried she; and then to Mr. Henry: "There is none but me to know one thing—that you were a traitor to him in your heart."

"God knows," groans he, "it was lost love on both sides."

Time went by in the house after that, without much change; only they were now three instead of four, which was a perpetual reminder of their loss. Miss Alison's money, you are to bear in mind, was highly needful for the estates; and the one brother being dead, my old lord soon set his heart upon her marrying the other. Day in, day out, he would work upon her, sitting by the chimney-side with his finger in his Latin book, and his eyes set upon her face with a kind of pleasant intentness that became the old gentleman very well. If she wept, he would condole with her, like an ancient man that has seen worse times and begins to think lightly even of sorrow; if she raged, he would fall to reading again in his Latin book, but always with some civil excuse; if she offered (as she often did) to let them have her money in a gift, he would show her how little it consisted with his honour, and remind her, even if he should consent, that Mr. Henry would certainly refuse. *Non vi sed sæpe cadendo* was a favorite word of his; and no doubt this quiet persecution wore away much of her resolve; no doubt, besides, he had a great influence on the girl, having stood in the place of both her parents; and for that matter, she was herself filled with the spirit of the Duries, and would have gone a great way for the glory of Durrisdeer; but not so far, I think, as to marry my poor patron, had it not been (strangely enough) for the circumstance of his extreme unpopularity.

This was the work of Tam Macmorland. There was not much harm in Tam; but he had that grievous weakness, a long tongue; and as the only man in that country who had been out (or rather who had come in again) he was sure of listeners. Those that have the underhand in any fighting, I have observed, are ever anxious to persuade themselves they were betrayed. By Tam's account of it, the rebels had been betrayed at every turn and by every officer they had; they had been betrayed at Derby, and betrayed at Falkirk; the night march was a step of treachery of my Lord George's; and Culloden was lost by the treachery of the Macdonalds. This habit of imputing treason grew upon the fool, till at last he must have in Mr. Henry also. Mr. Henry (by his account) had betrayed the lads of Durrisdeer; he had promised to follow with more men, and instead of that he had ridden to King George. "Ay, and the next day!" Tam would cry. "The puir, bonnie Master and the puir, kind lads that rade wi' him, were hardly ower the scaur, or he was aff—the Judis! Ay, weel—he has his way o't: he's to be my lord, nae less, and there's money a cauld corp amang the Hieland heather!" And at this, if Tam had been drinking, he would begin to weep.

Let any one speak long enough, he will get believers. This view of Mr. Henry's behaviour crept about the country by little and little; it was talked upon by folk that knew the contrary but were short of topics; and it was heard and believed and given out for gospel by the ignorant and the ill-willing. Mr. Henry began to be shunned; yet awhile, and the commons began to murmur as he went by, and the women (who are always the most bold because they are the most safe) to cry out their reproaches to his face. The Master was cried up for a saint. It was remembered how he had never any hand in pressing the tenants; as, indeed, no more he had, except to spend the money. He was a little wild perhaps, the folk said; but how much better was a natural, wild lad that would soon have settled down, than a skinflint and a sneckdraw, sitting, with his nose in an account-book, to persecute poor tenants. One trollop, who had had a child to the Master and by all accounts been very badly used, yet made herself a kind of champion of his memory. She flung a stone one day at Mr. Henry.

"Whaur's the bonnie lad that trustit ye?" she cried.

Mr. Henry reined in his horse and looked upon her, the blood flowing from his lip. "Ay, Jess?" says he. "You too? And yet ye should ken me better." For it was he who had helped her with money.

The woman had another stone ready, which she made as if she would cast; and he, to ward himself, threw up the hand that held his riding rod.

"What, would ye beat a lassie, ye ugly——?" cries she, and ran away screaming as though he had struck her.

Next day word went about the country like wildfire that Mr. Henry had beaten Jessie Broun within an inch of her life. I give it as one instance of how this snowball grew and one calumny

brought another; until my poor patron was so perished in reputation that he began to keep the house like my lord. All this while,
you may be very sure he uttered no complaints at home; the very
ground of the scandal was too sore a matter to be handled; and
Mr. Henry was very proud and strangely obstinate in silence. My
old lord must have heard of it, by John Paul, if by no one else;
and he must at least have remarked the altered habits of his son.
Yet even he, it is probable, knew not how high the feeling ran;
and as for Miss Alison, she was ever the last person to hear news,
and the least interested when she heard them.

In the height of the ill-feeling (for it died away as it came, no
man could say why) there was an election forward in the town of
St. Bride's, which is the next to Durrisdeer, standing on the Water
of Swift; some grievance was fermenting, I forget what, if ever I
heard; and it was currently said there would be broken heads
ere night, and that the sheriff had sent as far as Dumfries for soldiers. My lord moved that Mr. Henry should be present; assuring
him it was necessary to appear, for the credit of the house. "It
will soon be reported," said he, "that we do not take the lead in
our own country."

"It is a strange lead that I can take," said Mr. Henry; and when
they had pushed him further, "I tell you the plain truth," he said,
"I dare not show my face."

"You are the first of the house that ever said so," cries Miss
Alison.

"We will go all three," said my lord; and sure enough he got
into his boots (the first time in four years—a sore business John
Paul had to get them on) and Miss Alison into her riding coat,
and all three rode together to St. Bride's.

The streets were full of the riff-raff of all the country-side, who
had no sooner clapped eyes on Mr. Henry than the hissing began,
and the hooting, and the cries of "Judas!" and "Where was the
Master?" and "Where were the poor lads that rode with him?"
Even a stone was cast; but the more part cried shame at that, for
my old lord's sake and Miss Alison's. It took not ten minutes to
persuade my lord that Mr. Henry had been right. He said never
a word, but turned his horse about, and home again, with his
chin upon his bosom. Never a word said Miss Alison; no doubt
she thought the more; no doubt her pride was stung, for she was
a bone-bred Durie; and no doubt her heart was touched to see her

cousin so unjustly used. That night she was never in bed; I have often blamed my lady—when I call to mind that night, I readily forgive her all; and the first thing in the morning, she came to the old lord in his usual seat.

"If Henry still wants me," said she, "he can have me now." To himself she had a different speech: "I bring you no love, Henry; but God knows, all the pity in the world."

June the first, 1748, was the day of their marriage. It was December of the same year that first saw me alighting at the doors of the great house; and from there I take up the history of events as they befell under my own observation, like a witness in a court.

I made the last of my journey in the cold end of December, in a mighty dry day of frost; and who should be my guide but Patey Macmorland, brother of Tam? For a tow-headed, bare-legged brat of ten, he had more ill tales upon his tongue than ever I heard the match of; having drunken betimes in his brother's cup. I was still not so old myself; pride had not yet the upper-hand of curiosity; and indeed it would have taken any man, that cold morning, to hear all the old clashes of the country and be shown all the places by the way where strange things had fallen out. I had tales of Claverhouse as we came through the bogs, and tales of the devil as we came over the top of the scaur. As we came in by the abbey I heard somewhat of the old monks, and more of the freetraders, who use its ruins for a magazine, landing for that cause within a cannon-shot of Durrisdeer; and along all the road, the Duries and poor Mr. Henry were in the first rank of slander. My mind was thus highly prejudiced against the family I was about to serve; so that I was half surprised, when I beheld Durrisdeer itself, lying in a pretty, sheltered bay, under the Abbey Hill; the house most commodiously built in the French fashion or perhaps Italianate, for I have no skill in these arts; and the place the most beautified with gardens, lawns, shrubberies, and trees I had ever seen. The money sunk here unproductively would have quite restored the family; but as it was, it cost a revenue to keep it up.

Mr. Henry came himself to the door to welcome me: a tall, dark young gentleman (the Duries are all black men) of a plain and not cheerful face, very strong in body but not so strong in health: taking me by the hand without any pride, and putting me at home with plain, kind speeches. He led me into the hall, booted as I was,

to present me to my lord. It was still daylight; and the first thing
I observed was a lozenge of clear glass in the midst of the shield
in the painted window, which I remember thinking a blemish on
a room otherwise so handsome, with its family portraits, and the
pargetted ceiling with pendants, and the carved chimney, in one
corner of which my old lord sat reading in his Livy. He was like
Mr. Henry, with much the same plain countenance, only more
subtle and pleasant, and his talk a thousand times more entertaining. He had many questions to ask me, I remember, of Edinburgh College, where I had just received my mastership of arts,
and of the various professors, with whom and their proficiency he
seemed well acquainted; and thus, talking of things that I knew,
I soon got liberty of speech in my new home.

In the midst of this, came Mrs. Henry into the room: she was
very far gone, Miss Katharine being due in about six weeks, which
made me think less of her beauty at the first sight; and she used
me with more of condescension than the rest; so that, upon all
accounts, I kept her in the third place of my esteem.

It did not take long before all Pate Macmorland's tales were
blotted out of my belief, and I was become, what I have ever since
remained, a loving servant of the house of Durrisdeer. Mr. Henry
had the chief part of my affection. It was with him I worked; and
I found him an exacting master, keeping all his kindness for those
hours in which we were unemployed, and in the steward's office
not only loading me with work but viewing me with a shrewd
supervision. At length one day, he looked up from his paper with a
kind of timidness, and says he, "Mr. Mackellar, I think I ought
to tell you that you do very well." That was my first word of commendation; and from that day his jealousy of my performance
was relaxed; soon it was "Mr. Mackellar" here, and "Mr. Mackellar" there, with the whole family; and for much of my service
at Durrisdeer, I have transacted everything at my own time and to
my own fancy, and never a farthing challenged. Even while he
was driving me, I had begun to find my heart go out to Mr.
Henry; no doubt, partly in pity, he was a man so palpably unhappy. He would fall into a deep muse over our accounts, staring
at the page or out of the window; and at those times the look
of his face, and the sigh that would break from him, awoke in me
strong feelings of curiosity and commiseration. One day, I remember, we were late upon some business in the steward's room. This

room is in the top of the house and has a view upon the bay, and over a little wooded cape, on the long sands; and there, right over against the sun which was then dipping, we saw the free-traders with a great force of men and horses, scouring on the beach. Mr. Henry had been staring straight west, so that I marvelled he was not blinded by the sun; suddenly he frowns, rubs his hand upon his brow, and turns to me with a smile.

"You would not guess what I was thinking," says he. "I was thinking I would be a happier man if I could ride and run the danger of my life, with these lawless companions."

I told him I had observed he did not enjoy good spirits; and that it was a common fancy to envy others and think we should be the better of some change; quoting Horace to the point, like a young man fresh from college.

"Why, just so," said he. "And with that we may get back to our accounts."

It was not long before I began to get wind of the causes that so much depressed him. Indeed a blind man must have soon discovered there was a shadow on the house, the shadow of the Master of Ballantrae. Dead or alive (and he was then supposed to be dead) that man was his brother's rival: his rival abroad, where there was never a good word for Mr. Henry and nothing but regret and praise for the Master; and his rival at home, not only with his father and his wife, but with the very servants.

They were two old serving men, that were the leaders. John Paul, a little, bald, solemn, stomachy man, a great professor of piety and (take him for all in all) a pretty faithful servant, was the chief of the Master's faction. None durst go so far as John. He took a pleasure in disregarding Mr. Henry publicly, often with a slighting comparison. My lord and Mrs. Henry took him up, to be sure, but never so resolutely as they should; and he had only to pull his weeping face and begin his lamentations for the Master— "his laddie," as he called him—to have the whole condoned. As for Henry, he let these things pass in silence, sometimes with a sad and sometimes with a black look. There was no rivalling the dead, he knew that; and how to censure an old serving man for a fault of loyalty, was more than he could see. His was not the tongue to do it.

Macconochie was chief upon the other sside; an old, ill-spoken, swearing, ranting, drunken dog; and I have often thought it an odd circumstance in human nature, that these two serving men should each have been the champion of his contrary, and blackened their own faults and made light of their own virtues when they beheld them in a master. Macconochie had soon smelled out my secret inclination, took me much into his confidence, and would rant against the Master by the hour, so that even my work suffered. "They're a' daft here," he would cry, "and be damned to them! The Master—the deil's in their thrapples that should call him sae! it's Mr. Henry should be Master now! They were nane sea fond o' the Master when they had him, I'll can tell ye that. Sorrow on his name! Never a guid word did I hear on his lips, nor naebody else, but just fleering and flyting and profane cursing—deil ha'e him! There's nane kent his wickedness: him a gentleman! Did ever ye hear tell, Mr. Mackellar, o' Wully White the wabster? No? Aweel, Wully was an unco praying kind o' man; a driegh body, nane o' my kind, I never could abide the sight o' him; onyway he was a great hand by his way of it, and he up and rebukit the Master for some of his on-goings. It was a grand thing for the Master o' Ball'ntrae to tak up a feud wi' a wabster, was nae't?" Macconochie would sneer: indeed he never took the full name upon his lips but with a sort of a whine of hatred. "But he did! A fine employ it was: chapping at the man's door, and crying 'boo' in his lum, and puttin' poother in his fire, and pee-oys* in his window; till the man thocht it was auld Hornie was come seekin' him. Weel, to mak a lang story short, Wully gaed gyte. At the hinder end, they couldnae get him fra his knees, but he just roared and prayed and grat straucht on, till he got his release. It was fair murder, a'body said that. Ask John Paul—he was brawly ashamed o' that game, him that's sic a Christian man! Grand doin's for the Master o' Ball'ntrae!" I asked him what the Master had thought of it himself. "How would I ken?" says he. "He never said naething." And on again in his usual manner of banning and swearing, with every now and again a "Master of Ballantrae" sneered through his nose. It was in one of these confidences, that he showed me the Carlisle letter, the print of the horse-shoe still stamped in the paper. Indeed that was our last confidence; for he then expressed himself so ill-naturedly of Mrs. Henry, that I had to reprimand him sharply, and must thenceforth hold him at a distance.

* A kind of firework made with damp powder.

My old lord was uniformly kind to Mr. Henry; he had even pretty ways of gratitude, and would sometimes clap him on the shoulder and say, as if to the world at large: "This is a very good son to me." And grateful he was no doubt, being a man of sense and justice. But I think that was all, and I am sure Mr. Henry thought so. The love was all for the dead son. Not that this was often given breath to; indeed with me but once. My lord had asked me one day how I got on with Mr. Henry, and I had told him the truth.

"Ay," said he, looking sideways on the burning fire, "Henry is a good lad, a very good lad," said he. "You have heard, Mr. Mackellar, that I had another son? I am afraid he was not so virtuous a lad as Mr. Henry; but dear me, he's dead, Mr. Mackellar! and while he lived we were all very proud of him, all very proud. If he was not all he should have been in some ways, well, perhaps we loved him better!" This last he said looking musingly in the fire; and then to me, with a great deal of briskness, "But I am rejoiced you do so well with Mr. Henry. You will find him a good master." And with that he opened his book, which was the customary signal of dismission. But it would be little that he read and less that he understood; Culloden field and the Master, these would be the burthen of his thought; and the burthen of mine was an unnatural jealousy of the dead man for Mr. Henry's sake, that had even then begun to grow on me.

I am keeping Mrs. Henry for the last so that this expression of my sentiment may seem unwarrantably strong: the reader shall judge for himself when I am done. But I must first tell of another matter, which was the means of bringing me more intimate. I had not yet been six months at Durrisdeer when it chanced that John Paul fell sick and must keep his bed; drink was the root of his malady, in my poor thought; but he was tended and indeed carried himself like an afflicted saint; and the very minister, who came to visit him, professed himself edified when he went away. The third morning of his sickness, Mr. Henry comes to me with something of a hang-dog look.

"Mackellar," says he, "I wish I could trouble you upon a little service. There is a pension we pay; it is John's part to carry it; and now that he is sick, I know not to whom I should look unless it was yourself. The matter is very delicate; I could not carry it with my own hand for a sufficient reason; I dare not send Macconochie who is a talker, and I am—I have—I am desirous this should not come to Mrs. Henry's ears," says he, and flushed to his neck as he said it.

To say truth, when I found I was to carry money to one Jessie Broun who was no better than she should be, I supposed it was some trip of his own that Mr. Henry was dissembling. I was the more impressed when the truth came out.

It was up a wynd off a side street in St. Bride's, that Jessie had her lodging. The place was very ill inhabited, mostly by the free trading sort; there was a man with a broken head at the entry; halfway up, in a tavern, fellows were roaring and singing, though it was not yet nine in the day. Altogether, I had never seen a worse neighbourhood even in the great city of Edinburgh, and I was in two minds to go back. Jessie's room was of a piece with her surroundings and herself no better. She would not give me the receipt (which Mr. Henry had told me to demand, for he was very methodical) until she had sent out for spirits and I had pledged her in a glass; and all the time she carried on in a light-headed, reckless way, now aping the manners of a lady, now breaking into unseemly mirth, now making coquettish advances that oppressed me to the ground. Of the money, she spoke more tragically.

"It's blood money," said she, "I take it for that: blood money for the betrayed. See what I'm brought down to! Ah, if the bonnie lad were back again, it would be changed days. But he's deid—he's lyin' deid amang the Hieland hills—the bonnie lad, the bonnie lad!"

She had a rapt manner of crying on the bonnie lad, clasping her hands and casting up her eyes, that I think she must have learned of strolling players; and I thought her sorrow very much of an affectation, and that she dwelled upon the business because her shame was now all she had to be proud of. I will not say I did not pity her, but it was a loathing pity at the best; and her last change of manner wiped it out. This was when she had had enough of me for an audience and had set her name at last to the receipt. "There!" says she, and taking the most unwomanly oaths upon her tongue, bade me begone and carry it to the Judas who had sent me. It was the first time I had heard the name applied to Mr. Henry; I was staggered besides at her sudden vehemence of word and manner; and got forth from the room, under this shower of curses, like a beaten dog. But even then I was not

quit; for the vixen threw up her window and, leaning forth, continued to revile me as I went up the wynd; the freetraders, coming to the tavern door, joined in the mockery; and one had even
the inhumanity to set upon me a very savage, small dog, which bit
me in the ankle. This was a strong lesson, had I required one, to
avoid ill company; and I rode home in much pain from the bite
and considerable indignation of mind.

Mr. Henry was in the steward's room, affecting employment, but
I could see he was only impatient to hear of my errand.

"Well?" says he, as soon as I came in; and when I had told him
something of what passed, and that Jessie seemed an undeserving
woman and far from grateful: "She is no friend to me," said he;
"but indeed, Mackellar, I have few friends to boast of; and Jessie
has some cause to be unjust. I need not dissemble what all the
country knows: she was not very well used by one of our family."
This was the first time I had heard him refer to the Master even
distantly; and I think he found his tongue rebellious, even for
that much; but presently he resumed. "This is why I would have
nothing said. It would give pain to Mrs. Henry . . . and to my
father," he added with another flush.

"Mr. Henry," said I, "if you will take a freedom at my hands,
I would tell you to let that woman be. What service is your money
to the like of her? She has no sobriety and no economy; as for
gratitude, you will as soon get milk from a whinstone; and if you
will pretermit your bounty, it will make no change at all but just
to save the ankles of your messengers."

Mr. Henry smiled. "But I am grieved about your ankle," said
he, the next moment, with a proper gravity.

"And observe," I continued, "I give you this advice upon consideration; and yet my heart was touched for the woman in the
beginning."

"Why there it is, you see!" said Mr. Henry. "And you are
to remember that I knew her once a very decent lass. Besides
which, although I speak little of my family, I think much of its
repute."

And with that he broke up the talk, which was the first we had
together in such confidence. But the same afternoon, I had the
proof that his father was perfectly acquainted with the business,
and that it was only from his wife that Mr. Henry kept it secret.

"I fear you had a painful errand to-day," says my lord to me:

"for which, as it enters in no way among your duties, I wish to thank you, and to remind you at the same time (in case Mr. Henry should have neglected) how very desirable it is that no word of it should reach my daughter. Reflections on the dead, Mr. Mackellar, are doubly painful."

Anger glowed in my heart; and I could have told my lord to his face how little he had to do, bolstering up the image of the dead in Mrs. Henry's heart, and how much better he were employed, to shatter that false idol. For by this time, I saw very well how the land lay between my patron and his wife.

My pen is clear enough to tell a plain tale; but to render the effect of an infinity of small things, not one great enough in itself to be narrated; and to translate the story of looks, and the message of voices when they are saying no great matter; and to put in half a page the essence of near eighteen months: this is what I despair to accomplish. The fault, to be very blunt, lay all in Mrs. Henry. She felt it a merit to have consented to the marriage, and she took it like a martyrdom; in which my old lord, whether he knew it or not, fomented her. She made a merit, besides, of her constancy to the dead; though its name, to a nicer conscience, should have seemed rather disloyalty to the living; and here also my lord gave her his countenance. I suppose he was glad to talk of his loss, and ashamed to dwell on it with Mr. Henry. Certainly, at least, he made a little coterie apart in that family of three, and it was the husband who was shut out. It seems it was an old custom when the family were alone in Durrisdeer, that my lord should take his wine to the chimney-side, and Miss Alison (instead of withdrawing) should bring a stool to his knee and chatter to him privately; and after she had become my patron's wife, the same manner of doing was continued. It should have been pleasant to behold this ancient gentleman so loving with his daughter; but I was too much a partisan of Mr. Henry's, to be anything but wroth at his exclusion. Many's the time I have seen him make an obvious resolve, quit the table, and go and join himself to his wife and my Lord Durrisdeer; and on their part, they were never backward to make him welcome, turned to him smilingly as to an intruding child, and took him into their talk with an effort so ill-concealed that he was soon back again beside me at the table; whence (so great is the hall of Durrisdeer) we could but hear the murmur of voices at the chimney. There he would sit and watch,

and I along with him; and sometimes by my lord's head sorrow-
fully shaken, or his hand laid on Mrs. Henry's head, or hers upon
his knee as if in consolation, or sometimes by an exchange of tearful looks, we would draw our conclusion that the talk had gone
to the old subject and the shadow of the dead was in the hall.

I have hours when I blame Mr. Henry for taking all too
patiently; yet we are to remember he was married in pity, and accepted his wife upon that term. And indeed he had small encouragement to make a stand. Once, I remember, he announced
he had found a man to replace the pane of the stained window;
which, as it was he that managed all the business, was a thing
clearly within his attributions. But to the Master's fanciers, that
pane was like a relic; and on the first word of any change, the
blood flew to Mrs. Henry's face.

"I wonder at you!" she cried.

"I wonder at myself," says Mr. Henry, with more of bitterness
than I had ever heard him to express.

Thereupon my old lord stepped in with his smooth talk, so that
before the meal was at an end all seemed forgotten; only that,
after dinner, when the pair had withdrawn as usual to the chimney-side, we could see her weeping with her head upon his knee.
Mr. Henry kept up the talk with me upon some topic of the
estates—he could speak of little else but business, and was never
the best of company; but he kept it up that day with more
continuity, his eye straying ever and again to the chimney and his
voice changing to another key, but without check of delivery. The
pane, however, was not replaced; and I believe he counted it a
great defeat.

Whether he was stout enough or no, God knows he was kind
enough. Mrs. Henry had a manner of condescension with him,
such as (in a wife) would have pricked my vanity into an ulcer; he
took it like a favour. She held him at the staff's end; forgot and
then remembered and unbent to him, as we do to children;
burthened him with cold kindness; reproved him with a change of
colour and a bitten lip, like one shamed by his disgrace; ordered
him with a look of the eye, when she was off her guard; when she
was on the watch, pleaded with him for the most natural attentions as though they were unheard of favours. And to all this,
he replied with the most unwearied service; loving, as folks say,
the very ground she trod on, and carrying that love in his eyes as

bright as a lamp. When Miss Katharine was to be born, nothing would serve but he must stay in the room behind the head of the bed. There he sat, as white (they tell me) as a sheet and the sweat dropping from his brow; and the handkerchief he had in his hand was crushed into a little ball no bigger than a musket bullet. Nor could he bear the sight of Miss Katharine for many a day; indeed I doubt if he was ever what he should have been to my young lady; for the which want of natural feeling, he was loudly blamed.

Such was the state of this family down to the 7th April, 1749, when there befell the first of that series of events which were to break so many hearts and lose so many lives.

On that day I was sitting in my room a little before supper, when John Paul burst open the door with no civility of knocking, and told me there was one below that wished to speak with the steward; sneering at the name of my office.

I asked what manner of man, and what his name was; and this disclosed the cause of John's ill-humour; for it appeared the visitor refused to name himself except to me, a sore affront to the major-domo's consequence.

"Well," said I, smiling a little, "I will see what he wants."

I found in the entrance hall a big man very plainly habited and wrapped in a sea-cloak, like one new landed, as indeed he was. Not far off Macconochie was standing, with his tongue out of his mouth and his hand upon his chin, like a dull fellow thinking hard; and the stranger, who had brought his cloak about his face, appeared uneasy. He had no sooner seen me coming than he went to meet me with an effusive manner.

"My dear man," said he, "a thousand apologies for disturbing you, but I'm in the most awkward position. And there's a son of a ramrod there that I should know the looks of, and more betoken I believe that he knows mine. Being in this family, sir, and in a place of some responsibility (which was the cause I took the liberty to send for you), you are doubtless of the honest party?"

"You may be sure at least," says I, "that all of that party are quite safe in Durrisdeer."

"My dear man, it is my very thought," says he. "You see I have just been set on shore here by a very honest man, whose name I cannot remember, and who is to stand off and on for me till morning, at some danger to himself; and, to be clear with you,

I am a little concerned lest it should be at some to me. I have saved my life so often, Mr.—I forget your name, which is a very good one—that, faith, I would be very loath to lose it after all. And the son of a ramrod, whom I believe I saw before Carlisle . . ."

"O, sir," said I, "you can trust Macconochie until to-morrow."

"Well, and it's a delight to hear you say so," says the stranger. "The truth is that my name is not a very suitable one in this country of Scotland. With a gentleman like you, my dear man, I would have no concealments of course; and by your leave, I'll just breathe it in your year. They call me Francis Burke: Colonel Francis Burke; and I am here, at a most damnable risk to myself, to see your masters—if you'll excuse me, my good man, for giving them the name, for I'm sure it's a circumstance I would never have guessed from your appearance. And if you would be just so very obliging as to take my name to them, you might say that I come bearing letters which I am sure they will be very rejoiced to have the reading of."

Colonel Francis Burke was one of the Prince's Irishmen, that did his cause such an infinity of hurt and were so much distasted of the Scots at the time of the rebellion; and it came at once into my mind, how the Master of Ballantrae had astonished all men by going with that party. In the same moment, a strong foreboding of the truth possessed my soul.

"If you will step in here," said I, opening a chamber door, "I will let my lord know."

"And I am sure it's very good of you, Mr. What-is-your-name," says the Colonel.

Up to the hall I went, slow footed. There they were all three, my old lord in his place, Mrs. Henry at work by the window, Mr. Henry (as was much his custom) pacing the low end. In the midst was the table laid for supper. I told them briefly what I had to say. My old lord lay back in his seat. Mrs. Henry sprang up standing with a mechanical motion, and she and her husband stared at each other's eyes across the room; it was the strangest, challenging look these two exchanged, and as they looked, the colour faded in their faces. Then Mr. Henry turned to me; not to speak, only to sign with his finger; but that was enough, and I went down again for the Colonel.

When we returned, these three were in much the same position I had left them in; I believe no word had passed.

"My Lord Durrisdeer no doubt?" says the Colonel, bowing, and my lord bowed in answer. "And this," continues the Colonel, "should be the Master of Ballantrae?"

"I have never taken that name," said Mr. Henry; "but I am Henry Durie at your service."

Then the Colonel turns to Mrs. Henry, bowing with his hat upon his heart and the most killing airs of gallantry. "There can be no mistake about so fine a figure of a lady," says he. "I address the seductive Miss Alison, of whom I have so often heard?"

Once more husband and wife exchanged a look.

"I am Mrs. Henry Durie," said she; "but before my marriage my name was Alison Graeme."

Then my lord spoke up. "I am an old man, Colonel Burke," said he, "and a frail one. It will be mercy on your part to be expeditious. Do you bring me news of—" he hesitated, and then the words broke from him with a singular change of voice—"my son?"

"My dear lord, I will be round with you like a soldier," said the Colonel. "I do."

My lord held out a wavering hand; he seemed to wave a signal, but whether it was to give him time or to speak on, was more than we could guess. At length, he got out the one word—"Good?"

"Why, the very best in the creation!" cries the Colonel. "For my good friend and admired comrade is at this hour in the fine city of Paris, and as like as not, if I know anything of his habits, he will be drawing in his chair to a piece of dinner.—Bedad, I believe the lady's fainting."

Mrs. Henry was indeed the colour of death, and drooped against the window-frame. But when Mr. Henry made a movement as if to run to her, she straightened with a sort of shiver. "I am well," she said, with her white lips.

Mr. Henry stopped, and his face had a strong twitch of anger. The next moment, he had turned to the Colonel. "You must not blame yourself," says he, "for this effect on Mrs. Durie. It is only natural; we were all brought up like brother and sister."

Mrs. Henry looked at her husband with something like relief or even gratitude. In my way of thinking, that speech was the first step he made in her good graces.

"You must try to forgive me, Mrs. Durie, for indeed and I am just an Irish savage," said the Colonel: "and I deserve to be shot for not breaking the matter more artistically to a lady. But here are the Master's own letters; one for each of the three of you; and to be sure (if I know anything of my friend's genius) he will tell his own story with a better grace."

He brought the three letters forth as he spoke, arranged them by their superscriptions, presented the first to my lord, who took it greedily, and advanced towards Mrs. Henry holding out the second.

But the lady waved it back. "To my husband," says she, with a choked voice.

The Colonel was a quick man, but at this he was somewhat nonplussed. "To be sure," says he, "how very dull of me! To be sure." But he still held the letter.

At last Mr. Henry reached forth his hand, and there was nothing to be done but give it up. Mr. Henry took the letters (both hers and his own) and looked upon their outside, with his brows knit hard as if he were thinking. He had surprised me all through by his excellent behaviour; but he was to excel himself now.

"Let me give you a hand to your room," said he to his wife. "This has come something of the suddenest; and at any rate, you will wish to read your letter by yourself."

Again she looked upon him with the same thought of wonder; but he gave her no time, coming straight to where she stood. "It will be better so, believe me," said he, "and Colonel Burke is too considerate not to excuse you." And with that he took her hand by the fingers, and led her from the hall.

Mrs. Henry returned no more that night; and when Mr. Henry went to visit her next morning, as I heard long afterwards, she gave him the letter again, still unopened.

"O, read it and be done!" he had cried.

"Spare me that," said she.

And by these two speeches, to my way of thinking, each undid a great part of what they had previously done well. But the letter, sure enough, came into my hands and by me was burned, unopened.

To be very exact as to the adventures of the Master after Culloden, I wrote not long ago to Colonel Burke, now a Chevalier of the Order of St. Louis, begging him for some notes in writing, since I could scarce depend upon my memory at so great an interval. To confess the truth, I have been somewhat embarrassed by his response; for he sent me the complete memoirs of his life, touching only in places on the Master; running to a much greater length than my whole story, and not everywhere (as it seems to me) designed for edification. He begged in his letter, dated from Ettenheim, that I would find a publisher for the whole, after I had made what use of it I required; and I think I shall best answer my own purpose and fulfill his wishes by printing certain parts of it in full. In this way my readers will have a detailed and I believe a very genuine account of some essential matters; and if any publisher should take a fancy to the Chevalier's manner of narration, he knows where to apply for the rest, of which there is plenty at his service. I put in my first extract here, so that it may stand in the place of what the Chevalier told us over our wine in the hall of Durrisdeer; but you are to suppose it was not the brutal fact, but a very varnished version that he offered to my lord.

The Master's Wanderings
FROM THE MEMOIRS OF THE
CHEVALIER DE BURKE

I LEFT RUTHVEN (IT'S HARDLY NECESSARY TO REMARK) WITH MUCH greater satisfaction than I had come to it; but whether I missed my way in the deserts, or whether my companions failed me, I soon found myself alone. This was a predicament very disagreeable; for I never understood this horrid country or savage people, and the last stroke of the Prince's withdrawal had made us of the Irish more unpopular than ever. I was reflecting on my poor chances, when I saw another horseman on the hill, whom I supposed at first to have been a phantom, the news of his death in the very front at Culloden being current in the army generally. This was the Master of Ballantrae, my Lord Durrisdeer's son, a young nobleman of the rarest gallantry and parts, and equally designed by nature to adorn a court and to reap laurels in the field. Our meeting was the more welcome to both, as he was one of the few Scots who had used the Irish with consideration and as he might now be of very high utility in aiding my escape. Yet what founded our particular friendship was a circumstance by itself, as romantic as any fable of King Arthur.

This was on the second day of our flight, after we had slept one night in the rain upon the inclination of a mountain. There was an Appin man, Alan Black Stewart (or some such name,* but I have seen him since in France), who chanced to be passing the same way, and had a jealousy of my companion. Very uncivil expressions were exchanged; and Stewart calls upon the Master to alight and have it out.

"Why, Mr. Stewart," says the Master, "I think at the present time I would prefer to run a race with you." And with the word claps spurs to his horse.

Stewart ran after us, a childish thing to do, for more than a mile; and I could not help laughing, as I looked back at last and saw him on a hill, holding his hand to his side and nearly burst with running.

"But all the same," I could not help saying to my companion, "I would let no man run after me for any such proper purpose, and not give him his desire. It was a good jest, but it smells a trifle cowardly."

He bent his brows at me. "I do pretty well," says he, "when I saddle myself with the most unpopular man in Scotland, and let that suffice for courage."

"O, bedad," says I, "I could show you a more unpopular with the naked eye. And if you like not my company, you can 'saddle' yourself on some one else."

"Colonel Burke," says he, "do not let us quarrel; and to that effect, let me assure you I am the least patient man in the world."

"I am as little patient as yourself," said I. "I care not who knows that."

"At this rate," says he, reining in, "we shall not go very far. And I propose we do one of two things upon the instant: either quarrel and be done; or make a sure bargain to bear everything at each other's hands."

"Like a pair of brothers?" said I.

"I said no such foolishness," he replied. "I have a brother of my

---

* NOTE BY MR. MACKELLAR. Should not this be Alan *Breck* Stewart, afterwards notorious as the Appin murderer? The Chevalier is sometimes very weak on names.

own, and I think no more of him than of a colewort. But if we are
to have our noses rubbed together in this course of flight, let
us each dare to be ourselves like savages, and each swear that he
will neither resent nor deprecate the other. I am a pretty bad
fellow at bottom, and I find the pretence of virtues very irksome."

"O, I am as bad as yourself," said I. "There is no skim milk in
Francis Burke. But which is it to be? Fight or make friends?"

"Why," says he, "I think it will be the best manner to spin a
coin for it."

This proposition was too highly chivalrous not to take my fancy;
and strange as it may seem of two well-born gentlemen of to-day,
we span a half-crown (like a pair of ancient paladins) whether
we were to cut each other's throats or be sworn friends. A more
romantic circumstance can rarely have occurred; and it is one of
those points in my memoirs by which we may see the old tales of
Homer and the poets are equally true to-day, at least of the noble
and genteel. The coin fell for peace, and we shook hands upon our
bargain. And then it was that my companion explained to me his
thought in running away from Mr. Stewart, which was certainly
worthy of his political intellect. The report of his death, he said,
was a great guard to him; Mr. Stewart having recognised him, had
become a danger; and he had taken the briefest road to that
gentleman's silence. "For," says he, "Alan Black is too vain a man
to narrate any such story of himself."

Towards afternoon, we came down to the shores of that loch for
which we were heading; and there was the ship but newly come to
anchor. She was the *Sainte-Marie-des-Anges*, out of the port of
Havre-de-Grace. The Master, after we had signalled for a boat,
asked me if I knew the captain. I told him he was a countryman of
mine, of the most unblemished integrity, but, I was afraid, a
rather timorous man.

"No matter," says he. "For all that, he should certainly hear the
truth."

I asked him if he meant about the battle? for if the captain
once knew the standard was down, he would certainly put to sea
again at once.

"And even then!" said he; "the arms are now of no sort of
utility."

"My dear man," said I, "who thinks of the arms? But to be
sure we must remember our friends. They will be close upon our

heels, perhaps the Prince himself, and if the ship be gone, a great number of valuable lives may be imperilled."

"The captain and the crew have lives also, if you come to that," says Ballantrae.

This I declared was but a quibble, and that I would not hear of the captain being told: and then it was that Ballantrae made me a witty answer for the sake of which (and also because I have been blamed myself in this business of the *Sainte-Marie-des-Anges*) I have related the whole conversation as it passed.

"Frank," says he, "remember our bargain. I must not object to your holding your tongue, which I hereby even encourage you to do; but by the same terms, you are not to resent my telling."

I could not help laughing at this; though I still forewarned him what would come of it.

"The devil may come of it for what I care," says the reckless fellow. "I have always done exactly as I felt inclined."

As is well known, my prediction came true. The captain had no sooner heard the news, than he cut his cable and to sea again; and before morning broke, we were in the Great Minch.

The ship was very old; and the skipper although the most honest of men (and Irish too) was one of the least capable. The wind blew very boisterous, and the sea raged extremely. All that day we had little heart whether to eat or drink; went early to rest in some concern of mind; and (as if to give us a lesson) in the night, the wind chopped suddenly into the north-east, and blew a hurricane. We were awaked by the dreadful thunder of the tempest and the stamping of the mariners on deck; so that I supposed our last hour was certainly come; and the terror of my mind was increased out of all measure by Ballantrae, who mocked at my devotions. It is in hours like these that a man of any piety appears in his true light, and we find (what we are taught as babes) the small trust that can be set in worldly friends: I would be unworthy of my religion, if I let this pass without particular remark. For three days we lay in the dark in the cabin, and had but a biscuit to nibble. On the fourth, the wind fell, leaving the ship dismasted and heaving on vast billows. The captain had not a guess of whither we were blown; he was stark ignorant of his trade, and could do naught but bless the Holy Virgin: a very good thing too, but scarce the whole of seamanship. It seemed our one hope was to be picked up by another vessel; and if that should prove to be an English ship, it might be no great blessing to the Master and myself.

The fifth and sixth days we tossed there helpless. The seventh, some sail was got on her, but she was an unwieldy vessel at the best, and we made little but leeway. All the time, indeed, we had been drifting to the south and west, and during the tempest must have driven in that direction with unheard of violence. The ninth dawn was cold and black, with a great sea running, and every mark of foul weather. In this situation, we were overjoyed to sight a small ship on the horizon, and to perceive her go about and head for the *Sainte-Marie*. But our gratification did not very long endure; for when she had laid to and lowered a boat, it was immediately filled with disorderly fellows, who sang and shouted as they pulled across to us, and swarmed in on our deck with bare cutlasses, cursing loudly. Their leader was a horrible villain, with his face blacked and his whiskers curled in ringlets: Teach, his name; a most notorious pirate. He stamped about the deck, raving and crying out that his name was Satan and his ship was called Hell. There was something about him like a wicked child or a half-witted person, that daunted me beyond expression. I whispered in the ear of Ballantrae, that I would not be the last to volunteer and only prayed God they might be short of hands: he approved my purpose with a nod.

"Bedad," said I, to Master Teach, "if you are Satan, here is a divil for ye."

The word pleased him; and (not to dwell upon these shocking incidents) Ballantrae and I and two others were taken for recruits, while the skipper and all the rest were cast into the sea by the method of walking the plank. It was the first time I had seen this done; my heart died within me at the spectacle; and Master Teach or one of his acolytes (for my head was too much lost to be precise) remarked upon my pale face in a very alarming manner. I had the strength to cut a step or two of a jig and cry out some ribaldry, which saved me for that time; but my legs were like water when I must get down into the skiff among these miscreants; and what with my horror of my company and fear of the monstrous billows, it was all I could do to keep an Irish tongue and break a jest or two as we were pulled aboard. By the blessing of God, there was a fiddle in the pirate ship, which I had no sooner seen than I fell upon; and in my quality of crowder, I had the heavenly good luck to get favour in their eyes. *Crowding Pat* was the name they dubbed me with; and it was little I cared for a name so long as my skin was whole.

What kind of a pandemonium that vessel was, I cannot describe, but she was commanded by a lunatic, and might be called a floating Bedlam. Drinking, roaring, singing, quarrelling, dancing, they were never all sober at one time; and there were days together, when if a squall had supervened, it must have sent us to the bottom, or if a king's ship had come along, it would have found us quite helpless for defence. Once or twice, we sighted a sail, and if we were sober enough, overhauled it, God forgive us! and if we were all too drunk, she got away, and I would bless the saints under my breath. Teach ruled, if you can call that rule which brought no order, by the terror he created; and I observed the man was very vain of his position. I have known marshals of France, ay, and even Highland chieftains that were less openly puffed up; which throws a singular light on the pursuit of honour and glory. Indeed the longer we live, the more we perceive the sagacity of Aristotle and the other old philosophers; and though I have all my life been eager for legitimate distinctions, I can lay my hand upon my heart, at the end of my career, and declare there is not one—no, nor yet life itself—which is worth acquiring or preserving at the slightest cost of dignity.

It was long before I got private speech of Ballantrae; but at length one night we crept out upon the boltsprit, when the rest were better employed, and commiserated our position.

"None can deliver us but the saints," said I.

"My mind is very different," said Ballantrae; "for I am going to deliver myself. This Teach is the poorest creature possible; we make no profit of him and lie continually open to capture; and," says he, "I am not going to be a tarry pirate for nothing, nor yet to hang in chains if I can help it." And he told me what was in his mind to better the state of the ship in the way of discipline, which would give us safety for the present, and a sooner hope of deliverance when they should have gained enough and should break up their company.

I confessed to him ingenuously that my nerve was quite shook amid these horrible surroundings, and I durst scarce tell him to count upon me.

"I am not very easy frightened," said he, "nor very easy beat."

A few days after, there befell an accident which had nearly hanged us all; and offers the most extraordinary picture of the folly that ruled in our concerns. We were all pretty drunk: and some bedlamite spying a sail, Teach put the ship about in chase without a glance, and we began to bustle up the arms and boast of the horrors that should follow. I observed Ballantrae stood quiet in the bows, looking under the shade of his hand; but for my part, true to my policy among these savages, I was at work with the busiest and passing Irish jests for their diversion.

"Run up the colours," cries Teach. "Show the ——s the Jolly Roger!"

It was the merest drunken braggadocio at such a stage, and might have lost us a valuable prize; but I thought it no part of mine to reason, and I ran up the black flag with my own hand.

Ballantrae steps presently aft with a smile upon his face.

"You may perhaps like to know, you drunken dog," says he, "that you are chasing a king's ship."

Teach roared him the lie; but he ran at the same time to the bulwarks, and so did they all. I have never seen so many drunken men struck suddenly sober. The cruiser had gone about, upon our impudent display of colours; she was just then filling on the new tack; her ensign blew out quite plain to see; and even as we stared, there came a puff of smoke, and then a report, and a shot plunged in the waves a good way short of us. Some ran to the ropes, and got the *Sarah* round with an incredible swiftness. One fellow fell on the rum barrel, which stood broached upon the deck, and rolled it promptly overboard. On my part, I made for the Jolly Roger, struck it, tossed it in the sea; and could have flung myself after, so vexed was I with our mismanagement. As for Teach, he grew as pale as death, and incontinently went down to his cabin. Only twice he came on deck that afternoon; went to the taffrail; took a long look at the king's ship, which was still on the horizon heading after us; and then, without speech, back to his cabin. You may say he deserted us; and if it had not been for one very capable sailor we had on board, and for the lightness of the airs that blew all day, we must certainly have gone to the yardarm.

It is to be supposed Teach was humiliated, and perhaps alarmed for his position with the crew; and the way in which he set about regaining what he had lost, was highly characteristic of the man. Early next day, we smelled him burning sulphur in his cabin and crying out of "Hell, hell!" which was well understood among the crew, and filled their minds with apprehension. Presently he comes on deck, a perfect figure of fun, his face blacked, his hair and whiskers curled, his belt stuck full of pistols; chewing bits of glass so that the blood ran down his chin, and brandishing a dirk. I do not know if he had taken these manners from the Indians of America, where he was a native; but such was his way, and he would always thus announce that he was wound up to horrid deeds. The first that came near him was the fellow who had sent the rum overboard the day before; him he stabbed to the heart, damning him for a mutineer; and then capered about the body, raving and swearing and daring us to come on. It was the silliest exhibition; and yet dangerous too, for the cowardly fellow was plainly working himself up to another murder.

All of a sudden, Ballantrae stepped forth. "Have done with this play-acting," says he. "Do you think to frighten us with making faces? We saw nothing of you yesterday when you were wanted; and we did well without you, let me tell you that."

There was a murmur and a movement in the crew, of pleasure and alarm, I thought, in nearly equal parts. As for Teach, he gave a barbarous howl, and swung his dirk to fling it, an art in which (like many seamen) he was very expert.

"Knock that out of his hand!" says Ballantrae, so sudden and sharp that my arm obeyed him before my mind had understood.

Teach stood like one stupid, never thinking on his pistols.

"Go down to your cabin," cries Ballantrae, "and come on deck again when you are sober. Do you think we are going to hang for you, you black-faced, half-witted, drunken brute and butcher? Go down!" And he stamped his foot at him with such a sudden smartness that Teach fairly ran for it to the companion.

"And now, mates," says Ballantrae, "a word with you. I don't know if you are gentlemen of fortune for the fun of the thing; but I am not. I want to make money, and get ashore again, and spend it like a man. And on one thing my mind is made up: I will not hang if I can help it. Come: give me a hint; I'm only a beginner! Is there no way to get a little discipline and common-sense about this business?"

One of the men spoke up: he said by rights they should have a quartermaster; and no sooner was the word out of his mouth, than they were all of that opinion. The thing went by acclamation,

Ballantrae was made quartermaster, the rum was put in his charge, laws were passed in imitation of those of a pirate by the name of Roberts; and the last proposal was to make an end of Teach. But Ballantrae was afraid of a more efficient captain, who might be a counterweight to himself, and he opposed this stoutly. Teach, he said, was good enough to board ships and frighten fools with his blacked face and swearing; we could scarce get a better man than Teach for that; and besides as the man was now disconsidered and as good as deposed, we might reduce his proportion of the plunder. This carried it; Teach's share was cut down to a mere derision, being actually less than mine; and there remained only two points: whether he would consent, and who was to announce to him this resolution.

"Do not let that stick you," says Ballantrae, "I will do that."

And he stepped to the companion and down alone into the cabin to face that drunken savage.

"This is the man for us," cries one of the hands. "Three cheers for the quartermaster!" which were given with a will, my own voice among the loudest, and I dare say these plaudits had their effect on Master Teach in the cabin, as we have seen of late days how shouting in the streets may trouble even the minds of legislators.

What passed precisely was never known, though some of the heads of it came to the surface later on; and we were all amazed as well as gratified, when Ballantrae came on deck with Teach upon his arm, and announced that all had been consented.

I pass swiftly over those twelve or fifteen months in which we continued to keep the sea in the North Atlantic, getting our food and water from the ships we overhauled and doing on the whole a pretty fortunate business. Sure no one could wish to read anything so ungenteel as the memoirs of a pirate, even an unwilling one like me! Things went extremely better with our designs, and Ballantrae kept his lead to my admiration from that day forth. I would be tempted to suppose that a gentleman must everywhere be first, even aboard a rover; but my birth is every whit as good as any Scottish lord's, and I am not ashamed to confess that I stayed Crowding Pat until the end, and was not much better than the crew's buffoon. Indeed it was no scene to bring out my merits. My health suffered from a variety of reasons; I was more at home to the last on a horse's back than a ship's deck; and to be ingenuous,

the fear of the sea was constantly in my mind, battling with the
fear of my companions. I need not cry myself up for courage; I
have done well on many fields under the eyes of famous generals,
and earned my late advancement by an act of the most distinguished valour before many witnesses. But when we must proceed on
one of our abordages, the heart of Francis Burke was in his boots;
the little egg-shell skiff in which we must set forth, the horrible
heaving of the vast billows, the height of the ship that we must
scale, the thought of how many might be there in garrison upon
their legitimate defence, the scowling heavens which (in that
climate) so often looked darkly down upon our exploits, and
the mere crying of the wind in my ears, were all considerations
most unpalatable to my valour. Besides which, as I was always
a creature of the nicest sensibility, the scenes that must follow on
our success tempted me as little as the chances of defeat. Twice
we found women on board; and though I have seen towns sacked,
and of late days in France some very horrid public tumults, there
was something in the smallest of the numbers engaged and the
bleak, dangerous sea-surroundings that made these acts of piracy
far the most revolting. I confess ingenuously I could never proceed, unless I was three parts drunk; it was the same even with the
crew; Teach himself was fit for no enterprise till he was full of
rum; and it was one of the most difficult parts of Ballantrae's
performance, to serve us with liquor in the proper quantities. Even
this he did to admiration; being upon the whole the most capable
man I ever met with, and the one of the most natural genius. He
did not even scrape favour with the crew, as I did, by continual
buffoonery made upon a very anxious heart; but preserved on
most occasions a great deal of gravity and distance; so that he was
like a parent among a family of young children or a schoolmaster
with his boys. What made his part the harder to perform, the men
were most inveterate grumblers; Ballantrae's discipline, little as
it was, was yet irksome to their love of license; and what was worse,
being kept sober they had time to think. Some of them accordingly
would fall to repenting their abominable crimes; one in particular,
who was a good Catholic and with whom I would sometimes steal
apart for prayer; above all in bad weather, fogs, lashing rain and
the like, when we would be the less observed; and I am sure no
two criminals in the cart have ever performed their devotions with
more anxious sincerity. But the rest having no such grounds of

hope, fell to another pastime, that of computation. All day long they would be telling up their shares or glooming over the result. I have said we were pretty fortunate. But an observation fails to be made: that in this world, in no business that I have tried, do the profits rise to a man's expectations. We found many ships and took many; yet few of them contained much money, their goods were usually nothing to our purpose—what did we want with a cargo of ploughs or even of tobacco?—and it is quite a painful reflection how many whole crews we have made to walk the plank for no more than a stock of biscuit or an anker or two of spirit.

In the meanwhile, our ship was growing very foul, and it was high time we should make for our *port de carrénage,* which was in the estuary of a river among swamps. It was openly understood that we should then break up and go and squander our propor-tions of the spoil; and this made every man greedy of a little more, so that our decision was delayed from day to day. What finally decided matters was a trifling accident, such as an ignorant person might suppose incidental to our way of life. But here I must ex-plain: on only one of all the ships we boarded, the first on which we found women, did we meet with any genuine resistance. On that occasion, we had two men killed, and several injured, and if it had not been for the gallantry of Ballantrae, we had surely been beat back at last. Everywhere else, the defence (where there was any at all) was what the worst troops in Europe would have laughed at; so that the most dangerous part of our employment was to clamber up the side of the ship; and I have even known the poor souls on board to cast us a line, so eager were they to volun-teer instead of walking the plank. This constant immunity had made our fellows very soft, so that I understood how Teach had made so deep a mark upon their minds; for indeed the company of that lunatic was the chief danger in our way of life. The acci-dent to which I have referred was this. We had sighted a little full-rigged ship very close under our board in a haze; she sailed near as well as we did—I should be nearer truth, if I said near as ill; and we cleared the bow-chaser to see if we could bring a spar or two about their ears. The swell was exceeding great; the motion of the ship beyond description; it was little wonder if our gunners should fire thrice and be still quite broad of what they aimed at. But in the meanwhile, the chase had cleared a stern gun, the thickness of the air concealing them; and being better marksmen, their first shot struck us in the bows, knocked our two gunners into mince meat, so that we were all sprinkled with the blood, and plunged through the deck into the forecastle, where we slept. Ballantrae would have held on; indeed there was nothing in this *contretemps* to affect the mind of any soldier; but he had a quick perception of the men's wishes, and it was plain this lucky shot had given them a sickener of their trade. In a moment, they were all of one mind: the chase was drawing away from us, it was needless to hold on, the *Sarah* was too foul to overhaul a bottle, it was mere foolery to keep the sea with her; and on these pretended grounds, her head was incontinently put about and the course laid for the river. It was strange to see what merriment fell on that ship's company, and how they stamped about the deck jesting, and each computing what increase had come to his share by the death of the two gunners.

We were nine days making our port, so light were the airs we had to sail on, so foul the ship's bottom; but early on the tenth, before dawn, and in a light, lifting haze, we passed the head. A little after, the haze lifted, and fell again, showing us a cruiser very close. This was a sore blow, happening so near out refuge. There was a great debate of whether she had seen us, and if so whether it was likely they had recognised the *Sarah*. We were very careful, by destroying every member of those crews we overhauled, to leave no evidence as to our own persons; but the appearance of the *Sarah* herself we could not keep so private; and above all of late, since she had been foul and we had pursued many ships without success, it was plain that her description had been often published. I suppose this alert would have made us separate upon the instant. But here again that original genius of Ballantrae's had a surprise in store for me. He and Teach (and it was the most remarkable step of this success) had gone hand in hand since the first day of his appointment. I often questioned him upon the fact and never got an answer but once, when he told me he and Teach had an understanding "which would very much surprise the crew if they should hear of it, and would surprise himself a good deal if it was carried out." Well, here again, he and Teach were of a mind; and by their joint procurement, the anchor was no sooner down, than the whole crew went off upon a scene of drunkenness indescribable. By afternoon we were a mere shipful of lunatical persons, throwing of things overboard, howling of different songs at the same time, quarrelling and falling together and then forgetting our quarrels to embrace. Ballantrae had bidden me drink nothing and feign drunkenness as I valued my life; and I have never passed a day so wearisomely, lying the best part of the time upon the forecastle and watching the swamps and thickets by which our little basin was entirely surrounded for the eye. A little after dusk, Ballantrae stumbled up to my side, feigned to fall, with a drunken laugh, and before he got his feet again, whispered me to "reel down into the cabin and seem to fall asleep upon a locker, for there would be need of me soon." I did as I was told, and coming into the cabin, where it was quite dark, let myself fall on the first locker. There was a man there already; by the way he stirred and threw me off, I could not think he was much in liquor; and yet when I had found another place, he seemed to continue to sleep on. My heart now beat very hard, for I saw some desperate matter was in act. Presently down came Ballantrae, lit the lamp, looked about the cabin, nodded as if pleased, and on deck again without a word. I peered out from between my fingers, and saw there were three of us slumbering, or feigning to slumber, on the lockers: myself, one Dutton and one Grady, both resolute men. On deck, the rest were got to a pitch of revelry quite beyond the bounds of what is human; so that no reasonable name can describe the sounds they were now making. I had heard many a drunken bout in my time, many on board that very *Sarah,* but never anything the least like this, which made me early suppose the liquor had been tampered with. It was a long while before the yells and howls died out into a sort of miserable moaning, and then to silence; and it seemed a long while after that, before Ballantrae came down again, this time with Teach upon his heels. The latter cursed at the sight of us three upon the lockers.

"Tut," says Ballantrae, "you might fire a pistol at their ears. You know what stuff they have been swallowing."

There was a hatch in the cabin floor, and under that the richest part of the booty was stored against the day of division. It fastened with a ring and three padlocks, the keys (for greater security) being divided; one to Teach, one to Ballantrae, and one to the mate, a man called Hammond. Yet I was amazed to see they were now all in the one hand; and yet more amazed (still looking through my fingers) to observe Ballantrae and Teach bring up several packets, four of them in all, very carefully made up and with a loop for carriage.

"And now," says Teach, "let us be going."

"One word," says Ballantrae, "I have discovered there is another man besides yourself who knows a private path across the swamp. And it seems it is shorter than yours."

Teach cried out, in that case, they were undone.

"I do not know for that," says Ballantrae. "For there are several other circumstances with which I must acquaint you. First of all, there is no bullet in your pistols which (if you remember) I was kind enough to load for both of us this morning. Secondly, as there is some one else who knows a passage, you must think it highly improbable I should saddle myself with a lunatic like you. Thirdly, these gentlemen (who need no longer pretend to be asleep) are those of my party, and will now proceed to gag and bind you to the mast; and when your men awaken (if they ever do awake after the drugs we have mingled in their liquor) I am sure they will be so obliging as to deliver you, and you will have no difficulty, I dare say, to explain the business of the keys."

Not a word said Teach, but looked at us like a frightened baby, as we gagged and bound him.

"Now you see, you moon-calf," says Ballantrae, "why we made four packets. Heretofore you have been called Captain Teach, but I think you are now rather Captain Learn."

That was our last word on board the *Sarah,* we four with our four packets lowered ourselves softly into a skiff, and left that ship behind us as silent as the grave, only for the moaning of some of the drunkards. There was a fog about breast-high on the waters; so that Dutton, who knew the passage, must stand on his feet to direct our rowing; and·this, as it forced us to row gently, was the means of our deliverance. We were yet but a little way from the ship, when it began to come grey, and the birds to fly abroad upon the water. All of a sudden, Dutton clapped down upon his hands, and whispered us to be silent for our lives, and hearken. Sure enough, we heard a little faint creak of oars upon one hand, and then again, and further off, a creak of oars upon the other. It was clear, we had been sighted yesterday in the morning; here were the cruiser's boats to cut us out; here were we defenceless in their very midst. Sure, never were poor souls more perilously placed; and as we lay there on our oars, praying God the mist might hold, the sweat poured from my brow. Presently we heard one of the boats, where we might have thrown a biscuit in her. "Softly, men," we heard an officer whisper; and I marvelled they could not hear the drumming of my heart.

"Never mind the path," says Ballantrae, "we must get shelter anyhow; let us pull straight ahead for the sides of the basin."

This we did with the most anxious precaution, rowing, as best we could, upon our hands, and steering at a venture in the fog which was (for all that) our only safety. But heaven guided us; we touched ground at a thicket; scrambled ashore with our treasure; and having no other way of concealment, and the mist beginning already to lighten, hove down the skiff and let her sink. We were still but new under cover when the sun rose; and at the same time, from the midst of the basin, a great shouting of seamen sprang up, and we knew the *Sarah* was being boarded. I heard afterwards the officer that took her got great honour; and it's true the approach was creditably managed, but I think he had an easy capture when he came to board.*

I was still blessing the saints for my escape; when I became aware we were in trouble of another kind. We were here landed at random in a vast and dangerous swamp; and how to come at the path was a concern of doubt, fatigue and peril. Dutton, indeed, was of opinion we should wait until the ship was gone, and fish up the skiff; for any delay would be more wise than to go blindly ahead in that morass. One went back accordingly to the basin-side and (peering throught the thicket) saw the fog already quite drunk up and English colours flying on the *Sarah,* but no movement made to get her under way. Our situation was now very doubtful. The swamp was an unhealthful place to linger in; we had been so greedy to bring treasures that we had brought but little food; it was highly desirable, besides, that we should get clear of the neighbourhood and into the settlements, before the news of the capture went abroad; and against all these considerations, there was only the peril of the passage on the other side. I think it not wonderful we decided on the active part.

*　* NOTE BY MR. MACKELLAR. This Teach of the *Sarah* must not be confused with the celebrated *Blackbeard.* The dates and facts by no means tally. It is possibl; the second Teach may have at once borrowed the name and imitated the mor; excessive part of his manners from the first. Even the Master of Ballantra; could make admirers.

It was already blistering hot, when we set forth to pass the marsh, or rather to strike the path, by compass. Dutton took the compass, and one or other of us three carried his proportion of the treasure; I promise you he kept a sharp eye to his rear, for it was like the man's soul that he must trust us with. The thicket was as close as a bush; the ground very treacherous, so that we often sank in the most terrifying manner, and must go round about; the heat, besides, was stifling, the air singularly heavy, and the stinging insects abounded in such myriads that each of us walked under his own cloud. It has often been commented on, how much better gentlemen of birth endure fatigue than persons of the rabble; so that walking officers, who must tramp in the dirt beside their men, shame them by their constancy. This was well to be observed in the present instance; for here were Ballantrae and I, two gentlemen of the highest breeding, on the one hand; and on the other, Grady, a common mariner, and a man nearly a giant in physical strength. The case of Dutton is not in point, for I confess he did as well as any of us.* But as for Grady he began early to lament his case, tailed in the rear, refused to carry Dutton's packet when it came his turn, clamoured continually for rum (of which we had too little) and at last even threatened us from behind with a cocked pistol, unless we should allow him rest. Ballantrae would have fought it out, I believe; but I prevailed with him the other way; and we made a stop and ate a meal. It seemed to benefit Grady little; he was in the rear again at once, growling and bemoaning his lot; and at last, by some carelessness, not having followed properly in our tracks, stumbled into a deep part of the slough where it was mostly water, gave some very dreadful screams, and before we could come to his aid, had sunk along with his booty. His fate and above all these screams of his appalled us to the soul; yet it was on the whole a fortunate circumstance and the means of our deliverance. For it moved Dutton to mount into a tree, whence he was able to perceive and to show me, who had climbed after him, a high piece of the wood which was a landmark for the path. He went forward the more carelessly, I must suppose; for presently we saw him sink a little down, draw

---

* NOTE BY MR. MACKELLAR. And is not this the whole explanation? since this Dutton, exactly like the officers, enjoyed the stimulus of some responsibility.

up his feet and sink again, and so twice. Then he turned his face to us, pretty white.

"Lend a hand," said he, "I am in a bad place."

"I don't know about that," says Ballantrae, standing still.

Dutton broke out into the most violent oaths, sinking a little lower as he did, so that the mud was nearly to his waist; and plucking a pistol from his belt, "Help me," he cries, "or die and be damned to you!"

"Nay," says Ballantrae, "I did but jest. I am coming." And he set down his own packet and Dutton's which he was then carrying. "Do not venture near till we see if you are needed," said he to me, and went forward alone to where the man was bogged. He was quiet now, though he still held the pistol; and the marks of terror in his countenance were very moving to behold.

"For the Lord's sake," says he, "look sharp."

Ballantrae was now got close up. "Keep still," says he and seemed to consider; and then "Reach out both your hands!"

Dutton laid down his pistol, and so watery was the top surface, that it went clear out of sight; with an oath, he stooped to snatch it; and as he did so, Ballantrae leaned forth and stabbed him between the shoulders. Up went his hands over his head, I know not whether with the pain or to ward himself; and the next moment he doubled forward in the mud.

Ballantrae was already over the ankles, but he plucked himself out and came back to me, where I stood with my knees smiting one another. "The devil take you, Francis!" says he. "I believe you are a half-hearted fellow after all. I have only done justice on a pirate. And here we are quite clear of the *Sarah!* Who shall now say that we have dipped our hands in any irregularities?"

I assured him he did me injustice; but my sense of humanity was so much affected by the horridness of the fact that I could scarce find breath to answer with.

"Come," said he, "you must be more resolved. The need for this fellow ceased when he had shown you where the path ran; and you cannot deny I would have been daft to let slip so fair an opportunity."

I could not deny but he was right in principle; nor yet could I refrain from shedding tears, of which I think no man of valour need have been ashamed; and it was not until I had a share of the rum that I was able to proceed. I repeat I am far from ashamed of my generous emotion; mercy is honourable in the warrior; and yet I cannot altogether censure Ballantrae, whose step was really fortunate, as we struck the path without further misadventure, and the same night, about sundown, came to the edge of the morass.

We were too weary to seek far; on some dry sands still warm with the day's sun, and close under a wood of pines, we lay down and were instantly plunged in sleep.

We awaked the next morning very early, and began with a sullen spirit a conversation that came near to end in blows. We were now cast on shore in the southern provinces, thousands of miles from any French settlement; a dreadful journey and a thousand perils lay in front of us; and sure, if there was ever need for amity, it was in such an hour. I must suppose that Ballantrae had suffered in his sense of what is truly polite; indeed, and there is nothing strange in the idea, after the sea-wolves we had consorted with so long; and as for myself he fubbed me off unhandsomely, and any gentleman would have resented his behaviour.

I told him in what light I saw his conduct; he walked a little off, I following to upbraid him; and at last he stopped me with his hand.

"Frank," says he, "you know what we swore; and yet there is no oath invented would induce me to swallow such expressions, if I did not regard you with sincere affection. It is impossible you should doubt me there: I have given proofs. Dutton I had to take, because he knew the pass, and Grady because Dutton would not move without him; but what call was there to carry you along? You are a perpetual danger to me with your cursed Irish tongue. By rights you should now be in irons in the cruiser. And you quarrel with me like a baby for some trinkets!"

I considered this one of the most unhandsome speeches ever made; and indeed to this day I can scarce reconcile it to my notion of a gentleman that was my friend. I retorted upon him with his Scotch accent, of which he had not so much as some, but enough to be very barbarous and disgusting, as I told him plainly; and the affair would have gone to a great length, but for an alarming intervention.

We had got some way off upon the sand. The place where we had slept, with the packets lying undone and the money scattered openly, was now between us and the pines; and it was out of these the stranger must have come. There he was at least, a great hulking fellow of the country, with a broad axe on his shoulder, looking open-mouthed, now at the treasure which was just at his feet, and now at our disputation in which we had gone far enough to have weapons in our hands. We had no sooner observed him than he found his legs and made off again among the pines.

This was no scene to put our minds at rest: a couple of armed men in sea-clothes found quarrelling over a treasure, not many miles from where a pirate had been captured—here was enough to bring the whole country about our ears. The quarrel was not even made up; it was blotted from our minds; and we got our packets together in the twinkling of an eye and made off running with the best will in the world. But the trouble was, we did not know in what direction, and must continually return upon our steps. Ballantrae had indeed collected what he could from Dutton; but it's hard to travel upon hearsay; and the estuary, which spreads into a vast irregular harbour, turned us off upon every side with a new stretch of water.

We were near beside ourselves and already quite spent with running, when coming to the top of a dune, we saw we were again cut off by another ramification of the bay. This was a creek, however, very different from those that had arrested us before; being set in rocks, and so precipitously deep, that a small vessel was able to lie alongside, made fast with a hawser; and her crew had laid a plank to the shore. Here they had lighted a fire and were sitting at their meal. As for the vessel herself, she was one of those they build in the Bermudas.

The love of gold and the great hatred that everybody has to pirates were motives of the most influential, and would certainly raise the country in our pursuit. Besides it was now plain we were on some sort of straggling peninsula like the fingers of a hand; and the wrist, or passage to the mainland, which we should have taken at the first, was by this time not improbably secured. These considerations put us on a bolder counsel. For as long as we dared, looking every moment to hear sounds of the chase, we lay among some bushes on the top of the dune; and having by this means secured a little breath and recomposed our appearance, we strolled down at last, with a great affectation of carelessness, to the party by the fire.

It was a trader and his Negroes, belonging to Albany in the Province of New York, and now on the way home from the Indies with a cargo; his name I cannot recall. We were amazed to learn he had put in here from terror of the *Sarah;* for we had no thought our exploits had been so notorious. As soon as the Albanian heard she had been taken the day before, he jumped to his feet, gave us a cup of spirits for our good news, and sent his Negroes to get sail on the Bermudan. On our side, we profited by the dram to become more confidential, and at last offered ourselves as passengers. He looked askance at our tarry clothes and pistols, and replied civilly enough that he had scarce accommodation for himself; nor could either our prayers or our offers of money, in which we advanced pretty far, avail to shake him.

"I see you think ill of us," says Ballantrae, "but I will show you how well we think of you by telling you the truth. We are Jacobite fugitives, and there is a price upon our heads."

At this, the Albanian was plainly moved a little. He asked us many questions as to the Scotch war, which Ballantrae very patiently answered. And then, with a wink, in a vulgar manner, "I guess you and your Prince Charlie got more than you cared about," said he.

"Bedad, and that we did," said I. "And, my dear man, I wish you would set a new example and give us just that much."

This I said in the Irish way, about which there is allowed to be something very engaging. It's a remarkable thing, and a testimony to the love with which our nation is regarded, that this address scarce ever fails in a handsome fellow. I cannot tell how often I have seen a private soldier escape the horse, or a beggar wheedle out a good alms, by a touch of the brogue. And, indeed, as soon as the Albanian had laughed at me I was pretty much at rest. Even then, however, he made many conditions and (for one thing) took away our arms, before he suffered us aboard; which was the signal to cast off; so that in a moment after, we were gliding down the bay with a good breeze and blessing the name of God for our deliverance. Almost in the mouth of the estuary, we passed the cruiser, and a little after, the poor *Sarah* with her prize crew; and these were both sights to make us tremble. The Bermudan seemed a very safe place to be in, and our bold stroke to have been fortunately played, when we were thus reminded of the case of our companions. For all that, we had only exchanged traps, jumped

out of the frying pan into the fire, run from the yard-arm to the
block, and escaped the open hostility of the man of war to lie at
the mercy of the doubtful faith of our Albanian merchant.

From many circumstances, it chanced we were safer than we
could have dared to hope. The town of Albany was at that time
much concerned in contraband trade across the desert with the
Indians and the French. This, as it was highly illegal, relaxed,
their loyalty, and as it brought them in relation with the politest
people on the earth, divided even their sympathies. In short they
were like all the smugglers in the world, spies and agents ready-
made for either party. Our Albanian besides was a very honest
man indeed, and very greedy; and to crown our luck, he conceived
a great delight in our society. Before we had reached the town of
New York, we had come to a full agreement: that he should carry
us as far as Albany upon his ship, and thence put us on a way to
pass the boundaries and join the French. For all this we were to
pay at a high rate; but beggars cannot be choosers, nor outlaws
bargainers.

We sailed, then, up the Hudson River, which, I protest, is a very
fine stream, and put up at the *King's Arms* in Albany. The town
was full of the militia of the province, breathing slaughter against
the French. Governor Clinton was there himself, a very busy man,
and by what I could learn, very near distracted by the factiousness
of his Assembly. The Indians on both sides were on the war path;
we saw parties of them bringing in prisoners and (what was much
worse) scalps, both male and female, for which they were paid at a
fixed rate; and I assure you the sight was not encouraging. Altogether we could scarce have come at a period more unsuitable
for our designs; our position in the chief inn was dreadfully conspicuous: our Albanian fubbed us off with a thousand delays and
seemed upon the point of a retreat from his engagements; nothing
but peril appeared to environ the poor fugitives; and for some
time, we drowned our concern in a very irregular course of living.

This too proved to be fortunate; and it's one of the remarks
that fall to be made upon our escape, how providentially our steps
were conducted to the very end. What a humiliation to the dignity
of man! My philosophy, the extraordinary genius of Ballantrae,
our valour, in which I grant that we were equal—all these might
have proved insufficient without the Divine Blessing on our efforts.
And how true it is, as the Church tells us, that the Truths of

Religion are after all quite applicable even to daily affairs! At least it was in the course of our revelry that we made the acquaintance of a spirited youth, by the name of Chew. He was one of the most daring of the Indian traders, very well acquainted with the secret paths of the wilderness, needy, dissolute, and by a last good fortune, in some disgrace with his family. Him we persuaded to come to our relief; he privately provided what was needful for our flight; and one day we slipped out of Albany, without a word to our former friend, and embarked, a little above, in a canoe.

To the toils and perils of this journey, it would require a pen more elegant than mine to do full justice. The reader must conceive for himself the dreadful wilderness which we had now to thread; its thickets, swamps, precipitous rocks, impetuous rivers, and amazing waterfalls. Among these barbarous scenes, we must toil all day, now paddling, now carrying our canoe upon our shoulders; and at night we slept about a fire, surrounded by the howling of wolves and other savage animals. It was our design to mount the head-waters of the Hudson, to the neighborhood of Crown Point; where the French had a strong place in the woods, upon Lake Champlain. But to have done this directly were too perilous; and it was accordingly gone upon by such a labyrinth of rivers, lakes and portages as makes my head giddy to remember. These paths were in ordinary times entirely desert; but the country was now up, the tribes on the war path, the woods full of Indian scouts. Again and again we came upon these parties, when we least expected them; and one day, in particular, I shall never forget; how, as dawn was coming in, we were suddenly surrounded by five or six of these painted devils, uttering a very dreary sort of cry and brandishing their hatchets. It passed off harmlessly indeed, as did the rest of our encounters; for Chew was well known and highly valued among the different tribes. Indeed he was a very gallant, respectable young man. But even with the advantage of his companionship, you must not think these meetings were without sensible peril. To prove friendship on our part, it was needful to draw upon our stock of rum—indeed, under whatever disguise, that is the true business of the Indian trader, to keep a traveling public house in the forest; and when once the braves had got their bottle of *scaura* (as they call this beastly liquor) it behooved us to set forth and paddle for our scalps. Once they were a little drunk, good-bye to any sense or decency; they had but the one thought, to get more *scaura;* they might easily take it to their heads to give us chase; and had we been overtaken, I had never written these memoirs.

We were come to the most critical portion of our course, where we might equally expect to fall into the hands of French or English, when a terrible calamity befell us. Chew was taken suddenly sick with symptoms like those of poison, and in the course of a few hours expired in the bottom of the canoe. We thus lost at once our guide, our interpreter, our boatman and our passport, for he was all these in one; and found ourselves reduced, at a blow, to the most desperate and irremediable distress. Chew, who took a great pride in his knowledge, had indeed often lectured us on the geography; and Ballantrae, I believe, would listen. But for my part I have always found such information highly tedious; and beyond the fact that we were now in the country of the Adirondack Indians, and not so distant from our destination, could we but have found our way, I was entirely ignorant. The wisdom of my course was soon the more apparent; for with all his pains, Ballantrae was no further advanced than myself. He knew we must continue to go up one stream; then, by way of a portage, down another; and then up a third. But you are to consider, in a mountain country, how many streams come rolling in from every hand. And how is a gentleman, who is a perfect stranger in that part of the world, to tell any one of them from any other? Nor was this our only trouble. We were great novices, besides, in handling a canoe; the portages were almost beyond our strength, so that I have seen us sit down in despair for half an hour at a time without one word; and the appearance of a single Indian, since we had now no means of speaking to them, would have been in all probability the means of our destruction. There is altogether some excuse if Ballantrae showed something of a gloomy disposition; his habit of imputing blame to others, quite as capable as himself, was less tolerable, and his language it was not always easy to accept. Indeed he had contracted on board the pirate ship a manner of address which was in a high degree unusual between gentlemen; and now, when you might say he was in a fever, it increased upon him hugely.

The third day of these wanderings, as we were carrying the canoe upon a rocky portage, she fell and was entirely bilged. The portage was between two lakes, both pretty extensive; the track, such as it was, opened at both ends upon the water, and on both hands was enclosed by the unbroken woods; and the sides of the lakes were quite impassable with bog; so that we beheld ourselves not only condemned to go without our boat and the greater part of our provisions, but to plunge at once into impenetrable thickets and to desert what little guidance we still had—the course of the river. Each stuck his pistols in his belt, shouldered an axe, made a pack of his treasure and as much food as he could stagger under; and deserting the rest of our possessions, even to our swords, which would have much embarrassed us among the woods, we set forth on this deplorable adventure. The labours of Hercules, so finely described by Homer, were a trifle to what we now underwent. Some parts of the forest were perfectly dense down to the ground, so that we must cut our way like mites in a cheese. In some the bottom was full of deep swamp, and the whole wood entirely rotten. I have leaped on a great fallen log and sunk to the knees in touchwood; I have sought to stay myself, in falling, against what looked to be a solid trunk, and the whole thing has whiffed away at my touch like a sheet of paper. Stumbling, falling, bogging to the knees, hewing our way, our eyes almost put out with twigs and branches, our clothes plucked from our bodies, we laboured all day, and it is doubtful if we made two miles. What was worse, as we could rarely get a view of the country and were perpetually justled from our path by obstacles, it was impossible even to have a guess in what direction we were moving.

A little before sundown, in an open place with a stream and set about with barbarous mountains, Ballantrae threw down his pack. "I will go no further," said he, and bade me light the fire, damning my blood in terms not proper for a chairman.

I told him to try to forget he had even been a pirate, and to remember he had been a gentleman.

"Are you mad?" he cried. "Don't cross me here!" And then, shaking his fist at the hills, "To think," cries he, "that I must leave my bones in this miserable wilderness! Would God I had died upon the scaffold like a gentleman!" This he said ranting like an actor; and then sat biting his fingers and staring on the ground, a most unchristian object.

I took a certain horror of the man, for I thought a soldier and a gentleman should confront his end with more philosophy. I made him no reply, therefore, in words; and presently the evening fell so chill that I was glad, for my own sake, to kindle a fire. And yet God knows, in such an open spot, and the country alive with savages, the act was little short of lunacy. Ballantrae seemed never to observe me; but at last, as I was about parching a little corn, he looked up.

"Have you ever a brother?" said he.

"By the blessing of heaven," said I, "not less than five."

"I have the one," said he, with a strange voice; and then presently, "He shall pay me for all this," he added. And when I asked him what was his brother's part in our distress, "What!" he cried, "he sits in my place, he bears my name, he courts my wife; and I am here alone with a damned Irishman in this tooth-chattering desert! O, I have been a common gull!" he cried.

The explosion was in all ways so foreign to my friend's nature, that I was daunted out of all my just susceptibility. Sure, an offensive expression, however vivacious, appears a wonderfully small affair in circumstances so extreme! But here there is a strange thing to be noted. He had only once before referred to the lady with whom he was contracted. That was when we came in view of the town of New York, when he had told me, if all had their rights, he was now in sight of his own property, for Miss Graeme enjoyed a large estate in the province. And this was certainly a natural occasion; but now here she was named a second time; and what is surely fit to be observed, in this very month, which was November, '47, and *I believe upon that very day as we sat among these barbarous mountains,* his brother and Miss Graeme were married. I am the least superstitious of men; but the hand of Province is here displayed too openly not to be remarked.*

The next day, and the next, were passed in similar labours; Ballantrae often deciding on our course by the spinning of a coin; and once, when I expostulated on this childishness, he had an odd remark that I have never forgotten. "I know no better way," said he, "to express my scorn of human reason." I think it was the third day, that we found the body of a Christian, scalped and most abominably mangled, and lying in a pudder of his blood; the birds of the desert screaming over him, as thick as flies. I cannot describe how dreadfully this sight affected us; but it robbed

---

* NOTE BY MR. MACKELLAR. A complete blunder: there was at this date no word of the marriage: see above in my own narration.

me of all strength and all hope for this world. The same day, and only a little after, we were scrambling over a part of the forest that had been burned, when Ballantrae, who was a little ahead, ducked suddenly behind a fallen trunk. I joined him in this shelter, whence we could look abroad without being seen ourselves; and in the bottom of the next vale, beheld a large war party of the savages going by across our line. There might be the value of a weak battalion present; all naked to the waist, blacked with grease and soot, and painted with white lead and vermilion, according to their beastly habits. They went one behind another like a string of geese, and at a quickish trot; so that they took but a little while to rattle by and disappear again among the woods. Yet I suppose we endured a greater agony of hesitation and suspense in these few minutes than goes usually to a man's whole life. Whether they were French or English Indians, whether they desired scalps or prisoners, whether we should declare ourselves upon the chance or lie quiet and continue the heart-breaking business of our journey: sure, I think, these were questions to have puzzled the brains of Aristotle himself. Ballantrae turned to me with a face all wrinkled up and his teeth showing in his mouth, like what I have read of people starving; he said no word, but his whole appearance was a kind of dreadful question.

"They may be of the English side," I whispered; "and think! the best we could then hope, is to begin this over again."

"I know, I know," he said. "Yet it must come to a plunge at last." And he suddenly plucked out his coin, shook it in his closed hands, looked at it, and then lay down with his face in the dust.

ADDITION BY MR. MACKELLAR. I drop the Chevalier's narration at this point because the couple quarrelled and separated the same day; and the Chevalier's account of the quarrel seems to me (I must confess) quite incompatible with the nature of either of the men. Henceforth, they wandered alone, undergoing extraordinary sufferings; until first one and then the other was picked up by a party from Fort St. Frederick. Only two things are to be noted. And first (as most important for my purpose) that the Master, in the course of his miseries, buried his treasure, at a point never since discovered, but of which he took a drawing in his own blood on the lining of his hat. And second, that on his coming thus penniless to the Fort, he was welcomed like a brother by the

Chevalier, who thence paid his way to France. The simplicity of Mr. Burke's character leads him at this point to praise the Master exceedingly; to an eye more worldly wise, it would seem it was the Chevalier alone that was to be commended. I have the more pleasure in pointing to this really very noble trait of my esteemed correspondent, as I fear I may have wounded him immediately before. I have refrained from comments on any of his extraordinary and (in my eyes) immoral opinions, for I know him to be jealous of respect. But his version of the quarrel is really more than I can reproduce; for I knew the Master myself, and a man more insusceptible of fear is not conceivable. I regret this oversight of the Chevalier's, and all the more because the tenor of his narrative (set aside a few flourishes) strikes me as highly ingenuous.

Persecutions Endured by Mr. Henry

YOU CAN GUESS ON WHAT PART OF HIS ADVENTURES THE COLONEL principally dwelled. Indeed, if we had heard it all, it is to be thought the current of this business had been wholly altered; but the pirate ship was very gently touched upon. Nor did I hear the Colonel to an end even of that which he was willing to disclose; for Mr. Henry, having for some while been plunged in a brown study, rose at last from his seat and (reminding the Colonel there were matters that he must attend to) bade me follow him immediately to the office.

Once there, he sought no longer to dissemble his concern, walking to and fro in the room with a contorted face, and passing his hand repeatedly upon his brow.

"We have some business," he began at last; and there broke off, declared we must have wine, and sent for a magnum of the best. This was extremely foreign to his habitudes; and what was still more so, when the wine had come, he gulped it down one glass upon another like a man careless of appearances. But the drink steadied him.

"You will scarce be surprised, Mackellar," says he, "when I tell you that my brother (whose safety we are all rejoiced to learn) stands in some need of money."

I told him I had misdoubted as much; but the time was not very fortunate as the stock was low.

"Not mine," said he. "There is the money for the mortgage."
I reminded him it was Mrs. Henry's.

"I will be answerable to my wife," he cried violently.

"And then," said I, "there is the mortgage."

"I know," said he, "it is on that I would consult you."

I showed him how unfortunate a time it was to divert this money from its destination; and how by so doing we must lose the profit of our past economies, and plunge back the estate into the mire. I even took the liberty to plead with him; and when he still opposed me with a shake of the head and a bitter dogged smile, my zeal quite carried me beyond my place. "This is midsummer madness," cried I; "and I for one will be no party to it."

"You speak as though I did it for my pleasure," says he. "But I have a child now; and besides I love order; and to say the honest truth, Mackellar, I had begun to take a pride in the estates." He gloomed for a moment. "But what would you have?" he went on. "Nothing is mine, nothing. This day's news has knocked the bottom out of my life. I have only the name and the shadow of things; only the shadow; there is no substance in my rights."

"They will prove substantial enough before a court," said I.

He looked at me with a burning eye, and seemed to repress the word upon his lips; and I repented what I had said, for I saw that while he spoke of the estate he had still a side-thought to his marriage. And then, of a sudden, he twitched the letter from his pocket, where it lay all crumpled, smoothed it violently on the table, and read these words to me with a trembling tongue. " 'My dear Jacob'—This is how he begins" cries he—" 'My dear Jacob, I once called you so, you may remember; and you have now done the business, and flung my heels as high as Criffel.' What do you think of that, Mackellar," says he, "from an only brother? I declare to God I liked him very well; I was always staunch to him; and this is how he writes! But I will not sit down under the imputation—" (walking to and fro)—"I am as good as he, I am a better man than he, I call on God to prove it! I cannot give him all the monstrous sum he asks; he knows the estate to be incompetent; but I will give him what I have, and it is more than he expects. I have borne all this too long. See what he writes further on; read it for yourself: 'I know you are a niggardly dog.' A niggardly dog! I, niggardly? Is that true, Mackellar? You think it is?" I really thought he would have struck me at that. "O you all think so! Well, you shall see, and he shall see, and God shall see. If I ruin the estate and go barefoot, I shall stuff this bloodsucker. Let him ask all—all, and he shall have it! It is all his by rights. Ah!" he cried, "and I foresaw all this and worse, when he would not let me go." He poured out another glass of wine and was about to carry it to his lips, when I made so bold as lay a finger on his arm. He stopped a moment. "You are right," said he, and flung glass and all in the fireplace. "Come, let us count the money."

I durst no longer oppose him; indeed I was very much affected by the sight of so much disorder in a man usually so controlled; and we sat down together, counted the money, and made it up in packets for the greater ease of Colonel Burke, who was to be the bearer. This done, Mr. Henry returned to the hall, where he and my old lord sat all night through with their guest.

A little before dawn I was called and set out with the Colonel. He would scarce have liked a less responsible convoy, for he was a man who valued himself; nor could we afford him one more dignified, for Mr. Henry must not appear with the freetraders. It was a very bitter morning of wind, and as we went down through the long shrubbery, the Colonel held himself muffled in his cloak.

"Sir," said I, "this is a great sum of money that your friend requires. I must suppose his necessities to be very great."

"We must suppose so," says he, I thought drily, but perhaps it was the cloak about his mouth.

"I am only a servant of the family," said I. "You may deal openly with me. I think we are likely to get little good by him?"

"My dear man," said the Colonel, "Ballantrae is a gentleman of the most eminent natural abilities, and a man that I admire and that I revere, to the very ground he treads on." And then he seemed to me to pause like one in a difficulty.

"But for all that," said I, "we are likely to get little good by him?"

"Sure, and you can have it your own way, my dear man," says the Colonel.

By this time we had come to the side of the creek, where the boat awaited him. "Well," said he, "I am sure I am very much your debtor for all your civility, Mr. Whatever-your-name-is; and just as a last word, and since you show so much intelligent interest, I will mention a small circumstance that may be of use to the family. For I believe my friend omitted to mention that he has the largest pension on the Scots Fund of any refugee in Paris; and it's the more disgraceful, sir," cries the Colonel, warming, "because there's not one dirty penny for myself."

He cocked his hat at me, as if I had been to blame for this partiality; then changed again into his usual swaggering civility, shook me by the hand, and set off down to the boat, with the money under his arms, and whistling as he went the pathetic air of *Shule Aroon*. It was the first time I had heard that tune; I was to hear it again, words and all, as you shall learn; but I remember how that little stave of it ran in my head, after the freetraders had bade him "Wheesht, in the deil's name," and the grating of the oars had taken its place, and I stood and watched the dawn creeping on the sea, and the boat drawing away, and the lugger lying with her foresail backed awaiting it.

The gap made in our money was a sore embarrassment; and among other consequences, it had this: that I must ride to Edinburgh, and there raise a new loan on very questionable terms to keep the old afloat; and was thus, for close upon three weeks, absent from the house of Durrisdeer.

What passed in the interval, I had none to tell me; but I found Mrs. Henry, upon my return, much changed in her demeanour; the old talks with my lord for the most part pretermitted; a certain deprecation visible towards her husband, to whom I thought she addressed herself more often; and for one thing, she was now greatly wrapped up in Miss Katharine. You would think the change was agreeable to Mr. Henry! no such matter! To the contrary, every circumstance of alteration was a stab to him; he read in each the avowal of her truant fancies—that constancy to the Master of which she was proud while she supposed him dead, she had to blush for now she knew he was alive: and these blushes were the hated spring of her new conduct. I am to conceal no truth; and I will here say plainly, I think this was the period in which Mr. Henry showed the worst. He contained himself, indeed, in public; but there was a deep-seated irritation visible underneath. With me, from whom he had less concealment, he was often grossly unjust; and even for his wife, he would sometimes have a sharp retort: perhaps when she had ruffled him with some unwonted kindness; perhaps upon no tangible occasion, the mere habitual tenor of the man's annoyance bursting spontaneously forth. When he would thus forget himself (a thing so strangely out of keeping with the terms of their relation), there went a shock through the whole company; and the pair would look upon each other in a kind of pained amazement.

All the time too, while he was injuring himself by this defect of temper, he was hurting his position by a silence, of which I scarce know whether to say it was the child of generosity or pride. The freetraders came again and again, bringing messengers from the Master, and none departed empty-handed. I never durst reason with Mr. Henry; he gave what was asked of him in a kind of noble rage. Perhaps because he knew he was by nature inclining to the parsimonious, he took a back-foremost pleasure in the recklessness with which he supplied his brother's exigence. Perhaps the falsity of the position would have spurred a humbler man into the same excesses. But the estate (if I may say so) groaned under it; our daily expenses were shorn lower and lower; the stables were emptied, all but four roadsters; servants were discharged, which raised a dreadful murmuring in the country and heated up the old disfavour upon Mr. Henry; and at last the yearly visit to Edinburgh must be discontinued.

This was in 1756. You are to suppose that for seven years this bloodsucker had been drawing the life's blood from Durrisdeer; and that all this time, my patron had held his peace. It was an effect of devilish malice in the Master, that he addressed Mr. Henry alone upon the matter of his demands; and there was never a word to my lord. The family had looked on wondering at our economies. They had lamented, I have no doubt, that my patron had become so great a miser; a fault always despicable, but in the young abhorrent; and Mr. Henry was not yet thirty years of age. Still he had managed the business of Durrisdeer almost from a boy; and they bore with these changes in a silence as proud and bitter as his own, until the coping stone of the Edinburgh visit.

At this time, I believe my patron and his wife were rarely together save at meals. Immediately on the back of Colonel Burke's announcement, Mrs. Henry made palpable advances; you might say she had laid a sort of timid court to her husband, different indeed from her former manner of unconcern and distance. I never had the heart to blame Mr. Henry because he recoiled from these advances; nor yet to censure the wife, when she was cut to the quick by their rejection. But the result was an entire estrangement, so that (as I say) they rarely spoke except at meals. Even the matter of the Edinburgh visit was first broached at table; and it chanced that Mrs. Henry was that day ailing and querulous. She had no sooner understood her husband's meaning, than the red flew in her face.

"At last," she cried, "this is too much! Heaven knows what pleasure I have in my life, that I should be denied my only consolation. These shameful proclivities must be trod down; we are already a mark and an eyesore in the neighbourhood; I will not endure this fresh insanity."

"I cannot afford it," says Mr. Henry.

"Afford?" she cried. "For shame! But I have money of my own."

"That is all mine, madam, by marriage," he snarled, and instantly left the room.

My old lord threw up his hands to heaven, and he and his daughter, withdrawing to the chimney, gave me a broad hint to be gone. I found Mr. Henry in his usual retreat, the steward's room, perched on the end of the table and plunging his penknife in it, with a very ugly countenance.

"Mr. Henry," said I, "you do yourself too much injustice; and it is time this should cease."

"O!" cries he, "nobody minds here. They think it only natural. I have shameful proclivities. I am a niggardly dog," and he drove his knife up to the hilt. "But I will show that fellow," he cried with an oath, "I will show him which is the more generous."

"This is no generosity," said I, "this is only pride."

"Do you think I want morality?" he asked.

I thought he wanted help, and I should give it him, willy-nilly; and no sooner was Mrs. Henry gone to her room, than I presented myself at her door and sought admittance.

She openly showed her wonder. "What do you want with me, Mr. Mackellar?" said she.

"The Lord knows, madam," says I, "I have never troubled you before with any freedoms; but this thing lies too hard upon my conscience, and it will out. Is it possible that two people can be so blind as you and my lord? and have lived all these years with a noble gentleman like Mr. Henry, and understand so little of his nature?"

"What does this mean?" she cried.

"Do you not know where his money goes to? his—and yours— and the money for the very wine he does not drink at table?" I went on. "To Paris—to that man! Eight thousand pounds has he had of us in seven years, and my patron fool enough to keep it secret!"

"Eight thousand pounds!" she repeated. "It is impossible, the estate is not sufficient."

"God knows how we have sweated farthings to produce it," said I. "But eight thousand and sixty is the sum, beside odd shillings. And if you can think my patron miserly after that, this shall be my last interference."

"You need say no more, Mr. Mackellar," said she. "You have done most properly in what you too modestly call your inter- ference. I am much to blame; you must think me indeed a very unobservant wife"—(looking upon me with a strange smile)— "but I shall put this right at once. The Master was always of a very thoughtless nature; but his heart is excellent; he is the soul of generosity. I shall write to him myself. You cannot think how you have pained me by this communication."

"Indeed, madam, I had hoped to have pleased you," said I, for I raged to see her still thinking of the Master.

"And pleased," said she, "and pleased me of course."

That same day (I will not say but what I watched) I had the satisfaction to see Mr. Henry come from his wife's room in a state most unlike himself; for his face was all bloated with weeping, and yet he seemed to me to walk upon the air. By this, I was sure his wife had made him full amends for once; "Ah," thought I, to myself, "I have done a brave stroke this day."

On the morrow, as I was seated at my books, Mr. Henry came in softly behind me, took me by the shoulders and shook me in a manner of playfulness. "I find you are a faithless fellow after all," says he; which was his only reference to my part, but the tone he spoke in was more to me than any eloquence of protestation. Nor was this all I had effected; for when the next messenger came (as he did not long afterwards) from the Master, he got nothing away with him but a letter. For some while back, it had been I myself who had conducted these affairs; Mr. Henry not setting pen to paper, and I only in the dryest and most formal terms. But this letter I did not even see; it would scarce be pleasant reading, for

Mr. Henry felt he had his wife behind him for once, and I observed, on the day it was despatched, he had a very gratified expression.

Things went better now in the family, though it could scarce be pretended they went well. There was now at least no misconception; there was kindness upon all sides; and I believe my patron and his wife might again have drawn together, if he could but have pocketed his pride, and she forgot (what was the ground of all) her brooding on another man. It is wonderful how a private thought leaks out; it is wonderful to me now, how we should all have followed the current of her sentiments; and though she bore herself quietly, and had a very even disposition, yet we should have known whenever her fancy ran to Paris. And would not any one have thought that my disclosure must have rooted up that idol? I think there is the devil in women: all these years passed, never a sight of the man, little enough kindness to remember (by all accounts) even while she had him, the notion of his death intervening, his heartless rapacity laid bare to her: that all should not do, and she must still keep the best place in her heart for this accursed fellow, is a thing to make a plain man rage. I had never much natural sympathy for the passion of love; but this unreason in my patron's wife disgusted me outright with the whole matter. I remember checking a maid, because she sang some bairnly kickshaw while my mind was thus engaged; and my asperity brought about my ears the enmity of all the petticoats about the house; of which I recked very little, but it amused Mr. Henry, who rallied me much upon our joint unpopularity. It is strange enough (for my own mother was certainly one of the salt of the earth and my aunt Dickson, who paid my fees at the University, a very notable woman), but I have never had much toleration for the female sex, possibly not much understanding; and being far from a bold man, I have ever shunned their company. Not only do I see no cause to regret this diffidence in myself, but have invariably remarked the most unhappy consequences follow those who were less wise. So much I thought proper to set down, lest I show myself unjust to Mrs. Henry. And besides the remark arose naturally, on a reperusal of the letter which was the next step in these affairs, and reached me to my sincere astonishment by a private hand some week or so after the departure of the last messenger.

Troyes in Champagne,
July 12, 1756.

My Dear Sir:—You will doubtless be surprised to receive a communication from one so little known to you; but on the occasion I had the good fortune to rencounter you at Durrisdeer, I remarked you for a young man of a solid gravity of character: a qualification which I profess I admire and revere next to natural genius or the bold chivalrous spirit of the soldier. I was besides interested in the noble family which you have the honour to serve or (to speak more by the book) to be the humble and respected friend of; and a conversation I had the pleasure to have with you very early in the morning has remained much upon my mind.

Being the other day in Paris, on a visit from this famous city where I am in garrison, I took occasion to inquire your name (which I profess I had forgot) at my friend, the Master of B.; and a fair opportunity occurring, I write to inform you of what's new.

The Master of B. (when we had last some talk of him together) was in receipt, as I think I then told you, of a highly advantageous pension on the Scots Fund. He next received a company, and was soon after advanced to a regiment of his own. My dear Sir, I do not offer to explain this circumstance; any more than why I myself, who have rid at the right hand of Princes, should be fubbed off with a pair of colours and sent to rot in a hole at the bottom of the province. Accustomed as I am to courts, I cannot but feel it is no atmosphere for a plain soldier; and I could never hope to advance by similar means, even could I stoop to the endeavour. But our friend has a particular aptitude to succeed by the means of ladies; and if all be true that I have heard, he enjoyed a remarkable protection. It is like this turned against him; for whom I had the honour to shake him by the hand, he was but newly released from the Bastille where he had been cast on a sealed letter; and though now released, has both lost his regiment and his pension. My dear Sir, the loyalty of a plain Irishman will ultimately succeed in the place of craft; as I am sure a gentleman of your probity will agree.

Now, Sir, the Master is a man whose genius I admire beyond expression, and besides he is my friend; but I thought a little word of this revolution in his fortunes would not come amiss, for in my opinion, the man's desperate. He spoke when I saw him of a trip to India (whither I am myself in some hope of accompanying my illustrious countryman, Mr. Lally); but for this he would require (as I understood) more money than was readily at his command. You may have heard a military proverb; that it is a good thing to make a bridge of gold to a flying enemy? I trust you will take my meaning;—and I subscribe myself, with proper respects to my Lord Durrisdeer, to his son, and to the beauteous Mrs. Durie,

My dear Sir,
Your obedient humble servant,
Francis Burke

This missive I carried at once to Mr. Henry; and I think there was but the one thought between the two of us: that it had come a week too late. I made haste to send an answer to Colonel Burke, in which I begged him, if he should see the Master, to assure him his next messenger would be attended to. But with all my haste I was not in time to avert what was impending; the arrow had been drawn, it must now fly. I could almost doubt the power of Providence (and certainly his will) to stay the issue of events; and it is a strange thought, how many of us had been storing up the elements of this catastrophe, for how long a time, and with how blind an ignorance of what we did.

From the coming of the Colonel's letter, I had a spy-glass in my room, began to drop questions to the tenant folk, and as there was no great secrecy observed and the freetrade (in our part) went by force as much as stealth, I had soon got together a knowledge of the signals in use, and knew pretty well to an hour when any messenger might be expected. I say I questioned the tenants; for with the traders themselves, desperate blades that went habitually armed, I could never bring myself to meddle willingly. Indeed, by what proved in the sequel an unhappy chance, I was an object of scorn to some of these braggadocios; who had not only gratified me with a nickname, but catching me one night upon a by-path and being all (as they would have said) somewhat merry, had caused me to dance for their diversion. The method employed was that of cruelly chipping at my toes with naked cutlasses, shouting at the same time "Squaretoes"; and though they did me no bodily mischief, I was none the less deplorably affected and was indeed for several days confined to my bed: a scandal on the state of Scotland on which no comment is required.

It happened on the afternoon of November 7th, in this same unfortunate year, that I espied, during my walk, the smoke of a beacon fire upon the Muckleross. It was drawing near time for my return; but the uneasiness upon my spirits was that day so great, that I must burst through the thickets to the edge of what they call the Craig Head. The sun was already down, but there was still a broad light in the west, which showed me some of the smugglers treading out their signal fire upon the Ross, and in the bay the lugger lying with her sails brailed up. She was plainly but new come to anchor, and yet the skiff was already lowered and pulling for the landing place at the end of the long shrubbery. And this I knew could signify but one thing, the coming of a messenger for Durrisdeer.

I laid aside the remainder of my terrors, clambered down the brae—a place I had never ventured through before, and was hid among the shoreside thickets in time to see the boat touch. Captain Crail himself was steering, a thing not usual; by his side there sat a passenger; and the men gave way with difficulty, being hampered with near upon half-a-dozen portmanteaus, great and small. But the business of landing was briskly carried through; and presently the baggage was all tumbled on shore, the boat on its return voyage to the lugger, and the passenger standing alone upon the point of rock, a tall slender figure of a gentleman, habited in black, with a sword by his side and a walking cane upon his wrist. As he so stood, he waved the cane to Captain Crail by way of salutation, with something both of grace and mockery that wrote the gesture deeply on my mind.

No sooner was the boat away with my sworn enemies, than I took a sort of half courage, came forth to the margin of the thicket, and there halted again, my mind being greatly pulled about between natural diffidence and a dark foreboding of the truth. Indeed I might have stood there swithering all night, had not the stranger turned, spied me through the mists, which were beginning to fall, and waved and cried on me to draw near. I did so with a heart like lead.

"Here, my good man," said he, in the English accent, "here are some things for Durrisdeer."

I was now near enough to see him, a very handsome figure and countenance, swarthy, lean, long, with a quick, alert, black look, as of one who was a fighter and accustomed to command; upon one cheek, he had a mole, not unbecoming; a large diamond sparkled on his hand; his clothes, although of the one hue, were of a French and foppish design; his ruffles, which he wore longer than common, of exquisite lace; and I wondered the more to see him in such a guise, when he was but newly landed from a dirty smuggling lugger. At the same time he had a better look at me, toised me a second time sharply, and then smiled.

"I wager, my friend," says he, "that I know both your name and your nickname. I divined these very clothes upon your hand of writing, Mr. Mackellar."

At these words, I fell to shaking.

"O," says he, "you need not be afraid of me. I bear no malice for your tedious letters; and it is my purpose to employ you a good deal. You may call me Mr. Bally: it is the name I have assumed; or rather (since I am addressing so great a precision) it is so I have curtailed my own. Come now, pick up that and that"—indicating two of the portmanteaus. "That will be as much as you are fit to bear, and the rest can very well wait. Come, lose no more time, if you please."

His tone was so cutting that I managed to do as he bid by a sort of instinct, my mind being all the time quite lost. No sooner had I picked up the portmanteaus, than he turned his back and marched off through the long shrubbery; where it began already to be dusk, for the wood is thick and evergreen. I followed behind, loaded almost to the dust, though I profess I was not conscious of the burthen; being swallowed up in the monstrosity of this return and my mind flying like a weaver's shuttle.

On a sudden I set the portmanteaus to the ground and halted. He turned and looked back at me.

"Well?" said he.

"You are the Master of Ballantrae?"

"You will do me the justice to observe," says he, "that I have made no secret with the astute Mackellar."

"And in the name of God," cries I, "what brings you here? Go back, while it is yet time."

"I thank you," said he. "Your master has chosen this way, and not I; but since he has made the choice, he (and you also) must abide by the result. And now pick up these things of mine, which you have set down in a very boggy place, and attend to that which I have made your business."

But I had no thought now of obedience; I came straight up to him. "If nothing will move you to go back," said I; "though sure, under all the circumstances, any Christian or even any gentleman would scruple to go forward . . ."

"These are gratifying expressions," he threw in.

"If nothing will move you to go back," I continued, "there are still some decencies to be observed. Wait here with your baggage, and I will go forward and prepare your family. Your father is an old man; and . . ." I stumbled . . . "there are decencies to be observed"

"Truly," said he, "this Mackellar improves upon acquaintance. But look you here, my man, and understand it once for all—you waste your breath upon me, and I go my own way with inevitable motion."

"Ah!" says I. "Is that so? We shall see then!"

And I turned and took to my heels for Durrisdeer. He clutched at me and cried out angrily, and then I believe I heard him laugh, and then I am certain he pursued me for a step or two, and (I suppose) desisted. One thing at least is sure, that I came but a few minutes later to the door of the great house, nearly strangled for the lack of breath but quite alone. Straight up the stair I ran, and burst into the hall, and stopped before the family without the power of speech; but I must have carried my story in my looks, for they rose out of their places and stared on me like changelings.

"He has come," I panted out at last.

"He?" said Mr. Henry.

"Himself," said I.

"My son?" cried my lord. "Imprudent, imprudent boy! O, could he not stay where he was safe!"

Never a word said Mrs. Henry; nor did I look at her, I scarce knew why.

"Well," said Mr. Henry, with a very deep breath, "and where is he?"

"I left him in the long shrubbery," said I.

"Take me to him," said he.

So we went out together, he and I, without another word from any one; and in the midst of the gravelled plot, encountered the Master strolling up, whistling as he came and beating the air with his cane. There was still light enough overhead to recognise though not to read a countenance.

"Ah, Jacob!" says the Master. "So here is Esau back."

"James," says Mr. Henry, "for God's sake, call me by my name. I will not pretend that I am glad to see you; but I would fain make you as welcome as I can in the house of our fathers."

"Or in *my* house? or *yours*?" says the Master. "Which was you about to say? But this is an old sore, and we need not rub it. If you would not share with me in Paris, I hope you will yet scarce deny your elder brother a corner of the fire at Durrisdeer?"

"That is very idle speech," replied Mr. Henry. "And you understand the power of your position excellently well."

"Why, I believe I do," said the other with a little laugh. And this, though they had never touched hands, was (as we may say) the end of the brothers' meeting; for at this, the Master turned to me and bade me fetch his baggage.

I, on my side, turned to Mr. Henry for a confirmation; perhaps with some defiance.

"As long as the Master is here, Mr. Mackellar, you will very much oblige me by regarding his wishes as you would my own," says Mr. Henry. "We are constantly troubling you: will you be so good as send one of the servants?"—with an accent on the word.

If this speech were anything at all, it was surely a well-deserved reproof upon the stranger; and yet, so devilish was his impudence, he twisted it the other way.

"And shall we be common enough to say 'Sneck up'!" inquires he softly, looking upon me sideways.

Had a kingdom depended on the act, I could not have trusted myself in words; even to call a servant was beyond me; I had rather serve the man myself than speak; and I turned away in silence and went into the long shrubbery, with a heart full of anger and despair. It was dark under the trees, and I walked before me and forgot what business I was come upon, till I near broke my shin on the portmanteaus. Then it was that I remarked a strange particular; for whereas I had before carried both and scarce observed it, it was now as much as I could do to manage one. And this, as it forced me to make two journeys, kept me the longer from the hall.

When I got there the business of welcome was over long ago; the company was already at supper; and by an oversight that cut me to the quick, my place had been forgotten. I had seen one side of the Master's return; now I was to see the other. It was he who first remarked my coming in and standing back (as I did) in some annoyance. He jumped from his seat.

"And if I have not got the good Mackellar's place!" cries he. "John, lay another for Mr. Bally; I protest he will disturb no one, and your table is big enough for all."

I could scarce credit my ears; nor yet my senses when he took me by the shoulders and thrust me laughing into my own place; such an affectionate playfulness was in his voice. And while John laid the fresh place for him (a thing on which he still insisted) he went and leaned on his father's chair and looked down upon him, and the old man turned about and looked upwards on his son, with such a pleasant mutual tenderness, that I could have carried my hand to my head in mere amazement.

Yet all was of a piece. Never a harsh word fell from him, never a sneer showed upon his lip. He had laid aside even his cutting English accent, and spoke with the kindly Scots tongue, that sets a value on affectionate words; and though his manners had a graceful elegance mighty foreign to our ways in Durrisdeer, it was still a homely courtliness, that did not shame but flattered us. All that he did throughout the meal, indeed, drinking wine with me with a notable respect, turning about for a pleasant word with John, fondling his father's hand, breaking into little merry tales of his adventures, calling up the past with happy reference—all he did was so becoming, and himself so handsome, that I could scarce wonder if my lord and Mrs. Henry sat about the board with radiant faces, or if John waited behind with dropping tears.

As soon as supper was over, Mrs. Henry rose to withdraw.

"This was never your way, Alison," said he.

"It is my way now," she replied: which was notoriously false, "and I will give you a good-night, James, and a welcome—from the dead," said she, and her voice drooped and trembled.

Poor Mr. Henry, who had made rather a heavy figure through the meal, was more concerned than ever: pleased to see his wife withdraw, and yet half displeased, as he thought upon the cause of it;

and the next moment altogether dashed by the fervour of her speech.

On my part, I thought I was now one too many; and was stealing after Mrs. Henry, when the Master saw me.

"Now, Mr. Mackellar," says he, "I take this near on an unfriendliness. I cannot have you go: this is to make a stranger of the prodigal son—and let me remind you where—in his own father's house! Come, sit ye down, and drink another glass with Mr. Bally."

"Ay, ay, Mr. Mackellar," says my lord, "we must not make a stranger either of him or you. I have been telling my son," he added, his voice brightening as usual on the word, "how much we valued all your friendly service."

So I sat there silent till my usual hour; and might have been almost deceived in the man's nature, but for one passage in which his perfidy appeared too plain. Here was the passage; of which, after what he knows of the brothers' meeting, the reader shall consider for himself. Mr. Henry sitting somewhat dully, in spite of his best endeavours to carry things before my lord, up jumps the Master, passes about the board, and claps his brother on the shoulder.

"Come, come, *Hairry lad*," says he, with a broad accent such as they must have used together when they were boys, "you must not be downcast because your brother has come home. All's yours, that's sure enough, and little I grudge it you. Neither must you grudge me my place beside my father's fire."

"And that is too true, Henry," says my old lord with a little frown, a thing rare with him. "You have been the elder brother of the parable in the good sense; you must be careful of the other."

"I am easily put in the wrong," said Mr. Henry.

"Who puts you in the wrong?" cried my lord, I thought very tartly for so mild a man. "You have earned my gratitude and your brother's many thousand times; you may count on its endurance; and let that suffice."

"Ay, Harry, that you may," said the Master; and I thought Mr. Henry looked at him with a kind of wildness in his eye.

On all the miserable business that now followed, I have four questions that I asked myself often at the time and ask myself still. Was the man moved by a particular sentiment against Mr. Henry?

or by what he thought to be his interest? or by a mere delight in cruelty such as cats display and theologians tell us of the devil? or by what he would have called love? My common opinion halts among the three first; but perhaps there lay at the spring of his behaviour an element of all. As thus: Animosity to Mr. Henry would explain his hateful usage of him when they were alone; the interests he came to serve would explain his very different attitude before my lord; that and some spice of a design of gallantry, his care to stand well with Mrs. Henry; and the pleasure of malice for itself, the pains he was continually at to mingle and oppose these lines of conduct.

Partly because I was a very open friend to my patron, partly because in my letters to Paris I had often given myself some freedom of remonstrance, I was included in his diabolical amusement. When I was alone with him, he pursued me with sneers; before the family, he used me with the extreme of friendly condescension. This was not only painful in itself; not only did it put me continually in the wrong; but there was in it an element of insult indescribable. That he should thus leave me out in his dissimulation, as though even my testimony were too despicable to be considered, galled me to the blood. But what it was to me is not worth notice. I make but memorandum of it here; and chiefly for this reason, that it had one good result, and gave me the quicker sense of Mr. Henry's martyrdom.

It was on him the burthen fell. How was he to respond to the public advances of one who never lost a chance of gibing him in private? How was he to smile back on the deceiver and the insulter? He was condemned to seem ungracious. He was condemned to silence. Had he been less proud, had he spoken, who would have credited the truth? The acted calumny had done its work; my lord and Mrs. Henry were the daily witnesses of what went on; they could have sworn in court that the Master was a model of long-suffering good-nature and Mr. Henry a pattern of jealousy and thanklessness. And ugly enough as these must have appeared in any one, they seemed tenfold uglier in Mr. Henry; for who could forget that the Master lay in peril of his life, and that he had already lost his mistress, his title and his fortune?

"Henry, will you ride with me?" asks the Master one day.

And Mr. Henry, who had been goaded by the man all morning, raps out: "I will not."

"I sometimes wish you would be kinder, Henry," says the other wistfully.

I give this for a specimen; but such scenes befell continually. Small wonder if Mr. Henry was blamed; small wonder if I fretted myself into something near upon a bilious fever; nay, and at the mere recollection feel a bitterness in my blood.

Sure, never in this world was a more diabolical contrivance: so perfidious, so simple, so impossible to combat. And yet I think again, and I think always, Mrs. Henry might have read between the lines; she might have had more knowledge of her husband's nature; after all these years of marriage, she might have commanded or captured his confidence. And my old lord too, that very watchful gentleman, where was all his observation? But for one thing, the deceit was practised by a master hand, and might have gulled an angel. For another (in the case of Mrs. Henry), I have observed there are no persons so far away as those who are both married and estranged, so that they seem out of earshot or to have no common tongue. For a third (in the case of both of these spectators), they were blinded by old, ingrained predilection. And for a fourth, the risk the Master was supposed to stand in (supposed, I say—you will soon hear why) made it seem the more ungenerous to criticise; and keeping them in a perpetual tender solicitude about his life, blinded them the more effectually to his faults.

It was during this time that I perceived most clearly the effect of manner, and was led to lament most deeply the plainness of my own. Mr. Henry had the essence of a gentleman; when he was moved, when there was any call of circumstance, he could play his part with dignity and spirit; but in the day's commerce (it is idle to deny it) he fell short of the ornamental. The Master (on the other hand) had never a movement but it commended him. So it befell, that when the one appeared gracious and the other ungracious, every trick of their bodies seemed to call out confirmation. Nor that alone: but the more deeply Mr. Henry floundered in his brother's toils, the more clownish he grew; and the more the Master enjoyed his spiteful entertainment, the more engagingly, the more smilingly, he went! So that the plot, by its own scope and progress, furthered and confirmed itself.

It was one of the man's arts to use the peril in which (as I say) he was supposed to stand. He spoke of it to those who loved him

with a gentle pleasantry, which made it the more touching. To Mr.
Henry, he used it as a cruel weapon of offence. I remember his laying his finger on the clean lozenge of the painted window, one
day when we three were alone together in the hall. "Here went
your lucky guinea, Jacob," said he. And when Mr. Henry only
looked upon him darkly, "O," he added, "you need not look such
impotent malice, my good fly. You can be rid of your spider when
you please. How long, O Lord? When are you to be wrought to
the point of a denunciation, scrupulous brother? It is one of my
interests in this dreary hole. I ever loved experiment." Still Mr.
Henry only stared upon him with a glooming brow, and a changed
colour; and at last the Master broke out in a laugh and clapped
him on the shoulder, calling him a sulky dog. At this my patron
leaped back with a gesture I thought very dangerous; and I must
suppose the Master thought so too; for he looked the least in the
world discountenanced, and I do not remember him again to have
laid hands on Mr. Henry.

But though he had his peril always on his lips in the one way or
the other, I thought his conduct strangely incautious, and began
to fancy the government (who had set a price upon his head) was
gone sound asleep. I did not deny I was tempted with the wish to
denounce him; but two thoughts withheld me: one, that if he
were thus to end his life upon an honourable scaffold, the man
would be canonised for good in the minds of his father and my
patron's wife: the other, that if I was anyway mingled in the matter, Mr. Henry himself would scarce escape some glancings of
suspicion. And in the meanwhile our enemy went in and out
more than I could have thought possible, the fact that he was home
again was buzzed about all the country-side; and yet he was never
stirred. Of all these so many and so different persons who were
acquainted with his presence, none had the least greed (as I used
to say, in my annoyance) or the least loyalty; and the man rode
here and there—fully more welcome, considering the lees of old
unpopularity, than Mr. Henry—and considering the freetraders,
far safer than myself.

Not but what he had a trouble of his own; and this, as it brought
about the gravest consequences, I must now relate. The reader will
scarce have forgotten Jessie Broun; her way of life was much
among the smuggling party; Captain Crail himself was of her
intimates; and she had early word of Mr. Bally's presence at the

house. In my opinion she had long ceased to care two straws for the Master's person; but it was become her habit to connect herself continually with the Master's name; that was the ground of all her play-acting; and so, now when he was back, she thought she owed it to herself to grow a haunter of the neighbourhood of Durrisdeer. The Master could scarce go abroad but she was there in wait for him; a scandalous figure of a woman, not often sober; hailing him wildly as "her bonnie laddie," quoting pedlar's poetry, and as I receive the story, even seeking to weep upon his neck. I own I rubbed my hands over this persecution; but the Master, who laid so much upon others, was himself the least patient of men. There were strange scenes enacted in the policies. Some say he took his cane to her, and Jessie fell back upon her former weapon, stones. It is certain at least that he made a motion to Captain Crail to have the woman trepanned, and that the Captain refused the proposition with uncommon vehemence. And the end of the matter was victory for Jessie. Money was got together; an interview took place in which my proud gentleman must consent to be kissed and wept upon; and the woman was set up in a public of her own, somewhere on Solway side (but I forget where) and by the only news I ever had of it, extremely ill-frequented.

This is to look forward. After Jessie had been but a little while upon his heels, the Master comes to me one day in the steward's office, and with more civility than usual, "Mackellar," says he, "there is a damned crazy wench comes about here. I cannot well move in the matter myself, which brings me to you. Be so good as see to it: the men must have a strict injunction to drive the wench away."

"Sir," said I, trembling a little, "you can do your own dirty errands for yourself."

He said not a word to that, and left the room.

Presently came Mr. Henry. "Here is news!" cried he. "It seems all is not enough, and you must add to my wretchedness. It seems you have insulted Mr. Bally."

"Under your kind favour, Mr. Henry," said I, "it was he that insulted me, and as I think grossly. But I may have been careless of your position when I spoke; and if you think so when you know all, my dear patron, you have but to say the word. For you I would obey in any point whatever, even to sin, God pardon me!" And thereupon I told him what had passed.

Mr. Henry smiled to himself; a grimmer smile I never witnessed. "You did exactly well," said he. "He shall drink his Jessie Broun to the dregs." And then, spying the Master outside he opened the window, and crying to him by the name of Mr. Bally, asked him to step up and have a word.

"James," said he, when our persecutor had come in and closed the door behind him, looking at me with a smile as if he thought I was to be humbled, "you brought me a complaint against Mr. Mackellar into which I have inquired. I need not tell you I would always take his word against yours; for we are alone, and I am going to use something of your own freedom. Mr. Mackellar is a gentleman I value; and you must contrive, so long as you are under this roof, to bring yourself into no more collisions with one whom I will support at any possible cost to me or mine. As for the errand upon which you came to him, you must deliver yourself from the consequences of your own cruelty, and none of my servants shall be at all employed in such a case."

"My father's servants, I believe," says the Master.

"Go to him with this tale," said Mr. Henry.

The Master grew very white. He pointed at me with his finger. "I want that man discharged," he said.

"He shall not be," said Mr. Henry.

"You shall pay pretty dear for this," says the Master.

"I have paid so dear already for a wicked brother," said Mr. Henry, "that I am bankrupt even of fears. You have no place left where you can strike me."

"I will show you about that," says the Master, and went softly away.

"What will he do next, Mackellar?" cries Mr. Henry.

"Let me go away," said I. "My dear patron, let me go away; I am but the beginning of fresh sorrows."

"Would you leave me quite alone?" said he.

We were not long in suspense as to the nature of the new assault. Up to that hour, the Master had played a very close game with Mrs. Henry; avoiding pointedly to be alone with her, which I took at the time for an effect of decency, but now think to be a most insidious art; meeting her, you may say, at mealtime only; and behaving, when he did so, like an affectionate brother. Up to that hour, you may say he had scarce directly interfered between

Mr. Henry and his wife; except in so far as he had manœuvred the one quite forth from the good graces of the other. Now, all that was to be changed; but whether really in revenge, or because he was wearying of Durrisdeer and looked about for some diversion, who but the devil shall decide?

From that hour at least, began the siege of Mrs. Henry; a thing so deftly carried on that I scarce know if she was aware of it herself, and that her husband must look on in silence. The first parallel was opened (as was made to appear) by accident. The talk fell, as it did often, on the exiles in France; so it glided to the matter of their songs.

"There is one," says the Master, "if you are curious in these matters, that has always seemed to me very moving. The poetry is harsh; and yet, perhaps because of my situation, it has always found the way to my heart. It is supposed to be sung, I should tell you, by an exile's sweetheart; and represents, perhaps, not so much the truth of what she is thinking, as the truth of what he hopes of her, poor soul! in these far lands." And here the Master sighed. "I protest it is a pathetic sight when a score of rough Irish, all common sentinels, get to this song; and you may see by their falling tears, how it strikes home to them. It goes thus, father," says he, very adroitly taking my lord for his listener, "and if I cannot get to the end of it, you must think it is a common case with us exiles." And thereupon he struck up the same air as I had heard the Colonel whistle; but now to words, rustic indeed, yet most pathetically setting forth a poor girl's aspirations for an exiled lover: of which one verse indeed (or something like it) still sticks by me:

> O, I will dye my petticoat red,
> With my dear boy I'll beg my bread,
> Though all my friends should wish me dead,
>   For Willie among the rushes, O!

He sang it well even as a song; but he did better yet as a performer. I have heard famous actors, when there was not a dry eye in the Edinburgh theatre; a great wonder to behold; but no more wonderful than how the Master played upon that little ballad and on those who heard him like an instrument, and seemed now upon the point of failing, and now to conquer his distress, so that words and music seemed to pour out of his own heart and his own past, and to be aimed direct at Mrs. Henry. And his art went further yet; for all was so delicately touched, it seemed impossible to suspect him of the least design; and so far from making a parade of emotion, you would have sworn he was striving to be calm. When it came to an end, we all sat silent for a time; he had chosen the dusk of the afternoon, so that none could see his neighbour's face; but it seemed as if we held our breathing, only my old lord cleared his throat. The first to move was the singer, who got to his feet suddenly and softly, and went and walked softly to and fro in the low end of the hall, Mr. Henry's customary place. We were to suppose that he there struggled down the last of his emotion; for he presently returned and launched into a disquisition on the nature of the Irish (always so much miscalled, and whom he defended) in his natural voice; so that, before the lights were brought, we were in the usual course of talk. But even then, methought Mrs. Henry's face was a shade pale; and for another thing, she withdrew almost at once.

The next sign was a friendship this insidious devil struck up with innocent Miss Katharine; so that they were always together, hand in hand, or she climbing on his knee, like a pair of children. Like all his diabolical acts, this cut in several ways. It was the last stroke to Mr. Henry, to see his own babe debauched against him; it made him harsh with the poor innocent, which brought him still a peg lower in his wife's esteem; and (to conclude) it was a bond of union between the lady and the Master. Under this influence, their old reserve melted by daily stages. Presently there came walks in the long strubbery, talks in the Belvedere, and I know not what tender familiarity. I am sure Mrs. Henry was like many a good woman; she had a whole conscience, but perhaps by the means of a little winking. For even to so dull an observer as myself, it was plain her kindness was of a more moving nature than the sisterly. The tones of her voice appeared more numerous; she had a light and softness in her eye; she was more gentle with all of us, even with Mr. Henry, even with myself; methought she breathed of some quiet melancholy happiness.

To look on at this, what a torment it was for Mr. Henry! And yet it brought our ultimate deliverance, as I am soon to tell.

The purport of the Master's stay was no more noble (gild it as they might) than to wring money out. He had some design of a fortune in the French Indies, as the Chevalier wrote me; and it was the sum required for this that he came seeking. For the rest of the family it spelled ruin; but my lord, in his incredible partiality, pushed ever for the granting. The family was now so narrowed down (indeed there were no more of them than just the father and the two sons), that it was possible to break the entail, and alienate a piece of land. And to this, at first by hints, and then by open pressure, Mr. Henry was brought to consent. He never would have done so, I am very well assured, but for the weight of the distress under which he laboured. But for his passionate eagerness to see his brother gone, he would not thus have broken with his own sentiment and the traditions of his house. And even so, he sold them his consent at a dear rate, speaking for once openly and holding the business up in its own shameful colours.

"You will observe," he said, "this is an injustice to my son, if ever I have one."

"But that you are not likely to have," said my lord.

"God knows!" says Mr. Henry. "And considering the cruel falseness of the position in which I stand to my brother, and that you, my lord, are my father and have the right to command me, I set my hand to this paper. But one thing I will say first: I have been ungenerously pushed, and when next, my lord, you are tempted to compare your sons, I call on you to remember what I have done and what he has done. Acts are the fair test."

My lord was the most uneasy man I ever saw; even in his old face the blood came up. "I think this is not a very wisely chosen moment, Henry, for complaints," said he. "This takes away from the merit of your generosity."

"Do not deceive yourself, my lord," said Mr. Henry. "This injustice is not done from generosity to him, but in obedience to yourself."

"Before strangers . . ." begins my lord, still more unhappily affected.

"There is no one but Mackellar here," said Mr. Henry; "he is my friend. And, my lord, as you make him no stranger to your frequent blame, it were hard if I must keep him one to a thing so rare as my defence."

Almost I believe my lord would have rescinded his decision; but the Master was on the watch.

"Ah, Henry, Henry," says he, "you are the best of us still. Rugged and true! Ah, man, I wish I was as good."

And at that instance of his favourite's generosity, my lord desisted from his hesitation, and the deed was signed.

As soon as it could be brought about, the land of Ochterhall was sold for much below its value, and the money paid over to our leech and sent by some private carriage into France. Or so he said; though I have suspected since it did not go so far. And now here was all the man's business brought to a successful head, and his pockets once more bulging with our gold; and yet the point for which we had consented to this sacrifice was still denied us, and the visitor still lingered on at Durrisdeer. Whether in malice, or because the time was not yet come for his adventures to the Indies, or because he had hopes of his design on Mrs. Henry, or from the orders of the government, who shall say? but linger he did and that for weeks.

You will observe I say: from the orders of government; for about this time, the man's disreputable secret trickled out.

The first hint I had was from a tenant, who commented on the Master's stay and yet more on his security; for this tenant was a Jacobitish sympathiser, and had lost a son at Culloden, which gave him the more critical eye. "There is one thing," said he, "that I cannot but think strange; and that is how he got to Cockermouth."

"To Cockermouth?" said I, with a sudden memory of my first wonder on beholding the man disembark so *point-de-vice* after so long a voyage.

"Why, yes," says the tenant, "it was there he was picked up by Captain Crail. You thought he had come from France by sea? And so we all did."

I turned this news a little in my head, and then carried it to Mr. Henry. "Here is an odd circumstance," said I, and told him.

"What matters how he came, Mackellar, so long as he is here?" groans Mr. Henry.

"No, sir," said I, "but think again! Does not this smack a little of some government connivance? You know how much we have wondered already at the man's security."

"Stop," said Mr. Henry. "Let me think of this." And as he thought there came that grim smile upon his face that was a little like the Master's. "Give me paper," said he. And he sat without another word and wrote to a gentleman of his acquaintance—I will name no unnecessary names, but he was one in a high place. This letter I despatched by the only hand I could depend upon in such a case, Macconochie's; and the old man rode hard, for he was back with the reply, before even my eagerness had ventured to expect him. Again, as he read it, Mr. Henry had the same grim smile.

"This is the best you have done for me yet, Mackellar," says he. "With this in my hand, I will give him a shog. Watch for us at dinner."

At dinner accordingly, Mr. Henry proposed some very public appearance for the Master; and my lord, as he had hoped, objected to the danger of the course.

"O," says Mr. Henry, very easily, "you need no longer keep this up with me. I am as much in the secret as yourself."

"In the secret?" says my lord. "What do you mean, Henry? I give you my word I am in no secret from which you are excluded."

The Master had changed countenance, and I saw he was struck in a joint of his harness.

"How?" says Mr. Henry, turning to him with a huge appearance of surprise. "I see you serve your masters very faithfully; but I had thought you would have been humane enough to set your father's mind at rest."

"What are you talking of? I refuse to have my business publicly discussed. I order this to cease," cries the Master very foolishly and passionately, and indeed more like a child than a man.

"So much discretion was not looked for at your hands, I can assure you," continued Mr. Henry. "For see what my correspondent writes"—unfolding the paper—" 'It is, of course, in the interests both of the government and the gentleman whom we may perhaps best continue to call Mr. Bally, to keep this understanding secret; but it was never meant his own family should continue to endure the suspense you paint so feelingly; and I am pleased mine should be the hand to set these fears at rest. Mr. Bally is as safe in Great Britain as yourself.' "

"Is this possible?" cries my lord, looking at his son, with a great deal of wonder and still more of suspicion in his face.

"My dear father," says the Master, already much recovered, "I am overjoyed that this may be disclosed. My own instructions direct from London bore a very contrary sense, and I was charged to keep the indulgence secret from every one, yourself not excepted, and indeed yourself expressly named—as I can show in black and white, unless I have destroyed the letter. They must have changed their mind very swiftly, for the whole matter is still quite fresh; or rather Henry's correspondent must have misconceived that part, as he seems to have misconceived the rest. To tell you the truth, sir," he continued, getting visibly more easy, "I had supposed this unexplained favour to a rebel was the effect of some application from yourself; and the injunction to secrecy among my family the result of a desire on your part to conceal your kindness. Hence I was the more careful to obey orders. It remains now to guess by what other channel indulgence can have flowed on so notorious an offender as myself; for I do not think your son need defend himself from what seems hinted at in Henry's letter. I have never yet heard of a Durrisdeer who was a turncoat or a spy," says he, proudly.

And so it seemed he had swum out of this danger unharmed; but this was to reckon without a blunder he had made, and without the pertinacity of Mr. Henry, who was now to show he had something of his brother's spirit.

"You say the matter is still fresh," says Mr. Henry.

"It is recent," says the Master, with a fair show of stoutness and yet not without a quaver.

"Is it so recent as that?" asked Mr. Henry, like a man a little puzzled, and spreading his letter forth again.

In all the letter there was no word as to the date; but how was the Master to know that?

"It seemed to come late enough for me," says he, with a laugh. And at the sound of that laugh, which rang false like a cracked bell, my lord looked at him again across the table, and I saw his old lips draw together close.

"No," said Mr. Henry, still glancing on his letter, "but I remember your expression. You said it was very fresh."

And here we had a proof of our victory, and the strongest instance yet of my lord's incredible indulgence; for what must he do but interfere to save his favourite from exposure!

"I think, Henry," says he, with a kind of pitiful eagerness, "I think we need dispute no more. We are all rejoiced at last to find

your brother safe; we are all at one on that; and as grateful subjects, we can do no less than drink to the King's health and
bounty."

Thus was the Master extricated; but at least he had been put
to his defence, he had come lamely out, and the attraction of his
personal danger was now publicly plucked away from him. My
lord, in his heart of hearts, now knew his favourite to be a government spy; and Mrs. Henry (however she expiained the tale) was
notably cold in her behaviour to the discredited hero of romance.
Thus in the best fabric of duplicity, there is some weak point, if
you can strike it, which will loosen all; and if, by this fortunate
stroke, we had not shaken the idol, who can say how it might have
gone with us at the catastrophe?

And yet at the time we seemed to have accomplished nothing.
Before a day or two he had wiped off the ill-results of his discomfiture, and to all appearance, stood as high as ever. As for my
Lord Durrisdeer, he was sunk in parental partiality; it was not so
much love, which should be an active quality, as an apathy and
torpor of his other powers; and forgiveness (so to misapply a noble
word) flowed from him in sheer weakness, like the tears of senility.
Mrs. Henry's was a different case; and heaven alone knows what
he found to say to her or how he persuaded her from her contempt.
It is one of the worst things of sentiment, that the voice grows to
be more important than the words, and the speaker than that
which is spoken. But some excuse the Master must have found, or
perhaps he had even struck upon some art to wrest this exposure to his own advantage; for after a time of coldness, it seemed
as if things went worse than ever between him and Mrs. Henry.
They were then constantly together. I would not be thought to
cast one shadow of blame, beyond what is due to a half-wilful
blindness, on that unfortunate lady; but I do think, in these last
days, she was playing very near the fire; and whether I be wrong or
not in that, one thing is sure and quite sufficient: Mr. Henry
thought so. The poor gentleman sat for days in my room, so great
a picture of distress that I could never venture to address him; yet
it is to be thought he found some comfort even in my presence
and the knowledge of my sympathy. There were times, too, when
we talked, and a strange manner of talk it was; there was never a
person named, nor an individual circumstance referred to; yet we

had the same matter in our minds, and we were each aware of it. It is a strange art that can thus be practised: to talk for hours of a thing, and never name nor yet so much as hint at it. And I remember I wondered if it was by some such natural skill that the Master made love to Mrs. Henry all day long (as he manifestly did), yet never startled her into reserve.

To show how far affairs had gone with Mr. Henry, I will give some words of his, uttered (as I have cause not to forget) upon the 26th of February, 1757. It was unseasonable weather, a cast back into Winter: windless, bitter cold, the world all white with rime, the sky low and grey; the sea black and silent like a quarry hole. Mr. Henry sat close by the fire and debated (as was now common with him) whether "a man" should "do things," whether "interference was wise," and the like general propositions, which each of us particularly applied. I was by the window looking out, when there passed below me the Master, Mrs. Henry and Miss Katharine, that now constant trio. The child was running to and fro delighted with the frost; the Master spoke close in the lady's ear with what seemed (even from so far) a devilish grace of insinuation; and she on her part looked on the ground like a person lost in listening. I broke out of my reserve.

"If I were you, Mr. Henry," said I, "I would deal openly with my lord."

"Mackellar, Mackellar," said he, "you do not see the weakness of my ground. I can carry no such base thoughts to any one: to my father least of all; that would be to fall into the bottom of his scorn. The weakness of my ground," he continued, "lies in myself, that I am not one who engages love. I have their gratitude, they all tell me that: I have a rich estate of it! But I am not present in their minds; they are moved neither to think with me nor to think for me. There is my loss!" He got to his feet and trod down the fire. "But some method must be found, Mackellar," said he, looking at me suddenly over his shoulder; "some way must be found. I am a man of a great deal of patience—far too much—far too much. I begin to despise myself. And yet sure never was a man involved in such a toil!" He fell back to his brooding.

"Cheer up," said I. "It will burst of itself."

"I am far past anger now," says he, which had so little coherency with my own observation, that I let both fall.

Account of All That Passed on the Night of February 27th, 1757

ON THE EVENING OF THE INTERVIEW REFERRED TO, THE MASTER went abroad; he was abroad a great deal of the next day also, that fatal 27th; but where he went or what he did, we never concerned ourselves to ask until next day. If we had done so, and by any chance found out, it might have changed all. But as all we did was done in ignorance, and should be so judged, I shall so narrate these passages as they appeared to us in the moment of their birth, and reserve all that I since discovered for the time of its discovery. For I have now come to one of the dark parts of my narrative, and must engage the reader's indulgence for my patron.

All the 27th, that rigorous weather endured: a stifling cold; the folk passing about like smoking chimneys; the wide hearth in the hall piled high with fuel; some of the spring birds that had already blundered north into our neighbourhood, besieging the windows of the house or trotting on the frozen turf like things distracted. About noon there came a blink of sunshine; showing a very pretty, wintry, frosty landscape of white hills and woods, with Crail's lugger waiting for a wind under the Craig Head, and the smoke mounting straight into the air from every farm and cottage. With the coming of night, the haze closed in overhead; it fell dark and still and starless and exceedingly cold: a night the most unseasonable, fit for strange events.

Mrs. Henry withdrew, as was now her custom, very early. We had set ourselves of late to pass the evening with a game of cards; another mark that our visitor was wearying mightily of the life at Durrisdeer; and we had not been long at this, when my old lord slipped from his place beside the fire, and was off without a word to seek the warmth of bed. The three thus left together had neither love nor courtesy to share; not one of us would have sat up one instant to oblige another; yet from the influence of custom and as the cards had just been dealt, we continued the form of playing out the round. I should say we were late sitters; and though my lord had departed earlier than was his custom, twelve was already gone some time upon the clock, and the servants long ago in bed. Another thing I should say, that although I never saw the Master anyway affected with liquor, he had been drinking freely and was perhaps (although he showed it not) a trifle heated.

Anyway, he now practised one of his transitions; and so soon as the door closed behind my lord, and without the smallest change of voice, shifted from ordinary civil talk into a stream of insult.

"My dear Henry, it is yours to play," he had been saying, and now continued: "It is a very strange thing how, even in so small a matter as a game of cards, you display your rusticity. You play, Jacob, like a bonnet laird, or a sailor in a tavern. The same dulness, the same petty greed, *cette lenteur d'hébété qui me fait rager;* it is strange I should have such a brother. Even Squaretoes has a certain vivacity when his stake is imperilled; but the dreariness of a game with you, I positively lack language to depict."

Mr. Henry continued to look at his cards, as though very maturely considering some play; but his mind was elsewhere.

"Dear God, will this never be done?" cries the Master. *"Quel lourdeau!* But why do I trouble you with French expressions, which are lost on such an ignoramus? A *lourdeau,* my dear brother, is as we might say a bumpkin, a clown, a clodpole: a fellow without grace, lightness, quickness; any gift of pleasing, any natural brilliancy: such a one as you shall see, when you desire, by looking in the mirror. I tell you these things for your good, I assure you; and besides, Squaretoes" (looking at me and stifling a yawn), "it is one of my diversions in this very dreary spot, to toast you and your master at the fire like chestnuts. I have great pleasure in your case, for I observe the nickname (rustic as it is) has always the power to make you writhe. But sometimes I have more trouble with this dear fellow here, who seems to have gone to sleep upon his cards. Do you not see the applicability of the epithet I have just explained, dear Henry? Let me show you. For instance, with all those solid qualities which I delight to recognise in you, I never knew a woman who did not prefer me—nor, I think," he continued, with the most silken deliberation, "I think—who did not continue to prefer me."

Mr. Henry laid down his cards. He rose to his feet very softly, and seemed all the while like a person in deep thought. "You coward!" he said gently, as if to himself. And then, with neither hurry nor any particular violence, he struck the Master in the mouth.

The Master sprang to his feet like one transfigured; I had never seen the man so beautiful. "A blow!" he cried. "I would not take a blow from God Almighty."

"Lower your voice," said Mr. Henry. "Do you wish my father to interfere for you again?"

"Gentlemen, gentlemen," I cried, and sought to come between them.

The Master caught me by the shoulder, held me at arm's length, and still addressing his brother, "Do you know what this means?" said he.

"It was the most deliberate act of my life," says Mr. Henry.

"I must have blood, I must have blood for this," says the Master.

"Please God, it shall be yours," said Mr. Henry; and he went to the wall and took down a pair of swords that hung there with others, naked. These he presented to the Master by the points. "Mackellar shall see us play fair," said Mr. Henry. "I think it very needful."

"You need insult me no more," said the Master, taking one of the swords at random. "I have hated you all my life."

"My father is but newly gone to bed," said Mr. Henry. "We must go somewhere forth of the house."

"There is an excellent place in the long shrubbery," said the Master.

"Gentlemen," said I, "shame upon you both! Sons of the same mother, would you turn against the life she gave you?"

"Even so, Mackellar," said Mr. Henry, with the same perfect quietude of manner he had shown throughout.

"It is what I will prevent," said I.

And now here is a blot upon my life. At these words of mine, the Master turned his blade against my bosom; I saw the light run along the steel; and I threw up my arms and fell to my knees before him on the floor. "No, no," I cried, like a baby.

"We shall have no more trouble with him," said the Master. "It is a good thing to have a coward in the house."

"We must have light," said Mr. Henry, as though there had been no interruption.

"This trembler can bring a pair of candles," said the Master.

To my shame be it said, I was still so blinded with the flashing of that bare sword, that I volunteered to bring a lantern.

"We do not need a l-l-lantern," says the Master, mocking me.

"There is no breath of air. Come, get to your feet, take a pair of lights, and go before. I am close behind with this—" making the blade glitter as he spoke.

I took up the candlesticks and went before them, steps that I would give my hand to recall; but a coward is a slave at the best; and even as I went, my teeth smote each other in my mouth. It was as he had said, there was no breath stirring: a windless stricture of frost had bound the air; and as we went forth in the shine of the candles, the blackness was like a roof over our heads. Never a word was said, there was never a sound but the creaking of our steps along the frozen path. The cold of the night fell about me like a bucket of water; I shook as I went with more than terror; but my companions, bareheaded like myself and fresh from the warm hall, appeared not even conscious of the change.

"Here is the place," said the Master. "Set down the candles."

I did as he bid me, and presently the flames went up as steady as in a chamber in the midst of the frosted trees, and I beheld these two brothers take their places.

"The light is something in my eyes," said the Master.

"I will give you every advantage," replied Mr. Henry, shifting his ground, "for I think you are about to die." He spoke rather sadly than otherwise, yet there was a ring in his voice.

"Henry Durie," said the Master, "two words before I begin. You are a fencer, you can hold a foil; you little know what a change it makes to hold a sword! And by that I know you are to fall. But see how strong is my situation! If you fall, I shift out of this country to where my money is before me. If I fall, where are you? My father, your wife who is in love with me—as you very well know—your child even who prefers me to yourself:—how will these avenge me! Had you thought of that, dear Henry?" He looked at his brother with a smile; then made a fencing-room salute.

Never a word said Mr. Henry, but saluted too, and the swords rang together.

I am no judge of the play, my head besides was gone with cold and fear and horror; but it seems that Mr. Henry took and kept the upper-hand from the engagement, crowding in upon his foe with a contained and glowing fury. Nearer and nearer he crept upon the man till, of a sudden, the Master leaped back with a little sobbing oath; and I believe the movement brought the light once more against his eyes. To it they went again, on the fresh ground;

but now methought closer, Mr. Henry pressing more outrageously, the Master beyond doubt with shaken confidence. For it is beyond doubt he now recognized himself for lost, and had some taste of the cold agony of fear; or he had never attempted the foul stroke. I cannot say I followed it, my untrained eye was never quick enough to seize details, but it appears he caught his brother's blade with his left hand, a practice not permitted. Certainly Mr. Henry only saved himself by leaping on one side; as certainly the Master, lunging in the air, stumbled on his knee, and before he could move, the sword was through his body.

I cried out with a stifled scream, and ran in; but the body was already fallen to the ground, where it writhed a moment like a trodden worm, and then lay motionless.

"Look at his left hand," said Mr. Henry.

"It is all bloody," said I.

"On the inside?" said he.

"It is cut on the inside," said I.

"I thought so," said he, and turned his back.

I opened the man's clothes; the heart was quite still, it gave not a flutter.

"God forgive us, Mr. Henry!" said I. "He is dead."

"Dead?" he repeated, a little stupidly; and then with a rising tone, "Dead? dead?" says he, and suddenly cast his bloody sword upon the ground.

"What must we do?" said I. "Be yourself, sir. It is too late now: you must be yourself."

He turned and stared at me. "O, Mackellar!" says he, and put his face in his hands.

I plucked him by the coat. "For God's sake, for all our sakes, be more courageous!" said I. "What must we do?"

He showed me his face with the same stupid stare. "Do?" says he. And with that his eye fell on the body, and "O!" he cries out, with his hand to his brow, as if he had never remembered; and turning from me, made off towards the house of Durrisdeer at a strange stumbling run.

I stood a moment mused; then it seemed to me my duty lay most plain on the side of the living; and I ran after him, leaving the candles on the frosty ground and the body lying in their light under the trees. But run as I pleased, he had the start of me, and was got into the house, and up to the hall, where I found him standing before the fire with his face once more in his hands, and as he so stood, he visibly shuddered.

"Mr. Henry, Mr. Henry," I said, "this will be the ruin of us all."

"What is this that I have done?" cries he, and then, looking upon me with a countenance that I shall never forget, "Who is to tell the old man?" he said.

The word knocked at my heart; but it was no time for weakness. I went and poured him out a glass of brandy. "Drink that," said I, "drink it down." I forced him to swallow it like a child; and, being still perished with the cold of the night, I followed his example.

"It has to be told, Mackellar," said he. "It must be told." And he fell suddenly in a seat—my old lord's seat by the chimney-side —and was shaken with dry sobs.

Dismay came upon my soul; it was plain there was no help in Mr. Henry. "Well," said I, "sit there, and leave all to me." And taking a candle in my hand, I set forth out of the room in the dark house. There was no movement; I must suppose that all had gone unobserved; and I was now to consider how to smuggle through the rest with the like secrecy. It was no hour for scruples; and I opened my lady's door without so much as a knock, and passed boldly in.

"There is some calamity happened," she cried, sitting up in bed.

"Madam," said I, "I will go forth again into the passage; and do you get as quickly as you can into your clothes. There is much to be done."

She troubled me with no questions, nor did she keep me waiting. Ere I had time to prepare a word of that which I must say to her, she was on the threshold signing me to enter.

"Madam," said I, "if you cannot be very brave, I must go else-where; for if no one helps me tonight, there is an end of the house of Durrisdeer."

"I am very courageous," said she; and she looked at me with a sort of smile, very painful to see, but very brave too.

"It has come to a duel," said I.

"A duel?" she repeated. "A duel! Henry and——"

"And the Master," said I. "Things have been borne so long, things of which you know nothing, which you would not believe if I should tell. But to-night it went too far, and when he insulted you——"

"Stop," said she. "He? Who?"

"O madam!" cried I, my bitterness breaking forth, "do you ask me such a question? Indeed, then, I may go elsewhere for help; there is none here!"

"I do not know in what I have offended you," said she. "Forgive me; put me out of this suspense."

But I dared not tell her yet; I felt not sure of her; and at the doubt and under the sense of impotence it brought with it, I turned on the poor woman with something near to anger.

"Madam," said I, "we are speaking of two men: one of them insulted you, and you ask me which. I will help you to the answer. With one of these men you have spent all your hours: has the other reproached you? To one you have been always kind; to the other, as God sees me and judges between us two, I think not always: has his love ever failed you? To-night one of these two men told the other, in my hearing—the hearing of a hired stranger—that you were in love with him. Before I say one word, you shall answer your own question: Which was it? Nay, madam, you shall answer me another: If it has come to this dreadful end, whose fault is it?"

She stared at me like one dazzled. "Good God!" she said once, in a kind of bursting exclamation; and then a second time, in a whisper to herself, "Great God!—In the name of mercy, Mackellar, what is wrong?" she cried. "I am made up; I can hear all."

"You are not fit to hear," said I. "Whatever it was, you shall say first it was your fault."

"Oh!" she cried, with a gesture of wringing her hands, "this man will drive me mad! Can you not put *me* out of your thoughts?"

"I think not once of you," I cried. "I think of none but my dear unhappy master."

"Ah!" she cried, with her hand to her heart, "is Henry dead?"

"Lower your voice," said I. "The other."

I saw her sway like something stricken by the wind; and I know not whether in cowardice or misery, turned aside and looked upon the floor. "These are dreadful tidings," said I at length, when her silence began to put me in some fear; "and you and I behove to be the more bold if the house is to be saved." Still she answered nothing. "There is Miss Katharine besides," I added: "unless we bring this matter through, her inheritance is like to be of shame."

I do not know if it was the thought of her child or the naked word shame, that gave her deliverance; at least I had no sooner spoken than a sound passed her lips, the like of it I never heard; it was as though she had lain buried under a hill and sought to move that burthen. And the next moment she had found a sort of voice.

"It was a fight," she whispered. "It was not——?" and she paused upon the word.

"It was a fair fight on my dear master's part," said I. "As for the other, he was slain in the very act of a foul stroke."

"Not now!" she cried.

"Madam," said I, "hatred of that man glows in my bosom like a burning fire; ay, even now he is dead. God knows, I would have stopped the fighting, had I dared. It is my shame I did not. But when I saw him fall, if I could have spared one thought from pitying of my master, it had been to exult in that deliverance."

I do not know if she marked; but her next words were: "My lord?"

"That shall be my part," said I.

"You will not speak to him as you have to me?" she asked.

"Madam," said I, "have you not some one else to think of? Leave my lord to me."

"Some one else?" she repeated.

"Your husband," said I. She looked at me with a countenance illegible. "Are you going to turn your back on him?" I asked.

Still she looked at me; then her hand went to her heart again. "No," said she.

"God bless you for that word!" I said. "Go to him now where he sits in the hall; speak to him—it matters not what you say; give him your hand; say, 'I know all'—if God gives you grace enough, say, 'Forgive me.' "

"God strengthen you, and make you merciful," said she. "I will go to my husband."

"Let me light you there," said I, taking up the candle.

"I will find my way in the dark," she said, with a shudder, and I think the shudder was at me.

So we separated, she down-stairs to where a little light glimmered in the hall-door, I along the passage to my lord's room. It seems hard to say why, but I could not burst in on the old man as I could on the young woman; with whatever reluctance, I must knock. But his old slumbers were light, or perhaps he slept not; and at the first summons I was bidden enter.

He too sat up in bed; very aged and bloodless he looked; and whereas he had a certain largeness of appearance when dressed, for daylight, he now seemed frail and little, and his face (the wig being laid aside) not bigger than a child's. This daunted me; nor less, the haggard surmise of misfortune in his eye. Yet his voice was even peaceful as he inquired my errand. I sat my candle down upon a chair, leaned on the bed-foot, and looked at him.

"Lord Durrisdeer," said I, "it is very well known to you that I am a partisan in your family."

"I hope we are none of us partisans," said he. "That you love my son sincerely, I have always been glad to recognise."

"O, my lord, we are past the hour of these civilities," I replied. "If we are to save anything out of the fire, we must look the fact in its bare countenance. A partisan I am; partisans we have all been; it is as a partisan that I am here in the middle of the night to plead before you. Hear me; before I go, I will tell you why."

"I would always hear you, Mr. Mackellar," said he, "and that at any hour, whether of the day or night, for I would be always sure you had a reason. You spoke once before to very proper purpose; I have not forgotten that."

"I am here to plead the cause of my master," I said. "I need not tell you how he acts. You know how he is placed. You know with what generosity he has always met your other—met your wishes," I corrected myself, stumbling at that name of son. "You know—you must know—what he has suffered—what he has suffered about his wife."

"Mr. Mackellar!" cried my lord, rising in bed like a bearded lion.

"You said you would hear me," I continued. "What you do not know, what you should know, one of the things I am here to speak of—is the persecution he must bear in private. Your back is not turned, before one whom I dare not name to you falls upon him with the most unfeeling taunts; twits him—pardon me, my lord! twits him with your partiality, calls him Jacob, calls him clown, pursues him with ungenerous raillery, not to be borne by man. And let but one of you appear, instantly he changes; and my master must smile and courtesy to the man who has been feeding him with insults; I know—for I have shared in some of it, and I tell you the life is insupportable. All these months it has endured; it began with the man's landing; it was by the name of Jacob that my master was greeted the first night."

My lord made a movement as if to throw aside the clothes and rise. "If there be any truth in this——" said he.

"Do I look like a man lying?" I interrupted, checking him with my hand.

"You should have told me at first," he said.

"Ah, my lord, indeed I should, and you may well hate the face of this unfaithful servant!" I cried.

"I will take order," said he, "at once." And again made the movement to rise.

Again I checked him. "I have not done," said I. "Would God I had! All this my dear, unfortunate patron has endured without help or countenance. Your own best word, my lord, was only gratitude. Oh, but he was your son, too! He had no other father. He was hated in the country, God knows how unjustly. He had a loveless marriage. He stood on all hands without affection or support, dear, generous, ill-fated, noble heart."

"Your tears do you much honor and me much shame," says my lord, with a palsied trembling. "But you do me some injustice. Henry has been ever dear to me, very dear. James (I do not deny it, Mr. Mackellar), James is perhaps dearer; you have not seen my James in quite a favourable light; he has suffered under his misfortunes; and we can only remember how great and how unmerited these were. And even now his is the more affectionate nature. But I will not speak of him. All that you say of Henry is most true; I do not wonder, I know him to be very magnanimous; you will say I trade upon the knowledge? It is possible; there are dangerous virtues, virtues that tempt the encroacher. Mr. Mackellar, I will make it up to him; I will take order with all this. I have been weak; and what is worse, I have been dull."

"I must not hear you blame yourself, my lord, with that which I have yet to tell upon my conscience," I replied. "You have not been weak; you have been abused by a devilish dissembler. You saw yourself how he had deceived you in the matter of his danger; he has deceived you throughout in every step of his career. I wish to pluck him from your heart; I wish to force your eyes upon your other son; ah, you have a son there!"

"No, no," said he, "two sons—I have two sons."

I made some gesture of despair that struck him; he looked at me with a changed face. "There is much worse behind?" he asked, his voice dying as it rose upon the question.

"Much worse," I answered. "This night he said these words to Mr. Henry: 'I have never known a woman who did not prefer me to you, and I think who did not continue to prefer me.' "

"I will hear nothing against my daughter," he cried; and from his readiness to stop me in this direction, I conclude his eyes were not so dull as I had fancied, and he had looked on not without anxiety upon the siege of Mrs. Henry.

"I think not of blaming her," cried I. "It is not that. These words were said in my hearing to Mr. Henry; and if you find them not yet plain enough, these others but a little after: 'Your wife who is in love with me.' "

"They have quarrelled?" he said.

I nodded.

"I must fly to them," he said, beginning once again to leave his bed.

"No, no!" I cried, holding forth my hands.

"You do not know," said he. "These are dangerous words."

"Will nothing make you understand, my lord?" said I.

His eyes besought me for the truth.

I flung myself on my knees by the bedside. "O my lord," cried I, "think on him you have left, think of this poor sinner whom you begot, whom your wife bore to you, whom we have none of us strengthened as we could; think of him, not of yourself; he is the other sufferer—think of him! That is the door for sorrow, Christ's door, God's door: O, it stands open. Think of him, even as he thought of you. *Who is to tell the old man?*—these were his words. It was for that I came; that is why I am here pleading at your feet."

"Let me get up," he cried, thrusting me aside, and was on his feet before myself. His voice shook like a sail in the wind, yet he spoke with a good loudness; his face was like the snow, but his eyes were steady and dry. "Here is too much speech!" said he. "Where was it?"

"In the shrubbery," said I.

"And Mr. Henry?" he asked. And when I had told him he knotted his old face in thought.

"And Mr. James?" says he.

"I have left him lying," said I, "beside the candles."

"Candles?" he cried. And with that he ran to the window,

opened it, and looked abroad. "It might be spied from the road."

"Where none goes by at such an hour," I objected.

"It makes no matter," he said. "One night. Hark!" cries he. "What is that?"

It was the sound of men very guardedly rowing in the bay; and I told him so.

"The freetraders," said my lord. "Run at once, Mackellar, put these candles out. I will dress in the meanwhile; and when you return we can debate on what is wisest."

I groped my way down-stairs, and out at the door. From quite a far way off a sheen was visible, making points of brightness in the shrubbery; in so black a night it might have been remarked for miles; and I blamed myself bitterly for my incaution: how much more sharply when I reached the place! One of the candle-sticks was overthrown, and that taper quenched. The other burned steadily by itself, and made a broad space of light upon the frosted ground. All within that circle seemed, by the force of contrast and the overhanging blackness, brighter than by day. And there was the bloodstain in the midst; and a little further off Mr. Henry's sword, the pommel of which was a sliver; but of the body not a trace. My heart thumped upon my ribs, the hair stirred upon my scalp, as I stood there staring; so strange was the sight, so dire the fears it wakened. I looked right and left; the ground was so hard it told no story. I stood and listened till my ears ached, but the night was hollow about me like an empty church; not even a ripple stirred upon the shore; it seemed you might have heard a pin drop in the county.

I put the candle out, and the blackness fell about me groping dark; it was like a crowd surrounding me; and I went back to the house of Durrisdeer, with my chin upon my shoulder, startling, as I went, with craven suppositions. In the door a figure moved to meet me, and I had near screamed with terror ere I recognised Mrs. Henry.

"Have you told him?" says she.

"It was he who sent me," said I. "It is gone. But why are you here?"

"It is gone!" she repeated. "What is gone?"

"The body," said I. "Why are you not with your husband?"

"Gone?" said she. "You cannot have looked. Come back."

"There is no light now," said I. "I dare not."

"I can see in the dark. I have been standing here so long—so long," said she. "Come; give me your hand."

We returned to the shrubbery hand in hand, and to the fatal place.

"Take care of the blood," said I.

"Blood?" she cried, and started violently back.

"I suppose it will be," said I. "I am like a blind man."

"No," said she, "nothing! Have you not dreamed?"

"Ah, would to God we had!" cried I.

She spied the sword, picked it up, and, seeing the blood, let it fall again with her hands thrown wide. "Ah!" she cried. And then, with an instant courage, handled it the second time and thrust it to the hilt into the frozen ground. "I will take it back and clean it properly," says she, and again looked about her on all sides. "It cannot be that he was dead?" she added.

"There was no flutter of his heart," said I, and then remembering: "Why are you not with your husband?"

"It is no use," she said, "he will not speak to me."

"Not speak to you?" I repeated. "O, you have not tried!"

"You have a right to doubt me," she replied, with a gentle dignity.

At this, for the first time, I was seized with sorrow for her. "God knows, madam," I cried, "God knows I am not so hard as I appear; on this dreadful night, who can veneer his words? But I am a friend to all who are not Henry Durie's enemies!"

"It is hard, then, you should hesitate about his wife," said she.

I saw all at once, like the rending of a veil, how nobly she had borne this unnatural calamity, and how generously my reproaches.

"We must go back and tell this to my lord," said I.

"Him I cannot face," she cried.

"You will find him the least moved of all of us," said I.

"And yet I cannot face him," said she.

"Well," said I, "you can return to Mr. Henry; I will see my lord."

As we walked back, I bearing the candlesticks, she the sword—a strange burthen for that woman—she had another thought. "Should we tell Henry?" she asked.

"Let my lord decide," said I.

My lord was nearly dressed when I came to his chamber. He

heard me with a frown. "The freetraders," said he. "But whether dead or alive?"

"I thought him—" said I, and paused, ashamed of the word.

"I know; but you may very well have been in error. Why should they remove him if not living?" he asked. "O, here is a great door of hope. It must be given out that he departed—as he came—without any note of preparation. We must save all scandal."

I saw he had fallen, like the rest of us, to think mainly of the house. Now that all the living members of the family were plunged in irremediable sorrow, it was strange how we turned to that conjoint abstraction of the family itself, and sought to bolster up the airy nothing of its reputation: not the Duries only, but the hired steward himself.

"Are we to tell Mr. Henry?" I asked him.

"I will see," said he. "I am going first to visit him, then I go forth with you to view the shrubbery and consider."

We went down-stairs into the hall. Mr. Henry sat by the table with his head upon his hand, like a man of stone. His wife stood a little back from him, her hand at her mouth; it was plain she could not move him. My old lord walked very steadily to where his son was sitting; he had a steady countenance, too, but methought a little cold; when he was come quite up, he held out both his hands and said: "My son!"

With a broken, strangled cry, Mr. Henry leaped up and fell on his father's neck, crying and weeping, the most pitiful sight that ever a man witnessed. "O father," he cried, "you know I loved him; you know I loved him in the beginning; I could have died for him—you know that! I would have given my life for him and you. O say you know that! O say you can forgive me! O father, father, what have I done, what have I done? and we used to be bairns together!" and wept and sobbed, and fondled the old man, and clutched him about the neck, with the passion of a child in terror.

And then he caught sight of his wife, you would have thought for the first time, where she stood weeping to hear him; and in a moment had fallen at her knees. "And O my lass," he cried, "you must forgive me, too! Not your husband—I have only been the ruin of your life. But you knew me when I was a lad; there was no harm in Henry Durie then; he meant aye to be a friend to you. It's him—it's the old bairn that played with you—O can ye never, never forgive him?"

Throughout all this my lord was like a cold, kind spectator with his wits about him. At the first cry, which was indeed enough to call the house about us, he had said to me over his shoulder, "Close the door." And now he nodded to himself.

"We may leave him to his wife now," says he. "Bring a light, Mr. Mackellar."

Upon my going forth again with my lord, I was aware of a strange phenomenon; for though it was quite dark, and the night not yet old, methought I smelt the morning. At the same time there went a tossing through the branches of the evergreens, so that they sounded like a quiet sea; and the air puffed at times against our faces, and the flame of the candle shook. We made the more speed, I believe, being surrounded by this bustle; visited the scene of the duel, where my lord looked upon the blood with stoicism; and passing farther on toward the landing-place, came at last upon some evidences of the truth. For first of all, where there was a pool across the path, the ice had been trodden in, plainly by more than one man's weight; next, and but a little further, a young tree was broken; and down by the landing-place, where the trader's boats were usually beached, another stain of blood marked where the body must have been infallibly set down to rest the bearers.

This stain we set ourselves to wash away with the sea-water, carrying it in my lord's hat; and as we were thus engaged, there came up a sudden, moaning gust and left us instantly benighted.

"It will come to snow," says my lord; "and the best thing that we could hope. Let us go back now; we can do nothing in the dark."

As we went houseward, the wind being again subsided, we were aware of a strong pattering noise about us in the night; and when we issued from the shelter of the trees, we found it raining smartly.

Throughout the whole of this, my lord's clearness of mind, no less than his activity of body, had not ceased to minister to my amazement. He set the crown upon it in the council we held on our return. The freetraders had certainly secured the Master, though whether dead or alive we were still left to our conjectures; the rain would, long before day, wipe out all marks of the transaction; by this we must profit: the Master had unexpectedly come after the fall of night, it must now be given out he had as suddenly departed before the break of day; and to make all this plausible, it now only remained for me to mount into the man's chamber, and pack and conceal his baggage. True, we still lay at the discretion of the traders; but that was the incurable weakness of our guilt.

I heard him, as I said, with wonder, and hastened to obey. Mr. and Mrs. Henry were gone from the hall; my lord, for warmth's sake, hurried to his bed; there was still no sign of stir among the servants, and as I went up the tower stair, and entered the dead man's room, a horror of solitude weighed upon my mind. To my extreme surprise, it was all in the disorder of departure. Of his three portmanteaus, two were ready locked, the third lay open and near full. At once there flashed upon me some suspicion of the truth. The man had been going after all; he had but waited upon Crail, as Crail waited upon the wind; early in the night, the seamen had perceived the weather changing; the boat had come to give notice of the change and call the passenger aboard, and the boat's crew had stumbled on him lying in his blood. Nay, and there was more behind. This prearranged departure shed some light upon his inconceivable insult of the night before; it was a parting shot; hatred being no longer checked by policy. And for another thing, the nature of that insult, and the conduct of Mrs. Henry, pointed to one conclusion: which I have never verified, and can now never verify until the great assize: the conclusion that he had at last forgotten himself, had gone too far in his advances, and had been rebuffed. It can never be verified, as I say; but as I thought of it that morning among his baggage, the thought was sweet to me like honey.

Into the open portmanteau I dipped a little ere I closed it. The most beautiful lace and linen, many suits of those fine plain clothes in which he loved to appear; a book or two, and those of the best, Cæsar's "Commentaries," a volume of Mr. Hobbes, the "Henriade" of M. de Voltaire, a book upon the Indies, one on the mathematics, far beyond where I have studied: these were what I observed with very mingled feelings. But in the open portmanteau, no papers of any description. This set me musing. It was possible the man was dead; but, since the traders had carried him away, not likely. It was possible he might still die of his wound:

but it was also possible he might not. And in this latter case I was determined to have the means of some defence.

One after another I carried his portmanteaus to a loft in the top of the house which we kept locked; went to my own room for my keys, and, returning to the loft, had the gratification to find two that fitted pretty well. In one of the portmanteaus there was a shagreen letter-case, which I cut open with my knife; and thenceforth (so far as any credit went) the man was at my mercy. Here was a vast deal of gallant correspondence, chiefly of his Paris days; and what was more to the purpose, here were the copies of his own reports to the English secretary, and the originals of the secretary's answers: a most damning series: such as to publish would be to wreck the Master's honour and to set a price upon his life. I chuckled to myself as I ran through the documents; I rubbed my hands, I sang aloud in my glee. Day found me at the pleasing task; nor did I then remit my diligence, except in so far as I went to the window—looked out for a moment, to see the frost quite gone, the world turned black again, and the rain and the wind driving in the bay—and to assure myself that the lugger was gone from its anchorage, and the Master (whether dead or alive) now tumbling on the Irish Sea.

It is proper I should add in this place the very little I have subsequently angled out upon the doings of that night. It took me a long while to gather it; for we dared not openly ask, and the freetraders regarded me with enmity, if not with scorn. It was near six months before we ever knew for certain that the man survived; and it was years before I learned from one of Crail's men, turned publican on his ill-gotten gain, some particulars which smack to me of truth. It seems the traders found the Master struggled on one elbow, and now staring round him, and now gazing at the candle or at his hand which was all bloodied, like a man stupid. Upon their coming, he would seem to have found his mind, bade them carry him aboard and hold their tongues; and on the captain asking how he had come in such a pickle, replied with a burst of passionate swearing, and incontinently fainted. They held some debate, but they were momently looking for a wind, they were highly paid to smuggle him to France, and did not care to delay. Besides which, he was well enough liked by these abominable wretches: they supposed him under capital sentence, knew not in what mischief he might have got his wound, and judged it a piece of good nature to remove him out of the way of danger. So he was taken aboard, recovered on the passage over, and was set ashore a convalescent at the Havre de Grace. What is truly notable: he said not a word to any one of the duel, and not a trader knows to this day in what quarrel, or by the hand of what adversary, he fell. With any other man I should have set this down to natural decency; with him, to pride. He could not bear to avow, perhaps even to himself, that he had been vanquished by one whom he had so much insulted and whom he so cruelly despised.

Summary of Events During the Master's Second Absence

OF THE HEAVY SICKNESS WHICH DECLARED ITSELF NEXT MORNING, I can think with equanimity as of the last unmingled trouble that befell my master; and even that was perhaps a mercy in disguise; for what pains of the body could equal the miseries of the mind? Mrs. Henry and I had the watching by the bed. My old lord called from time to time to take the news, but would not usually pass the door. Once, I remember, when hope was nigh gone, he stepped to the bedside, looked awhile in his son's face, and turned away with a singular gesture of the head and hand thrown up, that remains upon my mind as something tragic; such grief and such a scorn of sublunary things were there expressed. But the most of the time, Mrs. Henry and I had the room to ourselves, taking turns by night and bearing each other company by day, for it was dreary watching. Mr. Henry, his shaven head bound in a napkin, tossed to and fro without remission, beating the bed with his hands. His tongue never lay; his voice ran continuously like a river; so that my heart was weary with the sound of it. It was notable, and to me inexpressibly mortifying, that he spoke all the while on matters of no import: comings and goings, horses— which he was ever calling to have saddled, thinking perhaps (the poor soul!) that he might ride away from his discomfort—matters of the garden, the salmon nets, and (what I particularly raged to hear) continually of his affairs, cyphering figures and holding disputation with the tenantry. Never a word of his father or his wife, nor of the Master, save only for a day or two, when his mind dwelled entirely in the past and he supposed himself a boy again and upon some innocent child's play with his brother. What made this the more affecting: it appeared the Master had then run some peril of his life, for there was a cry—"O, Jamie will be drowned—O, save Jamie!" which he came over and over with a great deal of passion.

This, I say, was affecting, both to Mrs. Henry and myself; but the balance of my master's wanderings did him little justice. It seemed he had set out to justify his brother's calumnies; as though he was bent to prove himself a man of a dry nature, immersed in money-getting. Had I been there alone, I would not have troubled my thumb; but all the while, as I listened, I was estimating the effect on the man's wife, and telling myself that he fell lower every day. I was the one person on the surface of the globe that comprehended him, and I was bound there should be yet another. Whether he was to die there and his virtues perish; or whether he should save his days and come back to that inheritance of sorrows, his right memory: I was bound he should be heartily lamented in the one case and unaffectedly welcomed in the other, by the person he loved the most, his wife.

Finding no occasion of free speech, I bethought me at last of a kind of documentary disclosure; and for some nights, when I was off duty and should have been asleep, I gave my time to the preparation of that which I may call my budget. But this I found to be the easiest portion of my task, and that which remained, namely the presentation to my lady, almost more than I had fortitude to overtake. Several days I went about with my papers under my arm, spying for some juncture of talk to serve as introduction. I will not deny but that some offered; only when they did, my tongue clove to the roof of my mouth; and I think I might have been carrying about my packet till this day, had not a fortunate accident delivered me from all my hesitations. This was at night, when I was once more leaving the room, the thing not yet done, and myself in despair at my own cowardice.

"What do you carry about with you, Mr. Mackellar?" she asked. "These last days, I see you always coming in and out with the same armful."

I returned upon my steps without a word, laid the papers before her on the table, and left her to her reading. Of what that was, I am now to give you some idea; and the best will be to re-

produce a letter of my own which came first in the budget and of
which (according to an excellent habitude) I have preserved the
scroll. It will show too the moderation of my part in these affairs,
a thing which some have called recklessly in question.

DURRISDEER.

1757.

Honoured Madam,—I trust I would not step out of my place
without occasion; but I see how much evil has flowed in the
past to all of your noble house from that unhappy and secretive
fault of reticency, and the papers on which I venture to call your
attention are family papers and all highly worthy your acquaintance.

    I append a schedule with some necessary observations
           And am,
              Honoured Madam,
                Your ladyship's obliged, obedient servant,

Ephraim Mackellar.

SCHEDULE OF PAPERS.

A. Scroll of ten letters from Ephraim Mackellar to the Hon.
James Durie, Esq., by courtesy Master of Ballantrae during the
latter's residence in Paris: under dates . . . (*follow the dates*)
. . . *Nota:* to be read in connection with B. and C.

B. Seven original letters from the said M^r of Ballantrae to the
said E. Mackellar, under dates . . . (*follow the dates*).

C. Three original letters from the said M^r of Ballantrae to the
Hon. Henry Durie, Esq., under dates . . . (*follow the dates*)
. . . *Nota:* given me by Mr. Henry to answer: copies of my
answers A 4, A 5, and A 9 of these productions. The purport of
Mr. Henry's communications, of which I can find no scroll, may
be gathered from those of his unnatural brother.

D. A correspondence, original and scroll, extending over a
period of three years till January of the current year, between
the said M^r of Ballantrae and——, Under Secretary of State;
twenty-seven in all. *Nota:* found among the Master's papers.

Weary as I was with watching and distress of mind, it was impossible for me to sleep. All night long, I walked in my chamber,
revolving what should be the issue and sometimes repenting the
temerity of my immixture in affairs so private; and with the first

peep of the morning, I was at the sick-room door. Mrs. Henry had thrown open the shutters and even the window, for the temperature was mild. She looked steadfastly before her; where was nothing to see, or only the blue of the morning creeping among the woods. Upon the stir of my entrance, she did not so much as turn about her face: a circumstance from which I augured very ill.

"Madam," I began; and then again, "Madam;" but could make no more of it. Nor yet did Mrs. Henry come to my assistance with a word. In this pass I began gathering up the papers where they lay scattered on the table; and the first thing that struck me, their bulk appeared to have diminished. Once I ran them through, and twice; but the correspondence with the secretary of state, on which I had reckoned so much against the future, was nowhere to be found. I looked in the chimney; amid the smouldering embers, black ashes of paper fluttered in the draught; and at that my timidity vanished.

"Good God, madam," cried I, in a voice not fitting for a sick-room, "Good God, madam, what have you done with my papers?"

"I have burned them," said Mrs. Henry, turning about. "It is enough, it is too much, that you and I have seen them."

"This is a fine night's work that you have done!" cried I. "And all to save the reputation of a man that ate bread by the shedding of his comrades' blood, as I do by the shedding ink."

"To save the reputation of that family in which you are a servant, Mr. Mackellar," she returned, "and for which you have already done so much."

"It is a family I will not serve much longer," I cried, "for I am driven desperate. You have stricken the sword out of my hands; you have left us all defenceless. I had always these letters I could shake over his head; and now—what is to do? We are so falsely situate, we dare not show the man the door; the country would fly on fire against us; and I had this one hold upon him—and now it is gone—now he may come back to-morrow, and we must all sit down with him to dinner, go for a stroll with him on the terrace, or take a hand at cards, of all things, to divert his leisure! No, madam; God forgive you, if he can find it in his heart; for I cannot find it in mine."

"I wonder to find you so simple, Mr. Mackellar," said Mrs. Henry. "What does this man value reputation? But he knows how high we prize it; he knows we would rather die than make these letters public; and do you suppose he would not trade upon the knowledge? What you call your sword, Mr. Mackellar, and which had been one indeed against a man of any remnant of propriety, would have been but a sword of paper against him. He would smile in your face at such a threat. He stands upon his degradation, he makes that his strength; it is in vain to struggle with such characters." She cried out this last a little desperately, and then with more quiet: "No, Mr. Mackellar, I have thought upon this matter all night, and there is no way out of it. Papers or no papers, the door of this house stands open for him; he is the rightful heir, forsooth! If we sought to exclude him, all would redound against poor Henry, and I should see him stoned again upon the streets. Ah! if Henry dies, it is a different matter! They have broke the entail for their own good purposes; the estate goes to my daughter; and I shall see who sets a foot upon it. But if Henry lives, my poor Mr. Mackellar, and that man returns, we must suffer: only this time, it will be together."

On the whole, I was well pleased with Mrs. Henry's attitude of mind; nor could I even deny there was some cogency in that which she advanced about the papers.

"Let us say no more about it," said I. "I can only be sorry I trusted a lady with the originals, which was an unbusinesslike proceeding at the best. As for what I said of leaving the service of the family, it was spoken with the tongue only; and you may set your mind at rest. I belong to Durrisdeer, Mrs. Henry, as if I had been born there."

I must do her the justice to say she seemed perfectly relieved; so that we began this morning, as we were to continue for so many years, on a proper ground of mutual indulgence and respect.

The same day, which was certainly prededicate to joy, we observed the first signal of recovery in Mr. Henry; and about three of the following afternoon, he found his mind again, recognising me by name with the strongest evidences of affection. Mrs. Henry was also in the room, at the bed-foot: but it did not appear that he observed her. And indeed (the fever being gone) he was so weak that he made but the one effort and sank again into a lethargy. The course of his restoration was now slow but equal; every day, his appetite improved; every week, we were able to remark an increase both of strength and flesh; and before the end of the month, he was out of bed and had even begun to be carried in his chair upon the terrace.

It was perhaps at this time that Mrs. Henry and I were the most uneasy in mind. Apprehension for his days was at an end; and a worse fear succeeded. Every day we drew consciously nearer to a day of reckoning; and the days passed on, and still there was nothing. Mr. Henry bettered in strength, he held long talks with us on a great diversity of subjects, his father came and sat with him and went again; and still there was no reference to the late tragedy or to the former troubles which had brought it on. Did he remember, and conceal his dreadful knowledge? or was the whole blotted from his mind? this was the problem that kept us watching and trembling all day when we were in his company, and held us awake at night when we were in our lonely beds. We knew not even which alternative to hope for, both appearing so unnatural and pointing so directly to an unsound brain. Once this fear offered, I observed his conduct with sedulous particularity. Something of the child he exhibited: a cheerfulness quite foreign to his previous character, an interest readily aroused, and then very tenacious, in small matters which he had heretofore despised. When he was stricken down, I was his only confidant, and I may say his only friend, and he was on terms of division with his wife; upon his recovery, all was changed, the past forgotten, the wife first and even single in his thoughts. He turned to her with all his emotions like a child to its mother, and seemed secure of sympathy; called her in all his needs with something of that querulous familiarity that marks a certainty of indulgence; and I must say, in justice to the woman, he was never disappointed. To her, indeed, this changed behaviour was inexpressibly affecting; and I think she felt it secretly as a reproach; so that I have seen her, in early days, escape out of the room that she might indulge herself in weeping. But to me, the change appeared not natural; and viewing it along with all the rest, I began to wonder, with many head-shakings, whether his reason were perfectly erect.

As this doubt stretched over many years, endured indeed until my master's death, and clouded all our subsequent relations, I may well consider of it more at large. When he was able to resume some charge of his affairs, I had many opportunities to try him with precision. There was no lack of understanding, nor yet of authority; but the old continuous interest had quite departed; he grew readily fatigued and fell to yawning; and he carried into money relations, where it is certainly out of place, a facility that bordered upon slackness. True, since we had no longer the exactions of the Master to contend against, there was the less occasion to raise strictness into principle or do battle for a farthing. True again, there was nothing excessive in these relaxations, or I would have been no party to them. But the whole thing marked a change, very slight yet very perceptible; and though no man could say my master had gone at all out of his mind, no man could deny that he had drifted from his character. It was the same to the end, with his manner and appearance. Some of the heat of the fever lingered in his veins: his movements a little hurried, his speech notably more voluble, yet neither truly amiss. His whole mind stood open to happy impressions, welcoming these and making much of them; but the smallest suggestion of trouble or sorrow he received with visible impatience and dismissed again with immediate relief. It was to this temper that he owed the felicity of his later days; and yet here it was, if anywhere, that you could call the man insane. A great part of this life consists in contemplating what we cannot cure; but Mr. Henry, if he could not dismiss solicitude by an effort of the mind, must instantly and at whatever cost annihilate the cause of it; so that he played alternately the ostrich and the bull. It is to this strenuous cowardice of pain that I have to set down all the unfortunate and excessive steps of his subsequent career. Certainly this was the reason of his beating McManus, the groom, a thing so much out of all his former practice and which awakened so much comment at the time. It is to this again, that I must lay the total loss of near upon two hundred pounds, more than the half of which I could have saved if his impatience would have suffered me. But he preferred loss or any desperate extreme to a continuance of mental suffering.

All this has led me far from our immediate trouble: whether he remembered or had forgotten his late dreadful act; and if he remembered, in what light he viewed it. The truth burst upon us suddenly, and was indeed one of the chief surprises of my life. He had been several times abroad, and was now beginning to walk a little with an arm, when it chanced I should be left alone with him upon the terrace. He turned to me with a singular furtive smile, such as schoolboys use when in fault; and says he, in a private whisper and without the least preface: "Where have you buried him?"

I could not make one sound in answer.

"Where have you buried him?" he repeated. "I want to see his grave."

I conceived I had best take the bull by the horns. "Mr. Henry," said I, "I have news to give that will rejoice you exceedingly. In all human likelihood, your hands are clear of blood. I reason from certain indices; and by these it should appear your brother was not dead, but was carried in a swound on board the lugger. By now, he may be perfectly recovered."

What there was in his countenance, I could not read. "James?" he asked.

"Your brother James," I answered. "I would not raise a hope that may be found deceptive; but in my heart, I think it very probable he is alive."

"Ah!" says Mr. Henry; and suddenly rising from his seat with more alacrity than he had yet discovered, set one finger on my breast, and cried at me in a kind of screaming whisper, "Mackellar"—these were his words—"nothing can kill that man. He is not mortal. He is bound upon my back to all eternity—to all God's eternity!" says he, and, sitting down again, fell upon a stubborn silence.

A day or two after, with the same secret smile, and first looking about as if to be sure we were alone, "Mackellar," said he, "when you have any intelligence, be sure and let me know. We must keep an eye upon him, or he will take us when we least expect."

"He will not show face here again," said I.

"O yes, he will," said Mr. Henry. "Wherever I am there will he be." And again he looked all about him.

"You must not dwell upon this thought, Mr. Henry," said I.

"No," said he, "that is a very good advice. We will never think of it, except when you have news. And we do not know yet," he added: "he may be dead."

The manner of his saying this convinced me thoroughly of what I had scarce ventured to suspect: that so far from suffering any penitence from the attempt, he did but lament his failure. This was a discovery I kept to myself, fearing it might do him a prejudice with his wife. But I might have saved myself the trouble;

she had divined it for herself, and found the sentiment quite natural. Indeed I could not but say that there were three of us all of the same mind; nor could any news have reached Durrisdeer more generally welcome than tidings of the Master's death.

This brings me to speak of the exception, my old lord. As soon as my anxiety for my own master began to be relaxed, I was aware of a change in the old gentleman, his father, that seemed to threaten mortal consequences.

His face was pale and swollen; as he sat in the chimney-side with his Latin, he would drop off sleeping and the book roll in the ashes; some days he would drag his foot, others stumble in speaking. The amenity of his behaviour appeared more extreme; full of excuses for the least trouble, very thoughtful for all; to myself, of a most flattering civility. One day, that he had sent for his lawyer and remained a long while private, he met me as he was crossing the hall with painful footsteps, and took me kindly by the hand. "Mr. Mackellar," said he, "I have had many occasions to set a proper value on your services; and to-day, when I recast my will, I have taken the freedom to name you for one of my executors. I believe you bear love enough to our house to render me this service." At that very time, he passed the greater portion of his days in slumber, from which it was often difficult to rouse him; seemed to have lost all count of years and had several times (particularly on waking) called for his wife and for an old servant whose very gravestone was now green with moss. If I had been put to my oath, I must have declared he was incapable of testing; and yet there was never a will drawn more sensible in every trait, or showing a more excellent judgment both of persons and affairs.

His dissolution, though it took not very long, proceeded by infinitesimal gradations. His faculties decayed together steadily; the power of his limbs was almost gone, he was extremely deaf, his speech had sunk into mere mumblings; and yet to the end he managed to discover something of his former courtesy and kindness, pressing the hand of any that helped him, presenting me with one of his Latin books in which he had laboriously traced my name, and in a thousand ways reminding us of the greatness of that loss, which it might almost be said we had already suffered. To the end, the power of articulation returned to him in flashes: it seemed he had only forgotten the art of speech as a child forgets his lesson, and at times he would call some part of it to mind. On the last night of his life, he suddenly broke silence with these words from Virgil: "Gnatique patrisque, alma, precor, miserere," perfectly uttered and with a fitting accent. At the sudden clear sound of it, we started from our several occupations; but it was in vain we turned to him; he sat there silent and to all appearance fatuous. A little later, he was had to bed with more difficulty than ever before; and some time in the night, without any mortal violence, his spirit fled.

At a far later period, I chanced to speak of these particulars with a doctor of medicine, a man of so high a reputation that I scruple to adduce his name. By his view of it, father and son both suffered from the same affection: the father from the strain of his unnatural sorrows, the son perhaps in the excitation of the fever, each had ruptured a vessel on the brain; and there was probably (my doctor added) some predisposition in the family to accidents of that description. The father sank, the son recovered all the externals of a healthy man; but it is like there was some destruction in those delicate tissues where the soul resides and does her earthly business; her heavenly, I would fain hope, cannot be thus obstructed by material accidents. And yet upon a more mature opinion, it matters not one jot; for He who shall pass judgment on the records of our life is the same that formed us in frailty.

The death of my old lord was the occasion of a fresh surprise to us who watched the behaviour of his successor. To any considering mind, the two sons had between them slain their father; and he who took the sword might be even said to have slain him with his hand. But no such thought appeared to trouble my new lord. He was becomingly grave; I could scarce say sorrowful, or only with a pleasant sorrow; talking of the dead with a regretful cheerfulness, relating old examples of his character, smiling at them with a good conscience; and when the day of the funeral came round, doing the honours with exact propriety. I could perceive besides, that he found a solid gratification in his accession to the title; the which he was punctilious in exacting.

And now there came upon the scene a new character, and one that played his part too in the story; I mean the present lord, Alexander, whose birth (17th July, 1757) filled the cup of my poor master's happiness. There was nothing then left him to wish for; nor yet leisure to wish for it. Indeed there never was a parent so

fond and doting as he showed himself. He was continually uneasy
in his son's absence. Was the child abroad? the father would be
watching the clouds in case it rained. Was it night? he would rise
out of his bed to observe its slumbers. His conversation grew even
wearyful to strangers, since he talked of little but his son. In
matters relating to the estate, all was designed with a particular
eye to Alexander; and it would be—"Let us put it in hand at
once, that the wood may be grown against Alexander's majority;"
or "this will fall in again handsomely for Alexander's marriage."
Every day this absorption of the man's nature became more observable, with many touching and some very blameworthy particulars. Soon the child could walk abroad with him, at first on the
terrace hand in hand, and afterward at large about the policies;
and this grew to be my lord's chief occupation. The sound of their
two voices (audible a great way off, for they spoke loud) became
familiar in the neighbourhood; and for my part I found it more
agreeable than the sound of birds. It was pretty to see the pair
returning, full of briers, and the father as flushed and sometimes
as bemuddied as the child: they were equal sharers in all sorts of
boyish entertainment, digging in the beach, damming of streams,
and what not; and I have seen them gaze through a fence at cattle
with the same childish contemplation.

The mention of these rambles brings me to a strange scene of
which I was a witness. There was one walk I never followed myself
without emotion, so often had I gone there upon miserable
errands, so much had there befallen against the house of Durrisdeer. But the path lay handy from all points beyond the
Muckleross; and I was driven, although much against my will, to
take my use of it perhaps once in the two months. It befell when
Mr. Alexander was of the age of seven or eight, I had some business on the far side in the morning, and entered the shrubbery on
my homeward way, about nine of a bright forenoon. It was that
time of year when the woods are all in their spring colours, the
thorns all in flower, and the birds in the high season of their
singing. In contrast to their merriment, the shrubbery was only
the more sad and I the more oppressed by its associations. In this
situation of spirit, it struck me disagreeably to hear voices a little
way in front, and to recognise the tones of my lord and Mr.
Alexander. I pushed ahead, and came presently into their view.
They stood together in the open space where the duel was, my

lord with his hand on his son's shoulder and speaking with some gravity. At least, as he raised his head upon my coming, I thought I could perceive his countenance to lighten.

"Ah," says he, "here comes the good Mackellar. I have just been telling Sandie the story of this place, and how there was a man whom the devil tried to kill, and how near he came to kill the devil instead."

I had thought it strange enough he should bring the child into that scene; that he should actually be discoursing of his act, passed measure. But the worst was yet to come; for he added, turning to his son: "You can ask Mackellar; he was here and saw it."

"Is it true, Mr. Mackellar?" asked the child. "And did you really see the devil?"

"I have not heard the tale," I replied; "and I am in a press of business." So far I said a little sourly, fencing with the embarrassment of the position; and suddenly the bitterness of the past and the terror of that scene by candlelight rushed in upon my mind; I bethought me that, for a difference of a second's quickness in parade, the child before me might have never seen the day; and the emotion that always fluttered round my heart in that dark shrubbery burst forth in words. "But so much is true," I cried, "that I have met the devil in these woods and seen him foiled here; blessed be God that we escaped with life—blessed be God that one stone yet stands upon another in the walls of Durrisdeer! and O, Mr. Alexander, if ever you come by this spot, though it was a hundred years hence and you came with the gayest and the highest in the land, I would step aside and remember a bit prayer."

My lord bowed his head gravely. "Ah," says he, "Mackellar is always in the right. Come, Alexander, take your bonnet off." And with that he uncovered and held out his hand. "O Lord," said he, "I thank thee, and my son thanks thee, for thy manifold great mercies. Let us have peace for a little; defend us from the evil man. Smite him, O Lord, upon the lying mouth!" The last broke out of him like a cry; and at that, whether remembered anger choked his utterance, or whether he perceived this was a singular sort of prayer, at least he came suddenly to a full stop; and after a moment, set back his hat upon his head.

"I think you have forgot a word, my lord," said I. "Forgive us our trespasses as we forgive them that trespass against us. For thine is the kingdom, and the power, and the glory, for ever and ever. Amen."

"Ah, that is easy saying," said my lord. "That is very easy saying, Mackellar. But for me to forgive?—I think I would cut a very silly figure, if I had the affectation to pretend it."

"The bairn, my lord," said I with some severity, for I thought his expressions little fitted for the ears of children.

"Why, very true," said he. "This is dull work for a bairn. Let's go nesting."

I forget if it was the same day, but it was soon after, my lord, finding me alone, opened himself a little more on the same head. "Mackellar," he said, "I am now a very happy man."

"I think so indeed, my lord," said I, "and the sight of it gives me a light heart."

"There is an obligation in happiness, do you not think so?" says he, musingly.

"I think so indeed," says I, "and one in sorrow too. If we are not here to try to do the best, in my humble opinion, the sooner we are away the better for all parties."

"Ah, but if you were in my shoes, would you forgive him?" asks my lord.

The suddenness of the attack a little gravelled me. "It is a duty laid upon us strictly," said I.

"Hut!" said he. "These are expressions! Do you forgive the man yourself?"

"Well—no!" said I. "God forgive me, I do not."

"Shake hands upon that!" cries my lord, with a kind of joviality.

"It is an ill sentiment to shake hands upon," said I, "for Christian people. I think I will give you mine on some more evangelical occasion."

This I said smiling a little; but as for my lord, he went from the room laughing aloud.

For my lord's slavery to the child, I can find no expression adequate. He lost himself in that continual thought: business, friends and wife being all alike forgotten or only remembered with a painful effort, like that of one struggling with a posset. It was most notable in the matter of his wife. Since I had known Durrisdeer, she had been the burthen of his thought and the loadstone of his eyes; and now, she was quite cast out. I have seen him come to the door of a room, look round, and pass my lady over as though she were a dog before the fire:—it would be Alexander he was seeking, and my lady knew it well. I have heard him speak of her so ruggedly, that I nearly found it in my heart to intervene: the cause would still be the same, that she had in some way thwarted Alexander. Without doubt this was in the nature of a judgment on my lady. Without doubt she had the tables turned upon her as only Providence can do it; she who had been cold so many years to every mark of tenderness, it was her part now to be neglected: the more praise to her that she played it well.

An odd situation resulted: that we had once more two parties in the house, and that now I was of my lady's. Not that ever I lost the love I bore my master. But for one thing, he had the less use for my society. For another, I could not but compare the case of Mr. Alexander with that of Miss Katharine; for whom my lord had never found the least attention. And for a third, I was wounded by the change he discovered to his wife, which struck me in the nature of an infidelity. I could not but admire besides the constancy and kindness she displayed. Perhaps her sentiment to my lord, as it had been founded from the first in pity, was that rather of a mother than a wife; perhaps it pleased her (if I may so say) to behold her two children so happy in each other: the more as one had suffered so unjustly in the past. But for all that, and though I could never trace in her one spark of jealousy, she must fall back for society on poor, neglected Miss Katharine; and I, on my part, came to pass my spare hours more and more with the mother and daughter. It would be easy to make too much of this division, for it was a pleasant family as families go; still the thing existed; whether my lord knew it or not, I am in doubt, I do not think he did, he was bound up so entirely in his son; but the rest of us knew it and (in a manner) suffered from the knowledge.

What troubled us most, however, was the great and growing danger to the child. My lord was his father over again; it was to be feared the son would prove a second Master. Time has proved these fears to have been quite exaggerate. Certainly there is no more worthy gentleman today in Scotland than the seventh Lord Durrisdeer. Of my own exodus from his employment, it does not become me to speak, above all in a memorandum written only to justify his father. . . .

[*Editor's Note. Five pages of Mr. Mackellar's MS. are here omitted. I have gathered from their perusal an impression that Mr. Mackellar, in his old age, was rather an exacting servant. Against the seventh Lord Durrisdeer (with whom at any rate we have no concern) nothing material is alleged.—R. L. S.*]

. . . But our fear at the time was lest he should turn out, in the person of his son, a second edition of his brother. My lady had tried to interject some wholesome discipline; she had been glad to give that up, and now looked on with secret dismay; sometimes she even spoke of it by hints; and sometimes when there was brought to her knowledge some monstrous instance of my lord's indulgence, she would betray herself in a gesture or perhaps an exclamation. As for myself, I was haunted by the thought both day and night: not so much for the child's sake as for the father's. The man had gone to sleep, he was dreaming a dream, and any rough wakening must infallibly prove mortal. That he should survive its death was inconceivable; and the fear of its dishonour made me cover my face.

It was this continual preoccupation that screwed me up at last to a remonstrance: a matter worthy to be narrated in detail. My lord and I sat one day at the same table upon some tedious business of detail; I have said that he had lost his former interest in such occupations; he was plainly itching to be gone, and he looked fretful, weary and methought older than I had ever previously observed. I suppose it was the haggard face that put me suddenly upon my enterprise.

"My lord," said I, with my head down, and feigning to continue my occupation—"or rather let me call you again by the name of Mr. Henry, for I fear your anger and want you to think upon old times——"

"My good Mackellar!" said he; and that in tones so kindly that I had near forsook my purpose. But I called to mind that I was speaking for his good, and stuck to my colours.

"Has it never come in upon your mind what you are doing?" I asked.

"What I am doing?" he repeated, "I was never good at guessing riddles."

"What you are doing with your son," said I.

"Well," said he, with some defiance in his tone, "and what am I doing with my son?"

"Your father was a very good man," says I, straying from the direct path. "But do you think he was a wise father?"

There was a pause before he spoke, and then: "I say nothing against him," he replied. "I had the most cause perhaps; but I say nothing."

"Why, there it is," said I. "You had the cause at least. And yet your father was a good man; I never knew a better, save on the one point, nor yet a wiser. Where he stumbled, it is highly possible another man should fall. He had the two sons——"

My lord rapped suddenly and violently on the table.

"What is this?" cried he. "Speak out!"

"I will, then," said I, my voice almost strangled with the thumping of my heart. "If you continue to indulge Mr. Alexander, you are following in your father's footsteps: Beware, my lord, lest (when he grows up) your son should follow in the Master's."

I had never meant to put the thing so crudely; but in the extreme of fear, there comes a brutal kind of courage, the most brutal indeed of all; and I burnt my ships with that plain word. I never had the answer. When I lifted my head, my lord had risen to his feet, and the next moment he fell heavily on the floor. The fit or seizure endured not very long; he came to himself vacantly, put his hand to his head, which I was then supporting, and says he, in a broken voice: "I have been ill," and a little after: "Help me." I got him to his feet, and he stood pretty well, though he kept hold of the table. "I have been ill, Mackellar," he said again. "Something broke, Mackellar—or was going to break, and then all swam away. I think I was very angry. Never you mind, Mackellar, never you mind, my man. I wouldnae hurt a hair upon your head. Too much has come and gone. It's a certain thing between us two. But I think, Mackellar, I will go to Mrs. Henry—I think I will go to Mrs. Henry," said he, and got pretty steadily from the room, leaving me overcome with penitence.

Presently the door flew open, and my lady swept in with flashing eyes. "What is all this?" she cried. "What have you done to my husband? Will nothing teach you your position in this house? Will you never cease from making and meddling?"

"My lady," said I, "since I have been in this house, I have had plenty of hard words. For awhile they were my daily diet, and I swallowed them all. As for to-day, you may call me what you please; you will never find the name hard enough for such a blunder. And yet I meant it for the best."

I told her all with ingenuity, even as it is written here; and when she had heard me out, she pondered, and I could see her animosity fall. "Yes," she said, "you meant well indeed. I have had the same thought myself, or the same temptation rather, which makes me pardon you. But, dear God, can you not understand that he can bear no more? He can bear no more!" she cried. "The cord is stretched to snapping. What matters the future, if he have one or two good days?"

"Amen," said I. "I will meddle no more. I am pleased enough that you should recognise the kindness of my meaning."

"Yes," said my lady, "but when it came to the point, I have to suppose your courage failed you; for what you said was said cruelly." She paused, looking at me; then suddenly smiled a little, and said a singular thing: "Do you know what you are, Mr. Mackellar? You are an old maid."

No more incident of any note occurred in the family until the return of that ill-starred man, the Master. But I have to place here a second extract from the memoirs of Chevalier Burke, interesting in itself and highly necessary for my purpose. It is our only sight of the Master on his Indian travels; and the first word in these pages of Secundra Dass. One fact, it is to observe, appears here very clearly, which if we had known some twenty years ago, how many calamities and sorrows had been spared!—that Secundra Dass spoke English.

Adventure of Chevalier Burke in India
EXTRACTED FROM HIS MEMOIRS

HERE WAS I, THEREFORE, ON THE STREETS OF THAT CITY, THE NAME of which I cannot call to mind, while even then I was so ill acquainted with its situation that I knew not whether to go south or north. The alert being sudden, I had run forth without shoes or stockings; my hat had been struck from my head in the mellay; my kit was in the hands of the English; I had no companion but the cipaye, no weapon but my sword, and the devil a coin in my pocket. In short I was for all the world like one of those calenders with whom Mr. Galland had made us acquainted in his elegant tales. These gentlemen, you will remember, were for ever falling in with extraordinary incidents; and I was myself upon the brink of one so astonishing that I protest I cannot explain it to this day.

The cipaye was a very honest man, he had served many years with the French colours, and would have let himself be cut to pieces for any of the brave countrymen of Mr. Lally. It is the same fellow (his name has quite escaped me) of whom I have narrated already a surprising instance of generosity of mind: when he found Mr. de Fessac and myself upon the ramparts, entirely overcome with liquor, and covered us with straw while the commandant was passing by. I consulted him therefore with perfect freedom. It was a fine question what to do; but we decided at last to escalade a garden wall, where we could certainly sleep in the shadow of the trees, and might perhaps find an occasion to get hold of a pair of slippers and a turban. In that part of the city we had only the difficulty of the choice, for it was a quarter consisting entirely of walled gardens, and the lanes which divided them were at that hour of the night deserted. I gave the cipaye a back, and we had soon dropped into a large enclosure full of trees. The place was soaking with the dew which, in that country, is exceedingly unwholesome, above all to whites; yet my fatigue was so extreme that I was already half asleep, when the cipaye recalled me to my senses. In the far end of the enclosure a bright light had suddenly shone out, and continued to burn steadily among the leaves. It was a circumstance highly unusual in such a place and hour; and in our situation, it behoved us to proceed with some timidity. The cipaye was sent to reconnoitre, and pretty soon returned with the intelligence that we had fallen extremely amiss, for the house belonged to a white man who was in all likelihood English.

"Faith," says I, "if there is a white man to be seen, I will have a look at him; for the Lord be praised! there are more sorts than the one!"

The cipaye led me forward accordingly to a place from which I had a clear view upon the house. It was surrounded with a wide verandah; a lamp, very well trimmed, stood upon the floor of it; and on either side of the lamp there sat a man, cross-legged after the oriental manner. Both, besides, were bundled up in muslin like two natives; and yet one of them was not only a white man, but a man very well known to me and the reader: being indeed that very Master of Ballantrae of whose gallantry and genius I have had to speak so often. Word had reached me that he was come to the Indies; though we had never met at least and I heard little of his occupations. But sure, I had no sooner recognised him, and found myself in the arms of so old a comrade, than I supposed my tribulations were quite done. I stepped plainly forth into the light of the moon, which shone exceeding strong, and hailing Ballantrae by name, made him in a few words master of my grievous situation. He turned, started the least thing in the world, looked me fair in the face while I was speaking, and when I had done, addressed himself to his companion in the barbarous native dialect. The second person, who was of an extraordinary delicate appearance, with legs like walking canes and fingers like the stalk of a tobacco pipe * now rose to his feet.

"The Sahib," says he, "understands no English language. I understand it myself, and I see you make some small mistake—O, which may happen very often! But the Sahib would be glad to know how you come in a garden."

"Ballantrae!" I cried. "Have you the damned impudence to deny me to my face?"

Ballantrae never moved a muscle, staring at me like an image in a pagoda.

"The Sahib understands no English language," says the native, as glib as before. "He be glad to know how you come in a garden."

"O, the divil fetch him!" says I. "He would be glad to know how I come in a garden, would he? Well now, my dear man, just have the civility to tell the Sahib, with my kind love, that we are two soldiers here whom he never met and never heard of, but the cipaye is a broth of a boy, and I am a broth of a boy myself; and if we don't get a full meal of meat, and a turban, and slippers, and the value of a gold mohur in small change as a matter of convenience, bedad, my friend, I could lay my finger on a garden where there is going to be trouble."

They carried their comedy so far as to converse awhile in Hindustanee; and then, says the Hindu, with the same smile, but sighing as if he were tired of the repetition. "The Sahib would be glad to know how you come in a garden."

* *Note by Mr. Mackellar.* Plainly Secundra Dass.—E. McK.

"Is that the way of it?" says I, and laying my hand on my sword-hilt, I bade the cipaye draw.

Ballantrae's Hindu, still smiling, pulled out a pistol from his bosom, and though Ballantrae himself never moved a muscle, I knew him well enough to be sure he was prepared.

"The Sahib thinks you better go away," says the Hindu.

Well, to be plain, it was what I was thinking myself; for the report of a pistol would have been, under Providence, the means of hanging the pair of us.

"Tell the Sahib, I consider him no gentleman," says I, and turned away with a gesture of contempt.

I was not gone three steps when the voice of the Hindu called me back. "The Sahib would be glad to know if you are a damn, low Irishman," says he; and at the words Ballantrae smiled and bowed very low.

"What is that?" says I.

"The Sahib say you ask your friend Mackellar," says the Hindu. "The Sahib he cry quits."

"Tell the Sahib I will give him a cure for the Scots fiddle when next we meet," cried I.

The pair were still smiling as I left.

There is little doubt some flaws may be picked in my own behaviour; and when a man, however gallant, appeals to posterity with an account of his exploits, he must almost certainly expect to share the fate of Cæsar and Alexander, and to meet with some detractors. But there is one thing that can never be laid at the door of Francis Burke: he never turned his back on a friend. . . .

(Here follows a passage which the Chevalier Burke has been at the pains to delete before sending me his manuscript. Doubtless it was some very natural complaint of what he supposed to be an indiscretion on my part; though, indeed, I can call none to mind. Perhaps Mr. Henry was less guarded; or it is just possible the Master found the means to examine my correspondence, and himself read the letter from Troyes: in revenge for which this cruel jest was perpetrated on Mr. Burke in his extreme necessity. The Master, for all his wickedness, was not without some natural affection; I believe he was sincerely attached to Mr. Burke in the beginning; but the thought of treachery dried up the springs of his very shallow friendship, and his detestable nature appeared naked.— E. McK.)

The Enemy in the House

IT IS A STRANGE THING THAT I SHOULD BE AT A STICK FOR A DATE —the date, besides, of an incident that changed the very nature of my life, and sent us all into foreign lands. But the truth is I was stricken out of all my habitudes, and find my journals very ill redd-up,* the day not indicated sometimes for a week or two together, and the whole fashion of the thing like that of a man near desperate. It was late in March at least, or early in April, 1764. I had slept heavily and wakened with a premonition of some evil to befall. So strong was this upon my spirit, that I hurried down-stairs in my shirt and breeches, and my hand (I remember) shook upon the rail. It was a cold, sunny morning with a thick white frost; the blackbirds sang exceeding sweet and loud about the house of Durrisdeer, and there was a noise of the sea in all the chambers. As I came by the doors of the hall, another sound arrested me, of voices talking. I drew nearer and stood like a man dreaming. Here was certainly a human voice, and that in my own master's house, and yet I knew it not; certainly human speech, and that in my native land; and yet listen as I pleased, I could not catch one syllable. An old tale started up in my mind of a fairy wife (or perhaps only a wandering stranger), that came to the place of my fathers some generations back, and stayed the matter of a week, talking often in a tongue that signified nothing to the hearers; and went again as she had come, under cloud of night, leaving not so much as a name behind her. A little fear I had, but more curiosity; and I opened the hall door, and entered.

The supper things still lay upon the table; the shutters were still closed, although day peeped in the divisions; and the great room was lighted only with a single taper and some lurching reverberation of the fire. Close in the chimney sat two men. The one that was wrapped in a cloak and wore boots, I knew at once: it was the bird of ill omen back again. Of the other, who was set close to the red embers, and made up into a bundle like a mummy, I could but see that he was an alien, of a darker hue than any man of Europe, very frailly built, with a singular tall forehead, and a secret eye. Several bundles and a small valise were on the floor; and to judge by the smallness of this luggage, and by the condition

* Ordered.

of the Master's boots, grossly patched by some unscrupulous country cobbler, evil had not prospered.

He rose upon my entrance; our eyes crossed; and I know not why it should have been, but my courage rose like a lark on a May morning.

"Ha!" said I, "is this you?"—and I was pleased with the unconcern of my own voice.

"It is even myself, worthy Mackellar," says the Master.

"This time you have brought the black dog visibly upon your back," I continued.

"Referring to Secundra Dass?" asked the Master. "Let me present you. He is a native gentleman of India."

"Hum!" said I. "I am no great lover either of you or your friends, Mr. Bally. But I will let a little daylight in and have a look at you." And so saying, I undid the shutters of the eastern window.

By the light of the morning, I could perceive the man was changed. Later, when we were all together, I was more struck to see how lightly time had dealt with him; but the first glance was otherwise.

"You are getting an old man," said I.

A shade came upon his face. "If you could see yourself," said he, "you would perhaps not dwell upon the topic."

"Hut!" I returned, "old age is nothing to me. I think I have been always old; and I am now, I thank God, better known and more respected. It is not every one that can say that, Mr. Bally! The lines in *your* brow are calamities; your life begins to close in upon you like a prison; death will soon be rapping at the door; and I see not from what source you are to draw your consolations."

Here the Master addressed himself to Secundra Dass in Hindustanee; from which I gathered (I freely confess, with a high degree of pleasure) that my remarks annoyed him. All this while, you may be sure, my mind had been busy upon other matters even while I rallied my enemy; and chiefly as to how I should communicate secretly and quickly with my lord. To this, in the breathing-space now given me, I turned all the forces of my mind; when, suddenly shifting my eyes, I was aware of the man himself standing in the doorway, and to all appearance quite composed. He had no sooner met my looks than he stepped across the threshold.

The Master heard him coming, and advanced upon the other side; about four feet apart, these brothers came to a full pause and stood exchanging steady looks and then my lord smiled, bowed a little forward, and turned briskly away.

"Mackellar," says he, "we must see to breakfast for these travellers."

It was plain the Master was a trifle disconcerted; but he assumed the more impudence of speech and manner. "I am as hungry as a hawk," says he. "Let it be something good, Henry."

My lord turned to him with the same hard smile. "Lord Durrisdeer," says he.

"Oh, never in the family!" returned the Master.

"Every one in this house renders me my proper title," says my lord. "If it please you to make an exception, I will leave you to consider what appearance it will bear to strangers, and whether it may not be translated as an effect of impotent jealousy."

I could have clapped my hands together with delight: the more so as my lord left no time for any answer, but, bidding me with a sign to follow him, went straight out of the hall.

"Come quick," says he, "we have to sweep vermin from the house." And he sped through the passages with so swift a step that I could scarce keep up with him, straight to the door of John Paul, the which he opened without summons and walked in. John was to all appearance sound asleep, but my lord made no pretence of waking him.

"John Paul," said he, speaking as quietly as ever I heard him, "you served my father long, or I would pack you from the house like a dog. If in half an hour's time I find you gone, you shall continue to receive your wages in Edinburgh. If you linger here or in St. Bride's—old man, old servant, and altogether—I shall find some very astonishing way to make you smart for your disloyalty. Up, and begone. The door you let them in by will serve for your departure. I do not choose my son shall see your face again."

"I am rejoiced to find you bear the thing so quietly," said I, when we were forth again by ourselves.

"Quietly!" cries he, and put my hand suddenly against his heart, which struck upon his bosom like a sledge.

At this revelation I was filled with wonder and fear. There was no constitution could bear so violent a strain—his least of all, that was unhinged already; and I decided in my mind that we must bring this monstrous situation to an end.

"It would be well, I think, if I took word to my lady," said I. Indeed, he should have gone himself, but I counted (not in vain) on his indifference.

"Aye," says he, "do. I will hurry breakfast: we must all appear at the table, even Alexander; it must appear we are untroubled."

I ran to my lady's room, and, with no preparatory cruelty, disclosed my news.

"My mind was long ago made up," said she. "We must make our packets secretly to-day, and leave secretly to-night. Thank Heaven, we have another house! The first ship that sails shall bear us to New York."

"And what of him?" I asked.

"We leave him Durrisdeer," she cried. "Let him work his pleasure upon that."

"Not so, by your leave," said I. "There shall be a dog at his heels that can hold fast. Bed he shall have, and board, and a horse to ride upon, if he behave himself; but the keys (if you think well of it, my lady) shall be left in the hands of one Mackellar. There will be good care taken; trust him for that."

"Mr. Mackellar," she cried, "I thank you for that thought! All shall be left in your hands. If we must go into a savage country, I bequeath it to you to take our vengeance. Send Macconochie to St. Bride's, to arrange privately for horses and to call the lawyer. My lord must leave procuration."

At that moment my lord came to the door, and we opened our plan to him.

"I will never hear of it," he cried; "he would think I feared him. I will stay in my own house, please God, until I die. There lives not the man can beard me out of it. Once and for all, here I am and here I stay, in spite of all the devils in hell." I can give no idea of the vehemency of his words and utterance; but we both stood aghast, and I in particular, who had been a witness of his former self-restraint.

My lady looked at me with an appeal that went to my heart and recalled me to my wits. I made her a private sign to go, and, when my lord and I were alone, went up to him where he was racing to and fro in one end of the room like a half-lunatic, and set my hand firmly on his shoulder.

"My lord," says I, "I am going to be the plain-dealer once more; if for the last time, so much the better, for I am grown weary of the part."

"Nothing will change me," he answered. "God forbid I should refuse to hear you; but nothing will change me." This he said firmly, with no signal of the former violence, which already raised my hopes.

"Very well," said I. "I can afford to waste my breath." I pointed to a chair, and he sat down and looked at me. "I can remember a time when my lady very much neglected you," said I.

"I never spoke of it while it lasted," returned my lord, with a high flush of colour; "and it is all changed now."

"Do you know how much?" I said. "Do you know how much it is all changed? The tables are turned, my lord! It is my lady that now courts you for a word, a look, ay, and courts you in vain. Do you know with whom she passes her days while you are out gallivanting in the policies? My word, she is glad to pass them with a certain dry old grieve * of the name of Ephraim Mackellar; and I think you may be able to remember what that means, for I am the more in a mistake or you were once driven to the same company yourself."

"Mackellar!" cries my lord, getting to his feet. "O my God, Mackellar!"

"It is neither the name of Mackellar nor the name of God that can change the truth," said I; "and I am telling you the fact. Now, for you, that suffered so much, to deal out the same suffering to another, is that the part of any Christian? But you are so swallowed up in your new friend that the old are all forgotten. They are all clean vanished from your memory. And yet they stood by you at the darkest; my lady not the least. And does my lady ever cross your mind? Does it ever cross your mind what she went through that night?—or what manner of a wife she has been to you thenceforward?—or in what kind of a position she finds herself to-day? Never. It is your pride to stay and face him out, and she must stay along with you. O, my lord's pride—that's the great affair! And yet she is the woman, and you are a great, hulking man!

* Land steward.

She is the woman that you swore to protect; and, more betoken, the own mother of that son of yours!"

"You are speaking very bitterly, Mackellar," said he; "but, the Lord knows, I fear you are speaking very true. I have not proved worthy of my happiness. Bring my lady back."

My lady was waiting near at hand to learn the issue. When I brought her in, my lord took a hand of each of us and laid them both upon his bosom. "I have had two friends in my life," said he. "All the comfort ever I had, it came from one or other. When you two are in a mind, I think I would be an ungrateful dog——" He shut his mouth very hard, and looked on us with swimming eyes. "Do what ye like with me," says he, "only don't think——" He stopped again. "Do what ye please with me: God knows I love and honour you." And dropping our two hands, he turned his back and went and gazed out of the window. But my lady ran after, calling his name, and threw herself upon his neck in a passion of weeping.

I went out and shut the door behind me, and stood and thanked God from the bottom of my heart.

At the breakfast board, according to my lord's design, we were all met. The Master had by that time plucked off his patched boots and made a toilet suitable to the hour; Secundra Dass was no longer bundled up in wrappers, but wore a decent plain black suit, which misbecame him strangely; and the pair were at the great window looking forth, when the family entered. They turned; and the black man (as they had already named him in the house) bowed almost to his knees, but the Master was for running forward like one of the family. My lady stopped him, curtseying low from the far end of the hall, and keeping her children at her back. My lord was a little in front: so there were the three cousins of Durrisdeer face to face. The hand of time was very legible on all; I seemed to read in their changed faces a *memento mori;* and what affected me still more, it was the wicked man that bore his years the handsomest. My lady was quite transfigured into the matron, a becoming woman for the head of a great tableful of children and dependents. My lord was grown slack in his limbs; he stooped; he walked with a running motion, as though he had learned again from Mr. Alexander; his face was drawn; it seemed a trifle longer than of old; and it wore at times a smile very singularly mingled, and which (in my eyes) appeared both bitter and pathetic. But the Master still bore himself erect, although perhaps with effort; his brow barred about the centre with imperious lines, his mouth set as for command. He had all the gravity and something of the splendor of Satan in the "Paradise Lost." I could not help but see the man with admiration, and was only surprised that I saw him with so little fear.

But indeed (as long as we were at the table) it seemed as if his authority were quite vanished and his teeth all drawn. We had known him a magician that controlled the elements; and here he was, transformed into an ordinary gentleman, chatting like his neighbours at the breakfast board. For now the father was dead, and my lord and lady reconciled, in what ear was he to pour his calumnies? It came upon me in a kind of vision how hugely I had overrated the man's subtlety. He had his malice still, he was false as ever; and, the occasion being gone that made his strength, he sat there impotent; he was still the viper, but now spent his venom on a file. Two more thoughts occurred to me while yet we sat at breakfast: the first, that he was abashed—I had almost said distressed—to find his wickedness quite unavailing; the second, that perhaps my lord was in the right, and we did amiss to fly from our dismasted enemy. But my poor master's leaping heart came in my mind, and I remembered it was for his wife we played the coward.

When the meal was over, the Master followed me to my room, and, taking a chair (which I had never offered him), asked me what was to be done with him.

"Why, Mr. Bally," said I, "the house will still be open to you for a time."

"For a time?" says he. "I do not know if I quite take your meaning."

"It is plain enough," said I. "We keep you for our reputation; as soon as you shall have publicly disgraced yourself by some of your misconduct, we shall pack you forth again."

"You are become an impudent rogue," said the Master, bending his brows at me dangerously.

"I learned in a good school," I returned. "And you must have perceived yourself, that with my old lord's death your power is quite departed. I do not fear you now, Mr. Bally; I think even—

God forgive me—that I take a certain pleasure in your company."

He broke out in a burst of laughter, which I clearly saw to be assumed.

"I have come with empty pockets," says he, after a pause.

"I do not think there will be any money going," I replied. "I would advise you not to build on that."

"I shall have something to say on the point," he returned.

"Indeed?" said I. "I have not a guess what it will be, then."

"Oh, you affect confidence," said the Master. "I have still one strong position,—that you people fear a scandal, and I enjoy it."

"Pardon me, Mr. Bally," says I. "We do not in the least fear a scandal against you."

He laughed again. "You have been studying repartee," he said. "But speech is very easy, and sometimes very deceptive. I warn you fairly: you will find me vitriol in the house. You would do wiser to pay money down, and see my back." And with that, he waved his hand to me and left the room.

A little after, my lord came with the lawyer, Mr. Carlyle; a bottle of old wine was brought, and we all had a glass before we fell to business. The necessary deeds were then prepared and executed, and the Scotch estates made over in trust to Mr. Carlyle and myself.

"There is one point, Mr. Carlyle," said my lord, when these affairs had been adjusted, "on which I wish that you would do us justice. This sudden departure coinciding with my brother's return will be certainly commented on. I wish you would discourage any conjunction of the two."

"I will make a point of it, my lord," said Mr. Carlyle. "The Mas —Mr. Bally does not then accompany you?"

"It is a point I must approach," said my lord. "Mr. Bally remains at Durrisdeer under the care of Mr. Mackellar; and I do not mean that he shall even know our destination."

"Common report, however——" began the lawyer.

"Ah, but, Mr. Carlyle, this is to be a secret quite among ourselves," interrupted my lord. "None but you and Mackellar are to be made acquainted with my movements."

"And Mr. Bally stays here? Quite so," said Mr. Carlyle. "The powers you leave——" Then he broke off again. "Mr. Mackellar, we have a rather heavy weight upon us."

"No doubt, sir," said I.

"No doubt," said he. "Mr. Bally will have no voice?"

"He will have no voice," said my lord, "and I hope no influence. Mr. Bally is not a good adviser."

"I see," said the lawyer. "By the way, has Mr. Bally means?"

"I understand him to have nothing," replied my lord. "I give him table, fire, and candle in this house."

"And in the matter of an allowance?—if I am to share the responsibility, you will see how highly desirable it is that I should understand your views," said the lawyer. "On the question of an allowance?"

"There will be no allowance," said my lord. "I wish Mr. Bally to live very private. We have not always been gratified with his behaviour."

"And in the matter of money," I added, "he has shown himself an infamous bad husband. Glance your eye upon that docket, Mr. Carlyle, where I have brought together the different sums the man has drawn from the estate in the last fifteen or twenty years. The total is pretty."

Mr. Carlyle made the motion of whistling. "I had no guess of this," said he. "Excuse me once more, my lord, if I appear to push you; but it is really desirable I should penetrate your intentions: Mr. Mackellar might die, when I should find myself alone upon this trust. Would it not be rather your lordship's preference that Mr. Bally should—ahem—should leave the country?"

My lord looked at Mr. Caryle. "Why do you ask that?" said he.

"I gather, my lord, that Mr. Bally is not a comfort to his family," says the lawyer with a smile.

My lord's face became suddenly knotted. "I wish he was in hell," cried he, and filled himself a glass of wine, but with a hand so tottering that he spilled the half into his bosom. This was the second time that, in the midst of the most regular and wise behaviour, his animosity had spirted out. It startled Mr. Carlyle, who observed my lord thenceforth with covert curiosity, and to me it restored the certainty that we were acting for the best in view of my lord's health and reason.

Except for this explosion, the interview was very successfully conducted. No doubt Mr. Carlyle would talk; as lawyers do, little by little. We could thus feel we had laid the foundations of a better feeling in the country; and the man's own misconduct would certainly complete what we had begun. Indeed, before his departure, the lawyer showed us there had already gone aboard some glimmerings of the truth.

"I should perhaps explain to you, my lord," said he, pausing, with his hat in his hand, "that I have not been altogether surprised with your lordship's dispositions in the case of Mr. Bally. Something of this nature oozed out when he was last in Durrisdeer. There was some talk of a woman at St. Bride's, to whom you had behaved extremely handsome, and Mr. Bally with no small degree of cruelty. There was the entail again, which was much controverted. In short, there was no want of talk, back and forward; and some of our wiseacres took up a strong opinion. I remained in suspense, as became one of my cloth; but Mr. Mackellar's docket here has finally opened my eyes. I do not think, Mr. Mackellar, that you and I will give him that much rope."

The rest of that important day passed prosperously through. It was our policy to keep the enemy in view, and I took my turn to be his watchman with the rest. I think his spirits rose as he perceived us to be so attentive: and I know that mine insensibly declined. What chiefly daunted me was the man's singular dexterity to worm himself into our troubles. You may have felt (after a horse accident) the hand of a bone-setter artfully divide and interrogate the muscles, and settle strongly on the injured place? It was so with the Master's tongue that was so cunning to question, and his eyes that were so quick to observe. I seemed to have said nothing, and yet to have let all out. Before I knew where I was, the man was condoling with me on my lord's neglect of my lady and myself, and his hurtful indulgence to his son. On this last point I perceived him (with panic fear) to return repeatedly. The boy had displayed a certain shrinking from his uncle; it was strong in my mind his father had been fool enough to indoctrinate the same, which was no wise beginning: and when I looked upon the man before me, still so handsome, so apt a speaker, with so great a variety of fortunes to relate, I saw he was the very personage to captivate a boyish fancy. John Paul had left only that morning; it was not to be supposed he had been altogether dumb upon his favourite subject; so that here would be Mr. Alexander in the part of Dido, with a curiosity inflamed to hear; and there would be the Master like a diabolical Æneas, full of matter the most pleasing in the world to any youthful ear, such as battles, sea-disasters, flights, the forests of the west, and (since his later voyage) the ancient cities of the Indies. How cunningly these baits might be employed, and what an empire might be so founded, little by little, in the mind of any boy, stood obviously clear to me. There was no inhibition, so long as the man was in the house, that would be strong enough to hold these two apart; for if it be hard to charm serpents, it is not very difficult thing to cast a glamour on a little chip of manhood not very long in breeches. I recalled an ancient sailor-man who dwelt in a lone house beyond the Figgate Whins (I believe he called it after Portobello), and how the boys would troop out of Leith on a Saturday, and sit and listen to his swearing tales, as thick as crows about a carrion: a thing I often remarked as I went by, a young student, on my own more mediative holiday diversion. Many of these boys went, no doubt, in the face of an express command; many feared and even hated the old brute of whom they made their hero; and I have seen them flee from him when he was tipsy, and stone him when he was drunk. And yet there they came each Saturday! How much more easily would a boy like Mr. Alexander fall under the influence of a high-looking, high-spoken gentleman-adventurer, who should conceive the fancy to entrap him; and, the influence gained, how easy to employ it for the child's perversion!

I doubt if our enemy had named Mr. Alexander three times, before I perceived which way his mind was aiming—all this train of thought and memory passed in one pulsation through my own—and you may say I started back as though an open hole had gaped across a pathway. Mr. Alexander: there was the weak point, there was the Eve in our perishable paradise; and the serpent was already hissing on the trail.

I promise you I went the more heartily about the preparations; my last scruple gone, the danger of delay written before me in huge characters. From that moment forth, I seem not to have sat down or breathed. Now I would be at my post with the Master and his Indian; now in the garret buckling a valise; now sending forth Macconochie by the side postern and the wood-path to bear it to the trysting-place; and again, snatching some words of counsel with my lady. This was the *verso* of our life in Durrisdeer that day, but on the *recto* all appeared quite settled, as of a family at home in its paternal seat; and what perturbation may have been observable, the Master would set down to the blow of his unlooked for coming and the fear he was accustomed to inspire.

Supper went creditably off, cold salutations passed, and the company trooped to their respective chambers. I attended the Master to the last. We had put him next door to his Indian, in the north wing; because that was the most distant and could be severed from the body of the house with doors. I saw he was a kind friend or a good master (whichever it was) to his Secundra Dass: seeing to his comfort; mending the fire with his own hand, for the Indian complained of cold; inquiring as to the rice on which the stranger made his diet; talking with him pleasantly in the Hindustanee, while I stood by, my candle in my hand, and affected to be overcome with slumber. At length the Master observed my signals of distress. "I perceive," says he, "that you have all your ancient habits: early to bed and early to rise. Yawn yourself away!"

Once in my own room, I made the customary motions of undressing, so that I might time myself; and when the cycle was complete, set my tinder-box ready and blew out my taper. The matter of an hour afterward, I made a light again, put on my shoes of list that I had worn by my lord's sick-bed, and set forth into the house to call the voyagers. All were dressed and waiting—my lord, my lady, Miss Katharine, Mr. Alexander, my lady's woman Christie; and I observed the effect of secrecy even upon quite innocent persons, that one after another showed in the chink of the door a face as white as paper. We slipped out of the side postern into a night of darkness, scarce broken by a star or two; so that at first we groped and stumbled and fell among the bushes. A few hundred yards up the wood-path, Macconochie was waiting us with a great lantern; so the rest of the way we went easy enough, but still in a kind of guilty silence. A little beyond the abbey, the path debouched on the main road; and some quarter of a mile farther, at the place called Eagles, where the moors begin, we saw the lights of the two carriages stand shining by the wayside. Scarce a word or two was uttered at our parting, and these regarded business: a silent grasping of hands, a turning of faces aside, and the thing was over; the horses broke into a trot, the lamplight sped like Will o' the Wisp upon the broken moorland, it dipped beyond Stony Brae; and there were Macconochie and I alone with our lantern on the road. There was one thing more to wait for; and that was the reappearance of the coach upon Cartmore. It seems they must have pulled up upon the summit, looked back for a last time, and seen our lantern not yet moved away from the place of separation.

For a lamp was taken from a carriage, and waved three times up and down by way of a farewell. And then they were gone indeed, having looked their last on the kind roof of Durrisdeer, their faces toward a barbarous country. I never knew, before, the greatness of that vault of night in which we too poor serving men, the one old and the one elderly, stood for the first time deserted; I had never felt, before, my own dependency upon the countenance of others. The sense of isolation burned in my bowels like a fire. It seemed that we who remained at home were the true exiles; and that Durrisdeer, and Solwayside, and all that made my country native, its air good to me, and its language welcome, had gone forth and was far over the sea with my old masters.

The remainder of that night I paced to and fro on the smooth highway, reflecting on the future and the past. My thoughts, which at first dwelled tenderly on those who were just gone, took a more manly temper as I considered what remained for me to do. Day came upon the inland mountaintops, and the fowls began to cry and the smoke of homesteads to arise in the brown bosom of the moors, before I turned my face homeward and went down the path to where the roof of Durrisdeer shone in the morning by the sea.

At the customary hour I had the Master called, and awaited his coming in the hall with a quiet mind. He looked about him at the empty room and the three covers set.

"We are a small party," said he. "How comes that!"

"This is the party to which we must grow accustomed," I replied.

He looked at me with a sudden sharpness. "What is all this?" said he.

"You and I and your friend Mr. Dass are now all the company," I replied. "My lord, my lady, and the children are gone upon a voyage."

"Upon my word!" said he. "Can this be possible? I have indeed fluttered your Volscians in Corioli! But this is no reason why our breakfast should go cold. Sit down, Mr. Mackellar, if you please"—taking, as he spoke, the head of the table, which I had designed to occupy myself—"and as we eat, you can give me the details of this evasion."

I could see he was more affected than his language carried, and I determined to equal him in coolness. "I was about to ask you to take the head of the table," said I; "for though I am now thrust into the position of your host, I could never forget that you were, after all, a member of the family."

For awhile he played the part of entertainer, giving directions to Macconochie, who received them with an evil grace, and attending specially upon Secundra. "And where has my good family with-drawn to?" he asked carelessly.

"Ah, Mr. Bally, that is another point!" said I. "I have no orders to communicate their destination."

"To me," he corrected.

"To any one," said I.

"It is the less pointed," said the Master; *"c'est de bon ton*: my brother improves as he continues. And I, dear Mr. Mackellar?"

"You will have bed and board, Mr. Bally," said I. "I am permitted to give you the run of the cellar, which is pretty reasonably stocked. You have only to keep well with me, which is no very difficult matter, and you shall want neither for wine nor a saddle-horse."

He made an excuse to send Macconochie from the room.

"And for money?" he inquired. "Have I to keep well with my good friend Mackellar for my pocket-money also? This is a pleasing return to the principles of boyhood."

"There was no allowance made," said I; "but I will take it on myself to see you are supplied in moderation."

"In moderation?" he repeated. "And you will take it on your-self?" He drew himself up and looked about the hall at the dark rows of portraits. "In the name of my ancestors, I thank you," says he; and then, with a return to irony: "But there must certainly be an allowance for Secundra Dass?" he said. "It is not possible they have omitted that."

"I will make a note of it and ask instructions when I write," said I.

And he, with a sudden change of manner, and leaning forward with an elbow on the table: "Do you think this entirely wise?"

"I execute my orders, Mr. Bally," said I.

"Profoundly modest," said the Master: "perhaps not equally in-genuous. You told me yesterday my power was fallen with my father's death. How comes it, then, that a peer of the realm flees under cloud of night out of a house in which his fathers have stood several sieges? that he conceals his address, which must be a matter of concern to his Gracious Majesty and to the whole republic? and that he should leave me in possession, and under the paternal charge of his invaluable Mackellar? This smacks to me of a very considerable and genuine apprehension."

I sought to interrupt him with some not very truthful denegation; but he waved me down and pursued his speech.

"I say it smacks of it," he said, "but I will go beyond that, for I think the apprehension grounded. I came to this house with some reluctancy. In view of the manner of my last departure, nothing but necessity could have induced me to return. Money, however, is that which I must have. You will not give with a good grace; well, I have the power to force it from you. Inside of a week, without leaving Durrisdeer, I will find out where these fools are fled to. I will follow; and when I have run my quarry down, I will drive a wedge into that family that shall once more burst it into shivers. I shall see then whether my Lord Durrisdeer" (said with indescribable scorn and rage) "will choose to buy my absence; and you will all see whether, by that time, I decide for profit or revenge."

I was amazed to hear the man so open. The truth is, he was consumed with anger at my lord's successful flight, felt himself to figure as a dupe, and was in no humour to weigh language.

"Do you consider *this* entirely wise?" said I, copying his words.

"These twenty years I have lived by my poor wisdom," he answered with a smile that seemed almost foolish in its vanity.

"And come out a beggar in the end," said I, "if beggar be a strong enough word for it."

"I would have you to observe, Mr. Mackellar," cried he, with a sudden, imperious heat in which I could not but admire him, "that I am scrupulously civil: copy me in that, and we shall be the better friends."

Throughout this dialogue I had been incommoded by the observation of Secundra Dass. Not one of us, since the first word, had made a feint of eating: our eyes were in each other's faces—you might say, in each other's bosoms; and those of the Indian troubled me with a certain changing brightness, as of comprehension. But I brushed the fancy aside: telling myself once more he understood no English; only, from the gravity of both voices and the occasional scorn and anger in the Master's, smelled out there was something of import in the wind.

For the matter of three weeks we continued to live together in the house of Durrisdeer: the beginning of that most singular chapter of my life—what I must call my intimacy with the Master. At first he was somewhat changeable in his behaviour: now civil, now returning to his old manner of flouting me to my face; and in both I met him half-way. Thanks be to Providence, I had now no measure to keep with the man; and I was never afraid of black brows, only of naked swords. So that I found a certain entertainment in these bouts of incivility, and was not always ill-inspired in my rejoinders. At last (it was at supper) I had a droll expression that entirely vanquished him. He laughed again and again; and "Who would have guessed," he cried, "that this old wife had any wit under his petticoats?"

"It is no wit, Mr. Bally," said I: "a dry Scot's humour, and something of the dryest." And indeed I never had the least pretension to be thought a wit.

From that hour he was never rude with me, but all passed between us in a manner of pleasantry. One of our chief times of daffing * was when he required a horse, another bottle, or some money; he would approach me then after the manner of a schoolboy, and I would carry it on by way of being his father: on both sides, with an infinity of mirth. I could not but perceive that he thought more of me, which tickled that poor part of mankind, the vanity. He dropped besides (I must suppose unconsciously) into a manner that was not only familiar, but even friendly; and this, on the part of one who had so long detested me, I found the more insidious. He went little abroad; sometimes even refusing invitations. "No," he would say, "what do I care for these thick-headed bonnet-lairds? I will stay at home, Mackellar; and we shall share a bottle quietly and have one of our good talks." And indeed mealtime at Durrisdeer must have been a delight to any one, by reason of the brilliancy of the discourse. He would often express wonder at his former indifference to my society. "But you see," he would add, "we were upon opposite sides. And so we are to-day; but let us never speak of that. I would think much less of you if you were not staunch to your employer." You are to consider, he seemed to me quite impotent for any evil; and how it is a most engaging form of flattery when (after many years) tardy justice is done to a man's character and parts. But I have no thought to excuse

* Fooling.

myself. I was to blame; I let him cajole me; and, in short, I think the watchdog was going sound asleep, when he was suddenly aroused.

I should say the Indian was continually travelling to and fro in the house. He never spoke, save in his own dialect and with the Master; walked without sound; and was always turning up where you would least expect him, fallen into a deep abstraction, from which he would start (upon your coming) to mock you with one of his grovelling obeisances. He seemed so quiet, so frail, and so wrapped in his own fancies, that I came to pass him over without much regard, or even to pity him for a harmless exile from his country. And yet without doubt the creature was still eavesdropping; and without doubt it was through his stealth and my security that our secret reached the Master.

It was one very wild night, after supper, and when we had been making more than usually merry, that the blow fell on me.

"This is all very fine," says the Master, "but we should do better to be buckling our valise."

"Why so?" I cried. "Are you leaving?"

"We are all leaving to-morrow in the morning," said he. "For the port of Glasgow first: thence for the province of New York."

I suppose I must have groaned aloud.

"Yes," he continued, "I boasted: I said a week, and it has taken me near twenty days. But never mind: I shall make it up; I will go the faster."

"Have you the money for this voyage?" I asked.

"Dear and ingenuous personage, I have," said he. "Blame me, if you choose, for my duplicity; but while I have been wringing shillings from my daddy, I had a stock of my own put by against a rainy day. You will pay for your own passage, if you choose to accompany us on our flank march; I have enough for Secundra and myself, but not more: enough to be dangerous, not enough to be generous. There is, however, an outside seat upon the chaise which I will let you have upon a moderate commutation; so that the whole menagerie can go together, the house-dog, the monkey, and the tiger."

"I go with you," said I.

"I count upon it," said the Master. "You have seen me foiled, I mean you shall see me victorious. To gain that I will risk wetting you like a sop in this wild weather."

"And at least," I added, "you know very well you could not throw me off."

"Not easily," said he. "You put your finger on the point with your usual excellent good sense. I never fight with the inevitable."

"I suppose it is useless to appeal to you," said I.

"Believe me, perfectly," said he.

"And yet if you would give me time, I could write———" I began.

"And what would be my Lord Durrisdeer's answer?" asks he.

"Aye," said I, "that is the rub."

"And at any rate, how much more expeditious that I should go myself!" says he. "But all this is quite a waste of breath. At seven to-morrow the chaise will be at the door. For I start from the door, Mackellar; I do not skulk through woods and take my chaise upon the wayside—shall we say, at Eagles?"

My mind was now thoroughly made up. "Can you spare me quarter of an hour at St. Bride's?" said I. "I have a little necessary business with Carlyle."

"An hour, if you prefer," said he. "I do not seek to deny that the money for your seat is an object to me; and you could always get the first to Glascow with saddle-horses."

"Well," said I, "I never thought to leave old Scotland."

"It will brisken you up," says he.

"This will be an ill journey for some one," I said. "I think, sir, for you. Something speaks in my bosom; and so much it says plain, That this is an ill-omened journey."

"If you take to prophecy," says he, "listen to that."

There came up a violent squall off the open Solway, and the rain was dashed on the great windows.

"Do ye ken what that bodes, warlock?" said he, in a broad accent: "that there'll be a man Mackellar unco sick at sea."

When I got to my chamber, I sat there under a painful excitation, hearkening to the turmoil of the gale which struck full upon that gable of the house. What with the pressure on my spirits, the eldritch cries of the wind among the turret-tops, and the perpetual trepidation of the masoned house, sleep fled my eyelids utterly. I sat by my taper, looking on the black panes of the window where the storm appeared continually on the point of bursting in its entrance; and upon that empty field I beheld a perspective of consequences that made the hair to rise upon my scalp. The child corrupted, the home broken up, my master dead or worse than dead, my mistress plunged in desolation—all these I saw before me painted brightly on the darkness; and the outcry of the wind appeared to mock at my inaction.

Mr. Mackellar's Journey with the Master

THE CHAISE CAME TO THE DOOR IN A STRONG DRENCHING MIST. We took our leave in silence: the house of Durrisdeer standing with dropping gutters and windows closed, like a place dedicate to melancholy. I observed the Master kept his head out, looking back on these splashed walls and glimmering roofs, till they were suddenly swallowed in the mist; and I must suppose some natural sadness fell upon the man at this departure; or was it some prevision of the end? At least, upon our mounting the long brae from Durrisdeer, as we walked side by side in the wet, he began first to whistle and then to sing the saddest of our country tunes, which sets folk weeping in a tavern, *Wandering Willie*. The set of words he used with it, I have not heard elsewhere, and could never come by any copy; but some of them which were the most appropriate to our departure linger in my memory. One verse began:

> Home was home then, my dear, full of kindly faces;
> Home was home then, my dear, happy for the child.

And ended somewhat thus:

> Now, when day dawns on the brow of the moorland,
> Lone stands the house and the chimney-stone is cold.
> Lone let it stand, now the folks are all departed,
> The kind hearts, the true hearts, that loved the place
> of old.

I could never be a judge of the merit of these verses; they were so hallowed by the melancholy of the air, and were sung (or rather "soothed") to me by a master singer at a time so fitting. He looked in my face when he had done, and saw that my eyes watered.

"Ah, Mackellar," said he, "do you think I have never a regret?"

"I do not think you could be so bad a man," said I, "if you had not all the machinery to be a good one."

"No, not all," says he: "not all. You are there in error. The malady of not wanting, my evangelist." But methought he sighed as he mounted again into the chaise.

All day long we journeyed in the same miserable weather: the mist besetting us closely, the heavens incessantly weeping on my head. The road lay over moorish hills, where was no sound but the crying of moor-fowl in the wet heather and the pouring of the swollen burns. Sometimes I would doze off in slumber, when I would find myself plunged at once in some foul and ominous nightmare, from the which I would awaken strangling. Sometimes, if the way was steep and the wheels turning slowly, I would overhear the voices from within, talking in that tropical tongue which was to me as inarticulate as the piping of the fowls. Sometimes, at a longer ascent, the Master would set foot to the ground and walk by my side, mostly without speech. And all the time, sleeping or waking, I beheld the same black perspective of approaching ruin; and the same pictures rose in my view, only they were now painted upon hillside mist. One, I remember, stood before me with the colours of a true illusion. It showed me my lord seated at a table in a small room; his head, which was at first buried in his hands, he slowly raised, and turned upon me a countenance from which hope had fled. I saw it first on the black window-panes, my last night in Durrisdeer; it haunted and returned upon me half the voyage through; and yet it was no effect of lunacy, for I have come to a ripe old age with no decay of my intelligence; nor yet (as I was then tempted to suppose) a heaven-sent warning of the future, for all manner of calamities befell, not that calamity—and I saw many pitiful sights, but never that one.

It was decided we should travel on all night; and it was singular, once the dusk had fallen, my spirits somewhat rose. The bright lamps, shining forth into the mist and on the smoking horses and the hodding post-boy, gave me perhaps an outlook intrinsically more cheerful than what day had shown; or perhaps my mind had become wearied of its melancholy. At least, I spent some waking hours, not without satisfaction in my thoughts, although wet and weary in my body; and fell at last into a natural slumber without dreams. Yet I must have been at work even in the deepest of my sleep; and at work with at least a measure of intelligence. For I started broad awake, in the very act of crying out to myself

Home was home then, my dear, happy for the child,

stricken to find in it an appropriateness, which I had not yesterday observed, to the Master's detestable purpose in the present journey.

We were then close upon the city of Glascow, where we were soon breakfasting together at an inn, and where (as the devil would have it) we found a ship in the very article of sailing. We took our places in the cabin; and, two days after, carried our effects on board. Her name was the *Nonesuch,* a very ancient ship and very happily named. By all accounts this should be her last voyage; people shook their heads upon the quays, and I had several warnings offered me by strangers in the street, to the effect that she was rotten as a cheese, too deeply loaden, and must infallibly founder if we met a gale. From this it fell out we were the only passengers; the captain, McMurtrie, was a silent, absorbed man with the Glascow or Gaelic accent; the mates ignorant, rough seafarers, come in through the hawsehole; and the Master and I were cast upon each other's company.

The *Nonesuch* carried a fair wind out of the Clyde, and for near upon a week we enjoyed bright weather and a sense of progress. I found myself (to my wonder) a born seaman, in so far at least as I was never sick; yet I was far from tasting the usual serenity of my health. Whether it was the motion of the ship on the billows, the confinement, the salted food, or all of these together, I suffered from a blackness of spirit and a painful strain upon my temper. The nature of my errand on that ship perhaps contributed; I think it did no more: the malady (whatever it was) sprang from my environment; and if the ship were not to blame, then it was the Master. Hatred and fear are ill bedfellows; but (to my shame be it spoken) I have tasted those in other places, lain down and got up with them, and eaten and drunk with them, and yet never before, nor after, have I been so poisoned through and through, in soul and body, as I was on board the *Nonesuch.* I freely confess my enemy set me a fair example of forbearance; in our worst days displayed the most patient geniality, holding me in conversation as long as I would suffer, and when I had rebuffed his civility, stretching himself on deck to read. The book he had on board with him was Mr. Richardson's famous *Clarissa;* and among other small attentions he would read me passages aloud; nor could any elocutionist have given with greater potency the pathetic portions of that work. I would retort upon him with passages out of the Bible, which was all my library—and very fresh to me, my religious duties (I grieve to say it) being always and even to this day extremely neglected. He tasted the merits of the work like the connoisseur he was; and would sometimes take it from my hand, turn the leaves over like a man that knew his way, and give me, with his fine declamation, a Roland for my Oliver. But it was singular how little he applied his reading to himself; it passed high above his head like summer thunder: Lovelace and Clarissa, the tales of David's generosity, the psalms of his penitence, the solemn questions of the book of Job, the touching poetry of Isaiah —they were to him a source of entertainment only, like the scraping of a fiddle in a change-house. This outer sensibility and inner toughness set me against him; it seemed of a piece with that impudent grossness which I knew to underlie the veneer of his fine manners; and sometimes my gorge rose against him as though he were deformed—and sometimes I would draw away as though from something partly spectral. I had moments when I thought of him as of a man of pasteboard—as though, if one should strike smartly through the buckram of his countenance, there would be found a mere vacuity within. This horror (not merely fanciful, I think) vastly increased my detestation of his neighbourhood; I began to feel something shiver within me on his drawing near; I had at times a longing to cry out; there were days when I thought I could have struck him. This frame of mind was doubtless helped by shame, because I had dropped during our last days at Durrisdeer into a certain toleration of the man; and if any one had then told me I should drop into it again, I must have laughed in his face. It is possible he remained unconscious of this extreme fever of my resentment; yet I think he was too quick; and rather that he had fallen, in a long life of idleness, into a positive need of company, which obliged him to confront and tolerate my unconcealed aversion. Certain at least, that he loved the note of his own tongue, as indeed he entirely loved all the parts and properties of himself: a sort of imbecility which almost necessarily attends on wickedness. I have seen him driven, when I proved recalcitrant, to long discourses with the skipper: and this, although the man plainly testified his weariness, fiddling miserably with both hand and foot, and replying only with a grunt.

After the first week out, we fell in with foul winds and heavy weather. The sea was high. The *Nonesuch,* being an old-fashioned ship and badly loaden, rolled beyond belief; so that the skipper trembled for his masts and I for my life. We made no progress on our course. An unbearable ill-humour settled on the ship; men, mates and master, girding at one another all day long. A saucy word on the one hand, and a blow on the other, made a daily incident. There were times when the whole crew refused their duty; and we of the afterguard were twice got under arms (being the first time that ever I bore weapons) in the fear of mutiny.

In the midst of our evil season sprang up a hurricane of wind; so that all supposed she must go down. I was shut in the cabin from noon of one day till sundown of the next; the Master was somewhere lashed on deck. Secundra had eaten of some drug and lay insensible; so you may say I passed these hours in an unbroken solitude. At first I was terrified beyond motion and almost beyond thought, my mind appearing to be frozen. Presently there stole in on me a ray of comfort. If the *Nonesuch* foundered, she would carry down with her into the deeps of that unsounded sea the creature whom we all so feared and hated; there would be no more Master of Ballantrae, the fish would sport among his ribs; his schemes all brought to nothing, his harmless enemies at peace. At first, I have said, it was but a ray of comfort; but it had soon grown to be broad sunshine. The thought of the man's death, of his deletion from this world which he embittered for so many, took possession of my mind. I hugged it, I found it sweet in my belly. I conceived the ship's last plunge, the sea bursting upon all sides into the cabin, the brief mortal conflict there, all by myself, in that closed place; I numbered the horrors, I had almost said with satisfaction; I felt I could bear all and more, if the *Nonesuch* carried down with her, overtook by the same ruin, the enemy of my poor master's house. Towards noon of the second day, the screaming of the wind abated; the ship lay not so perilously over; and it began to be clear to me that we were past the height of the tempest. As I hope for mercy, I was singly disappointed. In the selfishness of that vile, absorbing passion of hatred, I forgot the case of our innocent shipmates and thought but of myself and my enemy. For myself, I was already old, I had never been young, I was not formed for the world's pleasures, I had few affections; it mattered not the toss of a silver tester whether I was drowned there and then in the Atlantic, or dribbled out a few more years, to die, perhaps no less terribly, in a deserted sickbed. Down I went upon my knees—holding on by the locker, or else I had been instantly dashed across the tossing cabin—and, lifting up my voice in the midst of that clamour of the abating hurricane, impiously prayed for my own death. "O God," I cried, "I would be liker a man if I rose and struck this creature down; but thou madest me a coward from my mother's womb. O Lord, thou madest me so, thou knowest my weakness, thou knowest that any face of death will set me shaking in my shoes. But lo! here is thy servant ready, his mortal weakness laid aside. Let me give my life for this creature's; take the two of them, Lord! take the two, and have mercy on the innocent!" In some such words as these, only yet more irreverent and with more sacred adjurations, I continued to pour forth my spirit; God heard me not, I must suppose in mercy; and I was still absorbed in my agony of supplication, when some one, removing the tarpaulin cover, let the light of the sunset pour into the cabin. I stumbled to my feet ashamed, and was seized with surprise to find myself totter and ache like one that had been stretched upon the rack. Secundra Dass, who had slept off the effects of his drug, stood in a corner not far off, gazing at me with wild eyes; and from the open skylight the captain thanked me for my supplications.

"It's you that saved the ship, Mr. Mackellar," says he. "There is no craft of seamanship that could have kept her floating: well may we say: 'Except the Lord the city keep, the watchmen watch in vain!' "

I was abashed by the captain's error; abashed, also, by the surprise and fear with which the Indian regarded me at first, and the obsequious civilities with which he soon began to cumber me. I know now that he must have overheard and comprehended the peculiar nature of my prayers. It is certain, of course, that he at once disclosed the matter to his patron; and looking back with greater knowledge, I can now understand, what so much puzzled me at the moment, those singular and (so to speak) approving smiles with which the Master honoured me. Similarly, I can understand a word that I remember to have fallen from him in conversation that same night; when, holding up his hand and smiling, "Ah, Mackellar," said he, "not every man is so great a coward as he thinks he is—nor yet so good a Christian." He did not guess how true he spoke! For the fact is, the thoughts which had come to me in the violence of the storm retained their hold upon my spirit; and the words that rose to my lips unbidden in the instancy of prayer continued to sound in my ears: with what shameful consequences, it is fitting I should honestly relate; for I could not support a part of such disloyalty as to describe the sins of others and conceal my own.

The wind fell, but the sea hove ever the higher. All night the *Nonesuch* rolled outrageously; the next day dawned, and the next, and brought no change. To cross the cabin was scarce possible; old, experienced seamen were cast down upon the deck, and one cruelly mauled in the concussion; every board and block in the old ship cried out aloud; and the great bell by the anchor-bitts continually and dolefully rang. One of these days the Master and I sate alone together at the break of the poop. I should say the *Nonesuch* carried a high, raised poop. About the top of it ran considerable bulwarks, which made the ship unweatherly; and these, as they approached the front on each side, ran down in a fine, old-fashioned, carven scroll to join the bulwarks of the waist. From this disposition, which seems designed rather for ornament than use, it followed there was a discontinuance of protection: and that, besides, at the very margin of the elevated part where (in certain movements of the ship) it might be the most needful. It was here we were sitting: our feet hanging down, the Master betwixt me and the side, and I holding on with both hands to the grating of the cabin skylight; for it struck me it was a dangerous position, the more so as I had continually before my eyes a measure of our evolutions in the person of the Master, which stood out in the break of the bulwarks against the sun. Now his head would be in the zenith and his shadow fall quite beyond the *Nonesuch* on the further side; and now he would swing down till he was underneath my feet, and the line of the sea leaped high above him like the ceiling of a room. I looked on upon this with a growing fascination, as birds are said to look on snakes. My mind besides was troubled with an astonishing diversity of noises; for now that we had all sails spread in the vain hope to bring her to the sea, the ship sounded like a factory with their reverberations. We spoke first of the mutiny with which we had been threatened; this led us on to the topic of assassination; and that offered a temptation to the Master more strong than he was able to resist. He must tell me a tale, and show me at the same time how clever he was and how wicked. It was a thing he did always with affectation and display; generally with a good effect. But this tale, told in a high key in the midst of so great a tumult, and by a narrator who was one moment looking down at me from the skies and the next peering up from under the soles of my feet—this particular tale, I say, took hold upon me in a degree quite singular.

"My friend the count," it was thus that he began his story, "had for an enemy a certain German baron, a stranger in Rome. It matters not what was the ground of the count's enmity; but as he had a firm design to be revenged, and that with safety to himself, he kept it secret even from the baron. Indeed that is the first principle of vengeance; and hatred betrayed is hatred impotent. The count was a man of a curious, searching mind; he had something of the artist; if anything fell for him to do, it must always be done with an exact perfection, not only as to the result but in the very means and instruments, or he thought the thing miscarried. It chanced he was one day riding in the outer suburbs, when he came to a disused by-road branching off into the moor which lies about Rome. On the one hand was an ancient Roman tomb; on the other a deserted house in a garden of evergreen trees. This road brought him presently into a field of ruins, in the midst of which, in the side of a hill, he saw an open door and (not far off) a single stunted pine no greater than a currant-bush. The place was desert and very secret: a voice spoke in the count's bosom that there was something here to his advantage. He tied his horse to the pine-tree, took his flint and steel in his hand to make a light, and entered into the hill. The doorway opened on a passage of old Roman masonry, which shortly after branched in two. The count took the turning to the right, and followed it, groping forward in the dark, till he was brought up by a kind of fence, about elbow-high, which extended quite across the passage. Sounding forward with his foot, he found an edge of polished stone, and then vacancy. All his curiosity was now awakened, and, getting some rotten sticks that lay about the floor, he made a fire. In front of him was a profound well: doubtless some neighbouring peasant had once used it for his water, and it was he that had set up the fence. A long while the count stood leaning on the rail and looking down into the pit. It was of Roman foundation, and, like all that nation set their hands to, built as for eternity: the sides were still straight and the joints smooth; to a man who should fall in, no escape was possible. 'Now,' the count was thinking, 'a strong impulsion brought me to this place: what for? what have I gained? why should I be sent to gaze into this well?'—when the rail of the fence gave suddenly under his weight, and he came within an ace of falling headlong in. Leaping back to save himself, he trod out the last flicker of his fire, which gave him thenceforward no more light, only an incommoding smoke. 'Was I sent here to my death?' says he, and shook from head to foot. And then a thought flashed in his mind. He crept forth on hands and knees to the brink of the pit and felt above him in the air. The rail had been fast to a pair of uprights; it had only broken from the one, and still depended from the other. The count set it back again as he had found it, so that the place meant death to the first comer; and groped out of the catacomb like a sick man. The next day, riding in the Corso with the baron, he purposely betrayed a strong preoccupation. The other (as he had designed) inquired into the cause; and he (after some fencing) admitted that his spirits had been dashed by an unusual dream. This was calculated to draw on the baron—a superstitious man who affected the scorn of superstition. Some rallying followed; and then the count (as if suddenly carried away) called on his friend to beware, for it was of him that he had dreamed. You know enough of human nature, my excellent Mackellar, to be certain of one thing: I mean, that the baron did not rest till he had heard the dream. The count (sure that he would never desist) kept him in play till his curiosity was highly inflamed, and then suffered himself with seeming reluctance to be overborne. 'I warn you,' says he, 'evil will come of it; something tells me so. But since there is to be no peace either for you or me except on this condition, the blame be on your own head! This was the dream. I beheld you riding, I know not where, yet I think it must have been near Rome, for on your one hand was an ancient tomb and on the other a garden of evergreen trees. Methought I cried and cried upon you to come back in a very agony of terror; whether you heard me, I know not, but you went doggedly on. The road brought you to a desert place among ruins: where was a door in a hillside, and hard by the door a misbegotten pine. Here you dismounted (I still crying on you to beware), tied your horse to the pine-tree, and entered resolutely in by the door. Within it was dark; but in my dream I could still see you, and still besought you to hold back. You felt your way along the right-hand wall, took a branching passage to the right, and came to a little chamber, where was a well with a railing. At this (I know not why) my alarm for you increased a thousandfold, so that I seemed to scream myself hoarse with warnings, crying it was still time and bidding you begone at once from that vestibule. Such was the word I used in my dream, and it seemed then to have a clear significancy; but to-day and awake, I profess I know not what it means. To all my outcry you rendered not the least attention, leaning the while upon the rail and looking down intently in the water. And then there was made to you a communication, I do not think I even gathered what it was, but the fear of it plucked me clean out of my slumber, and I awoke shaking and sobbing. And now,' continues the count, 'I thank you from my heart for your insistency. This dream lay on me like a load; and now I have told it in plain words and in the broad daylight, it seems no great matter.'—'I do not know,' says the baron. 'It is in some points strange. A communication, did you say? Oh, it is an odd dream. It will make a story to amuse our friends.'—'I am not so sure,' says the count. 'I am sensible of some reluctancy. Let us rather forget it.'—'By all means,' says the baron. And (in fact) the dream was not again referred to. Some days after, the count proposed a ride in the fields, which the baron (since they were daily growing faster friends) very readily accepted. On the way back to Rome, the count led them insensibly by a particular route. Presently he reined in his horse, clapped his hand before his eyes, and cried out aloud. Then he showed his face again (which was now quite white, for he was a consummate actor) and stared upon the baron. 'What ails you?' cries the baron. 'What is wrong with you?' —'Nothing,' cries the count. 'It is nothing. A seizure, I know not what. Let us hurry back to Rome.' But in the meanwhile the baron had looked about him; and there, on the left-hand side of the way as they went back to Rome, he saw a dusty by-road with a tomb upon the one hand and a garden of evergreen trees upon the other.—'Yes,' says he, with a changed voice. 'Let us by all means hurry back to Rome. I fear you are not well in health.'—'Oh, for God's sake!' cries the count, shuddering. 'Back to Rome and let me get to bed.' They made their return with scarce a word; and the count, who should by rights have gone into society, took to his bed and gave out he had a touch of country fever. The next day the baron's horse was found tied to the pine, but himself was never heard of from that hour.—And now, was that a murder?" says the Master, breaking sharply off.

"Are you sure he was a count?" I asked.

"I am not certain of the title," said he, "but he was a gentleman of family: and the Lord deliver you, Mackellar, from an enemy so subtile!"

These last words he spoke down at me smiling, from high above; the next, he was under my feet. I continued to follow his evolutions with a childish fixity; they made me giddy and vacant, and I spoke as in a dream.

"He hated the baron with a great hatred?" I asked.

"His belly moved when the man came near him," said the Master.

"I have felt that same," said I.

"Verily!" cries the Master. "Here is news indeed! I wonder—do I flatter myself? or am I the cause of these ventral perturbations?"

He was quite capable of choosing out a graceful posture, even with no one to behold him but myself, and all the more if there were any element of peril. He sat now with one knee flung across the other, his arms on his bosom, fitting the swing of the ship with an exquisite balance, such as a featherweight might overthrow. All at once I had the vision of my lord at the table with his head upon his hands; only now, when he showed me his countenance, it was heavy with reproach. The words of my own prayer—*I were liker a man if I struck this creature down*—shot at the same time into my memory. I called my energies together, and (the ship then heeling downward toward my enemy) thrust at him swiftly with my foot. It was written I should have the guilt of this attempt without the profit. Whether from my own uncertainty or his incredible quickness, he escaped the thrust, leaping to his feet and catching hold at the same moment of a stay.

I do not know how long a time passed by: I lying where I was upon the deck, overcome with terror and remorse and shame: he standing with the stay in his hand, backed against the bulwarks, and regarding me with an expression singularly mingled. At last he spoke.

"Mackellar," said he, "I make no reproaches, but I offer you a bargain. On your side, I do not suppose you desire to have this exploit made public; on mine, I own to you freely I do not care to draw my breath in a perpetual terror of assassination by the man I sit at meat with. Promise me—but no," says he, breaking off, "you are not yet in the quiet possession of your mind; you might think I had extorted the promise from your weakness; and I would leave no door open for casuistry to come in—that dishonesty of the conscientious. Take time to meditate."

With that he made off up the sliding deck like a squirrel and plunged into the cabin. About half an hour later he returned: I still lying as he had left me.

"Now," says he, "will you give me your troth as a Christian and a faithful servant of my brother's, that I shall have no more to fear from your attempts?"

"I give it you," said I.

"I shall require your hand upon it," says he.

"You have the right to make conditions," I replied, and we shook hands.

He sat down at once in the same place and the old perilous attitude.

"Hold on!" cried I, covering my eyes. "I cannot bear to see you in that posture. The least irregularity of the sea might plunge you overboard."

"You are highly inconsistent," he replied, smiling, but doing as I asked. "For all that, Mackellar, I would have you to know you have risen forty feet in my esteem. You think I cannot set a price upon fidelity? But why do you suppose I carry that Secundra Dass about the world with me? Because he would die or do murder for me tomorrow; and I love him for it. Well, you may think it odd, but I like you the better for this afternoon's performance. I thought you were magnetised with the Ten Commandments; but no—God damn my soul!"—he cries, "the old wife has blood in his body after all!—Which does not change the fact," he continued, smiling again, "that you have done well to give your promise; for I doubt if you would ever shine in your new trade."

"I suppose," said I, "I should ask your pardon and God's for my attempt. At any rate I have passed my word, which I will keep faithfully. But when I think of those you persecute——" I paused.

"Life is a singular thing," said he, "and mankind a very singular people. You suppose yourself to love my brother. I assure you it is merely custom. Interrogate your memory; and when first you came to Durrisdeer, you will find you considered him a dull, ordinary youth. He is as dull and ordinary now, though not so young. Had you instead fallen in with me, you would to-day be as strong upon my side."

"I would never say you were ordinary, Mr. Bally," I returned;

"but here you prove yourself dull. You have just shown your reliance on my word. In other terms, that is my conscience—the same which starts instinctively back from you, like the eye from a strong light."

"Ah!" says he, "but I mean otherwise. I mean, had I met you in my youth. You are to consider I was not always as I am to-day; nor (had I met in with a friend of your description) should I have ever been so."

"Hut, Mr. Bally," says I, "you would have made a mock of me —you would never have spent ten civil words on such a square-toes."

But he was now fairly started on his new course of justification, with which he wearied me throughout the remainder of the passage. No doubt in the past he had taken pleasure to paint himself unnecessarily black, and made a vaunt of his wickedness, bearing it for a coat of arms. Nor was he so illogical as to abate one item of his old confessions. "But now that I know you are a human being," he would say, "I can take the trouble to explain myself. For I assure you I am human too, and have my virtues like my neighbours." I say he wearied me, for I had only the one word to say in answer: twenty times I must have said it: "Give up your present purpose and return with me to Durrisdeer; then I will believe you."

Thereupon he would shake his head at me. "Ah, Mackellar, you might live a thousand years and never understand my nature," he would say. "This battle is now committed, the hour of reflection quite past, the hour for mercy not yet come. It began between us when we span a coin in the hall of Durrisdeer now twenty years ago; we have had our ups and downs, but never either of us dreamed of giving in; and as for me, when my glove is cast, life and honour go with it."

"A fig for your honour!" I would say. "And by your leave, these warlike similitudes are something too high-sounding for the matter in hand. You want some dirty money, there is the bottom of your contention; and as for your means, what are they?—to stir up sorrow in a family that never harmed you, to debauch (if you can) your own born nephew, and to wring the heart of your born brother! A footpad that kills an old granny in a woollen mutch with a dirty bludgeon, and that for a shilling-piece and a paper of snuff—there is all the warrior that you are."

When I would attack him thus (or somewhat thus) he would smile and sigh like a man misunderstood. Once, I remember, he defended himself more at large, and had some curious sophistries, worth repeating for a light upon his character.

"You are very like a civilian to think war consists in drums and banners," said he. "War (as the ancients said very wisely) is *ultima ratio*. When we take our advantage unrelentingly, then we make war. Ah, Mackellar, you are a devil of a soldier in the steward's room at Durrisdeer, or the tenants do you sad injustice!"

"I think little of what war is or is not," I replied. "But you weary me with claiming my respect. Your brother is a good man, and you are a bad one—neither more nor less."

"Had I been Alexander——" he began.

"It is so we all dupe ourselves," I cried. "Had I been St. Paul, it would have been all one; I would have made the same hash of that career that you now see me making of my own."

"I tell you," he cried, bearing down my interruption, "had I been the least petty chieftain in the highlands, had I been the least king of naked Negroes in the African desert, my people would have adored me. A bad man, am I? Ah, but I was born for a good tyrant! Ask Secundra Dass; he will tell you I treat him like a son. Cast in your lot with me to-morrow, become my slave, my chattel, a thing I can command as I command the powers of my own limbs and spirit—you will see no more that dark side that I turn upon the world in anger. I must have all or none. But where all is given, I give it back with usury. I have a kingly nature: there is my loss!"

"It has been hitherto rather the loss of others," I remarked: "which seems a little on the hither side of royalty."

"Tilly-vally!" cried he. "Even now, I tell you I would spare that family in which you take so great an interest: yes, even now—to-morrow I would leave them to their petty welfare, and disappear in that forest of cut-throats and thimble-riggers that we call the world. I would do it tomorrow!" says he. "Only—only——"

"Only what?" I asked.

"Only they must beg it on their bended knees. I think in public too," he added, smiling. "Indeed, Mackellar, I doubt if there be a hall big enough to serve my purpose for that act of reparation."

"Vanity, vanity!" I moralised. "To think that this great force for evil should be swayed by the same sentiment that sets a lassie mincing to her glass!"

"O, there are double words for everything; the word that swells, the word that belittles: you cannot fight me with a word!" said he. "You said the other day that I relied on your conscience: were I in your humour of detraction, I might say I built upon your vanity. It is your pretension to be *un homme de parole;* 't is mine not to accept defeat. Call it vanity, call it virtue, call it greatness of soul—what signifies the expression? But recognise in each of us a common strain; that we both live for an idea."

It will be gathered from so much familiar talk, and so much patience on both sides, that we now lived together upon excellent terms. Such was again the fact, and this time more seriously than before. Apart from disputations such as that which I have tried to reproduce, not only consideration reigned, but I am tempted to say even kindness. When I fell sick (as I did shortly after our great storm) he sat by my berth to entertain me with his conversation, and treated me with excellent remedies, which I accepted with security. Himself commented on the circumstance. "You see," says he, "you begin to know me better. A very little while ago, upon this lonely ship, where no one but myself has any smattering of science, you would have made sure I had designs upon your life. And observe, it is since I found you had designs upon my own, that I have shown you most respect. You will tell me if this speaks of a small mind." I found little to reply. In so far as regarded myself, I believed him to mean well; I am perhaps the more a dupe of his dissimulation, but I believed (and I still believe) that he regarded me with genuine kindness. Singular and sad fact! so soon as this change began, my animosity abated, and these haunting visions of my master passed utterly away. So that, perhaps, there was truth in the man's last vaunting word to me, uttered on the second day of July, when our long voyage was at last brought almost to an end, and we lay becalmed at the sea-end of the vast harbour of New York in a gasping heat which was presently exchanged for a surprising waterfall of rain. I stood on the poop regarding the green shores near at hand, and now and then the light smoke of the little town, our destination. And as I was even then devising how to steal a march on my familiar enemy, I was conscious of a shade of embarrassment when he approached me with his hand extended.

"I am now to bid you farewell," said he, "and that for ever. For now you go among my enemies, where all your former prejudices will revive. I never yet failed to charm a person when I wanted; even you, my good friend—to call you so for once—even you have now a very different portrait of me in your memory, and one that you will never quite forget. The voyage has not lasted long enough, or I should have wrote the impression deeper. But now all is at an end, and we are again at war. Judge by this little interlude how dangerous I am; and tell those fools"—pointing with his finger to the town—"to think twice and thrice before they set me at defiance."

Passages at New York

I HAVE MENTIONED I WAS RESOLVED TO STEAL A MARCH UPON THE Master; and this, with the complicity of Captain MacMurtrie, was mighty easily effected: a boat being partly loaded on the one side of our ship and the Master placed on board of it, the while a skiff put off from the other carrying me alone. I had no more trouble in finding a direction to my lord's house, whither I went at top speed, and which I found to be on the outskirts of the place, a very suitable mansion, in a fine garden, with an extraordinary large barn, byre and stable all in one. It was here my lord was walking when I arrived; indeed it had become his chief place of frequentation, and his mind was now filled with farming. I burst in upon him breathless, and gave him my news: which was indeed no news at all, several ships having outsailed the *Nonesuch* in the interval.

"We have been expecting you long," said my lord; "and indeed, of late days, ceased to expect you any more. I am glad to take your hand again, Mackellar. I thought you had been at the bottom of the sea."

"Ah, my lord, would God I had!" cried I. "Things would have been better for yourself."

"Not in the least," says he grimly. "I could not ask better. There is a long score to pay, and now—at—last—I can begin to pay it."

I cried out against his security.

"O," says he, "this is not Durrisdeer, and I have taken my precautions. His reputation awaits him, I have prepared a welcome for my brother. Indeed fortune has served me; for I found here a merchant of Albany who knew him after the '45 and had mighty convenient suspicions of a murder: some one of the name of Chew it was, another Albanian. No one here will be surprised if I deny him my door; he will not be suffered to address my children, nor even to salute my wife: as for myself, I make so much exception for a brother that he may speak to me. I should lose my pleasure else," says my lord, rubbing his palms.

Presently he bethought himself, and set men off running, with billets, to summon the magnates of the province I cannot recall what pretext he employed; at least it was successful; and when our ancient enemy appeared upon the scene, he found my lord pacing in front of his house under some trees of shade, with the governor upon one hand and various notables upon the other. My lady, who was seated in the verandah, rose with a very pinched expression and carried her children into the house.

The Master, well dressed and with an elegant walking-sword, bowed to the company in a handsome manner and nodded to my lord with familiarity. My lord did not accept the salutation, but looked upon his brother with bended brows.

"Well, sir," says he, at last, "what ill wind brings you hither of all places, where (to our common disgrace) your reputation has preceded you?"

"Your lordship is pleased to be civil," cries the Master, with a fine start.

"I am pleased to be very plain," returned my lord; "because it is needful you should clearly understand your situation. At home, where you were so little known, it was still possible to keep appearances: that would be quite vain in this province; and I have to tell you that I am quite resolved to wash my hands of you. You have already ruined me almost to the door, as you ruined my father before me—whose heart you also broke. Your crimes escape the law; but my friend the governor has promised protection to my family. Have a care, sir!" cries my lord, shaking his cane at him: "if you are observed to utter two words to any of my innocent household, the law shall be stretched to make you smart for it."

"Ah!" says the Master, very slowly. "And so this is the advantage of a foreign land! These gentlemen are unacquainted with our story, I perceive. They do not know that I am the Lord Durrisdeer; they do not know you are my younger brother, sitting in my place under a sworn family compact; they do not know (or they would not be seen with you in familiar correspondence) that every acre is mine before God Almighty—and every doit of the money you withhold from me, you do it as a thief, a perjurer and a disloyal brother!"

"General Clinton," I cried, "do not listen to his lies. I am the steward of the estate, and there is not one word of truth in it. The man is a forfeited rebel turned into a hired spy: there is his story in two words."

It was thus that (in the heat of the moment) I let slip his infamy.

"Fellow," said the governor, turning his face sternly on the Master, "I know more of you than you think for. We have some broken ends of your adventures in the provinces, which you will do very well not to drive me to investigate. There is the disappearance of Mr. Jacob Chew with all his merchandise; there is the matter of where you came ashore from with so much money and jewels, when you were picked up by a Bermudan out of Albany. Believe me, if I let these matters lie, it is in commiseration for your family and out of respect for my valued friend, Lord Durrisdeer."

There was a murmur of applause from the provincials.

"I should have remembered how a title would shine out in such a hole as this," says the Master, white as a sheet: "no matter how unjustly come by. It remains for me then to die at my lord's door, where my dead body will form a very cheerful ornament."

"Away with your affectations!" cries my lord. "You know very well I have no such meaning; only to protect myself from calumny and my home from your intrusion. I offer you a choice. Either I shall pay your passage home on the first ship, when you may perhaps be able to resume your occupations under government, although God knows I would rather see you on the highway! Or, if that likes you not, stay here and welcome! I have inquired the least sum on which body and soul can be decently kept together in New York; so much you shall have, paid weekly; and if you cannot labour with your hands to better it, high time you should betake yourself to learn! The condition is, that you speak with no member of my family except myself," he added.

I do not think I have ever seen any man so pale as was the Master; but he was erect and his mouth firm.

"I have been met here with some very unmerited insults," said he, "from which I have certainly no idea to take refuge by flight. Give me your pittance; I take it without shame, for it is mine already—like the shirt upon your back, and I choose to stay until these gentlemen shall understand me better. Already they must spy the cloven hoof; since with all your pretended eagerness for the family honour, you take a pleasure to degrade it in my person."

"This is all very fine," says my lord; "but to us who know you of old, you must be sure it signifies nothing. You take that alternative out of which you think that you can make the most. Take it, if you can, in silence: it will serve you better in the long run, you may believe me, than this ostentation of ingratitude."

"O, gratitude, my lord!" cries the Master, with a mounting intonation and his forefinger very conspicuously lifted up. "Be at rest: it will not fail you. It now remains that I should salute these gentlemen whom we have wearied with our family affairs."

And he bowed to each in succession, settled his walking-sword, and took himself off, leaving every one amazed at his behaviour, and me not less so at my lord's.

We were now to enter on a changed phase of this family division. The Master was by no manner of means so helpless as my lord supposed, having at his hand and entirely devoted to his service an excellent artist in all sorts of goldsmith work. With my lord's allowance, which was not so scanty as he had described it, the pair could support life; and all the earnings of Secundra Dass might be laid upon one side for any future purpose. That this was done, I have no doubt. It was in all likelihood the Master's design to gather a sufficiency, and then proceed in quest of that treasure which he had buried long before among the mountains; to which, if he had confined himself, he would have been more happily inspired. But unfortunately for himself and all of us, he took counsel of his anger. The public disgrace of his arrival (which I sometimes wonder he could manage to survive) rankled in his bones; he was in that humour when a man (in the words of the old adage) will cut off his nose to spite his face; and he must make himself a public spectacle, in the hopes that some of the disgrace might spatter on my lord.

He chose, in a poor quarter of the town, a lonely, small house of boards, overhung with some acacias. It was furnished in front with a sort of hutch opening, like that of a dog's kennel, but about as high as a table from the ground, in which the poor man that built it had formerly displayed some wares; and it was this which took the Master's fancy and possibly suggested his proceedings. It appears, on board the pirate ship, he had acquired some quickness with the needle: enough at least to play the part of tailor in the public eye; which was all that was required by the nature of his vengeance. A placard was hung above the hutch, bearing these words in something of the following disposition:

JAMES DURIE

FORMERLY MASTER OF BALLANTRAE

CLOTHES NEATLY CLOUTED

———

SECUNDRA DASS

DECAYED GENTLEMAN OF INDIA

FINE GOLDSMITH WORK.

Underneath this, when he had a job, my gentleman sat withinside tailor-wise and busily stitching. I say, when he had a job, but such customers as came were rather for Secundra, and the Master's sewing would be more in the manner of Penelope's. He could never have designed to gain even butter to his bread by such a means of livelihood: enough for him, that there was the name of Durie dragged in the dirt on the placard, and the sometime heir of that proud family set up cross-legged in public for a reproach upon his brother's meanness. And in so far his device succeeded, that there was murmuring in the town and a party formed highly inimical to my lord. My lord's favour with the governor laid him more open on the other side; my lady (who was never so well received in the colony) met with painful innuendoes; in a party of women, where it would be the topic most natural to introduce, she was almost debarred from the naming of needlework; and I have seen her return with a flushed countenance and vow that she would go abroad no more.

In the meanwhile, my lord dwelled in his decent mansion, immersed in farming: a popular man with his intimates, and careless or unconscious of the rest. He laid on flesh; had a bright, busy face; even the heat seemed to prosper with him; and my lady (in despite of her own annoyances) daily blessed heaven her father should have left her such a paradise. She had looked on from a window upon the Master's humiliation; and from that hour appeared to feel at ease. I was not so sure myself; as time went on there seemed to me a something not quite wholesome in my lord's condition; happy he was, beyond a doubt, but the grounds of this felicity were secret; even in the bosom of his family, he brooded with manifest delight upon some private thought; and I conceived at last the suspicion (quite unworthy of us both) that he kept a mistress somewhere in the town. Yet he went little abroad, and his day was very fully occupied; indeed there was but a single period, and that pretty early in the morning while Mr. Alexander was at his lessonbook, of which I was not certain of the disposition. It should be borne in mind, in the defence of that which I now did, that I was always in some fear my lord was not quite justly in his reason; and with our enemy sitting so still in the same town with us, I did well to be upon my guard. Accordingly I made a pretext, had the hour changed at which I taught Mr. Alexander the foundation of cyphering and the mathematic, and set myself instead to dog my master's footsteps.

Every morning, fair or foul, he took his gold-headed cane, set his hat on the back of his head—a recent habitude, which I thought to indicate a burning brow—and betook himself to make a certain circuit. At the first his way was among pleasant trees and beside a graveyard, where he would sit awhile, if the day were fine, in meditation. Presently the path turned down to the waterside and came back along the harbour front and past the Master's booth. As he approached this second part of his circuit, my Lord Durrisdeer began to pace more leisurely, like a man delighted with the air and scene; and before the booth, half-way between that and the water's edge, would pause a little leaning on his staff. It was the hour when the Master sate within upon his board and plied his needle. So these two brothers would gaze upon each other with hard faces; and then my lord move on again, smiling to himself.

It was but twice that I must stoop to that ungrateful necessity of playing spy. I was then certain of my lord's purpose in his rambles and of the secret source of his delight. Here was his mistress: it was hatred and not love that gave him healthful colours. Some moralists might have been relieved by the discovery; I confess that I was dismayed. I found this situation of two brethren not only odious in itself, but big with possibilities of further evil; and I made it my practice, in so far as many occupations would allow, to go by a shorter path and be secretly present at their meeting.

Coming down one day a little late, after I had been near a week prevented, I was struck with surprise to find a new development. I should say there was a bench against the Master's house, where customers might sit to parley with the shopman; and here I found my lord seated, nursing his cane and looking pleasantly forth upon the bay. Not three feet from him sate the Master stitching. Neither spoke; nor (in this new situation) did my lord so much as cast a glance upon his enemy. He tasted his neighbourhood, I must suppose, less indirectly in the bare proximity of person; and without doubt, drank deep of hateful pleasures.

He had no sooner come away than I openly joined him.

"My lord, my lord," said I, "this is no manner of behaviour."

"I grow fat upon it," he replied; and not merely the words, which were strange enough, but the whole character of his expression shocked me.

"I warn you, my lord, against this indulgency of evil feeling," said I. "I know not to which it is more perilous, the soul or the reason: but you go the way to murder both."

"You cannot understand," said he. "You had never such mountains of bitterness upon your heart."

"And if it were no more," I added, "you will surely goad the man to some extremity."

"To the contrary: I am breaking his spirit," says my lord.

Every morning for hard upon a week, my lord took his same place upon the bench. It was a pleasant place, under the green acacias, with a sight upon the bay and shipping, and a sound (from some way off) of mariners singing at their employ. Here the two sate without speech or any external movement, beyond that of the needle or the Master biting off a thread, for he still clung to his pretence of industry; and here I made a point to join them, wondering at myself and my companions. If any of my lord's friends went by, he would hail them cheerfully, and cry out he was there to give some good advice to his brother, who was now (to his delight) grown quite industrious. And even this, the Master accepted with a steady countenance: what was in his mind, God knows, or perhaps Satan only.

All of a sudden, on a still day of what they call the Indian Summer, when the woods were changed into gold and pink and scarlet, the Master laid down his needle and burst into a fit of merriment. I think he must have been preparing it a long while in silence, for the note in itself was pretty naturally pitched; but breaking suddenly from so extreme a silence and in circumstances so averse from mirth, it sounded ominously on my ear.

"Henry," said he, "I have for once made a false step, and for once you have had the wit to profit by it. The farce of the cobbler ends to-day; and I confess to you (with my compliments) that you have had the best of it. Blood will out; and you have certainly a choice idea of how to make yourself unpleasant."

Never a word said my lord; it was just as though the Master had not broken silence.

"Come," resumed the Master, "do not be sulky, it will spoil your attitude. You can now afford (believe me) to be a little gracious; for I have not merely a defeat to accept. I had meant to continue this performance till I had gathered enough money for a certain purpose; I confess ingenuously, I have not the courage. You naturally desire my absence from this town; I have come round by another way to the same idea. And I have a proposition to make; or if your lordship prefers, a favour to ask."

"Ask it," says my lord.

"You may have heard that I had once in this country a considerable treasure," returned the Master: "it matters not whether or no—such is the fact; and I was obliged to bury it in a spot of which I have sufficient indications. To the recovery of this, has my ambition now come down; and as it is my own, you will not grudge it me."

"Go and get it," says my lord. "I make no opposition."

"Yes," said the Master, "but to do so I must find men and carriage. The way is long and rough, and the country infested with wild Indians. Advance me only so much as shall be needful: either as a lump sum, in lieu of my allowance; or if you prefer it, as a loan, which I shall repay on my return. And then, if you so decide, you may have seen the last of me."

My lord stared him steadily in the eyes; there was a hard smile upon his face, but he uttered nothing.

"Henry," said the Master, with a formidable quietness, and drawing at the same time somewhat back—"Henry, I had the honour to address you."

"Let us be stepping homeward," says my lord to me, who was plucking at his sleeve; and with that he rose, stretched himself, settled his hat, and still without a syllable of response, began to walk steadily along the shore.

I hesitated awhile between the two brothers, so serious a climax did we seem to have reached. But the Master had resumed his occupation, his eyes lowered, his hand seemingly as deft as ever; and I decided to pursue my lord.

"Are you mad?" I cried, so soon as I had overtook him. "Would you cast away so fair an opportunity?"

"Is it possible you should still believe in him?" inquired my lord, almost with a sneer.

"I wish him forth of this town," I cried. "I wish him anywhere and anyhow but as he is."

"I have said my say," returned my lord, "and you have said yours. There let it rest."

But I was bent on dislodging the Master. That sight of him patiently returning to his needlework was more than my imagination could digest. There was never a man made, and the Master the least of any, that could accept so long a series of insults. The air smelt blood to me. And I vowed there should be no neglect of mine if, through any chink of possibility, crime could yet be turned aside. That same day, therefore, I came to my lord in his business room, where he sat upon some trivial occupation.

"My lord," said I, "I have found a suitable investment for my small economies. But these are unhappily in Scotland; it will take some time to lift them, and the affair presses. Could your lordship see his way to advance me the amount against my note?"

He read me awhile with keen eyes. "I have never inquired into the state of your affairs, Mackellar," says he. "Beyond the amount of your caution, you may not be worth a farthing, for what I know."

"I have been a long while in your service, and never told a lie, nor yet asked a favour for myself," said I, "until to-day."

"A favour for the Master," he returned quietly. "Do you take me for a fool, Mackellar? Understand it once and for all; I treat this beast in my own way; fear nor favour shall not move me; and before I am hoodwinked, it will require a trickster less transparent than yourself. I ask service, loyal service; not that you should make and mar behind my back, and steal my own money to defeat me."

"My lord," said I, "these are very unpardonable expressions."

"Think once more, Mackellar," he replied; "and you will see they fit the fact. It is your own subterfuge that is unpardonable. Deny (if you can) that you designed this money to evade my orders with, and I will ask your pardon freely. If you cannot, you must have the resolution to hear your conduct go by its own name."

"If you think I had any design but to save you . . ." I began.

"O, my old friend," said he, "you know very well what I think! Here is my hand to you with all my heart; but of money, not one rap."

Defeated upon this side, I went straight to my room, wrote a letter, ran with it to the harbour, for I knew a ship was on the point of sailing: and came to the Master's door a little before dusk. Entering without the form of any knock, I found him sitting with his Indian at a simple meal of maize porridge with some milk. The house within was clean and poor; only a few books upon a shelf distinguished it, and (in one corner) Secundra's little bench.

"Mr. Bally," said I, "I have near five hundred pounds laid by in Scotland, the economies of a hard life. A letter goes by yon ship to have it lifted; have so much patience till the return ship comes in, and it is all yours, upon the same condition you offered to my lord this morning."

He rose from the table, came forward, took me by the shoulders, and looked me in the face, smiling.

"And yet you are very fond of money!" said he. "And yet you love money beyond all things else, except my brother!"

"I fear old age and poverty," said I, "which is another matter."

"I will never quarrel for a name. Call it so!" he replied. "Ah, Mackellar, Mackellar, if this were done from any love to me, how gladly would I close upon your offer!"

"And yet," I eagerly answered—"I say it to my shame, but I cannot see you in this poor place without compunction. It is not my single thought, nor my first; and yet it's there! I would gladly see you delivered. I do not offer it in love, and far from that; but as God judges me—and I wonder at it too!—quite without enmity."

"Ah," says he, still holding my shoulders and now gently shaking me, "you think of me more than you suppose. 'And I wonder at it too,'" he added, repeating my expression and I suppose something of my voice. "You are an honest man, and for that cause I spare you."

"Spare me?" I cried.

"Spare you," he repeated, letting me go and turning away. And then, fronting me once more: "You little know what I would do with it, Mackellar! Did you think I had swallowed my defeat indeed? Listen: my life has been a series of unmerited cast-backs. That fool, Prince Charlie, mismanaged a most promising affair: there fell my first fortune. In Paris I had my foot once more high upon the ladder: that time it was an accident, a letter came to the wrong hand, and I was bare again. A third time, I found my opportunity; I built up a place for myself in India with an infinite patience; and then Clive came, my rajah was swallowed up, and I escaped out of the convulsion, like another Æneas, with Secundra Dass upon my back. Three times I have had my hand upon the highest station; and I am not yet three and forty. I know the world as few men know it when they come to die, court and camp, the east and west; I know where to go, I see a thousand openings. I am now at the height of my resources, sound of health, of inordinate ambition. Well, all this I resign; I care not if I die and the world never hear of me; I care only for one thing, and that I will have. Mind yourself: lest, when the roof falls, you too should be crushed under the ruins."

As I came out of his house, all hope of intervention quite destroyed, I was aware of a stir on the harbour-side, and raising my eyes, there was a great ship newly come to anchor. It seems strange I could have looked upon her with so much indifference, for she brought death to the brothers of Durrisdeer. After all the desperate episodes of this contention, the insults, the opposing interests, the fraternal duel in the shrubbery, it was reserved for some poor devil in Grub Street, scribbling for his dinner and not caring what he scribbled, to cast a spell across four thousand miles of the salt sea, and send forth both these brothers into savage and wintry deserts, there to die. But such a thought was distant from my mind; and while all the provincials were fluttered about me by the unusual animation of their port, I passed throughout their midst on my return homeward, quite absorbed in the recollection of my visit and the Master's speech.

The same night there was brought to us from the ship a little packet of pamphlets. The next day, my lord was under engagement to go with the governor upon some party of pleasure; the time was nearly due, and I left him for a moment alone in his room and skimming through the pamphlets. When I returned his head had fallen upon the table, his arms lying abroad amongst the crumpled papers.

"My lord, my lord!" I cried as I ran forward, for I supposed he was in some fit.

He sprang up like a figure upon wires, his countenance deformed with fury, so that in a strange place I should scarce have known him. His hand at the same time flew above his head, as though to strike me down. "Leave me alone!" he screeched; and I fled, as fast as my shaking legs would bear me, for my lady. She too lost no time; but when we returned he had the door locked within, and only cried to us from the other side to leave him be. We looked in each other's faces, very white: each supposing the blow had come at last.

"I will write to the governor to excuse him," says she. "We must keep our strong friends." But when she took up the pen, it flew out of her fingers. "I cannot write," said she. "Can you?"

"I will make a shift, my lady," said I.

She looked over me as I wrote. "That will do," she said, when I had done. "Thank God, Mackellar, I have you to lean upon! But what can it be now? what, what can it be?"

In my own mind, I believed there was no explanation possible, and none required: it was my fear that the man's madness had now simply burst forth its way, like the long-smothered flames of a volcano; but to this (in mere mercy to my lady) I durst not give expression.

"It is more to the purpose to consider our own behaviour," said I. "Must we leave him there alone?"

"I do not dare disturb him," she replied. "Nature may know best; it may be nature that cries to be alone—and we grope in the dark. O yes, I would leave him as he is."

"I will then despatch this letter, my lady, and return here, if you please, to sit with you," said I.

"Pray do," cries my lady.

All afternoon we sat together, mostly in silence, watching my lord's door. My own mind was busy with the scene that had just passed, and its singular resemblance to my vision. I must say a word upon this, for the story has gone abroad with great exaggeration, and I have even seen it printed and my own name referred to for particulars. So much was the same: here was my lord in a room, with his head upon the table, and when he raised his face, it wore such an expression as distressed me to the soul. But the room was different, my lord's attitude at the table not at all the same, and his face, when he disclosed it, expressed a painful degree of fury instead of that haunting despair which had always (except once, already referred to) characterised it in the vision. There is the whole truth at last before the public; and if the differences be great, the coincidence was yet enough to fill me with uneasiness. All afternoon, as I say, I sat and pondered upon this quite to myself; for my lady had trouble of her own, and it was my last thought to vex her with fancies. About the midst of our time of waiting, she conceived an ingenious scheme, had Mr. Alexander fetched and bid him knock at his father's door. My lord sent the boy about his business, but without the least violence whether of manner or expression; so that I began to entertain a hope the fit was over.

At last, as the night fell and I was lighting a lamp that stood there trimmed, the door opened and my lord stood within upon the threshold. The light was not so strong that we could read his countenance; when he spoke, methought his voice a little altered but yet perfectly steady.

"Mackellar," said he, "carry this note to its destination with your own hand. It is highly private. Find the person alone when you deliver it."

"Henry," says my lady, "you are not ill?"

"No, no," says he, querulously, "I am occupied. Not at all; I am only occupied. It is a singular thing a man must be supposed to be ill when he has any business! Send me supper to this room, and a basket of wine: I expect the visit of a friend. Otherwise I am not to be disturbed."

And with that he once more shut himself in.

The note was addressed to one Captain Harris, at a tavern on the portside. I knew Harris (by reputation) for a dangerous adventurer, highly suspected of piracy in the past, and now following the rude business of an Indian trader. What my lord should have to say to him, or he to my lord, it passed my imagination to conceive: or yet how my lord had heard of him, unless by a disgraceful trial from which the man was recently escaped. Altogether I went upon the errand with reluctance, and from the little I saw of the captain, returned from it with sorrow. I found him in a foul-smelling chamber, sitting by a guttering candle and an empty bottle; he had the remains of a military carriage, or rather perhaps it was an affectation, for his manners were low.

"Tell my lord, with my service, that I will wait upon his lordship in the inside of half an hour," says he, when he had read the note; and then had the servility, pointing to his empty bottle, to propose that I should buy him liquor.

Although I returned with my best speed, the Captain followed close upon my heels, and he stayed late into the night. The cock was crowing a second time when I saw (from my chamber window) my lord lighting him to the gate, both men very much affected with their potations and sometimes leaning one upon the other to confabulate. Yet the next morning my lord was abroad again early with a hundred pounds of money in his pocket. I never supposed that he returned with it; and yet I was quite sure it did not find its way to the Master, for I lingered all morning within view of the booth. That was the last time my Lord Durrisdeer passed his own enclosure till we left New York; he walked in his barn or sat and talked with his family, all much as usual; but the town saw nothing of him, and his daily visits to the Master seemed forgotten. Nor yet did Harris reappear; or not until the end.

I was now much oppressed with a sense of the mysteries in which we had begun to move. It was plain, if only from his change of habitude, my lord had something on his mind of a grave nature; but what it was, whence it sprang, or why he should now keep the house and garden, I could make no guess at. It was clear, even to probation, the pamphlets had some share in this revolution; I read all I could find, and they were all extremely insignificant and of the usual kind of party scurrility; even to a high politician, I could spy out no particular matter of offence, and my lord was a man rather indifferent on public questions. The truth is, the pamphlet which was the spring of this affair, lay all the time on my lord's bosom. There it was that I found it at last, after he was dead, in the midst of the north wilderness: in such a place, in such dismal circumstances, I was to read for the first time these idle, lying words of a whig pamphleteer declaiming against indulgency to Jacobites: "Another notorious Rebel, the M——r of B——e, is to have his Title restored," the passage ran. "This Business has been long in hand, since he rendered some very disgraceful Services in Scotland and France. His Brother, L——d D——r, is known to be no better than himself in Inclination; and the supposed Heir, who is now to be set aside, was bred up in the most detestable Principles. In the old Phrase, it is *six of the one and half a dozen of the other;* but the Favour of such a Reposition is too extreme to be passed over." A man in his right wits could not have cared two straws for a tale so manifestly false; that government should ever entertain the notion, was inconceivable to any reasoning creature, unless possibly the fool that penned it; and my lord, though never brilliant, was ever remarkable for sense. That he should credit such a rodomontade, and carry the pamphlet on his bosom and the words in his heart, is the clear proof of the man's lunacy. Doubtless the mere mention of Mr. Alexander, and the threat directly held out against the child's succession, precipitated that which had so long impended. Or else my master had been truly mad for a long time, and we were too dull or too much used to him, and did not perceive the extent of his infirmity.

About a week after the day of the pamphlets I was late upon the harbour-side, and took a turn towards the Master's, as I often did. The door opened, a flood of light came forth upon the road, and I beheld a man taking his departure with friendly salutations. I cannot say how singularly I was shaken to recognise the adventurer Harris. I could not but conclude it was the hand of my lord that had brought him there; and prolonged my walk in very serious and apprehensive thought. It was late when I came home, and there was my lord making up his portmanteau for a voyage.

"Why do you come so late?" he cried. "We leave to-morrow for Albany, you and I together; and it is high time you were about your preparations."

"For Albany, my lord?" I cried. "And for what earthly purpose?"

"Change of scene," said he.

And my lady, who appeared to have been weeping, gave me the signal to obey without more parley. She told me a little later (when we found occasion to exchange some words) that he had suddenly announced his intention after a visit from Captain Harris, and her best endeavours, whether to dissuade him from the journey or to elicit some explanation of its purpose, had alike proved unavailing.

The Journey in the Wilderness

WE MADE A PROSPEROUS VOYAGE UP THAT FINE RIVER OF THE Hudson, the weather grateful, the hills singularly beautified with the colours of the autumn. At Albany we had our residence at an inn, where I was not so blind and my lord not so cunning but what I could see he had some design to hold me prisoner. The work he found for me to do was not so pressing that we should transact it apart from necessary papers in the chamber of an inn; nor was it of such importance that I should be set upon as many as four or five scrolls of the same document. I submitted in appearance; but I took private measures on my own side, and had the news of the town communicated to me daily by the politeness of our host. In this way I received at last a piece of intelligence for which, I may say, I had been waiting. Captain Harris (I was told) with "Mr. Mountain the trader" had gone by up the river in a boat. I would have feared the landlord's eye, so strong the sense of some complicity upon my master's part oppressed me. But I made out to say I had some knowledge of the captain, although none of Mr. Mountain, and to inquire who else was of the party. My informant knew not; Mr. Mountain had come ashore upon some needful purchases; had gone round the town buying, drinking, and prating; and it seemed the party went upon some likely venture, for he had spoken much of great things he would do when he returned. No more was known, for none of the rest had come ashore, and it seemed they were pressed for time to reach a certain spot before the snow should fall.

And sure enough, the next day, there fell a sprinkle even in Albany; but it passed as it came, and was but a reminder of what lay before us. I thought of it lightly then, knowing so little as I did of that inclement province: the retrospect is different; and I wonder at times if some of the horror of these events which I must now rehearse flowed not from the foul skies and savage winds to which we were exposed, and the agony of cold that we must suffer.

The boat having passed by, I thought at first we should have left the town. But no such matter. My lord continued his stay in Albany, where he had no ostensible affairs, and kept me by him, far from my due employment, and making a pretence of occupation. It is upon this passage I expect, and perhaps deserve, censure. I was not so dull but what I had my own thoughts. I could not see the master entrust himself into the hands of Harris, and not suspect some under-hand contrivance. Harris bore a villainous reputation, and he had been tampered with in private by my lord; Mountain the trader proved, upon inquiry, to be another of the same kidney; the errand they were all gone upon, being the recovery of ill-gotten treasures, offered in itself a very strong incentive to foul play; and the character of the country where they journeyed promised impunity to deeds of blood. Well: it is true I had all these thoughts and fears, and guesses of the Master's fate. But you are to consider I was the same man that sought to dash him from the bulwarks of a ship in the mid-sea; the same that, a little before, very impiously but sincerely offered God a bargain, seeking to hire God to be my bravo. It is true again that I had a good deal melted toward our enemy. But this I always thought of as a weakness of the flesh and even culpable; my mind remaining steady and quite bent against him. True yet again, that it was one thing to assume on my own shoulders the guilt and danger of a criminal attempt, and another to stand by and see my lord imperil and besmirch himself. But this was the very ground of my inaction. For (should I anyway stir in the business) I might fail indeed to have the Master, but I could not miss to make a by-word of my lord.

Thus it was that I did nothing; and upon the same reasons, I am still strong to justify my course. We lived meanwhile in Albany, but though alone together in a strange place, had little traffic beyond formal salutations. My lord had carried with him several introductions to chief people of the town and neighbourhood; others he had before encountered in New York: with this consequence, that he went much abroad, and I am sorry to say was altogether too convivial in his habits. I was often in bed, but never asleep, when he returned; and there was scarce a night when he did not betray the influence of liquor. By day he would still lay upon me endless tasks, which he showed considerable ingenuity to fish up and to renew, in the manner of Penelope's web. I never refuse, as I say, for I was hired to do his bidding; but I took no pains to keep my penetration under a bushel, and would sometimes smile in his face.

"I think I must be the devil and you Michael Scott," I said to him one day. "I have bridged Tweed and split the Eildons; and now you set me to the rope of sand."

He looked at me with shining eyes and looked away again, his jaw chewing; but without words.

"Well, well, my lord," said I, "your will is my pleasure. I will do this thing for the fourth time; but I would beg of you to invent another task against to-morrow, for by my troth, I am weary of this one."

"You do not know what you are saying," returned my lord, putting on his hat and turning his back to me. "It is a strange thing you should take a pleasure to annoy me. A friend—but that is a different affair. It is a strange thing. I am a man that has had ill-fortune all my life through. I am still surrounded by contrivances. I am always treading in plots," he burst out. "The whole world is banded against me."

"I would not talk wicked nonsense if I were you," said I; "but I will tell you what I *would* do—I would put my head in cold water, for you had more last night than you could carry."

"Do ye think that?" said he, with a manner of interest highly awakened. "Would that be good for me? It's a thing I never tried."

"I mind the days when you had no call to try, and I wish, my lord, that they were back again," said I. "But the plain truth is, if you continue to exceed, you will do yourself a mischief."

"I don't appear to carry drink the way I used to," said my lord. "I get overtaken, Mackellar. But I will be more upon my guard."

"That is what I would ask of you," I replied. "You are to bear in mind that you are Mr. Alexander's father: give the bairn a chance to carry his name with some responsibility."

"Ay, ay," said he. "Ye're a very sensible man, Mackellar, and have been long in my employ. But I think, if you have nothing more to say to me, I will be stepping. If you have nothing more to say?" he added, with that burning, childish eagerness that was now so common with the man.

"No, my lord, I have nothing more," said I, drily enough.

"Then I think I will be stepping," says my lord, and stood and looked at me fidgeting with his hat, which he had taken off again. "I suppose you will have no errands? No? I am to meet Sir William Johnson, but I will be more upon my guard." He was silent for a time, and then, smiling: "Do you call to mind a place, Mackellar—it's a little below Engles—where the burn runs very deep under a wood of rowans? I mind being there when I was a lad—dear, it comes over me like an old song!—I was after the fishing, and I made a bonny cast. Eh, but I was happy. I wonder, Mackellar, why I am never happy now?"

"My lord," said I, "if you would drink with more moderation you would have the better chance. It is an old by-word that the bottle is a false consoler."

"No doubt," said he, "no doubt. Well, I think I will be going."

"Good-morning, my lord," said I.

"Good-morning, good-morning," said he, and so got himself at last from the apartment.

I give that for a fair specimen of my lord in the morning; and I must have described my patron very ill if the reader does not perceive a notable falling off. To behold the man thus fallen; to know him accepted among his companions for a poor, muddled toper, welcome (if he were welcome at all) for the bare consideration of his title; and to recall the virtues he had once displayed against such odds of fortune: was not this a thing at once to rage and to be humbled at?

In his cups, he was more excessive. I will give but the one scene, close upon the end, which is strongly marked upon my memory to this day, and at the time affected me almost with horror.

I was in bed, lying there awake, when I heard him stumbling on the stair and singing. My lord had no gift of music, his brother had all the graces of the family, so that when I say singing, you are to understand a manner of high, carolling utterance, which was truly neither speech nor song. Something not unlike is to be heard upon the lips of children, ere they learn shame; from those of a man grown elderly, it had a strange effect. He opened the door with noisy precaution; peered in, shading his candle; conceived me to slumber; entered, set his light upon the table, and took off his hat. I saw him very plain; a high, feverish exultation appeared to boil in his veins, and he stood and smiled and smirked upon the candle. Presently he lifted up his arm, snapped his fingers, and fell to undress. As he did so, having once more forgot my presence, he took back to his singing; and now I could hear the words, which were those from the old song of the *Twa Corbies* endlessly repeated:

> And over his banes when they are bare
> The wind sall blaw for evermair!

I have said there was no music in the man. His strains had no logical succession except in so far as they inclined a little to the minor mode; but they exercised a rude potency upon the feelings, and followed the words, and signified the feelings of the singer with barbaric fitness. He took it first in the time and manner of a rant; presently this ill-favoured gleefulness abated, he began to dwell upon the notes more feelingly, and sank at last into a degree of maudlin pathos that was to me scarce bearable. By equal steps, the original briskness of his acts declined; and when he was stripped to his breeches, he sat on the bedside and fell to whimpering. I know nothing less respectable than the tears of drunkenness, and turned my back impatiently on this poor sight.

But he had started himself (I am to suppose) on that slippery descent of self-pity; on the which, to a man unstrung by old sorrows and recent potations, there is no arrest except exhaustion. His tears continued to flow, and the man to sit there, three parts naked, in the cold air of the chamber. I twitted myself alternately with inhumanity and sentimental weakness, now half rising in my bed to interfere, now reading myself lessons of indifference and courting slumber, until, upon a sudden, the *quantum mutatus ab illo* shot into my mind; and calling to remembrance his old wisdom, constancy, and patience, I was overborne with a pity almost approaching the passionate, not for my master alone but for the sons of man.

At this I leaped from my place, went over to his side and laid a hand on his bare shoulder, which was cold as stone. He uncovered his face and showed it me all swollen and begrutten* like a child's; and at the sight my impatience partially revived.

"Think shame to yourself," said I. "This is bairnly conduct. I might have been snivelling myself, if I had cared to swill my belly with wine. But I went to my bed sober like a man. Come: get into yours and have done with this pitiable exhibition."

"Oh, Mackellar," said he, "my heart is wae!"

"Wae?" cried I. "For a good cause, I think. What words were these you sang as you came in? Show pity to others, we then can talk of pity to yourself. You can be the one thing or the other, but I will be no party to half-way houses. If you're a striker, strike, and if you're a bleater, bleat!"

"Cry!" cries he, with a burst, "that's it—strike! that's talking!

* Tear-marked.

Man, I've stood it all too long. But when they laid a hand upon
the child, when the child's threatened"—his momentary vigour
whimpering off—"my child, my Alexander!"—and he was at his
tears again.

I took him by the shoulders and shook him. "Alexander!" said
I. "Do you even think of him? Not you! Look yourself in the face
like a brave man, and you'll find you're but a self-deceiver. The
wife, the friend, the child, they're all equally forgot, and you
sunk in a mere log of selfishness."

"Mackellar," said he, with a wonderful return to his old manner and appearance, "you may say what you will of me, but one
thing I never was—I was never selfish."

"I will open your eyes in your despite," said I. "How long have
we been here? and how often have you written to your family?
I think this is the first time you were ever separate: have you
written at all? Do they know if you are dead or living?"

I had caught him here too openly; it braced his better nature;
there was no more weeping, he thanked me very penitently, got
to bed and was soon fast asleep; and the first thing he did the
next morning was to sit down and begin a letter to my lady: a
very tender letter it was too, though it was never finished. Indeed
all communication with New York was transacted by myself; and
it will be judged I had a thankless task of it. What to tell my lady
and in what words, and how far to be false and how far cruel, was
a thing that kept me often from my slumber.

All this while, no doubt, my lord waited with growing im-
patiency for news of his accomplices. Harris, it is to be thought,
had promised a high degree of expedition; the time was already
overpast when word was to be looked for; and suspense was a very
evil counsellor to a man of an impaired intelligence. My lord's
mind throughout this interval dwelled almost wholly in the
Wilderness, following that party with whose deeds he had so
much concern. He continually conjured up their camps and prog-
resses, the fashion of the country, the perpetration in a thousand
different manners of the same horrid fact, and that consequent
spectacle of the Master's bones lying scattered in the wind. These
private, guilty considerations I would continually observe to peep
forth in the man's talk, like rabbits from a hill. And it is the less
wonder if the scene of his meditations began to draw him bodily.

It is well known what pretext he took. Sir William Johnson had a diplomatic errand in these parts; and my lord and I (from curiosity, as was given out) went in his company. Sir William was well attended and liberally supplied. Hunters brought us venison, fish was taken for us daily in the streams, and brandy ran like water. We proceeded by day and encamped by night in the military style; sentinels were set and changed; every man had his named duty; and Sir William was the spring of all. There was much in this that might at times have entertained me; but for our misfortune, the weather was extremely harsh, the days were in the beginning open, but the nights frosty from the first. A painful keen wind blew most of the time, so that we sat in the boat with blue fingers, and at night, as we scorched our faces at the fire, the clothes upon our back appeared to be of paper. A dreadful solitude surrounded our steps; the land was quite dispeopled, there was no smoke of fires, and save for a single boat of merchants on the second day, we met no travellers. The season was indeed late, but this desertion of the waterways impressed Sir William himself; and I have heard him more than once express a sense of intimidation. "I have come too late I fear; they must have dug up the hatchet," he said; and the future proved how justly he had reasoned.

I could never depict the blackness of my soul upon this journey. I have none of those minds that are in love with the unusual: to see the winter coming and to lie in the field so far from any house, oppressed me like a nightmare; it seemed, indeed, a kind of awful braving of God's power; and this thought, which I dare say only writes me down a coward, was greatly exaggerated by my private knowledge of the errand we were come upon. I was besides encumbered by my duties to Sir William, whom it fell upon me to entertain; for my lord was quite sunk into a state bordering on *pervigilium,* watching the woods with a rapt eye, sleeping scarce at all, and speaking sometimes not twenty words in a whole day. That which he said was still coherent; but it turned almost invariably upon the party for whom he kept his crazy lookout. He would tell Sir William often, and always as if it were a new communication, that he had "a brother somewhere in the woods," and beg that the sentinels should be directed "to inquire for him." "I am anxious for news of my brother," he would say. And sometimes, when we were under way, he would fancy he spied a canoe far off upon the water or a camp on the shore, and exhibit painful agitation. It was impossible but Sir William should be struck with these singularities; and at last he led me aside, and hinted his uneasiness. I touched my head and shook it; quite rejoiced to prepare a little testimony against possible disclosures.

"But in that case," cries Sir William, "is it wise to let him go at large?"

"Those that know him best," said I, "are persuaded that he should be humoured."

"Well, well," replied Sir William, "it is none of my affairs. But if I had understood, you would never have been here."

Our advance into this savage country had thus uneventfully proceeded for about a week, when we encamped for a night at a place where the river ran among considerable mountains clothed in wood. The fires were lighted on a level space at the water's edge; and we supped and lay down to sleep in the customary fashion. It chanced the night fell murderously cold; the stringency of the frost seized and bit me through my coverings, so that pain kept me wakeful; and I was afoot again before the peep of day, crouching by the fires or trotting to and fro at the stream's edge, to combat the aching of my limbs. At last dawn began to break upon hoar woods and mountains, the sleepers rolled in their robes, and the boisterous river dashing among spears of ice. I stood looking about me, swaddled in my stiff coat of a bull's fur, and the breath smoking from my scorched nostrils, when, upon a sudden, a singular, eager cry rang from the borders of the wood. The sentries answered it, the sleepers sprang to their feet; one pointed, the rest followed his direction with their eyes, and there, upon the edge of the forest and betwixt two trees, we beheld the figure of a man reaching forth his hands like one in ecstasy. The next moment he ran forward, fell on his knees at the side of the camp, and burst in tears.

This was John Mountain, the trader, escaped from the most horrid perils; and his first word, when he got speech, was to ask if we had seen Secundra Dass.

"Seen what?" cries Sir William.

"No," said I, "we have seen nothing of him. Why?"

"Nothing?" says Mountain. "Then I was right after all." With that he struck his palm upon his brow. "But what takes him back?" he cried. "What takes the man back among dead bodies? There is some damned mystery here."

This was a word which highly aroused our curiosity, but I shall be more perspicacious if I narrate these incidents in their true order. Here follows a narrative which I have compiled out of three sources, not very consistent in all points:

First, a written statement by Mountain, in which everything criminal is cleverly smuggled out of view;

Second, two conversations with Secundra Dass; and,

Third, many conversations with Mountain himself, in which he was pleased to be entirely plain; for the truth is he regarded me as an accomplice.

NARRATIVE OF THE TRADER, MOUNTAIN

The crew that went up the river under the joint command of Captain Harris and the Master numbered in all nine persons, of whom (if I except Secundra Dass) there was not one that had not merited the gallows. From Harris downward the voyagers were notorious in that colony for desperate, bloody-minded miscreants; some were reputed pirates, the most hawkers of rum; all ranters and drinkers; all fit associates, embarking together without remorse, upon this treacherous and murderous design. I could not hear there was much discipline or any set captain in the gang; but Harris and four others, Mountain himself, two Scotchmen— Pinkerton and Hastie—and a man of the name of Hicks, a drunken shoemaker, put their heads together and agreed upon the course. In a material sense, they were well enough provided; and the Master, in particular, brought with him a tent where he might enjoy some privacy and shelter.

Even this small indulgence told against him in the minds of his companions. But indeed he was in a position so entirely false (and even ridiculous) that all his habit of command and arts of pleasing were here thrown away. In the eyes of all, except Secundra Dass, he figured as a common gull and designated victim; going unconsciously to death; yet he could not but suppose himself the contriver and the leader of the expedition; he could scarce help but so conduct himself; and at the least hint of authority or condescension, his deceivers would be laughing in their sleeves. I was so used to see and to conceive him in a high, authoritative attitude, that when I had conceived his position on this journey, I was pained and could have blushed. How soon he may have entertained a first surmise, we cannot know; but it was long, and the party had advanced into the Wilderness beyond the reach of any help, ere he was fully awakened to the truth.

It fell thus. Harris and some others had drawn apart into the woods for consultation, when they were startled by a rustling in the brush. They were all accustomed to the arts of Indian warfare, and Mountain had not only lived and hunted, but fought and earned some reputation, with the savages. He could move in the woods without noise, and follow a trail like a hound; and upon the emergence of this alert, he was deputed by the rest to plunge into the thicket for intelligence. He was soon convinced there was a man in his close neighbourhood, moving with precaution but without art among the leaves and branches; and coming shortly to a place of advantage, he was able to observe Secundra Dass crawling briskly off with many backward glances. At this he knew not whether to laugh or cry; and his accomplices, when he had returned and reported, were in much the same dubiety. There was now no danger of an Indian onslaught; but on the other hand, since Secundra Dass was at the pains to spy upon them, it was highly probable he knew English, and if he knew English it was certain the whole of their design was in the Master's knowledge. There was one singularity in the position. If Secundra Dass knew and concealed his knowledge of English, Harris was a proficient in several of the tongues of India, and as his career in that part of the world had been a great deal worse than profligate, he had not thought proper to remark upon the circumstance. Each side had thus a spy-hole on the counsels of the other. The plotters, so soon as this advantage was explained, returned to camp; Harris, hearing the Hindustani was once more closeted with his master, crept to the side of the tent; and the rest, sitting about the fire with their tobacco, awaited his report with impatience. When he came at last, his face was very black. He had overheard enough to confirm the worst of his suspicions. Secundra Dass was a good English scholar; he had been some days creeping and listening, the Master was now fully informed of the conspiracy, and the pair proposed on the morrow to fall out of line at a carrying-place and plunge at a venture in the woods: preferring the full risk of famine, savage beasts, and savage men to their position in the midst of traitors.

What, then, was to be done? Some were for killing the Master on the spot; but Harris assured them that would be a crime without profit, since the secret of the treasure must die along with him that buried it. Others were for desisting at once from the whole enterprise and making for New York; but the appetising name of treasure, and the thought of the long way they had already travelled dissuaded the majority. I imagine they were dull fellows for the most part. Harris, indeed, had some acquirements, Mountain was no fool, Hastie was an educated man; but even these had manifestly failed in life, and the rest were the dregs of colonial rascality. The conclusion they reached, at least, was more the offspring of greed and hope, than reason. It was to temporise, to be wary and watch the Master, to be silent and supply no further aliment to his suspicions, and to depend entirely (as well as I make out) on the chance that their victim was as greedy, hopeful, and irrational as themselves, and might, after all, betray his life and treasure.

Twice, in the course of the next day, Secundra and the Master must have appeared to themselves to have escaped; and twice they were circumvented. The Master, save that the second time he grew a little pale, displayed no sign of disappointment, apologised for the stupidity with which he had fallen aside, thanked his recapturers as for a service, and rejoined the caravan with all his usual gallantry and cheerfulness of mien and bearing. But it is certain he had smelled a rat; for from thenceforth he and Secundra spoke only in each other's ear, and Harris listened and shivered by the tent in vain. The same night it was announced they were to leave the boats and proceed by foot: a circumstance which (as it put an end to the confusion of the portages) greatly lessened the chances of escape.

And now there began between the two sides a silent contest, for life on the one hand, for riches on the other. They were now near that quarter of the desert in which the Master himself must begin to play the part of guide; and using this for a pretext of prosecution, Harris and his men sat with him every night about the fire, and laboured to entrap him into some admission. If he let slip his secret, he knew well it was the warrant for his death; on the other hand, he durst not refuse their questions, and must appear to help them to the best of his capacity, or he practically published his mistrust. And yet Mountain assures me the man's brow was never ruffled. He sat in the midst of these jackals, his life depending by a thread, like some easy, witty householder at home by his own fire; an answer he had for everything—as often as not, a jesting answer; avoided threats, evaded insults; talked, laughed, and listened with an open countenance; and, in short, conducted himself in such a manner as must have disarmed suspicion, and went near to stagger knowledge. Indeed Mountain confessed to me they would soon have disbelieved the captain's story, and supposed their designated victim still quite innocent of their designs; but for the fact that he continued (however ingeniously) to give the slip to questions, and the yet stronger confirmation of his repeated efforts to escape. The last of these, which brought things to a head, I am now to relate. And first I should say that by this time the temper of Harris's companions was utterly worn out; civility was scarce pretended; and for one very significant circumstance, the Master and Secundra had been (on some pretext) deprived of weapons. On their side, however, the threatened pair kept up the parade of friendship handsomely; Secundra was all bows, the Master all smiles; and on the last night of the truce he had even gone so far as to sing for the diversion of the company. It was observed that he had also eaten with unusual heartiness, and drank deep: doubtless from design.

At least, about three in the morning, he came out of the tent into the open air, audibly mourning and complaining, with all the manner of a sufferer from surfeit. For some while, Secundra publicly attended on his patron, who at last became more easy, and fell asleep on the frosty ground behind the tent: the Indian returning within. Some time after, the sentry was changed; had the Master pointed out to him, where he lay in what is called a robe of buffalo; and thenceforth kept an eye upon him (he declared) without remission. With the first of the dawn, a draught of wind came suddenly and blew open one side the corner of the robe; and with the same puff, the Master's hat whirled in the air and fell some yards away. The sentry, thinking it remarkable the sleeper should not awaken, thereupon drew near; and the next moment, with a great shout, informed the camp their prisoner was escaped. He had left behind his Indian, who (in the first vivacity of the surprise) came near to pay the forfeit of his life, and was, in fact, inhumanly mishandled; but Secundra, in the midst of threats and cruelties, stuck to it with extraordinary loyalty, that he was quite ignorant of his master's plans, which might indeed be true, and of the manner of his escape, which was demonstrably false. Nothing was therefore left to the conspirators but to rely entirely on the skill of Mountain. The night had been frosty, the ground quite hard; and the sun was no sooner up than a strong thaw set in. It was Mountain's boast that few men could have followed that trail, and still fewer (even of the native Indians) found it. The Master had thus a long start before his pursuers had the scent, and he must have travelled with surprising energy for a pedestrian so unused, since it was near noon before Mountain had a view of him. At this conjuncture the trader was alone, all his companions following, at his own request, several hundred yards in the rear; he knew the Master was unarmed; his heart was besides heated with the exercise and lust of hunting; and seeing the quarry so close, so defenceless, and seemingly so fatigued, he vaingloriously determined to effect the capture with his single hand. A step or two further brought him to one margin of a little clearing; on the other, with his arms folded and his back to a huge stone, the Master sat. It is possible Mountain may have made a rustle, it is certain, at least, the Master raised his head and gazed directly at that quarter of the thicket where his hunter lay. "I could not be sure he saw me," Mountain said; "he just looked my way like a man with his mind made up, and all the courage ran out of me like rum out of a bottle." And presently, when the Master looked away again, and appeared to resume those meditations in which he had sat immersed before the trader's coming, Mountain slunk stealthily back and returned to seek the help of his companions.

And now began the chapter of surprises, for the scout had scarce informed the others of his discovery, and they were yet preparing their weapons for a rush upon the fugitive, when the man himself appeared in their midst, walking openly and quietly, with his hands behind his back.

"Ah, men!" says he, on his beholding them. "Here is a fortunate encounter. Let us get back to camp."

Mountain had not mentioned his own weakness or the Master's disconcerting gaze upon the thicket, so that (with all the rest) his return appeared spontaneous. For all that, a hubbub arose; oaths flew, fists were shaken, and guns pointed.

"Let us get back to camp," said the Master. "I have an explanation to make, but it must be laid before you all. And in the meanwhile I would put up these weapons, one of which might very easily go off and blow away your hopes of treasure. I would not kill," says he, smiling, "the goose with the golden eggs."

The charm of his superiority once more triumphed; and the party, in no particular order, set off on their return. By the way, he found occasion to get a word or two apart with Mountain.

"You are a clever fellow and a bold," says he, "but I am not so sure that you are doing yourself justice. I would have you to consider whether you would not do better, ay, and safer, to serve me instead of serving so commonplace a rascal as Mr. Harris. Consider of it," he concluded, dealing the man a gentle tap upon the shoulder, "and don't be in haste. Dead or alive, you will find me an ill man to quarrel with."

When they were come back to the camp, where Harris and Pinkerton stood guard over Secundra, these two ran upon the Master like viragoes, and were amazed out of measure when they were bidden by their comrades to "stand back and hear what the gentleman had to say." The Master had not flinched before their onslaught; nor, at this proof of the ground he had gained, did he betray the least sufficiency.

"Do not let us be in haste," says he. "Meat first and public speaking after."

With that they made a hasty meal: and as soon as it was done, the Master, leaning on one elbow, began his speech. He spoke long, addressing himself to each except Harris, finding for each (with the same exception) some particular flattery. He called them "bold, honest blades," declared he had never seen a more jovial company, work better done, or pains more merrily supported. "Well, then," says he, "some one asks me, Why the devil I ran away? But that is scarce worth answer, for I think you all know pretty well. But you know only pretty well: that is a point I shall arrive at presently, and be you ready to remark it when it comes. There is a traitor here: a double traitor: I will give you his name before I am done; and let that suffice for now. But here comes some other gentleman and asks me, Why in the devil I came back? Well, before I answer that question, I have one to put to you. It was this cur here, this Harris, that speaks Hindustani?" cries he, rising on one knee, and pointing fair at the man's face, with a gesture indescribably menacing; and when he had been answered in the affirmative, "Ah!" says he, "then are all my suspicions verified, and I did rightly to come back. Now, men, hear the truth for the first time." Thereupon he launched forth in a long story, told with extraordinary skill, how he had all along suspected Harris, how he had found the confirmation of his fears, and how Harris must have misrepresented what passed between Secundra and himself. At this point he made a bold stroke with excellent effect. "I suppose," says he, "you think you are going shares with Harris, I suppose you think you will see to that yourselves; you would naturally not think so flat a rogue could cozen you. But have a care! These half idiots have a sort of cunning, as the skunk has its stench; and it may be news to you that Harris has taken care of himself already. Yes, for him the treasure is all money in the bargain. You must find it or go starve. But he has been paid beforehand; my brother paid him to destroy me; look at him, if you doubt—look at him, grinning and gulping, a detected thief!" Thence, having made this happy impression, he explained how he had escaped, and thought better of it, and at last concluded to come back, lay the truth before the company, and take his chance with them once more: persuaded as he was, they would instantly depose Harris and elect some other leader. "There is the whole truth," said he: "and with one exception, I put myself entirely in your hands. What is the exception? There he sits," he cried, pointing once more to Harris; "a man that has to die! Weapons and conditions are all one to me; put me face to face with him, and if you give me nothing but a stick, in five minutes I will show you a sop of broken carrion, fit for dogs to roll in."

It was dark night when he made an end; they had listened in almost perfect silence; but the fire-light scarce permitted any one to judge, from the look of his neighbours, with what result of persuasion or conviction. Indeed, the Master had set himself in the brightest place, and kept his face there, to be the centre of man's eyes: doubtless on a profound calculation. Silence followed for awhile, and presently the whole party became involved in disputation: the Master lying on his back, with his hands knit under his head and one knee flung across the other, like a person unconcerned in the result. And here, I dare say, his bravado carried him too far and prejudiced his case. At least, after a cast or two back and forward, opinion settled finally against him. It's possible he hoped to repeat the business of the pirate ship, and be himself, perhaps, on hard enough conditions, elected leader; and things went so far that way, that Mountain actually threw out the proposition. But the rock he split upon was Hastie. This fellow was not well liked, being sour and slow, with an ugly, glowering disposition, but he had studied some time for the church at Edinburgh College, before ill-conduct had destroyed his prospects, and he now remembered and applied what he had learned. Indeed he had not proceeded very far, when the Master rolled carelessly upon one side, which was done (in Mountain's opinion) to conceal the beginnings of despair upon his countenance. Hastie dismissed the most of what they had heard as nothing to the matter; what they wanted was the treasure. All that was said of Harris might be true, and they would have to see to that in time. But what had that to do with the treasure? They had heard a vast of words; but the truth was just this, that Mr. Durie was damnably frightened and had several times run off. Here he was—whether caught or come back was all one to Hastie: the point was to make an end of the business. As for the talk of deposing and electing captains, he hoped they were all free men and could attend their own affairs. That was dust flung in their eyes, and so was the proposal to fight Harris. "He shall fight no one in the camp, I can tell him that," said Hastie. "We had trouble enough to get his arms away from him, and we should look pretty fools to give them back again. But if it's excitement the gentleman is after, I can supply him with more than perhaps he cares about. For I have no intention to spend the remainder of my life in these mountains; already I have been too long; and I propose that he should immediately tell us where that treasure is, or else immediately be shot. And there," says he, producing his weapon, "there is the pistol that I mean to use."

"Come, I call you a man," cries the Master, sitting up and looking at the speaker with an air of admiration.

"I didn't ask you to call me anything," returned Hastie; "which is it to be?"

"That's an idle question," said the Master. "Needs must when the devil drives. The truth is, we are within easy walk of the place, and I will show it you to-morrow."

With that, as if all were quite settled, and settled exactly to his mind, he walked off to his tent, whither Secundra had preceded him.

I cannot think of these last turns and wriggles of my old enemy except with admiration; scarce even pity is mingled with the sentiment, so strongly the man supported, so boldly resisted his misfortunes. Even at that hour, when he perceived himself quite lost, when he saw he had but effected an exchange of enemies, and overthrown Harris to set Hastie up, no sign of weakness appeared in his behaviour, and he withdrew to his tent, already determined (I must suppose) upon affronting the incredible hazard of his last expedient, with the same easy, assured, genteel expression and demeanour as he might have left a theatre withal to join a supper of the wits. But doubtless within, if we could see there, his soul trembled.

Early in the night, word went about the camp that he was sick; and the first thing the next morning he called Hastie to his side, and inquired most anxiously if he had any skill in medicine. As a matter of fact, this was a vanity of that fallen divinity student's, to which he had cunningly addressed himself. Hastie examined him; and being flattered, ignorant, and highly suspicious, knew not in the least whether the man was sick or malingering. In this state, he went forth again to his companions; and (as the thing which would give himself most consequence either way) announced that the patient was in a fair way to die.

"For all that," he added with an oath, "and if he bursts by the wayside, he must bring us this morning to the treasure."

But there were several in the camp (Mountain among the number) whom this brutality revolted. They would have seen the Master pistol'd, or pistol'd him themselves, without the smallest sentiment of pity; but they seem to have been touched by his gallant fight and unequivocal defeat the night before; perhaps, too, they were even already beginning to oppose themselves to their new leader: at least, they now declared that (if the man was sick) he should have a day's rest in spite of Hastie's teeth.

The next morning he was manifestly worse, and Hastie himself began to display something of humane concern, so easily does even the pretence of doctoring awaken sympathy. The third, the Master called Mountain and Hastie to the tent, announced himself to be dying, gave them full particulars as to the position of the cache, and begged them to set out incontinently on the quest, so that they might see if he deceived them, and (if they were at first unsuccessful) he should be able to correct their error.

But here arose a difficulty on which he doubtless counted. None of these men would trust another, none would consent to stay behind. On the other hand, although the Master seemed extremely low, spoke scarce above a whisper, and lay much of the time insensible, it was still possible it was a fraudulent sickness; and if all went treasure-hunting, it might prove they had gone upon a wild-goose chase, and return to find their prisoner flown. They concluded, therefore, to hang idling round the camp, alleging sympathy to their reason; and certainly, so mingled are our dispositions, several were sincerely (if not very deeply) affected by the natural peril of the man whom they callously designed to murder. In the afternoon, Hastie was called to the bedside to pray: the which (incredible as it must appear) he did with unction; about eight at night, the wailing of Secundra announced that all was over; and before ten, the Indian, with a link stuck in the ground, was toiling at the grave. Sunrise of next day beheld the Master's burial, all hands attending with great decency of demeanour; and the body was laid in the earth wrapped in a fur robe, with only the face uncovered; which last was of a waxy whiteness, and had the nostrils plugged according to some oriental habit of Secundra's. No sooner was the grave filled than the lamentations of the Indian once more struck concern to every heart; and it appears this gang of murderers, so far from resenting his outcries, although both distressful and (in such a country) perilous to their own safety, roughly but kindly endeavoured to console him.

But if human nature is even in the worst of men occasionally kind, it is still, and before all things, greedy; and they soon turned from the mourner to their own concerns. The cache of the treasure being hard by, although yet unidentified, it was concluded not to break camp; and the day passed, on the part of the voyagers, in unavailing exploration of the woods, Secundra the while lying on his master's grave. That night they placed no sentinel, but lay all together about the fire, in the customary woodman fashion, the heads outward, like the spokes of a wheel. Morning found them in the same disposition; only Pinkerton, who lay on Mountain's right, between him and Hastie, had (in the hours of darkness) been secretly butchered, and there lay, still wrapped as to his body in his mantle, but offering above that ungodly and horrific spectacle of the scalped head. The gang were that morning as pale as a company of phantoms, for the pertinacity of Indian war (or, to speak more correctly, Indian murder) was well known to all. But they laid the chief blame on their unsentinel'd posture; and fired with the neighbourhood of the treasure, determined to continue where they were. Pinkerton was buried hard by the Master; the survivors again passed the day in exploration, and returned in a mingled humour of anxiety and hope, being partly certain they were now close on the discovery of what they sought, and on the other hand (with the return of darkness) were infected with the fear of Indians. Mountain was the first sentry; he declares he neither slept nor yet sat down, but kept his watch with a perpetual and straining vigilance, and it was even with unconcern that (when he saw by the stars his time was up) he drew near the fire to waken his successor. This man (it was Hicks the shoemaker) slept on the lee side of the circle, something farther off in consequence than those to windward, and in a place darkened by the blowing smoke. Mountain stooped and took him by the shoulder; his hand was at once smeared by some adhesive wetness; and (the wind at the moment veering) the fire-light shone upon the sleeper and showed him, like Pinkerton, dead and scalped.

It was clear they had fallen in the hands of one of those matchless Indian bravos, that will sometimes follow a party for days. and in spite of indefatigable travel and unsleeping watch, continue to keep up with their advance and steal a scalp at every resting-place. Upon this discovery, the treasure-seekers, already reduced to a poor half-dozen, fell into mere dismay, seized a few necessaries, and deserting the remainder of their goods, fled outright into the forest. Their fire, they left still burning, and their dead comrade unburied. All day they ceased not to flee, eating by the way, from hand to mouth; and since they feared to sleep, continued to advance at random even in the hours of darkness. But the limit of man's endurance is soon reached; when they rested at last, it was to sleep profoundly; and when they woke, it was to find that the enemy was still upon their heels, and death and mutilation had once more lessened and deformed their company.

By this, they had become light-headed, they had quite missed their path in the Wilderness, their stores were already running low. With the further horrors, it is superfluous that I should swell this narrative, already too prolonged. Suffice it to say, that when at length a night passed by innocuous, and they might breathe again in the hope that the murderer had at last desisted from pursuit, Mountain and Secundra were alone. The trader is firmly persuaded their unseen enemy was some warrior of his own acquaintance, and that he himself was spared by favour. The mercy extended to Secundra he explains on the ground that the East Indian was thought to be insane; partly from the fact that, through all the horrors of the flight and while others were casting away their very food and weapons, Secundra continued to stagger forward with a mattock on his shoulder; and partly because, in the last days and with a great degree of heat and fluency, he perpetually spoke with himself in his own language. But he was sane enough when it came to English.

"You think he will be gone quite away?" he asked, upon their blest awakening in safety.

"I pray God so, I believe so, I dare to believe so," Mountain had replied almost with incoherence, as he described the scene to me.

And indeed he was so much distempered that until he met us, the next morning, he could scarce be certain whether he had dreamed, or whether it was a fact, that Secundra had thereupon turned directly about and returned without a word upon their footprints, setting his face for these wintry and hungry solitudes, along a path whose every stage was mile-stoned with a mutilated corpse.

The Journey in the Wilderness—Concluded

MOUNTAIN'S STORY, AS IT WAS LAID BEFORE SIR WILLIAM JOHNSON and my lord, was shorn, of course, of all the earlier particulars, and the expedition described to have proceeded uneventfully, until the Master sickened. But the latter part was very forcibly related, the speaker visibly thrilling to his recollections; and our then situation, on the fringe of the same desert, and the private interests of each, gave him an audience prepared to share in his emotions. For Mountain's intelligence not only changed the world for my Lord Durrisdeer, but materially affected the designs of Sir William Johnson.

These I find I must lay more at length before the reader. Word had reached Albany of dubious import; it had been rumoured some hostility was to be put in act; and the Indian diplomatist had thereupon sped into the Wilderness, even at the approach of winter, to nip that mischief in the bud. Here, on the borders, he learned that he was come too late; and a difficult choice was thus presented to a man (upon the whole) not any more bold than prudent. His standing with the painted braves may be compared to that of my Lord President Culloden among the chiefs of our own Highlanders at the 'forty-five; that is as much as to say, he was, to these men, reason's only speaking-trumpet, and counsels of peace and moderation, if they were to prevail at all, must prevail singly through his influence. If, then, he should return, the province must lie open to all the abominable tragedies of Indian war— the houses blaze, the wayfarer be cut off, and the men of the woods collect their usual disgusting spoil of human scalps. On the other side, to go further forth, to risk so small a party deeper in the desert, to carry words of peace among warlike savages already rejoicing to return to war: here was an extremity from which it was easy to perceive his mind revolted.

"I have come too late," he said more than once, and would fall into a deep consideration, his head bowed in his hands, his foot patting the ground.

At length he raised his face and looked upon us, that is to say, upon my lord, Mountain, and myself, sitting close round a small fire, which had been made for privacy in one corner of the camp.

"My lord, to be quite frank with you, I find myself in two minds," said he. "I think it very needful I should go on, but not at all proper I should any longer enjoy the pleasure of your company. We are here still upon the water-side; and I think the risk to southward no great matter. Will not yourself and Mr. Mackellar take a single boat's crew and return to Albany?"

My lord, I should say, had listened to Mountain's narrative regarding him throughout with a painful intensity of gaze; and since the tale concluded, had sat as in a dream. There was something very daunting in his look; something to my eyes not rightly human; the face, lean, and dark, and aged, the mouth painful, the teeth disclosed in a perpetual rictus; the eyeball swimming clear of the lids upon a field of blood-shot white. I could not behold him myself without a jarring irritation, such as (I believe) is too frequently the uppermost feeling on the sickness of those dear to us. Others, I could not but remark, were scarce able to support his neighbourhood—Sir William eviting to be near him, Mountain dodging his eye, and, when he met it, blenching and halting in his story. At this appeal, however, my lord appeared to recover his command upon himself.

"To Albany?" said he, with a good voice.

"Not short of it, at least," replied Sir William. "There is no safety nearer hand."

"I would be very sweir * to return," says my lord. "I am not afraid—of Indians," he added, with a jerk.

"I wish that I could say so much," returned Sir William, smiling; "although, if any man durst say it, it should be myself. But you are to keep in view my responsibility, and that as the voyage has now become highly dangerous, and your business—if you ever had any," says he, "brought quite to a conclusion by the distressing family intelligence you have received, I should be hardly justified if I even suffered you to proceed, and run the risk of some obloquy if anything regrettable should follow."

My lord turned to Mountain. "What did he pretend he died of?" he asked.

"I don't think I understand your honour," said the trader, pausing, like a man very much affected, in the dressing of some cruel frost-bites.

For a moment my lord seemed at a full stop; and then, with some irritation, "I ask you what he died of. Surely that's a plain question," said he.

"Oh, I don't know," said Mountain. "Hastie even never knew. He seemed to sicken natural, and just pass away."

"There it is, you see!" concluded my lord, turning to Sir William.

"Your lordship is too deep for me," replied Sir William.

"Why," says my lord, "this is a matter of succession; my son's title may be called in doubt; and the man being supposed to be dead of nobody can tell what, a great deal of suspicion would be naturally roused."

"But, God damn me, the man's buried!" cried Sir William.

"I will never believe that," returned my lord, painfully trembling. "I'll never believe it!" he cried again, and jumped to his feet. "Did he *look* dead?" he asked of Mountain.

"Look dead?" repeated the trader. "He looked white. Why, what would he be at? I tell you, I put the sods upon him."

My lord caught Sir William by the coat with a hooked hand.

* Unwilling.

"This man has the name of my brother," says he, "but it's well understood that he was never canny."

"Canny?" says Sir William. "What is that?"

"He's not of this world," whispered my lord, "neither him nor the black deil that serves him. I have struck my sword throughout his vitals," he cried, "I have felt the hilt dirl * on his breastbone, and the hot blood spirt in my very face, time and again, time and again!" he repeated, with a gesture indescribable. "But he was never dead for that," said he, and I sighed aloud. "Why should I think he was dead now? No, not till I see him rotting," says he.

Sir William looked across at me, with a long face. Mountain forgot his wounds, staring and gaping.

"My lord," said I, "I wish you would collect your spirits." But my throat was so dry, and my own wits so scattered, I could add no more.

"No," says my lord, "it's not to be supposed that he would understand me. Mackellar does, for he kens all, and has seen him buried before now. This is a very good servant to me, Sir William, this man Mackellar; he buried him with his own hands—he and my father—by the light of two siller candlesticks. The other man is a familiar spirit; he brought him from Coromandel. I would have told ye this long syne, Sir William, only it was in the family." These last remarks he made with a kind of a melancholy composure, and his time of aberration seemed to pass away. "You can ask yourself what it all means," he proceeded. "My brother falls sick, and dies, and is buried, as so they say; and all seems very plain. But why did the familiar go back? I think ye must see for yourself it's a point that wants some clearing."

"I will be at your service, my lord, in half a minute," said Sir William, rising. "Mr. Mackellar, two words with you," and he led me without the camp, the frost crunching in our steps, the trees standing at our elbow hoar with frost, even as on that night in the Long Shrubbery. "Of course, this is midsummer madness?" said Sir William, so soon as we were gotten out of hearing.

"Why, certainly," said I. "The man is mad. I think that manifest."

"Shall I seize and bind him?" asked Sir William. "I will upon your authority. If these are all ravings, that should certainly be done."

* Ring.

I looked down upon the ground, back at the camp with its bright fires and the folk watching us, and about me on the woods and mountains; there was just the one way that I could not look, and that was in Sir William's face.

"Sir William," said I at last, "I think my lord not sane, and have long thought him so. But there are degrees in madness; and whether he should be brought under restraint—Sir William, I am no fit judge," I concluded.

"I will be the judge," said he. "I ask for facts. Was there, in all that jargon, any word of truth or sanity? Do you hesitate?" he asked. "Am I to understand you have buried this gentleman before?"

"Not buried," said I; and then, taking up courage at last, "Sir William," said I, "unless I were to tell you a long story, which much concerns a noble family (and myself not in the least), it would be impossible to make this matter clear to you. Say the word, and I will do it, right or wrong. And, at any rate, I will say so much, that my lord is not so crazy as he seems. This is a strange matter, into the tail of which you are unhappily drifted."

"I desire none of your secrets," replied Sir William; "but I will be plain at the risk of incivility, and confess that I take little pleasure in my present company."

"I would be the last to blame you," said I, "for that."

"I have not asked either for your censure or your praise, sir," returned Sir William. "I desire simply to be quit of you; and to that effect, I put a boat and complement of men at your disposal."

"This is fairly offered," said I, after reflection. "But you must suffer me to say a word upon the other side. We have a natural curiosity to learn the truth of this affair; I have some of it myself; my lord (it is very plain) has but too much. The matter of the Indian's return is enigmatical."

"I think so myself," Sir William interrupted, "and I propose (since I go in that direction) to probe it to the bottom. Whether or not the man has gone like a dog to die upon his master's grave, his life, at least, is in great danger, and I propose, if I can, to save it. There is nothing against his character?"

"Nothing, Sir William," I replied.

"And the other?" he said. "I have heard my lord, of course; but, from the circumstances of his servant's loyalty, I must suppose he had some noble qualities."

"You must not ask me that!" I cried. "Hell may have noble flames. I have known him a score of years, and always hated, and always admired, and always slavishly feared him."

"I appear to intrude again upon your secrets," said Sir William, "believe me, inadvertently. Enough that I will see the grave, and (if possible) rescue the Indian. Upon these terms, can you persuade your master to return to Albany?"

"Sir William," said I, "I will tell you how it is. You do not see my lord to advantage; it will seem even strange to you that I should love him; but I do, and I am not alone. If he goes back to Albany, it must be by force, and it will be the death-warrant of his reason, and perhaps his life. That is my sincere belief; but I am in your hands, and ready to obey, if you will assume so much responsibility as to command."

"I will have no shred of responsibility; it is my single endeavour to avoid the same," cried Sir William. "You insist upon following this journey up; and be it so! I wash my hands of the whole matter."

With which word, he turned upon his heel and gave the order to break camp; and my lord, who had been hovering near by, came instantly to my side.

"Which is it to be?" said he.

"You are to have your way," I answered. "You shall see the grave."

The situation of the Master's grave was, between guides, easily described; it lay, indeed, beside a chief landmark of the Wilderness, a certain range of peaks, conspicuous by their design and altitude, and the source of many brawling tributaries to that inland sea, Lake Champlain. It was therefore possible to strike for it direct, instead of following back the blood-stained trail of the fugitives, and to cover, in some sixteen hours of march, a distance which their perturbed wanderings had extended over more than sixty. Our boats we left under a guard upon the river; it was, indeed, probable we should return to find them frozen fast; and the small equipment with which we set forth upon the expedition, included not only an infinity of furs to protect us from the cold, but an arsenal of snow-shoes to render travel possible, when the inevitable snow should fall. Considerable alarm was manifested at our departure; the march was conducted with soldierly precaution, the camp at night sedulously chosen and patrolled; and it was a consideration of this sort that arrested us, the second day, within not many hundred yards of our destination—the night being already imminent, the spot in which we stood well qualified to be a strong camp for a party of our numbers; and Sir William, therefore, on a sudden thought, arresting our advance.

Before us was the high range of mountains toward which we had been all day deviously drawing near. From the first light of the dawn, their silver peaks had been the goal of our advance across a tumbled lowland forest, thrid with rough streams, and strewn with monstrous boulders; the peaks (as I say) silver, for already at the higher altitudes the snow fell nightly; but the woods and the low ground only breathed upon with frost. All day heaven had been charged with ugly vapours, in the which the sun swam and glimmered like a shilling piece; all day the wind blew on our left cheek, barbarous cold, but very pure to breathe. With the end of the afternoon, however, the wind fell; the clouds, being no longer reinforced, were scattered or drunk up; the sun set behind us with some wintry splendour, and the white brow of the mountains shared its dying glow.

It was dark ere we had supper; we ate in silence, and the meal was scarce despatched before my lord slunk from the fireside to the margin of the camp; whither I made haste to follow him. The camp was on high ground, overlooking a frozen lake, perhaps a mile in its longest measurement; all about us, the forest lay in heights and hollows; above rose the white mountains; and higher yet, the moon rode in a fair sky. There was no breath of air; nowhere a twig creaked; and the sounds of our own camp were hushed and swallowed up in the surrounding stillness. Now that the sun and the wind were both gone down, it appeared almost warm, like a night of July: a singular illusion of the sense, when earth, air, and water were strained to bursting with the extremity of frost.

My lord (or what I still continued to call by his loved name) stood with his elbow in one hand, and his chin sunk in the other, gazing before him on the surface of the wood. My eyes followed his, and rested almost pleasantly upon the frosted contexture of the pines, rising in moonlit hillocks, or sinking in the shadow of small glens. Hard by, I told myself, was the grave of our enemy, now gone where the wicked cease from troubling, the earth heaped

for ever on his once so active limbs. I could not but think of him
as somehow fortunate, to be thus done with man's anxiety and
weariness, the daily expense of spirit, and that daily river of circumstance to be swum through, at any hazard, under the penalty
of shame or death. I could not but think how good was the end of
that long travel; and with that, my mind swung at a tangent to
my lord. For was not my lord dead also? a maimed soldier, looking
vainly for discharge, lingering derided in the line of battle? A kind
man, I remembered him; wise, with a decent pride, a son perhaps
too dutiful, a husband only too loving, one that could suffer and
be silent, one whose hand I loved to press. Of a sudden, pity
caught in my windpipe with a sob; I could have wept aloud to
remember and behold him; and standing thus by his elbow, under
the broad moon, I prayed fervently either that he should be
released, or I strengthened to persist in my affection.

"O God," said I, "this was the best man to me and to himself,
and now I shrink from him. He did no wrong, or not till he was
broke with sorrows; these are but his honourable wounds that
we begin to shrink from. O cover them up, O take him away,
before we hate him!"

I was still so engaged in my own bosom, when a sound broke
suddenly upon the night. It was neither very loud, nor very near;
yet, bursting as it did from so profound and so prolonged a silence,
it startled the camp like an alarm of trumpets. Ere I had taken
breath, Sir William was beside me, the main part of the voyagers
clustered at his back, intently giving ear. Methought, as I glanced
at them across my shoulder, there was a whiteness, other than
moonlight, on their cheeks; and the rays of the moon reflected
with a sparkle on the eyes of some, and the shadows lying black
under the brows of others (according as they raised or bowed the
head to listen) gave to the group a strange air of animation and
anxiety. My lord was to the front, crouching a little forth, his
hand raised as for silence: a man turned to stone. And still the
sounds continued, breathlessly renewed, with a precipitate rhythm.

Suddenly Mountain spoke in a loud, broken whisper, as of a
man relieved. "I have it now," he said; and, as we all turned to
hear him, "the Indian must have known the cache," he added.
"That is he—he is digging out the treasure."

"Why, to be sure!" exclaimed Sir William. "We were geese not
to have supposed so much."

"The only thing is," Mountain resumed, "the sound is very close to our old camp. And, again, I do not see how he is there before us, unless the man had wings!"

"Greed and fear are wings," remarked Sir William. "But this rogue has given us an alert, and I have a notion to return the compliment. What say you, gentlemen, shall we have a moonlight hunt?"

It was so agreed; dispositions were made to surround Secundra at his task; some of Sir William's Indians hastened in advance; and a strong guard being left at our headquarters, we set forth along the uneven bottom of the forest; frost crackling, ice sometimes loudly splitting underfoot; and overhead the blackness of pine-woods, and the broken brightness of the moon. Our way led down into a hollow of the land; and as we descended, the sounds diminished and had almost died away. Upon the other slope it was more open, only dotted with a few pines, and several vast and scattered rocks, that made inky shadows in the moonlight. Here the sounds began to reach us more distinctly; we could now perceive the ring of iron, and more exactly estimate the furious degree of haste with which the digger plied his instrument. As we neared the top of the ascent, a bird or two winged aloft and hovered darkly in the moonlight; and the next moment, we were gazing through a fringe of trees upon a singular picture.

A narrow plateau, overlooked by the white mountains, and encompassed nearer at hand by woods, lay bare to the strong radiance of the moon. Rough goods, such as make the wealth of foresters, were sprinkled here and there upon the ground in meaningless disarray. About the midst a tent stood, silvered with frost; the door open, gaping on the black interior. At the one end of this small stage, lay what seemed the tattered remnants of a man. Without doubt we had arrived upon the scene of Harris's encampment; there were the goods scattered in the panic of flight; it was in yon tent the Master breathed his last; and the frozen carrion that lay before us was the body of the drunken shoemaker. It was always moving to come upon the theatre of any tragic incident; to come upon it after so many days, and to find it (in the seclusion of a desert) still unchanged, must have impressed the mind of the most careless. And yet it was not that which struck us into pillars of stone; but the sight (which yet we had been half expecting) of Secundra, ankle deep in the grave of his late master. He had cast the main part of his raiment by, yet his frail arms and shoulders glistered in the moonlight with a copious sweat; his face was contracted with anxiety and expectation; his blows resounded on the grave, as thick as sobs; and behind him, strangely deformed and ink-black upon the frosty ground, the creature's shadow repeated and parodied his swift gesticulations. Some night birds arose from the boughs upon our coming, and then settled back; but Secundra, absorbed in his toil, heard or heeded not at all.

I heard Mountain whisper to Sir William: "Good God, it's the grave! He's digging him up!" It was what we had all guessed, and yet to hear it put in language thrilled me. Sir William violently started.

"You damned sacrilegious hound!" he cried. "What's this?"

Secundra leaped in the air, a little breathless cry escaped him, the tool flew from his grasp, and he stood one instant staring at the speaker. The next, swift as an arrow, he sped for the woods upon the farther side; and the next again, throwing up his hands with a violent gesture of resolution, he had begun already to retrace his steps.

"Well, then, you come, you help——" he was saying. But by now my lord had stepped beside Sir William; the moon shone fair upon his face, and the words were still upon Secundra's lips, when he beheld and recognised his master's enemy. "Him!" he screamed, clasping his hands and shrinking on himself.

"Come, come," said Sir William, "there is none here to do you harm, if you be innocent; and if you be guilty, your escape is quite cut off. Speak, what do you here among the graves of the dead and the remains of the unburied?"

"You no murderer?" inquired Secundra. "You true man? You see me safe?"

"I will see you safe if you be innocent," returned Sir William. "I have said the thing; I see not wherefore you should doubt it."

"There all murderers," cried Secundra, "that is why! He kill— murderer," pointing to Mountain; "there two hire-murderers,"— pointing to my lord and myself—"all gallows-murderers! Ah, I see you all swing in a rope. Now I go save the Sahib; he see you swing in a rope. The Sahib," he continued, pointing to the grave, "he not dead. He bury, he not dead."

My lord uttered a little noise, moved nearer to the grave, and stood and stared in it.

"Buried and not dead?" exclaimed Sir William. "What kind of rant is this?"

"See, Sahib!" said Secundra. "The Sahib and I alone with murderers; try all way to escape, no way good. Then try this way: good way in warm climate, good way in India; here in this damn cold place, who can tell? I tell you pretty good hurry: you help, you light a fire, help rub."

"What is the creature talking of?" cried Sir William. "My head goes round."

"I tell you I bury him alive," said Secundra. "I teach him swallow his tongue. Now dig him up pretty good hurry, and he not much worse. You light a fire."

Sir William turned to the nearest of his men. "Light a fire," said he. "My lot seems to be cast with the insane."

"You good man," returned Secundra. "Now I go dig the Sahib up."

He returned as he spoke to the grave, and resumed his former toil. My lord stood rooted, and I at my lord's side: fearing I knew not what.

The frost was not yet very deep, and presently the Indian threw aside his tool and began to scoop the dirt by handfuls. Then he disengaged a corner of a buffalo robe: and then I saw hair catch among his fingers; yet a moment more, and the moon shone on something white. Awhile Secundra crouched upon his knees, scraping with delicate fingers, breathing with puffed lips; and when he moved aside I beheld the face of the Master wholly disengaged. It was deadly white, the eyes closed, the ears and nostrils plugged, the cheeks fallen, the nose sharp as if in death; but for all he had lain so many days under the sod, corruption had not approached him and (what strangely affected all of us) his lips and chin were mantled with a swarthy beard.

"My God!" cried Mountain, "he was as smooth as a baby when we laid him there!"

"They say hair grows upon the dead," observed Sir William, but his voice was thick and weak.

Secundra paid no heed to our remarks, digging swift as a terrier, in the loose earth; every moment, the form of the Master, swathed in his buffalo robe, grew more distinct in the bottom of that shallow trough; the moon shining strong, and the shadows of the standers-by, as they drew forward and back, falling and flitting over his emergent countenance. The sight held us with a horror not before experienced, I dared not look my lord in the face, but for as long as it lasted, I never observed him to draw breath; and a little in the background one of the men (I know not whom) burst into a kind of sobbing.

"Now," said Secundra, "you help me lift him out."

Of the flight of time I have no idea; it may have been three hours, and it may have been five, that the Indian laboured to reanimate his master's body. One thing only I know, that it was still night, and the moon was not yet set, although it had sunk low, and now barred the plateau with long shadows, when Secundra uttered a small cry of satisfaction; and, leaning swiftly forth, I thought I could myself perceive a change upon that icy countenance of the unburied. The next moment I beheld his eyelids flutter; the next they rose entirely, and the week-old corpse looked me for a moment in the face.

So much display of life I can myself swear to. I have heard from others that he visibly strove to speak, that his teeth showed in his beard, and that his brow was contorted as with an agony of pain and effort. And this may have been; I know not, I was otherwise engaged. For, at that first disclosure of the dead man's eyes, my Lord Durrisdeer fell to the ground, and when I raised him up, he was a corpse.

Day came, and still Secundra could not be persuaded to desist from his unavailing efforts. Sir William, leaving a small party under my command, proceeded on his embassy with the first light; and still the Indian rubbed the limbs and breathed in the mouth of the dead body. You would think such labours might have vitalised a stone; but, except for that one moment (which was my lord's death), the black spirit of the Master held aloof from its discarded clay; and by about the hour of noon, even the faithful servant was at length convinced. He took it with unshaken quietude.

"Too cold," said he, "good way in India, no good here." And, asking for some food, which he ravenously devoured as soon as it was set before him, he drew near to the fire and took his place at my elbow. In the same spot, as soon as he had eaten, he stretched himself out, and fell into a childlike slumber, from which I must arouse him, some hours afterward, to take his part as one of the

mourners at the double funeral. It was the same throughout; he
seemed to have outlived at once and with the same effort, his grief
for his master and his terror of myself and Mountain.

One of the men left with me was skilled in stone-cutting; and
before Sir William returned to pick us up, I had chiselled on a
boulder this inscription, with a copy of which I may fitly bring
my narrative to a close:

J. D.,

HEIR TO A SCOTTISH TITLE,

A MASTER OF THE ARTS AND GRACES,

ADMIRED IN EUROPE, ASIA, AMERICA,

IN WAR AND PEACE,

IN THE TENTS OF SAVAGE HUNTERS AND THE

CITADELS OF KINGS, AFTER SO MUCH

ACQUIRED, ACCOMPLISHED, AND

ENDURED, LIES HERE FOR-

GOTTEN.

———

H. D.,

HIS BROTHER,

AFTER A LIFE OF UNMERITED DISTRESS,

BRAVELY SUPPORTED,

DIED ALMOST IN THE SAME HOUR,

AND SLEEPS IN THE SAME GRAVE

WITH HIS FRATERNAL ENEMY.

THE PIETY OF HIS WIFE AND ONE OLD

SERVANT RAISED THIS STONE

TO BOTH.

Weir of Hermiston

To My Wife

I saw rain falling and the rainbow drawn
On Lammermuir. Hearkening I heard again
In my precipitous city beaten bells
Winnow the keen sea wind. And here afar,
Intent on my own race and place, I wrote.
Take thou the writing: thine it is. For who
Burnished the sword, blew on the drowsy coal,
Held still the target higher, chary of praise
And prodigal of counsel—who but thou?
So now, in the end, if this the least be good,
If any deed be done, if any fire
Burn in the imperfect page, the praise be thine.

Introductory

In the wild end of a moorland parish, far out of the sight of any house, there stands a cairn among the heather, and a little by east of it, in the going down of the braeside, a monument with some verses half defaced. It was here that Claverhouse shot with his own hand the Praying Weaver of Balweary, and the chisel of Old Mortality has clinked on that lonely gravestone. Public and domestic history have thus marked with a bloody finger this hollow among the hills; and since the Cameronian gave his life there, two hundred years ago, in a glorious folly, and without comprehension or regret, the silence of the moss has been broken once again by the report of firearms and the cry of the dying.

The Deil's Hags was the old name. But the place is now called Francie's Cairn. For a while it was told that Francie walked. Aggie Hogg met him in the gloaming by the cairnside, and he spoke to her, with chattering teeth, so that his words were lost. He pursued Rob Todd (if anyone could have believed Robbie) for the space of half a mile with pitiful entreaties. But the age is one of incredulity; these superstitious decorations speedily fell off; and the facts of the story itself, like the bones of a giant buried there and half dug up, survived, naked and imperfect, in the memory of the scattered neighbours. To this day, of winter nights, when the sleet is on the window and the cattle are quiet in the byre, there will be told again, amid the silence of the young and the additions and corrections of the old, the tale of the Justice-Clerk and of his son, young Hermiston, that vanished from men's knowledge; of the two Kirsties and the Four Black Brothers of the Cauldstaneslap; and of Frank Innes, "the young fool advocate," that came into these moorland parts to find his destiny.

Contents

1. *Life and Death of Mrs. Weir*

THE LORD JUSTICE-CLERK WAS A STRANGER IN THAT PART OF THE country; but his lady wife was known there from a child, as her race had been before her. The old "riding Rutherfords of Hermiston," of whom she was the last descendant, had been famous men of yore, ill neighbours, ill subjects, and ill husbands to their wives though not their properties. Tales of them were rife for twenty miles about; and their name was even printed in the page of our Scots histories, not always to their credit. One bit the dust at Flodden; one was hanged at his peel door by James the Fifth; another fell dead in a carouse with Tom Dalzell; while a fourth (and that was Jean's own father) died presiding at a Hell-Fire Club, of which he was the founder. There were many heads shaken in Crossmichael at that judgment; the more so as the man had a villainous reputation among high and low, and both with the godly and the worldly. At that very hour of his demise, he had ten going pleas before the session, eight of them oppressive. And the same doom extended even to his agents; his grieve, that had been his right hand in many a left-hand business, being cast from his horse one night and drowned in a peat-hag on the Kye skairs; and his very doer (although lawyers have long spoons) surviving him not long, and dying on a sudden in a bloody flux.

In all these generations, while a male Rutherford was in the saddle with his lads, or brawling in a change-house, there would be always a white-faced wife immured at home in the old peel or the later mansion-house. It seemed this succession of martyrs bided long, but took their vengeance in the end, and that was in the person of the last descendant, Jean. She bore the name of the Rutherfords, but she was the daughter of their trembling wives. At the first she was not wholly without charm. Neighbours recalled in her, as a child, a strain of elfin wilfulness, gentle little mutinies, sad little gaieties, even a morning gleam of beauty that was not to be fulfilled. She withered in the growing, and (whether it was the sins of her sires or the sorrows of her mothers) came to her maturity depressed, and, as it were, defaced; no blood of life in her, no grasp or gaiety; pious, anxious, tender, tearful, and incompetent.

It was a wonder to many that she had married—seeming so

wholly of the stuff that makes old maids. But chance cast her in
the path of Adam Weir, then the new Lord-Advocate, a recognised, risen man, the conqueror of many obstacles, and thus late in
the day beginning to think upon a wife. He was one who looked
rather to obedience than beauty, yet it would seem he was struck
with her at the first look. "Wha's she?" he said, turning to his host;
and, when he had been told, "Ay," says he, "she looks menseful.
She minds me——"; and then, after a pause (which some have been
daring enough to set down to sentimental recollections), "Is she
releegious?" he asked, and was shortly after, at his own request,
presented. The acquaintance, which it seems profane to call a
courtship, was pursued with Mr. Weir's accustomed industry, and
was long a legend, or rather a source of legends, in the Parliament
House. He was described coming, rosy with much port, into the
drawing-room, walking direct up to the lady, and assailing her
with pleasantries, to which the embarrassed fair one responded, in
what seemed a kind of agony, "Eh, Mr. Weir!" or "O, Mr. Weir!" or
"Keep me, Mr. Weir!" On the very eve of their engagement it was
related that one had drawn near to the tender couple, and had
overheard the lady cry out, with the tones of one who talked for
the sake of talking, "Keep me, Mr. Weir, and what became of
him?" and the profound accents of the suitor's reply, "Haangit,
mem, haangit." The motives upon either side were much debated.
Mr. Weir must have supposed his bride to be somehow suitable;
perhaps he belonged to that class of men who think a weak head
the ornament of women—an opinion invariably punished in this
life. Her descent and her estate were beyond question. Her wayfar-
ing ancestors and her litigious father had done well by Jean. There
was ready money and there were broad acres, ready to fall wholly
to the husband, to lend dignity to his descendants, and to himself
a title, when he should be called upon the Bench. On the side of
Jean there was perhaps some fascination of curiosity as to this
unknown male animal that approached her with the roughness of
a ploughman and the *aplomb* of an advocate. Being so trenchantly
opposed to all she knew, loved, or understood, he may well have
seemed to her the extreme, if scarcely the ideal, of his sex. And
besides, he was an ill man to refuse. A little over forty at the period
of his marriage, he looked already older, and to the force of manhood added the senatorial dignity of years; it was, perhaps, with an
unreverend awe, but he was awful. The Bench, the Bar, and the

most experienced and reluctant witness, bowed to his authority—
and why not Jeannie Rutherford?

The heresy about foolish women is always punished, I have said,
and Lord Hermiston began to pay the penalty at once. His house
in George Square was wretchedly ill-guided; nothing answerable
to the expense of maintenance but the cellar, which was his own
private care. When things went wrong at dinner, as they continually did, my lord would look up the table at his wife: "I think
these broth would be better to swim in than to sup." Or else to the
butler: "Here, M'Killop, awa' wi' this Raadical gigot—tak' it to
the French, man, and bring me some puddocks! It seems rather a
sore kind of a business that I should be all day in Court haanging
Raadicals, and get nawthing to my denner." Of course this was but
a manner of speaking, and he had never hanged a man for being a
Radical in his life; the law, of which he was the faithful minister,
directing otherwise. And of course these growls were in the nature
of pleasantry, but it was of a recondite sort; and uttered as they
were in his resounding voice, and commented on by that expression which they called in the Parliament House "Hermiston's
hanging face"—they struck mere dismay into the wife. She sat
before him speechless and fluttering; at each dish, as at a fresh
ordeal, her eye hovered toward my lord's countenance and fell
again; if he but ate in silence, unspeakable relief was her portion;
if there were complaint, the world was darkened. She would seek
out the cook, who was always her *sister in the Lord*. "O, my dear,
this is the most dreidful thing that my lord can never be contented
in his own house!" she would begin; and weep and pray with the
cook; and then the cook would pray with Mrs. Weir; and the next
day's meal would never be a penny the better—and the next cook
(when she came) would be worse, if anything, but just as pious. It
was often wondered that Lord Hermiston bore it as he did; indeed
he was a stoical old voluptuary, contented with sound wine and
plenty of it. But there were moments when he overflowed. Perhaps
half-a-dozen times in the history of his married life—"Here! tak'
it awa', and bring me a piece bread and kebbuck!" he had exclaimed, with an appalling explosion of his voice and rare gestures.
None thought to dispute or to make excuses; the service was
arrested; Mrs. Weir sat at the head of the table whimpering without disguise; and his lordship opposite munched his bread and
cheese in ostentatious disregard. Once only, Mrs. Weir had ven-

tured to appeal. He was passing her chair on his way into the
study.

"O, Edom!" she wailed, in a voice tragic with tears, and reaching
out to him both hands, in one of which she held a sopping pocket-
handkerchief.

He paused and looked upon her with a face of wrath, into which
there stole, as he looked, a twinkle of humour.

"Noansense!" he said. "You and your noansense! What do I
want with a Christian faim'ly? I want Christian broth! Get me a
lass that can plain boil a potato, if she was a whüre off the streets."
And with these words, which echoed in her tender ears like blasphemy, he had passed on to his study and shut the door behind
him.

Such was the housewifery in George Square. It was better at
Hermiston, where Kirstie Elliott, the sister of a neighbouring
bonnet-laird, and an eighteenth cousin of the lady's, bore the
charge of all, and kept a trim house and a good country table.
Kirstie was a woman in a thousand, clean, capable, notable; once
a moorland Helen, and still comely as a blood horse and healthy
as the hill wind. High in flesh and voice and colour, she ran the
house with her whole intemperate soul, in a bustle, not without
buffets. Scarce more pious than decency in those days required, she
was the cause of many an anxious thought and many a tearful
prayer to Mrs. Weir. Housekeeper and mistress renewed the parts
of Martha and Mary; and though with a pricking conscience,
Mary reposed on Martha's strength as on a rock. Even Lord
Hermiston held Kirstie in a particular regard. There were few
with whom he unbent so gladly, few whom he favoured with so
many pleasantries. "Kirstie and me maun have our joke," he
would declare, in high good-humour, as he buttered Kirstie's
scones and she waited at table. A man who had no need either of
love or of popularity, a keen reader of men and of events, there
was perhaps only one truth for which he was quite unprepared:
he would have been quite unprepared to learn that Kirstie hated
him. He thought maid and master were well matched; hard,
handy, healthy, broad Scots folk, without a hair of nonsense to the
pair of them. And the fact was that she made a goddess and an
only child of the effete and tearful lady; and even as she waited at
table her hands would sometimes itch for my lord's ears.

Thus, at least, when the family were at Hermiston, not only my lord, but Mrs. Weir too, enjoyed a holiday. Free from the dreadful looking-for of the miscarried dinner, she would mind her seam, read her piety books, and take her walk (which was my lord's orders), sometimes by herself, sometimes with Archie, the only child of that scarce natural union. The child was her next bond to life. Her frosted sentiment bloomed again, she breathed deep of life, she let loose her heart, in that society. The miracle of her motherhood was ever new to her. The sight of the little man at her skirt intoxicated her with the sense of power, and froze her with the consciousness of her responsibility. She looked forward, and, seeing him in fancy grow up and play his diverse part on the world's theatre, caught in her breath and lifted up her courage with a lively effort. It was only with the child that she forgot herself and was at moments natural; yet it was only with the child that she had conceived and managed to pursue a scheme of conduct. Archie was to be a great man and a good; a minister if possible, a saint for certain. She tried to engage his mind upon her favourite books, Rutherford's *Letters,* Scougal's *Grace Abounding,* and the like. It was a common practice of hers (and strange to remember now) that she would carry the child to the Deil's Hags, sit with him on the Praying Weaver's stone and talk of the Covenanters till their tears ran down. Her view of history was wholly artless, a design in snow and ink; upon the one side, tender innocents with psalms upon their lips; upon the other, the persecutors, booted, bloody-minded, flushed with wine; a suffering Christ, a raging Beelzebub. *Persecutor* was a word that knocked upon the woman's heart; it was her highest thought of wickedness, and the mark of it was on her house. Her great-great-grandfather had drawn the sword against the Lord's anointed on the field of Rullion Green, and breathed his last (tradition said) in the arms of the detestable Dalzell. Nor could she blind herself to this, that had they lived in these old days, Hermiston himself would have been numbered alongside of Bloody MacKenzie and the politic Lauderdale and Rothes, in the band of God's immediate enemies. The sense of this moved her to the more fervour; she had a voice for that name of *persecutor* that thrilled in the child's marrow; and when one day the mob hooted and hissed them all in my lord's travelling-carriage, and cried, "Down with the persecutor! down with Hanging Hermiston!" and mamma covered her eyes and wept, and papa let down the glass and looked out upon the rabble

with his droll formidable face, bitter and smiling, as they said he
sometimes looked when he gave sentence, Archie was for the moment too much amazed to be alarmed, but he had scarce got his
mother by herself before his shrill voice was raised demanding an
explanation; why had they called papa a persecutor?

"Keep me, my precious!" she exclaimed. "Keep me, my dear!
this is poleetical. Ye must never ask me anything poleetical, Erchie.
Your faither is a great man, my dear, and it's no for me or you to
be judging him. It would be telling us all if we behaved ourselves
in our several stations the way your faither does in his high office;
and let me hear no more of any such disrespectful and undutiful
questions! No that you meant to be undutiful, my lamb; your
mother kens that—she kens it well, dearie!" and so slid off to safer
topics, and left on the mind of the child an obscure but ineradicable sense of something wrong.

Mrs. Weir's philosophy of life was summed in one expression—
tenderness. In her view of the universe, which was all lighted up
with a glow out of the doors of hell, good people must walk there
in a kind of ecstasy of tenderness. The beasts and plants had no
souls; they were here but for a day, and let their day pass gently!
And as for the immortal men, on what black, downward path
were many of them wending, and to what a horror of an immortality! "Are not two sparrows," "Whosoever shall smite thee," "God
sendeth His rain," "Judge not that ye be not judged"—these texts
made her body of divinity; she put them on in the morning with
her clothes and lay down to sleep with them at night; they haunted
her like a favourite air, they clung about her like a favourite
perfume. Their minister was a marrowy expounder of the law,
and my lord sat under him with relish; but Mrs. Weir respected
him from far off; heard him (like the cannon of a beleaguered city)
usefully booming outside on the dogmatic ramparts; and meanwhile, within and out of shot, dwelt in her private garden, which
she watered with grateful tears. It seems strange to say of this
colourless and ineffectual woman, but she was a true enthusiast,
and might have made the sunshine and the glory of a cloister. Perhaps none but Archie knew she could be eloquent; perhaps none
but he had seen her—her colour raised, her hands clasped or
quivering—glow with gentle ardour. There is a corner of the
policy of Hermiston, where you come suddenly in view of the
summit of Black Fell, sometimes like the mere grass top of a hill,

sometimes (and this is her own expression) like a precious jewel in the heavens. On such days, upon the sudden view of it, her hand would tighten on the child's fingers, her voice rise like a song. "I to the hills!" she would repeat. "And O, Erchie, are nae these like the hills of Naphtali?" and her easy tears would flow.

Upon an impressionable child the effect of this continual and pretty accompaniment to life was deep. The woman's quietism and piety passed on to his different nature undiminished; but whereas in her it was a native sentiment, in him it was only an implanted dogma. Nature and the child's pugnacity at times revolted. A cad from the Potterrow once struck him in the mouth; he struck back, the pair fought it out in the back stable lane towards the Meadows, and Archie returned with a considerable decline in the number of his front teeth, and unregenerately boasting of the losses of the foe. It was a sore day for Mrs. Weir; she wept and prayed over the infant backslider until my lord was due from court, and she must resume that air of tremulous composure with which she always greeted him. The Judge was that day in an observant mood, and remarked upon the absent teeth.

"I am afraid Erchie will have been fechting with some of they blagyard lads," said Mrs. Weir.

My lord's voice rang out as it did seldom in the privacy of his own house. "I'll have nonn of that, sir!" he cried. "Do you hear me?—nonn of that! No son of mine shall be speldering in the glaur with any dirty raibble."

The anxious mother was grateful for so much support; she had even feared the contrary. And that night when she put the child to bed—"Now, my dear, ye see!" she said, "I told you what your faither would think of it, if he heard ye had fallen into this dreidful sin; and let you and me pray to God that ye may be keepit from the like temptation or stren'thened to resist it!"

The womanly falsity of this was thrown away. Ice and iron cannot be welded; and the points of view of the Justice-Clerk and Mrs. Weir were not less unassimilable. The character and position of his father had long been a stumbling-block to Archie, and with every year of his age the difficulty grew more instant. The man was mostly silent; when he spoke at all, it was to speak of the things of the world, always in a worldly spirit, often in language that the child had been schooled to think coarse, and sometimes with words that he knew to be sins in themselves. Tenderness was the first duty, and my lord was invariably harsh. God was love; the name of my lord (to all who knew him) was fear. In the world, as schematised for Archie by his mother, the place was marked for such a creature. There were some whom it was good to pity and well (though very likely useless) to pray for; they were named reprobates, goats, God's enemies, brands for the burning; and Archie tallied every mark of identification, and drew the inevitable private inference that the Lord Justice-Clerk was the chief of sinners.

The mother's honesty was scarce complete. There was one influence she feared for the child and still secretly combated; that was my lord's; and half unconsciously, half in a wilful blindness, she continued to undermine her husband with his son. As long as Archie remained silent, she did so ruthlessly, with a single eye to heaven and the child's salvation; but the day came when Archie spoke. It was 1801, and Archie was seven, and beyond his years for curiosity and logic, when he brought the case up openly. If judging were sinful and forbidden, how came papa to be a judge? to have that sin for a trade? to bear the name of it for a distinction?

"I can't see it," said the little Rabbi, and wagged his head.

Mrs. Weir abounded in commonplace replies.

"No, I cannae see it," reiterated Archie. "And I'll tell you what, mamma, I don't think you and me's justifeed in staying with him."

The woman awoke to remorse; she saw herself disloyal to her man, her sovereign and bread-winner, in whom (with what she had of worldliness) she took a certain subdued pride. She expatiated in reply on my lord's honour and greatness; his useful services in this world of sorrow and wrong, and the place in which he stood, far above where babes and innocents could hope to see or criticise. But she had builded too well—Archie had his answers pat: Were not babes and innocents the type of the kingdom of heaven? Were not honour and greatness the badges of the world? And at any rate, how about the mob that had once seethed about the carriage?

"It's all very fine," he concluded, "but in my opinion, papa has no right to be it. And it seems that's not the worst yet of it. It seems he's called 'the Hanging Judge'—it seems he's crooool. I'll tell you what it is, mamma, there's a tex' borne in upon me: it were better for that man if a milestone were bound upon his back and him flung into the deepestmost pairts of the sea."

"O, my lamb, ye must never say the like of that!" she cried. "Ye're to honour faither and mother, dear, that your days may be long in the land. It's Atheists that cry out against him—French Atheists, Erchie! Ye would never surely even yourself down to be saying the same thing as French Atheists? It would break my heart to think that of you. And O, Erchie, here arena *you* setting up to *judge?* And have ye no forgot God's plain command—the First with Promise, dear? Mind you upon the beam and the mote!"

Having thus carried the war into the enemy's camp, the terrified lady breathed again. And no doubt it is easy thus to circumvent a child with catchwords, but it may be questioned how far it is effectual. An instinct in his breast detects the quibble, and a voice condemns it. He will instantly submit, privately hold the same opinion. For even in this simple and antique relation of the mother and the child, hypocrisies are multiplied.

When the Court rose that year and the family returned to Hermiston, it was a common remark in all the country that the lady was sore failed. She seemed to loose and seize again her touch with life, now sitting inert in a sort of durable bewilderment, anon waking to feverish and weak activity. She dawdled about the lassies at their work, looking stupidly on; she fell to rummaging in old cabinets and presses, and desisted when half through; she would begin remarks with an air of animation and drop them without a struggle. Her common appearance was of one who has forgotten something and is trying to remember; and when she overhauled, one after another, the worthless and touching mementoes of her youth, she might have been seeking the clue to that lost thought. During this period she gave many gifts to the neighbours and house lassies, giving them with a manner of regret that embarrassed the recipients.

The last night of all she was busy on some female work, and toiled upon it with so manifest and painful a devotion that my lord (who was not often curious) inquired as to its nature.

She blushed to the eyes. "O, Edom, it's for you!" she said. "It's slippers. I—I hae never made ye any."

"Ye daft auld wife!" returned his lordship. "A bonny figure I would be, palmering about in bauchles!"

The next day, at the hour of her walk, Kirstie interfered. Kirstie took this decay of her mistress very hard; bore her a grudge, quarrelled with and railed upon her, the anxiety of a genuine love wearing the disguise of temper. This day of all days she insisted disrespectfully, with rustic fury, that Mrs. Weir should stay at home. But "No, no," she said, "it's my lord's orders," and set forth as usual. Archie was visible in the acre bog, engaged upon some childish enterprise, the instrument of which was mire; and she stood and looked at him awhile like one about to call; then thought otherwise, sighed, and shook her head, and proceeded on her rounds alone. The house lassies were at the burnside washing, and saw her pass with her loose, weary, dowdy gait.

"She's a terrible feckless wife, the mistress!" said the one.

"Tut," said the other, "the wumman's seeck."

"Weel, I canna see nae differ in her," returned the first. "A füshionless quean, a feckless carline."

The poor creature thus discussed rambled awhile in the grounds without a purpose. Tides in her mind ebbed and flowed, and carried her to and fro like seaweed. She tried a path, paused, returned, and tried another; questing, forgetting her quest; the spirit of choice extinct in her bosom, or devoid of sequency. On a sudden, it appeared as though she had remembered, or had formed a resolution, wheeled about, returned with hurried steps, and appeared in the dining-room, where Kirstie was at the cleaning, like one charged with an important errand.

"Kirstie!" she began, and paused; and then with conviction, "Mr. Weir isna speeritually minded, but he has been a good man to me."

It was perhaps the first time since her husband's elevation that she had forgotten the handle to his name, of which the tender, inconsistent woman was not a little proud. And when Kirstie looked up at the speaker's face she was aware of a change.

"Godsake, what's the maitter wi' ye, mem?" cried the housekeeper, starting from the rug.

"I do not ken," answered her mistress, shaking her head. "But he is not speeritually minded, my dear."

"Here, sit down with ye! Godsake, what ails the wife?" cried Kirstie, and helped and forced her into my lord's own chair by the cheek of the hearth.

"Keep me, what's this?" she gasped. "Kirstie, what's this? I'm frich'ened."

They were her last words.

It was the lowering nightfall when my lord returned. He had

the sunset in his back, all clouds and glory; and before him, by the wayside, spied Kirstie Elliott waiting. She was dissolved in tears, and addressed him in a high, false note of barbarous mourning, such as still lingers modified among Scots heather.

"The Lord peety ye, Hermiston! the Lord prepare ye!" she keened out. "Weary upon me, that I should have to tell it!"

He reined in his horse and looked upon her with the hanging face.

"Has the French landit?" cried he.

"Man, man," she said, "is that a' ye can think of? The Lord prepare ye, the Lord comfort and support ye!"

"Is onybody deid?" says his lordship. "It's no Erchie?"

"Bethankit, no!" exclaimed the woman, startled into a more natural tone. "Na, na, it's no sae bad as that. It's the mistress, my lord; she just fair flittit before my e'en. She just gi'ed a sab and was by with it. Eh, my bonny Miss Jeannie, that I mind sae weel!" And forth again upon that pouring tide of lamentation in which women of her class excel and overabound.

Lord Hermiston sat in the saddle beholding her. Then he seemed to recover command upon himself.

"Weel, it's something of the suddenest," said he. "But she was a dwaibly body from the first."

And he rode home at a precipitate amble with Kirstie at his horse's heels.

Dressed as she was for her last walk, they had laid the dead lady on her bed. She was never interesting in life; in death she was not impressive; and as her husband stood before her, with his hands crossed behind his powerful back, that which he looked upon was the very image of the insignificant.

"Her and me were never cut out for one another," he remarked at last. "It was a daft-like marriage." And then, with a most unusual gentleness of tone, "Puir bitch," said he, "puir bitch!" Then suddenly: "Where's Erchie?"

Kirstie had decoyed him to her room and given him "a jeely-piece."

"Ye have some kind of gumption, too," observed the Judge, and considered his housekeeper grimly. "When all's said," he added, "I micht have done waur—I micht have been marriet upon a skirling Jezebel like you!"

"There's naebody thinking of you, Hermiston!" cried the offended woman. "We think of her that's out of her sorrows. And could *she* have done waur? Tell me that, Hermiston—tell me that before her clay-cauld corp!"

"Weel, there's some of them gey an' ill to please," observed his lordship.

2.   *Father and Son*

MY LORD JUSTICE-CLERK WAS KNOWN TO MANY; THE MAN ADAM Weir perhaps to none. He had nothing to explain or to conceal; he sufficed wholly and silently to himself; and that part of our nature which goes out (too often with false coin) to acquire glory or love, seemed in him to be omitted. He did not try to be loved, he did not care to be; it is probable the very thought of it was a stranger to his mind. He was an admired lawyer, a highly unpopular judge; and he looked down upon those who were his inferiors in either distinction, who were lawyers of less grasp or judges not so much detested. In all the rest of his days and doings, not one trace of vanity appeared; and he went on through life with a mechanical movement, as of the unconscious, that was almost august.

He saw little of his son. In the childish maladies with which the boy was troubled, he would make daily inquiries and daily pay him a visit, entering the sick-room with a facetious and appalling countenance, letting off a few perfunctory jests, and going again swiftly, to the patient's relief. Once, a court holiday falling opportunely, my lord had his carriage, and drove the child himself to Hermiston, the customary place of convalescence. It is conceivable he had been more than usually anxious, for that journey always remained in Archie's memory as a thing apart, his father having related to him from beginning to end, and with much detail, three authentic murder cases. Archie went the usual round of other Edinburgh boys, the high school and the college; and Hermiston looked on, or rather looked away, with scarce an affectation of interest in his progress. Daily, indeed, upon a signal after dinner, he was brought in, given nuts and a glass of port, regarded sardonically, sarcastically questioned. "Well, sir, and what have you donn with your book to-day?" my lord might begin, and

set him posers in law Latin. To a child just stumbling into Cor-
derius, Papinian and Paul proved quite invincible. But papa had
memory of no other. He was not harsh to the little scholar, having
a vast fund of patience learned upon the Bench, and was at no
pains whether to conceal or to express his disappointment. "Well,
ye have a long jaunt before ye yet!" he might observe, yawning,
and fall back on his own thoughts (as like as not) until the time
came for separation, and my lord would take the decanter and
the glass, and be off to the back chamber looking on the Meadows,
where he toiled on his cases till the hours were small. There was
no "fuller man" on the Bench; his memory was marvellous, though
wholly legal; if he had to "advise" extempore, none did it better;
yet there was none who more earnestly prepared. As he thus
watched in the night, or sat at table and forgot the presence of his
son, no doubt but he tasted deeply of recondite pleasures. To be
wholly devoted to some intellectual exercise is to have succeeded
in life; and perhaps only in law and the higher mathematics may
this devotion be maintained, suffice to itself without reaction, and
find continual rewards without excitement. This atmosphere of
his father's sterling industry was the best of Archie's education.
Assuredly it did not attract him; assuredly it rather rebutted and
depressed. Yet it was still present, unobserved like the ticking of
a clock, an arid ideal, a tasteless stimulant in the boy's life.

But Hermiston was not all of one piece. He was, besides, a
mighty toper; he could sit at wine until the day dawned, and pass
directly from the table to the Bench with a steady hand and a clear
head. Beyond the third bottle, he showed the plebeian in a larger
print; the low, gross accent, the low, foul mirth, grew broader and
commoner; he became less formidable, and infinitely more disgusting. Now, the boy had inherited from Jean Rutherford a
shivering delicacy, unequally mated with potential violence. In
the playing-fields, and amongst his own companions, he repaid a
coarse expression with a blow; at his father's table (when the time
came for him to join these revels) he turned pale and sickened in
silence. Of all the guests whom he there encountered, he had
toleration for only one: David Keith Carnegie, Lord Glenalmond.
Lord Glenalmond was tall and emaciated, with long features and
long delicate hands. He was often compared with the statue of
Forbes of Culloden in the Parliament House; and his blue eye, at

more than sixty, preserved some of the fire of youth. His exquisite disparity with any of his fellow guests, his appearance as of
an artist and an aristocrat stranded in rude company, riveted the
boy's attention; and as curiosity and interest are the things in the
world that are the most immediately and certainly rewarded, Lord
Glenalmond was attracted to the boy.

"And so this is your son, Hermiston?" he asked, laying his hand
on Archie's shoulder. "He's getting a big lad."

"Hout!" said the gracious father, "just his mother over again
—daurna say boo to a goose!"

But the stranger retained the boy, talked to him, drew him out,
found in him a taste for letters, and a fine, ardent, modest, youthful soul; and encouraged him to be a visitor on Sunday evenings
in his bare, cold, lonely dining-room, where he sat and read in the
isolation of a bachelor grown old in refinement. The beautiful
gentleness and grace of the old Judge, and the delicacy of his
person, thoughts, and language, spoke to Archie's heart in its own
tongue. He conceived the ambition to be such another; and, when
the day came for him to choose a profession, it was in emulation of
Lord Glenalmond, not of Lord Hermiston, that he chose the Bar.
Hermiston looked on at this friendship with some secret pride, but
openly with the intolerance of scorn. He scarce lost an opportunity
to put them down with a rough jape; and, to say truth, it was
not difficult, for they were neither of them quick. He had a word
of contempt for the whole crowd of poets, painters, fiddlers, and
their admirers, the bastard race of amateurs, which was continually
on his lips. "Signor Feedle-eerie!" he would say. "Oh, for Goad's
sake, no more of the signor!"

"You and my father are great friends, are you not?" asked Archie
once.

"There is no man that I more respect, Archie," replied Lord
Glenalmond. "He is two things of price. He is a great lawyer,
and he is upright as the day."

"You and he are so different," said the boy, his eyes dwelling on
those of his old friend, like a lover's on his mistress's.

"Indeed so," replied the Judge; "very different. And so I fear
are you and he. Yet I would like it very ill if my young friend
were to misjudge his father. He has all the Roman virtues: Cato
and Brutus were such; I think a son's heart might well be proud
of such an ancestry of one."

"And I would sooner he were a plaided herd," cried Archie, with sudden bitterness.

"And that is neither very wise, nor I believe entirely true," returned Glenalmond. "Before you are done you will find some of these expressions rise on you like a remorse. They are merely literary and decorative; they do not aptly express your thought, nor is your thought clearly apprehended, and no doubt your father (if he were here) would say 'Signor Feedle-eerie!' "

With the infinitely delicate sense of youth, Archie avoided the subject from that hour. It was perhaps a pity. Had he but talked—talked freely—let himself gush out in words (the way youth loves to do and should), there might have been no tale to write upon the Weirs of Hermiston. But the shadow of a threat of ridicule sufficed; in the slight tartness of these words he read a prohibition; and it is likely that Glenalmond meant it so.

Besides the veteran, the boy was without confidant or friend. Serious and eager, he came through school and college, and moved among a crowd of the indifferent, in the seclusion of his shyness. He grew up handsome, with an open, speaking countenance, with graceful, youthful ways; he was clever, he took prizes, he shone in the Speculative Society.* It should seem he must become the centre of a crowd of friends; but something that was in part the delicacy of his mother, in part the austerity of his father, held him aloof from all. It is a fact, and a strange one, that among his contemporaries Hermiston's son was thought to be a chip of the old block. "You're a friend of Archie Weir's?" said one to Frank Innes; and Innes replied, with his usual flippancy and more than his usual insight: "I know Weir, but I never met Archie." No one had met Archie, a malady most incident to only sons. He flew his private signal, and none heeded it; it seemed he was abroad in a world from which the very hope of intimacy was banished; and he looked round about him on the concourse of his fellow-students, and forward to the trivial days and acquaintances that were to come, without hope or interest.

As time went on, the tough and rough old sinner felt himself drawn to the son of his loins and sole continuator of his new family, with softnesses of sentiment that he could hardly credit and was wholly impotent to express. With a face, voice, and manner trained through forty years to terrify and repel, Rhadamanthus

* A famous debating society of the students of Edinburgh University.

may be great, but he will scarce be engaging. It is a fact that he tried to propitiate Archie, but a fact that cannot be too lightly taken; the attempt was so unconspicuously made, the failure so stoically supported. Sympathy is not due to the steadfast iron natures. If he failed to gain his son's friendship, or even his son's toleration, on he went up the great, bare staircase of his duty, uncheered and undepressed. There might have been more pleasure in his relations with Archie, so much he may have recognised at moments; but pleasure was a by-product of the singular chemistry of life, which only fools expected.

An idea of Archie's attitude, since we are all grown up and have forgotten the days of our youth, it is more difficult to convey. He made no attempt whatsoever to understand the man with whom he dined and breakfasted. Parsimony of pain, glut of pleasure, these are the two alternating ends of youth; and Archie was of the parsimonious. The wind blew cold out of a certain quarter—he turned his back upon it; stayed as little as was possible in his father's presence; and when there, averted his eyes as much as was decent from his father's face. The lamp shone for many hundred days upon these two at table—my lord ruddy, gloomy, and un-reverent; Archie with a potential brightness that was always dimmed and veiled in that society; and there were not, perhaps, in Christendom two men more radically strangers. The father, with a grand simplicity, either spoke of what interested himself, or maintained an unaffected silence. The son turned in his head for some topic that should be quite safe, that would spare him fresh evidences either of my lord's inherent grossness or of the in-nocence of his inhumanity; treading gingerly the ways of inter-course, like a lady gathering up her skirts in a by-path. If he made a mistake, and my lord began to abound in matter of offence, Archie drew himself up, his brow grew dark, his share of the talk expired; but my lord would faithfully and cheerfully continue to pour out the worst of himself before his silent and offended son.

"Well, it's a poor hert that never rejoices," he would say, at the conclusion of such a nightmare interview. "But I must get to my plew-stilts." And he would seclude himself as usual in the back room, and Archie go forth into the night and the city quivering with animosity and scorn.

3. *In the Matter of the Hanging of Duncan Jopp*

IT CHANCED IN THE YEAR 1813 THAT ARCHIE STRAYED ONE DAY into the Judiciary Court. The macer made room for the son of the presiding judge. In the dock, the centre of men's eyes, there stood a whey-coloured, misbegotten caitiff, Duncan Jopp, on trial for his life. His story, as it was raked out before him in that public scene, was one of disgrace and vice and cowardice, the very naked-ness of crime; and the creature heard and it seemed at times as though he understood—as if at times he forgot the horror of the place he stood in, and remembered the shame of what had brought him there. He kept his head bowed and his hands clutched upon the rail; his hair dropped in his eyes and at times he flung it back; and now he glanced about the audience in a sudden fellness of terror, and now looked in the face of his judge and gulped. There was pinned about his throat a piece of dingy flannel; and this it was perhaps that turned the scale in Archie's mind between disgust and pity. The creature stood in a vanishing point; yet a little while, and he was still a man, and had eyes and apprehension; yet a little longer, and with a last sordid piece of pageantry, he would cease to be. And here, in the meantime, with a trait of human nature that caught at the beholder's breath, he was tending a sore throat.

Over against him, my Lord Hermiston occupied the Bench in the red robes of criminal jurisdiction, his face framed in the white wig. Honest all through, he did not affect the virtue of impar-tiality; this was no case for refinement; there was a man to be hanged, he would have said, and he was hanging him. Nor was it possible to see his lordship, and acquit him of gusto in the task. It was plain he gloried in the exercise of his trained faculties, in the clear sight which pierced at once into the joint of fact, in the rude, unvarnished jibes with which he demolished every figment of defence. He took his ease and jested, unbending in that solemn place with some of the freedom of the tavern; and the rag of man with the flannel round his neck was hunted gallowsward with jeers.

Duncan had a mistress, scarce less forlorn and greatly older than himself, who came up, whimpering and curtseying, to add the weight of her betrayal. My lord gave her the oath in his most roaring voice and added an intolerant warning.

"Mind what ye say now, Janet," said he. "I have an e'e upon ye; I'm ill to jest with."

Presently, after she was tremblingly embarked on her story, "And what made ye do this, ye auld runt?" the Court interposed. "Do ye mean to tell me ye was the pannel's mistress?"

"If you please, ma loard," whined the female.

"Godsake! ye made a bonny couple," observed his lordship; and there was something so formidable and ferocious in his scorn that not even the galleries thought to laugh.

The summing up contained some jewels.

"These two peetiable creatures seem to have made up thegither, it's not for us to explain why."—"The pannel, who (whatever else he may be) appears to be equally ill set out in mind and boady."— "Neither the pannel nor yet the old wife appears to have had so much common-sense as even to tell a lie when it was necessary." And in the course of sentencing, my lord had this *obiter dictum*: "I have been the means, under God, of haanging a great number, but never just such a disjaskit rascal as yourself." The words were strong in themselves; the light and heat and detonation of their delivery, and the savage pleasure of the speaker in his task, made them tingle in the ears.

When all was over, Archie came forth again into a changed world. Had there been the least redeeming greatness in the crime, any obscurity, any dubiety, perhaps he might have understood. But the culprit stood, with his sore throat, in the sweat of his mortal agony, without defense or excuse; a thing to cover up with blushes; a being so much sunk beneath the zones of sympathy that pity might seem harmless. And the Judge had pursued him with a monstrous, relishing gaiety, horrible to be conceived, a trait for nightmares. It is one thing to spear a tiger, another to crush a toad; there are æsthetics even of the slaughterhouse; and the loathsomeness of Duncan Jopp enveloped and infected the image of his judge.

Archie passed by his friends in the High Street with incoherent words and gestures. He saw Holyrood in a dream, remembrance of its romance awoke in him and faded; he had a vision of the old radiant stories, of Queen Mary and Prince Charlie, of the hooded stag, of the splendour and crime, the velvet and bright iron of the past; and dismissed them with a cry of pain. He lay and moaned in the Hunter's Bog, and the heavens were dark above him and the grass of the field an offence. "This is my father," he said. "I draw my life from him; the flesh upon my bones is his, the bread I am fed with is the wages of these horrors." He recalled his mother, and ground his forehead in the earth. He thought of flight, and where was he to flee to? of other lives, but was there any life worth living in this den of savage and jeering animals?

The interval before the execution was like a violent dream. He met his father; he would not look at him, he could not speak to him. It seemed there was no living creature but must have been swift to recognise that imminent animosity, but the hide of the Lord Justice-Clerk remained impenetrable. Had my lord been talkative, the truce could never have subsisted; but he was by fortune in one of his humours of sour silence; and under the very guns of his broadside Archie nursed the enthusiasm of rebellion. It seemed to him, from the top of his nineteen years' experience, as if he were marked at birth to be the perpetrator of some signal action, to set back fallen Mercy, to overthrow the usurping devil that sat, horned and hoofed, on her throne. Seductive Jacobin figments, which he had often refuted at the Speculative, swam up in his mind and startled him as with voices; and he seemed to himself to walk accompanied by an almost tangible presence of new beliefs and duties.

On the named morning he was at the place of execution. He saw the fleering rabble the flinching wretch produced. He looked on for awhile at a certain parody of devotion, which seemed to strip the wretch of his last claim to manhood. Then followed the brutal instant of extinction, and the paltry dangling of the remains like broken jumping-jack. He had been prepared for something terrible, not for this tragic meanness. He stood a moment silent, and then—"I denounce this God-defying murder," he shouted; and his father, if he must have disclaimed the sentiment, might have owned the stentorian voice with which it was uttered.

Frank Innes dragged him from the spot. The two handsome lads followed the same course of study and recreation, and felt a certain mutual attraction, founded mainly on good looks. It had never gone deep; Frank was by nature a thin, jeering creature, not truly susceptible whether of feeling or inspiring friendship; and the relation between the pair was altogether on the outside, a thing of common knowledge and the pleasantries that spring from a common acquaintance. The more credit to Frank that he was appalled by Archie's outburst, and at least conceived the design of keeping him in sight, and, if possible, in hand, for the day. But Archie, who had just defied—was it God or Satan?—would not listen to the word of a college companion.

"I will not go with you," he said. "I do not desire your company, sir; I would be alone."

"Here, Weir, man, don't be absurd," said Innes, keeping a tight hold upon his sleeve. "I will not let you go until I know what you mean to do with yourself; it's no use brandishing that staff." For indeed at that moment Archie had made a sudden—perhaps a warlike—movement. "This has been the most insane affair; you know it has. You know very well that I'm playing the good Samaritan. All I wish is to keep you quiet."

"If quietness is what you wish, Mr. Innes," said Archie, "and you will promise to leave me entirely to myself, I will tell you so much, that I am going to walk in the country and admire the beauties of nature."

"Honour bright?" asked Frank.

"I am not in the habit of lying, Mr. Innes," retorted Archie. "I have the honour of wishing you good-day."

"You won't forget the Spec.?" asked Innes.

"The Spec.?" said Archie. "Oh, no, I won't forget the Spec."

And the one young man carried his tortured spirit forth of the city and all the day long, by one road and another, in an endless pilgrimage of misery; while the other hastened smilingly to spread the news of Weir's access of insanity, and to drum up for that night a full attendance at the Speculative, where farther eccentric developments might certainly be looked for. I doubt if Innes had the least belief in his prediction; I think it flowed rather from a wish to make the story as good and the scandal as great as possible; not from any ill-will to Archie—from the mere pleasure of beholding interested faces. But for all that his words were prophetic. Archie did not forget the Spec.; he put in an appearance there at the due time, and, before the evening was over, had dealt a memorable shock to his companions. It chanced he was the president of the night. He sat in the same room where the society still meets—only the portraits were not there; the men who afterwards sat for them were then but beginning their career.

The same lustre of many tapers shed its light over the meeting; the same chair, perhaps, supported him that so many of us have sat in since. At times he seemed to forget the business of the evening, but even in these periods he sat with a great air of energy and determination. At times he meddled bitterly and launched with defiance those fines which are the precious and rarely used artillery of the president. He little thought, as he did so, how he resembled his father, but his friends remarked upon it, chuckling. So far, in his high place above his fellow-students, he seemed set beyond the possibility of any scandal; but his mind was made up—he was determined to fulfil the sphere of his offence. He signed to Innes (whom he had just fined, and who just impeached his ruling) to succeed him in the chair, stepped down from the platform, and took his place by the chimney-piece, the shine of many wax tapers from above illuminating his pale face, the glow of the great red fire relieving from behind his slim figure. He had to propose, as an amendment to the next subject in the case book, "Whether capital punishment be consistent with God's will or man's policy?"

A breath of embarrassment, of something like alarm, passed round the room, so daring did these words appear upon the lips of Hermiston's only son. But the amendment was not seconded; the previous question was promptly moved and unanimously voted, and the momentary scandal smuggled by. Innes triumphed in the fulfilment of his prophecy. He and Archie were now become the heroes of the night; but whereas every one crowded about Innes, when the meeting broke up, but one of all his companions came to speak to Archie.

"Weir, man! that was an extraordinary raid of yours!" observed this courageous member, taking him confidentially by the arm as they went out.

"I don't think it a raid," said Archie grimly. "More like a war. I saw that poor brute hanged this morning, and my gorge rises at it yet."

"Hut-tut!" returned his companion, and, dropping his arm like something hot, he sought the less tense society of others.

Archie found himself alone. The last of the faithful—or was it only the boldest of the curious?—had fled. He watched the black huddle of his fellow-students draw off down and up the street, in whispering or boisterous gangs. And the isolation of the moment weighed upon him like an omen and an emblem of his destiny in life. Bred up in unbroken fear himself, among trembling servants, and in a house which (at the least ruffle in the master's voice) shuddered into silence, he saw himself on the brink of the red valley of war, and measured the danger and length of it with awe. He made a détour in the glimmer and shadow of the streets, came into the back stable lane, and watched for a long while the light burn steady in the Judge's room. The longer he gazed upon that illuminated window-blind, the more blank became the picture of the man who sat behind it, endlessly turning over sheets of process, pausing to sip a glass of port, or rising and passing heavily about his book-lined walls to verify some reference. He could not combine the brutal judge and the industrious, dispassionate student; the connecting link escaped him; from such a dual nature, it was impossible he should predict behaviour; and he asked himself if he had done well to plunge into a business of which the end could not be foreseen; and presently after, with a sickening decline of confidence, if he had done loyally to strike his father. For he had struck him—defied him twice over and before a cloud of witnesses —struck him a public buffet before crowds. Who had called him to judge his father in these precarious and high questions? The office was usurped. It might have become a stranger; in a son—there was no blinking it—in a son, it was disloyal. And now, between these two natures so antipathetic, so hateful to each other, there was depending an unpardonable affront: and the providence of God alone might foresee the manner in which it would be resented by Lord Hermiston.

These misgivings tortured him all night and arose with him in the winter's morning; they followed him from class to class, they made him shrinkingly sensitive to every shade of manner in his companions, they sounded in his ears through the current voice of the professor; and he brought them home with him at night unabated and indeed increased. The cause of this increase lay in a chance encounter with the celebrated Dr. Gregory. Archie stood looking vaguely in the lighted window of a book shop, trying to nerve himself for the approaching ordeal. My lord and he had met and parted in the morning as they had now done for long, with scarcely the ordinary civilities of life; and it was plain to the son that nothing had yet reached the father's ears. Indeed, when he recalled the awful countenance of my lord, a timid hope sprang up in him that perhaps there would be found no one bold enough to carry tales. If this were so, he asked himself, would he begin again? and he found no answer. It was at this moment that a hand was laid upon his arm, and a voice said in his ear, "My dear Mr. Archie, you had better come and see me."

He started, turned around, and found himself face to face with Dr. Gregory. "And why should I come to see you?" he asked, with the defiance of the miserable.

"Because you are looking exceedingly ill," said the doctor, "and you very evidently want looking after, my young friend. Good folk are scarce, you know; and it is not every one that would be quite so much missed as yourself. It is not every one that Hermiston would miss."

And with a nod and smile, the doctor passed on.

A moment after, Archie was in pursuit, and had in turn, but more roughly, seized him by the arm.

"What do you mean? what did you mean by saying that? What makes you think that Hermis—my father would have missed me?"

The doctor turned about and looked him all over with a clinical eye. A far more stupid man than Dr. Gregory might have guessed the truth; but ninety-nine out of a hundred, even if they had been equally inclined to kindness, would have blundered by some touch of charitable exaggeration. The doctor was better inspired. He knew the father well; in that white face of intelligence and suffering, he divined something of the son; and he told, without apology or adornment, the plain truth.

"When you had the measles, Mr. Archibald, you had them gey and ill; and I thought you were going to slip between my fingers," he said. "Well, your father was anxious. How did I know it? says you. Simply because I am a trained observer. The sign that I saw him make, ten thousand would have missed; and perhaps—*perhaps,* I say, because he's a hard man to judge of—but perhaps he never made another. A strange thing to consider! It was this. One day I came to him: 'Hermiston,' said I, 'there's a change.' He never said a word, just glowered at me (if ye'll pardon the phrase) like a wild beast. 'A change for the better,' said I. And I distinctly heard him take his breath."

The doctor left no opportunity for anti-climax; nodding his cocked hat (a piece of antiquity to which he clung) and repeating "Distinctly" with raised eyebrows, he took his departure, and left Archie speechless in the street.

The anecdote might be called infinitely little, and yet its meaning for Archie was immense. "I did not know the old man had so much blood in him." He had never dreamed this sire of his, this aboriginal antique, this adamantine Adam, had even so much of a heart as to be moved in the least degree for another—and that other himself, who had insulted him! With the generosity of youth, Archie was instantly under arms upon the other side: had instantly created a new image of Lord Hermiston, that of a man who was all iron without and all sensibility within. The mind of the vile jester, the tongue that had pursued Duncan Jopp with unmanly insults, the unbeloved countenance that he had known and feared for so long, were all forgotten; and he hastened home, impatient to confess his misdeeds, impatient to throw himself on the mercy of this imaginary character.

He was not to be long without a rude awakening. It was in the gloaming when he drew near the doorstep of the lighted house, and was aware of the figure of his father approaching from the opposite side. Little daylight lingered; but on the door being opened, the strong yellow shine of the lamp gushed out upon the landing and shone full on Archie, as he stood, in the old-fashioned observance of respect, to yield precedence. The Judge came without haste, stepping stately and firm; his chin raised, his face (as he entered the lamplight) strongly illumined, his mouth set hard. There was never a wink of change in his expression; without looking to the right or left, he mounted the stair, passed close to Archie, and entered the house. Instinctively, the boy, upon his first coming, had made a movement to meet him; instinctively, he recoiled against the railing, as the old man swept by him in a pomp of indignation. Words were needless; he knew all—perhaps more than all—and the hour of judgment was at hand.

It is possible that, in this sudden revulsion of hope and before these symptoms of impending danger, Archie might have fled. But not even that was left to him. My lord, after hanging up his cloak and hat, turned round in the lighted entry, and made him an imperative and silent gesture with his thumb, and with the strange instinct of obedience, Archie followed him into the house.

All dinner time there reigned over the Judge's table a palpable silence, and as soon as the solids were despatched he rose to his feet.

"M'Killop, tak' the wine into my room," said he; and then to his son: "Archie, you and me has to have a talk."

It was at this sickening moment that Archie's courage, for the first and last time, entirely deserted him. "I have an appointment," said he.

"It'll have to be broken, then," said Hermiston, and led the way into his study.

The lamp was shaded, the fire trimmed to a nicety, the table covered deep with orderly documents, the backs of law books made a frame upon all sides that was only broken by the window and the doors.

For a moment Hermiston warmed his hands at the fire, presenting his back to Archie; then suddenly disclosed on him the terrors of the Hanging Face.

"What's this I hear of ye!" he asked.

There was no answer possible to Archie.

"I'll have to tell ye, then," pursued Hermiston. "It seems ye've been skirling against the father that begot ye, and one of His Maijesty's Judges in this land; and that in the public street, and while an order of the Court was being executit. Forbye which, it would appear that ye've been airing your opeenions in a Coallege Debatin' Society," he paused a moment: and, then, with extraordinary bitterness, added: "Ye damned eediot."

"I had meant to tell you," stammered Archie. "I see you are well informed."

"Muckle obleeged to ye," said his lordship, and took his usual seat. "And so you disapprove of caapital punishment?" he added.

"I am sorry, sir, I do," said Archie.

"I am sorry, too," said his lordship. "And now, if you please, we shall approach this business with a little more parteecularity. I hear that at the hanging of Duncan Jopp—and, man! ye had a fine client there—in the middle of all the riff-raff of the ceety, ye thought fit to cry out, 'This is a damned murder, and my gorge rises at the man that haangit him.'"

"No, sir, these were not my words," cried Archie.

"What were ye'r words, then?" asked the Judge.

"I believe I said, 'I denounce it as a murder!'" said the son, "I beg your pardon—a God-defying murder. I have no wish to conceal the truth," he added, and looked his father for a moment in the face.

"God, it would only need that of it next!" cried Hermiston. "There was nothing about your gorge rising, then?"

"That was afterwards, my lord, as I was leaving the Speculative. I said I had been to see the miserable creature hanged, and my gorge rose at it."

"Did ye, though?" said Hermiston. "And I suppose ye knew who haangit him?"

"I was present at the trial, I ought to tell you that, I ought to explain. I ask your pardon beforehand for any expression that may seem undutiful. The position in which I stand is wretched," said the unhappy hero, now fairly face to face with the business he had chosen. "I have been reading some of your cases. I was present while Jopp was tried. It was a hideous business. Father, it was a hideous thing! Grant he was vile, why should you hunt him with a vileness equal to his own? It was done with glee—that is the word—you did it with glee; and I looked on, God help me! with horror."

"You're a young gentleman that doesna approve of caapital punishment," said Hermiston. "Weel, I'm an auld man that does. I was glad to get Jopp haangit, and what for would I pretend I wasna? You're all for honesty, it seems; you couldn't even steik your mouth on the public street. What for should I steik mines upon the Bench, the King's officer, bearing the sword, a dreid to evil-doers, as I was from the beginning, and as I will be to the end! Mair than enough of it! Heedious! I never gave twa thoughts to heediousness, I have no call to be bonny. I'm a man that gets through with my day's business, and let that suffice."

The ring of sarcasm had died out of his voice as he went on; the plain words became invested with some of the dignity of the justice-seat.

"It would be telling you if you could say as much," the speaker resumed. "But ye cannot. Ye've been reading some of my cases, ye say. But it was not for the law in them, it was to spy out your faither's nakedness, a fine employment in a son. You're splairging; you're running at lairge in life like a wild nowt. It's impossible you should think any longer of coming to the Bar. You're not fit for it; no splairger is. And another thing: son of mines or no son of mines, you have flung fylement in public on one of the Senators of the Coallege of Justice, and I would make it my business to see that ye were never admitted there yourself. There is a kind of a decency to be observit. Then comes the next of it—what am I to do with ye next? Ye'll have to find some kind of a trade, for I'll never support ye in idleset. What do ye fancy ye'll be fit for? The pulpit? Na, they could never get diveenity into that bloackhead. Him that the law of man whammles is no likely to do muckle better by the law of God. What would ye make of hell? Wouldna your gorge rise at that? Na, there's no room for splairgers under the fower quarters of John Calvin. What else is there? Speak up. Have ye got nothing of your own?"

"Father, let me go to the Peninsula," said Archie. "That's all I'm fit for—to fight."

"All? quo' he!" returned the Judge. "And it would be enough too, if I thought it. But I'll never trust ye so near the French, you that's so Frenchifeed."

"You do me injustice there, sir," said Archie. "I am loyal; I will not boast; but any interest I may have ever felt in the French——"

"Have ye been so loyal to me?" interrupted his father.

There came no reply.

"I think not," continued Hermiston. "And I would send no man to be a servant to the King, God bless him! that has proved such a shauchling son to his own faither. You can splairge here on Edinburgh street, and where's the hairm? It doesna pay buff on me! And if there were twenty thousand eediots like yourself, sorrow a Duncan Jopp would hang the fewer. But there's no splairging possible in a camp; and if you were to go to it, you would find out for yourself whether Lord Well'n'ton approves of caapital punishment or not. You a sodger!" he cried, with a sudden burst of scorn. "Ye auld wife, the sodgers would bray at ye like cuddies!"

As at the drawing of a curtain, Archie was aware of some illogicality in his position, and stood abashed. He had a strong impression, besides, of the essential valour of the old gentleman before him, how conveyed it would be hard to say.

"Well, have ye no other proposeetion?" said my lord again.

"You have taken this so calmly, sir, that I cannot but stand ashamed," began Archie.

"I'm nearer voamiting, though, than you would fancy," said my lord.

The blood rose to Archie's brow.

"I beg your pardon, I should have said that you had accepted my affront. . . . I admit it was an affront; I did not think to apologise, but I do, I ask your pardon; it will not be so again, I pass you my word of honour. . . . I should have said that I admired your magnanimity with—this—offender," Archie concluded with a gulp.

"I have no other son, ye see," said Hermiston. "A bonny one I have gotten! But I must just do the best I can wi' him, and what am I to do? If ye had been younger, I would have wheepit ye for this rideeculous exhibeetion. The way it is, I have just to grin and bear. But one thing is to be clearly understood. As a faither, I must grin and bear it; but if I had been the Lord Advocate instead of the Lord Justice-Clerk, son or no son, Mr. Erchibald Weir would have been in a jyle the night."

Archie was now dominated. Lord Hermiston was coarse and cruel; and yet the son was aware of a bloomless nobility, an ungracious abnegation of the man's self in the man's office. At every word, this sense of the greatness of Lord Hermiston's spirit struck more home; and along with it that of his own impotence, who had struck—and perhaps basely struck—at his own father, and not reached so far as to have even nettled him.

"I place myself in your hands without reserve," he said.

"That's the first sensible word I've had of ye the night," said Hermiston. "I can tell ye, that would have been the end of it, the one way or the other; but it's better ye should come there yourself, than what I would have had to hirstle ye. Weel, by my way of it—and my way is the best—there's just the one thing it's possible that ye might be with decency, and that's a laird. Ye'll be out of hairm's way at the least of it. If ye have to rowt, ye can rowt amang the kye; and the maist feck of the caapital punishment ye're like to come across'll be guddling trouts. Now, I'm for no idle lairdies; every man has to work, if it's only at peddling ballants; to work, or to be wheeped, or to be haangit. If I set ye down at Hermiston, I'll have to see you work that place the way it has never been workit yet; ye must ken about the sheep like a herd; ye must be my grieve there, and I'll see that I gain by ye. Is that understoood?"

"I will do my best," said Archie.

"Well, then, I'll send Kirstie word the morn, and ye can go yourself the day after," said Hermiston. "And just try to be less of an eediot!" he concluded, with a freezing smile, and turned immediately to the papers on his desk.

4. *Opinion of the Bench*

LATE THE SAME NIGHT, AFTER A DISORDERED WALK, ARCHIE WAS admitted into Lord Glenalmond's dining-room where he sat, with a book upon his knee, beside three frugal coals of fire. In his robes upon the Bench, Glenalmond had a certain air of burliness: plucked of these, it was a may-pole of a man that rose unsteadily from his chair to give his visitor welcome. Archie had suffered much in the last days, he had suffered again that evening; his face was white and drawn, his eyes wild and dark. But Lord Glenalmond greeted him without the least mark of surprise or curiosity.

"Come in, come in," said he. "Come in and take a seat. Carstairs" (to his servant), "make up the fire, and then you can bring a bit of supper," and again to Archie, with a very trivial accent: "I was half expecting you," he added.

"No supper," said Archie. "It is impossible that I should eat."

"Not impossible," said the tall old man, laying his hand upon his shoulder, "and, if you will believe me, necessary."

"You know what brings me?" said Archie, as soon as the servant had left the room.

"I have a guess, I have a guess," replied Glenalmond. "We will talk of it presently—when Carstairs has come and gone, and you have had a piece of my good Cheddar cheese and a pull at the porter tankard: not before."

"It is impossible I should eat," repeated Archie.

"Tut, tut!" said Lord Glenalmond. "You have eaten nothing to-day, and, I venture to add, nothing yesterday. There is no case that may not be made worse; this may be a very disagreeable business, but if you were to fall sick and die, it would be still more so, and for all concerned—for all concerned."

"I see you must know all," said Archie. "Where did you hear it?"

"In the mart of scandal, in the Parliament House," said Glenalmond. "It runs riot below among the Bar and the public, but it sifts up to us upon the Bench, and rumour has some of her voices even in the divisions."

Carstairs returned at this moment, and rapidly laid out a little supper; during which Lord Glenalmond spoke at large and a little vaguely on indifferent subjects, so that it might be rather said of him that he made a cheerful noise, than that he contributed to human conversation; and Archie sat upon the other side, not heeding him, brooding over his wrongs and errors.

But so soon as the servant was gone, he broke forth again at once. "Who told my father? Who dared to tell him? Could it have been you?"

"No, it was not me," said the Judge; "although—to be quite frank with you, and after I had seen and warned you—it might have been me. I believe it was Glenkindie."

"That shrimp!" cried Archie.

"As you say, that shrimp," returned my lord; "although really it is scarce a fitting mode of expression for one of the Senators of the College of Justice. We were hearing the parties in a long, crucial case, before the fifteen; Creech was moving at some length for an infeftment; when I saw Glenkindie lean forward to Hermiston with his hand over his mouth and make him a secret communication. No one could have guessed its nature from your father; from Glenkindie, yes, his malice sparkled out of him a little grossly. But your father, no. A man of granite. The next moment he pounced upon Creech. 'Mr. Creech,' says he, 'I'll take a look of that sasine,' and for thirty minutes after," said Glenalmond, with a smile, "Messrs. Creech and Co. were fighting a pretty up-hill battle, which resulted, I need hardly add, in their total rout. The case was dismissed. No, I doubt if ever I heard Hermiston better inspired. He was literally rejoicing *in apicibus juris.*"

Archie was able to endure no longer. He thrust his plate away and interrupted the deliberate and insignificant stream of talk. "Here," he said, "I have made a fool of myself, if I have not made something worse. Do you judge between us—judge between a father and a son. I can speak to you; it is not like . . . I will tell you what I feel and what I mean to do; and you shall be the judge," he repeated.

"I decline jurisdiction," said Glenalmond with extreme seriousness. "But, my dear boy, if it will do you any good to talk, and if it will interest you at all to hear what I may choose to say when I have heard you, I am quite at your command. Let an old man say it, for once, and not need to blush: I love you like a son."

There came a sudden sharp sound in Archie's throat. "Ay," he cried, "and there it is! Love! Like a son! And how do you think I love my father?"

"Quietly, quietly," says my lord.

"I will be very quiet," replied Archie. "And I will be baldly frank. I do not love my father; I wonder sometimes if I do not hate him. There's my shame; perhaps my sin; at least, and in the sight of God, not my fault. How was I to love him? He has never spoken to me, never smiled upon me; I do not think he ever touched me. You know the way he talks? You do not talk so, yet you can sit and hear him without shuddering, and I cannot. My soul is sick when he begins with it; I could smite him in the mouth. And all that's nothing. I was at the trial of this Jopp. You were not there, but you must have heard him often; the man's notorious for it, for being—look at my position! he's my father and this is how I have to speak of him—notorious for being a brute and cruel and a coward. Lord Glenalmond, I give you my word, when I came out of that Court, I longed to die—the shame of it was beyond my strength: but I—I——" he rose from his seat and began to pace the room in a disorder. "Well, who am I? A boy, who have never been tried, have never done anything except this twopenny impotent folly with my father. But I tell you, my lord, and I know myself, I am at least that kind of a man—or that kind of a boy, if you prefer it—that I could die in torments rather than that any one should suffer as that scoundrel suffered. Well, and what have I done? I see it now. I have made a fool of myself, as I said in the beginning; and I have gone back, and asked my father's pardon, and placed myself wholly in his hands—and he has sent me to Hermiston," with a wretched smile, "for life, I suppose—and what can I say? he strikes me as having done quite right, and let me off better than I had deserved."

"My poor, dear boy!" observed Glenalmond. "My poor dear and, if you will allow me to say so, very foolish boy! You are only discovering where you are; to one of your temperament, or of mine, a painful discovery. The world was not made for us; it was made for ten hundred millions of men, all different from each other and from us; there's no royal road there, we just have to sclamber and tumble. Don't think that I am at all disposed to be surprised; don't suppose that I ever think of blaming you; indeed I rather admire! But there fall to be offered one or two observations on the case which occur to me and which (if you will listen to them dispassionately) may be the means of inducing you to view the matter more calmly. First of all, I cannot acquit you of a good deal of what is called intolerance. You seem to have been very much offended because your father talks a little sculduddery after dinner, which it is perfectly licit for him to do, and which (although I am not very fond of it myself) appears to be entirely an affair of taste. Your father, I scarcely like to remind you, since it is so trite a commonplace, is older than yourself. At least, he is *major* and *sui juris,* and may please himself in the matter of his conversation. And, do you know, I wonder if he might not have as good an answer against you and me? We say we sometimes find him coarse, but I suspect he might retort that he finds us always dull. Perhaps a relevant exception."

He beamed on Archie, but no smile could be elicited.

"And now," proceeded the Judge, "for 'Archibald on Capital Punishment.' This is a very plausible academic opinion; of course I do not and I cannot hold it; but that's not to say that many able and excellent persons have not done so in the past. Possibly, in the past also, I may have a little dipped myself in the same heresy. My third client, or possibly my fourth, was the means of a return in my opinions. I never saw the man I more believed in; I would have put my hand in the fire, I would have gone to the cross for him; and when it came to trial he was gradually pictured before me, by undeniable probation, in the light of so gross, so cold-blooded, and so black-hearted a villain, that I had a mind to have cast my brief upon the table. I was then boiling against the man with even a more tropical temperature than I had been boiling for him. But I said to myself: 'No, you have taken up his case; and because you have changed your mind it must not be suffered to let drop. All that rich tide of eloquence that you prepared last night with so much enthusiasm is out of place, and yet you must not desert him, you must say something.' So I said something, and I got him off. It made my reputation. But an experience of that kind is formative. A man must not bring his passions to the Bar—or to the Bench."

This story had slightly rekindled Archie's interest. "I could never deny," he began—"I mean I can conceive that some men would be better dead. But who are we to know all the springs of God's unfortunate creatures? Who are we to trust ourselves where it seems that God himself must think twice before He treads, and to do it with delight? Yes, with delight. *Tigris ut aspera.*"

"Perhaps not a pleasant spectacle," said Glenalmond. "And yet, do you know, I think somehow a great one."

"I've had a long talk with him to-night," said Archie.

"I was supposing so," said Glenalmond.

"And he struck me—I cannot deny that he struck me as something very big," pursued the son. "Yes, he is big. He never spoke about himself; only about me. I suppose I admired him. The dreadful part——"

"Suppose we did not talk about that," interrupted Glenalmond. "You know it very well, it cannot in any way help that you should brood upon it, and I sometimes wonder whether you and I—who are a pair of sentimentalists—are quite good judges of plain men."

"How do you mean?" asked Archie.

"*Fair* judges, I mean," replied Glenalmond. "Can we be just to them? Do we not ask too much? There was a word of yours just now that impressed me a little when you asked me who we were to know all the springs of God's unfortunate creatures. You applied that, as I understood, to capital cases only. But does it—I ask myself—does it not apply all through? Is it any less difficult to judge of a good man or of a half-good man, than of the worst criminal at the Bar? And may not each have relevant excuses?"

"Ah, but we do not talk of punishing the good," cried Archie.

"No, we do not talk of it," said Glenalmond. "But I think we do it. Your father, for instance."

"You think I have punished him?" cried Archie.

Lord Glenalmond bowed his head.

"I think I have," said Archie. "And the worst is, I think he feels it! How much, who can tell, with such a being? But I think he does."

"And I am sure of it," said Glenalmond.

"Has he spoken to you, then?" cried Archie.

"Oh, no," replied the Judge.

"I tell you honestly," said Archie, "I want to make it up to him. I will go, I have already pledged myself to go, to Hermiston. That was to him. And now I pledge myself to you, in the sight of God, that I will close my mouth on capital punishment and all other subjects where our views may clash, for—how long shall I say? when shall I have sense enough?—ten years. Is that well?"

"It is well," said my lord.

"As far as it goes," said Archie. "It is enough as regards myself, it is to lay down enough of my conceit. But as regards him, whom

I have publicly insulted? What am I to do to him? How do you pay attentions to a—an Alp like that?"

"Only in one way," replied Glenalmond. "Only by obedience, punctual, prompt, and scrupulous."

"And I promise that he shall have it," answered Archie. "I offer you my hand in pledge of it."

"And I take your hand as a solemnity," replied the Judge. "God bless you, my dear, and enable you to keep your promise. God guide you in the true way, and spare your days, and preserve to you your honest heart." At that, he kissed the young man upon the forehead in a gracious, distant, antiquated way; and instantly launched, with a marked change of voice, into another subject. "And now, let us replenish the tankard; and I believe, if you will try my Cheddar again, you would find you had a better appetite. The Court has spoken, and the case is dismissed."

"No, there is one thing I must say," cried Archie. "I must say it in justice to himself. I know—I believe faithfully, slavishly, after our talk—he will never ask me anything unjust. I am proud to feel it, that we have that much in common, I am proud to say it to you."

The Judge, with shining eyes, raised his tankard. "And I think perhaps that we might permit ourselves a toast," said he. "I should like to propose the health of a man very different from me and very much my superior—a man from whom I have often differed, who has often (in the trivial expression) rubbed me the wrong way, but whom I have never ceased to respect and, I may add, to be not a little afraid of. Shall I give you his name?"

"The Lord Justice-Clerk, Lord Hermiston," said Archie, almost with gaiety; and the pair drank the toast deeply.

It was not precisely easy to re-establish, after these emotional passages, the natural flow of conversation. But the Judge eked out what was wanting with kind looks, produced his snuff-box (which was very rarely seen) to fill in a pause, and at last, despairing of any further social success, was upon the point of getting down a book to read a favourite passage, when there came a rather startling summons at the front door, and Carstairs ushered in my Lord Glenkindie, hot from a midnight supper. I am not aware that Glenkindie was ever a beautiful object, being short, and gross-bodied, and with an expression of sensuality comparable to a bear's. At that moment, coming in hissing from many potations, with a flushed countenance and blurred eyes, he was strikingly contrasted with the tall, pale, kingly figure of Glenalmond. A rush of confused thought came over Archie—of shame that this was one of his father's elect friends; of pride, that at the least of it Hermiston could carry his liquor; and last of all, of rage, that he should have here under his eye the man that had betrayed him. And then that too passed away; and he sat quiet, biding his opportunity.

The tipsy Senator plunged at once into an explanation with Glenalmond. There was a point reserved yesterday, he had been able to make neither head nor tail of it, and seeing lights in the house, he had just dropped in for a glass of porter—and at this point he became aware of the third person. Archie saw the cod's mouth and the blunt lips of Glenkindie gape at him for a mo-ment, and the recognition twinkle in his eyes.

"Who's this?" said he. "What? is this possibly you, Don Quick-shot? And how are ye? And how's your father? And what's all this we hear of you? It seems you're a most extraordinary leveller, by tall tales. No king, no parliaments, and your gorge rises at the macers, worthy men! Hoot, too! Dear, dear me! Your father's son too! Most rideekulous!"

Archie was on his feet, flushing a little at the reappearance of his unhappy figure of speech, but perfectly self-possessed. "My lord —and you, Lord Glenalmond, my dear friend," he began, "this is a happy chance for me, that I can make my confession and offer my apologies to two of you at once."

"Ah, but I don't know about that. Confession? It'll be judeecial, my young friend," cried the jocular Glenkindie. "And I'm afraid to listen to ye. Think if ye were to make me a coanvert!"

"If you would allow me, my lord," returned Archie, "what I have to say is very serious to me; and be pleased to be humourous after I am gone."

"Remember, I'll hear nothing against the macers!" put in the incorrigible Glenkindie.

But Archie continued as though he had not spoken. "I have played, both yesterday and today, a part for which I can only offer the excuse of youth. I was so unwise as to go to an execution; it seems, I made a scene at the gallows; not content with which, I spoke the same night in a college society against capital punishment. This is the extent of what I have done, and in case you hear more alleged against me, I protest my innocence. I have ex-

pressed my regret already to my father, who is so good as to pass
my conduct over—in a degree, and upon the condition that I am
to leave my law studies."

5. *Winter on the Moors*
I. AT HERMISTON

THE ROAD TO HERMISTON RUNS FOR A GREAT PART OF THE WAY
up the valley of a stream, a favourite with anglers and with
midges, full of falls and pools, and shaded by willows and natural
woods of birch. Here and there, but at great distances, a byway branches off, and a gaunt farmhouse may be descried above in
a fold of the hill; but the more part of the time, the road would be
quite empty of passage and the hills of habitation. Hermiston
parish is one of the least populous in Scotland; and, by the time
you came that length, you would scarce be surprised at the inimitable smallness of the kirk, a dwarfish, ancient place seated for
fifty, and standing in a green by the burnside among twoscore
gravestones. The manse close by, although no more than a cottage,
is surrounded by the brightness of a flower-garden and the straw
roofs of bees; and the whole colony, kirk and manse, garden and
graveyard, finds harbourage in a grove of rowans, and is all the
year round in a great silence broken only by the drone of the bees,
the tinkle of the burn, and the bell on Sundays. A mile beyond the
kirk the road leaves the valley by a precipitous ascent, and brings
you a little after to the place of Hermiston, where it comes to an
end in the back-yard before the coach-house. All beyond and about
is the great field of the hills; the plover, the curlew, and the lark
cry there; the wind blows as it blows in a ship's rigging, hard and
cold and pure; and the hilltops huddle one behind another like a
herd of cattle into the sunset.

The house was sixty years old, unsightly, comfortable; a farm-
yard and a kitchen garden on the left, with a fruit wall where
little hard green pears came to their maturity about the end of
October.

The policy (as who should say the park) was of some extent,
but very ill reclaimed; heather and moorfowl had crossed the
boundary wall and spread and roosted within; and it would have
tasked a landscape gardener to say where policy ended and un-

policied nature began. My lord had been led by the influence of Mr. Sheriff Scott into a considerable design of planting; many acres were accordingly set out with fir, and the little feathery besoms gave a false scale and lent a strange air of a toy-shop to the moors. A great, rooty sweetness of bogs was in the air, and at all seasons an infinite melancholy piping of hill birds. Standing so high and with so little shelter, it was a cold, exposed house, splashed by showers, drenched by continuous rains that made the gutters to spout, beaten upon and buffeted by all the winds of heaven; and the prospect would be often black with tempest, and often white with the snows of winter. But the house was wind and weather proof, the hearths were kept bright, and the rooms pleasant with live fires of peat; and Archie might sit of an evening and hear the squalls bugle on the moorland, and watch the fire prosper in the earthly fuel, and the smoke winding up the chimney, and drink deep of the pleasures of shelter.

Solitary as the place was, Archie did not want neighbours. Every night, if he chose, he might go down to the manse and share a "brewst" of toddy with the minister—a hare-brained ancient gentleman, long and light and still active, though his knees were loosened with age, and his voice broke continually in childish trebles—and his lady wife, a heavy, comely dame, without a word to say for herself beyond good-even and good-day. Harum-scarum, clodpole young lairds of the neighbourhood paid him the compliment of a visit. Young Hay of Romanes rode down to call, on his crop-eared pony; young Pringle of Drumanno came up on his bony grey. Hay remained on the hospitable field, and must be carried to bed; Pringle got somehow to his saddle about 3 A.M., and (as Archie stood with the lamp on the upper doorstep) lurched, uttered a senseless view halloa, and vanished out of the small circle of illumination like a wraith. Yet a minute or two longer the clatter of his break-neck flight was audible, then it was cut off by the intervening steepness of the hill; and again, a great while after, the renewed beating of phantom horse-hoofs, far in the valley of the Hermiston, showed that the horse at least, if not his rider, was still on the homeward way.

There was a Tuesday Club at the "Crosskeys" in Crossmichael, where the young bloods of the country-side congregated and drank deep on a percentage of the expense, so that he was left gainer who should have drunk the most. Archie had no great mind to this diversion, but he took it like a duty laid upon him, went with a decent regularity, did his manfullest with the liquor, held up his head in the local jests, and got home again and was able to put up his horse, to the admiration of Kirstie and the lass that helped her. He dined at Driffel, supped at Windielaws. He went to the new year's ball at Huntsfield and was made welcome, and thereafter rode to hounds with my Lord Muirfell, upon whose name, as that of a legitimate Lord of Parliament, in a work so full of Lords of Session, my pen should pause reverently. Yet the same fate attended him here as in Edinburgh. The habit of solitude tends to perpetuate itself, and an austerity of which he was quite unconscious, and a pride which seemed arrogance, and perhaps was chiefly shyness, discouraged and offended his new companions. Hay did not return more than twice, Pringle never at all, and there came a time when Archie even desisted from the Tuesday Club, and became in all things—what he had had the name of almost from the first—the Recluse of Hermiston. High-nosed Miss Pringle of Drumanno and high-stepping Miss Marshall of the Mains were understood to have had a difference of opinion about him the day after the ball—he was none the wiser, he could not suppose himself to be remarked by these entrancing ladies. At the ball itself my Lord Muirfell's daughter, the Lady Flora, spoke to him twice, and the second time with a touch of appeal, so that her colour rose and her voice trembled a little in his ear, like a passing grace in music. He stepped back with a heart on fire, coldly and not ungracefully excused himself, and a little after watched her dancing with young Drumanno of the empty laugh, and was harrowed at the sight, and raged to himself that this was a world in which it was given to Drumanno to please, and to himself only to stand aside and envy. He seemed excluded, as of right, from the favour of such society—seemed to extinguish mirth wherever he came, and was quick to feel the wound, and desist, and retire into solitude. If he had but understood the figure he presented, and the impression he made on these bright eyes and tender hearts; if he had but guessed that the Recluse of Hermiston, young, graceful, well spoken, but always cold, stirred the maidens of the county with the charm of Byronism when Byronism was new, it may be questioned whether his destiny might not even yet have been modified. It may be questioned, and I think it should be doubted. It was in his horoscope to be parsimonious of pain to himself, or of the chance of pain, even to the avoidance of any opportunity of pleasure; to have a Roman sense of duty, an instinctive aristocracy of manners and taste; to be the son of Adam Weir and Jean Rutherford.

II. KIRSTIE

KIRSTIE was now over fifty, and might have sat to a sculptor. Long of limb and still light of foot, deep-breasted, robust-loined, her golden hair not yet mingled with any trace of silver, the years had but caressed and embellished her. By the lines of a rich and vigorous maternity, she seemed destined to be the bride of heroes and the mother of their children; and behold, by the iniquity of fate, she had passed through her youth alone, and drew near to the confines of age, a childless woman. The tender ambitions that she had received at birth had been, by time and disappointment, diverted into a certain barren zeal of industry and fury of interference. She carried her thwarted ardours into housework, she washed floors with her empty heart. If she could not win the love of one with love, she must dominate all by her temper. Hasty, wordy, and wrathful, she had a drawn quarrel with most of her neighbours, and with the others not much more than armed neutrality. The grieve's wife had been "sneisty"; the sister of the gardener, who kept house for him, had shown herself "upsitten"; and she wrote to Lord Hermiston about once a year demanding the discharge of the offenders, and justifying the demand by much wealth of detail. For it must not be supposed that the quarrel rested with the wife and did not take in the husband also—or with the gardener's sister, and did not speedily include the gardener himself. As the upshot of all this petty quarrelling and intemperate speech, she was practically excluded (like a lightkeeper on his tower) from the comforts of human association; except with her own indoor drudge, who, being but a lassie and entirely at her mercy, must submit to the shifty weather of "the mistress's" moods without complaint, and be willing to take buffets or caresses according to the temper of the hour. To Kirstie, thus situate and in the Indian summer of her heart, which was slow to submit to age, the gods sent this equivocal good thing of Archie's presence. She had known him in the cradle and paddled him when he misbehaved; and yet, as she had not so much as set eyes on him since

he was eleven and had his last serious illness, the tall, slender, refined, and rather melancholy young gentleman of twenty came
upon her with the shock of a new acquaintance. He was "Young
Hermiston," "the laird himsel' "; he had an air of distinctive
superiority, a cold straight glance of his black eyes, that abashed
the woman's tantrums in the beginning, and therefore the possibility of any quarrel was excluded. He was new, and therefore
immediately aroused her curiosity; he was reticent, and kept it
awake. And lastly he was dark and she fair, and he was male and
she female, the everlasting fountains of interest.

Her feeling partook of the loyalty of a clanswoman, the hero-
worship of a maiden aunt, and the idolatry due to a god. No matter what he had asked of her, ridiculous or tragic, she would have
done it and joyed to do it. Her passion, for it was nothing less, entirely filled her. It was a rich physical pleasure to make his bed or
light his lamp for him when he was absent, to pull off his wet boots
or wait on him at dinner when he returned. A young man who
should have so doted on the idea, moral and physical, of any
woman, might be properly described as being in love, head and
heels, and would have behaved himself accordingly. But Kirstie—
though her heart leaped at his coming footsteps—though, when he
patted her shoulder, her face brightened for the day—had not a
hope or thought beyond the present moment and its perpetuation
to the end of time. Till the end of time she would have had nothing altered, but still continue delightedly to serve her idol, and be
repaid (say twice in the month) with a clap on the shoulder.

I have said her heart leaped—it is the accepted phrase. But
rather, when she was alone in any chamber of the house, and heard
his foot passing on the corridors, something in her bosom rose
slowly until her breath was suspended, and as slowly fell again
with a deep sigh, when the steps had passed and she was disappointed of her eyes' desire. This perpetual hunger and thirst of
his presence kept her all day on the alert. When he went forth at
morning, she would stand and follow him with admiring looks.
As it grew late and drew to the time of his return, she would steal
forth to a corner of the policy wall and be seen standing there
sometimes by the hour together, gazing with shaded eyes, waiting
the exquisite and barren pleasure of his view a mile off on the
mountains. When at night she had trimmed and gathered the fire,
turned down his bed, and laid out his night-gear—when there

was no more to be done for the king's pleasure, but to remember him fervently in her usually very tepid prayers, and go to bed brooding upon his perfections, his future career, and what she should give him the next day for dinner—there still remained before her one more opportunity; she was still to take in the tray to say good-night. Sometimes Archie would glance up from his book with a preoccupied nod and a perfunctory salutation which was in truth a dismissal; sometimes—and by degrees more often— the volume would be laid aside, he would meet her coming with a look of relief; and the conversation would be engaged, last out the supper, and be prolonged till the small hours by the waning fire. It was no wonder that Archie was fond of company after his solitary days; and Kirstie, upon her side, exerted all the arts of her vigorous nature to ensnare his attention. She would keep back some piece of news during dinner to be fired off with the entrance of the supper tray, and form as it were the *lever de rideau* of the evening's entertainment. Once he had heard her tongue wag, she made sure of the result. From one subject to another she moved by insidious transitions, fearing the least silence, fearing almost to give him time for an answer lest it should slip into a hint of separa- tion. Like so many people of her class, she was a brave narrator; her place was on the hearth-rug and she made it a rostrum, miming her stories as she told them, fitting them with vital detail, spinning them out with endless "quo' he's" and "quo' she's," her voice sink- ing into a whisper over the supernatural or the horrific; until she would suddenly spring up in affected surprise, and pointing to the clock, "Mercy, Mr. Archie!" she would say, "Whatten a time o' night is this of it! God forgive me for a daft wife!" So it befell, by good management, that she was not only the first to begin these nocturnal conversations, but invariably the first to break them off; so she managed to retire and not to be dismissed.

III. A BORDER FAMILY

Such an unequal intimacy has never been uncommon in Scot- land, where the clan spirit survives; where the servant tends to spend her life in the same service, a helpmeet at first, then a tyrant, and at last a pensioner; where, besides, she is not necessarily desti- tute of the pride of birth, but is, perhaps, like Kirstie, a connection of her master's, and at least knows the legend of her own family, and may count kinship with some illustrious dead. For that is the mark of the Scot of all classes: that he stands in an attitude towards the past unthinkable to Englishmen, and remembers and cherishes the memory of his forbears, good or bad; and there burns alive in him a sense of identity with the dead even to the twentieth generation. No more characteristic instance could be found than in the family of Kirstie Elliott. They were all, and Kirstie the first of all, ready and eager to pour forth the particulars of their genealogy, embellished with every detail that memory had handed down or fancy fabricated; and, behold! from every ramification of that tree there dangled a halter. The Elliotts themselves have had a chequered history; but these Elliotts deduced, besides, from three of the most unfortunate of the border clans—the Nicksons, the Ellwalds, and the Crozers. One ancestor after another might be seen appearing a moment out of the rain and the hill mist upon his furtive business, speeding home, perhaps, with a paltry booty of lame horses and lean kine, or squealing and dealing death in some moorland feud of the ferrets and the wildcats. One after another closed his obscure adventures in mid-air, triced up to the arm of the royal gibbet or the Baron's dule-tree. For the rusty blunderbuss of Scots criminal justice, which usually hurts nobody but jurymen, became a weapon of precision for the Nicksons, the Ellwalds, and the Crozers. The exhilaration of their exploits seemed to haunt the memories of their descendants alone, and the shame to be forgotten. Pride glowed in their bosoms to publish their relationship to "Andrew Ellwald of the Laverockstanes, called 'Unchancy Dand,' who was justifeed wi' seeven mair of the same name as Jeddart in the days of King James the Sax." In all this tissue of crime and misfortune, the Elliotts of Cauldstaneslap had one boast which must appear legitimate: the males were gallows-birds, born outlaws, petty thieves, and deadly brawlers; but according to the same tradition, the females were all chaste and faithful. The power of ancestry on the character is not limited to the inheritance of cells. If I buy ancestors by the gross from the benevolence of Lion King at Arms, my grandson (if he is Scottish) will feel a quickening emulation of their deeds. The men of the Elliotts were proud, lawless, violent as of right, cherishing and prolonging a tradition. In like manner with the women. And the woman, essentially passionate and reckless, who crouched on the rug, in the shine of the peat fire, telling these tales, had cherished through life a wild integrity of virtue.

Her father Gilbert had been deeply pious, a savage disciplinarian in the antique style, and withal a notorious smuggler. "I mind when I was a bairn getting mony a skelp and being shoo'd to bed like pou'try," she would say. "That would be when the lads and their bit kegs were on the road. We've had the riffraff of two-three counties in our kitchen, mony's the time, betwix' the twelve and the three; and their lanterns would be standing in the forecourt, ay, a score o' them at once. But there was nae ungodly talk permitted at Cauldstaneslap; my faither was a consistent man in walk and conversation; just let slip an aith, and there was the door to ye! He had that zeal for the Lord, it was a fair wonder to hear him pray, but the faimily has aye had a gift that way." This father was twice married, once to a dark woman of the old Ellwald stock, by whom he had Gilbert, presently of Cauldstaneslap; and, secondly, to the mother of Kirstie. "He was an auld man when he married her, a fell auld man wi' a muckle voice—you could hear him rowting from the top o' the kye-stairs," she said; "but for her, it appears, she was a perfit wonder. It was gentle blood she had, Mr. Archie, for it was your ain. The country-side gaed gyte about her and her gowden hair. Mines is no to be mentioned wi' it, and there's few weemen has mair hair than what I have, or yet a bonnier colour. Often would I tell my dear Miss Jeannie—that was your mother, dear, she was cruel ta'en up about her hair, it was unco tender, ye see—'Houts, Miss Jeannie,' I would say, 'just fling your washes and your French dentifrishes in the back o' the fire, for that's the place for them; and awa' down to a burnside, and wash yersel in cauld hill water, and dry your bonny hair in the caller wind o' the muirs, the way that my mother aye washed hers, and that I have aye made it a practice to have washen mines—just you do what I tell ye, my dear, and ye'll give me news of it! Ye'll have hair, and routh of hair, a pigtail as thick's my arm,' I said, 'and the bonniest colour like the clear gowden guineas, so as the lads in kirk'll no can keep their eyes off it!' Weel, it lasted out her time, puir thing! I cuttit a lock of it upon her corp that was lying there sae cauld. I'll show it ye some of thir days if ye're good. But, as I was sayin', my mither——"

On the death of the father there remained golden-haired Kirstie, who took service with her distant kinsfolk, the Rutherfords, and black-a-vised Gilbert, twenty years older, who farmed the Cauldstaneslap, married, and begot four sons between 1773 and 1784, and a daughter, like a postscript, in '97, the year of Camperdown and Cape St. Vincent. It seemed it was a tradition of the family to wind up with a belated girl. In 1804, at the age of sixty, Gilbert met an end that might be called heroic. He was due home from market any time from eight at night till five in the morning, and in any condition from the quarrelsome to the speechless, for he maintained to that age the goodly customs of the Scots farmer. It was known on this occasion that he had a good bit of money to bring home; the word had gone round loosely. The laird had shown his guineas, and if anybody had but noticed it, there was an ill-looking, vagabond crew, the scum of Edinburgh, that drew out of the market long ere it was dusk and took the hill-road by Hermiston, where it was not to be believed that they had lawful business. One of the country-side, one Dickieson, they took with them to be their guide, and dear he paid for it! Of a sudden, in the ford of the Broken Dykes, this vermin clan fell on the laird, six to one, and him three parts asleep, having drunk hard. But it is ill to catch an Elliott. For awhile, in the night and the black water that was deep as to his saddle-girths, he wrought with his staff like a smith at his stithy, and great was the sound of oaths and blows. With that the ambuscade was burst, and he rode for home with a pistol-ball in him, three knife-wounds, the loss of his front teeth, a broken rib and bridle, and a dying horse. That was a race with death that the laird rode! In the mirk night, with his broken bridle and his head swimming, he dug his spurs to the rowels in the horse's side, and the horse, that was even worse off than himself, the poor creature! screamed out loud like a person as he went, so that the hills echoed with it, and the folks at Cauldstaneslap got to their feet about the table and looked at each other with white faces. The horse fell dead at the yard gate, the laird won the length of the house and fell there on the threshold. To the son that raised him he gave the bag of money. "Hae," said he. All the way up the thieves had seemed to him to be at his heels, but now the hallucination left him—he saw them again in the place of the ambuscade—and the thirst of vengeance seized on his dying mind. Raising himself and pointing with an imperious finger into the black night from which he had come, he uttered the single com-

mand, "Brocken Dykes," and fainted. He had never been loved,
but he had been feared in honour. At that sight, at that word,
gasped out at them from a toothless and bleeding mouth, the old
Elliott spirit awoke with a shout in the four sons. "Wanting the
hat," continues my author, Kirstie, whom I but haltingly follow,
for she told this tale like one inspired, "wanting guns, for there
wasnae twa grains o' pouder in the house, wi' nae mair weepons
than their sticks into their hands, the fower o' them took the road.
Only Hob, and that was the eldest, hunkered at the door-sill where
the blood had rin, fyled his hand wi' it, and haddit it up to
Heeven in the way o' the auld Border aith. 'Hell shall have her ain
again this nicht!' he raired, and rode forth upon his errand." It
was three miles to Broken Dykes, down-hill, and a sore road.
Kirstie has seen men from Edinburgh dismounting there in plain
day to lead their horses. But the four brothers rode it as if Auld
Hornie were behind and Heaven in front. Come to the ford, and
there was Dickieson. By all tales, he was not dead, but breathed
and reared upon his elbow, and cried out to them for help. It was
at a graceless face that he asked mercy. As soon as Hob saw, by the
glint of the lantern, the eyes shining and the whiteness of the teeth
in the man's face, "Damn you!" says he; "ye hae your teeth, hae
ye?" and rode his horse to and fro upon that human remnant. Beyond that, Dandie must dismount with the lantern to be their
guide; he was the youngest son, scarce twenty at the time. "A'
nicht long they gaed in the wet heath and jennipers, and whaur
they gaed they neither knew nor cared, but just followed the
bluidstains and the footprints o' their faither's murderers. And a'
nicht Dandie had his nose to the grund like a tyke, and the ithers
followed and spak' naething, neither black nor white. There was
nae noise to be heard, but just the sough of the swalled burns, and
Hob, the dour yin, risping his teeth as he gaed." With the first
glint of the morning they saw they were on the drove road, and at
that the four stopped and had a dram to their breakfasts, for they
knew that Dand must have guided them right, and the rogues
could be but little ahead, hot foot for Edinburgh by the way of the
Pentland Hills. By eight o'clock they had word of them—a shepherd had seen four men "uncoly mishandled" go by in the last
hour. "That's yin a piece," says Clem, and swung his cudgel. "Five
o' them!" says Hob. "God's death, but the faither was a man! And
him drunk!" And then there befell them what my author termed

"a sair misbegowk," for they were overtaken by a posse of mounted neighbours come to aid in the pursuit. Four sour faces looked on the reinforcement. "The deil's broughten you!" said Clem, and they rode thenceforward in the rear of the party with hanging heads. Before ten they had found and secured the rogues, and by three of the afternoon, as they rode up the Vennel with their prisoners, they were aware of a concourse of people bearing in their midst something that dripped. "For the boady of the saxt," pursued Kirstie, "wi' his head smashed like a hazelnit, had been a' that nicht in the chairge o' Hermiston Water, and it dunting it on the stanes, and grunding it on the shallows, and flinging the deid thing heels-ower-hurdie at the Fa's o' Spango; and in the first o' the day Tweed had got a hold o' him and carried him off like a wind, for it was uncoly swalled and raced wi' him, bobbing under braesides, and was long playing with the creature in the drumlie lynns under the castle, and at the hinder end of all cuist him up on the starling of Crossmichael brig. Sae there they were a' thegither at last (for Dickieson had been brought in on a cart long syne), and folk could see what mainner o' man my brither had been that had held his head again sax and saved the siller, and him drunk!" Thus died of honourable injuries and in the savour of fame Gilbert Elliott of the Cauldstaneslap; but his sons had scarce less glory out of the business. Their savage haste, the skill with which Dand had found and followed the trail, the barbarity to the wounded Dickieson (which was like an open secret in the county) and the doom which it was currently supposed they had intended for the others, struck and stirred popular imagination. Some century earlier the last of the minstrels might have fashioned the last of the ballads out of that Homeric fight and chase; but the spirit was dead, or had been reincarnated already in Mr. Sheriff Scott, and the degenerate moorsmen must be content to tell the tale in prose and to make of the "Four Black Brothers" a unit after the fashion of the "Twelve Apostles" or the "Three Musketeers."

Robert, Gilbert, Clement, and Andrew—in the proper Border diminutive, Hob, Gib, Clem, and Dand Elliott—these ballad heroes had much in common; in particular, their high sense of the family and the family honour; but they went diverse ways, and prospered and failed in different businesses. According to Kirstie, "they had a' bees in their bonnets but Hob." Hob the laird was, indeed, essentially a decent man. An elder of the Kirk, nobody had heard an oath upon his lips, save, perhaps, thrice or so at the sheep-washing, since the chase of his father's murderers. The figure he had shown on that eventful night disappeared as if swallowed by a trap. He who had ecstatically dipped his hand in the red blood, he who had ridden down Dickieson, became, from that moment on, a stiff and rather graceless model of the rustic proprieties; cannily profiting by the high war prices, and yearly stowing away a little nest-egg in the bank against calamity; approved of and sometimes consulted by the greater lairds for the massive and placid sense of what he said, when he could be induced to say anything; and particularly valued by the minister, Mr. Torrance, as a right-hand man in the parish, and a model to parents. The transfiguration had been for the moment only; some Barbarossa, some old Adam of our ancestors, sleeps in all of us till the fit circumstance shall call it into action; and for as sober as he now seemed, Hob had given once for all the measure of the devil that haunted him. He was married, and, by reason of the effulgence of that legendary night, was adored by his wife. He had a mob of little lusty, bare-foot children who marched in a caravan the long miles to school, the stages of whose pilgrimage were marked by acts of spoliation and mischief, and who were qualified in the country-side as "fair pests." But in the house, if "faither was in," they were quiet as mice. In short, Hob moved through life in a great peace—the reward of any one who shall have killed his man, with any formidable and figurative circumstance, in the midst of a country gagged and swaddled with civilisation.

It was a current remark that the Elliotts were "guid and bad, like sanguishes"; and certainly there was a curious distinction, the men of business coming alternately with the dreamers. The second brother, Gib, was a weaver by trade, had gone out early into the world to Edinburgh, and come home again with his wings singed. There was an exaltation in his nature which had led him to embrace with enthusiasm the principles of the French Revolution, and had ended by bringing him under the hawse of my Lord Hermiston in that furious onslaught of his upon the Liberals, which sent Muir and Palmer into exile and dashed the party into chaff. It was whispered that my lord, in his great scorn for the movement, and prevailed upon a little by a sense of neighbourliness, had given Gib a hint. Meeting him one day in the Potterrow, my lord had stopped in front of him. "Gib, ye eediot," he had said, "what's this I hear of you? Poalitics, poalitics, poalitics weaver's poalitics, is the way of it, I hear. If ye are nae a' thegether dozened with eediocy, ye'll gang your ways back to Cauldstaneslap, and ca' your loom, and ca' your loom, man!" And Gilbert had taken him at the word and returned, with an expedition almost to be called flight, to the house of his father. The clearest of his inheritance was that family gift of prayer of which Kirstie had boasted; and the baffled politician now turned his attention to religious matters— or, as others said, to heresy and schism. Every Sunday morning he was in Crossmichael, where he had gathered together, one by one, a sect of about a dozen persons, who called themselves "God's Remnant of the True Faithful," or, for short, "God's Remnant." To the profane, they were known as "Gib's Deils." Baillie Sweedie, a noted humourist in the town, vowed that the proceedings always opened to the tune of "The Deil Fly Away with the Exciseman," and that the sacrament was dispensed in the form of hot whisky toddy; both wicked hits at the evangelist, who had been suspected of smuggling in his youth, and had been overtaken (as the phrase went) on the streets of Crossmichael one Fair day. It was known that every Sunday they prayed for a blessing on the arms of Bonaparte. For this, "God's Remnant," as they were "skailing" from the cottage that did duty for a temple, had been repeatedly stoned by the bairns, and Gib himself hooted by a squadron of Border volunteers in which his own brother, Dand, rode in a uniform and with a drawn sword. The "Remnant" were believed, besides, to be "antinomian in principle," which might otherwise have been a serious charge, but the way public opinion then blew it was quite swallowed up and forgotten in the scandal about Bonaparte. For the rest, Gilbert had set up his loom in an outhouse at Cauldstaneslap, where he laboured assiduously six days of the week. His brothers, appalled by his political opinions and willing to avoid dissension in the household, spoke but little to him; he less to them, remaining absorbed in the study of the Bible and almost constant prayer. The gaunt weaver was dry-nurse at Cauldstaneslap, and the bairns loved him dearly. Except when he was carrying an infant in his arms, he was rarely seen to smile—as, indeed, there were few smilers in that family. When his sister-in-law rallied him, and proposed that he should get a wife and bairns of his own, since he was so fond of them, "I have no

clearness of mind upon that point," he would reply. If nobody
called him in to dinner, he stayed out. Mrs. Hob, a hard, unsympathetic woman, once tried the experiment. He went without food
all day, but at dusk, as the light began to fail him, he came into
the house of his own accord, looking puzzled. "I've had a great
gale of prayer upon my speerit," said he. "I canna mind sae
muckle's what I had for denner." The creed of God's Remnant
was justified in the life of its founder. "And yet I dinna ken," said
Kirstie. "He's maybe no more stockfish than his neeghbours! He
rode wi' the rest o' them, and had a good stamach to the work, by
a' that I hear! God's Remnant! The deil's clavers! There wasna
muckle Christianity in the way Hob guided Johnny Dickieson, at
the least of it; but Guid kens! Is he a Christian even? He might
be a Mahommedan or a Deevil or a Fireworshiper, for what I
ken."

The third brother had his name on a door-plate, no less, in the
city of Glasgow. "Mr. Clement Elliott," as long as your arm. In
his case, that spirit of innovation which had shown itself timidly
in the case of Hob by the admission of new manures, and which
had run to waste with Gilbert in subversive politics and heretical
religions, bore useful fruit in many ingenious mechanical improvements. In boyhood, from his addiction to strange devices of
sticks and string, he had been counted the most eccentric of the
family. But that was all by now, and he was a partner of his firm,
and looked to die a baillie. He too had married, and was rearing
a plentiful family in the smoke and din of Glasgow; he was
wealthy, and could have bought out his brother, the cock-laird,
six times over, it was whispered; and when he slipped away to
Cauldstaneslap for a well-earned holiday, which he did as often as
he was able, he astonished the neighbours with his broadcloth, his
beaver hat, and the ample plies of his neck-cloth. Though an
eminently solid man at bottom, after the pattern of Hob, he had
contracted a certain Glasgow briskness and *aplomb* which set him
off. All the other Elliotts were as lean as a rake, but Clement was
laying on fat, and he panted sorely when he must get into his
boots. Dand said, chuckling: "Ay, Clem has the elements of a corporation." "A provost and corporation," returned Clem. And his
readiness was much admired.

The fourth brother, Dand, was a shepherd to his trade, and by
starts, when he could bring his mind to it, excelled in the busi-

ness. Nobody could train a dog like Dandie; nobody, through the peril of great storms in the winter time, could do more gallantly. But if his dexterity were exquisite, his diligence was but fitful; and he served his brother for bed and board, and a trifle of pocket-money when he asked for it. He loved money well enough, knew very well how to spend it, and could make a shrewd bargain when he liked. But he preferred a vague knowledge that he was well to windward to any counted coins in the pocket; he felt himself richer so. Hob would expostulate: "I'm an amateur herd," Dand would reply: "I'll keep your sheep to you when I'm so minded, but I'll keep my liberty too. Thir 's no man can coandescend on what I'm worth." Clem would expound to him the miraculous results of compound interest, and recommend investments. "Ay, man?" Dand would say, "and do you think, if I took Hob's siller, that I wouldna drink it or wear it on the lassies? And, anyway, my king-dom is no of the world. Either I'm a poet or else I'm nothing." Clem would remind him of old age. "I'll die young, like Robbie Burns," he would say stoutly. No question but he had a certain accomplishment in minor verse. His "Hermiston Burn," with its pretty refrain—

> I love to gang thinking whaur ye gang linking,
> Hermiston burn, in the howe;

his "Auld, auld Elliotts, clay-cauld Elliotts, dour, bauld Elliotts of auld," and his really fascinating piece about the Praying Weaver's Stone, had gained him in the neighbourhood the reputa-tion, still possible in Scotland, of a local bard; and, though not printed himself, he was recognised by others who were and who had become famous. Walter Scott owed to Dandie the text of the "Raid of Wearie" in the *Minstrelsy* and made him welcome at his house, and appreciated his talents, such as they were, with all his usual generosity. The Ettrick Shepherd was his sworn crony; they would meet, drink to excess, roar out their lyrics in each other's faces, and quarrel and make it up again till bedtime. And besides these recognitions, almost to be called official, Dandie was made welcome for the sake of his gift through the farmhouses of several contiguous dales, and was thus exposed to manifold temptations which he rather sought than fled. He had figured on the stool of repentance, for once fulfilling to the letter the tradition of his hero and model. His humourous verses to Mr. Torrance on that occasion—"Kenspeckle here my lane I stand"—unfortunately too indelicate for further citation, ran through the country like a fiery cross; they were recited, quoted, paraphrased, and laughed over as far away as Dumfries on the one hand and Dunbar on the other.

These four brothers were united by a close bond, the bond of that mutual admiration—or rather mutual hero-worship—which is so strong among the members of secluded families who have much ability and little culture. Even the extremes admired each other. Hob, who had as much poetry as the tongs, professed to find pleasure in Dand's verses; Clem, who had no more religion than Claverhouse, nourished a heartfelt, at least an open-mouthed, admiration of Gib's prayers; and Dandie followed with relish the rise of Clem's fortunes. Indulgence followed hard on the heels of admiration. The laird, Clem, and Dand, who were Tories and patriots of the hottest quality, excused to themselves, with a certain bashfulness, the radical and revolutionary heresies of Gid. By another division of the family, the laird, Clem, and Gib, who were men exactly virtuous, swallowed the dose of Dand's irregularities as a kind of clog or drawback in the mysterious providence of God affixed to bards, and distinctly probative of poetical genius. To appreciate the simplicity of their mutual admiration, it was necessary to hear Clem, arrived upon one of his visits, and dealing in a spirit of continuous irony with the affairs and personalities of that great city of Glasgow where he lived and transacted business. The various personages, ministers of the church, municipal officers, mercantile big-wigs, whom he had occasion to introduce, were all alike denigrated, all served but as reflectors to cast back a flattering side-light on the house of Cauldstaneslap. The Provost, for whom Clem by exception entertained a measure of respect, he would liken to Hob. "He minds me o' the laird there," he would say. "He has some of Hob's grand, whum-stane sense, and the same way with him of steiking his mouth when he's no very pleased." And Hob, all unconscious, would draw down his upper lip and produce, as if for comparison, the formidable grimace referred to. The unsatisfactory incumbent of St. Enoch's Kirk was thus briefly dismissed: "If he had but twa fingers o' Gib's he would waken them up." And Gib, honest man! would look down and secretly smile. Clem was a spy whom they had sent out into the world of men. He had come back with the good news that there was nobody to com-

pare with the Four Black Brothers, no position that they would
not adorn, no official that it would not be well they should replace, no interest of mankind, secular or spiritual, which would
not immediately bloom under their supervision. The excuse of
their folly is in two words: scarce the breadth of a hair divided
them from the peasantry. The measure of their sense is this: that
these symposia of rustic vanity were kept entirely within the
family, like some secret ancestral practice. To the world their
serious faces were never deformed by the suspicion of any simper
of self-contentment. Yet it was known. "They hae a guid pride o'
themsel's!" was the word in the country-side.

Lastly, in a Border story, there should be added their "two-
names." Hob was The Laird. "Roy ne puis, prince ne daigne"; he
was the laird of Cauldstaneslap—say fifty acres—*ipsissimus*. Clement was Mr. Elliott, as upon his door-plate, the earlier Dafty
having been discarded as no longer applicable, and indeed only
a reminder of misjudgment and the imbecility of the public; and
the youngest, in honour of his perpetual wanderings, was known
by the sobriquet of Randy Dand.

It will be understood that not all this information was communicated by the aunt, who had too much of the family failing
herself to appreciate it thoroughly in others. But as time went
on, Archie began to observe an omission in the family chronicle.

"Is there not a girl too?" he asked.

"Ay. Kirstie. She was named from me, or my grandmother at
least—it's the same thing," returned the aunt, and went on again
about Dand, whom she secretly preferred by reason of his gal-
lantries.

"But what is your niece like?" said Archie at the next opportunity.

"Her? As black's your hat! But I dinna suppose she would
maybe be what you would ca' *ill-looked* a' thegither. Na, she's a
kind of handsome jaud—a kind o' gipsy," said the aunt, who had
two sets of scales for men and women—or perhaps it would be
more fair to say that she had three, and the third and the most
loaded was for girls.

"How comes it that I never see her in church?" said Archie.

" 'Deed, and I believe she's in Glesgie with Clem and his wife.
A heap good she's like to get of it! I dinna say for men folk, but
where weemen folk are born, there let them bide. Glory to God,
I was never far'er from here than Crossmichael."

In the meantime it began to strike Archie as strange, that while she thus sang the praises of her kinsfolk, and manifestly relished their virtues and (I may say) their vices like a thing creditable to herself, there should appear not the least sign of cordiality between the house of Hermiston and that of Cauldstaneslap. Going to church of a Sunday, as the lady housekeeper stepped with her skirts kilted, three tucks of her white petticoat showing below, and her best India shawl upon her back (if the day were fine) in a pattern of radiant dyes, she would sometimes overtake her relatives preceding her more leisurely in the same direction. Gib of course was absent: by skriegh of day he had been gone to Crossmichael and his fellow heretics; but the rest of the family would be seen marching in open order: Hob and Dand, stiff-necked, straight-backed six-footers, with severe dark faces, and their plaids about their shoulders; the convoy of children scattering (in a state of high polish) on the wayside, and every now and again collected by the shrill summons of the mother; and the mother herself, by a suggestive circumstance which might have afforded matter of thought to a more experienced observer than Archie, wrapped in a shawl nearly identical with Kirstie's but a thought more gaudy and conspicuously newer. At the sight, Kirstie grew more tall—Kirstie showed her classical profile, nose in air and nostril spread, the pure blood came in her cheek evenly in a delicate living pink.

"A braw day to ye, Mistress Elliott," said she, and hostility and gentility were nicely mingled in her tones. "A fine day, mem," the laird's wife would reply with a miraculous curtsey, spreading the while her plumage—setting off, in other words, and with arts unknown to the mere man, the pattern of her India shawl. Behind her, the whole Cauldstaneslap contingent marched in closer order, and with an indescribable air of being in the presence of the foe; and while Dandie saluted his aunt with a certain familiarity as of one who was well in court, Hob marched on in awful immobility. There appeared upon the face of this attitude in the family the consequences of some dreadful feud. Presumably the two women had been principals in the original encounter, and the laird had probably been drawn into the quarrel by the ears, too late to be included in the present skin-deep reconciliation.

"Kirstie," said Archie one day, "what is this you have against your family?"

"I dinna complean," said Kirstie, with a flush. "I say naething."

"I see you do not—not even good-day to your own nephew," said he.

"I hae naething to be ashaimed of," said she. "I can say the Lord's prayer with a good grace. If Hob was ill, or in preeson or poverty, I would see to him blithely. But for curtchying and complimenting and colloguing, thank ye kindly!"

Archie had a bit of a smile: he leaned back in his chair. "I think you and Mrs. Robert are not very good friends," says he slyly, "when you have your India shawls on?"

She looked upon him in silence, with a sparkling eye but an indecipherable expression; and that was all that Archie was ever destined to learn of the battle of the India shawls.

"Do none of them ever come here to see you?" he inquired.

"Mr. Archie," said she, "I hope that I ken my place better. It would be a queer thing, I think, if I was to clamjamfry up your faither's house . . . that I should say it!—wi' a dirty, black-avised clan, no ane o' them it was worth while to mar soap upon but just mysel'! Na, they 're all damnifeed wi' the black Ellwalds. I have nae patience wi' black folks." Then, with a sudden consciousness of the case of Archie, "No that it maitters for men sae muckle," she made haste to add, "but there's naebody can deny that it's unwomanly. Long hair is the ornament o' woman ony way; we've good warrandise for that—it's in the Bible—and wha can doubt that the Apostle had some gowden-haired lassie in his mind—Apostle and all, for what was he but just a man like yersel'?"

6. *A Leaf from Christina's Psalm-Book*

ARCHIE WAS SEDULOUS AT CHURCH. SUNDAY AFTER SUNDAY HE SAT down and stood up with that small company, heard the voice of Mr. Torrance leaping like an ill-played clarionet from key to key, and had an opportunity to study his moth-eaten gown and the black thread mittens that he joined together in prayer, and lifted up with a reverent solemnity in the act of benediction. Hermiston pew was a little square box, dwarfish in proportion with the kirk itself, and enclosing a table not much bigger than a footstool. There sat Archie an apparent prince, the only undeniable gentleman and the only great heritor in the parish, taking his ease in the only pew, for no other in the kirk had doors. Thence he might command an undisturbed view of that congregation of solid plaided men, strapping wives and daughters, oppressed children, and uneasy sheep-dogs. It was strange how Archie missed the look of race; except the dogs, with their refined foxy faces and inimitably curling tails, there was no one present with the least claim to gentility. The Cauldstaneslap party was scarcely an exception; Dandie perhaps, as he amused himself making verses through the interminable burthen of the service, stood out a little by the glow in his eye and a certain superior animation of face and alertness of body; but even Dandie slouched like a rustic. The rest of the congregation, like so many sheep, oppressed him with a sense of hob-nailed routine, day following day—of physical labour in the open air, oatmeal porridge, peas bannock, the somnolent fireside in the evening, and the night-long nasal slumbers in a box-bed. Yet he knew many of them to be shrewd and humourous, men of character, notable women, making a bustle in the world and radiating an influence from their low-browed doors. He knew besides they were like other men; below the crust of custom, rapture found a way; he had heard them beat the timbrel before Bacchus —had heard them shout and carouse over their whisky toddy; and not the most Dutch-bottomed and severe faces among them all, not even the solemn elders themselves, but were capable of singular gambols at the voice of love. Men drawing near to an end of life's adventurous journey—maids thrilling with fear and curiosity on the threshold of entrance—women who had borne and perhaps buried children, who could remember the clinging of the small dead hands and the patter of the little feet now silent—he marvelled that among all those faces there should be no face of expectation, none that was mobile, none into which the rhythm and poetry of life had entered. "O for a live face," he thought; and at times he had a memory of Lady Flora; and at times he would study the living gallery before him with despair, and would see himself go on to waste his days in that joyless, pastoral place, and death come to him, and his grave be dug under the rowans, and the Spirit of the Earth laugh out in a thunder-peal at the huge fiasco.

On this particular Sunday, there was no doubt but that the spring had come at last. It was warm, with a latent shiver in the air that made the warmth only the more welcome. The shallows of the stream glittered and tinkled among bunches of primrose. Vagrant scents of the earth arrested Archie by the way with moments of ethereal intoxication. The grey, Quakerish dale was still only awakened in places and patches from the sobriety of its wintry colouring; and he wondered at its beauty; an essential beauty of the old earth it seemed to him, not resident in particulars but breathing to him from the whole. He surprised himself by a sudden impulse to write poetry—he did so sometimes, loose, galloping octosyllabics in the vein of Scott—and when he had taken his place on a boulder, near some fairy falls and shaded by a whip of a tree that was already radiant with new leaves, it still more surprised him that he should find nothing to write. His heart perhaps beat in time to some vast indwelling rhythm of the universe. By the time he came to a corner of the valley and could see the kirk, he had so lingered by the way that the first psalm was finishing. The nasal psalmody, full of turns and trills and graceless graces, seemed the essential voice of the kirk itself upraised in thanksgiving. "Everything's alive," he said; and again cries it aloud, "Thank God, everything's alive!" He lingered yet awhile in the kirk-yard. A tuft of primroses was blooming hard by the leg of an old, black table tombstone, and he stopped to contemplate the random apologue. They stood forth on the cold earth with a trenchancy of contrast; and he was struck with a sense of incompleteness in the day, the season, and the beauty that surrounded him—the chill there was in the warmth, the gross black clods about the opening primroses, the damp earthy smell that was everywhere intermingled with the scents. The voice of the aged Torrance within rose in an ecstasy. And he wondered if Torrance also felt in his old bones the joyous influence of the spring morning; Torrance, or the shadow of what once was Torrance, that must come so soon to lie outside here in the sun and rain with all his rheumatisms, while a new minister stood in his room and thundered from his own familiar pulpit? The pity of it, and something of the chill of the grave, shook him for a moment as he made haste to enter.

He went up the aisle reverently and took his place in the pew with lowered eyes, for he feared he had already offended the kind old gentleman in the pulpit, and was sedulous to offend no farther. He could not follow the prayer, not even the heads of it. Brightnesses of azure, clouds of fragrance, a tinkle of falling water and singing birds, rose like exhalations from some deeper, aboriginal memory, that was not his, but belonged to the flesh on his bones. His body remembered; and it seemed to him that his body was in no way gross, but ethereal and perishable like a strain of music; and he felt for it an exquisite tenderness as for a child, an innocent, full of beautiful instincts and destined to an early death. And he felt for old Torrance—of the many supplications, of the few days—a pity that was near to tears. The prayer ended. Right over him was a tablet in the wall, the only ornament in the roughly masoned chapel—for it was no more; the tablet commemorated, I was about to say the virtues, but rather the existence of a former Rutherford of Hermiston; and Archie, under that trophy of his long descent and local greatness, leaned back in the pew and contemplated vacancy with the shadow of a smile between playful and sad, that became him strangely. Dandie's sister, sitting by the side of Clem in her new Glasgow finery, chose that moment to observe the young laird. Aware of the stir of his entrance, the little formalist had kept her eyes fastened and her face prettily composed during the prayer. It was not hypocrisy, there was no one farther from a hypocrite. The girl had been taught to behave: to look up, to look down, to look unconscious, to look seriously impressed in church, and in every conjuncture to look her best. That was the game of female life, and she played it frankly. Archie was the one person in church who was of interest, who was somebody new, reputed eccentric, known to be young, and a laird, and still unseen by Christina. Small wonder that, as she stood there in her attitude of pretty decency, her mind should run upon him! If he spared a glance in her direction, he should know she was a well-behaved young lady who had been to Glasgow. In reason he must admire her clothes, and it was possible that he should think her pretty. At that her heart beat the least thing in the world; and she proceeded, by way of a corrective, to call up and dismiss a series of fancied pictures of the young man who should now, by rights, be looking at her. She settled on the plainest of them, a pink short young man with a dish face and no figure, at whose admiration she could afford to smile; but for all that, the consciousness of his gaze (which was really fixed on Torrance and his mittens) kept her in something of a flutter till the word Amen. Even then, she was far too well-bred to gratify her curiosity with any impatience. She resumed her seat languidly

—this was a Glasgow touch—she composed her dress, rearranged her nosegay of primroses, looked first in front, then behind upon the other side, and at last allowed her eyes to move, without hurry, in the direction of the Hermiston pew. For a moment, they were riveted. Next she had plucked her gaze home again like a tame bird who should have meditated flight. Possibilities crowded on her; she hung over the future and grew dizzy; the image of this young man, slim, graceful, dark, with the inscrutable half-smile, attracted and repelled her like a chasm. "I wonder, will I have met my fate?" she thought, and her heart swelled.

Torrance was got some way into his first exposition, positing a deep layer of texts as he went along, laying the foundations of his discourse, which was to deal with a nice point in divinity, before Archie suffered his eyes to wander. They fell first of all on Clem, looking insupportably prosperous and patronising Torrance with the favour of a modified attention, as of one who was used to better things in Glasgow. Though he had never before set eyes on him, Archie had no difficulty in identifying him, and no hesitation in pronouncing him vulgar, the worst of the family. Clem was leaning lazily forward when Archie first saw him. Presently he leaned nonchalantly back; and that deadly instrument, the maiden, was suddenly unmasked in profile. Though not quite in the front of the fashion (had anybody cared!), certain artful Glasgow mantua-makers, and her own inherent taste, had arrayed her to great advantage. Her accoutrement was, indeed, a cause of heart-burning, and almost of scandal, in that infinitesimal kirk company. Mrs. Hob had said her say at Cauldstaneslap. "Daft-like!" she had pronounced it. "A jaiket that'll no meet! Whaur's the sense of a jaiket that'll no button upon you, if it should come to be weet? What do ye ca' thir things? Demmy brokens, d' ye say? They'll be brokens wi' a vengeance or ye can win back! Weel, I have naething to do wi' it—it's no good taste." Clem, whose purse had thus metamorphosed his sister, and who was not insensible to the advertisement, had come to the rescue with a "Hoot, woman! What do you ken of good taste that has never been to the ceety?" And Hob, looking on the girl with pleased smiles, as she timidly displayed her finery in the midst of the dark kitchen, had thus ended the dispute: "The cutty looks weel," he had said, "and it's no very like rain. Wear them the day, hizzie; but it's no a thing to make a practice o'." In the breasts of her rivals, coming to the kirk very conscious of white under-linen, and their faces splendid with much soap, the sight of the toilet had raised a storm of varying emotion, from the mere unenvious admiration that was expressed in the long-drawn "Eh!" to the angrier feeling that found vent in an emphatic "Set her up!" Her frock was of straw-coloured jaconet muslin, cut low at the bosom and short at the ankle, so as to display her *demi-broquins* of Regency violet, crossing with many straps upon a yellow cobweb stocking. According to the pretty fashion in which our grandmothers did not hesitate to appear, and our great-aunts went forth armed for the pursuit and capture of our great-uncles, the dress was drawn up so as to mould the contour of both breasts, and in the nook between a cairngorm brooch maintained it. Here, too, surely in a very enviable position, trembled the nosegay of primroses. She wore on her shoulders— or rather, on her back and not her shoulders, which it scarcely passed—a French coat of sarsenet, tied in front with Margate braces, and of the same colour with her violet shoes. About her face clustered a disorder of dark ringlets, a little garland of yellow French roses surmounted her brow, and the whole was crowned by a village hat of chipped straw. Amongst all the rosy and all the weathered faces that surrounded her in church, she glowed like an open flower—girl and raiment, and the cairngorm that caught the daylight and returned it in a fiery flash, and the threads of bronze and gold that played in her hair.

Archie was attracted by the bright thing like a child. He looked at her again and yet again, and their looks crossed. The lip was lifted from her little teeth. He saw the red blood work vividly under her tawny skin. Her eye, which was great as a stag's, struck and held his gaze. He knew who she must be—Kirstie, she of the harsh diminutive, his housekeeper's niece, the sister of the rustic prophet, Gib—and he found in her the answer to his wishes.

Christina felt the shock of their encountering glances, and seemed to rise, clothed in smiles, into a region of the vague and bright. But the gratification was not more exquisite than it was brief. She looked away abruptly, and immediately began to blame herself for that abruptness. She knew what she should have done, too late—turned slowly with her nose in the air. And meantime his look was not removed, but continued to play upon her like a battery of cannon constantly aimed, and now seemed to isolate her alone with him, and now seemed to uplift her, as on a pillory, before the congregation. For Archie continued to drink her in with his eyes, even as a wayfarer comes to a well-head on a mountain, and stoops his face, and drinks with thirst unassuageable. In the cleft of her little breasts the fiery eye of the topaz and the pale florets of primrose fascinated him. He saw the breasts heave, and the flowers shake with the heaving, and marvelled what should so much discompose the girl. And Christina was conscious of his gaze —saw it, perhaps, with the dainty plaything of an ear that peeped among her ringlets; she was conscious of changing colour, conscious of her unsteady breath. Like a creature tracked, run down, surrounded, she sought in a dozen ways to give herself a countenance. She used her handkerchief—it was a really fine one—then she desisted in a panic: "He would only think I was too warm." She took to reading in the metrical psalms, and then remembered it was sermon-time. Last she put a "sugar-bool" in her mouth, and the next moment repented of the step. It was such a homely-like thing! Mr. Archie would never be eating sweeties in kirk; and, with a palpable effort, she swallowed it whole, and her colour flamed high. At this signal of distress Archie awoke to a sense of his ill-behaviour. What had he been doing? He had been exquisitely rude in church to the niece of his housekeeper; he had stared like a lackey and a libertine at a beautiful and modest girl. It was possible, it was even likely, he would be presented to her after service in the kirk-yard, and then how was he to look? And there was no excuse. He had marked the tokens of her shame, of her increasing indignation, and he was such a fool that he had not understood them. Shame bowed him down, and he looked resolutely at Mr. Torrance; who little supposed, good, worthy man, as he continued to expound justification by faith, what was his true business: to play the part of derivative to a pair of children at the old game of falling in love.

Christina was greatly relieved at first. It seemed to her that she was clothed again. She looked back on what had passed. All would have been right if she had not blushed, a silly fool! There was nothing to blush at, if she *had* taken a sugar-bool. Mrs. Mac-Taggart, the elder's wife in St. Enoch's, took them often. And if he had looked at her, what was more natural than that a young gentleman should look at the best-dressed girl in church? And at the same time, she knew far otherwise, she knew there was nothing casual or ordinary in the look, and valued herself on its memory like a decoration. Well, it was a blessing he had found something else to look at! And presently she began to have other thoughts. It was necessary, she fancied, that she should put herself right by a repetition of the incident, better managed. If the wish was father to the thought, she did not know or she would not recognize it. It was simply as a manœuvre of propriety, as something called for to lessen the significance of what had gone before, that she should a second time meet his eyes, and this time without blushing. And at the memory of the blush, she blushed again, and became one general blush burning from head to foot. Was ever anything so indelicate, so forward, done by a girl before? And here she was, making an exhibition of herself before the congregation about nothing! She stole a glance upon her neighbours, and behold! they were steadily indifferent, and Clem had gone to sleep. And still the one idea was becoming more and more potent with her, that in common prudence she must look again before the service ended. Something of the same sort was going forward in the mind of Archie, as he struggled with the load of penitence. So it chanced that, in the flutter of the moment when the last psalm was given out, and Torrance was reading the verse, and the leaves of every psalm-book in church were rustling under busy fingers, two stealthy glances were sent out like antennæ among the pews and on the indifferent and absorbed occupants, and drew timidly nearer to the straight line between Archie and Christina. They met, they lingered together for the least fraction of time, and that was enough. A charge as of electricity passed through Christina, and behold! the leaf of her psalm-book was torn across.

Archie was outside by the gate of the graveyard, conversing with Hob and the minister and shaking hands all round with the scattering congregation, when Clem and Christina were brought up to be presented. The laird took off his hat and bowed to her with grace and respect. Christina made her Glasgow curtsey to the laird, and went on again up the road for Hermiston and Cauldstaneslap, walking fast, breathing hurriedly with a heightened colour, and in this strange frame of mind, that when she was alone she seemed in high happiness, and when any one addressed her she resented it like a contradiction. A part of the way she had the company of some neighbour girls and a loutish young man; never had they seemed so insipid, never had she made herself so disagreeable. But these struck aside to their various destinations or were out-walked and left behind; and when she had driven off with sharp words the proffered convoy of some of her nephews and nieces, she was free to go on alone up Hermiston brae, walking on air, dwelling intoxicated among clouds of happiness. Near to the summit she heard steps behind her, a man's steps, light and very rapid. She knew the foot at once and walked the faster. "If it's me he's wanting he can run for it," she thought, smiling.

Archie overtook her like a man whose mind was made up.

"Miss Kirstie," he began.

"Miss Christina, if you please, Mr. Weir," she interrupted. "I canna bear the contraction."

"You forget it has a friendly sound for me. Your aunt is an old friend of mine and a very good one. I hope we shall see much of you at Hermiston?"

"My aunt and my sister-in-law doesna agree very well. Not that I have much ado with it. But still when I'm stopping in the house, if I was to be visiting my aunt, it would not look considerate-like."

"I am sorry," said Archie.

"I thank you kindly, Mr. Weir," she said. "I whiles think myself it's a great peety."

"Ah, I am sure your voice would always be for peace!" he cried.

"I wouldna be too sure of that," she said. "I have my days like other folk, I suppose."

"Do you know, in our old kirk, among our good old grey dames, you made an effect like sunshine."

"Ah, but that would be my Glasgow clothes!"

"I did not think I was so much under the influence of pretty frocks."

She smiled with a half look at him. "There's more than you!" she said. "But you see I'm only Cinderella. I'll have to put all these things by in my trunk; next Sunday I'll be as grey as the rest. They're Glasgow clothes, you see, and it would never do to make a practice of it. It would seem terrible conspicuous."

By that they were come to the place where their ways severed. The grey moors were all about them; in the midst a few sheep wandered; and they could see on the one hand the straggling caravan scaling the braes in front of them for Cauldstaneslap, and on the other, the contingent from Hermiston bending off and beginning to disappear by detachments into the policy gate. It was in these circumstances that they turned to say farewell, and deliberately exchanged a glance as they shook hands. All passed as it should, genteelly; and in Christina's mind, as she mounted the first steep ascent for Cauldstaneslap, a gratifying sense of triumph prevailed over the recollection of minor lapses and mistakes. She had kilted her gown, as she did usually at that rugged pass; but when she spied Archie still standing and gazing after her, the skirts came down again as if by enchantment. Here was a piece of nicety for that upland parish, where the matrons marched with their coats kilted in the rain, and the lasses walked barefoot to kirk through the dust of summer, and went bravely down by the burnside, and sat on stones to make a public toilet before entering! It was perhaps an air wafted from Glasgow; or perhaps it marked a stage of that dizziness of gratified vanity, in which the instinctive act passed unperceived. He was looking after! She unloaded her bosom of a prodigious sigh that was all pleasure, and betook herself to run. When she had overtaken the stragglers of her family, she caught up the niece whom she had so recently repulsed, and kissed and slapped her, and drove her away again, and ran after her with pretty cries and laughter. Perhaps she thought the laird might still be looking! But it chanced the little scene came under the view of eyes less favourable; for she overtook Mrs. Hob marching with Clem and Dand.

"You're shürely fey,* lass!" quoth Dandie.

"Think shame to yersel', miss!" said the strident Mrs. Hob. "Is this the gait to guide yersel' on the way home frae kirk? You're shürely no sponsible the day. And anyway I would mind my guid claes."

"Hoot!" said Christina, and went on before them head in air, treading the rough track with the tread of a wild doe.

She was in love with herself, her destiny, the air of the hills, the benediction of the sun. All the way home, she continued under the intoxication of these sky-scraping spirits. At table she could talk freely of young Hermiston; gave her opinion of him off-hand and with a loud voice, that he was a handsome young gentleman, real well-mannered and sensible-like, but it was a pity he looked doleful. Only—the moment after—a memory of his eyes in church embarrassed her. But for this inconsiderable check, all through

* Unlike yourself, strange, as persons are observed to be in the hour of approaching death or calamity.

mealtime she had a good appetite, and she kept them laughing at table, until Gib (who had returned before them from Crossmichael and his separative worship) reproved the whole of them for their levity.

Singing "in to herself" as she went, her mind still in the turmoil of glad confusion, she rose and tripped up-stairs to a little loft, lighted by four panes in the gable, where she slept with one of her nieces. The niece, who followed her, presuming on "Auntie's" high spirits, was flounced out of the apartment with small ceremony, and retired, smarting and half tearful, to bury her woes in the byre among the hay. Still humming, Christina divested herself of her finery, and put her treasures one by one in her great green trunk. The last of these was the psalm-book; it was a fine piece, the gift of Mistress Clem, in distinct old-faced type, on paper that had begun to grow foxy in the warehouse—not by service—and she was used to wrap it in a handkerchief every Sunday after its period of service was over, and bury it end-wise at the head of her trunk. As she now took it in hand the book fell open where the leaf was torn, and she stood and gazed upon that evidence of her by-gone discomposure. There returned again the vision of the two brown eyes staring at her, intent and bright, out of that dark corner of the kirk. The whole appearance and attitude, the smile, the suggested gesture of young Hermiston came before her in a flash at the sight of the torn page. "I was surely fey!" she said, echoing the words of Dandie, and at the suggested doom her high spirits deserted her. She flung herself prone upon the bed, and lay there, holding the psalm-book in her hands for hours, for the more part in a mere stupor of unconsenting pleasure and unreasoning fear. The fear was superstitious; there came up again and again in her memory Dandie's ill-omened words, and a hundred grisly and black tales out of the immediate neighbourhood read her a commentary on their force. The pleasure was never realised. You might say the joints of her body thought and remembered, and were gladdened, but her essential self, in the immediate theatre of consciousness, talked feverishly of something else, like a nervous person at a fire. The image that she most complacently dwelt on was that of Miss Christina in her character of the Fair Lass of Cauldstaneslap, carrying all before her in the straw-coloured frock, the violet mantle, and the yellow cobweb stockings. Archie's image, on the other hand, when it presented itself was never welcomed—

far less welcomed with any ardour, and it was exposed at times to merciless criticism. In the long, vague dialogues she held in her mind, often with imaginary, often with unrealised interlocutors, Archie, if he were referred to at all, came in for savage handling. He was described as "looking like a stork," "staring like a caulf," "a face like a ghaist's." "Do you call that manners?" she said; or, "I soon put him in his place." " '*Miss Christina, if you please, Mr. Weir!*' says I, and just flyped up my skirt tails." With gabble like this she would entertain herself long whiles together, and then her eye would perhaps fall on the torn leaf, and the eyes of Archie would appear again from the darkness of the wall, and the voluble words deserted her, and she would lie still and stupid, and think upon nothing with devotion, and be sometimes raised by a quiet sigh. Had a doctor of medicine come into that loft, he would have diagnosed a healthy, well-developed, eminently vivacious lass lying on her face in the fit of the sulks; not one who had just contracted, or was just contracting, a mortal sickness of the mind which should yet carry her towards death and despair. Had it been a doctor of psychology, he might have been pardoned for divining in the girl a passion of childish vanity, self-love *in excelsis,* and no more. It is to be understood that I have been painting chaos and describing the inarticulate. Every lineament that appears is too precise, almost every word used too strong. Take a finger-post in the mountains on a day of rolling mists; I have but copied the names that appear upon the pointers, the names of definite and famous cities far distant, and now perhaps basking in sunshine; but Christina remained all these hours, as it were, at the foot of the post itself, not moving, and enveloped in mutable blinding wreaths of haze.

The day was growing late and the sunbeams long and level, when she sat suddenly up, and wrapped in its handkerchief and put by that psalm-book which had already played a part so decisive in the first chapter of her love-story. In the absence of the mesmerist's eye, we are told nowadays that the head of a bright nail may fill his place, if it be steadfastly regarded. So that torn page had riveted her attention on what might else have been but little, and perhaps soon forgotten; while the ominous words of Dandie—heard, not heeded, and still remembered—had lent to her thoughts, or rather to her mood, a cast of solemnity, and that idea of Fate—a pagan Fate, uncontrolled by any Christian deity, obscure, lawless, and august—moving indissuadably in the affairs of Christian men. Thus even that phenomenon of love at first sight, which is so rare and seems so simple and violent, like a disruption of life's tissue, may be decomposed into a sequence of accidents happily concurring.

She put on a grey frock and a pink kerchief, looked at herself a moment with approval in the small square of glass that served her for a toilet mirror, and went softly down-stairs through the sleeping house that resounded with the sound of afternoon snoring. Just outside the door Dandie was sitting with a book in his hand, not reading, only honouring the Sabbath by a sacred vacancy of mind. She came near him and stood still.

"I'm for off up the muirs, Dandie," she said.

There was something unusually soft in her tones that made him look up. She was pale, her eyes dark and bright; no trace remained of the levity of the morning.

"Ay, lass? Ye'll have ye're ups and downs like me, I'm thinkin'," he observed.

"What for do ye say that?" she asked.

"O, for naething," says Dand. "Only I think ye're mair like me than the lave of them. Ye've mair of the poetic temper, tho' Guid kens little enough of the poetic taalent. It's an ill gift at the best. Look at yoursel'. At denner you were all sunshine and flowers and laughter, and now you're like the star of evening on a lake."

She drank in this hackneyed compliment like wine, and it glowed in her veins.

"But I'm saying, Dand"—she came nearer him—"I'm for the muirs. I must have a braith of air. If Clem was to be speiring for me, try and quaiet him, will ye no?"

"What way?" said Dandie. "I ken but the ae way, and that's leein'. I'll say ye had a sair heed, if ye like."

"But I havena," she objected.

"I daur say not," he returned. "I said I would say ye had; and if ye like to nay-say me when ye come back, it'll no matteerially maitter, for my chara'ter's clean gane a'ready past reca'."

"O, Dand, are ye a leear?" she asked, lingering.

"Folks say sae," replied the bard.

"Wha says sae?" she pursued.

"Them that should ken the best," he responded. "The lassies, for ane."

"But, Dand, you would never lee to me?" she asked.

"I'll leave that for your pairt of it, ye girzie," said he. "Ye'll lee to me fast eneuch, when ye hae gotten a jo. I'm tellin' ye and it's true; when you have a jo, Miss Kirstie, it'll be for guid and ill. I ken: I was made that way mysel', but the deil was in my luck! Here, gang awa wi' ye to your muirs, and let me be; I'm in an hour of inspirautien, ye upsetting tawpie!"

But she clung to her brother's neighbourhood, she knew not why.

"Will ye no gie 's a kiss, Dand?" she said. "I aye likit ye fine."

He kissed her and considered her a moment; he found something strange in her. But he was a libertine through and through, nourished equal contempt and suspicion of all womankind, and paid his way among them habitually with idle compliments.

"Gae wa' wi' ye!" said he. "Ye're a dentie baby, and be content wi' that!"

That was Dandie's way; a kiss and a comfit to Jenny—a bawbee and my blessing to Jill—and good-night to the whole clan of ye, my dears! When anything approached the serious, it became a matter for men, he both thought and said. Women, when they did not absorb, were only children to be shoo'd away. Merely in his character of connoisseur, however, Dandie glanced carelessly after his sister, as she crossed the meadow. "The brat 's no that bad!" he thought with surprise, for though he had just been paying her compliments, he had not really looked at her. "Hey! what's yon?" For the grey dress was cut with short sleeves and skirts, and displayed her trim strong legs clad in pink stockings of the same shade as the kerchief she wore round her shoulders, and that shimmered as she went. This was not her way in undress; he knew her ways and the ways of the whole sex in the country-side, no one better; when they did not go barefoot, they wore stout "rig and furrow" woollen hose of an invisible blue mostly, when they were not black outright; and Dandie, at the sight of this daintiness, put two and two together. It was a silk handkerchief, then they would be silken hose; they matched—then the whole outfit was a present of Clem's, a costly present, and not something to be worn through bog and brier, or on a late afternoon of Sunday. He whistled. "My denty May, either your heid's fair turned, or there's some on-goings!" he observed, and dismissed the subject.

She went slowly at first, but ever straighter and faster for the Cauldstaneslap, a pass among the hills to which the farm owed its name. The Slap opened like a doorway between two rounded hillocks; and through this ran the short cut to Hermiston. Immediately on the other side it went down through the Deil's Hags, a considerable marshy hollow of the hilltops, full of springs, and crouching junipers, and pools where the black peat-water slumbered. There was no view from here. A man might have sat upon the Praying Weaver's Stone a half-century, and seen none but the Cauldstaneslap children twice in the twenty-four hours on their way to the school and back again, an occasional shepherd, the irruption of a clan of sheep, or the birds who haunted about the springs, drinking and shrilly piping. So, when she had once passed the Slap, Kirstie was received into seclusion. She looked back a last time at the farm. It still lay deserted except for the figure of Dandie, who was now seen to be scribbling in his lap, the hour of expected inspiration having come to him at last. Thence she passed rapidly through the morass, and came to the further end of it, where a sluggish burn discharges, and the path for Hermiston accompanies it on the beginning of its downward path. From this corner a wide view was opened to her of the whole stretch of braes upon the other side, still sallow and in places rusty with the winter, with the path marked boldly, here and there by the burnside a tuft of birches, and—three miles off as the crow flies—from its enclosures and young plantations, the windows of Hermiston glittering in the western sun.

Here she sat down and waited, and looked for a long time at these far-away bright panes of glass. It amused her to have so extended a view, she thought. It amused her to see the house of Hermiston—to see "folk"; and there was an indistinguishable human unit, perhaps the gardener, visibly sauntering on the gravel paths.

By the time the sun was down and all the easterly braes lay plunged in clear shadow, she was aware of another figure coming up the path at a most unequal rate of approach, now half running, now pausing and seeming to hesitate. She watched him at first with a total suspension of thought. She held her thought as a person holds his breathing. Then she consented to recognise him. "He'll no be coming here, he canna be; it's no possible." And there began to grow upon her a subdued choking suspense. He *was* coming; his hesitations had quite ceased, his step grew firm and swift; no doubt remained; and the question loomed up before her instant: what was she to do? It was all very well to say that her brother was a laird himself; it was all very well to speak of casual intermarriages and to count cousinship, like Auntie Kirstie. The difference in their social station was trenchant; propriety, prudence, all that she had ever learned, all that she knew, bade her flee. But on the other hand the cup of life now offered to her was too enchanting. For one moment, she saw the question clearly, and definitely made her choice. She stood up and showed herself an instant in the gap relieved upon the sky line; and the next, fled trembling and sat down glowing with excitement on the Weaver's Stone. She shut her eyes, seeking, praying for composure. Her hand shook in her lap, and her mind was full of incongruous and futile speeches. What was there to make a work about? She could take care of herself, she supposed! There was no harm in seeing the laird. It was the best thing that could happen. She would mark a proper distance to him once and for all. Gradually the wheels of her nature ceased to go round so madly, and she sat in passive expectation, a quiet, solitary figure in the midst of the grey moss. I have said she was no hypocrite, but here I am at fault. She never admitted to herself that she had come up the hill to look for Archie. And perhaps after all she did not know, perhaps came as a stone falls. For the steps of love in the young, and especially in girls, are instinctive and unconscious.

In the meantime Archie was drawing rapidly near, and he at least was consciously seeking her neighbourhood. The afternoon had turned to ashes in his mouth; the memory of the girl had kept him from reading and drawn him as with cords; and at last, as the cool of the evening began to come on, he had taken his hat and set forth, with a smothered ejaculation, by the moor path to Cauld-staneslap. He had no hope to find her; he took the off chance without expectation of result and to relieve his uneasiness. The greater was his surprise, as he surmounted the slope and came into the hollow of the Deil's Hags, to see there, like an answer to his wishes, the little womanly figure in the grey dress and the pink kerchief sitting little, and low, and lost, and acutely solitary, in these desolate surroundings and on the weather-beaten stone of the dead weaver. Those things that still smacked of winter were all rusty about her, and those things that already relished of the spring had put forth the tender and lively colours of the season. Even in the unchanging face of the death-stone changes were to be

remarked; and in the channelled-lettering, the moss began to renew itself in jewels of green. By an after-thought that was a stroke
of art, she had turned up over her head the back of the kerchief;
so that it now framed becomingly her vivacious and yet pensive
face. Her feet were gathered under her on the one side, and she
leaned on her bare arm, which showed out strong and round,
tapered to a slim wrist, and shimmered in the fading light.

Young Hermiston was struck with a certain chill. He was reminded that he now dealt in serious matters of life and death.
This was a grown woman he was approaching, endowed with her
mysterious potencies and attractions, the treasury of the continued
race, and he was neither better nor worse than the average of his
sex and age. He had a certain delicacy which had preserved him
hitherto unspotted, and which (had either of them guessed it)
made him a more dangerous companion when his heart should be
really stirred. His throat was dry as he came near; but the appealing sweetness of her smile stood between them like a guardian
angel.

For she turned to him and smiled, though without rising. There
was a shade in this cavalier greeting that neither of them perceived: neither he, who simply thought it gracious and charming
as herself; nor yet she, who did not observe (quick as she was) the
difference between rising to meet the laird and remaining seated to
receive the expected admirer.

"Are ye stepping west, Hermiston?" said she, giving him his
territorial name after the fashion of the country-side.

"I was," said he a little hoarsely, "but I think I will be about the
end of my stroll now. Are you like me, Miss Christina? the house
would not hold me. I came here seeking air."

He took his seat at the other end of the tombstone and studied
her, wondering what was she. There was infinite import in the
question alike for her and him.

"Ay," she said. "I couldna bear the roof either. It's a habit of
mine to come up here about the gloaming when it's quaiet and
caller."

"It was a habit of my mother's also," he said gravely. The recollection half startled him as he expressed it. He looked around.
"I have scarce been here since. It's peaceful," he said, with a long
breath.

"It's no like Glasgow," she replied. "A weary place, yon Glasgow! But what a day have I had for my hame-coming, and what a bonny evening!"

"Indeed, it was a wonderful day," said Archie. "I think I will remember it years and years until I come to die. On days like this —I do not know if you feel as I do—but everything appears so brief, and fragile, and exquisite, that I am afraid to touch life. We are here for so short a time; and all the old people before us— Rutherfords of Hermiston, Elliotts of the Cauldstaneslap—that were here but awhile since, riding about and keeping up a great noise in this quiet corner—making love too, and marrying—why, where are they now? It's deadly commonplace, but after all, the commonplaces are the great poetic truths."

He was sounding her, semi-consciously, to see if she could understand him; to learn if she were only an animal the colour of flowers, or had a soul in her to keep her sweet. She, on her part, her means well in hand, watched, womanlike, for any opportunity to shine, to abound in his humour, whatever that might be. The dramatic artist, that lies dormant or only half awake in most human beings, had in her sprung to his feet in a divine fury, and chance had served her well. She looked upon him with a subdued twilight look that became the hour of the day and the train of thought; earnestness shone through her like stars in the purple west; and from the great but controlled upheaval of her whole nature there passed into her voice, and rang in her lightest words, a thrill of emotion.

"Have you mind of Dand's song?" she answered. "I think he'll have been trying to say what you have been thinking."

"No, I never heard it," he said. "Repeat it to me, can you?"

"It's nothing wanting the tune," said Kirstie.

"Then sing it me," said he.

"On the Lord's Day? That would never do, Mr. Weir!"

"I am afraid I am not so strict a keeper of the Sabbath, and there is no one in this place to hear us, unless the poor old ancient under the stone."

"No that I'm thinking that really," she said. "By my way of thinking, it's just as serious as a psalm. Will I sooth it to ye, then?"

"If you please," said he, and, drawing near to her on the tombstone, prepared to listen.

She sat up as if to sing. "I'll only can sooth it to ye," she explained. "I wouldna like to sing out loud on the Sabbath. I think the birds would carry news of it to Gilbert," and she smiled. "It's about the Elliotts," she continued, "and I think there's few bonnier bits in the book-poets, though Dand has never got printed yet."

And she began, in the low, clear tones of her half-voice, now sinking almost to a whisper, now rising to a particular note which was her best, and which Archie learned to wait for with growing emotion:

> O they rade in the rain, in the days that are gane,
>   In the rain and the wind and the lave,
> They shoutit in the ha' and they routit on the hill,
>   But they're a' quaitit noo in the grave.
> Auld, auld Elliotts, clay-cauld Elliotts, dour, bauld Elliotts of auld!

All the time she sang she looked steadfastly before her, her knees straight, her hands upon her knee, her head cast back and up. The expression was admirable throughout, for had she not learned it from the lips and under the criticism of the author? When it was done, she turned upon Archie a face softly bright, and eyes gently suffused and shining in the twilight, and his heart rose and went out to her with boundless pity and sympathy. His question was answered. She was a human being tuned to a sense of the tragedy of life; there were pathos and music and a great heart in the girl.

He arose instinctively, she also; for she saw she had gained a point, and scored the impression deeper, and she had wit enough left to flee upon a victory. They were but commonplaces that remained to be exchanged, but the low, moved voices in which they passed made them sacred in the memory. In the falling greyness of the evening he watched her figure winding through the morass, saw it turn a last time and wave a hand, and then pass through the Slap; and it seemed to him as if something went along with her out of the deepest of his heart. And something surely had come, and come to dwell there. He had retained from childhood a picture, now half obliterated by the passage of time and the multitude of fresh impressions, of his mother telling him, with the fluttered earnestness of her voice, and often with dropping tears, the tale of the "Praying Weaver," on the very scene of his brief tragedy and long repose. And now there was a companion piece; and he beheld, and he should behold for ever, Christina perched on the same tomb, in the grey colours of the evening, gracious, dainty, perfect as a flower, and she also singing—

> Of old, unhappy far-off things,
> And battles long ago,

—of their common ancestors now dead, of their rude wars composed, their weapons buried with them, and of these strange changelings, their descendants, who lingered a little in their places, and would soon be gone also, and perhaps sung of by others at the gloaming hour. By one of the unconscious arts of tenderness the two women were enshrined together in his memory. Tears, in that hour of sensibility, came into his eyes indifferently at the thought of either, and the girl, from being something merely bright and shapely, was caught up into the zone of things serious as life and death and his dead mother. So that in all ways and on either side, Fate played his game artfully with this poor pair of children. The generations were prepared, the pangs were made ready, before the curtain rose on the dark drama.

In the same moment of time that she disappeared from Archie there opened before Kirstie's eyes the cup-like hollow in which the farm lay. She saw, some five hundred feet below her, the house making itself bright with candles, and this was a broad hint to her to hurry. For they were only kindled on a Sabbath night with a view to that family worship which rounded in the incomparable tedium of the day and brought on the relaxation of supper. Already she knew that Robert must be within-sides at the head of the table, "waling the portions"; for it was Robert in his quality of family priest and judge, not the gifted Gilbert, who officiated. She made good time accordingly down the steep ascent, and came up to the door panting as the three younger brothers, all roused at last from slumber, stood together in the cool and the dark of the evening with a fry of nephews and nieces about them, chatting and awaiting the expected signal. She stood back; she had no mind to direct attention to her late arrival or to her labouring breath.

"Kirstie, ye have shaved it this time, my lass," said Clem. "Whaur were ye?"

"O, just taking a dander by mysel'," said Kirstie.

And the talk continued on the subject of the American war, without further reference to the truant who stood by them in the covert of the dusk, thrilling with happiness and the sense of guilt.

The signal was given, and the brothers began to go in one after another, amid the jostle and throng of Hob's children.

Only Dandie, waiting till the last, caught Kirstie by the arm. "When did ye begin to dander in pink hosen, Mistress Elliott?" he whispered slyly.

She looked down; she was one blush. "I maun have forgotten to change them," said she; and went in to prayers in her turn with a troubled mind, between anxiety as to whether Dand should have observed her yellow stockings at church, and should thus detect her in a palpable falsehood, and shame that she had already made good his prophecy.

She remembered the words of it, how it was to be when she had gotten a jo, and that that would be for good and evil. "Will I have gotten my jo now?" she thought with a secret rapture.

And all through prayers, where it was her principal business to conceal the pink stockings from the eyes of the indifferent Mrs. Hob—and all through supper, as she made a feint of eating, and sat at the table radiant and constrained—and again when she had left them and come into her chamber, and was alone with her sleeping niece, and could at last lay aside the armour of society—the same words sounded within her, the same profound note of happiness, of a world all changed and renewed, of a day that had been passed in Paradise, and of a night that was to be heaven opened. All night she seemed to be conveyed smoothly upon a shallow stream of sleep and waking, and through the bowers of Beulah; all night she cherished to her heart that exquisite hope; and if, towards morning, she forgot it awhile in a more profound unconsciousness, it was to catch again the rainbow thought with her first moment of awaking.

7. *Enter Mephistopheles*

TWO DAYS LATER A GIG FROM CROSSMICHAEL DEPOSITED FRANK Innes at the doors of Hermiston. Once in a way, during the past winter, Archie, in some acute phase of boredom, had written him a letter. It had contained something in the nature of an invitation, or a reference to an invitation—precisely what, neither of them now remembered. When Innes had received it, there had been nothing further from his mind than to bury himself in the moors with Archie; but not even the most acute political heads are guided through the steps of life with unerring directness. That would require a gift of prophecy which has been denied to man. For instance, who could have imagined that, not a month after he had received the letter, and turned it into mockery, and put off answering it, and in the end lost it, misfortunes of a gloomy cast should begin to thicken over Frank's career? His case may be briefly stated. His father, a small Morayshire laird with a large family, became recalcitrant and cut off the supplies; he had fitted himself out with the beginnings of quite a good law library, which, upon some sudden losses on the turf, he had been obliged to sell before they were paid for; and his bookseller, hearing some rumour of the event, took out a warrant for his arrest. Innes had early word of it, and was able to take precautions. In this immediate welter of his affairs, with an unpleasant charge hanging over him, he had judged it the part of prudence to be off instantly, had written a fervid letter to his father at Inverauld, and put himself in the coach for Crossmichael. Any port in a storm! He was manfully turning his back on the Parliament House and its gay babble, on porter and oysters, the racecourse and the ring; and manfully prepared, until these clouds should have blown by, to share a living grave with Archie Weir at Hermiston.

To do him justice, he was no less surprised to be going than Archie was to see him come; and he carried off his wonder with an infinitely better grace.

"Well, here I am!" said he, as he alighted. "Pylades has come to Orestes at last. By the way, did you get my answer? No? How very provoking! Well, here I am to answer for myself, and that's better still."

"I am very glad to see you, of course," said Archie. "I make you heartily welcome, of course. But you surely have not come to stay, with the courts still sitting; is that not most unwise?"

"Damn the courts!" says Frank. "What are the courts to friendship and a little fishing?"

And so it was agreed that he was to stay, with no term to the visit but the term which he had privily set to it himself—the day, namely, when his father should have come down with the dust, and he should be able to pacify the bookseller. On such vague conditions there began for these two young men (who were not even friends) a life of great familiarity and, as the days grew on, less and less intimacy. They were together at meal times, together o' nights when the hour had come for whisky toddy; but it might have been noticed (had there been any one to pay heed) that they were rarely so much together by day. Archie had Hermiston to attend to, multifarious activities in the hills, in which he did not require, and had even refused, Frank's escort. He would be off sometimes in the morning and leave only a note on the breakfast table to announce the fact; and sometimes, with no notice at all, he would not return for dinner until the hour was long past. Innes groaned under these desertions; it required all his philosophy to sit down to a solitary breakfast with composure, and all his unaffected good-nature to be able to greet Archie with friendliness on the more rare occasions when he came home late for dinner.

"I wonder what on earth he finds to do, Mrs. Elliott?" said he one morning, after he had just read the hasty billet and sat down to table.

"I suppose it will be business, sir," replied the housekeeper drily, measuring his distance off to him by an indicated curtsey.

"But I can't imagine what business!" he reiterated.

"I suppose it will be *his* business," retorted the austere Kirstie.

He turned to her with that happy brightness that made the charm of his disposition, and broke into a peal of healthy and natural laughter.

"Well played, Mrs. Elliott!" he cried, and the housekeeper's face relaxed into the shadow of an iron smile. "Well played indeed!" said he. "But you must not be making a stranger of me like that. Why, Archie and I were at the High School together, and we've been to college together, and we were going to the Bar together, when—you know! Dear, dear me! what a pity that was! A life spoiled, a fine young fellow as good as buried here in the wilderness with rustics; and all for what? A frolic, silly, if you like, but no more. God, how good your scones are, Mrs. Elliott!"

"They're no mines, it was the lassie made them," said Kirstie; "and, saving your presence, there's little sense in taking the Lord's name in vain about idle vivers that you fill your kyte wi'."

"I dare say you're perfectly right, ma'am," quoth the imperturbable Frank. "But, as I was saying, this is a pitiable business, this about poor Archie; and you and I might do worse than put our heads together, like a couple of sensible people, and bring it to an end. Let me tell you, ma'am, that Archie is really quite a promis-

ing young man, and in my opinion he would do well at the Bar.
As for his father, no one can deny his ability, and I don't fancy
any one would care to deny that he has the deil's own temper——"

"If you'll excuse me, Mr. Innes, I think the lass is crying on me,"
said Kirstie, and flounced from the room.

"The damned, cross-grained, old broom-stick!" ejaculated Innes.

In the meantime, Kirstie had escaped into the kitchen, and before her vassal gave vent to her feelings.

"Here, ettercap! Ye'll have to wait on yon Innes! I canna haud
myself in. 'Puir Erchie'! I'd 'puir Erchie' him, if I had my way!
And Hermiston with the deil's ain temper! God, let him take
Hermiston's scones out of his mouth first. There's no a hair on
ayther o' the Weirs that hasna mair spunk and dirdum to it than
what he has in his hale dwaibly body! Setting' up his snash to me!
Let him gang to the black toon where he's mebbe wantit—birling
in a curricle—wi' pimatum on his heid—making a mess o' himsel'
wi' nesty hizzies—a fair disgrace!" It was impossible to hear without admiration Kirstie's graduated disgust, as she brought forth,
one after another, these somewhat baseless charges. Then she remembered her immediate purpose, and turned again on her fascinated auditor. "Do ye no hear me, tawpie? Do ye no hear what
I'm tellin' ye? Will I have to shoo ye in to him? If I come to attend
to ye, mistress!" And the maid fled the kitchen, which had become
practically dangerous, to attend on Innes' wants in the front parlour.

Tantæne iræ? Has the reader perceived the reason? Since Frank's
coming there were no more hours of gossip over the supper tray!
All his blandishments were in vain; he had started handicapped
on the race for Mrs. Elliott's favour.

But it was a strange thing how misfortune dogged him in his
efforts to be genial. I must guard the reader against accepting
Kirstie's epithets as evidence; she was more concerned for their
vigour than for their accuracy. Dwaibly, for instance; nothing
could be more calumnious. Frank was the very picture of good
looks, good-humour, and manly youth. He had bright eyes with a
sparkle and a dance to them, curly hair, a charming smile, brilliant
teeth, an admirable carriage of the head, the look of a gentleman,
the address of one accustomed to please at first sight and to im-
prove the impression. And with all these advantages, he failed with
every one about Hermiston; with the silent shepherd, with the obse-

quious grieve, with the groom who was also the ploughman, with the gardener and the gardener's sister—a pious, down-hearted woman with a shawl over her ears—he failed equally and flatly. They did not like him, and they showed it. The little maid, indeed, was an exception; she admired him devoutly, probably dreamed of him in her private hours; but she was accustomed to play the part of silent auditor to Kirstie's tirades and silent recipient of Kirstie's buffets, and she had learned not only to be a very capable girl of her years, but a very secret and prudent one besides. Frank was thus conscious that he had one ally and sympathiser in the midst of that general union of disfavour that surrounded, watched, and waited on him in the house of Hermiston; but he had little comfort of society from that alliance, and the demure little maid (twelve on her last birthday) preserved her own counsel, and tripped on his service, brisk, dumbly responsive, but inexorably unconversational. For the others, they were beyond hope and beyond endurance. Never had a young Apollo been cast among such rustic barbarians. But perhaps the cause of his ill-success lay in one trait which was habitual and unconscious with him, yet diagnostic of the man. It was his practice to approach any one person at the expense of some one else. He offered you an alliance against the some one else; he flattered you by slighting him; you were drawn into a small intrigue against him before you knew how. Wonderful are the virtues of this process generally; but Frank's mistake was in the choice of the some one else. He was not politic in that; he listened to the voice of irritation. Archie had offended him at first by what he had felt to be rather a dry reception; had offended him since by his frequent absences. He was besides the one figure continually present in Frank's eye; and it was to his immediate dependents that Frank could offer the snare of his sympathy. Now the truth is that the Weirs, father and son, were surrounded by a posse of strenuous loyalists. Of my lord they were vastly proud. It was a distinction in itself to be one of the vassals of the "Hanging Judge," and his gross, formidable joviality was far from unpopular in the neighbourhood of his home. For Archie they had, one and all, a sensitive affection and respect which recoiled from a word of belittlement.

Nor was Frank more successful when he went farther afield. To the Four Black Brothers, for instance, he was antipathetic in the highest degree. Hob thought him too light, Gib too profane. Clem, who saw him but for a day or two before he went to Glasgow, wanted to know what the fule's business was, and whether he meant to stay here all session time! "Yon's a drone," he pronounced. As for Dand, it will be enough to describe their first meeting, when Frank had been whipping a river and the rustic celebrity chanced to come along the path.

"I'm told you are quite a poet," Frank had said.

"Wha tell's ye that, mannie?" had been the unconciliating answer.

"O, everybody," says Frank.

"God! Here's fame!" said the sardonic poet, and he had passed on his way.

Come to think of it, we have here perhaps a truer explanation of Frank's failures. Had he met Mr. Sheriff Scott he could have turned a neater compliment, because Mr. Scott would have been a friend worth making. Dand, on the other hand, he did not value sixpence, and he showed it even while he tried to flatter. Condescension is an excellent thing, but it is strange how one-sided the pleasure of it is! He who goes fishing among the Scots peasantry with condescension for a bait will have an empty basket by evening.

In proof of this theory Frank made a great success of it at the Crossmichael Club, to which Archie took him immediately on his arrival; his own last appearance on that scene of gaiety. Frank was made welcome there at once, continued to go regularly, and had attended a meeting (as the members ever after loved to tell) on the evening before his death. Young Hay and young Pringle appeared again. There was another supper at Windielaws, another dinner at Driffel; and it resulted in Frank being taken to the bosom of the county people as unreservedly as he had been repudiated by the country folk. He occupied Hermiston after the manner of an invader in a conquered capital. He was perpetually issuing from it, as from a base, to toddy parties, fishing parties, and dinner parties, to which Archie was not invited, or to which Archie would not go. It was now that the name of The Recluse became general for the young man. Some say that Innes invented it; Innes, at least, spread it abroad.

"How's all with your Recluse to-day?" people would ask.

"O, reclusing away!" Innes would declare, with his bright air of saying something witty; and immediately interrupt the general laughter which he had provoked much more by his air than his words, "Mind you, it's all very well laughing, but I'm not very well pleased. Poor Archie is a good fellow, an excellent fellow, a fellow I aways liked. I think it small of him to take his little disgrace so hard and shut himself up. 'Grant that it is a ridiculous story, painfully ridiculous,' I keep telling him. 'Be a man! Live it down, man!' But not he. Of course it's just solitude, and shame, and all that. But I confess I'm beginning to fear the result. It would be all the pities in the world if a really promising fellow like Weir was to end ill. I'm seriously tempted to write to Lord Hermiston, and put it plainly to him."

"I would if I were you," some of his auditors would say, shaking the head, sitting bewildered and confused at this new view of the matter, so deftly indicated by a single word. "A capital idea!" they would add, and wonder at the *aplomb* and position of this young man, who talked as a matter of course of writing to Hermiston and correcting him upon his private affairs.

And Frank would proceed, sweetly confidential: "I'll give you an idea, now. He's actually sore about the way that I'm received and he's left out in the county—actually jealous and sore. I've rallied him and I've reasoned with him, told him that every one was most kindly inclined towards him, told him even that I was received merely because I was his guest. But it's no use. He will neither accept the invitations he gets, nor stop brooding about the ones where he's left out. What I'm afraid of is that the wound's ulcerating. He had always one of those dark, secret, angry natures —a little underhand and plenty of bile—you know the sort. He must have inherited it from the Weirs, whom I suspect to have been a worthy family of weavers somewhere; what's the cant phrase?—sedentary occupation. It's precisely the kind of character to go wrong in a false position like what his father's made for him, or he's making for himself, whichever you like to call it. And for my part, I think it a disgrace," Frank would say generously.

Presently the sorrow and anxiety of this disinterested friend took shape. He began in private, in conversations of two, to talk vaguely of bad habits and low habits. "I must say I'm afraid he's going wrong altogether," he would say. "I'll tell you plainly, and between ourselves, I scarcely like to stay there any longer; only, man, I'm positively afraid to leave him alone. You'll see, I shall be blamed for it later on. I'm staying at a great sacrifice. I'm hindering my chances at the Bar, and I can't blind my eyes to it. And what I'm afraid of is that I'm going to get kicked for it all round before all's done. You see, nobody believes in friendship nowadays."

"Well, Innes,' his interlocutor would reply, "it's very good of you, I must say that. If there's any blame going you'll always be sure of *my* good word, for one thing."

"Well," Frank would continue, "candidly, I don't say it's pleasant. He has a very rough way with him; his father's son, you know. I don't say he's rude—of course, I couldn't be expected to stand that—but he steers very near the wind. No, it's not pleasant; but I tell ye, man, in conscience I don't think it would be fair to leave him. Mind you, I don't say there's anything actually wrong. What I say is that I don't like the looks of it, man!" and he would press the arm of his momentary confidant.

In the early stages I am persuaded there was no malice. He talked but for the pleasure of airing himself. He was essentially glib, as becomes the young advocate, and essentially careless of the truth, which is the mark of the young ass; and so he talked at random. There was no particular bias, but that one which is indigenous and universal, to flatter himself and to please and interest the present friend. And by thus milling air out of his mouth, he had presently built up a presentation of Archie which was known and talked of in all corners of the county. Wherever there was a residential house and a walled garden, wherever there was a dwarfish castle and a park, wherever a quadruple cottage by the ruins of a peel-tower showed an old family going down, and wherever a handsome villa with a carriage approach and a shrubbery marked the coming up of a new one—probably on the wheels of machinery—Archie began to be regarded in the light of a dark, perhaps a vicious mystery, and the future developments of his career to be looked for with uneasiness and confidential whispering. He had done something disgraceful, my dear. What, was not precisely known, and that good kind young man, Mr. Innes, did his best to make light of it. But there it was. And Mr. Innes was very anxious about him now; he was really uneasy, my dear; he was positively wrecking his own prospects because he dared not leave him alone. How wholly we all lie at the mercy of a single prater, not needfully with any malign purpose! And if a man but talks of himself in the right spirit, refers to his virtuous actions by the way, and never applies to them the name of virtue, how easily his evidence is accepted in the court of public opinion!

All this while, however, there was a more poisonous ferment at work between the two lads, which came late indeed to the surface, but had modified and magnified their dissensions from the first. To an idle, shallow, easy-going customer like Frank, the smell of a mystery was attractive. It gave his mind something to play with, like a new toy to a child; and it took him on the weak side, for like many young men coming to the Bar, and before they have been tried and found wanting, he flattered himself he was a fellow of unusual quickness and penetration. They knew nothing of Sherlock Holmes in these days, but there was a good deal said of Talleyrand. And if you could have caught Frank off his guard, he would have confessed with a smirk. that, if he resembled any one, it was the Marquis de Talleyrand-Périgord. It was on the occasion of Archie's first absence that this interest took root. It was vastly deepened when Kirstie resented his curiosity at breakfast, and that same afternoon there occurred another scene which clinched the business. He was fishing Swingleburn, Archie accompanying him, when the latter looked at his watch.

"Well, good-bye," said he. "I have something to do. See you at dinner."

"Don't be in such a hurry," cries Frank. "Hold on till I get my rod up. I'll go with you; I'm sick of flogging this ditch."

And he began to reel up his line.

Archie stood speechless. He took a long while to recover his wits under this direct attack; but by the time he was ready with his answer, and the angle was almost packed up, he had become completely Weir, and the hanging face gloomed on his young shoulders. He spoke with a laboured composure, a laboured kindness even; but a child could see that his mind was made up.

"I beg your pardon, Innes; I don't want to be disagreeable, but let us understand one another from the beginning. When I want your company, I'll let you know."

"Oh!" cries Frank, "you don't want my company, don't you?"

"Apparently not just now," replied Archie. "I even indicated to you when I did, if you'll remember—and that was at dinner. If we two fellows are to live together pleasantly—and I see no reason why we should not—it can only be by respecting each other's privacy. If we begin intruding——"

"Oh, come! I'll take this at no man's hands. Is this the way you treat a guest and an old friend?" cried Innes.

"Just go home and think over what I said by yourself," continued Archie, "whether it's reasonable, or whether it's really offensive or not; and let's meet at dinner as though nothing had happened. I'll put it this way, if you like—that I know my own character, that I'm looking forward (with great pleasure, I assure you) to a long visit from you, and that I'm taking precautions at the first. I see the thing that we—that I, if you like—might fall out upon, and I step in and *obsto principiis*. I wager you five pounds you'll end by seeing that I mean friendliness, and I assure you, Francie, I do," he added, relenting.

Bursting with anger, but incapable of speech, Innes shouldered his rod, made a gesture of farewell, and strode off down the burn-side. Archie watched him go without moving. He was sorry, but quite unashamed. He hated to be inhospitable, but in one thing he was his father's son. He had a strong sense that his house was his own and no man else's; and to lie at a guest's mercy was what he refused. He hated to seem harsh. But that was Frank's look-out. If Frank had been commonly discreet, he would have been decently courteous. And there was another consideration. The secret he was protecting was not his own merely; it was hers; it belonged to that inexpressible she who was fast taking possession of his soul, and whom he would soon have defended at the cost of burning cities. By the time he had watched Frank as far as the Swingleburnfoot, appearing and disappearing in the tarnished heather, still stalking at a fierce gait but already dwindled in the distance into less than the smallness of Lilliput, he could afford to smile at the occurrence. Either Frank would go, and that would be a relief—or he would continue to stay, and his host must continue to endure him. And Archie was now free—by devious paths, behind hillocks and in the hollow of burns—to make for the trysting-place where Kirstie, cried about by the curlew and the plover, waited and burned for his coming by the Covenanter's stone.

Innes went off down-hill in a passion of resentment, easy to be understood, but which yielded progressively to the needs of his situation. He cursed Archie for a cold-hearted, unfriendly, rude dog; and himself still more passionately for a fool in having come to Hermiston when he might have sought refuge in almost any other house in Scotland, but the step once taken was practically irretrievable. He had no more ready money to go anywhere else; he would have to borrow from Archie the next club-night; and ill as he thought of his host's manners, he was sure of his practical generosity. Frank's resemblance of Talleyrand strikes me as imaginary; but at least not Talleyrand himself could have more obediently taken his lesson from the facts. He met Archie at dinner without resentment, almost with cordiality. You must take your friends as you find them, he would have said. Archie couldn't help being his father's son, or his grandfather's, the hypothetical weaver's, grandson. The son of a hunks, he was still a hunks at heart, incapable of true generosity and consideration; but he had other qualities with which Frank could divert himself in the meanwhile, and to enjoy which it was necessary that Frank should keep his temper.

So excellently was it controlled that he awoke next morning with his head full of a different, though a cognate subject. What was Archie's little game? Why did he shun Frank's company? What was he keeping secret? Was he keeping tryst with somebody, and was it a woman? It would be a good joke and a fair revenge to discover. To that task he set himself with a great deal of patience, which might have surprised his friends, for he had been always credited not with patience so much as brilliancy; and little by little, from one point to another, he at last succeeded in piecing out the situation. First he remarked that, although Archie set out in all the directions of the compass, he always came home again from some point between the south and west. From the study of a map, and in consideration of the great expanse of untenanted moorland running in that direction towards the sources of the Clyde, he laid his finger on Cauldstaneslap and two other neighbouring farms, Kingsmuirs and Polintarf. But it was difficult to advance farther. With his rod for a pretext, he vainly visited each of them in turn; nothing was to be seen suspicious about this trinity of moorland settlements. He would have tried to follow Archie, had it been the least possible, but the nature of the land precluded the idea. He did the next best, ensconced himself in a quiet corner, and pursued his movements with a telescope. It was equally in vain, and he soon wearied of his futile vigilance, left the telescope at home, and had almost given the matter up in despair, when, on the twenty-seventh day of his visit, he was suddenly confronted with the person whom he sought. The first

Sunday Kirstie had managed to stay away from kirk on some pretext of indisposition, which was more truly modesty; the pleasure of beholding Archie seeming too sacred, too vivid for that public place. On the two following Frank had himself been absent on some of his excursions among the neighbouring families. It was not until the fourth, accordingly, that Frank had occasion to set eyes on the enchantress. With the first look, all hesitation was over. She came with the Cauldstaneslap party; then she lived at Cauldstaneslap. Here was Archie's secret, here was the woman, and more than that—though I have need here of every manageable attenuation of language—with the first look, he had already entered himself as rival. It was a good deal in pique, it was a little in revenge, it was much in genuine admiration: the devil may decide the proportions; I cannot, and it is very likely that Frank could not.

"Mighty attractive milkmaid," he observed, on the way home.

"Who?" said Archie.

"O, the girl you're looking at—aren't you? Forward there on the road. She came attended by the rustic bard; presumably, therefore, belongs to his exalted family. The single objection! for the Four Black Brothers are awkward customers. If anything were to go wrong, Gib would gibber, and Clem would prove inclement; and Dand fly in danders, and Hob blow up in gobbets. It would be a Helliott of a business!"

"Very humourous, I am sure," said Archie.

"Well, I am trying to be so," said Frank. "It's none too easy in this place, and with your solemn society, my dear fellow. But confess that the milkmaid has found favour in your eyes or resign all claim to be a man of taste."

"It is no matter," returned Archie.

But the other continued to look at him, steadily and quizzically, and his colour slowly rose and deepened under the glance, until not impudence itself could have denied that he was blushing. And at this Archie lost some of his control. He changed his stick from one hand to the other, and—"O, for God's sake, don't be an ass!" he cried.

"Ass? That's the retort delicate without doubt," says Frank. "Beware of the homespun brothers, dear. If they come into the dance, you'll see who's an ass. Think now, if they only applied (say) a quarter as much talent as I have applied to the question of what

Mr. Archie does with his evening hours, and why he is so un-affectedly nasty when the subject's touched on——"

"You are touching on it now," interrupted Archie with a wince.

"Thank you. That was all I wanted, an articulate confession," said Frank.

"I beg to remind you——" began Archie.

But he was interrupted in turn. "My dear fellow, don't. It's quite needless. The subject's dead and buried."

And Frank began to talk hastily on other matters, an art in which he was an adept, for it was his gift to be fluent on anything or nothing. But although Archie had the grace or the timidity to suffer him to rattle on, he was by no means done with the subject. When he came home to dinner, he was greeted with a sly demand, how things were looking "Cauldstaneslap ways." Frank took his first glass of port out after dinner to the toast of Kirstie, and later in the evening he returned to the charge again.

"I say, Weir, you'll excuse me for returning again to this affair. I've been thinking it over, and I wish to beg you very seriously to be more careful. It's not a safe business. Not safe, my boy," says he.

"What?" said Archie.

"Well, it's your own fault if I must put a name on the thing; but really, as a friend, I cannot stand by and see you rushing head down into these dangers. My dear boy," said he, holding up a warning cigar, "consider what is to be the end of it?"

"The end of what?"—Archie, helpless with irritation, persisted in this dangerous and ungracious guard.

"Well, the end of the milkmaid; or, to speak more by the card, the end of Miss Christina Elliott of the Cauldstaneslap?"

"I assure you," Archie broke out, "this is all a figment of your imagination. There is nothing to be said against that young lady; you have no right to introduce her name into the conversation."

"I'll make a note of it," said Frank. "She shall henceforth be nameless, nameless, nameless, Grigalach! I make a note besides of your valuable testimony to her character. I only want to look at this thing as a man of the world. Admitted she's an angel—but, my good fellow, is she a lady?"

This was torture to Archie. "I beg your pardon," he said, struggling to be composed, "but because you have wormed yourself into my confidence——"

"O, come!" cried Frank. "Your confidence? It was rosy but un-consenting. Your confidence, indeed? Now, look! This is what I must say, Weir, for it concerns your safety and good character, and therefore my honour as your friend. You say I wormed myself into your confidence. Wormed is good. But what have I done? I have put two and two together, just as the parish will be doing to-morrow, and the whole of Tweeddale in two weeks, and the Black Brothers—well, I won't put a date on that; it will be a dark and stormy morning. Your secret, in other words, is poor Poll's. And I want to ask of you as a friend whether you like the prospect? There are two horns to your dilemma, and I must say for myself I should look mighty ruefully on either. Do you see yourself ex-plaining to the Four Black Brothers? or do you see yourself pre-senting the milkmaid to papa as the future lady of Hermiston? Do you? I tell you plainly, I don't."

Archie rose. "I will hear no more of this," he said in a trembling voice.

But Frank again held up his cigar. "Tell me one thing first. Tell me if this is not a friend's part that I am playing?"

"I believe you think it so," replied Archie. "I can go as far as that. I can do so much justice to your motives. But I will hear no more of it. I am going to bed."

"That's right, Weir," said Frank, heartily. "Go to bed and think over it; and, I say, man, don't forget your prayers! I don't often do the moral—don't go in for that sort of thing—but when I do there's one thing sure, that I mean it."

So Archie marched off to bed, and Frank sat alone by the table for another hour or so, smiling to himself richly. There was noth-ing vindictive in his nature; but, if revenge came in his way, it might as well be good, and the thought of Archie's pillow reflec-tions that night was indescribably sweet to him. He felt a pleasant sense of power. He looked down on Archie as on a very little boy whose strings he pulled—as on a horse whom he had backed and bridled by sheer power of intelligence, and whom he might ride to glory or the grave at pleasure. Which was it to be? He lingered along, relishing the details of schemes that he was too idle to pursue. Poor cork upon a torrent, he tasted that night the sweets of omnipotence, and brooded like a deity over the strands of that intrigue which was to shatter him before the summer waned.

8.   *A Nocturnal Visit*

KIRSTIE HAD MANY CAUSES OF DISTRESS. MORE AND MORE AS WE grow old—and yet more and more as we grow old and are women, frozen by the fear of age—we come to rely on the voice as the single outlet of the soul. Only thus, in the curtailment of our means, can we relieve the straitened cry of the passion within us; only thus, in the bitter and sensitive shyness of advancing years, can we maintain relations with those vivacious figures of the young that still show before us, and tend daily to become no more than the moving wall-paper of life. Talk is the last link, the last relation. But with the end of the conversation, when the voice stops and the bright face of the listener is turned away, solitude falls again on the bruised heart. Kirstie had lost her "cannie hour at e'en"; she could no more wander with Archie, a ghost, if you will, but a happy ghost, in fields Elysian. And to her it was as if the whole world had fallen silent; to him, but an unremarkable change of amusements. And she raged to know it. The effervescency of her passionate and irritable nature rose within her at times to bursting point.

This is the price paid by age for unseasonable ardours of feeling. It must have been so for Kirstie at any time when the occasion chanced; but it so fell out that she was deprived of this delight in the hour when she had most need of it, when she had most to say, most to ask, and when she trembled to recognise her sovereignty not merely in abeyance but annulled. For, with the clairvoyance of a genuine love, she had pierced the mystery that had so long embarrassed Frank. She was conscious, even before it was carried out, even on that Sunday night when it began, of an invasion of her rights; and a voice told her the invader's name. Since then, by arts, by accident, by small things observed, and by the general drift of Archie's humour, she had passed beyond all possibility of doubt. With a sense of justice that Lord Hermiston might have envied, she had that day in church considered and admitted the attractions of the younger Kirstie; and with the profound humanity and sentimentality of her nature, she had recognised the coming of fate. Not thus would she have chosen. She had seen, in imagination, Archie wedded to some tall, powerful, and rosy heroine of the golden locks, made in her own image, for whom she would have strewed the bride-bed with delight; and now she could have wept to see the ambition falsified. But the gods had pronounced, and her doom was otherwise.

She lay tossing in bed that night, besieged with feverish thoughts. There were dangerous matters pending, a battle was toward, over the fate of which she hung in jealousy, sympathy, fear, and alternate loyalty and disloyalty to either side. Now she was re-incarnated in her niece, and now in Archie. Now she saw, through the girl's eyes, the youth on his knees to her, heard his persuasive instances with a deadly weakness, and received his over-mastering caresses. Anon, with a revulsion, her temper raged to see such utmost favours of fortune and love squandered on a brat of a girl, one of her own house, using her own name—a deadly in-gredient—and that "didnae ken her ain mind an' was as black's your hat." Now she trembled lest her deity should plead in vain, loving the idea of success for him like a triumph of nature; anon, with returning loyalty to her own family and sex, she trembled for Kirstie and the credit of the Elliotts. And again she had a vision of herself, the day over for her old-world tales and local gossip, bidding farewell to her last link with life and brightness and love; and behind and beyond, she saw but the blank butt-end where she must crawl to die. Had she then come to the lees? she, so great, so beautiful, with a heart as fresh as a girl's and strong as woman-hood? It could not be, and yet it was so; and for a moment her bed was horrible to her as the sides of the grave. And she looked for-ward over a waste of hours, and saw herself go on to rage and tremble, and be softened, and rage again, until the day came and the labours of the day must be renewed.

Suddenly she heard feet on the stairs—his feet, and soon after the sound of a window-sash flung open. She sat up with her heart beating. He had gone to his room alone, and he had not gone to bed. She might again have one of her night cracks; and at the en-trancing prospect, a change came over her mind; with the approach of this hope of pleasure, all the baser metal became immediately obliterated from her thoughts. She rose, all woman, and all the best of woman, tender, pitiful, hating the wrong, loyal to her own sex—and all the weakest of that dear miscellany, nourishing, cher-ishing next her soft heart, voicelessly flattering, hopes that she would have died sooner than have acknowledged. She tore off her nightcap, and her hair fell about her shoulders in profusion.

Undying coquetry awoke. By the faint light of her nocturnal rush, she stood before the looking-glass, carried her shapely arms above her head, and gathered up the treasures of her tresses. She was never backward to admire herself; that kind of modesty was a stranger to her nature; and she paused, struck with a pleased wonder at the sight. "Ye daft auld wife!" she said, answering a thought that was not; and she blushed with the innocent consciousness of a child. Hastily she did up the massive and shining coils, hastily donned a wrapper, and with the rush-light in her hand, stole into the hall. Below stairs she heard the clock ticking the deliberate seconds, and Frank jingling with the decanters in the dining-room. Aversion rose in her, bitter and momentary. "Nesty, tippling puggy!" she thought; and the next moment she had knocked guardedly at Archie's door and was bidden enter.

Archie had been looking out into the ancient blackness, pierced here and there with a rayless star; taking the sweet air of the moors and the night into his bosom deeply; seeking, perhaps finding, peace after the manner of the unhappy. He turned round as she came in, and showed her a pale face against the window-frame.

"Is that you, Kirstie?" he asked. "Come in!"

"It's unco late, my dear," said Kirstie, affecting unwillingness.

"No, no," he answered, "not at all. Come in, if you want a crack. I am not sleepy, God knows."

She advanced, took a chair by the toilet table and the candle, and set the rush-light at her foot. Something—it might be in the comparative disorder of her dress, it might be the emotion that now welled in her bosom—had touched her with a wand of transformation, and she seemed young with the youth of goddesses.

"Mr. Erchie," she began, "what's this that's come to ye?"

"I am not aware of anything that has come," said Archie, and blushed and repented bitterly that he had let her in.

"Oh, my dear, that'll no dae!" said Kirstie. "It's ill to blind the eyes of love. Oh, Mr. Erchie, tak' a thocht ere it's ower late. Ye shouldnae be impatient o' the braws o' life, they'll a' come in their saison, like the sun and the rain. Ye're young yet; ye've mony cantie years afore ye. See and dinnae wreck yersel at the outset like sae mony ithers! Hae patience—they telled me aye that was the owercome o' life—hae patience, there's a braw day coming yet. Gude kens it never cam to me; and here I am wi' nayther man nor bairn to ca' my ain, wearying a' folks wi' my ill tongue, and you just the first, Mr. Erchie?"

"I have a difficulty in knowing what you mean," said Archie.

"Weel, and I'll tell ye," she said. "It's just this, that I'm feared. I'm feared for ye, my dear. Remember, your faither is a hard man, reaping where he hasnae sowed and gaithering where he hasnae strawed. It's easy speakin', but mind! Ye'll have to look in the gurly face o'm, where it's ill to look, and vain to look for mercy. Ye mind me o' a bonny ship pitten oot into the black and gowsty seas—ye're a' safe still sittin' quait and crackin' wi' Kirstie in your lown chalmer; but whaur will ye be the morn, and in whatten horror o' the fearsome tempest, cryin' on the hills to cover ye?"

"Why, Kirstie, you're very enigmatical tonight—and very eloquent," Archie put in.

"And, my dear Mr. Erchie," she continued, with a change of voice, "ye mauna think that I canna sympathise wi' ye. Ye mauna think that I havena been young mysel'. Langsyne, when I was a bit lassie, no twenty yet——" She paused and sighed. "Clean and caller, wi' a fit like the hinney bee," she continued. "I was aye big and buirdly, ye maun understand; a bonny figure o' a woman, though I say it that suldna—built to rear bairns—brak bairns they suld hae been, and grand I would hae likit it! But I was young, dear, wi' the bonny glint o' youth in my e'en, and little I dreamed I'd ever be tellin' ye this, an auld, lanely, rudas wife! Weel, Mr. Erchie, there was a lad cam' courtin' me, as was but naetural. Mony had come before, and I would nane o' them. But this yin had a tongue to wile the birds frae the lift and the bees frae the fox-glove bells. Deary me, but it's lang syne. Folk have deed sinsyne and been buried, and are forgotten, and bairns been born and got merrit and got bairns o' their ain. Sinsyne woods have been plantit, and have grown up and are bonny trees, and the joes sit in their shadow, and sinsyne auld estates have changed hands, and there have been wars and rumours of wars on the face of the earth. And here I'm still—like an auld droopit craw—lookin' on and craikin'? But, Mr. Erchie, do ye no think that I have mind o' it a' still? I was dwalling then in my faither's house; and it's a curious thing that we were whiles trysted in the Deil's Hags. And do ye no think that I have mind of the bonny simmer days, the lang miles, o' the bluid-red heather, the cryin' o' the whaups, and the lad and the lassie that was trysted? Do ye no think that I mind how the hilly sweetness ran about my hairt? Ay, Mr. Erchie, I ken the way o' it—fine do I ken the way—how the grace o' God takes them like Paul of Tarsus, when they think o' it least, and drives the pair o' them into a land which is like a dream, and the world and the folks in't are nae mair than clouds to the puir lassie, and Heeven nae mair than windle-straes, if she can but pleesure him! Until Tam deed—that was my story," she broke off to say, "he deed, and I wasna at the buryin'. But while he was here, I could take care o' mysel'. And can yon puir lassie?"

Kirstie, her eyes shining with unshed tears, stretched out her hand towards him appealingly; the bright and the dull gold of her hair flashed and smouldered in the coils behind her comely head, like the rays of an eternal youth; the pure colour had risen in her face; and Archie was abashed alike by her beauty and her story. He came towards her slowly from the window, took up her hand in his and kissed it.

"Kirstie," he said hoarsely, "you have misjudged me sorely. I have always thought of her, I wouldna harm her for the universe, my woman."

"Eh, lad, and that's easy sayin'," cried Kirstie, "but it's nane sae easy doin'! Man, do ye no comprehend that it's God's wull we should be blendit and glamoured, and have nae command over our ain members at a time like that? My bairn," she cried, still holding his hand, "think o' the puir lass! have pity upon her, Erchie! and O, be wise for twa! Think o' the risk she rins! I have seen ye, and what's to prevent ithers? I saw ye once in the Hags, in my ain howi, and I was wae to see ye there—in pairt for the omen, for I think there's a weird on the place—and in pairt for puir nakit envy and bitterness o' hairt. It's strange ye should forgather there tae! God! but yon puir, thrawn, auld Covenanter's seen a heap o' human natur since he lookit his last on the musket barrels, if he never saw nane afore," she added with a kind of wonder in her eyes.

"I swear by my honour I have done her no wrong," said Archie. "I swear by my honour and the redemption of my soul that there shall none be done her. I have heard of this before. I have been foolish, Kirstie, not unkind and, above all, not base."

"There's my bairn!" said Kirstie, rising. "I'll can trust ye noo, I'll can gang to my bed wi' an easy hairt." And then she saw in a flash

how barren had been her triumph. Archie had promised to spare
the girl, and he would keep it; but who had promised to spare
Archie? What was to be the end of it? Over a maze of difficulties
she glanced, and saw, at the end of every passage, the flinty
countenance of Hermiston. And a kind of horror fell upon her at
what she had done. She wore a tragic mask. "Erchie, the Lord peety
you, dear, and peety me! I have buildit on this foundation,"—
laying her hand heavily on his shoulder—"and buildit hie, and pit
my hairt in the buildin' of it. If the hale hypothec were to fa', I
think, laddie, I would dee! Excuse a daft wife that loves ye, and
that kenned your mither. And for His name's sake keep yersel' frae
inordinate desires; haud your heart in baith your hands, carry it
canny and laigh; dinna send it up like a bairn's kite into the collieshangie o' the wunds? Mind, Maister Erchie dear, that this life's
a disappointment, and a mouthfu' o' mools is the appointed end."

"Ay, but, Kirstie, my woman, you're asking me ower much at
last," said Archie, profoundly moved, and lapsing into the broad
Scots. "Ye're asking what nae man can grant ye, what only the
Lord of heaven can grant ye if He see fit. Ay! And can even he? I
can promise ye what I shall do, and you can depend on that. But
how I shall feel—my woman, that is long past thinking of!"

They were both standing by now opposite each other. The face
of Archie wore the wretched semblance of a smile; hers was convulsed for a moment.

"Promise me ae thing," she cried, in a sharp voice. "Promise me
ye'll never do naething without telling me."

"No, Kirstie, I canna promise ye that," he replied. "I have
promised enough, God kens!"

"May the blessing of God lift and rest upon ye, dear!" she said.

"God bless ye, my old friend," said he.

9. *At the Weaver's Stone*

IT WAS LATE IN THE AFTERNOON WHEN ARCHIE DREW NEAR BY THE
hill path to the Praying Weaver's Stone. The Hags were in
shadow. But still, through the gate of the Slap, the sun shot a last
arrow, which spread far and straight across the surface of the moss,
here and there touching and shining on a tussock, and lighted at
length on the gravestone and the small figure awaiting him there.

The emptiness and solitude of the great moors seemed to be con-
centred there, and Kirstie pointed out by that figure of sunshine
for the only inhabitant. His first sight of her was thus excruci-
atingly sad, like a glimpse of a world from which all light, comfort,
and society were on the point of vanishing. And the next moment,
when she had turned her face to him and the quick smile had enlightened it, the whole face of nature smiled upon him in her
smile of welcome. Archie's slow pace was quickened; his legs
hasted to her though his heart was hanging back. The girl, upon
her side, drew herself together slowly and stood up, expectant;
she was all langour, her face was gone white; her arms ached for
him, her soul was on tiptoes. But he deceived her, pausing a few
steps away, not less white than herself, and holding up his hand
with a gesture of denial.

"No, Christina, not to-day," he said. "To-day I have to talk to
you seriously. Sit ye down, please, there where you were. Please!"
he repeated.

The revulsion of feeling in Christina's heart was violent. To
have longed and waited these weary hours for him, rehearsing her
endearments—to have seen him at last come—to have been ready
there, breathless, wholly passive, his to do what he would with—
and suddenly to have found herself confronted with a grey-faced,
harsh schoolmaster—it was too rude a shock. She could have wept,
but pride withheld her. She sat down on the stone, from which
she had arisen, part with the instinct of obedience, part as though
she had been thrust there. What was this? Why was she rejected?
Had she ceased to please? She stood here offering her wares, and he
would none of them! And yet they were all his! His to take and
keep, not his to refuse though! In her quick petulant nature, a
moment ago on fire with hope, thwarted love and wounded vanity
wrought. The schoolmaster that there is in all men, to the despair
of all girls and most women, was now completely in possession of
Archie. He had passed a night of sermons; a day of reflection; he
had come wound up to do his duty; and the set mouth, which in
him only betrayed the effort of his will, to her seemed the expression of an averted heart. It was the same with his constrained
voice and embarrassed utterance; and if so—if it was all over—the
pang of the thought took away from her the power of thinking.

He stood before her some way off. "Kirstie, there's been too
much of this. We've seen too much of each other." She looked up

quickly and her eyes contracted. "There's no good ever comes of these secret meetings. They're not frank, not honest truly, and I ought to have seen it. People have begun to talk; and it's not right of me. Do you see?"

"I see somebody will have been talking to ye," she said sullenly.

"They have, more than one of them," replied Archie.

"And whae were they?" she cried. "And what kind o' love do ye ca' that, that's ready to gang round like a whirligig at folk talking? Do ye think they havena talked to me?"

"Have they indeed?" said Archie, with a quick breath. "That is what I feared. Who were they? Who has dared——"

Archie was on the point of losing his temper.

As a matter of fact, not any one had talked to Christina on the matter; and she strenuously repeated her own first question in a panic of self-defence.

"Ah, well! what does it matter?" he said. "They were good folk that wished well to us, and the great affair is that there are people talking. My dear girl, we have to be wise. We must not wreck our lives at the outset. They may be long and happy yet, and we must see to it, Kirstie, like God's rational creatures and not like fool children. There is one thing we must see to before all. You're worth waiting for, Kirstie! worth waiting for a generation; it would be enough reward."—And here he remembered the schoolmaster again, and very unwisely took to following wisdom. "The first thing that we must see to, is that there shall be no scandal about for my father's sake. That would ruin all; do ye no see that?"

Kirstie was a little pleased, there had been some show of warmth of sentiment in what Archie had said last. But the dull irritation still persisted in her bosom; with the aboriginal instinct, having suffered herself, she wished to make Archie suffer.

And besides, there had come out the word she had always feared to hear from his lips, the name of his father. It is not to be supposed that, during so many days with a love avowed between them, some reference had not been made to their conjoint future. It had in fact been often touched upon, and from the first had been the sore point. Kirstie had wilfully closed the eye of thought; she would not argue even with herself; gallant, desperate little heart, she had accepted the command of that supreme attraction like the call of fate and marched blindfold on her doom. But Archie, with his masculine sense of responsibility, must reason; he must dwell on some future good, when the present good was all in all to Kirstie; he must talk—and talk lamely, as necessity drove him—of what was to be. Again and again he had touched on marriage; again and again been driven back into indistinctness by a memory of Lord Hermiston. And Kirstie had been swift to understand and quick to choke down and smother the understanding; swift to leap up in flame at a mention of that hope, which spoke volumes to her vanity and her love, that she might one day be Mrs. Weir of Hermiston; swift, also, to recognise in his stumbling or throttled utterance the death-knell of these expectations, and constant, poor girl! in her large-minded madness, to go on and to reck nothing of the future. But these unfinished references, these blinks in which his heart spoke, and his memory and reason rose up to silence it before the words were well uttered, gave her unqualifiable agony. She was raised up and dashed down again bleeding. The recurrence of the subject forced her, for however short a time, to open her eyes on which she did not wish to see; and it had invariably ended in another disappointment. So now again, at the mere wind of its coming, at the mere mention of his father's name—who might seem indeed to have accompanied them in their whole moorland courtship, an awful figure in a wig with an ironical and bitter smile, present to guilty consciousness—she fled from it head down.

"Ye havena told me yet," she said, "who was it spoke?"

"Your aunt for one," said Archie.

"Auntie Kirstie?" she cried. "And what do I care for my auntie Kirstie?"

"She cares a great deal for her niece," replied Archie, in kind reproof.

"Troth, and it's the first I've heard of it," retorted the girl.

"The question here is not who it is, but what they say, what they have noticed," pursued the lucid schoolmaster. "That is what we have to think of in self-defence."

"Auntie Kirstie, indeed! A bitter, thrawn auld maid that's fomented trouble in the country before I was born, and will be doing it still, I daur say, when I'm deid! It's in her nature; it's as natural for her as it's for a sheep to eat."

"Pardon me, Kirstie, she was not the only one," interposed Archie. "I had two warnings, two sermons, last night, both most kind and considerate. Had you been there, I promise you you would have grat, my dear! And they opened my eyes. I saw we were going a wrong way."

"Who was the other one?" Kirstie demanded.

By this time Archie was in the condition of a hunted beast. He had come, braced and resolute; he was to trace out a line of conduct for the pair of them in a few cold, convincing sentences; he had now been there some time, and he was still staggering round the outworks and undergoing what he felt to be a savage cross-examination.

"Mr. Frank!" she cried. "What nex', I would like to ken?"

"He spoke most kindly and truly."

"What like did he say?"

"I am not going to tell you; you have nothing to do with that," cried Archie, startled to find he had admitted so much.

"O, I have naething to do with it!" she repeated, springing to her feet. "A'body at Hermiston's free to pass their opinions upon me, but I have naething to do wi' it! Was this at prayers like? Did ye ca' the grieve into the consultation? Little wonder if a'body's talking, when ye make a'body ye're confidants! But as you say, Mr. Weir—most kindly, most considerately, most truly, I'm sure—I have naething to do with it. And I think I'll better be going. I'll be wishing you good-evening, Mr. Weir." And she made him a stately curtsey, shaking as she did so from head to foot, with the barren ecstasy of temper.

Poor Archie stood dumfounded. She had moved some steps away from him before he recovered the gift of articulate speech.

"Kirstie!" he cried. "O, Kirstie woman!"

There was in his voice a ring of appeal, a clang of mere astonishment that showed the schoolmaster was vanquished.

She turned round on him. "What do ye Kirstie me for?" she retorted. "What have ye to do wi' me? Gang to your ain freends and deave them!"

He could only repeat the appealing "Kirstie!"

"Kirstie, indeed!" cried the girl, her eyes blazing in her white face. "My name is Miss Christina Elliott, I would have ye to ken, and I daur ye to ca' me out of it. If I canna get love, I'll have respect, Mr. Weir. I'm come of decent people, and I'll have respect. What have I done that ye should lightly me? What have I done? What have I done? O, what have I done?" and her voice rose upon the third repetition. "I thocht—I thocht—I thocht I was sae happy!" and the first sob broke from her like the paroxysm of some mortal sickness.

Archie ran to her. He took the poor child in his arms, and she nestled to his breast as to a mother's, and clasped him in hands that were strong like vices. He felt her whole body shaken by the throes of distress, and had pity upon her beyond speech. Pity, and at the same time a bewildered fear of this explosive engine in his arms, whose works he did not understand, and yet had been tampering with. There arose from before him the curtains of boyhood, and he saw for the first time the ambiguous face of woman as she is. In vain he looked back over the interview; he saw not where he had offended. It seemed unprovoked, a wilful convulsion of brute nature. . . .

The last words of the incomplete novel, *Weir of Hermiston*, were written on the day of Robert Louis Stevenson's death, December 3, 1894.—Ed.

GLOSSARY

al, *one*

antinomian, *one of a sect which holds that under the Gospel dispensation the moral law is not obligatory.*

Auld Hornie, *the Devil.*

ballant, *ballad.*
bauchles, *brogues, old shoes.*
bees in their bonnet, *fads.*
birling, *whirling.*
black-a-vised, *dark-complexioned.*
bonnet-laird, *small landed proprietor.*
bool, *ball.*
brae, *rising ground.*
butt end, *end of a cottage.*
byre, *cow-house.*

ca', *drive.*
caller, *fresh.*
canna, *cannot.*
canny, *careful, shrewd.*
cantie, *cheerful.*
carline, *an old woman.*
chalmer, *chamber.*
claes, *clothes.*
clamjamfry, *crowd.*
clavers, *idle talk.*
cock-laird, *a yeoman.*
collieshangie, *turmoil.*
crack, *to converse.*
cuddy, *donkey.*
cuist, *cast.*
cutty, *slut.*

daft, *mad, frolicsome.*
dander, *to saunter.*
danders, *cinders.*

daurna, *dare not.*
deave, *to deafen.*
demmy brokens, *demi-broquins.*
dirdum, *vigour.*
disjaskit, *worn out, disreputable-look-ing.*
doer, *law agent.*
dour, *hard.*
drumlie, *dark.*
dule-tree, *the tree of lamentation, the hanging tree*: dule *is also Scots for boundary, and it may mean the boundary tree, the tree on which the baron hung interlopers.*
dunting, *knocking.*
dwaibly, *infirm, rickety.*

earrand, *errand.*
ettercap, *vixen.*

fetching, *fighting.*
feck, *quantity, portion.*
feckless, *feeble, powerless.*
fell, *strong and fiery.*
fey, *unlike yourself, strange, as persons are observed to be in the hour of ap-proaching death or disaster.*
fit, *foot.*
flyped, *turned up, turned inside out.*
forgather, *to fall in with.*
fule, *fool.*
füshionless, *pithless, weak.*
fyle, *to soil, to defile.*
fylement, *obloquy, defilement.*

gaed, *went.*
gey an', *very.*

gigot, *leg of mutton.*

girzie, *lit. diminutive of Grizel, here a playful nickname.*

glaur, *mud.*

glint, *glance, sparkle.*

gloaming, *twilight.*

glower, *to scowl.*

gobbets, *small lumps.*

gowden, *golden.*

gowsty, *gusty.*

grat, *wept.*

grieve, *land-steward.*

guddle, *to catch fish with the hands by groping under the stones or banks.*

guid, *good.*

gumption, *common sense, judgment.*

gurley, *stormy, surly.*

gyte, *beside itself.*

haddit, *held.*

hae, *have, take.*

hale, *whole.*

heels-ower-hurdie, *heels over head.*

hinney, *honey.*

hirstle, *to bustle.*

hizzie, *wench.*

howl, *hovel.*

hunkered, *crouched.*

hypothec, *lit. a term in Scots law meaning the security given by a tenant to a landlord, as furniture, produce, etc.; by metonymy and colloquially, "the whole structure," "the whole affair."*

idleset, *idleness.*

infeftment, *a term in Scots law originally synonymous with investiture.*

jelly-piece, *a slice of bread and jelly.*

jennipers, *juniper.*

jo, *sweetheart.*

justifeed, *executed, made the victim of justice.*

jyle, *jail.*

kebbuck, *cheese.*

ken, *to know.*

kenspeckle, *conspicuous.*

kilted, *tucked up.*

kyte, *belly.*

laigh, *low.*

laird, *landed proprietor.*

lane, *alone.*

lave, *rest, remainder.*

lown, *lonely, still.*

lynn, *cataract.*

macers, *officers of the court* [cf. *Guy Mannering,* last chapter].

maun, *must.*

menseful, *of good manners.*

mirk, *dark.*

misbegowk, *deception, disappointment.*

mools, *mould, earth.*

muckle, *much, great, big.*

my lane, *by myself.*

nowt, *black cattle.*

palmering, *walking infirmly.*

panel, *in Scots law, the accused person in a criminal action, the prisoner.*

peel, *a fortified watch-tower.*

plew-stilts, *plough-handles.*

policy, *ornamental grounds of a country mansion.*

puddock, *frog.*

quean, *wench.*

riffraff, *rabble.*

risping, *grating.*

rowt, *to roar, to rant.*

rowth, *abundance.*

rudas, *haggard old woman.*

runt, *an old cow past breeding; opprobriously, an old woman.*

sab, *sob.*

sanguishes, *sandwiches.*

sasine, *in Scots law, the act of giving legal possession of feudal property, or, colloquially, the deed by which that possession is proved.*

sclamber, *to scramble.*

sculduddery, *impropriety, grossness.*

session, *the Court of Session, the supreme court of Scotland.*

shauchling, *shuffling.*

shoo, *to chase gently.*

siller, *money.*

sinsyne, *since then.*

skailing, *dispersing.*

skelp, *slap.*

skirling, *screaming.*

skreigh-o'-day, *daybreak.*

snash, *abuse.*

sneisty, *supercilious.*

sooth, *to hum.*
speir, *to ask.*
speldering, *sprawling.*
splairge, *to splash.*
spunk, *spirit, fire.*
steik, *to shut.*
sugar-bool, *sugar-plum.*

tawpie, *a slow, foolish slut.*
telling you, *a good thing for you.*
thir, *these.*
thrawn, *cross-grained.*
toon, *town.*
two-names, *local sobriquets in addition to patronymic.*
tyke, *dog.*

unchancy, *unlucky.*
unco, *strange, extraordinary, very.*
upsitten, *impertinent.*

vivers, *victuals.*

waling, *choosing.*
warrandise, *warranty.*
waur, *worse.*
weird, *destiny.*
whammle, *to upset.*
whaup, *curlew.*
windlestrae, *crested dog's tail grass.*

yin, *one.*

SHORT
STORIES

Strange Case of Dr. Jekyll and Mr. Hyde

To Katharine De Mattos

It's ill to loose the bands that God decreed to bind;
Still will we be the children of the heather and the wind.
Far away from home, O it's still for you and me
That the broom is blowing bonnie in the north countrie.

Story of the Door

MR. UTTERSON THE LAWYER WAS A MAN OF A RUGGED COUNTE-
nance, that was never lighted by a smile; cold, scanty, and
embarrassed in discourse; backward in sentiment; lean, long,
dusty, dreary, and yet somehow lovable. At friendly meetings, and
when the wine was to his taste, something eminently human
beaconed from his eye; something indeed which never found its
way into his talk, but which spoke not only in these silent symbols
of the after-dinner face, but more often and loudly in the acts of
his life. He was austere with himself; drank gin when he was
alone, to mortify a taste for vintages; and though he enjoyed the
theatre, had not crossed the doors of one for twenty years. But he
had an approved tolerance for others; sometimes wondering, almost with envy, at the high pressure of spirits involved in their
misdeeds; and in any extremity inclined to help rather than to
reprove. "I incline to Cain's heresy," he used to say quaintly: "I let
my brother go to the devil in his own way." In this character, it
was frequently his fortune to be the last reputable acquaintance
and the last good influence in the lives of down-going men. And
to such as these, so long as they came about his chambers, he never
marked a shade of change in his demeanour.

No doubt the feat was easy to Mr. Utterson; for he was un-demonstrative at the best, and even his friendship seemed to be founded in a similar catholicity of good-nature. It is the mark of a modest man to accept his friendly circle ready-made from the hands of opportunity; and that was the lawyer's way. His friends were those of his own blood or those whom he had known the longest; his affections, like ivy, were the growth of time, they implied no aptness in the object. Hence, no doubt, the bond that united him to Mr. Richard Enfield, his distant kinsman, the well-known man about town. It was a nut to crack for many, what these two could see in each other, or what subject they could find in common. It was reported by those who encountered them in their Sunday walks, that they said nothing, looked singularly dull, and would hail with obvious relief the appearance of a friend. For all that, the two men put the greatest store by these excursions, counted them the chief jewel of each week, and not only set aside occasions of pleasure, but even resisted the calls of business, that they might enjoy them uninterrupted.

It chanced on one of these rambles that their way led them down a by-street in a busy quarter of London. The street was small and what is called quiet, but it drove a thriving trade on the week-days. The inhabitants were all doing well, it seemed, and all emulously hoping to do better still, and laying out the surplus of their gains in coquetry; so that the shop fronts stood along that thoroughfare with an air of invitation, like rows of smiling saleswomen. Even on Sunday, when it veiled its more florid charms and lay comparatively empty of passage, the street shone out in contrast to its dingy neighbourhood, like a fire in a forest; and with its freshly painted shutters, well-polished brasses, and general cleanliness and gaiety of note, instantly caught and pleased the eye of the passenger.

Two doors from one corner, on the left hand going east, the line was broken by the entry of a court; and just at that point, a certain sinister block of building thrust forward its gable on the street. It was two storeys high; showed no window, nothing but a door on the lower storey and a blind forehead of discoloured wall on the upper; and bore in every feature the marks of prolonged and sordid negligence. The door, which was equipped with neither bell nor knocker, was blistered and distained. Tramps slouched into the recess and struck matches on the panels; children kept shop upon the steps; the schoolboy had tried his knife on the mouldings; and for close on a generation, no one had appeared to drive away these random visitors or to repair their ravages.

Mr. Enfield and the lawyer were on the other side of the by-street; but when they came abreast of the entry, the former lifted up his cane and pointed.

"Did you ever remark that door?" he asked; and when his companion had replied in the affirmative, "It is connected in my mind," added he, "with a very odd story."

"Indeed?" said Mr. Utterson, with a slight change of voice, "and what was that?"

"Well, it was this way," returned Mr. Enfield: "I was coming home from some place at the end of the world, about three o'clock of a black winter morning, and my way lay through a part of town where there was literally nothing to be seen but lamps. Street after street, and all the folks asleep—street after street, all lighted up as if for a procession and all as empty as a church—till at last I got into that state of mind when a man listens and listens and begins to long for the sight of a policeman. All at once, I saw two figures: one a little man who was stumping along eastward at a good walk, and the other a girl of maybe eight or ten who was running as hard as she was able down a cross street. Well, sir, the two ran into one another naturally enough at the corner; and then came the horrible part of the thing; for the man trampled calmly over the child's body and left her screaming on the ground. It sounds nothing to hear, but it was hellish to see. It wasn't like a man; it was like some damned Juggernaut. I gave a view halloa, took to my heels, collared my gentleman, and brought him back to where there was already quite a group about the screaming child. He was perfectly cool and made no resistance, but gave me one look, so ugly that it brought out the sweat on me like running. The people who had turned out were the girl's own family; and pretty soon, the doctor, for whom she had been sent, put in his appearance. Well, the child was not much the worse, more frightened, according to the Sawbones; and there you might have supposed would be an end to it. But there was one curious circumstance. I had taken a loathing to my gentleman at first sight. So had the child's family, which was only natural. But the doctor's case was what struck me. He was the usual cut-and-dry apothecary, of no particular age and colour, with a strong Edinburgh accent,

and about as emotional as a bagpipe. Well, sir, he was like the
rest of us; every time he looked at my prisoner, I saw that Sawbones turn sick and white with the desire to kill him. I knew what
was in his mind, just as he knew what was in mine; and killing
being out of the question, we did the next best. We told the man
we could and would make such a scandal out of this, as should
make his name stink from one end of London to the other. If he
had any friends or any credit, we undertook that he should lose
them. And all the time, as we were pitching it in red hot, we were
keeping the women off him as best we could, for they were as
wild as harpies. I never saw a circle of such hateful faces; and
there was the man in the middle, with a kind of black, sneering
coolness—frightened too, I could see that—but carrying it off, sir,
really like Satan. 'If you choose to make capital out of this accident,' said he, 'I am naturally helpless. No gentleman but wishes
to avoid a scene,' says he. 'Name your figure.' Well, we screwed him
up to a hundred pounds for the child's family; he would have
clearly liked to stick out; but there was something about the lot
of us that meant mischief, and at last he struck. The next thing
was to get the money; and where do you think he carried us but
to that place with the door?—whipped out a key, went in, and
presently came back with the matter of ten pounds in gold and a
cheque for the balance on Coutts's, drawn payable to bearer and
signed with a name that I can't mention, though it's one of the
points of my story, but it was a name at least very well known and
often printed. The figure was stiff; but the signature was good for
more than that, if it was only genuine. I took the liberty of pointing out to my gentleman that the whole business looked apocry-
phal, and that a man does not, in real life, walk into a cellar door
at four in the morning and come out of it with another man's
cheque for close upon a hundred pounds. But he was quite easy
and sneering. 'Set your mind at rest,' says he, 'I will stay with you
till the banks open and cash the cheque myself.' So we all set off,
the doctor, and the child's father, and our friend and myself, and
passed the rest of the night in my chambers; and next day, when we
had breakfasted, went in a body to the bank. I gave in the cheque
myself, and said I had every reason to believe it was a forgery. Not
a bit of it. The cheque was genuine."

"Tut-tut," said Mr. Utterson.

"I see you feel as I do," said Mr. Enfield. "Yes, it's a bad story. For my man was a fellow that nobody could have to do with, a really damnable man; and the person that drew the cheque is the very pink of the proprieties, celebrated too, and (what makes it worse) one of your fellows who do what they call good. Black mail, I suppose; an honest man paying through the nose for some of the capers of his youth. Black Mail House is what I call that place with the door, in consequence. Though even that, you know, is far from explaining all," he added, and with the words fell into a vein of musing.

From this he was recalled by Mr. Utterson asking rather suddenly: "And you don't know if the drawer of the cheque lives there?"

"A likely place, isn't it?" returned Mr. Enfield. "But I happen to have noticed his address; he lives in some square or other."

"And you never asked about the—place with the door?" said Mr. Utterson.

"No, sir: I had a delicacy," was the reply. "I feel very strongly about putting questions; it partakes too much of the style of the day of judgment. You start a question, and it's like starting a stone. You sit quietly on the top of a hill; and away the stone goes, starting others; and presently some bland old bird (the last you would have thought of) is knocked on the head in his own back garden and the family have to change their name. No, sir, I make it a rule of mine: the more it looks like Queer Street, the less I ask."

"A very good rule, too," said the lawyer.

"But I have studied the place for myself," continued Mr. Enfield. "It seems scarcely a house. There is no other door, and nobody goes in or out of that one but, once in a great while, the gentleman of my adventure. There are three windows looking on the court on the first floor; none below; the windows are always shut, but they're clean. And then there is a chimney which is generally smoking; so somebody must live there. And yet it's not so sure; for the buildings are so packed together about that court, that it's hard to say where one ends and another begins."

The pair walked on again for awhile in silence; and then "Enfield," said Mr. Utterson, "that's a good rule of yours."

"Yes, I think it is," returned Enfield.

"But for all that," continued the lawyer, "there's one point I want to ask: I want to ask the name of that man who walked over the child."

"Well," said Mr. Enfield, "I can't see what harm it would do. It was a man of the name of Hyde."

"H'm," said Mr. Utterson. "What sort of a man is he to see?"

"He is not easy to describe. There is something wrong with his appearance; something displeasing, something downright detestable. I never saw a man I so disliked, and yet I scarce know why. He must be deformed somewhere; he gives a strong feeling of deformity, although I couldn't specify the point. He's an extraordinary looking man, and yet I really can name nothing out of the way. No, sir; I can make no hand of it; I can't describe him. And it's not want of memory; for I declare I can see him this moment."

Mr. Utterson again walked some way in silence and obviously under a weight of consideration. "You are sure he used a key?" he inquired at last.

"My dear sir . . ." began Enfield, surprised out of himself.

"Yes, I know," said Utterson; "I know it must seem strange. The fact is, if I do not ask you the name of the other party, it is because I know it already. You see, Richard, your tale has gone home. If you have been inexact in any point, you had better correct it."

"I think you might have warned me," returned the other with a touch of sullenness. "But I have been pedantically exact, as you call it. The fellow had a key; and what's more, he has it still. I saw him use it, not a week ago."

Mr. Utterson sighed deeply but said never a word; and the young man presently resumed. "Here is another lesson to say nothing," said he. "I am ashamed of my long tongue. Let us make a bargain never to refer to this again."

"With all my heart," said the lawyer. "I shake hands on that, Richard."

Search for Mr. Hyde

That evening Mr. Utterson came home to his bachelor house in sombre spirits and sat down to dinner without relish. It was his

custom of a Sunday, when this meal was over, to sit close by the
fire, a volume of some dry divinity on his reading-desk, until the
clock of the neighbouring church rang out the hour of twelve,
when he would go soberly and gratefully to bed. On this night,
however, as soon as the cloth was taken away, he took up a candle
and went into his business room. There he opened his safe, took
from the most private part of it a document endorsed on the envelope as Dr. Jekyll's Will, and sat down with a clouded brow
to study its contents. The will was holograph, for Mr. Utterson,
though he took charge of it now that it was made, had refused to
lend the least assistance in the making of it; it provided not only
that, in case of the decease of Henry Jekyll, M.D., D.C.L., LL.D.,
F.R.S., etc., all his possessions were to pass into the hands of his
"friend and benefactor Edward Hyde," but that in case of Dr.
Jekyll's "disappearance or unexplained absence for any period exceeding three calendar months," the said Edward Hyde should step
into the said Henry Jekyll's shoes without further delay and free
from any burthen or obligation, beyond the payment of a few
small sums to the members of the doctor's household. This document had long been the lawyer's eyesore. It offended him both as
a lawyer and as a lover of the sane and customary sides of life, to
whom the fanciful was the immodest. And hitherto it was his ignorance of Mr. Hyde that had swelled his indignation; now, by a
sudden turn, it was his knowledge. It was already bad enough
when the name was but a name of which he could learn no more.
It was worse when it began to be clothed upon with detestable attributes; and out of the shifting, insubstantial mists that had so
long baffled his eye, there leaped up the sudden, definite present-
ment of a fiend.

"I thought it was madness," he said, as he replaced the obnoxious paper in the safe, "and now I begin to fear it is disgrace."

With that he blew out his candle, put on a great-coat, and set
forth in the direction of Cavendish Square, that citadel of medicine, where his friend, the great Dr. Lanyon, had his house and
received his crowding patients. "If any one knows, it will be Lanyon," he had thought.

The solemn butler knew and welcomed him; he was subjected
to no stage of delay, but ushered direct from the door to the
dining-room where Dr. Lanyon sat alone over his wine. This was a
hearty, healthy, dapper, red-faced gentleman, with a shock of hair

prematurely white, and a boisterous and decided manner. At sight of Mr. Utterson, he sprang up from his chair and welcomed him with both hands. The geniality, as was the way of the man, was somewhat theatrical to the eye; but it reposed on genuine feeling. For these two were old friends, old mates both at school and college, both thorough respecters of themselves and of each other, and, what does not always follow, men who thoroughly enjoyed each other's company.

After a little rambling talk, the lawyer led up to the subject which so disagreeably preoccupied his mind.

"I suppose, Lanyon," said he, "you and I must be the two oldest friends that Henry Jekyll has?"

"I wish the friends were younger," chuckled Dr. Lanyon. "But I suppose we are. And what of that? I see little of him now."

"Indeed?" said Utterson. "I thought you had a bond of common interest."

"We had," was the reply. "But it is more than ten years since Henry Jekyll became too fanciful for me. He began to go wrong, wrong in mind; and though of course I continue to take an interest in him for old sake's sake, as they say, I see and I have seen devilish little of the man. Such unscientific balderdash," added the doctor, flushing suddenly purple, "would have estranged Damon and Pythias."

This little spirit of temper was somewhat of a relief to Mr. Utterson. "They have only differed on some point of science," he thought; and being a man of no scientific passions (except in the matter of conveyancing), he even added: "It is nothing worse than that!" He gave his friend a few seconds to recover his composure, and then approached the question he had come to put. "Did you ever come across a protégé of his—one Hyde?" he asked.

"Hyde?" repeated Lanyon. "No. Never heard of him. Since my time."

That was the amount of information that the lawyer carried back with him to the great, dark bed on which he tossed to and fro, until the small hours of the morning began to grow large. It was a night of little ease to his toiling mind, toiling in mere darkness and besieged by questions.

Six o'clock struck on the bells of the church that was so conveniently near to Mr. Utterson's dwelling, and still he was digging at the problem. Hitherto it had touched him on the intellectual side alone; but now his imagination also was engaged, or rather enslaved; and as he lay and tossed in the gross darkness of the night and the curtained room, Mr. Enfield's tale went by before his mind in a scroll of lighted pictures. He would be aware of the great field of lamps of a nocturnal city; then of the figure of a man walking swiftly; then of a child running from the doctor's; and then these met, and that human Juggernaut trod the child down and passed on regardless of her screams. Or else he would see a room in a rich house, where his friend lay asleep, dreaming and smiling at his dreams; and then the door of that room would be opened, the curtains of the bed plucked apart, the sleeper re-called, and lo! there would stand by his side a figure to whom power was given, and even at that dead hour, he must rise and do its bidding. The figure in these two phases haunted the lawyer all night; and if at any time he dozed over, it was but to see it glide more stealthily through sleeping houses, or move the more swiftly and still the more swiftly, even to dizziness, through wider labyrinths of lamp-lighted city, and at every street corner crush a child and leave her screaming. And still the figure had no face by which he might know it; even in his dreams, it had no face, or one that baffled him and melted before his eyes; and thus it was that there sprang up and grew apace in the lawyer's mind a singu-larly strong, almost an inordinate, curiosity to behold the features of the real Mr. Hyde. If he could but once set eyes on him, he thought the mystery would lighten and perhaps roll altogether away, as was the habit of mysterious things when well examined. He might see a reason for his friend's strange preference or bond-age (call it which you please) and even for the startling clause of the will. At least it would be a face worth seeing: the face of a man who was without bowels of mercy: a face which had but to show itself to raise up in the mind of the unimpressionable En-field a spirit of enduring hatred.

From that time forward, Mr. Utterson began to haunt the door in the by-street of shops. In the morning before office hours, at noon when business was plenty, and time scarce, at night under the face of the fogged city moon, by all lights and at all hours of solitude or concourse, the lawyer was to be found on his chosen post.

"If he be Mr. Hyde," he had thought, "I shall be Mr. Seek."

And at last his patience was rewarded. It was a fine dry night;

frost in the air; the streets as clean as a ball-room floor; the lamps, unshaken by any wind, drawing a regular pattern of light and shadow. By ten o'clock, when the shops were closed, the by-street was very solitary and, in spite of the low growl of London from all round, very silent. Small sounds carried far; domestic sounds out of the houses were clearly audible on either side of the road-way; and the rumour of the approach of any passenger preceded him by a long time. Mr. Utterson had been some minutes at his post, when he was aware of an odd, light footstep drawing near. In the course of his nightly patrols, he had long grown accustomed to the quaint effect with which the footfalls of a single person, while he is still a great way off, suddenly spring out distinct from the vast hum and clatter of the city. Yet his attention had never before been so sharply and decisively arrested; and it was with a strong, superstitious prevision of success that he withdrew into the entry of the court.

The steps drew swiftly nearer, and swelled out suddenly louder as they turned the end of the street. The lawyer, looking forth from the entry, could soon see what manner of man he had to deal with. He was small and very plainly dressed, and the look of him, even at that distance, went somehow strongly against the watcher's inclination. But he made straight for the door, crossing the roadway to save time; and as he came, he drew a key from his pocket like one approaching home.

Mr. Utterson stepped out and touched him on the shoulder as he passed. "Mr. Hyde, I think?"

Mr. Hyde shrank back with a hissing intake of the breath. But his fear was only momentary; and though he did not look the lawyer in the face, he answered coolly enough: "That is my name. What do you want?"

"I see you are going in," returned the lawyer. "I am an old friend of Dr. Jekyll's—Mr. Utterson of Gaunt Street—you must have heard my name; and meeting you so conveniently, I thought you might admit me."

"You will not find Dr. Jekyll; he is from home," replied Mr. Hyde, blowing in the key. And then suddenly, but still without looking up, "How did you know me?" he asked.

"On your side," said Mr. Utterson, "will you do me a favour?"

"With pleasure," replied the other. "What shall it be?"

"Will you let me see your face?" asked the lawyer.

Mr. Hyde appeared to hesitate, and then, as if upon some sudden reflection, fronted about with an air of defiance; and the pair stared at each other pretty fixedly for a few seconds. "Now I shall know you again," said Mr. Utterson. "It may be useful."

"Yes," returned Mr. Hyde, "it is as well we have met; and *à propos*, you should have my address." And he gave a number of a street in Soho.

"Good God!" thought Mr. Utterson, "can he, too, have been thinking of the will?" But he kept his feelings to himself and only grunted in acknowledgment of the address.

"And now," said the other, "how did you know me?"

"By description," was the reply.

"Whose description?"

"We have common friends," said Mr. Utterson.

"Common friends?" echoed Mr. Hyde, a little hoarsely. "Who are they?"

"Jekyll, for instance," said the lawyer.

"He never told you," cried Mr. Hyde, with a flush of anger. "I did not think you would have lied."

"Come," said Mr. Utterson, "that is not fitting language."

The other snarled aloud into a savage laugh; and the next moment, with extraordinary quickness, he had unlocked the door and disappeared into the house.

The lawyer stood awhile when Mr. Hyde had left him, the picture of disquietude. Then he began slowly to mount the street, pausing every step or two and putting his hand to his brow like a man in mental perplexity. The problem he was thus debating as he walked, was one of a class that is rarely solved. Mr. Hyde was pale and dwarfish, he gave an impression of deformity without any nameable malformation, he had a displeasing smile, he had borne himself to the lawyer with a sort of murderous mixture of timidity and boldness, and he spoke with a husky, whispering and somewhat broken voice; all these were points against him, but not all of these together could explain the hitherto unknown disgust, loathing, and fear with which Mr. Utterson regarded him. "There must be something else," said the perplexed gentleman. "There *is* something more, if I could find a name for it. God bless me, the man seems hardly human! Something troglodytic, shall we say? or can it be the old story of Dr. Fell? or is it the mere radiance of a foul soul that thus transpires through, and transfigures, its clay continent? The last, I think; for, O my poor old Harry Jekyll, if ever I read Satan's signature upon a face, it is on that of your new friend."

Round the corner from the by-street, there was a square of ancient, handsome houses, now for the most part decayed from their high estate and let in flats and chambers to all sorts and conditions of men: map-engravers, architects, shady lawyers and the agents of obscure enterprises. One house, however, second from the corner, was still occupied entire; and at the door of this, which wore a great air of wealth and comfort, though it was now plunged in darkness except for the fanlight, Mr. Utterson stopped and knocked. A well-dressed, elderly servant opened the door.

"Is Dr. Jekyll at home, Poole?" asked the lawyer.

"I will see, Mr. Utterson," said Poole, admitting the visitor, as he spoke, into a large, low-roofed, comfortable hall, paved with flags, warmed (after the fashion of a country house) by a bright, open fire, and furnished with costly cabinets of oak. "Will you wait here by the fire, sir? or shall I give you a light in the dining-room?"

"Here, thank you," said the lawyer, and he drew near and leaned on the tall fender. This hall, in which he was now left alone, was a pet fancy of his friend the doctor's; and Utterson himself was wont to speak of it as the pleasantest room in London. But to-night there was a shudder in his blood; the face of Hyde sat heavy on his memory; he felt (what was rare with him) a nausea and distaste of life; and in the gloom of his spirits, he seemed to read a menace in the flickering of the firelight on the polished cabinets and the uneasy starting of the shadow on the roof. He was ashamed of his relief, when Poole presently returned to announce that Dr. Jekyll was gone out.

"I saw Mr. Hyde go in by the old dissecting-room door, Poole," he said. "Is that right, when Dr. Jekyll is from home?"

"Quite right, Mr. Utterson, sir," replied the servant. "Mr. Hyde has a key."

"Your master seems to repose a great deal of trust in that young man, Poole," resumed the other musingly.

"Yes, sir, he do indeed," said Poole. "We have all orders to obey him."

"I do not think I ever met Mr. Hyde?" asked Utterson.

"O, dear no, sir. He never *dines* here," replied the butler. "Indeed we see very little of him on this side of the house; he mostly comes and goes by the laboratory."

"Well, good-night, Poole."

"Good-night, Mr. Utterson."

And the lawyer set out homeward with a very heavy heart. "Poor Harry Jekyll," he thought, "my mind misgives me he is in deep waters! He was wild when he was young; a long while ago to be sure; but in the law of God, there is no statute of limitations. Ay, it must be that; the ghost of some old sin, the cancer of some concealed disgrace: punishment coming, *pede claudo,* years after memory has forgotten and self-love condoned the fault." The lawyer, scared by the thought, brooded awhile on his own past, groping in all the corners of memory, lest by chance some Jack-in-the-Box of an old iniquity should leap to light there. His past was fairly blameless; few men could read the rolls of their life with less apprehension; yet he was humbled to the dust by the many ill things he had done, and raised up again into a sober and fearful gratitude by the many that he had come so near to doing, yet avoided. And then by a return on his former subject, he conceived a spark of hope. "This Master Hyde, if he were studied," thought he, "must have secrets of his own; black secrets, by the look of him; secrets compared to which poor Jekyll's worst would be like sunshine. Things cannot continue as they are. It turns me cold to think of this creature stealing like a thief to Harry's bedside; poor Harry, what a wakening! And the danger of it; for if this Hyde suspects the existence of the will, he may grow impatient to inherit. Ay, I must put my shoulder to the wheel—if Jekyll will but let me," he added, "if Jekyll will only let me." For once more he saw before his mind's eye, as clear as a transparency, the strange clauses of the will.

Dr. Jekyll Was Quite at Ease

A fortnight later, by excellent good fortune, the doctor gave one of his pleasant dinners to some five or six old cronies, all intelligent, reputable men and all judges of good wine; and Mr. Utterson so contrived that he remained behind after the others had departed. This was no new arrangement, but a thing that had befallen many scores of times. Where Utterson was liked, he was well liked. Hosts loved to detain the dry lawyer, when the light-hearted and the loose-tongued had already their foot on the threshold; they liked to sit awhile in his unobtrusive company, practising for solitude, sobering their minds in the man's rich silence after the expense and strain of gaiety. To this rule, Dr. Jekyll was no exception; and as he now sat on the opposite side of the fire—a large, well-made, smooth-faced man of fifty, with something of a slyish cast perhaps, but every mark of capacity and kindness—you could see by his looks that he cherished for Mr. Utterson a sincere and warm affection.

"I have been wanting to speak to you, Jekyll," began the latter. "You know that will of yours?"

A close observer might have gathered that the topic was distasteful; but the doctor carried it off gaily. "My poor Utterson," said he, "you are unfortunate in such a client. I never saw a man so distressed as you were by my will; unless it were that hide-bound pedant, Lanyon, at what he called my scientific heresies. O, I know he's a good fellow—you needn't frown—an excellent fellow, and I always mean to see more of him; but a hide-bound pedant for all that; an ignorant, blatant pedant. I was never more disappointed in any man than Lanyon."

"You know I never approved of it," pursued Utterson, ruthlessly disregarding the fresh topic.

"My will? Yes, certainly, I know that," said the doctor, a trifle sharply. "You have told me so."

"Well, I tell you so again," continued the lawyer. "I have been learning something of young Hyde."

The large handsome face of Dr. Jekyll grew pale to the very lips, and there came a blackness about his eyes. "I do not care to hear more," said he. "This is a matter I thought we had agreed to drop."

"What I heard was abominable," said Utterson.

"It can make no change. You do not understand my position," returned the doctor, with a certain incoherency of manner. "I am painfully situated, Utterson; my position is a very strange—a very strange one. It is one of those affairs that cannot be mended by talking."

"Jekyll," said Utterson, "you know me: I am a man to be trusted. Make a clean breast of this in confidence; and I make no doubt I can get you out of it."

"My good Utterson," said the doctor, "this is very good of you, this is downright good of you, and I cannot find words to thank you in. I believe you fully; I would trust you before any man alive, ay, before myself, if I could make the choice; but indeed it isn't what you fancy; it is not so bad as that; and just to put your good heart at rest, I will tell you one thing: the moment I choose, I can be rid of Mr. Hyde. I give you my hand upon that; and I thank you again and again; and I will just add one little word, Utterson, that I'm sure you'll take in good part: this is a private matter, and I beg of you to let it sleep."

Utterson reflected a little, looking in the fire.

"I have no doubt you are perfectly right," he said at last, getting to his feet.

"Well, but since we have touched upon this business, and for the last time I hope," continued the doctor, "there is one point I should like you to understand. I have really a very great interest in poor Hyde. I know you have seen him; he told me so; and I fear he was rude. But I do sincerely take a great, a very great interest in that young man; and if I am taken away, Utterson, I wish you to promise me that you will bear with him and get his rights for him. I think you would, if you knew all; and it would be a weight off my mind if you would promise."

"I can't pretend that I shall ever like him," said the lawyer.

"I don't ask that," pleaded Jekyll, laying his hand upon the other's arm; "I only ask for justice; I only ask you to help him for my sake, when I am no longer here."

Utterson heaved an irrepressible sigh. "Well," said he, "I prom- ise."

The Carew Murder Case

Nearly a year later, in the month of October, 18—, London was startled by a crime of singular ferocity and rendered all the more notable by the high position of the victim. The details were few and startling. A maid servant, living alone in a house not far from the river, had gone up-stairs to bed about eleven. Although a fog rolled over the city in the small hours, the early part of the night was cloudless, and the lane, which the maid's window overlooked, was brilliantly lit by the full moon. It seems she was romantically given, for she sat down upon her box, which stood immediately under the window, and fell into a dream of musing. Never (she used to say, with streaming tears, when she narrated that experience), never had she felt more at peace with all men or thought more kindly of the world. And as she so sat she became aware of an aged and beautiful gentleman with white hair, drawing near along the lane; and advancing to meet him, another and very small gentleman, to whom at first she paid less attention. When they had come within speech (which was just under the maid's eyes) the older man bowed and accosted the other with a very pretty manner of politeness. It did not seem as if the subject of his address were of great importance; indeed, from his pointing, it sometimes appeared as if he were only inquiring his way; but the moon shone on his face as he spoke, and the girl was pleased to watch it, it seemed to breathe such an innocent and old-world kindness of disposition, yet with something high too, as of a well-founded self-content. Presently her eye wandered to the other, and she was surprised to recognise in him a certain Mr. Hyde, who had once visited her master and for whom she had conceived a dislike. He had in his hand a heavy cane, with which he was trifling; but he answered never a word, and seemed to listen with an ill-contained impatience. And then all of a sudden he broke out in a great flame of anger, stamping with his foot, brandishing the cane, and carrying on (as the maid described it) like a madman. The old gentleman took a step back, with the air of one very much surprised and a trifle hurt; and at that Mr. Hyde broke out of all bounds and clubbed him to the earth. And next moment, with ape-like fury, he was trampling his victim underfoot and hailing down a storm of blows, under which the bones were audibly shattered and the body jumped upon the roadway. At the horror of these sights and sounds, the maid fainted.

It was two o'clock when she came to herself and called for the police. The murderer was gone long ago; but there lay his victim in the middle of the lane, incredibly mangled. The stick with which the deed had been done, although it was of some rare and very tough and heavy wood, had broken in the middle under the stress of this insensate cruelty; and one splintered half had rolled in the neighbouring gutter—the other, without doubt, had been carried away by the murderer. A purse and a gold watch were found upon the victim: but no cards or papers, except a sealed and stamped envelope, which he had been probably carrying to the post, and which bore the name and address of Mr. Utterson.

This was brought to the lawyer the next morning, before he was out of bed; and he had no sooner seen it, and been told the circumstances, than he shot out a solemn lip. "I shall say nothing till I have seen the body," said he; "this may be very serious. Have the kindness to wait while I dress." And with the same grave countenance he hurried through his breakfast and drove to the police station, whither the body had been carried. As soon as he came into the cell, he nodded.

"Yes," said he, "I recognise him. I am sorry to say that this is Sir Danvers Carew."

"Good God, sir," exclaimed the officer, "is it possible?" And the next moment his eye lighted up with professional ambition. "This will make a deal of noise," he said. "And perhaps you can help us to the man." And he briefly narrated what the maid had seen, and showed the broken stick.

Mr. Utterson had already quailed at the name of Hyde; but when the stick was laid before him, he could doubt no longer; broken and battered as it was, he recognised it for one that he had himself presented many years before to Henry Jekyll.

"Is this Mr. Hyde a person of small stature?" he inquired.

"Particularly small and particularly wicked-looking, is what the maid calls him," said the officer.

Mr. Utterson reflected; and then, raising his head, "If you will come with me to my cab," he said, "I think I can take you to his house."

It was by this time about nine in the morning, and the first fog of the season. A great chocolate-coloured pall lowered over heaven, but the wind was continually charging and routing these embattled vapours; so that as the cab crawled from street to street, Mr. Utterson beheld a marvellous number of degrees and hues of twilight; for here it would be dark like the back-end of evening; and there would be a glow of a rich, lurid brown, like the light of some strange conflagration; and here, for a moment, the fog would be quite broken up, and a haggard shaft of daylight would glance in between the swirling wreaths. The dismal quarter of Soho seen under these changing glimpses, with its muddy ways, and slatternly passengers, and its lamps, which had never been extinguished or had been kindled afresh to combat this mournful reinvasion of darkness, seemed, in the lawyer's eyes, like a district of some city in a nightmare. The thoughts of his mind, besides, were of the gloomiest dye; and when he glanced at the companion of his drive, he was conscious of some touch of that terror of the law and the law's officers, which may at times assail the most honest.

As the cab drew up before the address indicated, the fog lifted a little and showed him a dingy street, a gin palace, a low French eating-house, a shop for the retail of penny numbers and two-penny salads, many ragged children huddled in the doorways, and many women of many different nationalities passing out, key in hand, to have a morning glass; and the next moment the fog settled down again upon that part, as brown as umber, and cut him off from his blackguardly surroundings. This was the home of Henry Jekyll's favourite; of a man who was heir to quarter of a million sterling.

An ivory-faced and silvery-haired old woman opened the door. She had an evil face, smoothed by hypocrisy; but her manners were excellent. Yes, she said, this was Mr. Hyde's, but he was not at home; he had been in that night very late, but had gone away again in less than an hour; there was nothing strange in that; his habits were very irregular, and he was often absent; for instance, it was nearly two months since she had seen him till yesterday.

"Very well, then, we wish to see his rooms," said the lawyer; and when the woman began to declare it was impossible, "I had better tell you who this person is," he added. "This is Inspector Newcomen of Scotland Yard."

A flash of odious joy appeared upon the woman's face. "Ah!" said she, "he is in trouble! What has he done?"

Mr. Utterson and the inspector exchanged glances. "He don't seem a very popular character," observed the latter. "And now, my good woman, just let me and this gentleman have a look about us."

In the whole extent of the house, which but for the old woman remained otherwise empty, Mr. Hyde had only used a couple of rooms; but these were furnished with luxury and good taste. A closet was filled with wine; the plate was of silver, the napery elegant; a good picture hung upon the walls, a gift (as Utterson supposed) from Henry Jekyll, who was much of a connoisseur; and the carpets were of many plies and agreeable in colour. At this moment, however, the rooms bore every mark of having been recently and hurriedly ransacked; clothes lay about the floor, with their pockets inside out; lock-fast drawers stood open; and on the hearth there lay a pile of grey ashes, as though many papers had been burned. From these embers the inspector disinterred the butt end of a green cheque book, which had resisted the action of the fire; the other half of the stick was found behind the door; and as this clinched his suspicions, the officer declared himself delighted. A visit to the bank, where several thousand pounds were found to be lying to the murderer's credit, completed his gratification.

"You may depend upon it, sir," he told Mr. Utterson: "I have him in my hand. He must have lost his head, or he never would have left the stick or, above all, burned the cheque book. Why, money's life to the man. We have nothing to do but wait for him at the bank, and get out the handbills."

This last, however, was not so easy of accomplishment; for Mr. Hyde had numbered few familiars—even the master of the servant maid had only seen him twice; his family could nowhere be traced; he had never been photographed; and the few who could describe him differed widely, as common observers will. Only on one point, were they agreed; and that was the haunting sense of unexpressed deformity with which the fugitive impressed his beholders.

Incident of the Letter

It was late in the afternoon, when Mr. Utterson found his way to Dr. Jekyll's door, where he was at once admitted by Poole, and carried down by the kitchen offices and across a yard which had once been a garden, to the building which was indifferently known as the laboratory or the dissecting-rooms. The doctor had bought the house from the heirs of a celebrated surgeon; and his own tastes being rather chemical than anatomical, had changed the destination of the block at the bottom of the garden. It was the first time that the lawyer had been received in that part of his friend's quarters; and he eyed the dingy, windowless structure with curiosity, and gazed round with a distasteful sense of strangeness as he crossed the theatre, once crowded with eager students and now lying gaunt and silent, the tables laden with chemical apparatus, the floor strewn with crates and littered with packing straw, and the light falling dimly through the foggy cupola. At the further end, a flight of stairs mounted to a door covered with red baize; and through this, Mr. Utterson was at last received into the doctor's cabinet. It was a large room, fitted round with glass presses, furnished, among other things, with a cheval-glass and a business table, and looking out upon the court by three dusty windows barred with iron. A fire burned in the grate; a lamp was set lighted on the chimney shelf, for even in the houses the fog began to lie thickly; and there, close up to the warmth, sat Dr. Jekyll, looking deadly sick. He did not rise to meet his visitor, but held out a cold hand and bade him welcome in a changed voice.

"And now," said Mr. Utterson, as soon as Poole had left them, "you have heard the news?"

The doctor shuddered. "They were crying it in the square," he said. "I heard them in my dining-room."

"One word," said the lawyer. "Carew was my client, but so are you, and I want to know what I am doing. You have not been mad enough to hide this fellow?"

"Utterson, I swear to God," cried the doctor, "I swear to God I will never set eyes on him again. I bind my honour to you that I am done with him in this world. It is all at an end. And indeed he does not want my help; you do not know him as I do; he is safe, he is quite safe; mark my words, he will never more be heard of."

The lawyer listened gloomily; he did not like his friend's feverish manner. "You seem pretty sure of him," said he; "and for your sake, I hope you may be right. If it came to a trial, your name might appear."

"I am quite sure of him," replied Jekyll; "I have grounds for certainty that I cannot share with any one. But there is one thing on which you may advise me. I have—I have received a letter; and I am at a loss whether I should show it to the police. I should like to leave it in your hands, Utterson; you would judge wisely, I am sure; I have so great a trust in you."

"You fear, I suppose, that it might lead to his detection?" asked the lawyer.

"No," said the other. "I cannot say that I care what becomes of Hyde; I am quite done with him. I was thinking of my own character, which this hateful business has rather exposed."

Utterson ruminated awhile; he was surprised at his friend's selfishness, and yet relieved by it. "Well," said he, at last, "let me see the letter."

The letter was written in an odd, upright hand and signed "Edward Hyde": and it signified, briefly enough, that the writer's benefactor, Dr. Jekyll, whom he had long so unworthily repaid for a thousand generosities, need labour under no alarm for his safety, as he had means of escape on which he placed a sure dependence. The lawyer liked this letter well enough; it put a better colour on the intimacy than he had looked for; and he blamed himself for some of his past suspicions.

"Have you the envelope?" he asked.

"I burned it," replied Jekyll, "before I thought what I was about. But it bore no postwark. The note was handed in."

"Shall I keep this and sleep upon it?" asked Utterson.

"I wish you to judge for me entirely," was the reply. "I have lost confidence in myself."

"Well, I shall consider," returned the lawyer. "And now one word more: it was Hyde who dictated the terms in your will about that disappearance?"

The doctor seemed seized with a qualm of faintness; he shut his mouth tight and nodded.

"I knew it," said Utterson. "He meant to murder you. You have had a fine escape."

"I have had what is far more to the purpose," returned the doctor solemnly: "I have had a lesson—O God, Utterson, what a lesson I have had!" And he covered his face for a moment with his hands.

On his way out the lawyer stopped and had a word or two with Poole. "By-the-bye," said he, "there was a letter handed in to-day: what was the messenger like?" But Poole was positive nothing had come except by post; "and only circulars by that," he added.

This news sent off the visitor with his fears renewed. Plainly the letter had come by the laboratory door; possibly, indeed, it had been written in the cabinet; and if that were so, it must be differently judged, and handled with the more caution. The newsboys, as he went, were crying themselves hoarse along the footways: "Special edition. Shocking murder of an M.P." That was the funeral oration of one friend and client; and he could not help a certain apprehension lest the good name of another should be sucked down in the eddy of the scandal. It was, at least, a ticklish decision that he had to make; and self-reliant as he was by habit, he began to cherish a longing for advice. It was not to be had directly; but perhaps, he thought, it might be fished for.

Presently after, he sat on one side of his own hearth, with Mr. Guest, his head clerk, upon the other, and midway between, at a nicely calculated distance from the fire, a bottle of a particular old wine that had long dwelt unsunned in the foundations of his house. The fog still slept on the wing above the drowned city, where the lamps glimmered like carbuncles; and through the muffle and smother of these fallen clouds, the procession of the town's life was still rolling in through the great arteries with a sound as of a mighty wind. But the room was gay with firelight. In the bottle the acids were long ago resolved; the imperial dye had softened with time, as the colour grows richer in stained windows; and the glow of hot autumn afternoons on hillside vineyards, was ready to be set free and to disperse the fogs of London. Insensibly the lawyer melted. There was no man from whom he kept fewer secrets than Mr. Guest; and he was not always sure that he kept as many as he meant. Guest had often been on business to the doctor's; he knew Poole; he could scarce have failed to hear of Mr. Hyde's familiarity about the house; he might draw conclusions: was it not as well, then, that he should see a letter which put that mystery to rights? and above all since Guest, being a great student and critic of handwriting, would consider the step natural and obliging? The clerk, besides, was a man of counsel; he would scarce read so strange a document without dropping a remark; and by that remark Mr. Utterson might shape his future course.

"This is a sad business about Sir Danvers," he said.

"Yes, sir, indeed. It has elicited a great deal of public feeling," returned Guest. "The man, of course, was mad."

"I should like to hear your views on that," replied Utterson. "I have a document here in his handwriting; it is between ourselves, for I scarce know what to do about it; it is an ugly business at the best. But there it is; quite in your way: a murder's autograph."

Guest's eyes brightened, and he sat down at once and studied it with passion. "No, sir," he said: "not mad; but it is an odd hand."

"And by all accounts a very odd writer," added the lawyer.

Just then the servant entered with a note.

"Is that from Dr. Jekyll, sir?" inquired the clerk. "I thought I knew the writing. Anything private, Mr. Utterson?"

"Only an invitation to dinner. Why? Do you want to see it?"

"One moment. I thank you, sir"; and the clerk laid the two sheets of paper alongside and sedulously compared their contents. "Thank you, sir," he said at last, returning both; "it's a very interesting autograph."

There was a pause, during which Mr. Utterson struggled with himself. "Why did you compare them, Guest?" he inquired suddenly.

"Well, sir," returned the clerk, "there's a rather singular resemblance; the two hands are in many points identical: only differently sloped."

"Rather quaint," said Utterson.

"It is, as you say, rather quaint," returned Guest.

"I wouldn't speak of this note, you know," said the master.

"No, sir," said the clerk. "I understand."

But no sooner was Mr. Utterson alone that night than he locked the note into his safe, where it reposed from that time forward. "What!" he thought. "Henry Jekyll forge for a murderer!" And his blood ran cold in his veins.

Remarkable Incident of Dr. Lanyon

Time ran on; thousands of pounds were offered in reward, for the death of Sir Danvers was resented as a public injury; but Mr. Hyde had disappeared out of the ken of the police as though he had never existed. Much of his past was unearthed, indeed, and all disreputable: tales came out of the man's cruelty, at once so callous and violent; of his vile life, of his strange associates, of the hatred that seemed to have surrounded his career; but of his present whereabouts, not a whisper. From the time he had left the house in Soho on the morning of the murder, he was simply blotted out; and gradually, as time drew on, Mr. Utterson began to recover from the hotness of his alarm, and to grow more at quiet with himself. The death of Sir Danvers was, to his way of thinking, more than paid for by the disappearance of Mr. Hyde. Now that that evil influence had been withdrawn, a new life began for Dr. Jekyll. He came out of his seclusion, renewed relations with his friends, became once more their familiar guest and entertainer; and whilst he had always been known for charities, he was now no less distinguished for religion. He was busy, he was much in the open air, he did good; his face seemed to open and brighten, as if with an inward consciousness of service; and for more than two months, the doctor was at peace.

On the 8th of January Utterson had dined at the doctor's with a small party; Lanyon had been there; and the face of the host had looked from one to the other as in the old days when the trio were inseparable friends. On the 12th, and again on the 14th, the door was shut against the lawyer. "The doctor was confined to the house," Poole said, "and saw no one." On the 15th, he tried again, and was again refused; and having now been used for the last two months to see his friend almost daily, he found this return of solitude to weigh upon his spirits. The fifth night he had in Guest to dine with him; and the sixth he betook himself to Dr. Lanyon's.

There at least he was not denied admittance; but when he came in, he was shocked at the change which had taken place in the doctor's appearance. He had his death-warrant written legibly upon his face. The rosy man had grown pale; his flesh had fallen away; he was visibly balder and older; and yet it was not so much these tokens of a swift physical decay that arrested the lawyer's notice, as a look in the eye and quality of manner that seemed to testify to some deep-seated terror of the mind. It was unlikely that the doctor should fear death; and yet that was what Utterson was tempted to suspect. "Yes," he thought; "he is a doctor, he must know his own state and that his days are counted; and the knowledge is more than he can bear." And yet when Utterson remarked on his ill-looks, it was with an air of great firmness that Lanyon declared himself a doomed man.

"I have had a shock," he said, "and I shall never recover. It is a question of weeks. Well, life has been pleasant; I liked it; yes, sir, I used to like it. I sometimes think if we knew all, we should be more glad to get away."

"Jekyll is ill, too," observed Utterson. "Have you seen him?"

But Lanyon's face changed, and he held up a trembling hand. "I wish to see or hear no more of Dr. Jekyll," he said in a loud, unsteady voice. "I am quite done with that person; and I beg that you will spare me any allusion to one whom I regard as dead."

"Tut-tut," said Mr. Utterson; and then after a considerable pause, "Can't I do anything?" he inquired. "We are three very old friends, Lanyon; we shall not live to make others."

"Nothing can be done," returned Lanyon; "ask himself."

"He will not see me," said the lawyer.

"I am not surprised at that," was the reply. "Some day, Utterson, after I am dead, you may perhaps come to learn the right and wrong of this. I cannot tell you. And in the meantime, if you can sit and talk with me of other things, for God's sake, stay and do so; but if you cannot keep clear of this accursed topic, then, in God's name, go, for I cannot bear it."

As soon as he got home, Utterson sat down and wrote to Jekyll, complaining of his exclusion from the house, and asking the cause of this unhappy break with Lanyon; and the next day brought him a long answer, often very pathetically worded, and sometimes darkly mysterious in drift. The quarrel with Lanyon was incurable. "I do not blame our old friend," Jekyll wrote, "but I share his view that we must never meet. I mean from henceforth to lead a life of extreme seclusion; you must not be surprised, nor must you doubt my friendship, if my door is often shut even to you. You must suffer me to go my own dark way. I have brought on myself a punishment and a danger that I cannot name. If I am the chief of sinners, I am the chief of sufferers also. I could not think that this earth contained a place for sufferings and terrors so unmanning; and you can do but one thing, Utterson, to lighten this destiny, and that is to respect my silence." Utterson was amazed; the dark influence of Hyde had been withdrawn, the doctor had returned to his old tasks and amities; a week ago, the prospect had smiled with every promise of a cheerful and an honoured age; and now in a moment, friendship, and peace of mind, and the whole tenor of his life were wrecked. So great and unprepared a change pointed to madness; but in view of Lanyon's manner and words, there must lie for it some deeper ground.

A week afterwards Dr. Lanyon took to his bed, and in something less than a fortnight he was dead. The night after the funeral, at which he had been sadly affected, Utterson locked the door of his business room, and sitting there by the light of a melancholy candle, drew out and set before him an envelope addressed by the hand and sealed with the seal of his dead friend. "Private: for the hands of G. J. Utterson alone, and in case of his

predecease *to be destroyed unread*," so it was emphatically super-
scribed; and the lawyer dreaded to behold the contents. "I have
buried one friend to-day," he thought: "what if this should cost
me another?" And then he condemned the fear as a disloyalty, and
broke the seal. Within there was another enclosure, likewise
sealed, and marked upon the cover as "not to be opened till the
death or disappearance of Dr. Henry Jekyll." Utterson could not
trust his eyes. Yes, it was disappearance; here again, as in the mad
will which he had long ago restored to its author, here again were
the idea of a disappearance and the name of Henry Jekyll bracketed. But, in the will, that idea had sprung from the sinister suggestion of the man Hyde; it was set there with a purpose all too
plain and horrible. Written by the hand of Lanyon, what should
it mean? A great curiosity came on the trustee, to disregard the
prohibition and dive at once to the bottom of these mysteries;
but professional honour and faith to his dead friend were stringent
obligations; and the packet slept in the inmost corner of his
private safe.

It is one thing to mortify curiosity, another to conquer it; and
it may be doubted if, from that day forth, Utterson desired the
society of his surviving friend with the same eagerness. He thought
of him kindly; but his thoughts were disquieted and fearful. He
went to call indeed; but he was perhaps relieved to be denied admittance; perhaps, in his heart, he preferred to speak with Poole
upon the doorstep and surrounded by the air and sounds of the
open city, rather than to be admitted into that house of voluntary
bondage, and to sit and speak with its inscrutable recluse. Poole
had, indeed, no very pleasant news to communicate. The doctor,
it appeared, now more than ever confined himself to the cabinet
over the laboratory, where he would sometimes even sleep; he was
out of spirits, he had grown very silent, he did not read; it seemed
as if he had something on his mind. Utterson became so used to
the unvarying character of these reports, that he fell off little by
little in the frequency of his visits.

Incident at the Window

It chanced on Sunday, when Mr. Utterson was on his usual walk
with Mr. Enfield, that their way lay once again through the by-

street; and that when they came in front of the door, both stopped to gaze on it.

"Well," said Enfield, "that story's at an end at least. We shall never see more of Mr. Hyde."

"I hope not," said Utterson. "Did I ever tell you that I once saw him, and shared your feeling of repulsion?"

"It was impossible to do the one without the other," returned Enfield. "And by the way, what an ass you must have thought me, not to know that this was a back way to Dr. Jekyll's! It was partly your own fault that I found it out, even when I did."

"So you found it out, did you?" said Utterson. "But if that be so, we may step into the court and take a look at the windows. To tell you the truth, I am uneasy about poor Jekyll; and even outside, I feel as if the presence of a friend might do him good."

The court was very cool and a little damp, and full of premature twilight, although the sky, high up overhead, was still bright with sunset. The middle one of the three windows was half-way open; and sitting close beside it, taking the air with an infinite sadness of mien, like some disconsolate prisoner, Utterson saw Dr. Jekyll.

"What! Jekyll!" he cried. "I trust you are better."

"I am very low, Utterson," replied the doctor, drearily, "very low. It will not last long, thank God."

"You stay too much indoors," said the lawyer. "You should be out, whipping up the circulation like Mr. Enfield and me. (This is my cousin—Mr. Enfield—Dr. Jekyll.) Come now; get your hat and take a quick turn with us."

"You are very good," sighed the other. "I should like to very much; but no, no, no, it is quite impossible; I dare not. But indeed, Utterson, I am very glad to see you; this is really a great pleasure; I would ask you and Mr. Enfield up, but the place is really not fit."

"Why then," said the lawyer, good-naturedly, "the best thing we can do is to stay down here and speak with you from where we are."

"That is just what I was about to venture to propose," returned the doctor with a smile. But the words were hardly uttered, before the smile was struck out of his face and succeeded by an expression of such abject terror and despair, as froze the very blood of the two gentlemen below. They saw it but for a glimpse, for the window was instantly thrust down; but that glimpse had been sufficient, and they turned and left the court without a word. In silence, too, they traversed the by-streets; and it was not until they had come into a neighbouring thoroughfare, where even upon a Sunday there were still some stirrings of life, that Mr. Utterson at last turned and looked at his companion. They were both pale; and there was an answering horror in their eyes.

"God forgive us, God forgive us," said Mr. Utterson.

But Mr. Enfield only nodded his head very seriously, and walked on once more in silence.

The Last Night

Mr. Utterson was sitting by his fireside one evening after dinner, when he was surprised to receive a visit from Poole.

"Bless me, Poole, what brings you here?" he cried; and then taking a second look at him, "What ails you?" he added; "is the doctor ill?"

"Mr. Utterson," said the man, "there is something wrong."

"Take a seat, and here is a glass of wine for you," said the lawyer. "Now, take your time, and tell me plainly what you want."

"You know the doctor's ways, sir," replied Poole, "and how he shuts himself up. Well, he's shut up again in the cabinet; and I don't like it, sir—I wish I may die if I like it. Mr. Utterson, sir, I'm afraid."

"Now, my good man," said the lawyer, "be explicit. What are you afraid of?"

"I've been afraid for about a week," returned Poole, doggedly disregarding the question, "and I can bear it no more."

The man's appearance amply bore out his words; his manner was altered for the worse; and except for the moment when he had first announced his terror, he had not once looked the lawyer in the face. Even now, he sat with the glass of wine untasted on his knee, and his eyes directed to a corner of the floor. "I can bear it no more," he repeated.

"Come," said the lawyer, "I see you have some good reason, Poole; I see there is something seriously amiss. Try to tell me what it is."

"I think there's been foul play," said Poole, hoarsely.

"Foul play!" cried the lawyer, a good deal frightened and rather inclined to be irritated in consequence. "What foul play? What does the man mean?"

"I dare n't say, sir," was the answer; "but will you come along with me and see for yourself?"

Mr. Utterson's only answer was to rise and get his hat and great-coat; but he observed with wonder the greatness of the relief that appeared upon the butler's face, and perhaps with no less, that the wine was still untasted when he set it down to follow.

It was a wild, cold, seasonable night of March, with a pale moon, lying on her back as though the wind had tilted her, and a flying wrack of the most diaphanous and lawny texture. The wind made talking difficult, and flecked the blood into the face. It seemed to have swept the streets unusually bare of passengers, be-sides; for Mr. Utterson thought he had never seen that part of London so deserted. He could have wished it otherwise; never in his life had he been conscious of so sharp a wish to see and touch his fellow-creatures; for struggle as he might, there was borne in upon his mind a crushing anticipation of calamity. The square, when they got there, was all full of wind and dust, and the thin trees in the garden were lashing themselves along the railing. Poole, who had kept all the way a pace or two ahead, now pulled up in the midle of the pavement, and in spite of the biting weather, took off his hat and mopped his brow with a red pocket-handkerchief. But for all the hurry of his coming, these were not the dews of exertion that he wiped away, but the moisture of some strangling anguish; for his face was white and his voice, when he spoke, harsh and broken.

"Well, sir," he said, "here we are, and God grant there be noth-ing wrong."

"Amen, Poole," said the lawyer.

Thereupon the servant knocked in a very guarded manner; the door was opened on the chain; and a voice asked from within, "Is that you, Poole?"

"It's all right," said Poole. "Open the door."

The hall, when they entered it, was brightly lighted up; the fire was built high; and about the hearth the whole of the servants, men and women, stood huddled together like a flock of sheep. At the sight of Mr. Utterson, the housemaid broke into hysterical whimpering; and the cook, crying out, "Bless God! it's Mr. Utter-son," ran forward as if to take him in her arms.

"What, what? Are you all here?" said the lawyer peevishly·

"Very irregular, very unseemly; your master would be far from pleased."

"They're all afraid," said Poole.

Blank silence followed, no one protesting; only the maid lifted up her voice and now wept loudly.

"Hold your tongue!" Poole said to her, with a ferocity of accent that testified to his own jangled nerves; and indeed, when the girl had so suddenly raised the note of her lamentation, they had all started and turned towards the inner door with faces of dreadful expectation. "And now," continued the butler, addressing the knife-boy, "reach me a candle, and we'll get this through hands at once." And then he begged Mr. Utterson to follow him, and led the way to the back garden.

"Now, sir," said he, "you come as gently as you can. I want you to hear, and I don't want you to be heard. And see here, sir, if by any chance he was to ask you in, don't go."

Mr. Utterson's nerves, at this unlooked-for termination, gave a jerk that nearly threw him from his balance; but he recollected his courage and followed the butler into the laboratory building and through the surgical theatre, with its lumber of crates and bottles, to the foot of the stair. Here Poole motioned him to stand on one side and listen; while he himself, setting down the candle and making a great and obvious call on his resolution, mounted the steps and knocked with a somewhat uncertain hand on the red baize of the cabinet door.

"Mr. Utterson, sir, asking to see you," he called; and even as he did so, once more violently signed to the lawyer to give ear.

A voice answered from within: "Tell him I cannot see any one," it said complainingly.

"Thank you, sir," said Poole, with a note of something like triumph in his voice; and taking up his candle, he led Mr. Utterson back across the yard and into the great kitchen, where the fire was out and the beetles were leaping on the floor.

"Sir," he said, looking Mr. Utterson in the eyes, "was that my master's voice?"

"It seems much changed," replied the lawyer, very pale, but giving look for look.

"Changed? Well, yes, I think so," said the butler. "Have I been twenty years in this man's house, to be deceived about his voice? No, sir; master's made away with; he was made away with, eight days ago, when we heard him cry out upon the name of God; and *who*'s in there instead of him, and *why* it stays there, is a thing that cries to Heaven, Mr. Utterson!"

"This is a very strange tale, Poole; this is rather a wild tale, my man," said Mr. Utterson, biting his finger. "Suppose it were as you suppose, supposing Dr. Jekyll to have been—well, murdered, what could induce the murderer to stay? That won't hold water; it does n't commend itself to reason."

"Well, Mr. Utterson, you are a hard man to satisfy, but I'll do it yet," said Poole. "All this last week (you must know) him, or it, or whatever it is that lives in that cabinet, has been crying night and day for some sort of medicine and cannot get it to his mind. It was sometimes his way—the master's, that is—to write his orders on a sheet of paper and throw it on the stair. We've had nothing else this week back; nothing but papers, and a closed door, and the very meals left there to be smuggled in when nobody was looking. Well, sir, every day, ay, and twice and thrice in the same day, there have been orders and complaints, and I have been sent flying to all the wholesale chemists in town. Every time I brought the stuff back, there would be another paper telling me to return it, because it was not pure, and another order to a different firm. This drug is wanted bitter bad, sir, whatever for."

"Have you any of these papers?" asked Mr. Utterson.

Poole felt in his pocket and handed out a crumpled note, which the lawyer, bending nearer to the candle, carefully examined. Its contents ran thus: "Dr. Jekyll presents his compliments to Messrs. Maw. He assures them that their last sample is impure and quite useless for his present purpose. In the year 18—, Dr. J. purchased a somewhat large quantity from Messrs. M. He now begs them to search with the most sedulous care, and should any of the same quality be left, to forward it to him at once. Expense is no consideration. The importance of this to Dr. J. can hardly be exaggerated." So far the letter had run composedly enough, but here with a sudden splutter of the pen, the writer's emotion had broken loose. "For God's sake," he had added, "find me some of the old."

"This is a strange note," said Mr. Utterson; and then sharply, "How do you come to have it open?"

"The man at Maw's was main angry, sir, and he threw it back to me like so much dirt," returned Poole.

"This is unquestionably the doctor's hand, do you know?" resumed the lawyer.

"I thought it looked like it," said the servant rather sulkily; and then, with another voice, "But what matters hand of write?" he said. "I've seen him!"

"Seen him?" repeated Mr. Utterson. "Well?"

"That's it!" said Poole. "It was this way. I came suddenly into the theatre from the garden. It seems he had slipped out to look for this drug or whatever it is; for the cabinet door was open, and there he was at the far end of the room digging among the crates. He looked up when I came in, gave a kind of cry, and whipped up-stairs into the cabinet. It was but for one minute that I saw him, but the hair stood upon my head like quills. Sir, if that was my master, why had he a mask upon his face? If it was my master, why did he cry out like a rat, and run from me? I have served him long enough. And then . . ." The man paused and passed his hand over his face.

"These are all very strange circumstances," said Mr. Utterson, "but I think I begin to see daylight. Your master, Poole, is plainly seized with one of those maladies that both torture and deform the sufferer; hence, for aught I know, the alteration of his voice; hence the mask and the avoidance of his friends; hence his eagerness to find this drug, by means of which the poor soul retains some hope of ultimate recovery—God grant that he be not deceived! There is my explanation; it is sad enough, Poole, ay, and appalling to consider; but it is plain and natural, hangs well together, and delivers us from all exorbitant alarms."

"Sir," said the butler, turning to a sort of mottled pallor, "that thing was not my master, and there's the truth. My master"—here he looked round him and began to whisper—"is a tall, fine build of a man, and this was more of a dwarf." Utterson attempted to protest. "O, sir," cried Poole, "do you think I do not know my master after twenty years? Do you think I do not know where his head comes to in the cabinet door, where I saw him every morning of my life? No, sir, that thing in the mask was never Dr. Jekyll—God knows what it was, but it was never Dr. Jekyll; and it is the belief of my heart that there was murder done."

"Poole," replied the lawyer, "if you say that, it will become my duty to make certain. Much as I desire to spare your master's feelings, much as I am puzzled by this note which seems to prove him to be still alive, I shall consider it my duty to break in that door."

"Ah, Mr. Utterson, that's talking!" cried the butler.

"And now comes the second question," resumed Utterson: "Who is going to do it?"

"Why, you and me," was the undaunted reply.

"That's very well said," returned the lawyer; "and whatever comes of it, I shall make it my business to see you are no loser."

"There is an axe in the theatre," continued Poole; "and you might take the kitchen poker for yourself."

The lawyer took that rude but weighty instrument into his hand, and balanced it. "Do you know, Poole," he said, looking up, "that you and I are about to place ourselves in a position of some peril?"

"You may say so, sir, indeed," returned the butler.

"It is well, then, that we should be frank," said the other. "We both think more than we have said; let us make a clean breast. This masked figure that you saw, did you recognise it?"

"Well, sir, it went so quick, and the creature was so doubled up, that I could hardly swear to that," was the answer. "But if you mean, was it Mr. Hyde?—why, yes, I think it was! You see it was much of the same bigness; and it had the same quick, light way with it; and then who else could have got in by the laboratory door? You have not forgot, sir, that at the time of the murder he had still the key with him? But that's not all. I don't know, Mr. Utterson, if ever you met this Mr. Hyde?"

"Yes," said the lawyer, "I once spoke with him."

"Then you must know as well as the rest of us that there was something queer about that gentleman—something that gave a man a turn—I don't know rightly how to say it, sir, beyond this: that you felt it in your marrow kind of cold and thin."

"I own I felt something of what you describe," said Mr. Utterson.

"Quite so, sir," returned Poole. "Well, when that masked thing like a monkey jumped from among the chemicals and whipped into the cabinet, it went down my spine like ice. O, I know it's not evidence, Mr. Utterson; I'm book-learned enough for that; but a man has his feelings, and I give you my bible-word it was Mr. Hyde!"

"Ay, ay," said the lawyer. "My fears incline to the same point.

Evil, I fear, founded—evil was sure to come—of that connection Ay, truly, I believe you; I believe poor Harry is killed; and I believe his murderer (for what purpose, God alone can tell) is still lurking in his victim's room. Well, let our name be vengeance. Call Bradshaw."

The footman came at the summons, very white and nervous.

"Put yourself together, Bradshaw," said the lawyer. "This suspense, I know, is telling upon all of you; but it is now our intention to make an end of it. Poole, here, and I am going to force our way into the cabinet. If all is well, my shoulders are broad enough to bear the blame. Meanwhile, lest anything should really be amiss, or any malefactor seek to escape by the back, you and the boy must go round the corner with a pair of good sticks and take your post at the laboratory door. We give you ten minutes, to get to your stations."

As Bradshaw left, the lawyer looked at his watch. "And now, Poole, let us get to ours," he said; and taking the poker under his arm, led the way into the yard. The scud had banked over the moon, and it was now quite dark. The wind, which only broke in puffs and draughts into that deep well of building, tossed the light of the candle to and fro about their steps, until they came into the shelter of the theatre, where they sat down silently to wait. London hummed solemnly all around; but nearer at hand, the stillness was only broken by the sounds of a footfall moving to and fro along the cabinet floor.

"So it will walk all day, sir," whispered Poole; "ay, and the better part of the night. Only when a new sample comes from the chemist, there's a bit of a break. Ah, it's an ill-conscience that's such an enemy to rest! Ah, sir, there's blood foully shed in every step of it! But hark again, a little closer—put your heart in your ears, Mr. Utterson, and tell me, is that the doctor's foot?"

The steps fell lightly and oddly, with a certain swing, for all they went so slowly; it was different indeed from the heavy creaking tread of Henry Jekyll. Utterson sighed. "Is there never anything else?" he asked.

Poole nodded. "Once," he said. "Once I heard it weeping!"

"Weeping? how that?" said the lawyer, conscious of a sudden chill of horror.

"Weeping like a woman or a lost soul," said the butler. "I came away with that upon my heart, that I could have wept too."

But now the ten minutes drew to an end. Poole disinterred the axe from under a stack of packing straw; the candle was set upon the nearest table to light them to the attack; and they drew near with bated breath to where that patient foot was still going up and down, up and down, in the quiet of the night.

"Jekyll," cried Utterson, with a loud voice, "I demand to see you." He paused a moment, but there came no reply. "I give you fair warning, our suspicions are aroused, and I must and shall see you," he resumed; "if not by fair means, then by foul—if not of your consent, then by brute force!"

"Utterson," said the voice, "for God's sake, have mercy!"

"Ah, that's not Jekyll's voice—it's Hyde's!" cried Utterson. "Down with the door, Poole!"

Poole swung the axe over his shoulder; the blow shook the building, and the red baize door leaped against the lock and hinges. A dismal screech, as of mere animal terror, rang from the cabinet. Up went the axe again, and again the panels crashed and the frame bounded; four times the blow fell; but the wood was tough and the fittings were of excellent workmanship; and it was not until the fifth, that the lock burst in sunder and the wreck of the door fell inwards on the carpet.

The besiegers, appalled by their own riot and the stillness that had succeeded, stood back a little and peered in. There lay the cabinet before their eyes in the quiet lamplight, a good fire glowing and chattering on the hearth, the kettle singing its thin strain, a drawer or two open, papers neatly set forth on the business table, and nearer the fire, the things laid out for tea: the quietest room, you would have said, and, but for the glazed presses full of chemicals, the most commonplace that night in London.

Right in the midst there lay the body of a man sorely contorted and still twitching. They drew near on tiptoe, turned it on its back and beheld the face of Edward Hyde. He was dressed in clothes far too large for him, clothes of the doctor's bigness; the cords of his face still moved with the semblance of life, but life was quite gone: and by the crushed phial in the hand and the strong smell of kernels that hung upon the air, Utterson knew that he was looking on the body of a self-destroyer.

"We have come too late," he said sternly, "whether to save or punish. Hyde is gone to his account; and it only remains for us to find the body of your master."

The far greater proportion of the building was occupied by the theatre, which filled almost the whole ground storey and was lighted from above, and by the cabinet, which formed an upper storey at one end and looked upon the court. A corridor joined the theatre to the door on the by-street; and with this the cabinet communicated separately by a second flight of stairs. There were besides a few dark closets and a spacious cellar. All these they now thoroughly examined. Each closet needed but a glance, for all were empty, and all, by the dust that fell from their doors, had stood long unopened. The cellar, indeed, was filled with crazy lumber, mostly dating from the times of the surgeon who was Jekyll's predecessor; but even as they opened the door they were advertised of the uselessness of further search, by the fall of a perfect mat of cobweb which had for years sealed up the entrance. Nowhere was there any trace of Henry Jekyll, dead or alive.

Poole stamped on the flags of the corridor. "He must be buried here," he said, hearkening to the sound.

"Or he may have fled," said Utterson, and he turned to examine the door in the by-street. It was locked; and lying near by on the flags, they found the key, already stained with rust.

"This does not look like use," observed the lawyer.

"Use!" echoed Poole. "Do you not see, sir, it is broken? much as if a man had stamped on it."

"Ay," continued Utterson, "and the fractures, too, are rusty." The two men looked at each other with a scare. "This is beyond me, Poole," said the lawyer. "Let us go back to the cabinet."

They mounted the stair in silence, and still with an occasional awestruck glance at the dead body, proceeded more thoroughly to examine the contents of the cabinet. At one table, there were traces of chemical work, various measured heaps of some white salt being laid on glass saucers, as though for an experiment in which the unhappy man had been prevented.

"That is the same drug that I was always bringing him," said Poole; and even as he spoke, the kettle with a startling noise boiled over.

This brought them to the fireside, where the easy-chair was drawn cosily up, and the tea things stood ready to the sitter's elbow, the very sugar in the cup. There were several books on a shelf; one lay beside the tea things open, and Utterson was amazed to find it a copy of a pious work, for which Jekyll had several times expressed a great esteem, annotated, in his own hand, with startling blasphemies.

Next, in the course of their review of the chamber, the searchers came to the cheval glass, into whose depths they looked with an involuntary horror. But it was so turned as to show them nothing but the rosy glow playing on the roof, the fire sparkling in a hundred repetitions along the glazed front of the presses, and their own pale and fearful countenances stooping to look in.

"This glass has seen some strange things, sir," whispered Poole.

"And surely none stranger than itself," echoed the lawyer in the same tones. "For what did Jekyll"—he caught himself up at the word with a start, and then conquering the weakness—"what could Jekyll want with it?" he said.

"You may say that!" said Poole.

Next they turned to the business table. On the desk, among the neat array of papers, a large envelope was uppermost, and bore, in the doctor's hand, the name of Mr. Utterson. The lawyer unsealed it, and several enclosures fell to the floor. The first was a will, drawn in the same eccentric terms as the one which he had returned six months before, to serve as a testament in case of death and as a deed of gift in case of disappearance; but in place of the name of Edward Hyde, the lawyer, with indescribable amazement, read the name of Gabriel John Utterson. He looked at Poole, and then back at the paper, and last of all at the dead malefactor stretched upon the carpet.

"My head goes round," he said. "He has been all these days in possession; he had no cause to like me; he must have raged to see himself displaced; and he has not destroyed this document."

He caught up the next paper; it was a brief note in the doctor's hand and dated at the top. "O Poole!" the lawyer cried, "he was alive and here this day. He cannot have been disposed of in so short a space; he must be still alive, he must have fled! And then, why fled? and how? and in that case, can we venture to declare this suicide? O, we must be careful. I foresee that we may yet involve your master in some dire catastrophe."

"Why don't you read it, sir?" asked Poole.

"Because I fear," replied the lawyer solemnly. "God grant I have no cause for it!" And with that he brought the paper to his eyes and read as follows:

"*My dear Utterson,*—When this shall fall into your hands, I shall have disappeared, under what circumstances I have not the penetration to foresee, but my instinct and all the circumstances of my nameless situation tell me that the end is sure and must be early. Go then, and first read the narrative which Lanyon warned me he was to place in your hands; and if you care to hear more, turn to the confession of

"Your unworthy and unhappy friend,

"*Henry Jekyll*"

"There was a third enclosure?" asked Utterson.

"Here, sir," said Poole, and gave into his hands a considerable packet sealed in several places.

The lawyer put it in his pocket. "I would say nothing of this paper. If your master has fled or is dead, we may at least save his credit. It is now ten; I must go home and read these documents in quiet; but I shall be back before midnight, when we shall send for the police."

They went out, locking the door of the theatre behind them; and Utterson, once more leaving the servants gathered about the fire in the hall, trudged back to his office to read the two narratives in which this mystery was now to be explained.

Dr. Lanyon's Narrative

On the ninth of January, now four days ago, I received by the evening delivery a registered envelope, addressed in the hand of my colleague and old school-companion, Henry Jekyll. I was a good deal surprised by this; for we were by no means in the habit of correspondence; I had seen the man, dined with him, indeed, the night before; and I could imagine nothing in our intercourse that should justify formality of registration. The contents increased my wonder; for this is how the letter ran:

"10th December, 18—.

Dear Lanyon,

"You are one of my oldest friends; and although we may have differed at times on scientific questions, I cannot remember, at least on my side, any break in our affection. There was never a day when, if you had said to me, 'Jekyll my life, my honour, my reason, depend upon you,' I would not have sacrificed my left hand to help you. Lanyon, my life, my honour, my reason, are all at your mercy; if you fail me to-night I am lost. You might suppose, after this preface, that I am going to ask you for something dishonourable to grant. Judge for yourself.

"I want you to postpone all other engagements for to-night—ay, even if you were summoned to the bedside of an emperor; to take a cab, unless your carriage should be actually at the door; and with this letter in your hand for consultation, to drive straight to my house. Poole, my butler, has his orders; you will find him waiting your arrival with a locksmith. The door of my cabinet is then to be forced: and you are to go in alone; to open the glazed press (letter E) on the left hand, breaking the lock if it be shut; and to draw out, *with all its contents as they stand,* the fourth drawer from the top or (which is the same thing) the third from the bottom. In my extreme distress of mind, I have a morbid fear of misdirecting you; but even if I am in error, you may know the right drawer by its contents: some powders, a phial and a paper book. This drawer I beg of you to carry back with you to Cavendish Square exactly as it stands.

"That is the first part of the service: now for the second. You should be back, if you set out at once on the receipt of this, long before midnight; but I will leave you that amount of margin, not only in the fear of one of those obstacles that can neither be prevented nor foreseen, but because an hour when your servants are in bed is to be preferred for what will then remain to do. At midnight, then, I have to ask you to be alone in your consulting-room, to admit with your own hand into the house a man who will present himself in my name, and to place in his hands the drawer that you will have brought with you from my cabinet. Then you will have played your part and earned my gratitude completely. Five minutes afterwards, if you insist upon an explanation, you will have understood that these arrangements are of capital importance; and that by the neglect of one of them, fantastic as they must appear, you might have charged your conscience with my death or the shipwreck of my reason.

"Confident as I am that you will not trifle with this appeal, my heart sinks and my hand trembles at the bare thought of such a possibility. Think of me at this hour, in a strange place, labouring under a blackness of distress that no fancy can exaggerate, and yet well aware that, if you will but punctually serve me, my troubles will roll away like a story that is told. Serve me, my dear Lanyon, and save

"Your friend,

"H. J.

"P. S. I had already sealed this up when a fresh terror struck upon my soul. It is possible that the post-office may fail me, and this letter not come into your hands until to-morrow morning. In that case, dear Lanyon, do my errand when it shall be most convenient for you in the course of the day; and once more expect my messenger at midnight. It may then already be too late; and if that night passes without event, you will know that you have seen the last of Henry Jekyll."

Upon the reading of this letter, I made sure my colleague was insane; but till that was proved beyond the possibility of doubt, I felt bound to do as he requested. The less I understood of this farrago, the less I was in a position to judge of its importance; and an appeal so worded could not be set aside without a grave responsibility. I rose accordingly from table, got into a hansom, and drove straight to Jekyll's house. The butler was awaiting my arrival, he had received by the same post as mine a registered letter of instruction, and had sent at once for a locksmith and a carpenter. The tradesmen came while we were yet speaking; and we moved in a body to old Dr. Denman's surgical theatre, from which (as you are doubtless aware) Jekyll's private cabinet is most conveniently entered. The door was very strong, the lock excellent; the carpenter avowed he would have great trouble and have to do much damage, if force were to be used; and the locksmith was near despair. But this last was a handy fellow, and after two hours' work, the door stood open. The press marked E was unlocked; and I took out the drawer, had it filled up with straw and tied in a sheet, and returned with it to Cavendish Square.

Here I proceeded to examine its contents. The powders were neatly enough made up, but not with the nicety of the dispensing chemist; so that it was plain they were of Jekyll's private manufacture: and when I opened one of the wrappers I found what seemed to me a simple crystalline salt of a white colour. The phial, to which I next turned my attention, might have been about half full of a blood-red liquor, which was highly pungent to the sense of smell and seemed to me to contain phosphorous and some volatile ether. At the other ingredients I could make no guess. The book was an ordinary version book and contained little but a series of dates. These covered a period of many years, but I observed that the entries ceased nearly a year ago and quite abruptly. Here and there a brief remark was appended to a date, usually no more than a single word: "double" occurring perhaps six times in a total of several hundred entries; and once very early in the list and followed by several marks of exclamation, "total failure!!!" All this, though it whetted my curiosity, told me little that was definite. Here were a phial of some tincture, a paper of some salt, and the record of a series of experiments that had led (like too many of Jekyll's investigations) to no end of practical usefulness. How could the presence of these articles in my house affect either the honour, the sanity, or the life of my flighty colleague? If his messenger could go to one place, why could he not go to another? And even granting some impediment, why was this gentleman to be received by me in secret? The more I reflected the more convinced I grew that I was dealing with a case of cerebral disease; and though I dismissed my servants to bed, I loaded an old revolver, that I might be found in some posture of self-defence.

Twelve o'clock had scarce rung out over London, ere the knocker sounded very gently on the door. I went myself at the summons, and found a small man crouching against the pillars of the portico.

"Are you come from Dr. Jekyll?" I asked.

He told me "yes" by a constrained gesture; and when I had bidden him enter, he did not obey me without a searching backward glance into the darkness of the square. There was a policeman not far off, advancing with his bull's-eye open; and at the sight, I thought my visitor started and made greater haste.

These particulars struck me, I confess, disagreeably; and as I followed him into the bright light of the consulting-room, I kept my hand ready on my weapon. Here, at last, I had a chance of clearly seeing him. I had never set eyes on him before, so much was certain. He was small, as I have said; I was struck besides with the shocking expression of his face, with his remarkable com-

bination of great muscular activity and great apparent debility of
constitution, and—last but not least—with the odd, subjective
disturbance caused by his neighbourhood. This bore some resemblance to incipient rigour, and was accompanied by a marked
sinking of the pulse. At the time, I set it down to some idiosyn-
cratic, personal distaste, and merely wondered at the acuteness of
the symptoms; but I have since had reason to believe the cause to
lie much deeper in the nature of man, and to turn on some nobler
hinge than the principle of hatred.

This person (who had thus, from the first moment of his entrance, struck in me what I can only describe as a disgustful
curiosity) was dressed in a fashion that would have made an ordinary person laughable; his clothes, that is to say, although they
were of rich and sober fabric, were enormously too large for him
in every measurement—the trousers hanging on his legs and rolled
up to keep them from the ground, the waist of the coat below his
haunches, and the collar sprawling wide upon his shoulders.
Strange to relate, this ludicrous accoutrement was far from moving
me to laughter. Rather, as there was something abnormal and misbegotten in the very essence of the creature that now faced me—
something seizing, surprising, and revolting—this fresh disparity
seemed but to fit in with and to reinforce it; so that to my interest
in the man's nature and character, there was added a curiosity
as to his origin, his life, his fortune and status in the world.

These observations, though they have taken so great a space to
be set down in, were yet the work of a few seconds. My visitor was,
indeed, on fire with sombre excitement.

"Have you got it?" he cried. "Have you got it?" And so lively
was his impatience that he even laid his hand upon my arm and
sought to shake me.

I put him back, conscious at his touch of a certain icy pang
along my blood. "Come, sir," said I. "You forget that I have not
yet the pleasure of your acquaintance. Be seated, if you please."
And I showed him an example, and sat down myself in my customary seat and with as fair an imitation of my ordinary manner
to a patient, as the lateness of the hour, the nature of my preoccupations, and the horror I had of my visitor, would suffer me
to muster.

"I beg your pardon, Dr. Lanyon," he replied civilly enough.

"What you say is very well founded; and my impatience has shown its heels to my politeness. I come here at the instance of your colleague, Dr. Henry Jekyll, on a piece of business of some moment; and I understood . . ." He paused and put his hand to his throat, and I could see, in spite of his collected manner, that he was wrestling against the approaches of the hysteria—"I understood, a drawer . . ."

But here I took pity on my visitor's suspense, and some perhaps on my own growing curiosity.

"There it is, sir," said I, pointing to the drawer, where it lay on the floor behind a table and still covered with the sheet.

He sprang to it, and then paused, and laid his hand upon his heart: I could hear his teeth grate with the convulsive action of his jaws; and his face was so ghastly to see that I grew alarmed both for his life and reason.

"Compose yourself," said I.

He turned a dreadful smile to me, and as if with the decision of despair, plucked away the sheet. At sight of the contents, he uttered one loud sob of such immense relief that I sat petrified. And the next moment, in a voice that was already fairly well under control, "Have you a graduated glass?" he asked.

I rose from my place with something of an effort and gave him what he asked.

He thanked me with a smiling nod, measured out a few minims of the red tincture and added one of the powders. The mixture, which was at first of a reddish hue, began, in proportion as the crystals melted, to brighten in colour, to effervesce audibly, and to throw off small fumes of vapour. Suddenly and at the same moment, the ebullition ceased and the compound changed to a dark purple, which faded again more slowly to a watery green. My visitor, who had watched these metamorphoses with a keen eye, smiled, set down the glass upon the table, and then turned and looked upon me with an air of scrutiny.

"And now," said he, "to settle what remains. Will you be wise? will you be guided? will you suffer me to take this glass in my hand and to go forth from your house without further parley? or has the greed of curiosity too much command of you? Think before you answer, for it shall be done as you decide. As you decide, you shall be left as you were before, and neither richer nor wiser, unless the sense of service rendered to a man in mortal distress may be counted as a kind of riches of the soul. Or, if you shall so prefer to choose, a new province of knowledge and new avenues to fame and power shall be laid open to you, here, in this room, upon the instant; and your sight shall be blasted by a prodigy to stagger the unbelief of Satan."

"Sir," said I, affecting a coolness that I was far from truly possessing, "you speak enigmas, and you will perhaps not wonder that I hear you with no very strong impression of belief. But I have gone too far in the way of inexplicable services to pause before I see the end."

"It is well," replied my visitor. "Lanyon, you remember your vows: what follows is under the seal of our profession. And now, you who have so long been bound to the most narrow and material views, you who have denied the virtue of transcendental medicine, you who have derided your superiors—behold!"

He put the glass to his lips and drank at one gulp. A cry followed; he reeled, staggered, clutched at the table and held on, staring with injected eyes, gasping with open mouth; and as I looked there came, I thought, a change—he seemed to swell—his face became suddenly black and the features seemed to melt and alter—and the next moment I had sprung to my feet and leaped back against the wall, my arm raised to shield me from that prodigy, my mind submerged in terror.

"O God!" I screamed, and "O God!" again and again; for there before my eyes—pale and shaken, and half fainting, and groping before him with his hands, like a man restored from death—there stood Henry Jekyll!

What he told me in the next hour, I cannot bring my mind to set on paper. I saw what I saw, I heard what I heard, and my soul sickened at it; and yet now when that sight has faded from my eyes, I ask myself if I believe it, and I cannot answer. My life is shaken to its roots; sleep has left me; the deadliest terror sits by me at all hours of the day and night; I feel that my days are numbered, and that I must die; and yet I shall die incredulous. As for the moral turpitude that man unveiled to me, even with tears of penitence, I cannot, even in memory, dwell on it without a start of horror. I will say but one thing, Utterson, and that (if you can bring your mind to credit it) will be more than enough. The creature who crept into my house that night was, on Jekyll's own confession, known by the name of Hyde and hunted for in every corner of the land as the murderer of Carew.

HASTIE LANYON

Henry Jekyll's Full Statement of the Case

I was born in the year 18— to a large fortune, endowed besides with excellent parts, inclined by nature to industry, fond of the respect of the wise and good among my fellow-men, and thus, as might have been supposed, with every guarantee of an honourable and distinguished future. And indeed the worst of my faults was a certain impatient gaiety of disposition, such as has made the happiness of many, but such as I found it hard to reconcile with my imperious desire to carry my head high, and wear a more than commonly grave countenance before the public. Hence it came about that I concealed my pleasures; and that when I reached years of reflection, and began to look round me and take stock of my progress and position in the world, I stood already committed to a profound duplicity of life. Many a man would have even blazoned such irregularities as I was guilty of; but from the high views that I had set before me, I regarded and hid them with an almost morbid sense of shame. It was thus rather the exacting nature of my aspirations than any particular degradation in my faults, that made me what I was, and, with even a deeper trench than in the majority of men, severed in me those provinces of good and ill which divide and compound man's dual nature. In this case, I was driven to reflect deeply and inveterately on that hard law of life, which lies at the root of religion and is one of the most plentiful springs of distress. Though so profound a double-dealer, I was in no sense a hypocrite; both sides of me were in dead earnest; I was no more myself when I laid aside restraint and plunged in shame, than when I laboured, in the eye of day, at the furtherance of knowledge or the relief of sorrow and suffering. And it chanced that the direction of my scientific studies, which led wholly towards the mystic and the transcendental, reacted and shed a strong light on this consciousness of the perennial war among my members. With every day, and from both sides of my intelligence, the moral and the intellectual, I thus drew steadily nearer to that truth, by whose partial discovery I have been

doomed to such a dreadful shipwreck: that man is not truly one,
but truly two. I say two, because the state of my own knowledge
does not pass beyond that point. Others will follow, others will
outstrip me on the same lines; and I hazard the guess that man
will be ultimately known for a mere polity of multifarious, incongruous, and independent denizens. I for my part, from the nature of my life, advanced infallibly in one direction and in one
direction only. It was on the moral side, and in my own person,
that I learned to recognise the thorough and primitive duality of
man; I saw that, of the two natures that contended in the field of
my consciousness, even if I could rightly be said to be either, it
was only because I was radically both; and from an early date,
even before the course of my scientific discoveries had begun to
suggest the most naked possibility of such a miracle, I had learned
to dwell with pleasure, as a beloved day-dream, on the thought of
the separation of these elements. If each, I told myself, could but
be housed in separate identities, life would be relieved of all that
was unbearable; the unjust might go his way, delivered from the
aspirations and remorse of his more upright twin; and the just
could walk steadfastly and securely on his upward path, doing the
good things in which he found his pleasure, and no longer exposed to disgrace and penitence by the hands of this extraneous
evil. It was the curse of mankind that these incongruous faggots
were thus bound together—that in the agonised womb of consciousness, these polar twins should be continuously struggling.
How, then, were they dissociated?

I was so far in my reflections when, as I have said, a side light
began to shine upon the subject from the laboratory table. I began
to perceive more deeply than it has ever yet been stated, the trembling immateriality, the mist-like transience, of this seemingly so
solid body in which we walk attired. Certain agents I found to
have the power to shake and to pluck back that fleshly vestment,
even as a wind might toss the curtains of a pavilion. For two good
reasons, I will not enter deeply into this scientific branch of my
confession. First, because I have been made to learn that the doom
and burthen of our life is bound for ever on man's shoulders, and
when the attempt is made to cast it off, it but returns upon us with
more unfamiliar and more awful pressure. Second, because, as my
narrative will make, alas! too evident, my discoveries were incomplete. Enough, then, that I not only recognised my natural body

for the mere aura and effulgence of certain of the powers that made up my spirit, but managed to compound a drug by which these powers should be dethroned from their supremacy, and a second form and countenance substituted, none the less natural to me because they were the expression, and bore the stamp, of lower elements in my soul.

I hesitated long before I put this theory to the test of practice. I knew well that I risked death; for any drug that so potently controlled and shook the very fortress of identity, might by the least scruple of an overdose or at the least inopportunity in the moment of exhibition, utterly blot out that immaterial tabernacle which I looked to it to change. But the temptation of a discovery so singular and profound, at last overcame the suggestions of alarm. I had long since prepared my tincture; I purchased at once, from a firm of wholesale chemists, a large quantity of a particular salt which I knew, from my experiments, to be the last ingredient required; and late one accursed night, I compounded the elements, watched them boil and smoke together in the glass, and when the ebullition had subsided, with a strong glow of courage, drank off the potion.

The most racking pangs succeeded: a grinding in the bones, deadly nausea, and a horror of the spirit that cannot be exceeded at the hour of birth or death. Then these agonies began swiftly to subside, and I came to myself as if out of a great sickness. There was something strange in my sensations, something indescribably new and, from its very novelty, incredibly sweet. I felt younger, lighter, happier in body; within I was conscious of a heady recklessness, a current of disordered sensual images running like a mill race in my fancy, a solution of the bonds of obligation, an unknown but not an innocent freedom of the soul. I knew myself, at the first breath of this new life, to be more wicked, tenfold more wicked, sold a slave to my original evil; and the thought, in that moment, braced and delighted me like wine. I stretched out my hands, exulting in the freshness of these sensations; and in the act, I was suddenly aware that I had lost in stature.

There was no mirror, at that date, in my room; that which stands beside me as I write, was brought there later on for the very purpose of these transformations. The night, however, was far gone into the morning—the morning, black as it was, was nearly ripe for the conception of the day—the inmates of my house were

locked in the most rigorous hours of slumber; and I determined,
flushed as I was with hope and triumph, to venture in my new
shape as far as to my bedroom. I crossed the yard, wherein the
constellations looked down upon me, I could have thought, with
wonder, the first creature of that sort that their unsleeping vigilance had yet disclosed to them; I stole through the corridors, a
stranger in my own house; and coming to my room, I saw for the
first time the appearance of Edward Hyde.

I must here speak by theory alone, saying not that which I know,
but that which I suppose to be most probable. The evil side of my
nature, to which I had now transferred the stamping efficacy, was
less robust and less developed than the good which I had just
deposed. Again, in the course of my life, which had been, after all,
nine-tenths a life of effort, virtue, and control, it had been much
less exercised and much less exhausted. And hence, as I think, it
came about that Edward Hyde was so much smaller, slighter, and
younger than Henry Jekyll. Even as good shone upon the countenance of the one, evil was written broadly and plainly on the face
of the other. Evil besides (which I must still believe to be the lethal
side of man) had left on that body an imprint of deformity and
decay. And yet when I looked upon that ugly idol in the glass,
I was conscious of no repugnance, rather of a leap of welcome.
This, too, was myself. It seemed natural and human. In my eyes
it bore a livelier image of the spirit, it seemed more express and
single, than the imperfect and divided countenance I had been
hitherto accustomed to call mine. And in so far I was doubtless
right. I have observed that when I wore the semblance of Edward
Hyde, none could come near to me at first without a visible mis-
giving of the flesh. This, as I take it, was because all human beings,
as we meet them, are commingled out of good and evil: and Edward Hyde, alone in the ranks of mankind, was pure evil.

I lingered but a moment at the mirror: the second and conclu-
sive experiment had yet to be attempted; it yet remained to be
seen if I had lost my identity beyond redemption and must flee
before daylight from a house that was no longer mine; and hurrying back to my cabinet, I once more prepared and drank the cup,
once more suffered the pangs of dissolution, and came to myself
once more with the character, the stature, and the face of Henry
Jekyll.

That night I had come to the fatal cross roads. Had I approached my discovery in a more noble spirit, had I risked the experiment while under the empire of generous of pious aspirations, all must have been otherwise, and from these agonies of death and birth, I had come forth an angel instead of a fiend. The drug had no discriminating action; it was neither diabolical nor divine; it but shook the doors of the prison house of my disposition; and like the captives of Philippi, that which stood within ran forth. At that time my virtue slumbered; my evil, kept awake by ambition, was alert and swift to seize the occasion; and the thing that was projected was Edward Hyde. Hence, although I had now two characters as well as two appearances, one was wholly evil, and the other was still the old Henry Jekyll, that incongruous compound of whose reformation and improvement I had already learned to despair. The movement was thus wholly towards the worse.

Even at that time, I had not yet conquered my aversion to the dryness of a life of study. I would still be merrily disposed at times; and as my pleasures were (to say the least) undignified, and I was not only well known and highly considered, but growing towards the elderly man, this incoherency of my life was daily growing more unwelcome. It was on this side that my new power tempted me until I fell in slavery. I had but to drink the cup, to doff at once the body of the noted professor, and to assume, like a thick cloak, that of Edward Hyde. I smiled at the notion; it seemed to me at the time to be humourous; and I made my preparations with the most studious care. I took and furnished the house in Soho, to which Hyde was tracked by the police; and engaged as housekeeper a creature whom I well knew to be silent and unscrupulous. On the other side, I announced to my servants that a Mr. Hyde (whom I described) was to have full liberty and power about my house in the square; and to parry mishaps, I even called and made myself a familiar object, in my second character. I next drew up that will to which you so much objected; so that if anything befell me in the person of Dr. Jekyll, I could enter on that of Edward Hyde without pecuniary loss. And thus fortified, as I supposed, on very side, I began to profit by the strange immunities of my position.

Men have before hired bravos to transact their crimes, while their own person and reputation sat under shelter. I was the first that ever did so for his pleasures. I was the first that could thus plod in the public eye with a load of genial respectability, and in a moment, like a schoolboy, strip off these lendings and spring head-long into the sea of liberty. But for me, in my impenetrable mantle, the safety was complete. Think of it—I did not even exist! Let me but escape into my laboratory door, give me but a second or two to mix and swallow the draught that I had always standing ready; and whatever he had done, Edward Hyde would pass away like the stain of breath upon a mirror; and there in his stead, quietly at home, trimming the midnight lamp in his study, a man who could afford to laugh at suspicion, would be Henry Jekyll.

The pleasures which I made haste to seek in my disguise were, as I have said, undignified; I would scarce use a harder term. But in the hands of Edward Hyde, they soon began to turn towards the monstrous. When I would come back from these excursions, I was often plunged into a kind of wonder at my vicarious depravity. This familiar that I called out of my own soul, and sent forth alone to do his good pleasure, was a being inherently malign and villainous; his every act and thought centred on self; drinking pleasure with bestial avidity from any degree of torture to another; relentless like a man of stone. Henry Jekyll stood at times aghast before the acts of Edward Hyde; but the situation was apart from ordinary laws, and insidiously relaxed the grasp of conscience. It was Hyde, after all, and Hyde alone, that was guilty. Jekyll was no worse; he woke again to his good qualities seemingly unimpaired; he would even make haste, where it was possible, to undo the evil done by Hyde. And thus his conscience slumbered.

Into the details of the infamy at which I thus connived (for even now I can scarce grant that I committed it) I have no design of entering; I mean but to point out the warnings and the successive steps with which my chastisement approached. I met with one accident which, as it brought on no consequence, I shall no more than mention. An act of cruelty to a child aroused against me the anger of a passer-by, whom I recognised the other day in the person of your kinsman; the doctor and the child's family joined him; there were moments when I feared for my life; and at last, in order to pacify their too just resentment, Edward Hyde had to bring them to the door, and pay them in a cheque drawn in the name of Henry Jekyll. But this danger was easily eliminated from the future, by opening an account at another bank in the name of Edward Hyde himself; and when, by sloping my own hand backward, I had supplied my double with a signature, I thought I sat beyond the reach of fate.

Some two months before the murder of Sir Danvers, I had been out for one of my adventures, had returned at a late hour, and woke the next day in bed with somewhat odd sensations. It was in vain I looked about me; in vain I saw the decent furniture and tall proportions of my room in the square; in vain that I recognised the pattern of the bed curtains and the design of the mahogany frame; something still kept insisting that I was not where I was, that I had not wakened where I seemed to be, but in the little room in Soho where I was accustomed to sleep in the body of Edward Hyde. I smiled to myself, and, in my psychological way began lazily to inquire into the elements of this illusion, occasionally, even as I did so, dropping back into a comfortable morning doze. I was still so engaged when, in one of my more wakeful moments, my eyes fell upon my hand. Now the hand of Henry Jekyll (as you have often remarked) was professional in shape and size: it was large, firm, white, and comely. But the hand which I now saw, clearly enough, in the yellow light of a mid-London morning, lying half shut on the bed clothes, was lean, corded, knuckly, of a dusky pallor, and thickly shaded with a swart growth of hair. It was the hand of Edward Hyde.

I must have stared upon it for near half a minute, sunk as I was in the mere stupidity of wonder, before terror woke up in my breast as sudden and startling as the crash of cymbals; and bounding from my bed, I rushed to the mirror. At the sight that met my eyes, my blood was changed into something exquisitely thin and icy. Yes, I had gone to bed Henry Jekyll, I had awakened Edward Hyde. How was this to be explained? I asked myself; and then, with another bound of terror—how was it to be remedied? It was well on in the morning; the servants were up; all my drugs were in the cabinet—a long journey down two pair of stairs, through the back passage, across the open court and through the anatomical theatre, from where I was then standing horror-struck. It might indeed be possible to cover my face; but of what use was that, when I was unable to conceal the alteration in my stature? And then with an overpowering sweetness of relief, it came back upon my mind that the servants were already used to the coming and going of my second self. I had soon dressed, as well as I was able, in clothes of my own size; had soon passed through the house,

where Bradshaw stared and drew back at seeing Mr. Hyde at such
an hour and in such a strange array; and ten minutes later, Dr.
Jekyll had returned to his own shape and was sitting down, with a
darkened brow, to make a feint of breakfasting.

Small indeed was my appetite. This inexplicable incident, this
reversal of my previous experience, seemed, like the Babylonian
finger on the wall, to be spelling out the letters of my judgment;
and I began to reflect more seriously than ever before on the issues
and possibilities of my double existence. That part of me which
I had the power of projecting, had lately been much exercised and
nourished; it had seemed to me of late as though the body of
Edward Hyde had grown in stature, as though (when I wore that
form) I were conscious of a more generous tide of blood; and I
began to spy a danger that, if this were much prolonged, the
balance of my nature might be permanently overthrown, the
power of voluntary change be forfeited, and the character of Edward Hyde become irrevocably mine. The power of the drug had
not been always equally displayed. Once, very early in my career,
it had totally failed me; since then I had been obliged on more
than one occasion to double, and once, with infinite risk of death,
to treble the amount; and these rare uncertainties had cast hitherto the sole shadow on my contentment. Now, however, and in
the light of that morning's accident, I was led to remark that
whereas, in the beginning, the difficulty had been to throw off the
body of Jekyll, it had of late gradually but decidedly transferred
iself to the other side. All things therefore seemed to point to this:
that I was slowly losing hold of my original and better self, and becoming slowly incorporated with my second and worse.

Between these two, I now felt I had to choose. My two natures
had memory in common, but all other faculties were most unequally shared between them. Jekyll (who was composite) now
with the most sensitive apprehensions, now with a greedy gusto,
projected and shared in the pleasures and adventures of Hyde; but
Hyde was indifferent to Jekyll, or but remembered him as the
mountain bandit remembers the cavern in which he conceals himself from pursuit. Jekyll had more than a father's interest; Hyde
had more than a son's indifference. To cast in my lot with Jekyll,
was to die to those appetites which I had long secretly indulged
and had of late begun to pamper. To cast it in with Hyde, was to
die to a thousand interests and aspirations, and to become, at a

blow and for ever, despised and friendless. The bargain might appear unequal; but there was still another consideration in the scales; for while Jekyll would suffer smartingly in the fires of abstinence, Hyde would be not even conscious of all that he had lost. Strange as my circumstances were, the terms of this debate are as old and commonplace as man; much the same inducements and alarms cast the die for any tempted and trembling sinner; and it fell out with me, as it falls with so vast a majority of my fellows, that I chose the better part and was found wanting in the strength to keep to it.

Yes, I preferred the elderly and discontented doctor, surrounded by friends and cherishing honest hopes; and bade a resolute fare-well to the liberty, the comparative youth, the light step, leaping impulses and secret pleasures, that I had enjoyed in the disguise of Hyde. I made this choice perhaps with some unconscious reserva-tion, for I neither gave up the house in Soho, nor destroyed the clothes of Edward Hyde, which still lay ready in my cabinet. For two months, however, I was true to my determination; for two months I led a life of such severity as I had never before attained to, and enjoyed the compensations of an approving conscience. But time began at last to obliterate the freshness of my alarm; the praises of conscience began to grow into a thing of course; I began to be tortured with throes and longings, as of Hyde struggling after freedom; and at last, in an hour of moral weakness, I once again compounded and swallowed the transforming draught.

I do not suppose that, when a drunkard reasons with himself upon his vice, he is once out of five hundred times affected by the dangers that he runs through his brutish, physical insensibility; neither had I, long as I had considered my position, made enough allowance for the complete moral insensibility and insensate readi-ness to evil, which were the leading characters of Edward Hyde. Yet it was by these that I was punished. My devil had been long caged, he came out roaring. I was conscious, even when I took the draught, of a more unbridled, a more furious propensity to ill. It must have been this, I suppose, that stirred in my soul that tempest of impatience with which I listened to the civilities of my unhappy victim; I declare, at least, before God, no man morally sane could have been guilty of that crime upon so pitiful a provo-cation; and that I struck in no more reasonable spirit than that in which a sick child may break a plaything. But I had voluntarily stripped myself of all those balancing instincts by which even the worst of us continues to walk with some degree of steadiness among temptations; and in my case, to be tempted, however slightly, was to fall.

Instantly the spirit of hell awoke in me and raged. With a transport of glee, I mauled the unresisting body, tasting delight from every blow; and it was not till weariness had begun to succeed, that I was suddenly, in the top fit of my delirium, struck through the heart by a cold thrill of terror. A mist dispersed; I saw my life to be forfeit; and fled from the scene of these excesses, at once glorifying and trembling, my lust of evil gratified and stimulated, my love of life screwed to the topmost peg. I ran to the house in Soho, and (to make assurance doubly sure) destroyed my papers; thence I set out through the lamplit streets, in the same divided ecstasy of mind, gloating on my crime, light-headedly devising others in the future, and yet still hastening and still hearkening in my wake for the steps of the avenger. Hyde had a song upon his lips as he compounded the draught, and as he drank it, pledged the dead man. The pangs of transformation had not done tearing him, before Henry Jekyll, with streaming tears of gratitude and remorse, had fallen upon his knees and lifted his clasped hands to God. The veil of self-indulgence was rent from head to foot. I saw my life as a whole: I followed it up from the days of childhood, when I had walked with my father's hand, and through the self-denying toils of my professional life, to arrive again and again, with the same sense of unreality, at the damned horrors of the evening. I could have screamed aloud; I sought with tears and prayers to smother down the crowd of hideous images and sounds with which my memory swarmed against me; and still, between the petitions, the ugly face of my iniquity stared into my soul. As the acuteness of this remorse began to die away, it was succeeded by a sense of joy. The problem of my conduct was solved. Hyde was thenceforth impossible; whether I would or not, I was now confined to the better part of my existence; and O, how I rejoiced to think it! with what willing humility, I embraced anew the restrictions of natural life! with what sincere renunciation, I locked the door by which I had so often gone and come, and ground the key under my heel!

The next day, came the news that the murder had been over-looked, that the guilt of Hyde was patent to the world. and that the victim was a man high in public estimation. It was not only a crime, it had been a tragic folly. I think I was glad to know it; I think I was glad to have my better impulses thus buttressed and guarded by the terrors of the scaffold. Jekyll was now my city of refuge; let but Hyde peep out an instant, and the hands of all men would be raised to take and slay him.

I resolved in my future conduct to redeem the past; and I can say with honesty that my resolve was fruitful of some good. You know yourself how earnestly in the last months of last year, I laboured to relieve suffering; you know that much was done for others, and that the days passed quietly, almost happily for myself. Nor can I truly say that I wearied of this beneficent and innocent life; I think instead that I daily enjoyed it more completely; but I was still cursed with my duality of purpose; and as the first edge of my penitence wore off, the lower side of me, so long indulged, so recently chained down, began to growl for license. Not that I dreamed of resuscitating Hyde; the bare idea of that would startle me to frenzy: no, it was in my own person, that I was once more tempted to trifle with my conscience; and it was as an ordinary secret sinner, that I at last fell before the assaults of temptation.

There comes an end to all things; the most capacious measure is filled at last; and this brief condescension to my evil finally destroyed the balance of my soul. And yet I was not alarmed; the fall seemed natural, like a return to the old days before I had made my discovery. It was a fine, clear, January day, wet underfoot where the frost had melted, but cloudless overhead; and the Regent's Park was full of winter chirrupings and sweet with spring odours. I sat in the sun on a bench; the animal within me licking the chops of memory; the spiritual side a little drowsed, promising subsequent penitence, but not yet moved to begin. After all, I reflected, I was like my neighbours; and then I smiled, comparing myself with other men, comparing my active good-will with the lazy cruelty of their neglect. And at the very moment of that vainglorious thought, a qualm came over me, a horrid nausea and the most deadly shuddering. These passed away, and left me faint; and then as in its turn the faintness subsided, I began to be aware of a change in the temper of my thoughts, a greater boldness, a contempt of danger, a solution of the bonds of obligation. I looked down; my clothes hung formlessly on my shrunken limbs; the hand that lay on my knee was corded and hairy. I was once more Edward Hyde. A moment before I had been safe of all men's respect, wealthy, beloved—the cloth laying for me in the dining-room at home; and now I was the common quarry of mankind, hunted, houseless, a known murderer, thrall to the gallows.

My reason wavered, but it did not fail me utterly. I have more than once observed that, in my second character, my faculties seemed sharpened to a point and my spirits more tensely elastic; thus it came about that, where Jekyll perhaps might have succumbed, Hyde rose to the importance of the moment. My drugs were in one of the presses of my cabinet; how was I to reach them? That was the problem that (crushing my temples in my hands) I set myself to solve. The laboratory door I had closed. If I sought to enter by the house, my own servants would consign me to the gallows. I saw I must employ another hand, and thought of Lanyon. How was he to be reached? how persuaded? Supposing that I escaped capture in the streets, how was I to make my way into his presence? and how should I, an unknown and displeasing visitor, prevail on the famous physician to rifle the study of his colleague, Dr. Jekyll? Then I remembered that of my original character, one part remained to me: I could write my own hand; and once I had conceived that kindling spark, the way that I must follow became lighted up from end to end.

Thereupon I arranged my clothes as best I could, and summoning a passing hansom, drove to an hotel in Portland Street, the name of which I chanced to remember. At my appearance (which was indeed comical enough, however tragic a fate these garments covered) the driver could not conceal his mirth. I gnashed my teeth upon him with a gust of devilish fury; and the smile withered from his face—happily for him—yet more happily for myself, for in another instant I had certainly dragged him from his perch. At the inn, as I entered, I looked about me with so black a countenance as made the attendants tremble; not a look did they exchange in my presence; but obsequiously took my orders, led me to a private room, and brought me wherewithal to write. Hyde in danger of his life was a creature new to me; shaken with inordinate anger, strung to the pitch of murder, lusting to inflict pain. Yet the creature was astute; mastered his fury with a great effort of the will; composed his two important letters, one to Lanyon and one to Poole; and that he might receive actual evidence of their being posted, sent them out with directions that they should be registered.

Thenceforward, he sat all day over the fire in the private room, gnawing his nails; there he dined, sitting alone with his fears, the waiter visibly quailing before his eye; and thence, when the night was fully come, he set forth in the corner of a closed cab, and was driven to and fro about the streets of the city. He, I say—I cannot say, I. That child of Hell had nothing human; nothing lived in him but fear and hatred. And when at last, thinking the driver had begun to grow suspicious, he discharged the cab and ventured on foot, attired in his misfitting clothes, an object marked out for observation, into the midst of the nocturnal passengers, these two base passions raged within him like a tempest. He walked fast, hunted by his fears, chattering to himself, skulking through the less frequented thoroughfares, counting the minutes that still divided him from midnight. Once a woman spoke to him, offering, I think, a box of lights. He smote her in the face, and she fled.

When I came to myself at Lanyon's, the horror of my old friend perhaps affected me somewhat: I do not know; it was at least but a drop in the sea to the abhorrence with which I looked back upon these hours. A change had come over me. It was no longer the fear of the gallows, it was the horror of being Hyde that racked me. I received Lanyon's condemnation partly in a dream; it was partly in a dream that I came home to my own house and got into bed. I slept after the prostration of the day, with a stringent and profound slumber which not even the nightmares that wrung me could avail to break. I awoke in the morning shaken, weakened, but refreshed. I still hated and feared the thought of the brute that slept within me, and I had not of course forgotten the appalling dangers of the day before; but I was once more at home, in my own house and close to my drugs; and gratitude for my escape shone so strong in my soul that it almost rivalled the brightness of hope.

I was stepping leisurely across the court after breakfast, drinking the chill of the air with pleasure, when I was seized again with those indescribable sensations that heralded the change; and I had but the time to gain the shelter of my cabinet, before I was once again raging and freezing with the passions of Hyde. It took on this occasion a double dose to recall me to myself; and alas! six hours after, as I sat looking sadly in the fire, the pangs returned,

and the drug had to be readministered. In short, from that day
forth it seemed only by a great effort as of gymnastics, and only
under the immediate stimulation of the drug, that I was able to
wear the countenance of Jekyll. At all hours of the day and night,
I would be taken with the premonitory shudder; above all, if I
slept, or even dozed for a moment in my chair, it was always as
Hyde that I awakened. Under the strain of this continually impending doom and by the sleeplessness to which I now condemned
myself, ay, even beyond what I had thought possible to man, I
became, in my own person, a creature eaten up and emptied by
fever, languidly weak both in body and mind, and solely occupied
by one thought: the horror of my other self. But when I slept, or
when the virtue of the medicine wore off, I would leap almost
without transition (for the pangs of transformation grew daily less
marked) into the possession of a fancy brimming with images of terror, a soul boiling with causeless hatreds, and a body that seemed
not strong enough to contain the raging energies of life. The
powers of Hyde seemed to have grown with the sickliness of Jekyll.
And certainly the hate that now divided them was equal on each
side. With Jekyll, it was a thing of vital instinct. He had now seen
the full deformity of that creature that shared with him some
of the phenomena of consciousness, and was co-heir with him to
death: and beyond these links of community, which in themselves
made the most poignant part of his distress, he thought of Hyde,
for all his energy of life, as of something not only hellish but
inorganic. This was the shocking thing; that the slime of the pit
seemed to utter cries and voices; that the amorphous dust gesticu-
lated and sinned; that what was dead, and had no shape, should
usurp the offices of life. And this again, that that insurgent horror
was knit to him closer than a wife, closer than an eye; lay caged
in his flesh, where he heard it mutter and felt it struggle to be
born; and at every hour of weakness, and in the confidence of
slumber, prevailed against him, and deposed him out of life. The
hatred of Hyde for Jekyll, was of a different order. His terror of
the gallows drove him continually to commit temporary suicide,
and return to his subordinate station of a part instead of a person;
but he loathed the necessity, he loathed the despondency into
which Jekyll was now fallen, and he resented the dislike with
which he was himself regarded. Hence the apelike tricks that he

would play me, scrawling in my own hand blasphemies on the
pages of my books, burning the letters and destroying the portrait
of my father; and indeed, had it not been for his fear of death, he
would long ago have ruined himself in order to involve me in the
ruin. But his love of life is wonderful; I go further: I, who sicken
and freeze at the mere thought of him, when I recall the abjection
and passion of this attachment, and when I know how he fears my
power to cut him off by suicide, I find it in my heart to pity him.

It is useless, and the time awfully fails me, to prolong this description; no one has ever suffered such torments, let that suffice;
and yet even to these, habit brought—no, not alleviation—but a
certain callousness of soul, a certain acquiescence of despair; and
my punishment might have gone on for years, but for the last
calamity which has now fallen, and which has finally severed me
from my own face and nature. My provision of the salt, which had
never been renewed since the date of the first experiment, began
to run low. I sent out for a fresh supply, and mixed the draught;
the ebullition followed, and the first change of colour, not the
second; I drank it and it was without efficiency. You will learn
from Poole how I have had London ransacked: it was in vain; and
I am now persuaded that my first supply was impure, and that it
was that unknown impurity which lent efficacy to the draught.

About a week has passed, and I am now finishing this statement
under the influence of the last of the old powders. This, then, is
the last time, short of a miracle, that Henry Jekyll can think his
own thoughts or see his own face (now how sadly altered!) in the
glass. Nor must I delay too long to bring my writing to an end;
for if my narrative has hitherto escaped destruction, it has been by
a combination of great prudence and great good luck. Should the
throes of change take me in the act of writing it, Hyde will tear
it in pieces; but if some time shall have elapsed after I have laid
it by, his wonderful selfishness and circumscription to the moment
will probably save it once again from the action of his apelike
spite. And indeed the doom that is closing on us both, has already
changed and crushed him. Half an hour from now, when I shall
again and for ever reindue that hated personality, I know how I
shall sit shuddering and weeping in my chair, or continue, with
the most strained and fearstruck ecstasy of listening, to pace up
and down this room (my last earthly refuge) and give ear to every

sound of menace. Will Hyde die upon the scaffold? or will he find courage to release himself at the last moment? God knows; I am careless; this is my true hour of death, and what is to follow concerns another than myself. Here then, as I lay down the pen and proceed to seal up my confession, I bring the life of that unhappy Henry Jekyll to an end.

The Suicide Club

Story of the Young Man with the Cream Tarts

DURING HIS RESIDENCE IN LONDON, THE ACCOMPLISHED PRINCE Florizel of Bohemia gained the affection of all classes by the seduction of his manner and by a well-considered generosity. He was a remarkable man even by what was known of him; and that was but a small part of what he actually did. Although of a placid temper in ordinary circumstances, and accustomed to take the world with as much philosophy as any ploughman, the Prince of Bohemia was not without a taste for ways of life more adventurous and eccentric than that to which he was destined by his birth. Now and then, when he fell into a low humour, when there was no laughable play to witness in any of the London theatres, and when the season of the year was unsuitable to these field sports in which he excelled all competitors, he would summon his confidant and Master of the Horse, Colonel Geraldine, and bid him prepare himself against an evening ramble. The Master of the Horse was a young officer of a brave and even temerarious disposition. He greeted the news with delight, and hastened to make ready. Long practice and a varied acquaintance of life had given him a singular facility in disguise; he could adapt not only his face and bearing, but his voice and almost his thoughts, to those of any rank, character, or nation; and in this way he diverted attention from the Prince, and sometimes gained admission for the pair into strange societies. The civil authorities were never taken into the secret of these adventures; the imperturbable courage of the one and the ready invention and chivalrous devotion of the other had brought them through a score of dangerous passes; and they grew in confidence as time went on.

One evening in March they were driven by a sharp fall of sleet into an Oyster Bar in the immediate neighbourhood of Leicester Square. Colonel Geraldine was dressed and painted to represent a person connected with the Press in reduced circumstances; while the Prince had, as usual, travestied his appearance by the addition of false whiskers and a pair of large adhesive eyebrows. These lent him a shaggy and weather-beaten air, which, for one of his urbanity, formed the most impenetrable disguise. Thus equipped, the commander and his satellite sipped their brandy and soda in security.

The bar was full of guests, both male and female; but though more than one of these offered to fall into talk with our adventurers, none of them promised to grow interesting upon a nearer acquaintance. There was nothing present but the lees of London and the commonplace of disrespectability; and the Prince had already fallen to yawning, and was beginning to grow weary of the whole excursion, when the swing doors were pushed violently open, and a young man, followed by a couple of commissionaires, entered the bar. Each of the commissionaires carried a large dish of cream tarts under a cover, which they at once removed; and the young man made the round of the company, and pressed these confections upon every one's acceptance with an exaggerated courtesy. Sometimes his offer was laughingly accepted; sometimes it was firmly, or even harshly, rejected. In these latter cases the newcomer always ate the tart himself, with some more or less humourous commentary.

At last he accosted Prince Florizel.

"Sir," said he, with a profound obeisance, proffering the tart at the same time between his thumb and forefinger, "will you so far honour an entire stranger? I can answer for the quality of the pastry, having eaten two dozen and three of them myself since five o'clock."

"I am in the habit," replied the Prince, "of looking not so much to the nature of a gift as to the spirit in which it is offered."

"The spirit, sir," returned the young man, with another bow, "is one of mockery."

"Mockery?" repeated Florizel. "And whom do you propose to mock?"

"I am not here to expound my philosophy," replied the other, "but to distribute these cream tarts. If I mention that I heartily include myself in the ridicule of the transaction, I hope you will consider honour satisfied and condescend. If not, you will constrain me to eat my twenty-eighth, and I own to being weary of the exercise."

"You touch me," said the Prince, "and I have all the will in the world to rescue you from this dilemma, but upon one condition. If my friend and I eat your cakes—for which we have neither of us any natural inclination—we shall expect you to join us at supper, by way of recompense."

The young man seemed to reflect.

"I have still several dozen upon hand," he said at last; "and that will make it necessary for me to visit several more bars before my great affair is concluded. This will take some time; and if you are hungry——"

The Prince interrupted him with a polite gesture.

"My friend and I will accompany you," he said: "for we have already a deep interest in your very agreeable mode of passing an evening. And now that the preliminaries of peace are settled, allow me to sign the treaty for both."

And the Prince swallowed the tart with the best grace imaginable.

"It is delicious," said he.

"I perceive you are a connoisseur," replied the young man.

Colonel Geraldine likewise did honour to the pastry; and every one in that bar having now either accepted or refused his delicacies, the young man with the cream tarts led the way to another and similar establishment. The two commissionaires, who seemed to have grown accustomed to their absurd employment, followed immediately after; and the Prince and the Colonel brought up the rear, arm in arm, and smiling to each other as they went. In this order the company visited two other taverns, where scenes were enacted of a like nature to that already described—some refusing, some accepting, the favours of this vagabond hospitality, and the young man himself eating each rejected tart.

On leaving the third saloon the young man counted his store. There were but nine remaining, three in one tray and six in the other.

"Gentlemen," said he, addressing himself to his two new followers, "I am unwilling to delay your supper. I am positively sure you must be hungry. I feel that I owe you a special consideration. And on this great day for me, when I am closing a career of folly by my most conspicuously silly action, I wish to behave handsomely to all who give me countenance. Gentlemen, you shall wait no longer. Although my constitution is shattered by previous excesses, at the risk of my life I liquidate the suspensory condition."

With these words he crushed the nine remaining tarts into his mouth, and swallowed them at a single movement each. Then, turning to the commissionaires, he gave them a couple of sovereigns.

"I have to thank you," said he, "for your extraordinary patience."

And he dismissed them with a bow apiece. For some seconds he stood looking at the purse from which he had just paid his assistants, then, with a laugh, he tossed it into the middle of the street, and signified his readiness for supper.

In a small French restaurant in Soho, which had enjoyed an exaggerated reputation for some little while, but had already begun to be forgotten, and in a private room up two pair of stairs, the three companions made a very elegant supper, and drank three or four bottles of champagne, talking the while upon indifferent subjects. The young man was fluent and gay, but he laughed louder than was natural in a person of polite breeding; his hands trembled violently, and his voice took sudden and surprising inflections, which seemed to be independent of his will. The dessert had been cleared away, and all three had lighted their cigars, when the Prince addressed him in these words:

"You will, I am sure, pardon my curiosity. What I have seen of you has greatly pleased but even more puzzled me. And though I should be loath to seem indiscreet, I must tell you that my friend and I are persons very well worthy to be entrusted with a secret. We have many of our own, which we are continually revealing to improper ears. And if, as I suppose, your story is a silly one, you need have no delicacy with us, who are two of the silliest men in England. My name is Godall, Theophilus Godall; my friend is Major Alfred Hammersmith—or at least, such is the name by which he chooses to be known. We pass our lives entirely in the search for extravagant adventures; and there is no extravagance with which we are not capable of sympathy."

"I like you, Mr. Godall," returned the young man; "you inspire me with a natural confidence; and I have not the slightest objection to your friend, the Major; whom I take to be a nobleman in masquerade. At least, I am sure he is no soldier."

The Colonel smiled at this compliment to the perfection of his art; and the young man went on in a more animated manner.

"There is every reason why I should not tell you my story. Perhaps that is just the reason why I am going to do so. At least, you seem so well prepared to hear a tale of silliness that I cannot find it in my heart to disappoint you. My name, in spite of your example, I shall keep to myself. My age is not essential to the narrative. I am descended from my ancestors by ordinary generation, and from them I inherited the very eligible human tenement which I still occupy and a fortune of three hundred pounds a year. I suppose they also handed on to me a hare-brain humour, which it has been my chief delight to indulge. I received a good education. I can play the violin nearly well enough to earn money in the orchestra of a penny gaff, but not quite. The same remark applies to the flute and the French horn. I learned enough of whist to lose about a hundred a year at that scientific game. My acquaintance with French was sufficient to enable me to squander money in Paris with almost the same facility as in London. In short, I am a person full of manly accomplishments. I have had every sort of adventure, including a duel about nothing. Only two months ago I met a young lady exactly suited to my taste in mind and body; I found my heart melt; I saw that I had come upon my fate at last, and was in the way to fall in love. But when I came to reckon up what remained to me of my capital, I found it amounted to something less than four hundred pounds! I ask you fairly—can a man who respects himself fall in love on four hundred pounds? I concluded, certainly not; left the presence of my charmer, and slightly accelerating my usual rate of expenditure, came this morning to my last eighty pounds. This I divided into two equal parts; forty I reserved for a particular purpose; the remaining forty I was to dissipate before the night. I have passed a very entertaining day; and played many farces besides that of the cream tarts which procured me the advantage of your acquaintance; for I was determined, as I told you, to bring a foolish career to a still more foolish conclusion; and when you saw me throw my purse into the street, the forty pounds were at an end. Now you know me as well as I know myself: a fool but consistent in his folly; and, as I will ask you to believe, neither a whimperer nor a coward."

From the whole tone of the young man's statement it was plain that he harboured very bitter and contemptuous thoughts about himself. His auditors were led to imagine that his love affair was nearer his heart than he admitted, and that he had a design on his own life. The farce of the cream tarts began to have very much the air of a tragedy in disguise.

"Why, is this not odd," broke out Geraldine, giving a look to Prince Florizel, "that we three fellows should have met by the merest accident in so large a wilderness as London, and should be so nearly in the same condition?"

"How?" cried the young man. "Are you, too, ruined? Is this supper a folly like my cream tarts? Has the devil brought three of his own together for a last carouse?"

"The devil, depend upon it, can sometimes do a very gentle-manly thing," returned Prince Florizel; "and I am so much touched by this coincidence, that although we are not entirely in the same case, I am going to put an end to the disparity. Let your heroic treatment of the last cream tarts be my example."

So saying, the Prince drew out his purse and took from it a small bundle of bank-notes.

"You see, I was a week or so behind you, but I mean to catch you up and come neck and neck into the winning-post," he continued. "This," laying one of the notes upon the table, "will suffice for the bill. As for the rest——"

He tossed them into the fire, and they went up the chimney in a single blaze.

The young man tried to catch his arm, but as the table was between them his interference came too late.

"Unhappy man," he cried, "you should not have burned them all! You should have kept forty pounds."

"Forty pounds!" repeated the Prince. "Why, in heaven's name, forty pounds?"

"Why not eighty?" cried the Colonel; "for to my certain knowl-edge there must have been a hundred in the bundle."

"It was only forty pounds he needed," said the young man gloomily. "But without them there is no admission. The rule is strict. Forty pounds for each. Accursed life, where a man cannot even die without money!"

The Prince and the Colonel exchanged glances.

"Explain yourself," said the latter. "I have still a pocket-book tolerably well lined, and I need not say how readily I would share my wealth with Godall. But I must know to what end: you must certainly tell us what you mean."

The young man seemed to awaken; he looked uneasily from one to the other, and his face flushed deeply.

"You are not fooling me?" he asked. "You are indeed ruined men like me?"

"Indeed, I am for my part," replied the Colonel.

"And for mine," said the Prince, "I have given you proof. Who but a ruined man would throw his notes into the fire? The action speaks for itself."

"A ruined man—yes," returned the other suspiciously, "or else a millionaire."

"Enough, sir," said the Prince; "I have said so, and I am not accustomed to have my word remain in doubt."

"Ruined?" said the young man. "Are you ruined, like me? Are you, after a life of indulgence, come to such a pass that you can only indulge yourself in one thing more? Are you"—he kept lowering his voice as he went on—"are you going to give yourself that last indulgence? Are you going to avoid the consequences of your folly by the one infallible and easy path? Are you going to give the slip to the sheriff's officers of conscience by the one open door?"

Suddenly he broke off and attempted to laugh.

"Here is your health!" he cried, emptying his glass, "and good-night to you, my merry ruined men."

Colonel Geraldine caught him by the arm as he was about to rise.

"You lack confidence in us," he said, "and you are wrong. To all your questions I make answer in the affirmative. But I am not so timid, and can speak the Queen's English plainly. We too, like yourself, have had enough of life, and are determined to die. Sooner or later, alone or together, we meant to seek out death and beard him where he lies ready. Since we have met you, and your case is more pressing, let it be to-night—and at once—and, if you will, all three together. Such a penniless trio," he cried, "should go arm in arm into the halls of Pluto, and give each other some countenance among the shades!"

Geraldine had hit exactly on the manners and intonations that became the part he was playing. The Prince himself was disturbed, and looked over at his confidant with a shade of doubt. As for the young man, his flush came back darkly into his cheek, and his eyes threw out a spark of light.

"You are the men for me!" he cried, with an almost terrible gaiety. "Shake hands upon the bargain!" (his hand was cold and wet.) "You little know in what a company you will begin the march! You little know in what a happy moment for yourselves you partook of my cream tarts! I am only a unit, but I am a unit in an army. I know Death's private door. I am one of his familiars, and can show you into eternity without ceremony and yet without scandal."

They called upon him eagerly to explain his meaning.

"Can you muster eighty pounds between you?" he demanded.

Geraldine ostentatiously consulted his pocketbook, and replied in the affirmative.

"Fortunate beings!" cried the young man. "Forty pounds is the entry money of the Suicide Club."

"The Suicide Club," said the Prince, "why, what the devil is that?"

"Listen," said the young man; "this is the age of conveniences, and I have to tell you of the last perfection of the sort. We have affairs in different places; and hence railways were invented. Railways separated us infallibly from our friends; and so telegraphs were made that we might communicate speedily at great distances. Even in hotels we have lifts to spare us a climb of some hundred steps. Now, we know that life is only a stage to play the fool upon as long as the part amuses us. There was one more convenience lacking to modern comfort; a decent, easy way to quit that stage; the back stairs to liberty; or, as I said this moment, Death's private door. This, my two fellow-rebels, is supplied by the Suicide Club. Do not suppose that you and I are alone, or even exceptional, in the highly reasonable desire that we profess. A large number of our fellow-men, who have grown heartily sick of the performance in which they are expected to join daily and all their lives long, are only kept from flight by one or two considerations. Some have families who would be shocked, or even blamed, if the matter became public; others have a weakness at heart and recoil from the circumstances of death. This is, to some extent my own experience. I cannot put a pistol to my head and draw the trigger;

for something stronger than myself withholds the act; and although I loathe life, I have not strength enough in my body to take hold of death and be done with it. For such as I, and for all who desire to be out of the coil without posthumous scandal, the Suicide Club has been inaugurated. How this has been managed, what is its history, or what may be its ramifications in other lands, I am myself uninformed; and what I know of its constitution, I am not at liberty to communicate to you. To this extent, however, I am at your service. If you are truly tired of life, I will introduce you to-night to a meeting; and if not to-night, at least some time within the week, you will be easily relieved of your existences. It is now" (consulting his watch) "eleven; by half-past, at latest, we must leave this place; so that you have half an hour before you to consider my proposal. It is more serious than a cream tart," he added, with a smile; "and I suspect more palatable."

"More serious, certainly," returned Colonel Geraldine; "and as it is so much more so, will you allow me five minutes' speech in private with my friend, Mr. Godall?"

"It is only fair," answered the young man. "If you will permit, I will retire."

"You will be very obliging," said the Colonel.

As soon as the two were alone—"What," said Prince Florizel, "is the use of this confabulation, Geraldine? I see you are flurried, whereas my mind is very tranquilly made up. I will see the end of this."

"Your Highness," said the Colonel, turning pale, "let me ask you to consider the importance of your life, not only to your friends, but to the public interest. 'If not to-night,' said this madman; but supposing that to-night some irreparable disaster were to overtake your Highness's person, what, let me ask you, what would be my despair, and what the concern and disaster of a great nation?"

"I will see the end of this," repeated the Prince in his most deliberate tones; "and have the kindness, Colonel Geraldine, to remember and respect your word of honour as a gentleman. Under no circumstances, recollect, nor without my special authority, are you to betray the incognito under which I choose to go abroad. These were my commands, which I now reiterate. And now," he added, "let me ask you to call for the bill."

Colonel Geraldine bowed in submission; but he had a very white face as he summoned the young man of the cream tarts, and issued his directions to the waiter. The Prince preserved his undisturbed demeanour, and described a Palais Royal farce to the young suicide with great humour and gusto. He avoided the Colonel's appealing looks without ostentation, and selected another cheroot with more than usual care. Indeed, he was now the only man of the party who kept any command over his nerves.

The bill was discharged, the Prince giving the whole change of the note to the astonished waiter; and the three drove off in a four-wheeler. They were not long upon the way before the cab stopped at the entrance to a rather dark court. Here all descended.

After Geraldine had paid the fare, the young man turned, and addressed Prince Florizel as follows:

"It is still time, Mr. Godall, to make good your escape into thraldom. And for you too, Major Hammersmith. Reflect well before you take another step; and if your hearts say no—here are the cross-roads."

"Lead on, sir," said the Prince. "I am not the man to go back from a thing once said."

"Your coolness does me good," replied their guide. "I have never seen any one so unmoved at this conjuncture; and yet you are not the first whom I have escorted to this door. More than one of my friends has preceded me, where I knew I must shortly follow. But this is of no interest to you. Wait me here for only a few moments; I shall return as soon as I have arranged the preliminaries of your introduction."

And with that the young man, waving his hand to his companions, turned into the court, entered a doorway and disappeared.

"Of all our follies," said Colonel Geraldine in a low voice, "this is the wildest and most dangerous."

"I perfectly believe so," returned the Prince.

"We have still," pursued the Colonel, "a moment to ourselves. Let me beseech your Highness to profit by the opportunity and retire. The consequences of this step are so dark, and may be so grave, that I feel myself justified in pushing a little farther than usual the liberty which your Highness is so condescending as to allow me in private."

"Am I to understand that Colonel Geraldine is afraid?" asked his Highness, taking his cheroot from his lips, and looking keenly into the other's face.

"My fear is certainly not personal," replied the other proudly; "of that your Highness may rest well assured."

"I had supposed as much," returned the Prince, with undisturbed good humour; "but I was unwilling to remind you of the difference in our stations. No more—no more," he added, seeing Geraldine about to apologise, "you stand excused."

And he smoked placidly, leaning against a railing, until the young man returned.

"Well," he asked, "has our reception been arranged?"

"Follow me," was the reply. "The President will see you in the cabinet. And let me warn you to be frank in your answers. I have stood your guarantee; but the club requires a searching inquiry before admission; for the indiscretion of a single member would lead to the dispersion of the whole society for ever."

The Prince and Geraldine put their heads together for a moment. "Bear me out in this," said the one; and "bear me out in that," said the other; and by boldly taking up the characters of men with whom both were acquainted, they had come to an agreement in a twinkling, and were ready to follow their guide into the President's cabinet.

There were no formidable obstacles to pass. The outer door stood open; the door of the cabinet was ajar; and there, in a small but very high apartment, the young man left them once more.

"He will be here immediately," he said with a nod, as he disappeared.

Voices were audible in the cabinet through the folding-doors which formed one end; and now and then the noise of a champagne cork, followed by a burst of laughter, intervened among the sounds of conversation. A single tall window looked out upon the river and the embankment; and by the disposition of the lights they judged themselves not far from Charing Cross station. The furniture was scanty, and the coverings worn to the thread; and there was nothing movable except a hand-bell in the centre of a round table, and the hats and coats of a considerable party hung round the wall on pegs.

"What sort of a den is this?" said Geraldine.

"That is what I have come to see," replied the Prince. "If they keep live devils on the premises, the thing may grow amusing."

Just then the folding-door was opened no more than was necessary for the passage of a human body; and there entered at the same moment a louder buzz of talk, and the redoubtable President of the Suicide Club. The President was a man of fifty or upwards; large and rambling in his gait, with shaggy side-whiskers, a bald top to his head, and a veiled grey eye, which now and then emitted a twinkle. His mouth, which embraced a large cigar, he kept continually screwing round and round and from side to side, as he looked sagaciously and coldly at the strangers. He was dressed in light tweeds, with his neck very open, in a striped shirt collar; and carried a minute book under one arm.

"Good-evening," said he, after he had closed the door behind him. "I am told you wish to speak with me."

"We have a desire, sir, to join the Suicide Club," replied the Colonel.

The President rolled his cigar about in his mouth.

"What is that?" he said abruptly.

"Pardon me," returned the Colonel, "but I believe you are the person best qualified to give us information on that point."

"I?" cried the President. "A Suicide Club? Come, come! this is a frolic for All Fools' Day. I can make allowances for gentlemen who get merry in their liquor; but let there be an end to this."

"Call your Club what you will," said the Colonel, "you have some company behind these doors, and we insist on joining it."

"Sir," returned the President, curtly, "you have made a mistake. This is a private house, and you must leave it instantly."

The Prince had remained quietly in his seat throughout this little colloquy; but now, when the Colonel looked over to him, as much as to say, "Take your answer and come away, for God's sake!" he drew his cheroot from his mouth, and spoke.

"I have come here," said he, "upon the invitation of a friend of yours. He has doubtless informed you of my intention in thus intruding on your party. Let me remind you that a person in my circumstances has exceedingly little to bind him, and is not at all likely to tolerate much rudeness. I am a very quiet man, as a usual thing; but, my dear sir, you are either going to oblige me in the little matter of which you are aware, or you shall very bitterly repent that you ever admitted me to your ante-chamber."

The President laughed aloud.

"That is the way to speak," said he. "You are a man who is a man. You know the way to my heart, and can do what you like with me. Will you," he continued, addressing Geraldine, "will you step aside for a few minutes? I shall finish first with your companion, and some of the club's formalities require to be fulfilled in private."

With these words he opened the door of a small closet, into which he shut the Colonel.

"I believe in you," he said to Florizel, as soon as they were alone; "but are you sure of your friend?"

"Not so sure as I am of myself, though he has more cogent reasons," answered Florizel, "but sure enough to bring him here without alarm. He has had enough to cure the most tenacious man of life. He was cashiered the other day for cheating at cards."

"A good reason, I dare say," replied the President; "at least, we have another in the same case, and I feel sure of him. Have you also been in the Service, may I ask?"

"I have," was the reply; "but I was too lazy, I left it early."

"What is your reason for being tired of life?" pursued the President.

"The same, as near as I can make out," answered the Prince; "unadulterated laziness."

The President started. "D——n it," said he, "you must have something better than that."

"I have no more money," added Florizel. "That is also a vexation, wtihout doubt. It brings my sense of idleness to an acute point."

The President rolled his cigar round in his mouth for some seconds, directing his gaze straight into the eyes of this unusual neophyte; but the Prince supported his scrutiny with unabashed good temper.

"If I had not a deal of experience," said the President at last, "I should turn you off. But I know the world; and this much any way, that the most frivolous excuses for a suicide are often the toughest to stand by. And when I downright like a man, as I do you, sir, I would rather strain the regulation than deny him."

The Prince and the Colonel, one after the other, were subjected to a long and particular interrogatory: the Prince alone; but Geraldine in the presence of the Prince, so that the President might observe the countenance of the one while the other was being warmly cross-examined. The result was satisfactory; and the President, after having booked a few details of each case, produced a form of oath to be accepted. Nothing could be conceived more passive than the obedience promised, or more stringent than the terms by which the juror bound himself. The man who forfeited a pledge so awful could scarcely have a rag of honour or any of the consolations of religion left to him. Florizel signed the document, but not without a shudder; the Colonel followed his example with an air of great depression. Then the President received the entry money; and without more ado, introduced the two friends into the smoking-room of the Suicide Club.

The smoking-room of the Suicide Club was the same height as the cabinet into which it opened, but much larger, and papered from top to bottom with an imitation of oak wainscot. A large and cheerful fire and a number of gas-jets illuminated the company. The Prince and his follower made the number up to eighteen. Most of the party were smoking, and drinking champagne; a feverish hilarity reigned, with sudden and rather ghastly pauses.

"Is this a full meeting?" asked the Prince.

"Middling," said the President. "By the way," he added, "if you have any money, it is usual to offer some champagne. It keeps up a good spirit, and is one of my own little perquisites."

"Hammersmith," said Florizel, "I may leave the champagne to you."

And with that he turned away and began to go round among the guests. Accustomed to play the host in the highest circles, he charmed and dominated all whom he approached; there was something at once winning and authoritative in his address; and his extraordinary coolness gave him yet another distinction in this half-maniacal society. As he went from one to another he kept both his eyes and ears open, and soon began to gain a general idea of the people among whom he found himself. As in all other places of resort, one type predominated: people in the prime of youth, with every show of intelligence and sensibility in their appearance, but with little promise of strength or the quality that makes success. Few were much above thirty, and not a few were still in their teens. They stood, leaning on tables and shifting on their feet; sometimes they smoked extraordinarily fast, and sometimes they let their cigars go out; some talked well, but the conversation of others was plainly the result of nervous tension, and was equally without wit or purport. As each new bottle of champagne was opened, there was a manifest improvement in gaiety. Only two were seated—one in a chair in the recess of the window, with his head hanging and his hands plunged deep into his trouser pockets, pale, visibly moist with perspiration, saying never a word, a very wreck of soul and body; the other sat on the divan close by the chimney, and attracted notice by a trenchant dissimilarity from all the rest. He was probably upwards of forty, but he looked fully ten years older; and Florizel thought he had never seen a man more naturally hideous, nor one more ravaged by disease and ruinous excitements. He was no more than skin and bone, was partly paralysed, and wore spectacles of such unusual power, that his eyes appeared through the glasses greatly magnified and distorted in shape. Except the Prince and the President, he was the only person in the room who preserved the composure of ordinary life.

There was little decency among the members of the club. Some boasted of the disgraceful actions, the consequences of which had reduced them to seek refuge in death; and the others listened without disapproval. There was a tacit understanding against moral judgments; and whoever passed the club doors enjoyed already some of the immunities of the tomb. They drank to each other's memories, and to those of notable suicides in the past. They compared and developed their different views of death—some declaring that it was no more than blackness and cessation; others full of a hope that that very night they should be scaling the stars and commercing with the mighty dead.

"To the eternal memory of Baron Trenck, the type of suicides!" cried one. "He went out of a small cell into a smaller, that he might come forth again to freedom."

"For my part," said a second, "I wish no more than a bandage for my eyes and cotton for my ears. Only they have no cotton thick enough in this world."

A third was for reading the mysteries of life in a future state; and a fourth professed that he would never have joined the club, if he had not been induced to believe in Mr. Darwin.

"I could not bear," said this remarkable suicide, "to be descended from an ape."

Altogether, the Prince was disappointed by the bearing and conversation of the members.

"It does not seem to me," he thought, "a matter for so much disturbance. If a man has made up his mind to kill himself, let him do it, in God's name, like a gentleman. This flutter and big talk is out of place."

In the meanwhile Colonel Geraldine was a prey to the blackest apprehensions; the club and its rules were still a mystery, and he looked round the room for some one who should be able to set his mind at rest. In this survey his eye lighted on the paralytic person with the strong spectacles; and seeing him so exceedingly tranquil, he besought the President, who was going in and out of the room under a pressure of business, to present him to the gentleman on the divan.

The functionary explained the needlessness of all such formalities within the club, but nevertheless presented Mr. Hammersmith to Mr. Malthus.

Mr. Malthus looked at the Colonel curiously, and then requested him to take a seat upon his right.

"You are a new-comer," he said, "and wish information? You have come to the proper source. It is two years since I first visited this charming club."

The Colonel breathed again. If Mr. Malthus had frequented the place for two years there could be little danger for the Prince in a single evening. But Geraldine was none the less astonished, and began to suspect a mystification.

"What!" cried he, "two years! I thought—but indeed I see I have been made the subject of a pleasantry."

"By no means," replied Mr. Malthus mildly. "My case is peculiar. I am not, properly speaking, a suicide at all; but, as it were, an honorary member. I rarely visit the club twice in two months. My infirmity and the kindness of the President have procured me these little immunities, for which besides I pay at an advanced rate. Even as it is my luck has been extraordinary."

"I am afraid," said the Colonel, "that I must ask you to be more explicit. You must remember that I am still most imperfectly acquainted with the rules of the club."

"An ordinary member who comes here in search of death like yourself," replied the paralytic, "returns every evening until fortune favours him. He can, even if he is penniless, get board and lodging from the President: very fair, I believe, and clean, although, of course, not luxurious; that could hardly be, considering the exiguity (if I may so express myself) of the subscription. And then the President's company is a delicacy in itself."

"Indeed!" cried Geraldine, "he had not greatly prepossessed me."

"Ah!" said Mr. Malthus, "you do not know the man: the drollest fellow! What stories! What cynicism! He knows life to admiration and, between ourselves, is probably the most corrupt rogue in Christendom."

"And he also," asked the Colonel, "is a permanency—like yourself, if I may say so without offence?"

"Indeed, he is a permanency in a very different sense from me," replied Mr. Malthus. "I have been graciously spared, but I must go at last. Now he never plays. He shuffles and deals for the club, and makes the necessary arrangements. That man, my dear Mr. Hammersmith, is the very soul of ingenuity. For three years he has pursued in London his useful and, I think I may add, his artistic calling; and not so much as a whisper of suspicion has been once aroused. I believe him myself to be inspired. You doubtless remember the celebrated case, six months ago, of the gentleman who was accidentally poisoned in a chemist's shop? That was one of the least rich, one of the least racy, of his notions; but then, how simple! and how safe!"

"You astound me," said the Colonel. "Was that unfortunate gentleman one of the—" he was about to say "victims;" but bethinking himself in time, he substituted—"members of the club?"

In the same flash of thought it occurred to him that Mr. Malthus himself had not at all spoken in the tone of one who is in love with death; and he added hurriedly:

"But I perceive I am still in the dark. You speak of shuffling and dealing; pray for what end? And since you seem rather unwilling to die than otherwise, I must own that I cannot conceive what brings you here at all."

"You say truly that you are in the dark," replied Mr. Malthus with more animation. "Why, my dear sir, this club is the temple of intoxication. If my enfeebled health could support the excitement more often, you may depend upon it I should be more often here. It requires all the sense of duty engendered by a long habit of ill-health and careful regimen, to keep me from excess in this, which is, I may say, my last dissipation. I have tried them all, sir," he went on, laying his hand on Geraldine's arm, "all without exception, and I declare to you, upon my honour, there is not one of them that has not been grossly and untruthfully overrated. People trifle with love. Now, I deny that love is a strong passion. Fear is the strong passion; it is with fear that you must trifle, if you wish to taste the intense joys of living. Envy me—envy me, sir," he added with a chuckle, "I am a coward!"

Geraldine could scarcely repress a movement of repulsion for this deplorable wretch; but he commanded himself with an effort, and continued his inquiries.

"How, sir," he asked, "is the excitement so artfully prolonged? and where is there any element of uncertainty?"

"I must tell you how the victim for every evening is selected," returned Mr. Malthus; "and not only the victim, but another member, who is to be the instrument in the club's hands, and death's high priest for that occasion."

"Good God!" said the Colonel, "do they then kill each other?"

"The trouble of suicide is removed in that way," returned Malthus with a nod.

"Merciful Heavens!" ejaculated the Colonel, "and may you—may I—may the—my friend, I mean—may any of us be pitched upon this evening as the slayer of another man's body and immortal spirit? Can such things be possible among men born of women? Oh! infamy of infamies!"

He was about to rise in his horror, when he caught the Prince's eye. It was fixed upon him from across the room with a frowning and angry stare. And in a moment Geraldine recovered his composure.

"After all," he added, "why not? And since you say the game is interesting, *vogue la galère*—I follow the club!"

Mr. Malthus had keenly enjoyed the Colonel's amazement and disgust. He had the vanity of wickedness; and it pleased him to see another man give way to a generous movement, while he felt himself, in his entire corruption, superior to such emotions.

"You now, after your first moment of surprise," said he, "are in a position to appreciate the delights of our society. You can see how it combines the excitement of a gaming-table, a duel, and a Roman amphitheatre. The Pagans did well enough; I cordially admire the refinement of their minds; but it has been reserved for a Christian country to attain this extreme, this quintessence, this absolute of poignancy. You will understand how vapid are all amusements to a man who has acquired a taste for this one. The game we play," he continued, "is one of extreme simplicity. A full pack—but I perceive you are about to see the thing in progress. Will you lend me the help of your arm? I am unfortunately paralysed."

Indeed, just as Mr. Malthus was beginning his description, another pair of folding-doors was thrown open, and the whole club began to pass, not without some hurry, into the adjoining room. It was similar in every respect to the one from which it was entered, but somewhat differently furnished. The centre was occupied by a long green table, at which the President sat shuffling a pack of cards with great particularity. Even with the stick and the Colonel's arm, Mr. Malthus walked with so much difficulty that every one was seated before this pair and the Prince, who had waited for them, entered the apartment; and, in consequence, the three took seats close together at the lower end of the board.

"It is a pack of fifty-two," whispered Mr. Malthus. "Watch for the ace of spades, which is the sign of death, and the ace of clubs, which designates the official of the night. Happy, happy young men!" he added. "You have good eyes, and can follow the game. Alas! I cannot tell an ace from a deuce across the table."

And he proceeded to equip himself with a second pair of spectacles.

"I must at least watch the faces," he explained.

The Colonel rapidly informed his friend of all that he had learned from the honorary member, and of the horrible alternative that lay before them. The Prince was conscious of a deadly chill and a contraction about his heart; he swallowed with difficulty, and looked from side to side like a man in a maze.

"One bold stroke," whispered the Colonel, "and we may still escape."

But the suggestion recalled the Prince's spirits.

"Silence!" said he. "Let me see that you can play like a gentleman for any stake, however serious."

And he looked about him, once more to all appearance at his ease, although his heart beat thickly, and he was conscious of an unpleasant heat in his bosom. The members were all very quiet and intent; every one was pale, but none so pale as Mr. Malthus. His eyes protruded; his head kept nodding involuntarily upon his spine; his hands found their way, one after the other, to his mouth, where they made clutches at his tremulous and ashen lips. It was plain that the honorary member enjoyed his membership on very startling terms.

"Attention, gentlemen!" said the President.

And he began slowly dealing the cards about the table in the reverse direction, pausing until each man had shown his card. Nearly every one hesitated; and sometimes you would see a player's fingers stumble more than once before he could turn over the momentous slip of pasteboard. As the Prince's turn drew nearer, he was conscious of a growing and almost suffocating excitement; but he had somewhat of the gambler's nature, and recognised almost with astonishment that there was a degree of pleasure in his sensations. The nine of clubs fell to his lot; the three of spades was dealt to Geraldine; and the queen of hearts to Mr. Malthus, who was unable to suppress a sob of relief. The young man of the cream tarts almost immediately afterwards turned over the ace of clubs, and remained frozen with horror, the card still resting on his finger; he had not come there to kill, but to be killed; and the Prince, in his generous sympathy with his position, almost forgot the peril that still hung over himself and his friend.

The deal was coming round again, and still Death's card had not come out. The players held their respiration, and only breathed by gasps. The Prince received another club; Geraldine had a diamond; but when Mr. Malthus turned up his card a horrible noise, like that of something breaking, issued from his mouth; and he rose from his seat and sat down again, with no sign of his paralysis. It was the ace of spades. The honorary member had trifled once too often with his terrors.

Conversation broke out again almost at once. The players relaxed their rigid attitudes, and began to rise from the table and stroll back by twos and threes into the smoking-room. The President stretched his arms and yawned, like a man who had finished his day's work. But Mr. Malthus sat in his place, with his head in his hands, and his hands upon the table, drunk and motionless—a thing stricken down.

The Prince and Geraldine made their escape at once. In the cold night air their horror of what they had witnessed was redoubled.

"Alas!" cried the Prince, "to be bound by an oath in such a matter! to allow this wholesale trade in murder to be continued with profit and impunity! If I but dared to forfeit my pledge!"

"That is impossible for your Highness," replied the Colonel, "whose honour is the honour of Bohemia. But I dare, and may with propriety, forfeit mine."

"Geraldine," said the Prince, "if your honour suffers in any of the adventures into which you follow me, not only will I never pardon you, but—what I believe will much more sensibly affect you—I should never forgive myself."

"I receive your Highness's commands," replied the Colonel. "Shall we go from this accursed spot?"

"Yes," said the Prince. "Call a cab, in Heaven's name, and let me try to forget in slumber the memory of this night's disgrace." But it was notable that he carefully read the name of the court before he left it.

The next morning, as soon as the Prince was stirring, Colonel Geraldine brought him a daily newspaper, with the following paragraph marked:

"MELANCHOLY ACCIDENT.—This morning, about two o'clock, Mr. Bartholomew Malthus, of 16 Chepstow Place, Westbourne Grove, on his way home from a party at a friend's house, fell over the upper parapet in Trafalgar Square, fracturing his skull and breaking a leg and an arm. Death was instantaneous. Mr. Malthus, accompanied by a friend, was engaged in looking for a cab at the time of the unfortunate occurrence. As Mr. Malthus was paralytic, it is thought that his fall may have been occasioned by another seizure. The unhappy gentleman was well known in the most respectable circles, and his loss will be widely and deeply deplored."

"If ever a soul went straight to Hell," said Geraldine solemnly, "it was that paralytic man's."

The Prince buried his face in his hands, and remained silent.

"I am almost rejoiced," continued the Colonel, "to know that he is dead. But for our young man of the cream tarts I confess my heart bleeds."

"Geraldine," said the Prince, raising his face, "that unhappy lad was last night as innocent as you and I; and this morning the guilt of blood is on his soul. When I think of the President, my heart grows sick within me. I do not know how it shall be done, but I shall have that scoundrel at my mercy as there is a God in heaven. What an experience, what a lesson, was that game of cards!"

"One," said the Colonel, "never to be repeated."

The Prince remained so long without replying, that Geraldine grew alarmed.

"You cannot mean to return," he said. "You have suffered too much, and seen too much horror already. The duties of your high position forbid the repetition of the hazard."

"There is much in what you say," replied Prince Florizel, "and I am not altogether pleased with my own determination. Alas! in the clothes of the greatest potentate, what is there but a man? I never felt my weakness more acutely than now, Geraldine, but it is stronger than I. Can I cease to interest myself in the fortunes of the unhappy young man who supped with us some hours ago? Can I leave the President to follow his nefarious career unwatched? Can I begin an adventure so entrancing, and not follow it to an end? No, Geraldine; you ask of the Prince more than the man is able to perform. To-night, once more, we take our places at the table of the Suicide Club."

Colonel Geraldine fell upon his knees.

"Will your Highness take my life?" he cried. "It is his—his freely; but do not, O do not! let him ask me to countenance so terrible a risk."

"Colonel Geraldine," replied the Prince, with some haughtiness of manner, "your life is absolutely your own. I only looked for obedience; and when that is unwillingly rendered, I shall look for that no longer. I add one word: your importunity in this affair has been sufficient."

The Master of the Horse regained his feet at once. "Your Highness," he said, "may I be excused in my attendance this afternoon? I dare not, as an honourable man, venture a second time into that fatal house until I have perfectly ordered my affairs. Your Highness shall meet, I promise him, with no more opposition from the most devoted and grateful of his servants."

"My dear Geraldine," returned Prince Florizel, "I always regret when you oblige me to remember my rank. Dispose of your day as you think fit, but be here before eleven in the same disguise."

The club, on this second evening, was not so fully attended; and when Geraldine and the Prince arrived, there were not above half-a-dozen persons in the smoking-room. His Highness took the President aside and congratulated him warmly on the demise of Mr. Malthus.

"I like," he said, "to meet with capacity, and certainly find much of it in you. Your profession is of a very delicate nature, but I see you are well qualified to conduct it with success and secrecy."

The President was somewhat affected by these compliments from one of his Highness's superior bearing. He acknowledged them almost with humility.

"Poor Malthy!" he added, "I shall hardly know the club without him. The most of my patrons are boys, sir, and poetical boys, who are not much company for me. Not but what Malthy had some poetry, too; but it was of a kind that I could understand."

"I can readily imagine you should find yourself in sympathy with Mr. Malthus," returned the Prince. "He struck me as a man of a very original disposition."

The young man of the cream tarts was in the room, but painfully depressed and silent. His late companions sought in vain to lead him into conversation.

"How bitterly I wish," he cried, "that I had never brought you to this infamous abode! Begone, while you are clean-handed. If you could have heard the old man scream as he fell, and the noise of his bones upon the pavement! Wish me, if you have any kindness to so fallen a being—wish the ace of spades for me tonight!"

A few more members dropped in as the evening went on, but the club did not muster more than the devil's dozen when they took their places at the table. The Prince was again conscious of a certain joy in his alarms; but he was astonished to see Geraldine so much more self-possessed than on the night before.

"It is extraordinary," thought the Prince, "that a will, made or unmade, should so greatly influence a young man's spirit."

"Attention, gentlemen!" said the President, and he began to deal.

Three times the cards went all round the table, and neither of the marked cards had yet fallen from his hand. The excitement as he began the fourth distribution was overwhelming. There were just cards enough to go once more entirely round. The Prince, who sat second from the dealer's left, would receive, in the reverse mode of dealing practised at the club, the second last card. The third player turned up a black ace—it was the ace of clubs. The next received a diamond, the next a heart, and so on; but the ace of spades was still undelivered. At last Geraldine, who sat upon the Prince's left, turned his card; it was an ace, but the ace of hearts.

When Prince Florizel saw his fate upon the table in front of him, his heart stood still. He was a brave man, but the sweat poured off his face. There were exactly fifty chances out of a hundred that he was doomed. He reversed the card; it was the ace of spades. A loud roaring filled his brain, and the table swam before his eyes. He heard the player on his right break into a fit of laughter that sounded between mirth and disappointment; he saw the company rapidly dispersing, but his mind was full of other thoughts. He recognised how foolish, how criminal, had been his conduct. In perfect health, in the prime of his years, the heir to a throne, he had gambled away his future and that of a brave and loyal country. "God," he cried, "God forgive me!" And with that, the confusion of his senses passed away, and he regained his self-possession in a moment.

To his surprise Geraldine had disappeared. There was no one in the card-room but his destined butcher consulting with the President, and the young man of the cream tarts, who slipped up to the Prince and whispered in his ear:

"I would give a million, if I had it, for your luck."

His Highness could not help reflecting, as the young man departed, that he would have sold his opportunity for a much more moderate sum.

The whispered conference now came to an end. The holder of the ace of clubs left the room with a look of intelligence, and the President, approaching the unfortunate Prince, proffered him his hand.

"I am pleased to have met you, sir," said he, "and pleased to have been in a position to do you this trifling service. At least, you cannot complain of delay. On the second evening—what a stroke of luck!"

The Prince endeavoured in vain to articulate something in response, but his mouth was dry and his tongue seemed paralysed.

"You feel a little sickish?" asked the President, with some show of solicitude. "Most gentlemen do. Will you take a little brandy?"

The Prince signified in the affirmative, and the other immediately filled some of the spirit into a tumbler.

"Poor old Malthy!" ejaculated the President, as the Prince drained the glass. "He drank near upon a pint, and little enough good it seemed to do him!"

"I am more amenable to treatment," said the Prince, a good

deal revived. "I am my own man again at once, as you perceive. And so, let me ask you, what are my directions?"

"You will proceed along the Strand in the direction of the City, and on the left-hand pavement, until you meet the gentleman who has just left the room. He will continue your instructions, and him you will have the kindness to obey; the authority of the club is vested in his person for the night. And now," added the President, "I wish you a pleasant walk."

Florizel acknowledged the salutation rather awkwardly, and took his leave. He passed through the smoking-room, where the bulk of the players were still consuming champagne, some of which he had himself ordered and paid for; and he was surprised to find himself cursing them in his heart. He put on his hat and great-coat in the cabinet, and selected his umbrella from a corner. The familiarity of these acts, and the thought that he was about them for the last time, betrayed him into a fit of laughter which sounded unpleasantly in his own ears. He conceived a reluctance to leave the cabinet, and turned instead to the window. The sight of the lamps and the darkness recalled him to himself.

"Come, come, I must be a man," he thought, "and tear myself away."

At the corner of Box Court three men fell upon Prince Florizel and he was unceremoniously thrust into a carriage, which at once drove rapidly away. There was already an occupant.

"Will your Highness pardon my zeal?" said a well-known voice.

The Prince threw himself upon the Colonel's neck in a passion of relief.

"How can I ever thank you?" he cried. "And how was this effected?"

Although he had been willing to march upon his doom, he was overjoyed to yield to friendly violence, and return once more to life and hope.

"You can thank me effectually enough," replied the Colonel, "by avoiding all such dangers in the future. And as for your second question, all has been managed by the simplest means. I arranged this afternoon with a celebrated detective. Secrecy has been promised and paid for. Your own servants have been principally engaged in the affair. The house in Box Court has been surrounded since nightfall, and this, which is one of your own carriages, has been awaiting you for nearly an hour."

"And the miserable creature who was to have slain me—what of him?" inquired the Prince.

"He was pinioned as he left the club," replied the Colonel, "and now awaits your sentence at the Palace, where he will soon be joined by his accomplices."

"Geraldine," said the Prince, "you have saved me against my explicit orders, and you have done well. I owe you not only my life, but a lesson; and I should be unworthy of my rank if I did not show myself grateful to my teacher. Let it be yours to choose the manner."

There was a pause, during which the carriage continued to speed through the streets, and the two men were each buried in his own reflections. The silence was broken by Colonel Geraldine.

"Your Highness," said he, "has by this time a considerable body of prisoners. There is at least one criminal among the number to whom justice should be dealt. Our oath forbids us all recourse to law; and discretion would forbid it equally if the oath were loosened. May I inquire your Highness's intention?"

"It is decided," answered Florizel; "the President must fall in duel. It only remains to choose his adversary."

"Your Highness has permitted me to name my own recompense," said the Colonel. "Will he permit me to ask the appointment of my brother? It is an honourable post, but I dare assure your Highness that the lad will acquit himself with credit."

"You ask me an ungracious favour," said the Prince, "but I must refuse you nothing."

The Colonel kissed his hand with the greatest affection; and at that moment the carriage rolled under the archway of the Prince's splendid residence.

An hour after, Florizel in his official robes, and covered with all the orders of Bohemia, received the members of the Suicide Club.

"Foolish and wicked men," said he, "as many of you as have been driven into this strait by the lack of fortune shall receive employment and remuneration from my officers. Those who suffer under a sense of guilt must have recourse to a higher and more generous Potentate than I. I feel pity for all of you, deeper than you can imagine; to-morrow you shall tell me your stories; and as you answer more frankly, I shall be the more able to remedy your misfortunes. As for you," he added, turning to the President, "I should only offend a person of your parts by any offer of assistance; but I have instead a piece of diversion to propose to you. Here," laying his hand on the shoulder of Colonel Geraldine's young brother, "is an officer of mine who desires to make a little tour upon the Continent; and I ask you, as a favour, to accompany him on this excursion. Do you," he went on, changing his tone, "do you shoot well with the pistol? Because you may have need of that accomplishment. When two men go travelling together, it is best to be prepared for all. Let me add that, if by any chance you should lose young Mr. Geraldine upon the way, I shall always have another member of my household to place at your disposal; and I am known, Mr. President, to have long eyesight, and as long an arm."

With these words, said with much sternness, the Prince concluded his address. Next morning the members of the club were suitably provided for by his munificence, and the President set forth upon his travels, under the supervision of Mr. Geraldine, and a pair of faithful and adroit lackeys, well trained in the Prince's household. Not content with this, discreet agents were put in possession of the house of Box Court, and all letters of visitors for the Suicide Club or its officials were to be examined by Prince Florizel in person.

Here (*says my Arabian author*) ends THE STORY OF THE YOUNG MAN WITH THE CREAM TARTS, who is now a comfortable householder in Wigmore Street, Cavendish Square. The number, for obvious reasons, I suppress. Those who care to pursue the adventures of Prince Florizel and the President of the Suicide Club, may read the STORY OF THE PHYSICIAN AND THE SARATOGA TRUNK.

Story of the Physician and the Saratoga Trunk

Mr. Silas Q. Scuddamore was a young American of a simple and harmless disposition, which was the more to his credit as he came from New England—a quarter of the New World not precisely famous for those qualities. Although he was exceedingly rich, he kept a note of all his expenses in a little paper pocket-book; and he had chosen to study the attractions of Paris from the seventh story of what is called a furnished hotel, in the Latin Quarter. There was a great deal of habit in his penuriousness; and his virtue, which was very remarkable among his associates, was principally founded upon diffidence and youth.

The next room to his was inhabited by a lady, very attractive in her air and very elegant in toilette, whom, on his first arrival, he had taken for a Countess. In course of time he had learned that she was known by the name of Madame Zéphyrine, and that whatever station she occupied in life it was not that of a person of title. Madame Zéphyrine, probably in the hope of enchanting the young American, used to flaunt by him on the stairs with a civil inclination, a word of course, and a knock-down look out of her black eyes, and disappear in a rustle of silk, and with the revelation of an admirable foot and ankle. But these advances, so far from encouraging Mr. Scuddamore, plunged him into the depths of depression and bashfulness. She had come to him several times for a light, or to apologise for the imaginary depredations of her poodle; but his mouth was closed in the presence of so superior a being, his French promptly left him, and he could only stare and stammer until she was gone. The slenderness of their intercourse did not prevent him from throwing out insinuations of a very glorious order when he was safely alone with a few males.

The room on the other side of the American's—for there were three rooms on a floor in the hotel—was tenanted by an old English physician of rather doubtful reputation. Dr. Noel, for that was his name, had been forced to leave London, where he enjoyed a large and increasing practice; and it was hinted that the police had been the instigators of this change of scene. At least he, who had made something of a figure in earlier life, now dwelt in the Latin Quarter in great simplicity and solitude, and devoted much of his time to study. Mr. Scuddamore had made his acquaintance, and the pair would now and then dine together frugally in a restaurant across the street.

Silas Q. Scuddamore had many little vices of the more respectable order, and was not restrained by delicacy from indulging them in many rather doubtful ways. Chief among his foibles stood curiosity. He was a born gossip; and life, and especially those parts of it in which he had no experience, interested him to the degree of passion. He was a pert, invincible questioner, pushing his inquiries with equal pertinacity and indiscretion; he had been observed, when he took a letter to the post, to weigh it in his hand, to turn it over and over, and to study the address with care; and when he found a flaw in the partition between his room and Madame Zéphyrine's, instead of filling it up, he enlarged and improved the opening, and made use of it as a spy-hole on his neighbour's affairs.

One day, in the end of March, his curiosity growing as it was indulged, he enlarged the hole a little further, so that he might command another corner of the room. That evening, when he went as usual to inspect Madame Zéphyrine's movements, he was astonished to find the aperture obscured in an odd manner on the other side, and still more abashed when the obstacle was suddenly withdrawn and a titter of laughter reached his ears. Some of the plaster had evidently betrayed the secret of his spy-hole, and his neighbour had been returning the compliment in kind. Mr. Scuddamore was moved to a very acute feeling of annoyance; he condemned Madame Zéphyrine unmercifully; he even blamed himself; but when he found, next day, that she had taken no means to balk him of his favourite pastime, he continued to profit by her carelessness, and gratify his idle curiosity.

That next day Madame Zéphyrine received a long visit from a tall, loosely-built man of fifty or upwards, whom Silas had not hitherto seen. His tweed suit and coloured shirt, no less than his shaggy side-whiskers, identified him as a Britisher, and his dull grey eye affected Silas with a sense of cold. He kept screwing his mouth from side to side and round and round during the whole colloquy, which was carried on in whispers. More than once it seemed to the young New Englander as if their gestures indicated his own apartment; but the only thing definite he could gather by the most scrupulous attention was this remark made by the Englishman in a somewhat higher key, as if in answer to some reluctance or opposition:

"I have studied his taste to a nicety, and I tell you again and again you are the only woman of the sort that I can lay my hands on."

In answer to this, Madame Zéphyrine sighed, and appeared by a gesture to resign herself, like one yielding to unqualified authority.

That afternoon the observatory was finally blinded, a wardrobe having been drawn in front of it upon the other side, and while Silas was still lamenting over this misfortune, which he attributed to the Britisher's malign suggestion, the concierge brought him up a letter in a female handwriting. It was conceived in French of no very rigorous orthography, bore no signature, and in the most encouraging terms invited the young American to be present in a certain part of the Bullier Ball at eleven o'clock that night. Curiosity and timidity fought a long battle in his heart; sometimes he was all virtue, sometimes all fire and daring; and the result of it was that, long before ten, Mr. Silas Q. Scuddamore presented himself in unimpeachable attire at the door of the Bullier Ball Rooms, and paid his entry money with a sense of reckless deviltry that was not without its charm.

It was Carnival time, and the Ball was very full and noisy. The lights and the crowd at first rather abashed our young adventurer, and then, mounting to his brain with a sort of intoxication, put him in possession of more than his own share of manhood. He felt ready to face the devil, and strutted in the ballroom with the swagger of a cavalier. While he was thus parading, he became aware of Madame Zéphyrine and her Britisher in conference behind a pillar. The cat-like spirit of eavesdropping overcame him at once. He stole nearer and nearer on the couple from behind, until he was within earshot.

"That is the man," the Britisher was saying; "there—with the long blond hair—speaking to a girl in green."

Silas identified a very handsome young fellow of small stature, who was plainly the object of this designation.

"It is well," said Madame Zéphyrine. "I shall do my utmost. But, remember, the best of us may fail in such a matter."

"Tut!" returned her companion; "I answer for the result. Have I not chosen you from thirty? Go; but be wary of the Prince. I cannot think what cursed accident has brought him here tonight. As if there were not a dozen balls in Paris better worth his notice than this riot of students and counter-jumpers! See him where he sits, more like a reigning Emperor at home than a Prince upon his holidays!"

Silas was again lucky. He observed a person of rather a full build, strikingly handsome, and of a very stately and courteous demeanour, seated at table with another handsome young man, several years his junior, who addressed him with conspicuous deference. The name of Prince struck gratefully on Silas's Republican hearing, and the aspect of the person to whom that name was applied exercised its usual charm upon his mind. He left

Madame Zéphyrine and her Englishman to take care of each other, and threading his way through the assembly, approached the table which the Prince and his confidant had honoured with their choice.

"I tell you, Geraldine," the former was saying, "the action is madness. Yourself (I am glad to remember it) chose your brother for this perilous service, and you are bound in duty to have a guard upon his conduct. He has consented to delay so many days in Paris; that was already an imprudence, considering the character of the man he has to deal with; but now, when he is within eight and forty hours of his departure, when he is within two or three days of the decisive trial, I ask you, is this a place for him to spend his time? He should be in a gallery at practice; he should be sleeping long hours and taking moderate exercise on foot; he should be on a rigorous diet, without white wines or brandy. Does the dog imagine we are all playing comedy? The thing is deadly earnest, Geraldine."

"I know the lad too well to interfere," replied Colonel Geraldine, "and well enough not to be alarmed. He is more cautious than you fancy, and of an indomitable spirit. If it had been a woman I should not say so much, but I trust the President to him and the two valets without an instant's apprehension."

"I am gratified to hear you say so," replied the Prince; "but my mind is not at rest. These servants are well-trained spies, and already has not this miscreant succeeded three times in eluding their observation and spending several hours on end in private, and most likely dangerous, affairs? An amateur might have lost him by accident, but if Rudolph and Jérome were thrown off the scent, it must have been done on purpose, and by a man who had a cogent reason and exceptional resources."

"I believe the question is now one between my brother and myself," replied Geraldine, with a shade of offence in his tone.

"I permit it to be so, Colonel Geraldine," returned Prince Florizel. "Perhaps, for that very reason, you should be all the more ready to accept my counsels. But enough. That girl in yellow dances well."

And the talk veered into the ordinary topics of a Paris ballroom in the Carnival.

Silas remembered where he was, and that the hour was already near at hand when he ought to be upon the scene of his assignation. The more he reflected the less he liked the prospect, and as at that moment an eddy in the crowd began to draw him in the direction of the door, he suffered it to carry him away without resistance. The eddy stranded him in a corner under the gallery, where his ear was immediately struck with the voice of Madame Zéphyrine. She was speaking in French with the young man of the blond locks who had been pointed out by the strange Britisher not half an hour before.

"I have a character at stake," she said, "or I would put no other condition than my heart recommends. But you have only to say so much to the porter, and he will let you go by without a word."

"But why this talk of debt?" objected her companion.

"Heavens!" said she, "do you think I do not understand my own hotel?"

And she went by, clinging affectionately to her companion's arm.

This put Silas in mind of his billet.

"Ten minutes hence," thought he, "and I may be walking with as beautiful a woman as that, and even better dressed—perhaps a real lady, possibly a woman of title."

And then he remembered the spelling, and was a little downcast.

"But it may have been written by her maid," he imagined.

The clock was only a few minutes from the hour, and this immediate proximity set his heart beating at a curious and rather disagreeable speed. He reflected with relief that he was in no way bound to put in an appearance. Virtue and cowardice were together, and he made once more for the door, but this time of his own accord, and battling against the stream of people which was now moving in a contrary direction. Perhaps this prolonged resistance wearied him, or perhaps he was in that frame of mind when merely to continue in the same determination for a certain number of minutes produces a reaction and a different purpose. Certainly, at least, he wheeled about for a third time, and did not stop until he had found a place of concealment within a few yards of the appointed place.

Here he went through an agony of spirit, in which he several times prayed to God for help, for Silas had been devoutly educated. He had now not the least inclination for the meeting; nothing kept him from flight but a silly fear lest he should be thought unmanly; but this was so powerful that it kept head against all other motives; and although it could not decide him to advance, prevented him from definitely running away. At last the clock indicated ten minutes past the hour. Young Scuddamore's spirit began to rise; he peered round the corner and saw no one at the place of meeting; doubtless his unknown correspondent had wearied and gone away. He became as bold as he had formerly been timid. It seemed to him that if he came at all to the appointment, however late, he was clear from the charge of cowardice. Nay, now he began to suspect a hoax, and actually complimented himself on his shrewdness in having suspected and out-manœuvred his mystifiers. So very idle a thing is a boy's mind!

Armed with these reflections, he advanced boldly from his corner; but he had not taken above a couple of steps before a hand was laid upon his arm. He turned and beheld a lady cast in a very large mould and with somewhat stately features, but bearing no mark of severity in her looks.

"I see that you are a very self-confident lady-killer," said she; "for you make yourself expected. But I was determined to meet you. When a woman has once so far forgotten herself as to make the first advance, she has long ago left behind her all considerations of petty pride."

Silas was overwhelmed by the size and attractions of his correspondent and the suddenness with which she had fallen upon him. But she soon set him at his ease. She was very towardly and lenient in her behaviour; she led him on to make pleasantries, and then applauded him to the echo; and in a very short time, between blandishments and a liberal imbibition of warm brandy, she had not only induced him to fancy himself in love, but to declare his passion with the greatest vehemence.

"Alas!" she said; "I do not know whether I ought not to deplore this moment, great as is the pleasure you give me by your words. Hitherto I was alone to suffer; now, poor boy, there will be two. I am not my own mistress. I dare not ask you to visit me at my own house, for I am watched by jealous eyes. Let me see," she added; "I am older than you, although so much weaker; and while I trust in your courage and determination, I must employ my own knowledge of the world for our mutual benefit. Where do you live?"

He told her that he lodged in a furnished hotel, and named the street and number.

She seemed to reflect for some minutes, with an effort of mind.

"I see," she said at last. "You will be faithful and obedient, will you not?"

Silas assured her eagerly of his fidelity.

"To-morrow night, then," she continued, with an encouraging smile, "you must remain at home all the evening; and if any friends should visit you, dismiss them at once on any pretext that most readily presents itself. Your door is probably shut by ten?" she asked.

"By eleven," answered Silas.

"At a quarter-past eleven," pursued the lady, "leave the house. Merely cry for the door to be opened, and be sure you fall into no talk with the porter, as that might ruin everything. Go straight to the corner where the Luxembourg Gardens join the Boulevard; there you will find me waiting you. I trust you to follow my advice from point to point: and remember, if you fail me in only one particular, you will bring the sharpest trouble on a woman whose only fault is to have seen and loved you."

"I cannot see the use of all these instructions," said Silas.

"I believe you are already beginning to treat me as a master," she cried, tapping him with her fan upon the arm. "Patience, patience! that should come in time. A woman loves to be obeyed at first, although afterwards she finds her pleasure in obeying. Do as I ask you, for Heaven's sake, or I will answer for nothing. Indeed, now I think of it," she added, with the manner of one who had just seen further into a difficulty, "I find a better plan of keeping importunate visitors away. Tell the porter to admit no one for you, except a person who may come that night to claim a debt; and speak with some feeling, as though you feared the interview, so that he may take your words in earnest."

"I think you may trust me to protect myself against intruders," he said, not without a little pique.

"That is how I should prefer the thing arranged," she answered coldly. "I know you men; you think nothing of a woman's reputation."

Silas blushed and somewhat hung his head; for the scheme he had in view had involved a little vainglory before his acquaintances.

"Above all," she added, "do not speak to the porter as you come out."

"And why?" said he. "Of all your instructions, that seems to me the least important."

"You at first doubted the wisdom of some of the others, which you now see to be very necessary," she replied. "Believe me, this also has its uses; in time you will see them; and what am I to think of your affection, if you refuse me such trifles at our first interview?"

Silas confounded himself in explanations and apologies; in the middle of these she looked up at the clock and clapped her hands together with a suppressed scream.

"Heavens!" she cried, "is it so late? I have not an instant to lose. Alas, we poor women, what slaves we are! What have I not risked for you already?"

And after repeating her directions, which she artfully combined with caresses and the most abandoned looks, she bade him farewell and disappeared among the crowd.

The whole of the next day Silas was filled with a sense of great importance; he was now sure she was a countess; and when evening came he minutely obeyed her orders and was at the corner of the Luxembourg Gardens by the hour appointed. No one was there. He waited nearly half an hour, looking in the face of every one who passed or loitered near the spot; he even visited the neighbouring corners of the Boulevard and made a complete circuit of the garden railings; but there was no beautiful countess to throw herself into his arms. At last, and most reluctantly, he began to retrace his steps towards his hotel. On the way he remembered the words he had heard pass between Madame Zéphyrine and the blond young man, and they gave him an indefinite uneasiness.

"It appears," he reflected, "that every one has to tell lies to our porter."

He rang the bell, the door opened before him, and the porter in his bed-clothes came to offer him a light.

"Has he gone?" inquired the porter.

"He? Whom do you mean?" asked Silas, somewhat sharply, for he was irritated by his disappointment.

"I did not notice him go out," continued the porter, "but I trust you paid him. We do not care, in this house, to have lodgers who cannot meet their liabilities."

"What the devil do you mean?" demanded Silas, rudely. "I cannot understand a word of this farrago."

"The short blond young man who came for his debt," returned the other. "Him it is I mean. Who else should it be, when I had your orders to admit no one else?"

"Why, good God, of course he never came," retorted Silas.

"I believe what I believe," retorted the porter, putting his tongue into his cheek with a most roguish air.

"You are an insolent scoundrel," cried Silas, and, feeling that he had made a ridiculous exhibition of asperity, and at the same time bewildered by a dozen alarms, he turned and began to run up-stairs.

"Do you not want a light then?" cried the porter.

But Silas only hurried the faster, and did not pause until he had reached the seventh landing and stood in front of his own door. There he waited a moment to recover his breath, assailed by the worst forebodings and almost dreading to enter the room.

When at last he did so he was relieved to find it dark, and to all appearance untenanted. He drew a long breath. Here he was, home again in safety, and this should be his last folly as certainly as it had been his first. The matches stood on a little table by the bed, and he began to grope his way in that direction. As he moved, his apprehensions grew upon him once more, and he was pleased, when his foot encountered an obstacle, to find it nothing more alarming than a chair. At last he touched curtains. From the position of the window, which was faintly visible, he knew he must be at the foot of the bed, and had only to feel his way along it in order to reach the table in question.

He lowered his hand, but what he touched was not simply a counterpane—it was a counterpane with something underneath it like the outline of a human leg. Silas withdrew his arm and stood a moment petrified.

"What, what," he thought, "can this betoken?"

He listened intently, but there was no sound of breathing. Once more, with a great effort, he reached out the end of his finger to the spot he had already touched; but this time he leaped back half a yard, and stood shivering and fixed with terror. There was something in his bed. What it was he knew not, but there was something there.

It was some seconds before he could move. Then, guided by an instinct, he fell straight upon the matches, and keeping his back toward the bed, lighted a candle. As soon as the flame had kindled, he turned slowly round and looked for what he feared to see. Sure enough, there was the worst of his imaginations realised. The coverlid was drawn carefully up over the pillow, but it moulded the outline of a human body lying motionless; and when he dashed forward and flung aside the sheets, he beheld the blond young man whom he had seen in the Bullier Ball the night before, his eyes open and without speculation, his face swollen and blackened, and a thin stream of blood trickling from his nostrils.

Silas uttered a long tremulous wail, dropped the candle, and fell on his knees beside the bed.

Silas was awakened from the stupor into which his terrible discovery had plunged him, by a prolonged but discreet tapping at the door. It took him some seconds to remember his position; and when he hastened to prevent any one from entering it was already too late. Dr. Noel, in a tall nightcap, carrying a lamp which lighted up his long white countenance, sidling in his gait, and peering and cocking his head like some sort of bird, pushed the door slowly open, and advanced into the middle of the room.

"I thought I heard a cry," began the Doctor, "and fearing you might be unwell, I did not hesitate to offer this intrusion."

Silas, with a flushed face and a fearful beating heart, kept between the Doctor and the bed; but he found no voice to answer.

"You are in the dark," pursued the Doctor; "and yet you have not even begun to prepare for rest. You will not easily persuade me against my own eyesight; and your face declares most eloquently that you require either a friend or a physician—which is it to be? Let me feel your pulse, for that is often a just reporter of the heart."

He advanced to Silas, who still retreated before him backwards, and sought to take him by the wrist; but the strain on the young American's nerves had become too great for endurance. He avoided the Doctor with a febrile movement, and, throwing himself upon the floor, burst into a flood of weeping.

As soon as Dr. Noel perceived the dead man in the bed his face darkened; and hurrying back to the door which he had left ajar, he hastily closed and double-locked it.

"Up!" he cried, addressing Silas in strident tones. "This is no time for weeping. What have you done? How came this body in your room? Speak freely to one who may be helpful. Do you imagine I would ruin you? Do you think this piece of dead flesh on your pillow can alter in any degree the sympathy with which you have inspired me? Credulous youth, the horror with which blind and unjust law regards an action never attaches to the doer in the eyes of those who love him; and if I saw the friend of my heart return to me out of seas of blood he would be in no way changed in my affection. Raise yourself," he said; "good and ill are a chimera; there is naught in life except destiny, and however you may be circumstanced there is one at your side who will help you to the last."

Thus encouraged, Silas gathered himself together, and in a broken voice, and helped out by the Doctor's interrogations, contrived at last to put him in possession of the facts. But the conversation between the Prince and Geraldine he altogether omitted, as he had understood little of its purport, and had no idea that it was in any way related to his own misadventure.

"Alas!" cried Dr. Noel, "I am much abused, or you have fallen innocently into the most dangerous hands in Europe. Poor boy, what a pit has been dug for your simplicity! into what a deadly peril have your unwary feet been conducted! This man," he said, "this Englishman, whom you twice saw, and whom I suspect to be the soul of the contrivance, can you describe him? Was he young or old? tall or short?"

But Silas, who, for all his curiosity, had not a seeing eye in his head, was able to supply nothing but meagre generalities, which it was impossible to recognise.

"I would have it a piece of education in all schools!" cried the Doctor angrily. "Where is the use of eyesight and articulate speech if a man cannot observe and recollect the features of his enemy? I, who know all the gangs of Europe, might have identified him, and gained new weapons for your defence. Cultivate this art in future, my poor boy; you may find it of momentous service."

"The future!" repeated Silas. "What future is there left for me except the gallows?"

"Youth is but a cowardly season," returned the Doctor; "and a man's own troubles look blacker than they are. I am old, and yet I never despair."

"Can I tell such a story to the police?" demanded Silas.

"Assuredly not," replied the Doctor. "From what I see already of the machination in which you have been involved, your case is desperate upon that side; and for the narrow eye of the authorities you are infallibly the guilty person. And remember that we only know a portion of the plot; and the same infamous contrivers have doubtless arranged many other circumstances which would be elicited by a police inquiry, and help to fix the guilt more certainly upon your innocence."

"I am then lost, indeed!" cried Silas.

"I have not said so," answered Dr. Noel, "for I am a cautious man."

"But look at this!" objected Silas, pointing to the body. "Here is this object in my bed: not to be explained, not to be disposed of, not to be regarded without horror."

"Horror?" replied the Doctor. "No. When this sort of clock has run down, it is no more to me than an ingenious piece of mechanism, to be investigated with the bistery. When blood is once cold and stagnant, it is no longer human blood; when flesh is once dead, it is no longer that flesh which we desire in our lovers and respect in our friends. The grace, the attraction, the terror, have all gone from it with the animating spirit. Accustom yourself to look upon it with composure, for if my scheme is practicable you will have to live in constant proximity to that which now so greatly horrifies you."

"Your scheme?" cried Silas. "What is that? Tell me speedily, Doctor; for I have scarcely courage enough to continue to exist."

Without replying, Dr. Noel turned towards the bed, and proceeded to examine the corpse.

"Quite dead," he murmured. "Yes, as I had supposed, the pockets empty. Yes, and the name cut off the shirt. Their work has been done thoroughly and well. Fortunately he is of small stature."

Silas followed these words with an extreme anxiety. At last the Doctor, his autopsy completed, took a chair and addressed the young American with a smile.

"Since I came into your room," said he, "although my ears and my tongue have been so busy, I have not suffered my eyes to remain idle. I noted a little while ago that you have there, in the corner, one of those monstrous constructions which your fellow-countrymen carry with them into all quarters of the globe—in a word, a Saratoga trunk. Until this moment I have never been able

to conceive the utility of these erections; but then I began to have
a glimmer. Whether it was for convenience in the slave trade, or
to obviate the results of too ready an employment of the bowie-
knife, I cannot bring myself to decide. But one thing I see plainly
—the object of such a box is to contain a human body."

"Surely," cried Silas, "surely this is not a time for jesting."

"Although I may express myself with some degree of pleasantry,"
replied the Doctor, "the purport of my words is entirely serious.
And the first thing we have to do, my young friend, is to empty
your coffer of all it contains."

Silas, obeying the authority of Dr. Noel, put himself at his disposition. The Saratoga trunk was soon gutted of its contents,
which made a considerable litter on the floor; and then—Silas
taking the heels and the Doctor supporting the shoulders—the
body of the murdered man was carried from the bed, and, after
some difficulty, doubled up and inserted whole into the empty
box. With an effort on the part of both, the lid was forced down
upon this unusual baggage, and the trunk was locked and corded
by the Doctor's own hand, while Silas disposed of what had been
taken out between the closet and a chest of drawers.

"Now," said the Doctor, "the first step has been taken on the
way to your deliverance. To-morrow or rather to-day, it must be
your task to allay the suspicions of your porter, paying him all
that you owe; while you may trust me to make the arrangements
necessary to a safe conclusion. Meantime, follow me to my room,
where I shall give you a safe and powerful opiate; for, whatever
you do, you must have rest."

The next day was the longest in Silas's memory; it seemed as if
it would never be done. He denied himself to his friends, and sat
in a corner with his eyes fixed upon the Saratoga trunk in dismal
contemplation. His own former indiscretions were now returned
upon him in kind; for the observatory had been once more opened,
and he was conscious of an almost continual study from Madame
Zéphyrine's apartment. So distressing did this become, that he was
at last obliged to block up the spy-hole from his own side; and
when he was thus secured from observation he spent a considerable
portion of his time in contrite tears and prayer.

Late in the evening Dr. Noel entered the room carrying in his
hand a pair of sealed envelopes without address, one somewhat
bulky, and the other so slim as to seem without enclosure.

"Silas," he said, seating himself at the table, "the time has now come for me to explain my plan for your salvation. To-morrow morning, at an early hour, Prince Florizel of Bohemia returns to London, after having diverted himself for a few days with the Parisian Carnival. It was my fortune, a good while ago, to do Colonel Geraldine, his Master of the Horse, one of those services so common in my profession, which are never forgotten upon either side. I have no need to explain to you the nature of the obligation under which he was laid; suffice it to say that I knew him ready to serve me in any practicable manner. Now, it was necessary for you to gain London with your trunk unopened. To this the Custom House seemed to oppose a fatal difficulty; but I bethought me that the baggage of so considerable a person as the Prince is, as a matter of courtesy, passed without examination by the officers of Custom. I applied to Colonel Geraldine, and succeeded in obtaining a favourable answer. To-morrow, if you go before six to the hotel where the Prince lodges, your baggage will be passed over as a part of his, and you yourself will make the journey as a member of his suite."

"It seems to me, as you speak, that I have already seen both the Prince and Colonel Geraldine; I even overheard some of their conversation the other evening at the Bullier Ball."

"It is probable enough; for the Prince loves to mix with all societies," replied the Doctor. "Once arrived in London," he pursued, "your task is nearly ended. In this more bulky envelope I have given you a letter which I dare not address; but in the other you will find the designation of the house to which you must carry it along with your box, which will there be taken from you and not trouble you any more."

"Alas!" said Silas, "I have every wish to believe you; but how is it possible? You open up to me a bright prospect, but, I ask you, is my mind capable of receiving so unlikely a solution? Be more generous, and let me farther understand your meaning."

The Doctor seemed painfully impressed.

"Boy," he answered, "you do not know how hard a thing you ask of me. But be it so. I am now inured to humiliation; and it would be strange if I refused you this, after having granted you so much. Know, then, that although I now make so quiet an appearance—frugal, solitary, addicted to study—when I was younger, my name was once a rallying-cry among the most astute and dangerous spirits of London; and while I was outwardly an object for respect and consideration, my true power resided in the most secret, terrible, and criminal relations. It is to one of the persons who then obeyed me that I now address myself to deliver you from your burden. They were men of many different nations and dexterities, all bound together by a formidable oath, and working to the same purposes; the trade of the association was in murder; and I who speak to you, innocent as I appear, was the chieftain of this redoubtable crew."

"What?" cried Silas. "A murderer? And one with whom murder was a trade? Can I take your hand? Ought I to so much as accept your services? Dark and criminal old man, would you make an accomplice of my youth and my distress?"

The Doctor bitterly laughed.

"You are difficult to please, Mr. Scuddamore," said he; "but I now offer you your choice of company between the murdered man and the murderer. If your conscience is too nice to accept my aid, say so, and I will immediately leave you. Thenceforward you can deal with your trunk and its belongings as best suits your upright conscience."

"I own myself wrong," replied Silas. "I should have remembered how generously you offered to shield me, even before I had convinced you of my innocence, and I continue to listen to your counsels with gratitude."

"That is well," returned the Doctor; "and I perceive you are beginning to learn some of the lessons of experience."

"At the same time," resumed the New Englander, "as you confess yourself accustomed to this tragical business, and the people to whom you recommend me are your own former associates and friends, could you not yourself undertake the transport of the box, and rid me at once of its detested presence?"

"Upon my word," replied the Doctor, "I admire you cordially. If you do not think I have already meddled sufficiently in your concerns, believe me, from my heart I think the contrary. Take or leave my services as I offer them; and trouble me with no more words of gratitude, for I value your consideration even more lightly than I do your intellect. A time will come, if you should be spared to see a number of years in health and mind, when you will think differently of all this, and blush for your to-night's behaviour."

So saying, the Doctor arose from his chair, repeated his directions briefly and clearly, and departed from the room without permitting Silas any time to answer.

The next morning Silas presented himself at the hotel, where he was politely received by Colonel Geraldine, and relieved, from that moment, of all immediate alarm about his trunk and its grisly contents. The journey passed over without much incident, although the young man was horrified to overhear the sailors and railway porters complaining among themselves about the unusual weight of the Prince's baggage. Silas travelled in a carriage with the valets, for Prince Florizel chose to be alone with his Master of the Horse. On board the steamer, however, Silas attracted his Highness's attention by the melancholy of his air and attitude as he stood gazing at the pile of baggage; for he was still full of disquietude about the future.

"There is a young man," observed the Prince, "who must have some cause for sorrow."

"That," replied Geraldine, "is the American for whom I obtained permission to travel with your suite."

"You remind me that I have been remiss in courtesy," said Prince Florizel, and advancing to Silas, he addressed him with the most exquisite condescension in these words:

"I was charmed, young sir, to be able to gratify the desire you made known to me through Colonel Geraldine. Remember, if you please, that I shall be glad at any future time to lay you under a more serious obligation."

And then he put some questions as to the political condition of America, which Silas answered with sense and propriety.

"You are still a young man," said the Prince; "but I observe you to be very serious for your years. Perhaps you allow your attention to be too much occupied with grave studies. But, perhaps, on the other hand, I am myself indiscreet and touch upon a painful subject."

"I have certainly cause to be the most miserable of men," said Silas; "never has a more innocent person been more dismally abused."

"I will not ask you for your confidence," returned Prince Florizel. "But do not forget that Colonel Geraldine's recommendation is an unfailing passport; and that I am not only willing, but possibly more able than many others, to do you a service."

Silas was delighted with the amiability of this great personage; but his mind soon returned upon its gloomy preoccupations; for not even the favour of a Prince to a Republican can discharge a brooding spirit of its cares.

The train arrived at Charing Cross, where the officers of the Revenue respected the baggage of Prince Florizel in the usual manner. The most elegant equipages were in waiting; and Silas was driven, along with the rest, to the Prince's residence. There Colonel Geraldine sought him out, and expressed himself pleased to have been of any service to a friend of the physician's, for whom he professed a great consideration.

"I hope," he added, "that you will find none of your porcelain injured. Special orders were given along the line to deal tenderly with the Prince's effects."

And then, directing the servants to place one of the carriages at the young gentleman's disposal, and at once to charge the Saratoga trunk upon the dickey, the Colonel shook hands and excused himself on account of his occupations in the princely household.

Silas now broke the seal of the envelope containing the address, and directed the stately footman to drive him to Box Court, opening off the Strand. It seemed as if the place were not at all unknown to the man, for he looked startled and begged a repetition of the order. It was with a heart full of alarms, that Silas mounted into the luxurious vehicle, and was driven to his destination. The entrance to Box Court was too narrow for the passage of a coach; it was a mere footway between railings, with a post at either end. On one of these posts was seated a man, who at once jumped down and exchanged a friendly sign with the driver, while the footman opened the door and inquired of Silas whether he should take down the Saratoga trunk, and to what number it should be carried.

"If you please," said Silas. "To number three."

The footman and the man who had been sitting on the post, even with the aid of Silas himself, had hard work to carry in the trunk; and before it was deposited at the door of the house in question, the young American was horrified to find a score of loiterers looking on.

But he knocked with as good a countenance as he could muster up, and presented the other envelope to him who opened.

"He is not at home," said he, "but if you will leave your letter and return to-morrow early, I shall be able to inform you whether and when he can receive your visit. Would you like to leave your box?" he added.

"Dearly," cried Silas; and the next moment he repented his precipitation, and declared, with equal emphasis, that he would rather carry the box along with him to the hotel.

The crowd jeered at his indecision and followed him to the carriage with insulting remarks; and Silas, covered with shame and terror, implored the servants to conduct him to some quiet and comfortable house of entertainment in the immediate neighbourhood.

The Prince's equipage deposited Silas at the Craven Hotel in Craven Street, and immediately drove away, leaving him alone with the servants of the inn. The only vacant room, it appeared, was a little den up four pairs of stairs, and looking towards the back. To this hermitage, with infinite trouble and complaint, a pair of stout porters carried the Saratoga trunk. It is needless to mention that Silas kept closely at their heels throughout the ascent, and had his heart in his mouth at every corner. A single false step, he reflected, and the box might go over the banisters and land its fatal contents, plainly discovered, on the pavement of the hall.

Arrived in the room, he sat down on the edge of his bed to recover from the agony that he had just endured; but he had hardly taken his position when he was recalled to a sense of his peril by the action of the boots, who had knelt beside the trunk, and was proceeding officiously to undo its elaborate fastenings.

"Let it be!" cried Silas. "I shall want nothing from it while I stay here."

"You might have let it lie in the hall, then," growled the man; "a thing as big and heavy as a church. What you have inside, I cannot fancy. If it is all money, you are a richer man than me."

"Money?" repeated Silas, in a sudden perturbation. "What do you mean by money? I have no money, and you are speaking like a fool."

"All right, Captain," retorted the boots with a wink. "There's nobody will touch your lordship's money. I'm as safe as the bank," he added; "but as the box is heavy, I shouldn't mind drinking something to your lordship's health."

Silas pressed two Napoleons upon his acceptance, apologising, at the same time, for being obliged to trouble him with foreign money, and pleading his recent arrival for excuse. And the man, grumbling with even greater fervour, and looking contemptuously from the money in his hand to the Saratoga trunk and back again from the one to the other, at last consented to withdraw.

For nearly two days the dead body had been packed into Silas's box; and as soon as he was alone the unfortunate New Englander nosed all the cracks and openings with the most passionate attention. But the weather was cool, and the trunk still managed to contain his shocking secret.

He took a chair beside it, and buried his face in his hands, and his mind in the most profound reflection. If he were not speedily relieved, no question but he must be speedily discovered. Alone in a strange city, without friends or accomplices, if the Doctor's introduction failed him, he was indubitably a lost New Englander. He reflected pathetically over his ambitious designs for the future; he should not now become the hero and spokesman of his native place of Bangor, Maine; he should not, as he had fondly anticipated, move on from office to office, from honour to honour; he might as well divest himself at once of all hope of being acclaimed President of the United States, and leaving behind him a statue, in the worst possible style of art, to adorn the Capitol at Washington. Here he was, chained to a dead Englishman doubled up inside a Saratoga trunk; whom he must get rid of, or perish from the rolls of national glory!

I should be afraid to chronicle the language employed by this young man to the Doctor, to the murdered man, to Madame Zéphyrine, to the boots of the hotel, to the Prince's servants, and, in a word, to all who had been ever so remotely connected with his horrible misfortune.

He slunk down to dinner about seven at night; but the yellow coffee-room appalled him, the eyes of the other diners seemed to rest on his with suspicion, and his mind remained up-stairs with the Saratoga trunk. When the waiter came to offer him cheese, his nerves were already so much on edge that he leaped half-way out of his chair and upset the remainder of a pint of ale upon the table-cloth.

The fellow offered to show him the smoking-room when he had done; and although he would have much preferred to return at once to his perilous treasure, he had not the courage to refuse, and was shown down-stairs to the black, gas-lit cellar, which formed, and possibly still forms, the divan of the Craven Hotel.

Two very sad betting men were playing billiards, attended by a moist, consumptive marker; and for the moment Silas imagined that these were the only occupants of the apartment. But at the next glance his eye fell upon a person smoking in the farthest corner, with lowered eyes and a most respectable and modest aspect. He knew at once that he had seen the face before; and in spite of the entire change of clothes, recognised the man whom he had found seated on a post at the entrance to Box Court, and who had helped him to carry the trunk to and from the carriage. The New Englander simply turned and ran, nor did he pause until he had locked and bolted himself into his bedroom.

There, all night long, a prey to the most terrible imaginations, he watched beside the fatal boxful of dead flesh. The suggestion of the boots that his trunk was full of gold inspired him with all manner of new terrors, if he so much as dared to close an eye; and the presence in the smoking-room, and under an obvious disguise, of the loiterer from Box Court convinced him that he was once more the centre of obscure machination.

Midnight had sounded some time, when, impelled by uneasy suspicions, Silas opened his bedroom door and peered into the passage. It was dimly illuminated by a single jet of gas; and some distance off he perceived a man sleeping on the floor in the costume of an hotel under-servant. Silas drew near the man on tiptoe. He lay partly on his back, partly on his side, and his right forearm concealed his face from recognition. Suddenly, while the American was still bending over him, the sleeper removed his arm and opened his eyes, and Silas found himself once more face to face with the loiterer of Box Court.

"Good-night, sir," said the man, pleasantly.

But Silas was too profoundly moved to find an answer, and regained his room in silence.

Towards morning, worn out by apprehension, he fell asleep on his chair, with his head forward on the trunk. In spite of so constrained an attitude and such a grisly pillow, his slumber was sound and prolonged, and he was only awakened at a late hour and by a sharp tapping at the door.

He hurried to open, and found the boots without.

"You are the gentleman who called yesterday at Box Court?" he asked.

Silas, with a quaver, admitted that he had done so.

"Then this note is for you," added the servant, proffering a sealed envelope.

Silas tore it open, and found inside the words: "Twelve o'clock."

He was punctual to the hour; the trunk was carried before him by several stout servants; and he was himself ushered into a room, where a man sat warming himself before the fire with his back towards the door. The sound of so many persons entering and leaving, and the scraping of the trunk as it was deposited upon the bare boards, were alike unable to attract the notice of the occupant; and Silas stood waiting, in an agony of fear, until he should deign to recognise his presence.

Perhaps five minutes had elapsed before the man turned leisurely about, and disclosed the features of Prince Florizel of Bohemia.

"So, sir," he said with great severity, "this is the manner in which you abuse my politeness. You join yourself to persons of condition, I perceive, for no other purpose than to escape the consequences of your crimes; and I can readily understand your embarrassment when I addressed myself to you yesterday."

"Indeed," cried Silas, "I am innocent of everything except misfortune."

And in a hurried voice, and with the greatest ingenuousness, he recounted to the Prince the whole history of his calamity.

"I see I have been mistaken," said his Highness, when he had heard him to an end. "You are no other than a victim, and since I am not to punish you, you may be sure I shall do my utmost to help. And now," he continued, "to business. Open your box at once, and let me see what it contains."

Silas changed colour.

"I almost fear to look upon it," he exclaimed.

"Nay," replied the Prince, "have you not looked at it already? This is a form of sentimentality to be resisted. The sight of a sick man, whom we can still help, should appeal more directly to the feelings than that of a dead man who is equally beyond help or harm, love or hatred. Nerve yourself, Mr. Scuddamore," and then, seeing that Silas still hesitated, "I do not desire to give another name to my request," he added.

The young American awoke as if out of a dream, and with a shiver of repugnance addressed himself to loose the straps and open the lock of the Saratoga trunk. The Prince stood by, watching with a composed countenance and his hands behind his back. The body was quite stiff, and it cost Silas a great effort, both moral and physical, to dislodge it from its position, and discover the face.

Prince Florizel started back with an exclamation of painful surprise.

"Alas!" he cried, "you little know, Mr. Scuddamore, what a cruel gift you have brought me. This is a young man of my own suite, the brother of my trusted friend; and it was upon matters of my own service that he has thus perished at the hands of violent and treacherous men. Poor Geraldine," he went on, as if to himself, "in what words am I to tell you of your brother's fate? How can I excuse myself in your eyes, or in the eyes of God, for the presumptuous schemes that led him to this bloody and unnatural death? Ah, Florizel! Florizel! when will you learn the discretion that suits mortal life, and be no longer dazzled with the image of power at your disposal? Power!" he cried; "who is more powerless? I look upon this young man whom I have sacrificed, Mr. Scuddamore, and feel how small a thing it is to be a Prince."

Silas was moved at the sight of his emotion. He tried to murmur some consolatory words, and burst into tears. The Prince, touched by his obvious intention, came up to him and took him by the hand.

"Command yourself," said he. "We have both much to learn, and we shall both be better men for to-day's meeting."

Silas thanked him in silence, with an affectionate look.

"Write me the address of Dr. Noel on this piece of paper," continued the Prince, leading him towards the table; "and let me recommend you, when you are again in Paris, to avoid the society of that dangerous man. He has acted in this matter on a generous inspiration; that I must believe; had he been privy to young Geraldine's death he would never have despatched the body to the care of the actual criminal."

"The actual criminal!" repeated Silas in astonishment.

"Even so," returned the Prince. "This letter, which the disposition of Almighty Providence has so strangely delivered into my hands, was addressed to no less a person than the criminal himself, the infamous President of the Suicide Club. Seek to pry no further in these perilous affairs, but content yourself with your own miraculous escape, and leave this house at once. I have pressing affairs, and must arrange at once about this poor clay, which was so lately a gallant and handsome youth."

Silas took a grateful and submissive leave of Prince Florizel, but he lingered in Box Court until he saw him depart in a splendid carriage on a visit to Colonel Henderson, of the police. Republican as he was, the young American took off his hat with almost a sentiment of devotion to the retreating carriage. And the same night he started by rail on his return to Paris.

Here (*observes my Arabian author*) is the end of the STORY OF THE PHYSICIAN AND THE SARATOGA TRUNK. Omitting some reflections on the power of Providence, highly pertinent in the original, but little suited to our occidental taste, I shall only add that Mr. Scuddamore has already begun to mount the ladder of political fame, and by last advices was the Sheriff of his native town.

The Adventure of the Hansom Cab

Lieutenant Brackenbury Rich had greatly distinguished himself in one of the lesser Indian hill wars. He it was who took the chieftain prisoner with his own hand; his gallantry was universally applauded; and when he came home, prostrated by an ugly sabre cut and a protracted jungle fever, society was prepared to welcome the Lieutenant as a celebrity of minor lustre. But his was a character remarkable for unaffected modesty; adventure was dear to his heart, but he cared little for adulation; and he waited at foreign watering-places and in Algiers until the fame of his exploits had run through its nine days' vitality and begun to be forgotten. He arrived in London at last, in the early season, with as little observation as he could desire; and as he was an orphan and had none but distant relatives who lived in the provinces, it was almost as a foreigner that he installed himself in the capital of the country for which he had shed his blood.

On the day following his arrival he dined alone at a military club. He shook hands with a few old comrades, and received their congratulations; but as one and all had some engagement for the evening, he found himself left entirely to his own resources. He was in dress, for he had entertained the notion of visiting a theatre. But the great city was new to him; he had gone from a provincial school to a military college, and thence direct to the Eastern Empire; and he promised himself a variety of delights in this world for exploration. Swinging his cane, he took his way westward. It was a mild evening, already dark, and now and then threatening rain. The succession of faces in the lamplight stirred the Lieutenant's imagination; and it seemed to him as if he could walk for ever in that stimulating city atmosphere and surrounded by the mystery of four million private lives. He glanced at the houses, and marvelled what was passing behind those warmly-lighted windows; he looked into face after face, and saw them each intent upon some unknown interest, criminal or kindly.

"They talk of war," he thought, "but this is the great battlefield of mankind."

And then he began to wonder that he should walk so long in this complicated scene, and not chance upon so much as the shadow of an adventure for himself.

"All in good time," he reflected. "I am still a stranger, and perhaps wear a strange air. But I must be drawn into the eddy before long."

The night was already well advanced, when a plump of cold rain fell suddenly out of the darkness. Brackenbury paused under some trees, and as he did so he caught sight of a hansom cabman making him a sign that he was disengaged. The circumstance fell in so happily to the occasion that he at once raised his cane in answer, and had soon ensconced himself in the London gondola.

"Where to, sir?" asked the driver.

"Where you please," said Brackenbury.

And immediately, at a pace of surprising swiftness, the hansom drove off through the rain into a maze of villas. One villa was so like another, each with its front garden, and there was so little to distinguish the deserted lamp-lit streets and crescents through which the flying hansom took its way, that Brackenbury soon lost all idea of direction. He would have been contented to believe that the cabman was amusing himself by driving him round and round and in and out about a small quarter, but there was something businesslike in the speed which convinced him of the contrary. The man had an object in view, he was hastening towards a definite end; and Brackenbury was at once astonished at the fellow's skill in picking a way through such a labyrinth, and a little concerned to imagine what was the occasion of his hurry. He had heard tales of strangers falling ill in London. Did the driver belong to some bloody and treacherous association? and was he himself being whirled to a murderous death?

The thought had scarcely presented itself, when the cab swung sharply round a corner and pulled up before the garden gate of a villa in a long and wide road. The house was brilliantly lighted up. Another hansom had just driven away, and Brackenbury could see a gentleman being admitted at the front door and received by several liveried servants. He was surprised that the cabman should have stopped so immediately in front of a house where a reception was being held; but he did not doubt it was the result of accident, and sat placidly smoking where he was, until he heard the trap thrown open over his head.

"Here we are, sir," said the driver.

"Here!" repeated Brackenbury. "Where?"

"You told me to take you where I pleased, sir," returned the man with a chuckle, "and here we are."

It struck Brackenbury that the voice was wonderfully smooth and courteous for a man in so inferior a position; he remembered the speed at which he had been driven; and now it occurred to him that the hansom was more luxuriously appointed than the common run of public conveyances.

"I must ask you to explain," said he. "Do you mean to turn me out into the rain? My good man, I suspect the choice is mine."

"The choice is certainly yours," replied the driver; "but when I tell you all, I believe I know how a gentleman of your figure will decide. There is a gentleman's party in this house. I do not know whether the master be a stranger to London and without acquaintances of his own; or whether he is a man of odd notions. But certainly I was hired to kidnap single gentlemen in evening dress, as many as I pleased, but military officers by preference. You have simply to go in and say that Mr. Morris invited you."

"Are you Mr. Morris?" inquired the Lieutenant.

"Oh, no," replied the cabman. "Mr. Morris is the person of the house."

"It is not a common way of collecting guests," said Brackenbury; "but an eccentric man might very well indulge the whim without any intention to offend. And suppose that I refuse Mr. Morris's invitation," he went on, "what then?"

"My orders are to drive you back where I took you from," replied the man, "and set out to look for others up to midnight. Those who have no fancy for such an adventure, Mr. Morris said, were not the guests for him."

These words decided the Lieutenant on the spot.

"After all," he reflected, as he descended from the hansom, "I have not had long to wait for my adventure."

He had hardly found footing on the sidewalk, and was still feeling in his pocket for the fare, when the cab swung about and drove off by the way it came at the former break-neck velocity. Brackenbury shouted after the man, who paid no heed, and continued to drive away; but the sound of his voice was overheard in the house, the door was again thrown open, emitting a flood of light upon the garden, and a servant ran down to meet him holding an umbrella.

"The cabman has been paid," observed the servant in a very civil tone; and he proceeded to escort Brackenbury along the path and up the steps. In the hall several other attendants relieved him of his hat, cane, and paletot, gave him a ticket with a number in return, and politely hurried him up a stair adorned with tropical flowers, to the door of an apartment on the first story. Here a grave butler inquired his name, and announcing "Lieutenant Brackenbury Rich," ushered him into the drawing-room of the house.

A young man, slender and singularly handsome, came forward and greeted him with an air at once courtly and affectionate. Hundreds of candles, of the finest wax, lit up a room that was perfumed, like the staircase, with a profusion of rare and beautiful flowering shrubs. A side-table was loaded with tempting viands. Several servants went to and fro with fruits and goblets of champagne. The company was perhaps sixteen in number, all men, few beyond the prime of life, and with hardly an exception, of a dashing and capable exterior. They were divided into two groups, one about a roulette board, and the other surrounding a table at which one of their number held a bank of baccarat.

"I see," thought Brackenbury, "I am in a private gambling saloon, and the cabman was a tout."

His eye had embraced the details, and his mind formed the conclusion, while his host was still holding him by the hand; and to him his looks returned from this rapid survey. At a second view Mr. Morris surprised him still more than on the first. The easy elegance of his manners, the distinction, amiability, and courage that appeared upon his features, fitted very ill with the Lieutenant's preconceptions on the subject of the proprietor of a hell; and the tone of his conversation seemed to mark him out for a man of position and merit. Brackenbury found he had an instinctive liking for his entertainer; and though he chid himself for the weakness he was unable to resist a sort of friendly attraction for Mr. Morris's person and character.

"I have heard of you, Lieutenant Rich," said Mr. Morris, lowering his tone; "and believe me I am gratified to make your acquaintance. Your looks accord with the reputation that has preceded you from India. And if you will forget for awhile the irregularity of your presentation in my house, I shall feel it not only an honour, but genuine pleasure besides. A man who makes a mouthful of barbarian cavaliers," he added with a laugh, "should not be appalled by a breach of etiquette, however serious."

And he led him towards the sideboard and pressed him to partake of some refreshments.

"Upon my word," the Lieutenant reflected, "this is one of the pleasantest fellows and, I do not doubt, one of the most agreeable societies in London."

He partook of some champagne, which he found excellent; and observing that many of the company were already smoking, he lit one of his own Manilas, and strolled up to the roulette board, where he sometimes made a stake and sometimes looked on smilingly on the fortune of others. It was while he was thus idling that he became aware of a sharp scrutiny to which the whole of the guests were subjected. Mr. Morris went here and there, ostensibly busied on hospitable concerns; but he had ever a shrewd glance at disposal; not a man of the party escaped his sudden, searching looks; he took stock of the bearing of heavy losers, he valued the amount of the stakes, he paused behind couples who were deep in conversation; and, in a word, there was hardly a characteristic of any one present but he seemed to catch and make a note of it. Brackenbury began to wonder if this were indeed a gambling hell: it had so much the air of a private inquisition. He followed Mr. Morris in all his movements; and although the man had a ready smile, he seemed to perceive, as it were under a mask, a haggard, careworn, and preoccupied spirit. The fellows around him laughed and made their game; but Brackenbury had lost interest in the guests.

"This Morris," thought he, "is no idler in the room. Some deep purpose inspires him; let it be mine to fathom it."

Now and then Mr. Morris would call one of his visitors aside; and after a brief colloquy in an ante-room, he would return alone, and the visitors in question reappeared no more. After a certain number of repetitions, this performance excited Brackenbury's curiosity to a high degree. He determined to be at the bottom of this minor mystery at once; and strolling into the ante-room, found a deep window recess concealed by curtains of the fashionable green. Here he hurriedly ensconced himself; nor had he to wait long before the sound of steps and voices drew near him from the principal apartment. Peering through the division, he saw Mr. Morris escorting a fat and ruddy personage, with somewhat the look of a commercial traveller, whom Brackenbury had already remarked for his coarse laugh and under-bred behaviour at the table. The pair halted immediately before the window, so that Brackenbury lost not a word of the following discourse:

"I beg you a thousand pardons!" began Mr. Morris, with the most conciliatory manner; "and, if I appear rude, I am sure you will readily forgive me. In a place so great as London accidents must continually happen; and the best that we can hope is to remedy them with as small delay as possible. I will not deny that I fear you have made a mistake and honoured my poor house by inadvertence; for, to speak openly, I cannot at all remember your appearance. Let me put the question without unnecessary circumlocution—between gentlemen of honour a word will suffice— Under whose roof do you suppose yourself to be?"

"That of Mr. Morris," replied the other, with a prodigious display of confusion, which had been visibly growing upon him throughout the last few words.

"Mr. John or Mr. James Morris?" inquired the host.

"I really cannot tell you," returned the unfortunate guest. "I am not personally acquainted with the gentleman, any more than I am with yourself."

"I see," said Mr. Morris. "There is another person of the same name farther down the street; and I have no doubt the policeman will be able to supply you with his number. Believe me, I felicitate myself on the misunderstanding which has procured me the pleasure of your company for so long; and let me express a hope that we may meet again upon a more regular footing. Meantime, I would not for the world detain you longer from your friends. John," he added, raising his voice, "will you see that the gentleman finds his great-coat?"

And with the most agreeable air Mr. Morris escorted his visitor as far as the ante-room door, where he left him under conduct of the butler. As he passed the window, on his return to the drawing-room, Brackenbury could hear him utter a profound sigh, as though his mind was loaded with a great anxiety, and his nerves already fatigued with the task on which he was engaged.

For perhaps an hour the hansoms kept arriving with such frequency, that Mr. Morris had to receive a new guest for every old one that he sent away, and the company preserved its number undiminished. But towards the end of that time the arrivals grew few and far between, and at length ceased entirely, while the process of elimination was continued with unimpaired activity. The drawing-room began to look empty: the baccarat was discontinued for lack of a banker; more than one person said good-night of his own accord, and was suffered to depart without expostulation: and in the meanwhile Mr. Morris redoubled in agreeable attentions to those who stayed behind. He went from group to group and from person to person with looks of the readiest sympathy and the most pertinent and pleasing talk; he was not so much like a host as like a hostess, and there was a feminine coquetry and condescension in his manner which charmed the hearts of all.

As the guests grew thinner, Lieutenant Rich strolled for a moment out of the drawing-room into the hall in quest of fresher air. But he had no sooner passed the threshold of the ante-chamber than he was brought to a dead halt by a discovery of the most surprising nature. The flowering shrubs had disappeared from the staircase; three large furniture wagons stood before the garden gate; the servants were busy dismantling the house upon all sides; and some of them had already donned their great-coats and were preparing to depart. It was like the end of a country ball, where everything has been supplied by contract. Brackenbury had indeed some matter for reflection. First, the guests, who were no real guests after all, had been dismissed; and now the servants, who could hardly be genuine servants, were actively dispersing.

"Was the whole establishment a sham?" he asked himself. "The mushroom of a single night which should disappear before morning?"

Watching a favourable opportunity, Brackenbury dashed upstairs to the higher regions of the house. It was as he had expected. He ran from room to room, and saw not a stick of furniture nor so much as a picture on the walls. Although the house had been painted and papered, it was not only uninhabited at present, but plainly had never been inhabited at all. The young officer remembered with astonishment its spacious, settled, and hospitable air on his arrival. It was only at a prodigious cost that the imposture could have been carried out upon so great a scale.

Who, then, was Mr. Morris? What was his intention in thus playing the householder for a single night in the remote west of London? And why did he collect his visitors at hazard from the streets?

Brackenbury remembered that he had already delayed too long, and hastened to join the company. Many had left during his absence; and counting the Lieutenant and his host, there were not more than five persons in the drawing-room—recently so thronged. Mr. Morris greeted him, as he re-entered the apartment, with a smile, and immediately rose to his feet.

"It is now time, gentlemen," said he, "to explain my purpose in decoying you from your amusements. I trust you did not find the evening hang very dully on your hands; but my object, I will confess it, was not to entertain your leisure, but to help myself in an unfortunate necessity. You are all gentlemen," he continued, "your appearance does you that much justice, and I ask for no better security. Hence, I speak it without concealment, I ask you to render me a dangerous and delicate service; dangerous because you may run the hazard of your lives, and delicate because I must ask an absolute discretion upon all that you shall see or hear. From an utter stranger the request is almost comically extravagant; I am well aware of this; and I would add at once, if there be any one present who has heard enough, if there be one among the party who recoils from a dangerous confidence and a piece of Quixotic devotion to he knows not whom—here is my hand ready, and I shall wish him good-night and God-speed, with all the sincerity in the world."

A very tall, black man, with a heavy stoop, immediately responded to this appeal.

"I commend your frankness, sir," said he; "and, for my part, I go. I make no reflections; but I cannot deny that you fill me with suspicious thoughts. I go myself, as I say; and perhaps you will think I have no right to add words to my example."

"On the contrary," replied Mr. Morris, "I am obliged to you for all you say. It would be impossible to exaggerate the gravity of my proposal."

"Well, gentlemen, what do you say?" said the tall man, addressing the others. "We have had our evening's frolic; shall we go homeward peaceably in a body? You will think well of my suggestion in the morning, when you see the sun again in innocence and safety."

The speaker pronounced the last words with an intonation which added to their force; and his face wore a singular expression, full of gravity and significance. Another of the company rose hastily, and, with some appearance of alarm, prepared to take his leave. There were only two who held their ground, Brackenbury and an old red-nosed cavalry Major; but these two preserved a nonchalant demeanour, and, beyond a look of intelligence which they rapidly exchanged, appeared entirely foreign to the discussion that had just been terminated.

Mr. Morris conducted the deserters as far as the door, which he closed upon their heels; then he turned round disclosing a countenance of mingled relief and animation, and addressed the two officers as follows:

"I have chosen my men like Joshua in the Bible," said Mr. Morris, "and I now believe I have the pick of London. Your appearance pleased my hansom cabmen; then it delighted me; I have watched your behaviour in a strange company, and under the most unusual circumstances; I have studied how you played and how you bore your losses; lastly, I have put you to the test of a staggering announcement, and you received it like an invitation to dinner. It is not for nothing," he cried, "that I have been for years the companion and the pupil of the bravest and wisest potentate in Europe."

"At the affair of Bunderchang," observed the Major, "I asked for twelve volunteers, and every trooper in the ranks replied to my appeal. But a gaming party is not the same thing as a regiment under fire. You may be pleased, I suppose, to have found two, and two who will not fail you at a push. As for the pair who ran away, I count them among the most pitiful hounds I ever met with. Lieutenant Rich," he added, addressing Brackenbury, "I have heard much of you of late; and I cannot doubt but you have also heard of me. I am Major O'Rooke."

And the veteran tendered his hand, which was red and tremulous, to the young Lieutenant.

"Who has not?" answered Brackenbury.

"When this little matter is settled," said Mr. Morris, "you will think I have sufficiently rewarded you; for I could offer neither a more valuable service than to make him acquainted with the other."

"And now," said Major O'Rooke, "is it a duel?"

"A duel after a fashion," replied Mr. Morris, "a duel with unknown and dangerous enemies, and, as I gravely fear, a duel to the death. I must ask you," he continued, "to call me Morris no longer: call me, if you please, Hammersmith; my real name, as well as that of another person to whom I hope to present you before long, you will gratify me by not asking and not seeking to discover for yourselves. Three days ago the person of whom I speak disappeared suddenly from home; and, until this morning, I received no hint of his situation. You will fancy my alarm when I tell you that he is engaged upon a work of private justice. Bound by an unhappy oath, too lightly sworn, he finds it necessary, without the help of law, to rid the earth of an insidious and bloody villain. Already two of our friends, and one of them my own born brother, have perished in the enterprise. He himself, or I am much deceived, is taken in the same fatal toils. But at least he still lives and still hopes, as this billet sufficiently proves."

And the speaker, no other than Colonel Geraldine, proffered a letter, thus conceived:

"*Major Hammersmith*, On Wednesday, at 3 A.M., you will be admitted by the small door to the gardens of Rochester House, Regent's Park, by a man who is entirely in my interest. I must request you not to fail me by a second. Pray bring my case of swords, and, if you can find them, one or two gentlemen of conduct and discretion to whom my person is unknown. My name must not be used in this affair.

"T. Godall."

"From his wisdom alone, if he had no other title," pursued Colonel Geraldine, when the others had each satisfied his curiosity, "my friend is a man whose directions should implicitly be followed. I need not tell you, therefore, that I have not so much as visited the neighbourhood of Rochester House; and that I am still as wholly in the dark as either of yourselves as to the nature of my friend's dilemma. I betook myself, as soon as I had received this order, to a furnishing contractor, and, in a few hours, the house in which we now are had assumed its late air of festival. My scheme was at least original; and I am far from regretting an action which has procured me the services of Major O'Rooke and Lieutenant Brackenbury Rich. But the servants in the street will have a strange awakening. The house which this evening was full of lights and visitors they will find uninhabited and for sale tomorrow morning. Thus even the most serious concerns," added the Colonel, "have a merry side."

"And let us add a merry ending," said Brackenbury.

The Colonel consulted his watch.

"It is now hard on two," he said. "We have an hour before us, and a swift cab is at the door. Tell me if I may count upon your help."

"During a long life," replied Major O'Rooke, "I never took back my hand from anything, nor so much as hedged a bet."

Brackenbury signified his readiness in the most becoming terms; and after they had drunk a glass or two of wine, the Colonel gave each of them a loaded revolver, and the three mounted into the cab and drove off for the address in question.

Rochester House was a magnificent residence on the banks of the canal. The large extent of the garden isolated it in an unusual degree from the annoyances of neighbourhood. It seemed the *parc aux cerfs* of some great nobleman or millionaire. As far as could be seen from the street, there was not a glimmer of light in any of the numerous windows of the mansion; and the place had a look of neglect, as though the master had been long from home.

The cab was discharged, and the three gentlemen were not long in discovering the small door, which was a sort of postern in a lane between two garden walls. It still wanted ten or fifteen minutes of the appointed time; the rain fell heavily, and the adventurers sheltered themselves below some pendent ivy, and spoke in low tones of the approaching trial.

Suddenly Geraldine raised his finger to command silence, and all three bent their hearing to the utmost. Through the continuous noise of the rain, the steps and voices of two men became audible from the other side of the wall; and, as they drew nearer, Brackenbury, whose sense of hearing was remarkably acute, could even distinguish some fragments of their talk.

"Is the grave dug?" asked one.

"It is," replied the other; "behind the laurel hedge. When the job is done, we can cover it with a pile of stakes."

The first speaker laughed, and the sound of his merriment was shocking to the listeners on the other side.

"In an hour from now," he said.

And by the sounds of the steps it was obvious that the pair had separated, and were proceeding in contrary directions.

Almost immediately after the postern door was cautiously opened, a white face was protruded into the lane, and a hand was seen beckoning to the watchers. In dead silence the three passed the door, which was immediately locked behind them, and followed their guide through several garden alleys to the kitchen entrance of the house. A single candle burned in the great paved kitchen, which was destitute of the customary furniture; and as the party proceeded to ascend from thence by a flight of winding stairs, a prodigious noise of rats testified still more plainly to the dilapidation of the house.

Their conductor preceded them, carrying the candle. He was a lean man, much bent, but still agile; and he turned from time to time and admonished silence and caution by his gestures. Colonel Geraldine followed on his heels, the case of swords under one arm, and a pistol ready in the other. Brackenbury's heart beat thickly. He perceived that they were still in time; but he judged from the alacrity of the old man that the hour of action must be near at hand; the circumstances of this adventure were so obscure and menacing, the place seemed so well chosen for the darkest acts, that an older man than Brackenbury might have been pardoned a measure of emotion as he closed the procession up the winding stair.

At the top the guide threw open a door and ushered the three officers before him into a small apartment, lighted by a smoky lamp and the glow of a modest fire. At the chimney corner sat a man in the early prime of life, and of a stout but courtly and commanding appearance. His attitude and expression were those of the most unmoved composure; he was smoking a cheroot with much enjoyment and deliberation, and on a table by his elbow stood a long glass of some effervescing beverage, which diffused an agreeable odour through the room.

"Welcome," said he, extending his hand to Colonel Geraldine. "I knew I might count on your exactitude."

"On my devotion," replied the Colonel, with a bow.

"Present me to your friends," continued the first; and, when that ceremony had been performed, "I wish, gentlemen," he added, with the most exquisite affability, "that I could offer you a more cheerful programme; it is ungracious to inaugurate an acquaintance upon serious affairs; but the compulsion of events is stronger than the obligations of good-fellowship. I hope and believe you will be able to forgive me this unpleasant evening; and for men of your stamp it will be enough to know that you are conferring a considerable favour."

"Your Highness," said the Major, "must pardon my bluntness. I am unable to hide what I know. For some time back I have suspected Major Hammersmith, but Mr. Godall is unmistakable. To seek two men in London unacquainted with Prince Florizel of Bohemia was to ask too much at Fortune's hands."

"Prince Florizel!" cried Brackenbury in amazement.

And he gazed with the deepest interest on the features of the celebrated personage before him.

"I shall not lament the loss of my incognito," remarked the Prince, "for it enables me to thank you with the more authority. You would have done as much for Mr. Godall, I feel sure, as for the Prince of Bohemia; but the latter can perhaps do more for you. The gain is mine," he added, with a courteous gesture.

And the next moment he was conversing with the two officers about the Indian army and the native troops, a subject on which, as on all others, he had a remarkable fund of information and the soundest views.

There was something so striking in this man's attitude at a moment of deadly peril that Brackenbury was overcome with respectful admiration; nor was he less sensible to the charm of his conversation or the surprising amenity of his address. Every gesture, every intonation, was not only noble in itself, but seemed to ennoble the fortunate mortal for whom it was intended; and Brackenbury confessed to himself with enthusiasm that this was a sovereign for whom a brave man might thankfully lay down his life.

Many minutes had thus passed, when the person who had introduced them into the house, and who had sat ever since in a corner, and with his watch in his hand, arose and whispered a word into the Prince's ear.

"It is well, Dr. Noel," replied Florizel, aloud: and then addressing the others, "You will excuse me, gentlemen," he added, "if I have to leave you in the dark. The moment now approaches."

Dr. Noel extinguished the lamp. A faint, grey light, premonitory of the dawn, illuminated the window, but was not sufficient to illuminate the room; and when the Prince rose to his feet, it was impossible to distinguish his features or to make a guess at the nature of the emotion which obviously affected him as he spoke. He moved towards the door, and placed himself at one side of it in an attitude of the wariest attention.

"You will have the kindness," he said, "to maintain the strictest silence, and to conceal yourselves in the densest of the shadow."

The three officers and the physician hastened to obey, and for nearly ten minutes the only sound in Rochester House was occasioned by the excursions of the rats behind the woodwork. At the end of that period, a loud creak of a hinge broke in with surprising distinctness on the silence; and shortly after, the watchers could distinguish a slow and cautious tread approaching up the kitchen stair. At every second step the intruder seemed to pause and lend an ear, and during these intervals, which seemed of an incalculable duration, a profound disquiet possessed the spirit of the listeners. Dr. Noel, accustomed as he was to dangerous emotions, suffered an almost pitiful physical prostration; his breath whistled in his lungs, his teeth grated one upon another, and his joints cracked aloud as he nervously shifted his position.

At last a hand was laid upon the door, and the bolt shot back with a slight report. There followed another pause, during which Brackenbury could see the Prince draw himself together noiselessly as if for some unusual exertion. Then the door opened, letting in a little more of the light of the morning; and the figure of a man appeared upon the threshold and stood motionless. He was tall, and carried a knife in his hand. Even in the twilight they could see his upper teeth bare and glistening, for his mouth was open like that of a hound about to leap. The man had evidently been over the head in water but a minute or two before; and even while he stood there the drops kept falling from his wet clothes and pattered on the floor.

The next moment he crossed the threshold. There was a leap, a stifled cry, an instantaneous struggle; and before Colonel Geraldine could spring to his aid, the Prince held the man, disarmed and helpless, by the shoulders.

"Dr. Noel," he said, "you will be so good as to relight the lamp."

And relinquishing the charge of his prisoner to Geraldine and Brackenbury, he crossed the room and set his back against the chimney-piece. As soon as the lamp had kindled, the party beheld an unaccustomed sternness on the Prince's features. It was no longer Florizel, the careless gentleman; it was the Prince of Bohemia, justly incensed and full of deadly purpose, who now raised his head and addressed the captive President of the Suicide Club.

"President," he said, "you have laid your last snare, and your own feet are taken in it. The day is beginning; it is your last morning. You have just swum the Regent's Canal; it is your last bathe in this world. Your old accomplice, Dr. Noel, so far from betraying me, has delivered you into my hands for judgment. And the grave you had dug for me this afternoon shall serve, in God's almighty providence, to hide your own just doom from the curiosity of mankind. Kneel and pray, sir, if you have a mind that way; for your time is short, and God is weary of your iniquities."

The President made no answer either by word or sign; but continued to hang his head and gaze sullenly on the floor, as though he were conscious of the Prince's prolonged and unsparing regard.

"Gentlemen," continued Florizel, resuming the ordinary tone of his conversation, "this is a fellow who has long eluded me, but whom, thanks to Dr. Noel, I now have tightly by the heels. To tell the story of his misdeeds would occupy more time than we can now afford; but if the canal had contained nothing but the blood of his victims, I believe the wretch would have been no drier than you see him. Even in an affair of this sort I desire to preserve the forms of honour. But I make you the judges, gentlemen—this is more an execution than a duel; and to give the rogue his choice of weapons would be to push too far a point of etiquette. I cannot afford to lose my life in such a business," he continued, unlocking the case of swords; "and as a pistol-bullet travels so often on the wings of chance, and skill and courage may fall by the most trembling marksman, I have decided, and I feel sure you will approve my determination, to put this question to the touch of swords."

When Brackenbury and Major O'Rooke, to whom these remarks were particularly addressed, had each intimated his approval, "Quick, sir," added Prince Florizel to the President, "choose a blade and do not keep me waiting; I have an impatience to be done with you for ever."

For the first time since he was captured and disarmed the President raised his head, and it was plain that he began instantly to pluck up courage.

"Is it to be stand up?" he asked eagerly, "and between you and me?"

"I mean so far to honour you," replied the Prince.

"Oh, come!" cried the President. "With a fair field, who knows how things may happen? I must add that I consider it handsome behaviour on your Highness's part; and if the worst comes to the worst I shall die by one of the most gallant gentlemen in Europe."

And the President, liberated by those who had detained him, stepped up to the table and began, with minute attention, to select a sword. He was highly elated, and seemed to feel no doubt that he should issue victorious from the contest. The spectators grew alarmed in the face of so entire a confidence, and adjured Prince Florizel to reconsider his intention.

"It is but a farce," he answered; "and I think I can promise you, gentlemen, that it will not be long a-playing."

"Your Highness will be careful not to overreach," said Colonel Geraldine.

"Geraldine," returned the Prince, "did you ever know me fail in a debt of honour? I owe you this man's death, and you shall have it."

The President at last satisfied himself with one of the rapiers, and signified his readiness by a gesture that was not devoid of a rude nobility. The nearness of peril, and the sense of courage, even to this obnoxious villain, lent an air of manhood and a certain grace.

The Prince helped himself at random to a sword.

"Colonel Geraldine and Dr. Noel," he said, "will have the goodness to await me in this room. I wish no personal friend of mine to be involved in this transaction. Major O'Rooke, you are a man of some years and a settled reputation—let me recommend the President to your good graces. Lieutenant Rich will be so good as to lend me his attentions: a young man cannot have too much experience in such affairs."

"Your Highness," replied Brackenbury, "it is an honour I shall prize extremely."

"It is well," returned Prince Florizel; "I shall hope to stand your friend in more important circumstances."

And so saying he led the way out of the apartment and down the kitchen stairs.

The two men who were thus left alone threw open the window and leaned out, straining every sense to catch an indication of the tragical events that were about to follow. The rain was now over; day had almost come, and the birds were piping in the shrubbery and on the forest trees of the garden. The Prince and his companions were visible for a moment as they followed an alley between two flowering thickets; but at the first corner a clump of foliage intervened, and they were again concealed from view. This was all the Colonel and the physician had an opportunity to see, and the garden was so vast, and the place of combat evidently so remote from the house, that not even the noise of sword-play reached their ears.

"He has taken him towards the grave," said Dr. Noel, with a shudder.

"God," cried the Colonel, "God defend the right!"

And they awaited the event in silence, the Doctor shaking with fear, the Colonel in an agony of sweat. Many minutes must have elapsed, the day was sensibly broader, and the birds were singing more heartily in the garden before a sound of returning footsteps recalled their glances towards the door. It was the Prince and the two Indian officers who entered. God had defended the right.

"I am ashamed of my emotion," said Prince Florizel; "I feel it a weakness unworthy of my station, but the continued existence of that hound of hell had begun to play upon me like a disease, and his death has more refreshed me than a night of slumber. Look, Geraldine," he continued, throwing his sword upon the floor, "there is the blood of the man who killed your brother. It should be a welcome sight. And yet," he added, "see how strangely we men are made! my revenge is not yet five minutes old, and already

I am beginning to ask myself if even revenge be attainable on this precarious stage of life. The ill he did, who can undo it? The career in which he amassed a huge fortune (for the house itself in which he stayed belonged to him)—that career is now a part of the destiny of mankind for ever; and I might weary myself making thrusts in carte until the crack of judgment, and Geraldine's brother would be none the less dead, and a thousand other innocent persons would be none the less dishonoured and debauched! The existence of a man is so small a thing to take, so mighty a thing to employ! Alas!" he cried, "is there anything in life so disenchanting as attainment?"

"God's justice has been done," replied the Doctor. "So much I behold. The lesson, your Highness, has been a cruel one for me; and I await my own turn with deadly apprehension."

"What was I saying?" cried the Prince. "I have punished, and here is the man beside us who can help me to undo. Ah, Dr. Noel! you and I have before us many a day of hard and honourable toil; and perhaps, before we have done, you may have more than redeemed your early errors."

"And in the meantime," said the Doctor, "let me go and bury my oldest friend."

(And this, *observes the erudite Arabian,* is the fortunate conclusion of the tale. The Prince, it is superfluous to mention, forgot none of those who served him in this great exploit; and to this day his authority and influence help them forward in their public career, while his condescending friendship adds a charm to their private life. To collect, *continues the author,* all the strange events in which this Prince has played the part of Providence were to fill the habitable globe with books.)

The Bottle Imp

Note. Any student of that very unliterary product, the English drama of the early part of the century, will here recognise the name and the root idea of a piece once rendered popular by the redoubtable B. Smith. The root idea is there and identical, and yet I believe I have made it a new thing. And the fact that the tale has been designed and written for a Polynesian audience may lend it some extraneous interest nearer home.

R. L. S.

THERE WAS A MAN OF THE ISLAND OF HAWAII, WHOM I SHALL CALL Keawe; for the truth is, he still lives, and his name must be kept secret; but the place of his birth was not far from Honaunau, where the bones of Keawe the Great lie hidden in a cave. This man was poor, brave, and active; he could read and write like a schoolmaster; he was a first-rate mariner besides, sailed for some time in the island steamers, and steered a whale-boat on the Hamakua coast. At length it came in Keawe's mind to have a sight of the great world and foreign cities, and he shipped on a vessel bound to San Francisco.

This is a fine town, with a fine harbour, and rich people uncountable; and, in particular, there is one hill which is covered with palaces. Upon this hill Keawe was one day taking a walk, with his pocket full of money, viewing the great houses upon either hand with pleasure. "What fine houses there are!" he was thinking, "and how happy must these people be who dwell in them, and take no care for the morrow!" The thought was in his mind when he came abreast of a house that was smaller than some others, but all finished and beautiful like a toy; the steps of that house shone like silver, and the borders of the garden bloomed like garlands, and the windows were bright like diamonds; and Keawe stopped and wondered at the excellence of all he saw. So stopping, he was aware of a man that looked forth upon him through a window, so clear, that Keawe could see him as you see a fish in a pool upon the reef. The man was elderly, with a bald head and a black beard; and his face was heavy with sorrow, and he bitterly sighed. And the truth of it is, that as Keawe looked in upon the man, and the man looked out upon Keawe, each envied the other.

All of a sudden the man smiled and nodded, and beckoned Keawe to enter, and met him at the door of the house.

"This is a fine house of mine," said the man, and bitterly sighed. "Would you not care to view the chambers?"

So he led Keawe all over it, from the cellar to the roof, and there was nothing there that was not perfect of its kind, and Keawe was astonished.

"Truly," said Keawe, "this is a beautiful house; if I lived in the like of it, I should be laughing all day long. How comes it, then, that you should be sighing?"

"There is no reason," said the man, "why you should not have a house in all points similar to this, and finer, if you wish. You have some money, I suppose?"

"I have fifty dollars," said Keawe; "but a house like this will cost more than fifty dollars."

The man made a computation. "I am sorry you have no more," said he, "for it may raise you trouble in the future; but it shall be yours at fifty dollars."

"The house?" asked Keawe.

"No, not the house," replied the man; "but the bottle. For, I must tell you, although I appear to you so rich and fortunate, all my fortune, and this house itself and its garden, came out of a bottle not much bigger than a pint. This is it."

And he opened a lockfast place, and took out a round-bellied bottle with a long neck; the glass of it was white like milk, with changing rainbow colours in the grain. Withinsides something obscurely moved, like a shadow and a fire.

"This is the bottle," said the man; and, when Keawe laughed, "You do not believe me?" he added. "Try, then, for yourself. See if you can break it."

So Keawe took the bottle up and dashed it on the floor till he was weary; but it jumped on the floor like a child's ball, and was not injured.

"This is a strange thing," said Keawe. "For by the touch of it, as well as by the look, the bottle should be of glass."

"Of glass it is," replied the man, sighing more heavily than ever; "but the glass of it was tempered in the flames of hell. An imp lives in it, and that is the shadow we behold there moving; or, so I suppose. If any man buy this bottle the imp is at his command; all that he desires—love, fame, money, houses like this house, ay, or a city like this city—all are his at the word uttered. Napoleon had this bottle, and by it he grew to be the king of the world; but he sold it at the last and fell. Captain Cook had this bottle, and by it he found his way to so many islands; but he, too, sold it, and was slain upon Hawaii. For, once it is sold, the power goes and the protection; and unless a man remain content with what he has, ill will befall him."

"And yet you talk of selling it yourself?" Keawe said.

"I have all I wish, and I am growing elderly," replied the man. "There is one thing the imp cannot do—he cannot prolong life; and it would not be fair to conceal from you there is a drawback to the bottle; for if a man die before he sells it, he must burn in hell for ever."

"To be sure, that is a drawback and no mistake," cried Keawe. "I would not meddle with the thing. I can do without a house, thank God; but there is one thing I could not be doing with one particle, and that is to be damned."

"Dear me, you must not run away with things," returned the man. "All you have to do is to use the power of the imp in moderation, and then sell it to some one else, as I do to you, and finish your life in comfort."

"Well, I observe two things," said Keawe. "All the time you keep sighing like a maid in love, that is one; and, for the other, you sell this bottle very cheap."

"I have told you already why I sigh," said the man. "It is because I fear my health is breaking up; and, as you said yourself, to die and go to the devil is a pity for any one. As for why I sell so cheap, I must explain to you there is a peculiarity about the bottle. Long ago, when the devil brought it first upon earth, it was extremely expensive, and was sold first of all to Prester John for many millions of dollars; but it cannot be sold at all, unless sold at a loss. If you sell it for as much as you paid for it, back it comes to you again like a homing pigeon. It follows that the price has kept falling in these centuries, and the bottle is now remarkably cheap. I bought it myself from one of my great neighbours on this hill, and the price I paid was only ninety dollars. I could sell it for as high as eighty-nine dollars and ninety-nine cents, but not a penny dearer, or back the thing must come to me. Now, about this there are two bothers. First, when you offer a bottle so singular for eighty-odd dollars, people suppose you to be jesting. And second— but there is no hurry about that—and I need not go into it. Only remember it must be coined money that you sell it for."

"How am I to know that this is all true?" asked Keawe.

"Some of it you can try at once," replied the man. "Give me your fifty dollars, take the bottle, and wish your fifty dollars back into your pocket. If that does not happen, I pledge you my honour I will cry off the bargain and restore your money."

"You are not deceiving me?" said Keawe.

The man bound himself with a great oath.

"Well, I will risk that much," said Keawe, "for that can do no harm," and he paid over his money to the man, and the man handed him the bottle.

"Imp of the bottle," said Keawe, "I want my fifty dollars back." And sure enough, he had scarce said the word before his pocket was as heavy as ever.

"To be sure this is a wonderful bottle," said Keawe.

"And now good-morning to you, my fine fellow, and the devil go with you for me," said the man.

"Hold on," said Keawe, "I don't want any more of this fun. Here, take your bottle back."

"You have bought it for less than I paid for it," replied the man, rubbing his hands. "It is yours now; and, for my part, I am only concerned to see the back of you." And with that he rang for his Chinese servant, and had Keawe shown out of the house.

Now, when Keawe was in the street, with the bottle under his arm, he began to think. "If all is true about this bottle, I may have made a losing bargain," thinks he. "But, perhaps the man was only fooling me." The first thing he did was to count his money; the sum was exact—forty-nine dollars American money, and one Chili piece. "That looks like the truth," said Keawe. "Now I will try another part."

The streets in that part of the city were as clean as a ship's decks, and though it was noon, there were no passengers. Keawe set the bottle in the gutter and walked away. Twice he looked back, and there was the milky, round-bellied bottle where he left it. A third time he looked back, and turned a corner; but he had scarce done so, when something knocked upon his elbow, and behold! It was the long neck sticking up; and, as for the round belly, it was jammed into the pocket of his pilot-coat.

"And that looks like the truth," said Keawe.

The next thing he did was to buy a corkscrew in a shop, and go apart into a secret place in the fields. And there he tried to draw the cork, but as often as he put the screw in, out it came again, and the cork as whole as ever.

"This is some new sort of cork," said Keawe, and all at once he began to shake and sweat, for he was afraid of that bottle.

On his way back to the port-side he saw a shop where a man sold shells and clubs from the wild islands, old heathen deities, old coined money, pictures from China and Japan, and all manner of things that sailors bring in their sea-chests. And here he had an idea. So he went in and offered the bottle for a hundred dollars. The man of the shop laughed at him at first, and offered him five; but, indeed, it was a curious bottle, such glass was never blown in any human glassworks, so prettily the colours shone under the milky white, and so strangely the shadow hovered in the midst; so, after he had disputed awhile after the manner of his kind, the shopman gave Keawe sixty silver dollars for the thing and set it on a shelf in the midst of his window.

"Now," said Keawe, "I have sold that for sixty which I bought for fifty—or, to say truth, a little less, because one of my dollars was from Chili. Now I shall know the truth upon another point."

So he went back on board his ship, and when he opened his chest, there was the bottle, and had come more quickly than himself. Now Keawe had a mate on board whose name was Lopaka.

"What ails you," said Lopaka, "that you stare in your chest?"

They were alone in the ship's forecastle, and Keawe bound him to secrecy, and told all.

"This is a very strange affair," said Lopaka; "and I fear you will be in trouble about this bottle. But there is one point very clear— that you are sure of the trouble, and you had better have the profit in the bargain. Make up your mind what you want with it; give the order, and if it is done as you desire, I will buy the bottle myself; for I have an idea of my own to get a schooner, and go trading through the islands."

"That is not my idea," said Keawe; "but to have a beautiful house and garden on the Kona Coast, where I was born, the sun shining in at the door, flowers in the garden, glass in the windows, pictures on the walls, and toys and fine carpets on the tables, for all the world like the house I was in this day—only a story higher, and with balconies all about like the King's palace; and to live there without care and make merry with my friends and relatives."

"Well," said Lopaka, "let us carry it back with us to Hawaii; and if all comes true, as you suppose, I will buy the bottle, as I said, and ask a schooner."

Upon that they were agreed, and it was not long before the ship returned to Honolulu, carrying Keawe and Lopaka, and the bottle. They were scarce come ashore when they met a friend upon the beach, who began at once to condole with Keawe.

"I do not know what I am to be condoled about," said Keawe.

"Is it possible you have not heard," said the friend, "your uncle —that good old man—is dead, and your cousin—that beautiful boy—was drowned at sea?"

Keawe was filled with sorrow, and, beginning to weep and to lament, he forgot about the bottle. But Lopaka was thinking to himself, and presently, when Keawe's grief was a little abated, "I have been thinking," said Lopaka, "had not your uncle lands in Hawaii, in the district of Kau?"

"No," said Keawe, "not in Kau: they are on the mountain-side —a little by south Hookena."

"These lands will now be yours?" asked Lopaka.

"And so they will," says Keawe, and began again to lament for his relatives.

"No," said Lopaka, "do not lament at present. I have a thought in my mind. How if this should be the doing of the bottle? For here is the place ready for your house."

"If this be so," cried Keawe, "it is a very ill way to serve me by killing my relatives. But it may be, indeed; for it was in just such a station that I saw the house with my mind's eye."

"The house, however, is not yet built," said Lopaka.

"No, nor like to be!" said Keawe; "for though my uncle has some coffee and ava and bananas, it will not be more than will keep me in comfort; and the rest of that land is the black lava."

"Let us go to the lawyer," said Lopaka; "I have still this idea in my mind."

Now, when they came to the lawyer's, it appeared Keawe's uncle had grown monstrous rich in the last days, and there was a fund of money.

"And here is the money for the house!" cried Lopaka.

"If you are thinking of a new house," said the lawyer, "here is the card of a new architect, of whom they tell me great things."

"Better and better!" cried Lopaka. "Here is all made plain for us. Let us continue to obey orders."

So they went to the architect, and he had drawings of houses on his table.

"You want something out of the way," said the architect. "How do you like this?" and he handed a drawing to Keawe.

Now, when Keawe set eyes on the drawing, he cried out aloud, for it was the picture of his thought exactly drawn.

"I am in for this house," thought he. "Little as I like the way it comes to me, I am in for it now, and I may as well take the good along with the evil."

So he told the architect all that he wished, and how he would have that house furnished, and about the pictures on the wall and the knick-knacks on the tables; and he asked the man plainly for how much he would undertake the whole affair.

The architect put many questions, and took his pen and made a computation; and when he had done he named the very sum that Keawe had inherited.

Lopaka and Keawe looked at one another and nodded.

"It is quite clear," thought Keawe, "that I am to have this house, whether or no. It comes from the devil, and I fear I will get little good by that; and of one thing I am sure, I will make no more wishes as long as I have this bottle. But with the house I am saddled; and I may as well take the good along with the evil."

So he made his terms with the architect, and they signed a paper; and Keawe and Lopaka took ship again and sailed to Australia; for it was concluded between them they should not interfere at all, but leave the architect and the bottle-imp to build and to adorn that house at their own pleasure.

The voyage was a good voyage, only all the time Keawe was holding in his breath, for he had sworn he would utter no more wishes, and take no more favours, from the devil. The time was up when they got back. The architect told them that the house was ready, and Keawe and Lopaka took a passage in the *Hall,* and went down Kona way to view the house, and see if all had been done fitly according to the thought that was in Keawe's mind.

Now, the house stood on the mountain-side, visible to ships. Above, the forest ran up into the clouds of rain; below, the black lava fell in cliffs, where the kings of old lay buried. A garden bloomed about that house with every hue of flowers; and there was an orchard of papaia on the one hand and an orchard of herdprint on the other, and right in front, toward the sea, a ship's mast had been rigged up and bore a flag. As for the house, it was three stories high, with great chambers and broad balconies on each. The windows were of glass, so excellent that it was as clear as water and as bright as day. All manner of furniture adorned the chambers. Pictures hung upon the wall in golden frames—pictures of ships, and men fighting, and of the most beautiful women, and of singular places; nowhere in the world are there pictures of so bright a colour as those Keawe found hanging in his house. As for the knick-knacks they were extraordinarily fine: chiming clocks and musical boxes, little men with nodding heads, books filled with pictures, weapons of price from all quarters of the world, and the most elegant puzzles to entertain the leisure of a solitary man. And as no one would care to live in such chambers, only to walk through and view them, the balconies were made so broad that a whole town might have lived upon them in delight; and Keawe knew not which to prefer, whether the back porch, where you get the land-breeze, and looked upon the orchards and the flowers, or the front balcony, where you could drink the wind of the sea, and look down the steep wall of the mountain and see the *Hall* going by once a week or so between Hookena and the hills of Pele, or the schooners plying up the coast for wood and ava and bananas.

When they had viewed all, Keawe and Lopaka sat on the porch.

"Well," asked Lopaka, "is it all as you designed?"

"Words cannot utter it," said Keawe. "It is better than I dreamed, and I am sick with satisfaction."

"There is but one thing to consider," said Lopaka, "all this may be quite natural, and the bottle-imp have nothing whatever to say to it. If I were to buy the bottle, and got no schooner after all, I should have put my hand in the fire for nothing. I gave you my word, I know; but yet I think you would not grudge me one more proof."

"I have sworn I would take no more favours," said Keawe. "I have gone already deep enough."

"This is no favour I am thinking of," replied Lopaka. "It is only to see the imp himself. There is nothing to be gained by that, and so nothing to be ashamed of, and yet, if I once saw him, I should be sure of the whole matter. So indulge me so far, and let me see the imp; and, after that, here is the money in my hand, and I will buy it."

"There is only one thing I am afraid of," said Keawe. "The imp may be very ugly to view, and if you once set eyes upon him you might be very undesirous of the bottle."

"I am a man of my word," said Lopaka. "And here is the money betwixt us."

"Very well," replied Keawe, "I have a curiosity myself. So come, let us have one look at you, Mr. Imp."

Now as soon as that was said, the imp looked out of the bottle, and in again, swift as a lizard; and there sat Keawe and Lopaka turned to stone. The night had quite come, before either found a thought to say or voice to say it with; and then Lopaka pushed the money over and took the bottle.

"I am a man of my word," said he, "and had need to be so, or I would not touch this bottle with my foot. Well, I shall get my schooner and a dollar or two for my pocket; and then I will be rid of this devil as fast as I can. For to tell you the plain truth, the look of him has cast me down."

"Lopaka," said Keawe, "do not you think any worse of me than you can help; I know it is night, and the roads bad, and the pass by the tombs an ill place to go by so late, but I declare since I have seen that little face, I cannot eat or sleep or pray till it is gone from me. I will give you a lantern, and a basket to put the bottle in, and any picture or fine thing in all my house that takes your fancy; and be gone at once, and go sleep at Hookena with Nahinu."

"Keawe," said Lopaka, "many a man would take this ill; above all, when I am doing you a turn so friendly, as to keep my word and buy the bottle; and for that matter, the night and the dark, and the way by the tombs, must be all tenfold more dangerous to a man with such a sin upon his conscience, and such a bottle under his arm. But for my part, I am so extremely terrified myself, I have not the heart to blame you. Here I go, then; and I pray God you may be happy in your house, and I fortunate with my schooner, and both get to heaven in the end in spite of the devil and his bottle."

So Lopaka went down the mountain; and Keawe stood in his front balcony, and listened to the clink of the horse's shoes, and watched the lantern go shining down the path, and along the cliff of caves where the old dead are buried; and all the time he trembled and clasped his hands, and prayed for his friend, and gave glory to God that he himself was escaped out of that trouble.

But the next day came very brightly, and that new house of his was so delightful to behold that he forgot his terrors. One day followed another, and Keawe dwelt there in perpetual joy. He had his place on the back porch; it was there he ate and lived, and read the stories in the Honolulu newspapers; but when any one came by they would go in and view the chambers and the pictures. And the fame of the house went far and wide; it was called *Ka-Hale Nui*—the Great House—in all Kona; and sometimes the Bright House, for Keawe kept a Chinaman, who was all day dusting and furbishing; and the glass, and the gilt, and the fine stuffs, and the pictures, shone as bright as the morning. As for Keawe himself, he could not walk in the chambers without singing, his heart was so enlarged; and when ships sailed by upon the sea, he would fly his colours on the mast.

So time went by, until one day Keawe went upon a visit as far as Kailua to certain of his friends. There he was well feasted; and left as soon as he could the next morning, and rode hard, for he was impatient to behold his beautiful house; and, besides, the night then coming on was the night in which the dead of old days go abroad in the sides of Kona; and having already meddled with the devil, he was the more chary of meeting with the dead. A little beyond Honaunau, looking far ahead, he was aware of a woman bathing in the edge of the sea; and she seemed a well-grown girl, but he thought no more of it. Then he saw her white shift flutter as she put it on, and then her red holoku; and by the time he came abreast of her she was done with her toilet, and had come up from the sea, and stood by the trackside in her red holoku, and she was all freshened with the bath, and her eyes shone and were kind. Now Keawe no sooner beheld her than he drew rein.

"I thought I knew every one in this country," said he. "How comes it that I do not know you?"

"I am Kokua, daughter of Kiano," said the girl, "and I have just returned from Oahu. Who are you?"

"I will tell you who I am in a little," said Keawe, dismounting from his horse, "but not now. For I have a thought in my mind, and if you knew who I was, you might have heard of me, and would not give me a true answer. But tell me, first of all, one thing: are you married?"

At this Kokua laughed out aloud. "It is you who ask questions," she said. "Are you married yourself?"

"Indeed, Kokua, I am not," replied Keawe, "and never thought to be until this hour. But here is the plain truth. I have met you here at the roadside, and I saw your eyes, which are like the stars, and my heart went to you as swift as a bird. And so now, if you want none of me, say so, and I will go on to my own place; but if you think me no worse than any other young man, say so, too, and I will turn aside to your father's for the night, and to-morrow I will talk with the good man."

Kokua said never a word, but she looked at the sea and laughed.

"Kokua," said Keawe, "if you say nothing, I will take that for the good answer; so let us be stepping to your father's door."

She went on ahead of him, still without speech; only sometimes she glanced back and glanced away again, and she kept the strings of her hat in her mouth.

Now, when they had come to the door, Kiano came out on his veranda, and cried out and welcomed Keawe by name. At that the girl looked over, for the fame of the great house had come to her ears; and, to be sure, it was a great temptation. All that evening they were very merry together; and the girl was as bold as brass under the eyes of her parents, and made a mark of Keawe, for she had a quick wit. The next day he had a word with Kiano, and found the girl alone.

"Kokua," said he, "you made a mark of me all the evening; and it is still time to bid me go. I would not tell you who I was, because I have so fine a house, and I feared you would think too much of that house and too little of the man that loves you. Now you know all, and if you wish to have seen the last of me, say so at once."

"No," said Kokua, but this time she did not laugh, nor did Keawe ask for more.

This was the wooing of Keawe; things had gone quickly; but so an arrow goes, and the ball of a rifle swifter still, and yet both may strike the target. Things had gone fast, but they had gone far also, and the thought of Keawe rang in the maiden's head; she heard his voice in the breach of the surf upon the lava, and for this young man that she had seen but twice she would have left father and mother and her native islands. As for Keawe himself, his horse flew up the path of the mountain under the cliff of tombs, and the sound of the hoofs, and the sound of Keawe singing to himself for pleasure, echoed in the caverns of the dead. He came to the Bright House, and still he was singing. He sat and ate in the broad balcony, and the Chinaman wondered at his master, to hear how he sang between the mouthfuls. The sun went down into the sea, and the night came; and Keawe walked the balconies by lamp-light, high on the mountains, and the voice of his singing startled men on ships.

"Here am I now upon my high place," he said to himself. "Life may be no better; this is the mountain top; and all shelves about me toward the worse. For the first time I will light up the chambers, and bathe in my fine bath with the hot water and the cold, and sleep above in the bed of my bridal chamber."

So the Chinaman had word, and he must rise from sleep and light the furnaces; and as he walked below, beside the boilers, he heard his master singing and rejoicing above him in the lighted chambers. When the water began to be hot the Chinaman cried to his master: and Keawe went into the bath-room; and the Chinaman heard him sing as he filled the marble basin; and heard him sing, and the singing broken, as he undressed; until of a sudden, the song ceased. The Chinaman listened, and listened; he called up the house to Keawe to ask if all were well, and Keawe answered him "Yes," and bade him go to bed; but there was no more singing in the Bright House; and all night long the Chinaman heard his master's feet go round and round the balconies without repose.

Now, the truth of it was this: as Keawe undressed for his bath, he spied upon his flesh a patch like a patch of lichen on a rock, and it was then that he stopped singing. For he knew the likeness of that patch, and knew that he was fallen in the Chinese Evil.

Now, it is a sad thing for any man to fall into this sickness. And it would be a sad thing for any one to leave a house so beautiful and so commodious, and depart from all his friends to the north coast of Molokai, between the mighty cliff and the sea-breakers. But what was that to the case of the man Keawe, he who had met his love but yesterday, and won her but that morning, and now saw all his hopes break, in a moment, like a piece of glass?

Awhile he sat upon the edge of the bath, then sprang, with a cry, and ran outside; and to and fro, to and fro, along the balcony, like one despairing.

"Very willingly could I leave Hawaii, the home of my fathers," Keawe was thinking. "Very lightly could I leave my house, the high-placed, the many-windowed, here upon the mountains. Very bravely could I go to Molokai, to Kalaupapa by the cliffs, to live with the smitten and to sleep there, far from my fathers. But what wrong have I done, what sin lies upon my soul, that I should have encountered Kokua coming cool from the sea-water in the evening? Kokua, the soul ensnarer! Kokua, the light of my life! Her may I never wed, her may I look upon no longer, her may I no more handle with my loving hand; and it is for this, it is for you, O Kokua! that I pour my lamentations!"

Now you are to observe what sort of a man Keawe was, for he might have dwelt there in the Bright House for years, and no one been the wiser of his sickness; but he reckoned nothing of that, if he must lose Kokua. And again he might have wed Kokua even as he was; and so many would have done, because they have the souls of pigs; but Keawe loved the maid manfully, and he would do her no hurt and bring her in no danger.

A little beyond the midst of the night, there came in his mind the recollection of that bottle. He went round to the back porch, and called to memory the day when the devil had looked forth; and at the thought ice ran in his veins.

"A dreadful thing is the bottle," thought Keawe, "and dreadful is the imp, and it is a dreadful thing to risk the flames of hell. But what other hope have I to cure my sickness or to wed Kokua? What!" he thought, "would I beard the devil once, only to get me a house, and not face him again to win Kokua?"

Thereupon he called to mind it was the next day the *Hall* went by on her return to Honolulu. "There must I go first," he thought, "and see Lopaka. For the best hope that I have now is to find that same bottle I was so pleased to be rid of."

Never a wink could he sleep; the food stuck in his throat; but he sent a letter to Kiano, and about the time when the steamer would be coming, rode down beside the cliff of the tombs. It rained; his horse went heavily; he looked up at the black mouths of the caves, and he envied the dead that slept there and were done with trouble; and called to mind how he had galloped by the day before, and was astonished. So he came down to Hookena, and there was all the country gathered for the steamer as usual. In the shed before the store they sat and jested and passed the news; but there was no matter of speech in Keawe's bosom, and he sat in their midst and looked without on the rain falling on the houses, and the surf beating among the rocks, and the sighs arose in his throat.

"Keawe of the Bright House is out of spirits," said one to another. Indeed, and so he was, and little wonder.

Then the *Hall* came, and the whale-boat carried him on board. The after-part of the ship was full of Haoles—whites—who had been to visit the volcano, as their custom is; and the midst was crowded with Kanakas, and the fore-part with wild bulls from Hilo and horses from Kau; but Keawe sat apart from all in his sorrow, and watched for the house of Kiano. There it sat low upon the shore in the black rocks, and shaded by the coron palms, and there by the door was a red holoku, no greater than a fly, and going to and fro with a fly's busyness. "Ah, queen of my heart," he cried, "I'll venture my dear soul to win you!"

Soon after darkness fell and the cabins were lit up, and the Haoles sat and played at the cards and drank whiskey as their custom is; but Keawe walked the deck all night; and all the next day, as they steamed under the lea of Maui or of Molokai, he was still pacing to and fro like a wild animal in a menagerie.

Toward evening they passed Diamond Head, and came to the pier of Honolulu. Keawe stepped out among the crowd and began to ask for Lopaka. It seemed he had become the owner of a schooner—none better in the islands—and was gone upon an adventure as far as Pola-Pola or Kahiki; so there was no help to be looked for from Lopaka. Keawe called to mind a friend of his, a lawyer in the town (I must not tell his name), and inquired of him. They said he was grown suddenly rich, and had a fine new house upon Waikiki shore; and this put a thought in Keawe's head, and he called a hack and drove to the lawyer's house.

The house was all brand new, and the trees in the garden no greater than walking-sticks, and the lawyer, when he came, had the air of a man well pleased.

"What can I do to serve you?" said the lawyer.

"You are a friend of Lopaka's," replied Keawe, "and Lopaka purchased from me a certain piece of goods that I thought you might enable me to trace."

The lawyer's face became very dark. "I do not profess to misunderstand you, Mr. Keawe," said he, "though this is an ugly business to be stirring in. You may be sure I know nothing, but yet I have a guess, and if you would apply in a certain quarter I think you might have news."

And he named the name of a man, which, again, I had better not repeat. So it was for days, and Keawe went from one to another, finding everywhere new clothes and carriages, and fine new houses and men everywhere in great contentment, although, to be sure, when he hinted at his business their faces would cloud over.

"No doubt I am upon the track," thought Keawe. "These new clothes and carriages are all the gifts of the little imp, and these glad faces are the faces of men who have taken their profit and got rid of the accursed thing in safety. When I see pale cheeks and hear sighing, I shall know that I am near the bottle."

So it befell at last that he was recommended to a Haole in Beritania Street. When he came to the door, about the hour of the evening meal, there were the usual marks of the new house, and the young garden, and the electric light shining in the windows; but when the owner came, a shock of hope and fear ran through Keawe; for here was a young man, white as a corpse, and black about the eyes, the hair shedding from his head, and such a look in his countenance as a man may have when he is waiting for the gallows.

"Here it is, to be sure," thought Keawe, and so with this man he noways veiled his errand. "I am come to buy the bottle," said he.

At the word, the young Haole of Beritania Street reeled against the wall.

"The bottle!" he gasped. "To buy the bottle!" Then he seemed to choke, and seizing Keawe by the arm, carried him into a room and poured out wine in two glasses.

"Here is my respects," said Keawe, who had been much about with Haoles in his time. "Yes," he added, "I am come to buy the bottle. What is the price by now?"

At that word the young man let his glass slip through his fingers, and looked upon Keawe like a ghost.

"The price," says he; "the price! You do not know the price?"

"It is for that I am asking you," returned Keawe. "But why are you so much concerned? Is there anything wrong about the price?"

"It has dropped a great deal in value since your time, Mr. Keawe," said the young man, stammering.

"Well, well, I shall have the less to pay for it," says Keawe. "How much did it cost you?"

The young man was as white as a sheet. "Two cents," said he.

"What?" cried Keawe, "two cents? Why, then, you can only sell it for one. And he who buys it——" The words died upon Keawe's tongue; he who bought it could never sell it again, the bottle and the bottle imp must abide with him until he died, and when he died must carry him to the red end of hell.

The young man of Beritania Street fell upon his knees. "For God's sake, buy it!" he cried. "You can have all my fortune in the bargain. I was made when I bought it at that price. I had embezzled money at my store; I was lost else; I must have gone to jail."

"Poor creature," said Keawe, "you would risk your soul upon so desperate an adventure, and to avoid the proper punishment of your own disgrace; and you think I could hesitate with love in front of me. Give me the bottle, and the change which I make sure you have all ready. Here is a five-cent piece."

It was as Keawe supposed; the young man had the change ready in a drawer; the bottle changed hands, and Keawe's fingers were no sooner clasped upon the stalk than he had breathed his wish to be a clean man. And, sure enough, when he got home to his room, and stripped himself before a glass, his flesh was whole like an infant's. And here was the strange thing: he had no sooner seen this miracle than his mind was changed within him, and he cared naught for the Chinese Evil, and little enough for Kokua; and had but the one thought, that here he was bound to the bottle imp for time and for eternity, and had no better hope but to be a cinder for ever in the flames of hell. Away ahead of him he saw them blaze with his mind's eye, and his soul shrank, and darkness fell upon the light.

When Keawe came to himself a little, he was aware it was the night when the band played at the hotel. Thither he went, because he feared to be alone; and there, among happy faces, walked to and fro, and heard the tunes go up and down, and saw Berger beat the measure, and all the while he heard the flames crackle, and saw the red fire burning in the bottomless pit. Of a sudden the band played *Hiki-ao-ao;* that was a song that he had sung with Kokua, and at the strain courage returned to him.

"It is done now," he thought, "and once more let me take the good along with the evil."

So it befell that he returned to Hawaii by the first steamer, and as soon as it could be managed he was wedded to Kokua, and carried her up the mountain-side to the Bright House.

Now it was so with these two, that when they were together Keawe's heart was stilled; but as soon as he was alone he fell into a brooding horror, and heard the flames crackle, and saw the red fire burn in the bottomless pit. The girl, indeed, had come to him wholly; her heart leaped in her side at sight of him, her hand clung to his; and she was so fashioned, from the hair upon her head to the nails upon her toes, that none could see her without joy. She was pleasant in her nature. She had the good word always. Full of song she was, and went to and fro in the Bright House, the brightest thing in its three stories, carolling like the birds. And Keawe beheld and heard her with delight, and then must shrink upon one side, and weep and groan to think upon the price that he had paid for her; and then he must dry his eyes, and wash his face, and go and sit with her on the broad balconies, joining in her songs, and, with a sick spirit, answering her smiles.

There came a day when her feet began to be heavy and her songs more rare; and now it was not Keawe only that would weep apart, but each would sunder from the other and sit in opposite balconies with the whole width of the Bright House betwixt. Keawe was so sunk in his despair, he scarce observed the change, and was only glad he had more hours to sit alone and brood upon his destiny, and was not so frequently condemned to pull a smiling face on a sick heart. But one day, coming softly through the house, he heard the sound of a child sobbing, and there was Kokua rolling her face upon the balcony floor, and weeping like the lost.

"You do well to weep in this house, Kokua," he said. "And yet I would give the head off my body that you (at least) might have been happy."

"Happy!" she cried. "Keawe, when you lived alone in your Bright House you were the word of the island for a happy man; laughter and song were in your mouth, and your face was as bright as the sunrise. Then you wedded poor Kokua; and the good God knows what is amiss in her—but from that day you have not smiled. Oh!" she cried, "what ails me? I thought I was pretty, and I knew I loved him. What ails me, that I throw this cloud upon my husband?"

"Poor Kokua," said Keawe. He sat down by her side, and sought to take her hand; but that she plucked away. "Poor Kokua," he said, again. "My poor child—my pretty. And I had thought all this while to spare you! Well, you shall know all. Then, at least, you will pity poor Keawe; then you will understand how much he loved you in the past—that he dared hell for your possession—and how much he loves you still (the poor condemned one), that he can yet call up a smile when he beholds you."

With that, he told her all, even from the beginning.

"You have done this for me?" she cried. "Ah, well, then what do I care!" and she clasped and wept upon him.

"Ah, child!" said Keawe, "and yet, when I consider of the fire of hell, I care a good deal!"

"Never tell me," said she, "no man can be lost because he loved Kokua, and no other fault. I tell you, Keawe, I shall save you with these hands, or perish in your company. What! you loved me and gave your soul, and you think I will not die to save you in return?"

"Ah, my dear, you might die a hundred times, and what difference would that make?" he cried, "except to leave me lonely till the time comes of my damnation?"

"You know nothing," said she. "I was educated in a school in Honolulu; I am no common girl. And I tell you I shall save my lover. What is this you say about a cent? But all the world is not American. In England they have a piece they call a farthing, which is about half a cent. Ah! sorrow!" she cried, "that makes it scarcely better, for the buyer must be lost, and we shall find none so brave as my Keawe! But, then, there is France; they have a small coin there which they call a centime, and these go five to the cent or thereabout. We could not do better. Come, Keawe, let us go to the French islands; let us go to Tahiti, as fast as ships can bear us. There we have four centimes, three centimes, two centimes, one centime; four possible sales to come and go on; and two of us to push the bargain. Come, my Keawe! kiss me, and banish care. Kokua will defend you."

"Gift of God!" he cried. "I cannot think that God will punish me for desiring aught so good! Be it as you will, then, take me where you please: I put my life and my salvation in your hands."

Early the next day Kokua was about her preparations. She took Keawe's chest that he went with sailoring; and first she put the bottle in a corner, and then packed it with the richest of their clothes and the bravest of the knick-knacks in the house. "For," said she, "we must seem to be rich folks, or who will believe in the bottle?" All the time of her preparation she was as gay as a bird; only when she looked upon Keawe the tears would spring in her eye, and she must run and kiss him. As for Keawe, a weight was off his soul; now that he had his secret shared, and some hope in front of him, he seemed like a new man, his feet went lightly on the earth, and his breath was good to him again. Yet was terror still at his elbow; and ever and again, as the wind blows out a taper, hope died in him, and he saw the flames toss and the red fire burn in hell.

It was given out in the country they were gone pleasuring to the States, which was thought a strange thing, and yet not so strange as the truth, if any could have guessed it. So they went to Honolulu in the *Hall,* and thence in the *Umatilla* to San Francisco with a crowd of Haoles, and at San Francisco took their passage by the mail brigantine, the *Tropic Bird,* for Papeete, the chief place of the French in the south islands. Thither they came, after a pleasant voyage, on a fair day of the Trade wind, and saw the reef with the surf breaking and Motuiti with its palms, and the schooner riding withinside, and the white houses of the town low down along the shore among green trees, and overhead the mountains and the clouds of Tahiti, the wise island.

It was judged the most wise to hire a house, which they did accordingly, opposite the British Consul's, to make a great parade of money, and themselves conspicuous with carriages and horses. This it was very easy to do, so long as they had the bottle in their possession; for Kokua was more bold than Keawe, and, whenever she had a mind, called on the imp for twenty or a hundred dollars.

At this rate they soon grew to be remarked in the town; and the strangers from Hawaii, their riding and their driving, the fine holokus, and the rich lace of Kokua, became the matter of much talk.

They got on well after the first with the Tahitian language, which is indeed like to the Hawaiian, with a change of certain letters; and as soon as they had any freedom of speech, began to push the bottle. You are to consider it was not an easy subject to introduce; it was not easy to persuade people you are in earnest, when you offer to sell them for four centimes the spring of health and riches inexhaustible. It was necessary besides to explain the dangers of the bottle; and either people disbelieved the whole thing and laughed, or they thought the more of the darker part, became overcast with gravity, and drew away from Keawe and Kokua, as from persons who had dealings with the devil. So far from gaining ground, these two began to find they were avoided in the town; the children ran away from them screaming, a thing intolerable to Kokua; Catholics crossed themselves as they went by; and all persons began with one accord to disengage themselves from their advances.

Depression fell upon their spirits. They would sit at night in their new house, after a day's weariness, and not exchange one word, or the silence would be broken by Kokua bursting suddenly into sobs. Sometimes they would pray together; sometimes they would have the bottle out upon the floor, and sit all evening watching how the shadow hovered in the midst. At such times they would be afraid to go to rest. It was long ere slumber came to them, and, if either dozed off, it would be to wake and find the other silently weeping in the dark, or, perhaps, to wake alone, the other having fled from the house and the neighbourhood of that bottle, to pace under the bananas in the little garden, or to wander on the beach by moonlight.

One night it was so when Kokua awoke. Keawe was gone. She felt in the bed and his place was cold. Then fear fell upon her, and she sat up in bed. A little moonshine filtered through the shutters. The room was bright, and she could spy the bottle on the floor. Outside it blew high, the great trees of the avenue cried aloud, and the fallen leaves rattled in the veranda. In the midst of this Kokua was aware of another sound; whether of a beast or of a man she could scarce tell, but it was as sad as death, and cut

her to the soul. Softly she arose, set the door ajar, and looked forth
into the moonlit yard. There, under the bananas, lay Keawe, his
mouth in the dust, and as he lay he moaned.

It was Kokua's first thought to run forward and console him;
her second potently withheld her. Keawe had borne himself before his wife like a brave man; it became her little in the hour of
weakness to intrude upon his shame. With the thought she drew
back into the house.

"Heaven," she thought, "how careless have I been—how weak!
It is he, not I, that stands in this eternal peril; it was he, not I, that
took the curse upon his soul. It is for my sake, and for the love of
a creature of so little worth and such poor help, that he now beholds so close to him the flames of hell—ay, and smells the smoke
of it, lying without there in the wind and moonlight. Am I so dull
of spirit that never till now I have surmised my duty, or have I
seen it before and turned aside? But now, at least, I take up my
soul in both the hands of my affection; now I say farewell to the
white steps of heaven and the waiting faces of my friends. A love
for a love, and let mine be equalled with Keawe's! A soul for a
soul, and be it mine to perish!"

She was a deft woman with her hands, and was soon apparelled.
She took in her hands the change—the precious centimes they
kept ever at their side; for this coin is little used, and they had
made provision at a government office. When she was forth in the
avenue clouds came on the wind, and the moon was blackened.
The town slept, and she knew not whither to turn till she heard
one coughing in the shadow of the trees.

"Old man," said Kokua, "what do you here abroad in the cold
night?"

The old man could scarce express himself for coughing, but
she made out that he was old and poor, and a stranger in the
island.

"Will you do me a service?" said Kokua. "As one stranger to
another, and as an old man to a young woman, will you help a
daughter of Hawaii?"

"Ah," said the old man. "So you are the witch from the eight
islands, and even my old soul you seek to entangle. But I have
heard of you, and defy your wickedness."

"Sit down here," said Kokua, "and let me tell you a tale." And
she told him the story of Keawe from the beginning to the end.

"And now," said she, "I am his wife, whom he bought with his soul's welfare. And what should I do? If I went to him myself and offered to buy it, he will refuse. But if you go, he will sell it eagerly; I will await you here; you will buy it for four centimes, and I will buy it again for three. And the Lord strengthen a poor girl!"

"If you meant falsely," said the old man, "I think God would strike you dead."

"He would!" cried Kokua. "Be sure he would. I could not be so treacherous, God would not suffer it."

"Give me the four centimes and await me here," said the old man.

Now, when Kokua stood alone in the street, her spirit died. The wind roared in the trees, and it seemed to her the rushing of the flames of hell; the shadows towered in the light of the street lamp, and they seemed to her the snatching hands of evil ones. If she had had the strength, she must have run away, and if she had had the breath she must have screamed aloud; but, in truth, she could do neither, and stood and trembled in the avenue, like an affrighted child.

Then she saw the old man returning, and he had the bottle in his hand.

"I have done your bidding," said he, "I left your husband weeping like a child; to-night he will sleep easy." And he held the bottle forth.

"Before you give it me," Kokua panted, "take the good with the evil—ask to be delivered from your cough."

"I am an old man," replied the other, "and too near the gate of the grave to take a favour from the devil. But what is this? Why do you not take the bottle? Do you hesitate?"

"Not hesitate!" cried Kokua. "I am only weak. Give me a moment. It is my hand resists, my flesh shrinks back from the accursed thing. One moment only!"

The old man looked upon Kokua kindly. "Poor child!" said he, "you fear: your soul misgives you. Well, let me keep it. I am old, and can never more be happy in this world, and as for the next——"

"Give it me!" gasped Kokua. "There is your money. Do you think I am so base as that? Give me the bottle."

"God bless you, child," said the old man.

Kokua concealed the bottle under her holoku, said farewell to the old man, and walked off along the avenue, she cared not whither. For all roads were now the same to her, and led equally to hell. Sometimes she walked, and sometimes ran; sometimes she screamed out loud in the night, and sometimes lay by the wayside in the dust and wept. All that she had heard of hell came back to her; she saw the flames blaze, and she smelled the smoke, and her flesh withered on the coals.

Near day she came to her mind again, and returned to the house. It was even as the old man said—Keawe slumbered like a child. Kokua stood and gazed upon his face.

"Now, my husband," said she, "it is your turn to sleep. When you wake it will be your turn to sing and laugh. But for poor Kokua, alas! that meant no evil—for poor Kokua no more sleep, no more singing, no more delight, whether in earth or Heaven."

With that she lay down in the bed by his side, and her misery was so extreme that she fell in a deep slumber instantly.

Late in the morning her husband woke her and gave her the good news. It seemed he was silly with delight, for he paid no heed to her distress, ill though she dissembled it. The words stuck in her mouth, it mattered not; Keawe did the speaking. She ate not a bite, but who was to observe it? For Keawe cleared the dish. Kokua saw and heard him, like some strange thing in a dream; there were times when she forgot or doubted, and put her hands to her brow; to know herself doomed and hear her husband babble, seemed so monstrous.

All the while Keawe was eating and talking, and planning the time of their return, and thanking her for saving him, and fondling her, and calling her the true helper after all. He laughed at the old man that was fool enough to buy that bottle.

"A worthy old man he seemed," Keawe said. "But no one can judge by appearances. For why did the old reprobate require the bottle?"

"My husband," said Kokua, humbly, "his purpose may have been good."

Keawe laughed like an angry man.

"Fiddle-de-dee!" cried Keawe. "An old rogue, I tell you; and an old ass to boot. For the bottle was hard enough to sell at four centimes; and at three it will be quite impossible. The margin is not broad enough, the thing begins to smell of scorching—brrr!"

said he, and shuddered. "It is true I bought it myself at a cent, when I knew not there were smaller coins. I was a fool for my pains; there will never be found another, and whoever has that bottle now will carry it to the pit."

"O my husband!" said Kokua. "Is it not a terrible thing to save oneself by the eternal ruin of another? It seems to me I could not laugh. I would be humbled. I would be filled with melancholy. I would pray for the poor holder."

Then Keawe, because he felt the truth of what she said, grew the more angry. "Heighty-teighty!" cried he. "You may be filled with melancholy if you please. It is not the mind of a good wife. If you thought at all of me, you would sit shamed."

Thereupon he went out, and Kokua was alone.

What chance had she to sell that bottle at two centimes? None, she perceived. And if she had any, here was her husband hurrying her away to a country where there was nothing lower than a cent. And here—on the morrow of her sacrifice—was her husband leaving her and blaming her.

She would not even try to profit by what time she had, but sat in the house, and now had the bottle out and viewed it with unutterable fear, and now, with loathing, hid it out of sight.

By and by, Keawe came back, and would have her take a drive.

"My husband, I am ill," she said. "I am out of heart. Excuse me, I can take no pleasure."

Then was Keawe more wroth than ever. With her, because he thought she was brooding over the case of the old man; and with himself, because he thought she was right, and was ashamed to be so happy.

"This is your truth," cried he, "and this your affection! Your husband is just saved from eternal ruin, which he encountered for the love of you—and you can take no pleasure! Kokua, you have a disloyal heart."

He went forth again furious, and wandered in the town all day. He met friends, and drank with them; they hired a carriage and drove into the country, and there drank again. All the time Keawe was ill at ease, because he was taking this pastime while his wife was sad, and because he knew in his heart that she was more right than he; and the knowledge made him drink the deeper.

Now, there was an old brutal Haole drinking with him, one that had been a boatswain of a whaler—a runaway, a digger in gold mines, and convict in prisons. He had a low mind and a foul mouth; he loved to drink and to see others drunken; and he pressed the glass upon Keawe. Soon there was no more money in the company.

"Here, you!" says the boatswain, "you are rich, you have been always saying. You have a bottle or some foolishness."

"Yes," says Keawe, "I am rich; I will go back and get some money from my wife, who keeps it."

"That's a bad idea, mate," said the boatswain. "Never you trust a petticoat with dollars. They're all as false as water; you keep an eye on her."

Now, this word struck in Keawe's mind; for he was muddled with what he had been drinking.

"I should not wonder but she was false, indeed," thought he. "Why else should she be so cast down at my release? But I will show her I am not the man to be fooled. I will catch her in the act."

Accordingly, when they were back in town, Keawe bade the boatswain wait for him at the corner, by the old calaboose, and went forward up the avenue alone to the door of his house. The night had come again; there was a light within, but never a sound; and Keawe crept about the corner, opened the back door softly, and looked in.

There was Kokua on the floor, the lamp at her side; before her was a milk-white bottle, with a round belly and a long neck; and as she viewed it, Kokua wrung her hands.

A long time Keawe stood and looked in the doorway. At first he was struck stupid; and then fear fell upon him that the bargain had been made amiss, and the bottle had come back to him as it came at San Francisco; and at that his knees were loosened, and the fumes of the wine departed from his head like mists off a river in the morning. And then he had another thought; and it was a strange one, that made his cheeks to burn.

"I must make sure of this," thought he.

So he closed the door, and went softly round the corner again, and then came noisily in, as though he were but now returned. And, lo! by the time he opened the front door no bottle was to be seen; and Kokua sat in a chair and started up like one awakened out of sleep.

"I have been drinking all day and making merry," said Keawe.

"I have been with good companions, and now I only come back for money, and return to drink and carouse with them again."

Both his face and voice were as stern as judgment, but Kokua was too troubled to observe.

"You do well to use your own, my husband," said she, and her words trembled.

"Oh, I do well in all things," said Keawe, and he went straight to the chest and took out money. But he looked besides in the corner where they kept the bottle, and there was no bottle there.

At that the chest heaved upon the floor like a sea-billow, and the house span about him like a wreath of smoke, for he saw she was lost now, and there was no escape. "It is what I feared," he thought. "It is she who has bought it."

And then he came to himself a little and rose up; but the sweat streamed on his face as thick as the rain and as cold as the well-water.

"Kokua," said he, "I said to you to-day what ill became me. Now I return to house with my jolly companions," and at that he laughed a little quietly. "I will take more pleasure in the cup if you forgive me."

She clasped his knees in a moment; she kissed his knees with flowing tears.

"Oh," she cried, "I asked but a kind word!"

"Let us never one think hardly of the other," said Keawe, and was gone out of the house.

Now, the money that Keawe had taken was only some of that store of centime pieces they had laid in at their arrival. It was very sure he had no mind to be drinking. His wife had given her soul for him, now he must give his for hers; no other thought was in the world with him.

At the corner, by the old calaboose, there was the boatswain waiting.

"My wife has the bottle," said Keawe, "and, unless you help me to recover it, there can be no more money and no more liquor to-night."

"You do not mean to say you are serious about that bottle?" cried the boatswain.

"There is the lamp," said Keawe. "Do I look as if I was jesting?"

"That is so," said the boatswain. "You look as serious as a ghost."

"Well, then," said Keawe, "here are two centimes; you must go to my wife in the house, and offer her these for the bottle, which (if I am not much mistaken) she will give you instantly. Bring it to me here, and I will buy it back from you for one; for that is the law with this bottle, that it still must be sold for a less sum. But whatever you do, never breathe a word to her that you have come from me."

"Mate, I wonder are you making a fool of me?" asked the boatswain.

"It will do you no harm if I am," returned Keawe.

"That is so, mate," said the boatswain.

"And if you doubt me," added Keawe, "you can try. As soon as you are clear of the house, wish to have your pocket full of money, or a bottle of the best rum, or what you please, and you will see the virtue of the thing."

"Very well, Kanaka," says the boatswain. "I will try; but if you are having your fun out of me, I will take my fun out of you with a belaying-pin."

So the whaler-man went off up the avenue; and Keawe stood and waited. It was near the same spot where Kokua had waited the night before; but Keawe was more resolved, and never faltered in his purpose; only his soul was bitter with despair.

It seemed a long time he had to wait before he heard a voice singing in the darkness of the avenue. He knew the voice to be the boatswain's; but it was strange how drunken it appeared upon a sudden.

Next the man himself came stumbling into the light of the lamp. He had the devil's bottle buttoned in his coat; another bottle was in his hand; and even as he came in view he raised it to his mouth and drank.

"You have it," said Keawe. "I see that."

"Hands off!" cried the boatswain, jumping back. "Take a step near me, and I'll smash your mouth. You thought you could make a cat's paw of me, did you?"

"What do you mean?" cried Keawe.

"Mean?" cried the boatswain. "This is a pretty good bottle, this is; that's what I mean. How I got it for two centimes I can't make out; but I am sure you sha'n't have it for one."

"You mean you won't sell?" gasped Keawe.

"No, sir," cried the boatswain. "But I'll give you a drink of the rum, if you like."

"I tell you," said Keawe, "the man who has that bottle goes to hell."

"I reckon I'm going anyway," returned the sailor; "and this bottle's the best thing to go with I've struck yet. No, sir!" he cried again, "this is my bottle now, and you can go and fish for another."

"Can this be true?" Keawe cried. "For your own sake, I beseech you, sell it me!"

"I don't value any of your talk," replied the boatswain. "You thought I was a flat, now you see I'm not; and there's an end. If you won't have a swallow of the rum, I'll have one myself. Here's your health, and good-night to you!"

So off he went down the avenue toward town, and there goes the bottle out of the story.

But Keawe ran to Kokua light as the wind; and great was their joy that night; and great, since then, has been the peace of all their days in the Bright House.

The Body-Snatcher

EVERY NIGHT IN THE YEAR, FOUR OF US SAT IN THE SMALL PARLOUR of the George at Debenham—the undertaker, and the land-lord, and Fettes, and myself. Sometimes there would be more; but blow high, blow low, come rain or snow or frost, we four would be each planted in his own particular arm-chair. Fettes was an old drunken Scotchman, a man of education obviously, and a man of some property, since he lived in idleness. He had come to Deben-ham years ago, while still young, and by a mere continuance of living had grown to be an adopted townsman. His blue camlet cloak was a local antiquity, like the church-spire. His place in the parlour at the George, his absence from church, his old, crapulous, disreputable vices, were all things of course in Debenham. He had some vague Radical opinions and some fleeting infidelities, which he would now and again set forth and emphasise with tot-tering slaps upon the table. He drank rum—five glasses regularly every evening; and for the greater portion of his nightly visit to the George sat, with his glass in his right hand, in a state of melan-choly alcoholic saturation. We called him the Doctor, for he was supposed to have some special knowledge of medicine, and had been known, upon a pinch, to set a fracture or reduce a disloca-tion; but beyond these slight particulars, we had no knowledge of his character and antecedents.

One dark winter night—it had struck nine some time before the landlord joined us—there was a sick man in the George, a great neighbouring proprietor suddenly struck down with apoplexy on his way to Parliament; and the great man's still greater London doctor had been telegraphed to his bedside. It was the first time that such a thing had happened in Debenham, for the railway was but newly open, and we were all proportionately moved by the occurrence.

"He's come," said the landlord, after he had filled and lighted his pipe.

"He?" said I. "Who?—not the doctor?"

"Himself," replied our host.

"What is his name?"

"Dr. Macfarlane," said the landlord.

Fettes was far through his third tumbler, stupidly fuddled, now nodding over, now staring mazily around him; but at the last word he seemed to awaken, and repeated the name "Macfarlane" twice, quietly enough the first time, but with sudden emotion at the second.

"Yes," said the landlord, "that's his name, Dr. Wolfe Macfarlane."

Fettes became instantly sober; his eyes awoke, his voice became clear, loud, and steady, his language forcible and earnest. We were all startled by the transformation, as if a man had risen from the dead.

"I beg your pardon," he said, "I am afraid I have not been paying much attention to your talk. Who is this Wolfe Macfarlane?" And then, when he had heard the landlord out, "It cannot be, it cannot be," he added; "and yet I would like well to see him face to face."

"Do you know him, Doctor?" asked the undertaker, with a gasp.

"God forbid!" was the reply. "And yet the name is a strange one; it were too much to fancy two. Tell me, landlord, is he old?"

"Well," said the host, "he's not a young man, to be sure, and his hair is white; but he looks younger than you."

"He is older, though; years older. But," with a slap upon the table, "it's the rum you see in my face—rum and sin. This man, perhaps, may have an easy conscience and a good digestion. Conscience! Hear me speak. You would think I was some good, old, decent Christian, would you not? But no, not I; I never canted. Voltaire might have canted if he'd stood in my shoes; but the brains"—with a rattling fillip on his bald head—"the brains were clear and active, and I saw and made no deductions."

"If you know this doctor," I ventured to remark, after a somewhat awful pause, "I should gather that you do not share the landlord's good opinion."

Fettes paid no regard to me.

"Yes," he said, with sudden decision, "I must see him face to face."

There was another pause, and then a door was closed rather sharply on the first floor, and a step was heard upon the stair.

"That's the doctor," cried the landlord. "Look sharp, and you can catch him."

It was but two steps from the small parlour to the door of the old George Inn; the wide oak staircase landed almost in the street; there was room for a Turkey rug and nothing more between the threshold and the last round of the descent; but this little space was every evening brilliantly lit up, not only by the light upon the stair and the great signal-lamp below the sign, but by the warm radiance of the bar-room window. The George thus brightly advertised itself to passers-by in the cold street. Fettes walked steadily to the spot, and we, who were hanging behind, beheld the two men meet, as one of them had phrased it, face to face. Dr. Macfarlane was alert and vigorous. His white hair set off his pale and placid, although energetic, countenance. He was richly dressed in the finest of broadcloth and the whitest of linen, with a great gold watchchain, and studs and spectacles of the same precious material. He wore a broad-folded tie, white and speckled with lilac, and he carried on his arm a comfortable driving-coat of fur. There was no doubt but he became his years, breathing, as he did, of wealth and consideration; and it was a surprising contrast to see our parlour sot—bald, dirty, pimpled, and robed in his old camlet cloak—confront him at the bottom of the stairs.

"Macfarlane!" he said somewhat loudly, more like a herald than a friend.

The great doctor pulled up short on the fourth step, as though the familiarity of the address surprised and somewhat shocked his dignity.

"Toddy Macfarlane!" repeated Fettes.

The London man almost staggered. He stared for the swiftest of seconds at the man before him, glanced behind him with a sort of scare, and then in a startled whisper, "Fettes!" he said, "you!"

"Ay," said the other, "me! Did you think I was dead too? We are not so easy shut of our acquaintance."

"Hush, hush!" exclaimed the doctor. "Hush, hush! this meeting is so unexpected—I can see you are unmanned. I hardly knew you, I confess, at first; but I am overjoyed—overjoyed to have this opportunity. For the present it must be how-d'ye-do and good-bye in one, for my fly is waiting, and I must not fail the train; but you shall—let me see—yes—you shall give me your address, and you can count on early news of me. We must do something for you, Fettes. I fear you are out at elbows; but we must see to that for auld lang syne, as once we sang at suppers."

"Money!" cried Fettes; "money from you! The money that I had from you is lying where I cast it in the rain."

Dr. Macfarlane had talked himself into some measure of superiority and confidence, but the uncommon energy of this refusal cast him back into his first confusion.

A horrible, ugly look came and went across his almost venerable countenance. "My dear fellow," he said, "be it as you please; my last thought is to offend you. I would intrude on none. I will leave you my address, however——"

"I do not wish it—I do not wish to know the roof that shelters you," interrupted the other. "I heard your name; I feared it might be you; I wished to know if, after all, there were a God; I know now that there is none. Begone!"

He still stood in the middle of the rug, between the stair and doorway; and the great London physician, in order to escape, would be forced to step to one side. It was plain that he hesitated before the thought of this humiliation. White as he was, there was a dangerous glitter in his spectacles; but while he still paused uncertain, he became aware that the driver of his fly was peering in from the street at this unusual scene and caught a glimpse at the same time of our little body from the parlour, huddled by the corner of the bar. The presence of so many witnesses decided him at once to flee. He crouched together, brushing on the wainscot, and made a dart like a serpent, striking for the door. But his tribulation was not yet entirely at an end, for even as he was passing Fettes clutched him by the arm and these words came in a whisper, and yet painfully distinct, "Have you seen it again?"

The great rich London doctor cried out aloud with a sharp, throttling cry; he dashed his questioner across the open space, and, with his hands over his head, fled out of the door like a detected thief. Before it had occurred to one of us to make a movement the fly was already rattling toward the station. The scene was over like a dream, but the dream had left proofs and traces of its passage. Next day the servant found the fine gold spectacles broken on the threshold, and that very night we were all standing breathless by the bar-room window, and Fettes at our side, sober, pale, and resolute in look.

"God protect us, Mr. Fettes!" said the landlord, coming first into possession of his customary senses. "What in the universe is all this? These are strange things you have been saying."

Fettes turned toward us; he looked us each in succession in the face. "See if you can hold your tongues," said he. "That man Macfarlane is not safe to cross; those that have done so already have repented it too late."

And then, without so much as finishing his third glass, far less waiting for the other two, he bade us good-bye and went forth, under the lamp of the hotel, into the black night.

We three turned to our places in the parlour, with the big red fire and four clear candles; and as we recapitulated what had passed the first chill of our surprise soon changed into a glow of curiosity. We sat late; it was the latest session I have known in the old George. Each man, before we parted, had his theory that he was bound to prove; and none of us had any nearer business in this world than to track out the past of our condemned companion, and surprise the secret that he shared with the great London doctor. It is no great boast, but I believe I was a better hand at worming out a story than either of my fellows at the George; and perhaps there is now no other man alive who could narrate to you the following foul and unnatural events.

In his young days Fettes studied medicine in the schools of Edinburgh. He had talent of a kind, the talent that picks up swiftly what it hears and readily retails it for its own. He worked little at home; but he was civil, attentive, and intelligent in the presence of his masters. They soon picked him out as a lad who listened closely and remembered well; nay, strange as it seemed to me when I first heard it, he was in those days well favoured, and pleased by his exterior. There was, at that period, a certain extramural teacher of anatomy, whom I shall here designate by the letter K. His name was subsequently too well known. The man who bore it skulked through the streets of Edinburgh in disguise, while the mob that applauded at the execution of Burke called loudly for

the blood of his employer. But Mr. K—— was then at the top of
his vogue; he enjoyed a popularity due partly to his own talent
and address, partly to the incapacity of his rival, the university
professor. The students, at least, swore by his name, and Fettes
believed himself, and was believed by others, to have laid the
foundations of success when he had acquired the favour of this
meteorically famous man. Mr. K—— was a *bon vivant* as well as
an accomplished teacher; he liked a sly illusion no less than a
careful preparation. In both capacities Fettes enjoyed and deserved his notice, and by the second year of his attendance he
held the half-regular position of second demonstrator or sub-
assistant in his class.

In this capacity, the charge of the theatre and lecture-room de-
volved in particular upon his shoulders. He had to answer for the
cleanliness of the premises and the conduct of the other students,
and it was a part of his duty to supply, receive, and divide the
various subjects. It was with a view to this last—at that time very
delicate—affair that he was lodged by Mr. K—— in the same
wynd, and at last in the same building, with the dissecting-rooms.
Here, after a night of turbulent pleasures, his hand still tottering,
his sight still misty and confused, he would be called out of bed in
the black hours before the winter dawn by the unclean and desperate interlopers who supplied the table. He would open the
door to these men, since infamous throughout the land. He would
help them with their tragic burthen, pay them their sordid price,
and remain alone, when they were gone, with the unfriendly relics
of humanity. From such a scene he would return to snatch another
hour or two of slumber, to repair the abuses of the night, and refresh himself for the labours of the day.

Few lads could have been more insensible to the impressions of
a life thus passed among the ensigns of mortality. His mind was
closed against all general considerations. He was incapable of
interest in the fate and fortunes of another, the slave of his own
desires and low ambitions. Cold, light, and selfish in the last resort,
he had that modicum of prudence, miscalled morality, which keeps
a man from inconvenient drunkenness or punishable theft. He
coveted, besides, a measure of consideration from his masters and
his fellow-pupils, and he had no desire to fail conspicuously in the
external parts of life. Thus he made it his pleasure to gain some
distinction in his studies, and day after day rendered unimpeach-

able eye-service to his employer, Mr. K——. For his day of work he indemnified himself by nights of roaring, blackguardly enjoyment; and when that balance had been struck, the organ that he called his conscience declared itself content.

The supply of subjects was a continual trouble to him as well as to his master. In that large and busy class, the raw material of the anatomists kept perpetually running out; and the business thus rendered necessary was not only unpleasant in itself, but threatened dangerous consequences to all who were concerned. It was the policy of Mr. K—— to ask no questions in his dealings with the trade. "They bring the body, and we pay the price," he used to say, dwelling on the alliteration—"*quid pro quo*." And, again, and somewhat profanely, "Ask no questions," he would tell his assistants, "for conscience' sake." There was no understanding that the subjects were provided by the crime of murder. Had that idea been broached to him in words, he would have recoiled in horror; but the lightness of his speech upon so grave a matter was, in itself, an offense against good manners, and a temptation to the men with whom he dealt. Fettes, for instance, had often remarked to himself upon the singular freshness of the bodies. He had been struck again and again by the hang-dog, abominable looks of the ruffians who came to him before the dawn; and putting things together clearly in his private thoughts, he perhaps attributed a meaning too immoral and too categorical to the unguarded counsels of his master. He understood his duty, in short, to have three branches: to take what was brought, to pay the price, and to avert the eye from any evidence of crime.

One November morning this policy of silence was put sharply to the test. He had been awake all night with a racking toothache —pacing his room like a caged beast or throwing himself in fury on his bed—and had fallen at last into that profound, uneasy slumber that so often follows on a night of pain, when he was awakened by the third or fourth angry repetition of the concerted signal. There was a thin, bright moonshine; it was bitter cold, windy, and frosty; the town had not yet awakened, but an indefinable stir already preluded the noise and business of the day. The ghouls had come later than usual, and they seemed more than usually eager to be gone. Fettes, sick with sleep, lighted them upstairs. He heard their grumbling Irish voices through a dream; and as they stripped the sack from their sad merchandise he leaned dozing, with his shoulder propped against the wall; he had to shake himself to find the men their money. As he did so his eyes lighted on the dead face. He started; he took two steps nearer, with the candle raised.

"God Almighty!" he cried. "That is Jane Galbraith!"

The men answered nothing, but they shuffled nearer the door.

"I know her, I tell you," he continued. "She was alive and hearty yesterday. It's impossible she can be dead; it's impossible you should have got this body fairly."

"Sure, sir, you're mistaken entirely," said one of the men.

But the other looked Fettes darkly in the eyes, and demanded the money on the spot.

It was impossible to misconceive the threat or to exaggerate the danger. The lad's heart failed him. He stammered some excuses, counted out the sum, and saw his hateful visitors depart. No sooner were they gone than he hastened to confirm his doubts. By a dozen unquestionable marks he identified the girl he had jested with the day before, He saw, with horror, marks upon her body that might well betoken violence. A panic seized him, and he took refuge in his room. There he reflected at length over the discovery that he had made; considered soberly the bearing of Mr. K——'s instructions and the danger to himself of interference in so serious a business, and at last, in sore perlexity, determined to wait for the advice of his immediate superior, the class assistant.

This was a young doctor, Wolfe Macfarlane, a high favourite among all the reckless students, clever, dissipated, and unscrupulous to the last degree. He had travelled and studied abroad. His manners were agreeable and a little forward. He was an authority on the stage, skilful on the ice or the links with skate or golf-club; he dressed with nice audacity, and, to put the finishing touch upon his glory, he kept a gig and a strong trotting-horse. With Fettes he was on terms of intimacy; indeed, their relative positions called for some community of life; and when subjects were scarce the pair would drive far into the country in Macfarlane's gig, visit and desecrate some lonely graveyard, and return before dawn with their booty to the door of the dissecting-room.

On that particular morning Macfarlane arrived somewhat earlier than his wont. Fettes heard him, and met him on the stairs, told him his story, and showed him the cause of his alarm. Macfarlane examined the marks on her body.

"Yes," he said with a nod, "it looks fishy."

"Well, what should I do?" asked Fettes.

"Do?" repeated the other. "Do you want to do anything? Least said soonest mended, I should say."

"Some one else might recognise her," objected Fettes. "She was as well known as the Castle Rock."

"We'll hope not," said Macfarlane, "and if anybody does—well, you didn't, don't you see, and there's an end. The fact is, this has been going on too long. Stir up the mud, and you'll get K——into the most unholy trouble; you'll be in a shocking box yourself. So will I, if you come to that. I should like to know how any one of us would look, or what the devil we should have to say for ourselves, in any Christian witness-box. For me, you know there's one thing certain—that, practically speaking, all our subjects have been murdered."

"Macfarlane!" cried Fettes.

"Come now!" sneered the other. "As if you hadn't suspected it yourself!"

"Suspecting is one thing——"

"And proof another. Yes, I know; and I'm as sorry as you are this should have come here," tapping the body with his cane. "The next best thing for me is not to recognise it; and," he added coolly, "I don't. You may, if you please. I don't dictate, but I think a man of the world would do as I do; and I may add, I fancy that is what K—— would look for at our hands. The question is, Why did he choose us two for his assistants? And I answer, because he didn't want old wives."

This was the tone of all others to affect the mind of a lad like Fettes. He agreed to imitate Macfarlane. The body of the unfortunate girl was duly dissected, and no one remarked or appeared to recognise her.

One afternoon, when his day's work was over, Fettes dropped into a popular tavern and found Macfarlane sitting with a stranger. This was a small man, very pale and dark, with coal-black eyes. The cut of his features gave a promise of intellect and refinement which was but feebly realised in his manners, for he proved, upon a nearer acquaintance, coarse, vulgar, and stupid. He exercised, however, a very remarkable control over Macfarlane; issued orders like the Great Bashaw; became inflamed at the least discussion or delay, and commented rudely on the servility with which he was obeyed. This most offensive person took a fancy to Fettes on the spot, plied him with drinks, and honoured him with unusual confidences on his past career. If a tenth part of what he confessed were true, he was a very loathsome rogue; and the lad's vanity was tickled by the attention of so experienced a man.

"I'm a pretty bad fellow myself," the stranger remarked, "but Macfarlane is the boy—Toddy Macfarlane I call him. Toddy, order your friend another glass." Or it might be, "Toddy, you jump up and shut the door." "Toddy hates me," he said again. "Oh, yes, Toddy, you do!"

"Don't you call me that confounded name," growled Macfarlane.

"Hear him! Did you ever see the lads play knife? He would like to do that all over my body," remarked the stranger.

"We medicals have a better way than that," said Fettes. "When we dislike a dead friend of ours, we dissect him."

Macfarlane looked up sharply, as though this jest were scarcely to his mind.

The afternoon passed. Gray, for that was the stranger's name, invited Fettes to join them at dinner, ordered a feast so sumptuous that the tavern was thrown in commotion, and when all was done commanded Macfarlane to settle the bill. It was late before they separated; the man Gray was incapably drunk. Macfarlane, sobered by his fury, chewed the cud of the money he had been forced to squander and the slights he had been obliged to swallow. Fettes, with various liquors singing in his head, returned home with devious footsteps and a mind entirely in abeyance. Next day Macfarlane was absent from the class, and Fettes smiled to himself as he imagined him still squiring the intolerable Gray from tavern to tavern. As soon as the hour of liberty had struck he posted from place to place in quest of his last night's companions. He could find them, however, nowhere; so returned early to his rooms, went early to bed, and slept the sleep of the just.

At four in the morning he was awakened by the well-known signal. Descending to the door, he was filled with astonishment to find Macfarlane with his gig, and in the gig one of those long and ghastly packages with which he was so well acquainted.

"What?" he cried. "Have you been out alone? How did you manage?"

But Macfarlane silenced him roughly, bidding him turn to

business. When they had got the body up-stairs and laid it on the table, Macfarlane made at first as if he were going away. Then he paused and seemed to hesitate; and then, "You had better look at the face," said he, in tones of some constraint. "You had better," he repeated, as Fettes only stared at him in wonder.

"But where, and how, and when did you come by it?" cried the other.

"Look at the face," was the only answer.

Fettes was staggered; strange doubt assailed him. He looked from the young doctor to the body, and then back again. At last, with a start, he did as he was bidden. He had almost expected the sight that met his eyes, and yet the shock was cruel. To see, fixed in the rigidity of death and naked on that coarse layer of sack-cloth, the man whom he had left well clad and full of meat and sin upon the threshold of a tavern, awoke, even in the thoughtless Fettes, some of the terrors of the conscience. It was a *cras tibi* which re-echoed in his soul, that two whom he had known should have come to lie upon these icy tables. Yet these were only secondary thoughts. His first concern regarded Wolfe. Unprepared for a challenge so momentous, he knew not how to look his comrade in the face. He durst not meet his eye, and he had neither words nor voice at his command.

It was Macfarlane himself who made the first advance. He came up quietly behind and laid his hand gently but firmly on the other's shoulder.

"Richardson," said he, "may have the head."

Now Richardson was a student who had long been anxious for that portion of the human subject to dissect. There was no answer, and the murderer resumed: "Talking of business, you must pay me; your accounts, you see, must tally."

Fettes found a voice, the ghost of his own: "Pay you!" he cried. "Pay you for that?"

"Why, yes, of course you must. By all means and on every possible account, you must," returned the other. "I dare not give it for nothing, you dare not take it for nothing; it would compromise us both. This is another case like Jane Galbraith's. The more things are wrong the more we must act as if all were right. Where does old K—— keep his money?"

"There," answered Fettes hoarsely, pointing to a cupboard in the corner.

"Give me the key, then," said the other, calmly, holding out his hand.

There was an instant's hesitation, and the die was cast. Macfarlane could not suppress a nervous twitch, the infinitesimal mark of an immense relief, as he felt the key between his fingers. He opened the cupboard, brought out pen and ink and a paper-book that stood in one compartment, and separated from the funds in a drawer a sum suitable to the occasion.

"Now, look here," he said, "there is the payment made—first proof of your good faith: first step to your security. You have now to clinch it by a second. Enter the payment in your book, and then you for your part may defy the devil."

The next few seconds were for Fettes an agony of thought; but in balancing his terrors it was the most immediate that triumphed. Any future difficulty seemed almost welcome if he could avoid a present quarrel with Macfarlane. He set down the candle which he had been carrying all this time, and with a steady hand entered the date, the nature, and the amount of the transaction.

"And now," said Macfarlane, "it's only fair that you should pocket the lucre. I've had my share already. By the bye, when a man of the world falls into a bit of luck, has a few shillings extra in his pocket—I'm ashamed to speak of it, but there's a rule of conduct in the case. No treating, no purchase of expensive class-books, no squaring of old debts; borrow, don't lend."

"Macfarlane," began Fettes, still somewhat hoarsely, "I have put my neck in a halter to oblige you."

"To oblige me?" cried Wolfe. "Oh, come! You did, as near as I can see the matter, what you downright had to do in self-defence. Suppose I got into trouble, where would you be? This second little matter flows clearly from the first. Mr. Gray is the continuation of Miss Galbraith. You can't begin and then stop. If you begin, you must keep on beginning; that's the truth. No rest for the wicked."

A horrible sense of blackness and the treachery of fate seized hold upon the soul of the unhappy student.

"My God!" he cried, "but what have I done? and when did I begin? To be made a class assistant—in the name of reason, where's the harm in that? Service wanted the position; Service might have got it. Would *he* have been where *I* am now?"

"My dear fellow," said Macfarlane, "what a boy you are! What harm *has* come to you? What harm *can* come to you if you hold your tongue? Why, man, do you know what this life is? There are two squads of us—the lions and the lambs. If you're a lamb, you'll come to lie upon these tables like Gray or Jane Galbraith; if you're a lion, you'll live and drive a horse like me, like K——, like all the world with any wit or courage. You're staggered at the first. But look at K——! My dear fellow, you're clever, you have pluck. I like you, and K—— likes you. You were born to lead the hunt; and I tell you, on my honour and my experience of life, three days from now you'll laugh at all these scarecrows like a high-school boy at a farce."

And with that Macfarlane took his departure and drove off up the wynd in his gig to get under cover before daylight. Fettes was thus left alone with his regrets. He saw the miserable peril in which he stood involved. He saw, with inexpressible dismay, that there was no limit to his weakness, and that, from concession to concession, he had fallen from the arbiter of Macfarlane's destiny to his paid and helpless accomplice. He would have given the world to have been a little braver at the time, but it did not occur to him that he might still be brave. The secret of Jane Galbraith and the cursed entry in the daybook closed his mouth.

Hours passed; the class began to arrive; the members of the unhappy Gray were dealt out to one and to another, and received without remark. Richardson was made happy with the head; and before the hour of freedom rang Fettes trembled with exultation to perceive how far they had already gone toward safety.

For two days he continued to watch, with increasing joy, the dreadful process of disguise.

On the third day Macfarlane made his appearance. He had been ill, he said; but he made up for lost time by the energy with which he directed the students. To Richardson in particular he extended the most valuable assistance and advice, and that student, encouraged by the praise of the demonstrator, burned high with ambitious hopes, and saw the medal already in his grasp.

Before the week was out Macfarlane's prophecy had been fulfilled. Fettes had outlived his terrors and had forgotten his baseness. He began to plume himself upon his courage, and had so arranged the story in his mind that he could look back on these events with an unhealthy pride. Of his accomplice he saw but little. They met, of course, in the business of the class; they received their orders together from Mr. K——. At times they had a word or two in private, and Macfarlane was from first to last particularly kind and jovial. But it was plain that he avoided any reference to their common secret; and even when Fettes whispered to him that he had cast in his lot with the lions and forsworn the lambs, he only signed to him smilingly to hold his peace.

At length an occasion arose which threw the pair once more into a closer union. Mr. K—— was again short of subjects; pupils were eager, and it was a part of this teacher's pretensions to be always well supplied. At the same time there came the news of a burial in the rustic graveyard of Glencorse. Time has little changed the place in question. It stood then, as now, upon a crossroad, out of call of human habitations, and buried fathom deep in the foliage of six cedar trees. The cries of the sheep upon the neighbouring hills, the streamlets upon either hand, one loudly singing among pebbles, the other dripping furtively from pond to pond, the stir of the wind in mountainous old flowering chestnuts, and once in seven days the voice of the bell and the old tunes of the precentor, were the only sounds that disturbed the silence around the rural church. The Resurrection Man—to use a by-name of the period— was not to be deterred by any of the sanctities of customary piety. It was part of his trade to despise and desecrate the scrolls and trumpets of old tombs, the paths worn by the feet of worshippers and mourners, and the offerings and the inscriptions of bereaved affection. To rustic neighbourhoods, where love is more than commonly tenacious, and where some bonds of blood or fellowship unite the entire society of a parish, the body-snatcher, far from being repelled by natural respect, was attracted by the ease and safety of the task. To bodies that had been laid in earth, in joyful expectation of a far different awakening, there came that hasty, lamp-lit, terror-haunted resurrection of the spade and mattock. The coffin was forced, the cerements torn, and the melancholy relics, clad in sackcloth, after being rattled for hours on moonless by-ways, were at length exposed to uttermost indignities before a class of gaping boys.

Somewhat as two vultures may swoop upon a dying lamb, Fettes and Macfarlane were to be let loose upon a grave in that green and quiet resting-place. The wife of a farmer, a woman who had lived for sixty years, and been known for nothing but good butter and a godly conversation, was to be rooted from her grave at midnight and carried, dead and naked, to that far-away city that she had always honoured with her Sunday's best; the place beside her family was to be empty till the crack of doom; her innocent and almost venerable members to be exposed to that last curiosity of the anatomist.

Late one afternoon the pair set forth, well wrapped in cloaks and furnished with a formidable bottle. It rained without remission—a cold, dense, lashing rain. Now and again there blew a puff of wind, but these sheets of falling water kept it down. Bottle and all, it was a sad and silent drive as far as Penicuik, where they were to spend the evening. They stopped once, to hide their implements in a thick bush not far from the churchyard, and once again at the Fisher's Tryst, to have a toast before the kitchen fire and vary their nips of whisky with a glass of ale. When they reached their journey's end the gig was housed, the horse was fed and comforted, and the two young doctors in a private room sat down to the best dinner and the best wine the house afforded. The lights, the fire, the beating rain upon the window, the cold, incongruous work that lay before them, added zest to their enjoyment of the meal. With every glass their cordiality increased. Soon Macfarlane handed a little pile of gold to his companion.

"A compliment," he said. "Between friends these little d——d accommodations ought to fly like pipe-lights."

Fettes pocketed the money, and applauded the sentiment to the echo. "You are a philosopher," he cried. "I was an ass till I knew you. You and K—— between you, by the Lord Harry! but you'll make a man of me."

"Of course, we shall," applauded Macfarlane. "A man? I tell you, it required a man to back me up the other morning. There are some big, brawling, forty-year-old cowards who would have turned sick at the look of the d——d thing; but not you—you kept your head. I watched you."

"Well, and why not?" Fettes thus vaunted himself. "It was no affair of mine. There was nothing to gain on the one side but disturbance, and on the other I could count on your gratitude, don't you see?" And he slapped his pocket till the gold pieces rang.

Macfarlane somehow felt a certain touch of alarm at these unpleasant words. He may have regretted that he had taught his young companion so successfully, but he had no time to interfere, for the other noisily continued in this boastful strain:

"The great thing is not to be afraid. Now, between you and me, I don't want to hang—that's practical; but for all cant, Macfarlane, I was born with a contempt. Hell, God, Devil, right, wrong, sin, crime, and all the old gallery of curiosities—they may frighten boys, but men of the world, like you and me, despise them. Here's to the memory of Gray!"

It was by this time growing somewhat late. The gig, according to order, was brought round to the door with both lamps brightly shining, and the young men had to pay their bill and take the road. They announced that they were bound for Peebles, and drove in that direction till they were clear of the last houses of the town; then, extinguishing the lamps, returned upon their course, and followed a by-road toward Glencorse. There was no sound but that of their own passage, and the incessant, strident pouring of the rain. It was pitch dark; here and there a white gate or a white stone in the wall guided them for a short space across the night; but for the most part it was at a foot pace, and almost groping, that they picked their way through that resonant blackness to their solemn and isolated destination. In the sunken woods that traverse the neighbourhood of the burying-ground the last glimmer failed them, and it became necessary to kindle a match and reillumine one of the lanterns of the gig. Thus, under the dripping trees, and environed by huge and moving shadows, they reached the scene of their unhallowed labours.

They were both experienced in such affairs, and powerful with the spade; and they had scarce been twenty minutes at their task before they were rewarded by a dull rattle on the coffin lid. At the same moment Macfarlane, having hurt his hand upon a stone, flung it carelessly above his head. The grave, in which they now stood almost to the shoulders, was close to the edge of the plateau of the graveyard; and the gig lamp had been propped, the better to illuminate their labours, against a tree, and on the immediate verge of the steep bank descending to the stream. Chance had taken a sure aim with the stone. Then came a clang of broken glass; night fell upon them; sounds alternately dull and ringing announced the bounding of the lantern down the bank, and its occasional collision with the trees. A stone or two, which it had dislodged in its descent, rattled behind it into the profundities of the glen; and then silence, like night, resumed its sway; and they might bend their hearing to its utmost pitch, but naught was to be heard except the rain, now marching to the wind, now steadily falling over miles of open country.

They were so nearly at an end of their abhorred task that they judged it wisest to complete it in the dark. The coffin was exhumed and broken open; the body inserted in the dripping sack and carried between them to the gig; one mounted to keep it in its place, and the other, taking the horse by the mouth, groped along by wall and bush until they reached the wider road by the Fisher's Tryst. Here was a faint, diffused radiancy, which they hailed like daylight; by that they pushed the horse to a good pace and began to rattle along merrily in the direction of the town.

They had both been wetted to the skin during their operations, and now, as the gig jumped among the deep ruts, the thing that stood propped between them fell now upon one and now upon the other. At every repetition of the horrid contact each instinctively repelled it with the greater haste; and the process, natural although it was, began to tell upon the nerves of the companions. Macfarlane made some ill-favoured jest about the farmer's wife, but it came hollowly from his lips, and was allowed to drop in silence. Still their unnatural burthen bumped from side to side; and now the head would be laid, as if in confidence, upon their shoulders, and now the drenching sack-cloth would flap icily about their faces. A creeping chill began to possess the soul of Fettes. He peered at the bundle, and it seemed somehow larger than at first. All over the country-side, and from every degree of distance, the farm dogs accompanied their passage with tragic ululations; and it grew and grew upon his mind that some unnatural miracle had been accomplished, that some nameless change had befallen the dead body, and that it was in fear of their unholy burthen that the dogs were howling.

"For God's sake," said he, making a great effort to arrive at speech, "for God's sake, let's have a light!"

Seemingly Macfarlane was affected in the same direction; for, though he made no reply, he stopped the horse, passed the reins to his companion, got down, and proceeded to kindle the remaining lamp. They had by that time got no farther than the cross-road down to Auchenclinny. The rain still poured as though the deluge were returning, and it was no easy matter to make a light in such a world of wet and darkness. When at last the flickering blue flame had been transferred to the wick and began to expand and clarify, and shed a wide circle of misty brightness round the gig, it became possible for the two young men to see each other and the thing they had along with them. The rain had moulded the rough sacking to the outlines of the body underneath; the head was distinct from the trunk, the shoulders plainly modelled; something at once spectral and human riveted their eyes upon the ghastly comrade of their drive.

For some time Macfarlane stood motionless, holding up the lamp. A nameless dread was swathed, like a wet sheet, about the body, and tightened the white skin upon the face of Fettes; a fear that was meaningless, a horror of what could not be, kept mounting to his brain. Another beat of the watch, and he had spoken. But his comrade forestalled him.

"That is not a woman," said Macfarlane, in a hushed voice.

"It was a woman when we put her in," whispered Fettes.

"Hold that lamp," said the other. "I must see her face."

And as Fettes took the lamp his companion untied the fastenings of the sack and drew down the cover from the head. The light fell very clear upon the dark, well-moulded features and smooth-shaven cheeks of a too familiar countenance, often beheld in dreams of both of these young men. A wild yell rang up into the night; each leaped from his own side into the roadway; the lamp fell, broke, and was extinguished; and the horse, terrified by this unusual commotion, bounded and went off toward Edinburgh at a gallop, bearing along with it, sole occupant of the gig, the body of the dead and long-dissected Gray.

Providence and the Guitar

1.

MONSIEUR LEON BERTHELINI HAD A GREAT CARE OF HIS APPEARance, and sedulously suited his deportment to the costume of the hour. He affected something Spanish in his air, and something of the bandit, with a flavour of Rembrandt at home. In person he was decidedly small and inclined to be stout; his face was the picture of good humour; his dark eyes, which were very expressive, told of a kind heart, a brisk, merry nature, and the most indefatigable spirits. If he had worn the clothes of the period you would have set him down for a hitherto undiscovered hybrid between the barber, the innkeeper, and the affable dispensing chemist. But in the outrageous bravery of velvet jacket and flapped hat, with trousers that were more accurately described as fleshings, a white handkerchief cavalierly knotted at his neck, a shock of Olympian curls upon his brow, and his feet shod through all weathers in the slenderest of Molière shoes—you had but to look at him and you knew you were in the presence of a Great Creature. When he wore an overcoat he scorned to pass the sleeves; a single button held it round his shoulders; it was tossed backwards after the manner of a cloak, and carried with the gait and presence of an Almaviva. I am of opinion that M. Berthelini was nearing forty. But he had a boy's heart, gloried in his finery, and walked through life like a child in a perpetual dramatic performance. If he were not Almaviva after all, it was not for lack of making believe. And he enjoyed the artist's compensation. If he were not really Almaviva, he was sometimes just as happy as though he were.

I have seen him, at moments when he has fancied himself alone with his Maker, adopt so gay and chivalrous a bearing, and represent his own part with so much warmth and conscience, that the illusion became catching, and I believed implicitly in the Great Creature's pose.

But, alas! life cannot be entirely conducted on these principles; man cannot live by Almavivery alone; and the Great Creature, having failed upon several theatres, was obliged to step down every evening from his heights, and sing from a half-a-dozen to a dozen comic songs, twang a guitar, keep a country audience in good humour, and preside finally over the mysteries of a tombola.

Madame Berthelini, who was art and part with him in these undignified labours, had perhaps a higher position in the scale of beings, and enjoyed a natural dignity of her own. But her heart was not any more rightly placed, for that would have been impossible; and she had acquired a little air of melancholy, attractive enough in its way, but not good to see like the wholesome, sky-scraping, boyish spirits of her lord.

He, indeed, swam like a kite on a fair wind, high above earthly troubles. Detonations of temper were not unfrequent in the zones he travelled; but sulky fogs and tearful depressions were there alike unknown. A well-delivered blow upon a table, or a noble attitude, imitated from Mélingue or Frederic, relieved his irritation like a vengeance. Though the heaven had fallen, if he had played his part with propriety, Berthelini had been content! And the man's atmosphere, if not his example, reacted on his wife; for the couple doted on each other, and although you would have thought they walked in different worlds, yet continued to walk hand in hand.

It chanced one day that Monsieur and Madame Berthelini descended with two boxes and a guitar in a fat case at the station of the little town of Castel-le-Gâchis, and the omnibus carried them with their effects to the Hotel of the Black Head. This was a dismal, conventual building in a narrow street, capable of standing siege when once the gates were shut, and smelling strangely in the interior of straw and chocolate and old feminine apparel. Berthelini paused upon the threshold with a painful premonition. In some former state, it seemed to him, he had visited a hostelry that smelt not otherwise, and been ill received.

The landlord, a tragic person in a large felt hat, rose from a business table under the key-rack, and came forward, removing his hat with both hands as he did so.

"Sir, I salute you. May I inquire what is your charge for artists?" inquired Berthelini, with a courtesy at once splendid and insinuating.

"For artists?" said the landlord. His countenance fell and the smile of welcome disappeared. "Oh, artists!" he added brutally; "four francs a day." And he turned his back upon these inconsiderable customers.

A commercial traveller is received, he also, upon a reduction— yet is he welcome, yet can he command the fatted calf; but an artist, had he the manners of an Almaviva, were he dressed like Solomon in all his glory, is received like a dog and served like a timid lady travelling alone.

Accustomed as he was to the rubs of his profession, Berthelini was unpleasantly affected by the landlord's manner.

"Elvira," said he to his wife, "mark my words: Castel-le-Gâchis is a tragic folly."

"Wait till we see what we take," replied Elvira.

"We shall take nothing," returned Berthelini; "we shall feed upon insults. I have an eye, Elvira; I have a spirit of divination; and this place is accursed. The landlord has been discourteous, the Commissary will be brutal, the audience will be sordid and uproarious, and you will take a cold upon your throat. We have been besotted enough to come; the die is cast—it will be a second Sedan."

Sedan was a town hateful to the Berthelinis, not only from patriotism (for they were French, and answered after the flesh to the somewhat homely name of Duval), but because it had been the scene of their most sad reverses. In that place they had lain three weeks in pawn for their hotel bill, and had it not been for a surprising stroke of fortune they might have been lying there in pawn until this day. To mention the name of Sedan was for the Berthelinis to dip the brush in earthquake and eclipse. Count Almaviva slouched his hat with a gesture expressive of despair, and even Elvira felt as if ill-fortune had been personally invoked.

"Let us ask for breakfast," said she, with a woman's tact.

The Commissary of Police of Castel-le-Gâchis was a large red Commissary, pimpled, and subject to a strong cutaneous transpiration. I have repeated the name of his office because he was so very much more a Commissary than a man. The spirit of his dignity had entered into him. He carried his corporation as if it were something official. Whenever he insulted a common citizen it seemed to him as if he were adroitly flattering the Government by a side wind; in default of dignity he was brutal from an over-weening sense of duty. His office was a den, whence passers-by could hear rude accents laying down, not the law, but the good pleasure of the Commissary.

Six several times in the course of the day did M. Berthelini hurry thither in quest of the requisite permission for his evening's entertainment; six several times he found the official was abroad. Leon Berthelini began to grow quite a familiar figure in the streets of Castel-le-Gâchis; he became a local celebrity, and was pointed out as "the man who was looking for the Commissary." Idle children attached themselves to his footsteps, and trotted after him back and forward between the hotel and the office. Leon might try as he liked; he might roll cigarettes, he might straddle, he might cock his hat at a dozen different jaunty inclinations—the part of Almaviva was, under the circumstances, difficult to play.

As he passed the market-place upon the seventh excursion the Commissary was pointed out to him, where he stood, with his waistcoat unbuttoned and his hands behind his back, to superintend the sale and measurement of butter. Berthelini threaded his way through the market stalls and baskets, and accosted the dignitary with a bow which was a triumph of the histrionic art.

"I have the honour," he asked, "of meeting M. le Commissaire?"

The Commissary was affected by the nobility of his address. He excelled Leon in the depth if not in the airy grace of his salutation.

"The honour," said he, "is mine!"

"I am," continued the strolling-player, "I am, sir, an artist, and I have permitted myself to interrupt you on an affair of business. To-night I give a trifling musical entertainment at the Café of the Triumphs of the Plough—permit me to offer you this little programme—and I have come to ask you for the necessary authorisation."

At the word "artist," the Commissary had replaced his hat with the air of a person who, having condescended too far, should suddenly remember the duties of his rank.

"Go, go," said he, "I am busy—I am measuring butter."

"Heathen Jew!" thought Leon. "Permit me, sir," he resumed, aloud. "I have gone six times already——"

"Put up your bills if you choose," interrupted the Commissary. "In an hour or so I will examine your papers at the office. But now go; I am busy."

"Measuring butter?" thought Berthelini. "Oh, France, and it is for this that we made '93!"

The preparations were soon made; the bills posted, programmes laid on the dinner-table of every hotel in the town, and a stage erected at one end of the Café of the Triumphs of the Plough; but when Leon returned to the office, the Commissary was once more abroad.

"He is like Madame Benoîton," thought Leon. "Fichu Commissaire!"

And just then he met the man face to face.

"Here, sir," said he, "are my papers. Will you be pleased to verify?"

But the Commissary was now intent upon dinner.

"No use," he replied, "no use; I am busy; I am quite satisfied. Give your entertainment."

And he hurried on.

"Fichu Commissaire!" thought Leon.

2.

The audience was pretty large; and the proprietor of the café made a good thing of it in beer. But the Berthelinis exerted themselves in vain.

Leon was radiant in velveteen; he had a rakish way of smoking a cigarette between his songs that was worth money in itself; he underlined his comic points, so that the dullest numskull in Castel-le-Gâchis had a notion when to laugh; and he handled his guitar in a manner worthy of himself. Indeed his play with that instrument was as good as a whole romantic drama; it was so dashing, so florid, and so cavalier.

Elvira, on the other hand, sang her patriotic and romantic songs with more than usual expression; her voice had charm and plangency; and as Leon looked at her, in her low-bodied maroon dress, with her arms bare to the shoulder, and a red flower set provocatively in her corset, he repeated to himself for the many hundredth time that she was one of the loveliest creatures in the world of women.

Alas! when she went round with the tambourine, the golden youth of Castel-le-Gâchis turned from her coldly. Here and there a single halfpenny was forthcoming; the net result of a collection never exceeded half a franc: and the Maire himself, after seven different applications, had contributed exactly twopence. A certain chill began to settle upon the artists themselves; it seemed as if they were singing to slugs; Apollo himself might have lost heart with such an audience. The Berthelinis struggled against the impression; they put their back into their work, they sang loud and louder, the guitar twanged like a living thing; and at last Leon arose in his might, and burst with inimitable conviction into his great song, *"Y a des honnêtes gens partout!"* Never had he given more proof of his artistic mastery; it was his intimate, indefeasible conviction that Castel-le-Gâchis formed an exception to the law he was now lyrically proclaiming, and was peopled exclusively by thieves and bullies; and yet, as I say, he flung it down like a challenge, he trolled it forth like an article of faith; and his face so beamed the while that you would have thought he must make converts of the benches.

He was at the top of his register, with his head thrown back and his mouth open, when the door was thrown violently open, and a pair of newcomers marched noisily into the café. It was the Commissary followed by the Garde Champêtre.

The undaunted Berthelini still continued to proclaim, *"Y a des honnêtes gens partout!"* But now the sentiment produced an audible titter among the audience. Berthelini wondered why; he did not know the antecedents of the Garde Champêtre; he had never heard of a little story about postage stamps. But the public knew all about the postage stamps, and enjoyed the coincidence hugely.

The Commissary planted himself upon a vacant chair with somewhat the air of Cromwell visiting the Rump, and spoke in occasional whispers to the Garde Champêtre, who remained respectfully standing at his back. The eyes of both were directed upon Berthelini, who persisted in his statement.

"*Y a des honnêtes gens partout,*" he was just chanting for the twentieth time; when up got the Commissary upon his feet and waved brutally to the singer with his cane.

"Is it me you want?" inquired Leon, stopping in his song.

"It is you," replied the potentate.

"Fichu Commissaire!" thought Leon, and he descended from the stage and made his way to the functionary.

"How does it happen, sir," said the Commissary, swelling in person, "that I find you mountebanking in a public café without my permission?"

"Without?" cried the indignant Leon. "Permit me to remind you——"

"Come, come, sir!" said the Commissary, "I desire no explanations."

"I care nothing about what you desire," returned the singer. "I choose to give them, and I will not be gagged. I am an artist, sir, a distinction that you cannot comprehend. I received your permission and stand here upon the strength of it; interfere with me who dare."

"You have not got my signature, I tell you," cried the Commissary. "Show me my signature! Where is my signature?"

That was just the question; where was his signature? Leon recognised that he was in a hole; but his spirit rose with the occasion, and he blustered nobly, tossing back his curls. The Commissary played up to him in the character of tyrant; and as the one leaned farther forward, the other leaned farther back—majesty confronting fury. The audience had transferred their attention to this new performance, and listened with that silent gravity common to all Frenchmen in the neighbourhood of the police. Elvira had sat down, she was used to these distractions, and it was rather melancholy than fear that now oppressed her.

"Another word," cried the Commissary, "and I arrest you."

"Arrest me!" shouted Leon. "I defy you!"

"I am the Commissary of Police," said the official.

Leon commanded his feelings, and replied, with great delicacy of innuendo:

"So it would appear."

The point was too refined for Castel-le-Gâchis; it did not raise a smile; and as for the Commissary, he simply bade the singer follow him to his office, and directed his proud footsteps towards the door. There was nothing for it but to obey. Leon did so with a proper pantomime of indifference, but it was a leek to eat, and there was no denying it.

The Maire had slipped out and was already waiting at the Commissary's door. Now the Maire, in France, is the refuge of the oppressed. He stands between his people and the boisterous rigours of the Police. He can sometimes understand what is said to him; he is not always puffed up beyond measure by his dignity. 'T is a thing worth the knowledge of travellers. When all seems over, and a man has made up his mind to injustice, he has still, like the heroes of romance, a little bugle at his belt whereon to blow; and the Maire, a comfortable *deus ex machina,* may still descend to deliver him from the minions of the law. The Maire of Castel-le-Gâchis, although inaccessible to the charms of music as retailed by the Berthelinis, had no hesitation whatever as to the rights of the matter. He instantly fell foul of the Commissary in very high terms, and the Commissary, pricked by this humiliation, accepted battle on the point of fact. The argument lasted some little while with varying success, until at length victory inclined so plainly to the Commissary's side that the Maire was fain to re-assert himself by an exercise of authority. He had been outargued, but he was still the Maire. And so, turning from his interlocutor, he briefly but kindly recommended Leon to go back instanter to his concert.

"It is already growing late," he added.

Leon did not wait to be told twice. He returned to the Café of the Triumphs of the Plough with all expedition. Alas! the audience had melted away during his absence; Elvira was sitting in a very disconsolate attitude on the guitar-box; she had watched the company dispersing by twos and threes, and the prolonged spectacle had somewhat overwhelmed her spirits. Each man, she reflected, retired with a certain proportion of her earnings in his pockets, and she saw to-night's board and to-morrow's railway expenses, and finally even to-morrow's dinner, walk one after another out of the café door and disappear into the night.

"What was it?" she asked, languidly.

But Leon did not answer. He was looking round him on th?

scene of defeat. Scarce a score of listeners remained, and these of the least promising sort. The minute hand of the clock was already climbing upward towards eleven.

"It's a lost battle," said he, and then taking up the money-box he turned it out. "Three francs seventy-five!" he cried, "as against four of board and six of railway fares, and no time for the tombola! Elvira, this is Waterloo." And he sat down and passed both hands desperately among his curls. "O Fichu Commissaire!" he cried, "Fichu Commissaire!"

"Let us get the things together and be off," returned Elvira. "We might try another song, but there is not six halfpence in the room."

"Six halfpence?" cried Leon, "six hundred thousand devils! There is not a human creature in the town—nothing but pigs and dogs and commissaries! Pray heaven, we get safe to bed!"

"Don't imagine things!" exclaimed Elvira, with a shudder.

And with that they set to work on their preparations. The tobacco-jar, the cigarette-holder, the three papers of shirt-studs, which were to have been the prizes of the tombola had the tombola come off, were made into a bundle with the music; the guitar was stowed into the fat guitar-case; and Elvira having thrown a thin shawl about her neck and shoulders, the pair issued from the café and set off for the Black Head.

As they crossed the market-place the church bell rang out eleven. It was a dark, mild night, and there was no one in the streets.

"It is all very fine," said Leon: "but I have a presentiment. The night is not yet done."

3.

The Black Head presented not a single chink of light upon the street, and the carriage gate was closed.

"This is unprecedented," observed Leon. "An inn closed by five minutes after eleven! And there were several commercial travellers in the café up to a late hour. Elvira, my heart misgives me. Let us ring the bell."

The bell had a potent note; and being swung under the arch it filled the house from top to bottom with surly, clanging reverberations. The sound accentuated the conventual appearance of the building; a wintry sentiment, a thought of prayer and mortification, took hold upon Elvira's mind; and as for Leon, he seemed to be reading the stage directions for a lugubrious fifth act.

"This is your fault," said Elvira; "this is what comes of fancying things!"

Again Leon pulled the bell-rope; again the solemn tocsin awoke the echoes of the inn; and ere they had died away, a light glimmered in the carriage entrance, and a powerful voice was heard upraised and tremulous with wrath.

"What's all this?" cried the tragic host through the spars of the gate. "Hard upon twelve, and you come clamouring like Prussians at the door of a respectable hotel? Oh!" he cried, "I know you now! Common singers! People in trouble with the police! And you present yourselves at midnight like lords and ladies? Be off with you!"

"You will permit me to remind you," said Leon, in thrilling tones, "that I am a guest in your house, that I am properly inscribed, and that I have deposited baggage to the value of four hundred francs."

"You cannot get in at this hour," returned the man. "This is no thieves' tavern, for mohocks and night rakes and organ-grinders."

"Brute!" cried Elvira, for the organ-grinders touched her home.

"Then I demand my baggage," said Leon, with unabated dignity.

"I know nothing of your baggage," replied the landlord.

"You detain my baggage? You dare to detain my baggage?" cried the singer.

"Who are you?" returned the landlord. "It is dark—I cannot recognise you."

"Very well, then—you detain my baggage," concluded Leon. "You shall smart for this. I will weary out your life with persecutions; I will drag you from court to court; if there is justice to be had in France, it shall be rendered between you and me. And I will make you a by-word—I will put you in a song—a scurrilous song— an indecent song—a popular song—which the boys shall sing to you in the street, and come and howl through these spars at midnight!"

He had gone on raising his voice at every phrase, for all the while the landlord was very placidly retiring; and now, when the last glimmer of light had vanished from the arch, and the last foot-step died away in the interior, Leon turned to his wife with a heroic countenance.

"Elvira," said he, "I have now a duty in life. I shall destroy that man as Eugène Sue destroyed the concierge. Let us come at once to the Gendarmerie and begin our vengeance."

He picked up the guitar-case, which had been propped against the wall, and they set forth through the silent and ill-lighted town with burning hearts.

The Gendarmerie was concealed beside the telegraph office at the bottom of a vast court, which was partly laid out in gardens; and here all the shepherds of the public lay locked in grateful sleep. It took a deal of knocking to waken one; and he, when he came at last to the door, could find no other remark but that "it was none of his business." Leon reasoned with him, threatened him, besought him; here, he said, was Madame Berthelini in evening dress—a delicate woman—in an interesting condition—the last was thrown in, I fancy, for effect; and to all this the man-at-arms made the same answer:

"It is none of my business," said he.

"Very well," said Leon, "then we shall go to the Commissary." Thither they went; the office was closed and dark; but the house was close by, and Leon was soon swinging the bell like a madman. The Commissary's wife appeared at a window. She was a thread-paper creature, and informed them that the Commissary had not yet come home.

"Is he at the Maire's?" demanded Leon.

She thought that was not unlikely.

"Where is the Maire's house?" he asked.

And she gave him some rather vague information on that point.

"Stay you here, Elvira," said Leon, "lest I should miss him by the way. If, when I return, I find you here no longer, I shall follow at once to the Black Head."

And he set out to find the Maire's. It took him some ten minutes wandering among blind lanes, and when he arrived it was already half an hour past midnight. A long white garden wall overhung by some thick chestnuts, a door with a letter-box, and an iron bell-pull, that was all that could be seen of the Maire's domicile. Leon took the bell-pull in both hands, and danced furiously upon the sidewalk. The bell itself was just upon the other side of the wall, it responded to his activity, and scattered an alarming clangour far and wide into the night.

A window was thrown open in a house across the street, and a voice inquired the cause of this untimely uproar.

"I wish the Maire," said Leon.

"He has been in bed this hour," returned the voice.

"He must get up again," retorted Leon, and he was for tackling the bell-pull once more.

"You will never make him hear," responded the voice. "The garden is of great extent, the house is at the farther end, and both the Maire and his housekeeper are deaf."

"Aha!" said Leon, pausing. "The Maire is deaf, is he? That explains." And he thought of the evening's concert with a momentary feeling of relief. "Ah!" he continued, "and so the Maire is deaf, and the garden vast, and the house at the far end?"

"And you might ring all night," added the voice, "and be none the better for it. You would only keep me awake."

"Thank you, neighbour," replied the singer. "You shall sleep."

And he made off again at his best pace for the Commissary's. Elvira was still walking to and fro before the door.

"He has not come?" asked Leon.

"Not he," she replied.

"Good," returned Leon. "I am sure our man's inside. Let me see the guitar-case. I shall lay this siege in form, Elvira; I am angry; I am indignant; I am truculently inclined; but I thank my Maker I have still a sense of fun. The unjust judge shall be importuned in a serenade, Elvira. Set him up—and set him up."

He had the case opened by this time, struck a few chords, and fell into an attitude which was irresistibly Spanish.

"Now," he continued, "feel your voice. Are you ready? Follow me!"

The guitar twanged, and the two voices upraised, in harmony and with a startling loudness, the chorus of a song of old Béranger's:

> *"Commissaire! Commissaire!*
> *Colin bat sa menagère."*

The stones of Castel-le-Gâchis thrilled at this audacious innovation. Hitherto had the night been sacred to repose and nightcaps; and now what was this? Window after window was opened;

matches scratched, and candles began to flicker; swollen sleepy faces peered forth into the starlight. There were two figures before the Commissary's house, each bolt upright, with head thrown back and eyes interrogating the starry heavens; the guitar wailed, shouted, and reverberated like half an orchestra; and the voices, with a crisp and spirited delivery, hurled the appropriate burthen at the Commissary's window. All the echoes repeated the functionary's name. It was more like an entr'acte in a farce of Molière's than a passage of real life in Castel-le-Gâchis.

The Commissary, if he was not the first, was not the last of the neighbours to yield to the influence of music, and furiously throw open the window of his bedroom. He was beside himself with rage. He leaned far over the window-sill, raving and gesticulating; the tassel of his white nightcap danced like a thing of life; he opened his mouth to dimensions hitherto unprecedented, and yet his voice, instead of escaping from it in a roar, came forth shrill and choked and tottering. A little more serenading, and it was clear he would be better acquainted with the apoplexy.

I scorn to reproduce his language; he touched upon too many serious topics by the way for a quiet story-teller. Although he was known for a man who was prompt with his tongue, and had a power of strong expression at command, he excelled himself so remarkably this night, that one maiden lady, who had got out of bed like the rest to hear the serenade, was obliged to shut her window at the second clause. Even what she had heard disquieted her conscience; and next day she said she scarcely reckoned as a maiden lady any longer.

Leon tried to explain his predicament, but he received nothing but threats of arrest by way of answer.

"If I come down to you!" cried the Commissary.

"Aye," said Leon, "do!"

"I will not!" cried the Commissary.

"You dare not!" answered Leon.

At that the Commissary closed his window.

"All is over," said the singer. "The serenade was perhaps ill-judged. These boors have no sense of humour."

"Let us get away from here," said Elvira, with a shiver. "All these people looking—it is so rude and so brutal." And then giving way once more to passion—"Brutes!" she cried aloud to the candle-lit spectators—"brutes! brutes! brutes!"

"*Sauve qui peut,*" said Leon. "You have done it now!"

And taking the guitar in one hand and the case in the other, he led the way with something too precipitate to be merely called precipitation from the scene of this absurd adventure.

4.

To the west of Castel-le-Gâchis four rows of venerable lime-trees formed, in this starry night, a twilit avenue with two side aisles of pitch darkness. Here and there stone benches were disposed between the trunks. There was not a breath of wind; a heavy atmosphere of perfume hung about the alleys; and every leaf stood stock-still upon its twig. Hither, after vainly knocking at an inn or two, the Berthelinis came at length to pass the night. After an amiable contention, Leon insisted on giving his coat to Elvira, and they sat down together on the first bench in silence. Leon made a cigarette, which he smoked to an end, looking up into the trees, and, beyond them, at the constellations, of which he tried vainly to recall the names. The silence was broken by the church bell; it rang the four quarters on a light and tinkling measure; then followed a single deep stroke that died slowly away with a thrill; and stillness resumed its empire.

"One," said Leon. "Four hours till daylight. It is warm; it is starry; I have matches and tobacco. Do not let us exaggerate, Elvira—the experience is positively charming. I feel a glow within me; I am born again. This is the poetry of life. Think of Cooper's novels, my dear."

"Leon," she said, fiercely, "how can you talk such wicked, infamous nonsense? To pass all night out of doors—it is like a nightmare! We shall die."

"You suffer yourself to be led away," he replied, soothingly. "It is not unpleasant here; only you brood. Come, now, let us repeat a scene. Shall we try Alceste and Célimène? No? Or a passage from the 'Two Orphans'? Come, now, it will occupy your mind; I will play up to you as I never have played before; I feel art moving in my bones."

"Hold your tongue," she cried, "or you will drive me mad! Will nothing solemnise you—not even this hideous situation?"

"Oh, hideous!" objected Leon. "Hideous is not the word. Why,

where would you be? *'Dites, la jeune belle, où voulez-vous aller?'* "
he carolled. "Well, now," he went on, opening the guitar-case,
"there's another idea for you—sing. Sing *'Dites, la jeune belle!'* It
will compose your spirits, Elvira, I am sure."

And without waiting an answer he began to strum the sym-
phony. The first chords awoke a young man who was lying asleep
upon a neighbouring bench.

"Hullo!" cried the young man, "who are you?"

"Under which king, Bezonian?" declaimed the artist. "Speak or
die!"

Or if it was not exactly that, it was something to much the same
purpose from a French tragedy.

The young man drew near in the twilight. He was a tall, powerful, gentlemanly fellow, with a somewhat puffy face, dressed in a
grey tweed suit, with a deer-stalker hat of the same material; and
as he now came forward he carried a knapsack slung upon one
arm.

"Are you camping out here, too?" he asked, with a strong English accent. "I'm not sorry for company."

Leon explained their misadventure; and the other told them
that he was a Cambridge undergraduate on a walking tour, that
he had run short of money, could no longer pay for his night's
lodging, had already been camping out for two nights, and feared
he should require to continue the same manœuvre for at least two
nights more.

"Luckily, it's jolly weather," he concluded.

"You hear that, Elvira," said Leon. "Madame Berthelini," he
went on, "is ridiculously affected by this trifling occurrence. For
my part, I find it romantic and far from uncomfortable; or at
least," he added, shifting on the stone bench, "not quite so uncomfortable as might have been expected. But pray be seated."

"Yes," returned the undergraduate, sitting down, "it's rather
nice than otherwise when once you're used to it; only it's devilish
difficult to get washed. I like the fresh air and these stars and
things."

"Aha!" said Leon, "Monsieur is an artist."

"An artist?" returned the other, with a blank stare. "Not if I
know it!"

"Pardon me," said the actor. "What you said this moment about
the orbs of heaven———"

"Oh, nonsense!" cried the Englishman. "A fellow may admire the stars and be anything he likes."

"You have an artist's nature, however, Mr. —— I beg your pardon; may I, without indiscretion, inquire your name?" asked Leon.

"My name is Stubbs," replied the Englishman.

"I thank you," returned Leon. "Mine is Berthelini—Leon Berthelini, ex-artist of the theatres of Montrouge, Belleville, and Montmartre. Humble as you see me, I have created with applause more than one important *rôle.* The Press were unanimous in praise of my Howling Devil of the Mountains, in the piece of the same name. Madame, whom I now present to you, is herself an artist, and I must not omit to state, a better artist than her husband. She also is a creator; she created nearly twenty successful songs at one of the principal Parisian music-halls. But, to continue, I was saying you had an artist's nature, Monsieur Stubbs, and you must permit me to be a judge in such a question. I trust you will not falsify your instincts; let me beseech you to follow the career of an artist."

"Thank you," returned Stubbs, with a chuckle. "I'm going to be a banker."

"No," said Leon, "do not say so. Not that. A man with such a nature as yours should not derogate so far. What are a few privations here and there, so long as you are working for a high and noble goal?"

"This fellow's mad," thought Stubbs; "but the woman's rather pretty, and he's not bad fun for himself, if you come to that." What he said was different. "I thought you said you were an actor?"

"I certainly did so," replied Leon. "I am one, or, alas! I was."

"And so you want me to be an actor, do you?" continued the undergraduate. "Why, man, I could never so much as learn the stuff; my memory's like a sieve; and as for acting, I've no more idea than a cat."

"The stage is not the only course," said Leon. "Be a sculptor, be a dancer, be a poet or a novelist; follow your heart, in short, and do some thorough work before you die."

"And do you call these things *art?*" inquired Stubbs.

"Why, certainly!" returned Leon. "Are they not all branches?"

"Oh! I didn't know," replied the Englishman. "I thought an artist meant a fellow who painted."

The singer stared at him in some surprise.

"It is the difference of language," he said at last. "This Tower of Babel, when shall we have paid for it? If I could speak English you would follow me more readily."

"Between you and me, I don't believe I should," replied the other. "You seem to have thought a devil of a lot about this business. For my part, I admire the stars, and like to have them shining —it's so cheery—but hang me if I had an idea it had anything to do with art! It's not in my line, you see. I'm not intellectual; I have no end of trouble to scrape through my exams., I can tell you! But I'm not a bad sort at bottom," he added, seeing his interlocutor looked distressed even in the dim starshine, "and I rather like the play, and music, and guitars, and things."

Leon had a perception that the understanding was incomplete. He changed the subject.

"And so you travel on foot?" he continued. "How romantic! How courageous! And how are you pleased with my land? How does the scenery affect you among these wild hills of ours?"

"Well, the fact is," began Stubbs—he was about to say that he didn't care for scenery, which was not at all true, being, on the contrary, only an athletic undergraduate pretension; but he had begun to suspect that Berthelini liked a different sort of meat, and substituted something else—"The fact is, I think it jolly. They told me it was no good up here; even the guide-book said so; but I don't know what they meant. I think it is deuced pretty—upon my word, I do."

At this moment, in the most unexpected manner, Elvira burst into tears.

"My voice!" she cried. "Leon, if I stay here longer I shall lose my voice!"

"You shall not stay another moment," cried the actor. "If I have to beat in a door, if I have to burn the town, I shall find you shelter."

With that, he replaced the guitar, and comforting her with some caresses, drew her arm through his.

"Monsieur Stubbs," said he, taking off his hat, "the reception I offer you is rather problematical; but let me beseech you to give us the pleasure of your society. You are a little embarrassed for the moment; you must, indeed, permit me to advance what may be necessary. I ask it as a favour; we must not part so soon after having met so strangely."

"Oh, come, you know," said Stubbs, "I can't let a fellow like you——" And there he paused, feeling somehow or other on a wrong tack.

"I do not wish to employ menaces," continued Leon, with a smile; "but if you refuse, indeed I shall not take it kindly."

"I don't quite see my way out of it," thought the under-graduate; and then, after a pause, he said, aloud and ungraciously enough, "All right. I—I'm very much obliged, of course." And he proceeded to follow them, thinking in his heart, "But it's bad form, all the same, to force an obligation on a fellow."

5.

Leon strode ahead as if he knew exactly where he was going; the sobs of Madame were still faintly audible, and no one uttered a word. A dog barked furiously in a courtyard as they went by; then the church clock struck two, and many domestic clocks followed or preceded it in piping tones. And just then Berthelini spied a light. It burned in a small house on the outskirts of the town, and thither the party now directed their steps.

"It is always a chance," said Leon.

The house in question stood back from the street behind an open space, part garden, part turnip field; and several outhouses stood forward from either wing at right angles to the front. One of these had recently undergone some change. An enormous window, looking towards the north, had been effected in the wall and roof, and Leon began to hope it was a studio.

"If it's only a painter," he said, with a chuckle, "ten to one we get as good a welcome as we want."

"I thought painters were principally poor," said Stubbs.

"Ah," cried Leon, "you do not know the world as I do. The poorer the better for us."

And the trio advanced into the turnip field.

The light was in the ground floor; as one window was brightly illuminated and two others more faintly, it might be supposed that there was a single lamp in one corner of a large apartment; and a

certain tremulousness and temporary dwindling showed that a live
fire contributed to the effect. The sound of a voice now became
audible; and the trespassers paused to listen. It was pitched in
a high, angry key, but had still a good, full, and masculine note in
it. The utterance was voluble, too voluble even to be quite distinct; a stream of words, rising and falling, with ever and again a
phrase thrown out by itself, as if the speaker reckoned on its
virtue.

Suddenly another voice joined in. This time it was a woman's;
and if the man were angry, the woman was incensed to the degree
of fury. There was that absolutely blank composure known to
suffering males; that colourless unnatural speech which shows a
spirit accurately balanced between homicide and hysterics; the
tone in which the best of women sometimes utter words worse than
death to those most dear to them. If Abstract Bones-and-Sepulchre
were to be endowed with the gift of speech, thus, and not otherwise, would it discourse. Leon was a brave man, and I fear he was
somewhat sceptically given (he had been educated in a Papistical
country), but the habit of childhood prevailed, and he crossed
himself devoutly. He had met several women in his career. It was
obvious that his instinct had not deceived him, for the male voice
broke forth instantly in a towering passion.

The undergraduate, who had not understood the significance
of the woman's contribution, pricked up his ears at the change
upon the man.

"There's going to be a free fight," he opined.

There was another retort from the woman, still calm but a little
higher.

"Hysterics?" asked Leon of his wife. "Is that the stage direction?"

"How should I know?" returned Elvira, somewhat tartly.

"Oh, woman, woman!" said Leon, beginning to open the guitar-
case. "It is one of the burdens of my life, Monsieur Stubbs; they
support each other; they always pretend there is no system; they
say it's nature. Even Madame Berthelini, who is a dramatic artist!"

"You are heartless, Leon," said Elvira; "that woman is in
trouble."

"And the man, my angel?" inquired Berthelini, passing the ribbon of his guitar. "And the man, *m'amour?*"

"He is a man," she answered.

"You hear that?" said Leon to Stubbs. "It is not too late for you. Mark the intonation. And now," he continued, "what are we to give them?"

"Are you going to sing?" asked Stubbs.

"I am a troubadour," replied Leon. "I claim a welcome by and for my art. If I were a banker could I do as much?"

"Well, you wouldn't need, you know," answered the undergraduate.

"Egad," said Leon, "but that's true. Elvira, that is true."

"Of course it is," she replied. "Did you not know it?"

"My dear," answered Leon, impressively, "I know nothing but what is agreeable. Even my knowledge of life is a work of art superiorly composed. But what are we to give them? It should be something appropriate."

Visions of "Let dogs delight" passed through the undergraduate's mind; but it occurred to him that the poetry was English and that he did not know the air. Hence he contributed no suggestion.

"Something about our houselessness," said Elvira.

"I have it," cried Leon. And he broke forth into a song of Pierre Dupont's:

> *"Savez-vous où gîte*
> *Mai, ce joli mois?"*

Elvira joined in; so did Stubbs, with a good ear and voice, but an imperfect acquaintance with the music. Leon and the guitar were equal to the situation. The actor dispensed his throat-notes with prodigality and enthusiasm; and, as he looked up to heaven in his heroic way, tossing the black ringlets, it seemed to him that the very stars contributed a dumb applause to his efforts, and the universe lent him its silence for a chorus. That is one of the best features of the heavenly bodies, that they belong to everybody in particular; and a man like Leon, a chronic Endymion who managed to get along without encouragement, is always the world's centre for himself.

He alone—and it is to be noted, he was the worst singer of the three—took the music seriously to heart, and judged the serenade from a high artistic point of view. Elvira, on the other hand, was preoccupied about their reception; and, as for Stubbs, he considered the whole affair in the light of a broad joke.

"Know you the lair of May, the lovely month?" went the three voices in the turnip field.

The inhabitants were plainly fluttered; the light moved to and fro, strengthening in one window, paling in another; and then the door was thrown open, and a man in a blouse appeared on the threshold carrying a lamp. He was a powerful young fellow, with bewildered hair and beard, wearing his neck open; his blouse was stained with oil-colours in a harlequinesque disorder; and there was something rural in the droop and bagginess of his belted trousers.

From immediately behind him, and indeed over his shoulder, a woman's face looked out into the darkness; it was pale and a little weary, although still young; it wore a dwindling, disappearing prettiness, soon to be quite gone, and the expression was both gentle and sour, and reminded one faintly of the taste of certain drugs. For all that, it was not a face to dislike; when the prettiness had vanished, it seemed as if a certain pale beauty might step in to take its place; and as both the mildness and the asperity were characters of youth, it might be hoped that, with years, both would merge into a constant, brave, and not unkindly temper.

"What is all this?" cried the man.

6.

Leon had his hat in his hand at once. He came forward with his customary grace; it was a moment which would have earned him a round of cheering on the stage. Elvira and Stubbs advanced behind him, like a couple of Admetus's sheep following the god Apollo.

"Sir," said Leon, "the hour is unpardonably late, and our little serenade has the air of an impertinence. Believe me, sir, it is an appeal. Monsieur is an artist, I perceive. We are here three artists benighted and without shelter, one a woman—a delicate woman— in evening dress—in an interesting situation. This will not fail to touch the woman's heart of Madame, whom I perceive indistinctly behind Monsieur her husband, and whose face speaks eloquently of a well-regulated mind. Ah! Monsieur, Madame—one generous moment, and you make three people happy! Two or three hours beside your fire—I ask it of Monsieur in the name of Art—I ask it of Madame by the sanctity of womanhood."

The two, as by a tacit consent, drew back from the door.

"Come in," said the man.

"Entrez, Madame," said the woman.

The door opened directly upon the kitchen of the house, which was to all appearance the only sitting-room. The furniture was both plain and scanty; but there were one or two landscapes on the wall handsomely framed, as if they had already visited the committee rooms of an exhibition and been thence extruded. Leon walked up to the pictures and represented the part of a connoisseur before each in turn, with his usual dramatic insight and force. The master of the house, as if irresistibly attracted, followed him from canvas to canvas with the lamp. Elvira was led directly to the fire, where she proceeded to warm herself, while Stubbs stood in the middle of the floor and followed the proceedings of Leon with mild astonishment in his eyes.

"You should see them by daylight," said the artist.

"I promise myself that pleasure," said Leon. "You possess, sir, if you will permit me an observation, the art of composition to a T."

"You are very good," returned the other. "But should you not draw nearer to the fire?"

"With all my heart," said Leon.

And the whole party soon gathered at the table over a hasty and not an elegant cold supper, washed down with the least of small wines. Nobody liked the meal, but nobody complained; they put a good face upon it, one and all, and made a great clattering of knives and forks. To see Leon eating a single cold sausage was to see a triumph; by the time he had done he had got through as much pantomime as would have sufficed for a baron of beef, and he had the relaxed expression of the over-eaten.

As Elvira had naturally taken a place by the side of Leon, and Stubbs as naturally, although I believe unconsciously, by the side of Elvira, the host and hostess were left together. Yet it was to be noted that they never addressed a word to each other, nor so much as suffered their eyes to meet. The interrupted skirmish still survived in ill feeling; and the instant the guests departed it would break forth again as bitterly as ever. The talk wandered from this to that subject—for with one accord the party had declared it was too late to go to bed; but those two never relaxed towards each other; Goneril and Regan in a sisterly tiff were not more bent on enmity.

It chanced that Elvira was so much tired by all the little excitements of the night, that for once she laid aside her company manners, which were both easy and correct, and in the most natural manner in the world leaned her head on Leon's shoulder. At the same time, fatigue suggesting tenderness, she locked the fingers of her right hand into those of her husband's left; and, half closing her eyes, dozed off into a golden borderland between sleep and waking. But all the time she was not unaware of what was passing, and saw the painter's wife studying her with looks between contempt and envy.

It occurred to Leon that his constitution demanded the use of some tobacco; and he undid his fingers from Elvira's in order to roll a cigarette. It was gently done, and he took care that his indulgence should in no other way disturb his wife's position. But it seemed to catch the eye of the painter's wife with a special significancy. She looked straight before her for an instant, and then, with a swift and stealthy movement, took hold of her husband's hand below the table. Alas! she might have spared herself the dexterity. For the poor fellow was so overcome by this caress that he stopped with his mouth open in the middle of a word, and by the expression of his face plainly declared to all the company that his thoughts had been diverted into softer channels.

If it had not been rather amiable, it would have been absurdly droll. His wife at once withdrew her touch; but it was plain she had to exert some force. Thereupon the young man coloured and looked for a moment beautiful.

Leon and Elvira both observed the by-play, and a shock passed from one to the other; for they were inveterate match-makers, especially between those who were already married.

"I beg your pardon," said Leon, suddenly. "I see no use in pretending. Before we came in here we heard sounds indicating— if I may so express myself—an imperfect harmony."

"Sir——" began the man."

But the woman was beforehand.

"It is quite true," she said. "I see no cause to be ashamed. If my husband is mad I shall at least do my utmost to prevent the consequences. Picture to yourself, Monsieur and Madame," she went on, for she passed Stubbs over, "that this wretched person—a dauber, an incompetent, not fit to be a sign-painter—receives this morning an admirable offer from an uncle—an uncle of my own, my mother's brother, and tenderly beloved—of a clerkship with nearly a hundred and fifty pounds a year, and that he—picture to yourself!—he refused it! Why? For the sake of Art, he says. Look at his art, I say—look at it! Is it fit to be seen? Ask him—is it fit to be sold? And it is for this, Monsieur and Madame, that he condemns me to the most deplorable existence, without luxuries, without comforts, in a vile suburb of a country town. *O non!*" she cried, "*non—je ne me tairai pas—c'est plus fort que moi!* I take these gentlemen and this lady for judges—is this kind? is it decent? is it manly? Do I not deserve better at his hands after having married him and"—(a visible hitch)—"done everything in the world to please him?"

I doubt if there were ever a more embarrassed company at a table; every one looked like a fool; and the husband like the biggest.

"The art of Monsieur, however," said Elvira, breaking the silence, "is not wanting in distinction."

"It has this distinction," said the wife, "that nobody will buy it."

"I should have supposed a clerkship——" began Stubbs.

"Art is Art," swept in Leon. "I salute Art. It is the beautiful, the divine; it is the spirit of the world, and the pride of life. But——" And the actor paused.

"A clerkship——" began Stubbs.

"I'll tell you what it is," said the painter. "I am an artist, and as this gentleman says, Art is this and the other; but of course, if my wife is going to make my life a piece of perdition all day long, I prefer to go and drown myself out of hand."

"Go!" said his wife. "I should like to see you!"

"I was going to say," resumed Stubbs, "that a fellow may be a clerk and paint almost as much as he likes. I know a fellow in a bank who makes capital water-colour sketches; he even sold one for seven-and-six."

To both the women this seemed a plank of safety; each hopefully interrogated the countenance of her lord; even Elvira, an artist herself!—but indeed there must be something permanently mercantile in the female nature. The two men exchanged a glance; it was tragic; not otherwise might two philosophers salute, as at the end of a labourious life each recognised that he was still a mystery to his disciples.

Leon arose.

"Art is Art," he repeated, sadly. "It is not water-colour sketches, nor practising on a piano. It is a life to be lived."   .

"And in the meantime people starve!" observed the woman of the house. "If that's a life, it is not one for me."

"I'll tell you what," burst forth Leon; "you, Madame, go into another room and talk it over with my wife; and I'll stay here and talk it over with your husband. It may come to nothing, but let's try."

"I am very willing," replied the young woman; and she proceeded to light a candle. "This way, if you please." And she led Elvira up-stairs into a bedroom.

"The fact is," said she, sitting down, "that my husband cannot paint."

"No more can mine act," replied Elvira.

"I should have thought he could," returned the other; "he seems clever."

"He is so, and the best of men besides," said Elvira; "but he cannot act."

"At least he is not a sheer humbug like mine; he can at least sing."

"You mistake Leon," returned his wife, warmly. "He does not even pretend to sing; he has too fine a taste; he does so for a living. And, believe me, neither of the men are humbugs. They are people with a mission—which they cannot carry out."

"Humbug or not," replied the other, "you came very near passing the night in the fields; and, for my part, I live in terror of starvation. I should think it was a man's mission to think twice about his wife. But it appears not. Nothing is their mission but to play the fool. Oh!" she broke out, "is it not something dreary to think of that man of mine? If he could only do it, who would care? But no—not he—no more than I can!"

"Have you any children?" asked Elvira.

"No; but then I may."

"Children change so much," said Elvira, with a sigh.

And just then from the room below there flew up a sudden

snapping chord on the guitar; one followed after another; then the voice of Leon joined in; and there was an air being played and sung that stopped the speech of the two women. The wife of the painter stood like a person transfixed; Elvira, looking into her eyes, could see all manner of beautiful memories and kind thoughts that were passing in and out of her soul with every note; it was a piece of her youth that went before her; a green French plain, the smell of apple-flowers, the far and shining ringlets of a river, and the words and presence of love.

"Leon has hit the nail," thought Elvira to herself, "I wonder how."

The how was plain enough. Leon had asked the painter if there were no air connected with courtship and pleasant times; and having learned what he wished, and allowed an interval to pass, he had soared forth into

> *"O mon amante,*
> *O mon desir,*
> *Sachons cueillir*
> *L'heure charmante!"*

"Pardon me, Madame," said the painter's wife, "your husband sings admirably well."

"He sings that with some feeling," replied Elvira, critically, although she was a little moved herself, for the song cut both ways in the upper chamber; "but it is as an actor and not as a musician."

"Life is very sad," said the other; "it so wastes away under one's fingers."

"I have not found it so," replied Elvira. "I think the good parts of it last and grow greater every day."

"Frankly, how would you advise me?"

"Frankly, I would let my husband do what he wished. He is obviously a very loving painter; you have not yet tried him as a clerk. And you know—if it were only as the possible father of your children—it is as well to keep him at his best."

"He is an excellent fellow," said the wife.

They kept it up till sunrise with music and all manner of good-fellowship; and at sunrise, while the sky was still temperate and clear, they separated on the threshold with a thousand excellent wishes for each other's welfare. Castel-le-Gâchis was beginning to send up its smoke against the golden East; and the church bell was ringing six.

"My guitar is a familiar spirit," said Leon, as he and Elvira took the nearest way toward the inn; "it resuscitated a Commissary, created an English tourist, and reconciled a man and wife."

Stubbs, on his part, went off into the morning with reflections of his own.

"They are all mad," thought he, "all mad—but wonderfully decent."

The Sire De Malétroit's Door

D ENIS DE BEAULIEU WAS NOT YET TWO-AND-TWENTY, BUT HE counted himself a grown man, and a very accomplished cavalier into the bargain. Lads were early formed in that rough, warfaring epoch; and when one has been in a pitched battle and a dozen raids, has killed one's man in an honourable fashion, and knows a thing or two of strategy and mankind, a certain swagger in the gait is surely to be pardoned. He had put up his horse with due care, and supped with due deliberation; and then, in a very agreeable frame of mind, went out to pay a visit in the grey of the evening. It was not a very wise proceeding on the young man's part. He would have done better to remain beside the fire or go decently to bed. For the town was full of the troops of Burgundy and England under a mixed command; and though Denis was there on safe-conduct, his safe-conduct was like to serve him little on a chance encounter.

It was September, 1429; the weather had fallen sharp; a flighty piping wind, laden with showers, beat about the township; and the dead leaves ran riot along the streets. Here and there a window was already lighted up; and the noise of men-at-arms making merry over supper within, came forth in fits and was swallowed up and carried away by the wind. The night fell swiftly; the flag of England, fluttering on the spire-top, grew ever fainter and fainter against the flying clouds—a black speck like a swallow in the tumultuous, leaden chaos of the sky. As the night fell the wind rose, and began to hoot under archways and roar amid the tree-tops in the valley below the town.

Denis de Beaulieu walked fast and was soon knocking at his

friend's door; but though he promised himself to stay only a little while and make an early return, his welcome was so pleasant, and he found so much to delay him, that it was already long past midnight before he said good-bye upon the threshold. The wind had fallen again in the meanwhile; the night was as black as the grave; not a star, nor a glimmer of moonshine, slipped through the canopy of cloud. Denis was ill-acquainted with the intricate lanes of Chateau Landon; even by daylight he had found some trouble in picking his way; and in this absolute darkness he soon lost it altogether. He was certain of one thing only—to keep mounting the hill; for his friend's house lay at the lower end, or tail, of Chateau Landon, while the inn was up at the head, under the great church spire. With this clue to go upon he stumbled and groped forward, now breathing more freely in open places where there was a good slice of sky overhead, now feeling along the wall in stifling closes. It is an eerie and mysterious position to be thus submerged in opaque blackness in an almost unknown town. The silence is terrifying in its possibilities. The touch of cold window-bars to the exploring hand startles the man like the touch of a toad; the inequalities of the pavement shake his heart into his mouth; a piece of denser darkness threatens an ambuscade or a chasm in the pathway; and where the air is brighter, the houses put on strange and bewildering appearances, as if to lead him farther from his way. For Denis, who had to regain his inn without attracting notice, there was real danger as well as mere discomfort in the walk; and he went warily and boldly at once, and at every corner paused to make an observation.

He had been for some time threading a lane so narrow that he could touch a wall with either hand when it began to open out and go sharply downward. Plainly this lay no longer in the direction of his inn; but the hope of a little more light tempted him forward to reconnoitre. The lane ended in a terrace with a bartizan wall, which gave an outlook between high houses, as out of an embrasure, into the valley lying dark and formless several hundred feet below. Denis looked down, and could discern a few tree-tops waving and a single speck of brightness where the river ran across a weir. The weather was clearing up, and the sky had lightened, so as to show the outline of the heavier clouds and the dark margin of the hills. By the uncertain glimmer, the house on his left hand should be a place of some pretensions; it was sur-

mounted by several pinnacles and turret-tops; the round stern of
a chapel, with a fringe of flying buttresses, projected boldly from
the main block; and the door was sheltered under a deep porch
carved with figures and overhung by two long gargoyles. The
windows of the chapel gleamed through their intricate tracery with
a light as of many tapers, and threw out the buttresses and the
peaked roof in a more intense blackness against the sky. It was
plainly the hotel of some great family of the neighbourhood; and
as it reminded Denis of a town house of his own at Bourges, he
stood for some time gazing up at it and mentally gauging the skill
of the architects and the consideration of the two families.

There seemed to be no issue to the terrace but the lane by which
he had reached it; he could only retrace his steps, but he had
gained some notion of his whereabouts, and hoped by this means
to hit the main thoroughfare and speedily regain the inn. He was
reckoning without that chapter of accidents which was to make
this night memorable above all others in his career; for he had
not gone back above a hundred yards before he saw a light coming to meet him, and heard loud voices speaking together in the
echoing narrows of the lane. It was a party of men-at-arms going
the night round with torches. Denis assured himself that they had
all been making free with the wine-bowl, and were in no mood to
be particular about safe-conducts or the niceties of chivalrous war.
It was as like as not that they would kill him like a dog and leave
him where he fell. The situation was inspiriting but nervous.
Their own torches would conceal him from sight, he reflected;
and he hoped that they would drown the noise of his footsteps
with their own empty voices. If he were but fleet and silent, he
might evade their notice altogether.

Unfortunately, as he turned to beat a retreat, his foot rolled
upon a pebble; he fell against the wall with an ejaculation, and
his sword rang loudly on the stones. Two or three voices demanded
who went there—some in French, some in English; but Denis
made no reply, and ran the faster down the lane. Once upon the
terrace, he paused to look back. They still kept calling after him,
and just then began to double the pace in pursuit, with a considerable clank of armour, and great tossing of the torchlight to
and fro in the narrow jaws of the passage.

Denis cast a look around and darted into the porch. There he
might escape observation, or—if that were too much to expect—

was in a capital posture whether for parley or defence. So thinking, he drew his sword and tried to set his back against the door. To his surprise, it yielded behind his weight; and though he turned in a moment, continued to swing back on oiled and noiseless hinges, until it stood wide open on a black interior. When things fall out opportunely for the person concerned, he is not apt to be critical about the how or why, his own immediate personal convenience seeming a sufficient reason for the strangest oddities and revolutions in our sublunary things; and so Denis, without a moment's hesitation, stepped within and partly closed the door behind him to conceal his place of refuge. Nothing was further from his thoughts than to close it altogether; but for some inexplicable reason—perhaps by a spring or a weight—the ponderous mass of oak whipped itself out of his fingers and clanked to, with a formidable rumble and a noise like the falling of an automatic bar.

The round, at that very moment, debouched upon the terrace and proceeded to summon him with shouts and curses. He heard them ferreting in the dark corners; the stock of a lance even rattled along the outer surface of the door behind which he stood; but these gentlemen were in too high a humour to be long delayed, and soon made off down a corkscrew pathway which had escaped Denis's observation, and passed out of sight and hearing along the battlements of the town.

Denis breathed again. He gave them a few minutes' grace for fear of accidents, and then groped about for some means of opening the door and slipping forth again. The inner surface was quite smooth, not a handle, not a moulding, not a projection of any sort. He got his finger-nails round the edges and pulled, but the mass was immovable. He shook it, it was as firm as a rock. Denis de Beaulieu frowned and gave vent to a little noiseless whistle. What ailed the door? he wondered. Why was it open? How came it to shut so easily and so effectually after him? There was something obscure and under-hand about all this, that was little to the young man's fancy. It looked like a snare; and yet who could suppose a snare in such a quiet by-street and in a house of so prosperous and even noble an exterior? And yet—snare or no snare, intentionally or unintentionally—here he was, prettily trapped; and for the life of him he could see no way out of it again. The darkness began to weigh upon him. He gave ear; all was silence without, but within and close by he seemed to catch a faint sighing, a faint sobbing rustle, a little stealthy creak—as though many persons were at his side, holding themselves quite still, and governing even their respiration with the extreme of slyness. The idea went to his vitals with a shock, and he faced about suddenly as if to defend his life. Then, for the first time, he became aware of a light about the level of his eyes and at some distance in the interior of the house—a vertical thread of light, widening towards the bottom, such as might escape between two wings of arras over a doorway. To see anything was a relief to Denis; it was like a piece of solid ground to a man labouring in a morass; his mind seized upon it with avidity; and he stood staring at it and trying to piece together some logical conception of his surroundings. Plainly there was a flight of steps ascending from his own level to that of this illuminated doorway; and indeed he thought he could make out another thread of light, as fine as a needle, and as faint as phosphorescence, which might very well be reflected along the polished wood of a handrail. Since he had begun to suspect that he was not alone, his heart had continued to beat with smothering violence, and an intolerable desire for action of any sort had possessed itself of his spirit. He was in deadly peril, he believed. What could be more natural than to mount the staircase, lift the curtain, and confront his difficulty at once? At least he would be dealing with something tangible; at least he would be no longer in the dark. He stepped slowly forward with outstretched hands, until his foot struck the bottom step; then he rapidly scaled the stairs, stood for a moment to compose his expression, lifted the arras and went in.

He found himself in a large apartment of polished stone. There were three doors; one on each of three sides; all similarly curtained with tapestry. The fourth side was occupied by two large windows and a great stone chimney-piece, carved with the arms of the Malétroits. Denis recognised the bearings, and was gratified to find himself in such good hands. The room was strongly illuminated; but it contained little furniture except a heavy table and a chair or two, the hearth was innocent of fire, and the pavement was but sparsely strewn with rushes clearly many days old.

On a high chair beside the chimney, and directly facing Denis as he entered, sat a little old gentleman in a fur tippet. He sat with

his legs crossed and his hands folded, and a cup of spiced wine
stood by his elbow on a bracket on the wall. His countenance had
a strongly masculine cast; not properly human, but such as we see
in the bull, the goat, or the domestic boar; something equivocal
and wheedling, something greedy, brutal, and dangerous. The
upper lip was inordinately full, as though swollen by a blow or a
toothache; and the smile, the peaked eyebrows, and the small,
strong eyes were quaintly and almost comically evil in expression.
Beautiful white hair hung straight all round his head, like a
saint's, and fell in a single curl upon the tippet. His beard and
moustache were the pink of venerable sweetness. Age, probably in
consequence of inordinate precautions, had left no mark upon his
hands; and the Malétroit hand was famous. It would be difficult
to imagine anything at once so fleshy and so delicate in design;
the taper, sensual fingers were like those of one of Leonardo's
women; the fork of the thumb made a dimpled protuberance when
closed; the nails were perfectly shaped, and of a dead, surprising
whiteness. It rendered his aspect tenfold more redoubtable, that a
man with hands like these should keep them devoutly folded like
a virgin martyr—that a man with so intent and startling an expression of face should sit patiently on his seat and contemplate
people with an unwinking stare, like a god, or a god's statue. His
quiescence seemed ironical and treacherous, it fitted so poorly with
his looks.

Such was Alain, Sire de Malétroit.

Denis and he looked silently at each other for a second or two.

"Pray step in," said the Sire de Malétroit. "I have been expecting you all the evening."

He had not risen, but he accompanied his words with a smile
and a slight but courteous inclination of the head. Partly from the
smile, partly from the strange musical murmur with which the
Sire prefaced his observation, Denis felt a strong shudder of disgust go through his marrow. And what with disgust and honest
confusion of mind, he could scarcely get words together in reply.

"I fear," he said, "that this is a double accident. I am not the
person you suppose me. It seems you were looking for a visit; but
for my part, nothing was further from my thoughts—nothing
could be more contrary to my wishes—than this intrusion."

"Well, well," replied the old gentleman indulgently, "here you
are, which is the main point. Seat yourself, my friend, and put your-

self entirely at your ease. We shall arrange our little affairs presently."

Denis perceived that the matter was still complicated with some misconception, and he hastened to continue his explanations.

"Your door . . ." he began.

"About my door?" asked the other, raising his peaked eyebrows. "A little piece of ingenuity." And he shrugged his shoulders. "A hospitable fancy! By your own account, you were not desirous of making my acquaintance. We old people look for such reluctance now and then; when it touches our honour, we cast about until we find some way of overcoming it. You arrive uninvited, but believe me, very welcome."

"You persist in error, sir," said Denis. "There can be no question between you and me. I am a stranger in this country-side. My name is Denis, damoiseau de Beaulieu. If you see me in your house, it is only——"

"My young friend," interrupted the other, "you will permit me to have my own ideas on that subject. They probably differ from yours at the present moment," he added with a leer, "but time will show which of us is in the right."

Denis was convinced he had to do with a lunatic. He seated himself with a shrug, content to wait the upshot; and a pause ensued, during which he thought he could distinguish a hurried gabbling as of prayer from behind the arras immediately opposite him. Sometimes there seemed to be but one person engaged, sometimes two; and the vehemence of the voice, low as it was, seemed to indicate either great haste or an agony of spirit. It occurred to him that this piece of tapestry covered the entrance to the chapel he had noticed from without.

The old gentleman meanwhile surveyed Denis from head to foot with a smile, and from time to time emitted little noises like a bird or a mouse, which seemed to indicate a high degree of satisfaction. This state of matters became rapidly insupportable; and Denis, to put an end to it, remarked politely that the wind had gone down.

The old gentleman fell into a fit of silent laughter, so prolonged and violent that he became quite red in the face. Denis got upon his feet at once, and put on his hat with a flourish.

"Sir," he said, "if you are in your wits, you have affronted me grossly. If you are out of them, I flatter myself I can find better employment for my brains than to talk with lunatics. My conscience is clear; you have made a fool of me from the first moment; you have refused to hear my explanations; and now there is no power under God will make me stay here any longer; and if I cannot make my way out in a more decent fashion, I will hack your door in pieces with my sword."

The Sire de Malétroit raised his right hand and wagged it at Denis with the fore and little fingers extended.

"My dear nephew," he said, "sit down."

"Nephew!" retorted Denis, "you lie in your throat;" and he snapped his fingers in his face.

"Sit down, you rogue!" cried the old gentleman, in a sudden, harsh voice, like the barking of a dog. "Do you fancy," he went on, "that when I had made my little contrivance for the door I had stopped short with that? If you prefer to be bound hand and foot till your bones ache, rise and try to go away. If you choose to remain a free young buck, agreeably conversing with an old gentleman—why, sit where you are in peace, and God be with you."

"Do you mean I am a prisoner?" demanded Denis.

"I state the facts," replied the other. "I would rather leave the conclusion to yourself."

Denis sat down again. Externally he managed to keep pretty calm, but within, he was now boiling with anger, now chilled with apprehension. He no longer felt convinced that he was dealing with a madman. And if the old gentleman was sane, what, in God's name, had he to look for? What absurd or tragical adventure had befallen him? What countenance was he to assume?

While he was thus unpleasantly reflecting, the arras that overhung the chapel door was raised, and a tall priest in his robes came forth and, giving a long, keen stare at Denis, said something in an undertone to Sire de Malétroit.

"She is in a better frame of spirit?" asked the latter.

"She is more resigned, messire," replied the priest.

"Now the Lord help her, she is hard to please!" sneered the old gentleman. "A likely stripling—not ill-born—and of her own choosing, too? Why, what more would the jade have?"

"The situation is not usual for a young damsel," said the other, "and somewhat trying to her blushes."

"She should have thought of that before she began the dance.

It was none of my choosing, God knows that: but since she is in it, by our lady, she shall carry it to the end." And then addressing Denis, "Monsieur de Beaulieu," he asked, "may I present you to my niece? She has been waiting your arrival, I may say, with even greater impatience than myself."

Denis had resigned himself with a good grace—all he desired was to know the worst of it as speedily as possible; so he rose at once, and bowed in acquiescence. The Sire de Malétroit followed his example and limped, with the assistance of the chaplain's arm, towards the chapel-door. The priest pulled aside the arras, and all three entered. The building had considerable architectural pretensions. A light groining sprang from six stout columns, and hung down in two rich pendants from the centre of the vault. The place terminated behind the altar in a round end, embossed and honeycombed with a superfluity of ornament in relief, and pierced by many little windows shaped like stars, trefoils, or wheels. These windows were imperfectly glazed, so that the night air circulated freely in the chapel. The tapers, of which there must have been half a hundred burning on the altar, were unmercifully blown about; and the light went through many different phases of brilliancy and semi-eclipse. On the steps in front of the altar knelt a young girl richly attired as a bride. A chill settled over Denis as he observed her costume; he fought with desperate energy against the conclusion that was being thrust upon his mind; it could not— it should not—be as he feared.

"Blanche," said the Sire, in his most flute-like tones, "I have brought a friend to see you, my little girl; turn round and give him your pretty hand. It is good to be devout; but it is necessary to be polite, my niece."

The girl rose to her feet and turned toward the new-comers. She moved all of a piece; and shame and exhaustion were expressed in every line of her fresh young body; and she held her head down and kept her eyes upon the pavement, as she came slowly forward. In the course of her advance, her eyes fell upon Denis de Beaulieu's feet—feet of which he was justly vain, be it remarked, and wore in the most elegant accoutrement even while travelling. She paused—started, as if his yellow boots had conveyed some shocking meaning—and glanced suddenly up into the wearer's countenance. Their eyes met; shame gave place to horror and terror in her looks; the blood left her lips; with a piercing scream she covered her face with her hands and sank upon the chapel floor.

"That is not the man!" she cried. "My uncle, that is not the man!"

The Sire de Malétroit chirped agreeably. "Of course not," he said, "I expected as much. It was so unfortunate you could not remember his name."

"Indeed," she cried, "indeed, I have never seen this person till this moment—I have never so much as set eyes upon him—I never wish to see him again. Sir," she said, turning to Denis, "if you are a gentleman, you will bear me out. Have I ever seen you—have you ever seen me—before this accursed hour?"

"To speak for myself, I have never had that pleasure," answered the young man. "This is the first time, messire, that I have met with your engaging niece."

The old gentleman shrugged his shoulders.

"I am distressed to hear it," he said. "But it is never too late to begin. I had little more acquaintance with my own late lady ere I married her; which proves," he added, with a grimace, "that these impromptu marriages may often produce an excellent understanding in the long run. As the bridegroom is to have a voice in the matter, I will give him two hours to make up for lost time before we proceed with the ceremony." And he turned toward the door, followed by the clergyman.

The girl was on her feet in a moment. "My uncle, you cannot be in earnest," she said. "I declare before God I will stab myself rather than be forced on that young man. The heart rises at it; God forbids such marriages; you dishonour your white hair. Oh, my uncle, pity me! There is not a woman in all the world but would prefer death to such a nuptial. Is it possible," she added, faltering—"is it possible that you do not believe me—that you still think this"—and she pointed at Denis with a tremor of anger and contempt—"that you still think *this* to be the man?"

"Frankly," said the old gentleman, pausing on the threshold, "I do. But let me explain to you once for all, Blanche de Malétroit, my way of thinking about this affair. When you took it into your head to dishonour my family and the name that I have borne, in peace and war, for more than three-score years, you forfeited not only the right to question my designs, but that of looking me in the face. If your father had been alive, he would have spat on you and turned you out of doors. His was the hand of iron. You may bless your God you have only to deal with the hand of velvet, mademoiselle. It was my duty to get you married without delay. Out of pure good-will, I have tried to find your own gallant for you. And I believe I have succeeded. But before God and all the holy angels, Blanche de Malétroit, if I have not, I care not one jack-straw. So let me recommend you to be polite to our young friend; for upon my word, your next groom may be less appetising."

And with that he went out, with the chaplain at his heels; and the arras fell behind the pair.

The girl turned upon Denis with flashing eyes.

"And what, sir," she demanded, "may be the meaning of all this?"

"God knows," returned Denis, gloomily. "I am a prisoner in this house, which seems full of mad people. More I know not; and nothing do I understand."

"And pray how came you here?" she asked.

He told her as briefly as he could. "For the rest," he added, "perhaps you will follow my example, and tell me the answer to all these riddles, and what, in God's name, is like to be the end of it."

She stood silent for a little, and he could see her lips tremble and her tearless eyes burn with a feverish lustre. Then she pressed her forehead in both hands.

"Alas, how my head aches!" she said wearily—"to say nothing of my poor heart! But it is due to you to know my story, unmaidenly as it must seem. I am called Blanche de Malétroit; I have been without father or mother for—oh! for as long as I can recollect, and indeed I have been most unhappy all my life. Three months ago a young captain began to stand near me every day in church. I could see that I pleased him; I am much to blame, but I was so glad that any one should love me; and when he passed me a letter, I took it home with me and read it with great pleasure. Since that time he has written many. He was so anxious to speak with me, poor fellow! and kept asking me to leave the door open some evening that we might have two words upon the stair. For he knew how much my uncle trusted me." She gave something like a sob at that, and it was a moment before she could go on. "My uncle is a hard man, but he is very shrewd," she said at last. "He has performed many feats in war, and was a great person at court, and much trusted by Queen Isabeau in old days. How he came to suspect me I cannot tell; but it is hard to keep anything from his knowledge; and this morning, as we came from mass, he took my hand into his, forced it open, and read my little billet, walking by my side all the while. When he finished, he gave it back to me with great politeness. It contained another request to have the door left open; and this has been the ruin of us all. My uncle kept me strictly in my room until evening, and then ordered me to dress myself as you see me—a hard mockery for a young girl, do you not think so? I suppose, when he could not prevail with me to tell him the young captain's name, he must have laid a trap for him: into which, alas! you have fallen in the anger of God. I looked for much confusion; for how could I tell whether he was willing to take me for his wife on these sharp terms? He might have been trifling with me from the first; or I might have made myself too cheap in his eyes. But truly I had not looked for such a shameful punishment as this! I could not think that God would let a girl be so disgraced before a young man. And now I tell you all; and I can scarcely hope that you will not despise me."

Denis made her a respectful inclination.

"Madam," he said, "you have honoured me by your confidence. It remains for me to prove that I am not unworthy of the honour. Is Messire de Malétroit at hand?"

"I believe he is writing in the salle without," she answered.

"May I lead you thither, madam?" asked Denis, offering his hand with his most courtly bearing.

She accepted it; and the pair passed out of the chapel, Blanche in a very drooping and shamefast condition, but Denis strutting and ruffling in the consciousness of a mission, and the boyish certainty of accomplishing it with honour.

The Sire de Malétroit rose to meet them with an ironical obeisance.

"Sir," said Denis, with the grandest possible air, "I believe I am to have some say in the matter of this marriage; and let me tell you at once, I will be no party to forcing the inclination of this young lady. Had it been freely offered to me, I should have been proud to accept her hand, for I perceive she is as good as she is beautiful; but as things are, I have now the honour, messire, of refusing."

Blanche looked at him with gratitude in her eyes; but the old gentleman only smiled and smiled, until his smile grew positively sickening to Denis.

"I am afraid," he said, "Monsieur de Beaulieu, that you do not perfectly understand the choice I have offered you. Follow me, I beseech you, to this window." And he led the way to one of the large windows which stood open on the night. "You observe," he went on, "there is an iron ring in the upper masonry, and reeved through that, a very efficacious rope. Now, mark my words: if you should find your disinclination to my niece's person insurmountable, I shall have you hanged out of this window before sunrise. I shall only proceed to such an extremity with the greatest regret, you may believe me. For it is not at all your death that I desire, but my niece's establishment in life. At the same time, it must come to that if you prove obstinate. Your family, Monsieur de Beaulieu, is very well in its way; but if you sprang from Charlemagne, you should not refuse the hand of a Malétroit with impunity—not if she had been as common as the Paris road—not if she were as hideous as the gargoyle over my door. Neither my niece nor you, nor my own private feelings, move me at all in this matter. The honour of my house has been compromised; I believe you to be the guilty person, at least you are now in the secret; and you can hardly wonder if I request you to wipe out the stain. If you will not, your blood be on your own head! It will be no great satisfaction to me to have your interesting relics kicking their heels in the breeze below my windows, but half a loaf is better than no bread, and if I cannot cure the dishonour, I shall at least stop the scandal."

There was a pause.

"I believe there are other ways of settling such imbroglios among gentlemen," said Denis. "You wear a sword, and I hear you have used it with distinction."

The Sire de Malétroit made a signal to the chaplain, who crossed the room with long silent strides and raised the arras over the third of the three doors. It was only a moment before he let it fall again; but Denis had time to see a dusky passage full of armed men.

"When I was a little younger, I should have been delighted to honour you, Monsieur de Beaulieu," said Sire Alain; "but I am now too old. Faithful retainers are the sinews of age, and I must employ the strength I have. This is one of the hardest things to swallow as a man grows up in years; but with a little patience, even this becomes habitual. You and the lady seem to prefer the salle for what remains of your two hours; and as I have no desire to cross your preference, I shall resign it to your use with all the pleasure in the world. No haste!" he added, holding up his hand, as he saw a dangerous look come into Denis de Beaulieu's face. "If your mind revolt against hanging, it will be time enough two hours hence to throw yourself out of the window or upon the pikes of my retainers. Two hours of life are always two hours. A great many things may turn up in even as little a while as that. And, besides, if I understand her appearance, my niece has something to say to you. You will not disfigure your last hours by a want of politeness to a lady?"

Denis looked at Blanche, and she made him an imploring gesture.

It is likely that the old gentleman was hugely pleased at this symptom of an understanding; for he smiled on both, and added sweetly: "If you will give me your word of honour, Monsieur de Beaulieu, to await my return at the end of the two hours before attempting anything desperate, I shall withdraw my retainers, and let you speak in greater privacy with mademoiselle."

Denis again glanced at the girl, who seemed to beseech him to agree.

"I give you my word of honour," he said.

Messire de Malétroit bowed, and proceeded to limp about the apartment, clearing his throat the while with that odd musical chirp which had already grown so irritating in the ears of Denis de Beaulieu. He first possessed himself of some papers which lay upon the table; then he went to the mouth of the passage and appeared to give an order to the men behind the arras; and lastly he hobbled out through the door by which Denis had come in, turning upon the threshold to address a last smiling bow to the young couple, and followed by the chaplain with a hand-lamp.

No sooner were they alone than Blanche advanced towards Denis with her hands extended. Her face was flushed and excited, and her eyes shone with tears.

"You shall not die!" she cried, "you shall marry me after all."

"You seem to think, madam," replied Denis, "that I stand much in fear of death."

"Oh, no, no," she said, "I see you are no poltroon. It is for my own sake—I could not bear to have you slain for such a scruple."

"I am afraid," returned Denis, "that you underrate the difficulty, madam. What you may be too generous to refuse, I may be too proud to accept. In a moment of noble feeling towards me, you forgot what you perhaps owe to others."

He had the decency to keep his eyes on the floor as he said this, and after he had finished, so as not to spy upon her confusion. She stood silent for a moment, then walked suddenly away, and falling on her uncle's chair, fairly burst out sobbing. Denis was in the acme of embarrassment. He looked round, as if to seek for inspiration, and seeing a stool, plumped down upon it for something to do. There he sat playing with the guard of his rapier, and wishing himself dead a thousand times over, and buried in the nastiest kitchen-heap in France. His eyes wandered round the apartment, but found nothing to arrest them. There were such wide spaces between the furniture, the light fell so badly and cheerlessly over all, the dark outside air looked in so coldly through the windows that he thought he had never seen a church so vast, nor a tomb so melancholy. The regular sobs of Blanche de Malétroit measured out the time like the ticking of a clock. He read the device upon the shield over and over again, until his eyes became obscured; he stared into shadowy corners until he imagined they were swarming with horrible animals; and every now and again he awoke with a start, to remember that his last two hours were running, and death was on the march.

Oftener and oftener, as the time went on, did his glance settle on the girl herself. Her face was bowed forward and covered with her hands, and she was shaken at intervals by the convulsive hiccup of grief. Even thus she was not an unpleasant object to dwell upon, so plump and yet so fine, with a warm brown skin, and the most beautiful hair, Denis thought, in the whole world of womankind. Her hands were like her uncle's; but they were more in place at the end of her young arms, and looked infinitely soft and caressing. He remembered how her blue eyes had shone upon him, full of anger, pity, and innocence. And the more he dwelt on her perfections, the uglier death looked, and the more deeply was he smitten with penitence at her continued tears. Now he felt that no man could have the courage to leave a world which contained so beautiful a creature; and now he would have given forty minutes of his last hour to have unsaid his cruel speech.

Suddenly a hoarse and ragged peal of cockcrow rose to their ears from the dark valley below the windows. And this shattering noise in the silence of all around was like a light in a dark place, and shook them both out of their reflections.

"Alas, can I do nothing to help you?" she said, looking up.

"Madam," replied Denis, with a fine irrelevancy, "if I have said anything to wound you, believe me, it was for your own sake and not for mine."

She thanked him with a tearful look.

"I feel your position cruelly," he went on. "The world has been bitter hard on you. Your uncle is a disgrace to mankind. Believe me, madam, there is no young gentleman in all France but would be glad of my opportunity, to die in doing you a momentary service."

"I know already that you can be very brave and generous," she answered. "What I *want* to know is whether I can serve you—now or afterwards," she added, with a quaver.

"Most certainly," he answered with a smile. "Let me sit beside you as if I were a friend, instead of a foolish intruder; try to forget how awkwardly we are placed to one another; make my last moments go pleasantly; and you will do me the chief service possible."

"You are very gallant," she added, with a yet deeper sadness . . . "very gallant . . . and it somehow pains me. But draw nearer, if you please; and if you find anything to say to me, you will at least make certain of a very friendly listener. Ah! Monsieur de Beaulieu," she broke forth—"ah! Monsieur de Beaulieu, how can I look you in the face?" And she fell to weeping again with a renewed effusion.

"Madam," said Denis, taking her hand in both of his, "reflect on the little time I have before me, and the great bitterness into which I am cast by the sight of your distress. Spare me, in my last moments, the spectacle of what I cannot cure even with the sacrifice of my life."

"I am very selfish," answered Blanche. "I will be braver, Monsieur de Beaulieu, for your sake. But think if I can do you no kindness in the future—if you have no friends to whom I could carry your adieux. Charge me as heavily as you can; every burthen will lighten, by so little, the invaluable gratitude I owe you. Put it in my power to do something more for you than weep."

"My mother is married again, and has a young family to care for. My brother Guichard will inherit my fiefs; and if I am not in

error, that will content him amply for my death. Life is a little
vapour that passeth away, as we are told by those in holy orders.
When a man is in a fair way and sees all life open in front of him,
he seems to himself to make a very important figure in the world.
His horse whinnies to him; the trumpets blow and the girls look
out of window as he rides into town before his company; he receives many assurances of trust and regard—sometimes by express
in a letter—sometimes face to face, with persons of great consequence falling on his neck. It is not wonderful if his head is turned
for a time. But once he is dead, were he as brave as Hercules or
as wise as Solomon, he is soon forgotten. It is not ten years since
my father fell, with many other knights around him, in a very
fierce encounter, and I do not think any one of them, nor so much
as the name of the fight, is now remembered. No, no, madam, the
nearer you come to it, you see that death is a dark and dusty
corner, where a man gets into his tomb and has the door shut after
him till the Judgment Day. I have few friends just now, and once
I am dead I shall have none."

"Ah, Monsieur de Beaulieu!" she exclaimed, "you forget
Blanche de Malétroit."

"You have a sweet nature, madam, and you are pleased to estimate a little service far beyond its worth."

"It is not that," she answered. "You mistake me if you think I
am easily touched by my own concerns. I say so, because you are
the noblest man I have ever met; because I recognise in you a
spirit that would have made even a common person famous in the
land."

"And yet here I die in a mousetrap—with no more noise about
it than my own squeaking," answered he.

A look of pain crossed her face, and she was silent for a little
while. Then a light came into her eyes, and with a smile she spoke
again.

"I cannot have my champion think meanly of himself. Any one
who gives his life for another will be met in Paradise by all the
heralds and angels of the Lord God. And you have no such cause
to hang your head. For . . . pray, do you think me beautiful?"
she asked, with a deep flush.

"Indeed, madam, I do," he said.

"I am glad of that," she answered heartily. "Do you think there
are many men in France who have been asked in marriage by a

beautiful maiden—with her own lips—and who have refused her
to her face? I know you men would half despise such a triumph;
but believe me, we women know more of what is precious in love.
There is nothing that should set a person higher in his own
esteem; and we women would prize nothing more dearly."

"You are very good," he said; "but you cannot make me forget
that I was asked in pity and not for love."

"I am not so sure of that," she replied, holding down her head.
"Hear me to an end, Monsieur de Beaulieu. I know how you must
despise me; I feel you are right to do so; I am too poor a creature
to occupy one thought of your mind, although, alas! you must die
for me this morning. But when I asked you to marry me, indeed,
and indeed, it was because I respected and admired you, and
loved you with my whole soul, from the very moment that you
took my part against my uncle. If you had seen yourself, and how
noble you looked, you would pity rather than despise me. And
now," she went on, hurriedly checking him with her hand, "although I have laid aside all reserve and told you so much, remember that I know your sentiments towards me already. I would not,
believe me, being nobly born, weary you with importunities into
consent. I too have a pride of my own: and I declare before the
holy mother of God, if you should now go back from your word
already given, I would no more marry you than I would marry my
uncle's groom."

Denis smiled a little bitterly.

"It is a small love," he said, "that shies at a little pride."

She made no answer, although she probably had her own
thoughts.

"Come hither to the window," he said with a sigh. "Here is the
dawn."

And indeed the dawn was already beginning. The hollow of the
sky was full of essential daylight, colourless and clean; and the
valley underneath was flooded with a grey reflection. A few thin
vapours clung in the coves of the forest or lay along the winding
course of the river. The scene disengaged a surprising effect of
stillness, which was hardly interrupted when the cocks began once
more to crow among the steadings. Perhaps the same fellow who
had made so horrid a clangour in the darkness not half an hour
before, now sent up the merriest cheer to greet the coming day.
A little wind went bustling and eddying among the tree-tops un-

derneath the windows. And still the daylight kept flooding insensibly out of the east, which was soon to grow incandescent and cast up that red-hot cannon-ball, the rising sun.

Denis looked out over all this with a bit of a shiver. He had taken her hand, and retained it in his almost unconsciously.

"Has the day begun already?" she said; and then, illogically enough: "the night has been so long! Alas! what shall we say to my uncle when he returns?"

"What you will," said Denis, and he pressed her fingers in his. She was silent.

"Blanche," he said, with a swift, uncertain, passionate utterance, "you have seen whether I fear death. You must know well enough that I would as gladly leap out of that window into the empty air as to lay a finger on you without your free and full consent. But if you care for me at all, do not let me lose my life in a misapprehension; for I love you better than the whole world; and though I will die for you blithely, it would be like all the joys of Paradise to live on and spend my life in your service."

As he stopped speaking, a bell began to ring loudly in the interior of the house; and a clatter of armour in the corridor showed that the retainers were returning to their post, and the two hours were at an end.

"After all that you have heard?" she whispered, leaning towards him with her lips and eyes.

"I have heard nothing," he replied.

"The captain's name was Florimond de Champdivers," she said in his ear.

"I did not hear it," he answered, taking her supple body in his arms, and covering her wet face with kisses.

A melodious chirping was audible behind, followed by a beautiful chuckle, and the voice of Messire de Malétroit wished his new nephew a good-morning.

A Lodging for the Night

A STORY OF FRANCIS VILLON

✳

I T WAS LATE IN NOVEMBER, 1456. THE SNOW FELL OVER PARIS WITH rigorous, relentless persistence; sometimes the wind made a sally and scattered it in flying vortices; sometimes there was a lull, and flake after flake descended out of the black night air, silent, circuitous, interminable. To poor people, looking up under moist eyebrows, it seemed a wonder where it all came from. Master Francis Villon had propounded an alternative that afternoon, at a tavern window: was it only Pagan Jupiter plucking geese upon Olympus? or were the holy angels moulting? He was only a poor Master of Arts, he went on; and as the question somewhat touched upon divinity, he durst not venture to conclude. A silly old priest from Montargis, who was among the company, treated the young rascal to a bottle of wine in honour of the jest and grimaces with which it was accompanied, and swore on his own white beard that he had been just such another irreverent dog when he was Villon's age.

The air was raw and pointed, but not far below freezing; and the flakes were large, damp, and adhesive. The whole city was sheeted up. An army might have marched from end to end and not a foot fall given the alarm. If there were any belated birds in heaven, they saw the island like a large white patch, and the bridges like slim white spars, on the black ground of the river. High up overhead the snow settled among the tracery of the cathedral towers. Many a niche was drifted full; many a statue wore a long white bonnet on its grotesque or sainted head. The gargoyles had been transformed into great false noses, drooping towards the point. The crockets were like upright pillows swollen on one side. In the intervals of the wind, there was a dull sound of dripping about the precincts of the church.

The cemetery of St. John had taken its own share of the snow. All the graves were decently covered; tall white housetops stood around in grave array; worthy burghers were long ago in bed, benightcapped like their domiciles; there was no light in all the neigbourhood but a little peep from a lamp that hung swinging in the church choir, and tossed the shadows to and fro in time to its oscillations. The clock was hard on ten when the patrol went by with halberds and a lantern, beating their hands; and they saw nothing suspicious about the cemetery of St. John.

Yet there was a small house, backed up against the cemetery wall, which was still awake, and awake to evil purpose, in that snoring district. There was not much to betray it from without; only a stream of warm vapour from the chimney-top, a patch where the snow melted on the roof, and a few half-obliterated footprints at the door. But within, behind the shuttered windows, Master Francis Villon the poet, and some of the thievish crew with whom he consorted, were keeping the night alive and passing round the bottle.

A great pile of living embers diffused a strong and ruddy glow from the arched chimney. Before this straddled Dom Nicolas, the Picardy monk, with his skirts picked up and his fat legs bared to the comfortable warmth. His dilated shadow cut the room in half; and the firelight only escaped on either side of his broad person, and in a little pool between his outspread feet. His face had the beery, bruised appearance of the continual drinker's; it was covered with a network of congested veins, purple in ordinary circumstances, but now pale violet, for even with his back to the fire the cold pinched him on the other side. His cowl had half fallen back, and made a strange excrescence on either side of his bull neck. So he straddled, grumbling, and cut the room in half with the shadow of his portly frame.

On the right, Villon and Guy Tabary were huddled together over a scrap of parchment; Villon making a ballade which he was to call the "Ballade of Roast Fish," and Tabary spluttering admiration at his shoulder. The poet was a rag of a man, dark, little.

and lean, with hollow cheeks and thin black locks. He carried his four-and-twenty years with feverish animation. Greed had made folds about his eyes, evil smiles had puckered his mouth. The wolf and pig struggled together in his face. It was an eloquent, sharp, ugly, earthly countenance. His hands were small and prehensile, with fingers knotted like a cord; and they were continually flickering in front of him in violent and expressive pantomime. As for Tabary, a broad, complacent, admiring imbecility breathed from his squash nose and slobbering lips; he had become a thief, just as he might have become the most decent of burgesses, by the imperious chance that rules the lives of human geese and human donkeys.

At the monk's other hand, Montigny and Thevenin Pensete played a game of chance. About the first there clung some flavour of good birth and training, as about a fallen angel; something long, lithe, and courtly in the person; something acquiline and darkling in the face. Thevenin, poor soul, was in great feather: he had done a good stroke of knavery that afternoon in the Faubourg St. Jacques, and all night he had been gaining from Montigny. A flat smile illuminated his face; his bald head shone rosily in a garland of red curls; his little protuberant stomach shook with silent chucklings as he swept in his gains.

"Doubles or quits?" said Thevenin.

Montigny nodded grimly.

"*Some may prefer to dine in state,*" wrote Villon, "*On bread and cheese on silver plate.* Or, or—help me out, Guido!"

Tabary giggled.

"*Or parsley on a golden dish,*" scribbled the poet.

The wind was freshening without; it drove the snow before it, and sometimes raised its voice in a victorious whoop, and made sepulchral grumblings in the chimney. The cold was growing sharper as the night went on. Villon, protruding his lips, imitated the gust with something between a whistle and a groan. It was an eerie, uncomfortable talent of the poet's, much detested by the Picardy monk.

"Can't you hear it rattle in the gibbet?" said Villon. "They are all dancing the devil's jig on nothing, up there. You may dance, my gallants, you'll be none the warmer! Whew, what a gust! Down went somebody just now! A medlar the fewer on the three-legged medlar-tree!—I say, Dom Nicolas, it'll be cold to-night on the St. Denis Road?" he asked.

Dom Nicolas winked both his big eyes, and seemed to choke upon his Adam's apple. Montfaucon, the great grisly Paris gibbet, stood hard by the St. Denis Road, and the pleasantry touched him on the raw. As for Tabary, he laughed immoderately over the medlars; he had never heard anything more light-hearted; and he held his sides and crowed. Villon fetched him a fillip on the nose, which turned his mirth into an attack of coughing.

"Oh, stop that row," said Villon, "and think of rhymes to 'fish.' "

"Doubles or quits," said Montigny doggedly.

"With all my heart," quoth Thevenin.

"Is there any more in that bottle?" asked the monk.

"Open another," said Villon. "How do you ever hope to fill that big hogshead, your body, with little things like bottles? And how do you expect to get to heaven? How many angels, do you fancy, can be spared to carry up a single monk from Picardy? Or do you think yourself another Elias—and they'll send the coach for you?"

"Hominibus impossible," replied the monk as he filled his glass.

Tabary was in ecstasies.

Villon filiped his nose again.

"Laugh at my jokes, if you like," he said.

"It was very good," objected Tabary.

Villon made a face at him. "Think of rhymes to 'fish,' " he said. "What have you to do with Latin? You'll wish you knew none of it at the great assizes, when the devil calls for Guido Tabary, clericus —the devil with the hump-back and red-hot finger-nails. Talking of the devil," he added in a whisper, "look at Montigny!"

All three peered covertly at the gamester. He did not seem to be enjoying his luck. His mouth was a little to a side; one nostril nearly shut, and the other much inflated. The black dog was on his back, as people say, in terrifying nursery metaphor; and he breathed hard under the gruesome burthen.

"He looks as if he could knife him," whispered Tabary, with round eyes.

The monk shuddered, and turned his face and spread his open hands to the red embers. It was the cold that thus affected Dom Nicolas, and not any excess of moral sensibility.

"Come now," said Villon—"about this ballade. How does it run so far?" And beating time with his hand, he read it aloud to Tabary.

They were interrupted at the fourth rhyme by a brief and fatal movement among the gamesters. The round was completed, and Thevenin was just opening his mouth to claim another victory, when Montigny leaped up, swift as an adder, and stabbed him to the heart. The blow took effect before he had time to utter a cry, before he had time to move. A tremor or two convulsed his frame; his hands opened and shut, his heels rattled on the floor; then his head rolled backward over one shoulder with the eyes wide open; and Thevenin Pensete's spirit had returned to Him who made it.

Every one sprang to his feet; but the business was over in two twos. The four living fellows looked at each other in rather a ghastly fashion; the dead man contemplating a corner of the roof with a singular and ugly leer.

"My God!" said Tabary; and he began to pray in Latin.

Villon broke out into hysterical laughter. He came a step forward and ducked a ridiculous bow at Thevenin, and laughed still louder. Then he sat down suddenly, all of a heap, upon a stool, and continued laughing bitterly, as though he would shake himself to pieces.

Montigny recovered his composure first.

"Let's see what he has about him," he remarked, and he picked the dead man's pockets with a practised hand, and divided the money into four equal portions on the table. "There's for you," he said.

The monk received his share with a deep sigh, and a single stealthy glance at the dead Thevenin, who was beginning to sink into himself and topple sideways off the chair.

"We're all in for it," cried Villon, swallowing his mirth. "It's a hanging job for every man jack of us that's here—not to speak of those who aren't." He made a shocking gesture in the air with his raised right hand, and put out his tongue and threw his head on one side, so as to counterfeit the appearance of one who has been hanged. Then he pocketed his share of the spoil, and executed a shuffle with his feet as if to restore the circulation.

Tabary was the last to help himself; he made a dash at the money, and retired to the other end of the apartment.

Montigny stuck Thevenin upright in the chair, and drew out the dagger, which was followed by a jet of blood.

"You fellows had better be moving," he said, as he wiped the blade on his victim's doublet.

"I think we had," returned Villon, with a gulp. "Damn his fat head!" he broke out. "It sticks in my throat like phlegm. What right has a man to have red hair when he is dead?" And he fell all of a heap again upon the stool, and fairly covered his face with his hands.

Montigny and Dom Nicolas laughed aloud, even Tabary feebly chiming in.

"Cry baby," said the monk.

"I always said he was a woman," added Montigny, with a sneer. "Sit up, can't you?" he went on, giving another shake to the murdered body. "Tread out that fire, Nick!"

But Nick was better employed; he was quietly taking Villon's purse, as the poet sat, limp and trembling, on the stool where he had been making a ballade not three minutes before. Montigny and Tabary dumbly demanded a share of the booty, which the monk silently promised as he passed the little bag into the bosom of his gown. In many ways an artistic nature unfits a man for practical existence.

No sooner had the theft been accomplished than Villon shook himself, jumped to his feet, and began helping to scatter and extinguish the embers. Meanwhile Montigny opened the door and cautiously peered into the street. The coast was clear; there was no meddlesome patrol in sight. Still it was judged wiser to slip out severally; and as Villon was himself in a hurry to escape from the neighbourhood of the dead Thevenin, and the rest were in a still greater hurry to get rid of him before he should discover the loss of his money, he was the first by general consent to issue forth into the street.

The wind had triumphed and swept all the clouds from heaven. Only a few vapours, as thin as moonlight, fleeted rapidly across the stars. It was bitter cold; and by a common optical effect, things seemed almost more definite than in the broadest daylight. The sleeping city was absolutely still; a company of white hoods, a field full of little alps, below the twinkling stars. Villon cursed his fortune. Would it were still snowing! Now, wherever he went, he left an indelible trail behind him on the glittering streets; wherever he went he was still tethered to the house by the cemetery of St. John; wherever he went he must weave, with his own plodding feet, the rope that bound him to the crime and would bind him to the gallows. The leer of the dead man came back to him with a new significance. He snapped his fingers as if to pluck up his own spirits, and choosing a street at random, stepped boldly forward in the snow.

Two things preoccupied him as he went: the aspect of the gallows at Montfaucon in this bright, windy phase of the night's existence, for one; and for another, the look of the dead man with his bald head and garland of red curls. Both struck cold upon his heart, and he kept quickening his pace as if he could escape from unpleasant thoughts by mere fleetness of foot. Sometimes he looked back over his shoulder with a sudden nervous jerk; but he was the only moving thing in the white streets, except when the wind swooped round a corner and threw up the snow, which was beginning to freeze, in spouts of glittering dust.

Suddenly he saw, a long way before him, a black clump and a couple of lanterns. The clump was in motion, and the lanterns swung as though carried by men walking. It was a patrol. And though it was merely crossing his line of march he judged it wiser to get out of eyeshot as speedily as he could. He was not in the humour to be challenged, and he was conscious of making a very conspicuous mark upon the snow. Just on his left hand there stood a great hotel, with some turrets and a large porch before the door; it was half ruinous, he remembered, and had long stood empty; and so he made three steps of it, and jumped into the shelter of the porch. It was pretty dark inside, after the glimmer of the snowy streets, and he was groping forward with outspread hands, when he stumbled over some substance which offered an indescribable mixture of resistances, hard and soft, firm and loose. His heart gave a leap and he sprang two steps back and stared dreadfully at the obstacle. Then he gave a little laugh of relief. It was only a woman, and she dead. He knelt beside her to make sure upon this latter point. She was freezing cold, and rigid like a stick. A little ragged finery fluttered in the wind about her hair, and her cheeks had been heavily rouged that same afternoon. Her pockets were quite empty; but in her stocking, underneath the garter, Villon found two of the small coins that went by the name of whites. It was little enough; but it was always something; and the poet was moved with a deep sense of pathos that she should have died before she had spent her money. That seemed to him a dark and pitiable mystery; and he looked from the coins in his hand to the dead woman, and back again to the coins, shaking his head over the riddle of man's life. Henry V. of England, dying at Vincennes just after he had conquered France, and this poor jade cut off by a cold draught in a great man's doorway, before she had time to spend her couple of whites—it seemed a cruel way to carry on the world. Two whites would have taken such a little while to squander; and yet it would have been one more good taste in the mouth, one more smack of the lips, before the devil got the soul, and the body was left to birds and vermin. He would like to use all his tallow before the light was blown out and the lantern broken.

While these thoughts were passing through his mind, he was feeling, half mechanically, for his purse. Suddenly his heart stopped beating; a feeling of cold scales passed up the back of his legs, and a cold blow seemed to fall upon his scalp. He stood petrified for a moment; then he felt again with one feverish movement; and then his loss burst upon him, and he was covered at once with perspiration. To spendthrifts money is so living and actual—it is such a thin veil between them and their pleasures! There is only one limit to their fortune—that of time; and a spendthrift with only a few crowns is the Emperor of Rome until they are spent. For such a person to lose his money is to suffer the most shocking reverse, and fall from heaven to hell, from all to nothing, in a breath. And all the more if he has put his head in the halter for it; if he may be hanged to-morrow for that same purse, so dearly earned, so foolishly departed! Villon stood and cursed; he threw the two whites into the street; he shook his fist at heaven; he stamped, and was not horrified to find himself trampling the poor corpse. Then he began rapidly to retrace his steps towards the house beside the cemetery. He had forgotten all fear of the patrol, which was long gone by at any rate, and had no idea but that of his lost purse. It was in vain that he looked right and left upon the snow: nothing was to be seen. He had not dropped it in the streets. Had it fallen in the house? He would have liked dearly to go in and see; but the idea of the grisly occupant unmanned him. And he saw besides, as he drew near, that their efforts to put out the fire had been unsuccessful; on the contrary, it had broken into a blaze, and a changeful light played in the chinks of door and window, and revived his terror for the authorities and Paris gibbet.

He returned to the hotel with the porch, and groped about upon the snow for the money he had thrown away in his childish passion. But he could only find one white; the other had probably struck sideways and sunk deeply in. With a single white in his pocket, all his projects for a rousing night in some wild tavern vanished utterly away. And it was not only pleasure that fled laughing from his grasp; positive discomfort, positive pain, attacked him as he stood ruefully before the porch. His perspiration had dried upon him; and although the wind had now fallen, a binding frost was setting in stronger with every hour, and he felt benumbed and sick at heart. What was to be done? Late as was the hour, improbable as was success, he would try the house of his adopted father, the chaplain of St. Benoît.

He ran there all the way, and knocked timidly. There was no answer. He knocked again and again, taking heart with every stroke; and at last steps were heard approaching from within. A barred wicket fell open in the iron-studded door, and emitted a gush of yellow light.

"Hold up your face to the wicket," said the chaplain from within.

"It's only me," whimpered Villon.

"Oh, it's only you, is it?" returned the chaplain; and he cursed him with foul unpriestly oaths for disturbing him at such an hour, and bade him be off to hell, where he came from.

"My hands are blue to the wrist," pleaded Villon; "my feet are dead and full of twinges; my nose aches with the sharp air; the cold lies at my heart. I may be dead before morning. Only this once, father, and before God, I will never ask again!"

"You should have come earlier," said the ecclesiastic coolly. "Young men require a lesson now and then." He shut the wicket and retired deliberately into the interior of the house.

Villon was beside himself; he beat upon the door with his hands and feet, and shouted hoarsely after the chaplain.

"Wormy old fox!" he cried, "If I had my hand under your twist, I would send you flying headlong into the bottomless pit."

A door shut in the interior, faintly audible to the poet down long passages. He passed his hand over his mouth with an oath. And then the humour of the situation struck him, and he laughed and looked lightly up to heaven, where the stars seemed to be winking over his discomfiture.

What was to be done? It looked very like a night in the frosty streets. The idea of the dead woman popped into his imagination, and gave him a hearty fright; what had happened to her in the early night might very well well happen to him before morning. And he so young! and with such immense possibilities of disorderly amusement before him! He felt quite pathetic over the notion of his own fate, as if it had been some one else's, and made a little imaginative vignette of the scene in the morning when they should find his body.

He passed all his chances under review, turning the white between his thumb and forefinger. Unfortunately he was on bad terms with some old friends who would once have taken pity on him in such a plight. He had lampooned them in verses; he had beaten and cheated them; and yet now, when he was in so close a pinch, he thought there was at least one who might perhaps relent. It was a chance. It was worthy trying at least, and he would go and see.

On the way, two little accidents happened to him which coloured his musings in a very different manner. For, first, he fell in with the track of a patrol, and walked in it for some hundred yards, although it lay out of his direction. And this spirited him up; at least he had confused his trail; for he was still possessed with the idea of people tracking him all about Paris over the snow, and collaring him next morning before he was awake. The other matter affected him quite differently. He passed a street corner, where, not so long before, a woman and her child had been devoured by wolves. This was just the kind of weather, he reflected, when wolves might take it into their heads to enter Paris again; and a lone man in these deserted streets would run the chance of something worse than a mere scare. He stopped and looked upon the place with an unpleasant interest—it was a centre where several lanes intersected each other; and he looked down them all, one after another, and held his breath to listen, lest he should detect some galloping black things on the snow or hear the sound of howling between him and the river. He remembered his mother telling him the story and pointing out the spot, while he was yet a child. His mother! If he only knew where she lived, he might make sure at least of shelter. He determined he would inquire upon the morrow; nay, he would go and see her too, poor old girl! So thinking, he arrived at his destination—his last hope for the night.

The house was quite dark, like its neighbours; and yet after a few taps, he heard a movement overhead, a door opening, and a cautious voice asking who was there. The poet named himself in a loud whisper, and waited, not without some trepidation, the result. Nor had he to wait long. A window was suddenly opened, and a pailful of slops splashed down upon the doorstep. Villon had not been unprepared for something of the sort, and had put himself as much in shelter as the nature of the porch admitted; but for all that, he was deplorably drenched below the waist. His hose began to freeze almost at once. Death from cold and exposure stared him in the face; he remembered he was of phthisical tendency, and began coughing tentatively. But the gravity of the danger steadied his nerves. He stopped a few hundred yards from the door where he had been so rudely used, and reflected with his finger to his nose. He could only see one way of getting a lodging, and that was to take it. He had noticed a house not far away, which looked as if it might be easily broken into, and thither he betook himself promptly, entertaining himself on the way with the idea of a room still hot, with a table still loaded with the remains of supper, where he might pass the rest of the black hours and whence he should issue, on the morrow, with an armful of valuable plate. He even considered on what viands and what wines he should prefer; and as he was calling the roll of his favourite dainties, roast fish presented itself to his mind with an odd mixture of amusement and horror.

"I shall never finish that ballade," he thought to himself; and then, with another shudder at the recollection, "Oh, damn his fat head!" he repeated fervently, and spat upon the snow.

The house in question looked dark at first sight; but as Villon made a preliminary inspection in search of the handiest point of attack, a little twinkle of light caught his eye from behind a curtained window.

"The devil!" he thought. "People awake! Some student or some saint, confound the crew! Can't they get drunk and lie in bed snoring like their neighbours? What's the good of curfew, and poor devils of bell-ringers jumping at a rope's end in bell-towers? What's the use of day, if people sit up all night? The gripes to them!" He grinned as he saw where his logic was leading him. "Every man to his business, after all," added he, "and if they're awake, by the Lord, I may come by a supper honestly for once, and cheat the devil."

He went boldly to the door and knocked with an assured hand. On both previous occasions, he had knocked timidly and with some dread of attracting notice; but now when he had just discarded the thought of a burglarious entry, knocking at a door seemed a mighty simple and innocent proceeding. The sound of his blows echoed through the house with thin, phantasmal reverberations, as though it were quite empty; but these had scarcely died away before a measured tread drew near, a couple of bolts were withdrawn, and one wing was opened broadly, as though no guile or fear of guile were known to those within. A tall figure of a man, muscular and spare, but a little bent, confronted Villon. The head was massive in bulk, but finely sculptured; the nose blunt at the bottom, but refining upward to where it joined a pair of strong and honest eyebrows; the mouth and eyes surrounded with delicate markings, and the whole face based upon a thick white beard, boldly and squarely trimmed. Seen as it was by the light of a flickering hand-lamp, it looked perhaps nobler than it had a right to do; but it was a fine face, honourable rather than intelligent, strong, simple, and righteous.

"You knock late, sir," said the old man in resonant, courteous tones.

Villon cringed and brought up many servile words of apology; at a crisis of this sort the beggar was uppermost in him, and the man of genius hid his head with confusion.

"You are cold," repeated the old man, "and hungry? Well, step in." And he ordered him into the house with a noble enough gesture.

"Some great seigneur," thought Villon, as his host, setting down the lamp on the flagged pavement of the entry, shot the bolts once more into their places.

"You will pardon me if I go in front," he said, when this was done; and he preceded the poet up-stairs into a large apartment, warmed with a pan of charcoal and lit by a great lamp hanging from the roof. It was very bare of furniture; only some gold plate on a sideboard; some folios; and a stand of armour between the windows. Some smart tapestry hung upon the walls, representing the crucifixion of our Lord in one piece, and in another a scene of shepherds and shepherdesses by a running stream. Over the chimney was a shield of arms.

"Will you seat yourself," said the old man, "and forgive me if

I leave you? I am alone in my house to-night, and if you are to eat I must forage for you myself."

No sooner was his host gone than Villon leaped from the chair on which he had just seated himself, and began examining the room, with the stealth and passion of a cat. He weighed the gold flagons in his hand, opened all the folios, and investigated the arms upon the shield, and the stuff with which the seats were lined. He raised the window curtains, and saw that the windows were set with rich stained glass in figures, so far as he could see, of martial import. Then he stood in the middle of the room, drew a long breath, and retaining it with puffed cheeks, looked round and round him, turning on his heels, as if to impress every feature of the apartment on his memory.

"Seven pieces of plate," he said. "If there had been ten, I would have risked it. A fine house, and a fine old master, so help me all the saints!"

And just then, hearing the old man's tread returning along the corridor, he stole back to his chair, and began humbly toasting his wet legs before the charcoal pan.

His entertainer had a plate of meat in one hand and a jug of wine in the other. He set down the plate upon the table, motioning Villon to draw in his chair, and going to the sideboard, brought back two goblets which he filled.

"I drink your better fortune," he said gravely touching Villon's cup with his own.

"To our better acquaintance," said the poet, growing bold. A mere man of the people would have been awed by the courtesy of the old seigneur, but Villon was hardened in that matter; he had made mirth for great lords before now, and found them as black rascals as himself. And so he devoted himself to the viands with a ravenous gusto, while the old man, leaning backward, watched him with steady, curious eyes.

"You have blood on your shoulder, my man," he said.

Montigny must have laid his wet right hand upon him as he left the house. He cursed Montigny in his heart.

"It was none of my shedding," he stammered.

"I had not supposed so," returned his host quietly. "A brawl?"

"Well, something of that sort," Villon admitted with a quaver.

"Perhaps a fellow murdered?"

"Oh, no, not murdered," said the poet, more and more confused. "It was all fair play—murdered by accident. I had no hand in it, God strike me dead!" he added fervently.

"One rogue the fewer, I dare say," observed the master of the house.

"You may dare to say that," agreed Villon, infinitely relieved. "As big a rogue as there is between here and Jerusalem. He turned up his toes like a lamb. But it was a nasty thing to look at. I dare say you've seen dead men in your time, my lord?" he added, glancing at the armour.

"Many," said the old man. "I have followed the wars, as you imagine."

Villon laid down his knife and fork, which he had just taken up again.

"Were any of them bald?" he asked.

"Oh, yes, and with hair as white as mine."

"I don't think I should mind the white so much," said Villon. "His was red." And he had a return of his shuddering and tendency to laughter, which he drowned with a great draught of wine. "I'm a little put out when I think of it," he went on. "I knew him—damn him! And then the cold gives a man fancies—or the fancies give a man cold, I don't know which."

"Have you any money?" asked the old man.

"I have one white," returned the poet, laughing. "I got it out of a dead jade's stocking in a porch. She was as dead as Cæsar, poor wench, and as cold as a church, with bits of ribbon sticking in her hair. This is a hard world in winter for wolves and wenches and poor rogues like me."

"I," said the old man, "am Enguerrand de la Feuillée, seigneur de Brisetout, bailly du Patatrac. Who and what may you be?"

Villon rose and made a suitable reverence. "I am called Francis Villon," he said, "a poor Master of Arts of this university. I know some Latin, and a deal of vice. I can make chansons, ballades, lais, virelais, and roundels, and I am very fond of wine. I was born in a garret, and I shall not improbably die upon the gallows. I may add, my lord, that from this night forward I am your lordship's very obsequious servant to command."

"No servant of mine," said the knight; "my guest for this evening, and no more."

"A very grateful guest," said Villon politely, and he drank in dumb show to his entertainer.

"You are shrewd," began the old man, tapping his forehead, "very shrewd; you have learning; you are a clerk; and yet you take a small piece of money off a dead woman in the street. Is it not a kind of theft?"

"It is a kind of theft much practised in the wars, my lord."

"The wars are the field of honour," returned the old man proudly. "There a man plays his life upon the cast; he fights in the name of his lord the king, his Lord God, and all their lordships the holy saints and angels."

"Put it," said Villon, "that I were really a thief, should I not play my life also, and against heavier odds?"

"For gain but not for honour."

"Gain?" repeated Villon with a shrug. "Gain! The poor fellow wants supper, and takes it. So does the soldier in a campaign. Why, what are all these requisitions we hear so much about? If they are not gain to those who take them, they are loss enough to the others. The men-at-arms drink by a good fire, while the burgher bites his nails to buy them wine and wood. I have seen a good many ploughmen swinging on trees about the country; ay, I have seen thirty on one elm, and a very poor figure they made; and when I asked some one how all these came to be hanged, I was told it was because they could not scrape together enough crowns to satisfy the men-at-arms."

"These things are a necessity of war, which the low-born must endure with constancy. It is true that some captains drive over-hard; there are spirits in every rank not easily moved by pity; and indeed many follow arms who are no better than brigands."

"You see," said the poet, "you cannot separate the soldier from the brigand; and what is a thief but an isolated brigand with circumspect manners? I steal a couple of mutton chops, without so much as disturbing people's sleep; the farmer grumbles a bit, but sups none the less wholesomely on what remains. You come up blowing gloriously on a trumpet, take away the whole sheep, and beat the farmer pitifully into the bargain. I have no trumpet; I am only Tom, Dick, or Harry; I am a rogue and a dog, and hanging's too good for me—with all my heart; but just ask the farmer which of us he prefers, just find out which of us he lies awake to curse on cold nights."

"Look at us two," said his lordship. "I am old, strong, and honoured. If I were turned from my house to-morrow, hundreds would be proud to shelter me. Poor people would go out and pass the night in the streets with their children, if I merely hinted that I wished to be alone. And I find you up, wandering homeless, and picking farthings off dead women by the wayside! I fear no man and nothing; I have seen you tremble and lose countenance at a word. I wait God's summons contentedly in my own house, or, if it please the king to call me out again, upon the field of battle. You look for the gallows; a rough, swift death, without hope or honour. Is there no difference between these two?"

"As far as to the moon," Villon acquiesced. "But if I had been born lord of Brisetout, and you had been the poor scholar Francis, would the difference have been any the less? Should not I have been warming my knees at this charcoal pan, and would not you have been groping for farthings in the snow? Should not I have been the soldier, and you the thief?"

"A thief?" cried the old man. "I a thief! If you understood your words, you would repent them."

Villon turned out his hands with a gesture of inimitable impudence. "If your lordship had done me the honour to follow my argument!" he said.

"I do you too much honour in submitting to your presence," said the knight. "Learn to curb your tongue when you speak with old and honourable men, or some one hastier than I may reprove you in a sharper fashion." And he rose and paced the lower end of the apartment, struggling with anger and antipathy. Villon surreptitiously refilled his cup, and settled himself more comfortably in the chair, crossing his knees and leaning his head upon one hand and the elbow against the back of the chair. He was now replete and warm; and he was in nowise frightened for his host, having gauged him as justly as was possible between two such different characters. The night was far spent, and in a very comfortable fashion after all; and he felt morally certain of a safe departure on the morrow.

"Tell me one thing," said the old man, pausing in his walk. "Are you really a thief?"

"I claim the sacred rights of hospitality," returned the poet. "My lord, I am."

"You are very young," the knight continued.

"I should never have been so old," replied Villon, showing his fingers, "if I had not helped myself with these ten talents. They have been my nursing mothers and my nursing fathers."

"You may still repent and change."

"I repent daily," said the poet. "There are few people more given to repentance than poor Francis. As for change, let somebody change my circumstances. A man must continue to eat, if it were only that he may continue to repent."

"The change must begin in the heart," returned the old man solemnly.

"My dear lord," answered Villon, "do you really fancy that I steal for pleasure? I hate stealing, like any other piece of work of danger. My teeth chatter when I see a gallows. But I must eat, I must drink, I must mix in society of some sort. What the devil! Man is not a solitary animal—*Cui Deus fœminam tradit.* Make me king's pantler—make me abbot of St. Denis; make me bailly of the Patatrac; and then I shall be changed indeed. But as long as you leave me the poor scholar Francis Villon, without a farthing, why, of course, I remain the same."

"The grace of God is all-powerful."

"I should be a heretic to question it," said Francis. "It has made you lord of Brisetout and bailly of the Patatrac; it has given me nothing but the quick wits under my hat and these ten toes upon my hands. May I help myself to wine? I thank you respectfully. By God's grace, you have a very superior vintage."

The lord of Brisetout walked to and fro with his hands behind his back. Perhaps he was not yet quite settled in his mind about the parallel between thieves and soldiers; perhaps Villon had interested him by some cross-thread of sympathy; perhaps his wits were simply muddled by so much unfamiliar reasoning; but whatever the cause, he somehow yearned to convert the young man to a better way of thinking, and could not make up his mind to drive him forth again into the street.

"There is something more than I can understand in this," he said at length. "Your mouth is full of subtleties, and the devil has led you very far astray; but the devil is only a very weak spirit before God's truth, and all his subtleties vanish at a word of true honour, like darkness at morning. Listen to me once more. I learned long ago that a gentleman should live chivalrously and lovingly to God, and the king, and his lady; and though I have seen many strange things done, I have still striven to command my ways upon that rule. It is not only written in all noble histories, but in every man's heart, if he will take care to read. You speak of food and wine, and I know very well that hunger is a difficult trial to endure; but you do not speak of other wants; you say nothing of honour, of faith to God and other men, of courtesy, of love without reproach. It may be that I am not very wise—and yet I think I am—but you seem to me like one who has lost his way and made a great error in life. You are attending to the little wants, and you have totally forgotten the great and only real ones, like a man who should be doctoring toothache on the Judgment Day. For such things as honour and love and faith are not only nobler than food and drink, but indeed I think we desire them more, and suffer more sharply for their absence. I speak to you as I think you will most easily understand me. Are you not, while careful to fill your belly, disregarding another appetite in your heart, which spoils the pleasure of your life and keeps you continually wretched?"

Villon was sensibly nettled under all this sermonising. "You think I have no sense of honour!" he cried. "I'm poor enough, God knows! It's hard to see rich people with their gloves, and you blowing in your hands. An empty belly is a bitter thing, although you speak so lightly of it. If you had had as many as I, perhaps you would change your tune. Anyway I'm a thief—make the most of that—but I'm not a devil from hell, God strike me dead. I would have you to know I've an honour of my own, as good as yours, though I don't prate about it all day long, as if it was a God's miracle to have any. It seems quite natural to me; I keep it in its box till it's wanted. Why now, look you here, how long have I been in this room with you? Did you not tell me you were alone in the house? Look at your gold plate! You're strong, if you like, but you're old and unarmed, and I have my knife. What did I want but a jerk of the elbow and here would have been you with the cold steel in your bowels, and there would have been me, linking in the streets, with an armful of golden cups! Did you suppose I hadn't wit enough to see that? And I scorned the action. There are your damned goblets, as safe as in a church; there are you, with your heart ticking as good as new; and here am I, ready to go out again as poor as I came in, with my one white that you threw in my teeth! And you think I have no sense of honour— God strike me dead!"

The old man stretched out his right arm. "I will tell you what you are," he said. "You are a rogue, my man, an impudent and black-hearted rogue and vagabond. I have passed an hour with you. Oh! believe me, I feel myself disgraced! And you have eaten and drunk at my table. But now I am sick at your presence; the day has come, and the night-bird should be off to his roost. Will you go before, or after?"

"Which you please," returned the poet, rising. "I believe you to be strictly honourable." He thoughtfully emptied his cup. "I wish I could add you were intelligent," he went on, knocking on his head with his knuckles. "Age! age! the brains stiff and rheumatic."

The old man preceded him from a point of self-respect. Villon followed, whistling, with his thumbs in his girdle.

"God pity you," said the lord of Brisetout at the door.

"Good-bye, papa," returned Villon with a yawn. "Many thanks for the cold mutton."

The door closed behind him. The dawn was breaking over the white roofs. A chill, uncomfortable morning ushered in the day. Villon stood and heartily stretched himself in the middle of the road.

"A very dull old gentleman," he thought. "I wonder what his goblets may be worth."

Markheim

Y ES," SAID THE DEALER, "OUR WINDFALLS ARE OF VARIOUS KINDS. Some customers are ignorant, and then I touch a dividend of my superior knowledge. Some are dishonest," and here he held up the candle, so that the light fell strongly on his visitor, "and in that case," he continued, "I profit by my virtue."

Markheim had but just entered from the daylight streets, and his eyes had not yet grown familiar with the mingled shine and darkness in the shop. At these pointed words, and before the near presence of the flame, he blinked painfully and looked aside.

The dealer chuckled "You come to me on Christmas Day," he resumed, "when you know that I am alone in my house, put up my shutters, and make a point of refusing business. Well, you will have to pay for that; you will have to pay for my loss of time, when I should be balancing my books; you will have to pay, besides, for a kind of manner that I remark in you to-day very strongly. I am the essence of discretion, and ask no awkward questions; but when a customer cannot look me in the eye, he has to pay for it." The dealer once more chuckled; and then, changing to his usual business voice, though still with a note of irony, "You can give, as usual, a clear account of how you came into the possession of the object?" he continued. "Still your uncle's cabinet? A remarkable collector, sir!"

And the little pale, round-shouldered dealer stood almost on tiptoe, looking over the top of his gold spectacles, and nodding his head with every mark of disbelief. Markheim returned his gaze with one of infinite pity, and a touch of horror.

"This time," said he, "you are in error. I have not come to sell,

but to buy. I have no curios to dispose of; my uncle's cabinet is
bare to the wainscot; even were it still intact, I have done well on
the Stock Exchange, and should more likely add to it than otherwise, and my errand to-day is simplicity itself. I seek a Christmas
present for a lady," he continued, waxing more fluent as he struck
into the speech he had prepared; "and certainly I owe you every
excuse for thus disturbing you upon so small a matter. But the
thing was neglected yesterday; I must produce my little compliment at dinner; and, as you very well know, a rich marriage is not
a thing to be neglected."

There followed a pause, during which the dealer seemed to
weigh this statement incredulously. The ticking of many clocks
among the curious lumber of the shop, and the faint rushing of
the cabs in a near thoroughfare, filled up the interval of silence.

"Well, sir," said the dealer, "be it so. You are an old customer
after all; and if, as you say, you have the chance of a good marriage, far be it from me to be an obstacle. Here is a nice thing for
a lady now," he went on, "this hand glass—fifteenth century, war-
ranted; comes from a good collection, too; but I reserve the name,
in the interests of my customer, who was just like yourself, my dear
sir, the nephew and sole heir of a remarkable collector."

The dealer, while he thus ran on in his dry and biting voice,
had stooped to take the object from its place; and, as he had done
so, a shock had passed through Markheim, a start both of hand
and foot, a sudden leap of many tumultuous passions to the face.
It passed as swiftly as it came, and left no trace beyond a certain
trembling of the hand that now received the glass.

"A glass," he said hoarsely, and then paused, and repeated it
more clearly. "A glass? For Christmas? Surely not?"

"And why not?" cried the dealer. "Why not a glass?"

Markheim was looking upon him with an indefinable expression.
"You ask me why not?" he said. "Why, look here—look in it—
look at yourself! Do you like to see it? No! nor I—nor any man."

The little man had jumped back when Markheim had so suddenly confronted him with the mirror; but now, perceiving there
was nothing worse on hand, he chuckled. "Your future lady, sir,
must be pretty hard favoured," said he.

"I ask you," said Markheim, "for a Christmas present, and you
give me this—this damned reminder of years, and sins and follies—
this hand-conscience! Did you mean it? Had you a thought in your

mind? Tell me. It will be better for you if you do. Come, tell me about yourself. I hazard a guess now, that you are in secret a very charitable man?"

The dealer looked closely at his companion. It was very odd, Markheim did not appear to be laughing; there was something in his face like an eager sparkle of hope, but nothing of mirth.

"What are you driving at?" the dealer asked.

"Not charitable?" returned the other, gloomily. "Not charitable; not pious; not scrupulous; unloving, unbeloved; a hand to get money, a safe to keep it. Is that all? Dear God, man, is that all?"

"I will tell you what it is," began the dealer, with some sharpness, and then broke off again into a chuckle. "But I see this is a love match of yours. and you have been drinking the lady's health."

"Ah!" cried Markheim, with a strange curiosity. "Ah, have you been in love? Tell me about that."

"I," cried the dealer. "I in love! I never had the time, nor have I the time to-day for all this nonsense. Will you take the glass?"

"Where is the hurry?" returned Markheim. "It is very pleasant to stand here talking; and life is so short and insecure that I would not hurry away from any pleasure—no, not even from so mild a one as this. We should rather cling, cling to what little we can get, like a man at a cliff's edge. Every second is a cliff, if you think upon it—a cliff a mile high—high enough, if we fall, to dash us out of every feature of humanity. Hence it is best to talk pleasantly. Let us talk to each other; why should we wear this mask? Let us be confidential. Who knows, we might become friends?"

"I have just one word to say to you," said the dealer. "Either make your purchase, or walk out of my shop."

"True, true," said Markheim. "Enough fooling. To business. Show me something else."

The dealer stooped once more, this time to replace the glass upon the shelf, his thin blond hair falling over his eyes as he did so. Markheim moved a little nearer, with one hand in the pocket of his great-coat; he drew himself up and filled his lungs; at the same time many different emotions were depicted together on his face—terror, horror, and resolve, fascination and a physical repulsion; and through a haggard lift of his upper lip, his teeth looked out.

"This, perhaps, may suit," observed the dealer; and then, as he began to re-arise, Markheim bounded from behind upon his victim. The long, skewerlike dagger flashed and fell. The dealer struggled like a hen, striking his temple on the shelf, and then tumbled on the floor in heap.

Time had some score of small voices in that shop, some stately and slow as was becoming to their great age; others garrulous and hurried. All these told out the seconds in an intricate chorus of tickings. Then the passage of a lad's feet, heavily running on the pavement, broke in upon these smaller voices and startled Markheim into the consciousness of his surroundings. He looked about him awfully. The candle stood on the counter, its flame solemnly wagging in a draught; and by that inconsiderable movement, the whole room was filled with noiseless bustle and kept heaving like a sea: the tall shadows nodding, the gross blots of darkness swelling and dwindling as with respiration, the faces of the portraits and the china gods changing and wavering like images in water. The inner door stood ajar, and peered into that leaguer of shadows with a long slit of daylight like a pointing finger.

From these fear-stricken rovings, Markheim's eyes returned to the body of his victim, where it lay both humped and sprawling, incredibly small and strangely meaner than in life. In these poor, miserly clothes, in that ungainly attitude, the dealer lay like so much sawdust. Markheim had feared to see it, and, lo! it was nothing. And yet, as he gazed, this bundle of old clothes and pool of blood began to find eloquent voices. There it must lie; there was none to work the cunning hinges or direct the miracle of locomotion—there it must lie till it was found. Found! ay, and then? Then would this dead flesh lift up a cry that would ring over England, and fill the world with the echoes of pursuit. Ay, dead or not, this was still the enemy. "Time was that when the brains were out," he thought; and the first word struck into his mind. Time, now that the deed was accomplished—time, which had closed for the victim, had become instant and momentous for the slayer.

The thought was yet in his mind, when, first one and then another, with every variety of pace and voice—one deep as the bell from a cathedral turret, another ringing on its treble notes the prelude of a waltz—the clocks began to strike the hour of three in the afternoon.

The sudden outbreak of so many tongues in that dumb chamber staggered him. He began to bestir himself, going to and fro with the candle, beleaguered by moving shadows, and startled to the soul by chance reflections. In many rich mirrors, some of home designs, some from Venice or Amsterdam, he saw his face repeated and repeated, as it were an army of spies; his own eyes met and detected him; and the sound of his own steps, lightly as they fell, vexed the surrounding quiet. And still as he continued to fill his pockets, his mind accused him, with a sickening iteration, of the thousand faults of his design. He should have chosen a more quiet hour; he should have prepared an alibi; he should not have used a knife; he should have been more cautious, and only bound and gagged the dealer, and not killed him; he should have been more bold, and killed the servant also; he should have done all things otherwise; poignant regrets, weary, incessant toiling of the mind to change what was unchangeable, to plan what was now useless, to be the architect of the irrevocable past. Meanwhile, and behind all this activity, brute terrors, like the scurrying of rats in a deserted attic, filled the more remote chambers of his brain with riot; the hand of the constable would fall heavy on his shoulder, and his nerves would jerk like a hooked fish; or he beheld, in galloping defile, the dock, the prison, the gallows, and the black coffin.

Terror of the people in the street sat down before his mind like a besieging army. It was impossible, he thought, but that some rumour of the struggle must have reached their ears and set on edge their curiosity; and now, in all the neighbouring houses, he divined them sitting motionless and with uplifted ear—solitary people, condemned to spend Christmas dwelling alone on memories of the past, and now startlingly recalled from that tender exercise; happy family parties, struck into silence round the table, the mother still with raised finger: every degree and age and humour, but all, by their own hearts, prying and hearkening and weaving the rope that was to hang him. Sometimes it seemed to him he could not move too softly; the clink of the tall Bohemian goblets rang out loudly like a bell; and alarmed by the bigness of the ticking, he was tempted to stop the clocks. And then, again, with a swift transition of his terrors, the very silence of the place appeared a source of peril, and a thing to strike and freeze the passer-by; and he would step more boldly, and bustle aloud among the contents of the shop, and imitate, with elaborate bravado, the movements of a busy man at ease in his own house.

But he was now so pulled about by different alarms that, while one portion of his mind was still alert and cunning, another trembled on the brink of lunacy. One hallucination in particular took a strong hold on his credulity. The neighbour hearkening with white face beside his window, the passer-by arrested by a horrible surmise on the pavement—these could at worst suspect, they could not know; through the brick walls and shuttered windows only sounds could penetrate. But here, within the house, was he alone? He knew he was; he had watched the servant set forth sweethearting, in her poor best, "out for the day" written in every ribbon and smile. Yes, he was alone, of course; and yet, in the bulk of empty house above him, he could surely hear a stir of delicate footing—he was surely conscious, inexplicably conscious of some presence. Ay, surely; to every room and corner of the house his imagination followed it; and now it was a faceless thing, and yet had eyes to see with; and again it was a shadow of himself; and yet again behold the image of the dead dealer, reinspired with cunning and hatred.

At times, with a strong effort, he would glance at the open door which still seemed to repel his eyes. The house was tall, the skylight small and dirty, the day blind with fog; and the light that filtered down to the ground storey was exceedingly faint, and showed dimly on the threshold of the shop. And yet, in that strip of doubtful brightness, did there not hang wavering a shadow?

Suddenly, from the street outside, a very jovial gentleman began to beat with a staff on the shopdoor, accompanying his blows with shouts and railleries in which the dealer was continually called upon by name. Markheim, smitten into ice, glanced at the dead man. But no! he lay quite still; he was fled away far beyond earshot of these blows and shoutings; he was sunk beneath seas of silence; and his name, which would once have caught his notice above the howling of a storm, had become an empty sound. And presently the jovial gentleman desisted from his knocking and departed.

Here was a broad hint to hurry what remained to be done, to get forth from this accusing neighbourhood, to plunge into a bath of London multitudes, and to reach, on the other side of day, that haven of safety and apparent innocence—his bed. One visitor had come: at any moment another might follow and be more obstinate. To have done the deed, and yet not to reap the profit, would be too abhorrent a failure. The money, that was now Markheim's concern; and as a means to that, the keys.

He glanced over his shoulder at the open door, where the shadow was still lingering and shivering; and with no conscious repugnance of the mind, yet with a tremor of the belly, he drew near the body of his victim. The human character had quite departed. Like a suit half stuffed with bran, the limbs lay scattered, the trunk doubled, on the floor; and yet the thing repelled him. Although so dingy and inconsiderable to the eye, he feared it might have more significance to the touch. He took the body by the shoulders, and turned it on its back. It was strangely light and supple, and the limbs, as if they had been broken, fell into the oddest postures. The face was robbed of all expression; but it was as pale as wax, and shockingly smeared with blood about one temple. That was, for Markheim, the one displeasing circumstance. It carried him back, upon the instant, to a certain fair day in a fishers' village: a grey day, a piping wind, a crowd upon the street, the blare of brasses, the booming of drums, the nasal voice of a ballad singer; and a boy going to and fro, buried over head in the crowd and divided between interest and fear, until, coming out upon the chief place of concourse, he beheld a booth and a great screen with pictures, dismally designed, garishly coloured: Brownrigg with her apprentice; the Mannings with their murdered guest; Weare in the death-grip of Thurtell; and a score besides of famous crimes. The thing was as clear as an illusion; he was once again that little boy; he was looking once again, and with the same sense of physical revolt, at these vile pictures; he was still stunned by the thumping of the drums. A bar of that day's music returned upon his memory; and at that, for the first time, a qualm came over him, a breath of nausea, a sudden weakness of the joints, which he must instantly resist and conquer.

He judged it more prudent to confront than to flee from these considerations; looking the more hardily in the dead face, bending his mind to realise the nature and greatness of his crime. So little a while ago that face had moved with every change of sentiment, that pale mouth had spoken, that body had been all on fire with governable energies; and now, and by his act, that piece of life had been arrested, as the horologist, with interjected finger, arrests the beating of the clock. So he reasoned in vain; he could rise to no more remorseful consciousness; the same heart which had shuddered before the painted effigies of crime, looked on its reality unmoved. At best, he felt a gleam of pity for one who had been endowed in vain with all those faculties that can make the world a garden of enchantment, one who had never lived and who was now dead. But of penitence, no, not a tremor.

With that, shaking himself clear of these considerations, he found the keys and advanced towards the open door of the shop. Outside, it had begun to rain smartly; and the sound of the shower upon the roof had banished silence. Like some dripping cavern, the chambers of the house were haunted by an incessant echoing, which filled the ear and mingled with the ticking of the clocks. And, as Markheim approached the door, he seemed to hear, in answer to his own cautious tread, the steps of another foot withdrawing up the stair. The shadow still palpitated loosely on the threshold. He threw a ton's weight of resolve upon his muscles, and drew back the door.

The faint, foggy daylight glimmered dimly on the bare floor and stairs; on the bright suit of armour posted, halbert in hand, upon the landing; and on the dark wood-carvings, and framed pictures that hung against the yellow panels of the wainscot. So loud was the beating of the rain through all the house that, in Markheim's ears, it began to be distinguished into many different sounds. Footsteps and sighs, the tread of regiments marching in the distance, the chink of money in the counting, and the creaking of doors held stealthily ajar, appeared to mingle with the patter of the drops upon the cupola and the gushing of the water in the pipes. The sense that he was not alone grew upon him to the verge of madness. On every side he was haunted and begirt by presences. He heard them moving in the upper chambers; from the shop, he heard the dead man getting to his legs; and as he began with a great effort to mount the stairs, feet fled quietly before him and followed stealthily behind. If he were but deaf, he thought, how tranquilly he would possess his soul! And then again, and hearkening with ever fresh attention, he blessed himself for that unresting sense which held the outposts and stood a trusty sentinel upon his life. His head turned continually on his neck; his eyes, which seemed starting from their orbits, scouted on every side, and on every side were half rewarded as with the tail of something nameless vanishing. The four-and-twenty steps to the first floor were four-and-twenty agonies.

On that first storey, the doors stood ajar, three of them like three ambushes, shaking his nerves like the throats of cannon. He could never again, he felt, be sufficiently immured and fortified from men's observing eyes; he longed to be home, girt in by walls, buried among bedclothes, and invisible to all but God. And at that thought he wondered a little, recollecting tales of other murderers and the fear they were said to entertain of heavenly avengers. It was not so, at least, with him. He feared the laws of nature, lest, in their callous and immutable procedure, they should preserve some damning evidence of his crime. He feared tenfold more, with a slavish, superstitious terror, some scission in the continuity of man's experience, some wilful illegality of nature. He played a game of skill, depending on the rules, calculating consequence from cause; and what if nature, as the defeated tyrant overthrew the chess-board, should break the mould of their succession? The like had befallen Napoleon (so writers said) when the winter changed the time of its appearance. The like might befall Markheim: the solid walls might become transparent and reveal his doings like those of bees in a glass hive; the stout planks might yield under his foot like quicksands and detain him in their clutch; ay, and there were soberer accidents that might destroy him: if, for instance, the house should fall and imprison him beside the body of his victim; or the house next door should fly on fire, and the firemen invade him from all sides. These things he feared; and, in a sense, these things might be called the hands of God reached forth against sin. But about God himself he was at ease; his act was doubtless exceptional, but so were his excuses, which God knew; it was there, and not among men, that he felt sure of justice.

When he had got safe into the drawing-room, and shut the door behind him, he was aware of a respite from alarms. The room was quite dismantled, uncarpeted besides, and strewn with packing-cases and incongruous furniture; several great pier-glasses, in which he beheld himself at various angles, like an actor on a stage; many pictures, framed and unframed, standing, with their faces to the wall; a fine Sheraton sideboard, a cabinet of marquetry, and a great old bed, with tapestry hangings. The windows opened to the floor; but by great good-fortune the lower part of the shutters had been closed, and this concealed him from the neighbours. Here, then, Markheim drew in a packing-case before the cabinet, and began to search among the keys. It was a long business, for there were many; and it was irksome, besides; for, after all, there might be nothing in the cabinet, and time was on the wing. But the closeness of the occupation sobered him. With the tail of his eye he saw the door—even glanced at it from time to time directly, like a besieged commander pleased to verify the good estate of his defences. But in truth he was at peace. The rain falling in the street sounded natural and pleasant. Presently, on the other side, the notes of a piano were wakened to the music of a hymn, and the voices of many children took up the air and words. How stately, how comfortable was the melody! How fresh the youthful voices! Markheim gave ear to it smilingly, as he sorted out the keys; and his mind was thronged with answerable ideas and images; churchgoing children and the pealing of the high organ; children afield, bathers by the brookside, ramblers on the brambly common, kite-fliers in the windy and cloud-navigated sky; and then, at another cadence of the hymn, back again to church, and the somnolence of summer Sundays, and the high genteel voice of the parson (which he smiled a little to recall) and the painted Jacobean tombs, and the dim lettering of the Ten Commandments in the chancel.

And as he sat thus, at once busy and absent, he was startled to his feet. A flash of ice, a flash of fire, a bursting gush of blood, went over him, and then he stood transfixed and thrilling. A step mounted the stair slowly and steadily, and presently a hand was laid upon the knob, and the lock clicked, and the door opened.

Fear held Markheim in a vice. What to expect he knew not, whether the dead man walking, or the official ministers of human justice, or some chance witness blindly stumbling in to consign him to the gallows. But when a face was thrust into the aperture, glanced round the room, looked at him, nodded and smiled as if in friendly recognition, and then withdrew again, and the door closed behind it, his fear broke loose from his control in a hoarse cry. At the sound of this the visitant returned.

"Did you call me?" he asked, pleasantly, and with that he entered the room and closed the door behind him.

Markheim stood and gazed at him with all his eyes. Perhaps there was a film upon his sight, but the outlines of the newcomer seemed to change and waver like those of the idols in the wavering candle-light of the shop; and at times he thought he knew him; and at times he thought he bore a likeness to himself; and always, like a lump of living terror, there lay in his bosom the conviction that this thing was not of the earth and not of God.

And yet the creature had a strange air of the commonplace, as he stood looking on Markheim with a smile; and when he added: "You are looking for the money, I believe?" it was in the tones of every-day politeness.

Markheim made no answer.

"I should warn you," resumed the other, "that the maid has left her sweetheart earlier than usual and will soon be here. If Mr. Markheim be found in this house, I need not describe to him the consequences."

"You know me?" cried the murderer.

The visitor smiled. "You have long been a favourite of mine," he said; "and I have long observed and often sought to help you."

"What are you?" cried Markheim: "the devil?"

"What I may be," returned the other, "cannot affect the service I propose to render you."

"It can," cried Markheim; "it does! Be helped by you? No, never, not by you! You do not know me yet; thank God, you do not know me!"

"I know you," replied the visitant, with a sort of kind severity or rather firmness. "I know you to the soul."

"Know me!" cried Markheim. "Who can do so? My life is but a travesty and slander on myself. I have lived to belie my nature. All men do; all men are better than this disguise that grows about and stifles them. You see each dragged away by life, like one whom bravos have seized and muffled in a cloak. If they had their own control—if you could see their faces, they would be altogether different, they would shine out for heroes and saints! I am worse than most; my self is more overlaid; my excuse is known to me and God. But, had I the time, I could disclose myself."

"To me?" inquired the visitant.

"To you before all," returned the murderer. "I supposed you were intelligent. I thought—since you exist—you would prove a reader of the heart. And yet you would propose to judge me by my acts! Think of it; my acts! I was born and I have lived in a land of giants; giants have dragged me by the wrists since I was born out of my mother—the giants of circumstance. And you would judge me by my acts! But can you not look within? Can you not understand that evil is hateful to me? Can you not see within me the clear writing of conscience, never blurred by any wilful sophistry, although too often disregarded? Can you not read me for a thing that surely must be common as humanity—the unwilling sinner?"

"All this is very feelingly expressed," was the reply, "but it regards me not. These points of consistency are beyond my province, and I care not in the least by what compulsion you may have been dragged away, so as you are but carried in the right direction. But time flies; the servant delays, looking in the faces of the crowd and at the pictures on the hoardings, but still she keeps moving nearer; and remember, it is as if the gallows itself was striding towards you through the Christmas streets! Shall I help you; I, who know all? Shall I tell you where to find the money?"

"For what price?" asked Markheim.

"I offer you the service for a Christmas gift," returned the other.

Markheim could not refrain from smiling with a kind of bitter triumph. "No," said he, "I will take nothing at your hands; if I were dying of thirst, and it was your hand that put the pitcher to my lips, I should find the courage to refuse. It may be credulous, but I will do nothing to commit myself to evil."

"I have no objection to a death-bed repentance," observed the visitant.

"Because you disbelieve their efficacy!" Markheim cried.

"I do not say so," returned the other; "but I look on these things from a different side, and when the life is done my interest falls. The man has lived to serve me, to spread black looks under colour of religion, or to sow tares in the wheatfield, as you do, in a course of weak compliance with desire. Now that he draws so near to his deliverance, he can add but one act of service—to repent, to die smiling, and thus to build up in confidence and hope the more timorous of my surviving followers. I am not so hard a master. Try me. Accept my help. Please yourself in life as you have done hitherto; please yourself more amply, spread your elbows at the board; and when the night begins to fall and the curtains to be drawn, I tell you, for your greater comfort, that you will find it even easy to compound your quarrel with your conscience, and to make a truckling peace with God. I came but now from such a death-bed, and the room was full of sincere mourners, listening to the man's last words: and when I looked into that face, which had been set as a flint against mercy, I found it smiling with hope."

"And do you, then, suppose me such a creature?" asked Markheim. "Do you think I have no more generous aspirations than to sin, and sin, and sin, and at last, sneak into heaven? My heart rises at the thought. Is this, then, your experience of mankind? or is it because you find me with red hands that you presume such baseness? and is this crime of murder indeed so impious as to dry up the very springs of good?"

"Murder is to me no special category," replied the other. "All sins are murder, even as all life is war. I behold your race, like starving mariners on a raft, plucking crusts out of the hands of famine and feeding on each other's lives. I follow sins beyond the moment of their acting; I find in all that the last consequence is death; and to my eyes, the pretty maid who thwarts her mother with such taking graces on a question of a ball, drips no less visibly with human gore than such a murderer as yourself. Do I say that I follow sins? I follow virtues also; they differ not by the thickness of a nail, they are both scythes for the reaping angel of Death. Evil, for which I live, consists not in action but in character. The bad man is dear to me; not the bad act, whose fruits, if we could follow them far enough down the hurtling cataract of the ages, might yet be found more blessed than those of the rarest virtues. And it is not because you have killed a dealer, but because you are Markheim, that I offered to forward your escape."

"I will lay my heart open to you," answered Markheim. "This crime on which you find me is my last. On my way to it I have learned many lessons; itself is a lesson, a momentous lesson. Hitherto I have been driven with revolt to what I would not; I was a bond-slave to poverty, driven and scourged. There are robust virtues that can stand in these temptations; mine was not so: I had a thirst of pleasure. But to-day, and out of this deed, I pluck both warning and riches—both the power and a fresh resolve to be myself. I become in all things a free actor in the world; I begin to see myself all changed, these hands the agents of good, this heart at peace. Something comes over me out of the past; something of what I have dreamed on Sabbath evenings to the sound of the church organ, of what I forecast when I shed tears over noble books, or talked, an innocent child, with my mother. There lies my life; I have wandered a few years, but now I see once more my city of destination."

"You are to use this money on the Stock Exchange, I think?" remarked the visitor; "and there, if I mistake not, you have already lost some thousands?"

"Ah," said Markheim, "but this time I have a sure thing."

"This time, again, you will lose," replied the visitor quietly.

"Ah, but I keep back the half!" cried Markheim.

"That also you will lose," said the other.

The sweat started upon Markheim's brow. "Well, then, what matter?" he exclaimed. "Say it be lost, say I am plunged again in poverty, shall one part of me, and that the worst, continue until the end to override the better? Evil and good run strong in me, haling me both ways, I do not love the one thing, I love all. I can conceive great deeds, renunciations, martyrdoms; and though I be fallen to such a crime as murder, pity is no stranger to my thoughts. I pity the poor; who knows their trials better than my-self? I pity and help them; I prize love, I love honest laughter; there is no good thing nor true thing on earth but I love it from my heart. And are my vices only to direct my life, and my virtues to lie without effect, like some passive lumber of the mind? Not so; good, also, is a spring of acts."

But the visitant raised his finger. "For six-and-thirty years that you have been in this world," said he, "through many changes of fortune and varieties of humour, I have watched you steadily fall. Fifteen years ago you would have started at a theft. Three years back you would have blenched at the name of murder. Is there any crime, is there any cruelty of meanness, from which you still recoil?—five years from now I shall detect you in the fact! Down-ward, downward, lies your way; nor can anything but death avail to stop you."

"It is true," Markheim said huskily, "I have in some degree complied with evil. But it is so with all: the very saints, in the mere exercise of living, grow less dainty, and take on the tone of their surroundings."

"I will propound to you one simple question," said the other; "and as you answer, I shall read to you your moral horoscope. You have grown in many things more lax; possibly you do right to be so; and at any account, it is the same with all men. But granting that, are you in any one particular, however trifling, more difficult to please with your own conduct, or do you go in all things with a looser rein?"

"In any one?" repeated Markheim, with an anguish of consideration. "No," he added, with despair, "in none! I have gone down in all."

"Then," said the visitor, "content yourself with what you are, for you will never change; and the words of your part on this stage are irrevocably written down."

Markheim stood for a long while silent, and indeed it was the visitor who first broke the silence. "That being so," he said, "shall I show you the money?"

"And grace?" cried Markheim.

"Have you not tried it?" returned the other. "Two or three years ago, did I not see you on the platform of revival meetings, and was not your voice the loudest in the hymn?"

"It is true," said Markheim; "and I see clearly what remains for me by way of duty. I thank you for these lessons from my soul; my eyes are opened, and I behold myself at last for what I am."

At this moment, the sharp note of the doorbell rang through the house; and the visitant, as though this were some concerted signal for which he had been waiting, changed at once in his demeanour.

"The maid!" he cried. "She has returned, as I forewarned you, and there is now before you one more difficult passage. Her master. you must say, is ill; you must let her in, with an assured but rather serious countenance—no smiles, no overacting, and I promise you success! Once the girl within, and the door closed, the same dexterity that has already rid you of the dealer will relieve you of this last danger in your path. Thenceforward you have the whole evening—the whole night, if needful—to ransack the treasures of the house and to make good your safety. This is help that comes to you with the mask of danger. Up!" he cried: "up, friend; your life hangs trembling in the scales: up, and act!"

Markheim steadily regarded his counsellor. "If I be condemned to evil acts," he said, "there is still one door of freedom open—I can cease from action. If my life be an ill thing, I can lay it down. Though I be, as you say truly, at the beck of every small temptation, I can yet, by one decisive gesture, place myself beyond the reach of all. My love of good is damned to barrenness; it may, and let it be! But I have still my hatred of evil: and from that, to your galling disappointment, you shall see that I can draw both energy and courage."

The features of the visitor began to undergo a wonderful and lovely change: they brightened and softened with a tender triumph; and, even as they brightened, faded and dislimned. But Markheim did not pause to watch or understand the transformation. He opened the door and went down-stairs very slowly, thinking to himself. His past went soberly before him; he beheld it as it was, ugly and strenuous like a dream, random as chance-medley —a scene of defeat. Life, as he thus reviewed it, tempted him no longer; but on the further side he perceived a quiet haven for his bark. He paused in the passage, and looked into the shop, where the candle still burned by the dead body. It was strangely silent. Thoughts of the dealer swarmed into his mind, as he stood gazing. And then the bell once more broke out into impatient clamour.

He confronted the maid upon the threshold with something like a smile.

"You had better go for the police," said he: "I have killed your master."

Thrawn Janet

THE REVEREND MURDOCK SOULIS WAS LONG MINISTER OF THE moorland parish of Balweary, in the vale of Dule. A severe, bleak-faced old man, dreadful to his hearers, he dwelt in the last years of his life, without relative or servant or any human company, in the small and lonely manse under the Hanging Shaw. In spite of the iron composure of his features, his eye was wild, scared, and uncertain; and when he dwelt, in private admonitions, on the future of the impenitent, it seemed as if his eye pierced through the storms of time to the terrors of eternity. Many young persons, coming to prepare themselves against the season of the Holy Communion, were dreadfully affected by his talk. He had a sermon on 1st Peter, v. and 8th, "The devil as a roaring lion," on the Sunday after every seventeenth of August, and he was accustomed to surpass himself upon that text both by the appalling nature of the matter and the terror of his bearing in the pulpit. The children were frightened into fits, and the old looked more than usually oracular, and were, all that day, full of those hints that Hamlet deprecated. The manse itself, where it stood by the water of Dule among some thick trees, with the Shaw overhanging it on the one side, and on the other many cold, moorish hill-tops rising towards the sky, had begun, at a very early period of Mr. Soulis's ministry, to be avoided in the dusk hours by all who valued themselves upon their prudence; and guidmen sitting at the clachan alehouse shook their heads together at the thought of passing late by that uncanny neighbourhood. There was one spot, to be more particular, which was regarded with especial awe. The manse stood between the highroad and the water of Dule, with a gable to each;

its back was towards the kirktown of Balweary, nearly half a mile away; in front of it, a bare garden, hedged with thorn, occupied the land between the river and the road. The house was two storeys high, with two large rooms on each. It opened not directly on the garden, but on a causewayed path, or passage, giving on the road on the one hand, and closed on the other by the tall willows and elders that bordered on the stream. And it was this strip of causeway that enjoyed among the young parishioners of Balweary so infamous a reputation. The minister walked there often after dark, sometimes groaning aloud in the instancy of his unspoken prayers; and when he was from home, and the manse door was locked, the more daring schoolboys ventured, with beating hearts, to "follow my leader" across that legendary spot.

This atmosphere of terror, surrounding, as it did, a man of God of spotless character and orthodoxy, was a common cause of wonder and subject of inquiry among the few strangers who were led by chance or business into that unknown, outlying country. But many even of the people of the parish were ignorant of the strange events which had marked the first year of Mr. Soulis's ministrations; and among those who were better informed, some were naturally reticent, and others shy of that particular topic. Now and again, only, one of the older folk would warm into courage over his third tumbler, and recount the cause of the minister's strange looks and solitary life.

Fifty years syne, when Mr. Soulis cam' first into Ba'weary, he was still a young man—a callant, the folk said—fu' o' book learnin' and grand at the exposition, but, as was natural in sae young a man, wi' nae leevin' experience in religion. The younger sort were greatly taken wi' his gifts and his gab; but auld, concerned, serious men and women were moved even to prayer for the young man, whom they took to be a self-deceiver, and the parish that was like to be sae ill-supplied. It was before the days o' the moderates—weary fa' them; but ill things are like guid—they baith come bit by bit, a pickle at a time; and there were folk even then that said the Lord had left the college professors to their ain devices, an' the lads that went to study wi' them wad hae done mair and better sittin' in a peat-bog, like their forebears of the persecution, wi' a Bible under their oxter and a speerit o' prayer in their heart. There was nae doubt, onyway, but that Mr. Soulis

had been ower lang at the college. He was careful and troubled
for mony things besides the ae thing needful. He had a feck o'
books wi' him—mair than had ever been seen before in a' that
presbytery; and a sair wark the carrier had wi' them, for they were
a' like to have smoored in the Deil's Hag between this and
Kilmackerlie. They were books o' divinity, to be sure, or so they
ca'd them; but the serious were o' opinion there was little service
for sae mony, when the hail o' God's Word would gang in the neuk
of a plaid. Then he wad sit half the day and half the nicht forbye,
which was scant decent—writin', nae less; and first, they were
feared he wad read his sermons; and syne it proved he was writin'
a book himsel', which was surely no fittin' for ane of his years and
sma' experience.

Onway it behoved him to get an auld, decent wife to keep the
manse for him an' see to his bit denners; and he was recommended
to an auld limmer—Janet M'Clour, they ca'ed her—and sae far
left to himsel' as to be ower persuaded. There was mony advised
him to the contrar, for Janet was mair than suspeckit by the best
folk in Ba'weary. Lang or that, she had had a wean to a dragoon;
she hadnae come forrit * for maybe thretty year; and bairns had
seen her mumblin' to hersel' up on Key's Loan in the gloamin',
whilk was an unco time an' place for a God-fearin' woman. Howsoever, it was the laird himsel' that had first tauld the minister o'
Janet; and in thae days he wad have gane a far gate to pleesure the
laird. When folk tauld him that Janet was sib to the deil, it was
a' superstition by his way of it; an' when they cast up the Bible
to him an' the witch of Endor, he wad threep it doun their
thrapples that thir days were a' gane by, and the deil was merci-
fully restrained.

Weel, when it got about the clachan that Janet M'Clour was to
be servant at the manse, the folk were fair mad wi' her an' him
thegether; and some o' the guidwives had nae better to dae than
get round her door cheeks and chairge her wi' a' that was ken't
again her, frae the sodger's bairn to John Tamson's twa kye. She
was nae great speaker; folk usually let her gang her ain gate, an'
she let them gang theirs, wi' neither Fair-guideen nor Fair-guid-
day; but when she buckled to, she had a tongue to deave the
miller. Up she got, an' there wasnae an auld story in Ba'weary but
she gart somebody lowp for it that day; they couldnae say ae thing

* To come forrit—to offer oneself as a communicant.

but she could say twa to it; till, at the hinder end, the guidwives up and claught haud of her, and clawed the coats aff her back, and pu'd her doun the clachan to the water o' Dule, to see if she were a witch or no, soum or droun. The carline skirled till ye could hear her at the Hangin' Shaw, and she focht like ten; there was mony a guidwife bure the mark of her neist day an' mony a lang day after; and just in the hettest o' the collieshangie, wha suld come up (for his sins) but the new minister.

"Women," said he (and he had a grand voice), "I charge you in the Lord's name to let her go."

Janet ran to him—she was fair wud wi' terror—an' clang to him, an' prayed him, for Christ's sake, save her frae the cummers; an' they, for their pairt, tauld him a' that was ken't, and maybe mair.

"Woman," says he to Janet, "is this true?"

"As the Lord sees me," says she, "as the Lord made me, no a word o't. Forbye the bairn," says she, "I've been a decent woman a' my days."

"Will you," says Mr. Soulis, "in the name of God, and before me, His unworthy minister, renounce the devil and his works?"

Weel, it wad appear that when he askit that, she gave a girn that fairly frichtit them that saw her, an' they could hear her teeth play dirl thegether in her chafts; but there was naething for it but the ae way or the ither; an' Janet lifted up her hand and renounced the deil before them a'.

"And now," says Mr. Soulis to the guidwives, "home with ye, one and all, and pray to God for His forgiveness."

And he gied Janet his arm, though she had little on her but a sark, and took her up the clachan to her ain door like a leddy of the land; an' her scrieghin' and laughin' as was a scandal to be heard.

There were mony grave folk lang ower their prayers that nicht; but when the morn cam' there was sic a fear fell upon a' Ba'weary that the bairns hid theirsels, and even the men folk stood and keekit frae their doors. For there was Janet comin' doun the clachan—her or her likeness, nane could tell—wi' her neck thrawn, and her heid on ae side, like a body that has been hangit, and a girn on her face like an unstreakit corp. By an' by they got used wi' it, and even speered at her to ken what was wrang; but frae that day forth she couldnae speak like a Christian woman, but slavered and played click wi' her teeth like apair o' shears; and frae that day forth the name o' God cam' never on her lips. Whiles she wad try to say it, but it michtnae be. Them that kenned best said least; but they never gied that Thing the name o' Janet M'Clour; for the auld Janet, by their way o't, was in muckle hell that day. But the minister was neither to haud nor to bind; he preached about naething but the folk's cruelty that had gi'en her a stroke of the palsy; he skelpt the bairns that meddled her; and he had her up to the manse that same nicht, and dwalled there a' his lane wi' her under the Hangin' Shaw.

Weel, time gaed by: and the idler sort commenced to think mair lichtly o' that black business. The minister was weel thocht o'; he was aye late at the writing, folk wad see his can'le doon by the Dule water after twal' at e'en; and he seemed pleased wi' himsel' and upsitten as at first, though a' body could see that he was dwining. As for Janet she cam' an' she gaed; if she didnae speak muckle afore, it was reason she should speak less then; she meddled naebody; but she was an eldritch thing to see, an' name wad hae mistrysted wi' her for Ba'weary glebe.

About the end o' July there cam' a spell o' weather, the like o't never was in that country-side; it was lown an' het an' heartless; the herds couldnae win up the Black Hill, the bairns were ower weariet to play; an' yet it was gousty too, wi' claps o' het wund that rummled in the glens, and bits o' shouers that slockened naething. We aye thocht it but to thun'er on the morn; but the morn cam', an' the morn's morning, and it was aye the same un-canny weather, sair on folks and bestial. Of a' that were the waur, nane suffered like Mr. Soulis; he could neither sleep nor eat, he tauld his elders; an' when he wasnae writin' at his weary book, he wad be stravaguin' ower a' the country-side like a man possessed, when a' body else was blythe to keep caller ben the house.

Abune Hangin' Shaw, in the bield o' the Black Hill, there's a bit enclosed grund wi' an iron yett; and it seems, in the auld days, that was the kirkyaird a' Ba'weary, and consecrated by the Papists be-fore the blessed licht shone upon the kingdom. It was a great howff, o' Mr. Soulis's onyway; there he would sit an' consider his sermons; and inded it's a bieldy bit. Weel, as he cam' ower the wast end o' the Black Hill, ae day, he saw first twa, an' syne fower, an' syne seeven corbie craws fleein' round an' round abune the auld kirkyaird. They flew laigh and heavy, an' squawked to ither as they gaed; and it was clear to Mr. Soulis that something had put them frae their ordinar. He wasnae easy fleyed, an' gaed straucht up to the wa's; and what suld he find there but a man, or the appearance of a man, sittin' in the inside upon a grave. He was of a great stature, an' black as hell, and his e'en were singular to see.* Mr. Soulis had heard tell o' black men, mony's the time; but there was something unco about this black man that daunted him. Het as he was, he took a kind o' cauld grue in the marrow o' his banes; but up he spak for a' that; an' says he: "My friend, are you a stranger in this place?" The black man answered never a word; he got upon his feet, an' begude to hirsle to the wa' on the far side; but he aye lookit at the minister; an' the minister stood an' lookit back; till a' in a meenute the black man was ower the wa' an' rinnin' for the bield o' the trees. Mr. Soulis, he hardly kenned why, ran after him; but he was sair forjaskit wi' his walk an' the het, unhalesome weather; and rin as he likit, he got nae mair than a glisk o' the black man amang the birks, till he won doun to the foot o' the hillside, an' there he saw him ance mair, gaun, hap, step, an' lowp, ower Dule water to the manse.

Mr. Soulis wasnae weel pleased that this fearsome gangrel suld mak' sae free wi' Ba'weary manse; an' he ran the harder, an' wet shoon, ower the burn, an' up the walk; but the deil a black man was there to see. He stepped out upon the road, but there was naebody there; he gaed a' ower the gairden, but na, nae black man. At the hinder end, and a bit feared as was but natural, he lifted the hasp and into the manse; and there was Janet M'Clour before his een, wi' her thrawn craig, and nane sae pleased to see him. And he aye minded sinsyne, when first he set his een upon her, he had the same cauld and deidly grue.

"Janet," says he, "have you seen a black man?"

"A black man!" quo' she. "Save us a'! Ye're no wise, minister. There's nae black man in a' Ba'weary."

But she didnae speak plain, ye maun understand; but yam-yammered, like a powny wi' the bit in its moo.

"Weel," says he, "Janet, if there was nae black man, I have spoken with the Accuser of the Brethren."

* It was a common belief in Scotland that the devil appeared as a black man. This appears in several witch trials and I think in Law's *Memorials,* that delightful storehouse of the quaint and grisly.

And he sat doun like ane wi' a fever, an' his teeth chittered in his heid.

"Hoots," says she, "think shame to yoursel', minister"; and' gied him a drap brandy that she keept aye by her.

Syne Mr. Soulis gaed into his study amang a' his books. It's a lang, laigh, mirk chalmer, perishin' cauld in winter, an' no very dry even in th top o' the simmer, for the manse stands near the burn. Sae doun he sat, and thocht of a' that had come an' gane since he was in Ba'weary, an' his hame, an' the days when he was a bairn an' ran daffin' on the braes; and that black man aye ran in his heid like the owercomer of a sang. Aye the mair he thocht, the mair he thocht o' the black man. He tried the prayer, an' the words wouldnae come to him; an' he tried, they say, to write at his book, but he couldnae mak' nae mair o' that. There was whiles he thocht the black man was at his oxter, an' the swat stood upon him cauld as well-water; and there was other whiles, when he cam' to himsel' like a christened bairn and minded naething.

The upshot was that he gaed to the window an' stood glowrin' at Dule water. The trees are unco thick, an' water lies deep an' black under the manse; and there was Janet washin' the cla'es wi' her coats kilted. She had her back to the minister, an' he, for his pairt, hardly kenned what he was lookin' at. Syne she turned round, an' shawed her face; Mr. Soulis had the same cauld grue as twice that day afore, an' it was borne in upon him what folk said, that Janet was deid lang syne, an' this was a bogle in her clay-cauld flesh. He drew back a pickle and he scanned her narrowly. She was tramp-trampin' in the cla'es, croonin' to hersel'; and eh! Gude guide us, but it was a fearsome face. Whiles she sang louder, but there was nae man born o' woman that could tell the words o' her sang; an' whiles she lookit side-lang doun, but there was naething there for her to look at. There gaed a scunner through the flesh upon his banes; and that was Heeven's advertisement. But Mr. Soulis just blamed himsel', he said, to think sae ill of a puir, auld afflicted wife that hadnae a freend forbye himsel'; an' he put up a bit prayer for him an' her, an' drank a little caller water—for his heart rose again the meat—an' gaed up to his naked bed in the gloaming.

That was a nicht that has never been forgotten in Ba'weary, the nicht o' the seventeenth of August, seventeen hun'er' an' twal'. It had been het afore, as I hae said, but that nicht it was hetter than ever. The sun gaed doun amang unco-lookin' clouds; it fell as mirk as the pit; no a star, no a breath o' wund; ye couldnae see your han' afore your face, and even the auld folk cuist the covers frae their beds and lay pechin' for their breath. Wi' a' that he had upon his mind, it was gey and unlikely Mr. Soulis wad get muckle sleep. He lay an' he tummled; the gude, caller bed that he got into brunt his very banes; whiles he slept, and whiles he waukened; whiles he heard the time o' nicht, and whiles a tyke yowlin' up the muir, as if somebody was deid; whiles he thocht he heard bogles claverin' in his lug, an' whiles he saw spunkies in the room. He behoved, he judged, to be sick; an' sick he was—little he jaloosed the sickness.

At the hinder end, he got a clearness in his mind, sat up in his sark on the bed-side, and fell thinkin' ance mair o' the black man an' Janet. He couldnae weel tell how—maybe it was the cauld to his feet—but it cam' in upon him wi' a spate that there was some connection between thir twa, an' that either or baith o' them were bogles. And just at that moment, in Janet's room, which was neist to his, there cam' a stramp o' feet as if men were wars'lin', an' then a loud bang; an' then a wund gaed reishling round the fower quarters of the house; an' then a' was ance mair as seelent as the grave.

Mr. Soulis was feared for neither man nor deevil. He got his tinder-box, an' lit a can'le, an' made three steps o't ower to Janet's door. It was on the hasp, an' he pushed it open, an' keeked bauldly in. It was a big room, as big as the minister's ain, an' plenished wi' grand, auld, solid gear, for he had nathing else. There was a fower-posted bed wi' auld tapestry; and a braw cabinet of aik, that was fu' o' the minister's divinity books, an' put there to be out o' the gate; an' a wheen duds o' Janet's lying here and there about the floor. But nae Janet could Mr. Soulis see; nor ony sign of a contention. In he gaed (an' there's few that wad ha'e followed him) an' lookit a' round, an' listened. But there was naethin' to be heard, neither inside the manse nor in a' Ba'weary parish, an' naethin' to be seen but the muckle shadows turnin' round the can'le. An' then, a' at ance, the minister's heart played dunt an' stood stock-still; an' a cauld wund blew amang the hairs o' his heid. Whaten a weary sicht was that for the puir man's een! For there was Janet hangin' frae a nail beside the auld aik cabinet: her heid aye lay on her shouther, her een were steeked, the tongue projeckit frae her mouth, and her heels were twa feet clear abune the floor.

"God forgive us all!" thocht Mr. Soulis, "poor Janet's dead."

He cam' a step nearer to the corp; an' then his heart fair whammled in his inside. For by what cantrip it wad ill-beseem a man to judge, she was hingin' frae a single nail an' by a single wursted thread for darnin' hose.

It's a awfu' thing to be your lane at nicht wi' siccan prodigies o' darkness; but Mr. Soulis was strong in the Lord. He turned an' gaed his ways oot o' that room, and lockit the door ahint him; and step by step, doom the stairs, as heavy as leed; and set doon the can'le on the table at the stairfoot. He couldnae pray, he couldnae think, he was dreepin' wi' caul' swat, an' naething could he hear but the dunt-dunt-duntin' o' his ain heart. He micht maybe have stood there an hour, or maybe twa, he minded sae little; when a' o' a sudden, he heard a laigh, uncanny steer up-stairs; a foot gaed to an' fro in the chalmer whaur the corp was hingin'; syne the door was opened, though he minded weel that he had lockit it; an' syne there was a step upon the landin', an' it seemed to him as if the corp was lookin ower the rail and doun upon him whaur he stood.

He took up the can'le again (for he couldnae want the licht), and as saftly as ever he could, gaed straucht out o' the manse an' to the far end o' the causeway. It was aye pit-mirk; the flame o' the can'le, when he set it on the grund, brunt steedy and clear as in a room; naething moved, but the Dule water seepin' and sabbin' doon the glen, an' yon unhaly footstep that cam' ploddin' doun the stairs inside the manse. He kenned the foot ower weel, for it was Janet's; and at ilka step that cam' a wee thing nearer, the cauld got deeper in his vitals. He commended his soul to Him that made an' keepit him; "and O Lord," said he, "give me strength this night to war against the powers of evil."

By this time the foot was comin' through the passage for the door; he could hear a hand skirt alang the wa', as if the fearsome thing was feelin' for its way. The saughs tossed an' maned thegether, a long sigh cam' ower the hills, the flame o' the can'le was blawn aboot; an' there stood the corp of Thrawn Janet, wi' her grogram goun an' her black mutch, wi' the heid aye upon the shouther, an' the grin still upon the face o't—leevin', ye wad hae said—deid, as Mr. Soulis weel—kenned—upon the threshold o' the manse.

It's a strange thing that the saul of man should be that thirled into his perishable body; but the minister saw that, an' his heart didnae break.

She didnae stand there lang; she began to move again an' cam' slowly towards Mr. Soulis whaur he stood under the saughs. A' the life o' his body, a' the strength o' his speerit, were glowerin' frae his een. It seemed she was gaun to speak, but wanted words, an' made a sign wi' the left hand. There cam' a clap o' wund, like a cat's fuff; oot gaed the can'le, the saughs skrieghed like folk; an' Mr. Soulis kenned that, live or die, this was the end o't.

"Witch, beldame, devil!" he cried, "I charge you, by the power of God, begone—if you be dead, to the grave—if you be damned, to hell."

An' at that moment the Lord's ain hand out o' the Heevens struck the Horror whaur it stood; the auld, deid, desecrated corp o' the witch-wife, sae lang keepit frae the grave and hirsled round by deils, lowed up like a brunstane spunk and fell in ashes to the grund; the thunder followed, peal on dirling peal, the rairing rain upon the back o' that; and Mr. Soulis lowped through the garden hedge, and ran, wi' skelloch upon skelloch, for the clachan.

That same mornin', John Christie saw the Black Man pass the Muckle Cairn as it was chappin' six; before eicht, he gaed by the change-house at Knockdow; an' no lang after, Sandy M'Lellan saw him gaun linkin' doun the braes frae Kilmackerlie. There's little doubt but it was him that dwalled sae lang in Janet's body; but he was awa' at last; and sinsyne the deil has never fashed us in Ba'weary.

But it was a sair dispensation for the minister; lang, lang he lay ravin' in his bed; and frae that hour to this, he was the man ye ken the day.

THE BEACH OF FALESÁ

To

Those Old Shipments among the Islands
Harry Henderson
Ben Hird
Jack Buckland
Their Friend
R. L. S.

1. *A South-Sea Bridal*

I SAW THAT ISLAND FIRST WHEN IT WAS NEITHER NIGHT NOR MORNing. The moon was to the west, setting, but still broad and bright. To the east, and right amidships of the dawn, which was all pink, the day-star sparkled like a diamond. The land-breeze blew in our faces, and smelt strong of wild lime and vanilla; other things besides, but these were the most plain; and the chill of it set me sneezing. I should say I had been for years on a low island near the line, living for the most part solitary among natives. Here was a fresh experience; even the tongue would be quite strange to me; and the look of these woods and mountains, and the rare smell of them, renewed my blood.

The captain blew out the binnacle-lamp.

"There!" said he, "there goes a bit of smoke, Mr. Wiltshire, behind the break of the roof. That's Falesá, where your station is, the last village to the east; nobody lives to windward—I don't know why. Take my glass, and you can make the houses out."

I took the glass; and the shores leaped nearer, and I saw the tangle of the woods and the breach of the surf, and the brown roofs and the black insides of houses peeped among the trees.

"Do you catch a bit of white there to the east'ard?" the captain continued. "That's your house. Coral built, stands high, veranda you could walk on three abreast; best station in the South Pacific. When old Adams saw it, he took and shook me by the hand. 'I've dropped into a soft thing here,' says he. 'So you have,' says I, 'and time too!' Poor Johnny! I never saw him again but the once, and then he had changed his tune—couldn't get on with the natives, or the whites, or something; and the next time we came round there, he was dead and buried. I took and put up a bit of a stick to him: 'John Adams, *obit* eighteen and sixty-eight. Go thou and do likewise.' I missed that man. I never could see much harm in Johnny."

"What did he die of?" I inquired.

"Some kind of sickness," says the captain. "It appears it took him sudden. Seems he got up in the night, and filled up on Pain Killer and Kennedy's Discovery. No go—he was booked beyond Kennedy. Then he had tried to open a case of gin. No go again—not strong enough. Then he must have turned to and run out on the veranda, and capsized over the rail. When they found him, the next day, he was clean crazy—carried on all the time about somebody watering his copra. Poor John!"

"Was it thought to be the island?" I asked.

"Well, it was thought to be the island, or the trouble, or something," he replied. "I never could hear but what it was a healthy place. Our last man, Vigours, never turned a hair. He left because of the beach—said he was afraid of Black Jack and Case and Whistling Jimmie, who was still alive at the time, but got drowned soon afterward when drunk. As for old Captain Randall, he's been here any time since eighteen-forty, forty-five. I never could see much harm in Billy, nor much change. Seems as if he might live to be Old Kafoozleum. No, I guess it's healthy."

"There's a boat coming now," said I. "She's right in the pass; looks to be a sixteen-foot whale; two white men in the stern-sheets."

"That's the boat that drowned Whistling Jimmie!" cried the captain; "let's see the glass. Yes, that's Case, sure enough, and the darkie. They've got a gallows bad reputation, but you know what a place the beach is for talking. My belief, that Whistling Jimmie was the worst of the trouble; and he's gone to glory, you see. What'll you bet they ain't after gin? Lay you five to two they take six cases."

When these two traders came aboard I was pleased with the looks of them at once, or, rather, with the looks of both, and the speech of one. I was sick for white neighbours after my four years at the line, which I always counted years of prison; getting ta-booed, and going down to the Speak House to see and get it taken off; buying gin and going on a break, and then repenting; sitting in the house at night with the lamp for company; or walking on the beach and wondering what kind of a fool to call myself for being where I was. There were no other whites upon my island, and when I sailed to the next, rough customers made the most of the society. Now to see these two when they came aboard was a pleas-ure. One was a Negro, to be sure; but they were both rigged out smart in striped pajamas and straw hats, and Case would have passed muster in a city. He was yellow and smallish, had a hawk's nose to his face, pale eyes, and his beard trimmed with scissors. No man knew his country, beyond he was of English speech; and it was clear he came of a good family and was splendidly educated He was accomplished too; played the accordion first rate; and give him a piece of a string or a cork or a pack of cards, and he could show you tricks equal to any professional. He could speak, when he chose, fit for a drawing-room; and when he chose he could blaspheme worse than a Yankee boatswain, and talk smart to sicken a Kanaka. The way he thought would pay best at the mo-ment, that was Case's way, and it always seemed to come natural, and like as if he was born to it. He had the courage of a lion and the cunning of a rat; and if he's not in hell to-day, there's no such place. I know but one good point to the man—that he was fond of his wife, and kind to her. She was a Samoa woman, and dyed her hair red—Samoa style; and when he came to die (as I have to tell of) they found one strange thing—that he had made a will, like a Christian, and the widow got the lot; all his, they said, and all Black Jack's, and the most of Billy Randall's in the bargain, for it was Case that kept the books. So she went off home in the schooner *Manu'a,* and does the lady to this day in her own place.

But of all this on that first morning I knew no more than a fly. Case me like a gentleman and like a friend, made me welcome to Falesá, and put his services at my disposal, which was the more helpful from my ignorance of the natives. All the better part of the day we sat drinking better acquaintance in the cabin, and I never heard a man talk more to the point. There was no smarter trader, and none dodgier, in the islands. I though Falesá seemed to be the right kind of a place; and the more I drank the lighter my heart. Our last trader had fled the place at half an hour's notice, taking a chance passage in a labour ship from up west. The captain, when he came, had found the station closed, the keys left with the native pastor, and a letter from the runaway, confessing he was fairly frightened of his life. Since then the firm had not been represented, and of course there was no cargo. The wind, besides, was fair, the captain hoped he could make his next island by dawn, with a good tide, and the business of landing my trade was gone about lively. There was no call for me to fool with it, Case said; nobody would touch my things, every one was honest in Falesá, only about chickens or an odd knife or an odd stick of tobacco; and the best I could do was to sit quiet till the vessel left, then come straight to his house, see old Captain Randall, the father of the beach, take pot-luck, and go home to sleep when it got dark. So it was high noon, and the schooner was under way before I set my foot on shore at Falesá.

I had a glass or two on board; I was just off a long cruise, and the ground heaved under me like a ship's deck. The world was like all new painted; my foot went along to music; Falesá might have been Fiddler's Green, if there is such a place, and more's the pity if there isn't! It was good to foot the grass, to look aloft at the green mountains, to see the men with their green wreaths and the women in their bright dresses, red and blue. On we went, in the strong sun and the cool shadow, liking both; and all the children in the town came trotting after with their shaven heads and their brown bodies, and raising a thin kind of a cheer in our wake, like crowing poultry.

"By the bye," says Case, "we must get you a wife."

"That's so," said I; "I had forgotten."

There was a crowd of girls about us, and I pulled up and looked among them like a bashaw. They were all dressed out for the sake of the ship being in; and the women of Falesá are a handsome lot to see. If they have a fault, they are a trifle broad in the beam; and I was just thinking so when Case touched me.

"That's pretty," says he.

I saw one coming on the other side alone. She had been fishing; all she wore was a chemise, and it was wetted through. She was young and very slender for an island maid, with a long face, a high forehead, and a shy, strange, blindish look, between a cat's and a baby's.

"Who's she?" said I. "She'll do."

"That's Uma," said Case, and he called her up and spoke to her in the native. I didn't know what he said; but when he was in the midst she looked up at me quick and timid, like a child dodging a blow, then down again, and presently smiled. She had a wide mouth, the lips and the chin cut like any statue's; and the smile came out for a moment and was gone. Then she stood with her head bent, and heard Case to an end, spoke back in the pretty Polynesian voice, looking him full in the face, heard him again in answer, and then with an obeisance started off. I had just a share of the bow, but never another shot of her eye, and there was no more word of smiling.

"I guess it's all right," said Case. "I guess you can have her. I'll make it square with the old lady. You can have your pick of the lot for a plug of tobacco," he added, sneering.

I suppose it was the smile that stuck in my memory, for I spoke back sharp. "She doesn't look that sort," I cried.

"I don't know that she is," said Case. "I believe she's as right as the mail. Keeps to herself, don't go round with the gang, and that. Oh, no, don't you misunderstand me—Uma's on the square." He spoke eager, I thought, and that surprised and pleased me. "Indeed," he went on, "I shouldn't make so sure of getting her, only she cottoned to the cut of your jib. All you have to do is to keep dark and let me work the mother my own way; and I'll bring the girl round to the captain's for the marriage."

I didn't care for the word marriage, and I said so.

"Oh, there's nothing to hurt in the marriage," says he. "Black Jack's the chaplain."

By this time we had come in view of the house of these three white men; for a Negro is counted a white man, and so is a Chinese! A strange idea, but common in the islands. It was a board house with a strip of rickety veranda. The store was to the front, with a counter, scales, and the finest possible display of trade: a case or two of tinned meats; a barrel of hard bread, a few bolts of cotton stuff, not to be compared with mine; the only thing well represented being the contraband firearms and liquor. "If these are my only rivals," thinks I, "I should do well in Falesá." Indeed, there was only the one way they could touch me, and that was with the guns and drink.

In the back room was old Captain Randall, squatting on the floor native fashion, fat and pale, naked to the waist, grey as a badger, and his eyes set with drink. His body was covered with grey hair and crawled over by flies; one was in the corner of his eye—he never heeded; and mosquitoes hummed about the man like bees. Any clean-minded man would have had the creature out at once and buried him; and to see him, and think he was seventy, and remember he had once commanded a ship, and come ashore in his smart togs, and talked big in bars and consulates, and sat in club verandas, turned me sick and sober.

He tried to get up when I came in, but that was hopeless; so he reached me a hand instead, and stumbled out some salutation.

"Papa's pretty full this morning," observed Case. "We've had an epidemic here; and Captain Randall takes gin for a prophylactic—don't you, Papa?"

"Never took such a thing in my life!" cried the captain, indignantly. "Take gin for my health's sake, Mr. Wha's-ever-your name—'s a precautionary measure."

"That's all right, Papa," said Case. "But you'll have to brace up. There's going to be a marriage—Mr. Wilshire here is going to get spliced."

The old man asked to whom.

"To Uma," said Case.

"Uma!" cried the captain. "Wha' 's he want Uma for? 's he come here for his health, anyway? Wha' 'n hell 's he want Uma for?"

"Dry up, Papa," said Case. " 'Tain't you that's to marry her. I guess you're not her godfather and godmother. I guess Mr. Wiltshire's going to please himself."

With that he made an excuse to me that he must move about the marriage, and left me alone with the poor wretch that was his partner and (to speak truth) his gull. Trade and station belonged both to Randall; Case and the Negro were parasites; they crawled and fed upon him like the flies, he none the wiser. Indeed, I have no harm to say of Billy Randall beyond the fact that my gorge rose at him, and the time I now passed in his company was like a nightmare.

The room was stifling hot and full of flies, for the house was dirty and low and small, and stood in a bad place, behind the village, in the borders of the bush, and sheltered from the trade. The three men's beds were on the floor, and a litter of pans and dishes. There was no standing furniture; Randall, when he was violent, tearing it to laths. There I sat and had a meal which was served us by Case's wife; and there I was entertained all day by that remains of man, his tongue stumbling among low old jokes and long old stories, and his own wheezy laughter always ready, so that he had no sense of my depression. He was nipping gin all the while. Sometimes he fell asleep, and awoke again, whimpering and shivering, and every now and again he would ask me why I wanted to marry Uma. "My friend," I was telling myself all day, "you must not come to be an old gentleman like this."

It might be four in the afternoon, perhaps, when the back door was thrust slowly open, and a strange old native woman crawled into the house almost on her belly. She was swathed in black stuff to her heels; her hair was grey in swatches; her face was tattooed, which was not the practice in that island; her eyes big and bright and crazy. These she fixed upon me with a rapt expression that I saw to be part acting. She said no plain word, but smacked and mumbled with her lips, and hummed aloud, like a child over its Christmas pudding. She came straight across the house, heading for me, and, as soon as she was alongside, caught up my hand and purred and crooned over it like a great cat. From this she slipped into a kind of song.

"Who the devil's this?" cried I, for the thing startled me.

"It's Faavao," says Randall; and I saw he had hitched along the floor into the farthest corner.

"You ain't afraid of her?" I cried.

"Me 'fraid!" cried the captain. "My dear friend, I defy her! I don't let her put her foot in here, only I suppose's different to-day for the marriage. 'S Uma's mother."

"Well, suppose it is; what's she carrying on about?" I asked, more irritated, perhaps more frightened, than I cared to show; and the captain told me she was making up a quantity of poetry in my praise because I was to marry Uma. "All right, old lady," says I, with rather a failure of a laugh, "anything to oblige. But when you're done with my hand, you might let me know."

She did as though she understood; the song rose into a cry, and stopped; the woman crouched out of the house the same way that she came in, and must have plunged straight into the bush, for when I followed her to the door she had already vanished.

"These are rum manners," said I.

" 'S a rum crowd," said the captain, and, to my surprise, he made the sign of the cross on his bare bosom.

"Hillo!" says I, "are you a Papist?"

He repudiated the idea with contempt. "Hardshell Baptis'," said he. "But, my dear friend, the Papists got some good ideas too; and th' 's one of 'em. You take my advice, and whenever you come across Uma or Faavao or Vigours, or any of that crowd, you take a leaf out o' the priests, and do what I do. Savvy?" says he, repeated the sign, and winked his dim eye at me. *"No, sir!"* he broke out again, "no Papists here!" and for a long time entertained me with his religious opinions.

I must have been taken with Uma from the first, or I should certainly have fled from that house, and got into the clean air, and the clean sea, or some convenient river—though, it's true, I was committed to Case; and, besides, I could never have held my head up in that island if I had run from a girl upon my wedding-night.

The sun was down, the sky all on fire, and the lamp had been some time lighted, when Case came back with Uma and the Negro. She was dressed and scented; her kilt was of fine tapa, looking richer in the folds than any silk; her bust, which was of the colour of dark honey, she wore bare, only for some half-a-dozen necklaces of seeds and flowers; and behind her ears and in her hair she had the scarlet flowers of the hibiscus. She showed the best bearing for a bride conceivable, serious and still; and I thought shame to stand up with her in that mean house and before that grinning Negro. I thought shame, I say; for the mountebank was dressed with a big paper collar, the book he made believe to read from was an odd volume of a novel, and the words of his service not fit to be set down. My conscience smote me when we joined hands: and when she got her certificate I was tempted to throw up the bargain and confess. Here is the document. It was Case that wrote it, signatures and all, in a leaf out of the ledger:

This is to certify that Uma, daughter of Faavao of Falesá, Island of ——, is illegally married to Mr. John Wiltshire, and

Mr. John Wiltshire is at liberty to send her packing when he pleases.

JOHN BLACKAMOAR,
Chaplain to the Hulks.

Extracted from the Register
by William T. Randall,
Master Mariner.

A nice paper to put in a girl's hand and see her hide away like gold. A man might easily feel cheap for less. But it was the practice in these parts, and (as I told myself) not the least the fault of us white men, but of the missionaries. If they had let the natives be, I had never needed this deception, but taken all the wives I wished, and left them when I pleased, with a clear conscience.

The more ashamed I was, the more hurry I was in to be gone; and our desires thus jumping together, I made the less remark of a change in the traders. Case had been all eagerness to keep me; now, as though he had attained a purpose, he seemed all eagerness to have me go. Uma, he said, could show me to my house, and the three bade us farewell indoors.

The night was nearly come; the village smelt of trees and flowers and the sea and bread-fruit-cooking; there came a fine roll of sea from the reef, and from a distance, among the woods and houses, many pretty sounds of men and children. It did me good to breathe free air; it did me good to be done with the captain, and see, instead, the creature at my side. I felt for all the world as though she were some girl at home in the Old Country, and forgetting myself for the minute, took her hand to walk with. Her fingers nestled into mine, I heard her breathe deep and quick, and all at once she caught my hand to her face and pressed it there. "You good!" she cried, and ran ahead of me, and stopped and looked back and smiled, and ran ahead of me again, thus guiding me through the edge of the bush, and by a quiet way to my own house.

The truth is, Case had done the courting for me in style—told her I was mad to have her, and cared nothing for the consequences; and the poor soul, knowing that which I was still ignorant of, believed it, every word, and had her head nigh turned with vanity and gratitude. Now, of all this I had no guess; I was one of those most opposed to any nonsense about native women, having seen so many whites eaten up by their wives' relatives, and made fools of into the bargain; and I told myself I must make a stand at once, and bring her to her bearings. But she looked so quaint and pretty as she ran away and then awaited me, and the thing was done so like a child or a kind dog, that the best I could do was just to follow her whenever she went on, to listen for the fall of her bare feet, and to watch in the dusk for the shining of her body. And there was another thought came in my head. She played kitten with me now when we were alone; but in the house she had carried it the way a countess might, so proud and humble. And what with her dress—for all there was so little of it, and that native enough—what with her fine tapa and fine scents, and her red flowers and seeds, that were quite as bright as jewels, only larger—it came over me she was a kind of countess really, dressed to hear great singers at a concert, and no even mate for a poor trader like myself.

She was the first in the house; and while I was still without I saw a match flash and the lamplight kindle in the windows. The station was a wonderful fine place, coral built, with quite a wide veranda, and the main room high and wide. My chests and cases had been piled in, and made rather of a mess; and there, in the thick of the confusion, stood Uma by the table, awaiting me. Her shadow went all the way up behind her into the hollow of the iron roof; she stood against it bright, the lamplight shining on her skin. I stopped in the door, and she looked at me, not speaking, with eyes that were eager and yet daunted; then she touched herself on the bosom.

"Me—your wifie," she said. It had never taken me like that before; but the want of her took and shook all through me, like the wind in the luff of a sail.

I could not speak if I had wanted; and if I could, I would not. I was ashamed to be so much moved about a native, ashamed of the marriage too, and the certificate she had treasured in her kilt; and I turned aside and made believe to rummage among my cases. The first thing I lighted on was a case of gin, the only one that I had brought; and partly for the girl's sake, and partly for horror of the recollections of old Randall, took a sudden resolve. I pried the lid off. One by one I drew the bottles with a pocket cork-screw, and sent Uma out to pour the stuff from the veranda.

She came back after the last, and looked at me puzzled like.

"No good," said I, for I was now a little better master of my tongue. "Man he drink, he no good."

She agreed with this, but kept considering. "Why you bring him?" she asked, presently, "Suppose you no want drink, you no bring him, I think."

"That's all right," said I. "One time I want drink too much; now no want. You see, I no savvy, I get one little wifie. Suppose I drink gin, my little wifie be 'fraid."

To speak to her kindly was about more than I was fit for; I had made my vow I would never let on to weakness with a native, and I had nothing for it but to stop.

She stood looking gravely down at me where I sat by the open case. "I think you good man," she said. And suddenly she had fallen before me on the floor. "I belong you all-e-same pig!" she cried.

2. *The Ban*

I came on the veranda just before the sun rose on the morrow. My house was the last on the east; there was a cape of woods and cliffs behind that hid the sunrise. To the west, a swift, cold river ran down, and beyond was the green of the village, dotted with cocoa-palms and bread-fruits and houses. The shutters were some of them down and some open; I saw the mosquito bars still stretched, with shadows of people new-awakened sitting up inside; and all over the green others were stalking silent, wrapped in their many-coloured sleeping-clothes, like Bedouins in Bible pictures. It was mortal still and solemn and chilly, and the light of the dawn on the lagoon was like the shining of a fire.

But the thing that troubled me was nearer hand. Some dozen young men and children made a piece of a half-circle, flanking my house: the river divided them, some were on the near side, some on the far, and one on a boulder in the midst; and they all sat silent, wrapped in their sheets, and stared at me and my house as straight as pointer dogs. I thought it strange as I went out. When I had bathed and come back again, and found them all there, and two or three more along with them, I thought it stranger still. What could they see to gaze at in my house I wondered, and went in.

But the thought of these starers stuck in my mind, and presently I came out again. The sun was now up, but it was still behind the cape of woods. Say a quarter of an hour had come and gone. The crowd was greatly increased, the far bank of the river was lined for quite a way—perhaps thirty grown folk, and of children twice as many, some standing, some squatted on the ground, and all staring at my house. I have seen a house in a South-Sea village thus surrounded, but then a trader was thrashing his wife inside, and she singing out. Here was nothing—the stove was alight, the smoke going up in a Christian manner; all was shipshape and Bristol fashion. To be sure, there was a stranger come, but they had a chance to see that stranger yesterday, and took it quiet enough. What ailed them now? I leaned my arms on the rail and stared back. Devil a wink they had in them! Now and then I could see the children chatter, but they spoke so low not even the hum of their speaking came my length. The rest were like graven images: they stared at me, dumb and sorrowful, with their bright eyes; and it came upon me things would look not much different if I were on the platform of the gallows, and these good folk had come to see me hanged.

I felt I was getting daunted, and began to be afraid I looked it, which would never do. Up I stood, made believe to stretch myself, came down the veranda stair, and strolled toward the river. There went a short buzz from one to the other, like what you hear in theatres when the curtain goes up; and some of the nearest gave back the matter of a pace. I saw a girl lay one hand on a young man and make a gesture upward with the other; at the same time she said something in the native with a gasping voice. Three little boys sat beside my path, where I must pass within three feet of them. Wrapped in their sheets, with their shaved heads and bits of topknots, and queer faces, they looked like figures on a chimney-piece. Awhile they sat their ground, solemn as judges. I came up hand over fist, doing my five knots, like a man that meant business; and I thought I saw a sort of a wink and gulp in the three faces. Then one jumped up (he was the farthest off) and ran for his mammy. The other two, trying to follow suit, got foul, came to the ground together bawling, wriggled right out of their sheets, and in a moment there were all three of them scampering for their lives, and singing out like pigs. The natives, who would never let a joke slip, even at a burial, laughed and let up, as short as a dog's bark.

They say it scares a man to be alone. No such thing. What scares him in the dark or the high bush is that he can't make sure, and

there might be an army at his elbow. What scares him worst is to
be right in the midst of a crowd, and have no guess of what they're
driving at. When that laugh stopped, I stopped too. The boys
had not yet made their offing; they were still on the full stretch
going the one way, when I had already gone about ship and was
sheering off the other. Like a fool I had come out, doing my five
knots; like a fool I went back again. It must have been the funniest thing to see, and what knocked me silly, this time no one
laughed; only one old woman gave a kind of pious moan, the way
you have heard Dissenters in their chapels at the sermon.

"I never saw such fools of Kanakas as your people here," I said
once to Uma, glancing out of the window at the starers.

"Savvy nothing," says Uma, with a kind of disgusted air that she
was good at.

And that was all the talk we had upon the matter, for I was put
out, and Uma took the thing so much as a matter of course that I
was fairly ashamed.

All day, off and on, now fewer and now more, the fools sat about
the west end of my house and across the river, waiting for the
show, whatever that was—fire to come down from heaven, I suppose, and consume me, bones and baggage. But by evening, like
real islanders, they had wearied of the business, and got away, and
had a dance instead in the big house of the village, where I heard
them singing and clapping hands till, maybe, ten at night, and the
next day it seemed they had forgotten I existed. If fire had come
down from heaven or the earth opened and swallowed me, there
would have been nobody to see the sport or take the lesson, or
whatever you like to call it. But I was to find they hadn't forgot
either, and kept an eye lifting for phenomena over my way.

I was hard at it both these days getting my trade in order and
taking stock of what Vigours had left. This was a job that made
me pretty sick, and kept me from thinking on much else. Ben had
taken stock the trip before—I knew I could trust Ben—but it was
plain somebody had been making free in the meantime. I found
I was out by what might easily cover six months' salary and profit,
and I could have kicked myself all round the village to have been
such a blamed ass, sitting boozing with that Case instead of attending to my own affairs and taking stock.

However, there's no use crying over spilt milk. It was done now,
and couldn't be undone. All I could do was to get what was left of

it, and my new stuff (my own choice) in order, to go round and get
after the rats and cockroaches, and to fix up that store regular
Sydney style. A fine show I made of it; and the third morning,
when I had lit my pipe and stood in the doorway and looked in,
and turned and looked far up the mountain and saw the cocoa-
nuts waving and posted up the tons of copra, and over the village
green and saw the island dandies and reckoned up the yards of
print they wanted for their kilts and dresses, I felt as if I was in
the right place to make a fortune, and go home again and start a
public-house. There was I, sitting in that veranda, in as handsome
a piece of scenery as you could find, a splendid sun, and a fine,
fresh, healthy trade that stirred up a man's blood like sea-bathing;
and the whole thing was clean gone from me, and I was dreaming
England, which is, after all, a nasty, cold, muddy hole, with not
enough light to see to read by; and dreaming the looks of my
public, by a cant of a broad high-road like an avenue and with the
sign on a green tree.

So much for the morning, but the day passed and the devil any
one looked near me, and from all I knew of natives in other
islands I thought this strange. People laughed a little at our firm
and their fine stations, and at this station of Falesá in particular;
all the copra in the district wouldn't pay for it (I heard them say)
in fifty years, which I supposed was an exaggeration. But when
the day went, and no business came at all, I began to get down-
hearted; and, about three in the afternoon, I went out for a stroll
to cheer me up. On the green I saw a white man coming with a
cassock on, by which and by the face of him I knew he was a
priest. He was a good-natured old soul to look at, gone a little
grizzled, and so dirty you could have written with him on a piece
of paper.

"Good-day, sir," said I.

He answered me eagerly in native.

"Don't you speak any English?" said I.

"French," says he.

"Well," said I, "I'm sorry, but I can't do anything there."

He tried me awhile in the French, and then again in native,
which he seemed to think was the best chance. I made out he was
after more than passing the time of day with me, but had something to communicate, and I listened the harder. I heard the names
of Adams and Case and of Randall—Randall the oftenest—and

the word "poison," or something like it, and a native word that he said very often. I went home, repeating it to myself.

"What does fussy-ocky mean?" I asked of Uma, for that was as near at I could come to it.

"Make dead," said she.

"The devil it does!" says I. "Did ever you hear that Case had poisoned Johnny Adams?"

"Every man he savvy that," says Uma, scornful-like. "Give him white sand—bad sand. He got the bottle still. Suppose he give you gin, you no take him."

Now I had heard much the same sort of story in other islands, and the same white powder always to the front, which made me think the less of it. For all that, I went over to Randall's place to see what I could pick up, and found Case on the doorstep, cleaning a gun.

"Good shooting here?" says I.

"A 1," says he. "The bush is full of all kinds of birds. I wish copra was as plenty," says he— I thought, slyly—"but there don't seem anything doing."

I could see Black Jack in the store, serving a customer.

"That looks like business, though," said I.

"That's the first sale we've made in three weeks," said he.

"You don't tell me?" says I. "Three weeks? Well, well."

"If you don't believe me," he cries, a little hot, "you can go and look at the copra-house. It's half empty to this blessed hour."

"I shouldn't be much the better for that, you see," says I. "For all I can tell, it might have been whole empty yesterday."

"That's so," says he, with a bit of a laugh.

"By the bye," I said, "what sort of a party is the priest? Seems rather a friendly sort."

At this Case laughed right out loud. "Ah!" says he, "I see what ails you now. Galuchet's been at you." *Father Galoshes* was the name he went by most, but Case always gave it the French quirk, which was another reason we had for thinking him above the common.

"Yes, I have seen him," I says. "I made out he didn't think much of your Captain Randall."

"That he don't!" says Case. "It was the trouble about poor Adams. The last day, when he lay dying, there was young Buncombe round. Ever met Buncombe?"

I told him no.

"He's a cure, is Buncombe!" laughs Case. "Well, Buncombe took it in his head that, as there was no other clergyman about, bar Kanaka pastors, we ought to call in Father Galuchet, and have the old man administered and take the sacrament. It was all the same to me, you may suppose; but I said I thought Adams was the fellow to consult. He was jawing away about watered copra and a sight of foolery. 'Look here,' I said, 'you're pretty sick. Would you like to see Galoshes?' He sat right upon his elbow. 'Get the priest,' says he, 'get the priest; don't let me die here like a dog!' He spoke kind of fierce and eager, but sensible enough. There was nothing to say against that, so we sent and asked Galuchet if he would come. You bet he would. He jumped in his dirty linen at the thought of it. But we had reckoned without Papa. He's a hard-shelled Baptist, is Papa; no Papists need apply. And he took and locked the door. Buncombe told him he was bigoted, and I thought he would have had a fit. 'Bigoted!' he says. 'Me bigoted? Have I lived to hear it from a jackanapes like you?' And he made for Buncombe, and I had to hold them apart; and there was Adams in the middle, gone luny again, and carrying on about copra like a born fool. It was good as the play, and I was about knocked out of time with laughing, when all of a sudden Adams sat up, clapped his hands to his chest, and went into the horrors. He died hard, did John Adams," says Case, with a kind of a sudden sternness.

"And what became of the priest?" I asked.

"The priest?" says Case. "Oh! he was hammering on the door outside, and crying on the natives to come and beat it in, and singing out it was a soul he wished to save, and that. He was in a rare taking, was the priest. But what would you have? Johnny had slipped his cable; no more Johnny in the market; and the administration racket clean played out. Next thing, word came to Randall that the priest was praying upon Johnny's grave. Papa was pretty full, and got a club, and lit out straight for the place, and there was Galoshes on his knees, and a lot of natives looking on. You wouldn't think Papa cared that much about anything, unless it was liquor; but he and the priest stuck to it two hours, slanging each other in native, and every time Galoshes tried to kneel down Papa went for him with the club. There never were such larks at Falesá. The end of it was that Captain Randall knocked over with some kind of a fit or stroke, and the priest got in his goods after all. But he was the angriest priest you ever heard of, and complained to the chiefs about the outrage, as he called it. That was no account, for our chiefs are Protestant here; and, anyway, he had been making trouble about the drum for morning school, and they were glad to give him a wipe. Now he swears old Randall gave Adams poison or something, and when the two meet they grin at each other like baboons."

He told this story as natural as could be, and like a man that enjoyed the fun; though now I come to think of it after so long, it seems rather a sickening yarn. However, Case never set up to be soft, only to be square and hearty, and a man all round; and, to tell the truth, he puzzled me entirely.

I went home and asked Uma if she were a Popey, which I had made out to be the native word for Catholics.

"*E le ai!*" says she. She always used the native when she meant "no" more than usually strong, and, indeed, there's more of it. "No good Popey," she added.

Then I asked her about Adams and the priest, and she told me much the same yarn in her own way. So that I was left not much farther on, but inclined, upon the whole, to think the bottom of the matter was the row about the sacrament, and the poisoning only talk.

The next day was a Sunday, when there was no business to be looked for. Uma asked me in the morning if I was going to "pray;" I told her she bet not, and she stopped home herself, with no more words. I thought this seemed unlike a native, and a native woman, and a woman that had new clothes to show off; however, it suited me to the ground, and I made the less of it. The queer thing was that I came next door to going to church after all, a thing I'm little likely to forget. I had turned out for a stroll, and heard the hymn tune up. You know how it is. If you hear folk singing, it seems to draw you; and pretty soon I found myself alongside the church. It was a little, long, low place, coral built, rounded off at both ends like a whale-boat, a big native roof on the top of it, windows without sashes and doorways without doors. I stuck my head into one of the windows, and the sight was so new to me—for things went quite different in the islands I was acquainted with— that I stayed and looked on. The congregation sat on the floor on mats, the women on one side, the men on the other, all rigged out to kill—the women with dresses and trade hats, the men in white jackets and shirts. The hymn was over; the pastor, a big buck Kanaka, was in the pulpit, preaching for his life; and by the way he wagged his hand, and worked his voice, and made his points, and seemed to argue with the folk, I made out he was a gun at the business. Well, he looked up suddenly and caught my eye, and I give you my word he staggered in the pulpit; his eyes bulged out of his head, his hand rose and pointed at me like as if against his will, and the sermon stopped right there.

It isn't a fine thing to say for yourself, but I ran away; and, if the same kind of a shock was given me, I should run away again to-morrow. To see that palavering Kanaka struck all of a heap at the mere sight of me gave me a feeling as if the bottom had dropped out of the world. I went right home, and stayed there, and said nothing. You might think I would tell Uma, but that was against my system. You might have thought I would have gone over and consulted Case; but the truth was I was ashamed to speak of such a thing, I thought every one would blurt out laughing in my face. So I held my tongue, and thought all the more; and the more I thought, the less I liked the business.

By Monday night I got it clearly in my head I must be tabooed. A new store to stand open two days in a village and not a man or woman come to see the trade, was past believing.

"Uma," said I, "I think I'm tabooed."

"I think so," said she.

I thought awhile whether I should ask her more, but it's a bad idea to set natives up with any notion of consulting them, so I went to Case. It was dark, and he was sitting alone, as he did mostly, smoking on the stairs.

"Case," said I, "here's a queer thing. I'm tabooed."

"Oh, fudge!" says he; " 't ain't the practice in these islands."

"That may be, or it mayn't," said I. "It's the practice where I was before. You can bet I know what it's like; and I tell it you for a fact, I'm tabooed."

"Well," said he, "what have you been doing?"

"That's what I want to find out," said I.

"Oh, you can't be," said he; "it ain't possible. However, I'll tell you what I'll do. Just to put your mind at rest, I'll go round and find out for sure. Just you waltz in and talk to Papa."

"Thank you," I said, "I'd rather stay right out her on the veranda. Your house is so close."

"I'll call Papa out here, then," says he.

"My dear fellow," I says, "I wish you wouldn't. The fact is, I don't take to Mr. Randall."

Case laughed, took a lantern from the store, and set out into the village. He was gone perhaps a quarter of an hour, and he looked mighty serious when he came back.

"Well," said he, clapping down the lantern on the veranda steps, "I would never have believed it. I don't know where the impudence of these Kanakas'll go next; they seem to have lost all idea of respect for whites. What we want is a man-of-war—a German, if we could—they know how to manage Kanakas."

"I *am* tabooed, then?" I cried.

"Something of the sort," said he. "It's the worst thing of the kind I've heard of yet. But I'll stand by you, Wiltshire, man to man. You come round here to-morrow about nine, and we'll have it out with the chiefs. They're afraid of me, or they used to be; but their heads are so big by now, I don't know what to think. Understand me, Wiltshire; I don't count this your quarrel," he went on, with a great deal of resolution, "I count it all of our quarrel, I count it the White Man's Quarrel, and I'll stand to it through thick and thin, and there's my hand on it."

"Have you found out what's the reason?" I asked.

"Not yet," said Case. "But we'll fire them down to-morrow."

Altogether I was pretty well pleased with his attitude, and almost more the next day, when we met to go before the chiefs, to see him so stern and resolved. The chiefs awaited us in one of their big oval houses, which was marked out to us from a long way off by the crowd about the eaves, a hundred strong if there was one—men, women, and children. Many of the men were on their way to work and wore green wreaths, and it put me in thoughts of the first of May at home. This crowd opened and buzzed about the pair of us as we went in, with a sudden angry animation. Five chiefs were there; four mighty, stately men, the fifth old and puckered. They sat on mats in their white kilts and jackets; they had fans in their hands, like fine ladies; and two of the younger ones wore Catholic medals, which gave me matter of reflection. Our place was set, and the mats laid for us over against these grandees, on the near side of the house; the midst was empty; the crowd, close at our backs, murmured and craned and jostled to look on, and the shadows of them tossed in front of us on the clean pebbles of the floor. I was just a hair put out by the excitement of the commons, but the quiet, civil appearance of the chiefs reassured me, all the more when their spokesman began and made a long speech in a low voice, sometimes waving his hand toward Case, sometimes toward me, and sometimes knocking with his knuckles on the mat. One thing was clear: there was no sign of anger in the chiefs.

"What's he been saying?" I asked, when he had done.

"Oh, just that they're glad to see you, and they understand by me you wish to make some kind of complaint, and you're to fire away, and they'll do the square thing."

"It took a precious long time to say that," said I.

"Oh, the rest was sawder and *bonjour* and that," said Case. "You know what Kanakas are."

"Well, they don't get much *bonjour* out of me," said I. "You tell them who I am. I'm a white man, and a British subject, and no end of a big chief at home; and I've come here to do them good, and bring them civilisation; and no sooner have I got my trade sorted out than they go and taboo me, and no one dare come near my place! Tell them I don't mean to fly in the face of anything legal; and if what they want's a present, I'll do what's fair. I don't blame any man looking out for himself, tell them, for that's human nature; but if they think they're going to come any of their native ideas over me, they'll find themselves mistaken. And tell them plain that I demand the reason of this treatment as a white man and a British subject."

That was my speech. I knew how to deal with Kanakas: give them plain sense and fair dealings, and—I'll do them that much justice—they knuckle under every time. They haven't any real government or any real law, that's what you've got to knock into their heads; and even if they had, it would be a good joke if it was to apply to a white man. It would be a strange thing if we came all this way and couldn't do what we pleased. The mere idea has always put my monkey up, and I rapped my speech out pretty big. Then Case translated it—or made believe to, rather—and the first chief replied, and then a second, and a third, all in the same style —easy and genteel, but solemn underneath. Once a question was put to Case, and he answered it, and all hands (both chiefs and commons) laughed out aloud, and looked at me. Last of all, the puckered old fellow and the big young chief that spoke first started

in to put Case through a kind of catechism. Sometimes I made out
that Case was trying to fence, and they stuck to him like hounds,
and the sweat ran down his face, which was no very pleasant sight
to me, and at some of his answers the crowd moaned and murmured, which was a worse hearing. It's a cruel shame I knew no
native, for (as I now believe) they were asking Case about my
marriage, and he must have had a tough job of it to clear his feet.
But leave Case alone; he had the brains to run a parliament.

"Well, is that all?" I asked, when a pause came.

"Come along," says he, mopping his face; "I'll tell you outside."

"Do you mean they won't take the taboo off?" I cried.

"It's something queer," said he. "I'll tell you outside. Better
come away."

"I won't take it at their hands," cried I. "I ain't that kind of
a man. You don't find me turn my back on a parcel of Kanakas."

"You'd better," said Case.

He looked at me with a signal in his eye; and the five chiefs
looked at me civilly enough, but kind of pointed; and the people
looked at me and craned and jostled. I remembered the folks that
watched my house, and how the pastor had jumped in his pulpit
at the bare sight of me; and the whole business seemed so out of
the way that I rose and followed Case. The crowd opened again to
let us through, but wider than before, the children on the skirts
running and singing out, and as we two white men walked away
they all stood and watched us.

"And now," said I, "what is all this about?"

"The truth is I can't rightly make it out myself. They have a
down on you," says Case.

"Taboo a man because they have a down on him!" I cried. "I
never heard the like."

"It's worse than that, you see," said Case. "You ain't tabooed—
I told you that couldn't be. The people won't go near you,
Wiltshire, and there's where it is."

"They won't go near me? What do you mean by that? Why
won't they go near me?" I cried.

Case hesitated. "Seems they're frightened," says he, in a low
voice.

I stopped dead short. "Frightened?" I repeated. "Are you gone
crazy, Case? What are they frightened of?"

"I wish I could make out," Case answered, shaking his head.

"Appears like one of their tomfool superstitions. That's what I don't cotton to," he said. "It's like the business about Vigours."

"I'd like to know what you mean by that, and I'll trouble you to tell me," says I.

"Well, you know, Vigours lit out and left all standing," said he. "It was some superstition business—I never got the hang of it; but it began to look bad before the end."

"I've heard a different story about that," said I, "and I had better tell you so. I heard he ran away because of you."

"Oh! well, I suppose he was ashamed to tell the truth," says Case; "I guess he thought it silly. And it's a fact that I packed him off. 'What would you do, old man?' says he. 'Get,' says I, 'and not think twice about it.' I was the gladdest kind of man to see him clear away. It ain't my notion to turn my back on a mate when he's in a tight place, but there was that much trouble in the village that I couldn't see where it might likely end. I was a fool to be so much about with Vigours. They cast it up to me today. Didn't you hear Maea—that's the young chief, the big one—ripping out about 'Vika'? That was him they were after. They don't seem to forget it, somehow."

"This is all very well," said I, "but it don't tell me what's wrong; it don't tell me what they're afraid of—what their idea is."

"Well, I wish I knew," said Case. "I can't say fairer than that."

"You might have asked, I think," says I.

"And so I did," says he. "But you must have seen for yourself, unless you're blind, that the asking got the other way. I'll go as far as I dare for another white man; but when I find I'm in the scrape myself, I think first of my own bacon. The loss of me is I'm too good-natured. And I'll take the freedom of telling you you show a queer kind of gratitude to a man who's got into all this mess along of your affairs."

"There's a thing I'm thinking of," said I. "You were a fool to be so much about with Vigours. One comfort, you haven't been much about with me. I notice you've never been inside my house. Own up now; you had word of this before?"

"It's a fact I haven't been," said he. "It was an oversight, and I am sorry for it, Wiltshire. But about coming now, I'll be quite plain."

"You mean you won't?" I asked.

"Awfully sorry, old man, but that's the size of it," says Case.

"In short, you're afraid?" says I.

"In short, I'm afraid," says he.

"And I'm still to be tabooed for nothing?" I asked.

"I tell you you're not tabooed," said he. "The Kanakas won't go near you, that's all. And who's to make 'em? We traders have a lot of gall, I must say; we make these poor Kanakas take back their laws, and take up their taboos, and that, whenever it happens to suit us. But you don't mean to say you expect a law obliging people to deal in your store whether they want to or not? You don't mean to tell me you've got the gall for that? And if you had, it would be a queer thing to propose to me. I would just like to point out to you, Wiltshire, that I'm a trader myself."

"I don't think I would talk of gall if I was you," said I. "Here's about what it comes to, as well as I can make out: None of the people are to trade with me, and they're all to trade with you. You're to have the copra, and I'm to go to the devil and shake myself. And I don't know any native, and you're the only man here worth mention that speaks English, and you have the gall to up and hint to me my life's in danger, and all you've got to tell me is you don't know why!"

"Well, it *is* all I have to tell you," said he. "I don't know—I wish I did."

"And so you turn your back and leave me to myself! is that the position?" says I.

"If you like to put it nasty," says he. "I don't put it so. I say merely, 'I'm going to keep clear of you; or, if I don't, I'll get in danger for myself.'"

"Well," says I, "you're a nice kind of a white man!"

"Oh, I understand; you're riled," said he. "I would be myself. I can make excuses."

"All right," I said, "go and make excuses somewhere else. Here's my way, there's yours!"

With that we parted, and I went straight home, in a hot temper, and found Uma trying on a lot of trade goods like a baby.

"Here," I said, "you quit that foolery! Here's pretty mess to have made, as if I wasn't bothered enough anyway! And I thought I told you to get dinner!"

And then I believe I gave her a bit of the rough side of my

tongue, as she deserved. She stood up at once, like a sentry to his officer; for I must say she was always well brought up, and had a great respect for whites.

"And now," says I, "you belong round here, you're bound to understand this. What am I tabooed for, anyway? Or, if I ain't tabooed, what makes the folks afraid of me?"

She stood and looked at me with eyes like saucers.

"You no savvy?" she gasps at last.

"No," said I. "How would you expect me to? We don't have any such craziness where I come from."

"Ese no tell you?" she asked again.

(*Ese* was the name the natives had for Case; it may mean foreign, or extraordinary; or it might mean a mummy apple; but most like it was only his own name misheard and put in a Kanaka spelling.)

"Not much," said I.

"D—n Ese!" she cried.

You might think it funny to hear this Kanaka girl come out with a big swear. No such thing. There was no swearing in her—no, nor anger; she was beyond anger, and meant the word simple and serious. She stood there straight as she said it. I cannot justly say that I ever saw a woman look like that before or after, and it struck me mum. Then she made a kind of an obeisance, but it was the proudest kind, and threw her hands out open.

"I 'shamed," she said. "I think you savvy. Ese he tell me you savvy, he tell me you no mind, tell me you love me too much. Taboo belong me," she said, touching herself on the bosom, as she had done upon our wedding-night. "Now I go 'way, taboo he go 'way too. Then you get too much copra. You like more better, I think. *Tofá, alii,*" says she in the native—"Farewell, chief!"

"Hold on!" I cried. "Don't be in such a hurry."

She looked at me sidelong with a smile. "You see, you get copra," she said, the same as you might offer candies to a child.

"Uma," said I, "hear reason. I didn't know, and that's a fact; and Case seems to have played it pretty mean upon the pair of us. But I do know now, and I don't mind; I love you too much. You no go 'way, you no leave me, I too much sorry."

"You no love me," she cried, "you talk me bad words!" And she threw herself in a corner of the floor, and began to cry.

Well, I'm no scholar, but I wasn't born yesterday, and I thought the worst of that trouble was over. However, there she lay—her

back turned, her face to the wall—and shook with sobbing like a
little child, so that her feet jumped with it. It's strange how it hits
a man when he's in love; for there's no use mincing things; Kanaka
and all, I was in love with her, or just as good. I tried to take her
hand, but she would none of that. "Uma," I said, "there's no sense
in carrying on like this. I want you stop here, I want my little
wifie, I tell you true."

"No tell me true," she sobbed.

"All right," says I, "I'll wait till you're through with this." And
I sat right down beside her on the floor, and set to smooth her
hair with my hand. At first she wriggled away when I touched her;
then she seemed to notice me no more; then her sobs grew gradually less, and presently stopped; and the next thing I knew, she
raised her face to mine.

"You tell me true? You like me stop?" she asked.

"Uma," I said, "I would rather have you than all the copra in
the South Seas," which was a very big expression, and the strangest
thing was that I meant it.

She threw her arms about me, sprang close up, and pressed her
face to mine, in the island way of kissing, so that I was all wetted
with her tears, and my heart went out to her wholly. I never had
anything so near me as this little brown bit of a girl. Many things
went together, and all helped to turn my head. She was pretty
enough to eat; it seemed she was my only friend in that queer
place; I was ashamed that I had spoken rough to her: and she
was a woman, and my wife, and a kind of a baby besides that I
was sorry for; and the salt of her tears was in my mouth. And I
forgot Case and the natives; and I forgot that I knew nothing of
the story, or only remembered it to banish the remembrance; and
I forgot that I was to get no copra, and so could make no livelihood; and I forgot my employers, and the strange kind of service
I was doing them, when I preferred my fancy to their business; and
I forgot even that Uma was no true wife of mine, but just a maid
beguiled, and that in a pretty shabby style. But that is to look too
far on. I will come to that part of it next.

It was late before we thought of getting dinner. The stove was
out, and gone stone cold; but we fired up after awhile, and cooked
each a dish, helping and hindering each other, and making a play
of it like children. I was so greedy of her nearness that I sat down
to dinner with my lass upon my knee, made sure of her with one

hand, and ate with the other. Ay, and more than that. She was the worst cook I suppose God made; the things she set her hand to it would have sickened an honest horse to eat of; yet I made my meal that day on Uma's cookery, and can never call to mind to have been better pleased. I didn't pretend to myself, and I didn't pretend to her. I saw I was clean gone; and if she was to make a fool of me, she must. And I suppose it was this that set her talking, for now she made sure that we were friends. A lot she told me, sitting in my lap and eating my dish, as I ate hers, from foolery—a lot about herself and her mother and Case, all which would be very tedious, and fill sheets if I set it down in Beach de Mar, but which I must give a hint of in plain English, and one thing about myself, which had a very big effect on my concerns, as you are soon to hear.

It seems she was born in one of the Line Islands; had been only two or three years in these parts, where she had come with a white man, who was married to her mother and then died; and only the one year in Falesá. Before that they had been a good deal on the move, trekking about after the white man, who was one of those rolling stones that keep going round after a soft job. They talk about looking for gold at the end of a rainbow; but if a man wants an employment that'll last him till he dies, let him start out on the soft-job hunt. There's meat and drink in it too, and beer and skittles, for you never hear of them starving, and rarely see them sober; and as for steady sport, cock-fighting isn't in the same county with it. Anyway, this beach-comber carried the woman and her daughter all over the shop, but mostly to out-of-the-way islands, where there were no police, and he thought, perhaps, the soft job hung out. I've my own view of this old party; but I was just as glad he had kept Uma clear of Apia and Papeete and these flash towns. At last he struck Fale-alii on this island, got some trade—the Lord knows how!—muddled it all away in the usual style, and died worth next to nothing, bar a bit of land at Falesá that he had got for a bad debt, which was what put it in the minds of the mother and daughter to come there and live. It seems Case encouraged them all he could, and helped to get their house built. He was very kind those days, and gave Uma trade, and there is no doubt he had his eye on her from the beginning. However, they had scarce settled, when up turned a young man, a native, and wanted to marry her. He was a small chief, and had some fine mats and old songs in his family, and was "very pretty," Uma said; and, altogether, it was an extraordinary match for a penniless girl and an out-islander.

At the first word of this I got downright sick with jealousy.

"And you mean to say you would have married him?" I cried.

"*Ioe*, yes," said she. "I like too much!"

"Well!" I said. "And suppose I had come round after?"

"I like you more better now," said she. "But suppose I marry Ioane, I one good wife. I no common Kanaka. Good girl!" says she.

"Well, I had to be pleased with that; but I promise you I didn't care about the business one little bit. And I liked the end of that yarn no better than the beginning. For it seems this proposal of marriage was the start of all the trouble. It seems, before that, Uma and her mother had been looked down upon, of course, for kinless folk and out-islanders, but nothing to hurt; and, even when Ioane came forward, there was less trouble at first than might have been looked for. And then, all of a sudden, about six months before my coming, Ioane backed out and left that part of the island, and from that day to this Uma and her mother had found themselves alone. None called at their house—none spoke to them on the roads. If they went to church, the other women drew their mats away and left them in a clear place by themselves. It was a regular excommunication, like what you read of in the Middle Ages; and the cause or sense of it beyond guessing. It was some *talo pepelo,* Uma said, some lie, some calumny; and all she knew of it was that the girls who had been jealous of her luck with Ioane used to twit her with his desertion, and cry out, when they met her alone in the woods, that she would never be married. "They tell me no man he marry me. He too much 'fraid," she said.

The only soul that came about them after this desertion was Master Case. Even he was chary of showing himself, and turned up mostly by night; and pretty soon he began to table his cards and make up to Uma. I was still sore about Ioane, and when Case turned up in the same line of business I cut up downright rough.

"Well," I said, sneering, "and I suppose you thought Case 'very pretty' and 'liked too much'?"

"Now you talk silly," said she. "White man, he come here, I marry him all-e-same Kanaka; very well then, he marry me all-e-same white woman. Suppose he no marry, he go 'way, woman he

stop. All-e-same thief, empty hand, Tonga-heart—no can love!
Now you come marry me. You big heart—you no 'shamed island-
girl. That thing I love you far too much. I proud."

I don't know that ever I felt sicker all the days of my life. I laid
down my fork, and I put away the "island-girl;" I didn't seem
somehow to have any use for either, and I went and walked up and
down in the house, and Uma followed me with her eyes, for she
was troubled, and small wonder! But troubled was no word for it
with me. I so wanted, and so feared, to make a clean breast of the
sweep that I had been.

And just then there came a sound of singing out of the sea; it
sprang up suddenly clear and near, as the boat turned the headland, and Uma, running to the window, cried out it was "Misi"
come upon his rounds.

I thought it was a strange thing I should be glad to have a missionary; but, if it was strange, it was still true.

"Uma," said I, "you stop here in this room, and don't budge a
foot out of it till I come back."

3.   The Missionary

As I came out on the veranda, the mission-boat was shooting for
the mouth of the river. She was a long whale-boat painted white;
a bit of an awning astern; a native pastor crouched on the wedge
of poop, steering; some four-and-twenty paddles flashing and dipping, true to the boat-song; and the missionary under the awning,
in his white clothes, reading in a book; and set him up! It was
pretty to see and hear; there's no smarter sight in the islands than
a missionary boat with a good crew and a good pipe to them; and
I considered it for half a minute with a bit of envy perhaps, and
then strolled down toward the river.

From the opposite side there was another man aiming for the
same place, but he ran and got there first. It was Case; doubtless
his idea was to keep me apart from the missionary, who might
serve me as interpreter; but my mind was upon other things. I was
thinking how he had jockeyed us about the marriage, and tried
his hand on Uma before; and at the sight of him rage flew into my
nostrils.

"Get out of that, you low, swindling thief!" I cried.

"What's that you say?" says he.

I gave him the word again, and rammed it down with a good oath. "And if ever I catch you within six fathoms of my house," I cried, "I'll clap a bullet in your measly carcass."

"You must do as you like about your house," said he, "where I told you I have no thought of going; but this is a public place."

"It's a place where I have private business," said I. "I have no idea of a hound like you eavesdropping, and I give you notice to clear out."

"I don't take it, though," says Case.

"I'll show you then," said I.

"We'll have to see about that," said he.

He was quick with his hands, but he had neither the height nor the weight, being a flimsy creature alongside a man like me, and, besides, I was blazing to that height of wrath that I could have bit into a chisel. I gave him first the one and then the other, so that I could hear his head rattle and crack, and he went down straight.

"Have you had enough?" cries I. But he only looked up white and blank, and the blood spread upon his face like wine upon a napkin. "Have you had enough?" I cried again. "Speak up, and don't lie malingering there, or I'll take my feet to you."

He sat up at that, and held his head—by the look of him you could see it was spinning—and the blood poured on his pajamas.

"I've had enough for this time," says he, and he got up staggering, and went off by the way that he had come.

The boat was close in; I saw the missionary had laid his book to one side, and I smiled to myself. "He'll know I'm a man, anyway," thinks I.

This was the first time, in all my years in the Pacific, I had ever exchanged two words with any missionary, let alone asked one for a favour. I didn't like the lot, no trader does; they look down upon us, and make no concealment; and, besides, they're partly Kanakaised, and suck up with natives instead of with other white men like themselves. I had a rig of clean, striped pajamas—for, of course, I had dressed decent to go before the chiefs; but when I saw the missionary step out of his boat in the regular uniform, white duck clothes, pith helmet, white shirt and tie, and yellow boots to his feet, I could have bunged stones at him. As he came nearer, queering me pretty curious (because of the fight, I suppose), I saw he looked mortal sick, for the truth was he had a fever on, and had just had a chill in the boat.

"Mr. Tarleton, I believe?" says I, for I had got his name.

"And you, I suppose, are the new trader?" says he.

"I want to tell you first that I don't hold with missions," I went on, "and that I think you and the likes of you do a sight of harm, filling up the natives with old wives' tales and bumptiousness."

"You are perfectly entitled to your opinions," says he, looking a bit ugly, "but I have no call to hear them."

"It so happens that you've got to hear them," I said. "I'm no missionary, nor missionary lover; I'm no Kanaka, nor favourer of Kanakas—I'm just a trader; I'm just a common low God-damned white man and British subject, the sort you would like to wipe your boots on. I hope that's plain!"

"Yes, my man," said he. "It's more plain than creditable. When you are sober, you'll be sorry for this."

He tried to pass on, but I stopped him with my hand. The Kanakas were beginning to growl. Guess they didn't like my tone, for I spoke to that man as free as I would to you.

"Now, you can't say I've deceived you," said I, "and I can go on. I want a service—I want two services, in fact; and, if you care to give me them, I'll perhaps take more stock in what you call your Christianity."

He was silent for a moment. Then he smiled. "You are rather a strange sort of man," says he.

"I'm the sort of man God made me," says I. "I don't set up to be a gentleman," I said.

"I am not quite so sure," said he. "And what can I do for you, Mr. ——?"

"Wiltshire," I says, "though I'm mostly called Welsher; but Wiltshire is the way it's spelt, if the people on the beach could only get their tongues about it. And what do I want? Well, I'll tell you the first thing. I'm what you call a sinner—what I call a sweep— and I want you to help me make it up to a person I've deceived."

He turned and spoke to his crew in the native. "And now I am at your service," said he, "but only for the time my crew are dining. I must be much farther down the coast before night. I was delayed at Papa-malulu till this morning, and I have an engagement in Fale-alii to-morrow night."

I led the way to my house in silence, and rather pleased with myself for the way I had managed the talk, for I like a man to keep his self-respect.

"I was sorry to see you fighting," says he.

"Oh, that's part of the yarn I want to tell you," I said. "That's service number two. After you've heard it you'll let me know whether you're sorry or not."

We walked right in through the store, and I was surprised to find Uma had cleared away the dinner things. This was so unlike her ways that I saw she had done it out of gratitude, and liked her the better. She and Mr. Tarleton called each other by name, and he was very civil to her seemingly. But I thought little of that; they can always find civility for a Kanaka, it's us white men they lord it over. Besides, I didn't want much Tarleton just then. I was going to do my pitch.

"Uma," said I, "give us your marriage certificate." She looked put out. "Come," said I, "you can trust me. Hand it up."

She had it about her person, as usual; I believe she thought it was a pass to heaven, and if she died without having it handy she would go to hell. I couldn't see where she put it the first time, I couldn't see now where she took it from; it seemed to jump into her hand like that Blavatsky business in the papers. But it's the same way with all island women, and I guess they're taught it when young.

"Now," said I, with the certificate in my hand, "I was married to this girl by Black Jack, the Negro. The certificate was wrote by Case, and it's a dandy piece of literature, I promise you. Since then I've found that there's a kind of cry in the place against this wife of mine, and so long as I keep her I cannot trade. Now, what would any man do in my place, if he was a man?" I said. "The first thing he would do is this, I guess." And I took and tore up the certificate and bunged the pieces on the floor.

"Aue!" * cried Uma, and began to clap her hands; but I caught one of them in mine.

"And the second thing that he would do," said I, "if he was what I would call a man and you would call a man, Mr. Tarleton, is to bring the girl right before you or any other missionary, and to up and say: 'I was wrong married to this wife of mine, but I think a heap of her, and now I want to be married to her right.' Fire away, Mr. Tarleton. And I guess you'd better do it in native; it'll please

* Alas.

the old lady," I said, giving her the proper name of a man's wife upon the spot.

So we had in two of the crew for to witness, and were spliced in our own house; and the parson prayed a good bit, I must say—but not so long as some—and shook hands with the pair of us.

"Mr. Wiltshire," he says, when he had made out the lines and packed off the witnesses, "I have to thank you for a very lively pleasure. I have rarely performed the marriage ceremony with more grateful emotions."

That was what you would call talking. He was going on, besides, with more of it, and I was ready for as much taffy as he had in stock, for I felt good. But Uma had been taken up with something half through the marriage, and cut straight in.

"How your hand he get hurt?" she asked.

"You ask Case's head, old lady," says I.

She jumped with joy, and sang out.

"You haven't made much of a Christian of this one," says I to Mr. Tarleton.

"We didn't think her one of our worst," says he, "when she was at Fale-alii; and if Uma bears malice I shall be tempted to fancy she had good cause."

"Well, there we are at service number two," said I. "I want to tell you our yarn, and see if you can let a little daylight in."

"Is it long?" he asked.

"Yes," I cried; "it's a goodish bit of a yarn!"

"Well, I'll give you all the time I can spare," says he, looking at his watch. "But I must tell you fairly, I haven't eaten since five this morning, and, unless you can let me have something, I am not likely to eat again before seven or eight to-night."

"By God, we'll give you dinner!" I cried.

I was a little caught up at my swearing, just when all was going straight; and so was the missionary, I suppose, but he made believe to look out of the window, and thanked us.

So we ran him up a bit of a meal. I was bound to let the old lady have a hand in it, to show off, so I deputised her to brew the tea. I don't think I ever met such tea as she turned out. But that was not the worst, for she got round with the salt-box, which she considered an extra European touch, and turned my stew into sea-water. Altogether, Mr. Tarleton had a devil of a dinner of it; but he had plenty of entertainment by the way, for all the while that we were cooking, and afterward, when he was making believe to eat, I kept posting him up on Master Case and the beach of Falesá, and he putting questions that showed he was following close.

"Well," said he at last, "I am afraid you have a dangerous enemy. This man Case is very clever and seems really wicked. I must tell you I have had my eye on him for nearly a year, and have rather had the worst of our encounters. About the time when the last representative of your firm ran so suddenly away, I had a letter from Namu, the native pastor, begging me to come to Falesá at my earliest convenience, as his flock were all 'adopting Catholic practices.' I had great confidence in Namu; I fear it only shows how easily we are deceived. No one could hear him preach and not be persuaded he was a man of extraordinary parts. All our islanders easily acquire a kind of eloquence, and can roll out and illustrate, with a great deal of vigour and fancy, second-hand sermons; but Namu's sermons are his own, and I cannot deny that I have found them means of grace. Moreover, he has keen curiosity in secular things, does not fear work, is clever at carpentering, and has made himself so much respected among the neighbouring pastors that we call him, in a jest which is half serious, the Bishop of the East. In short, I was proud of the man; all the more puzzled by his letter, and took an occasion to come this way. The morning before my arrival, Vigours had been sent on board the Lion, and Namu was perfectly at his ease, apparently ashamed of his letter, and quite unwilling to explain it. This, of course, I could not allow, and he ended by confessing that he had been much concerned to find his people using the sign of the cross, but since he had learned the explanation his mind was satisfied. For Vigours had the Evil Eye, a common thing in a country of Europe called Italy, where men were often struck dead by that kind of devil, and it appeared the sign of the cross was a charm against its power.

" 'And I explain it, Misi,' said Namu, 'in this way: the country in Europe is a Popey country, and the devil of the Evil Eye may be a Catholic devil, or, at least, used to Catholic ways. So then I reasoned thus: if this sign of the cross were used in a Popey manner it would be sinful, but when it is used only to protect men from a devil, which is a thing harmless in itself, the sign too must be harmless. For the sign is neither good nor bad. But if the bottle be full of gin, the gin is bad; and if the sign made in idolatry be bad, so is the idolatry.' And, very like a native pastor, he had a text apposite about the casting out of devils.

" 'And who has been telling you about the Evil Eye?' I asked.

"He admitted it was Case. Now, I am afraid you will think me very narrow, Mr. Wiltshire, but I must tell you I was displeased, and cannot think a trader at all a good man to advise or have an influence upon my pastors. And, besides, there had been some flying talk in the country of old Adams and his being poisoned, to which I had paid no great heed; but it came back to me at the moment.

" 'And is this Case a man of a sanctified life?' I asked.

"He admitted he was not; for, though he did not drink, he was profligate with women, and had no religion.

" 'Then,' said I, 'I think the less you have to do with him the better.'

"But it is not easy to have the last word with a man like Namu. He was ready in a moment with an illustration. 'Misi,' said he, 'you have told me there were wise men, not pastors, not even holy, who knew many things useful to be taught—about trees, for instance, and beasts, and to print books, and about the stones that are burned to make knives of. Such men teach you in your college, and you learn for them, but take care not to learn to be unholy. Misi, Case is my college.'

"I knew not what to say. Mr. Vigours had evidently been driven out of Falesá by the machinations of Case and with something not very unlike the collusion of my pastor. I called to mind it was Namu who had reassured me about Adams and traced the rumour to the ill-will of the priest. And I saw I must inform myself more thoroughly from an impartial source. There is an old rascal of a chief here, Faiaso, whom I dare say you saw to-day at the council; he has been all his life turbulent and shy, a great fomenter of rebellions, and a thorn in the side of the mission and the island. For all that he is very shrewd, and, except in politics or about his own misdemeanours, a teller of the truth. I went to his house, told him what I had heard, and besought him to be frank. I do not think I had ever a more painful interview. Perhaps you will understand me, Mr. Wiltshire, if I tell you that I am perfectly serious in these old wives' tales with which you reproached me, and as anxious to do well for these islands as you can be to please and to protect your pretty wife. And you are to remember that I thought Namu a paragon, and was proud of the man as one of the first ripe fruits of the mission. And now I was informed that he had fallen in a sort of dependence upon Case. The beginning of it was not corrupt; it began, doubtless, in fear and respect, produced by trickery and pretence; but I was shocked to find that another element had been lately added, that Namu helped himself in the store, and was believed to be deep in Case's debt. Whatever the trader said, that Namu believed with trembling. He was not alone in this; many in the village lived in a similar subjection; but Namu's case was the most influential, it was through Namu that Case had wrought most evil; and with a certain following among the chiefs, and the pastor in his pocket, the man was as good as master of the village. You know something of Vigours and Adams, but perhaps you have never heard of old Underhill, Adams's predecessor. He was a quiet, mild old fellow, I remember, and we were told he had died suddenly: white men die very suddenly in Falesá. The truth, as I now heard it, made my blood run cold. It seems he was struck with a general palsy, all of him dead but one eye, which he continually winked. Word was started that the helpless old man was now a devil, and this vile fellow Case worked upon the natives' fears, which he professed to share, and pretended he durst not go into the house alone. At last a grave was dug, and the living body buried at the far end of the village. Namu, my pastor, whom I had helped to educate, offered up a prayer at the hateful scene.

"I felt myself in a very difficult position. Perhaps it was my duty to have denounced Namu and had him deposed. Perhaps I think so now, but at the time it seemed less clear. He had a great influence, it might prove greater than mine. The natives are prone to superstition; perhaps by stirring them up I might but ingrain and spread these dangerous fancies. And Namu besides, apart from this novel and accursed influence, was a good pastor, an able man, and spiritually minded. Where should I look for a better? How was I to find as good? At that moment, with Namu's failure fresh in my view, the work of my life appeared a mockery; hope was dead in me. I would rather repair such tools as I had than go abroad in quest of others that must certainly prove worse; and a scandal is, at the best, a thing to be avoided when humanly possible. Right or wrong, then, I determined on a quiet course. All that night I denounced and reasoned with the erring pastor, twitted him with his ignorance and want of faith, twitted him with his wretched attitude, making clean the outside of the cup and platter, callously helping at a murder, childishly flying in excitement about a few childish, unnecessary, and inconvenient gestures; and long before day I had him on his knees and bathed in the tears of what seemed a genuine repentance. On Sunday I took the pulpit in the morning, and preached from First Kings, nineteenth, on the fire, the earthquake, and the voice, distinguishing the true spiritual power, and referring with such plainness as I dared to recent events in Falesá. The effect produced was great, and it was much increased when Namu rose in his turn and confessed that he had been wanting in faith and conduct, and was convinced of sin. So far, then, all was well; but there was one unfortunate circumstance. It was nearing the time of our 'May' in the island, when the native contributions to the missions are received; it fell in my duty to make a notification on the subject, and this gave my enemy his chance, by which he was not slow to profit.

"News of the whole proceedings must have been carried to Case as soon as church was over, and the same afternoon he made an occasion to meet me in the midst of the village. He came up with so much intentness and animosity that I felt it would be damaging to avoid him.

"'So,' says he, in native, 'here is the holy man. He has been preaching against me, but that was not in his heart. He has been preaching upon the love of God; but that was not in his heart, it was between his teeth. Will you know what was in his heart?' cries he. 'I will show it to you!' And, making a snatch at my head, he made believe to pluck out a dollar, and held it in the air.

"There went that rumour through the crowd with which Polynesians receive a prodigy. As for myself, I stood amazed. The thing was a common conjuring trick which I have seen performed at home a score of times; but how was I to convince the villagers of that? I wished I had learned legerdemain instead of Hebrew, that I might have paid the fellow out with his own coin. But there I was; I could not stand there silent, and the best I could find to say was weak.

"'I will trouble you not to lay hands on me again,' said I.

"'I have no such thought,' said he, 'nor will I deprive you of your dollar. Here it is,' he said, and flung it at my feet. I am told it lay where it fell three days."

"I must say it was well played," said I.

"Oh! he is clever," said Mr. Tarleton, "and you can now see for yourself how dangerous. He was a party to the horrid death of the paralytic; he is accused of poisoning Adams; he drove Vigours out of the place by lies that might have led to murder; and there is no question but he has now made up his mind to rid himself of you. How he means to try we have no guess; only be sure, it's something new. There is no end to his readiness and invention."

"He gives himself a sight of trouble," said I. "And after all, what for?"

"Why, how many tons of copra may they make in this district?" asked the missionary.

"I dare say as much as sixty tons," says I.

"And what is the profit to the local trader?" he asked.

"You may call it three pounds," said I.

"Then you can reckon for yourself how much he does it for," said Mr. Tarleton. "But the more important thing is to defeat him. It is clear he spread some report against Uma, in order to isolate and have his wicked will of her. Failing of that, and seeing a new rival come upon the scene, he used her in a different way. Now, the first point to find out is about Namu. Uma, when people began to leave you and your mother alone, what did Namu do?"

"Stop away all-a-same," says Uma.

"I fear the dog has returned to his vomit," said Mr. Tarleton. "And now what am I to do for you? I will speak to Namu, I will warn him he is observed; it will be strange if he allow anything to go on amiss when he is put upon his guard. At the same time, this precaution may fail, and then you must turn elsewhere. You have two people at hand to whom you might apply. There is, first of all, the priest, who might protect you by the Catholic interest; they are a wretchedly small body, but they count two chiefs. And then there is old Faiaso. Ah! if it had been some years ago you would have needed no one else; but his influence is much reduced, it has gone into Maea's hands, and Maea, I fear, is one of Case's jackals. In fine, if the worst comes to the worst, you must send up or come yourself to Fale-alii, and, though I am not due at this end of the island for a month, I will just see what can be done."

So Mr. Tarleton said farewell; and half an hour later the crew were singing and the paddles flashing in the missionary boat.

4. *Devil-Work*

Near a month went by without much doing. The same night of our marriage Galoshes called round, and made himself mighty civil, and got into a habit of dropping in about dark and smoking his pipe with the family. He could talk to Uma, of course, and started to teach me native and French at the same time. He was a kind old buffer, though the dirtiest you would wish to see, and he muddled me up with foreign languages worse than the Tower of Babel.

That was one employment we had, and it made me feel less lonesome; but there was no profit in the thing, for though the priest came and sat and yarned, none of his folks could be enticed into my store, and if it hadn't been for the other occupation I struck out, there wouldn't have been a pound of copra in the house. This was the idea: Faavao (Uma's mother) had a score of bearing-trees. Of course we could get no labour, being all as good as tabooed, and the two women and I turned to and made copra with our own hands. It was copra to make your mouth water when it was done—I never understood how much the natives cheated me till I had made that four hundred pounds of my own hand—and it weighed so light I felt inclined to take and water it myself.

When we were at the job a good many Kanakas used to put in the best of the day looking on, and once that nigger turned up. He stood back with the natives and laughed and did the big don and the funny dog, till I began to get riled.

"Here, you nigger!" says I.

"I don't address myself to you, Sah," says the nigger. "Only speak to gen'le'um."

"I know," says I, "but it happens I was addressing myself to you, Mr. Black Jack. And all I want to know is just this: did you see Case's figure-head about a week ago?"

"No, Sah," says he.

"That's all right, then," says I; "for I'll show you the own brother to it, only black, in the inside of about two minutes."

And I began to walk toward him, quite slow, and my hands

down; only there was trouble in my eye, if anybody took the pains to look.

"You're a low, obstropulous fellow, Sah," says he.

"You bet!" says I.

By that time he thought I was about as near as convenient, and lit out so it would have done your heart good to see him travel. And that was all I saw of that precious gang until what I am about to tell you.

It was one of my chief employments these days to go pot-hunting in the woods, which I found (as Case had told me) very rich in game. I have spoken of the cape which shut up the village and my station from the east. A path went about the end of it, and led into the next bay. A strong wind blew here daily, and as the line of the barrier reef stopped at the end of the cape, a heavy surf ran on the shores of the bay. A little cliffy hill cut the valley in two parts, and stood close on the beach; and at high water the sea broke right on the face of it, so that all passage was stopped. Woody mountains hemmed the place all round; the barrier to the east was particularly steep and leafy, the lower parts of it, along the sea, falling in sheer black cliffs streaked with cinnabar; the upper part lumpy with the tops of the great trees. Some of the trees were bright green, and some red, and the sand of the beach as black as your shoes. Many birds hovered round the bay, some of them snow-white; and the flying-fox (or vampire) flew there in broad daylight, gnashing its teeth.

For a long while I came as far as this shooting, and went no farther. There was no sign of any path beyond, and the cocoa-palms in the front of the foot of the valley were the last this way. For the whole "eye" of the island, as natives call the windward end, lay desert. From Falesá round about to Papa-malulu, there was neither house, nor man, nor planted fruit-tree; and the reef being mostly absent, and the shores bluff, the sea beat direct among crags, and there was scarce a landing-place.

I should tell you that after I began to go in the woods, although no one appeared to come near my store, I found people willing enough to pass the time of day with me where nobody could see them; and as I had begun to pick up native, and most of them had a word or two of English, I began to hold little odds and ends of conversation, not to much purpose, to be sure, but they took off the worst of the feeling, for it's a miserable thing to be made a leper of.

It chanced one day, toward the end of the month, that I was sitting in this bay in the edge of the bush, looking east, with a Kanaka. I had given him a fill of tobacco, and we were making out to talk as best we could; indeed, he had more English than most.

I asked him if there was no road going eastward.

"One time one road," said he. "Now he dead."

"Nobody he go there?" I asked.

"No good," said he. "Too much devil he stop there."

"Oho!" says I, "got-um plenty devil, that bush?"

"Man devil, woman devil; too much devil," said my friend. "Stop there all-e-time. Man he go there, no come back."

I thought if this fellow was so well posted on devils and spoke of them so free, which is not common, I had better fish for a little information about myself and Uma.

"You think me one devil?" I asked.

"No think devil," said he, soothingly. "Think all-e-same fool."

"Uma, she devil?" I asked again.

"No, no; no devil. Devil stop bush," said the young man.

I was looking in front of me across the bay, and I saw the hanging front of the woods pushed suddenly open, and Case, with a gun in his hand, step forth into the sunshine on the black beach. He was got up in light pajamas, near white, his gun sparkled, he looked mighty conspicuous; and the land-crabs scuttled from all around him to their holes.

"Hullo, my friend!" says I, "you no talk all-e-same true. Ese he go, he come back."

"Ese no all-e-same; Ese *Tiapolo*," says my friend; and, with a "Good-bye," slunk off among the trees.

I watched Case all around the beach, where the tide was low; and let him pass me on the homeward way to Falesá. He was in deep thought, and the birds seemed to know it, trotting quite near him on the sand, or wheeling and calling in his ears. When he passed me I could see by the working of his lips that he was talking to himself, and what pleased me mightily, he had still my trademark on his brow. I tell you plain truth; I had a mind to give him a gunful in his ugly mug, but I thought better of it.

All this time, and all the time I was following home, I kept repeating that native word, which I remembered by "Polly, put the kettle on and make us all some tea," tea-a-pollo.

"Uma," says I, when I got back, "what does *Tiapolo* mean?"

"Devil," says she.

"I thought *aitu* was the word for that," I said.

"*Aitu* 'nother kind of devil," said she; "stop bush, eat Kanaka. Tiapolo big chief devil, stop home; all-e-same Christian devil."

"Well, then," said I, "I'm no farther forward. How can Case be Tiapolo?"

"No all-e-same," said she. "Ese belong Tiapolo. Tiapolo too much like; Ese all-e-same his son. Suppose Ese he wish something, Tiapolo he made him."

"That's mighty convenient for Ese," says I. "And what kind of things does he make for him?"

Well, out came a rigmarole of all sort of stories, many of which (like the dollar he took from Mr. Tarleton's head) were plain enough to me, but others I could make nothing of; and the thing that most surprised the Kanakas was what surprised me least— namely, that he would go in the desert among all the *aitus*. Some of the boldest, however, had accompanied him, and had heard him speak with the dead and give them orders, and, safe in his protection, had returned unscathed. Some said he had a church there, where he worshipped Tiapolo, and Tiapolo appeared to him; others swore that there was no sorcery at all, that he performed his miracles by the power of prayer, and the church was no church, but a prison, in which he had confined a dangerous *aitu*. Namu had been in the bush with him once, and returned glorifying God for these wonders. Altogether, I began to have a glimmer of the man's position, and the means by which he had acquired it, and though I saw he was a tough nut to crack, I was noways cast down.

"Very well," said I, "I'll have a look at Master Case's place of worship myself, and we'll see about the glorifying."

At this Uma fell in a terrible taking; if I went in the high bush I should never return; none could go there but by the protection of Tiapolo.

"I'll chance it on God's," said I. "I'm a good sort of a fellow, Uma, as fellows go, and I guess God'll con me through."

She was silent for awhile. "I think," said she, mighty solemn— and then, presently—"Victoreea, he big chief?"

"You bet!" said I.

"He like you too much?" she asked again. I told her, with a grin, I believed the old lady was rather partial to me.

"All right," said she. "Victoreea he big chief, like you too much. No can help you here in Falesá; no can do—too far off. Maea he be small chief—stop here. Suppose he like you—make you all right. All-e-same God and Tiapolo. Go he big chief—got too much work. Tiapolo he small chief—he like too much make-see, work very hard."

"I'll have to hand you over to Mr. Tarleton," said I. "Your theology's out of its bearings, Uma."

However, we stuck to this business all the evening, and, with the stories she told me of the desert and its dangers, she came near frightening herself into a fit. I don't remember half a quarter of them, of course, for I paid little heed; but two come back to me kind of clear.

About six miles up the coast there is a sheltered cove they call *Fanga-anaana*—"the haven full of caves." I've seen it from the sea myself, as near as I could get my boys to venture in; and it's a little strip of yellow sand, black cliffs overhang it, full of the black mouths of caves; great trees overhang the cliffs, and dangle-down lianas; and in one place, about the middle, a big brook pours over in a cascade. Well, there was a boat going by here, with six young men of Falesá, "all very pretty," Uma said, which was the loss of them. It blew strong, there was a heavy head sea, and by the time they opened Fanga-anaana, and saw the white cascade and the shady beach, they were all tired and thirsty, and their water had run out. One proposed to land and get a drink, and, being reckless fellows, they were all of the same mind except the youngest. Lotu was his name; he was a very good young gentleman, and very wise; and he held out that they were crazy, telling them the place was given over to spirits and devils and the dead, and there were no living folk nearer than six miles the one way, and maybe twelve the other. But they laughed at his words, and, being five to one, pulled in, beached the boat, and landed. It was a wonderful pleasant place, Lotu said, and the water excellent. They walked round the beach, but could see nowhere any way to mount the cliffs, which made them easier in their mind; and at last they sat down to make a meal on the food they had brought with them. They were scarce set, when there came out of the mouth of one of the black caves six of the most beautiful ladies ever seen; they had flowers in their hair, and the most beautiful breasts, and necklaces of scarlet seeds; and began to jest with these young gentlemen, and the young gentlemen to jest back with them, all but Lotu. As for Lotu, he saw there could be no living woman in such a place, and ran, and flung himself in the bottom of the boat, and covered his face, and prayed. All the time the business lasted Lotu made one clean break of prayer, and that was all he knew of it, until his friends came back, and made him sit up, and they put to sea again out of the bay, which was now quite desert, and no word of the six ladies. But, what frightened Lotu most, not one of the five remembered anything of what had passed, but they were all like drunken men, and sang and laughed in the boat, and skylarked. The wind freshened and came squally, and the sea rose extraordinary high; it was such weather as any man in the islands would have turned his back to and fled home to Falesá; but these five were like crazy folk, and cracked on all sail and drove their boat into the seas. Lotu went to the bailing; none of the others thought to help him, but sang and skylarked and carried on, and spoke singular things beyond a man's comprehension, and laughed out loud when they said them. So the rest of the day Lotu bailed for his life in the bottom of the boat, and was all drenched with sweat and cold sea-water; and none heeded him. Against all expectation, they came safe in a dreadful tempest to Papa-malulu, where the palms were singing out, and the cocoa-nuts flying like cannon-balls about the village green; and the same night the five young gentlemen sickened, and spoke never a reasonable word until they died.

"And do you mean to tell me you can swallow a yarn like that?" I asked.

She told me the thing was well known, and with handsome young men alone it was even common; but this was the only case where five had been slain the same day and in a company by the love of the women-devils; and it had made a great stir in the island, and she would be crazy if she doubted.

"Well, anyway," says I, "you needn't be frightened about me. I've no use for the women-devils. You're all the woman I want, and all the devil too, old lady."

To this she answered there were other sorts, and she had seen one with her own eyes. She had gone one day alone to the next bay, and, perhaps, got near the margin of the bad place. The boughs of the high bush overshadowed her from the cant of the hill, but she herself was outside on a flat place, very stony and growing full of young mummy-apples four and five feet high. It was a dark day in the rainy season, and now there came squalls that tore off the leaves and sent them flying, and now it was all still as in a house. It was in one of these still times that a whole gang of birds and flying-foxes came pegging out of the bush like creatures frightened. Presently after she heard a rustle nearer hand, and saw, coming out of the margin of the trees, among the mummy-apples, the appearance of a lean grey old boar. It seemed to think as it came, like a person; and all of a sudden, as she looked at it coming, she was aware it was no boar, but a thing that was a man with a man's thoughts. At that she ran, and the pig after her, and as the pig ran it holla'd aloud, so that the place rang with it.

"I wish I had been there with my gun," said I. "I guess that pig would have holla'd so as to surprise himself."

But she told me a gun was of no use with the likes of these, which were the spirits of the dead.

Well, this kind of talk put in the evening, which was the best of it. But of course it didn't change my notion, and the next day, with my gun and a good knife, I set off upon a voyage of discovery. I made, as near as I could, for the place where I had seen Case come out; for if it was true he had some kind of establishment in the bush I reckoned I should find a path. The beginning of the desert was marked off by a wall, to call it so, for it was more of a long mound of stones. They say it reaches right across the island, but how they know it is another question, for I doubt if any one has made the journey in a hundred years, the natives sticking chiefly to the sea and their little colonies along the coast, and that part being mortal high and steep and full of cliffs. Up to the west side of the wall the ground has been cleared, and there are cocoa-palms and mummy-apples and guavas, and lots of sensitive. Just across, the bush begins outright; high bush at that, trees going up like the masts of ships, and ropes of liana hanging down like a ship's rigging, and nasty orchids growing in the forks like funguses. The ground where there was no underwood looked to be a heap of boulders. I saw many green pigeons which I might have shot, only I was there with a different idea. A number of butterflies flopped up and down along the ground like dead leaves; sometimes

I would hear a bird calling, sometimes the wind overhead, and always the sea along the coast.

But the queerness of the place it's more difficult to tell of, unless to one who has been alone in the high bush himself. The brightest kind of a day it is always dim down there. A man can see to the end of nothing; whichever way he looks the wood shuts up, one bough folding with another like the fingers of your hand; and whenever he listens he hears always something new—men talking, children laughing, the strokes of an axe a far way ahead of him, and sometimes a sort of a quick, stealthy scurry near at hand that makes him jump and look to his weapons. It's all very well for him to tell himself that he's alone, bar trees and birds; he can't make out to believe it; whichever way he turns the whole place seems to be alive and looking on. Don't think it was Uma's yarns that put me out; I don't value native talk a fourpenny-piece; it's a thing that's natural in the bush, and that's the end of it.

As I got near the top of the hill, for the ground of the wood goes up in this place steep as a ladder, the wind began to sound straight on, and the leaves to toss and switch open and let in the sun. This suited me better; it was the same noise all the time, and nothing to startle. Well, I had got to a place where there was an underwood of what they call wild cocoa-nut—mighty pretty with its scarlet fruit—when there came a sound of singing in the wind that I thought I had never heard the like of. It was all very fine to tell myself it was the branches; I knew better. It was all very fine to tell myself it was a bird; I knew never a bird that sang like that. It rose and swelled, and died away and swelled again; and now I thought it was like some one weeping, only prettier; and now I thought it was like harps; and there was one thing I made sure of, it was a sight too sweet to be wholesome in a place like that. You may laugh if you like; but I declare I called to mind the six young ladies that came, with their scarlet necklaces, out of the cave at Fanga-anaana, and wondered if they sang like that. We laugh at the natives and their superstitions; but see how many traders take them up, splendidly educated white men, that have been bookkeepers (some of them) and clerks in the old country. It's my belief a superstition grows up in a place like the different kind of weeds; and as I stood there and listened to that wailing I twittered in my shoes.

You may call me a coward to be frightened; I thought myself brave enough to go on ahead. But I went mighty carefully, with

my gun cocked, spying all about me like a hunter, fully expecting
to see a handsome young woman sitting somewhere in the bush,
and fully determined (if I did) to try her with a charge of duck-
shot. And sure enough, I had not gone far when I met with a queer
thing. The wind came on the top of the wood in a strong puff, the
leaves in front of me burst open, and I saw for a second something
hanging in a tree. It was gone in a wink, the puff blowing by and
the leaves closing. I tell you the truth: I had made up my mind
to see an *aitu;* and if the thing had looked like a pig or a woman,
it wouldn't have given me the same turn. The trouble was that it
seemed kind of square, and the idea of a square thing that was
alive and sang knocked me sick and silly. I must have stood quite
awhile; and I made pretty certain it was right out of the same tree
that the singing came. Then I began to come to myself a bit.

"Well," says I, "if this is really so, if this is a place where there
are square things that sing, I'm going up anyway. Let's have my
fun for my money."

But I thought I might as well take the off-chance of a prayer
being any good; so I plumped on my knees and prayed out loud;
and all the time I was praying the strange sounds came out of the
tree, and went up and down, and changed, for all the world like
music, only you could see it wasn't human—there was nothing
there that you could whistle.

As soon as I had made an end in proper style, I laid down my
gun, stuck my knife between my teeth, walked right up to the tree
and began to climb. I tell you my heart was like ice. But presently,
as I went up, I caught another glimpse of the thing, and that relieved me, for I thought it seemed like a box; and when I had got
right up to it I near fell out of the tree with laughing.

A box it was, sure enough, and a candle-box at that, with the
brand upon the side of it; and it had banjo-strings stretched so as
to sound when the wind blew. I believe they call the thing a
Tyrolean* harp, whatever that may mean.

"Well, Mr. Case," said I, "you frightened me once, but I defy
you to frighten me again," I says, and slipped down the tree, and
set out again to find my enemy's head office, which I guessed would
not be far away.

The undergrowth was thick in this part; I couldn't see before my
nose, and must burst my way through by main force and ply the

---

* Æolian.

knife as I went, slicing the cords of the lianas and slashing down whole trees at a blow. I call them trees for the bigness, but in truth they were just big weeds, and sappy to cut through like a carrot. From all this crowd and kind of vegetation, I was just thinking to myself, the place might have once been cleared, when I came on my nose over a pile of stones, and saw in a moment it was some kind of a work of man. The Lord knows when it was made or when deserted, for this part of the island has lain undisturbed since long before the whites came. A few steps beyond I hit into the path I had been always looking for. It was narrow, but well beaten, and I saw that Case had plenty of disciples. It seems, indeed it was, a piece of fashionable boldness to venture up here with the trader, and a young man scarce reckoned himself grown till he had got his breech tattooed, for one thing, and seen Case's devils for another. This is mighty like Kanakas: but, if you look at it another way, it's mighty like white folks too.

A bit along the path I was brought to a clear stand, and had to rub my eyes. There was a wall in front of me, the path passing it by a gap; it was tumbledown and plainly very old, but built of big stones very well laid; and there is no native alive to-day upon that island that could dream of such a piece of building! Along all the top of it was a line of queer figures, idols or scarecrows, or what not. They had carved and painted faces ugly to view, their eyes and teeth were of shell, their hair and their bright clothes blew in the wind, and some of them worked with the tugging. There are islands up west where they make these kind of figures till to-day; but if ever they were made in this island, the practice and the very recollection of it are now long forgotten. And the singular thing was that all these bogies were as fresh as toys out of a shop.

Then it came in my mind that Case had let out to me the first day that he was a good forger of island curiosities—a thing by which so many traders turn an honest penny. And with that I saw the whole business, and how this display served the man a double purpose: first of all, to season his curiosities, and then to frighten those that came to visit him.

But I should tell you (what made the thing more curious) that all the time the Tyrolean harps were harping round me in the trees, and even while I looked, a green-and-yellow bird (that, I suppose, was building) began to tear the hair off the head of one of the figures.

A little farther on I found the best curiosity of the museum. The first I saw of it was a longish mound of earth with a twist to it. Digging off the earth with my hands, I found underneath tarpaulin stretched on boards, so that this was plainly the roof of the cellar. It stood right on the top of the hill, and the entrance was on the far side, between two rocks, like the entrance to a cave. I went as far in as the bend, and, looking round the corner, saw a shining face. It was big and ugly, like a pantomime mask, and the brightness of it waxed and dwindled, and at times it smoked.

"Oho!" says I, "luminous paint!"

And I must say I rather admired the man's ingenuity. With a box of tools and a few mighty simple contrivances he had made out to have a devil of a temple. Any poor Kanaka brought up here in the dark, with the harps whining all round him, and shown that smoking face in the bottom of a hole would make a kind of doubt but he had seen and heard enough devils for a lifetime. It's easy to find out what Kanakas think. Just go back to your self anyway round ten to fifteen years old, and there's an average Kanaka. There are some pious, just as there are pious boys; and the most of them, like the boys again, are middling honest and yet think it rather larks to steal, and are easy scared, and rather like to be so. I remember a boy I was at school with at home who played the Case business. He didn't know anything, that boy; he couldn't do anything; he had no luminous paint and no Tyrolean harps; he just boldly said he was a sorcerer, and frightened us out of our boots, and we loved it. And then it came in my mind how the master had once flogged that boy, and the surprise we were all in to see the sorcerer catch it and hum like anybody else. Thinks I to myself: "I must find some way of fixing it so for Master Case." And the next moment I had my idea.

I went back by the path, which, when once you had found it, was quite plain and easy walking; and when I stepped out on the black sands, who should I see but Master Case himself? I cocked my gun and held it handy, and we marched up and passed without a word, each keeping the tail of his eye on the other; and no sooner had we passed than we each wheeled round like fellows drilling, and stood face to face. We had each taken the same notion in his head, you see, that the other fellow might give him the load of his gun in the stern.

"You've shot nothing," says Case.

"I'm not on the shoot to-day," said I.

"Well, the devil go with you for me," says he.

"The same to you," says I.

But we stuck just the way we were; no fear of either of us moving.

Case laughed. "We can't stop here all day, though," said he.

"Don't let me detain you," says I.

He laughed again. "Look here, Wiltshire, do you think me a fool?" he asked.

"More of a knave, if you want to know," says I.

"Well, do you think it would better me to shoot you here, on this open beach?" said he. "Because I don't. Folks come fishing every day. There may be a score of them up the valley now, making copra; there might be half a dozen on the hill behind you, after pigeons; they might be watching us this minute, and I shouldn't wonder. I give you my word I don't want to shoot you. Why should I? You don't hinder me any. You haven't got one pound of copra but what you made with your own hands, like a Negro slave. You're vegetating—that's what I call it—and I don't care where you vegetate, nor yet how long. Give me your word you don't mean to shoot me, and I'll give you a lead and walk away."

"Well," said I, "you're frank and pleasant, ain't you? And I'll be the same. I don't mean to shoot you to-day. Why should I? This business is beginning; it ain't done yet, Mr. Case. I've given you one turn already. I can see the marks of my knuckles on your head to this blooming hour, and I've more cooking for you. I'm not a paralee, like Underhill. My name ain't Adams, and it ain't Vigours; and I mean to show you that you've met your match."

"This is a silly way to talk," said he. "This is not the talk to make me move on with."

"All right," said I, "stay where you are. I ain't in any hurry and you know it. I can put in a day on this beach and never mind. I ain't got any copra to bother with. I ain't got any luminous paint to see to."

I was sorry I said that last, but it whipped out before I knew. I could see it took the wind out of his sails, and he stood and stared at me with his brow drawn up. Then I suppose he made up his mind he must get to the bottom of this.

"I take you at your word," says he, and turned his back, and walked right into the devil's bush.

I let him go, of course, for I had passed my word. But I watched him as long as he was in sight, and after he was gone lit out for cover as lively as you would want to see, and went the rest of the way home under the bush, for I didn't trust him sixpence worth. One thing I saw, I had been ass enough to give him warning, and that which I meant to do I must do at once.

You would think I had had about enough excitement for one morning, but there was another turn waiting me. As soon as I got far enough round the cape to see my house I made out there were strangers there; a little farther, and no doubt about it. There was a couple of armed sentinels squatting at my door. I could only suppose the trouble about Uma must have come to a head, and the station been seized. For aught I could think, Uma was taken up already, and these armed men were waiting to do the like with me.   However, as I came nearer, which I did at top speed, I saw there was a third native sitting on the veranda like a guest, and Uma was talking with him like a hostess. Nearer still I made out it was the big young chief, Maea, and that he was smiling away and smoking. And what was he smoking? None of your European cigarettes fit for a cat, not even the genuine big, knock-me-down native article that a fellow can really put in the time with if his pipe is broke—but a cigar, and one of my Mexicans at that, that I could swear to. At sight of this my heart started beating, and I took a wild hope in my head that the trouble was over, and Maea had come round.

Uma pointed me out to him as I came up, and he met me at the head of my own stairs like a thorough gentleman.

"Vilivili," said he, which was the best they could make of my name, "I pleased."

There is no doubt when an island chief wants to be civil he can do it. I saw the way things were from the word go. There was no call for Uma to say to me: "He no 'fraid Ese now, come bring copra." I tell you I shook hands with that Kanaka like as if he was the best white man in Europe.

The fact was, Case and he had got after the same girl, or Maea suspected it, and concluded to make hay of the trader on the chance. He had dressed himself up, got a couple of his retainers cleaned and armed to kind of make the thing more public, and, just waiting till Case was clear of the village, came round to put the whole of his business my way. He was rich as well as powerful.

I suppose that man was worth fifty thousand nuts per annum. I
gave him the price of the beach and a quarter cent better, and as
for credit, I would have advanced him the inside of the store and
the fittings besides, I was so pleased to see him. I must say he
bought like a gentleman: rice and tins and biscuits enough for a
week's feast, and stuffs by the bolt. He was agreeable besides; he
had plenty fun to him; and we cracked jests together, mostly
through the interpreter, because he had mighty little English, and
my native was still off colour. One thing I made out: he could
never really have thought much harm of Uma; he could never have
been really frightened, and must just have made believe from
dodginess, and because he thought Case had a strong pull in the
village and could help him on.

This set me thinking that both he and I were in a tightish place.
What he had done was to fly in the face of the whole village, and
the thing might cost him his authority. More than that, after my
talk with Case on the beach, I thought it might very well cost me
my life. Case had as good as said he would pot me if ever I got
any copra; he would come home to find the best business in the
village had changed hands, and the best thing I thought I could
do was to get in first with the potting.

"See here, Uma," says I, "tell him I'm sorry I made him wait,
but I was up looking at Case's Tiapolo store in the bush."

"He want savvy if you no 'fraid?" translated Uma.

I laughed out. "Not much!" says I. "Tell him the place is a
blooming toy-shop! Tell him in England we give these things to the
kid to play with."

"He want savvy if you hear devil sing?" she asked next.

"Look here," I said, "I can't do it now, because I've got no
banjo-strings in stock; but the next time the ship comes round I'll
have one of these same contraptions right here in my veranda,
and he can see for himself how much devil there is to it. Tell him,
as soon as I can get the strings I'll make one for his pickaninnies.
The name of the concern is a Tyrolean harp; and you can tell him
the name means in English that nobody but dam-fools give a cent
for it."

This time he was so pleased he had to try his English again.
"You talk true?" says he.

"Rather!" said I. "Talk all-a-same Bible. Bring out a Bible here,
Uma, if you've got such a thing, and I'll kiss it. Or, I'll tell you

what's better still," says I, taking a header, "ask him if he's afraid
to go up there himself by day."

It appeared he wasn't; he could venture as far as that by day and
in company.

"That's the ticket, then!" said I. "Tell him the man's a fraud
and the place foolishness, and if he'll go up there to-morrow he'll
see all that's left of it. But tell him this, Uma, and mind he understands it: If he gets talking it's bound to come to Case, and I'm a
dead man! I'm playing his game, tell him, and if he says one word
my blood will be at his door and be the damnation of him here
and after."

She told him, and he shook hands with me up to the hilt, and,
says he: "No talk. Go up tomollow. You my friend?"

"No, sir," says I, "no such foolishness. I've come here to trade,
tell him, and not to make friends. But, as to Case, I'll send that
man to glory!"

So off Maea went, pretty well pleased, as I could see.

5. *Night in the Bush*

Well, I was committed now; Tiapolo had to be smashed up before
next day, and my hands were pretty full, not only with preparations, but with arguments. My house was like a mechanics' debating society. Uma was so made up that I shouldn't go into the
bush by night, or that, if I did, I was never to come back again.
You know her style of arguing: you've had a specimen about
Queen Victoria and the devil; and I leave you to fancy if I was
tired of it before dark.

At last I had a good idea. "What was the use of casting my pearls
before her?" I thought; some of her own chopped hay would be
likelier to do the business.

"I'll tell you what, then," said I. "You fish out your Bible, and
I'll take that up along with me. That'll make me right."

She swore a Bible was no use.

"That's just your Kanaka ignorance," said I. "Bring the Bible
out."

She brought it, and I turned to the title-page, where I thought
there would likely be some English, and so there was. "There!"

said I. "Look at that! *'London: Printed for the British and Foreign Bible Society, Blackfriars,'* and the date, which I can't read, owing to its being in these X's. There's no devil in hell can look near the Bible Society, Blackfriars. Why, you silly," I said, "how do you suppose we get along with our own *aitus* at home! All Bible Society!"

"I think you no got any," said she. "White man, he tell me you no got."

"Sounds likely, don't it?" I asked. "Why would these islands all be chock full of them and none in Europe?"

"Well, you no got bread-fruit," said she.

I could have torn my hair. "Now, look here, old lady," said I, "you dry up, for I'm tired of you. I'll take the Bible, which'll put me as straight as the mail, and that's the last word I've got to say."

The night fell extraordinary dark, clouds coming up with sundown and overspreading all; not a star showed; there was only an end of a moon, and that not due before the small hours. Round the village, what with the lights and the fires in the open houses, and the torches of many fishers moving on the reef, it kept as gay as an illumination; but the sea and the mountains and woods were all clean gone. I suppose it might be eight o'clock when I took the road, laden like a donkey. First there was that Bible, a book as big as your head, which I had let myself in for by my own tomfoolery. Then there was my gun, and knife, and lantern, and patent matches, all necessary. And then there was the real plant of the affair in hand, a mortal weight of gunpowder, a pair of dynamite fishing-bombs, and two or three pieces of slowmatch that I had hauled out of the tin cases and spliced together the best way I could; for the match was only trade stuff, and a man would be crazy that trusted it. Altogether, you see, I had the materials of a pretty good blow up! Expense was nothing to me; I wanted that thing done right.

As long as I was in the open, and had the lamp in my house to steer by, I did well. But when I got to the path, it fell so dark I could make no headway, walking into trees and swearing there, like a man looking for the matches in his bedroom. I knew it was risky to light up, for my lantern would be visible all the way to the point of the cape, and as no one went there after dark, it would be talked about, and come to Case's ears. But what was I to do? I had either to give the business over and lose caste with Maea, or light up, take my chance, and get through the thing the smartest I was able.

As long as I was on the path I walked hard, but when I came to the black beach I had to run. For the tide was now nearly flowed; and to get through with my powder dry between the surf and the steep hill, took all the quickness I possessed. As it was, even the wash caught me to the knees, and I came near falling on a stone. All this time the hurry I was in, and the free air and smell of the sea, kept my spirits lively: but when I was once in the bush and began to climb the path I took it easier. The fearsomeness of the wood had been a good bit rubbed off for me by Master Case's banjo-strings and graven images, yet I thought it was a dreary walk, and guessed, when the disciples went up there, they must be badly scared. The light of the lantern, striking among all these trunks and forked branches and twisted rope-ends of lianas, made the whole place, or all that you could see of it, a kind of a puzzle of turning shadows. They came to meet you, solid and quick like giants, and then spun off and vanished; they hove up over your head like clubs, and flew away into the night like birds. The floor of the bush glimmered with dead wood, the way the match-box used to shine after you had struck a lucifer. Big, cold drops fell on me from the branches overhead like sweat. There was no wind to mention; only a little icy breath of a land-breeze that stirred nothing; and the harps were silent.

The first landfall I made was when I got through the bush of wild cocoa-nuts, and came in view of the bogies on the wall. Mighty queer they looked by the shining of the lantern, with their painted faces and shell eyes, and their clothes, and their hair hanging. One after another I pulled them all up and piled them in a bundle on the cellar roof, so as they might go to glory with the rest. Then I chose a place behind one of the big stones at the entrance, buried my powder and the two shells, and arranged my match along the passage. And then I had a look at the smoking head, just for good-bye. It was doing fine.

"Cheer up," says I. "You're booked."

It was my first idea to light up and be getting homeward; for the darkness and the glimmer of the dead wood and the shadows of the lantern made me lonely. But I knew where one of the harps hung; it seemed a pity it shouldn't go with the rest; and at

the same time I couldn't help letting on to myself that I was
mortal tired of my employment, and would like best to be at
home and have the door shut. I stepped out of the cellar and
argued it fore and back. There was a sound of the sea far down
below me on the coast; nearer hand not a leaf stirred; I might have
been the only living creature this side of Cape Horn. Well, as I
stood there thinking, it seemed the bush woke and became full of
little noises. Little noises they were, and nothing to hurt; a bit of
a crackle, a bit of a rush; but the breath jumped right out of me
and my throat went as dry as a biscuit. It wasn't Case I was afraid
of, which would have been common-sense; I never thought of Case;
what took me, as sharp as the colic, was the old wives' tales—the
devil-women and the man-pigs. It was the toss of a penny whether
I should run; but I got a purchase on myself, and stepped out, and
held up the lantern (like a fool) and looked all round.

In the direction of the village and the path there was nothing to
be seen; but when I turned inland it's a wonder to me I didn't
drop. There, coming right up out of the desert and the bad bush
—there, sure enough, was a devil-woman, just as the way I had
figured she would look. I saw the light shine on her bare arms and
her bright eyes, and there went out of me a yell so big that I
thought it was my death.

"Ah! No sing out!" says the devil-woman, in a kind of a high
whisper. "Why you talk big voice? Put out light! Ese he come."

"My God Almighty, Uma, is that you?" says I.

*"Ioe,"** says she. "I come quick. Ese here soon."

"You come along?" I asked. "You no 'fraid?"

"Ah, too much 'fraid!" she whispered, clutching me. "I think
die."

"Well," says I, with a kind of a weak grin. "I'm not the one to
laugh at you, Mrs. Wiltshire, for I'm about the worst scared man
in the South Pacific myself."

She told me in two words what brought her. I was scarce gone,
it seems, when Faavao came in, and the old woman had met Black
Jack running as hard as he was fit from our house to Case's. Uma
neither spoke nor stopped, but lit right out to come and warn me.
She was so close at my heels that the lantern was her guide across
the beach, and afterward, by the glimmer of it in the trees, she got
her line up-hill. It was only when I had got to the top or was in

* Yes.

the cellar that she wandered—Lord knows where!—and lost a sight of precious time, afraid to call out lest Case was at the heels of her, and falling in the bush, so that she was all knocked and bruised. That must have been when she got too far to the south-ward, and how she came to take me in the flank at last and frighten me beyond what I've got the words to tell of.

Well, anything was better than a devil-woman, but I thought her yarn serious enough. Black Jack had no call to be about my house, unless he was set there to watch; and it looked to me as if my tom-fool word about the paint, and perhaps some chatter of Maea's, had got us all in a clove hitch. One thing was clear: Uma and I were here for the night; we daren't try to go home before day, and even then it would be safer to strike round up the mountain and come in by the back of the village, or we might walk into an ambuscade. It was plain, too, that the mine should be sprung im-mediately, or Case might be in time to stop it.

I marched into the tunnel, Uma keeping tight hold of me, opened my lantern and lit the match. The first length of it burned like a spill of paper, and I stood stupid, watching it burn, and thinking we were going aloft with Tiapolo, which was none of my views. The second took to a better rate, though faster than I cared about; and at that I got my wits again, hauled Uma clear of the passage, blew out and dropped the lantern, and the pair of us groped our way into the bush until I thought it might be safe, and lay down together by a tree.

"Old lady," I said, "I won't forget this night. You're a trump, and that's what's wrong with you."

She bumped herself close up to me. She had run out the way she was, with nothing on her but her kilt; and she was all wet with the dews and the sea on her black beach, and shook straight on with cold and the terror of the dark and the devils.

"Too much 'fraid," was all she said.

The far side of Case's hill goes down near as steep as a precipice into the next valley. We were on the very edge of it, and I could see the dead wood shine and hear the sea sound far below. I didn't care about the position, which left me no retreat, but I was afraid to change. Then I saw I had made a worse mistake about the lantern, which I should have left lighted, so that I could have had a crack at Case when he stepped into the shine of it. And since I hadn't had the wit to do that, it seemed a senseless thing to leave the good lantern to blow up with the graven images. The thing belonged to me, after all, and was worth money, and might come in handy. If I could have trusted the match, I might have run in still and rescued it. But who was going to trust to the match? You know what trade is. The stuff was good enough for Kanakas to go fishing with, where they've got to look lively anyway, and the most they risk is only to have their hand blown off. But for any one that wanted to fool around a blow up like mine that match was rubbish.

Altogether the best I could do was to lie still, see my shot-gun handy, and wait for the explosion. But it was a solemn kind of business. The blackness of the night was like solid; the only thing you could see was the nasty bogy glimmer of the dead wood, and that showed you nothing but itself; and as for sounds, I stretched my ears till I thought I could have heard the match burn in the tunnel, and that bush was as silent as a coffin. Now and then there was a bit of a crack; but whether it was near or far, whether it was Case stubbling his toes within a few yards of me, or a tree breaking miles away, I knew no more than the babe unborn.

And then, all of a sudden, Vesuvius went off. It was a long time coming; but when it came (though I say it that shouldn't) no man could ask to see a better. At first it was just a son of a gun of a row, and a spout of fire, and the wood lighted up so that you could see to read. And then the trouble began. Uma and I were half buried under a wagonful of earth, and glad it was no worse, for one of the rocks at the entrance of the tunnel was fired clean into the air, fell within a couple of fathoms of where we lay, and bounded over the edge of the hill, and went pounding down into the next valley. I saw I had rather undercalculated our distance, or overdone the dynamite and powder, which you please.

And presently I saw I had made another slip. The noise of the thing began to die off, shaking the island; the dazzle was over; and yet the night didn't come back the way I expected. For the whole wood was scattered with red coals and brands from the explosion; they were all round me on the flat, some had fallen below in the valley, and some stuck and flared in the tree-tops. I had no fear of fire, for these forests are too wet to kindle. But the trouble was that the place was all lit up—not very bright, but good enough to get a shot by; and the way the coals were scattered, it was just as likely Case might have the advantage as myself. I looked all round for his white face, you may be sure; but there was not a sign of him. As for Uma, the life seemed to have been knocked right out of her by the bang and blaze of it.

There was one bad point in my game. One of the blessed graven images had come down all afire, hair and clothes and body, not four yards away from me. I cast a mighty noticing glance all round; there was still no Case, and I made up my mind I must get rid of that burning stick before he came, or I should be shot there like a dog.

It was my first idea to have crawled, and then I thought speed was the main thing, and stood half up to make a rush. The same moment, from somewhere between me and the sea, there came a flash and a report, and a rifle-bullet screeched in my ear. I swung straight round and up with my gun, but the brute had a Winchester, and before I could as much as see him his second shot knocked me over like a ninepin. I seemed to fly in the air, then came down by the run and lay half a minute, silly; and then I found my hands empty, and my gun had flown over my head as I fell. It makes a man mighty wide awake to be in the kind of box that I was in. I scarcely knew where I was hurt, or whether I was hurt or not, but turned right over on my face to crawl after my weapon. Unless you have tried to get about with a smashed leg you don't know what pain is, and I let out a howl like a bullock's.

This was the unluckiest noise that ever I made in my life. Up to then Uma had stuck to her tree like a sensible woman, knowing she would be only in the way; but as soon as she heard me sing out she ran forward. The Winchester cracked again, and down she went.

I had sat up, leg and all, to stop her; but when I saw her tumble I clapped down again where I was, lay still, and felt the handle of my knife. I had been scurried and put out before. No more of that for me. He had knocked over my girl, I had got to fix him for it; and I lay there and gritted my teeth, and footed up the chances. My leg was broke, my gun was gone. Case had still ten shots in his Winchester. It looked a kind of hopeless business. But I never despaired nor thought upon despairing: that man had got to go.

For a goodish bit not one of us let on. Then I heard Case begin to move nearer in the bush, but mighty careful. The image had burned out, there were only a few coals left here and there, and the wood was main dark, but had a kind of a low glow in it like a fire on its last legs. It was by this that I made out Case's head looking at me over a big tuft of ferns, and at the same time the brute saw me and shouldered his Winchester. I lay quite still, and as good as looked into the barrel: it was my last chance, but I thought my heart would have come right out of its bearings. Then he fired. Lucky for me it was no shot-gun, for the bullet struck within an inch of me and knocked the dirt in my eyes.

Just you try and see if you can lie quiet, and let a man take a sitting shot at you and miss you by a hair. But I did, and lucky, too. Awhile Case stood with the Winchester at the port-arms; then he gave a little laugh to himself and stepped round the ferns.

"Laugh!" thought I. "If you had the wit of a louse you would be praying!"

I was all as taut as a ship's hawser or the spring of a watch, and as soon as he came within reach of me I had him by the ankle, plucked the feet right out from under him, laid him out, and was upon the top of him, broken leg and all, before he breathed. His Winchester had gone the same road as my shot-gun; it was nothing to me—I defied him now. I'm a pretty strong man anyway, but I never knew what strength was till I got hold of Case. He was knocked out of time by the rattle he came down with, and threw up his hands together, more like a frightened woman, so that I caught both of them with my left. This wakened him up, and he fastened his teeth in my forearm like a weasel. Much I cared. My leg gave me all the pain I had any use for, and I drew my knife and got it in the place.

"Now," said I, "I've got you; and you're gone up, and a good job too! Do you feel the point of that? That's for Underhill! And there's for Adams! And now here's for Uma, and that's going to knock your blooming soul right out of you!"

With that I gave him the cold steel for all I was worth. His body kicked under me like a spring sofa; he gave a dreadful kind of a long moan, and lay still.

"I wonder if you're dead? I hope so!" I thought, for my head was swimming. But I wasn't going to take chances; I had his own example too close before me for that; and I tried to draw the knife out to give it him again. The blood came over my hands, I remember, hot as tea; and with that I fainted clean away, and fell with my head on the man's mouth.

When I came to myself it was pitch dark; the cinders had burned out; there was nothing to be seen but the shine of the dead wood, and I couldn't remember where I was nor why I was in such pain, nor what I was all wetted with. Then it came back, and the first thing I attended to was to give him the knife again a half-a-dozen times up to the handle. I believe he was dead already, but it did him no harm and did me good.

"I bet you're dead now," I said, and then I called to Uma.

Nothing answered, and I made a move to go and grope for her, fouled my broken leg, and fainted again.

When I came to myself the second time the clouds had all cleared away, except a few that sailed there, white as cotton. The moon was up—a tropic moon. The moon at home turns a wood black, but even this old butt-end of a one showed up that forest as green as by day. The night birds—or, rather, they're a kind of early morning bird—sang out with their long, falling notes like nightingales. And I could see the dead man, that I was still half resting on, looking right up into the sky with his open eyes, no paler than when he was alive; and a little way off Uma tumbled on her side. I got over to her the best way I was able, and when I got there she was broad awake and crying, and sobbing to herself with no more noise than an insect. It appears she was afraid to cry out loud, because of the *aitus*. Altogether she was not much hurt, but scared beyond belief; she had come to her senses a long while ago, cried out to me, heard nothing in reply, made out we were both dead, and had lain there ever since, afraid to budge a finger. The ball had ploughed up her shoulder, and she had lost a main quantity of blood; but I soon had that tied up the way it ought to be with the tail of my shirt and a scarf I had on, got her head on my sound knee and my back against a trunk, and settled down to wait for morning. Uma was for neither use nor ornament, and could only clutch hold of me and shake and cry. I don't suppose there was ever anybody worse scared, and, to do her justice, she had had a lively night of it. As for me, I was in a good bit of pain and fever, but not so bad when I sat still; and every time I looked over to Case I could have sung and whistled. Talk about meat and drink! To see that man lying there dead as a herring filled me full.

The night birds stopped after awhile; and then the light began to change, the east came orange, the whole wood began to whirr with singing like a musical box, and there was the broad day.

I didn't expect Maea for a long while yet; and, indeed, I thought

there was an off-chance he might go back on the whole idea and
not come at all. I was the better pleased when, about an hour after
daylight, I heard sticks smashing and a lot of Kanakas laughing
and singing out to keep their courage up. Uma sat up quite brisk
at the first word of it; and presently we saw a party come stringing
out of the path, Maea in front, and behind him a white man in a
pith helmet. It was Mr. Tarleton, who had turned up late last
night in Falesá, having left his boat and walked the last stage with
a lantern.

They buried Case upon the field of glory, right in the hole where
he had kept the smoking head. I waited till the thing was done;
and Mr. Tarleton prayed, which I thought tomfoolery, but I'm
bound to say he gave a pretty sick view of the dear departed's
prospects, and seemed to have his own ideas of hell. I had it out
with him afterward, told him he had scamped his duty, and what
he had ought to have done was to up like a man and tell the
Kanakas plainly Case was damned, and a good riddance; but I
never could get him to see it my way. Then they made me a litter
of poles and carried me down to the station. Mr. Tarleton set my
leg, and made a regular missionary splice of it, so that I limp to
this day. That done, he took down my evidence, and Uma's, and
Maea's, wrote it all out fine, and had us sign it; and then he got the
chiefs and marched over to Papa Randall's to seize Case's papers.

All they found was a bit of a diary, kept for a good many years,
and all about the price of copra, and chickens being stolen, and
that; and the books of the business and the will I told you of in
the beginning, by both of which the whole thing (stock, lock, and
barrel) appeared to belong to the Samoa woman. It was I that
bought her out at a mighty reasonable figure, for she was in a
hurry to get home. As for Randall and the black, they had to
tramp; got into some kind of a station on the Papa-malulu side;
did very bad business, for the truth is neither of the pair was fit
for it, and lived mostly on fish, which was the means of Randall's
death. It seems there was a nice shoal in one day, and Papa went
after them with the dynamite; either the match burned too fast, or
Papa was full, or both, but the shell went off (in the usual way)
before he threw it, and where was Papa's hand? Well, there's nothing to hurt in that; the islands up north are all full of one-handed
men like the parties in the "Arabian Nights;" but either Randall
was too old, or he drank too much, and the short and the long of it

was that he died. Pretty soon after, the nigger was turned out of the island for stealing from white men, and went off to the west, where he found men of his own colour, in case he liked that, and the men of his own colour took and ate him at some kind of a corroborree, and I'm sure I hope he was to their fancy!

So there was I, left alone in my glory at Falesá; and when the schooner came round I filled her up, and gave her a deck cargo half as high as the house. I must say Mr. Tarleton did the right thing by us; but he took a meanish kind of a revenge.

"Now, Mr. Wiltshire," said he, "I've put you all square with everybody here. It wasn't difficult to do, Case being gone; but I have done it, and given my pledge besides that you will deal fairly with the natives. I must ask you to keep my word."

Well, so I did. I used to be bothered about my balances, but I reasoned it out this way. We all have queerish balances, and the natives all know it and water their copra in a proportion so that it's fair all round; but the truth is, it did use to bother me, and, though I did well in Falesá, I was half glad when the firm moved me on to another station, where I was under no kind of a pledge and could look my balances in the face.

As for the old lady, you know her as well as I do. She's only the one fault. If you don't keep your eye lifting she would give away the roof off the station. Well, it seems it's natural in Kanakas. She's turned a powerful big woman now, and could throw a London bobby over her shoulder. But that's natural in Kanakas too, and there's no manner of doubt that she's an A 1 wife.

Mr. Tarleton's gone home, his trick being over. He was the best missionary I ever struck, and now, it seems, he's parsonising down Somerset way. Well, that's best for him; he'll have no Kanakas there to get luny over.

My public-house? Not a bit of it, nor ever likely. I'm stuck here, I fancy. I don't like to leave the kids, you see: and—there's no use talking—they're better here than what they would be in a white man's country, though Ben took the eldest up to Auckland, where he's being schooled with the best. But what bothers me is the girls. They're only half-castes, of course; I know that as well as you do, and there's nobody thinks less of half-castes than I do; but they're mine, and about all I've got. I can't reconcile my mind to their taking up with Kanakas, and I'd like to know where I'm to find the whites?

ESSAYS

ESSAYS

Virginibus Puerisque

1.

WITH THE SINGLE EXCEPTION OF FALSTAFF, ALL SHAKESPEARE'S characters are what we call marrying men. Mercutio, as he was own cousin to Benedick and Biron, would have come to the same end in the long run. Even Iago had a wife, and, what is far stranger, he was jealous. People like Jacques and the Fool in *Lear,* although we can hardly imagine they would ever marry, kept single out of a cynical humour or for a broken heart, and not, as we do nowadays, from a spirit of incredulity and preference for the single state. For that matter, if you turn to George Sand's French version of *As You Like It* (and I think I can promise you will like it but little), you will find Jacques marries Celia just as Orlando marries Rosalind.

At least there seems to have been much less hesitation over marriage in Shakespeare's days; and what hesitation there was was of a laughing sort, and not much more serious, one way or the other, than that of Panurge. In modern comedies the heroes are mostly of Benedick's way of thinking, but twice as much in earnest, and not one quarter so confident. And I take this diffidence as a proof of how sincere their terror is. They know they are only human after all; they know what gins and pitfalls lie about their feet; and how the shadow of matrimony waits, resolute and awful, at the cross-roads. They would wish to keep their liberty; but if that may not be, why, God's will be done! "What, are you afraid of marriage?" asks Cécile, in *Maître Guerin*. "Oh, mon Dieu, non!" replies Arthur; "I should take chloroform."

They look forward to marriage much in the same way as they prepare themselves for death: each seems inevitable; each is a great Perhaps, and a leap into the dark, for which, when a man is in the blue devils, he has specially to harden his heart. That splendid scoundrel, Maxime de Trailles, took the news of marriages much as an old man hears the deaths of his contemporaries. "C'est désespérant," he cried, throwing himself down in the arm-chair at Madame Schontz's; "c'est désespérant, nous nous marions tous!" Every marriage was like another grey hair on his head; and the jolly church bells seemed to taunt him with his fifty years and fair round belly.

The fact is, we are much more afraid of life than our ancestors, and cannot find it in our hearts either to marry or not to marry. Marriage is terrifying, but so is a cold and forlorn old age. The friendships of men are vastly agreeable, but they are insecure. You know all the time that one friend will marry and put you to the door; a second accept a situation in China, and become no more to you than a name, a reminiscence, and an occasional crossed letter, very laborious to read; a third will take up with some religious crotchet and treat you to sour looks thenceforward. So, in one way or another, life forces men apart and breaks up the goodly fellowships for ever. The very flexibility and ease which make men's friendships so agreeable while they endure, make them the easier to destroy and forget. And a man who has a few friends, or one who has a dozen (if there be any one so wealthy on this earth), cannot forget on how precarious a base his happiness reposes; and how by a stroke or two of fate—a death, a few light words, a piece of stamped paper, a woman's bright eyes—he may be left, in a month, destitute of all. Marriage is certainly a perilous remedy. Instead of on two or three, you stake your happiness on one life only. But still, as the bargain is more explicit and complete on your part, it is more so on the other; and you have not to fear so many contingencies; it is not every wind that can blow you from your anchorage; and so long as Death withholds his sickle, you will always have a friend at home. People who share a cell in the Bastille, or are thrown together on an uninhabited island, if they do not immediately fall to fisticuffs, will find some possible ground of compromise. They will learn each other's ways and humours, so as to know where they must go warily, and where they may lean their whole weight. The discretion of the first years becomes the settled habit of the last; and so, with wisdom and patience, two lives may grow indissolubly into one.

But marriage, if comfortable, is not at all heroic. It certainly narrows and damps the spirits of generous men. In marriage, a man becomes slack and selfish, and undergoes a fatty degeneration of his moral being. It is not only when Lydgate misallies himself with Rosamond Vincy, but when Ladislaw marries above him with Dorothea, that this may be exemplified. The air of the fireside withers out all the fine wildings of the husband's heart. He is so comfortable and happy that he begins to prefer comfort and happiness to everything else on earth, his wife included. Yesterday he would have shared his last shilling; to-day "his first duty is to his family," and is fulfilled in large measure by laying down vintages and husbanding the health of an invaluable parent. Twenty years ago this man was equally capable of crime or heroism; now he is fit for neither. His soul is asleep, and you may speak without constraint; you will not wake him. It is not for nothing that Don Quixote was a bachelor and Marcus Aurelius married ill. For women, there is less of this danger. Marriage is of so much use to a woman, opens out to her so much more of life, and puts her in the way of so much more freedom and usefulness, that, whether she marry ill or well, she can hardly miss some benefit. It is true, however, that some of the merriest and most genuine of women are old maids; and that those old maids, and wives who are unhappily married, have often most of the true motherly touch. And this would seem to show, even for women, some narrowing influence in comfortable married life. But the rule is none the less certain: if you wish the pick of men and women, take a good bachelor and a good wife.

I am often filled with wonder that so many marriages are passably successful, and so few come to open failure, the more so as I fail to understand the principle on which people regulate their choice. I see women marrying indiscriminately with staring burgesses and ferret-faced, white-eyed boys, and men dwelling in contentment with noisy scullions, or taking into their lives acidulous vestals. It is a common answer to say the good people marry because they fall in love; and of course you may use and misuse a word as much as you please, if you have the world along with you. But love is at least a somewhat hyperbolical expression for such lukewarm preference. It is not here, anyway, that Love employs his golden shafts; he cannot be said, with any fitness of language, to reign here and revel. Indeed, if this be love at all, it is plain the poets have been fooling with mankind since the foundation of the world. And you have only to look these happy couples in the face, to see they have never been in love, or in hate, or in any other high passion, all their days. When you see a dish of fruit at dessert, you sometimes set your affections upon one particular peach or nectarine, watch it with some anxiety as it comes round the table, and feel quite a sensible disappointment when it is taken by some one else. I have used the phrase "high passion." Well, I should say this was about as high a passion as generally leads to marriage. One husband hears after marriage that some poor fellow is dying of his wife's love. "What a pity!" he exclaims; "you know I could so easily have got another!" And yet that is a very happy union. Or again: A young man was telling me the sweet story of his loves. "I like it well enough as long as her sisters are there," said this amorous swain; "but I don't know what to do when we're alone." Once more: A married lady was debating the subject with another lady. "You know, dear," said the first, "after ten years of marriage, if he is nothing else, your husband is always an old friend." "I have many old friends," returned the other, "but I prefer them to be nothing more." "Oh, perhaps I might *prefer* that also!" There is a common note in these three illustrations of the modern idyll; and it must be owned the god goes among us with a limping gait and blear eyes. You wonder whether it was so always; whether desire was always equally dull and spiritless, and possession equally cold. I cannot help fancying most people make, ere they marry, some such table of recommendations as Hannah Godwin wrote to her brother William anent her friend, Miss Gay. It is so charmingly comical, and so pat to the occasion, that I must quote a few phrases. "The young lady is in every sense formed to make one of your disposition really happy. She has a pleasing voice, with which she accompanies her musical instrument with judgment. She has an easy politeness in her manners, neither free nor reserved. She is a good housekeeper and a good economist, and yet of a generous disposition. As to her internal accomplishments, I have reason to speak still more highly of them: good sense without vanity, a penetrating judgment without a disposition to satire, with about as much religion as my William likes, struck me with a wish that she was my William's wife." That is about the tune: pleasing voice, moderate good looks, unimpeachable internal accomplishments after the style of the copy-book, with about as much religion as my William likes; and then, with all speed, to church.

To deal plainly, if they only married when they fell in love, most people would die unwed; and among the others, there would be not a few tumultuous households. The Lion is the King of Beasts, but he is scarcely suitable for a domestic pet. In the same way, I suspect love is rather too violent a passion to make, in all cases, a good domestic sentiment. Like other violent excitements, it throws up not only what is best, but what is worst and smallest, in men's characters. Just as some people are malicious in drink, or brawling and virulent under the influence of religious feeling, some are moody, jealous, and exacting when they are in love, who are honest, downright, good-hearted fellows enough in the everyday affairs and humours of the world.

How then, seeing we are driven to the hypothesis that people choose in comparatively cold blood, how is it they choose so well? One is almost tempted to hint that it does not much matter whom you marry; that, in fact, marriage is a subjective affection, and if you have made up your mind to it, and once talked yourself fairly over, you could "pull it through" with anybody. But even if we take matrimony at its lowest, even if we regard it as no more than a sort of friendship recognised by the police, there must be degrees in the freedom and sympathy realised, and some principle to guide simple folk in their selection. Now what should this principle be? Are there no more definite rules than are to be found in the Prayer-book? Law and religion forbid the bans on the ground of propinquity or consanguinity; society steps in to separate classes; and in all this most critical matter, has common-sense, has wisdom, never a word to say? In the absence of more magisterial teaching, let us talk it over between friends: even a few guesses may be of interest to youths and maidens.

In all that concerns eating and drinking, company, climate, and ways of life, community of taste is to be sought for. It would be trying, for instance, to keep bed and board with an early riser or a vegetarian. In matters of art and intellect, I believe it is of no consequence. Certainly it is of none in the companionships of men, who will dine more readily with one who has a good heart, a good cellar, and a humourous tongue, than with another who shares all their favourite hobbies and is melancholy withal. If your wife likes, Tupper, that is no reason why you should hang your head. She thinks with the majority, and has the courage of her opinions. I have always suspected public taste to be a mongrel product out of affectation by dogmatism; and felt sure, if you could only find an honest man of no special literary bent, he would tell you he thought much of Shakespeare bombastic and most absurd, and all of him written in very obscure English and wearisome to read. And not long ago I was able to lay by my lantern in content, for I found the honest man. He was a fellow of parts, quick, humourous, a clever painter, and with an eye for certain poetical effects of sea and ships. I am not much of a judge of that kind of thing, but a sketch of his comes before me sometimes at night. How strong, supple, and living the ship seems upon the billows! With what a dip and rake she shears the flying sea! I cannot fancy the man who saw this effect, and took it on the wing with so much force and spirit, was what you call commonplace in the last recesses of the heart. And yet he thought, and was not ashamed to have it known of him, that Ouida was better in every way than William Shakespeare. If there were more people of his honesty, this would be about the staple of lay criticism. It is not taste that is plentiful, but courage that is rare. And what have we in place? How many, who think no otherwise than the young painter, have we not heard disbursing second-hand hyperboles? Have you never turned sick at heart, O best of critics! when some of your own sweet adjectives were returned on you before a gaping audience? Enthusiasm about art is become a function of the average female being, which she performs with precision and a sort of haunting sprightliness, like an ingenious and well-regulated machine. Sometimes, alas! the calmest man is carried away in the torrent, bandies adjectives with the best, and out-Herods Herod for some shameful moments. When you remember that, you will be tempted to put things strongly, and say you will marry no one who is not like George the Second, and cannot state openly a distaste for poetry and painting.

The word "facts" is, in some ways, crucial. I have spoken with Jesuits and Plymouth Brethren, mathematicians and poets, dogmatic republicans and dear old gentlemen in bird's-eye neckcloths; and each understood the word "facts" in an occult sense of his own. Try as I might, I could get no nearer the principle of their division. What was essential to them, seemed to me trivial or untrue. We could come to no compromise as to what was, or what was not, important in the life of man. Turn as we pleased, we all stood back to back in a big ring, and saw another quarter of the heavens, with different mountain-tops along the sky-line and different constellations overhead. We had each of us some whimsy in the brain, which we believed more than anything else, and which discoloured all experience to its own shade. How would you have people agree, when one is deaf and the other blind? Now this is where there should be community between man and wife. They should be agreed on their catchword in *"facts of religion,"* or *"facts of science,"* or *"society, my dear"*; for without such an agreement all intercourse is a painful strain upon the mind. "About as much religion as my William likes," in short, that is what is necessary to make a happy couple of any William and his spouse. For there are differences which no habit nor affection can reconcile, and the Bohemian must not intermarry with the Pharisee. Imagine Consuelo as Mrs. Samuel Budgett, the wife of the successful merchant! The best of men and the best of women may sometimes live together all their lives, and, for want of some consent on fundamental questions, hold each other lost spirits to the end.

A certain sort of talent is almost indispensable for people who would spend years together and not bore themselves to death. But the talent, like the agreement, must be for and about life. To dwell happily together, they should be versed in the niceties of the heart, and born with a faculty for willing compromise. The woman must be talented as a woman, and it will not much matter although she is talented in nothing else. She must know her *métier de femme,* and have a fine touch for the affections. And it is more important that a person should be a good gossip, and talk pleasantly and smartly of common friends and the thousand and one nothings of the day and hour, than that she should speak with the tongues of men and angels; for awhile together by the fire, happens more frequently in marriage than the presence of a distinguished foreigner to dinner. That people should laugh over the same sort of jests, and have many a story of "grouse in the gun-room," many an old joke between them which time cannot wither nor custom stale, is a better preparation for life, by your leave, than many other things higher and better sounding in the world's ears. You could read Kant by yourself, if you wanted; but you must share a joke with some one else. You can forgive people who do not follow you through a philosophical disquisition; but to find your wife laughing when you had tears in your eyes, or staring when you were in a fit of laughter, would go some way towards a dissolution of the marriage.

I know a woman who, from some distaste or disability, could never so much as understand the meaning of the word *politics,* and has given up trying to distinguish Whigs from Tories; but take her on her own politics, ask her about other men or women and the chicanery of everyday existence—the rubs, the tricks, the vanities on which life turns—and you will not find many more shrewd, trenchant, and humourous. Nay, to make plainer what I have in mind, this same woman has a share of the higher and more poetical understanding, frank interest in things for their own sake, and enduring astonishment at the most common. She is not to be deceived by custom, or made to think a mystery solved when it is repeated. I have heard her say she could wonder herself crazy over the human eyebrow. Now in a world where most of us walk very contentedly in the little lit circle of their own reason, and have to be reminded of what lies without by specious and clamant exceptions—earthquakes, eruptions of Vesuvius, banjos floating in mid-air at a *séance,* and the like—a mind so fresh and unsophisticated is no despicable gift. I will own I think it a better sort of mind than goes necessarily with the clearest views on public business. It will wash. It will find something to say at an odd moment. It has in it the spring of pleasant and quaint fancies. Whereas I can imagine myself yawning all night long until my jaws ached and the tears came into my eyes, although my companion on the other side of the hearth held the most enlightened opinions on the franchise or the ballot.

The question of professions, in as far as they regard marriage, was only interesting to women until of late days, but it touches all of us now. Certainly, if I could help it, I would never marry a wife who wrote. The practice of letters is miserably harassing to the mind; and after an hour or two's work, all the more human portion of the author is extinct; he will bully, backbite, and speak daggers. Music, I hear, is not much better. But painting, on the contrary, is often highly sedative; because so much of the labour, after your picture is once begun, is almost entirely manual, and of that skilled sort of manual labour which offers a continual series of successes, and so tickles a man, through his vanity, into good-humour. Alas! in letters there is nothing of this sort. You may write as beautiful a hand as you will, you have always something else to think of, and cannot pause to notice your loops and flourishes; they are beside the mark, and the first law stationer could put you to the blush. Rousseau, indeed, made some account of penmanship, even made it a source of livelihood, when he copied out the *Héloïse* for *dilettante* ladies; and therein showed that strange eccentric prudence which guided him among so many thousand follies and insanities. It would be well for all of the *genus irritabile* thus to add something of skilled labour to intangible brain-work. To find the right word is so doubtful a success and lies so near to failure, that there is no satisfaction in a year of it; but we all know when we have formed a letter perfectly; and a stupid artist, right or wrong, is almost equally certain he has found a right tone or a right colour, or made a dexterous stroke with his brush. And, again, painters may work out of doors; and the fresh air, the deliberate seasons, and the "tranquillising influence" of the green earth, counterbalance the fever of thought, and keep them cool, placable, and prosaic.

A ship captain is a good man to marry if it is a marriage of love, for absences are a good influence in love and keep it bright and delicate; but he is just the worst man if the feeling is more pedestrian, as habit is too frequently torn open and the solder has never time to set. Men who fish, botanise, work with the turning-lathe, or gather sea-weeds, will make admirable husbands; and a little amateur painting in water-colours shows the innocent and quiet mind. Those who have a few intimates are to be avoided; while those who swim loose, who have their hat in their hand all along the street, who can number an infinity of acquaintances and are not chargeable with any one friend, promise an easy disposition and no rival to the wife's influence. I will not say they are the best of men, but they are the stuff out of which adroit and capable women manufacture the best of husbands. It is to be noticed that those who have loved once or twice already are so much the better educated to a woman's hand; the bright boy of fiction is an odd and most uncomfortable mixture of shyness and coarseness, and needs a deal of civilising. Lastly (and this is, perhaps, the golden rule), no woman should marry a tee-totaller, or a man who does not smoke. It is not for nothing that this "ignoble tabagie," as Michelet calls it, spreads over all the world. Michelet rails against it because it renders you happy apart from thought or work; to provident women this will seem no evil influence in married life. Whatever keeps a man in the front garden, whatever checks wandering fancy and all inordinate ambition, whatever makes for lounging and contentment, makes just so surely for domestic happiness.

These notes, if they amuse the reader at all, will probably amuse him more when he differs than when he agrees with them; at least they will do no harm, for nobody will follow my advice. But the last word is of more concern. Marriage is a step so grave and decisive that it attracts light-headed, variable men by its very awfulness. They have been so tried among the inconstant squalls and currents, so often sailed for islands in the air or lain becalmed with burning heart, that they will risk all for solid ground below their feet. Desperate pilots, they run their sea-sick, weary bark upon the dashing rocks. It seems as if marriage were the royal road through life, and realised, on the instant, what we have all dreamed on summer Sundays when the bells ring, or at night when we cannot sleep for the desire of living. They think it will sober and change them. Like those who join a brotherhood, they fancy it needs but an act to be out of the coil and clamour for ever. But this is a wile of the devil's. To the end, spring winds will sow disquietude, passing faces leave a regret behind them, and the whole world keep calling and calling in their ears. For marriage is like life in this— that it is a field of battle, and not a bed of roses.

2.

Hope, they say, deserts us at no period of our existence. From first to last, and in the face of smarting disillusions, we continue to expect good fortune, better health, and better conduct; and that so confidently, that we judge it needless to deserve them. I think it improbable that I shall ever write like Shakespeare, conduct an army like Hannibal, or distinguish myself like Marcus Aurelius in the paths of virtue; and yet I have my by-days, hope prompting, when I am very ready to believe that I shall combine all these various excellences in my own person, and go marching down to posterity with divine honours. There is nothing so monstrous but we can believe it of ourselves. About ourselves, about our aspirations and delinquencies, we have dwelt by choice in a delicious vagueness from our boyhood up. No one will have forgotten Tom Sawyer's aspiration: "Ah, if he could only die *temporarily!*" Or, perhaps, better still, the inward resolution of the two pirates, that "so long as they remained in that business, their piracies should not again be sullied with the crime of stealing." Here we recognise the thoughts of our boyhood; and our boyhood ceased—well, when?—not, I think, at twenty; nor, perhaps, altogether at twenty-five; nor yet at thirty; and possibly, to be quite frank, we are still in the thick of that Arcadian period. For as the race of man, after centuries of civilisation, still keeps some traits of their barbarian fathers, so man the individual is not altogether quit of youth, when he is already old and honoured, and Lord Chancellor of England. We advanced in years somewhat in the manner of an invading army in a barren land; the age that we have reached, as the phrase goes, we but hold with an outpost, and still keep open our communications with the extreme rear and first beginnings of the march. There is our true base; that is not only the beginning, but the perennial spring of our faculties; and grandfather William can retire upon occasion into the green enchanted forest of his boyhood.

The unfading boyishness of hope and its vigorous irrationality are nowhere better displayed than in questions of conduct. There is a character in the *Pilgrim's Progress,* one Mr. *Linger-after-Lust,* with whom I fancy we are all on speaking terms; one famous among the famous for ingenuity of hope up to and beyond the moment of defeat; one who, after eighty years of contrary experience, will believe it possible to continue in the business of piracy and yet avoid the guilt of theft. Every sin is our last; every 1st of January a remarkable turning-point in our career. Any overt act, above all, is felt to be alchemic in its power to change. A drunkard takes the pledge; it will be strange if that does not help him. For how many years did Mr. Pepys continue to make and break his little vows? And yet I have not heard that he was discouraged in the end. By such steps we think to fix a momentary resolution; as a timid fellow hies him to the dentist's while the tooth is stinging.

But, alas, by planting a stake at the top of flood, you can neither prevent nor delay the inevitable ebb. There is no hocus-pocus in morality; and even the "sanctimonious ceremony" of marriage leaves the man unchanged. This is a hard saying, and has an air of paradox. For there is something in marriage so natural and inviting, that the step has an air of great simplicity and ease; it offers to bury for ever many aching preoccupations; it is to afford us unfailing and familiar company through life; it opens up a smiling prospect of the blest and passive kind of love, rather than the blessing and active; it is approached not only through the delights of courtship, but by a public performance and repeated legal signatures. A man naturally thinks it will go hard with him if he cannot be good and fortunate and happy within such august circumvallations.

And yet there is probably no other act in a man's life so hotheaded and foolhardy as this one of marriage. For years, let us suppose, you have been making the most indifferent business of your career. Your experience has not, we may dare to say, been more encouraging than Paul's or Horace's; like them, you have seen and desired the good that you were not able to accomplish; like them, you have done the evil that you loathed. You have waked at night in a hot or a cold sweat, according to your habit of body, remembering, with dismal surprise, your own unpardonable acts and sayings. You have been sometimes tempted to withdraw entirely from this game of life; as a man who makes nothing but misses withdraws from that less dangerous one of billiards. You have fallen back upon the thought that you yourself most sharply smarted for your misdemeanours, or, in the old, plaintive phrase, that you were nobody's enemy but your own. And then you have been made aware of what was beautiful and amiable, wise and kind, in the other part of your behaviour; and it seemed as if nothing could reconcile the contradiction, as indeed nothing can. If you are a man, you have shut your mouth hard and said nothing; and if you are only a man in the making, you have recognised that yours was quite a special case, and you yourself not guilty of your own pestiferous career.

Granted, and with all my heart. Let us accept these apologies; let us agree that you are nobody's enemy but your own; let us agree that you are a sort of moral cripple, impotent for good; and let us regard you with the unmingled pity due to such a fate. But there is one thing to which, on these terms, we can never agree:— we can never agree to have you marry. What! you have had one life to manage, and have failed so strangely, and now can see nothing wiser than to conjoin with it the management of some one else's? Because you have been unfaithful in a very little, you propose yourself to be a ruler over ten cities. You strip yourself by such a step of all remaining consolations and excuses. You are no longer content to be your own enemy; you must be your wife's also. You have been hitherto in a mere subaltern attitude; dealing cruel blows about you in life, yet only half responsible, since you came there by no choice or movement of your own. Now, it appears, you must take things on your own authority: God made you, but you marry yourself; and for all that your wife suffers, no one is responsible but you. A man must be very certain of his knowledge ere he undertake to guide a ticket-of-leave man through a dangerous pass; you have eternally missed your way in life, with consequences that you still deplore, and yet you masterfully seize your wife's hand, and, blindfold, drag her after you to ruin. And it is your wife, you observe, whom you select. She, whose happiness you most desire, you choose to be your victim. You would earnestly warn her from a tottering bridge or bad investment. If she were to marry some one else, how you would tremble for her fate! If she were only your sister, and you thought half as much of her, how doubtfully would you entrust her future to a man no better than yourself!

Times are changed with him who marries; there are no more by-path meadows, where you may innocently linger, but the road lies long and straight and dusty to the grave. Idleness, which is often becoming and even wise in the bachelor, begins to wear a different aspect when you have a wife to support. Suppose, after you are married, one of those little slips were to befall you. What happened last November might surely happen February next. They may have annoyed you at the time, because they were not what you had meant; but how will they annoy you in the future, and how will they shake the fabric of your wife's confidence and peace! A thousand things unpleasing went on in the *chiaroscuro* of a life that you shrank from too particularly realising; you did not care, in those days, to make a fetish of your conscience; you would recognise your failures with a nod, and so, good-day. But the time for these reserves is over. You have wilfully introduced a witness into your life, the scene of these defeats, and can no longer close the mind's eye upon uncomely passages, but must stand up straight and put a name upon your actions. And your witness is not only the judge, but the victim of your sins; not only can she condemn you to the sharpest penalties, but she must herself share feelingly in their endurance. And observe, once more, with what temerity you have chosen precisely *her* to be your spy, whose esteem you value highest, and whom you have already taught to think you better than you are. You may think you had a conscience, and believed in God; but what is a conscience to a wife? Wise men of yore erected statues of their deities, and consciously performed their part in life before those marble eyes. A god watched them at the board, and stood by their bedside in the morning when they woke; and all about their ancient cities, where they bought and sold, or where they piped and wrestled, there would stand some symbol of the things that are outside of man. These were lessons, delivered in the quiet dialect of art, which told their story faithfully, but gently. It is the same lesson, if you will—but how harrowingly taught!—when the woman you respect shall weep from your unkindness or blush with shame at your misconduct. Poor girls in Italy turn their painted Madonnas to the wall: you cannot set aside your wife. To marry is to domesticate the Recording Angel. Once you are married, there is nothing left for you, not even suicide, but to be good.

And goodness in marriage is a more intricate problem than mere single virtue; for in marriage there are two ideals to be realised. A girl, it is true, has always lived in a glass house among reproving relatives, whose word was law; she has been bred up to sacrifice her judgments and take the key submissively from dear papa; and it is wonderful how swiftly she can change her tune into the husband's. Her morality has been, too often, an affair of precept and conformity. But in the case of a bachelor who has enjoyed some measure both of privacy and freedom, his moral judgments have been passed in some accordance with his nature. His sins were always sins in his own sight; he could then only sin when he did some act against his clear conviction; the light that he walked by was obscure, but it was single. Now, when two people of any grit and spirit put their fortunes into one, there succeeds to this comparative certainty a huge welter of competing jurisdictions. It no longer matters so much how life appears to one; one must consult another: one, who may be strong, must not offend the other, who is weak. The only weak brother I am willing to consider is (to make a bull for once) my wife. For her, and for her only, I must waive my righteous judgments, and go crookedly about my life.

How, then, in such an atmosphere of compromise, to keep honour bright and abstain from base capitulations? How are you to put aside love's pleadings? How are you, the apostle of laxity, to turn suddenly about into the rabbi of precision; and after these years of ragged practice, pose for a hero to the lackey who has found you out? In this temptation to mutual indulgence lies the particular peril to morality in married life. Daily they drop a little lower from the first ideal, and for awhile continue to accept these changelings with a gross complacency. At last Love wakes and looks about him; finds his hero sunk into a stout old brute, intent on brandy pawnee; finds his heroine divested of her angel brightness; and in the flash of that first disenchantment, flees for ever.

Again, the husband, in these unions, is usually a man, and the wife commonly enough a woman; and when this is the case, although it makes the firmer marriage, a thick additional veil of misconception hangs above the doubtful business. Women, I believe, are somewhat rarer than men; but then, if I were a woman myself, I dare say I should hold the reverse; and at least we all enter more or less wholly into one or other of these camps. A man who delights women by his feminine perceptions will often scatter his admirers by a chance explosion of the under side of man; and the most masculine and direct of women will some day, to your dire surprise, draw out like a telescope into successive lengths of personation. Alas! for the man, knowing her to be at heart more candid than himself, who shall flounder, panting, through these mazes in the quest for truth. The proper qualities of each sex are, indeed, eternally surprising to the other. Between the Latin and the Teuton races there are similar divergences, not to be bridged by the most liberal sympathy. And in the good, plain, cut-and-dry explanations of this life, which pass current among us as the wisdom of the elders, this difficulty has been turned with the aid of pious lies. Thus, when a young lady has angelic features, eats nothing to speak of, plays all day long on the piano, and sings ravishingly in church, it requires a rough infidelity, falsely called cynicism, to believe that she may be a little devil after all. Yet so it is: she may be a tale-bearer, a liar, and a thief; she may have a taste for brandy, and no heart. My compliments to George Eliot for her Rosamond Vincy; the ugly work of satire she has transmuted to the ends of art, by the companion figure of Lydgate; and the satire

was much wanted for the education of young men. That doctrine
of the excellence of women, however chivalrous, is cowardly as
well as false. It is better to face the fact, and know, when you
marry, that you take into your life a creature of equal, if of unlike,
frailties; whose weak human heart beats no more tunefully than
yours.

But it is the object of a liberal education not only to obscure the
knowledge of one sex by another, but to magnify the natural differences between the two. Man is a creature who lives not upon
bread alone, but principally by catchwords; and the little rift between the sexes is astonishingly widened by simply teaching one
set of catchwords to the girls and another to the boys. To the first,
there is shown but a very small field of experience, and taught a very
trenchant principle for judgment and action; to the other, the
world of life is more largely displayed, and their rule of conduct
is proportionally widened. They are taught to follow different
virtues, to hate different vices, to place their ideal, even for each
other, in different achievements. What should be the result of such
a course? When a horse has run away, and the two flustered people
in the gig have each possessed themselves of a rein, we know the
end of that conveyance will be in the ditch. So, when I see a raw
youth and a green girl, fluted and fiddled in a dancing measure
into that most serious contract, and setting out upon life's journey
with ideas so monstrously divergent, I am not surprised that some
make shipwreck, but that any come to port. What the boy does
almost proudly, as a manly peccadillo, the girl will shudder at as
a debasing vice; what is to her the mere common-sense of tactics, he
will spit out of his mouth as shameful. Through such a sea of
contrarities must this green couple steer their way; and contrive
to love each other; and to respect, forsooth; and be ready, when
the time arrives, to educate the little men and women who shall
succeed to their places and perplexities.

And yet, when all has been said, the man who should hold back
from marriage is in the same case with him who runs away from
battle. To avoid an occasion for our virtues is a worse degree of
failure than to push forward pluckily and make a fall. It is lawful
to pray God that we be not led into temptation; but not lawful to
skulk from those that come to us. The noblest passage in one of the
noblest books of this century, is where the old pope glories in the
trial, nay, in the partial fall and but imperfect triumph, of the

younger hero.* Without some such manly note, it were perhaps better to have no conscience at all. But there is a vast difference between teaching flight, and showing points of peril that a man may march the more warily. And the true conclusion of this paper is to turn our back on apprehensions, and embrace that shining and courageous virtue, Faith. Hope is the boy, a blind, headlong, pleasant fellow, good to chase swallows with the salt; Faith is the grave, experienced, yet smiling man. Hope lives on ignorance; open-eyed Faith is built upon a knowledge of our life, of the tyranny of circumstance and the frailty of human resolution. Hope looks for unqualified success; but Faith counts certainly on failure, and takes honourable defeat to be a form of victory. Hope is a kind old pagan; but Faith grew up in Christian days, and early learnt humility. In the one temper, a man is indignant that he cannot spring up in a clap to heights of elegance and virtue; in the other, out of a sense of his infirmities, he is filled with confidence because a year has come and gone, and he has still preserved some rags of honour. In the first, he expects an angel for a wife; in the last, he knows that she is like himself—erring, thoughtless, and untrue; but like himself also, filled with a struggling radiancy of better things, and adorned with ineffective qualities. You may safely go to school with hope; but ere you marry, should have learned the mingled lesson of the world: that dolls are stuffed with sawdust, and yet are excellent playthings; that hope and love address themselves to a perfection never realised, and yet, firmly held, become the salt and staff of life; that you yourself are compacted of infirmities, perfect, you might say, in imperfection, and yet you have a something in you lovable and worth preserving; and that, while the mass of mankind lies under this scurvy condemnation, you will scarce find one but, by some generous reading, will become to you a lesson, a model, and a noble spouse through life. So thinking, you will constantly support your own unworthiness, and easily forgive the failings of your friend. Nay, you will be wisely glad that you retain the sense of blemishes; for the faults of married people continually spur up each of them, hour by hour, to do better and to meet and love upon a higher ground. And ever, between the failures, there will come glimpses of kind virtues to encourage and console.

* Browning's *Ring and Book.*

3. *On Falling in Love*

"Lord, what fools these mortals be!"

There is only one event in life which really astonishes a man and startles him out of his prepared opinions. Everything else befalls him very much as he expected. Event succeeds to event, with an agreeable variety indeed, but with little that is either startling or intense; they form together no more than a sort of background, or running accompaniment to the man's own reflections; and he falls naturally into a cool, curious, and smiling habit of mind, and builds himself up in a conception of life which expects to-morrow to be after the pattern of to-day and yesterday. He may be accustomed to the vagaries of his friends and acquaintances under the influence of love. He may sometimes look forward to it for himself with an incomprehensible expectation. But it is a subject in which neither intuition nor the behaviour of others will help the philosopher to the truth. There is probably nothing rightly thought or rightly written on this matter of love that is not a piece of the person's experience. I remember an anecdote of a well-known French theorist, who was debating a point eagerly in his *cénacle*. It was objected against him that he had never experienced love. Whereupon he arose, left the society, and made it a point not to return to it until he considered that he had supplied the defect. "Now," he remarked, on entering, "now I am in a position to continue the discussion." Perhaps he had not penetrated very deeply into the subject after all; but the story indicates right thinking, and may serve as an apologue to readers of this essay.

When at last the scales fall from his eyes, it is not without something of the nature of dismay that the man finds himself in such changed conditions. He has to deal with commanding emotions instead of the easy dislikes and preferences in which he has hitherto passed his days; and he recognises capabilities for pain and pleasure of which he had not yet suspected the existence. Falling in love is the one illogical adventure, the one thing of which we are tempted to think as supernatural, in our trite and reasonable world. The effect is out of all proportion with the cause. Two persons, neither of them, it may be, very amiable or very beautiful, meet, speak a little, and look a little into each other's eyes.

That has been done a dozen or so of times in the experience of either with no great result. But on this occasion all is different. They fall at once into that state in which another person becomes to us the very gist and centrepoint of God's creation, and demolishes our labourious theories with a smile; in which our ideas are so bound up with the one master-thought that even the trivial cares of our own person become so many acts of devotion, and the love of life itself is translated into a wish to remain in the same world with so precious and desirable a fellow-creature. And all the while their acquaintances look on in stupor, and ask each other, with almost passionate emphasis, what so-and-so can see in that woman, or such-an-one in that man? I am sure, gentlemen, I cannot tell you. For my part, I cannot think what the women mean. It might be very well, if the Apollo Belvedere should suddenly glow all over into life, and step forward from the pedestal with that godlike air of his. But of the misbegotten changelings who call themselves men, and prate intolerably over dinner-tables, I never saw one who seemed worthy to inspire love—no, nor read of any, except Leonardo da Vinci, and perhaps Goethe in his youth. About women I entertain a somewhat different opinion; but there, I have the misfortune to be a man.

There are many matters in which you may waylay Destiny, and bid him stand and deliver. Hard work, high thinking, adventurous excitement, and a great deal more that forms a part of this or the other person's spiritual bill of fare, are within the reach of almost any one who can dare a little and be patient. But it is by no means in the way of every one to fall in love. You know the difficulty Shakespeare was put into when Queen Elizabeth asked him to show Falstaff in love. I do not believe that Henry Fielding was ever in love. Scott, if it were not for a passage or two in *Rob Roy,* would give me very much the same effect. These are great names and (what is more to the purpose) strong, healthy, high-strung, and generous natures, of whom the reverse might have been expected. As for the innumerable army of anæmic and tailorish persons who occupy the face of this planet with so much propriety, it is palpably absurd to imagine them in any such situation as a love-affair. A wet rag goes safely by the fire; and if a man is blind, he cannot expect to be much impressed by romantic scenery. Apart from all this, many lovable people miss each other in the world, or meet under some unfavorable star. There is the nice and critical moment of declaration to be got over. From timidity or lack of opportunity a good half of possible love cases never get so far, and at least another quarter do there cease and determine. A very adroit person, to be sure, manages to prepare the way and out with his declaration in the nick of time. And then there is a fine solid sort of man, who goes on from snub to snub; and if he has to declare forty times, will continue imperturbably declaring, amid the astonished consideration of men and angels, until he has a favourable answer. I dare say, if one were a woman, one would like to marry a man who was capable of doing this, but not quite one who had done so. It is just a little bit abject, and somehow just a little bit gross; and marriages in which one of the parties has been thus battered into consent scarcely form agreeable subjects for meditation. Love should run out to meet love with open arms. Indeed, the ideal story is that of two people who go into love step for step, with a fluttered consciousness, like a pair of children venturing together into a dark room. From the first moment when they see each other, with a pang of curiosity, through stage after stage of growing pleasure and embarrassment, they can read the expression of their own trouble in each other's eyes. There is here no declaration properly so called; the feeling is so plainly shared, that as soon as the man knows what it is in his own heart, he is sure of what it is in the woman's.

This simple accident of falling in love is as beneficial as it is astonishing. It arrests the petrifying influence of years, disproves cold-blooded and cynical conclusions, and awakens dormant sensibilities. Hitherto the man had found it a good policy to disbelieve the existence of any enjoyment which was out of his reach; and thus he turned his back upon the strong sunny parts of nature, and accustomed himself to look exclusively on what was common and dull. He accepted a prose ideal, let himself go blind of many sympathies by disuse; and if he were young and witty, or beautiful, wilfully forewent these advantages. He joined himself to the following of what, in the old mythology of love, was prettily called *nonchaloir;* and in an odd mixture of feelings, a fling of self-respect, a preference for selfish liberty, and a great dash of that fear with which honest people regard serious interests, kept himself back from the straightforward course of life among certain selected activities. And now, all of a sudden, he is unhorsed, like St. Paul, from his infidel affectation. His heart, which has been ticking

accurate seconds for the last year, gives a bound and begins to beat
high and irregularly in his breast. It seems as if he had never heard
or felt or seen until that moment; and by the report of his memory,
he must have lived his past life between sleep or waking, or with
the preoccupied attention of a brown study. He is practically incommoded by the generosity of his feelings, smiles much when he
is alone, and develops a habit of looking rather blankly upon the
moon and stars. But it is not at all within the province of a prose
essayist to give a picture of this hyperbolical frame of mind; and
the thing has been done already, and that to admiration. In
Adelaide, in Tennyson's *Maud,* and in some of Heine's songs, you
get the absolute expression of this midsummer spirit. Romeo and
Juliet were very much in love; although they tell me some German
critics are of a different opinion, probably the same who would
have us think Mercutio a dull fellow. Poor Antony was in love, and
no mistake. That lay figure Marius, in *Les Misérables,* is also a
genuine case in his own way, and worth observation. A good many
of George Sand's people are thoroughly in love; and so are a good
many of George Meredith's. Altogether, there is plenty to read on
the subject. If the root of the matter be in him, and if he has the
requisite chords to set in vibration, a young man may occasionally
enter, with the key of art, into that land of Beulah which is upon
the borders of Heaven and within sight of the City of Love. There
let him sit awhile to hatch delightful hopes and perilous illusions.

One thing that accompanies the passion in its first blush is certainly difficult to explain. It comes (I do not quite see how) that
from having a very supreme sense of pleasure in all parts of life—
in lying down to sleep, in waking, in motion, in breathing, in
continuing to be—the lover begins to regard his happiness as
beneficial for the rest of the world and highly meritorious in himself. Our race has never been able contentedly to suppose that the
noise of its wars, conducted by a few young gentlemen in a corner
of an inconsiderable star, does not re-echo among the courts of
Heaven with quite a formidable effect. In much the same taste,
when people find a great to-do in their own breasts, they imagine
it must have some influence in their neighbourhood. The presence
of the two lovers is so enchanting to each other that it seems as if
it must be the best thing possible for everybody else. They are half
inclined to fancy it is because of them and their love that the sky
is blue and the sun shines. And certainly the weather is usually fine

while people are courting. . . . In point of fact, although the happy man feels very kindly towards others of his own sex, there is apt to be something too much of the magnifico in his demeanour. If people grow presuming and self-important over such matters as a dukedom or the Holy See, they will scarcely support the dizziest elevation in life without some suspicion of a strut; and the dizziest elevation is to love and be loved in return. Consequently, accepted lovers are a trifle condescending in their address to other men. An over-weening sense of the passion and importance of life hardly conduces to simplicity of manner. To women, they feel very nobly, very purely, and very generously, as if they were so many Joan-of-Arcs; but this does not come out in their behaviour; and they treat them to Grandisonian airs marked with a suspicion of fatuity. I am not quite certain that women do not like this sort of thing; but really, after having bemused myself over *Daniel Deronda,* I have given up trying to understand what they like.

If it did nothing else, this sublime and ridiculous superstition, that the pleasure of the pair is somehow blessed to others, and everybody is made happier in their happiness, would serve at least to keep love generous and great-hearted. Nor is it quite a baseless superstition after all. Other lovers are hugely interested. They strike the nicest balance between pity and approval, when they see people aping the greatness of their own sentiments. It is an understood thing in the play, that while the young gentlefolk are courting on the terrace, a rough flirtation is being carried on, and a light, trivial sort of love is growing up, between the footman and the singing chambermaid. As people are generally cast for the leading parts in their own imaginations, the reader can apply the parallel to real life without much chance of going wrong. In short, they are quite sure this other love-affair is not so deep-seated as their own, but they like dearly to see it going forward. And love, considered as a spectacle, must have attractions for many who are not of the confraternity. The sentimental old maid is a commonplace of the novelists; and he must be rather a poor sort of human being, to be sure, who can look on at this pretty madness without indulgence and sympathy. For nature commends itself to people with a most insinuating art; the busiest is now and again arrested by a great sunset; and you may be as pacific or as cold-blooded as you will, but you cannot help some emotion when you read of well-disputed battles, or meet a pair of lovers in the lane.

Certainly, whatever it may be with regard to the world at large, this idea of beneficent pleasure is true as between the sweethearts. To do good and communicate is the lover's grand intention. It is the happiness of the other that makes his own most intense gratification. It is not possible to disentangle the different emotions, the pride, humility, pity and passion, which are excited by a look of happy love or an unexpected caress. To make one's self beautiful, to dress the hair, to excel in talk, to do anything and all things that puff out the character and attributes and make them imposing in the eyes of others, is not only to magnify one's self, but to offer the most delicate homage at the same time. And it is in this latter intention that they are done by lovers; for the essence of love is kindness; and indeed it may be best defined as passionate kindness: kindness, so to speak, run mad and become importunate and violent. Vanity in a merely personal sense exists no longer. The lover takes a perilous pleasure in privately displaying his weak points and having them, one after another, accepted and condoned. He wishes to be assured that he is not loved for this or that good quality, but for himself, or something as like himself as he can contrive to set forward. For, although it may have been a very difficult thing to paint the marriage of Cana, or write the fourth act of *Antony and Cleopatra*, there is a more difficult piece of art before every one in this world who cares to set about explaining his own character to others. Words and acts are easily wrenched from their true significance; and they are all the language we have to come and go upon. A pitiful job we make of it, as a rule. For better or worse, people mistake our meaning and take our emotions at a wrong valuation. And generally we rest pretty content with our failures; we are content to be misapprehended by cackling flirts; but when once a man is moonstruck with this affection of love, he makes it a point of honour to clear such dubieties away. He cannot have the Best of her Sex misled upon a point of this importance; and his pride revolts at being loved in a mistake.

He discovers a great reluctance to return on former periods of his life. To all that has not been shared with her, rights and duties, bygone fortunes and dispositions, he can look back only by a difficult and repugnant effort of the will. That he should have wasted some years in ignorance of what alone was really important, that he may have entertained the thought of other women with any show of complacency, is a burthen almost too heavy for his self-respect. But it is the thought of another past that rankles in his spirit like a poisoned wound. That he himself made a fashion of being alive in the bald, beggarly days before a certain meeting, is deplorable enough in all good conscience. But that She should have permitted herself the same liberty seems inconsistent with a Divine providence.

A great many people run down jealousy, on the score that it is an artificial feeling, as well as practically inconvenient. This is scarcely fair; for the feeling on which it merely attends, like an ill-humoured courtier, is itself artificial in exactly the same sense and to the same degree. I suppose what is meant by that objection is that jealousy has not always been a character of man; formed no part of that very modest kit of sentiments with which he is supposed to have begun the world; but waited to make its appearance in better days and among richer natures. And this is equally true of love, and friendship, and love of country, and delight in what they call the beauties of nature, and most other things worth having. Love, in particular, will not endure any historical scrutiny: to all who have fallen across it, it is one of the most incontestable facts in the world; but if you begin to ask what it was in other periods and countries, in Greece for instance, the strangest doubts begin to spring up, and everything seems so vague and changing that a dream is logical in comparison. Jealousy, at any rate, is one of the consequences of love; you may like it or not, at pleasure; but there it is.

It is not exactly jealousy, however, that we feel when we reflect on the past of those we love. A bundle of letters found after years of happy union creates no sense of insecurity in the present; and yet it will pain a man sharply. The two people entertain no vulgar doubt of each other: but this pre-existence of both occurs to the mind as something indelicate. To be altogether right, they should have had twin birth together, at the same moment with the feeling that unites them. Then indeed it would be simple and perfect and without reserve or afterthought. Then they would understand each other with a fulness impossible otherwise. There would be no barrier between them of associations that cannot be imparted. They would be led into none of those comparisons that send the blood back to the heart. And they would know that there had been no time lost, and they had been together as much as was possible. For besides terror for the separation that must follow some time or other in the future, men feel anger, and something like remorse, when they think of that other separation which endured until they met. Some one has written that love makes people believe in immortality, because there seems not to be room enough in life for so great a tenderness, and it is inconceivable that the most masterful of our emotions should have no more than the spare moments of a few years. Indeed, it seems strange; but if we call to mind analogies, we can hardly regard it as impossible.

"The blind bow-boy," who smiles upon us from the end of terraces in old Dutch gardens, laughingly hails his bird-bolts among a fleeting generation. But for as fast as ever he shoots, the game dissolves and disappears into eternity from under his falling arrows; this one is gone ere he is struck; the other has but time to make one gesture and give one passionate cry; and they are all the things of a moment. When the generation is gone, when the play is over, when the thirty years' panorama has been withdrawn in tatters from the stage of the world, we may ask what has become of these great, weighty, and undying loves, and the sweethearts who despised mortal conditions in a fine credulity; and they can only show us a few songs in a bygone taste, a few actions worth remembering, and a few children who have retained some happy stamp from the disposition of their parents.

4. *Truth of Intercourse*

Among sayings that have a currency in spite of being wholly false upon the face of them for the sake of a half-truth upon another subject which is accidentally combined with the error, one of the grossest and broadest conveys the monstrous proposition that it is easy to tell the truth and hard to tell a lie. I wish heartily it were. But the truth is one; it has first to be discovered, then justly and exactly uttered. Even with instruments specially contrived for such a purpose—with a foot rule, a level, or a theodolite—it is not easy to be exact; it is easier, alas! to be inexact. From those who mark the divisions on a scale to those who measure the boundaries of empires or the distance of the heavenly stars, it is by careful method and minute, unwearying attention that men rise even to material exactness or to sure knowledge even of external and constant things. But it is easier to draw the outline of a mountain than the changing appearance of a face; and truth in human relations is of this more intangible and dubious order: hard to seize, harder to communicate. Veracity to facts in a loose, colloquial sense—not to say that I have been in Malabar when as a matter of fact I was never out of England, not to say that I have read Cervantes in the original when as a matter of fact I know not one syllable of Spanish—this, indeed, is easy and to the same degree unimportant in itself. Lies of this sort, according to circumstances, may or may not be important; in a certain sense even they may or may not be false. The habitual liar may be a very honest fellow, and live truly with his wife and friends; while another man who never told a formal falsehood in his life may yet be himself one lie—heart and face, from top to bottom. This is the kind of lie which poisons intimacy. And, *vice versa*, veracity to sentiment, truth in a relation, truth to your own heart and your friends, never to feign or falsify emotion —that is the truth which makes love possible and mankind happy.

L'art de bien dire is but a drawing-room accomplishment unless it be pressed into the service of the truth. The difficulty of literature is not to write, but to write what you mean; not to affect your reader, but to affect him precisely as you wish. This is commonly understood in the case of books or set orations; even in making your will, or writing an explicit letter, some difficulty is admitted by the world. But one thing you can never make Philistine natures understand; one thing, which yet lies on the surface, remains as unseizable to their wits as a high flights of metaphysics—namely, that the business of life is mainly carried on by means of this difficult art of literature, and according to a man's proficiency in that art shall be the freedom and the fulness of his intercourse with other men. Anybody, it is supposed, can say what he means; and, in spite of their notorious experience to the contrary, people so continue to suppose. Now, I simply open the last book I have been reading— Mr. Leland's captivating *English Gipsies.* "It is said," I find on p. 7, "that those who can converse with Irish peasants in their own native tongue form far higher opinions of their appreciation of the beautiful, and of *the elements of humour and pathos in their hearts,* than do those who know their thoughts only through the medium of English. I know from my own observations that this is quite the case with the Indians of North America, and it is unquestionably so with the gipsy." In short, where a man has not a full possession of the language, the most important, because the most amiable, qualities of his nature have to lie buried and fallow; for the pleasure of comradeship, and the intellectual part of love, rest upon these very "elements of humour and pathos." Here is a man opulent in both, and for lack of a medium he can put none of it out to interest in the market of affection! But what is thus made plain to our apprehensions in the case of a foreign language is partially true even with the tongue we learned in childhood. Indeed, we all speak different dialects; one shall be copious and exact, another loose and meagre; but the speech of the ideal talker shall correspond and fit upon the truth of fact—not clumsily, obscuring lineaments, like a mantle, but cleanly adhering, like an athlete's skin. And what is the result? That the one can open himself more clearly to his friends, and can enjoy more of what makes life truly valuable—intimacy with those he loves. An orator makes a false step; he employs some trivial, some absurd, some vulgar phrase; in the turn of a sentence he insults, by a side wind, those whom he is labouring to charm; in speaking to one sentiment he unconsciously ruffles another in parenthesis; and you are not surprised, for you know his task to be delicate and filled with perils. "O frivolous mind of man, light ignorance!" As if yourself, when you seek to explain some misunderstanding or excuse some apparent fault, speaking swiftly and addressing a mind still recently incensed, were not harnessing for a more perilous adventure; as if yourself required less tact and eloquence; as if an angry friend or a suspicious lover were not more easy to offend than a meeting of indifferent politicians! Nay, and the orator treads in a beaten round; the matters he discusses have been discussed a thousand times before; language is ready-shaped to his purpose; he speaks out of a cut-and-dry vocabulary. But you—may it not be that your defence reposes on some subtlety of feeling, not so much as touched upon in Shakespeare, to express which, like a pioneer, you must venture forth into zones of thought still unsurveyed, and become yourself a literary innovator? For even in love there are unlovely humours; ambiguous acts, unpardonable words, may yet have sprung from a kind sentiment. If the injured one could read your heart, you may be sure that he would understand and pardon; but, alas! the heart cannot be shown—it has to be demonstrated in words. Do you think it is a hard thing to write poetry? Why, that is to write poetry, and of a high, if not the highest, order.

I should even more admire "the lifelong and heroic literary la-

bours" of my fellow-men, patiently clearing up in words their loves
and their contentions, and speaking their autobiography daily to
their wives, were it not for a circumstance which lessens their difficulty and my admiration by equal parts. For life, though largely,
is not entirely carried on by literature. We are subject to physical
passions and contortions; the voice breaks and changes, and speaks
by unconscious and winning inflections; we have legible countenances, like an open book; things that cannot be said look eloquently through the eyes; and the soul, not locked into the body as
a dungeon, dwells ever on the threshold with appealing signals.
Groans and tears, looks and gestures, a flush or a paleness, are often
the most clear reporters of the heart, and speak more directly to
the hearts of others. The message flies by these interpreters in the
least space of time, and the misunderstanding is averted in the moment of its birth. To explain in words takes time and a just and
patient hearing; and in the critical epochs of a close relation, patience and justice are not qualities on which we can rely. But the
look or the gesture explains things in a breath; they tell their message without ambiguity; unlike speech, they cannot stumble, by
the way, on a reproach or an illusion that should steel your friend
against the truth; and then they have a higher authority, for they
are the direct expression of the heart, not yet transmitted through
the unfaithful and sophisticating brain. Not long ago I wrote a letter to a friend which came near involving us in quarrel; but we
met, and in personal talk I repeated the worst of what I had written, and added worse to that; and with the commentary of the
body it seemed not unfriendly either to hear or say. Indeed, letters
are in vain for the purposes of intimacy; an absence is a dead break
in the relation; yet two who know each other fully and are bent on
perpetuity in love, may so preserve the attitude of their affections
that they may meet on the same terms as they had parted.

Pitiful is the case of the blind, who cannot read the face; pitiful
that of the deaf, who cannot follow the changes of the voice. And
there are others also to be pitied; for there are some of an inert,
uneloquent nature, who have been denied all the symbols of communication, who have neither a lively play of facial expression,
nor speaking gestures, nor a responsive voice, nor yet the gift of
frank, explanatory speech: people truly made of clay, people tied
for life into a bag which no one can undo. They are poorer than
the gipsy, for their heart can speak no language under heaven.

Such people we must learn slowly by the tenor of their acts, or through yea and nay communications; or we take them on trust on the strength of a general air, and now and again, when we see the spirit breaking through in a flash, correct or change our estimate. But these will be uphill intimacies, without charm or freedom, to the end; and freedom is the chief ingredient in confidence. Some minds, romantically dull, despise physical endowments. That is a doctrine for a misanthrope; to those who like their fellow-creatures it must always be meaningless; and, for my part, I can see few things more desirable, after the possession of such radical qualities as honour and humour and pathos, than to have a lively and not a stolid countenance; to have looks to correspond with every feeling; to be elegant and delightful in person, so that we shall please even in the intervals of active pleasing, and may never discredit speech with uncouth manners or become unconsciously our own burlesques. But of all unfortunates there is one creature (for I will not call him man) conspicuous in misfortune. This is he who has forfeited his birthright of expression, who has cultivated artful intonations, who has taught his face tricks, like a pet monkey, and on every side perverted or cut off his means of communication with his fellow-men. The body is a house of many windows: there we all sit, showing ourselves and crying on the passers-by to come and love us. But this fellow has filled his windows with opaque glass, elegantly coloured. His house may be admired for its design, the crowd may pause before the stained windows, but meanwhile the poor proprietor must lie languishing within, uncomforted, unchangeably alone.

Truth of intercourse is something more difficult than to refrain from open lies. It is possible to avoid falsehood and yet not tell the truth. It is not enough to answer formal questions. To reach the truth by yea and nay communications implies a questioner with a share of inspiration, such as is often found in mutual love. *Yea* and *nay* mean nothing; the meaning must have been related in the question. Many words are often necessary to convey a very simple statement; for in this sort of exercise we never hit the gold; the most that we can hope is by many arrows, more or less far off on different sides, to indicate, in the course of time, for what target we are aiming, and after an hour's talk, back and forward, to convey the purport of a single principle or a single thought. And yet while the curt, pithy speaker misses the point entirely, a wordy, prole-

gomenous babbler will often add three new offences in the process
of excusing one. It is really a most delicate affair. The world was
made before the English language, and seemingly upon a different
design. Suppose we held our converse not in words, but in music;
those who have a bad ear would find themselves cut off from all
near commerce, and no better than foreigners in this big world.
But we do not consider how many have "a bad ear" for words, nor
how often the most eloquent find nothing to reply. I hate ques-
tioners and questions; there are so few that can be spoken to without a lie. *"Do you forgive me?"* Madam and sweetheart, so far as I
have gone in life I have never yet been able to discover what forgiveness means. *"Is it still the same between us?"* Why, how can it
be? It is eternally different; and yet you are still the friend of my
heart. *"Do you understand me?"* God knows; I should think it
highly improbable.

The cruellest lies are often told in silence. A man may have sat
in a room for hours and not opened his teeth, and yet come out of
that room a disloyal friend or a vile calumniator. And how many
loves have perished because, from pride, or spite, or diffidence, or
that unmanly shame which withholds a man from daring to betray
emotion, a lover, at the critical point of the relation, has but hung
his head and held his tongue? And, again, a lie may be told by a
truth, or a truth conveyed through a lie. Truth to facts is not always truth to sentiment; and part of the truth, as often happens in
answer to a question, may be the foulest calumny. A fact may be
an exception; but the feeling is the law, and it is that which you
must neither garble nor belie. The whole tenor of a conversation
is a part of the meaning of each separate statement; the beginning
and the end define and travesty the intermediate conversation. You
never speak to God; you address a fellow-man, full of his own tem-
pers; and to tell truth, rightly understood, is not to state the true
facts, but to convey a true impression; truth in spirit, not truth to
letter, is the true veracity. To reconcile averted friends a Jesuitical
discretion is often needful, not so much to gain a kind hearing as
to communicate sober truth. Women have an ill name in this connection; yet they live in as true relations; the lie of a good woman
is the true index of her heart.

"It takes," says Thoreau, in the noblest and most useful passage
I remember to have read in any modern author,* "two to speak

* *A Week on the Concord and Merrimack Rivers,* Wednesday, p. 283.

truth—one to speak and another to hear." He must be very little experienced, or have no great zeal for truth, who does not recognise the fact. A grain of anger or a grain of suspicion produces strange acoustical effects, and makes the ear greedy to remark offence. Hence we find those who have once quarrelled carry themselves distantly, and are ever ready to break the truce. To speak truth there must be moral equality or else no respect; and hence between parent and child intercourse is apt to degenerate into a verbal fencing bout, and misapprehensions to become ingrained. And there is another side to this, for the parent begins with an imperfect notion of the child's character, formed in early years or during the equinoctial gales of youth; to this he adheres, noting only the facts which suit with his preconception; and wherever a person fancies himself unjustly judged, he at once and finally gives up the effort to speak truth. With our chosen friends, on the other hand, and still more between lovers (for mutual understanding is love's essence), the truth is easily indicated by the one and aptly comprehended by the other. A hint taken, a look understood, conveys the gist of long and delicate explanations; and where the life is known even *yea* and *nay* become luminous. In the closest of all relations—that of a love well founded and equally shared—speech is half discarded, like a roundabout, infantile process or a ceremony of formal etiquette; and the two communicate directly by their presences, and with few looks and fewer words contrive to share their good and evil and uphold each other's hearts in joy. For love rests upon a physical basis; it is a familiarity of nature's making and apart from voluntary choice. Understanding has in some sort outrun knowledge, for the affection perhaps began with the acquaintance; and as it was not made like other relations, so it is not, like them, to be perturbed or clouded. Each knows more than can be uttered; each lives by faith, and believes by a natural compulsion; and between man and wife the language of the body is largely developed and grown strangely eloquent. The thought that prompted and was conveyed in a caress would only lose to be set down in words—ay, although Shakespeare himself should be the scribe.

Yet it is in these dear intimacies, beyond all others, that we must strive and do battle for the truth. Let but a doubt arise, and alas! all the previous intimacy and confidence is but another charge against the person doubted. *"What a monstrous dishonesty is this if I have been deceived so long and so completely!"* Let but that thought gain entrance, and you plead before a deaf tribunal. Appeal to the past; why, that is your crime! Make all clear, convince the reason; alas! speciousness is but a proof against you. *"If you can abuse me now, the more likely that you have abused me from the first."*

For a strong affection such moments are worth supporting, and they will end well; for your advocate is in your lover's heart, and speaks her own language; it is not you but she herself who can defend and clear you of the charge. But in slighter intimacies, and for a less stringent union? Indeed, is it worth while? We are all *incompris,* only more or less concerned for the mischance; all trying wrongly to do right; all fawning at each other's feet like dumb, neglected lap-dogs. Sometimes we catch an eye—this is our opportunity in the ages—and we wag our tail with a poor smile. *"Is that all?"* All? If you only knew! But how can they know? They do not love us; the more fools we to squander life on the indifferent.

But the morality of the thing, you will be glad to hear, is excellent; for it is only by trying to understand others that we can get our own hearts understood; and in matters of human feeling the clement judge is the most successful pleader.

TALK AND TALKERS

"Sir, we had a good talk."—JOHNSON.

"As we must account for every idle word, so
we must for every idle silence."—FRANKLIN.

1

THERE CAN BE NO FAIRER AMBITION THAN TO EXCEL IN TALK; TO
be affable, gay, ready, clear, and welcome; to have a fact, a
thought, or an illustration, pat to every subject; and not only to
cheer the flight of time among our intimates, but bear our part in
that great international congress, always sitting, where public
wrongs are first declared, public errors first corrected, and the
course of public opinion shaped, day by day, a little nearer to the
right. No measure comes before Parliament but it has been long
ago prepared by the grand jury of the talkers; no book is written
that has not been largely composed by their assistance. Literature
in many of its branches is no other than the shadow of good talk;
but the imitation falls far short of the original in life, freedom, and
effect. There are always two to a talk, giving and taking, comparing experience, and according conclusions. Talk is fluid, tentative,
continually "in further search and progress"; while written words
remain fixed, become idols even to the writer, found wooden dog-
matisms, and preserve flies of obvious error in the amber of the
truth. Last and chief, while literature, gagged with linsey-woolsey,
can only deal with a fraction of the life of man, talk goes fancy
free and may call a spade a spade. Talk has none of the freezing
immunities of the pulpit. It cannot, even if it would, become
merely æsthetic or merely classical like literature. A jest intervenes,
the solemn humbug is dissolved in laughter, and speech runs forth

out of the contemporary groove into the open fields of nature, cheery and cheering, like schoolboys out of school. And it is in talk alone that we can learn our period and ourselves. In short, the first duty of a man is to speak; that is his chief business in this world; and talk, which is the harmonious speech of two or more, is by far the most accessible of pleasures. It costs nothing in money; it is all profit; it completes our education, founds and fosters our friendships, and can be enjoyed at any age and in almost any state of health.

The spice of life is battle; the friendliest relations are still a kind of contest; and if we would not forego all that is valuable in our lot, we must continually face some other person, eye to eye, and wrestle a fall whether in love or enmity. It is still by force of body, or power of character or intellect, that we attain to worthy pleasures. Men and women contend for each other in the lists of love, like rival mesmerists; the active and adroit decide their challenges in the sports of the body; and the sedentary sit down to chess or conversation. All sluggish and pacific pleasures are, to the same degree, solitary and selfish; and every durable bond between human beings is founded in or heightened by some element of competition. Now, the relation that has the least root in matter is undoubtedly that airy one of friendship; and hence, I suppose, it is that good talk most commonly arises among friends. Talk is, indeed, both the scene and instrument of friendship. It is in talk alone that the friends can measure strength, and enjoy that amicable counterassertion of personality which is the gauge of relations and the sport of life.

A good talk is not to be had for the asking. Humours must first be accorded in a kind of overture or prologue; hour, company, and circumstance be suited; and then, at a fit juncture, the subject, the quarry of two heated minds, spring up like a deer out of the wood. Not that the talker has any of the hunter's pride, though he has all and more than all his ardour. The genuine artist follows the stream of conversation as an angler follows the windings of a brook, not dallying where he fails to "kill." He trusts implicitly to hazard; and he is rewarded by continual variety, continual pleasure, and those changing prospects of the truth that are the best of education. There is nothing in a subject, so called, that we should regard it as an idol, or follow it beyond the promptings of desire. Indeed, there are few subjects; and so far as they are truly talkable,

more than the half of them may be reduced to three: that I am I,
that you are you, and that there are other people dimly understood to be not quite the same as either. Wherever talk may range,
it still runs half the time on these eternal lines. The theme being
set, each plays on himself as on an instrument; asserts and justifies
himself; ransacks his brain for instances and opinions, and brings
them forth new-minted, to his own surprise and the admiration of
his adversary. All natural talk is a festival of ostentation; and by
the laws of the game each accepts and fans the vanity of the other.
It is from that reason that we venture to lay ourselves so open, that
we dare to be so warmly eloquent, and that we swell in each other's
eyes to such a vast proportion. For talkers, once launched, begin to
overflow the limits of their ordinary selves, tower up to the height
of their secret pretensions, and give themselves out for the heroes,
brave, pious, musical, and wise, that in their most shining moments
they aspire to be. So they weave for themselves with words and for
awhile inhabit a palace of delights, temple at once and theatre,
where they fill the round of the world's dignities, and feast with
the gods, exulting in Kudos. And when the talk is over, each goes
his way, still flushed with vanity and admiration, still trailing
clouds of glory; each declines from the height of his ideal orgie,
not in a moment, but by slow declension. I remember, in the *entr'-
acte* of an afternoon performance, coming forth into the sunshine,
in a beautiful green, gardened corner of a romantic city; and as I
sat and smoked, the music moving in my blood, I seemed to sit
there and evaporate *The Flying Dutchman* (for it was that I had
been hearing) with a wonderful sense of life, warmth, well-being,
and pride; and the noises of the city, voices, bells, and marching
feet fell together in my ears like a symphonious orchestra. In the
same way, the excitement of a good talk lives for a long while after
in the blood, the heart still hot within you, the brain still simmer-
ing, and the physical earth swimming around you with the colours
of the sunset.

Natural talk, like ploughing, should turn up a large surface of
life, rather than dig mines into geological strata. Masses of experience, anecdote, incident, cross-lights, quotation, historical instances, the whole flotsam and jetsam of two minds forced in and
in upon the matter in hand from every point of the compass, and
from every degree of mental elevation and abasement—these are
the material with which talk is fortified, the food on which the

talkers thrive. Such argument as is proper to the exercise should still be brief and seizing. Talk should proceed by instances; by the apposite, not the expository. It should keep close along the lines of humanity, near the bosoms and businesses of men, at the level where history, fiction, and experience intersect and illuminate each other. I am I, and You are You, with all my heart; but conceive how these lean propositions change and brighten when, instead of words, the actual you and I sit cheek by jowl, the spirit housed in the live body, and the very clothes uttering voices to corroborate the story in the face. Not less surprising is the change when we leave off to speak of generalities—the bad, the good, the miser, and all the characters of Theophrastus—and call up other men, by anecdote or instance, in their very trick and feature; or trading on a common knowledge, toss each other famous names, still glowing with the hues of life. Communication is no longer by words, but by the instancing of whole biographies, epics, systems of philosophy, and epochs of history, in bulk. That which is understood excels that which is spoken in quantity and quality alike; ideas thus figured and personified, change hands, as we may say, like coin; and the speakers imply without effort the most obscure and intricate thoughts. Strangers who have a large common ground of reading will, for this reason, come the sooner to the grapple of genuine converse. If they know Othello and Napoleon, Consuelo and Clarissa Harlowe, Vautrin and Steenie Steenson, they can leave generalities and begin at once to speak by figures.

Conduct and art are the two subjects that arise most frequently and that embrace the widest range of facts. A few pleasures bear discussion for their own sake, but only those which are most social or most radically human; and even these can only be discussed among their devotees. A technicality is always welcome to the expert, whether in athletics, art, or law; I have heard the best kind of talk on technicalities from such rare and happy persons as both know and love their business. No human being ever spoke of scenery for above two minutes at a time, which makes me suspect we hear too much of it in literature. The weather is regarded as the very nadir and scoff of conversational topics. And yet the weather, the dramatic element in scenery, is far more tractable in language, and far more human both in import and suggestion than the stable features of the landscape. Sailors and shepherds, and the people generally of coast and mountain, talk well of it; and it is often excitingly presented in literature. But the tendency of all living talk draws it back and back into the common focus of humanity. Talk is a creature of the street and market-place, feeding on gossip; and its last resort is still in a discussion on morals. That is the heroic form of gossip; heroic in virtue of its high pretensions; but still gossip, because it turns on personalities. You can keep no men long, nor Scotchmen at all, off moral or theological discussion. These are to all the world what law is to lawyers; they are everybody's technicalities; the medium through which all consider life, and the dialect in which they express their judgments. I knew three young men who walked together daily for some two months in a solemn and beautiful forest and in cloudless summer weather; daily they talked with unabated zest, and yet scarce wandered that whole time beyond two subjects—theology and love. And perhaps neither a court of love nor an assembly of divines would have granted their premises or welcomed their conclusions.

Conclusions, indeed, are not often reached by talk any more than by private thinking. That is not the profit. The profit is in the exercise, and above all in the experience; for when we reason at large on any subject, we review our state and history in life. From time to time, however, and specially, I think, in talking art, talk becomes effective, conquering like war, widening the boundaries of knowledge like an exploration. A point arises; the question takes a problematical, a baffling, yet a likely air; the talkers begin to feel lively presentiments of some conclusion near at hand; towards this they strive with emulous ardour, each by his own path, and struggling for first utterance; and then one leaps upon the summit of that matter with a shout, and almost at the same moment the other is beside him; and behold they are agreed. Like enough, the progress is illusory, a mere cat's cradle having been wound and unwound out of words. But the sense of joint discovery is none the less giddy and inspiriting. And in the life of the talker such triumphs, though imaginary, are neither few nor far apart; they are attained with speed and pleasure, in the hour of mirth; and by the nature of the process, they are always worthily shared.

There is a certain attitude, combative at once and deferential, eager to fight yet most averse to quarrel, which marks out at once the talkable man. It is not eloquence, not fairness, not obstinacy, but a certain proportion of all of these that I love to encounter in my amicable adversaries. They must not be pontiffs holding doctrine, but huntsmen questing after elements of truth. Neither must they be boys to be instructed, but fellow-teachers with whom I may wrangle and agree on equal terms. We must reach some solution, some shadow of consent; for without that, eager talk becomes a torture. But we do not wish to reach it cheaply, or quickly, or without the tussle and effort wherein pleasure lies.

The very best talker, with me, is one whom I shall call Spring-Heel'd Jack. I say so, because I never knew any one who mingled so largely the possible ingredients of converse. In the Spanish proverb, the fourth man necessary to compound a salad, is a madman to mix it: Jack is that madman. I know not which is more remarkable; the insane lucidity of his conclusions, the humourous eloquence of his language, or his power of method, bringing the whole of life into the focus of the subject treated, mixing the conversational salad like a drunken god. He doubles like the serpent, changes and flashes like the shaken kaleidoscope, transmigrates bodily into the views of others, and so, in the twinkling of an eye and with a heady rapture, turns questions inside out and flings them empty before you on the ground, like a triumphant conjuror. It is my common practice when a piece of conduct puzzles me, to attack it in the presence of Jack with such grossness, such partiality, and such wearing iteration, as at length shall spur him up in its defence. In a moment he transmigrates, dons the required character, and with moonstruck philosophy justifies the act in question. I can fancy nothing to compare with the *vim* of these impersonations, the strange scale of language, flying from Shakespeare to Kant, and from Kant to Major Dyngwell—

"As fast as a musician scatters sounds
Out of an instrument—"

the sudden, sweeping generalisations, the absurd irrelevant particularities, the wit, wisdom, folly, humour, eloquence, and bathos, each startling in its kind, and yet all luminous in the admired disorder of their combination. A talker of a different calibre, though belonging to the same school, is Burly. Burly is a man of a great presence; he commands a larger atmosphere, gives the impression of a grosser mass of character than most men. It has been said of him that his presence could be felt in a room you entered blindfold; and the same, I think, has been said of other powerful constitutions condemned to much physical inaction. There is something boisterous and piratic in Burly's manner of talk which suits well enough with this impression. He will roar you down, he will bury his face in his hands, he will undergo passions of revolt and agony; and meanwhile his attitude of mind is really both conciliatory and receptive; and after Pistol has been out-Pistol'd, and the welkin rung for hours, you begin to perceive a certain subsidence in these spring torrents, points of agreement issue, and you end arm-in-arm, and in a glow of mutual admiration. The outcry only serves to make your final union the more unexpected and precious. Throughout there has been perfect sincerity, perfect intelligence, a desire to hear although not always to listen, and an unaffected eagerness to meet concessions. You have, with Burly, none of the dangers that attend debate with Spring-Heel'd Jack; who may at any moment turn his powers of transmigration on yourself, create for you a view you never held, and then furiously fall on you for holding it. These, at least, are my two favourites, and both are loud, copious, intolerant talkers. This argues that I myself am in the same category; for if we love talking at all, we love a bright, fierce adversary, who will hold his ground, foot by foot, in much our own manner, sell his attention dearly, and give us our full measure of the dust and exertion of battle. Both these men can be beat from a position, but it takes six hours to do it; a high and hard adventure, worth attempting. With both you can pass days in an enchanted country of the mind, with people, scenery, and manners of its own; live a life apart, more arduous, active, and glowing than any real existence; and come forth again when the talk is over, as out of a theatre or a dream, to find the east wind still blowing and the chimney-pots of the old battered city still around you. Jack has the far finer mind, Burly the far more honest; Jack gives us the animated poetry, Burly the romantic prose, of similar themes; the one glances high like a meteor and makes a light in darkness; the other, with many changing hues of fire, burns at the sea-level, like a conflagration; but both have the same humour and artistic interests, the same unquenched ardour in pursuit, the same gusts of talk and thunderclaps of contradiction.

Cockshot * is a different article, but vastly entertaining, and has been meat and drink to me for many a long evening. His manner is dry, brisk, and pertinacious, and the choice of words not much. The point about him is his extraordinary readiness and spirit. You

* The late Fleeming Jenkin.

can propound nothing but he has either a theory about it ready-made, or will have one instantly on the stocks, and proceed to lay its timbers and launch it in your presence. "Let me see," he will say. "Give me a moment. I *should* have some theory for that." A blither spectacle than the vigour with which he sets about the task, it were hard to fancy. He is possessed by a demoniac energy, welding the elements for his life, and bending ideas, as an athlete bends a horseshoe, with a visible and lively effort. He has, in theorising, a compass, an art; what I would call the synthetic gusto; something of a Herbert Spencer, who should see the fun of the thing. You are not bound, and no more is he, to place your faith in these brand-new opinions. But some of them are right enough, durable even for life; and the poorest serve for a cock-shy—as when idle people, after picnics, float a bottle on a pond and have an hour's diversion ere it sinks. Whichever they are, serious opinions or humours of the moment, he still defends his ventures with indefatigable wit and spirit, hitting savagely himself, but taking punishment like a man. He knows and never forgets that people talk, first of all, for the sake of talking; conducts himself in the ring, to use the old slang, like a thorough "glutton," and honestly enjoys a telling facer from his adversary. Cockshot is bottled effervescency, the sworn foe of sleep. Three-in-the-morning Cockshot, says a victim. His talk is like the driest of all imaginable dry champagnes. Sleight of hand and inimitable quickness are the qualities by which he lives. Athelred, on the other hand, presents you with the spectacle of a sincere and somewhat slow nature thinking aloud. He is the most unready man ı ever knew to shine in conversation. You may see him sometimes wrestle with a refractory jest for a minute or two together, and perhaps fail to throw it in the end. And there is something singularly engaging, often instructive, in the simplicity with which he thus exposes the process as well as the result, the works as well as the dial of the clock. Withal he has his hours of inspiration. Apt words come to him as if by accident, and, coming from deeper down, they smack the more personally, they have the more of fine old crusted humanity, rich in sediment and humour. There are sayings of his in which he has stamped himself into the very grain of the language; you would think he must have worn the words next his skin and slept with them. Yet it is not as a sayer of particular good things that Athelred is most to be regarded, rather as the stalwart woodman of thought. I have pulled on a light cord

often enough, while he has been wielding the broad-axe; and between us, on this unequal division, many a specious fallacy has
fallen. I have known him to battle the same question night after
night for years, keeping it in the reign of talk, constantly applying
it and re-applying it to life with humourous or grave intention,
and all the while, never hurrying, nor flagging, nor taking an unfair advantage of the facts. Jack at a given moment, when arising,
as it were, from the tripod, can be more radiantly just to those
from whom he differs; but then the tenor of his thoughts is even
calumnious; while Athelred, slower to forge excuses, is yet slower
to condemn, and sits over the welter of the world, vacillating but
still judicial, and still faithfully contending with his doubts.

Both the last talkers deal much in points of conduct and religion studied in the "dry light" of prose. Indirectly and as if against
his will the same elements from time to time appear in the troubled and poetic talk of Opalstein. His various and exotic knowledge, complete although unready sympathies, and fine, full, dis-
criminative flow of language, fit him out to be the best of talkers;
so perhaps he is with some, not *quite* with me—*proxime accessit*,
I should say. He sings the praises of the earth and the arts, flowers
and jewels, wine and music, in a moonlight, serenading manner,
as to the light guitar; even wisdom comes from his tongue like
singing; no one is, indeed, more tuneful in the upper notes. But
even while he sings the song of the Sirens, he still hearkens to the
barking of the Sphinx. Jarring Byronic notes interrupt the flow of
his Horatian humours. His mirth has something of the tragedy of
the world for its perpetual background; and he feasts like Don
Giovanni to a double orchestra, one lightly sounding for the
dance, one pealing Beethoven in the distance. He is not truly reconciled either with life or with himself; and this instant war in his
members sometimes divides the man's attention. He does not always, perhaps not often, frankly surrender himself in conversation.
He brings into the talk other thoughts than those which he expresses; you are conscious that he keeps an eye on something else,
that he does not shake off the world, nor quite forget himself.
Hence arise occasional disappointments; even an occasional un-
fairness for his companions, who find themselves one day giving
too much, and the next, when they are wary out of season, giving
perhaps too little. Purcel is in another class from any I have mentioned. He is no debater, but appears in conversation, as occasion

rises, in two distinct characters, one of which I admire and fear, and the other love. In the first, he is radiantly civil and rather silent, sits on a high, courtly hilltop, and from that vantage-ground drops you his remarks like favours. He seems not to share in our sublunary contentions; he wears no sign of interest; when on a sudden there falls in a crystal of wit, so polished that the dull do not perceive it, but so right that the sensitive are silenced. True talk should have more body and blood, should be louder, vainer and more declaratory of the man; the true talker should not hold so steady an advantage over whom he speaks with; and that is one reason out of a score why I prefer my Purcel is his second character, when he unbends into a strain of graceful gossip, singing like the fireside kettle. In these moods he has an elegant homeliness that rings of the true Queen Anne. I know another person who attains, in his moments, to the insolence of a Restoration comedy, speaking, I declare, as Congreve wrote; but that is a sport of nature, and scarce falls under the rubric, for there is none, alas! to give him answer.

One last remark occurs: It is the mark of genuine conversation that the sayings can scarce be quoted with their full effect beyond the circle of common friends. To have their proper weight they should appear in a biography, and with the portrait of the speaker. Good talk is dramatic; it is like an impromptu piece of acting where each should represent himself to the greatest advantage; and that is the best kind of talk where each speaker is most fully and candidly himself, and where, if you were to shift the speeches round from one to another, there would be the greatest loss in significance and perspicuity. It is for this reason that talk depends so wholly on our company. We should like to introduce Falstaff and Mercutio, or Falstaff and Sir Toby; but Falstaff in talk with Cordelia seems even painful. Most of us, by the Protean quality of man, can talk to some degree with all; but the true talk, that strikes out all the slumbering best of us, comes only with the peculiar brethren of our spirits, is founded as deep as love in the constitution of our being, and is a thing to relish with all our energy, while yet we have it, and to be grateful for for ever.

2.

In the last paper there was perhaps too much about mere debate; and there was nothing said at all about that kind of talk which is merely luminous and restful, a higher power of silence, the quiet of the evening shared by ruminating friends. There is something, aside from personal preference, to be alleged in support of this omission. Those who are no chimney-cornerers, who rejoice in the social thunderstorm, have a ground in reason for their choice. They get little rest indeed; but restfulness is a quality for cattle; the virtues are all active, life is alert, and it is in repose that men prepare themselves for evil. On the other hand, they are bruised into a knowledge of themselves and others; they have in a high degree the fencer's pleasure in dexterity displayed and proved; what they get they get upon life's terms, paying for it as they go; and once the talk is launched, they are assured of honest dealing from an adversary eager like themselves. The aboriginal man within us, the cave-dweller, still lusty as when he fought tooth and nail for roots and berries, scents this kind of equal battle from afar; it is like his old primæval days upon the crags, a return to the sincerity of savage life from the comfortable fictions of the civilised. And if it be delightful to the Old Man, it is none the less profitable to his younger brother, the conscientious gentleman. I feel never quite sure of your urbane and smiling coteries; I fear they indulge a man's vanities in silence, suffer him to encroach, encourage him on to be an ass, and send him forth again, not merely contemned for the moment, but radically more contemptible than when he entered. But if I have a flushed, blustering fellow for my opposite, bent on carrying a point, my vanity is sure to have its ears rubbed, once at least, in the course of the debate. He will not spare me when we differ; he will not fear to demonstrate my folly to my face.

For many natures there is not much charm in the still, chambered society, the circle of bland countenances, the digestive silence, the admired remark, the flutter of affectionate approval. They demand more atmosphere and exercise; "a gale upon their spirits," as our pious ancestors would phrase it; to have their wits well breathed in an uproarious Valhalla. And I suspect that the choice, given their character and faults, is one to be defended. The purely wise are silenced by facts; they talk in a clear atmosphere, problems lying around them like a view in nature; if they can be shown to be somewhat in the wrong, they digest the reproof like a thrashing, and make better intellectual blood. They stand corrected by a whisper; a word or a glance reminds them of the great eternal law. But it is not so with all. Others in conversation seek rather contact with their fellow-men than increase of knowledge or clarity of thought. The drama, not the philosophy, of life is the sphere of their intellectual activity. Even when they pursue truth, they desire as much as possible of what we may call human scenery along the road they follow. They dwell in the heart of life; the blood sounding in their ears, their eyes laying hold of what delights them with a brutal avidity that makes them blind to all besides, their interest riveted on people, living, loving, talking, tangible people. To a man of this description, the sphere of argument seems very pale and ghostly. By a strong expression, a perturbed countenance, floods of tears, an insult which his conscience obliges him to swallow, he is brought round to knowledge which no syllogism would have conveyed to him. His own experience is so vivid, he is so superlatively conscious of himself, that if, day after day, he is allowed to hector and hear nothing but approving echoes, he will lose his hold on the soberness of things and take himself in earnest for a god. Talk might be to such an one the very way of moral ruin; the school where he might learn to be at once intolerable and ridiculous.

This character is perhaps commoner than philosophers suppose. And for persons of that stamp to learn much by conversation, they must speak with their superiors, not in intellect, for that is a superiority that must be proved, but in station. If they cannot find a friend to bully them for their good, they must find either an old man, a woman, or some one so far below them in the artificial order of society, that courtesy may be particularly exercised.

The best teachers are the aged. To the old our mouths are always partly closed; we must swallow our obvious retorts and listen. They sit above our heads, on life's raised daïs, and appeal at once to our respect and pity. A flavour of the old school, a touch of something different in their manner—which is freer and rounder, if they come of what is called a good family, and often more timid and precise if they are of the middle class—serves, in these days, to accentuate the difference of age and add a distinction to grey hairs. But their superiority is founded more deeply than by outward marks or gestures. They are before us in the march of man; they have more or less solved the irking problem; they have battled through the equinox of life; in good and evil they have held their course; and now, without open shame, they near the crown and harbour. It may be we have been struck with one of fortune's darts; we can scarce be civil, so cruelly is our spirit tossed. Yet long be-

fore we were so much as thought upon, the like calamity befell the
old man or woman that now, with pleasant humour, rallies us
upon our inattention, sitting composed in the holy evening of
man's life, in the clear shining after rain. We grow ashamed of our
distresses, new and hot and coarse, like villainous roadside brandy;
we see life in aerial perspective, under the heavens of faith; and
out of the worst, in the mere presence of contented elders, look
forward and take patience. Fear shrinks before them "like a thing
reproved," not the flitting and ineffectual fear of death, but the instant, dwelling terror of the responsibilities and revenges of life.
Their speech, indeed, is timid; they report lions in the path; they
counsel a meticulous footing; but their serene, marred faces are
more eloquent and tell another story. Where they have gone, we
will go also, not very greatly fearing; what they have endured unbroken, we also, God helping us, will make a shift to bear.

Not only is the presence of the aged in itself remedial, but their
minds are stored with antidotes, wisdom's simples, plain considerations overlooked by youth. They have matter to communicate, be
they never so stupid. Their talk is not merely literature, it is great
literature; classic in virtue of the speaker's detachment, studded,
like a book of travel, with things we should not otherwise have
learnt. In virtue, I have said, of the speaker's detachment—and
this is why, of two old men, the one who is not your father speaks
to you with the more sensible authority; for in the paternal relation the oldest have lively interests and remain still young. Thus I
have known two young men great friends; each swore by the other's father; the father of each swore by the other lad; and yet each
pair of parent and child were perpetually by the ears. This is typical: it reads like the germ of some kindly comedy.

The old appear in conversation in two characters: the critically
silent and the garrulous anecdotic. The last is perhaps what we
look for; it is perhaps the more instructive. An old gentleman, well
on in years, sits handsomely and naturally in the bow-window of
his age, scanning experience with reverted eye; and chirping and
smiling, communicates the accidents and reads the lesson of his
long career. Opinions are strengthened, indeed, but they are also
weeded out in the course of years. What remains steadily present
to the eye of the retired veteran in his hermitage, what still ministers to his content, what still quickens his old honest heart—these
are "the real long-lived things" that Whitman tells us to prefer.

Where youth agrees with age, not where they differ, wisdom lies; and it is when the young disciple finds his heart to beat in tune with his grey-bearded teacher's that a lesson may be learned. I have known one old gentleman, whom I may name, for he is now gathered to his stock—Robert Hunter, Sheriff of Dunbarton, and author of an excellent law-book still re-edited and republished. Whether he was originally big or little is more than I can guess. When I knew him he was all fallen away and fallen in; crooked and shrunken; buckled into a stiff waistcoat for support; troubled by ailments, which kept him hobbling in and out of the room; one foot gouty; a wig for decency, not for deception, on his head; close shaved, except under his chin—and for that he never failed to apologise, for it went sore against the traditions of his life. You can imagine how he would fare in a novel by Miss Mather; yet this rag of a Chelsea veteran lived to his last year in the plenitude of all that is best in man, brimming with human kindness, and staunch as a Roman soldier under his manifold infirmities. You could not say that he had lost his memory, for he would repeat Shakespeare and Webster and Jeremy Taylor and Burke by the page together; but the parchment was filled up, there was no room for fresh inscriptions, and he was capable of repeating the same anecdote on many successive visits. His voice survived in its full power, and he took a pride in using it. On his last voyage as Commissioner of Lighthouses, he hailed a ship at sea and made himself clearly audible without a speaking-trumpet, ruffling the while with a proper vanity in his achievement. He had a habit of eking out his words with interrogative hems, which was puzzling and a little wearisome, suited ill with his appearance, and seemed a survival from some former stage of bodily portliness. Of yore, when he was a great pedestrian and no enemy to good claret, he may have pointed with these minute guns his allocutions to the bench. His humour was perfectly equable, set beyond the reach of fate; gout, rheumatism, stone, and gravel might have combined their forces against that frail tabernacle, but when I came round on Sunday evening, he would lay aside Jeremy Taylor's *Life of Christ* and greet me with the same open brow, the same kind formality of manner. His opinions and sympathies dated the man almost to a decade. He had begun life, under his mother's influence, as an admirer of Junius, but on maturer knowledge had transferred his admiration to Burke. He cautioned me, with entire gravity, to be punctilious

in writing English; never to forget that I was a Scotchman, that
English was a foreign tongue, and that if I attempted the colloquial, I should certainly be shamed: the remark was apposite, I
suppose, in the days of David Hume. Scott was too new for him;
he had known the author—known him, too, for a Tory; and to the
genuine classic a contemporary is always something of a trouble.
He had the old, serious love of the play; had even, as he was proud
to tell, played a certain part in the history of Shakespearian re-
vivals, for he had successfully pressed on Murray, of the old Edinburgh Theatre, the idea of producing Shakespeare's fairy pieces
with great scenic display. A moderate in religion, he was much
struck in the last years of his life by a conversation with two young
lads, revivalists. "H'm," he would say—"new to me. I have had—
h'm—no such experience." It struck him, not with pain, rather
with a solemn philosophic interest, that he, a Christian as he
hoped, and a Christian of so old a standing, should hear these
young fellows talking of his own subject, his own weapons that he
had fought the battle of life with—"and—h'm—not understand."
In this wise and graceful attitude he did justice to himself and
others, reposed unshaken in his old beliefs, and recognised their
limits without anger or alarm. His last recorded remark, on the
last night of his life, was after he had been arguing against Calvinism with his minister and was interrupted by an intolerable
pang. "After all," he said, "of all the 'isms, I know none so bad as
rheumatism." My own last sight of him was some time before,
when we dined together at an inn; he had been on circuit, for he
stuck to his duties like a chief part of his existence; and I remember it as the only occasion on which he ever soiled his lips with
slang—a thing he loathed. We were both Roberts; and as we took
our places at table, he addressed me with a twinkle: "We are just
what you would call two bob." He offered me port, I remember,
as the proper milk of youth; spoke of "twenty-shilling notes"; and
throughout the meal was full of old-world pleasantry and quaint-
ness, like an ancient boy on a holiday. But what I recall chiefly was
his confession that he had never read *Othello* to an end. Shakespeare was his continual study. He loved nothing better than to
display his knowledge and memory by adducing parallel passages
from Shakespeare, passages where the same word was employed, or
the same idea differently treated. But *Othello* had beaten him.
"That noble gentleman and that noble lady—h'm—too painful

for me." The same night the hoardings were covered with posters, "Burlesque of *Othello*," and the contrast blazed up in my mind like a bonfire. An unforgettable look it gave me into that kind man's soul. His acquaintance was indeed a liberal and pious education. All the humanities were taught in that bare dining-room beside his gouty footstool. He was a piece of good advice; he was himself the instance that pointed and adorned his various talk. Nor could a young man have found elsewhere a place so set apart from envy, fear, discontent, or any of the passions that debase; a life so honest and composed; a soul like an ancient violin, so subdued to harmony, responding to a touch in music—as in that dining-room, with Mr. Hunter chatting at the eleventh hour, under the shadow of eternity, fearless and gentle.

The second class of old people are not anecdotic; they are rather hearers than talkers, listening to the young with an amused and critical attention. To have this sort of intercourse to perfection, I think we must go to old ladies. Women are better hearers than men, to begin with; they learn, I fear in anguish, to bear with the tedious and infantile vanity of the other sex; and we will take more from a woman than even from the oldest man in the way of biting comment. Biting comment is the chief part, whether for profit or amusement, in this business. The old lady that I have in my eye is a very caustic speaker, her tongue, after years of practice, in absolute command, whether for silence or attack. If she chance to dislike you, you will be tempted to curse the malignity of age. But if you chance to please even slightly, you will be listened to with a particular laughing grace of sympathy, and from time to time chastised, as if in play, with a parasol as heavy as a pole-axe. It requires a singular art, as well as the vantage-ground of age, to deal these stunning corrections among the coxcombs of the young. The pill is disguised in sugar of wit; it is administered as a compliment—if you had not pleased, you would not have been censured; it is a personal affair—a hyphen, a *trait d'union,* between you and your censor; age's philandering, for her pleasure and your good. Incontestably the young man feels very much of a fool; but he must be a perfect Malvolio, sick with self-love, if he cannot take an open buffet and still smile. The correction of silence is what kills; when you know you have transgressed, and your friend says nothing and avoids your eye. If a man were made of gutta-percha, his heart would quail at such a moment. But when the word is out, the worst is over; and a fellow with any good-humour at all may pass through a perfect hail of witty criticism, every bare place on his soul hit to the quick with a shrewd missile, and reappear, as if after a dive, tingling with a fine moral reaction, and ready, with a shrinking readiness, one-third loath, for a repetition of the discipline.

There are few women, not well sunned and ripened, and perhaps toughened, who can thus stand apart from a man and say the true thing with a kind of genial cruelty. Still there are some—and I doubt if there be any man who can return the compliment. The class of man represented by Vernon Whitford in *The Egoist* says, indeed, the true thing, but he says it stockishly. Vernon is a noble fellow, and makes, by the way, a noble and instructive contrast to Daniel Deronda; his conduct is the conduct of a man of honour; but we agree with him, against our consciences, when he remorsefully considers "its astonishing dryness." He is the best of men, but the best of women manage to combine all that and something more. Their very faults assist them; they are helped even by the falseness of their position in life. They can retire into the fortified camp of the proprieties. They can touch a subject and suppress it. The most adroit employ a somewhat elaborate reserve as a means to be frank, much as they wear gloves when they shake hands. But a man has the full responsibility of his freedom, cannot evade a question, can scarce be silent without rudeness, must answer for his words upon the moment, and is not seldom left face to face with a damning choice, between the more or less dishonourable wriggling of Deronda and the downright woodenness of Vernon Whitford.

But the superiority of women is perpetually menaced; they do not sit throned on infirmities like the old; they are suitors as well as sovereigns; their vanity is engaged, their affections are too apt to follow; and hence much of the talk between the sexes degenerates into something unworthy of the name. The desire to please, to shine with a certain softness of lustre and to draw a fascinating picture of oneself, banishes from conversation all that is sterling and most of what is humourous. As soon as a strong current of mutual admiration begins to flow, the human interest triumphs entirely over the intellectual, and the commerce of words, consciously or not, becomes secondary to the commercing of eyes. But even where this ridiculous danger is avoided, and a man and woman converse equally and honestly, something in their nature or their education falsifies the strain. An instinct prompts them to agree; and where that is impossible, to agree to differ. Should they neglect the warning, at the first suspicion of an argument, they find themselves in different hemispheres. About any point of business or conduct, any actual affair demanding settlement, a woman will speak and listen, hear and answer arguments, not only with natural wisdom, but with candour and logical honesty. But if the subject of debate be something in the air, an abstraction, an excuse for talk, a logical Aunt Sally, then may the male debater instantly abandon hope; he may employ reason, adduce facts, be supple, be smiling, be angry, all shall avail him nothing; what the woman said first, that (unless she has forgotten it) she will repeat at the end. Hence, at the very junctures when a talk between men grows brighter and quicker and begins to promise to bear fruit, talk between the sexes is menaced with dissolution. The point of difference, the point of interest, is evaded by the brilliant woman, under a shower of irrelevant conversational rockets; it is bridged by the discreet woman with a rustle of silk, as she passes smoothly forward to the nearest point of safety. And this sort of prestidigitation, juggling the dangerous topic out of sight until it can be reintroduced with safety in an altered shape, is a piece of tactics among the true drawing-room queens.

The drawing-room is, indeed, an artificial place; it is so by our choice and for our sins. The subjection of women; the ideal imposed upon them from the cradle, and worn, like a hair-shirt, with so much constancy; their motherly, superior tenderness to man's vanity and self-importance; their managing arts—the arts of a civilised slave among good-natured barbarians—are all painful ingredients and all help to falsify relations. It is not till we get clear of that amusing artificial scene that genuine relations are founded, or ideas honestly compared. In the garden, on the road or the hillside, or *tête-à-tête* and apart from interruptions, occasions arise when we may learn much from any single woman; and nowhere more often than in married life. Marriage is one long conversation, chequered by disputes. The disputes are valueless; they but ingrain the difference; the heroic heart of woman prompting her at once to nail her colours to the mast. But in the intervals, almost unconsciously and with no desire to shine, the whole material of life is turned over and over, ideas are struck out and shared, the two persons more and more adapt their notions one to suit the other, and in process of time, without sound of trumpet, they conduct each other into new worlds of thought.

Father Damien

AN OPEN LETTER TO THE REVEREND DR. HYDE OF HONOLULU

✳

Sydney, February 25, 1890.

Sir,—It may probably occur to you that we have met, and visited, and conversed; on my side, with interest. You may remember that you have done me several courtesies, for which I was prepared to be grateful. But there are duties which come before gratitude, and offences which justly divide friends, far more acquaintances. Your letter to the Reverend H. B. Gage is a document, which, in my sight, if you had filled me with bread when I was starving, if you had sat up to nurse my father when he lay a-dying, would yet absolve me from the bonds of gratitude. You know enough, doubtless, of the process of canonisation to be aware that, a hundred years after the death of Damien, there will appear a man charged with the painful office of the *devil's advocate*. After that noble brother of mine, and of all frail clay, shall have lain a century at rest, one shall accuse, one defend him. The circumstance is unusual that the devil's advocate should be a volunteer, should be a member of a sect immediately rival, and should make haste to take upon himself his ugly office ere the bones are cold; unusual, and of a taste which I shall leave my readers free to qualify; unusual, and to me inspiring. If I have at all learned the trade of using words to convey truth and to arouse emotion, you have at last furnished me with a subject. For it is in the interest of all mankind and the cause of public decency in every quarter of the world, not only that Damien should be righted, but that you and your letter should be displayed at length, in their true colours, to the public eye.

To do this properly, I must begin by quoting you at large: I shall then proceed to criticise your utterance from several points of view, divine and human, in the course of which I shall attempt to draw again and with more specification the character of the dead saint whom it has pleased you to vilify: so much being done, I shall say farewell to you for ever.

> "*Honolulu, August* 2, 1889.
>
> "*Rev. H. B. Gage.*
>
> "*Dear Brother,*—In answer to your inquiries about Father Damien, I can only reply that we who knew the man are surprised at the extravagant newspaper laudations, as if he was a most saintly philanthropist. The simple truth is, he was a coarse, dirty man, headstrong and bigoted. He was not sent to Molokai, but went there without orders; did not stay at the leper settlement (before he became one himself), but circulated freely over the whole island (less than half the island is devoted to the lepers), and he came often to Honolulu. He had no hand in the reforms and improvements inaugurated, which were the work of our Board of Health, as occasion required and means were provided. He was not a pure man in his relations with women, and the leprosy of which he died should be attributed to his vices and carelessness. Others have done much for the lepers, our own ministers, the government physicians, and so forth, but never with the Catholic idea of meriting eternal life.—Yours, etc.,
>
> "*C. M. Hyde.*" *

To deal fitly with a letter so extraordinary, I must draw at the outset on my private knowledge of the signatory and his sect. It may offend others; scarcely you, who have been so busy to collect, so bold to publish, gossip on your rivals. And this is perhaps the moment when I may best explain to you the character of what you are to read: I conceive you as a man quite beyond and below the reticences of civility: with what measure you mete, with that shall it be measured you again; with you, at last, I rejoice to feel the button off the foil and to plunge home. And if in aught that I shall say I should offend others, your colleagues, whom I respect and remember with affection, I can but offer them my regret; I am not free, I am inspired by the consideration of interests far more large;

* From the Sydney *Presbyterian*, October 26, 1889.

and such pain as can be inflicted by anything from me must be indeed trifling when compared with the pain with which they read your letter. It is not the hangman, but the criminal, that brings dishonour on the house.

You belong, sir, to a sect—I believe my sect, and that in which my ancestors laboured—which has enjoyed, and partly failed to utilise, an exceptional advantage in the islands of Hawaii. The first missionaries came; they found the land already self-purged of its old and bloody faith; they were embraced, almost on their arrival, with enthusiasm; what troubles they supported came far more from whites than from Hawaiians; and to these last they stood (in a rough figure) in the shoes of God. This is not the place to enter into the degree or causes of their failure, such as it is. One element alone is pertinent, and must here be plainly dealt with. In the course of their evangelical calling, they—or too many of them— grew rich. It may be news to you that the houses of missionaries are a cause of mocking on the streets of Honolulu. It will as least be news to you, that when I returned your civil visit, the driver of my cab commented on the size, the taste, and the comfort of your home. It would have been news certainly to myself, had any one told me that afternoon that I should live to drag such matter into print. But you see, sir, how you degrade better men to your own level; and it is needful that those who are to judge betwixt you and me, betwixt Damien and the devil's advocate, should under- stand your letter to have been penned in a house which could raise, and that very justly, the envy and the comments of the passers-by. I think (to employ a phrase of yours which I admire) it "should be attributed" to you that you have never visited the scene of Damien's life and death. If you had, and had recalled it, and looked about your pleasant rooms, even your pen perhaps would have been stayed.

Your sect (and remember, as far as any sect avows me, it is mine) has not done ill in a worldly sense in the Hawaiian Kingdom. When calamity befell their innocent parishioners, when leprosy descended and took root in the Eight Islands, a *quid pro quo* was to be looked for. To that prosperous mission, and to you, as one of its adornments, God had sent at last an opportunity. I know I am touching here upon a nerve acutely sensitive. I know that others of your colleagues look back on the inertia of your Church, and the intrusive and decisive heroism of Damien, with something almost to be called remorse. I am sure it is so with yourself; I am persuaded your letter was inspired by a certain envy, not essentially ignoble, and the one human trait to be espied in that performance. You were thinking of the lost chance, the past day; of that which should have been conceived and was not; of the service due and not rendered. *Time was,* said the voice in your ear, in your pleasant room, as you sat raging and writing; and if the words written were base beyond parallel, the rage, I am happy to repeat—it is the only compliment I shall pay you—the rage was almost virtuous. But, sir, when we have failed, and another has succeeded; when we have stood by, and another has stepped in; when we sit and grow bulky in our charming mansions, and a plain, uncouth peasant steps into the battle, under the eyes of God, and succours the afflicted, and consoles the dying, and is himself afflicted in his turn, and dies upon the field of honour—the battle cannot be retrieved as your unhappy irritation has suggested. It is a lost battle, and lost for ever. One thing remained to you in your defeat—some rags of common honour; and these you have made haste to cast away.

Common honour; not the honour of having done anything right, but the honour of not having done aught conspicuously foul; the honour of the inert: that was what remained to you. We are not all expected to be Damiens; a man may conceive his duty more narrowly, he may love his comforts better; and none will cast a stone at him for that. But will a gentleman of your reverend profession allow me an example from the fields of gallantry? When two gentlemen compete for the favour of a lady, and the one succeeds and the other is rejected, and (as will sometimes happen) matter damaging to the successful rival's credit reaches the ear of the defeated, it is held by plain men of no pretensions that his mouth is, in the circumstances, almost necessarily closed. Your Church and Damien's were in Hawaii upon a rivalry to do well: to help, to edify, to set divine examples. You have (in one huge instance) failed, and Damien succeeded, I marvel it should not have occurred to you that you were doomed to silence; that when you had been outstripped in that high rivalry, and sat inglorious in the midst of your well-being, in your pleasant room—and Damien, crowned with glories and horrors, toiled and rotted in that pigstye of his under the cliffs of Kalawao—you, the elect who would not, were the last man on earth to collect and propagate gossip on the volunteer who would and did.

I think I see you—for I try to see you in the flesh as I write these sentences—I think I see you leap at the word pigstye, a hyperbolical expression at the best. "He had no hand in the reforms," he was "a coarse, dirty man"; these were your own words; and you may think it possible that I am come to support you with fresh evidence. In a sense, it is even so. Damien has been too much depicted with a conventional halo and conventional features; so drawn by men who perhaps had not the eye to remark or the pen to express the individual; or who perhaps were only blinded and silenced by generous admiration, such as I partly envy for myself—such as you, if your soul were enlightened, would envy on your bended knees. It is the least defect of such a method of portraiture that it makes the path easy for the devil's advocate, and leaves for the misuse of the slanderer a considerable field of truth. For the truth that is suppressed by friends is the readiest weapon of the enemy. The world, in your despite, may perhaps owe you something, if your letter be the means of substituting once for all a credible likeness for a wax abstraction. For, if that world at all remember you, on the day when Damien of Molokai shall be named Saint, it will be in virtue of one work: your letter to the Reverend H. B. Gage.

You may ask on what authority I speak. It was my inclement destiny to become acquainted, not with Damien, but with Dr. Hyde. When I visited the lazaretto Damien was already in his resting grave. But such information as I have, I gathered on the spot in conversation with those who knew him well and long: some indeed who revered his memory; but others who had sparred and wrangled with him, who beheld him with no halo, who perhaps regarded him with small respect, and through whose unprepared and scarcely partial communications the plain, human features of the man shone on me convincingly. These gave me what knowledge I possess; and I learnt it in that scene where it could be most completely and sensitively understood—Kalawao, which you have never visited, about which you have never so much as endeavoured to inform yourself: for, brief as your letter is, you have found the means to stumble into that confession. "*Less than one-half* of the island," you say, "is devoted to the lepers." Molokai—

"*Molokai ahima*," the "grey," lofty, and most desolate island—along all its northern side plunges in front of precipice into a sea of unusual profundity. This range of cliff is, from east to west, the true end and frontier of the island. Only in one spot there projects into the ocean a certain triangular and rugged down, grassy, stony, windy, and rising in the midst into a hill with a dead crater: the whole bearing to the cliff that overhangs it somewhat the same relation as a bracket to a wall. With this hint you will now be able to pick out the leper station on a map; you will be able to judge how much of Molokai is thus cut off between the surf and precipice, whether less than a half, or less than a quarter, or a fifth, or a tenth—or say, a twentieth; and the next time you burst into print you will be in a position to share with us the issue of your calculations.

I imagine you to be one of those persons who talk with cheerfulness of that place which oxen and wainropes could not drag you to behold. You, who do not even know its situation on the map, probably denounce sensational descriptions, stretching your limbs the while in your pleasant parlour on Beretania Street. When I was pulled ashore there one early morning, there sat with me in the boat two sisters, bidding farewell (in humble imitation of Damien) to the lights and joys of human life. One of these wept silently; I could not withhold myself from joining her. Had you been there, it is my belief that nature would have triumphed even in you; and as the boat drew but a little nearer, and you beheld the stairs crowded with abominable deformations of our common manhood, and saw yourself landing in the midst of such a population as only now and then surrounds us in the horror of a nightmare—what a haggard eye you would have rolled over your reluctant shoulder towards the house on Beretania Street! Had you gone on; had you found every fourth face a blot upon the landscape; had you visited the hospital and seen the butt-ends of human beings lying there almost unrecognisable, but still breathing, still thinking, still remembering; you would have understood that life in the lazaretto is an ordeal from which the nerves of a man's spirit shrink, even as his eye quails under the brightness of the sun; you would have felt it was (even to-day) a pitiful place to visit and a hell to dwell in. It is not the fear of possible infection. That seems a little thing when compared with the pain, the pity, and the disgust of the visitor's surroundings, and the atmosphere of affliction, disease, and physical disgrace in which he breathes. I do not think I am a man more than usually timid; but I never recall the days and nights I spent upon that island promontory (eight days and seven nights), without heartfelt thankfulness that I am somewhere else. I find in my diary that I speak of my stay as a "grinding experience": I have once jotted in the margin, *"Harrowing* is the word"; and when the *Mokolii* bore me at last towards the outer world, I kept repeating to myself, with a new conception of their pregnancy, those simple words of the song—

" 'Tis the most distressful country that ever yet was seen."

And observe: that which I saw and suffered from was a settlement purged, bettered, beautified; the new village built, the hospital and the Bishop-Home excellently arranged; the sisters, the doctor, and the missionaries, all indefatigable in their noble tasks. It was a different place when Damien came there, and made his great renunciation, and slept that first night under a tree amidst his rotting brethren: alone with pestilence; and looking forward (with what courage, with what pitiful sinkings of dread, God only knows) to a lifetime of dressing sores and stumps.

You will say, perhaps, I am too sensitive, that sights as painful abound in cancer hospitals and are confronted daily by doctors and nurses. I have long learned to admire and envy the doctors and the nurses. But there is no cancer hospital so large and populous as Kalawao and Kalaupapa; and in such a matter every fresh case, like every inch of length in the pipe of an organ, deepens the note of the impression; for what daunts the onlooker is that monstrous sum of human suffering by which he stands surrounded. Lastly, no doctor or nurse is called upon to enter once for all the doors of that gehenna; they do not say farewell, they need not abandon hope, on its sad threshold; they but go for a time to their high calling, and can look forward as they go to relief, to recreation, and to rest. But Damien shut to with his own hand the doors of his own sepulchre.

I shall now extract three passages from my diary at Kalawao.

A. "Damien is dead and already somewhat ungratefully remembered in the field of his labours and sufferings. 'He was a good man, but very officious,' says one. Another tells me he had fallen (as other priests so easily do) into something of the ways and habits of thought of a Kanaka; but he had the wit to recognise the fact, and the good sense to laugh at" [over] "it. A plain man it seems he was; I cannot find he was a popular."

B. "After Ragsdale's death" [Ragsdale was a famous Luna, or overseer, of the unruly settlement] "there followed a brief term of office by Father Damien which served only to publish the weakness of that noble man. He was rough in his ways, and he had no control. Authority was relaxed; Damien's life was threatened, and he was soon eager to resign."

C. "Of Damien I begin to have an idea. He seems to have been a man of the peasant class, certainly of the peasant type: shrewd; ignorant and bigoted, yet with an open mind, and capable of receiving and digesting a reproof if it were bluntly administered; superbly generous in the least thing as well as in the greatest, and as ready to give his last shirt (although not without human grumbling) as he had been to sacrifice his life; essentially indiscreet and officious, which made him a troublesome colleague; domineering in all his ways, which made him incurably unpopular with the Kanakas, but yet destitute of real authority, so that his boys laughed at him and he must carry out his wishes by the means of bribes. He learned to have a mania for doctoring; and set up the Kanakas against the remedies of his regular rivals: perhaps (if anything matter at all in the treatment of such a disease) the worst thing that he did, and certainly the easiest. The best and worst of the man appear very plainly in his dealings with Mr. Chapman's money; he had originally laid it out" [intended to lay it out] "entirely for the benefit of Catholics, and even so not wisely, but after a long, plain talk, he admitted his error fully and revised the list. The sad state of the boys' home is in part the result of his lack of control; in part, of his own slovenly ways and false ideas of hygiene. Brother officials used to call it 'Damien's Chinatown.' 'Well,' they would say, 'your Chinatown keeps growing.' And he would laugh with perfect good-nature, and adhere to his errors with perfect obstinacy. So much I have gathered of truth about this plain, noble human brother and father of ours; his imperfections are the traits of his face, by which we know him for our fellow; his martyrdom and his example nothing can lessen or annul; and only a person here on the spot can properly appreciate their greatness."

I have set down these private passages, as you perceive, without correction; thanks to you, the public has them in their bluntness. They are almost a list of the man's faults, for it is rather these that I was seeking: with his virtues, with the heroic profile of his life, I and the world were already sufficiently acquainted. I was besides a little suspicious of Catholic testimony; in no ill sense, but merely because Damien's admirers and disciples were the least likely to be critical. I know you will be more suspicious still; and the facts set down above were one and all collected from the lips of Protestants who had opposed the father in his life. Yet I am strangely deceived, or they build up the image of a man, with all his weaknesses, essentially heroic, and alive with rugged honesty, generosity and mirth.

Take it for what it is, rough private jottings of the worst sides of Damien's character, collected from the lips of those who had laboured with and (in your own phrase) "knew the man"—though I question whether Damien would have said that he knew you. Take it, and observe with wonder how well you were served by your gossips, how ill by your intelligence and sympathy; in how many points of fact we are at one, and how widely our appreciations vary. There is something wrong here; either with you or me. It is possible, for instance, that you, who seem to have so many ears in Kalawao, had heard of the affair of Mr. Chapman's money, and were singly struck by Damien's intended wrong-doing. I was struck with that also, and set it fairly down; but I was struck much more by the fact that he had the honesty of mind to be convinced. I may here tell you that it was a long business; that one of his colleagues sat with him late into the night, multiplying arguments and accusations; that the father listened as usual with "perfect good-nature and perfect obstinacy;" but at the last, when he was persuaded—"Yes," said he, "I am very much obliged to you; you have done me a service; it would have been a theft." There are many (not Catholics merely) who require their heroes and saints to be infallible; to these the story will be painful; not to the true lovers, patrons, and servants of mankind.

And I take it, this is a type of our division; that you are one of those who have an eye for faults and failures; that you take a pleasure to find and publish them; and that, having found them, you make haste to forget the overvailing virtues and the real success which had alone introduced them to your knowledge. It is a dangerous frame of mind. That you may understand how danger-

ous, and into what a situation it has already brought you, we will
(if you please) go hand-in-hand through the different phrases of
your letter, and candidly examine each from the point of view of
its truth, its appositeness, and its charity.

Damien was *coarse*.

It is very possible. You make us sorry for the lepers who had
only a coarse old peasant for their friend and father. But you,
who were so refined, why were you not there, to cheer them with
the lights of culture? Or may I remind you that we have some
reason to doubt if John the Baptist were genteel; and in the case
of Peter, on whose career you doubtless dwell approvingly in the
pulpit, no doubt at all he was a "coarse, headstrong" fisherman!
Yet even in our Protestant Bibles Peter is called Saint.

Damien was *dirty*.

He was. Think of the poor lepers annoyed with this dirty comrade! But the clean Dr. Hyde was at his food in a fine house.

Damien was *headstrong*.

I believe you are right again; and I thank God for his strong
head and heart.

Damien was *bigoted*.

I am not fond of bigots myself, because they are not fond of
me. But what is meant by bigotry, that we should regard it as a
blemish in a priest? Damien believed his own religion with the
simplicity of a peasant or a child; as I would I could suppose that
you do. For this, I wonder at him some way off; and had that been
his only character, should have avoided him in life. But the point
of interest in Damien, which has caused him to be so much talked
about and made him at last the subject of your pen and mine, was
that, in him, his bigotry, his intense and narrow faith, wrought
potently for good, and strengthened him to be one of the world's
heroes and exemplars.

Damien *was not sent to Molokai, but went there without orders.*

Is this a misreading? or do you really mean the words for blame?
I have heard Christ, in the pulpits of our Church, held up for
imitation on the ground that His sacrifice was voluntary. Does Dr.
Hyde think otherwise?

Damien *did not stay at the settlement, etc.*

It is true he was allowed many indulgences. Am I to understand that you blame the father for profiting by these, or the officers for granting them? In either case, it is a mighty Spartan standard to issue from the house on Beretania Street; and I am convinced you will find yourself with few supporters.

Damien *had no hand in the reforms, etc.*

I think even you will admit that I have already been frank in my description of the man I am defending; but before I take you up upon this head, I will be franker still, and tell you that perhaps nowhere in the world can a man taste a more pleasurable sense of contrast than when he passes from Damien's "Chinatown" at Kalawao to the beautiful Bishop-Home at Kalaupapa. At this point, in my desire to make all fair for you, I will break my rule and adduce Catholic testimony. Here is a passage from my diary about my visit to the Chinatown, from which you will see how it is (even now) regarded by its own officials: "We went round all the dormitories, refectories, etc.—dark and dingy enough, with a superficial cleanliness, which he" [Mr. Dutton, the lay brother] "did not seek to defend. 'It is almost decent,' said he; 'the sisters will make that all right when we get them here.'" And yet I gathered it was already better since Damien was dead, and far better than when he was there alone and had his own (not always excellent) way. I have now come far enough to meet you on a common ground of fact; and I tell you that, to a mind not prejudiced by jealousy, all the reforms of the lazaretto, and even those which he most vigorously opposed, are properly the work of Damien. They are the evidence of his success; they are what his heroism provoked from the reluctant and the careless. Many were before him in the field; Mr. Meyer, for instance, of whose faithful work we hear too little: there have been many since; and some had more worldly wisdom, though none had more devotion, than our saint. Before his day, even you will confess, they had effected little. It was his part, by one striking act of martyrdom, to direct all men's eyes on that distressful country. At a blow, and with the price of his life, he made the place illustrious and public. And that, if you will consider largely, was the one reform needful; pregnant of all that should succeed. It brought money; it brought (best individual addition of them all) the sisters; it brought supervision, for public opinion and public interest landed with the man at Kalawao. If ever any man brought reforms, and died to bring them, it was he. There is not a clean cup or towel in the Bishop-Home, but dirty Damien washed it.

Damien *was not a pure man in his relations with women, etc.*
How do you know that? Is this the nature of the conversation in that house on Beretania Street which the cabman envied, driving past?—racy details of the misconduct of the poor peasant priest, toiling under the cliffs of Molokai?

Many have visited the station before me; they seem not to have heard the rumour. When I was there I heard many shocking tales, for my informants were men speaking with the plainness of the laity; and I heard plenty of complaints of Damien. Why was this never mentioned? and how came it to you in the retirement of your clerical parlour?

But I must not even seem to deceive you. This scandal, when I read it in your letter, was not new to me. I had heard it once before; and I must tell you how. There came to Samoa a man from Honolulu; he, in a public-house on the beach, volunteered the statement that Damien had "contracted the disease from having connection with the female lepers"; and I find a joy in telling you how the report was welcomed in a public-house. A man sprang to his feet; I am not at liberty to give his name, but from what I heard I doubt if you would care to have him to dinner in Beretania Street. "You miserable little——" (here is a word I dare not print, it would so shock your ears). "You miserable little——," he cried, "if the story were a thousand times true, can't you see you are a million times a lower——for daring to repeat it?" I wish it could be told of you that when the report reached you in your house, perhaps after family worship, you had found in your soul enough holy anger to receive it with the same expressions: ay, even with that one which I dare not print; it would not need to have been blotted away, like Uncle Toby's oath, by the tears of the recording angel; it would have been counted to you for your brightest righteousness. But you have deliberately chosen the part of the man from Honolulu, and you have played it with improvements of your own. The man from Honolulu—miserable, leering creature—communicated the tale to a rude knot of beach-combing drinkers in a public-house, where (I will so far agree with your temperance opinions) man is not always at his noblest; and the man from Honolulu had himself been drinking—drinking, we may charitably fancy, to excess. It was to your "Dear Brother, the Reverend H. B. Gage," that you chose to communicate the sickening story; and the blue ribbon which adorns your portly bosom forbids me to allow you the extenuating plea that you were drunk when it was done. Your "dear brother"—a brother indeed—made haste to deliver up your letter (as a means of grace, perhaps) to the religious papers; where, after many months, I found and read and wondered at it; and whence I have now reproduced it for the wonder of others. And you and your dear brother have, by this cycle of operations, built up a contrast very edifying to examine in detail. The man whom you would not care to have to dinner, on the one side; on the other, the Reverend Dr. Hyde and the Reverend H. B. Gage: the Apia bar-room, the Honolulu manse.

But I fear you scarce appreciate how you appear to your fellow-men; and to bring it home to you, I will suppose your story to be true. I will suppose—and God forgive me for supposing it—that Damien faltered and stumbled in his narrow path of duty; I will suppose that, in the horror of his isolation, perhaps in the fever of incipient disease, he, who was doing so much more than he had sworn, failed in the letter of his priestly oath—he, who was so much a better man than either you or me, who did what we have never dreamed of daring—he too tasted of our common frailty. "O, Iago, the pity of it!" The least tender should be moved to tears; the most incredulous to prayer. And all that you could do was to pen your letter to the Reverend H. B. Gage!

Is it growing at all clear to you what a picture you have drawn of your own heart? I will try yet once again to make it clearer. You had a father: suppose this tale were about him, and some informant brought it to you, proof in hand: I am not making too high an estimate of your emotional nature when I suppose you would regret the circumstances? that you would feel the tale of frailty the more keenly since it shamed the author of your days? and that the last thing you would do would be to publish it in the religious press? Well, the man who tried to do what Damien did, is my father, and the father of the man in the Apia bar, and the father of all who love goodness; and he was your father too, if God had given you grace to see it.

An Apology for Idlers

> BOSWELL: We grow weary when idle.
>
> JOHNSON: That is, sir, because others being busy, we want company; but if we were idle, there would be no growing weary; we should all entertain one another.

JUST NOW, WHEN EVERY ONE IS BOUND, UNDER PAIN OF A DECREE in absence convicting them of *lèse*-respectability, to enter on some lucrative profession, and labour therein with something not far short of enthusiasm, a cry from the opposite party who are content when they have enough, and like to look on and enjoy in the meanwhile, savours a little of bravado and gasconade. And yet this should not be. Idleness so called, which does not consist in doing nothing, but in doing a great deal not recognised in the dogmatic formularies of the ruling class, has as good a right to state its position as industry itself. It is admitted that the presence of people who refuse to enter in the great handicap race for six-penny pieces, is at once an insult and a disenchantment for those who do. A fine fellow (as we see so many) takes his determination, votes for the sixpences, and in the emphatic Americanism, "goes for" them. And while such an one is ploughing distressfully up the road, it is not hard to understand his resentment, when he perceives cool persons in the meadows by the wayside, lying with a handkerchief over their ears and a glass at their elbow. Alexander is touched in a very delicate place by the disregard of Diogenes. Where was the glory of having taken Rome for these tumultuous barbarians, who poured into the Senate house, and found the Fathers sitting silent and unmoved by their success? It is a sore thing to have laboured along and scaled the arduous hilltops, and when all is done, find humanity indifferent to your achievement.

Hence physicists condemn the unphysical; financiers have only a superficial toleration for those who know little of stocks; literary persons despise the unlettered; and people of all pursuits combine to disparage those who have none.

But though this is one difficulty of the subject, it is not the greatest. You could not be put in prison for speaking against industry, but you can be sent to Coventry for speaking like a fool. The greatest difficulty with most subjects is to do them well; therefore, please to remember this is an apology. It is certain that much may be judiciously argued in favour of diligence; only there is something to be said against it, and that is what, on the present occasion, I have to say. To state one argument is not necessarily to be deaf to all others, and that a man has written a book of travels in Montenegro, is no reason why he should never have been to Richmond.

It is surely beyond a doubt that people should be a good deal idle in youth. For though here and there a Lord Macaulay may escape from school honours with all his wits about him, most boys pay so dear for their medals that they never afterwards have a shot in their locker, and begin the world bankrupt. And the same holds true during all the time a lad is educating himself, or suffering others to educate him. It must have been a very foolish old gentleman who addressed Johnson at Oxford in these words: "Young man, ply your book diligently now, and acquire a stock of knowledge; for when years come upon you, you will find that poring upon books will be but an irksome task." The old gentleman seems to have been unaware that many other things besides reading grow irksome, and not a few become impossible, by the time a man has to use spectacles and cannot walk without a stick. Books are good enough in their own way, but they are a mighty bloodless substitute for life. It seems a pity to sit, like the Lady of Shalott, peering into a mirror, with your back turned on all the bustle and glamour of reality. And if a man reads very hard, as the old anecdote reminds us, he will have little time for thoughts.

If you look back on your own education, I am sure it will not be the full, vivid, instructive hours of truantry that you regret; you would rather cancel some lack-lustre periods between sleep and waking in the class. For my own part, I have attended a good many lectures in my time. I still remember that the spinning of a top is a case of Kinetic Stability. I still remember that Emphyteusis is

not a disease, nor Stillicide a crime. But though I would not willingly part with such scraps of science, I do not set the same store
by them as by certain other odds and ends that I came by in the
open street while I was playing truant. This is not the moment to
dilate on that mighty place of education, which was the favourite
school of Dickens and of Balzac, and turns out yearly many inglorious masters in the Science of the Aspects of Life. Suffice it to
say this: if a lad does not learn in the streets, it is because he has
no faculty of learning. Nor is the truant always in the streets, for if
he prefers, he may go out by the gardened suburbs into the country. He may pitch on some tuft of lilacs over a burn, and smoke
innumerable pipes to the tune of the water on the stones. A bird
will sing in the thicket. And there he may fall into a vein of kindly
thought, and see things in a new perspective. Why, if this be not
education, what is? We may conceive Mr. Worldly Wiseman ac-
costing such an one, and the conversation that should thereupon
ensue:—

"How now, young fellow, what dost thou here?"

"Truly, sir, I take mine ease."

"Is not this the hour of the class? and should'st thou not be
plying thy Book with diligence, to the end thou mayest obtain
knowledge?"

"Nay, but thus also I follow after Learning, by your leave."

"Learning, quotha! After what fashion, I pray thee? Is it mathematics?"

"No, to be sure."

"Is it metaphysics?"

"Nor that."

"Is it some language?"

"Nay, it is no language."

"Is it a trade?"

"Nor a trade neither."

"Why, then, what is't?"

"Indeed, sir, as a time may soon come for me to go upon
Pilgrimage, I am desirous to note what is commonly done by
persons in my case, and where are the ugliest Sloughs and Thickets
on the Road; as also, what manner of Staff is of the best service.
Moreover, I lie here, by this water, to learn by root-of-heart a
lesson which my master teaches me to call Peace, or Contentment."

Hereupon Mr. Worldly Wiseman was much commoved with

passion, and shaking his cane with a very threatful countenance, broke forth upon this wise: "Learning, quotha!" said he; "I would have all such rogues scourged by the Hangman!"

And so he would go his way, ruffling out his cravat with a crackle of starch, like a turkey when it spread its feathers.

Now this, of Wiseman's, is the common opinion. A fact is not called a fact, but a piece of gossip, if it does not fall into one of your scholastic categories. An inquiry must be in some acknowledged direction, with a name to go by; or else you are not inquiring at all, only lounging; and the workhouse is too good for you. It is supposed that all knowledge is at the bottom of a well, or the far end of a telescope. Sainte-Beuve, as he grew older, came to regard all experience as a single great book, in which to study for a few years ere we go hence; and it seemed all one to him whether you should read in Chapter xx., which is the differential calculus, or in Chapter xxxix., which is hearing the band play in the gardens. As a matter of fact, an intelligent person, looking out of his eyes and hearkening in his ears, with a smile on his face all the time, will get more true education than many another in a life of heroic vigils. There is certainly some chill and arid knowledge to be found upon the summits of formal and laborious science; but it is all round about you, and for the trouble of looking, that you will acquire the warm and palpitating facts of life. While others are filling their memory with a lumber of words, one-half of which they will forget before the week be out, your truant may learn some really useful art: to play the fiddle, to know a good cigar, or to speak with ease and opportunity to all varieties of men. Many who have "plied their book diligently," and know all about some one branch or another of accepted lore, come out of the study with an ancient and owl-like demeanour, and prove dry, stockish, and dyspeptic in all the better and brighter parts of life. Many make a large fortune, who remain underbred and pathetically stupid to the last. And meantime there goes the idler, who began life along with them—by your leave, a different picture. He has had time to take care of his health and his spirits; he has been a great deal in the open air, which is the most salutary of all things for both body and mind; and if he has never read the great Book in very recondite places, he has dipped into it and skimmed it over to excellent purpose. Might not the student afford some Hebrew roots, and the business man some of his half-crowns, for a share of the idler's knowledge of life at large, and Art of Living? Nay, and the idler has another and more important quality than these. I mean his wisdom. He who has much looked on at the childish satisfaction of other people in their hobbies, will regard his own with only a very ironical indulgence. He will not be heard among the dogmatists. He will have a great and cool allowance for all sorts of people and opinions. If he finds no out-of-the-way truths, he will identify himself with no very burning falsehood. His way takes him along a by-road, not much frequented, but very even and pleasant, which is called Commonplace Lane, and leads to the Belvedere of Common-sense. Thence he shall command an agreeable, if no very noble prospect; and while others behold the East and West, the Devil and the Sunrise, he will be contentedly aware of a sort of morning hour upon all sublunary things, with an army of shadows running speedily and in many different directions into the great daylight of Eternity. The shadows and the generations, the shrill doctors and the plangent wars, go by into ultimate silence and emptiness; but underneath all this, a man may see, out of the Belvedere windows, much green and peaceful landscape; many firelit parlours; good people laughing, drinking, and making love as they did before the Flood or the French Revolution; and the old shepherd telling his tale under the hawthorn.

Extreme *busyness*, whether at school or college, kirk or market, is a symptom of deficient vitality; and a faculty for idleness implies a catholic appetite and a strong sense of personal identity. There is a sort of dead-alive, hackneyed people about, who are scarcely conscious of living except in the exercise of some conventional occupation. Bring these fellows into the country, or set them aboard ship, and you will see how they pine for their desk or their study. They have no curiosity; they cannot give themselves over to random provocations; they do not take pleasure in the exercise of their faculties for its own sake; and unless Necessity lays about them with a stick, they will even stand still. It is no good speaking to such folk: they *cannot* be idle, their nature is not generous enough; and they pass those hours in a sort of coma, which are not dedicated to furious moiling in the gold-mill. When they do not require to go to the office, when they are not hungry and have no mind to drink, the whole breathing world is a blank to them. If they have to wait an hour or so for a train, they fall into a stupid trance with their eyes open. To see them, you would suppose there was nothing to look at and no one to speak with; you would imagine they were paralysed or alienated; and yet very possibly they are hard workers in their own way, and have good eyesight for a flaw in a deed or a turn of the market. They have been to school and college, but all the time they had their eye on the medal; they have gone about in the world and mixed with clever people, but all the time they were thinking of their own affairs. As if a man's soul were not too small to begin with, they have dwarfed and narrowed theirs by a life of all work and no play; until here they are at forty, with a listless attention, a mind vacant of all material of amusement, and not one thought to rub against another, while they wait for the train. Before he was breeched, he might have clambered on the boxes; when he was twenty, he would have stared at the girls; but now the pipe is smoked out, the snuffbox empty, and my gentleman sits bolt upright upon a bench, with lamentable eyes. This does not appeal to me as being Success in Life.

But it is not only the person himself who suffers from his busy habits, but his wife and children, his friends and relations, and down to the very people he sits with in a railway carriage or an omnibus. Perpetual devotion to what a man calls his business, is only to be sustained by perpetual neglect of many other things. And it is not by any means certain that a man's business is the most important thing he has to do. To an impartial estimate it will seem clear that many of the wisest, most virtuous, and most beneficent parts that are to be played upon the Theatre of Life are filled by gratuitous performers, and pass, among the world at large, as phases of idleness. For in that Theatre, not only the walking gentlemen, singing chambermaids, and diligent fiddlers in the orchestra, but those who look on and clap their hands from the benches, do really play a part and fulfil important offices towards the general result. You are no doubt very dependent on the care of your lawyer and stockbroker, of the guards and signalmen who convey you rapidly from place to place, and the policemen who walk the streets for your protection; but is there not a thought of gratitude in your heart for certain other benefactors who set you smiling when they fall in your way, or season your dinner with good company? Colonel Newcome helped to lose his friend's money; Fred Bayham had an ugly trick of borrowing shirts; and yet they were better people to fall among than Mr. Barnes. And though Falstaff was neither sober nor very honest, I think I could name one or two long-faced Barabbases whom the world could better have done without. Hazlitt mentions that he was more sensible of obligation to Northcote, who had never done him any-thing he could call a service, than to his whole circle of ostenta-tious friends; for he thought a good companion emphatically the greatest benefactor. I know there are people in the world who can-not feel grateful unless the favour has been done them at the cost of pain and difficulty. But this is a churlish disposition. A man may send you six sheets of letter-paper covered with the most entertaining gossip, or you may pass half an hour pleasantly, per-haps profitably, over an article of his; do you think the service would be greater, if he had made the manuscript in his heart's blood, like a compact with the devil? Do you really fancy you should be more beholden to your correspondent, if he had been damning you all the while for your importunity? Pleasures are more beneficial than duties because, like the quality of mercy, they are not strained, and they are twice blest. There must always be two to a kiss, and there may be a score in a jest; but wherever there is an element of sacrifice, the favour is conferred with pain, and, among generous people, received with confusion. There is no duty we so much underrate as the duty of being happy. By being happy, we sow anonymous benefits upon the world, which remain un-known even to ourselves, or when they are disclosed, surprise no-body so much as the benefactor. The other day, a ragged, bare-foot boy ran down the street after a marble, with so jolly an air that he set every one he passed into a good-humour; one of these persons, who had been delivered from more than usually black thoughts, stopped the little fellow and gave him some money with this remark: "You see what sometimes comes of looking pleased." If he had looked pleased before, he had now to look both pleased and mystified. For my part, I justify this encouragement of smiling rather than tearful children; I do not wish to pay for tears any-where but upon the stage; but I am prepared to deal largely in the opposite commodity. A happy man or woman is a better thing to find than a five-pound note. He or she is a radiating focus of good-will; and their entrance into a room is as though another candle had been lighted. We need not care whether they could prove the forty-seventh proposition; they do a better thing than that, they practically demonstrate the great Theorem of the Live-ableness of Life. Consequently, if a person cannot be happy without remaining idle, idle he should remain. It is a revolutionary precept; but thanks to hunger and the workhouse, one not easily to be abused; and within practical limits, it is one of the most incontestable truths in the whole Body of Morality. Look at one of your industrous fellows for a moment, I beseech you. He sows hurry and reaps indigestion; he puts a vast deal of activity out to interest, and receives a large measure of nervous derangement in return. Either he absents himself entirely from all fellowship, and lives a recluse in a garret, with carpet slippers and a leaden inkpot; or he comes among people swiftly and bitterly, in a contraction of his whole nervous system, to discharge some temper before he returns to work. I do not care how much or how well he works, this fellow is an evil feature in other people's lives. They would be happier if he were dead. They could easier do without his services in the Circumlocution Office, than they can tolerate his fractious spirits. He poisons life at the well-head. It is better to be beggared out of hand by a scapegrace nephew, than daily hag-ridden by a peevish uncle.

And what, in God's name, is all this pother about? For what cause do they embitter their own and other people's lives? That a man should publish three or thirty articles a year, that he should finish or not finish his great allegorical picture, are questions of little interest to the world. The ranks of life are full; and although a thousand fall, there are always some to go into the breach. When they told Joan of Arc she should be at home minding women's work, she answered there were plenty to spin and wash. And so, even with your own rare gifts! When nature is "so careless of the single life," why should we coddle ourselves into the fancy that our own is of exceptional importance? Suppose Shakespeare had been knocked on the head some dark night in Sir Thomas Lucy's preserves, the world would have wagged on better or worse, the pitcher gone to the well, the scythe to the corn, and the student to his book; and no one been any the wiser of the loss. There are not many works extant, if you look the alternative all over, which are worth the price of a pound of tobacco to a man of limited means. This is a sobering reflection for the proudest of our earthly vanities. Even a tobacconist may, upon consideration, find no great cause for personal vainglory in the phrase; for al-

though tobacco is an admirable sedative, the qualities necessary
for retailing it are neither rare nor precious in themselves. Alas
and alas! you may take it how you will, but the services of no single
individual are indispensable. Atlas was just a gentleman with a
protracted nightmare! And yet you see merchants who go and
labour themselves into a great fortune and thence into the bank-
ruptcy court; scribblers who keep scribbling at little articles until
their temper is a cross to all who come about them, as though
Pharaoh should set the Israelites to make a pin instead of a pyramid; and fine young men who work themselves into a decline, and
are driven off in a hearse with white plumes upon it. Would you
not suppose these persons had been whispered, by the Master of
the Ceremonies, the promise of some momentous destiny? and that
this lukewarm bullet on which they play their farces was the bull's-
eye and centrepoint of all the universe? And yet it is not so. The
ends for which they give away their priceless youth, for all they
know, may be chimerical or hurtful; the glory and riches they expect may never come, or may find them indifferent; and they and
the world they inhabit are so inconsiderable that the mind freezes
at the thought.

Child's Play

T HE REGRET WE HAVE FOR OUR CHILDHOOD IS NOT WHOLLY JUSTI-
fiable: so much a man may lay down without fear of public
ribaldry; for although we shake our heads over the change, we
are not unconscious of the manifold advantages of our new state.
What we lose in generous impulse, we more than gain in the habit
of generously watching others; and the capacity to enjoy Shakespeare may balance a lost aptitude for playing at soldiers. Terror
is gone out of our lives, moreover; we no longer see the devil in
the bed-curtains nor lie awake to listen to the wind. We go to
school no more; and if we have only exchanged one drudgery for
another (which is by no means sure), we are set free for ever from
the daily fear of chastisement. And yet a great change has overtaken us; and although we do not enjoy ourselves less, at least we
take our pleasure differently. We need pickles nowadays to make
Wednesday's cold mutton please our Friday's appetite; and I can
remember the time when to call it red venison, and tell myself
a hunter's story, would have made it more palatable than the best
of sauces. To the grown person, cold mutton is cold mutton all the
world over; not all the mythology ever invented by man will make
it better or worse to him; the broad fact, the clamant reality, of the
mutton carries away before it such seductive figments. But for the
child it is still possible to weave an enchantment over eatables; and
if he has but read of a dish in a storybook, it will be heavenly
manna to him for a week.

If a grown man does not like eating and drinking and exercise,
if he is not something positive in his tastes, it means he has a feeble
body and should have some medicine; but children may be pure

spirits, if they will, and take their enjoyment in a world of moon-shine. Sensation does not count for so much in our first years as afterwards; something of the swaddling numbness of infancy clings about us; we see and touch and hear through a sort of golden mist. Children, for instance, are able enough to see, but they have no great faculty for looking; they do not use their eyes for the pleasure of using them, but for by-ends of their own; and the things I call to mind seeing most vividly, were not beautiful in themselves, but merely interesting or enviable to me as I thought they might be turned to practical account in play. Nor is the sense of touch so clean and poignant in children as it is in a man. If you will turn over your old memories, I think the sensations of this sort you remember will be somewhat vague, and come to not much more than a blunt, general sense of heat on summer days, or a blunt, general sense of wellbeing in bed. And here, of course, you will understand pleasurable sensations; for overmastering pain—the most deadly and tragical element in life, and the true commander of man's soul and body—alas! pain has its own way with all of us; it breaks in, a rude visitant, upon the fairy garden where the child wanders in a dream, no less surely than it rules upon the field of battle, or sends the immortal war-god whimpering to his father; and innocence, no more than philosophy, can protect us from this sting. As for taste, when we bear in mind the excesses of un-mitigated sugar which delight a youthful palate, "it is surely no very cynical asperity" to think taste a character of the maturer growth. Smell and hearing are perhaps more developed; I remem-ber many scents, many voices, and a great deal of spring singing in the woods. But hearing is capable of vast improvement as a means of pleasure; and there is all the world between gaping wonderment at the jargon of birds, and the emotion with which a man listens to articulate music.

At the same time, and step by step with this increase in the definition and intensity of what we feel which accompanies our growing age, another change takes place in the sphere of intellect, by which all things are transformed and seen through theories and associations as through coloured windows. We make to ourselves day by day, out of history, and gossip, and economical speculations, and God knows what, a medium in which we walk and through which we look abroad. We study shop windows with other eyes than in our childhood, never to wonder, not always to admire, but to make and modify our little incongruous theories about life. It is no longer the uniform of a soldier that arrests our attention; but perhaps the flowing carriage of a woman, or perhaps a countenance that has been vividly stamped with passion and carries an adventurous story written in its lines. The pleasure of surprise is passed away; sugar-loaves and water-carts seem mighty tame to encounter; and we walk the streets to make romances and to sociologise. Nor must we deny that a good many of us walk them solely for the purposes of transit or in the interest of a livelier digestion. These, indeed, may look back with mingled thoughts upon their childhood, but the rest are in a better case; they know more than when they were children, they understand better, their desires and sympathies answer more nimbly to the provocation of the senses, and their minds are brimming with interest as they go about the world.

According to my contention, this is a flight to which children cannot rise. They are wheeled in perambulators or dragged about by nurses in a pleasing stupor. A vague, faint, abiding wonderment possesses them. Here and there some specially remarkable circumstance, such as a water-cart or a guardsman, fairly penetrates into the seat of thought and calls them, for half a moment, out of themselves; and you may see them, still towed forward sideways by the inexorable nurse as by a sort of destiny, but still staring at the bright object in their wake. It may be some minutes before another such moving spectacle reawakens them to the world in which they dwell. For other children, they almost invariably show some intelligent sympathy. "There is a fine fellow making mud pies," they seem to say; "that I can understand, there is some sense in mud pies." But the doings of their elders, unless where they are speakingly picturesque or recommend themselves by the quality of being easily imitable, they let them go over their heads (as we say) without the least regard. If it were not for this perpetual imitation, we should be tempted to fancy they despised us outright, or only considered us in the light of creatures brutally strong and brutally silly; among whom they condescended to dwell in obedience like a philosopher at a barbarous court. At times, indeed, they display an arrogance of disregard that is truly staggering. Once, when I was groaning aloud with physical pain, a young gentleman came into the room and nonchalantly inquired if I had seen his bow and arrow. He made no account of my groans, which he accepted, as he had to accept so much else, as a piece of the inexplicable conduct of his elders; and like a wise young gentleman, he would waste no wonder on the subject. Those elders, who care so little for rational enjoyment, and are even the enemies of rational enjoyment for others, he had accepted without understanding and without complaint, as the rest of us accept the scheme of the universe.

We grown people can tell ourselves a story, give and take strokes until the bucklers ring, ride far and fast, marry, fall, and die; all the while sitting quietly by the fire or lying prone in bed. This is exactly what a child cannot do, or does not do, at least, when he can find anything else. He works all with lay figures and stage properties. When his story comes to the fighting, he must rise, get something by way of a sword and have a set-to with a piece of furniture, until he is out of breath. When he comes to ride with the king's pardon, he must bestride a chair, which he will so hurry and belabour and on which he will so furiously demean himself, that the messenger will arrive, if not bloody with spurring, at least fiery red with haste. If his romance involves an accident upon a cliff, he must clamber in person about the chest of drawers and fall bodily upon the carpet, before his imagination is satisfied. Lead soldiers, dolls, all toys, in short, are in the same category and answer the same end. Nothing can stagger a child's faith; he accepts the clumsiest substitutes and can swallow the most staring incongruities. The chair he has just been besieging as a castle, or valiantly cutting to the ground as a dragon, is taken away for the accommodation of a morning visitor, and he is nothing abashed; he can skirmish by the hour with a stationary coal-scuttle; in the midst of the enchanted pleasance, he can see, without sensible shock, the gardener soberly digging potatoes for the day's dinner. He can make abstraction of whatever does not fit into his fable; and he puts his eyes into his pocket, just as we hold our noses in an unsavoury lane. And so it is, that although the ways of children cross with those of their elders in a hundred places daily, they never go in the same direction nor so much as lie in the same element. So may the telegraph wires intersect the line of the highroad, or so might a landscape painter and a bagman visit the same country, and yet move in different worlds.

People struck with these spectacles, cry aloud about the power of imagination in the young. Indeed there may be two words to that.

It is, in some ways, but a pedestrian fancy that the child exhibits.
It is the grown people who make the nursery stories; all the children
do, is jealously to preserve the text. One out of a dozen reasons
why *Robinson Crusoe* should be so popular with youth, is that it
hits their level in this matter to a nicety; Crusoe was always at
makeshifts and had, in so many words, to *play* at a great variety
of professions; and then the book is all about tools, and there is
nothing that delights a child so much. Hammers and saws belong
to a province of life that positively calls for imitation. The juvenile
lyrical drama, surely of the most ancient Thespian model, wherein
the trades of mankind are successively simulated to the running
burthen "On a cold and frosty morning," gives a good instance of
the artistic taste in children. And this need for overt action and
lay figures testifies to a defect in the child's imagination which
prevents him from carrying out his novels in the privacy of his
own heart. He does not yet know enough of the world and men.
His experience is incomplete. That stage-wardrobe and scene-room
that we call the memory is so ill provided, that he can overtake few
combinations and body out few stories, to his own content, without
some external aid. He is at the experimental stage; he is not sure
how one would feel in certain circumstances; to make sure, he must
come as near trying it as his means permit. And so here is young
heroism with a wooden sword, and mothers practise their kind
vocation over a bit of jointed stick. It may be laughable enough
just now; but it is these same people and these same thoughts,
that not long hence, when they are on the theatre of life, will
make you weep and tremble. For children think very much the
same thoughts and dream the same dreams, as bearded men and
marriageable women. No one is more romantic. Fame and honour,
the love of young men and the love of mothers, the business man's
pleasure in method, all these and others they anticipate and rehearse in their play hours. Upon us, who are further advanced and
fairly dealing with the threads of destiny, they only glance from
time to time to glean a hint for their own mimetic reproduction.
Two children playing at soldiers are far more interesting to each
other than one of the scarlet beings whom both are busy imitating.
This is perhaps the greatest oddity of all. "Art for Art" is their
motto; and the doings of grown folk are only interesting as the raw
material for play. Not Théophile Gautier, not Flaubert, can look
more callously upon life, or rate the reproduction more highly

over the reality; and they will parody an execution, a deathbed, or the funeral of the young man of Nain, with all the cheerfulness in the world.

The true parallel for play is not to be found, of course, in conscious art, which, though it be derived from play, is itself an abstract, impersonal thing, and depends largely upon philosophical interests beyond the scope of childhood. It is when we make castles in the air and personate the leading character in our own romances, that we return to the spirit of our first years. Only, there are several reasons why the spirit is no longer so agreeable to indulge. Nowadays, when we admit this personal element into our divagations we are apt to stir up uncomfortable and sorrowful memories, and remind ourselves sharply of old wounds. Our day-dreams can no longer lie all in the air like a story in the *Arabian Nights;* they read to us rather like the history of a period in which we ourselves had taken part, where we come across many unfortunate passages and find our own conduct smartly reprimanded. And then the child, mind you, acts his parts. He does not merely repeat them to himself; he leaps, he runs, and sets the blood agog over all his body. And so his play breathes him; and he no sooner assumes a passion than he gives it vent. Alas! when we betake ourselves to our intellectual form of play, sitting quietly by the fire or lying prone in bed, we rouse many hot feelings for which we can find no outlet. Substitutes are not acceptable to the mature mind, which desires the thing itself; and even to rehearse a triumphant dialogue with one's enemy, although it is perhaps the most satisfactory piece of play still left within our reach, is not entirely satisfying, and is even apt to lead to a visit and an interview which may be the reverse of triumphant after all.

In the child's world of dim sensation, play is all in all. "Making believe" is the gist of his whole life, and he cannot so much as take a walk except in character. I could not learn my alphabet without some suitable *mise-en-scène,* and had to act a business man in an office before I could sit down to my book. Will you kindly question your memory, and find out how much you did, work or pleasure, in good faith and soberness, and for how much you had to cheat yourself with some invention? I remember, as though it were yesterday, the expansion of spirit, the dignity and self-reliance, that came with a pair of mustachios in burnt cork, even when there was none to see. Children are even content to forego what we call the realities, and prefer the shadow to the substance. When they might be speaking intelligibly together, they chatter senseless gibberish by the hour, and are quite happy because they are making believe to speak French. I have said already how even the imperious appetite of hunger suffers itself to be gulled and led by the nose with the fag end of an old song. And it goes deeper than this: when children are together even a meal is felt as an interruption in the business of life; and they must find some imaginative sanction, and tell themselves some sort of story, to account for, to colour, to render entertaining, the simple processes of eating and drinking. What wonderful fancies I have heard evolved out of the pattern upon tea-cups!—from which there followed a code of rules and a whole world of excitement, until tea-drinking began to take rank as a game. When my cousin and I took our porridge of a morning, we had a device to enliven the course of the meal. He ate his with sugar, and explained it to be a country continually buried under snow. I took mine with milk, and explained it to be a country suffering gradual inundation. You can imagine us exchanging bulletins; how here was an island still unsubmerged, here a valley not yet covered with snow; what inventions were made; how his population lived in cabins on perches and travelled on stilts, and how mine was always in boats; how the interest grew furious, as the last corner of safe ground was cut off on all sides and grew smaller every moment; and how, in fine, the food was of altogether secondary importance, and might even have been nauseous, so long as we seasoned it with these dreams. But perhaps the most exciting moments I ever had over a meal, were in the case of calves' feet jelly. It was hardly possible not to believe—and you may be sure, so far from trying, I did all I could to favour the illusion—that some part of it was hollow, and that sooner or later my spoon would lay open the secret tabernacle of the golden rock. There, might some miniature *Red Beard* await his hour; there, might one find the treasures of the *Forty Thieves,* and bewildered Cassim beating about the walls. And so I quarried on slowly, with bated breath, savouring the interest. Believe me, I had little palate left for the jelly; and though I preferred the taste when I took cream with it, I used often to go without, because the cream dimmed the transparent fractures.

Even with games, this spirit is authoritative with right-minded children. It is thus that hide-and-seek has so pre-eminent a sovereignty, for it is the well-spring of romance, and the actions and the excitement to which it gives rise lend themselves to almost any sort of fable. And thus cricket, which is a mere matter of dexterity, palpably about nothing and for no end, often fails to satisfy infantile craving. It is a game, if you like, but not a game of play. You cannot tell yourself a story about cricket; and the activity it calls forth can be justified on no rational theory. Even football, although it admirably simulates the tug and the ebb and flow of battle, has presented difficulties to the mind of young sticklers after verisimilitude; and I knew at least one little boy who was mightily exercised about the presence of the ball, and had to spirit himself up, whenever he came to play, with an elaborate story of enchantment, and take the missile as a sort of talisman bandied about in conflict between two Arabian nations.

To think of such a frame of mind, is to become disquieted about the bringing up of children. Surely they dwell in a mythological epoch, and are not the contemporaries of their parents. What can they think of them? what can they make of these bearded or petticoated giants who look down upon their games? who move upon a cloudy Olympus, following unknown designs apart from rational enjoyment? who profess the tenderest solicitude for children, and yet every now and again reach down out of their altitude and terribly vindicate the prerogatives of age? Off goes the child, corporally smarting, but morally rebellious. Were there ever such unthinkable deities as parents? I would give a great deal to know what, in nine cases out of ten, is the child's unvarnished feeling. A sense of past cajolery; a sense of personal attraction, at best very feeble; above all, I should imagine, a sense of terror for the untried residue of mankind: go to make up the attraction that he feels. No wonder, poor little heart, with such a weltering world in front of him, if he clings to the hand he knows! The dread irrationality of the whole affair, as it seems to children, is a thing we are all too ready to forget. "O, why," I remember passionately wondering, "why can we not all be happy and devote ourselves to play?" And when children do philosophise, I believe it is usually to very much the same purpose.

One thing, at least, comes very clearly out of these considerations; that whatever we are to expect at the hands of children, it should not be any peddling exactitude about matters of fact. They walk in a vain show, and among mists and rainbows; they are passionate after dreams and unconcerned about realities; speech is a difficult art not wholly learned; and there is nothing in their own tastes or purposes to teach them what we mean by abstract truthfulness. When a bad writer is inexact, even if he can look back on half a century of years, we charge him with incompetence and not with dishonesty. And why not extend the same allowance to imperfect speakers? Let a stockbroker be dead stupid about poetry, or a poet inexact in the details of business, and we excuse them heartily from blame. But show us a miserable, unbreeched, human entity, whose whole profession it is to take a tub for a fortified town and a shaving-brush for the deadly stiletto, and who passes three-fourths of his time in a dream and the rest in open self-deception, and we expect him to be as nice upon a matter of fact as a scientific expert bearing evidence. Upon my heart, I think it less than decent. You do not consider how little the child sees, or how swift he is to weave what he has seen into bewildering fiction; and that he cares no more for what you call truth, than you for a gingerbread dragoon.

I am reminded, as I write, that the child is very inquiring as to the precise truth of stories. But indeed this is a very different matter, and one bound up with the subject of play, and the precise amount of playfulness, or playability, to be looked for in the world. Many such burning questions must arise in the course of nursery education. Among the fauna of this planet, which already embraces the pretty soldier and the terrifying Irish beggarman, is, or is not, the child to expect a Bluebeard or a Cormoran? Is he, or is he not, to look out for magicians, kindly and potent? May he, or may he not, reasonably hope to be cast away upon a desert island, or turned to such diminutive proportions that he can live on equal terms with his lead soldiery, and go a cruise in his own toy schooner? Surely all these are practical questions to a neophyte entering upon life with a view to play. Precision upon such a point, the child can understand. But if you merely ask him of his past behaviour, as to who threw such a stone, for instance, or struck such and such a match; or whether he had looked into a parcel or gone by a forbidden path—why, he can see no moment in the inquiry, and it is ten to one, he has already half forgotten and half bemused himself with subsequent imaginings.

It would be easy to leave them in their native cloud-land, where they figure so prettily—pretty like flowers and innocent like dogs. They will come out of their gardens soon enough, and have to go into offices and the witness-box. Spare them yet awhile, O conscientious parent! Let them doze among their playthings yet a little! for who knows what a rough, warfaring existence lies before them in the future?

Æs Triplex

THE CHANGES WROUGHT BY DEATH ARE IN THEMSELVES SO SHARP
and final, and so terrible and melancholy in their consequences, that the thing stands alone in man's experience, and has
no parallel upon earth. It outdoes all other accidents because it is
the last of them. Sometimes it leaps suddenly upon its victims, like
a Thug; sometimes it lays a regular siege and creeps upon their
citadel during a score of years. And when the business is done,
there is sore havoc made in other people's lives, and a pin knocked
out by which many subsidiary friendships hung together. There
are empty chairs, solitary walks, and single beds at night. Again,
in taking away our friends, death does not take them away utterly,
but leaves behind a mocking, tragical, and soon intolerable residue, which must be hurriedly concealed. Hence a whole chapter
of sights and customs striking to the mind, from the pyramids of
Egypt to the gibbets and dule trees of mediæval Europe. The
poorest persons have a bit of pageant going towards the tomb;
memorial stones are set up over the least memorable; and, in order
to preserve some show of respect for what remains of our old loves
and friendships, we must accompany it with much grimly ludicrous
ceremonial, and the hired undertaker parades before the door. All
this, and much more of the same sort, accompanied by the eloquence of poets, has gone a great way to put humanity in error;
nay, in many philosophies the error has been embodied and laid
down with every circumstance of logic; although in real life the
bustle and swiftness, in leaving people little time to think, have not
left them time enough to go dangerously wrong in practice.

As a matter of fact, although few things are spoken of with more

fearful whisperings than this prospect of death, few have less influence on conduct under healthy circumstances. We have all heard
of cities in South America built upon the side of fiery mountains,
and how, even in this tremendous neighbourhood, the inhabitants
are not a jot more impressed by the solemnity of mortal conditions
than if they were delving gardens in the greenest corner of England. There are serenades and suppers and much gallantry among
the myrtles overhead; and meanwhile the foundation shudders
underfoot, the bowels of the mountain growl, and at any moment
living ruin may leap sky-high into the moonlight, and tumble man
and his merry-making in the dust. In the eyes of very young people, and very dull old ones, there is something indescribably reckless and desperate in such a picture. It seems not credible that
respectable married people, with umbrellas, should find appetite
for a bit of supper within quite a long distance of a fiery mountain;
ordinary life begins to smell of high-handed debauch when it is
carried on so close to a catastrophe; and even cheese and salad,
it seems, could hardly be relished in such circumstances without
something like a defiance of the Creator. It should be a place for
nobody but hermits dwelling in prayer and maceration, or mere
born-devils drowning care in a perpetual carouse.

And yet, when one comes to think upon it calmly, the situation
of these South American citizens forms only a very pale figure for
the state of ordinary mankind. This world itself, travelling blindly
and swiftly in overcrowded space, among a million other worlds
travelling blindly and swiftly in contrary directions, may very well
come by a knock that would set it into explosion like a penny
squib. And what, pathologically looked at, is the human body with
all its organs, but a mere bagful of petards? The least of these is as
dangerous to the whole economy as the ship's powder-magazine to
the ship; and with every breath we breathe, and every meal we eat,
we are putting one or more of them in peril. If we clung as de-
votedly as some philosophers pretend we do to the abstract idea
of life, or were half as frightened as they make out we are, for the
subversive accident that ends it all, the trumpets might sound by
the hour and no one would follow them into battle—the blue-
peter might fly at the truck, but who would climb into a sea-going
ship? Think (if these philosophers were right) with what a preparation of spirit we should affront the daily peril of the dinner-table:
a deadlier spot than any battle-field in history, where the far

greater proportion of our ancestors have miserably left their bones!
What woman would ever be lured into marriage, so much more
dangerous than the wildest sea? And what would it be to grow old?
For, after a certain distance, every step we take in life we find the
ice growing thinner below our feet, and all around us and behind
us we see our contemporaries going through. By the time a man
gets well into the seventies, his continued existence is a mere miracle; and when he lays his old bones in bed for the night, there is an
overwhelming probability that he will never see the day. Do the
old men mind it, as a matter of fact? Why, no. They were never
merrier; they have their grog at night, and tell the raciest stories;
they hear of the death of people about their own age, or even
younger, not as if it was a grisly warning, but with a simple childlike pleasure at having outlived some one else; and when a draught
might puff them out like a guttering candle, or a bit of a stumble
shatter them like so much glass, their old hearts keep sound and
unaffrighted, and they go on, bubbling with laughter, through
years of man's age compared to which the valley at Balaclava was
as safe and peaceful as a village cricket-green on Sunday. It may
fairly be questioned (if we look to the peril only) whether it was
a much more daring feat for Curtius to plunge into the gulf, than
for any old gentleman of ninety to doff his clothes and clamber
into bed.

Indeed, it is a memorable subject for consideration, with what
unconcern and gaiety mankind pricks on along the Valley of the
Shadow of Death. The whole way is one wilderness of snares, and
the end of it, for those who fear the last pinch, is irrevocable ruin.
And yet we go spinning through it all, like a party for the Derby.
Perhaps the reader remembers one of the humourous devices of
the deified Caligula: how he encouraged a vast concourse of holi-
day-makers on to his bridge over Baiæ bay; and when they were in
the height of their enjoyment, turned loose the Prætorian guards
among the company, and had them tossed into the sea. This is no
bad miniature of the dealings of nature with the transitory race of
man. Only, what a chequered picnic we have of it, even while it
lasts! and into what great waters, not to be crossed by any swimmer,
God's pale Prætorian throws us over in the end!

We live the time that a match flickers; we pop the cork of a
ginger-beer bottle, and the earthquake swallows us on the instant.
Is it not odd, is it not incongruous, is it not, in the highest sense

of human speech, incredible, that we should think so highly of the ginger-beer, and regard so little the devouring earthquake? The love of Life and the fear of Death are two famous phrases that grow harder to understand the more we think about them. It is a well-known fact that an immense proportion of boat accidents would never happen if people held the sheet in their hands instead of making it fast; and yet, unless it be some martinet of a professional mariner or some landsman with shattered nerves, every one of God's creatures makes it fast. A strange instance of man's unconcern and brazen boldness in the face of death!

We confound ourselves with metaphysical phrases, which we import into daily talk with noble inappropriateness. We have no idea of what death is, apart from its circumstances and some of its consequences to others; and although we have some experience of living, there is not a man on earth who has flown so high into abstraction as to have any practical guess at the meaning of the word *life*. All literature, from Job and Omar Khayyam to Thomas Carlyle or Walt Whitman, is but an attempt to look upon the human state with such largeness of view as shall enable us to rise from the consideration of living to the Definition of Life. And our sages give us about the best satisfaction in their power when they say that it is a vapour, or a show, or made out of the same stuff with dreams. Philosophy, in its more rigid sense, has been at the same work for ages; and after a myriad bald heads have wagged over the problem, and piles of words have been heaped one upon another into dry and cloudy volumes without end, philosophy has the honour of laying before us, with modest pride, her contribution towards the subject: that life is a Permanent Possibility of Sensation. Truly a fine result! A man may very well love beef, or hunting, or a woman; but surely, surely, not a Permanent Possibility of Sensation! He may be afraid of a precipice, or a dentist, or a large enemy with a club, or even an undertaker's man; but not certainly of abstract death. We may trick with the word life in its dozen senses until we are weary of tricking; we may argue in terms of all the philosophies on earth, but one fact remains true throughout—that we do not love life, in the sense that we are greatly preoccupied about its conservation; that we do not, properly speaking, love life at all, but living. Into the views of the least careful there will enter some degree of providence; no man's eyes are fixed entirely on the passing hour; but although we have some anticipation

of good health, good weather, wine, active employment, love, and
self-approval, the sum of these anticipations does not amount to
anything like a general view of life's possibilities and issues; nor
are those who cherish them most vividly, at all the most scrupulous
of their personal safety. To be deeply interested in the accidents of
our existence, to enjoy keenly the mixed texture of human experience, rather leads a man to disregard precautions, and risk his
neck against a straw. For surely the love of living is stronger in an
Alpine climber roping over a peril, or a hunter riding merrily at a
stiff fence, than in a creature who lives upon a diet and walks a
measured distance in the interest of his constitution.

There is a great deal of very vile nonsense talked upon both
sides of the matter: tearing divines reducing life to the dimensions
of a mere funeral procession, so short as to be hardly decent; and
melancholy unbelievers yearning for the tomb as if it were a world
too far away. Both sides must feel a little ashamed of their per-
formances now and again when they draw in their chairs to dinner.
Indeed, a good meal and a bottle of wine is an answer to most
standard works upon the question. When a man's heart warms to
his viands, he forgets a great deal of sophistry, and soars into a rosy
zone of contemplation. Death may be knocking at the door, like the
Commander's statue; we have something else in hand, thank God,
and let him knock. Passing bells are ringing all the world over.
All the world over, and every hour, some one is parting company
with all his aches and ecstasies. For us also the trap is laid. But we
are so fond of life that we have no leisure to entertain the terror of
death. It is a honeymoon with us all through, and none of the
longest. Small blame to us if we give our whole hearts to this glowing bride of ours, to the appetites, to honour, to the hungry curiosity of the mind, to the pleasure of the eyes in nature, and the
pride of our own nimble bodies.

We all of us appreciate the sensations; but as for caring about
the Permanence of the Possibility, a man's head is generally very
bald, and his senses very dull, before he comes to that. Whether
we regard life as a lane leading to a dead wall—a mere bag's end,
as the French say—or whether we think of it as a vestibule or
gymnasium, where we wait our turn and prepare our faculties for
some more noble destiny; whether we thunder in a pulpit, or pule
in little atheistic poetry-books, about its vanity and brevity;
whether we look justly for years of health and vigour, or are about

to mount into a Bath-chair, as a step towards the hearse; in each and all of these views and situations there is but one conclusion possible: that a man should stop his ears against paralysing terror, and run the race that is set before him with a single mind. No one surely could have recoiled with more heartache and terror from the thought of death than our respected lexicographer; and yet we know how little it affected his conduct, how wisely and boldly he walked, and in what a fresh and lively vein he spoke of life. Already an old man, he ventured on his Highland tour; and his heart, bound with triple brass, did not recoil before twenty-seven individual cups of tea. As courage and intelligence are the two qualities best worth a good man's cultivation, so it is the first part of intelligence to recognise our precarious estate in life, and the first part of courage to be not at all abashed before the fact. A frank and somewhat headlong carriage, not looking too anxiously before, not dallying in maudlin regret over the past, stamps the man who is well armoured for this world.

And not only well armoured for himself, but a good friend and a good citizen to boot. We do not go to cowards for tender dealing; there is nothing so cruel as panic; the man who has least fear for his own carcass, has most time to consider others. That eminent chemist who took his walks abroad in tin shoes, and subsisted wholly upon tepid milk, had all his work cut out for him in considerate dealings with his own digestion. So soon as prudence has begun to grow up in the brain, like a dismal fungus, it finds its first expression in a paralysis of generous acts. The victim begins to shrink spiritually; he develops a fancy for parlours with a regulated temperature, and takes his morality on the principle of tin shoes and tepid milk. The care of one important body or soul becomes so engrossing, that all the noises of the outer world begin to come thin and faint into the parlour with the regulated temperature; and the tin shoes go equably forward over blood and rain. To be overwise is to ossify; and the scruple-monger ends by standing stockstill. Now the man who has his heart on his sleeve, and a good whirling weathercock of a brain, who reckons his life as a thing to be dashingly used and cheerfully hazarded, makes a very different acquaintance of the world, keeps all his pulses going true and fast, and gathers impetus as he runs, until, if he be running towards anything better than wildfire, he may shoot up and become a constellation in the end. Lord look after his health, Lord have a care of his soul, says he; and he has at the key of the position, and swashes through incongruity and peril towards his aim. Death is on all sides of him with pointed batteries, as he is on all sides of all of us; unfortunate surprises gird him round; mimmouthed friends and relations hold up their hands in quite a little elegiacal synod about his path: and what cares he for all this? Being a true lover of living, a fellow with something pushing and spontaneous in his inside, he must, like any other soldier, in any other stirring, deadly warfare, push on at his best pace until he touch the goal. "A peerage or Westminster Abbey!" cried Nelson in his bright, boyish, heroic manner. These are great incentives; not for any of these, but for the plain satisfaction of living, of being about their business in some sort or other, do the brave, serviceable men of every nation tread down the nettle danger, and pass flyingly over all the stumbling-blocks of prudence. Think of the heroism of Johnson, think of that superb indifference to mortal limitation that set him upon his dictionary, and carried him through triumphantly until the end! Who, if he were wisely considerate of things at large, would ever embark upon any work much more considerable than a halfpenny post card? Who would project a serial novel, after Thackeray and Dickens had each fallen in mid-course? Who would find heart enough to begin to live, if he dallied with the consideration of death?

And, after all, what sorry and pitiful quibbling all this is! To forego all the issues of living in a parlour with a regulated temperature—as if that were not to die a hundred times over, and for ten years at a stretch! As if it were not to die in one's own lifetime, and without even the sad immunities of death! As if it were not to die, and yet be the patient spectators of our own pitiable change! The Permanent Possibility is preserved, but the sensations carefully held at arm's length, as if one kept a photographic plate in a dark chamber. It is better to lose health like a spendthrift than to waste it like a miser. It is better to live and be done with it, than to die daily in the sickroom. By all means begin your folio; even if the doctor does not give you a year, even if he hesitates about a month, make one brave push and see what can be accomplished in a week. It is not only in finished undertakings that we ought to honour useful labour. A spirit goes out of the man who means execution, which outlives the most untimely ending. All who have meant good work with their whole hearts, have done good work, although they may die before they have the time to sign it. Every heart that has beat strong and cheerfully has left a hopeful impulse behind it in the world, and bettered the tradition of mankind. And even if death catch people, like an open pitfall, and in mid-career, laying out vast projects, and planning monstrous foundations, flushed with hope, and their mouths full of boastful language, they should be at once tripped up and silenced: is there not something brave and spirited in such a termination? and does not life go down with a better grace, foaming in full body over a precipice, than miserably straggling to an end in sandy deltas? When the Greeks made their fine saying that those whom the gods love die young, I cannot help believing they had this sort of death also in their eye. For surely, at whatever age it overtake the man, this is to die young. Death has not been suffered to take so much as an allusion from his heart. In the hot-fit of life, a-tiptoe on the highest point of being, he passes at a bound on to the other side. The noise of the mallet and chisel is scarcely quenched, the trumpets are hardly done blowing, when, trailing with him clouds of glory, this happy-starred, full-blooded spirit shoots into the spiritual land.

Old Mortality

1

THERE IS A CERTAIN GRAVEYARD, LOOKED UPON ON THE ONE SIDE BY a prison, on the other by the windows of a quiet hotel; below, under a steep cliff, it beholds the traffic of many lines of rail, and the scream of the engine and the shock of meeting buffers mount to it all day long. The aisles are lined with the inclosed sepulchres of families, door beyond door, like houses in a street; and in the morning the shadow of the prison turrets, and of many tall memorials, fall upon the graves. There, in the hot fits of youth, I came to be unhappy. Pleasant incidents are woven with my memory of the place. I here made friends with a certain plain old gentleman, a visitor on sunny mornings, gravely cheerful, who, with one eye upon the place that awaited him, chirped about his youth like winter sparrows; a beautiful housemaid of the hotel once, for some days together, dumbly flirted with me from a window and kept my wild heart flying; and once—she possibly remembers—the wise Eugenia followed me to that austere inclosure. Her hair came down, and in the shelter of the tomb my trembling fingers helped her to repair the braid. But for the most part I went there solitary and, with irrevocable emotion, pored on the names of the forgotten. Name after name, and to each the conventional attributions and the idle dates: a regiment of the unknown that had been the joy of mothers, and had thrilled with the illusions of youth, and at last, in the dim sick-room, wrestled with the pangs of old mortality. In that whole crew of the silenced there was but one of whom my fancy had received a picture; and he, with his comely, florid countenance, bewigged and habited in scarlet, and in his day combining fame and popularity, stood forth, like a taunt, among that company of phantom appellations. It was then possible to leave behind us something more explicit than these severe, monotonous, and lying epitaphs; and the thing left, the memory of a painted picture and what we call the immortality of a name, was hardly more desirable than mere oblivion. Even David Hume, as he lay composed beneath that "circular idea," was fainter than a dream; and when the housemaid, broom in hand, smiled and beckoned from the open window, the fame of that bewigged philosopher melted like a raindrop in the sea.

And yet in soberness I cared as little for the housemaid as for David Hume. The interests of youth are rarely frank; his passions, like Noah's dove, come home to roost. The fire, sensibility, and volume of his own nature, that is all that he has learned to recognise. The tumultuary and grey tide of life, the empire of routine, the unrejoicing faces of his elders, fill him with contemptuous surprise; there also he seems to walk among the tombs of spirits; and it is only in the course of years, and after much rubbing with his fellowmen, that he begins by glimpses to see himself from without and his fellows from within: to know his own for one among the thousand undenoted countenances of the city street, and to divine in others the throb of human agony and hope. In the meantime he will avoid the hospital doors, the pale faces, the cripple, the sweet whiff of chloroform—for there, on the most thoughtless, the pains of others are burned home; but he will continue to walk, in a divine self-pity, the aisles of the forgotten graveyard. The length of man's life, which is endless to the brave and busy, is scorned by his ambitious thought. He cannot bear to have come for so little, and to go again so wholly. He cannot bear, above all, in that brief scene, to be still idle, and by way of cure, neglects the little that he has to do. The parable of the talent is the brief epitome of youth. To believe in immortality is one thing, but it is first needful to believe in life. Denunciatory preachers seem not to suspect that they may be taken gravely and in evil part; that young men may come to think of time as of a moment, and with the pride of Satan wave back the inadequate gift. Yet here is a true peril; this it is that sets them to pace the graveyard alleys and to read, with strange extremes of pity and derision, the memorials of the dead.

Books were the proper remedy: books of vivid human import,

forcing upon their minds the issues, pleasures, busyness, importance, and immediacy of that life in which they stand; books of
smiling or heroic temper, to excite or to console; books of a large
design, shadowing the complexity of that game of consequences to
which we all sit down, the hanger-back not least. But the average
sermon flees the point, disporting itself in that eternity of which
we know, and need to know, so little; avoiding the bright, crowded,
and momentous fields of life where destiny awaits us. Upon the
average book a writer may be silent; he may set it down to his ill-
hap that when his own youth was in the acrid fermentation, he
should have fallen and fed upon the cheerless fields of Obermann.
Yet to Mr. Arnold, who led him to these pastures, he still bears a
grudge. The day is perhaps not far off when people will begin to
count *Moll Flanders*, ay, or *The Country Wife*, more wholesome
and more pious diet than these guidebooks to consistent egoism.

But the most inhuman of boys soon wearies of the inhumanity of
Obermann. And even while I still continued to be a haunter of the
graveyard, I began insensibly to turn my attention to the grave-
diggers, and was weaned out of myself to observe the conduct of
visitors. This was day-spring, indeed, to a lad in such great darkness. Not that I began to see men, or to try to see them, from
within, nor to learn charity and modesty and justice from the
sight; but still stared at them externally from the prison windows
of my affectation. Once I remember to have observed two working-
women with a baby halting by a grave; there was something mon-
umental in the grouping, one upright carrying the child, the other
with bowed face crouching by her side. A wreath of immortelles
under a glass dome had thus attracted them; and, drawing near, I
overheard their judgment on that wonder. "Eh! what extravagance!" To a youth afflicted with the callosity of sentiment, this
quaint and pregnant saying appeared merely base.

My acquaintance with grave-diggers, considering its length, was
unremarkable. One, indeed, whom I found plying his spade in the
red evening, high above Allan Water and in the shadow of Dun-
blane Cathedral, told me of his acquaintance with the birds that
still attended on his labours; how some would even perch about
him, waiting for their prey; and in a true Sexton's Calendar, how
the species varied with the season of the year. But this was the very
poetry of the profession. The others whom I knew were somewhat
dry. A faint flavour of the gardener hung about them, but sophis-

ticated and disbloomed. They had engagements to keep, not alone
with the deliberate series of the seasons, but with mankind's clocks
and hour-long measurement of time. And thus there was no leisure
for the relishing pinch, or the hour-long gossip, foot on spade.
They were men wrapped up in their grim business; they liked well
to open long-closed family vaults, blowing in the key and throwing
wide the grating; and they carried in their minds a calendar of
names and dates. It would be "in fifty-twa" that such a tomb was
last opened for "Miss Jemimy." It was thus they spoke of their past
patients—familiarly but not without respect, like old family servants. Here is indeed a servant, whom we forget that we possess;
who does not wait at the bright table, or run at the bell's summons,
but patiently smokes his pipe beside the mortuary fire, and in his
faithful memory notches the burials of our race. To suspect
Shakespeare in his maturity of a superficial touch savours of
paradox; yet he was surely in error when he attributed insensibility
to the digger of the grave. But perhaps it is on Hamlet that the
charge should lie; or perhaps the English sexton differs from the
Scotch. The "goodman delver," reckoning up his years of office,
might have at least suggested other thoughts. It is a pride common
among sextons. A cabinet-maker does not count his cabinets, nor
even an author his volumes, save when they stare upon him from
the shelves; but the grave-digger numbers his graves. He would
indeed be something different from human if his solitary open-air
and tragic labours left not a broad mark upon his mind. There, in
his tranquil aisle, apart from city clamour, among the cats and
robins and the ancient effigies and legends of the tomb, he waits
the continual passage of his contemporaries, falling like minute
drops into eternity. As they fall, he counts them; and this enumera-
tion, which was at first perhaps appalling to his soul, in the process
of years and by the kindly influence of habit grows to be his pride
and pleasure. There are many common stories telling how he
piques himself on crowded cemeteries. But I will rather tell of the
old grave-digger of Monkton, to whose unsuffering bedside the
minister was summoned. He dwelt in a cottage built into the wall
of the churchyard; and through a bull's-eye pane above his bed he
could see, as he lay dying, the rank grasses and the upright and
recumbent stones. Dr. Laurie was, I think, a Moderate: 'tis certain,
at least, that he took a very Roman view of death-bed dispositions;
for he told the old man that he had lived beyond man's natural

years, that his life had been easy and reputable, that his family had all grown up and been a credit to his care, and that it now behoved him unregretfully to gird his loins and follow the majority. The grave-digger heard him out; then he raised himself upon one elbow, and with the other hand pointed through the window to the scene of his life-long labours. "Doctor," he said, "I ha'e laid three hunner and fowerscore in that kirkyaird; an it had been His wull," indicating Heaven, "I would ha'e likit weel to ha'e made out the fower hunner." But it was not to be; this tragedian of the fifth act had now another part to play; and the time had come when others were to gird and carry him.

2

I would fain strike a note that should be more heroical; but the ground of all youth's suffering, solitude, hysteria, and haunting of the grave, is nothing else than naked, ignorant selfishness. It is himself that he sees dead; those are his virtues that are forgotten; his is the vague epitaph. Pity him but the more, if pity be your cue; for where a man is all pride, vanity, and personal aspiration, he goes through fire unshielded. In every part and corner of your life, to lose oneself is to be gainer; to forget oneself is to be happy; and his poor, laughable, and tragic fool has not yet learned the rudiments; himself, giant Prometheus, is still ironed on the peaks of Caucasus. But by-and-by his truant interests will leave that tortured body, slip abroad, and gather flowers. Then shall death appear before him in an altered guise; no longer as a doom peculiar to himself, whether fate's crowning injustice or his own last vengeance upon those who fail to value him; but now as a power that wounds him far more tenderly, not without solemn compensations, taking and giving, bereaving and yet storing up.

The first step for all is to learn to the dregs our own ignoble fallibility. When we have fallen through storey after storey of our vanity and aspiration, and sit rueful among the ruins, then it is that we begin to measure the stature of our friends: how they stand between us and our own contempt, believing in our best; how, linking us with others, and still spreading wide the influential circle, they weave us in and in with the fabric of contemporary life; and to what petty size they dwarf the virtues and the vices that appeared gigantic in our youth. So that at the last, when such

a pin falls out—when there vanishes in the least breath of time one
of those rich magazines of life on which we drew for our supply—
when he who had first dawned upon us as a face among the faces
of the city, and, still growing, came to bulk on our regard with
those clear features of the loved and living man, falls in a breath
to memory and shadow, there falls along with him a whole wing
of the palace of our life.

3

One such face I now remember; one such blank some half a
dozen of us labour to dissemble. In his youth he was most beautiful
in person, most serene and genial by disposition; full of racy words
and quaint thoughts. Laughter attended on his coming. He had
the air of a great gentleman, jovial and royal with his equals, and
to the poorest student gentle and attentive. Power seemed to reside
in him exhaustless; we saw him stoop to play with us, but held
him marked for higher destinies; we loved his notice; and I have
rarely had my pride more gratified than when he sat at my father's
table, my acknowledged friend. So he walked among us, both
hands full of gifts, carrying with nonchalance the seeds of a most
influential life.

The powers and the ground of friendship is a mystery; but,
looking back, I can discern that, in part, we loved the thing he
was, for some shadow of what he was to be. For with all his beauty,
power, breeding, urbanity, and mirth, there was in those days
something soulless in our friend. He would astonish us by sallies,
witty, innocent, and inhumane; and by a misapplied Johnsonian
pleasantry, demolish honest sentiment. I can still see and hear him,
as he went his way along the lamplit streets, *Là ci darem la mano*
on his lips, a noble figure of a youth, but following vanity and
incredulous of good; and sure enough, somewhere on the high seas
of life, with his health, his hopes, his patrimony, and his self-
respect, miserably went down.

From this disaster, like a spent swimmer, he came desperately
ashore, bankrupt of money and consideration; creeping to the
family he had deserted; with broken wing, never more to rise. But
in his face there was a light of knowledge that was new to it. Of
the wounds of his body he was never healed; died of them gradually, with clear-eyed resignation; of his wounded pride, we knew

only from his silence. He returned to that city where he had
lorded it in his ambitious youth; lived there alone, seeing few;
striving to retrieve the irretrievable; at times still grappling with
that mortal frailty that had brought him down; still joying in
his friend's successes; his laugh still ready but with kindlier music;
and over all his thoughts the shadow of that unalterable law which
he had disavowed and which had brought him low. Lastly, when
his bodily evils had quite disabled him, he lay a great while dying,
still without complaint, still finding interests; to his last step gentle,
urbane, and with the will to smile.

The tale of this great failure is, to those who remained true to
him, the tale of a success. In his youth he took thought for no one
but himself; when he came ashore again, his whole armada lost,
he seemed to think of none but others. Such was his tenderness
for others, such his instinct of fine courtesy and pride, that of that
impure passion of remorse he never breathed a syllable; even regret
was rare with him, and pointed with a jest. You would not have
dreamed, if you had known him then, that this was that great failure, that beacon to young men, over whose fall a whole society
had hissed and pointed fingers. Often have we gone to him, red-
hot with our own hopeful sorrows, railing on the rose-leaves in our
princely bed of life, and he would patiently give ear and wisely
counsel; and it was only upon some return of our own thoughts
that we were reminded what manner of man this was to whom we
disembosomed: a man, by his own fault, ruined; shut out of the
garden of his gifts; his whole city of hope both ploughed and
salted; silently awaiting the deliverer. Then something took us
by the throat; and to see him there, so gentle, patient, brave, and
pious, oppressed but not cast down, sorrow was so swallowed up
in admiration that we could not dare to pity him. Even if the
old fault flashed out again, it but awoke our wonder that, in that
lost battle, he should have still the energy to fight. He had gone to
ruin with a kind of kindly *abandon,* like one who condescended;
but once ruined, with the lights all out, he fought as for a kingdom.
Most men, finding themselves the authors of their own disgrace,
rail the louder against God or destiny. Most men, when they repent, oblige their friends to share the bitterness of that repentance.
But he had held an inquest and passed sentence: *mene, mene;* and
condemned himself to smiling silence. He had given trouble

enough; had earned misfortune amply, and foregone the right to murmur.

Thus was our old comrade, like Samson, careless in his days of strength; but on the coming of adversity, and when that strength was gone that had betrayed him—"for our strength is weakness"—he began to blossom and bring forth. Well, now, he is out of the fight: the burthen that he bore thrown down before the great deliverer. We

> "in the vast cathedral leave him:
> God accept him,
> Christ receive him!"

4

If we go now and look on these innumerable epitaphs, the pathos and the irony are strangely fled. They do not stand merely to the dead, these foolish monuments; they are pillars and legends set up to glorify the difficult but not desperate life of man. This ground is hallowed by the heroes of defeat.

I see the indifferent pass before my friend's last resting-place; pause, with a shrug of pity, marvelling that so rich an argosy had sunk. A pity, now that he is done with suffering, a pity most uncalled for, and an ignorant wonder. Before those who loved him, his memory shines like a reproach; they honour him for silent lessons; they cherish his example; and in what remains before them of their toil, fear to be unworthy of the dead. For this proud man was one of those who prospered in the valley of humiliation—of whom Bunyan wrote that, "Though Christian had the hard hap to meet in the valley with Apollyon, yet I must tell you, that in former times men have met with angels here; have found pearls here; and have in this place found the words of life."

On the Enjoyment of Unpleasant Places

I T IS A DIFFICULT MATTER TO MAKE THE MOST OF ANY GIVEN PLACE, and we have much in our own power. Things looked at patiently from one side after another generally end by showing a side that is beautiful. A few months ago some words were said in the *Portfolio* as to an "austere regimen in scenery"; and such a discipline was then recommended as "healthful and strengthening to the taste." That is the text, so to speak, of the present essay. This discipline in scenery, it must be understood, is something more than a mere walk before breakfast to whet the appetite. For when we are put down in some unsightly neighbourhood, and especially if we have come to be more or less dependent on what we see, we must set ourselves to hunt out beautiful things with all the ardour and patience of a botanist after a rare plant. Day by day we perfect ourselves in the art of seeing Nature more favourably. We learn to live with her, as people learn to live with fretful or violent spouses: to dwell lovingly on what is good, and shut our eyes against all that is bleak or inharmonious. We learn, also, to come to each place in the right spirit. The traveller, as Brantôme quaintly tells us, *"fait des discours en soi pour se soutenir en chemin";* and into these discourses he weaves something out of all that he sees and suffers by the way; they take their tone greatly from the varying character of the scene; a sharp ascent brings different thoughts from a level road; and the man's fancies grow lighter as he comes out of the wood into a clearing. Nor does the scenery any more affect the thoughts than the thoughts affect the scenery. We see places through our humours as through differently coloured glasses. We are ourselves a term in the equation, a note of the chord, and make discord or harmony almost at will. There is no fear for the result, if we can but surrender ourselves sufficiently to the country that surrounds and follows us, so that we are ever thinking suitable thoughts or telling ourselves some suitable sort of story as we go. We become thus, in some sense, a centre of beauty; we are provocative of beauty, much as a gentle and sincere character is provocative of sincerity and gentleness in others. And even where there is no harmony to be elicited by the quickest and most obedient of spirits, we may still embellish a place with some attraction of romance. We may learn to go far afield for associations, and handle them lightly when we have found them. Sometimes an old print comes to our aid; I have seen many a spot lit up at once with picturesque imaginations, by a reminiscence of Callot, or Sadeler, or Paul Brill. Dick Turpin has been my lay figure for many an English lane. And I suppose the Trossachs would hardly be the Trossachs for most tourists if a man of admirable romantic instinct had not peopled it for them with harmonious figures, and brought them thither with minds rightly prepared for the impression. There is half the battle in this preparation. For instance: I have rarely been able to visit, in the proper spirit, the wild and inhospitable places of our own Highlands. I am happier where it is tame and fertile, and not readily pleased without trees. I understand that there are some phases of mental trouble that harmonise well with such surroundings, and that some persons, by the dispensing power of the imagination, can go back several centuries in spirit, and put themselves into sympathy with the hunted, houseless, unsociable way of life that was in its place upon these savage hills. Now, when I am sad, I like nature to charm me out of my sadness, like David before Saul; and the thought of these past ages strikes nothing in me but an unpleasant pity; so that I can never hit on the right humour for this sort of landscape, and lose much pleasure in consequence. Still, even here, if I were only let alone, and time enough were given, I should have all manner of pleasures, and take many clear and beautiful images away with me when I left. When we cannot think ourselves into sympathy with the great features of a country, we learn to ignore them, and put our head among the grass for flowers, or pore, for long times together, over the changeful current of a stream. We come down to the sermon in stones, when we are shut out from any poem in the spread landscape. We begin to peep and botanise, we take an interest in birds and insects, we find many things beautiful in miniature. The reader will recollect the little summer scene in *Wuthering Heights*—the one warm scene, perhaps, in all that powerful, miserable novel—and the great feature that is made therein by grasses and flowers and a little sunshine: this is in the spirit of which I now speak. And, lastly, we can go indoors; interiors are sometimes as beautiful, often more picturesque, than the shows of the open air, and they have that quality of shelter of which I shall presently have more to say.

With all this in mind, I have often been tempted to put forth the paradox that any place is good enough to live a life in, while it is only in a few, and those highly favoured, that we can pass a few hours agreeably. For, if we only stay long enough, we become at home in the neighbourhood. Reminiscences spring up, like flowers, about uninteresting corners. We forget to some degree the superior loveliness of other places, and fall into a tolerant and sympathetic spirit which is its own reward and justification. Looking back the other day on some recollections of my own, I was astonished to find how much I owed to such a residence; six weeks in one unpleasant country-side had done more, it seemed, to quicken and educate my sensibilities than many years in places that jumped more nearly with my inclination.

The country to which I refer was a level and treeless plateau, over which the winds cut like a whip. For miles on miles it was the same. A river, indeed, fell into the sea near the town where I resided; but the valley of the river was shallow and bald, for as far up as ever I had the heart to follow it. There were roads, certainly, but roads that had no beauty or interest; for, as there was no timber, and but little irregularity of surface, you saw your whole walk exposed to you from the beginning: there was nothing left to fancy, nothing to expect, nothing to see by the wayside, save here and there an unhomely-looking homestead, and here and there a solitary, spectacled stonebreaker; and you were only accompanied, as you went doggedly forward, by the gaunt telegraph-posts and the hum of the resonant wires in the keen sea-wind. To one who had learned to know their song in warm pleasant places by the Mediterranean, it seemed to taunt the country, and make it still bleaker by suggested contrast. Even the waste places by the side of the road were not, as Hawthorne liked to put it, "taken back to Nature" by any decent covering of vegetation. Wherever the land had the chance, it seemed to lie fallow. There is a certain tawny nudity of the South, bare sunburnt plains, coloured like a lion, and hills clothed only in the blue transparent air; but this was of another description—this was the nakedness of the North; the earth seemed to know that it was naked, and was ashamed and cold.

It seemed to be always blowing on that coast. Indeed, this had passed into the speech of the inhabitants, and they saluted each other when they met with "Breezy, breezy," instead of the customary "Fine day" of farther south. These continual winds were not like the harvest breeze, that just keeps an equable pressure against your face as you walk, and serves to set all the trees talking over your head, or bring round you the smell of the wet surface of the country after a shower. They were of the bitter, hard, persistent sort, that interferes with sight and respiration, and makes the eyes sore. Even such winds as these have their own merit in proper time and place. It is pleasant to see them brandish great masses of shadow. And what a power they have over the colour of the world! How they ruffle the solid woodlands in their passage, and make them shudder and whiten like a single willow! There is nothing more vertiginous than a wind like this among the woods, with all its sights and noises; and the effect gets between some painters and their sober eyesight, so that, even when the rest of their picture is calm, the foliage is coloured like foliage in a gale. There was nothing, however, of this sort to be noticed in a country where there were no trees and hardly any shadows, save the passive shadows of clouds or those of rigid houses and walls. But the wind was nevertheless an occasion of pleasure; for nowhere could you taste more fully the pleasure of a sudden lull, or a place of opportune shelter. The reader knows what I mean; he must remember how, when he has sat himself down behind a dyke on a hillside, he delighted to hear the wind hiss vainly through the crannies at his back; how his body tingled all over with warmth, and it began to dawn upon him, with a sort of slow surprise, that the country was beautiful, the heather purple, and the far-away hills all marbled with sun and shadow. Wordsworth, in a beautiful passage of the "Prelude," has used this as a figure for the feeling struck in us by the quiet by-streets of London after the uproar of the great thoroughfares; and the comparison may be turned the other way with as good effect:

"Meanwhile the roar continues, till at length,
Escaped as from an enemy, we turn
Abruptly into some sequester'd nook,
Still as a shelter'd place when winds blow loud!"

I remember meeting a man once, in a train, who told me of what must have been quite the most perfect instance of this pleasure of escape. He had gone up, one sunny, windy morning, to the top of a great cathedral somewhere abroad; I think it was Cologne Cathedral, the great unfinished marvel by the Rhine; and after a long while in dark stairways, he issued at last into the sunshine, on a platform high above the town. At that elevation it was quite still and warm; the gale was only in the lower strata of the air, and he had forgotten it in the quiet interior of the church and during his long ascent; and so you may judge of his surprise when, resting his arms on the sunlit balustrade and looking over into the *Place* far below him, he saw the good people holding on their hats and leaning hard against the wind as they walked. There is something, to my fancy, quite perfect in this little experience of my fellow-traveller's. The ways of men seem always very trivial to us when we find ourselves alone on a church-top, with the blue sky and a few tall pinnacles, and see far below us the steep roofs and foreshortened buttresses, and the silent activity of the city streets; but how much more must they not have seemed so to him as he stood, not only above other men's business, but above other men's climate, in a golden zone like Apollo's!

This was the sort of pleasure I found in the country of which I write. The pleasure was to be out of the wind, and to keep it in memory all the time, and hug oneself upon the shelter. And it was only by the sea that any such sheltered places were to be found. Between the black worm-eaten headlands there are little bights and havens, well screened from the wind and the commotion of the external sea, where the sand and weeds look up into the gazer's face from a depth of tranquil water, and the sea-birds, screaming and flickering from the ruined crags, alone disturb the silence and the sunshine. One such place has impressed itself on my memory beyond all others. On a rock by the water's edge, old fighting men of the Norse breed had planted a double castle; the two stood wall to wall like semi-detached villas; and yet feud had run so high between their owners, that one, from out of a window, shot the other as he stood in his own doorway. There is something in the juxtaposition of these two enemies full of tragic irony. It is grim to think of bearded men and bitter women taking hateful counsel together about the two hall-fires at night, when the sea boomed against the foundations and the wild winter wind was loose over the battlements. And in the study we may reconstruct for ourselves some pale figure of what life then was. Not so when we are there; when we are there such thoughts come to us only to intensify a contrary impression, and association is turned against itself. I remember walking thither three afternoons in succession, my eyes weary with being set against the wind, and how, dropping suddenly over the edge of the down, I found myself in a new world of warmth and shelter. The wind, from which I had escaped, "as from an enemy," was seemingly quite local. It carried no clouds with it, and came from such a quarter that it did not trouble the sea within view. The two castles, black and ruinous as the rocks about them, were still distinguishable from these by something more insecure and fantastic in the outline, something that the last storm had left imminent and the next would demolish entirely. It would be difficult to render in words the sense of peace that took possession of me on these three afternoons. It was helped out, as I have said, by the contrast. The shore was battered and be-mauled by previous tempests; I had the memory at heart of the insane strife of the pigmies who had erected these two castles and lived in them in mutual distrust and enmity, and knew I had only to put my head out of this little cup of shelter to find the hard wind blowing in my eyes; and yet there were the two great tracts of motionless blue air and peaceful sea looking on, unconcerned and apart, at the turmoil of the present moment and the memorials of the precarious past. There is ever something transitory and fret-ful in the impression of a high wind under a cloudless sky; it seems to have no root in the constitution of things; it must speedily begin to faint and wither away like a cut flower. And on those days the thought of the wind and the thought of human life came very near together in my mind. Our noisy years did indeed seem moments in the being of the eternal silence: the wind, in the face of that great field of stationary blue, was as the wind of a butterfly's wing. The placidity of the sea was a thing likewise to be remembered. Shelley speaks of the sea as "hungering for calm," and in this place one learned to understand the phrase. Looking down into these green waters from the broken edge of the rock, or swimming leisurely in the sunshine, it seemed to me that they were enjoying their own tranquillity; and when now and again it was disturbed by a wind ripple on the surface, or the quick black passage of a fish far below, they settled back again (one could fancy) with relief.

On shore too, in the little nook of shelter, everything was so subdued and still that the least particular struck in me a pleasurable surprise. The desultory crackling of the whin-pods in the afternoon sun usurped the ear. The hot, sweet breath of the bank, that had been saturated all day long with sunshine, and now exhaled it into my face, was like the breath of a fellow-creature. I remember that I was haunted by two lines of French verse; in some dumb way they seemed to fit my surroundings and give expression to the contentment that was in me, and I kept repeating to myself—

> "Mon cœur est un luth suspendu,
>   Sitôt qu'on le touche, il résonne."

I can give no reason why these lines came to me at this time; and for that very cause I repeat them here. For all I know, they may serve to complete the impression in the mind of the reader, as they were certainly a part of it for me.

And this happened to me in the place of all others where I liked least to stay. When I think of it I grow ashamed of my own ingratitude. "Out of the strong came forth sweetness." There, in the bleak and gusty North, I received, perhaps, my strongest impression of peace. I saw the sea to be great and calm; and the earth, in that little corner, was all alive and friendly to me. So, wherever a man is, he will find something to please and pacify him: in the town he will meet pleasant faces of men and women, and see beautiful flowers at a window, or hear a cage-bird singing at the corner of the gloomiest street; and for the country, there is no country without some amenity—let him only look for it in the right spirit, and he will surely find.

A Humble Remonstrance

1

WE HAVE RECENTLY * ENJOYED A QUITE PECULIAR PLEASURE: hearing, in some detail, the opinions, about the art they practise, of Mr. Walter Besant and Mr. Henry James; two men certainly of very different calibre: Mr. James so precise of outline, so cunning of fence, so scrupulous of finish, and Mr. Besant so genial, so friendly, with so persuasive and humourous a vein of whim: Mr. James the very type of the deliberate artist, Mr. Besant the impersonation of good-nature. That such doctors should differ will excite no great surprise; but one point in which they seem to agree fills me, I confess, with wonder. For they are both content to talk about the "art of fiction"; and Mr. Besant, waxing exceedingly bold, goes on to oppose this so-called "art of fiction" to the "art of poetry." By the art of poetry he can mean nothing but the art of verse, an art of handicraft, and only comparable with the art of prose. For that heat and height of sane emotion which we agree to call by the name of poetry, is but a libertine and vagrant quality; present, at times, in any art, more often absent from them all; too seldom present in the prose novel, too frequently absent from the ode and epic. Fiction is in the same case; it is no substantive art, but an element which enters largely into all the arts but architecture. Homer, Wordsworth, Phidias, Hogarth, and Salvini, all deal in fiction; and yet I do not suppose that either Hogarth or Salvini, to mention but these two, entered in any degree into the scope of Mr. Besant's interesting lecture or

* 1884.

915

Mr. James's charming essay. The art of fiction, then, regarded as a definition, is both too ample and too scanty. Let me suggest another; let me suggest that what both Mr. James and Mr. Besant had in view was neither more nor less than the art of narrative.

But Mr. Besant is anxious to speak solely of "the modern English novel," the stay and breadwinner of Mr. Mudie; and in the author of the most pleasing novel on that roll, *All Sorts and Conditions of Men,* the desire is natural enough. I can conceive, then, that he would hasten to propose two additions, and read thus: the art of *fictitious narrative in prose.*

Now the fact of the existence of the modern English novel is not to be denied; materially, with its three volumes, leaded type, and gilded lettering, it is easily distinguishable from other forms of literature; but to talk at all fruitfully of any branch of art, it is needful to build our definitions on some more fundamental ground than binding. Why, then, are we to add "in prose"? *The Odyssey* appears to me the best of romances; *The Lady of the Lake* to stand high in the second order; and Chaucer's tales and prologues to contain more of the matter and art of the modern English novel than the whole treasury of Mr. Mudie. Whether a narrative be written in blank verse or the Spenserian stanza, in the long period of Gibbon or the chipped phrase of Charles Reade, the principles of the art of narrative must be equally observed. The choice of a noble and swelling style in prose affects the problem of narration in the same way, if not to the same degree, as the choice of measured verse; for both imply a closer synthesis of events, a higher key of dialogue, and a more picked and stately strain of words. If you are to refuse *Don Juan,* it is hard to see why you should include *Zanoni* or (to bracket works of very different value) *The Scarlet Letter;* and by what discrimination are you to open your doors to *The Pilgrim's Progress* and close them on *The Faery Queen?* To bring things closer home, I will here propound to Mr. Besant a conundrum. A narrative called *Paradise Lost* was written in English verse by one John Milton; what was it then? It was next translated by Chateaubriand into French prose; and what was it then? Lastly, the French translation was, by some inspired compatriot of George Gilfillan (and of mine) turned bodily into an English novel; and, in the name of clearness, what was it then?

But, once more, why should we add "fictitious"? The reason

why is obvious. The reason why not, if something more recondite, does not want for weight. The art of narrative, in fact, is the same, whether it is applied to the selection and illustration of a real series of events or of an imaginary series. Boswell's *Life of Johnson* (a work of cunning and inimitable art) owes its success to the same technical manœuvres as (let us say) *Tom Jones:* the clear conception of certain characters of man, the choice and presentation of certain incidents out of a great number that offered, and the invention (yes, invention) and preservation of a certain key in dialogue. In which these things are done with the more art—in which with the greater air of nature—readers will differently judge. Boswell's is, indeed, a very special case, and almost a generic; but it is not only in Boswell, it is in every biography with any salt of life, it is in every history where events and men, rather than ideas, are presented—in Tacitus, in Carlyle, in Michelet, in Macaulay—that the novelist will find many of his own methods most conspicuously and adroitly handled. He will find besides that he, who is free—who has the right to invent or steal a missing incident, who has the right, more precious still, of wholesale omission—is frequently defeated, and, with all his advantages, leaves a less strong impression of reality and passion. Mr. James utters his mind with a becoming fervour on the sanctity of truth to the novelist; on a more careful examination truth will seem a word of very debatable propriety, not only for the labours of the novelist, but for those of the historian. No art—to use the daring phrase of Mr. James—can successfully "compete with life"; and the art that seeks to do so is condemned to perish *montibus aviis.* Life goes before us, infinite in complication; attended by the most various and surprising meteors; appealing at once to the eye, to the ear, to the mind—the seat of wonder, to the touch—so thrillingly delicate, and to the belly—so imperious when starved. It combines and employs in its manifestation the method and material, not of one art only, but of all the arts. Music is but an arbitrary trifling with a few of life's majestic chords; painting is but a shadow of its pageantry of light and colour; literature does but drily indicate that wealth of incident, of moral obligation, of virtue, vice, action, rapture, and agony, with which it teems. To "compete with life," whose sun we cannot look upon, whose passions and diseases waste and slay us—to compete with the flavour of wine, the beauty of the dawn, the scorching of fire, the bitterness of death and separation—here is, indeed, a projected escalade of heaven; here are, indeed, labours for a Hercules in a dress coat, armed with a pen and a dictionary to depict the passions, armed with a tube of superior flake-white to paint the portrait of the insufferable sun. No art is true in this sense: none can "compete with life": not even history, built indeed of indisputable facts, but these facts robbed of their vivacity and sting; so that even when we read of the sack of a city or the fall of an empire, we are surprised, and justly commend the author's talent, if our pulse be quickened. And mark, for a last differentia, that this quickening of the pulse is, in almost every case, purely agreeable; that these phantom reproductions of experience, even at their most acute, convey decided pleasure; while experience itself, in the cockpit of life, can torture and slay.

What, then, is the object, what the method, of an art, and what the source of its power? The whole secret is that no art does "compete with life." Man's one method, whether he reasons or creates, is to half-shut his eyes against the dazzle and confusion of reality. The arts, like arithmetic and geometry, turn away their eyes from the gross, coloured, and mobile nature at our feet, and regard instead a certain figmentary abstraction. Geometry will tell us of a circle, a thing never seen in nature; asked about a green circle or an iron circle, it lays its hand upon its mouth. So with the arts. Painting, ruefully comparing sunshine and flakewhite, gives up truth of colour, as it had already given up relief and movement; and instead of vying with nature, arranges a scheme of harmonious tints. Literature, above all in its most typical mood, the mood of narrative, similarly flees the direct challenge and pursues instead an independent and creative aim. So far as it imitates at all, it imitates not life but speech: not the facts of human destiny, but the emphasis and the suppressions with which the human actor tells of them. The real art that dealt with life directly was that of the first men who told their stories round the savage camp-fire. Our art is occupied, and bound to be occupied, not so much in making stories true as in making them typical; not so much in capturing the lineaments of each fact, as in marshalling all of them towards a common end. For the welter of impressions, all forcible but all discreet, which life presents, it substitutes a certain artificial series of impressions, all indeed most feebly represented, but all aiming at the same effect, all eloquent of the same idea, all chiming together like consonant notes in music or like the graduated tints in a good picture. From all its chapters, from all its pages, from all its sentences, the well-written novel echoes and re-echoes its one creative and controlling thought; to this must every incident and character contribute; the style must have been pitched in unison with this; and if there is anywhere a word that looks another way, the book would be stronger, clearer, and (I had almost said) fuller without it. Life is monstrous, infinite, illogical, abrupt, and poignant; a work of art, in comparison, is neat, finite, self-contained, rational, flowing, and emasculate. Life imposes by brute energy, like inarticulate thunder; art catches the ear, among the far louder noises of experience, like an air artificially made by a discreet musician. A proposition of geometry does not compete with life; and a proposition of geometry is a fair and luminous parallel for a work of art. Both are reasonable, both untrue to the crude fact; both inhere in nature, neither represents it. The novel, which is a work of art, exists, not by its resemblances to life, which are forced and material, as a shoe must still consist of leather, but by its immeasurable difference from life, which is designed and significant, and is both the method and the meaning of the work.

The life of man is not the subject of novels, but the inexhaustible magazine from which subjects are to be selected; the name of these is legion; and with each new subject—for here again I must differ by the whole width of heaven from Mr. James —the true artist will vary his method and change the point of attack. That which was in one case an excellence, will become a defect in another; what was the making of one book, will in the next be impertinent or dull. First each novel, and then each class of novels, exists by and for itself. I will take, for instance, three main classes, which are fairly distinct: first, the novel of adventure, which appeals to certain almost sensual and quite illogical tendencies in man; second, the novel of character, which appeals to our intellectual appreciation of man's foibles and mingled and inconstant motives; and third, the dramatic novel, which deals with the same stuff as the serious theatre, and appeals to our emotional nature and moral judgment.

And first for the novel of adventure. Mr. James refers, with singular generosity of praise, to a little book about a quest for hidden treasure; but he lets fall, by the way, some rather startling words. In this book he misses what he calls the "immense luxury" of being able to quarrel with his author. The luxury, to most of us, is to lay by our judgment, to be submerged by the tale as by a billow, and only to awake, and begin to distinguish and find fault, when the piece is over and the volume laid aside. Still more remarkable is Mr. James's reason. He cannot criticise the author, as he goes, "because," says he, comparing it with another work, *"I have been a child, but I have never been on a quest for buried treasure."* Here is, indeed, a wilful paradox; for if he has never been on a quest for buried treasure, it can be demonstrated that he has never been a child. There never was a child (unless Master James) but has hunted gold, and been a pirate, and a military commander, and a bandit of the mountains; but has fought, and suffered shipwreck and prison, and imbrued its little hands in gore, and gallantly retrieved the lost battle, and triumphantly protected innocence and beauty. Elsewhere in his essay Mr. James has protested with excellent reason against too narrow a conception of experience; for the born artist, he contends, the "faintest hints of life" are converted into revelations; and it will be found true, I believe, in a majority of cases, that the artist writes with more gusto and effect of those things which he has only wished to do, than of those which he has done. Desire is a wonderful telescope, and Pisgah the best observatory. Now, while it is true that neither Mr. James nor the author of the work in question has ever, in the fleshly sense, gone questing after gold, it is probable that both have ardently desired and fondly imagined the details of such a life in youthful day-dreams; and the author, counting upon that, and well aware (cunning and low-minded man!) that this class of interest, having been frequently treated, finds a readily accessible and beaten road to the sympathies of the reader, addressed himself throughout to the building up and circumstantiation of this boyish dream. Character to the boy is a sealed book; for him, a pirate is a beard, a pair of wide trousers, and a liberal complement of pistols. The author, for the sake of circumstantiation and because he was himself more or less grown up, admitted character, within certain limits, into his design; but only within certain limits. Had the same puppets figured in a scheme of another sort, they had been drawn to very different purpose; for in this elementary novel of adventure, the characters need to be presented with but one class of qualities—the warlike and formidable. So as they appear insidious in deceit and fatal in the combat, they have served their end. Danger is the matter with which this class of novel deals; fear, the passion with which it idly trifles; and the characters are portrayed only so far as they realise the sense of danger and provoke the sympathy of fear. To add more traits, to be too clever, to start the hare of moral or intellectual interest while we are running the fox of material interest, is not to enrich but to stultify your tale. The stupid reader will only be offended, and the clever reader lose the scent.

The novel of character has this difference from all others: that it requires no coherency of plot, and for this reason, as in the case of *Gil Blas,* it is sometimes called the novel of adventure. It turns on the humours of the persons represented; these are, to be sure, embodied in incidents, but the incidents themselves, being tributary, need not march in a progression; and the characters may be statically shown. As they enter, so they may go out; they must be consistent, but they need not grow. Here Mr. James will recognise the note of much of his own work: he treats, for the most part, the statics of character, studying it at rest or only gently moved; and, with his usual delicate and just artistic instinct, he avoids those stronger passions which would deform the attitudes he loves to study, and change his sitters from the humourists of ordinary life to the brute forces and bare types of more emotional moments. In his recent *The Author of Beltraffio,* so just in conception, so nimble and neat in workmanship, strong passion is indeed employed; but observe that it is not displayed. Even in the heroine the working of the passion is suppressed; and the great struggle, the true tragedy, the *scène-à-faire,* passes unseen behind the panels of a locked door. The delectable invention of the young visitor is introduced, consciously or not, to this end: that Mr. James, true to his method, might avoid the scene of passion. I trust no reader will suppose me guilty of undervaluing this little masterpiece. I mean merely that it belongs to one marked class of novel, and that it would have been very differently conceived and treated had it belonged to that other marked class, of which I now proceed to speak.

I take pleasure in calling the dramatic novel by that name, because it enables me to point out by the way a strange and peculiarly English misconception. It is sometimes supposed that the drama consists of incident. It consists of passion, which gives the actor his opportunity; and that passion must progressively increase, or the actor, as the piece proceeded, would be unable to carry the audience from a lower to a higher pitch of interest and emotion. A good serious play must therefore be founded on one of the passionate *cruces* of life, where duty and inclination come nobly to the grapple; and the same is true of what I call, for that reason, the dramatic novel. I will instance a few worthy specimens, all of our own day and language; Meredith's *Rhoda Fleming,* that wonderful and painful book, long out of print,* and hunted for at book-stalls like an Aldine; Hardy's *Pair of Blue Eyes;* and two of Charles Reade's, *Griffith Gaunt* and *The Double Marriage,* originally called *White Lies,* and founded (by an accident quaintly favourable to my nomenclature) on a play by Maquet, the partner of the great Dumas. In this kind of novel the closed door of *The Author of Beltraffio* must be broken open; passion must appear upon the scene and utter its last word; passion is the be-all and the end-all, the plot and the solution, the protagonist and the *deus ex machina* in one. The characters may come anyhow upon the stage: we do not care; the point is, that, before they leave it, they shall become transfigured and raised out of themselves by passion. It may be part of the design to draw them with detail; to depict a full-length character, and then behold it melt and change in the furnace of emotion. But there is no obligation of the sort; nice portraiture is not required; and we are content to accept mere abstract types, so they be strongly and sincerely moved. A novel of this class may be even great, and yet contain no individual figure; it may be great, because it displays the workings of the perturbed heart and the impersonal utterance of passion; and with an artist of the second class it is, indeed, even more likely to be great, when the issue has thus been narrowed and the whole force of the writer's mind directed to passion alone. Cleverness again, which has its fair field in the novel of character, is debarred all entry upon this more solemn theatre. A far-fetched motive, an ingenious evasion of the issue, a witty instead of a passionate turn, offend us like an insincerity. All should be plain, all straight-forward to the end. Hence it is that, in *Rhoda Fleming,* Mrs. Lovel raises such resentment in the reader; her motives are too flimsy, her ways are too equivocal, for the weight and strength of her surroundings. Hence the hot indignation of the reader when Balzac, after having begun the *Duchesse*

* Now no longer so, thank Heaven!

de Langeais in terms of strong if somewhat swollen passion, cuts
the knot by the derangement of the hero's clock. Such personages
and incidents belong to the novel of character; they are out of
place in the high society of the passions; when the passions are introduced in art at their full height, we look to see them, not baffled
and impotently striving, as in life, but towering above circumstance
and acting substitutes for fate.

And here I can imagine Mr. James, with his lucid sense, to intervene. To much of what I have said he would apparently demur;
in much he would, somewhat impatiently, acquiesce. It may be
true; but it is not what he desired to say or to hear said. He spoke
of the finished picture and its worth when done; I, of the brushes,
the palette, and the north light. He uttered his views in the tone
and for the ear of good society; I, with the emphasis and technicalities of the obtrusive student. But the point, I may reply, is not
merely to amuse the public, but to offer helpful advice to the
young writer. And the young writer will not so much be helped by
genial pictures of what an art may aspire to at its highest, as by a
true idea of what it must be on the lowest terms. The best that we
can say to him is this: Let him choose a motive, whether of character or passion; carefully construct his plot so that every incident
is an illustration of the motive, and every property employed shall
bear to it a near relation of congruity or contrast; avoid a sub-plot,
unless, as sometimes in Shakespeare, the sub-plot be a reversion or
complement of the main intrigue; suffer not his style to flag below
the level of the argument; pitch the key of conversation, not with
any thought of how men talk in parlours, but with a single eye to
the degree of passion he may be called on to express; and allow
neither himself in the narrative nor any character in the course of
the dialogue, to utter one sentence that is not part and parcel of
the business of the story or the discussion of the problem involved.
Let him not regret if this shortens his book; it will be better so;
for to add irrelevant matter is not to lengthen but to bury. Let
him not mind if he miss a thousand qualities, so that he keeps
unflaggingly in pursuit of the one he has chosen. Let him not care
particularly if he miss the tone of conversation, the pungent material detail of the day's manners, the reproduction of the atmosphere and the environment. These elements are not essential: a
novel may be excellent, and yet have none of them; a passion or a
character is so much the better depicted as it rises clearer from

material circumstance. In this age of the particular, let him remember the ages of the abstract, the great books of the past, the brave men that lived before Shakespeare and before Balzac. And as the root of the whole matter, let him bear in mind that his novel is not a transcript of life, to be judged by its exactitude; but a simplification of some side or point of life, to stand or fall by its significant simplicity. For although, in great men, working upon great motives, what we observe and admire is often their complexity, yet underneath appearances the truth remains unchanged: that simplification was their method, and that simplicity is their excellence.

2

Since the above was written another novelist has entered repeatedly the lists of theory: one well worthy of mention, Mr. W. D. Howells; and none ever couched a lance with narrower convictions. His own work and those of his pupils and masters singly occupy his mind; he is the bondslave, the zealot of his school; he dreams of an advance in art like what there is in science; he thinks of past things as radically dead; he thinks a form can be outlived: a strange immersion in his own history; a strange forgetfulness of the history of the race! Meanwhile, by a glance at his own works (could he see them with the eager eyes of his readers) much of this illusion would be dispelled. For while he holds all the poor little orthodoxies of the day—no poorer and no smaller than those of yesterday or to-morrow, poor and small, indeed, only so far as they are exclusive—the living quality of much that he has done is of a contrary, I had almost said of a heretical, complexion. A man, as I read him, of an originally strong romantic bent—a certain glow of romance still resides in many of his books, and lends them their distinction. As by accident he runs out and revels in the exceptional; and it is then, as often as not, that his reader rejoices—justly, as I contend. For in all this excessive eagerness to be centrally human, is there not one central human thing that Mr. Howells is too often tempted to neglect: I mean himself? A poet, a finished artist, a man in love with the appearances of life, a cunning reader of the mind, he has other passions and aspirations than those he loves to draw. And why should he suppress himself and do such reverence to the Lemuel Barkers? The obvious is not of necessity the normal; fashion rules and deforms; the majority fall tamely into the contemporary shape, and thus attain, in the eyes of the true observer, only a higher power of insignificance; and the danger is lest, in seeking to draw the normal, a man should draw the null, and write the novel of society instead of the romance of man.

BOOKS
OF TRAVEL

Travels with a Donkey in the Cevennes

My dear Sidney Colvin,

The journey which this little book is to describe was very agreeable and fortunate for me. After an uncouth beginning, I had the best of luck to the end. But we are all travellers in what John Bunyan calls the wilderness of this world—all, too, travellers with a donkey; and the best that we find in our travels is an honest friend. He is a fortunate voyager who finds many. We travel, indeed, to find them. They are the end and the reward of life. They keep us worthy of ourselves; and when we are alone, we are only nearer to the absent.

Every book is, in an intimate sense, a circular letter to the friends of him who writes it. They alone take his meaning; they find private messages, assurances of love, and expressions of gratitude, dropped for them in every corner. The public is but a generous patron who defrays the postage. Yet though the letter is directed to all, we have an old and kindly custom of addressing it on the outside to one. Of what shall a man be proud, if he is not proud of his friends? And so, my dear Sidney Colvin, it is with pride that I sign myself affectionately yours,

R. L. S.

Velay

*'Many are the mighty things, and nought is
more mighty than man. . . . He masters by his
devices the tenant of the fields.'*—Sophocles.
'Who hath loosed the bands of the wild ass?'
—Job.

✴

The Donkey, the Pack, and the Pack-saddle

IN A LITTLE PLACE CALLED LE MONASTIER, IN A PLEASANT HIGH-land valley fifteen miles from Le Puy, I spent about a month of fine days. Monastier is notable for the making of lace, for drunkenness, for freedom of language, and for unparalleled political dissension. There are adherents of each of the four French parties—Legitimists, Orleanists, Imperialists, and Republicans—in this little mountain-town; and they all hate, loathe, decry, and calumniate each other. Except for business purposes, or to give each other the lie in a tavern brawl, they have laid aside even the civility of speech. 'Tis a mere mountain Poland. In the midst of this Babylon I found myself a rallying-point; every one was anxious to be kind and helpful to the stranger. This was not merely from the natural hospitality of mountain people, nor even from the surprise with which I was regarded as a man living of his own free will in Le Monastier, when he might just as well have lived anywhere else in this big world; it arose a good deal from my projected excursion southward through the Cevennes. A traveller of my sort was a thing hitherto unheard of in that district. I was looked upon with contempt, like a man who should project a journey to the moon, but yet with a respectful interest, like one setting forth for the inclement Pole. All were ready to help in my

931

preparations; a crowd of sympathisers supported me at the critical moment of a bargain; not a step was taken but was heralded by glasses round and celebrated by a dinner or a breakfast.

It was already hard upon October before I was ready to set forth, and at the high altitudes over which my road lay there was no Indian summer to be looked for. I was determined, if not to camp out, at least to have the means of camping out in my possession; for there is nothing more harassing to an easy mind than the necessity of reaching shelter by dusk, and the hospitality of a village inn is not always to be reckoned sure by those who trudge on foot. A tent, above all for a solitary traveller, is troublesome to pitch, and troublesome to strike again; and even on the march it forms a conspicuous feature in your baggage. A sleeping-sack, on the other hand, is always ready—you have only to get into it; it serves a double purpose—a bed by night, a portmanteau by day; and it does not advertise your intention of camping out to every curious passer-by. This is a huge point. If the camp is not secret, it is but a troubled resting-place; you become a public character; the convivial rustic visits your bedside after an early supper; and you must sleep with one eye open, and be up before the day. I decided on a sleeping-sack; and after repeated visits to Le Puy, and a deal of high living for myself and my advisers, a sleeping-sack was designed, constructed, and triumphally brought home.

This child of my invention was nearly six feet square, exclusive of two triangular flaps to serve as a pillow by night and as the top and bottom of the sack by day. I call it "the sack," but it was never a sack by more than courtesy: only a sort of long roll or sausage, green water-proof cart-cloth without and blue sheep's fur within. It was commodious as a valise, warm and dry for a bed. There was luxurious turning room for one; and at a pinch the thing might serve for two. I could bury myself in it up to the neck; for my head I trusted to a fur cap, with a hood to fold down over my ears, and a band to pass under my nose like a respirator; and in case of heavy rain I proposed to make myself a little tent, or tentlet, with my water-proof coat, three stones, and a bent branch.

It will readily be conceived that I could not carry this huge package on my own, merely human, shoulders. It remained to choose a beast of burden. Now, a horse is a fine lady among animals, flighty, timid, delicate in eating, of tender health; he is too valuable and too restive to be left alone, so that you are chained to your brute as to a fellow galley-slave; a dangerous road puts him out of his wits; in short, he's an uncertain and exacting ally, and adds thirty-fold to the troubles of the voyager. What I required was something cheap and small and hardy, and of a stolid and peaceful temper; and all these requisites pointed to a donkey.

There dwelt an old man in Monastier, of rather unsound intellect according to some, much followed by street-boys, and known to fame as Father Adam. Father Adam had a cart, and to draw the cart a diminutive she-ass, not much bigger than a dog, the colour of a mouse, with a kindly eye and a determined under-jaw. There was something neat and high-bred, a quakerish elegance, about the rogue that hit my fancy on the spot. Our first interview was in Monastier market-place. To prove her good temper, one child after another was set upon her back to ride, and one after another went head over heels into the air; until a want of confidence began to reign in youthful bosoms, and the experiment was discontinued from a dearth of subjects. I was already backed up by a deputation of my friends; but as if this were not enough, all the buyers and sellers came round and helped me in the bargain; and the ass and I and Father Adam were the centre of a hubbub for near half an hour. At length she passed into my service for the consideration of sixty-five francs and a glass of brandy. The sack had already cost eighty francs and two glasses of beer; so that Modestine, as I instantly baptised her, was upon all accounts the cheaper article. Indeed, that was as it should be; for she was only an appurtenance of my mattress, or self-acting bedstead on four castors.

I had a last interview with Father Adam in a billiard-room at the witching hour of dawn, when I administered the brandy. He professed himself greatly touched by the separation, and declared he had often bought white bread for the donkey when he had been content with black bread for himself; but this, according to the best authorities, must have been a flight of fancy. He had a name in the village for brutally misusing the ass; yet it is certain that he shed a tear, and the tear made a clean mark down one cheek.

By the advice of a fallacious local saddler, a leather pad was made for me with rings to fasten on my bundle; and I thoughtfully completed my kit and arranged my toilette. By way of armoury and utensils, I took a revolver, a little spirit-lamp and pan, a lantern and some halfpenny candles, a jack-knife and a large leather flask. The main cargo consisted of two entire changes of warm clothing—besides my travelling wear of country velveteen, pilot-coat, and knitted spencer—some books, and my railway-rug, which, being also in the form of a bag, made me a double castle for cold nights. The permanent larder was represented by cakes of chocolate and tins of Bologna sausage. All this, except what I carried about my person, was easily stowed into the sheepskin bag; and by good fortune I threw in my empty knapsack, rather for convenience of carriage than from any thought that I should want it on my journey. For more immediate needs, I took a leg of cold mutton, a bottle of Beaujolais, an empty bottle to carry milk, an egg-beater, and a considerable quantity of black bread and white, like Father Adam, for myself and donkey, only in my scheme of things the destinations were reversed.

Monastrians, of all shades of thought in politics, had agreed in threatening me with many ludicrous misadventures, and with sudden death in many surprising forms. Cold, wolves, robbers, above all the nocturnal practical joker, were daily and eloquently forced on my attention. Yet in these vaticinations, the true, patent danger was left out. Like Christian, it was from my pack I suffered by the way. Before telling my own mishaps, let me, in two words, relate the lesson of my experience. If the pack is well strapped at the ends, and hung at full length—not doubled, for your life—across the pack-saddle, the traveller is safe. The saddle will certainly not fit, such is the imperfection of our transitory life; it will assuredly topple and tend to overset; but there are stones on every roadside, and a man soon learns the art of correcting any tendency to overbalance with a well-adjusted stone.

On the day of my departure I was up a little after five; by six, we began to load the donkey; and ten minutes after, my hopes were in the dust. The pad would not stay on Modestine's back for half a moment. I returned it to its maker, with whom I had so contumelious a passage that the street outside was crowded from wall to wall with gossips looking on and listening. The pad changed hands with much vivacity; perhaps it would be more descriptive to say that we threw it at each other's heads; and, at any rate, we were very warm and unfriendly, and spoke with a deal of freedom.

I had a common donkey pack-saddle—a *barde,* as they call it—fitted upon Modestine; and once more loaded her with my effects. The doubled sack, my pilot-coat (for it was warm, and I was to walk in my waistcoat), a great bar of black bread, an open basket containing the white bread, the mutton, and the bottles, were all corded together in a very elaborate system of knots, and I looked on the result with fatuous content. In such a monstrous deck-cargo, all poised *above* the donkey's shoulders, with nothing below to balance, on a brand-new pack-saddle that had not yet been worn to fit the animal, and fastened with brand-new girths that might be expected to stretch and slacken by the way, even a very careless traveller should have seen disaster brewing. That elaborate system of knots, again, was the work of too many sympathisers to be very artfully designed. It is true they tightened the cords with a will; as many as three at a time would have a foot against Modestine's quarters, and be hauling with clenched teeth; but I learned afterwards that one thoughtful person, without any exercise of force, can make a more solid job than half a dozen heated and enthusiastic grooms. I was then but a novice; even after the misadventure of the pad nothing could disturb my security, and I went forth from the stable-door as an ox goeth to the slaughter.

The Green Donkey-Driver

The bell of Monastier was just striking nine as I got quit of these preliminary troubles and descended the hill through the common. As long as I was within sight of the windows, a secret shame and the fear of some laughable defeat withheld me from tampering with Modestine. She tripped along upon her four small hoofs with a sober daintiness of gait; from time to time she shook her ears or her tail; and she looked so small under the bundle that my mind misgave me. We got across the ford without difficulty—there was no doubt about the matter, she was docility itself—and once on the other bank, where the road begins to mount through pine-woods, I took in my right hand the unhallowed staff, and with a quaking spirit applied it to the donkey. Modestine brisked up her pace for perhaps three steps, and then relapsed into her former minuet. Another application had the same effect, and so with the third. I am worthy the name of an Englishman, and it goes against my conscience to lay my hand rudely on a female. I desisted, and looked her all over from head to foot; the poor brute's knees were trembling and her breathing was distressed; it was plain that she could go no faster on a hill. God forbid, thought I, that I should brutalise this innocent creature; let her go at her own pace, and let me patiently follow.

What that pace was, there is no word mean enough to describe; it was something as much slower than a walk as a walk is slower than a run; it kept me hanging on each foot for an incredible length of time; in five minutes it exhausted the spirit and set up a fever in all the muscles of the leg. And yet I had to keep close at hand and measure my advance exactly upon hers; for if I dropped a few yards into the rear, or went on a few yards ahead, Modestine came instantly to a halt and began to browse. The thought that this was to last from here to Alais nearly broke my heart. Of all conceivable journeys, this promised to be the most tedious. I tried to tell myself it was a lovely day; I tried to charm my foreboding spirit with tobacco; but I had a vision ever present to me of the long, long roads, up hill and down dale, and a pair of figures ever infinitesimally moving, foot by foot, a yard to the minute, and, like things enchanted in a nightmare, approaching no nearer to the goal.

In the mean time there came up behind us a tall peasant, perhaps forty years of age, of an ironical snuffy countenance, and arrayed in the green tail-coat of the country. He overtook us hand over hand, and stopped to consider our pitiful advance.

"Your donkey," says he, "is very old?"

I told him, I believed not.

Then, he supposed, we had come far.

I told him, we had but newly left Monastier.

"*Et vous marchez comme ça!*" cried he; and, throwing back his head, he laughed long and heartily. I watched him, half prepared to feel offended, until he had satisfied his mirth; and then, "You must have no pity on these animals," said he; and, plucking a switch out of a thicket, he began to lace Modestine about the stern-works, uttering a cry. The rogue pricked up her ears and broke into a good round pace, which she kept up without flagging, and without exhibiting the least symptom of distress, as long as the peasant kept beside us. Her former panting and shaking had been, I regret to say, a piece of comedy.

My *deus ex machinâ*, before he left me, supplied some excellent, if inhumane, advice; presented me with the switch, which he declared she would feel more tenderly than my cane; and finally taught me the true cry or masonic word of donkey-drivers, "Proot!" All the time, he regarded me with a comical incredulous air, which was embarrassing to confront; and smiled over my donkey-driving, as I might have smiled over his orthography, or his green tail-coat. But it was not my turn for the moment.

I was proud of my new lore, and thought I had learned the art to perfection. And certainly Modestine did wonders for the rest of the forenoon, and I had a breathing space to look about me. It was Sabbath; the mountain-fields were all vacant in the sunshine; and as we came down through St. Martin de Frugères, the church was crowded to the door, there were people kneeling without upon the steps, and the sound of the priest's chanting came forth out of the dim interior. It gave me a home feeling on the spot; for I am a countryman of the Sabbath, so to speak, and all Sabbath observances, like a Scotch accent, strike in me mixed feelings, grateful and reverse. It is only a traveller, hurrying by like a person from another planet, who can rightly enjoy the peace and beauty of the great ascetic feast. The sight of the resting country does his spirit good. There is something better than music in the wide unusual silence; and it disposes him to amiable thoughts, like the sound of a little river or the warmth of sunlight.

In this pleasant humour I came down the hill to where Goudet stands in a green end of a valley, with Château Beaufort opposite upon a rocky steep, and the stream, as clear as crystal, lying in a deep pool between them. Above and below, you may hear it wimpling over the stones, an amiable stripling of a river, which it seems absurd to call the Loire. On all sides, Goudet is shut in by mountains; rocky foot-paths, practicable at best for donkeys, join it to the outer world of France; and the men and women drink and swear, in their green corner, or look up at the snow-clad peaks in winter from the threshold of their homes, in an isolation, you would think, like that of Homer's Cyclops. But it is not so; the postman reaches Goudet with the letter-bag; the aspiring youth of Goudet are within a day's walk of the railway at Le Puy; and here in the inn you may find an engraved portrait of the host's nephew, Régis Senac, "Professor of Fencing and Champion of the two Americas," a distinction gained by him, along with the sum of five hundred dollars, at Tammany Hall, New York, on the 10th April 1876.

I hurried over my midday meal, and was early forth again. But, alas, as we climbed the interminable hill upon the other side, "Proot!" seemed to have lost its virtue. I prooted like a lion, I prooted mellifluously like a sucking-dove; but Modestine would be neither softened nor intimidated. She held doggedly to her pace; nothing but a blow would move her, and that only for a second. I must follow at her heels, incessantly belabouring. A moment's pause in this ignoble toil, and she relapsed into her own private gait. I think I never heard of any one in as mean a situation. I must reach the lake of Bouchet, where I meant to camp, before sundown, and, to have even a hope of this, I must instantly maltreat this uncomplaining animal. The sound of my own blows sickened me. Once, when I looked at her, she had a faint resemblance to a lady of my acquaintance who formerly loaded me with kindness; and this increased my horror of my cruelty.

To make matters worse, we encountered another donkey, ranging at will upon the roadside; and this donkey chanced to be a gentleman. He and Modestine met nickering for joy, and I had to separate the pair and beat down their young romance with a renewed and feverish bastinado. If the other donkey had had the heart of a male under his hide, he would have fallen upon me tooth and hoof; and this was a kind of consolation—he was plainly unworthy of Modestine's affection. But the incident saddened me, as did everything that spoke of my donkey's sex.

It was blazing hot up the valley, windless, with vehement sun upon my shoulders; and I had to labour so consistently with my stick that the sweat ran into my eyes. Every five minutes, too, the pack, the basket, and the pilot-coat would take an ugly slew to one side or the other; and I had to stop Modestine, just when I had got her to a tolerable pace of about two miles an hour, to tug, push, shoulder, and readjust the load. And at last, in the village of Ussel, saddle and all, the whole hypothec turned round and grovelled in the dust below the donkey's belly. She, none better pleased, incontinently drew up and seemed to smile; and a party of one man, two women, and two children came up, and, standing round me in a half-circle, encouraged her by their example.

I had the devil's own trouble to get the thing righted; and the instant I had done so, without hesitation, it toppled and fell down upon the other side. Judge if I was hot! And yet not a hand was offered to assist me. The man, indeed, told me I ought to have a

package of a different shape. I suggested, if he knew nothing better
to the point in my predicament, he might hold his tongue. And the
good-natured dog agreed with me smilingly. It was the most despicable fix. I must plainly content myself with the pack for Modestine, and take the following items for my own share of the portage:
a cane, a quart flask, a pilot-jacket heavily weighted in the pockets,
two pounds of black bread, and an open basket full of meats and
bottles. I believe I may say I am not devoid of greatness of soul;
for I did not recoil from this infamous burden. I disposed it,
Heaven knows how, so as to be mildly portable, and then proceeded
to steer Modestine through the village. She tried, as was indeed her
invariable habit, to enter every house and every courtyard in the
whole length; and, encumbered as I was, without a hand to help
myself, no words can render an idea of my difficulties. A priest,
with six or seven others, was examining a church in process of
repair, and he and his acolytes laughed loudly as they saw my
plight. I remembered having laughed myself when I had seen
good men struggling with adversity in the person of a jackass, and
the recollection filled me with penitence. That was in my old light
days, before this trouble came upon me. God knows at least that I
shall never laugh again, thought I. But O, what a cruel thing is a
farce to those engaged in it!

A little out of the village, Modestine, filled with the demon, set
her heart upon a by-road, and positively refused to leave it. I
dropped all my bundles, and, I am ashamed to say, struck the poor
sinner twice across the face. It was pitiful to see her lift up her
head with shut eyes, as if waiting for another blow. I came very
near crying; but I did a wiser thing than that, and sat squarely
down by the roadside to consider my situation under the cheerful
influence of tobacco and a nip of brandy. Modestine, in the mean
while, munched some black bread with a contrite hypocritical air.
It was plain that I must make a sacrifice to the gods of shipwreck.
I threw away the empty bottle destined to carry milk; I threw
away my own white bread, and, disdaining to act by general
average, kept the black bread for Modestine; lastly, I threw away
the cold leg of mutton and the egg-whisk, although this last was
dear to my heart. Thus I found room for everything in the basket,
and even stowed the boating-coat on the top. By means of an end
of cord I slung it under one arm; and although the cord cut my

shoulder, and the jacket hung almost to the ground, it was with a heart greatly lightened that I set forth again.

I had now an arm free to thrash Modestine, and cruelly I chastised her. If I were to reach the lakeside before dark, she must bestir her little shanks to some tune. Already the sun had gone down into a windy-looking mist; and although there were still a few streaks of gold far off to the east on the hills and the black fir-woods, all was cold and gray about our onward path. An infinity of little country by-roads led hither and thither among the fields. It was the most pointless labyrinth. I could see my destination overhead, or rather the peak that dominates it; but choose as I pleased, the roads always ended by turning away from it, and sneaking back towards the valley, or northward along the margin of the hills. The failing light, the waning colour, the naked, unhomely, stony country through which I was travelling, threw me into some despondency. I promise you, the stick was not idle; I think every decent step that Modestine took must have cost me at least two emphatic blows. There was not another sound in the neighbourhood but that of my unwearying bastinado.

Suddenly, in the midst of my toils, the load once more bit the dust, and, as by enchantment, all the cords were simultaneously loosened, and the road scattered with my dear possessions. The packing was to begin again from the beginning; and as I had to invent a new and better system, I do not doubt but I lost half an hour. It began to be dusk in earnest as I reached a wilderness of turf and stones. It had the air of being a road which should lead everywhere at the same time; and I was falling into something not unlike despair when I saw two figures stalking towards me over the stones. They walked one behind the other like tramps, but their pace was remarkable. The son led the way, a tall, ill-made, sombre, Scotch-looking man; the mother followed, all in her Sunday's best, with an elegantly-embroidered ribbon to her cap, and a new felt hat atop, and proffering, as she strode along with kilted petticoats, a string of obscene and blasphemous oaths.

I hailed the son and asked him my direction. He pointed loosely west and northwest, muttered an inaudible comment, and, without slacking his pace for an instant, stalked on, as he was going, right athwart my path. The mother followed without so much as raising her head. I shouted and shouted after them, but they continued to scale the hillside, and turned a deaf ear to my outcries. At last, leaving Modestine by herself, I was constrained to run after them, hailing the while. They stopped as I drew near, the mother still cursing; and I could see she was a handsome, motherly, respectable-looking woman. The son once more answered me roughly and inaudibly, and was for setting out again. But this time I simply collared the mother, who was nearest me, and, apologising for my violence, declared that I could not let them go until they had put me on my road. They were neither of them offended—rather mollified than otherwise; told me I had only to follow them; and then the mother asked me what I wanted by the lake at such an hour. I replied, in the Scotch manner, by inquiring if she had far to go herself. She told me, with another oath, that she had an hour and a half's road before her. And then, without salutation, the pair strode forward again up the hillside in the gathering dusk.

I returned for Modestine, pushed her briskly forward, and, after a sharp ascent of twenty minutes, reached the edge of a plateau. The view, looking back on my day's journey, was both wild and sad. Mount Mézenc and the peaks beyond St. Julien stood out in trenchant gloom against a cold glitter in the east; and the intervening field of hills had fallen together into one broad wash of shadow, except here and there the outline of a wooded sugar-loaf in black, here and there a white irregular patch to represent a cultivated farm, and here and there a blot where the Loire, the Gazeille, or Laussonne wandered in a gorge.

Soon we were on a high-road, and surprise seized on my mind as I beheld a village of some magnitude close at hand; for I had been told that the neighbourhood of the lake was uninhabited except by trout. The road smoked in the twilight with children driving home cattle from the fields; and a pair of mounted stride-legged women, hat and cap and all, dashed past me at a hammering trot from the canton where they had been to church and market. I asked one of the children where I was. At Bouchet St. Nicolas, he told me. Thither, about a mile south of my destination, and on the other side of a respectable summit, had these confused roads and treacherous peasantry conducted me. My shoulder was cut, so that it hurt sharply; my arm ached like toothache from perpetual beating; I gave up the lake and my design to camp, and asked for the *auberge*.

I Have a Goad

The *auberge* of Bouchet St. Nicolas was among the least preten-
tious I have ever visited; but I saw many more of the like upon
my journey. Indeed, it was typical of these French highlands.
Imagine a cottage of two stories, with a bench before the door; the
stable and kitchen in a suite, so that Modestine and I could hear
each other dining; furniture of the plainest, earthern floors, a
single bedchamber for travellers, and that without any convenience
but beds. In the kitchen cooking and eating go forward side by
side, and the family sleep at night. Any one who has a fancy to
wash must do so in public at the common table. The food is
sometimes spare; hard fish and omelette have been my portion
more than once; the wine is of the smallest, the brandy abominable
to man; and the visit of a fat sow, grouting under the table and
rubbing against your legs, is no impossible accompaniment to
dinner.

But the people of the inn, in nine cases out of ten, show themselves friendly and considerate. As soon as you cross the doors you
cease to be a stranger; and although these peasantry are rude and
forbidding on the highway, they show a tincture of kind breeding
when you share their hearth. At Bouchet, for instance, I uncorked
my bottle of Beaujolais, and asked the host to join me. He would
take but little.

"I am an amateur of such wine, do you see?" he said, "and I am
capable of leaving you not enough."

In these hedge-inns the traveller is expected to eat with his own
knife; unless he asks, no other will be supplied: with a glass, a
whang of bread, and an iron fork, the table is completely laid. My
knife was cordially admired by the landlord of Bouchet, and the
spring filled him with wonder.

"I should never have guessed that," he said. "I would bet," he
added, weighing it in his hand, "that this cost you not less than five
francs."

When I told him it had cost me twenty, his jaw dropped.

He was a mild, handsome, sensible, friendly old man, astonishingly ignorant. His wife, who was not so pleasant in her manners,
knew how to read, although I do not suppose she ever did so. She

had a share of brains and spoke with a cutting emphasis, like one
who ruled the roast.

"My man knows nothing," she said, with an angry nod; "he is
like the beasts."

And the old gentleman signified acquiescence with his head.
There was no contempt on her part, and no shame on his; the
facts were accepted loyally, and no more about the matter.

I was tightly cross-examined about my journey; and the lady
understood in a moment, and sketched out what I should put into
my book when I got home. "Whether people harvest or not in
such or such a place; if there were forests; studies of manners;
what, for example, I and the master of the house say to you; the
beauties of Nature, and all that." And she interrogated me with a
look.

"It is just that," said I.

"You see," she added to her husband, "I understood that."

They were both much interested by the story of my misadventures.

"In the morning," said the husband, "I will make you something
better than your cane. Such a beast as that feels nothing; it is in
the proverb—*dur comme un âne;* you might beat her insensible
with a cudgel, and yet you would arrive nowhere."

Something better! I little knew what he was offering.

The sleeping-room was furnished with two beds. I had one; and
I will own I was a little abashed to find a young man and his wife
and child in the act of mounting into the other. This was my first
experience of the sort; and if I am always to feel equally silly and
extraneous, I pray God it be my last as well. I kept my eyes to
myself, and know nothing of the woman except that she had
beautiful arms, and seemed no whit embarrassed by my appearance. As a matter of fact, the situation was more trying to me than
to the pair. A pair keep each other in countenance; it is the single
gentleman who has to blush. But I could not help attributing my
sentiments to the husband, and sought to conciliate his tolerance
with a cup of brandy from my flask. He told me that he was a
cooper of Alais travelling to St. Etienne in search of work, and
that in his spare moments he followed the fatal calling of a maker
of matches. Me he readily enough divined to be a brandy merchant.

I was up first in the morning (Monday, September 23d), and hastened my toilette guiltily, so as to leave a clear field for madam, the cooper's wife. I drank a bowl of milk, and set off to explore the neighbourhood of Bouchet. It was perishing cold, a gray, windy, wintry morning; misty clouds flew fast and low; the wind piped over the naked platform; and the only speck of colour was away behind Mount Mézenc and the eastern hills, where the sky still wore the orange of the dawn.

It was five in the morning, and four thousand feet above the sea; and I had to bury my hands in my pockets and trot. People were trooping out to the labours of the field by twos and threes, and all turned round to stare upon the stranger. I had seen them coming back last night, I saw them going afield again; and there was the life of Bouchet in a nutshell.

When I came back to the inn for a bit of breakfast, the landlady was in the kitchen combing out her daughter's hair; and I made her my compliments upon its beauty.

"Oh, no," said the mother; "it is not so beautiful as it ought to be. Look, it is too fine."

Thus does a wise peasantry console itself under adverse physical circumstances, and, by a startling democratic process, the defects of the majority decide the type of beauty.

"And where," said I, "is monsieur?"

"The master of the house is up-stairs," she answered, "making you a goad."

Blessed be the man who invented goads! Blessed the innkeeper of Bouchet St. Nicolas, who introduced me to their use! This plain wand, with an eighth of an inch of pin, was indeed a sceptre when he put it in my hands. Thenceforward Modestine was my slave. A prick, and she passed the most inviting stable-door. A prick, and she broke forth into a gallant little trotlet that devoured the miles. It was not a remarkable speed, when all was said; and we took four hours to cover ten miles at the best of it. But what a heavenly change since yesterday! No more wielding of the ugly cudgel; no more flailing with an aching arm; no more broadsword exercise, but a discreet and gentlemanly fence. And what although now and then a drop of blood should appear on Modestine's mouse-coloured wedge-like rump? I should have preferred it otherwise, indeed; but yesterday's exploits had purged my heart of all humanity. The perverse little devil, since she would not be taken with kindness, must even go with pricking.

It was bleak and bitter cold, and, except a cavalcade of stride-legged ladies and a pair of post-runners, the road was dead solitary all the way to Pradelles. I scarce remember an incident but one. A handsome foal with a bell about his neck came charging up to us upon a stretch of common, sniffed the air martially as one about to do great deeds, and, suddenly thinking otherwise in his green young heart, put about and galloped off as he had come, the bell tinkling in the wind. For a long while afterwards I saw his noble attitude as he drew up, and heard the note of his bell; and when I struck the high-road, the song of the telegraph-wires seemed to continue the same music.

Pradelles stands on a hillside, high above the Allier, surrounded by rich meadows. They were cutting aftermath on all sides, which gave the neighbourhood, this gusty autumn morning, an untimely smell of hay. On the opposite bank of the Allier the land kept mounting for miles to the horizon: a tanned and sallow autumn landscape, with black blots of fir-wood and white roads wandering through the hills. Over all this the clouds shed a uniform and purplish shadow, sad and somewhat menacing, exaggerating height and distance, and throwing into still higher relief the twisted ribbons of the highway. It was a cheerless prospect, but one stimulating to a traveller. For I was now upon the limit of Velay, and all that I beheld lay in another country—wild Gévaudan, mountainous, uncultivated, and but recently disforested from terror of the wolves.

Wolves, alas, like bandits, seem to flee the traveller's advance; and you may trudge through all our comfortable Europe, and not meet with an adventure worth the name. But here, if anywhere, a man was on the frontiers of hope. For this was the land of the ever-memorable BEAST, the Napoléon Buonaparte of wolves. What a career was his! He lived ten months at free quarters in Gévaudan and Vivarais; he ate women and children and "shepherdesses celebrated for their beauty;" he pursued armed horsemen; he has been seen at broad noonday chasing a postchaise and outrider along the king's high-road and chaise and outrider fleeing before him at the gallop. He was placarded like a political offender, and ten thousand francs were offered for his head. And yet, when he was shot and sent to Versailles, behold! a common wolf, and even small for that. "Though I could reach from pole to pole," sang Alexander Pope; the Little Corporal shook Europe; and if all wolves had been as this wolf, they would have changed the history of man. M. Elie Berthet has made him the hero of a novel, which I have read, and do not wish to read again.

I hurried over my lunch, and was proof against the landlady's desire that I should visit our Lady of Pradelles, "who performed many miracles, although she was of wood;" and before three-quarters of an hour I was goading Modestine down the steep descent that leads to Langogne on the Allier. On both sides of the road, in big dusty fields, farmers were preparing for next Spring. Every fifty yards a yoke of great-necked stolid oxen were patiently haling at the plough. I saw one of these mild formidable servants of the glebe, who took a sudden interest in Modestine and me. The furrow down which he was journeying lay at an angle to the road, and his head was solidly fixed to the yoke like those of caryatides below a ponderous cornice; but he screwed round his big honest eyes and followed us with a ruminating look, until his master bade him turn the plough and proceed to reascend the field. From all these furrowing ploughshares, from the feet of oxen, from a labourer here and there who was breaking the dry clods with a hoe, the wind carried away a thin dust like so much smoke. It was a fine, busy, breathing, rustic landscape; and as I continued to descend, the highlands of Gévaudan kept mounting in front of me against the sky.

I had crossed the Loire the day before; now I was to cross the Allier; so near are these two confluents in their youth. Just at the bridge of Langogne, as the long-promised rain was beginning to fall, a lassie of some seven or eight addressed me in the sacramental phrase, *"D'où 'st que vous venez?"* She did it with so high an air that she set me laughing; and this cut her to the quick. She was evidently one who reckoned on respect, and stood looking after me in silent dudgeon, as I crossed the bridge and entered the county of Gévaudan.

Upper Gévaudan

"The way also here was very wearisome through dirt and slabbiness; nor was there on all this ground so much as one inn or victualling-house wherein to refresh the feebler sort."

Pilgrim's Progress.

A Camp in the Dark

THE NEXT DAY (TUESDAY, SEPTEMBER 24TH), IT WAS TWO O'CLOCK IN the afternoon before I got my journal written up and my knapsack repaired, for I was determined to carry my knapsack in the future and have no more ado with baskets; and half an hour afterwards I set out for Le Cheylard l'Evêque, a place on the borders of the forest of Mercoire. A man, I was told, should walk there in an hour and a half; and I thought it scarce too ambitious to suppose that a man encumbered with a donkey might cover the same distance in four hours.

All the way up the long hill from Langogne it rained and hailed alternately; the wind kept freshening steadily, although slowly; plentiful hurrying clouds—some dragging veils of straight rain-shower, others massed and luminous as though promising snow—careered out of the north and followed me along my way. I was soon out of the cultivated basin of the Allier, and away from the ploughing oxen, and such-like sights of the country. Moor, heathery marsh, tracts of rock and pines, woods of birch all jewelled with the autumn yellow, here and there a few naked cottages and bleak fields,—these were the characters of the country. Hill and valley followed valley and hill; the little green and stony cattle-tracks wandered in and out of one another, split into three or four, died away in marshy hollows, and began again sporadically on hillsides or at the borders of a wood.

There was no direct road to Cheylard, and it was no easy affair to make a passage in this uneven country and through this intermittent labyrinth of tracks. It must have been about four when I struck Sagnerousse, and went on my way rejoicing in a sure point of departure. Two hours afterwards, the dusk rapidly falling, in a lull of the wind, I issued from a fir-wood where I had long been wandering, and found, not the looked-for village, but another marish bottom among rough-and-tumble hills. For some time past I had heard the ringing of cattle-bells ahead; and now, as I came out of the skirts of the wood, I saw near upon a dozen cows and perhaps as many more black figures, which I conjectured to be children, although the mist had almost unrecognisably exaggerated their forms. These were all silently following each other round and round in a circle, now taking hands, now breaking up with chains and reverences. A dance of children appeals to very innocent and lively thoughts; but, at nightfall on the marshes, the thing was eerie and fantastic to behold. Even I, who am well enough read in Herbert Spencer, felt a sort of silence fall for an instant on my mind. The next, I was pricking Modestine forward, and guiding her like an unruly ship through the open. In a path, she went doggedly ahead of her own accord, as before a fair wind; but once on the turf or among heather, and the brute became demented. The tendency of lost travellers to go round in a circle was developed in her to the degree of passion, and it took all the steering I had in me to keep even a decently straight course through a single field.

While I was thus desperately tacking through the bog, children and cattle began to disperse, until only a pair of girls remained behind. From these I sought direction on my path. The peasantry in general were but little disposed to counsel a wayfarer. One old devil simply retired into his house, and barricaded the door on my approach; and I might beat and shout myself hoarse, he turned a deaf ear. Another, having given me a direction which, as I found afterwards, I had misunderstood, complacently watched me going wrong without adding a sign. He did not care a stalk of parsley if I wandered all night upon the hills! As for these two girls, they were a pair of impudent sly sluts, with not a thought but mischief. One put out her tongue at me, the other bade me follow the cows; and they both giggled and jogged each other's elbows. The Beast of Gévaudan ate about a hundred children of this district: I began to think of him with sympathy.

Leaving the girls, I pushed on through the bog, and got into another wood and upon a well-marked road. It grew darker and darker. Modestine, suddenly beginning to smell mischief, bettered the pace of her own accord, and from that time forward gave me no trouble. It was the first sign of intelligence I had occasion to remark in her. At the same time, the wind freshened into half a gale, and another heavy discharge of rain came flying up out of the north. At the other side of the wood I sighted some red windows in the dusk. This was the hamlet of Fouzilhic; three houses on a hillside, near a wood of birches. Here I found a delightful old man, who came a little way with me in the rain to put me safely on the road for Cheylard. He would hear of no reward; but shook his hands above his head almost as if in menace, and refused volubly and shrilly, in unmitigated *patois*.

All seemed right at last. My thoughts began to turn upon dinner and a fireside, and my heart was agreeably softened in my bosom. Alas, and I was on the brink of new and greater miseries! Suddenly, at a single swoop, the night fell. I have been abroad in many a black night, but never in a blacker. A glimmer of rocks, a glimmer of the track where it was well beaten, a certain fleecy density, or night within night, for a tree—this was all that I could discriminate. The sky was simply darkness overhead; even the flying clouds pursued their way invisibly to human eyesight. I could not distinguish my hand at arm's length from the track, nor my goad, at the same distance, from the meadows or the sky.

Soon the road that I was following split, after the fashion of the country, into three or four in a piece of rocky meadow. Since Modestine had shown such a fancy for beaten roads, I tried her instinct in this predicament. But the instinct of an ass is what might be expected from the name; a half a minute she was clambering round and round among some boulders, as lost a donkey as you would wish to see. I should have camped long before had I been properly provided; but as this was to be so short a stage, I had brought no wine, no bread for myself and little over a pound for my lady-friend. Add to this, that I and Modestine were both handsomely wetted by the showers. But now, if I could have found some water, I should have camped at once in spite of all. Water, however, being entirely absent, except in the form of rain, I determined to return to Fouzilhic, and ask a guide a little further on my way—"a little farther lend thy guiding hand."

The thing was easy to decide, hard to accomplish. In this sensible roaring blackness I was sure of nothing but the direction of the wind. To this I set my face; the road had disappeared, and I went across country, now in marshy opens, now baffled by walls unscalable to Modestine, until I came once more in sight of some red windows. This time they were differently disposed. It was not Fouzilhic, but Fouzilhac, a hamlet little distant from the other in space, but worlds away in the spirit of its inhabitants. I tied Modestine to a gate, and groped forward, stumbling among rocks, plunging mid-leg in bog, until I gained the entrance of the village. In the first lighted house there was a woman who would not open to me. She could do nothing, she cried to me through the door, being alone and lame; but if I would apply at the next house, there was a man who could help me if he had a mind.

They came to the next door in force, a man, two women, and a girl, and brought a pair of lanterns to examine the wayfarer. The man was not ill-looking, but had a shifty smile. He leaned against the doorpost, and heard me state my case. All I asked was a guide as far as Cheylard.

"*C'est que, voyez-vous, il fait noir,*" said he.

I told him that was just my reason for requiring help.

"I understand that," said he, looking uncomfortable; "*mais— c'est—de la peine.*"

I was willing to pay, I said. He shook his head. I rose as high as ten francs; but he continued to shake his head. "Name your own price, then," said I.

"*Ce n'est pas ça,*" he said at length, and with evident difficulty; "but I am not going to cross the door—*mais je ne sortirai pas de la porte.*"

I grew a little warm, and asked him what he proposed that I should do.

"Where are you going beyond Cheylard?" he asked by way of answer.

"That is no affair of yours," I returned, for I was not going to indulge his bestial curiosity; "it changes nothing in my present predicament."

"*C'est vrai, ça,*" he acknowledged, with a laugh; "*oui, c'est vrai. Et d'où venez vous?*"

A better man than I might have felt nettled.

"Oh," said I, "I am not going to answer any of your questions, so you may spare yourself the trouble of putting them. I am late enough already; I want help. If you will not guide me yourself, at least help me to find some one else who will."

"Hold on," he cried suddenly. "Was it not you who passed in the meadow while it was still day?"

"Yes, yes," said the girl, whom I had not hitherto recognised; "it was monsieur; I told him to follow the cow."

"As for you, mademoiselle," said I, "you are a *farceuse.*"

"And," added the man, "what the devil have you done to be still here?"

What the devil, indeed! But there I was. "The great thing," said I, "is to make an end of it;" and once more proposed that he should help me to find a guide.

"*C'est que,*" he said again, "*c'est que—il fait noir.*"

"Very well," said I; "take one of your lanterns."

"No," he cried, drawing a thought backward, and again intrenching himself behind one of his former phrases; "I will not cross the door."

I looked at him. I saw unaffected terror struggling on his face with unaffected shame; he was smiling pitifully and wetting his lip with his tongue, like a detected schoolboy. I drew a brief picture of my state, and asked him what I was to do.

"I don't know," he said; "I will not cross the door."

Here was the Beast of Gévaudan, and no mistake.

"Sir," said I, with my most commanding manners, "you are a coward."

And with that I turned my back upon the family party, who hastened to retire within their fortifications; and the famous door was closed again, but not till I had overheard the sound of laughter. *Filia barbara pater barbarior.* Let me say it in the plural: the Beasts of Gévaudan.

The lanterns had somewhat dazzled me, and I ploughed distressfully among stones and rubbish-heaps. All the other houses in the village were both dark and silent; and though I knocked at here and there a door, my knocking was unanswered. It was a bad business; I gave up Fouzilhac with my curses. The rain had stopped, and the wind, which still kept rising, began to dry my coat and trousers. "Very well," thought I, "water or no water, I must camp." But the first thing was to return to Modestine. I am pretty sure I was twenty minutes groping for my lady in the dark; and if it had not been for the unkindly services of the bog, into which I once more stumbled, I might have still been groping for her at the dawn. My next business was to gain the shelter of a wood, for the wind was cold as well as boisterous. How, in this well-wooded district, I should have been so long in finding one, is another of the insoluble mysteries of this day's adventures; but I will take my oath that I put near an hour to the discovery.

At last black trees began to show upon my left, and, suddenly crossing the road, made a cave of unmitigated blackness right in front. I call it a cave without exaggeration; to pass below that arch of leaves was like entering a dungeon. I felt about until my hand encountered a stout branch, and to this I tied Modestine, a haggard, drenched, desponding donkey. Then I lowered my pack, laid it along the wall on the margin of the road, and unbuckled the straps. I knew well enough where the lantern was; but where were the candles? I groped and groped among the tumbled articles, and, while I was thus groping, suddenly I touched the spirit-lamp. Salvation! This would serve my turn as well. The wind roared unwearyingly among the trees; I could hear the boughs tossing and the leaves churning through half a mile of forest; yet the scene of my encampment was not only as black as the pit, but admirably sheltered. At the second match the wick caught flame. The light was both livid and shifting; but it cut me off from the universe, and doubled the darkness of the surrounding night.

I tied Modestine more conveniently for herself, and broke up half the black bread for her supper, reserving the other half against the morning. Then I gathered what I should want within reach, took off my wet boots and gaiters, which I wrapped in my waterproof, arranged my knapsack for a pillow under the flap of my sleeping-bag, insinuated my limbs into the interior, and buckled myself in like a bambino. I opened a tin of Bologna sausage and broke a cake of chocolate, and that was all I had to eat. It may sound offensive, but I ate them together, bite by bite, by way of bread and meat. All I had to wash down this revolting mixture was neat brandy: a revolting beverage in itself. But I was rare and hungry; ate well, and smoked one of the best cigarettes in my experience. Then I put a stone in my straw hat, pulled the flap of my fur cap over my neck and eyes, put my revolver ready to my hand, and snuggled well down among the sheepskins.

I questioned at first if I were sleepy, for I felt my heart beating faster than usual, as if with an agreeable excitement to which my mind remained a stranger. But as soon as my eyelids touched, that subtle glue leaped between them, and they would no more come separate. The wind among the trees was my lullaby. Sometimes it sounded for minutes together with a steady even rush, not rising nor abating; and again it would swell and burst like a great crashing breaker, and the trees would patter me all over with big drops from the rain of the afternoon. Night after night, in my own bedroom in the country, I have given ear to this perturbing concert of the wind among the woods; but whether it was a difference in the trees, or the lie of the ground, or because I was myself outside and in the midst of it, the fact remains that the wind sang to a different tune among these woods of Gévaudan. I hearkened and hearkened; and meanwhile sleep took gradual possession of my body and subdued my thoughts and senses; but still my last waking effort was to listen and distinguish, and my last conscious state was one of wonder at the foreign clamour in my ears.

Twice in the course of the dark hours—once when a stone galled me underneath the sack, and again when the poor patient Modestine, growing angry, pawed and stamped upon the road— I was recalled for a brief while to consciousness, and saw a star or two overhead, and the lace-like edge of the foliage against the sky. When I awoke for the third time (Wednesday, September 25th), the world was flooded with a blue light, the mother of the dawn. I saw the leaves labouring in the wind and the ribbon of the road; and, on turning my head, there was Modestine tied to a beech, and standing half across the path in an attitude of inimitable patience. I closed my eyes again, and set to thinking over the experience of the night. I was surprised to find how easy and pleasant it had been, even in this tempestuous weather. The stone which annoyed me would not have been there, had I not been forced to camp blindfold in the opaque night; and I had felt no other inconvenience except when my feet encountered the lantern or the second volume of Peyrat's *Pastors of the Desert* among the mixed contents of my sleeping-bag; nay more, I had felt not a touch of cold, and awakened with unusually lightsome and clear sensations.

With that, I shook myself, got once more into my boots and gaiters, and breaking up the rest of the bread for Modestine, strolled about to see in what part of the world I had awakened. Ulysses, left on Ithaca, and with a mind unsettled by the goddess, was not more pleasantly astray. I have been after an adventure all my life, a pure dispassionate adventure, such as befell early and heroic voyagers; and thus to be found by morning in a random woodside nook in Gévaudan—not knowing north from south, as strange to my surroundings as the first man upon the earth, an inland castaway—was to find a fraction of my day-dreams realised. I was on the skirts of a little wood of birch, sprinkled with a few beeches; behind, it adjoined another wood of fir; and in front, it broke up and went down in open order into a shallow and meadowy dale. All round there were bare hill-tops, some near, some far away, as the perspective closed or opened, but none apparently much higher than the rest. The wind huddled the trees. The golden specks of autumn in the birches tossed shiveringly. Overhead the sky was full of strings and shreds of vapour, flying, vanishing, reappearing, and turning about an axis like tumblers, as the wind hounded them through heaven. It was wild weather and famishing cold. I ate some chocolate, swallowed a mouthful of brandy, and smoked a cigarette before the cold should have time to disable my fingers. And by the time I had got all this done, and had made my pack and bound it on the pack-saddle, the day was tiptoe on the threshold of the east. We had not gone many steps along the lane, before the sun, still invisible to me, sent a glow of gold over some cloud mountains that lay ranged along the eastern sky.

The wind had us on the stern, and hurried us bitingly forward. I buttoned myself into my coat, and walked on in a pleasant frame of mind with all men, when suddenly, at a corner, there was Fouzilhic once more in front of me. Not only that, but there was the old gentleman who had escorted me so far the night before, running out of his house at sight of me, with hands upraised in horror.

"My poor boy!" he cried, "what does this mean?"

I told him what had happened. He beat his old hands like clappers in a mill, to think how lightly he had let me go; but when he heard of the man of Fouzilhac, anger and depression seized upon his mind.

"This time, at least," said he, "there shall be no mistake."

And he limped along, for he was very rheumatic, for about half a mile, and until I was almost within sight of Cheylard, the destination I had hunted for so long.

Cheylard and Luc

Candidly, it seemed little worthy of all this searching. A few broken ends of village, with no particular street, but a succession of open places heaped with logs and fagots; a couple of tilted crosses, a shrine to our Lady of all Graces on the summit of a little hill; and all this, upon a rattling highland river, in the corner of a naked valley. What went ye out for to see? thought I to myself. But the place had a life of its own. I found a board commemorating the liberalities of Cheylard for the past year, hung up, like a banner, in the diminutive and tottering church. In 1877, it appeared, the inhabitants subscribed forty-eight francs ten centimes for the "Work of the Propagation of the Faith." Some of this, I could not help hoping, would be applied to my native land. Cheylard scrapes together halfpence for the darkened souls in Edinburgh; while Balquidder and Dunrossness bemoan the ignorance of Rome. Thus, to the high entertainment of the angels, do we pelt each other with evangelists, like schoolboys bickering in the snow.

The inn was again singularly unpretentious. The whole furniture of a not ill-to-do family was in the kitchen: the beds, the cradle, the clothes, the plate-rack, the meal-chest, and the photograph of the parish priest. There were five children, one of whom was set to its morning prayers at the stair-foot soon after my arrival, and a sixth would erelong be forthcoming. I was kindly received by these good folk. They were much interested in my misadventure. The wood in which I had slept belonged to them; the man of Fouzilhac they thought a monster of iniquity, and counselled me warmly to summon him at law—"because I might have died." The good wife was horror-stricken to see me drink over a pint of uncreamed milk.

"You will do yourself an evil," she said. "Permit me to boil it for you."

After I had begun the morning on this delightful liquor, she having an infinity of things to arrange, I was permitted, nay requested, to make a bowl of chocolate for myself. My boots and gaiters were hung up to dry, and, seeing me trying to write my journal on my knee, the eldest daughter let down a hinged table in the chimney-corner for my convenience. Here I wrote, drank my chocolate, and finally ate an omelette before I left. The table was thick with dust; for, as they explained, it was not used except in winter weather. I had a clear look up the vent, through brown agglomerations of soot and blue vapour, to the sky; and whenever a handful of twigs was thrown on to the fire, my legs were scorched by the blaze.

The husband had begun life as a mule-teer, and when I came to charge Modestine showed himself full of the prudence of his art. "You will have to change this package," said he; "it ought to be in two parts, and then you might have double the weight."

I explained that I wanted no more weight; and for no donkey hitherto created would I cut my sleeping-bag in two.

"It fatigues her, however," said the innkeeper; "it fatigues her greatly on the march. Look."

Alas, there were her two forelegs no better than raw beef on the inside, and blood was running from under her tail. They told me when I left, and I was ready to believe it, that before a few days I should come to love Modestine like a dog. Three days had passed, we had shared some misadventures, and my heart was still as cold as a potato towards my beast of burden. She was pretty enough to look at; but then she had given proof of dead stupidity, redeemed indeed by patience, but aggravated by flashes of sorry and ill-judged light-heartedness. And I own this new discovery seemed another point against her. What the devil was the good of a she-ass if she could not carry a sleeping-bag and a few necessaries? I saw the end of the fable rapidly approaching, when I should have to carry Modestine. Æsop was the man to know the world! I assure you I set out with heavy thoughts upon my short day's march.

It was not only heavy thoughts about Modestine that weighted me upon the way; it was a leaden business altogether. For first, the wind blew so rudely that I had to hold on the pack with one hand from Cheylard to Luc; and second, my road lay through one of the most beggarly countries in the world. It was like the worst of the Scotch Highlands, only worse; cold, naked, and ignoble, scant of wood, scant of heather, scant of life. A road and some fences broke the unvarying waste, and the line of the road was marked by upright pillars, to serve in time of snow.

Why any one should desire to visit either Luc or Cheylard is more than my much-inventing spirit can suppose. For my part, I travel not to go anywhere, but to go. I travel for travel's sake. The great affair is to move; to feel the needs and hitches of our life more nearly; to come down off this feather-bed of civilisation, and find the globe granite underfoot and strewn with cutting flints. Alas, as we get up in life, and are more preoccupied with our affairs, even a holiday is a thing that must be worked for. To hold a pack upon a pack-saddle against a gale out of the freezing north is no high industry, but it is one that serves to occupy and compose the mind. And when the present is so exacting, who can annoy himself about the future?

I came out at length above the Allier. A more unsightly prospect at this season of the year it would be hard to fancy. Shelving hills rose round it on all sides, here dabbled with wood and fields, there rising to peaks alternately naked and hairy with pines. The colour throughout was black or ashen, and came to a point in the ruins of the castle of Luc, which pricked up impudently from below my feet, carrying on a pinnacle a tall white statue of Our Lady, which, I heard with interest, weighed fifty quintals, and was to be dedicated on the 6th of October. Through this sorry landscape trickled the Allier and a tributary of nearly equal size, which came down to join it through a broad nude valley in Vivarais. The weather had somewhat lightened, and the clouds massed in squadron; but the fierce wind still hunted them through heaven, and cast great ungainly splashes of shadow and sunlight over the scene.

Luc itself was a straggling double file of houses wedged between hill and river. It had no beauty, nor was there any notable feature, save the old castle overhead with its fifty quintals of brand-new Madonna. But the inn was clean and large. The kitchen, with its two box-beds hung with clean check curtains, with its wide stone chimney, its chimney-shelf four yards long and garnished with lanterns and religious statuettes, its array of chests and pair of ticking clocks, was the very model of what a kitchen ought to be; a melodrama kitchen, suitable for bandits or noblemen in disguise. Nor was the scene disgraced by the landlady, a handsome, silent, dark old woman, clothed and hooded in black like a nun. Even the public bedroom had a character of its own, with the long deal tables and benches, where fifty might have dined, set out as for a harvest-home, and the three box-beds along the wall. In one of these, lying on straw and covered with a pair of table-napkins, did I do penance all night long in goose-flesh and chattering teeth, and sigh from time to time as I awakened for my sheepskin sack and the lee of some great wood.

Our Lady of the Snows

"I behold
The House, the Brotherhood austere—
And what am I, that I am here?"
MATTHEW ARNOLD.

Father Apollinaris

NEXT MORNING (THURSDAY, 26TH SEPTEMBER) I TOOK THE ROAD IN a new order. The sack was no longer doubled, but hung at full length across the saddle, a green sausage six feet long with a tuft of blue wool hanging out of either end. It was more picturesque, it spared the donkey, and, as I began to see, it would insure stability, blow high, blow low. But it was not without a pang that I had so decided. For although I had purchased a new cord, and made all as fast as I was able, I was yet jealously uneasy lest the flaps should tumble out and scatter my effects along the line of march.

My way lay up the bald valley of the river, along the march of Vivarais and Gévaudan. The hills of Gévaudan on the right were a little more naked, if anything, than those of Vivarais upon the left, and the former had a monopoly of a low dotty underwood that grew thickly in the gorges and died out in solitary burrs upon the shoulders and the summits. Black bricks of fir-wood were plastered here and there upon both sides, and here and there were cultivated fields. A railway ran beside the river; the only bit of railway in Gévaudan, although there are many proposals afoot and surveys being made, and even, as they tell me, a station standing ready built in Mende. A year or two hence and this may be another world. The desert is beleaguered. Now may some Languedocian Wordsworth turn the sonnet into *patois:* "Mountains and vales and floods, heard YE that whistle?"

At a place called La Bastide I was directed to leave the river, and follow a road that mounted on the left among the hills of Vivarais, the modern Ardèche; for I was now come within a little way of my strange destination, the Trappist monastery of our Lady of the Snows. The sun came out as I left the shelter of a pine-wood, and I beheld suddenly a fine wild landscape to the south. High rocky hills, as blue as sapphire, closed the view, and between these lay ridge upon ridge, heathery, craggy, the sun glittering on veins of rock, the underwood clambering in the hollows, as rude as God made them at the first. There was not a sign of man's hand in all the prospect; and indeed not a trace of his passage, save where generation after generation had walked in twisted footpaths, in and out among the beeches, and up and down upon the channelled slopes. The mists, which had hitherto beset me, were now broken into clouds, and fled swiftly and shone brightly in the sun. I drew a long breath. It was grateful to come, after so long, upon a scene of some attraction for the human heart. I own I like definite form in what my eyes are to rest upon; and if landscapes were sold, like the sheets of characters of my boyhood, one penny plain and twopence coloured, I should go the length of two-pence every day of my life.

But if things had grown better to the south, it was still desolate and inclement near at hand. A spidery cross on every hill-top marked the neighbourhood of a religious house; and a quarter of a mile beyond, the outlook southward opening out and growing bolder with every step, a white statue of the Virgin at the corner of a young plantation directed the traveller to our Lady of the Snows. Here, then, I struck leftward, and pursued my way, driving my secular donkey before me, and creaking in my secular boots and gaiters, towards the asylum of silence.

I had not gone very far ere the wind brought to me the clanging of a bell, and somehow, I can scarce tell why, my heart sank within me at the sound. I have rarely approached anything with more unaffected terror than the monastery of our Lady of the Snows. This it is to have had a Protestant education. And suddenly, on turning a corner, fear took hold on me from head to foot—slavish superstitious fear; and though I did not stop in my advance, yet I went on slowly, like a man who should have passed a bourne unnoticed, and strayed into the country of the dead. For there upon the narrow new-made road, between the stripling pines, was a mediæval friar, fighting with a barrowful of turfs. Every Sunday of my childhood I used to study the Hermits of Marco Sadeler—enchanting prints, full of wood and field and mediæval landscapes, as large as a country, for the imagination to go a travelling in; and here, sure enough, was one of Marco Sadeler's heroes. He was robed in white like any spectre, and the hood falling back, in the instancy of his contention with the barrow, disclosed a pate as bald and yellow as a skull. He might have been buried any time these thousand years, and all the lively parts of him resolved into earth and broken up with the farmer's harrow.

I was troubled besides in my mind as to etiquette. Durst I address a person who was under a vow of silence? Clearly not. But drawing near, I doffed my cap to him with a far-away superstitious reverence. He nodded back, and cheerfully addressed me. Was I going to the monastery? Who was I? An Englishman? Ah, an Irishman, then?

"No," I said, "a Scotsman."

A Scotsman? Ah, he had never seen a Scotsman before. And he looked me all over, his good, honest, brawny countenance shining with interest, as a boy might look upon a lion or an alligator. From him I learned with disgust that I could not be received at our Lady of the Snows; I might get a meal, perhaps, but that was all. And then, as our talk ran on, and it turned out that I was not a pedlar, but a literary man, who drew landscapes and was going to write a book, he changed his manner of thinking as to my reception (for I fear they respect persons even in a Trappist monastery), and told me I must be sure to ask for the Father Prior, and state my case to him in full. On second thoughts he determined to go down with me himself; he thought he could manage for me better. Might he say that I was a geographer?

No; I thought, in the interests of truth, he positively might not.

"Very well, then" (with disappointment), "an author."

It appeared he had been in a seminary with six young Irishmen, all priests long since, who had received newspapers and kept him informed of the state of ecclesiastical affairs in England. And he asked me eagerly after Dr. Pusey, for whose conversion the good man had continued ever since to pray night and morning.

"I thought he was very near the truth," he said; "and he will reach it yet; there is so much virtue in prayer."

He must be a stiff ungodly Protestant who can take anything but pleasure in this kind and hopeful story. While he was thus near the subject, the good father asked me if I were a Christian; and when he found I was not, or not after his way, he glossed it over with great good-will.

The road which we were following, and which this stalwart father had made with his own two hands within the space of a year, came to a corner, and showed us some white buildings a little further on beyond the wood. At the same time, the bell once more sounded abroad. We were hard upon the monastery. Father Apollinaris (for that was my companion's name) stopped me.

"I must not speak to you down there," he said. "Ask for the Brother Porter, and all will be well. But try to see me as you go out again through the wood, where I may speak to you. I am charmed to have made your acquaintance."

And then suddenly raising his arms, flapping his fingers, and crying out twice, "I must not speak, I must not speak!" he ran away in front of me and disappeared into the monastery-door.

I own this somewhat ghastly eccentricity went a good way to revive my terrors. But where one was so good and simple, why should not all be alike? I took heart of grace, and went forward to the gate as fast as Modestine, who seemed to have a disaffection for monasteries, would permit. It was the first door, in my acquaintance of her, which she had not shown an indecent haste to enter. I summoned the place in form, though with a quaking heart. Father Michael, the Father Hospitaller, and a pair of brown-robed brothers came to the gate and spoke with me awhile. I think my sack was the great attraction; it had already beguiled the heart of poor Apollinaris, who had charged me on my life to show it to the Father Prior. But whether it was my address, or the sack, or the idea speedily published among that part of the brotherhood who attended on strangers that I was not a pedlar after all, I found no difficulty as to my reception. Modestine was led away by a layman to the stables, and I and my pack were received into our Lady of the Snows.

The Monks

Father Michael, a pleasant, fresh-faced, smiling man, perhaps of thirty-five, took me to the pantry, and gave me a glass of liqueur to stay me until dinner. We had some talk, or rather I should say he listened to my prattle indulgently enough, but with an abstracted air, like a spirit with a thing of clay. And truly when I remember that I descanted principally on my appetite, and that it must have been by that time more than eighteen hours since Father Michael had so much as broken bread, I can well understand that he would find an earthly savour in my conversation. But his manner, though superior, was exquisitely gracious; and I find I have a lurking curiosity as to Father Michael's past.

The whet administered, I was left alone for a little in the monastery garden. This is no more than the main court, laid out in sandy paths and beds of particoloured dahlias, and with a fountain and a black statue of the Virgin in the centre. The buildings stand around it four-square, bleak, as yet unseasoned by the years and weather, and with no other features than a belfry and a pair of slated gables. Brothers in white, brothers in brown, passed silently along the sanded alleys; and when I first came out, three hooded monks were kneeling on the terrace at their prayers. A naked hill commands the monastery upon one side, and the wood commands it on the other. It lies exposed to wind; the snow falls off and on from October to May, and sometimes lies six weeks on end; but if they stood in Eden, with a climate like heaven's, the buildings themselves would offer the same wintry and cheerless aspect; and for my part, on this wild September day, before I was called to dinner, I felt chilly in and out.

When I had eaten well and heartily, Brother Ambrose, a hearty conversible Frenchman (for all those who wait on strangers have the liberty to speak), led me to a little room in that part of the building which is set apart for *MM. les retraitants.* It was clean and whitewashed, and furnished with strict necessaries, a crucifix, a bust of the late Pope, the *Imitation* in French, a book of religious meditations, and the life of Elizabeth Seton, evangelist, it would appear, of North America and of New England in particular. As far as my experience goes, there is a fair field for some more evangelisation in these quarters; but think of Cotton

Mather! I should like to give him a reading of this little work in heaven, where I hope he dwells; but perhaps he knows all that already, and much more; and perhaps he and Mrs. Seton are the dearest friends, and gladly unite their voices in the everlasting psalm. Over the table, to conclude the inventory of the room, hung a set of regulations for *MM. les retraitants*: what services they should attend, when they were to tell their beads or meditate, and when they were to rise and go to rest. At the foot was a notable N.B.: *"Le temps libre est employé à l'examen de conscience, à la confession, à faire de bonnes résolutions, &c."* To make good resolutions, indeed! You might talk as fruitfully of making the hair grow on your head.

I had scarce explored my niche when Brother Ambrose returned. An English boarder, it appeared, would like to speak with me. I professed my willingness, and the friar ushered in a fresh, young, little Irishman of fifty, a deacon of the Church, arrayed in strict canonicals, and wearing on his head what, in default of knowledge, I can only call the ecclesiastical shako. He had lived seven years in retreat at a convent of nuns in Belgium, and now five at our Lady of the Snows; he never saw an English newspaper; he spoke French imperfectly, and had he spoken it like a native, there was not much chance of conversation where he dwelt. With this, he was a man eminently sociable, greedy of news, and simple-minded like a child. If I was pleased to have a guide about the monastery, he was no less delighted to see an English face and hear an English tongue.

He showed me his own room, where he passed his time among breviaries, Hebrew Bibles, and the Waverley novels. Thence he led me to the cloisters, into the chapter-house, through the vestry, where the brothers' gowns and broad straw hats were hanging up, each with his religious name upon a board—names full of legendary suavity and interests, such as Basil, Hilarion, Raphael, or Pacifique; into the library, where were all the works of Veuillot and Chateaubriand, and the *Odes et Ballades,* if you please, and even Molière, to say nothing of innumerable fathers and a great variety of local and general historians. Thence my good Irishman took me round the workshops, where brothers bake bread, and make cartwheels, and take photographs; where one superintends a collection of curiosities, and another a gallery of rabbits. For in a Trappist monastery each monk has an occupation of his own choice, apart from his religious duties and the general labours of the house. Each must sing in the choir, if he has a voice and ear, and join in the haymaking if he has a hand to stir; but in his private hours, although he must be occupied, he may be occupied on what he likes. Thus I was told that one brother was engaged with literature; while Father Apollinaris busies himself in making roads, and the Abbot employs himself in binding books. It is not so long since this Abbot was consecrated, by the way; and on that occasion, by a special grace, his mother was permitted to enter the chapel and witness the ceremony of consecration. A proud day for her to have a son a mitred abbot; it makes you glad to think they let her in.

In all these journeyings to and fro, many silent fathers and brethren fell in our way. Usually they paid no more regard to our passage than if we had been a cloud; but sometimes the good deacon had a permission to ask of them, and it was granted by a peculiar movement of the hands, almost like that of a dog's paws in swimming, or refused by the usual negative signs, and in either case with lowered eyelids and a certain air of contrition, as of a man who was steering very close to evil.

The monks, by special grace of their Abbot, were still taking two meals a day; but it was already time for their grand fast, which begins somewhere in September and lasts till Easter, and during which they eat but once in the twenty-four hours, and that at two in the afternoon, twelve hours after they have begun the toil and vigil of the day. Their meals are scanty, but even of these they eat sparingly; and though each is allowed a small carafe of wine, many refrain from this indulgence. Without doubt, the most of mankind grossly overeat themselves; our meals serve not only for support, but as a hearty and natural diversion from the labour of life. Yet, though excess may be hurtful, I should have thought this Trappist regimen defective. And I am astonished, as I look back, at the freshness of face and cheerfulness of manner of all whom I beheld. A happier nor a healthier company I should scarce suppose that I have ever seen. As a matter of fact, on this bleak upland, and with the incessant occupation of the monks, life is of an uncertain tenure, and death no infrequent visitor, at our Lady of the Snows. This, at least, was what was told me. But if they die easily, they must live healthily in the mean time, for they seemed all firm of flesh and high in colour; and the only morbid sign that I could observe, an unusual brilliancy of eye, was one that served rather to increase the general impression of vivacity and strength.

Those with whom I spoke were singularly sweet-tempered, with what I can only call a holy cheerfulness in air and conversation. There is a note, in the direction to visitors, telling them not to be offended at the curt speech of those who wait upon them, since it is proper to monks to speak little. The note might have been spared; to a man the hospitallers were all brimming with innocent talk, and, in my experience of the monastery, it was easier to begin than to break off a conversation. With the exception of Father Michael, who was a man of the world, they showed themselves full of kind and healthy interest in all sorts of subjects—in politics, in voyages, in my sleeping-sack—and not without a certain pleasure in the sound of their own voices.

As for those who are restricted to silence, I can only wonder how they bear their solemn and cheerless isolation. And yet, apart from any view of mortification, I can see a certain policy, not only in the exclusion of women, but in this vow of silence. I have had some experience of lay phalansteries, of an artistic, not to say a bacchanalian, character; and seen more than one association easily formed and yet more easily dispersed. With a Cistercian rule, perhaps they might have lasted longer. In the neighbourhood of women it is but a touch-and-go association that can be formed among defenceless men; the stronger electricity is sure to triumph; the dreams of boyhood, the schemes of youth, are abandoned after an interview of ten minutes, and the arts and sciences, and professional male jollity, deserted at once for two sweet eyes and a caressing accent. And next after this, the tongue is the great divider.

I am almost ashamed to pursue this worldly criticism of a religious rule; but there is yet another point in which the Trappist order appeals to me as a model of wisdom. By two in the morning the clapper goes upon the bell, and so on, hour by hour, and sometimes quarter by quarter, till eight, the hour of rest; so infinitesimally is the day divided among different occupations. The man who keeps rabbits, for example, hurries from his hutches to the chapel, the chapter-room, or the refectory, all day long: every hour he has an office to sing, a duty to perform; from two, when he rises in the dark, till eight, when he returns to receive the comfortable gift of sleep, he is upon his feet and occupied with manifold and changing business. I know many persons, worth several thousands in the year, who are not so fortunate in the disposal of their lives. Into how many houses would not the note of the monastery-bell, dividing the day into manageable portions, bring peace of mind and healthful activity of body! We speak of hardships, but the true hardship is to be a dull fool, and permitted to mismanage life in our own dull and foolish manner.

From this point of view, we may perhaps better understand the monk's existence. A long novitiate and every proof of constancy of mind and strength of body is required before admission to the order; but I could not find that many were discouraged. In the photographer's studio, which figures so strangely among the outbuildings, my eye was attracted by the portrait of a young fellow in the uniform of a private of foot. This was one of the novices, who came of the age for service, and marched and drilled and mounted guard for the proper time among the garrison of Algiers. Here was a man who had surely seen both sides of life before deciding; yet as soon as he was set free from service he returned to finsh his novitiate.

This austere rule entitles a man to heaven as by right. When the Trappist sickens, he quits not his habit; he lies in the bed of death as he has prayed and laboured in his frugal and silent existence; and when the Liberator comes, at the very moment, even before they have carried him in his robe to lie his little last in the chapel among continual chantings, joy-bells break forth, as if for a marriage, from the slated belfry, and proclaim throughout the neighbourhood that another soul has gone to God.

At night, under the conduct of my kind Irishman, I took my place in the gallery to hear compline and *Salve Regina,* with which the Cistercians bring every day to a conclusion. There were none of those circumstances which strike the Protestant as childish or as tawdry in the public offices of Rome. A stern simplicity, heightened by the romance of the surroundings, spoke directly to the heart. I recall the white-washed chapel, the hooded figures in the choir, the lights alternately occluded and revealed, the strong manly singing, the silence that ensued, the sight of cowled heads bowed in prayer, and then the clear trenchant beating of the bell, breaking in to show that the last office was over and the hour of sleep had come; and when I remember, I am not surprised that I made my escape into the court with somewhat whirling fancies, and stood like a man bewildered in the windy starry night.

But I was weary; and when I had quieted my spirits with Elizabeth Seton's memoirs—a dull work—the cold and the raving of the wind among the pines—for my room was on that side of the monastery which adjoins the woods—disposed me readily to slumber. I was wakened at black midnight, as it seemed, though it was really two in the morning, by the first stroke upon the bell. All the brothers were then hurrying to the chapel; the dead in life, at this untimely hour, were already beginning the uncomforted labours of their day. The dead in life—there was a chill reflection. And the words of a French song came back into my memory, telling of the best of our mixed existence.

> *"Que t'as de belles filles,*
> *Giroflé!*
> *Girofla!*
> *Que t'as de belles filles,*
> *L'Amour les comptera!"*

And I blessed God that I was free to wander free to hope, and free to love.

The Boarders

But there was another side to my residence at our Lady of the Snows. At this late season there were not many boarders; and yet I was not alone in the public part of the monastery. This itself is hard by the gate, with a small dining-room on the ground-floor, and a whole corridor of cells similar to mine up-stairs. I have stupidly forgotten the board for a regular *retraitant;* but it was somewhere between three and five francs a day, and I think most probably the first. Chance visitors like myself might give what they chose as a free-will offering, but nothing was demanded. I may mention that when I was going away, Father Michael refused twenty francs as excessive. I explained the reasoning which led me to offer him so much; but even then, from a curious point of honour, he would not accept it with his own hand. "I have no right to refuse for the monastery," he explained, "but I should prefer if you would give it to one of the brothers."

I had dined alone, because I arrived late; but at supper I found two other guests. One was a country parish priest, who had walked over that morning from the seat of his cure near Mende to enjoy four days of solitude and prayer. He was a grenadier in person, with the hale colour and circular wrinkles of a peasant; and as he complained much of how he had been impeded by his skirts upon the march, I have a vivid fancy portrait of him, striding along, upright, big-boned, with kilted cassock, through the bleak hills of Gévaudan. The other was a short, grizzling, thick-set man, from forty-five to fifty, dressed in tweed with a knitted spencer, and the red ribbon of a decoration in his button-hole. This last was a hard person to classify. He was an old soldier, who had seen service and risen to the rank of commandant; and he retained some of the brisk decisive manners of the camp. On the other hand, as soon as his resignation was accepted, he had come to our Lady of the Snows as a boarder, and, after a brief experience of its ways, had decided to remain as a novice. Already the new life was beginning to modify his appearance; already he had acquired somewhat of the quiet and smiling air of the breth-ren; and he was as yet neither an officer nor a Trappist, but partook of the character of each. And certainly here was a man in an interesting nick of life. Out of the noise of cannon and trumpets, he was in the act of passing into this still country bordering on the grave, where men sleep nightly in their grave-clothes, and, like phantoms, communicate by signs.

At supper we talked politics. I make it my business, when I am in France, to preach political good-will and moderation, and to dwell on the example of Poland, much as some alarmists in Eng-land dwell on the example of Carthage. The priest and the Com-mandant assured me of their sympathy with all I said, and made a heavy sighing over the bitterness of contemporary feeling.

"Why, you cannot say anything to a man with which he does not absolutely agree," said I, "but he flies up at you in a temper."

They both declared that such a state of things was antichristian.

While we were thus agreeing, what should my tongue stumble upon but a word in praise of Gambetta's moderation. The old soldier's countenance was instantly suffused with blood; with the palms of his hands he beat the table like a naughty child.

"*Comment, monsieur?*" he shouted. "*Comment? Gambetta* moderate? Will you dare to justify these words?*"

But the priest had not forgotten the tenor of our talk. And suddenly, in the height of his fury, the old soldier found a warning look directed on his face; the absurdity of his behaviour was brought home to him in a flash; and the storm came to an abrupt end, without another word.

It was only in the morning, over our coffee (Friday, September 27th), that this couple found out I was a heretic. I suppose I had misled them by some admiring expressions as to the monastic life around us; and it was only by a point-blank question that the truth came out. I had been tolerantly used both by simple Father Apollinaris and astute Father Michael; and the good Irish deacon, when he heard of my religious weakness, had only patted me upon the shoulder and said, "You must be a Catholic and come to heaven." But I was now among a different sect of orthodox. These two men were bitter and upright and narrow, like the worst of Scotsmen, and indeed, upon my heart, I fancy they were worse. The priest snorted aloud like a battle-horse.

"*Et vous prétendez mourir dans cette espèce de croyance?*" he demanded; and there is no type used by mortal printers large enough to qualify his accent.

I humbly indicated that I had no design of changing.

But he could not away with such a monstrous attitude. "No, no," he cried; "you must change. You have come here, God has led you here, and you must embrace the opportunity."

I made a slip in policy; I appealed to the family affections, though I was speaking to a priest and a soldier, two classes of men circumstantially divorced from the kind and homely ties of life.

"Your father and mother?" cried the priest. "Very well; you will convert them in their turn when you go home."

I think I see my father's face! I would rather tackle the Gætulian lion in his den than embark on such an enterprise against the family theologian.

But now the hunt was up; priest and soldier were in full cry for my conversion; and the Work of the Propagation of the Faith, for which the people of Cheylard subscribed forty-eight francs ten centimes during 1877, was being gallantly pursued against myself. It was an odd but most effective proselytising. They never sought to convince me in argument, where I might have attempted some defence; but took it for granted that I was both ashamed and terrified at my position, and urged me solely on the point of time. Now, they said, when God had led me to our Lady of the Snows, now was the appointed hour.

"Do not be withheld by false shame," observed the priest, for my encouragement.

For one who feels very similarly to all sects of religion, and who has never been able, even for a moment, to weigh seriously the merit of this or that creed on the eternal side of things, however much he may see to praise or blame upon the secular and temporal side, the situation thus created was both unfair and painful. I committed my second fault in tact, and tried to plead that it was all the same thing in the end, and we were all drawing near by different sides to the same kind and undiscriminating Friend and Father. That, as it seems to lay-spirits, would be the only gospel worthy of the name. But different men think differently; and this revolutionary aspiration brought down the priest with all the terrors of the law. He launched into harrowing details of hell. The damned, he said—on the authority of a little book which he had read not a week before, and which, to add conviction to conviction, he had fully intended to bring along with him in his pocket—were to occupy the same attitude through all eternity in the midst of dismal tortures. And as he thus expatiated, he grew in nobility of aspect with his enthusiasm.

As a result the pair concluded that I should seek out the Prior, since the Abbot was from home, and lay my case immediately before him.

"*C'est mon conseil comme ancien militaire,*" observed the Commandant; "*et celui de monsieur comme pêtre.*"

"*Oui,*" added the curé, sententiously nodding; "*comme ancien militaire—et comme pêtre.*"

At this moment, whilst I was somewhat embarrassed how to answer, in came one of the monks, a little brown fellow, as lively as a grig, and with an Italian accent, who threw himself at once into the contention, but in a milder and more persuasive vein, as befitted one of these pleasant brethren. Look at *him,* he said. The rule was very hard; he would have dearly liked to stay in his own country, Italy—it was well known how beautiful it was, the beautiful Italy; but then there were no Trappists in Italy; and he had a soul to save; and here he was.

I am afraid I must be at bottom, what a cheerful Indian critic has dubbed me, "a faddling hedonist;" for this description of the brother's motives gave me somewhat of a shock. I should have preferred to think he had chosen the life for its own sake, and not for ulterior purposes; and this shows how profoundly I was out of sympathy with these good Trappists, even when I was doing my best to sympathise. But to the curé the argument seemed decisive.

"Hear that!" he cried. "And I have seen a marquis here, a marquis, a marquis"—he repeated the holy word three times over —"and other persons high in society; and generals. And here, at your side, is this gentleman, who has been so many years in armies —decorated, an old warrior. And here he is, ready to dedicate himself to God."

I was by this time so thoroughly embarrassed that I pled cold feet, and made my escape from the apartment. It was a furious windy morning, with a sky much cleared, and long and potent intervals of sunshine; and I wandered until dinner in the wild country towards the east, sorely staggered and beaten upon by the gale, but rewarded with some striking views.

At dinner the Work of the Propagation of the Faith was recommenced, and on this occasion still more distastefully to me. The priest asked me many questions as to the contemptible faith of my fathers, and received my replies with a kind of ecclesiastical titter.

"Your sect," he said once; "for I think you will admit it would be doing it too much honour to call it a religion."

"As you please, monsieur," said I. *"La parole est à vous."*

At length I grew annoyed beyond endurance; and although he was on his own ground and, what is more to the purpose, an old man, and so holding a claim upon my toleration, I could not avoid a protest against this uncivil usage. He was sadly discountenanced.

"I assure you," he said, "I have no inclination to laugh in my heart. I have no other feeling but interest in your soul."

And there ended my conversion. Honest man! he was no dangerous deceiver; but a country parson, full of zeal and faith. Long may he tread Gévaudan with his kilted skirts—a man strong to walk and strong to comfort his parishioners in death! I daresay he would beat bravely through a snowstorm where his duty called him; and it is not always the most faithful believer who makes the cunningest apostle.

Upper Gévaudan

(Continued)

> *"The bed was made, the room was fit,*
> *By punctual eve the stars were lit;*
> *The air was still, the water ran;*
> *No need there was for maid or man,*
> *When we put up, my ass and I,*
> *At God's green caravanserai."*
>
> Old Play.

Across the Goulet

THE WIND FELL DURING DINNER, AND THE SKY REMAINED CLEAR; so it was under better auspices that I loaded Modestine before the monastery-gate. My Irish friend accompanied me so far on the way. As we came through the wood, there was Père Apollinaire hauling his barrow; and he too quitted his labours to go with me for perhaps a hundred yards, holding my hand between both of his in front of him. I parted first from one and then from the other with unfeigned regret, but yet with the glee of the traveller who shakes off the dust of one stage before hurrying forth upon another. Then Modestine and I mounted the course of the Allier, which here led us back into Gévaudan towards its sources in the forest of Mercoire. It was but an inconsiderable burn before we left its guidance. Thence, over a hill, our way lay through a naked plateau, until we reached Chasseradès at sundown.

The company in the inn-kitchen that night were all men employed in survey for one of the projected railways. They were intelligent and conversible, and we decided the future of France over hot wine, until the state of the clock frightened us to rest.

There were four beds in the little up-stairs room; and we slept six. But I had a bed to myself, and persuaded them to leave the window open.

"Hé, bourgeois; il est cinq heures!" was the cry that wakened me in the morning (Saturday, September 28th). The room was full of a transparent darkness, which dimly showed me the other three beds and the five different nightcaps on the pillows. But out of the window the dawn was growing ruddy in a long belt over the hill-tops, and day was about to flood the plateau. The hour was inspiriting; and there seemed a promise of calm weather, which was perfectly fulfilled. I was soon under way with Modestine. The road lay for awhile over the plateau, and then descended through a precipitous village into the valley of the Chassezac. This stream ran among green meadows, well hidden from the world by its steep banks; the broom was in flower, and here and there was a hamlet sending up its smoke.

At last the path crossed the Chassezac upon a bridge, and, forsaking this deep hollow, set itself to cross the mountain of La Goulet. It wound up through Lestampes by upland fields and woods of beech and birch, and with every corner brought me into an acquaintance with some new interest. Even in the gully of the Chassezac my ear had been struck by a noise like that of a great bass bell ringing at the distance of many miles; but this, as I continued to mount and draw nearer to it, seemed to change in character, and I found at length that it came from some one leading flocks afield to the note of a rural horn. The narrow street of Lestampes stood full of sheep, from wall to wall—black sheep and white, bleating with one accord like the birds in spring, and each one accompanying himself upon the sheep-bell round his neck. It made a pathetic concert, all in treble. A little higher, and I passed a pair of men in a tree with pruning-hooks, and one of them was singing the music of a bourrée. Still further, and when I was already threading the birches, the crowing of cocks came cheerfully up to my ears, and along with that the voice of a flute discoursing a deliberate and plaintive air from one of the upland villages. I pictured to myself some grizzled, apple-cheeked, country schoolmaster fluting in his bit of a garden in the clear autumn sunshine. All these beautiful and interesting sounds filled my heart with an unwonted expectation; and it appeared to me that, once past this range which I was mounting, I should descend into the garden of the world. Nor was I deceived, for I was now done with rains and winds and a bleak country. The first part of my journey ended here; and this was like an induction of sweet sounds into the other and more beautiful.

There are other degrees of *feyness*, as of punishment, besides the capital; and I was now led by my good spirits into an adventure which I relate in the interest of future donkey-drivers. The road zigzagged so widely on the hillside, that I chose a short cut by map and compass, and struck through the dwarf woods to catch the road again upon a higher level. It was my one serious conflict with Modestine. She would none of my short cut; she turned in my face, she backed, she reared; she, whom I had hitherto imagined to be dumb, actually brayed with a loud hoarse flourish, like a cock crowing for the dawn. I plied the goad with one hand; with the other, so steep was the ascent, I had to hold on the pack-saddle. Half a dozen times she was nearly over backwards on the top of me; half a dozen times, from sheer weariness of spirit, I was nearly giving it up, and leading her down again to follow the road. But I took the thing as a wager, and fought it through. It was surprised, as I went on my way again, by what appeared to be chill rain-drops falling on my hand, and more than once looked up in wonder at the cloudless sky. But it was only sweat which came dropping from my brow.

Over the summit of the Goulet there was no marked road—only upright stones posted from space to space to guide the drovers. The turf underfoot was springy and well scented. I had no company but a lark or two, and met but one bullock-cart between Lestampes and Bleymard. In front of me I saw a shallow valley, and beyond that the range of the Lozère, sparsely wooded and well enough modelled in the flanks, but straight and dull in outline. There was scarce a sign of culture; only about Bleymard, the white high-road from Villefort to Mende traversed a range of meadows, set with spiry poplars, and sounding from side to side with the bells of flocks and herds.

A Night among the Pines

From Bleymard after dinner, although it was already late, I set out to scale a portion of the Lozère. An ill-marked stony drove road guided me forward; and I met nearly half a dozen bullock-carts descending from the woods, each laden with a whole pine-tree for the winter's firing. At the top of the woods, which do not climb very high upon this cold ridge, I struck leftward by a path among the pines, until I hit on a dell of green turf, where a streamlet made a little spout over some stones to serve me for a water-tap. "In a more sacred or sequestered bower . . . nor nymph, nor faunus, haunted." The trees were not old, but they grew thickly round the glade: there was no outlook, except north-eastward upon distant hill-tops, or straight upward to the sky; and the encampment felt secure and private like a room. By the time I had made my arrangements and fed Modestine, the day was already beginning to decline. I buckled myself to the knees into my sack and made a hearty meal; and as soon as the sun went down, I pulled my cap over my eyes and fell asleep.

Night is a dead monotonous period under a roof; but in the open world it passes lightly, with its stars and dews and perfumes, and the hours are marked by changes in the face of Nature. What seems a kind of temporal death to people choked between walls and curtains, is only a light and living slumber to the man who sleeps a-field. All night long he can hear Nature breathing deeply and freely; even as she takes her rest, she turns and smiles; and there is one stirring hour unknown to those who dwell in houses, when a wakeful influence goes abroad over the sleeping hemi-sphere, and all the outdoor world are on their feet. It is then that the cock first crows, not this time to announce the dawn, but like a cheerful watchman speeding the course of night. Cattle awake on the meadows; sheep break their fast on dewy hillsides; and change to a new lair among the ferns; and houseless men, who have lain down with the fowls, open their dim eyes and behold the beauty of the night.

At what inaudible summons, at what gentle touch of Nature, are all these sleepers thus recalled in the same hour to life? Do the stars rain down an influence, or do we share some thrill of mother earth below our resting bodies? Even shepherds and old country-folk, who are the deepest read in these arcana, have not a guess as to the means or purpose of this nightly resurrection. Towards two in the morning they declare the thing takes place; and neither know nor inquire further. And at least it is a pleasant incident. We are disturbed in our slumber only, like the luxurious Montaigne, "that we may the better and more sensibly relish it." We have a moment to look upon the stars. And there is a special pleasure for some minds in the reflection that we share the impulse with all outdoor creatures in our neighbourhood, that we have escaped out of the Bastille of civilisation, and are become, for the time being, a mere kindly animal and a sheep of Nature's flock.

When that hour came to me among the pines, I wakened thirsty. My tin was standing by me half full of water. I emptied it at a draught; and feeling broad awake after this internal cold aspersion, sat upright to make a cigarette. The stars were clear, coloured, and jewel-like, but not frosty. A faint silvery vapour stood for the Milky Way. All around me the black fir-points stood upright and stock-still. By the whiteness of the pack-saddle, I could see Modestine walking round and round at the length of her tether; I could hear her steadily munching at the sward; but there was not another sound, save the indescribable quiet talk of the runnel over the stones. I lay lazily smoking and studying the colour of the sky, as we call the void of space, from where it showed a reddish gray behind the pines to where it showed a glossy blue-black between the stars. As if to be more like a pedlar, I wear a silver ring. This I could see faintly shining as I raised or lowered the cigarette; and at each whiff the inside of my hand was illuminated, and became for a second the highest light in the landscape.

A faint wind, more like a moving coolness than a stream of air, passed down the glade from time to time; so that even in my great chamber the air was being renewed all night long. I thought with horror of the inn at Chasseradès and the congregated nightcaps; with horror of the nocturnal prowesses of clerks and students, of hot theatres and pass-keys and close rooms. I have not often enjoyed a more serene possession of myself, nor felt more independent of material aids. The outer world, from which we cower into our houses, seemed after all a gentle habitable place; and night after night a man's bed, it seemed, was laid and waiting for him in the fields, where God keeps an open house. I thought I had rediscovered one of those truths which are revealed to savages and hid from political economists: at the least, I had discovered a new pleasure for myself. And yet even while I was exulting in my solitude I became aware of a strange lack. I wished a companion to lie near me in the starlight, silent and not moving, but ever within touch. For there is a fellowship more quiet even than solitude, and which, rightly understood, is solitude made perfect. And to live out of doors with the woman a man loves is of all lives the most complete and free.

As I thus lay, between content and longing, a faint noise stole towards me through the pines. I thought, at first, it was the crowing of cocks or the barking of dogs at some very distant farm; but steadily and gradually it took articulate shape in my ears, until I became aware that a passenger was going by upon the high-road in the valley, and singing loudly as he went. There was more of good-will than grace in his performance; but he trolled with ample lungs; and the sound of his voice took hold upon the hillside and set the air shaking in the leafy glens. I have heard people passing by night in sleeping cities; some of them sang; one, I remember, played loudly on the bagpipes. I have heard the rattle of a cart or carriage spring up suddenly after hours of stillness, and pass, for some minutes, within the range of my hearing as I lay abed. There is a romance about all who are abroad in the black hours, and with something of a thrill we try to guess their business. But here the romance was double: first, this glad passenger, lit internally with wine, who sent up his voice in music through the night; and then I, on the other hand, buckled into my sack, and smoking alone in the pine-woods between four and five thousand feet towards the stars.

When I awoke again (Sunday, 29th September), many of the stars had disappeared; only the stronger companions of the night still burned visibly overhead; and away towards the east I saw a faint haze of light upon the horizon, such as had been the Milky Way when I was last awake. Day was at hand. I lit my lantern, and by its glowworm light put on my boots and gaiters; then I broke up some bread for Modestine, filled my can at the water-tap, and lit my spirit-lamp to boil myself some chocolate. The blue darkness lay long in the glade where I had so sweetly slumbered; but soon there was a broad streak of orange melting into gold along the mountain-tops of Vivarais. A solemn glee possessed my mind at this gradual and lovely coming in of day. I heard the runnel with delight; I looked round me for something beautiful and unexpected; but the still black pine-trees, the hollow glade, the munching ass, remained unchanged in figure. Nothing had altered but the light, and that, indeed, shed over all a spirit of life and of breathing peace, and moved me to a strange exhilaration.

I drank my water chocolate, which was hot if it was not rich, and strolled here and there, and up and down about the glade. While I was thus delaying, a gush of steady wind, as long as a heavy sigh, poured direct out of the quarter of the morning. It was cold, and set me sneezing. The trees near at hand tossed their black plumes in its passage; and I could see the thin distant spires of pine along the edge of the hill rock slightly to and fro against the golden east. Ten minutes after, the sunlight spread at a gallop along the hillside, scattering shadows and sparkles, and the day had come completely.

I hastened to prepare my pack, and tackle the steep ascent that lay before me; but I had something on my mind. It was only a fancy; yet a fancy will sometimes be importunate. I had been most hospitably received and punctually served in my green caravanserai. The room was airy, the water excellent, and the dawn had called me to a moment. I say nothing of the tapestries or the inimitable ceiling, nor yet of the view which I commanded from the windows; but I felt I was in some one's debt for all this liberal entertainment. And so it pleased me, in a half-laughing way, to leave pieces of money on the turf as I went along, until I had left enough for my night's lodging. I trust they did not fall to some rich and churlish drover.

The Country of the Camisards

"We travelled in the print of olden wars;
Yet all the land was green;
And love we found, and peace,
Where fire and war had been.
They pass and smile, the children of the sword—
No more the sword they wield;
And O, how deep the corn
Along the battlefield!"

W. P. BANNATYNE.

Across the Lozère

THE TRACK THAT I HAD FOLLOWED IN THE EVENING SOON DIED out, and I continued to follow over a bald turf ascent a row of stone pillars, such as had conducted me across the Goulet. It was already warm. I tied my jacket on the pack, and walked in my knitted waistcoat. Modestine herself was in high spirits, and broke of her own accord, for the first time in my experience, into a jolting trot that set the oats swashing in the pocket of my coat. The view, back upon the northern Gévaudan, extended with every step; scarce a tree, scarce a house, appeared upon the fields of wild hill that ran north, east, and west, all blue and gold in the haze and sunlight of the morning. A multitude of little birds kept sweeping and twittering about my path; they perched on the stone pillars, they pecked and strutted on the turf, and I saw them circle in volleys in the blue air, and show, from time to time, translucent flickering wings between the sun and me.

Almost from the first moment of my march, a faint large noise, like a distant surf, had filled my ears. Sometimes I was tempted to think it the voice of a neighbouring waterfall, and sometimes a subjective result of the utter stillness of the hill. But as I continued to advance, the noise increased and became like the hissing of an enormous tea-urn, and at the same time breaths of cool air began to reach me from the direction of the summit. At length I understood. It was blowing stiffly from the south upon the other slope of the Lozère, and every step that I took I was drawing nearer to the wind.

Although it had been long desired, it was quite unexpectedly at last that my eyes rose above the summit. A step that seemed no way more decisive than many other steps that had preceded it— and, "like stout Cortez when, with eagle eyes, he stared on the Pacific," I took possession, in my own name, of a new quarter of the world. For behold, instead of the gross turf rampart I had been mounting for so long, a view into the hazy air of heaven, and a land of intricate blue hills below my feet.

The Lozère lies nearly east and west, cutting Gévaudan into two unequal parts; its highest point, this *Pic de Finiels,* on which I was then standing, rises upwards of five thousand six hundred feet above the sea, and in clear weather commands a view over all lower Languedoc to the Mediterranean Sea. I have spoken with people who either pretend or believe that they had seen, from the *Pic de Finiels,* white ships sailing by Montpellier and Cette. Behind was the upland northern country through which my way had lain, peopled by a dull race, without wood, without much grandeur of hill-form, and famous in the past for little beside wolves. But in front of me, half veiled in sunny haze, lay a new Gévaudan, rich, picturesque, illustrious for stirring events. Speaking largely, I was in the Cevennes at Monastier, and during all my journey; but there is a strict and local sense in which only this confused and shaggy country at my feet has any title to the name, and in this sense the peasantry employ the word. These are the Cevennes with an emphasis: the Cevennes of the Cevennes. In that undecipherable labyrinth of hills, a war of bandits, a war of wild beasts, raged for two years between the Grand Monarch with all his troops and marshals on the one hand, and a few thousand Protestant mountaineers upon the other. A hundred and eighty years ago, the Camisards held a station even on the Lozère, where I stood; they had an organisation, arsenals, a military and religious hierarchy; their affairs were "the discourse of every coffee-house" in London; England sent fleets in their support; their leaders prophesied and murdered; with colours and drums, and the singing of old French psalms, their bands some-times affronted daylight, marched before walled cities, and dispersed the generals of the king; and sometimes at night, or in masquerade, possessed themselves of strong castles, and avenged treachery upon their allies and cruelty upon their foes. There, a hundred and eighty years ago, was the chivalrous Roland, "Count and Lord Roland, generalissimo of the Protestants in France," grave, silent, imperious, pock-marked ex-dragoon, whom a lady followed in his wanderings out of love. There was Cavalier, a baker's apprentice with a genius for war, elected brigadier of Camisards at seventeen, to die at fifty-five the English governor of Jersey. There again was Castanet, a partisan leader in a voluminous peruke and with a taste for controversial divinity. Strange generals, who moved apart to take counsel with the God of Hosts, and fled or offered battle, set sentinels or slept in an unguarded camp, as the Spirit whispered to their hearts! And there, to follow these and other leaders, was the rank and file of prophets and disciples, bold, patient, indefatigable, hardy to run upon the mountains, cheering their rough life with psalms, eager to fight, eager to pray, listening devoutly to the oracles of brainsick children, and mystically putting a grain of wheat among the pewter balls with which they charged their muskets.

I had travelled hitherto through a dull district, and in the track of nothing more notable than the child-eating Beast of Gévaudan, the Napoléon Buonaparte of wolves. But now I was to go down into the scene of a romantic chapter—or, better, a romantic footnote—in the history of the world. What was left of all this bygone dust and heroism? I was told that Protestantism still survived in this head seat of Protestant resistance; so much the priest himself had told me in the monastery parlour. But I had yet to learn if it were a bare survival, or a lively and generous tradition. Again, if in the northern Cevennes the people are narrow in religious judgments, and more filled with zeal than charity, what was I to look for in this land of persecution and reprisal—in a land where the tyranny of the Church produced the Camisards rebellion, and the terror of the Camisards threw the Catholic peasantry into legalised revolt upon the other side, so that Camisard and Florentin skulked for each other's lives among the mountains?

Just on the brow of the hill, where I paused to look before me, the series of stone pillars came abruptly to an end; and only a little below, a sort of track appeared and began to go down a breakneck slope, turning like a corkscrew as it went. It led into a valley between falling hills, stubbly with rocks like a reaped field of corn, and floored further down with green meadows. I followed the track with precipitation; the steepness of the slope, the continual agile turning of the line of the descent, and the old unwearied hope of finding something new in a new country, all conspired to lend me wings. Yet a little lower and a stream began, collecting itself together out of many fountains, and soon making a glad noise among the hills. Sometimes it would cross the track in a bit of waterfall, with a pool, in which Modestine refreshed her feet.

The whole descent is like a dream to me, so rapidly was it accomplished. I had scarcely left the summit ere the valley had closed round my path, and the sun beat upon me, walking in a stagnant lowland atmosphere. The track became a road, and went up and down in easy undulations. I passed cabin after cabin, but all seemed deserted; and I saw not a human creature, nor heard any sound except that of the stream. I was, however, in a different country from the day before. The stony skeleton of the world was here vigorously displayed to sun and air. The slopes were steep and changeful. Oak-trees clung along the hills, well grown, wealthy in leaf, and touched by the autumn with strong and luminous colours. Here and there another stream would fall in from the right or the left, down a gorge of snow-white and tumultuary boulders. The river in the bottom (for it was rapidly growing a river, collecting on all hands as it trotted on its way) here foamed awhile in desperate rapids, and there lay in pools of the most enchanting sea-green shot with watery browns. As far as I have gone, I have never seen a river of so changeful and delicate a hue; crystal was not more clear, the meadows were not by half so green; and at every pool I saw I felt a thrill of longing to be out of these hot, dusty, and material garments, and bathe my naked body in the mountain air and water. All the time as I went on I never forgot it was the Sabbath; the stillness was a perpetual reminder; and I heard in spirit the church-bells clamouring all over Europe, and the psalms of a thousand churches.

At length a human sound struck upon my ear—a cry strangely modulated between pathos and derision; and looking across the valley, I saw a little urchin sitting in a meadow, with his hands about his knees, and dwarfed to almost comical smallness by the distance. But the rogue had picked me out as I went down the road, from oak-wood on to oak-wood, driving Modestine; and he made me the compliments of the new country in this tremulous high-pitched salutation. And as all noises are lovely and natural at a sufficient distance, this also, coming through so much clean hill air and crossing all the green valley, sounded pleasant to my ear, and seemed a thing rustic, like the oaks or the river.

A little after, the stream that I was following fell into the Tarn at Pont de Montvert of bloody memory.

Pont de Montvert

One of the first things I encountered in Pont de Montvert was, if I remember rightly, the Protestant temple; but this was but the type of other novelties. A subtle atmosphere distinguishes a town in England from a town in France, or even in Scotland. At Carlisle you can see you are in one country; at Dumfries, thirty miles away, you are as sure that you are in the other. I should find it difficult to tell in what particulars Pont de Montvert differed from Monastier or Langogne, or even Bleymard; but the difference existed, and spoke eloquently to the eyes. The place, with its houses, its lanes, its glaring river-bed, wore an indescribable air of the South.

All was Sunday bustle in the streets and in the public-house, as all had been Sabbath peace among the mountains. There must have been near a score of us at dinner by eleven before noon; and after I had eaten and drunken, and sat writing up my journal, I suppose as many more came dropping in one after another, or by twos and threes. In crossing the Lozère I had not only come among new natural features, but moved into the territory of a different race. These people, as they hurriedly despatched their viands in an intricate sword-play of knives, questioned and answered me with a degree of intelligence which excelled all that I had met, except among the railway folk at Chasseradès. They had open telling faces, and were lively both in speech and manner. They not only entered thoroughly into the spirit of my little trip, but more than one declared, if he were rich enough, he would like to set forth on such another.

Even physically there was a pleasant change. I had not seen a pretty woman since I left Monastier, and there but one. Now of the three who sat down with me to dinner, one was certainly not beautiful—a poor timid thing of forty, quite troubled at this roaring *table d'hôte,* whom I squired and helped to wine, and pledged and tried generally to encourage, with quite a contrary effect; but the other two, both married, were both more handsome than the average of women. And Clarisse? What shall I say of Clarisse? She waited the table with a heavy placable nonchalance, like a performing cow; her great gray eyes were steeped in amorous langour; her features, although fleshy, were of an original and accurate design; her mouth had a curl; her nostril spoke of dainty pride; her cheek fell into strange and interesting lines. It was a face capable of strong emotion, and, with training, it offered the promise of delicate sentiment. It seemed pitiful to see so good a model left to country admirers and a country way of thought. Beauty should at least have touched society; then, in a moment, it throws off a weight that lay upon it, it becomes conscious of itself, it puts on an elegance, learns a gait and a carriage of the head, and, in a moment, *patet dea.* Before I left I assured Clarisse of my hearty admiration. She took it like milk, without embarrassment or wonder, merely looking at me steadily with her great eyes; and I own the result upon myself was some confusion. If Clarisse could read English, I should not dare to add that her figure was unworthy of her face. Hers was a case for stays; but that may perhaps grow better as she gets up in years.

Pont de Montvert, or Greenhill Bridge, as we might say at home, is a place memorable in the story of the Camisards. It was here that the war broke out; here that these southern Covenanters slew their Archbishop Sharpe. The persecution on the one hand, the febrile enthusiasm on the other, are almost equally difficult to understand in these quiet modern days, and with our easy modern beliefs and disbeliefs. The Protestants were one and all beside their right minds with zeal and sorrow. They were all prophets and prophetesses. Children at the breast would exhort their parents to good works. "A child of fifteen months at Quissac spoke from it's mother's arms, agitated and sobbing, distinctly and with a loud voice." Marshal Villars has seen a town where all the women "seemed possessed by the devil," and had trembling fits, and uttered prophecies publicly upon the streets. A prophetess of Vivarais was hanged at Montpellier because blood flowed from her eyes and nose, and she declared that she was weeping tears of blood for the misfortunes of the Protestants. And it was not only women and children. Stalwart dangerous fellows, used to swing the sickle or to wield the forest axe, were likewise shaken with strange paroxysms, and spoke oracles with sobs and streaming tears. A persecution unsurpassed in violence had lasted near a score of years, and this was the result upon the persecuted; hanging, burning, breaking on the wheel, had been in vain; the dragoons had left their hoofmarks over all the country-side; there were men rowing in the galleys, and women pining in the prisons of the Church; and not a thought was changed in the heart of any upright Protestant.

Now the head and forefront of the persecution—after Lamoignon de Bâvile—François de Langlade du Chayla (pronounce *Chéïla*), Archpriest of the Cevennes and Inspector of Missions in the same country, had a house in which he sometimes dwelt in the town of Pont de Montvert. He was a conscientious person, who seems to have been intended by nature for a pirate, and now fifty-five, an age by which a man has learned all the moderation of which he is capable. A missionary in his youth in China, he there suffered martyrdom, was left for dead, and only succoured and brought back to life by the charity of a pariah. We must suppose the pariah devoid of second sight, and not purposely malicious in this act. Such an experience, it might be thought, would have cured a man of the desire to persecute; but the human spirit is a thing strangely put together; and, having been a Christian martyr, Du Chayla became a Christian persecutor. The Work of the Propagation of the Faith went roundly forward in his hands. His house in Pont de Montvert served him as a prison. There he plucked out the hairs of the beard, and closed the hands of his prisoners upon live coal, to convince them that they were deceived in their opinions. And yet had not he himself tried and proved the inefficacy of these carnal arguments among the Boodhists in China?

Not only was life made intolerable in Languedoc, but flight was rigidly forbidden. One Massip, a muleteer, and well acquainted with the mountain-paths, had already guided several troops of fugitives in safety to Geneva; and on him, with another convoy, consisting mostly of women dressed as men, Du Chayla, in an evil hour for himself, laid his hands. The Sunday following, there was a conventicle of Protestants in the woods of Altefage upon Mount Bougès; where there stood up one Séguier—Spirit Séguier, as his companions called him—a woolcarder, tall, black-faced, and toothless, but a man full of prophecy. He declared, in the name of God, that the time for submission had gone by, and they must betake themselves to arms for the deliverance of their brethren and the destruction of the priests.

The next night, 24th July 1702, a sound disturbed the Inspector of Missions as he sat in his prison-house at Pont de Montvert; the voices of many men upraised in psalmody drew nearer and nearer through the town. It was ten at night; he had his court about him, priests, soldiers, and servants, to the number of twelve or fifteen; and now dreading the insolence of a conventicle below his very windows, he ordered forth his soldiers to report. But the psalm-singers were already at his door, fifty strong, led by the inspired Séguier, and breathing death. To their summons, the archpriest made answer like a stout old persecutor, and bade his garrison fire upon the mob. One Camisard (for, according to some, it was in this night's work that they came by the name) fell at this discharge; his comrades burst in the door with hatchets and a beam of wood, overran the lower storey of the house, set free the prisoners, and finding one of them in the vine, a sort of Scavenger's Daughter of the place and period, redoubled in fury against Du Chayla, and sought by repeated assaults to carry the upper floors. But he, on his side, had given absolution to his men, and they bravely held the staircase.

"Children of God," cried the prophet, "hold your hands. Let us burn the house, with the priest and the satellites of *Baal.*"

The fire caught readily. Out of an upper window Du Chayla and his men lowered themselves into the garden by means of knotted sheets; some escaped across the river under the bullets of the insurgents; but the archpriest himself fell, broke his thigh, and could only crawl into the hedge. What were his reflections as this second martyrdom drew near? A poor, brave, besotted, hateful man, who had done his duty resolutely according to his light both in the Cevennes and China. He found at least one telling word to say in his defence; for when the roof fell in and the upbursting flames discovered his retreat, and they came and dragged him to the public place of the town, raging and calling him damned— "If I be damned," said he, "why should you also damn yourselves?"

Here was a good reason for the last; but in the course of his inspectorship he had given many stronger which all told in a contrary direction; and these he was now to hear. One by one, Séguier first, the Camisards drew near and stabbed him. "This," they said, "is for my father broken on the wheel. This for my brother in the galleys. That for my mother or my sister imprisoned in your cursed convents." Each gave his blow and his reason; and then all kneeled and sang psalms around the body till the dawn. With the dawn, still singing, they defiled away towards Frugères, further up the Tarn, to pursue the work of vengeance, leaving Du Chayla's prison-house in ruins, and his body pierced with two-and-fifty wounds upon the public place.

'Tis a wild night's work, with its accompaniment of psalms; and it seems as if a psalm must always have a sound of threatening in that town upon the Tarn. But the story does not end, even so far as concerns Pont de Montvert, with the departure of the Camisards. The career of Séguier was brief and bloody. Two more priests and a whole family at Ladevèze, from the father to the servants, fell by his hand or by his orders; and yet he was but a day or two at large, and restrained all the time by the presence of the soldiery. Taken at length by a famous soldier of fortune, Captain Poul, he appeared unmoved before his judges.

"Your name?" they asked.

"Pierre Séguier."

"Why are you called Spirit?"

"Because the Spirit of the Lord is with me."

"Your domicile?"

"Lately in the desert, and soon in heaven."

"Have you no remorse for your crimes?"

"I have committed none. *My soul is like a garden full of shelter and of fountains.*"

At Pont de Montvert, on the 12th of August, he had his right hand stricken from his body, and was burned alive. And his soul was like a garden? So perhaps was the soul of Du Chayla, the Christian martyr. And perhaps if you could read in my soul, or I could read in yours, our own composure might seem little less surprising.

Du Chayla's house still stands, with a new roof, beside one of the bridges of the town; and if you are curious you may see the terrace-garden into which he dropped.

In the Valley of the Tarn

A new road leads from Pont de Montvert to Florac by the valley of the Tarn; a smooth sandy ledge, it runs about half-way between the summit of the cliffs and the river in the bottom of the valley; and I went in and out, as I followed it, from bays of shadow into promontories of afternoon sun. This was a pass like that of Killie-crankie; a deep turning gully in the hills, with the Tarn making a wonderful hoarse uproar far below, and craggy summits stand-ing in the sunshine high above. A thin fringe of ash-trees ran about the hilltops, like ivy on a ruin; but on the lower slopes, and far up every glen, the Spanish chestnut-trees stood each four-square to heaven under its tented foliage. Some were planted, each on its own terrace no larger than a bed; some, trusting in their roots, found strength to grow and prosper and be straight and large upon the rapid slopes of the valley; others, where there was a margin to the river, stood marshalled in a line and mighty like cedars of Lebanon. Yet even where they grew most thickly they were not to be thought of as a wood, but as a herd of stalwart individuals; and the dome of each tree stood forth separate and large, and as it were a little hill, from among the domes of its companions. They gave forth a faint sweet perfume which per-vaded the air of the afternoon; autumn had put tints of gold and tarnish in the green; and the sun so shone through and kindled the broad foliage, that each chestnut was relieved against another, not in shadow, but in light. A humble sketcher here laid down his pencil in despair.

I wish I could convey a notion of the growth of these noble trees; of how they strike out boughs like the oak, and trail sprays of drooping foliage like the willow; of how they stand on up-right fluted columns like the pillars of a church; or like the olive, from the most shattered bole can put out smooth and youthful shoots, and begin a new life upon the ruins of the old. Thus they partake of the nature of many different trees; and even their prickly topknots, seen near at hand against the sky, have a certain palm-like air that impresses the imagination. But their individuality, although compounded of so many elements, is but the richer and the more original. And to look down upon a level filled with these knolls of foliage, or to see a clan of old unconquerable chestnuts cluster "like herded elephants" upon the spur of a mountain, is to rise to higher thoughts of the powers that are in Nature.

Between Modestine's laggard humour and the beauty of the scene, we made little progress all that afternoon; and at last finding the sun, although still far from setting, was already beginning to desert the narrow valley of the Tarn, I began to cast about for a place to camp in. This was not easy to find; the terraces were too narrow, and the ground, where it was unterraced, was usually too steep for a man to lie upon. I should have slipped all night, and awakened towards morning with my feet or my head in the river.

After perhaps a mile, I saw, some sixty feet above the road, a little plateau large enough to hold my sack, and securely parapeted by the trunk of an aged and enormous chestnut. Thither, with infinite trouble, I goaded and kicked the reluctant Modestine, and there I hastened to unload her. There was only room for myself upon the plateau, and I had to go nearly as high again before I found so much as standing room for the ass. It was on a heap of rolling stones, on an artificial terrace, certainly not five feet square in all. Here I tied her to a chestnut, and having given her corn and bread and made a pile of chestnut-leaves, of which I found her greedy, I descended once more to my own encampment.

The position was unpleasantly exposed. One or two carts went by upon the road; and as long as daylight lasted I concealed myself, for all the world like a hunted Camisard, behind my fortification of vast chestnut trunk; for I was passionately afraid of discovery and the visit of jocular persons in the night. Moreover, I saw that I must be early awake; for these chestnut gardens had been the scene of industry no farther gone than on the day before. The slope was strewn with lopped branches, and here and there a great package of leaves was propped against a trunk; for even the leaves are serviceable, and the peasants use them in winter by way of fodder for their animals. I picked a meal in fear and trembling, half lying down to hide myself from the road; and I daresay I was as much concerned as if I had been a scout from Joani's band above upon the Lozère, or from Salomon's across the Tarn, in the old times of psalm-singing and blood. Or, indeed, perhaps more; for the Camisards had a remarkable confidence in God; and a tale comes back into my memory of how the Count of Gévaudan, riding with a party of dragoons and a notary at his saddlebow to enforce the oath of fidelity in all the country hamlets, entered a valley in the woods, and found Cavalier and his men at dinner, gaily seated on the grass, and their hats crowned with box-tree garlands, while fifteen women washed their linen in the stream. Such was a field festival in 1703; at that date Antony Watteau would be painting similar subjects.

This was a very different camp from that of the night before in the cool and silent pine-woods. It was warm and even stifling in the valley. The shrill song of frogs, like the tremolo note of a whistle with a pea in it, rang up from the riverside before the sun was down. In the growing dusk, faint rustlings began to run to and fro among the fallen leaves; from time to time a faint chirping or cheeping noise would fall upon my ear; and from time to time I thought I could see the movement of something swift and indistinct between the chestnuts. A profusion of large ants swarmed upon the ground; bats whisked by, and mosquitoes droned overhead. The long boughs with their bunches of leaves hung against the sky like garlands; and those immediately above and around me had somewhat the air of a trellis which should have been wrecked and half overthrown in a gale of wind.

Sleep for a long time fled my eyelids; and just as I was beginning to feel quiet stealing over my limbs, and settling densely on my mind, a noise at my head startled me broad awake again, and, I will frankly confess it, brought my heart into my mouth. It was such a noise as a person would make scratching loudly with a fingernail, it came from under the knapsack which served me for a pillow, and it was thrice repeated before I had time to sit up and turn about. Nothing was to be seen, nothing more was to be heard, but a few of these mysterious rustlings far and near, and the ceaseless accompaniment of the river and the frogs. I learned next day that the chestnut gardens are infested by rats; rustling, chirping, and scraping were probably all due to these; but the puzzle, for the moment, was insoluble, and I had to compose myself for sleep, as best I could, in wondering uncertainly about my neighbours.

I was wakened in the gray of the morning (Monday, 30th September) by the sound of footsteps not far off upon the stones, and opening my eyes, I beheld a peasant going by among the chestnuts by a footpath that I had not hitherto observed. He turned his head neither to the right nor to the left, and disappeared in a few strides among the foliage. Here was an escape! But it was plainly more than time to be moving. The peasantry were abroad; scarce less terrible to me in my nondescript position than the soldiers of Captain Poul to an undaunted Camisard. I fed Modestine with what haste I could; but as I was returning to my sack, I saw a man and a boy come down the hillside in a direction crossing mine. They unintelligibly hailed me, and I replied with inarticulate but cheerful sounds, and hurried forward to get into my gaiters.

The pair, who seemed to be father and son, came slowly up to the plateau, and stood close beside me for some time in silence. The bed was open, and I saw with regret my revolver lying patently disclosed on the blue wool. At last, after they had looked me all over, and the silence had grown laughably embarrassing, the man demanded in what seemed unfriendly tones:

"You have slept here?"

"Yes," said I. "As you see."

"Why?" he asked.

"My faith," I answered lightly, "I was tired."

He next inquired where I was going and what I had had for dinner; and then, without the least transition, "*C'est bien,*" he added, "come along." And he and his son, without another word, turned off to the next chestnut-tree but one, which they set to pruning. The thing had passed off more simply than I hoped. He was a grave respectable man; and his unfriendly voice did not imply that he thought he was speaking to a criminal, but merely to an inferior.

I was soon on the road, nibbling a cake of chocolate and seriously occupied with a case of conscience. Was I to pay for my night's lodging? I had slept ill, the bed was full of fleas in the shape of ants, there was no water in the room, the very dawn had neglected to call me in the morning. I might have missed a train, had there been any in the neighbourhood to catch. Clearly, I was dissatisfied with my entertainment; and I decided I should not pay unless I met a beggar.

The valley looked even lovelier by morning; and soon the road descended to the level of the river. Here, in a place where many straight and prosperous chestnuts stood together, making an aisle upon a swarded terrace, I made my morning toilette in the water of the Tarn. It was marvellously clear, thrillingly cool; the soap-suds disappeared as if by magic in the swift current, and the white boulders gave one a model for cleanliness. To wash in one of God's rivers in the open air seems to me a sort of cheerful solemnity or semi-pagan act of worship. To dabble among dishes in a bedroom may perhaps make clean the body; but the imagination takes no share in such a cleansing. I went on with a light and peaceful heart, and sang psalms to the spiritual ear as I advanced.

Suddenly up came an old woman, who point-blank demanded alms.

"Good," thought I; "here comes the waiter with the bill."

And I paid for my night's lodging on the spot. Take it how you please, but this was the first and the last beggar that I met with during all my tour.

A step or two farther I was overtaken by an old man in a brown nightcap, clear-eyed, weather-beaten, with a faint excited smile. A little girl followed him, driving two sheep and a goat; but she kept in our wake, while the old man walked beside me and talked about the morning and the valley. It was not much past six; and for healthy people who have slept enough, that is the hour of expansion and of open and trustful talk.

"*Connaissez-vous le Seigneur?*" he said at length.

I asked him what Seigneur he meant; but he only repeated the question with more emphasis and a look in his eyes denoting hope and interest.

"Ah," said I, pointing upwards, "I understand you now. Yes, I know Him; He is the best of acquaintances."

The old man said he was delighted. "Hold," he added, striking his bosom; "it makes me happy here." There were a few who knew the Lord in these valleys, he went on to tell me; not many, but a few. "Many are called," he quoted, "and few chosen."

"My father," said I, "it is not easy to say who know the Lord; and it is none of our business. Protestants and Catholics, and even those who worship stones, may know Him and be known by Him; for He has made all."

I did not know I was so good a preacher.

The old man assured me he thought as I did, and repeated his expressions of pleasure at meeting me. "We are so few," he said. "They call us Moravians here; but down in the department of Gard, where there are also a good number, they are called Derbists, after an English pastor."

I began to understand that I was figuring, in questionable taste, as a member of some sect to me unknown; but I was more pleased with the pleasure of my companion than embarrassed by my own equivocal position. Indeed I can see no dishonesty in not avowing a difference; and especially in these high matters, where we have all a sufficient assurance that, whoever may be in the wrong, we ourselves are not completely in the right. The truth is much talked about; but this old man in a brown nightcap showed himself so simple, sweet, and friendly that I am not unwilling to profess myself his convert. He was, as a matter of fact, a Plymouth Brother. Of what that involves in the way of doctrine I have no idea nor the time to inform myself; but I know right well that we are all embarked upon a troublesome world, the children of one Father, striving in many essential points to do and to become the same. And although it was somewhat in a mistake that he shook hands with me so often and showed himself so ready to receive my words, that was a mistake of the truth-finding sort. For charity begins blindfold; and only through a series of similar misapprehensions rises at length into a settled principle of love and patience, and a firm belief in all our fellowmen. If I deceived this good old man, in the like manner I would willingly go on to deceive others. And if ever at length, out of our separate and sad ways, we should all come together into one common house, I have a hope, to which I cling dearly, that my mountain Plymouth Brother will hasten to shake hands with me again.

Thus, talking like Christian and Faithful by the way, he and I came down upon a hamlet by the Tarn. It was but a humble place, called La Vernède, with less than a dozen houses, and a Protestant chapel on a knoll. Here he dwelt; and here, at the inn, I ordered my breakfast. The inn was kept by an agreeable young man, a stone-breaker on the road, and his sister, a pretty and engaging girl. The village schoolmaster dropped in to speak with the stranger. And these were all Protestants—a fact which pleased me more than I should have expected; and, what pleased me still more, they seemed all upright and simple people. The Plymouth Brother hung round me with a sort of yearning interest, and returned at least thrice to make sure I was enjoying my meal. His behaviour touched me deeply at the time, and even now moves me in recollection. He feared to intrude, but he would not willingly forego one moment of my society; and he seemed never weary of shaking me by the hand.

When all the rest had drifted off to their day's work, I sat for near half an hour with the young mistress of the house, who talked pleasantly over her seam of the chestnut harvest, and the beauties of the Tarn, and old family affections, broken up when young folk go from home, yet still subsisting. Hers, I am sure, was a sweet nature, with a country plainness and much delicacy underneath; and he who takes her to his heart will doubtless be a fortunate young man.

The valley below La Vernède pleased me more and more as I went forward. Now the hills approached from either hand, naked and crumbling, and walled in the river between cliffs; and now the valley widened and became green. The road led me past the old castle of Miral on a steep; past a battlemented monastery, long since broken up and turned into a church and parsonage; and past a cluster of black roofs, the village of Cocurès, sitting among vineyards and meadows and orchards thick with red apples, and where, along the highway, they were knocking down walnuts from the roadside trees, and gathering them in sacks and baskets. The hills, however much the vale might open, were still tall and bare, with cliffy battlements and here and there a pointed summit; and the Tarn still rattled through the stones with a mountain noise. I had been led, by bagmen of a picturesque turn of mind, to expect a horrific country after the heart of Byron; but to my Scotch eyes it seemed smiling and plentiful, as the weather still gave an impression of high summer to my Scotch body; although the chestnuts were already picked out by the autumn, and the poplars, that here began to mingle with them, had turned into pale gold against the approach of winter.

There was something in this landscape, smiling although wild, that explained to me the spirit of the Southern Covenanters. Those who took to the hills for conscience' sake in Scotland had all gloomy and bedevilled thoughts; for once that they received God's comfort they would be twice engaged with Satan; but the Camisards had only bright and supporting visions. They dealt much more in blood, both given and taken; yet I find no obsession of the Evil One in their records. With a light conscience, they pursued their life in these rough times and circumstances. The soul of Séguier, let us not forget, was like a garden. They knew they were on God's side, with a knowledge that has no parallel among the Scots; for the Scots, although they might be certain of the cause, could never rest confident of the person.

"We flew," says one old Camisard, "when we heard the sound of psalm-singing, we flew as if with wings. We felt within us an animating ardour, a transporting desire. The feeling cannot be expressed in words. It is a thing that must have been experienced to be understood. However weary we might be, we thought no more of our weariness and grew light, so soon as the psalms fell upon our ears."

The valley of the Tarn and the people whom I met at La Vernède not only explain to me this passage, but the twenty years of suffering which those, who were so stiff and so bloody when once they betook themselves to war, endured with the meekness of children and the constancy of saints and peasants.

Florac

On a branch of the Tarn stands Florac, the seat of a subprefecture, with an old castle, an alley of planes, many quaint street-corners, and a live fountain welling from the hill. It is notable, besides, for handsome women, and as one of the two capitals, Alais being the other, of the country of the Camisards.

The landlord of the inn took me, after I had eaten, to an adjoining café, where I, or rather my journey, became the topic of the afternoon. Every one had some suggestion for my guidance; and the subprefectorial map was fetched from the subprefecture itself, and much thumbed among coffee-cups and glasses of liqueur. Most of these kind advisers were Protestant, though I observed that Protestant and Catholic intermingled in a very easy manner; and it surprised me to see what a lively memory still subsisted of the religious war. Among the hills of the south-west, by Mauchline,

Cumnock, or Carsphairn, in isolated farms or in the manse, serious Presbyterian people still recall the days of the great persecution, and the graves of local martyrs are still piously regarded. But in towns and among the so-called better classes, I fear that these old doings have become an idle tale. If you met a mixed company in the King's Arms at Wigton, it is not likely that the talk would run on Covenanters. Nay, at Muirkirk of Glenluce, I found the beadle's wife had not so much as heard of Prophet Peden. But these Cévenols were proud of their ancestors in quite another sense; the war was their chosen topic; its exploits were their own patent of nobility; and where a man or a race has had but one adventure, and that heroic, we must expect and pardon some prolixity of reference. They told me the country was still full of legends hitherto uncollected; I heard from them about Cavalier's descendants—not direct descendants, be it understood, but only cousins or nephews—who were still prosperous people in the scene of the boy-general's exploits; and one farmer had seen the bones of old combatants dug up into the air of an afternoon in the nineteenth century, in a field where the ancestors had fought, and the great-grandchildren were peaceably ditching.

Later in the day one of the Protestant pastors was so good as to visit me: a young man, intelligent and polite, with whom I passed an hour or two in talk. Florac, he told me, is part Protestant, part Catholic; and the difference in religion is usually doubled by a difference in politics. You may judge of my surprise, coming as I did from such a babbling purgatorial Poland of a place as Monastier, when I learned that the population lived together on very quiet terms; and there was even an exchange of hospitalities between households thus doubly separated. Black Camisard and White Camisard, militiaman and Miquelet and dragoon, Protestant prophet and Catholic cadet of the White Cross, they had all been sabreing and shooting, burning, pillaging, and murdering, their hearts hot with indignant passion; and here, after a hundred and seventy years, Protestant is still Protestant, Catholic still Catholic, in mutual toleration and mild amity of life. But the race of man, like that indomitable nature whence it sprang, has medicating virtues of its own; the years and seasons bring various harvests; the sun returns after the rain; and mankind outlives sæcular animosities, as a single man awakens from the passions of a day. We judge our ancestors from a more divine position; and the dust being a little laid with several centuries, we can see both sides adorned with human virtues and fighting with a show of right.

I have never thought it easy to be just, and find it daily even harder than I thought. I own I met these Protestants with delight and a sense of coming home. I was accustomed to speak their language, in another and deeper sense of the word than that which distinguishes between French and English; for the true babel is a divergence upon morals. And hence I could hold more free communication with the Protestants, and judge them more justly, than the Catholics. Father Apollinaris may pair off with my mountain Plymouth Brother as two guileless and devout old men; yet I ask myself if I had as ready a feeling for the virtues of the Trappist; or had I been a Catholic, if I should have felt so warmly to the dissenter of La Vernède. With the first I was on terms of mere forbearance; but with the other, although only on a misunderstanding and by keeping on selected points, it was still possible to hold converse and exchange some honest thoughts. In this world of imperfection we gladly welcome even partial intimacies. And if we find but one to whom we can speak out of our heart freely, with whom we can walk in love and simplicity without dissimulation, we have no ground of quarrel with the world or God.

In the Valley of the Mimente

On Tuesday, 1st October, we left Florac late in the afternoon, a tired donkey and tired donkey-driver. A little way up the Tarnon, a covered bridge of wood introduced us into the valley of the Mimente. Steep rocky red mountains overhung the stream; great oaks and chestnuts grew upon the slopes or in stony terraces; here and there was a red field of millet or a few apple-trees studded with red apples; and the road passed hard by two black hamlets, one with an old castle atop to please the heart of the tourist.

It was difficult here again to find a spot fit for my encampment. Even under the oaks and chestnuts the ground had not only a very rapid slope, but was heaped with loose stones; and where there was no timber the hills descended to the stream in a red precipice tufted with heather. The sun had left the highest peak in front of me, and the valley was full of the lowing sound of herdsmen's horns as they recalled the flocks into the stable, when I spied a bight of meadow some way below the roadway in an angle of the river. Thither I descended, and, tying Modestine provisionally to a tree, proceeded to investigate the neighbourhood. A gray pearly evening shadow filled the glen; objects at a little distance grew indistinct and melted bafflingly into each other; and the darkness was rising steadily like an exhalation. I approached a great oak which grew in the meadow, hard by the river's brink; when to my disgust the voices of children fell upon my ear, and I beheld a house round the angle on the other bank. I had half a mind to pack and begone again, but the growing darkness moved me to remain. I had only to make no noise until the night was fairly come, and trust to the dawn to call me early in the morning. But it was hard to be annoyed by neighbours in such a great hotel.

A hollow underneath the oak was my bed. Before I had fed Modestine and arranged my sack, three stars were already brightly shining, and the others were beginning dimly to appear. I slipped down to the river, which looked very black among its rocks, to fill my can; and dined with a good appetite in the dark, for I scrupled to light a lantern while so near a house. The moon, which I had seen, a pallid crescent, all afternoon, faintly illuminated the summit of the hills, but not a ray fell into the bottom of the glen where I was lying. The oak rose before me like a pillar of darkness; and overhead the heartsome stars were set in the face of the night. No one knows the stars who has not slept, as the French happily put it, *à la belle étoile.* He may know all their names and distances and magnitudes, and yet be ignorant of what alone concerns mankind, their serene and gladsome influence on the mind. The greater part of poetry is about the stars; and very justly, for they are themselves the most classical of poets. These same far-away worlds, sprinkled like tapers or shaken together like a diamond dust upon the sky, had looked not otherwise to Roland or Cavalier, when, in the words of the latter, they had "no other tent but the sky, and no other bed than my mother earth."

All night a strong wind blew up the valley, and the acorns fell pattering over me from the oak. Yet, on this first night of October, the air was as mild as May, and I slept with the fur thrown back.

I was much disturbed by the barking of a dog, an animal that I fear more than any wolf. A dog is vastly braver, and is besides supported by the sense of duty. If you kill a wolf, you meet with encouragement and praise; but if you kill a dog, the sacred rights of property and the domestic affections come clamouring round you for redress. At the end of a fagging day, the sharp cruel note of a dog's bark is in itself a keen annoyance; and to a tramp like myself, he represents the sedentary and respectable world in its most hostile form. There is something of the clergyman or the lawyer about this engaging animal; and if he were not amenable to stones, the boldest man would shrink from travelling aloof. I respect dogs much in the domestic circle; but on the highway or sleeping a-field, I both detest and fear them.

I was wakened next morning (Wednesday, October 2d) by the same dog—for I knew his bark—making a charge down the bank, and then, seeing me sit up, retreating again with great alacrity. The stars were not yet quite extinguished. The heaven was of that enchanting mild gray-blue of the early morn. A still clear light began to fall, and the trees on the hillside were outlined sharply against the sky. The wind had veered more to the north, and no longer reached me in the glen; but as I was going on with my preparations, it drove a white cloud very swiftly over the hill-top; and looking up, I was surprised to see the cloud dyed with gold. In these high regions of the air, the sun was already shining as at noon. If only the clouds travelled high enough, we should see the same thing all night long. For it is always daylight in the fields of space.

As I began to go up the valley, a draught of wind came down it out of the seat of the sunrise, although the clouds continued to run overhead in an almost contrary direction. A few steps farther, and I saw a whole hillside gilded with the sun; and still a little beyond, between two peaks, a centre of dazzling brilliancy appeared floating in the sky, and I was once more face to face with the big bonfire that occupies the kernel of our system.

I met but one human being that forenoon, a dark military-looking wayfarer, who carried a gamebag on a baldric; but he made a remark that seems worthy of record. For when I asked him if he were Protestant or Catholic—

"Oh," said he, "I make no shame of my religion. I am a Catholic."

He made no shame of it! The phrase is a piece of natural statistics; for it is the language of one in a minority. I thought with a smile of Bavile and his dragoons, and how you may ride rough-shod over a religion for a century, and leave it only the more lively for the friction. Ireland is still Catholic; the Cevennes still Prot-estant. It is not a basketful of law-papers, nor the hoofs and pistol-butts of a regiment of horse, that can change one tittle of a plough-man's thoughts. Outdoor rustic people have not many ideas, but such as they have are hardy plants and thrive flourishingly in persecution. One who has grown a long while in the sweat of laborious noons, and under the stars at night, a frequenter of hills and forests, an old honest countryman, has, in the end, a sense of communion with the powers of the universe, and amicable re-lations towards his God. Like my mountain Plymouth Brother, he knows the Lord. His religion does not repose upon a choice of logic; it is the poetry of the man's experience, the philosophy of the history of his life. God, like a great power, like a great shining sun, has appeared to this simple fellow in the course of years, and become the ground and essence of his least reflections; and you may change creeds and dogmas by authority, or proclaim a new religion with the sound of trumpets, if you will; but here is a man who has his own thoughts, and will stubbornly adhere to them in good and evil. He is a Catholic, a Protestant, or a Plymouth Brother, in the same indefeasible sense that a man is not a woman, or a woman not a man. For he could not vary from his faith, un-less he could eradicate all memory of the past, and, in a strict and not a conventional meaning, change his mind.

The Heart of the Country

I was now drawing near to Cassagnas, a cluster of black roofs upon the hillside, in this wild valley, among chestnut gardens, and looked upon in a clear air by many rocky peaks. The road along the Mimente is yet new, nor have the mountaineers recovered their surprise when the first cart arrived at Cassagnas. But al-though it lay thus apart from the current of men's business, this hamlet had already made a figure in the history of France. Hard by, in caverns of the mountain, was one of the five arsenals of the Camisards; where they laid up clothes and corn and arms against necessity, forged bayonets and sabres, and made themselves gunpowder with willow charcoal and saltpetre boiled in kettles. To the same caves, amid this multifarious industry, the sick and wounded were brought up to heal; and there they were visited by the two surgeons, Chabrier and Tavan, and secretly nursed by women of the neighbourhood.

Of the five legions into which the Camisards were divided, it was the oldest and the most obscure that had its magazines by Cassagnas. This was the band of Spirit Séguier; men who had joined their voices with his in the 68th Psalm as they marched down by night on the archpriest of the Cevennes. Séguier, promoted to heaven, was succeeded by Salomon Couderc, whom Cavalier treats in his memoirs as chaplain-general to the whole army of the Camisards. He was a prophet; a great reader of the heart, who admitted people to the sacrament or refused them by "intentively viewing every man" between the eyes; and had the most of the Scriptures off by rote. And this was surely happy; since in a surprise in August 1703, he lost his mule, his portfolios, and his Bible. It is only strange that they were not surprised more often and more effectually; for this legion of Cassagnas was truly patriarchal in its theory of war, and camped without sentries, leaving that duty to the angels of the God for whom they fought. This is a token, not only of their faith, but of the trackless country where they harboured. M. de Caldon, taking a stroll one fine day, walked without warning into their midst, as he might have walked into "a flock of sheep in a plain," and found some asleep and some awake and psalm-singing. A traitor had need of no recommendation to insinuate himself among their ranks, beyond "his faculty of singing psalms;" and even the prophet Salomon "took him into a particular friendship." Thus, among their intricate hills, the rustic troop subsisted; and history can attribute few exploits to them but sacraments and ecstasies.

People of this tough and simple stock will not, as I have just been saying, prove variable in religion; nor will they get nearer to apostasy than a mere external conformity like that of Naaman in the house of Rimmon. When Louis XVI., in the words of the edict, "convinced by the uselessness of a century of persecutions, and rather from necessity than sympathy," granted at last a royal grace of toleration, Cassagnas was still Protestant; and to a man, it is so to this day. There is, indeed, one family that is not Protestant, but neither is it Catholic. It is that of a Catholic curé in revolt, who has taken to his bosom a schoolmistress. And his conduct, it's worth noting, is disapproved by the Protestant villagers.

"It is a bad idea for a man," said one, "to go back from his engagements."

The villagers whom I saw seemed intelligent after a countrified fashion, and were all plain and dignified in manner. As a Protestant myself, I was well looked upon, and my acquaintance with history gained me farther respect. For we had something not unlike a religious controversy at table, a gendarme and a merchant with whom I dined being both strangers to the place and Catholics. The young men of the house stood round and supported me; and the whole discussion was tolerantly conducted, and surprised a man brought up among the infinitesimal and contentious differences of Scotland. The merchant, indeed, grew a little warm, and was far less pleased than some others with my historical acquirements. But the gendarme was mighty easy over it all.

"It's a bad idea for a man to change," said he; and the remark was generally applauded.

That was not the opinion of the priest and soldier at our Lady of the Snows. But this is a different race; and perhaps the same great-heartedness that upheld them to resist, now enables them to differ in a kind spirit. For courage respects courage; but where a faith has been trodden out, we may look for a mean and narrow population. The true work of Bruce and Wallace was the union of the nations; not that they should stand apart a while longer, skirmishing upon their borders; but that, when the time came, they might unite with self-respect.

The merchant was much interested in my journey, and thought it dangerous to sleep a-field.

"There are the wolves," said he; "and then it is known you are an Englishman. The English have always long purses, and it might very well enter into some one's head to deal you an ill blow some night."

I told him I was not much afraid of such accidents; and at any rate judged it unwise to dwell upon alarms or consider small perils in the arrangement of life. Life itself, I submitted, was a far too risky business as a whole to make each additional particular of danger worth regard. "Something," said I, "might burst in your inside any day of the week, and there would be an end of you, if you were locked into your room with three turns of the key."

"*Cependant,*" said he, "*coucher dehors!*"

"God," said I, "is everywhere."

"*Cependant, coucher dehors!*" he repeated, and his voice was eloquent of terror.

He was the only person, in all my voyage, who saw anything hardy in so simple a proceeding; although many considered it superfluous. Only one, on the other hand, professed much delight in the idea; and that was my Plymouth Brother, who cried out, when I told him I sometimes preferred sleeping under the stars to a close and noisy alehouse, "Now I see that you know the Lord!"

The merchant asked me for one of my cards as I was leaving, for he said I should be something to talk of in the future, and desired me to make a note of his request and reason; a desire with which I have thus complied.

A little after two I struck across the Mimente, and took a rugged path southward up a hillside covered with loose stones and tufts of heather. At the top, as is the habit of the country, the path disappeared; and I left my she-ass munching heather, and went forward alone to seek a road.

I was now on the separation of two vast watersheds; behind me all the streams were bound for the Garonne and the Western Ocean; before me was the basin of the Rhone. Hence, as from the Lozère, you can see in clear weather the shining of the Gulf of Lyons; and perhaps from here the soldiers of Salomon may have watched for the topsails of Sir Cloudesley Shovel, and the long-promised aid from England. You may take this ridge as lying in the heart of the country of the Camisards; four of the five legions camped all round it and almost within view—Salomon and Joani to the north, Castanet and Roland to the south; and when Julien had finished his famous work, the devastation of the High Cevennes, which lasted all through October and November 1703, and during which four hundred and sixty villages and hamlets were, with fire and pickaxe, utterly subverted, a man standing on this eminence would have looked forth upon a silent, smokeless, and dispeopled land. Time and man's activity have now repaired these ruins; Cassagnas is once more roofed and sending up domestic smoke; and in the chestnut gardens, in low and leafy corners, many a prosperous farmer returns, when the day's work is done, to his children and bright hearth. And still it was perhaps the wildest view of all my journey. Peak upon peak, chain upon chain of hills ran surging southward, channelled and sculptured by the winter streams, feathered from head to foot with chestnuts, and here and there breaking out into a coronal of cliffs. The sun, which was still far from setting, sent a drift of misty gold across the hill-tops, but the valleys were already plunged in a profound and quiet shadow.

A very old shepherd, hobbling on a pair of sticks and wearing a black cap of liberty, as if in honour of his nearness to the grave, directed me to the road for St. Germain de Calberte. There was something solemn in the isolation of this infirm and ancient creature. Where he dwelt, how he got upon this high ridge, or how he proposed to get down again, were more than I could fancy. Not far off upon my right was the famous Plan de Font Morte, where Poul with his Armenian sabre slashed down the Camisards of Séguier. This, methought, might be some Rip van Winkle of the war, who had lost his comrades, fleeing before Poul, and wandered ever since upon the mountains. It might be news to him that Cavalier had surrendered, or Roland had fallen fighting with his back against an olive. And while I was thus working on my fancy, I heard him hailing in broken tones, and saw him waving me to come back with one of his two sticks. I had already got some way past him; but, leaving Modestine once more, retraced my steps.

Alas, it was a very commonplace affair. The old gentleman had forgot to ask the peddler what he sold, and wished to remedy this neglect.

I told him sternly, "Nothing."

"Nothing?" cried he.

I repeated "Nothing," and made off.

It's odd to think of, but perhaps I thus became as inexplicable to the old man as he had been to me.

The road lay under chestnuts, and though I saw a hamlet or two below me in the vale, and many lone houses of the chestnut farmers, it was a very solitary march all afternoon; and the evening began early underneath the trees. But I heard the voice of a woman singing some sad, old, endless ballad not far off. It seemed to be about love and a *bel amoureux*, her handsome sweet-heart; and I wished I could have taken up the strain and answered her, as I went on upon my invisible woodland way, weav ing, like Pippa in the poem, my own thoughts with hers. What could I have told her? Little enough; and yet all the heart requires. How the world gives and takes away, and brings sweethearts near, only to separate them again into distant and strange lands; but to love is the great amulet which makes the world a garden; and "hope, which comes to all," outwears the accidents of life, and reaches with tremulous hand beyond the grave and death. Easy to say: yea, but also, by God's mercy, both easy and grateful to believe!

We struck at last into a wide white high road carpeted with noiseless dust. The night had come; the moon had been shining for a long while upon the opposite mountain; when on turning a corner my donkey and I issued ourselves into her light. I had emptied out my brandy at Florac, for I could bear the stuff no longer, and replaced it with some generous and scented Volnay; and now I drank to the moon's sacred majesty upon the road. It was but a couple of mouthfuls; yet I became thenceforth unconscious of my limbs, and my blood flowed with luxury. Even Modestine was inspired by this purified nocturnal sunshine, and bestirred her little hoofs as to a livelier measure. The road wound and descended swiftly among masses of chestnuts. Hot dust rose from our feet and flowed away. Our two shadows—mine deformed with the knapsack, hers comically bestridden by the pack—now lay before us clearly outlined on the road, and now, as we turned a corner, went off into the ghostly distance, and sailed along the mountain like clouds. From time to time a warm wind rustled down the valley, and set all the chestnuts dangling their bunches of foliage and fruit; the ear was filled with whispering music, and the shadows danced in tune. And next moment the breeze had gone by, and in all the valley nothing moved except our travelling feet. On the opposite slope, the monstrous ribs and gullies of the mountain were faintly designed in the moonshine; and high overhead, in some lone house, there burned one lighted window, one square spark of red in the huge field of sad nocturnal colouring.

At a certain point, as I went downward, turning many acute angles, the moon disappeared behind the hill; and I pursued my way in great darkness, until another turning shot me without preparation into St. Germain de Calberte. The place was asleep and silent, and buried in opaque night. Only from a single open door, some lamplight escaped upon the road to show me that I was come among men's habitations. The two last gossips of the evening, still talking by a garden wall, directed me to the inn. The landlady was getting her chicks to bed; the fire was already out, and had, not without grumbling, to be rekindled; half an hour later, and I must have gone supperless to roost.

The Last Day

When I awoke (Thursday, 2d October), and, hearing a great flourishing of cocks and chuckling of contented hens, betook me to the window of the clean and comfortable room where I had slept the night, I looked forth on a sunshiny morning in a deep vale of chestnut gardens. It was still early, and the cockcrows, and the slanting lights, and the long shadows encouraged me to be out and look round me.

St. Germain de Calberte is a great parish nine leagues round about. At the period of the wars, and immediately before the devastation, it was inhabited by two hundred and seventy-five families, of which only nine were Catholic; and it took the curé seventeen September days to go from house to house on horseback for a census. But the place itself, although capital of a canton, is scarce larger than a hamlet. It lies terraced across a steep slope in the midst of mighty chestnuts. The Protestant chapel stands below upon a shoulder; in the midst of the town is the quaint old Catholic church.

It was here that poor Du Chayla, the Christian martyr, kept his library and held a court of missionaries; here he had built his tomb, thinking to lie among a grateful population whom he had redeemed from error; and hither on the morrow of his death they brought the body, pierced with two-and-fifty wounds, to be interred. Clad in his priestly robes, he was laid out in state in the church. The curé, taking his text from Second Samuel, twentieth chapter and twelfth verse, "And Amasa wallowed in his blood in the highway," preached a rousing sermon, and exhorted his brethren to die each at his post, like their unhappy and illustrious superior. In the midst of this eloquence there came a breeze that Spirit Séquier was near at hand; and behold! all the assembly took to their horses' heels, some east, some west, and the curé himself as far as Alais.

Strange was the position of this little Catholic metropolis, a thimbleful of Rome, in such a wild and contrary neighbourhood. On the one hand, the legion of Salomon overlooked it from Cassagnas; on the other, it was cut off from assistance by the legion of Roland at Mialet. The curé, Louvrelenil, although he took a panic at the archpriest's funeral, and so hurriedly decamped to Alais, stood well by his isolated pulpit, and thence uttered ful minations against the crimes of the Protestants. Salomon besieged the village for an hour and a half, but was beat back. The militia-men, on guard before the curé's door, could be heard, in the black hours, singing Protestant psalms and holding friendly talk with the insurgents. And in the morning, although not a shot had been fired, there would not be a round of powder in their flasks. Where was it gone? All handed over to the Camisards for a consideration. Untrusty guardians for an isolated priest!

That these continual stirs were once busy in St. Germain de Calberte, the imagination with difficulty receives; all is now so quiet, the pulse of human life now beats so low and still in this hamlet of the mountains. Boys followed me a great way off, like a timid sort of lion-hunters; and people turned round to have a second look, or came out of their houses, as I went by. My passage was the first event, you would have fancied, since the Camisards. There was nothing rude or forward in this observation; it was but a pleased and wondering scrutiny, like that of oxen or the human infant; yet it wearied my spirits, and soon drove me from the street.

I took refuge on the terraces, which are here greenly carpeted with sward, and tried to imitate with a pencil the inimitable attitudes of the chestnuts as they bear up their canopy of leaves. Ever and again a little wind went by, and the nuts dropped all around me, with a light and dull sound, upon the sward. The noise was as of a thin fall of great hailstones; but there went with it a cheerful human sentiment of an approaching harvest and farmers rejoicing in their gains. Looking up, I could see the brown nut peering through the husk, which was already gaping; and between the stems the eye embraced an amphitheatre of hill, sun-lit and green with leaves.

I have not often enjoyed a place more deeply. I moved in an atmosphere of pleasure, and felt light and quiet and content. But perhaps it was not the place alone that so disposed my spirit.

Perhaps some one was thinking of me in another country; or perhaps some thought of my own had come and gone unnoticed, and yet done me good. For some thoughts, which sure would be the most beautiful, vanish before we can rightly scan their features; as though a god, travelling by our green highways, should but ope the door, give one smiling look into the house, and go again for ever. Was it Apollo, or Mercury, or Love with folded wings? Who shall say? But we go the lighter about our business, and feel peace and pleasure in our hearts.

I dined with a pair of Catholics. They agreed in the condemnation of a young man, a Catholic, who had married a Protestant girl and gone over to the religion of his wife. A Protestant born they could understand and respect; indeed, they seemed to be of the mind of an old Catholic woman, who told me that same day there was no difference between the two sects, save that "wrong was more wrong for the Catholic," who had more light and guidance; but this of a man's desertion filled them with contempt.

"It is a bad idea for a man to change," said one.

It may have been accidental, but you see how this phrase pursued me; and for myself, I believe it is the current philosophy in these parts. I have some difficulty in imagining a better. It's not only a great flight of confidence for a man to change his creed and go out of his family for heaven's sake; but the odds are—nay, and the hope is—that, with all this great transition in the eyes of man, he has not changed himself a hair's-breadth to the eyes of God. Honour to those who do so, for the wrench is sore. But it argues something narrow, whether of strength or weakness, whether of the prophet or the fool, in those who can take a sufficient interest in such infinitesimal and human operations, or who can quit a friendship for a doubtful process of the mind. And I think I should not leave my old creed for another, changing only words for other words; but by some brave reading, embrace it in spirit and truth, and find wrong as wrong for me as for the best of other communions.

The phylloxera was in the neighbourhood; and instead of wine we drank at dinner a more economical juice of the grape—La Parisienne, they call it. It is made by putting the fruit whole into a cask with water; one by one the berries ferment and burst; what is drunk during the day is supplied at night in water; so, with ever another pitcher from the well, and ever another grape exploding and giving out its strength, one cask of Parisienne may last a family till spring. It is, as the reader will anticipate, a feeble beverage, but very pleasant to the taste.

What with dinner and coffee, it was long past three before I left St. Germain de Calberte. I went down beside the Gardon of Mialet, a great glaring watercourse devoid of water, and through St. Etienne de Vallée Française, or Val Francesque, as they used to call it; and towards evening began to ascend the hill of St. Pierre. It was a long and steep ascent. Behind me an empty carriage returning to St. Jean du Gard kept hard upon my tracks, and near the summit overtook me. The driver, like the rest of the world, was sure I was a pedlar; but, unlike others, he was sure of what I had to sell. He had noticed the blue wool which hung out of my pack at either end; and from this he had decided, beyond my power to alter his decision, that I dealt in blue-wool collars, such as decorate the neck of the French draught-horse.

I had hurried to the topmost powers of Modestine, for I dearly desired to see the view upon the other side before the day had faded. But it was night when I reached the summit; the moon was riding high and clear; and only a few gray streaks of twilight lingered in the west. A yawning valley, gulfed in blackness, lay like a hole in created nature at my feet; but the outline of the hills was sharp against the sky. There was Mount Aigoal, the stronghold of Castanet. And Castanet, not only as an active undertaking leader, deserves some mention among Camisards; for there is a spray of rose among his laurel; and he showed how, even in a public tragedy, love will have its way. In the high tide of war he married, in his mountain citadel, a young and pretty lass called Mariette. There were great rejoicings; and the bridegroom released five-and-twenty prisoners in honour of the glad event. Seven months afterwards Mariette, the Princess of the Cevennes, as they called her in derision, fell into the hands of the authorities, where it was like to have gone hard with her. But Castanet was a man of execution, and loved his wife. He fell on Valleraugue, and got a lady there for a hostage; and for the first and last time in that war there was an exchange of prisoners. Their daughter, pledge of some starry night upon Mount Aigoal, has left descendants to this day.

Modestine and I—it was our last meal together—had a snack upon the top of St. Pierre, I on a heap of stones, she standing by me in the moonlight and decorously eating bread out of my hand. The poor brute would eat more heartily in this manner; for she had a sort of affection for me, which I was soon to betray.

It was a long descent upon St. Jean du Gard, and we met no one but a carter, visible afar off by the glint of the moon on his extinguished lantern.

Before ten o'clock we had got in and were at supper; fifteen miles and a stiff hill in little beyond six hours!

Farewell, Modestine

On examination, on the morning of October 3d, Modestine was pronounced unfit for travel. She would need at least two days' repose according to the ostler; but I was now eager to reach Alais for my letters; and, being in a civilised country of stage-coaches, I determined to sell my lady-friend and be off by the diligence that afternoon. Our yesterday's march, with the testimony of the driver who had pursued us up the long hill of St. Pierre, spread a favourable notion of my donkey's capabilities. Intending purchasers were aware of an unrivalled opportunity. Before ten I had an offer of twenty-five francs; and before noon, after a desperate engagement, I sold her, saddle and all, for five-and-thirty. The pecuniary gain is not obvious, but I had bought freedom into the bargain.

St. Jean du Gard is a large place and largely Protestant. The *maire,* a Protestant, asked me to help him in a small matter which is itself characteristic of the country. The young women of the Cevennes profit by the common religion and the difference of the language to go largely as governesses into England; and here was one, a native of Mialet, struggling with English circulars from two different agencies in London. I gave what help I could; and volunteered some advice, which struck me as being excellent.

One thing more I note. The phylloxera has ravaged the vineyards in this neighbourhood; and in the early morning, under some chestnuts by the river, I found a party of men working with a cider-press. I could not at first make out what they were after, and asked one fellow to explain.

"Making cider," he said. *"Oui, c'est comme ça. Comme dans le nord!"*

There was a ring of sarcasm in his voice: the country was going to the devil.

It was not until I was fairly seated by the driver, and rattling through a rocky valley with dwarf olives, that I became aware of my bereavement. I had lost Modestine. Up to that moment I had thought I hated her; but now she was gone,

> "And, O,
> The difference to me!"

For twelve days we had been fast companions; we had travelled upwards of a hundred and twenty miles, crossed several respectable ridges, and jogged along with our six legs by many a rocky and many a boggy by-road. After the first day, although sometimes I was hurt and distant in manner, I still kept my patience; and as for her, poor soul! she had come to regard me as a god. She loved to eat out of my hand. She was patient, elegant in form, the colour of an ideal mouse, and inimitably small. Her faults were those of her race and sex; her virtues were her own. Farewell, and if for ever—

Father Adam wept when he sold her to me; after I had sold her in my turn, I was tempted to follow his example; and being alone with a stage-driver and four or five agreeable young men, I did not hesitate to yield to my emotion.

The Royal Sport Nautique*

THE RAIN TOOK OFF NEAR LAEKEN. BUT THE SUN WAS ALREADY down; the air was chill; and we had scarcely a dry stitch between the pair of us. Nay, now we found ourselves near the end of the Allée Verte, and on the very threshold of Brussels we were confronted by a serious difficulty. The shores were closely lined by canal boats waiting their turn at the lock. Nowhere was there any convenient landing-place; nowhere so much as a stable-yard to leave the canoes in for the night. We scrambled ashore and entered an *estaminet* where some sorry fellows were drinking with the landlord. The landlord was pretty round with us; he knew of no coach-house or stable-yard, nothing of the sort; and seeing we had come with no mind to drink, he did not conceal his impatience to be rid of us. One of the sorry fellows came to the rescue. Somewhere in the corner of the basin there was a slip, he informed us, and something else besides, not very clearly defined by him, but hopefully construed by his hearers.

Sure enough there was the slip in the corner of the basin; and at the top of it two nice-looking lads in boating-clothes. The *Arethusa* addressed himself to these. One of them said there would be no difficulty about a night's lodging for our boats; and the other, taking a cigarette from his lips, inquired if they were made by Searle & Son. The name was quite an introduction. Half-a-dozen other young men came out of a boat-house bearing the superscription ROYAL SPORT NAUTIQUE, and joined in the talk.

* Typical of the casual chronicle of their canoe trip through Belgium is this commentary on the reception given *Cigarette*, Sir Walter Grindley Simpson, and his companion *Arethusa*, Robert Louis Stevenson, as recorded in *An Inland Voyage*.—Ed.

They were all very polite, voluble, and enthusiastic; and their discourse was interlarded with English boating-terms, and the names of English boat-builders and English clubs. I do not know, to my shame, any spot in my native land, where I should have been so warmly received by the same number of people. We wer English boating-men, and the Belgian boating-men fell upon our necks. I wonder if French Huguenots were as cordially greeted by English Protestants when they came across the Channel out of great tribulation. But, after all, what religion knits people so closely as common sport?

The canoes were carried into the boat-house; they were washed down for us by the club servants, the sails were hung out to dry, and everything made as snug and tidy as a picture. And in the meanwhile we were led upstairs by our new-found brethren, for so more than one of them stated the relationship, and made free of their lavatory. This one lent us soap, that one a towel, a third and fourth helped us to undo our bags. And all the time such questions, such assurances of respect and sympathy! I declare I never knew what glory was before.

"Yes, yes, the *Royal Sport Nautique* is the oldest club in Belgium."

"We number two hundred."

"We"—this is not a substantive speech, but an abstract of many speeches, the impression left upon my mind after a great deal of talk; and very youthful, pleasant, natural, and patriotic it seems to me to be—"We have gained all races, except those where we were cheated by the French."

"You must leave all your wet things to be dried."

"O! *entre frères!* In any boat-house in England we should find the same." (I cordially hope they might.)

"*En Angleterre, vous employez des sliding-seats, n'est-ce pas?*"

"We are all employed in commerce during the day; but in the evening, *voyez-vous, nous sommes sérieux.*"

These were the words. They were all employed over the frivolous mercantile concerns of Belgium during the day; but in the evening they found some hours for the serious concerns of life. I may have a wrong idea of wisdom, but I think that was a very wise remark. People connected with literature and philosophy are busy all their days in getting rid of second-hand notions and false standards. It is their profession, in the sweat of their brows, by dogged thinking, to recover their old fresh view of life, and distinguish what they really and originally like from what they have only learned to tolerate perforce. And these Royal Nautical Sportsmen had the distinction still quite legible in their hearts. They had still those clean perceptions of what is nice and nasty, what is interesting and what is dull, which envious old gentlemen refer to as illusions. The nightmare illusion of middle age, the bear's hug of custom gradually squeezing the life out of a man's soul, had not yet begun for these happy-star'd young Belgians. They still knew that the interest they took in their business was a trifling affair compared to their spontaneous, long-suffering affection for nautical sports. To know what you prefer, instead of humbly saying Amen to what the world tells you you ought to prefer, is to have kept your soul alive. Such a man may be generous; he may be honest in something more than the commercial sense; he may love his friends with an elective, personal sympathy, and not accept them as an adjunct of the station to which he has been called. He may be a man, in short, acting on his own instincts, keeping in his own shape that God made him in; and not a mere crank in the social engine-house, welded on principles that he does not understand, and for purposes that he does not care for.

For will any one dare to tell me that business is more entertaining than fooling among boats? He must have never seen a boat, or never seen an office, who says so. And for certain the one is a great deal better for the health. There should be nothing so much a man's business as his amusements. Nothing but money-grubbing can be put forward to the contrary; no one but

> Mammon, the least erected spirit that fell
> From Heaven,

durst risk a word in answer. It is but a lying cant that would represent the merchant and the banker as people disinterestedly toiling for mankind, and then most useful when they are most absorbed in their transactions; for the man is more important than his services. And when my Royal Nautical Sportsman shall have so far fallen from his hopeful youth that he cannot pluck up an enthusiasm over anything but his ledger, I venture to doubt whether he will be near so nice a fellow, and whether he would welcome, with so good a grace, a couple of drenched Englishmen paddling into Brussels in the dusk.

When we had changed our wet clothes and drunk a glass of pale ale to the club's prosperity, one of their number escorted us to a hotel. He would not join us at our dinner, but he had no objection to a glass of wine. Enthusiasm is very wearing; and I begin to understand why prophets were unpopular in Judæa, where they were best known. For three stricken hours did this excellent young man sit beside us to dilate on boats and boat-races; and before he left, he was kind enough to order our bedroom candles.

We endeavoured now and again to change the subject; but the diversion did not last a moment: the Royal Nautical Sportsman bridled, shied, answered the question, and then breasted once more into the swelling tide of his subject. I call it his subject; but I think it was he who was subjected. The *Arethusa*, who holds all racing as a creature of the devil, found himself in a pitiful dilemma. He durst not own his ignorance for the honour of old England, and spoke away about English clubs and English oarsmen whose fame had never before come to his ears. Several times, and once, above all, on the question of sliding-seats, he was within an ace of exposure. As for the *Cigarette*, who has rowed races in the heat of his blood, but now disowns these slips of his wanton youth, his case was still more desperate; for the Royal Nautical proposed that he should take an oar in one of their eights on the morrow, to compare the English with the Belgian stroke. I could see my friend perspiring in his chair whenever that particular topic came up. And there was yet another proposal which had the same effect on both of us. It appeared that the champion canoeist of Europe (as well as most other champions) was a Royal Nautical Sportsman. And if we would only wait until the Sunday, this infernal paddler would be so condescending as to accompany us on our next stage. Neither of us had the least desire to drive the coursers of the sun against Apollo.

When the young man was gone, we countermanded our candles, and ordered some brandy and water. The great billows had gone over our head. The Royal Nautical Sportsmen were as nice young fellows as a man would wish to see, but they were a trifle too young and a thought too nautical for us. We began to see that we were old and cynical; we liked ease and the agreeable rambling of the human mind about this and the other subject; we did not want to disgrace our native land by messing at eight, or toiling pitifully in the wake of the champion canoeist. In short, we had recourse to flight. It seemed ungrateful, but we tried to make that good on a card loaded with sincere compliments. And indeed it was no time for scruples; we seemed to feel the hot breath of the champion on our necks.

The Silverado Squatters

"Vixerunt nonnulli in agris, delectati re sua familiari. His idem propositum fuit quod regibus, ut ne qua re agerent, ne cui parerent, libertate uterentur: cujus proprium est sic vivere ut velis."

Cic., *De Off.,* I. xx.

To

Virgil Williams
and
Dora Norton Williams

These sketches are affectionately
dedicated by their friend

THE AUTHOR

T HE SCENE OF THIS LITTLE BOOK IS ON A HIGH MOUNTAIN. THERE are, indeed, many higher; there are many of a nobler outline. It is no place of pilgrimage for the summary globe-trotter; but to one who lives upon its sides, Mount Saint Helena soon becomes a centre of interest. It is the Mont Blanc of one section of the Californian Coast Range, none of its near neighbours rising to one-half its altitude. It looks down on much green, intricate country. It feeds in the spring-time many splashing brooks. From its summit you must have an excellent lesson of geography: seeing, to the south, San Francisco Bay, with Tamalpais on the one hand and Monte Diablo on the other; to the west and thirty miles away, the open ocean; eastward, across the cornlands and thick tule swamps of Sacramento Valley, to where the Central Pacific Railroad begins to climb the sides of the Sierras; and northward, for what I know, the white head of Shasta looking down on Oregon. Three counties, Napa County, Lake County, and Sonoma County, march across its cliffy shoulders. Its naked peak stands nearly four thousand five hundred feet above the sea; its sides are fringed with forest; and the soil, where it is bare, glows warm with cinnabar.

Life in its shadow goes rustically forward. Bucks, and bears, and rattlesnakes, and former mining operations, are the staple of men's talk. Agriculture has only begun to mount above the valley. And though in a few years from now the whole district may be smiling with farms, passing trains shaking the mountain to the heart, many-windowed hotels lighting up the night like factories, and a prosperous city occupying the site of sleepy Calistoga; yet in the meantime, around the foot of that mountain the silence of nature reigns in a great measure unbroken, and the people of hill and valley go sauntering about their business as in the days before the flood.

To reach Mount Saint Helena from San Francisco, the traveller has twice to cross the bay: once by the busy Oakland Ferry, and again, after an hour or so of the railway, from Vallejo Junction to Vallejo. Thence he takes rail once more to mount the long green strath of Napa Valley.

In all the contractions and expansions of that inland sea, the Bay of San Francisco, there can be few drearier scenes than the Vallejo Ferry. Bald shores and a low, bald islet enclose the sea; through the narrows the tide bubbles, muddy like a river. When we made the passage (bound, although yet we knew it not, for Silverado) the steamer jumped, and the black buoys were dancing in the jabble; the ocean breeze blew killing chill; and, although the upper sky was still unflecked with vapour, the sea-fogs were pouring in from seaward, over the hilltops of Marin County, in one great, shapeless, silver cloud.

South Vallejo is typical of many Californian towns. It was a blunder; the site has proved untenable; and although it is still such a young place by the scale of Europe, it has already begun to be deserted for its neighbour and namesake, North Vallejo. A long pier, a number of drinking-saloons, a hotel of a great size, marshy pools where the frogs keep up their croaking, and even at high noon the entire absence of any human face or voice—these are the marks of South Vallejo. Yet there was a tall building beside the pier, labelled the *Star Flour Mills;* and sea-going, full-rigged ships lay close alongshore, waiting for their cargo. Soon these would be plunging round the Horn, soon the flour from the *Star Flour Mills* would be landed on the wharves of Liverpool. For that, too, is one of England's outposts; thither, to this gaunt mill, across the Atlantic and Pacific deeps and round about the icy Horn, this crowd of great, three-masted, deep-sea ships come, bringing nothing, and return with bread.

The Frisby House, for that was the name of the hotel, was a place of fallen fortunes, like the town. It was now given up to labourers, and partly ruinous. At dinner there was the ordinary display of what is called in the west a two-bit house: the tablecloth checked red and white, the plague of flies, the wire hencoops over the dishes, the great variety and invariable vileness of the food and the rough coatless men devouring it in silence. In our bed-room, the stove would not burn, though it would smoke; and while one window would not open, the other would not shut. There was a view on a bit of empty road, a few dark houses, a donkey wandering with its shadow on a slope, and a blink of sea, with a tall ship lying anchored in the moonlight. All about that dreary inn frogs sang their ungainly chorus.

Early the next morning we mounted the hill along a wooden footway, bridging one marish spot after another. Here and there, as we ascended, we passed a house embowered in white roses. More of the bay became apparent, and soon the blue peak of Tamalpais rose above the green level of the island opposite. It told us we were still but a little way from the city of the Golden Gates, already, at that hour, beginning to awake among the sand-hills. It called to us over the waters as with the voice of a bird. Its stately head, blue as a sapphire on the paler azure of the sky, spoke to us of wider outlooks and the bright Pacific. For Tamalpais stands sentry, like a lighthouse, over the Golden Gates, between the bay and the open ocean, and looks down indifferently on both. Even as we saw and hailed it from Vallejo, seamen, far out at sea, were scanning it with shaded eyes; and, as if to answer to the thought, one of the great ships below began silently to clothe her-self with white sails, homeward bound for England.

For some way beyond Vallejo the railway led us through bald green pastures. On the west the rough highlands of Marin shut off the ocean; in the midst, in long, straggling, gleaming arms, the

Lay died out among the grass; there were few trees and few enclosures; the sun shone wide over open uplands, the displumed
hills stood clear against the sky. But by-and-by these hills began
to draw nearer on either hand, and first thicket and then wood
began to clothe their sides; and soon we were away from all signs
of the sea's neighbourhood, mounting an inland, irrigated valley.
A great variety of oaks stood, now severally, now in a becoming
grove, among the fields and vineyards. The towns were compact, in
about equal proportions, of bright new wooden houses and great
and growing forest trees; and the chapel bell on the engine
sounded most festally that sunny Sunday, as we drew up at one
green town after another, with the townsfolk trooping in their
Sunday's best to see the strangers, with the sun sparkling on the
clean houses, and great domes of foliage humming overhead in
the breeze.

This pleasant Napa Valley is, at its north end, blockaded by our
mountain. There, at Calistoga, the railroad ceases, and the traveller who intends faring farther, to the Geysers or to the springs in
Lake County, must cross the spurs of the mountain by stage. Thus,
Mount Saint Helena is not only a summit, but a frontier; and up
to the time of writing it has stayed the progress of the iron horse.

IN THE VALLEY

1. *Calistoga*

IT IS DIFFICULT FOR A EUROPEAN TO IMAGINE CALISTOGA, THE
whole place is so new, and of such an occidental pattern; the
very name, I hear, was invented at a supper-party by the man who
found the springs.

The railroad and the highway come up the valley about parallel to one another. The street of Calistoga joins them, perpen-

dicular to both—a wide street, with bright, clean, low houses, here and there a veranda over the sidewalk, here and there a horse-post, here and there lounging townsfolk. Other streets are marked out, and most likely named; for these towns in the New World began with a firm resolve to grow larger, Washington and Broadway, and then First and Second, and so forth, being boldly plotted out as soon as the community indulges in a plan. But, in the meanwhile, all the life and most of the houses of Calistoga are concentrated upon that street between the railway station and the road. I never heard it called by any name, but I will hazard a guess that it is either Washington or Broadway. Here are the blacksmith's, the chemist's, the general merchant's, and Kong Sam Kee, the Chinese laundryman's; here, probably, is the office of the local paper (for the place has a paper—they all have papers); and here certainly is one of the hotels, Cheeseborough's, whence the daring Foss, a man dear to legend, starts his horses for the Geysers.

It must be remembered that we are here in a land of stage-drivers and highwaymen: a land, in that sense, like England a hundred years ago. The highway robber—road-agent, he is quaintly called—is still busy in these parts. The fame of Vasquez is still young. Only a few years ago, the Lakeport stage was robbed a mile or two from Calistoga. In 1879, the dentist of Mendocino City, fifty miles away upon the coast, suddenly threw off the garments of his trade, like Grindoff, in *The Miller and His Men,* and flamed forth in his second dress as a captain of banditti. A great robbery was followed by a long chase, a chase of days if not of weeks, among the intricate hill-country; and the chase was followed by much desultory fighting, in which several—and the dentist, I believe, amongst the number—bit the dust. The grass was springing for the first time, nourished upon their blood, when I arrived in Calistoga. I am reminded of another highwayman of that same year. "He had been unwell," so ran his humourous defence, "and the doctor told him to take something, so he took the express box."

The cultus of the stage-coachman always flourishes highest where there are thieves on the road, and where the guard travels armed, and the stage is not only a link between country and city, and the vehicle of news, but has a faint warfaring aroma, like a man who should be brother to a soldier. California boasts her famous stage-drivers, and among the famous Foss is not forgotten. Along the unfenced, abominabie mountain roads, he launches his team with small regard to human life or the doctrine of probabilities. Flinching travellers, who behold themselves coasting eternity at every corner, look with natural admiration at the driver's huge, impassive, fleshy countenance. He has the very face for the driver in Sam Weller's anecdote, who upset the election party at the required point. Wonderful tales are current of his readiness and skill. One in particular, of how one of his horses fell at a ticklish passage of the road, and how Foss let slip the reins, and, driving over the fallen animal, arrived at the next stage with only three. This I relate as I heard it, without guarantee.

I only saw Foss once, though, strange as it may sound, I have twice talked with him. He lives out of Calistoga, at a ranche called Fossville. One evening, after he was long gone home, I dropped into Cheeseborough's, and was asked if I should like to speak with Mr. Foss. Supposing that the interview was impossible, and that I was merely called upon to subscribe the general sentiment, I boldly answered "Yes." Next moment, I had one instrument at my ear, another at my mouth, and found myself, with nothing in the world to say, conversing with a man several miles off among desolate hills. Foss rapidly and somewhat plaintively brought the conversation to an end; and he returned to his night's grog at Fossville, while I strolled forth again on Calistoga high street. But it was an odd thing that here, on what we are accustomed to consider the very skirts of civilisation, I should have used the telephone for the first time in my civilised career. So it goes in these young countries; telephones, and telegraphs, and newspapers, and advertisements running far ahead among the Indians and the grizzly bears.

Alone, on the other side of the railway, stands the Springs Hotel, with its attendant cottages. The floor of the valley is extremely level to the very roots of the hills; only here and there a hillock, crowned with pines, rises like the barrow of some chieftain famed in war; and right against one of these hillocks of the Springs Hotel—is or was; for since I was there the place has been destroyed by fire, and has risen again from its ashes. A lawn runs about the house, and the lawn is in its turn surrounded by a system of little five-roomed cottages, each with a veranda and a weedy palm before the door. Some of the cottages are let to residents, and these are wreathed in flowers. The rest are occupied by ordinary visitors to the hotel; and a very pleasant way this is, by which you have a little country cottage of your own, without domestic burthens, and by the day or week.

The whole neighbourhood of Mount Saint Helena is full of sulphur and of boiling springs. The Geysers are famous; they were the great health resort of the Indians before the coming of the whites. Lake County is dotted with spas; Hot Springs and White Sulphur Springs are the names of two stations on the Napa Valley Railroad; and Calistoga itself seems to repose on a mere film above a boiling, subterranean lake. At one end of the hotel enclosure are the springs from which it takes its name, hot enough to scald a child seriously while I was there. At the other end, the tenant of a cottage sank a well, and there also the water came up boiling. It keeps this end of the valley as warm as a toast. I have gone across to the hotel a little after five in the morning, when a sea-fog from the Pacific was hanging thick and grey, and dark and dirty overhead, and found the thermometer had been up before me, and had already climbed among the nineties; and in the stress of the day it was sometimes too hot to move about.

But in spite of this heat from above and below, doing one on both sides, Calistoga was a pleasant place to dwell in; beautifully green, for it was then that favoured moment in the Californian year, when the rains are over and the dusty summer has not yet set in; often visited by fresh airs, now from the mountain, now across Sonoma from the sea; very quiet, very idle, very silent but for the breezes and the cattle bells afield. And there was something satisfactory in the sight of that great mountain that enclosed us to the north: whether it stood, robed in sunshine, quaking to its topmost pinnacle with the heat and brightness of the day; or whether it set itself to weaving vapours, wisp after wisp growing, trembling, fleeting, and fading in the blue.

The tangled, woody, and almost trackless foothills that enclose the valley, shutting it off from Sonoma on the west, and from Yolo on the east—rough as they were in outline, dug out by winter streams, crowned by cliffy bluffs and nodding pine-trees— were dwarfed into satellites by the bulk and bearing of Mount Saint Helena. She over-towered them by two-thirds of her own stature. She excelled them by the boldness of her profile. Her

great bald summit, clear of trees and pasture, a cairn of quartz
and cinnabar, rejected kinship with the dark and shaggy wilderness of lesser hilltops.

2. *The Petrified Forest*

We drove off from the Springs Hotel about three in the afternoon. The sun warmed me to the heart. A broad, cool wind
streamed pauselessly down the valley, laden with perfume. Up at
the top stood Mount Saint Helena, a bulk of mountain, bare atop,
with tree-fringed spurs, and radiating warmth. Once we saw it
framed in a grove of tall and exquisitely graceful white oaks,
in line and colour a finished composition. We passed a cow
stretched by the roadside, her bell slowly beating time to the
movement of her ruminating jaws, her big red face crawled over
by half-a-dozen flies, a monument of content.

A little farther, and we struck to the left up a mountain road,
and for two hours threaded one valley after another, green,
tangled, full of noble timber, giving us every now and again a
sight of Mount Saint Helena and the blue hilly distance, and
crossed by many streams, through which we splashed to the
carriage-step. To the right or the left, there was scarce any
trace of man but the road we followed; I think we passed but one
ranchero's house in the whole distance, and that was closed and
smokeless. But we had the society of these bright streams—daz-
zlingly clear, as is their wont, splashing from the wheels in
diamonds, and striking a lively coolness through the sunshine.
And what with the innumerable variety of greens, the masses of
foliage tossing in the breeze, the glimpses of distance, the descents
into seemingly impenetrable thickets, the continual dodging of
the road, which made haste to plunge again into the covert, we
had a fine sense of woods, and spring-time, and the open air.

Our driver gave me a lecture by the way on Californian trees—
a thing I was much in need of, having fallen among painters
who know the name of nothing, and Mexicans who know the
name of nothing in English. He taught me the madrona, the manzanita, the buckeye, the maple; he showed me the crested mountain quail; he showed me where some young redwoods were already spiring heavenwards from the ruins of the old; for in this

district all had already perished: redwoods and redskins, the two noblest indigenous living things, alike condemned.

At length, in a lonely dell, we came on a huge wooden gate with a sign upon it like an inn. "The Petrified Forest. Proprietor: C. Evans," ran the legend. Within, on a knoll of sward, was the house of the proprietor, and another smaller house hard by to serve as a museum, where photographs and petrifactions were retailed. It was a pure little isle of touristry among these solitary hills.

The proprietor was a brave old white-faced Swede. He had wandered this way, Heaven knows how, and taken up his acres— I forget how many years ago—all alone, bent double with sciatica, and with six bits in his pocket and an axe upon his shoulder. Long, useless years of seafaring had thus discharged him at the end, penniless and sick. Without doubt he had tried his luck at the diggings, and got no good from that; without doubt he had loved the bottle, and lived the life of Jack ashore. But at the end of these adventures, here he came; and, the place hitting his fancy, down he sat to make a new life of it, far from crimps and the salt sea. And the very sight of his ranche had done him good. It was "the handsomest spot in the Californy mountains." "Isn't it handsome, now?" he said. Every penny he makes goes into that ranche to make it handsomer. Then the climate, with the sea-breeze every afternoon in the hottest summer weather, had gradually cured the sciatica; and his sister and niece were now domesticated with him for company—or, rather, the niece came only once in the two days, teaching music the meanwhile in the valley. And then, for a last piece of luck, "the handsomest spot in the Californy mountains" had produced a petrified forest, which Mr. Evans now shows at the modest figure of half a dollar a head, or two-thirds of his capital when he first came there with an axe and a sciatica.

This tardy favourite of fortune—hobbling a little, I think, as if in memory of the sciatica, but with not a trace that I can remember of the sea—thoroughly ruralised from head to foot, proceeded to escort us up the hill behind his house.

"Who first found the forest?" asked my wife.

"The first? I was that man," said he. "I was cleaning up the pasture for my beasts, when I found *this*"—kicking a great redwood, seven feet in diameter, that lay there on its side, hollow heart, clinging lumps of bark, all changed into grey stone, with veins of quartz between what had been the layers of the wood.

"Were you surprised?"

"Surprised? No! What would I be surprised about? What did I know about petrifactions—following the sea? Petrifaction! There was no such word in my language! I knew about putre-faction, though! I thought it was a stone; so would you, if you was cleaning up pasture."

And now he had a theory of his own, which I did not quite grasp, except that the trees had not "grewed" there. But he mentioned, with evident pride, that he differed from all the scientific people who had visited the spot; and he flung about such words as "tufa" and "silica" with careless freedom.

When I mentioned I was from Scotland, "My old country," he said; "my old country"—with a smiling look and a tone of real affection in his voice. I was mightily surprised, for he was obvi-ously Scandinavian, and begged him to explain. It seemed he had learned his English and done nearly all his sailing in Scotch ships. "Out of Glasgow," said he, "or Greenock; but that's all the same—they all hail from Glasgow." And he was so pleased with me for being a Scotsman, and his adopted compatriot, that he made me a present of a very beautiful piece of petrifaction—I believe the most beautiful and portable he had.

Here was a man, at least, who was a Swede, a Scot, and an American, acknowledging some kind allegiance to three lands. Mr. Wallace's Scoto-Circassian will not fail to come before the reader. I have myself met and spoken with a Fifeshire German, whose combination of abominable accents struck me dumb. But, indeed, I think we all belong to many countries. And perhaps this habit of much travel, and the engendering of scattered friend-ships, may prepare the euthanasia of ancient nations.

And the forest itself? Well, on a tangled, briery hillside—for the pasture would bear a little further cleaning up, to my eyes —there lie scattered thickly various lengths of petrified trunk, such as the one already mentioned. It is very curious, of course, and ancient enough, if that were all. Doubtless, the heart of the geologist beats quicker at the sight; but, for my part, I was mightily unmoved. Sight-seeing is the art of disappointment.

> "There's nothing under heaven so blue
> That's fairly worth the travelling to."

But, fortunately, Heaven rewards us with many agreeable prospects and adventures by the way; and sometimes, when we go out to see a petrified forest, prepares a far more delightful curiosity in the form of Mr. Evans, whom may all prosperity attend throughout a long and green old age.

3. *Napa Wine*

I was interested in Californian wine. Indeed, I am interested in all wines, and have been all my life, from the raisin wine that a school-fellow kept secreted in his play-box up to my last discovery, those notable Valtellines that once shone upon the board of Cæsar.

Some of us, kind old Pagans, watch with dread the shadows falling on the age: how the unconquerable worm invades the sunny terraces of France, and Bordeaux is no more, and the Rhone a mere Arabia Petræa. Château Neuf is dead, and I have never tasted it; Hermitage—a hermitage indeed from all life's sorrows—lies expiring by the river. And in the place of these imperial elixirs, beautiful to every sense, gem-hued, flower-scented, dream-compellers:—behold upon the quays at Cette the chemicals arrayed; behold the analyst at Marseilles, raising hands in obsecration, attesting god Lyœus, and the vats staved in, and the dishonest wines poured forth among the sea. It is not Pan only; Bacchus, too, is dead.

If wine is to withdraw its most poetic countenance, the sun of the white dinner-cloth, a deity to be invoked by two or three, all fervent, hushing their talk, degusting tenderly, and storing reminiscences—for a bottle of good wine, like a good act, shines ever in the retrospect—if wine is to desert us, go thy ways, old Jack! Now we begin to have compunctions, and look back at the brave bottles squandered upon dinner-parties, where the guests drank grossly, discussing politics the while, and even the schoolboy "took his whack," like liquorice water. And at the same time, we look timidly forward, with a spark of hope, to where the new lands, already weary of producing gold, begin to green with vineyards. A nice point in human history falls to be decided by Californian and Australian wines.

Wine in California is still in the experimental stage; and when you taste a vintage, grave economical questions are involved. The beginning of vine-planting is like the beginning of mining for the precious metals: the wine-grower also "prospects." One corner of land after another is tried with one kind of grape after another. This is a failure; that is better; a third best. So, bit by bit, they grope about for their Clos Vougeot and Lafite. Those lodes and pockets of earth, more precious than the precious ores, that yield inimitable fragrance and soft fire; whose virtuous Bonanzas, where the soil has sublimated under sun and stars to something finer, and the wine is bottled poetry: these still lie undiscovered; chaparral conceals, thicket embowers them; the miner chips the rock and wanders farther, and the grizzly muses undisturbed. But there they bide their hour, awaiting their Columbus; and nature nurses and prepares them. The smack of Californian earth shall linger on the palate of your grandson.

Meanwhile the wine is merely a good wine; the best that I have tasted better than a Beaujolais, and not unlike. But the trade is poor; it lives from hand to mouth, putting its all into experiments, and forced to sell its vintages. To find one properly matured, and bearing its own name, is to be fortune's favourite.

Bearing its own name, I say, and dwell upon the innuendo.

"You want to know why California wine is not drunk in the States?" a San Francisco wine merchant said to me, after he had shown me through his premises. "Well, here's the reason."

And opening a large cupboard, fitted with many little drawers, he proceeded to shower me all over with a great variety of gorgeously tinted labels, blue, red, or yellow, stamped with crown or coronet, and hailing from such a profusion of *clos* and *châteaux*, that a single department could scarce have furnished forth the names. But it was strange that all looked unfamiliar.

"Château X——?" said I. "I never heard of that."

"I dare say not," said he. "I had been reading one of X——'s novels."

They were all castles in Spain! But that sure enough is the reason why California wine is not drunk in the States.

Napa Valley has been long a seat of the wine-growing industry. It did not here begin, as it does too often, in the low valley lands along the river, but took at once to the rough foot-hills, where alone it can expect to prosper. A basking inclination, and stones, to be a reservoir of the day's heat, seem necessary to the soil for wine; the grossness of the earth must be evaporated, its marrow daily melted and refined for ages; until at length these clods that break below our footing, and to the eye appear but common earth, are truly and to the perceiving mind, a masterpiece of nature. The dust of Richebourg, which the wind carries away, what an apotheosis of the dust! Not man himself can seem a stranger child of that brown, friable powder, than the blood and sun in that old flask behind the faggots.

A Californian vineyard, one of man's outposts in the wilderness, has features of its own. There is nothing here to remind you of the Rhine or Rhone, of the low *côte d'or,* or the infamous and scabby deserts of Champagne; but all is green, solitary, covert. We visited two of them, Mr. Schram's and Mr. M'Eckron's, sharing the same glen.

Some way down the valley below Calistoga, we turned sharply to the south and plunged into the thick of the wood. A rude trail rapidly mounting; a little stream tinkling by on the one hand, big enough perhaps after the rains, but already yielding up its life; overhead and on all sides a bower of green and tangled thicket, still fragrant and still flower-bespangled by the early season, where thimble-berry played the part of our English hawthorn, and the buckeyes were putting forth their twisted horns of blossom: through all this, we struggled toughly upwards, canted to and fro by the roughness of the trail, and continually switched across the face by sprays of leaf or blossom. The last is no great inconvenience at home; but here in California it is a matter of some moment. For in all woods and by every wayside there prospers an abominable shrub or weed, called poison oak, whose very neighbourhood is venomous to some, and whose actual touch is avoided by the most impervious.

The two houses, with their vineyards, stood each in a green niche of its own in this steep and narrow forest dell. Though they were so near, there was already a good difference in level; and Mr. M'Eckron's head must be a long way under the feet of Mr. Schram. No more had been cleared than was necessary for cultivation; close around each oasis ran the tangled wood; the glen enfolds them; there they lie basking in sun and silence, concealed from all but the clouds and the mountain birds.

Mr. M'Eckron's is a bachelor establishment; a little bit of a wooden house, a small cellar hard by in the hillside, and a patch of vines planted and tended single-handed by himself. He had but recently begun; his vines were young, his business young also; but I thought he had the look of the man who succeeds. He hailed from Greenock: he remembered his father putting him inside Mons Meg, and that touched me home; and we exchanged a word or two of Scotch, which pleased me more than you would fancy.

Mr. Schram's, on the other hand, is the oldest vineyard in the valley, eighteen years old, I think; yet he began a penniless barber, and even after he had broken ground up here with his black malvoisies, continued for long to tramp the valley with his razor. Now, his place is the picture of prosperity: stuffed birds in the veranda, cellars far dug into the hillside, and resting on pillars like a bandit's cave:—all trimness, varnish, flowers, and sunshine, among the tangled wildwood. Stout, smiling Mrs. Schram, who has been to Europe and apparently all about the States for pleasure, entertained Fanny in the veranda, while I was tasting wines in the cellar. To Mr. Schram this was a solemn office; his serious gusto warmed my heart; prosperity had not yet wholly banished a certain neophite and girlish trepidation, and he followed every sip and read my face with proud anxiety. I tasted all. I tasted every variety and shade of Schramberger, red and white Schramberger, Burgundy Schramberger, Schramberger Hock, Schramberger Golden Chasselas, the latter with a notable bouquet, and I fear to think how many more. Much of it goes to London—most, I think; and Mr. Schram has a great notion of the English taste.

In this wild spot, I did not feel the sacredness of ancient cultivation. It was still raw, it was no Marathon, and no Johannisberg; yet the stirring sunlight, and the growing vines, and the vats and bottles in the cavern, made a pleasant music for the mind. Here, also, earth's cream was being skimmed and garnered; and the London customers can taste, such as it is, the tang of the earth in this green valley. So local, so quintessential is a wine, that it seems the very birds in the veranda might communicate a flavour, and that romantic cellar influence the bottle next to be uncorked in Pimlico, and the smile of jolly Mr. Schram might mantle in the glass.

But these are but experiments. All things in this new land are moving farther on: the wine-vats and the miner's blasting tools

but picket for a night, like Bedouin pavilions; and to-morrow, to
fresh woods! This stir of change and these perpetual echoes of
the moving footfall, haunt the land. Men move eternally, still
chasing Fortune; and, fortune found, still wander. As we drove
back to Calistoga, the road lay empty of mere passengers, but its
green side was dotted with the camps of travelling families: one
cumbered with a great waggonful of household stuff, settlers going to occupy a ranche they had taken up in Mendocino, or perhaps Tehama County; another, a party in dust-coats, men and
women, whom we found camped in a grove on the roadside, all
on pleasure bent, with a Chinaman to cook for them, and who
waved their hands to us as we drove by.

4.   *The Scot Abroad*

A few pages back, I wrote that a man belonged in these days, to
a variety of countries; but the old land is still the true love, the
others are but pleasant infidelities. Scotland is indefinable; it
has no unity except upon the map. Two languages, many dialects,
innumerable forms of piety, and countless local patriotisms and
prejudices, part us among ourselves more widely than the extreme east and west of that great continent of America. When I
am at home, I feel a man from Glasgow to be something like a
rival, a man from Barra to be more than half a foreigner. Yet
let us meet in some far country, and, whether we hail from the
braes of Manor or the braes of Mar, some ready-made affection
joins us on the instant. It is not race. Look at us. One is Norse,
one Celtic, and another Saxon. It is not community of tongue. We
have it not among ourselves; and we have it almost to perfection,
with English, or Irish, or American. It is no tie of faith, for we
detest each other's errors. And yet somewhere, deep down in the
heart of each one of us, something yearns for the old land, and the
old kindly people.

Of all mysteries of the human heart, this is perhaps the most
inscrutable. There is no special loveliness in that grey country,
with its rainy, sea-beat archipelago; its fields of dark mountains;
its unsightly places, black with coal; its treeless, sour, unfriendly-
looking corn-lands; its quaint, grey, castled city, where the bells
clash of a Sunday, and the wind squalls, and the salt showers

fly and beat. I do not even know if I desire to live there; but let me hear, in some far land, a kindred voice sing out, "Oh, why left I my hame?" and it seems at once as if no beauty under the kind heavens, and no society of the wise and good, can repay me for my absence from my country. And though I think I would rather die elsewhere, yet in my heart of hearts I long to be buried among good Scots clods. I will say it fairly, it grows on me with every year: there are no stars so lovely as Edinburgh street-lamps. When I forget thee, auld Reekie, may my right hand forget its cunning!

The happiest lot on earth is to be born a Scotchman. You must pay for it in many ways, as for all other advantages on earth. You have to learn the paraphrases and the shorter catechism; you generally take to drink; your youth, as far as I can find out, is a time of louder war against society, of more outcry and tears and turmoil, than if you had been born, for instance, in England. But somehow life is warmer and closer; the hearth burns more redly; the lights of home shine softer on the rainy street; the very names, endeared in verse and music, cling nearer round our hearts. An Englishman may meet an Englishman to-morrow, upon Chimborazo, and neither of them care; but when the Scotch wine-grower told me of Mons Meg, it was like magic.

> "From the dim shieling on the misty island
>   Mountains divide us, and a world of seas;
>   Yet still our hearts are true, our hearts are Highland,
>   And we, in dreams, behold the Hebrides."

And, Highland and Lowland, all our hearts are Scotch.

Only a few days after I had seen M'Eckron, a message reached me in my cottage. It was a Scotchman who had come down a long way from the hills to market. He had heard there was a country-man in Calistoga, and came round to the hotel to see him. We said a few words to each other; we had not much to say—should never have seen each other had we stayed at home, separated alike in space and in society; and then we shook hands, and he went his way again to his ranche among the hills, and that was all.

Another Scotchman there was, a resident, who for the mere love of the common country, douce, serious, religious man, drove me all about the valley, and took as much interest in me as if I had been his son: more, perhaps; for the son has faults too keenly felt, while the abstract countryman is perfect—like a whiff of peats.

And there was yet another. Upon him I came suddenly, as he was calmly entering my cottage, his mind quite evidently bent on plunder: a man of about fifty, filthy, ragged, roguish, with a chimney-pot hat and a tail coat, and a pursing of his mouth that might have been envied by an elder of the kirk. He had just such a face as I have seen a dozen times behind the plate.

"Hullo, sir!" I cried. "Where are you going?"

He turned round without a quiver.

"You are a Scotchman, sir?" he said gravely. "So am I; I come from Aberdeen. This is my card," presenting me with a piece of pasteboard which he had raked out of some gutter in the period of the rains. "I was just examining this palm," he continued, indicating the misbegotten plant before our door, "which is the largest specimen I have yet observed in Califoarnia."

There were four or five larger within sight. But where was the use of argument? He produced a tape-line, made me help him to measure the tree at the level of the ground, and entered the figures in a large and filthy pocket-book, all with the gravity of Solomon. He then thanked me profusely, remarking that such little services were due between countrymen; shook hands with me, "for auld lang syne," as he said; and took himself solemnly away, radiating dirt and humbug as he went.

A month or two after this encounter of mine, there came a Scot to Sacramento—perhaps from Aberdeen. Anyway, there never was any one more Scotch in this wide world. He could sing and dance, and drink, I presume; and he played the pipes with vigour and success. All the Scotch in Sacramento became infatuated with him, and spent their spare time and money, driving him about in an open cab, between drinks, while he blew himself scarlet at the pipes. This is a very sad story. After he had borrowed money from every one, he and his pipes suddenly disappeared from Sacramento, and when I last heard, the police were looking for him.

I cannot say how this story amused me, when I felt myself so thoroughly ripe on both sides to be duped in the same way.

It is at least a curious thing, to conclude, that the races which wander widest, Jews and Scotch, should be the most clannish in the world. But perhaps these two are cause and effect: "For ye were strangers in the land of Egypt."

WITH THE CHILDREN OF ISRAEL

---- ✕ ----

1. To Introduce Mr. Kelmar

ONE THING IN THIS NEW COUNTRY VERY PARTICULARLY STRIKES a stranger, and that is the number of antiquities. Already there have been many cycles of population succeeding each other, and passing away and leaving behind them relics. These, standing on into changed times, strike the imagination as forcibly as any pyramid or feudal tower. The towns, like the vineyards, are experimentally founded: they grow great and prosper by passing occasions; and when the lode comes to an end, and the miners move elsewhere, the town remains behind them, like Palmyra in the desert. I suppose there are, in no country in the world, so many deserted towns as here in California.

The whole neighbourhood of Mount Saint Helena, now so quiet and sylvan, was once alive with mining camps and villages. Here there would be two thousand souls under canvas; there one thousand or fifteen hundred ensconced, as if for ever, in a town of comfortable houses. But the luck had failed, the mines petered out; and the army of miners had departed, and left this quarter of the world to the rattlesnakes and deer and grizzlies, and to the slower but steadier advance of husbandry.

It was with an eye on one of these deserted places, Pine Flat, on the Geysers road, that we had come first to Calistoga. There is something singularly enticing in the idea of going, rent-free, into a ready-made house. And to the British merchant, sitting at home at ease, it may appear that, with such a roof over your head and a spring of clear water hard by, the whole problem of the squatter's existence would be solved. Food, however, has yet to be considered. I will go as far as most people on tinned meats; some of the brightest moments of my life were passed over tinned mulligatawney in the cabin of a sixteen-ton schooner, storm-stayed in Portree Bay; but after suitable experiments, I pronounce authoritatively that man cannot live by tins alone. Fresh meat must be had on an occasion. It is true that the great Foss, driving by along the Geysers road, wooden-faced, but glorified with legend, might have been induced to bring us meat, but the great Foss could hardly bring us milk. To take a cow would have involved taking a field of grass and a milkmaid; after which it would have been hardly worth while to pause, and we might have added to our colony a flock of sheep and an experienced butcher.

It is really very disheartening how we depend on other people in this life. "Mihi est propositum," as you may see by the motto, "id quod regibus"; and behold it cannot be carried out, unless I find a neighbour rolling in cattle.

Now, my principal adviser in this matter was one whom I will call Kelmar. That was not what he called himself, but as soon as I set eyes on him, I knew it was or ought to be his name; I am sure it will be his name among the angels. Kelmar was the store-keeper, a Russian Jew, good-natured, in a very thriving way of business, and, on equal terms, one of the most serviceable of men. He also had something of the expression of a Scotch country elder, who, by some peculiarity, should chance to be a Hebrew. He had a projecting under lip, with which he continually smiled, or rather smirked. Mrs. Kelmar was a singularly kind woman; and the oldest son had quite a dark and romantic bearing, and might be heard on summer evenings playing sentimental airs on the violin.

I had no idea, at the time I made his acquaintance, what an important person Kelmar was. But the Jew store-keepers of California, profiting at once by the needs and habits of the people, have made themselves in too many cases the tyrants of the rural population. Credit is offered, is pressed on the new customer, and when once he is beyond his depth, the tune changes, and he is from thenceforth a white slave. I believe, even from the little I saw, that Kelmar, if he choose to put on the screw, could send half the settlers packing in a radius of seven or eight miles round Calistoga. These are continually paying him, but are never suffered to get out of debt. He palms dull goods upon them, for they dare not refuse to buy; he goes and dines with them when he is on an outing, and no man is loudlier welcomed; he is their family friend, the director of their business, and, to a degree elsewhere unknown in modern days, their king.

For some reason, Kelmar always shook his head at the mention of Pine Flat, and for some days I thought he disapproved of the whole scheme and was proportionately sad. One fine morning, however, he met me, wreathed in smiles. He had found the very place for me—Silverado, another old mining town, right up the mountain. Rufe Hanson, the hunter, could take care of us—fine people, the Hansoms; we should be close to the Toll House, where the Lakeport stage called daily; it was the best place for my health, besides. Rufe had been consumptive, and was now quite a strong man, ain't it? In short, the place and all its accompaniments seemed made for us on purpose.

He took me to his back door, whence, as from every point of Calistoga, Mount Saint Helena could be seen towering in the air. There, in the nick, just where the eastern foot-hills joined the mountain, and she herself began to rise above the zone of forest —there was Silverado. The name had already pleased me; the high station pleased me still more. I began to inquire with some eagerness. It was but a little while ago that Silverado was a great place. The mine—a silver mine, of course—had promised great things. There was quite a lively population, with several hotels and boarding-houses; and Kelmar himself had opened a branch store, and done extremely well—"Ain't it?" he said, appealing to his wife. And she said, "Yes; extremely well." Now there was no one living in the town but Rufe the hunter; and once more I heard Rufe's praises by the yard, and this time sung in chorus.

I could not help perceiving at the time that there was something underneath; that no unmixed desire to have us comfortably settled had inspired the Kelmars with this flow of words. But I was impatient to be gone, to be about my kingly project; and when we were offered seats in Kelmar's waggon, I accepted on the spot. The plan of their next Sunday's outing took them, by good fortune, over the border into Lake County. They would carry us so far, drop us at the Toll House, present us to the Hansons, and call for us again on Monday morning early.

2.   *First Impressions of Silverado*

We were to leave by six precisely; that was solemnly pledged on
both sides; and a messenger came to us the last thing at night, to
remind us of the hour. But it was eight before we got clear of
Calistoga: Kelmar, Mrs. Kelmar, a friend of theirs whom we
named Abramina, her little daughter, my wife, myself, and,
stowed away behind us, a cluster of ship's coffee-kettles. These last
were highly ornamental in the sheen of their bright tin, but I
could invent no reason for their presence. Our carriageful reckoned up, as near as we could get at it, some three hundred years
to the six of us. Four of the six, besides, were Hebrews. But I
never, in all my life, was conscious of so strong an atmosphere of
holiday. No word was spoken but of pleasure; and even when we
drove in silence, nods and smiles went round the party like refreshments.

The sun shone out of a cloudless sky. Close at the zenith rode
the belated moon, still clearly visible, and, along one margin,
even bright. The wind blew a gale from the north; the trees
roared; the corn and the deep grass in the valley fled in whitening surges; the dust towered into the air along the road and dispersed like the smoke of battle. It was clear in our teeth from
the first, and for all the windings of the road it managed to
keep clear in our teeth until the end.

For some two miles we rattled through the valley, skirting the
eastern foot-hills; then we struck off to the right, through haugh-
land, and presently, crossing a dry watercourse, entered the Toll
road, or, to be more local, entered on "the grade." The road
mounts the near shoulder of Mount Saint Helena, bound northward into Lake County. In one place it skirts along the edge of a
narrow and deep cañon, filled with trees, and I was glad, indeed,
not to be driven at this point by the dashing Foss. Kelmar, with
his unvarying smile, jogging to the motion of the trap, drove for
all the world like a good, plain, country clergyman at home; and
I profess I blessed him unawares for his timidity.

Vineyards and deep meadows, islanded and framed with thicket,
gave place more and more as we ascended to woods of oak and
madrona, dotted with enormous pines. It was these pines, as they
shot above the lower wood, that produced that pencilling of

single trees I had so often remarked from the valley. Thence, looking up and from however far, each fir stands separate against the sky no bigger than an eyelash; and all together lend a quaint, fringed aspect to the hills. The oak is no baby; even the madrona, upon these spurs of Mount Saint Helena, comes to a fine bulk and ranks with forest trees; but the pines look down upon the rest for underwood. As Mount Saint Helena among her foot-hills, so these dark giants out-top their fellow-vegetables. Alas! if they had left the redwoods, the pines, in turn, would have been dwarfed. But the redwoods, fallen from their high estate, are serving as family bedsteads, or yet more humbly as field fences, along all Napa Valley.

A rough smack of resin was in the air, and a crystal mountain purity. It came pouring over these green slopes by the oceanful. The woods sang aloud, and gave largely of their healthful breath. Gladness seemed to inhabit these upper zones, and we had left indifference behind us in the valley. "I to the hills will lift mine eyes!" There are days in a life when thus to climb out of the lowlands seems like scaling heaven.

As we continued to ascend, the wind fell upon us with increasing strength. It was a wonder how the two stout horses managed to pull us up that steep incline and still face the athletic opposition of the wind, or how their great eyes were able to endure the dust. Ten minutes after we went by, a tree fell, blocking the road; and even before us leaves were thickly strewn, and boughs had fallen, large enough to make the passage difficult. But now we were hard by the summit. The road crosses the ridge, just in the nick that Kelmar showed me from below, and then, without pause, plunges down a deep, thickly wooded glen on the farther side. At the highest point a trail strikes up the main hill to the leftward; and that leads to Silverado. A hundred yards beyond, and in a kind of elbow of the glen, stands the Toll House Hotel. We came up the one side, were caught upon the summit by the whole weight of the wind as it poured over into Napa Valley, and a minute after had drawn up in shelter, but all buffeted and breathless, at the Toll House door.

A water-tank, and stables, and a grey house of two stories, with gable ends and a veranda, are jammed hard against the hillside, just where a stream has cut for itself a narrow cañon, filled with pines. The pines go right up overhead; a little more and the stream might have played, like a fire-hose, on the Toll House roof. In front the ground drops as sharply as it rises behind. There is just room for the road and a sort of promontory of croquet ground, and then you can lean over the edge and look deep below you through the wood. I said croquet *ground,* not *green;* for the surface was of brown, beaten earth. The toll-bar itself was the only other note of originality: a long beam, turning on a post, and kept slightly horizontal by a counterweight of stones. Regularly about sundown this rude barrier was swung, like a derrick, across the road and made fast, I think, to a tree upon the farther side.

On our arrival there followed a gay scene in the bar. I was presented to Mr. Corwin, the landlord; to Mr. Jennings, the engineer, who lives there for his health; to Mr. Hoddy, a most pleasant little gentleman, once a member of the Ohio legislature, again the editor of a local paper, and now, with undiminished dignity, keeping the Toll House bar. I had a number of drinks and cigars bestowed on me, and enjoyed a famous opportunity of seeing Kelmar in his glory, friendly, radiant, smiling, steadily edging one of the ship's kettles on the reluctant Corwin. Corwin, plainly aghast, resisted gallantly, and for that bout victory crowned his arms.

At last we set forth for Silverado on foot. Kelmar and his jolly Jew girls were full of the sentiment of Sunday outings, breathed geniality and vagueness, and suffered a little vile boy from the hotel to lead them here and there about the woods. For three people all so old, so bulky in body, and belonging to a race so venerable, they could not but surprise us by their extreme and almost imbecile youthfulness of spirit. They were only going to stay ten minutes at the Toll House; had they not twenty long miles of road before them on the other side? Stay to dinner? Not they! Put up the horses? Never. Let us attach them to the veranda by a wisp of straw rope, such as would not have held a person's hat on that blustering day. And with all these protestations of hurry, they proved irresponsible like children. Kelmar himself, shrewd old Russian Jew, with a smirk that seemed just to have concluded a bargain to its satisfaction, intrusted himself and us devoutly to that boy. Yet the boy was patently fallacious; and for that matter a most unsympathetic urchin, raised apparently on gingerbread. He was bent on his own pleasure, nothing else; and Kelmar followed him to his ruin, with the same shrewd smirk. If the boy said there was "a hole there in the hill" —a hole, pure and simple, neither more nor less—Kelmar and his Jew girls would follow him a hundred yards to look complacently down that hole. For two hours we looked for houses; and for two hours they followed us, smelling trees, picking flowers, foisting false botany on the unwary. Had we taken five, with that vile lad to head them off on idle divagations, for five they would have smiled and stumbled through the woods.

However, we came forth at length, and as by accident, upon a lawn, sparse planted like an orchard, but with forest instead of fruit trees. That was the site of Silverado mining town. A piece of ground was levelled up, where Kelmar's store had been; and facing that we saw Rufe Hanson's house, still bearing on its front the legend *Silverado Hotel*. Not another sign of habitation. Silverado town had all been carted from the scene; one of the houses was now the schoolhouse far down the road; one was gone here, one there, but all were gone away. It was now a sylvan solitude, and the silence was unbroken but by the great, vague voice of the wind. Some days before our visit, a grizzly bear had been sporting round the Hansons' chicken-house.

Mrs. Hanson was at home alone, we found. Rufe had been out after a "bar," had risen late, and was now gone, it did not clearly appear whither. Perhaps he had had wind of Kelmar's coming, and was now ensconced among the underwood, or watching us from the shoulder of the mountain. We, hearing there were no houses to be had, were for immediately giving up all hopes of Silverado. But this, somehow, was not to Kelmar's fancy. He first proposed that we should "camp someveres around, ain't it?" waving his hand cheerily as though to weave a spell; and when that was firmly rejected, he decided that we must take up house with the Hansons. Mrs. Hanson had been, from the first, flustered, subdued, and a little pale; but from this proposition she recoiled with haggard indignation. So did we, who would have preferred, in a manner of speaking, death. But Kelmar was not to be put by. He edged Mrs. Hanson into a corner, where for a long time he threatened her with his forefinger, like a character in Dickens; and the poor woman, driven to her entrenchments, at last remembered with a shriek that there were still some houses at the tunnel.

Thither we went; the Jews, who should already have been miles into Lake County, still cheerily accompanying us. For about a furlong we followed a good road along the hillside through the forest, until suddenly that road widened out and came abruptly to an end. A cañon, woody below, red, rocky, and naked overhead, was here walled across by a dump of rolling stones, dangerously steep, and from twenty to thirty feet in height. A rusty iron chute on wooden legs came flying, like a monstrous gargoyle, across the parapet. It was down this that they poured the precious ore; and below here the carts stood to wait their lading, and carry it millward down the mountain.

The whole cañon was so entirely blocked, as if by some rude guerrilla fortification, that we could only mount by lengths of wooden ladder, fixed in the hillside. These led us round the farther corner of the dump; and when they were at an end, we still persevered over loose rubble and wading deep in poison oak, till we struck a triangular platform, filling up the whole glen, and shut in on either hand by bold projections of the mountain. Only in front the place was open like the proscenium of a theatre, and we looked forth into a great realm of air, and down upon treetops and hilltops, and far and near on wild and varied country. The place still stood as on the day it was deserted: a line of iron rails with a bifurcation; a truck in working order; a world of lumber, old wood, old iron; a blacksmith's forge on one side, half buried in the leaves of dwarf madronas; and on the other, an old brown wooden house.

Fanny and I dashed at the house. It consisted of three rooms, and was so plastered against the hill, that one room was right atop of another, that the upper floor was more than twice as large as the lower, and that all three apartments must be entered from a different side and level. Not a window-sash remained. The door of the lower room was smashed, and one panel hung in splinters. We entered that, and found a fair amount of rubbish: sand and gravel that had been sifted in there by the mountain winds; straw, sticks, and stones; a table, a barrel; a plate-rack on the wall; two home-made boot-jacks, signs of miners and their boots; and a pair of papers pinned on the boarding, headed respectively "Funnel No. 1," and "Funnel No. 2," but with the tails torn away. The window, sashless of course, was choked with the green and sweetly smelling foliage of a bay; and through a chink in the floor, a spray of poison oak had shot up and was handsomely prospering in the interior. It was my first care to cut away that poison oak, Fanny standing by at a respectful distance. That was our first improvement by which we took possession.

The room immediately above could only be entered by a plank propped against the threshold, along which the intruder must foot it gingerly, clutching for support to sprays of poison oak, the proper product of the country. Herein was, on either hand, a triple tier of beds, where miners had once lain; and the other gable was pierced by a sashless window and a doorless doorway opening on the air of heaven, five feet above the ground. As for the third room, which entered squarely from the ground level, but higher up the hill and further up the cañon, it contained only rubbish and the uprights for another triple tier of beds.

The whole building was overhung by a bold, lion-like, red rock. Poison oak, sweet bay trees, calycanthus, brush, and chaparral, grew freely but sparsely all about it. In front, in the strong sunshine, the platform lay overstrewn with busy litter, as though the labours of the mine might begin again to-morrow in the morning.

Following back into the cañon, among the mass of rotting plant and through the flowering bushes, we came to a great crazy staging, with a wry windlass on the top; and clambering up, we could look into an open shaft, leading edgeways down into the bowels of the mountain, trickling with water, and lit by some stray sungleams, whence I know not. In that quiet place the still, far-away tinkle of the water-drops was loudly audible. Close by, another shaft led edgeways up into the superincumbent shoulder of the hill. It lay partly open; and sixty or a hundred feet above our head, we could see the strata propped apart by solid wooden wedges, and a pine, half undermined, precariously nodding on the verge. Here also a rugged, horizontal tunnel ran straight into the unsunned bowels of the rock. This secure angle in the mountain's flank was, even on this wild day, as still as my lady's chamber. But in the tunnel a cold, wet draught tempestuously blew. Nor have I ever known that place otherwise than cold and windy.

Such was our first prospect of Juan Silverado. I own I had looked for something different: a clique of neighbourly houses on a village green, we shall say, all empty to be sure, but swept and varnished; a trout stream brawling by; great elms or chestnuts, humming with bees and nested in by song-birds; and the moun-

tains standing round about, as at Jerusalem. Here, mountain and
house and the old tools of industry were all alike rusty and down-
falling. The hill was here wedged up, and there poured forth its
bowels in a spout of broken mineral; man with his picks and
powder, and nature with her own great blasting tools of sun and
rain, labouring together at the ruin of that proud mountain. The
view up the cañon was a glimpse of devastation; dry red minerals
sliding together, here and there a crag, here and there dwarf
thicket clinging in the general glissade, and over all a broken outline trenching on the blue of heaven. Downwards indeed, from
our rock eyrie, we beheld the greener side of nature; and the bearing of the pines and the sweet smell of bays and nutmegs commended themselves gratefully to our senses. One way and another,
now the die was cast. Silverado be it!

After we had got back to the Toll House, the Jews were not
long of striking forward. But I observed that one of the Hanson
lads came down, before their departure, and returned with a
ship's kettle. Happy Hansons! Nor was it until after Kelmar was
gone, if I remember rightly, that Rufe put in an appearance to
arrange the details of our installation.

The latter part of the day, Fanny and I sat in the veranda of
the Toll House, utterly stunned by the uproar of the wind among
the trees on the other side of the valley. Sometimes, we would
have it it was like a sea, but it was not various enough for that;
and again, we thought it like the roar of a cataract, but it was
too changeful for the cataract; and then we would decide, speaking in sleepy voices, that it could be compared with nothing but
itself. My mind was entirely preoccupied by the noise. I hearkened
to it by the hour, gapingly hearkened, and let my cigarette go
out. Sometimes the wind would make a sally nearer hand, and
send a shrill, whistling crash among the foliage on our side of the
glen; and sometimes a backdraught would strike into the elbow
where we sat, and cast the gravel and torn leaves into our faces.
But for the most part, this great, streaming gale passed unweariedly by us into Napa Valley, not two hundred yards away
visible by the tossing boughs, stunningly audible, and yet not
moving a hair upon our heads. So it blew all night long while I
was writing up my journal, and after we were in bed, under a
cloudless, starset heaven; and so it was blowing still next morning
when we rose.

It was a laughable thought to us, what had become of our cheerful, wandering Hebrews. We could not suppose they had reached a destination. The meanest boy could lead them miles out of their way to see a gopher-hole. Boys we felt to be their special danger; none others were of that exact pitch of cheerful irrelevancy to exercise a kindred sway upon their minds: but before the attractions of a boy their most settled resolutions would be wax. We thought we could follow in fancy these three aged Hebrew truants wandering in and out on hilltop and in thicket, a demon boy trotting far ahead, their will-o'-the-wisp conductor; and at last about midnight, the wind still roaring in the darkness, we had a vision of all three on their knees upon a mountain-top around a glow-worm.

3. *The Return*

Next morning we were up by half-past five, according to agreement, and it was ten by the clock before our Jew boys returned to pick us up: Kelmar, Mrs. Kelmar, and Abramina, all smiling from ear to ear, and full of tales of the hospitality they had found on the other side. It had not gone unrewarded; for I observed with interest that the ship's kettles, all but one, had been "placed." Three Lake County families, at least, endowed for life with a ship's kettle. Come, this was no misspent Sunday. The absence of the kettles told its own story: our Jews said nothing about them; but, on the other hand, they said many kind and comely things about the people they had met. The two women, in particular, had been charmed out of themselves by the sight of a young girl surrounded by her admirers; all evening, it appeared, they had been triumphing together in the girl's innocent successes, and to this natural and unselfish joy they gave expression in language that was beautiful by its simplicity and truth.

Take them for all in all, few people have done my heart more good; they seemed so thoroughly entitled to happiness, and to enjoy it in so large a measure and so free from after-thought; almost they persuaded me to be a Jew. There was, indeed, a chink of money in their talk. They particularly commended people who were well to do. "*He* don't care—ain't it?" was their highest word of commendation to an individual fate; and here I seem to grasp the root of their philosophy—it was to be free from care, to be free to make these Sunday wanderings, that they so eagerly pursued after wealth; and all this carefulness was to be careless. The fine good-humour of all three seemed to declare they had attained their end. Yet there was the other side to it; and the recipients of kettles perhaps cared greatly.

No sooner had they returned, than the scene of yesterday began again. The horses were not even tied with a straw rope this time— it was not worth while; and Kelmar disappeared into the bar, leaving them under a tree on the other side of the road. I had to devote myself. I stood under the shadow of that tree for, I suppose, hard upon an hour, and had not the heart to be angry. Once some one remembered me, and brought me out a half a tumblerful of the playful, innocuous American cocktail. I drank it, and lo! veins of living fire ran down my legs; and then a focus of conflagration remained seated in my stomach, not unpleasantly, for quarter of an hour. I love these sweet, fiery pangs, but I will not court them. The bulk of the time I spent in repeating as much French poetry as I could remember to the horses, who seemed to enjoy it hugely. And now it went—

> "O ma vieille Font-georges
> Où volent les rouges-gorges":

and again, to a more trampling measure—

> "Et tout tremble, Irun, Coïmbre,
> Santander, Almodovar,
> Sitôt qu'on entend le timbre
> Des cymbales de Bivar."

The redbreasts and the brooks of Europe, in that dry and songless land; brave old names and wars, strong cities, cymbals, and bright armour, in that nook of the mountain, sacred only to the Indian and the bear! This is still the strangest thing in all man's travelling, that he should carry about with him incongruous memories. There is no foreign land; it is the traveller only that is foreign, and now and again, by a flash of recollection, lights up the contrasts of the earth.

But while I was thus wandering in my fancy, great feats had been transacted in the bar. Corwin the bold had fallen, Kelmar was again crowned with laurels, and the last of the ship's kettles had changed hands. If I had ever doubted the purity of Kelmar's motives, if I had ever suspected him of a single eye to business in his eternal dallyings, now at least, when the last kettle was disposed of, my suspicions must have been allayed. I dare not guess how much more time was wasted; nor how often we drove off, merely to drive back again and renew interrupted conversations about nothing, before the Toll House was fairly left behind. Alas! and not a mile down the grade there stands a ranche in a sunny vineyard, and here we must all dismount again and enter.

Only the old lady was at home, Mrs. Guele, a brown old Swiss dame, the picture of honesty; and with her we drank a bottle of wine and had an age-long conversation, which would have been highly delightful if Fanny and I had not been faint with hunger. The ladies each narrated the story of her marriage, our two Hebrews with the prettiest combination of sentiment and financial bathos. Abramina, specially, endeared herself with every word. She was as simple, natural, and engaging as a kid that should have been brought up to the business of a money-changer. One touch was so resplendently Hebraic that I cannot pass it over. When her "old man" wrote home for her from America, her old man's family would not entrust her with the money for the passage, till she had bound herself by an oath—on her knees, I think she said—not to employ it otherwise. This had tickled Abramina hugely, but I think it tickled me fully more.

Mrs. Guele told of her homesickness up here in the long winters; of her honest, country-woman troubles and alarms upon the journey; how in the bank at Frankfort she had feared lest the banker, after having taken her cheque, should deny all knowledge of it—a fear I have myself every time I go to a bank; and how crossing the Luneburger Heath, an old lady, witnessing her trouble and finding whither she was bound, had given her "the blessing of a person eighty years old, which would be sure to bring her safely to the States. And the first thing I did," added Mrs. Guele, "was to fall down-stairs."

At length we got out of the house, and some of us into the trap, when—judgment of Heaven!—here came Mr. Guele from his vineyard. So another quarter of an hour went by; till at length, at our earnest pleading, we set forth again in earnest, Fanny and I white-faced and silent, but the Jews still smiling. The heart fails me. There was yet another stoppage! And we drove at last into

Calistoga past two in the afternoon, Fanny and I having breakfasted at six in the morning, eight mortal hours before. We were a pallid couple; but still the Jews were smiling.

So ended our excursion with the village usurers; and, now that it was done, we had no more idea of the nature of the business, nor of the part we had been playing in it, than the child unborn. That all the people we had met were the slaves of Kelmar, though in various degrees of servitude; that we ourselves had been sent up the mountain in the interests of none but Kelmar; that the money we laid out, dollar by dollar, cent by cent, and through the hands of various intermediaries, should all hop ultimately into Kelmar's till—these were facts that we only grew to recognise in the course of time and by the accumulation of evidence. At length all doubt was quieted, when one of the kettle-holders confessed. Stopping his trap in the moonlight, a little way out of Calistoga, he told me, in so many words, that he dare not show face there with an empty pocket. "You see, I don't mind if it was only five dollars, Mr. Stevens," he said, "but I must give Mr. Kelmar *something*."

Even now, when the whole tyranny is plain to me, I cannot find it in my heart to be as angry as perhaps I should be with the Hebrew tyrant. The whole game of business is beggar my neighbour; and though perhaps that game looks uglier when played at such close quarters and on so small a scale, it is none the more intrinsically inhumane for that. The village usurer is not so sad a feature of humanity and human progress as the millionaire manufacturer, fattening on the toil and loss of thousands, and yet declaiming from the platform against the greed and dishonesty of landlords. If it were fair for Cobden to buy up land from owners whom he thought unconscious of its proper value, it was fair enough for my Russian Jew to give credit to his farmers. Kelmar, if he was unconscious of the beam in his own eye, was at least silent in the matter of his brother's mote.

The Act of Squatting

There were four of us squatters—myself and my wife, the King and Queen of Silverado; Sam, the Crown Prince; and Chuchu, the Grand Duke. Chuchu, a setter crossed with spaniel, was the most unsuited for a rough life. He had been nurtured tenderly in the society of ladies; his heart was large and soft; he regarded the sofa-cushion as a bed-rock necessary of existence. Though about the size of a sheep, he loved to sit in ladies' laps; he never said a bad word in all his blameless days; and if he had seen a flute, I am sure he could have played upon it by nature. It may seem hard to say it of a dog, but Chuchu was a tame cat.

The king and queen, the grand duke, and a basket of cold provender for immediate use, set forth from Calistoga in a double buggy; the crown prince, on horseback, led the way like an outrider. Bags and boxes and a second-hand stove were to follow close upon our heels by Hanson's team.

It was a beautiful still day; the sky was one field of azure. Not a leaf moved, not a speck appeared in heaven. Only from the summit of the mountain one little snowy wisp of cloud after another kept detaching itself, like smoke from a volcano, and blowing southward in some high stream of air: Mount Saint Helena still at her interminable task, making the weather, like a Lapland witch.

By noon we had come in sight of the mill: a great brown building, half-way up the hill, big as a factory, two stories high, and with tanks and ladders along the roof; which, as a pendicle of Silverado mine, we held to be an outlying province of our own. Thither, then, we went, crossing the valley by a grassy trail; and there lunched out of the basket, sitting in a kind of portico, and wondering, while we ate, at this great bulk of useless building. Through a chink we could look far down into the interior, and see sunbeams floating in the dust and striking on tier after tier of silent, rusty machinery. It cost six thousand dollars, twelve hundred English sovereigns; and now, here it stands deserted, like the temple of a forgotten religion, the busy millers toiling somewhere else. All the time we were there, mill and mill town showed no sign of life; that part of the mountainside, which is very open and green, was tenanted by no living creature but ourselves and the insects; and nothing stirred but the cloud manufactory upon the mountain summit. It was odd to compare this with the former days, when the engine was in full blast, the mill palpitating to its strokes, and the carts came rattling down from Silverado, charged with ore.

By two we had been landed at the mine, the buggy was gone

again, and we were left to our own reflections and the basket of cold provender, until Hanson should arrive. Hot as it was by the sun, there was something chill in such a homecoming, in that world of wreck and rust, splinter and rolling gravel, where for so many years no fire had smoked.

Silverado platform filled the whole width of the cañon. Above, as I have said, this was a wild, red, stony gully in the mountains; but below it was a wooded dingle. And through this, I was told, there had gone a path between the mine and the Toll House— our natural north-west passage to civilisation. I found and fol lowed it, clearing my way as I went through fallen branches and dead trees. It went straight down that steep cañon, till it brought you out abruptly over the roofs of the hotel. There was nowhere any break in the descent. It almost seemed as if, were you to drop a stone down the old iron chute at our platform, it would never rest until it hopped upon the Toll House shingles. Signs were not wanting of the ancient greatness of Silverado. The footpath was well marked, and had been well trodden in the old days by thirsty miners. And far down, buried in foliage, deep out of sight of Silverado, I came on a last outpost of the mine—a mound of gravel, some wreck of wooden aqueduct, and the mouth of a tunnel, like a treasure grotto in a fairy story. A stream of water, fed by the invisible leakage from our shaft, and dyed red with cinnabar or iron, ran trippingly forth out of the bowels of the cave; and, looking far under the arch, I could see something like an iron lantern fastened on the rocky wall. It was a promising spot for the imagination. No boy could have left it unexplored.

The stream thenceforward stole along the bottom of the dingle, and made, for that dry land, a pleasant warbling in the leaves. Once, I suppose, it ran splashing down the whole length of the cañon, but now its head waters had been tapped by the shaft at Silverado, and for a great part of its course it wandered sunless among the joints of the mountain. No wonder that it should better its pace when it sees, far before it, daylight whitening in the arch, or that it should come trotting forth into the sunlight with a song.

The two stages had gone by when I got down, and the Toll House stood, dozing in sun and dust and silence, like a place enchanted. My mission was after hay for bedding, and that I was readily promised. But when I mentioned that we were waiting for

Rufe, the people shook their heads. Rufe was not a regular man anyway, it seemed; and if he got playing poker——Well, poker was too many for Rufe. I had not yet heard them bracketed together; but it seemed a natural conjunction, and commended itself swiftly to my fears; and as soon as I returned to Silverado and had told my story, we practically gave Hanson up, and set ourselves to do what we could find do-able in our desert-island state.

The lower room had been the assayer's office. The floor was thick with *débris*—part human, from the former occupants; part natural, sifted in by mountain winds. In a sea of red dust there swam or floated sticks, boards, hay, straw, stones, and paper; ancient newspapers, above all—for the newspaper, especially when torn, soon becomes an antiquity—and bills of the Silverado boarding house, some dated Silverado, some Calistoga Mine. Here is one, verbatim; and if any one can calculate the scale of charges, he has my envious admiration.

Calistoga Mine, May 3rd, 1875.

John Stanley
      To S. Chapman, Cr.

To board from April 1st, to April 30	$25 75
" " " May 1st, to 3rd	2 00
	27 75

Where is John Stanley mining now? Where is S. Chapman, within whose hospitable walls we were to lodge? The date was but five years old, but in that time the world had changed for Silverado; like Palmyra in the desert, it had outlived its people and its purpose; we camped, like Layard, amid ruins, and these names spoke to us of prehistoric time. A boot-jack, a pair of boots, a dog-hutch, and these bills of Mr. Chapman's were the only speaking relics that we disinterred from all that vast Silverado rubbish-heap; but what would I not have given to unearth a letter, a pocket-book, a diary, only a ledger, or a roll of names, to take me back, in a more personal manner, to the past? It pleases me, besides, to fancy that Stanley or Chapman, or one of their companions, may light upon this chronicle, and be struck by the name, and read some news of their anterior home, coming, as it were, out of a subsequent epoch of history in that quarter of the world.

As we were tumbling the mingled rubbish on the floor, kicking it with our feet, and groping for these written evidences of the past, Sam, with a somewhat whitened face, produced a paper bag. "What's this?" said he. It contained a granulated powder, something the colour of Gregory's Mixture, but rosier; and as there were several of the bags, and each more or less broken, the powder was spread widely on the floor. Had any of us ever seen giant powder? No, nobody had; and instantly there grew up in my mind a shadowy belief, verging with every moment nearer to certitude, that I had somewhere heard somebody describe it as just such a powder as the one around us. I have learnt since that it is a substance not unlike tallow, and is made up in rolls for all the world like tallow candles.

Fanny, to add to our happiness, told us a story of a gentleman who had camped one night, like ourselves, by a deserted mine. He was a handy, thrifty fellow, and looked right and left for plunder, but all he could lay his hands on was a can of oil. After dark he had to see to the horses with a lantern; and not to miss an opportunity, filled up his lamp from the oil can. Thus equipped, he set forth into the forest. A little while after, his friends heard a loud explosion; the mountain echoes bellowed, and then all was still. On examination, the can proved to contain oil, with the trifling addition of nitro-glycerine; but no research disclosed a trace of either man or lantern.

It was a pretty sight, after this anecdote, to see us sweeping out the giant powder. It seemed never to be far enough away. And, after all, it was only some rock pounded for assay.

So much for the lower room. We scraped some of the rougher dirt off the floor, and left it. That was our sitting-room and kitchen, though there was nothing to sit upon but the table, and no provision for a fire except a hole in the roof of the room above, which had once contained the chimney of a stove.

To that upper room we now proceeded. There were the eighteen bunks in a double tier, nine on either hand, where from eighteen to thirty-six miners had once snored together all night long, John Stanley, perhaps, snoring loudest. There was the roof, with a hole in it through which the sun now shot an arrow. There was the floor, in much the same state as the one below, though, perhaps, there was more hay, and certainly there was the added ingredient of broken glass, the man who stole the window-frames having apparently made a miscarriage with this one. Without a broom, without hay or bedding, we could but look about us with a beginning of despair. The one bright arrow of day, in that gaunt and shattered barrack, made the rest look dirtier and darker, and the sight drove us at last into the open.

Here, also, the handiwork of man lay ruined: but the plants were all alive and thriving; the view below was fresh with the colours of nature; and we had exchanged a dim, human garret for a corner, even although it were untidy, of the blue hall of heaven. Not a bird, not a beast, not a reptile. There was no noise in that part of the world, save when we passed beside the staging, and heard the water musically falling in the shaft.

We wandered to and fro. We searched among that drift of lumber—wood and iron, nails and rails, and sleepers and the wheels of trucks. We gazed up the cleft into the bosom of the mountain. We sat by the margin of the dump and saw, far below us, the green treetops standing still in the clear air. Beautiful perfumes, breaths of bay, resin, and nutmeg, came to us more often and grew sweeter and sharper as the afternoon declined. But still there was no word of Hanson.

I set to with pick and shovel, and deepened the pool behind the shaft, till we were sure of sufficient water for the morning; and by the time I had finished, the sun had begun to go down behind the mountain shoulder, the platform was plunged in quiet shadow, and a chill descended from the sky. Night began early in our cleft. Before us, over the margin of the dump, we could see the sun still striking aslant into the wooded nick below, and on the battlemented, pine-bescattered ridges on the farther side.

There was no stove, of course, and no hearth in our lodging, so we betook ourselves to the blacksmith's forge across the platform. If the platform be taken as a stage, and the out-curving margin of the dump to represent the line of the footlights, then our house would be the first wing on the actor's left, and this blacksmith's forge, although no match for it in size, the foremost on the right. It was a low, brown cottage, planted close against the hill, and overhung by the foliage and peeling boughs of a madrona thicket. Within it was full of dead leaves and mountain dust, and rubbish from the mine. But we soon had a good fire brightly blazing, and sat close about it on impromptu seats. Chuchu, the slave of sofa-cushions, whimpered for a softer bed; but the rest of us were greatly revived and comforted by that good creature—fire, which gives us warmth and light and companionable sounds, and colours up the emptiest building with better than frescoes. For awhile it was even pleasant in the forge, with the blaze in the midst, and a look over our shoulders on the woods and mountains where the day was dying like a dolphin.

It was between seven and eight before Hanson arrived, with a waggonful of our effects and two of his wife's relatives to lend him a hand. The elder showed surprising strength. He would pick up a huge packing-case, full of books of all things, swing it on his shoulder, and away up the two crazy ladders and the breakneck spout of rolling mineral, familiarly termed a path, that led from the car-track to our house. Even for a man unburthened, the ascent was toilsome and precarious; but Irvine scaled it with a light foot, carrying box after box, as the hero whisks the stage child up the practicable footway beside the waterfall of the fifth act. With so strong a helper, the business was speedily transacted. Soon the assayer's office was thronged with our belongings, piled higgledy-piggledy, and upside down, about the floor. There were our boxes, indeed, but my wife had left her keys in Calistoga. There was the stove, but, alas! our carriers had forgot the chimney, and lost one of the plates along the road. The Silverado problem was scarce solved.

Rufe himself was grave and good-natured over his share of blame; he even, if I remember right, expressed regret. But his crew, to my astonishment and anger, grinned from ear to ear, and laughed aloud at our distress. They thought it "real funny" about the stovepipe they had forgotten; "real funny" that they should have lost a plate. As for hay, the whole party refused to bring us any till they should have supped. See how late they were! Never had there been such a job as coming up that grade! Nor often, I suspect, such a game of poker as that before they started. But about nine, as a particular favour, we should have some hay.

So they took their departure, leaving me still staring, and we resigned ourselves to wait for their return. The fire in the forge had been suffered to go out, and we were one and all too weary to kindle another. We dined, or, not to take that word in vain, we ate after a fashion, in the nightmare disorder of the assayer's office, perched among boxes. A single candle lighted us. It could scarce be called a house-warming; for there was, of course, no fire, and with the two open doors and the open window gaping on the night, like breaches in a fortress, it began to grow rapidly chill. Talk ceased; nobody moved but the unhappy Chuchu, still in quest of sofa-cushions, who tumbled complainingly among the trunks. It required a certain happiness of disposition to look forward hopefully, from so dismal a beginning, across the brief hours of night, to the warm shining of to-morrow's sun.

But the hay arrived at last, and we turned, with our last spark of courage, to the bedroom. We had improved the entrance, but it was still a kind of rope-walking; and it would have been droll to see us mounting, one after another, by candlelight, under the open stars.

The western door—that which looked up the cañon, and through which we entered by our bridge of flying plank—was still entire, a handsome, panelled door, the most finished piece of carpentry in Silverado. And the two lowest bunks next to this we roughly filled with hay for that night's use. Through the opposite, or eastern-looking gable, with its open door and window, a faint, diffused starshine came into the room like mist; and when we were once in bed, we lay, awaiting sleep, in a haunted, incomplete obscurity. At first the silence of the night was utter. Then a high wind began in the distance among the treetops, and for hours continued to grow higher. It seemed to me much such a wind as we had found on our visit; yet here in our open chamber we were fanned only by gentle and refreshing draughts, so deep was the cañon, so close our house was planted under the overhanging rock.

THE HUNTER'S FAMILY

There is quite a large race or class of people in America, for whom we scarcely seem to have a parallel in England. Of pure white blood, they are unknown or unrecognisable in towns; inhabit the fringe of settlements and the deep, quiet places of the country; rebellious to all labour, and pettily thievish, like the English gipsies; rustically ignorant, but with a touch of woodlore and the dexterity of the savage. Whence they came is a moot point. At the time of the war, they poured north in crowds to escape conscription; lived during summer on fruits, wild animals,

and petty theft; and at the approach of winter, when these supplies failed, built great fires in the forest, and there died stoically
by starvation. They are widely scattered, however, and easily
recognised. Loutish, but not ill-looking, they will sit all day,
swinging their legs on a field fence, the mind seemingly as devoid
of all reflection as a Suffolk peasant's, careless of politics, for the
most part incapable of reading, but with a rebellious vanity and a
strong sense of independence. Hunting is their most congenial
business, or, if the occasion offers, a little amateur detection. In
tracking a criminal, following a particular horse along a beaten
highway, and drawing inductions from a hair or a footprint, one
of those somnolent, grinning Hodges will suddenly display activity of body and finesse of mind. By their names ye may know
them, the women figuring as Loveina, Larsenia, Serena, Leanna,
Orreana; the men answering to Alvin, Alva, or Orion, pronounced Orrion, with the accent on the first. Whether they are
indeed a race, or whether this is the form of degeneracy common
to all backwoodsmen, they are at least known by a generic by-
word, as Poor Whites or Low-downers.

I will not say that the Hanson family was Poor White, because
the name savours of offence; but I may go as far as this—they
were, in many points, not unsimilar to the people usually so
called. Rufe himself combined two of the qualifications, for he
was both a hunter and an amateur detective. It was he who
pursued Russel and Dollar, the robbers of the Lake Port stage,
and captured them the very morning after the exploit, while they
were still sleeping in a hayfield. Russel, a drunken Scotch carpenter, was even an acquaintance of his own, and he expressed much
grave commiseration for his fate. In all that he said and did, Rufe
was grave. I never saw him hurried. When he spoke, he took out
his pipe with ceremonial deliberation, looked east and west, and
then, in quiet tones and few words, stated his business or told his
story. His gait was to match; it would never have surprised you if,
at any step, he had turned round and walked away again, so
warily and slowly, and with so much seeming hesitation did he go
about. He lay long in bed in the morning—rarely, indeed, rose
before noon; he loved all games, from poker to clerical croquet;
and in the Toll House croquet ground I have seen him toiling at
the latter with the devotion of a curate. He took an interest in
education, was an active member of the local school-board, and

when I was there, he had recently lost the schoolhouse key. His waggon was broken, but it never seemed to occur to him to mend it. Like all truly idle people, he had an artistic eye. He chose the print stuff for his wife's dresses, and counselled her in the making of a patchwork quilt, always, as she thought, wrongly, but to the more educated eye, always with bizarre and admirable taste—the taste of an Indian. With all this, he was a perfect, unoffending gentleman in word and act. Take his clay pipe from him, and he was fit for any society but that of fools. Quiet as he was, there burned a deep, permanent excitement in his dark blue eyes; and when this grave man smiled, it was like sunshine in a shady place.

Mrs. Hanson (*née,* if you please, Lovelands) was more commonplace than her lord. She was a comely woman, too, plump, fair-coloured, with wonderful white teeth; and in her print dresses (chosen by Rufe) and with a large sun-bonnet shading her valued complexion, made, I assure you, a very agreeable figure. But she was on the surface, what there was of her, out-spoken and loud-spoken. Her noisy laughter had none of the charm of one of Hanson's rare, slow-spreading smiles; there was no reticence, no mystery, no manner about the woman: she was a first-class dairy-maid, but her husband was an unknown quantity between the savage and the nobleman. She was often in and out with us, merry, and healthy, and fair; he came far seldomer—only, indeed, when there was business, or now and again, to pay a visit of ceremony, brushed up for the occasion, with his wife on his arm, and a clean clay pipe in his teeth. These visits, in our forest state, had quite the air of an event, and turned our red cañon into a salon.

Such was the pair who ruled in the old Silverado Hotel, among the windy trees, on the mountain shoulder overlooking the whole length of Napa Valley, as the man aloft looks down on the ship's deck. There they kept house, with sundry horses and fowls, and a family of sons, Daniel Webster, and I think George Washington, among the number. Nor did they want visitors. An old gentleman, of singular stolidity, and called Breedlove—I think he had crossed the plains in the same caravan with Rufe—housed with them for awhile during our stay; and they had besides a permanent lodger, in the form of Mrs. Hanson's brother, Irvine Lovelands. I spell Irvine by guess; for I could get no information on the subject, just as I could never find out, in spite of many inquiries, whether or not Rufe was a contraction for Rufus. They were all cheerfully at sea about their names in that generation. And this is surely the more notable where the names are all so strange, and even the family names appear to have been coined. At one time, at least, the ancestors of all these Alvins and Alvas, Loveinas, Lovelands, and Breedloves, must have taken serious council and found a certain poetry in these denominations; that must have been, then, their form of literature. But still times change; and their next descendants, the George Washingtons and Daniel Websters, will at least be clear upon the point. And anyway, and however his name should be spelt, this Irvine Lovelands was the most unmitigated Caliban I ever knew.

Our very first morning at Silverado, when we were full of business, patching up doors and windows, making beds and seats, and getting our rough lodging into shape, Irvine and his sister made their appearance together, she for neighbourliness and general curiosity; he, because he was working for me, to my sorrow, cutting firewood at I forget how much a day. The way that he set about cutting wood was characteristic. We were at that moment patching up and unpacking in the kitchen. Down he sat on one side, and down sat his sister on the other. Both were chewing pine-tree gum, and he, to my annoyance, accompanied that simple pleasure with profuse expectoration. She rattled away, talking up hill and down dale, laughing, tossing her head, showing her brilliant teeth. He looked on in silence, now spitting heavily on the floor, now putting his head back and uttering a loud, discordant, joyless laugh. He had a tangle of shock hair, the colour of wool; his mouth was a grin; although as strong as a horse, he looked neither heavy nor yet adroit, only leggy, coltish, and in the road. But it was plain he was in high spirits, thoroughly enjoying his visit; and he laughed frankly whenever we failed to accomplish what we were about. This was scarcely helpful: it was even, to amateur carpenters, embarrassing; but it lasted until we knocked off work and began to get dinner. Then Mrs. Hanson remembered she should have been gone an hour ago; and the pair retired, and the lady's laughter died away among the nutmegs down the path. That was Irvine's first day's work in my employment—the devil take him!

The next morning he returned and, as he was this time alone, he bestowed his conversation upon us with great liberality. He prided himself on his intelligence; asked us if we knew the school-ma'am. *He* didn't think much of her, anyway. He had tried her, he had. He had put a question to her. If a tree a hundred feet high were to fall a foot a day, how long would it take to fall right down? She had not been able to solve the problem. "She don't know nothing," he opined. He told us how a friend of his kept a school with a revolver, and chuckled mightily over that; his friend could teach school, he could. All the time he kept chewing gum and spitting. He would stand awhile looking down; and then he would toss back his shock of hair, and laugh hoarsely, and spit, and bring forward a new subject. A man, he told us, who bore a grudge against him, had poisoned his dog. "That was a low thing for a man to do now, wasn't it? It wasn't like a man, that, nohow. But I got even with him: I pisoned *his* dog." His clumsy utterance, his rude embarrassed manner, set a fresh value on the stupidity of his remarks. I do not think I ever appreciated the meaning of two words until I knew Irvine—the verb, loaf, and the noun, oaf; between them, they complete his portrait. He could lounge, and wriggle, and rub himself against the wall, and grin, and be more in everybody's way than any other two people that I ever set my eyes on. Nothing that he did became him; and yet you were conscious that he was one of your own race, that his mind was cumbrously at work, revolving the problem of existence like a quid of gum, and in his own cloudy manner enjoying life, and passing judgment on his fellows. Above all things, he was de-lighted with himself. You would not have thought it, from his uneasy manners and troubled, struggling utterance; but he loved himself to the marrow, and was happy and proud like a peacock on a rail.

His self-esteem was, indeed, the one joint in his harness. He could be got to work, and even kept at work, by flattery. As long as my wife stood over him, crying out how strong he was, so long exactly he would stick to the matter in hand; and the moment she turned her back, or ceased to praise him, he would stop. His physical strength was wonderful; and to have a woman stand by and admire his achievements, warmed his heart like sunshine. Yet he was as cowardly as he was powerful, and felt no shame in own-ing to the weakness. Something was once wanted from the crazy platform over the shaft, and he at once refused to venture there—

"did not like," as he said, "foolin' round them kind o' places,"
and let my wife go instead of him, looking on with a grin. Vanity,
where it rules, is usually more heroic: but Irvine steadily approved himself, and expected others to approve him; rather looked
down upon my wife, and decidedly expected her to look up to
him, on the strength of his superior prudence.

Yet the strangest part of the whole matter was perhaps this, that
Irvine was as beautiful as a statue. His features were, in themselves, perfect; it was only his cloudy, uncouth, and coarse expression that disfigured them. So much strength residing in so
spare a frame was proof sufficient of the accuracy of his shape. He
must have been built somewhat after the pattern of Jack Shep-
pard; but the famous housebreaker, we may be certain, was no
lout. It was by the extraordinary powers of his mind no less than
by the vigour of his body, that he broke his strong prison with
such imperfect implements, turning the very obstacles to service.
Irvine, in the same case, would have sat down and spat, and
grumbled curses. He had the soul of a fat sheep, but, regarded as
an artist's model, the exterior of a Greek God. It was a cruel
thought to persons less favoured in their birth, that this creature,
endowed—to use the language of theatres—with extraordinary
"means," should so manage to misemploy them that he looked
ugly and almost deformed. It was only by an effort of abstraction,
and after many days, that you discovered what he was.

By playing on the oaf's conceit, and standing closely over him,
we got a path made round the corner of the dump to our door, so
that we could come and go with decent ease; and he even enjoyed the work, for in that there were boulders to be plucked up
bodily, bushes to be uprooted, and other occasions for athletic
display: but cutting wood was a different matter. Anybody could
cut wood; and, besides, my wife was tired of supervising him, and
had other things to attend to. And in short, days went by, and
Irvine came daily, and talked and lounged and spat; but the
firewood remained intact as sleepers on the platform or growing
trees upon the mountain-side. Irvine, as a woodcutter, we could
tolerate; but Irvine as a friend of the family, at so much a day,
was too bald an imposition, and at length, on the afternoon of
the fourth or fifth day of our connection, I explained to him, as
clearly as I could, the light in which I had grown to regard his
presence. I pointed out to him that I could not continue to give

him a salary for spitting on the floor; and this expression, which came after a good many others, at last penetrated his obdurate wits. He rose at once, and said if that was the way he was going to be spoke to, he reckoned he would quit. And, no one interposing, he departed.

So far, so good. But we had no firewood. The next afternoon, I strolled down to Rufe's and consulted him on the subject. It was a very droll interview, in the large, bare north room of the Silverado Hotel, Mrs. Hanson's patchwork on a frame, and Rufe, and his wife, and I, and the oaf himself, all more or less embarrassed. Rufe announced there was nobody in the neighbourhood but Irvine who could do a day's work for anybody. Irvine, thereupon, refused to have any more to do with my service; he "wouldn't work no more for a man as had spoke to him 's I had done." I found myself on the point of the last humiliation—driven to beseech the creature whom I had just dismissed with insult: but I took the high hand in despair, said there must be no talk of Irvine coming back unless matters were to be differently managed; that I would rather chop firewood for myself than be fooled; and, in short, the Hansons being eager for the lad's hire, I so imposed upon them with merely affected resolution, that they ended by begging me to re-employ him again, on a solemn promise that he should be more industrious. The promise, I am bound to say, was kept. We soon had a fine pile of firewood at our door; and if Caliban gave me the cold shoulder and spared me his conversation, I thought none the worse of him for that, nor did I find my days much longer for the deprivation.

The leading spirit of the family was, I am inclined to fancy, Mrs. Hanson. Her social brilliancy somewhat dazzled the others, and she had more of the small change of sense. It was she who faced Kelmar, for instance; and perhaps if she had been alone, Kelmar would have had no rule within her doors. Rufe, to be sure, had a fine, sober, open-air attitude of mind, seeing the world without exaggeration—perhaps, we may even say, without enough; for he lacked, along with the others, that commercial idealism which puts so high a value on time and money. Sanity itself is a kind of convention. Perhaps Rufe was wrong; but, looking on life plainly, he was unable to perceive that croquet or poker were in any way less important than, for instance, mending his waggon. Even his own profession, hunting, was dear to him mainly as a sort of play; even that he would have neglected, had it not appealed to his imagination. His hunting-suit, for instance, had cost I should be afraid to say how many bucks—the currency in which he paid his way: it was all befringed, after the Indian fashion, and it was dear to his heart. The pictorial side of his daily business was never forgotten. He was even anxious to stand for his picture in those buckskin hunting clothes; and I remember how he once warmed almost into enthusiasm, his dark blue eyes growing perceptibly larger, as he planned the composition in which he should appear, "with the horns of some real big bucks, and dogs, and a camp on a crick" (creek, stream).

There was no trace in Irvine of his woodland poetry. He did not care for hunting, nor yet for buckskin suits. He had never observed scenery. The world, as it appeared to him, was almost obliterated by his own great grinning figure in the foreground: Caliban Malvolio. And it seems to me as if, in the persons of these brothers-in-law, we had the two sides of rusticity fairly well represented: the hunter living really in nature; the clodhopper living merely out of society: the one bent up in every corporal agent to capacity in one pursuit, doing at least one thing keenly and thoughtfully, and thoroughly alive to all that touches it; the other in the inert and bestial state, walking in a faint dream, and taking so dim an impression of the myriad sides of life that he is truly conscious of nothing but himself. It is only in the fastnesses of nature, forests, mountains, and the back of man's beyond, that a creature endowed with five senses can grow up into the perfection of this crass and earthy vanity. In towns or the busier country sides, he is roughly reminded of other men's existence; and if he learns no more, he learns at least to fear contempt. But Irvine had come scathless through life, conscious only of himself, of his great strength and intelligence; and in the silence of the universe, to which he did not listen, dwelling with delight on the sound of his own thoughts.

THE SEA-FOGS

A change in the colour of the light usually called me in the morning. By a certain hour, the long, vertical chinks in our western gable, where the boards had shrunk and separated, flashed suddenly into my eyes as stripes of dazzling blue, at once so dark and splendid that I used to marvel how the qualities could be combined. At an earlier hour, the heavens in that quarter were still quietly coloured, but the shoulder of the mountain which shuts in the cañon already glowed with sunlight in a wonderful compound of gold and rose and green; and this too would kindle, although more mildly and with rainbow tints, the fissures of our crazy gable. If I were sleeping heavily, it was the bold blue that struck me awake; if more lightly, then I would come to myself in that earlier and fairier light.

One Sunday morning, about five, the first brightness called me. I rose and turned to the east, not for my devotions, but for air. The night had been very still. The little private gale that blew every evening in our cañon, for ten minutes or perhaps a quarter of an hour, had swiftly blown itself out; in the hours that followed not a sigh of wind had shaken the treetops; and our barrack, for all its breaches, was less fresh that morning than of wont. But I had no sooner reached the window than I forgot all else in the sight that met my eyes, and I made but two bounds into my clothes, and down the crazy plank to the platform.

The sun was still concealed below the opposite hilltops, though it was shining already, not twenty feet above my head, on our own mountain slope. But the scene, beyond a few near features, was entirely changed. Napa Valley was gone; gone were all the lower slopes and woody foot-hills of the range; and in their place, not a thousand feet below me, rolled a great level ocean. It was as though I had gone to bed the night before, safe in a nook of in-land mountains, and had awakened in a bay upon the coast. I had seen these inundations from below; at Calistoga I had risen and gone abroad in the early morning, coughing and sneezing, under fathoms on fathoms of grey sea-vapour, like a cloudy sky—a dull sight for the artist, and a painful experience for the invalid. But to sit aloft one's self in the pure air and under the unclouded dome of heaven, and thus look down on the submergence of the valley, was strangely different and even delightful to the eyes. Far away were hilltops like little islands. Nearer, a smoky surf beat about the foot of precipices and poured into all the coves of these rough mountains. The colour of that fog ocean was a thing never to be forgotten. For an instant, among the Hebrides and just about sundown, I have seen something like it on the sea itself. But the white was not so opaline; nor was there, what surprisingly increased the effect, that breathless, crystal stillness over all. Even in its gentlest moods the salt sea travails, moaning among the weeds or lisping on the sand; but that vast fog ocean lay in a trance of silence, nor did the sweet air of the morning tremble with a sound.

As I continued to sit upon the dump, I began to observe that this sea was not so level as at first sight it appeared to be. Away in the extreme south, a little hill of fog arose against the sky above the general surface, and as it had already caught the sun, it shone on the horizon like the topsails of some giant ship. There were huge waves, stationary, as it seemed, like waves in a frozen sea; and yet, as I looked again, I was not sure but they were moving after all, with a slow and august advance. And while I was yet doubting, a promontory of the hills some four or five miles away, conspicuous by a bouquet of tall pines, was in a single instant overtaken and swallowed up. It reappeared in a little, with its pines, but this time as an islet, and only to be swallowed up once more and then for good. This set me looking nearer, and I saw that in every cove along the line of mountains the fog was being piled in higher and higher, as though by some wind that was inaudible to me. I could trace its progress, one pine-tree first growing hazy and then disappearing after another; although sometimes there was none of this fore-running haze, but the whole opaque white ocean gave a start and swallowed a piece of mountain at a gulp. It was to flee these poisonous fogs that I had left the seaboard, and climbed so high among the mountains. And now, behold, here came the fog to besiege me in my chosen altitudes, and yet came so beautifully that my first thought was of welcome.

The sun had now gotten much higher, and through all the gaps of the hills it cast long bars of gold across that white ocean. An eagle, or some other very great bird of the mountain, came wheeling over the nearer pine-tops, and hung, poised and something sideways, as if to look abroad on that unwonted desolation, spying perhaps with terror, for the eyries of her comrades. Then, with a long cry, she disappeared again towards Lake County and the clearer air. At length it seemed to me as if the flood were beginning to subside. The old landmarks, by whose disappearance I had measured its advance, here a crag, there a brave pine tree, now began, in the inverse order, to make their reappearance into daylight. I judged all danger of the fog was over. This was not

Noah's flood; it was but a morning spring, and would now drift out seaward whence it came. So, mightily relieved, and a good deal exhilarated by the sight, I went into the house to light the fire.

I suppose it was nearly seven when I once more mounted the platform to look abroad. The fog ocean had swelled up enormously since last I saw it; and a few hundred feet below me, in the deep gap where the Toll House stands and the road runs through into Lake County, it had already topped the slope, and was pouring over and down the other side like driving smoke. The wind had climbed along with it; and though I was still in calm air, I could see the trees tossing below me, and their long, strident sighing mounted to me where I stood.

Half an hour later, the fog had surmounted all the ridge on the opposite side of the gap, though a shoulder of the mountain still warded it out of our cañon. Napa Valley and its bounding hills were now utterly blotted out. The fog, sunny white in the sunshine, was pouring over into Lake County in a huge, ragged cataract, tossing treetops appearing and disappearing in the spray. The air struck with a little chill, and set me coughing. It smelt strong of the fog, like the smell of a washing-house, but with a shrewd tang of the sea salt.

Had it not been for two things—the sheltering spur which answered as a dyke, and the great valley on the other side which rapidly engulfed whatever mounted—our own little platform in the cañon must have been already buried a hundred feet in salt and poisonous air. As it was, the interest of the scene entirely occupied our minds. We were set just out of the wind, and but just above the fog; we could listen to the voice of the one as to music on the stage; we could plunge our eyes down into the other, as into some flowing stream from over the parapet of a bridge; thus we looked on upon a strange, impetuous, silent, shifting exhibition of the powers of nature, and saw the familiar landscape changing from moment to moment like figures in a dream.

The imagination loves to trifle with what is not. Had this been indeed the deluge, I should have felt more strongly, but the emotion would have been similar in kind. I played with the idea, as the child flees in delighted terror from the creations of his fancy. The look of the thing helped me. And when at last I began to flee up the mountain, it was indeed partly to escape from the raw air that kept me coughing, but it was also part in play.

As I ascended the mountain-side, I came once more to overlook the upper surface of the fog; but it wore a different appearance from what I had beheld at daybreak. For, first, the sun now fell on it from high overhead, and its surface shone and undulated like a great nor'land moor country, sheeted with untrodden morning snow. And next the new level must have been a thousand or fifteen hundred feet higher than the old, so that only five or six points of all the broken country below me, still stood out. Napa Valley was now one with Sonoma on the west. On the hither side, only a thin scattered fringe of bluffs was unsubmerged; and through all the gaps the fog was pouring over, like an ocean, into the blue clear sunny country on the east. There it was soon lost; for it fell instantly into the bottom of the valleys, following the water-shed; and the hilltops in that quarter were still clear cut upon the eastern sky.

Through the Toll House gap and over the near ridges on the other side, the deluge was immense. A spray of thin vapour was thrown high above it, rising and falling, and blown into fantastic shapes. The speed of its course was like a mountain torrent. Here and there a few treetops were discovered and then whelmed again; and for one second, the bough of a dead pine beckoned out of the spray like the arm of a drowning man. But still the imagination was dissatisfied, still the ear waited for something more. Had this indeed been water (as it seemed so, to the eye), with what a plunge of reverberating thunder would it have rolled upon its course, disembowelling mountains and deracinating pines! And yet water it was, and sea-water at that—true Pacific billows, only somewhat rarefied, rolling in mid-air among the hilltops.

I climbed still higher, among the red rattling gravel and dwarf underwood of Mount Saint Helena, until I could look right down upon Silverado, and admire the favoured nook in which it lay. The sunny plain of fog was several hundred feet higher; behind the protecting spur a gigantic accumulation of cottony vapour threatened, with every second, to blow over and submerge our homestead; but the vortex setting past the Toll House was too strong; and there lay our little platform, in the arms of the deluge, but still enjoying its unbroken sunshine. About eleven, however, thin spray came flying over the friendly buttress, and I began to think the fog had hunted out its Jonah after all. But it was the last effort. The wind veered while we were at dinner, and began to blow squally from the mountain summit; and by half-past one, all that world of sea-fogs was utterly routed and flying here and there into the south in little rags of cloud. And instead of a lone seabeach, we found ourselves once more inhabiting a high mountain-side, with the clear green country far below us, and the light smoke of Calistoga blowing in the air.

This was the great Russian campaign for that season. Now and then, in the early morning, a little white lakelet of fog would be seen far down in Napa Valley; but the heights were not again assailed, nor was the surrounding world again shut off from Silverado.

THE TOLL HOUSE

The Toll House, standing alone by the wayside under nodding pines, with its streamlet and water-tank; its backwoods, toll-bar, and well-trodden croquet ground; the ostler standing by the stable door, chewing a straw; a glimpse of the Chinese cook in the back parts; and Mr. Hoddy in the bar, gravely alert and serviceable, and equally anxious to lend or borrow books;—dozed all day in the dusty sunshine, more than half asleep. There were no neighbours, except the Hansons up the hill. The traffic on the road was infinitesimal; only, at rare intervals, a couple in a waggon, or a dusty farmer on a spring-board, toiling over "the grade" to that metropolitan hamlet, Calistoga; and, at the fixed hours, the passage of the stages.

The nearest building was the schoolhouse, down the road; and the school-ma'am boarded at the Toll House, walking thence in the morning to the little brown shanty, where she taught the young ones of the district, and returning thither pretty weary in the afternoon. She had chosen this outlying situation, I understood, for her health. Mr. Corwin was consumptive; so was Rufe; so was Mr. Jennings, the engineer. In short, the place was a kind of small Davos: consumptive folk consorting on a hilltop in the most unbroken idleness. Jennings never did anything that I could see, except now and then to fish, and generally to sit about in the bar and the veranda, waiting for something to happen. Corwin and

Rufe did as little as possible; and if the school-ma'am, poor lady, had to work pretty hard all morning, she subsided when it was over into much the same dazed beatitude as all the rest.

Her special corner was the parlour—a very genteel room, with Bible prints, a crayon portrait of Mrs. Corwin in the height of fashion, a few years ago, another of her son (Mr. Corwin was not represented), a mirror, and a selection of dried grasses. A large book was laid religiously on the table—"From Palace to Hovel," I believe, its name—full of the raciest experiences in England. The author had mingled freely with all classes, the nobility particularly meeting him with open arms; and I must say that traveller had ill requited his reception. His book, in short, was a capital instance of the Penny Messalina school of literature; and there arose from it, in that cool parlour, in that silent, wayside, mountain inn, a rank atmosphere of gold and blood and "Jenkins," and the "Mysteries of London," and sickening, inverted snobbery, fit to knock you down. The mention of this book reminds me of another and far racier picture of our island life. The latter parts of *Rocambole* are surely too sparingly consulted in the country which they celebrate. No man's education can be said to be complete, nor can he pronounce the world yet emptied of enjoyment, till he has made the acquaintance of "the Reverend Patterson, director of the Evangelical Society." To follow the evolutions of that reverend gentleman, who goes through scenes in which even Mr. Duffield would hesitate to place a bishop, is to rise to new ideas. But, alas! there was no Patterson about the Toll House. Only, alongside of "From Palace to Hovel," a sixpenny "Ouida" figured. So literature, you see, was not unrepresented.

The school-ma'am had friends to stay with her, other school-ma'ams enjoying their holidays, quite a bevy of damsels. They seemed never to go out, or not beyond the veranda, but sat close in the little parlour, quietly talking or listening to the wind among the trees. Sleep dwelt in the Toll House, like a fixture: summer sleep, shallow, soft, and dreamless. A cuckoo clock, a great rarity in such a place, hooted at intervals about the echoing house; and Mr. Jennings would open his eyes for a moment in the bar, and turn the leaf of a newspaper, and the resting school-ma'ams in the parlour would be recalled to the consciousness of their inaction.

Busy Mrs. Corwin and her busy Chinaman might be heard indeed, in the penetralia, pounding dough or rattling dishes; or perhaps Rufe had called up some of the sleepers for a game of croquet, and the hollow strokes of the mallet sounded far away among the woods: but with these exceptions, it was sleep and sunshine and dust, and the wind in the pine-trees, all day long.

A little before stage time, that castle of indolence awoke. The ostler threw his straw away and set to his preparations. Mr. Jennings rubbed his eyes; happy Mr. Jennings, the something he had been waiting for all day about to happen at last! The boarders gathered in the veranda, silently giving ear, and gazing down the road with shaded eyes. And as yet there was no sign for the senses, not a sound, not a tremor of the mountain road. The birds, to whom the secret of the hooting cuckoo is unknown, must have set down to instinct this premonitory bustle.

And then the first of the two stages swooped upon the Toll House with a roar and in a cloud of dust; and the shock had not yet time to subside, before the second was abreast of it. Huge concerns they were, well horsed and loaded, the men in their shirt-sleeves, the women swathed in veils, the long whip cracking like a pistol; and as they charged upon that slumbering hostelry, each shepherding a dust storm, the dead place blossomed into life and talk and clatter. This the Toll House?—with its city throng, its jostling shoulders, its infinity of instant business in the bar? The mind would not receive it! The heartfelt bustle of that hour is hardly credible; the thrill of the great shower of letters from the post-bag, the childish hope and interest with which one gazed in all these strangers' eyes. They paused there but to pass: the blue-clad China-boy, the San Francisco magnate, the mystery in the dust-coat, the secret memoirs in tweed, the ogling, well-shod lady with her troop of girls; they did but flash and go; they were hull-down for us behind life's ocean, and we but hailed their topsails on the line. Yet, out of our great solitude of four and twenty mountain hours, we thrilled to their momentary presence; gauged and divined them, loved and hated; and stood light-headed in that storm of human electricity. Yes, like Piccadilly Circus, this is also one of life's crossing-places. Here I beheld one man, already famous or infamous, a centre of pistol-shots: and another who, if not yet known to rumour, will fill a column of the

Sunday paper when he comes to hang—a burly, thick-set, powerful Chinese desperado, six long bristles upon either lip; redolent of whisky, playing-cards, and pistols; swaggering in the bar with the lowest assumption of the lowest European manners; rapping out blackguard English oaths in his canorous oriental voice; and combining in one person the depravities of two races and two civilisations. For all his lust and vigour, he seemed to look cold upon me from the valley of the shadow of the gallows. He imagined a vain thing; and while he drained his cocktail, Holbein's death was at his elbow. Once, too, I fell in talk with another of these flitting strangers—like the rest, in his shirt-sleeves and all begrimed with dust—and the next minute we were discussing Paris and London, theatres and wines. To him, journeying from one human place to another, this was a trifle; but to me! No, Mr. Lillie, I have not forgotten it.

And presently the city-tide was at its flood and began to ebb. Life runs in Piccadilly Circus, say, from nine to one, and then, there also, ebbs into the small hours of the echoing policeman and the lamps and stars. But the Toll House is far up stream, and near its rural springs; the bubble of the tide but touches it. Before you had yet grasped your pleasure, the horses were put to, the loud whips volleyed, and the tide was gone. North and south had the two stages vanished, the towering dust subsided in the woods; but there was still an interval before the flush had fallen on your cheeks, before the ear became once more contented with the silence, or the seven sleepers of the Toll House dozed back to their accustomed corners. Yet a little, and the ostler would swing round the great barrier across the road; and in the golden evening, that dreamy inn begin to trim its lamps and spread the board for supper.

As I recall the place—the green dell below; the spires of pine; the sun-warm, scented air; that grey, gabled inn, with its faint stirrings of life amid the slumber of the mountains—I slowly awake to a sense of admiration, gratitude, and almost love. A fine place, after all, for a wasted life to doze away in—the cuckoo clock hooting of its far home country; the croquet mallets, eloquent of English lawns; the stages daily bringing news of the turbulent world away below there; and perhaps once in the summer, a salt fog pouring overhead with its tale of the Pacific.

A STARRY DRIVE

In our rule at Silverado, there was a melancholy interregnum. The queen and the crown prince with one accord fell sick; and, as I was sick to begin with, our lone position on Mount Saint Helena was no longer tenable, and we had to hurry back to Calistoga and a cottage on the green. By that time we had begun to realise the difficulties of our position. We had found what an amount of labour it cost to support life in our red cañon; and it was the dearest desire of our hearts to get a China-boy to go along with us when we returned. We could have given him a whole house to himself, self-contained, as they say in the advertisements; and on the money question we were prepared to go far. Kong Sam Kee, the Calistoga washerman, was entrusted with the affair; and from day to day it languished on, with protestations on our part and mellifluous excuses on the part of Kong Sam Kee.

At length, about half-past eight of our last evening, with the waggon ready harnessed to convey us up the grade, the washerman, with a somewhat sneering air, produced the boy. He was a handsome, gentlemanly lad, attired in rich dark blue, and shod with snowy white; but, alas! he had heard rumours of Silverado. He knew it for a lone place on the mountain-side, with no friendly wash-house near by, where he might smoke a pipe of opium o' nights with other China-boys, and lose his little earnings at the game of tan; and he first backed out for more money; and then, when that demand was satisfied, refused to come point-blank. He was wedded to his wash-houses; he had no taste for the rural life; and we must go to our mountain servantless. It must have been near half an hour before we reached that conclusion, standing in the midst of Calistoga high street under the stars, and the China-boy and Kong Sam Kee singing their pigeon English in the sweetest voices and with the most musical inflections.

We were not, however, to return alone; for we brought with us Joe Strong, the painter, a most good-natured comrade and a capital hand at an omelette. I do not know in which capacity he was most valued—as a cook or a companion; and he did excellently well in both.

The Kong Sam Kee negotiation had delayed us unduly; it

must have been half-past nine before we left Calistoga, and night came fully ere we struck the bottom of the grade. I have never seen such a night. It semed to throw calumny in the teeth of all the painters that ever dabbled in starlight. The sky itself was of a ruddy, powerful, nameless, changing colour, dark and glossy like a serpent's back. The stars, by innumerable millions, stuck boldly forth like lamps. The milky way was bright, like a moonlit cloud; half heaven seemed milky way. The greater luminaries shone each more clearly than a winter's moon. Their light was dyed in every sort of colour—red, like fire; blue, like steel; green, like the tracks of sunset; and so sharply did each stand forth in its own lustre that there was no appearance of that flat, star-spangled arch we know so well in pictures, but all the hollow of heaven was one chaos of contesting luminaries—a hurly-burly of stars. Against this the hills and rugged treetops stood out redly dark.

As we continued to advance, the lesser lights and milky ways first grew pale, and then vanished; the countless hosts of heaven dwindled in number by successive millions; those that still shone had tempered their exceeding brightness and fallen back into their customary wistful distance; and the sky declined from its first bewildering splendour into the appearance of a common night. Slowly this change proceeded, and still there was no sign of any cause. Then a whiteness like mist was thrown over the spurs of the mountain. Yet awhile, and, as we turned a corner, a great leap of silver light and net of forest shadows fell across the road and upon our wondering waggonful; and, swimming low among the trees, we beheld a strange, misshapen, waning moon, half tilted on her back.

"Where are ye when the moon appears?" so the old poet sang, half taunting, to the stars, bent upon a courtly purpose.

"As the sunlight round the dim earth's midnight tower of shadow
                                                            pours,
    Streaming past the dim, wide portals,
    Viewless to the eyes of mortals,
Till it floods the moon's pale islet or the morning's golden
                                                            shores."

So sings Mr. Trowbridge, with a noble inspiration. And so had the sunlight flooded that pale islet of the moon, and her lit face put out, one after another, that galaxy of stars. The wonder of the drive was over; but, by some nice conjunction of clearness in the air and fit shadow in the valley where we travelled, we had seen for a little while that brave display of the midnight heavens. It was gone, but it had been; nor shall I ever again behold the stars with the same mind. He who has seen the sea commoved with a great hurricane, thinks of it very differently from him who has seen it only in a calm. And the difference between a calm and a hurricane is not greatly more striking than that between the ordinary face of night and the splendour that shone upon us in that drive. Two in our waggon knew night as she shines upon the tropics, but even that bore no comparison. The nameless colour of the sky, the hues of the star-fire, and the incredible projection of the stars themselves, starting from their orbits, so that the eye seemed to distinguish their positions in the hollow of space—these were things that we had never seen before and shall never see again.

Meanwhile, in this altered night, we proceeded on our way among the scents and silence of the forest, reached the top of the grade, wound up by Hanson's, and came at last to a stand under the flying gargoyle of the chute. Sam, who had been lying back, fast asleep, with the moon on his face, got down, with the remark that it was pleasant "to be home." The waggon turned and drove away, the noise gently dying in the woods, and we clambered up the rough path, Caliban's great feat of engineering, and came home to Silverado.

The moon shone in at the eastern doors and windows, and over the lumber on the platform. The one tall pine beside the ledge was steeped in silver. Away up the cañon, a wild cat welcomed us with three discordant squalls. But once we had lit a candle, and began to review our improvements, homely in either sense, and count our stores, it was wonderful what a feeling of possession and permanence grew up in the hearts of the lords of Silverado. A bed had still to be made up for Strong, and the morning's water to be fetched, with clinking pail; and as we set about these household duties, and showed off our wealth and conveniences before the stranger, and had a glass of wine, I think, in honour of our return, and trooped at length one after another up the flying bridge of plank, and lay down to sleep in our shattered, moon-pierced barrack, we were among the happiest sovereigns in the world, and certainly ruled over the most contented people. Yet, in our absence, the palace had been sacked. Wild cats, so the Hansons said, had broken in and carried off a side of bacon, a hatchet, and two knives.

EPISODES IN THE STORY OF A MINE

No one could live at Silverado and not be curious about the story of the mine. We were surrounded by so many evidences of expense and toil, we lived so entirely in the wreck of that great enterprise, like mites in the ruins of a cheese, that the idea of the old din and bustle haunted our repose. Our own house, the forge, the dump, the chutes, the rails, the windlass, the mass of broken plant; the two tunnels, one far below in the green dell, the other on the platform where we kept our wine; the deep shaft, with the sun-glints and the water-drops; above all, the ledge, that great gaping slice out of the mountain shoulder, propped apart by wooden wedges, on whose immediate margin, high above our heads, the one tall pine precariously nodded—these stood for its greatness; while the dog-hutch, boot-jacks, old boots, old tavern bills, and the very beds that we inherited from by-gone miners, put in human touches and realised for us the story of the past.

I have sat on an old sleeper, under the thick madronas near the forge, with just a look over the dump on the green world below, and seen the sun lying broad among the wreck, and heard the silence broken only by the tinkling water in the shaft, or a stir of the royal family about the battered palace, and my mind has gone back to the epoch of the Stanleys and the Chapmans, with a grand *tutti* of pick and drill, hammer and anvil, echoing about the cañon; the assayer hard at it in our dining room; the carts below on the road, and their cargo of red mineral bounding and thundering down the iron chute. And now all gone—all fallen away into this sunny silence and desertion: a family of squatters dining in the assayer's office, making their beds in the big sleeping room erstwhile so crowded, keeping their wine in the tunnel that once rang with picks.

But Silverado itself, although now fallen in its turn into decay, was once but a mushroom, and had succeeded to other mines and other flitting cities. Twenty years ago, away down the glen on the Lake County side there was a place, Jonestown by name, with two thousand inhabitants dwelling under canvas, and one roofed house for the sale of whisky. Round on the western side of Mount Saint Helena, there was at the same date, a second large encampment, its name, if it ever had one, lost for me. Both of these have perished, leaving not a stick and scarce a memory behind them. Tide after tide of hopeful miners have thus flowed and ebbed about the mountain, coming and going, now by lone prospectors, now with a rush. Last, in order of time came Silverado, reared the big mill, in the valley, founded the town which is now represented, monumentally, by Hanson's, pierced all these slaps and shafts and tunnels, and in turn declined and died away.

> "Our noisy years seem moments in the wake
> Of the eternal silence."

As to the success of Silverado in its time of being, two reports were current. According to the first, six hundred thousand dollars were taken out of that great upright seam, that still hung open above us on crazy wedges. Then the ledge pinched out, and there followed, in quest of the remainder, a great drifting and tunnelling in all directions, and a great consequent effusion of dollars, until, all parties being sick of the expense, the mine was deserted, and the town decamped. According to the second version, told me with much secrecy of manner, the whole affair, mine, mill, and town, were parts of one majestic swindle. There had never come any silver out of any portion of the mine; there was no silver to come. At midnight trains of packhorses might have been observed winding by devious tracks about the shoulder of the mountain. They came from far away, from Amador or Placer, laden with silver in "old cigar boxes." They discharged their load at Silverado, in the hour of sleep; and before the morning they were gone again with their mysterious drivers to their unknown source. In this way, twenty thousand pounds' worth of silver was smuggled in under cover of night, in these old cigar boxes; mixed with Silverado mineral; carted down to the mill; crushed, amalgamated, and refined, and despatched to the city as the proper product of the mine. Stock-jobbing, if it can cover such expenses, must be a profitable business in San Francisco.

I give these two versions as I got them. But I place little reliance on either, my belief in history having been greatly shaken. For it chanced that I had come to dwell in Silverado at a critical hour; great events in its history were about to happen—did happen, as I am led to believe; nay, and it will be seen that I played a part in that revolution myself. And yet from first to last I never had a glimmer of an idea what was going on; and even now, after full reflection, profess myself at sea. That there was some obscure intrigue of the cigar-box order, and that I, in the character of a wooden puppet, set pen to paper in the interest of somebody, so much, and no more, is certain.

Silverado, then under my immediate sway, belonged to one whom I will call a Mr. Ronalds. I only knew him through the extraordinarily distorting medium of local gossip, now as a momentous jobber; now as a dupe to point an adage; and again, and much more probably, as an ordinary Christian gentleman like you or me, who had opened a mine and worked it for awhile with better and worse fortune. So, through a defective window-pane, you may see the passer-by shoot up into a hunchbacked giant, or dwindle into a potbellied dwarf.

To Ronalds, at least, the mine belonged; but the notice by which he held it would run out upon the 30th of June—or rather, as I suppose, it had run out already, and the month of grace would expire upon that day, after which any American citizen might post a notice of his own, and make Silverado his. This, with a sort of quiet slyness, Rufe told me at an early period of our acquaintance. There was no silver, of course; the mine "wasn't worth nothing, Mr. Stevens," but there was a deal of old iron and wood around, and to gain possession of this old wood and iron, and get a right to the water, Rufe proposed, if I had no objections, to "jump the claim."

Of course, I had no objection. But I was filled with wonder. If all he wanted was the wood and iron, what, in the name of fortune, was to prevent him taking them? "His right there was none to dispute." He might lay hands on all to-morrow, as the wild cats had laid hands upon our knives and hatchet. Besides, was this mass of heavy mining plant worth transportation? If it was, why had not the rightful owners carted it away? If it was, would they not preserve their title to these movables, even after they had lost their title to the mine? And if it were not, what the better was Rufe? Nothing would grow at Silverado; there was even no wood to cut; beyond a sense of property, there was nothing to be gained. Lastly, was it at all credible that Ronalds would forget what Rufe remembered? The days of grace were not yet over: any fine morning he might appear, paper in hand, and enter for another year on his inheritance. However, it was none of my business; all seemed legal; Rufe or Ronalds, all was one to me.

On the morning of the 27th, Mrs. Hanson appeared with the milk as usual, in her sun-bonnet. The time would be out on Tuesday, she reminded us, and bade me be in readiness to play my part, though I had no idea what it was to be. And suppose Ronalds came? we asked. She received the idea with derision, laughing aloud with all her fine teeth. He could not find the mine to save his life, it appeared, without Rufe to guide him. Last year, when he came, they heard him "up and down the road a hollerin' and a raisin' Cain." And at last he had to come to the Hansons in despair, and bid Rufe, "Jump into your pants and shoes, and show me where this old mine is, anyway!" Seeing that Ronalds had laid out so much money in the spot, and that a beaten road led right up to the bottom of the dump, I thought this a remarkable example. The sense of locality must be singularly in abeyance in the case of Ronalds.

That same evening, supper comfortably over, Joe Strong busy at work on a drawing of the dump and the opposite hills, we were all out on the platform together, sitting there, under the tented heavens, with the same sense of privacy as if we had been cabined in a parlour, when the sound of brisk footsteps came mounting up the path. We pricked our ears at this, for the tread seemed lighter and firmer than was usual with our country neighbours. And presently, sure enough, two town gentlemen, with cigars and kid gloves, came debouching past the house. They looked in that place like a blasphemy.

"Good-evening," they said. For none of us had stirred; we all sat stiff with wonder.

"Good-evening," I returned; and then, to put them at their ease, "A stiff climb," I added.

"Yes," replied the leader; "but we have to thank you for this path."

I did not like the man's tone. None of us liked it. He did not seem embarrassed by the meeting, but threw up his remarks like favours, and strode magisterially by us towards the shaft and tunnel.

Presently we heard his voice raised to his companion. "We drifted every sort of way, but couldn't strike the ledge." Then again: "It pinched out here." And once more: "Every miner that ever worked upon it says there's bound to be a ledge somewhere."

These were the snatches of his talk that reached us, and they had a damning significance. We, the lords of Silverado, had come face to face with our superior. It is the worst of all quaint and of all cheap ways of life that they bring us at last to the pinch of some humiliation. I liked well enough to be a squatter when there was none but Hanson by; before Ronalds, I will own, I somewhat quailed. I hastened to do him fealty, said I gathered he was the Squattee, and apologised. He threatened me with ejection, in a manner grimly pleasant—more pleasant to him, I fancy, than to me; and then he passed off into praises of the former state of Silverado. "It was the busiest little mining town you ever saw": a population of between a thousand and fifteen hundred souls, the engine in full blast, the mill newly erected; nothing going but champagne, and hope the order of the day. Ninety thousand dollars came out; a hundred and forty thousand were put in, making a net loss of fifty thousand. The last days, I gathered, the days of John Stanley, were not so bright; the champagne had ceased to flow, the population was already moving elsewhere, and Silverado had begun to wither in the branch before it was cut at the root. The last shot that was fired knocked over the stove chimney, and made that hole in the roof of our barrack, through which the sun was wont to visit slug-a-beds towards afternoon. A noisy last shot, to inaugurate the days of silence.

Throughout this interview, my conscience was a good deal exercised; and I was moved to throw myself on my knees and own the intended treachery. But then I had Hanson to consider. I was in much the same position as Old Rowley, that royal humourist, whom "the rogue had taken into his confidence." And again, here was Ronalds on the spot. He must know the day of the month as well as Hanson and I. If a broad hint were necessary, he had the broadest in the world. For a large board had been nailed by the crown prince on the very front of our house, between the door and window, painted in cinnabar—the pigment of the country—with doggrel rhymes and contumelious pictures, and announcing, in terms unnecessarily figurative, that the trick was already played, the claim already jumped, and Master Sam the legitimate successor of Mr. Ronalds. But no, nothing could save that man; *quem deus vult perdere, prius dementat.* As he came so he went, and left his rights depending.

Late at night, by Silverado reckoning, and after we were all abed, Mrs. Hanson returned to give us the newest of her news. It was like a scene in a ship's steerage: all of us abed in our different tiers, the single candle struggling with the darkness, and this plump, handsome woman, seated on an upturned valise beside the bunks, talking and showing her fine teeth, and laughing till the rafters rang. Any ship, to be sure, with a hundredth part as many holes in it as our barrack, must long ago have gone to her last port. Up to that time I had always imagined Mrs. Hanson's loquacity to be mere incontinence, that she said what was uppermost for the pleasure of speaking, and laughed and laughed again as a kind of musical accompaniment. But I now found there was an art in it. I found it less communicative than silence itself. I wished to know why Ronalds had come; how he had found his way without Rufe; and why, being on the spot, he had not refreshed his title. She talked interminably on, but her replies were never answers. She fled under a cloud of words; and when I had made sure that she was purposely eluding me, I dropped the subject in my turn, and let her rattle where she would.

She had come to tell us that, instead of waiting for Tuesday, the claim was to be jumped on the morrow. How? If the time were not out, it was impossible. Why? If Ronalds had come and gone, and done nothing, there was the less cause for hurry. But again I could reach no satisfaction. The claim was to be jumped next morning, that was all that she would condescend upon.

And yet it was not jumped the next morning, nor yet the next, and a whole week had come and gone before we heard more of this exploit. That day week, however, a day of great heat, Hanson, with a little roll of paper in his hand, and the eternal pipe alight; Breedlove, his large, dull friend, to act, I suppose, as witness; Mrs. Hanson, in her Sunday best; and all the children, from the oldest to the youngest;—arrived in a procession, tailing one behind another up the path. Caliban was absent, but he had been chary of his friendly visits since the row; and with that exception, the whole family was gathered together as for a marriage or a christening. Strong was sitting at work, in the shade of the dwarf madronas near the forge; and they planted themselves about him in a circle, one on a stone, another on the waggon rails, a third on a piece of plank. Gradually the children stole away up the cañon to where there was another chute, somewhat smaller than the one across the dump; and down this chute, for the rest of the afternoon, they poured one avalanche of stones after another, waking the echoes of the glen. Meantime we elders sat together on the platform, Hanson and his friend smoking in silence like Indian sachems, Mrs. Hanson rattling on as usual with an adroit volubility, saying nothing, but keeping the party at their ease like a courtly hostess.

Not a word occurred about the business of the day. Once, twice, and thrice I tried to slide the subject in, but was discouraged by the stoic apathy of Rufe, and beaten down before the pouring verbiage of his wife. There is nothing of the Indian brave about me, and I began to grill with impatience. At last, like a highway robber, I cornered Hanson, and bade him stand and deliver his business. Thereupon he gravely rose, as though to hint that this was not a proper place, nor the subject one suitable for squaws, and I, following his example, led him up the plank into our barrack. There he bestowed himself on a box, and unrolled his papers with fastidious deliberation. There were two sheets of note-paper, and an old mining notice, dated May 30th, 1879, part print, part manuscript, and the latter much obliterated by the rains. It was by this identical piece of paper that the mine had been held last year. For thirteen months it had endured the weather and the change of seasons on a cairn behind the shoulder of the cañon; and it was now my business, spreading it before me on the table, and sitting on a valise, to copy its terms with some necessary changes, twice over on the two sheets of note-paper. One was then to be placed on the same cairn—a "mound of rocks" the notice put it; and the other to be lodged for registration.

Rufe watched me, silently smoking, till I came to the place for the locator's name at the end of the first copy; and when I proposed that he should sign, I thought I saw a scare in his eye. "I don't think that'll be necessary," he said slowly; "just you write it down." Perhaps this mighty hunter, who was the most active member of the local school board, could not write. There would be nothing strange in that. The constable of Calistoga is, and has been for years, a bed-ridden man, and, if I remember rightly, blind. He had more need of the emoluments than another, it was explained; and it was easy for him to "depytise," with a strong accent on the last. So friendly and so free are popular institutions.

When I had done my scrivening, Hanson strolled out, and addressed Breedlove, "Will you step up here a bit?" and after they had disappeared a little while into the chaparral and madrona thicket, they came back again, minus a notice, and the deed was done. The claim was jumped; a tract of mountainside, fifteen hundred feet long by six hundred wide, with all the earth's precious bowels, had passed from Ronalds to Hanson, and, in the passage, changed its name from the "Mammoth" to the "Calistoga." I had tried to get Rufe to call it after his wife, after himself, and after Garfield, the Republican Presidential candidate of the hour —since then elected, and, alas! dead—but all was in vain. The claim had once been called the Calistoga before, and he seemed to feel safety in returning to that.

And so the history of that mine became once more plunged in darkness, lit only by some monster pyrotechnical displays of gossip. And perhaps the most curious feature of the whole matter is this: that we should have dwelt in this quiet corner of the mountains, with not a dozen neighbours, and yet struggled all the while, like desperate swimmers, in this sea of falsities and contradictions. Wherever a man is, there will be a lie.

TOILS AND PLEASURES

I must try to convey some notion of our life, of how the days passed and what pleasure we took in them, of what there was to do and how we set about doing it, in our mountain hermitage. The house, after we had repaired the worst of the damages, and filled in some of the doors and windows with white cotton cloth, became a healthy and a pleasant dwelling-place, always airy and dry, and haunted by the outdoor perfumes of the glen. Within, it had the look of habitation, the human look. You had only to go into the third room, which we did not use, and see its stones, its sifting earth, its tumbled litter; and then return to our lodging, with the beds made, the plates on the rack, the pail of bright water behind the door, the stove crackling in a corner, and perhaps the table roughly laid against a meal,—and man's order, the little clean spots that he creates to dwell in, were at once contrasted with the rich passivity of nature. And yet our house was everywhere so wrecked and shattered, the air came and went so freely, the sun found so many portholes, the golden outdoor glow shone in so many open chinks, that we enjoyed, at the same time, some of the comforts of a roof and much of the gaiety and brightness of al fresco life. A single shower of rain, to be sure, and we should have been drowned out like mice. But ours was a Californian summer, and an earthquake was a far likelier accident than a shower of rain.

Trustful in this fine weather, we kept the house for kitchen and bedroom, and used the platform as our summer parlour. The sense of privacy, as I have said already, was complete. We could look over the dump on miles of forest and rough hilltop; our eyes commanded some of Napa Valley, where the train ran, and the little country townships sat so close together along the line of the rail. But here there was no man to intrude. None but the Hansons were our visitors. Even they came but at long intervals, or twice daily, at a stated hour, with milk. So our days, as they were never interrupted, drew out to the greater length; hour melted insensibly into hour; the household duties, though they were many, and some of them laborious, dwindled into mere isiets of business in a sea of sunny daytime; and it appears to me, looking back, as though the far greater part of our life at Silverado had been passed, propped upon an elbow, or seated on a plank, listening to the silence that there is among the hills.

My work, it is true, was over early in the morning. I rose before any one else, lit the stove, put on the water to boil, and strolled forth upon the platform to wait till it was ready. Silverado would then be still in shadow, the sun shining on the mountain higher up. A clean smell of trees, a smell of the earth at morning, hung in the air. Regularly, every day, there was a single bird, not singing, but awkwardly chirruping among the green madronas, and the sound was cheerful, natural, and stirring. It did not hold the attention, nor interrupt the thread of meditation, like a blackbird or a nightingale; it was mere woodland prattle, of which the mind was conscious like a perfume. The freshness of these morning seasons remained with me far on into the day.

As soon as the kettle boiled, I made porridge and coffee; and that, beyond the literal drawing of water, and the preparation of kindling, which it would be hyperbolical to call the hewing of wood, ended my domestic duties for the day. Thenceforth my wife laboured single-handed in the palace, and I lay or wandered on the platform at my own sweet will. The little corner near the forge, where we found a refuge under the madronas from the unsparing early sun, is indeed connected in my mind with some nightmare encounters over Euclid, and the Latin Grammar. These were known as Sam's lessons. He was supposed to be the victim and the sufferer; but here there must have been some misconception, for whereas I generally retired to bed after one of these engagements, he was no sooner set free than he dashed up to the Chinaman's house, where he had installed a printing-press, that great element of civilisation, and the sound of his labours would be faintly audible about the cañon half the day.

To walk at all was a laborious business; the foot sank and slid, the boots were cut to pieces, among sharp, uneven, rolling stones. When we crossed the platform in any direction, it was usual to lay a course, following as much as possible the line of waggon rails. Thus, if water were to be drawn, the water-carrier left the house along some tilting planks that we had laid down, and not laid down very well. These carried him to that great highroad, the railway; and the railway served him as far as to the head of the shaft. But from thence to the spring and back again he made the best of his unaided way, staggering among the stones, and wading in low growth of the calycanthus, where the rattlesnakes lay hissing at his passage. Yet I liked to draw water. It was pleasant to dip the grey metal pail into the clean, colourless, cool water; pleasant to carry it back, with the water lipping at the edge, and a broken sunbeam quivering in the midst.

But the extreme roughness of the walking confined us in common practice to the platform, and indeed to those parts of it that were most easily accessible along the line of rails. The rails came straight forward from the shaft, here and there overgrown with little green bushes, but still entire, and still carrying a truck, which it was Sam's delight to trundle to and fro by the hour with various ladings. About midway down the platform, the railroad trended to the right, leaving our house and coasting along the far side within a few yards of the madronas and the forge, and not far off the latter, ended in a sort of platform on the edge of the dump. There, in old days, the trucks were tipped, and their load sent thundering down the chute. There, besides, was the only spot where we could approach the margin of the dump. Anywhere else, you took your life in your right hand when you came within a yard and a half to peer over. For at any moment the dump might begin to slide and carry you down and bury you below its ruins. Indeed, the neighbourhood of an old mine is a place beset with dangers. For as still as Silverado was, at any moment the report of rotten wood might tell us that the platform had fallen into the shaft; the dump might begin to pour into the road below; or a wedge slip in the great upright seam, and hundreds of tons of mountain bury the scene of our encampment.

I have already compared the dump to a rampart, built certainly by some rude people, and for prehistoric wars. It was likewise a frontier. All below was green and woodland, the tall pines soaring one above another, each with a firm outline and full spread of bough. All above was arid, rocky, and bald. The great spout of broken mineral, that had dammed the cañon up, was a creature of man's handiwork, its material dug out with a pick and powder, and spread by the service of the trucks. But nature herself, in that upper district, seemed to have had an eye to nothing besides mining; and even the natural hillside was all sliding gravel and precarious boulder. Close at the margin of the well leaves would decay to skeletons and mummies, which at length some stronger gust would carry clear of the cañon and scatter in the subjacent woods. Even moisture and decaying vegetable matter could not, with all nature's alchemy, concoct enough soil to nourish a few poor grasses. It is the same, they say, in the neighbourhood of all silver mines; the nature of that precious rock being stubborn with quartz and poisonous with cinnabar. Both were plenty in our Silverado. The stones sparkled white in the sunshine with quartz; they were all stained red with cinnabar. Here, doubtless, came the Indians of yore to paint their faces for the war-path; and cinnabar, if I remember rightly, was one of the few articles of Indian commerce. Now, Sam had it in his undisturbed possession, to pound down and slake, and paint his rude designs with. But to me it had always a fine flavour of poetry, compounded out of Indian story and Hawthornden's allusion:

> "Desire, alas! desire a Zeuxis new,
>   From Indies borrowing gold, from Eastern skies
>   Most bright cinoper . . ."

Yet this is but half the picture; our Silverado platform has another side to it. Though there was no soil, and scarce a blade of grass, yet out of these tumbled gravel-heaps and broken boulders, a flower garden bloomed as at home in a conservatory. Calycanthus crept, like a hardy weed, all over our rough parlour, choking the railway, and pushing forth its rusty, aromatic cones from between two blocks of shattered mineral. Azaleas made a big snow-bed just above the well. The shoulder of the hill waved white with Mediterranean heath. In the crannies of the ledge and about the spurs of the tall pine, a red flowering stone-plant hung in clusters. Even the low, thorny chaparral was thick with pea-like blossom. Close at the foot of our path nutmegs prospered, delightful to the sight and smell. At sunrise, and again late at night, the scent of the sweet baytrees filled the cañon, and the down-blowing night wind must have borne it hundreds of feet into the outer air.

All this vegetation, to be sure, was stunted. The madrona was here no bigger than the manzanita; the bay was but a stripling shrub; the very pines, with four or five exceptions in all our upper cañon, were not so tall as myself, or but a little taller, and the most of them came lower than my waist. For a prosperous forest tree, we must look below, where the glen was crowded with green spires. But for flowers and ravishing perfume, we had none to envy: our heap of road-metal was thick with bloom, like a hawthorn in the front of June; our red, baking angle in the mountain, a laboratory of poignant scents. It was an endless wonder to my mind, as I dreamed about the platform, following the progress of the shadows, where the madrona with its leaves, the azalea and calycanthus with their blossoms, could find moisture to support such thick, wet, waxy growths, or the bay-tree collect the ingredients of its perfume. But there they all grew together, healthy, happy, and happy-making, as though rooted in a fathom of black soil.

Nor was it only vegetable life that prospered. We had, indeed, few birds, and none that had much of a voice or anything worthy to be called a song. My morning comrade had a thin chirp, unmusical and monotonous, but friendly and pleasant to hear. He had but one rival: a fellow with an ostentatious cry of near an octave descending, not one note of which properly followed another. This is the only bird I ever knew with a wrong ear; but

there was something enthralling about his performance. You
listened and listened, thinking each time he must surely get it
right; but no, it was always wrong, and always wrong the same
way. Yet he seemed proud of his song, delivered it with execution
and a manner of his own, and was charming to his mate. A very in-
correct, incessant human whistler had thus a chance of knowing
how his own music pleased the world. Two great birds—eagles,
we thought—dwelt at the top of the cañon, among the crags that
were printed on the sky. Now and again, but very rarely, they
wheeled high over our heads in silence, or with a distant, dying
scream; and then, with a fresh impulse, winged fleetly forward,
dipped over a hilltop, and were gone. They seemed solemn and
ancient things, sailing the blue air: perhaps coeval with the
mountain where they haunted, perhaps emigrants from Rome,
where the glad legions may have shouted to behold them on the
morn of battle.

But if birds were rare, the place abounded with rattlesnakes—
the rattlesnakes' nest, it might have been named. Wherever we
brushed among the bushes, our passage woke their angry buzz.
One dwelt habitually in the wood-pile, and sometimes, when we
came for firewood, thrust up his small head between two logs, and
hissed at the intrusion. The rattle has a legendary credit; it is
said to be awe-inspiring, and, once heard, to stamp itself for ever
in the memory. But the sound is not at all alarming; the hum of
many insects, and the buzz of the wasp convince the ear of danger
quite as readily. As a matter of fact, we lived for weeks in Silverado, coming and going, with rattles sprung on every side, and it
never occurred to us to be afraid. I used to take sun-baths and do
calisthenics in a certain pleasant nook among azalea and calycanthus, the rattles whizzing on every side like spinning-wheels,
and the combined hiss or buzz rising louder and angrier at any
sudden movement; but I was never in the least impressed, nor
ever attacked. It was only towards the end of our stay, that a man
down at Calistoga, who was expatiating on the terrifying nature
of the sound, gave me at last a very good imitation; and it burst
on me at once that we dwelt in the very metropolis of deadly
snakes, and that the rattle was simply the commonest noise in
Silverado. Immediately on our return, we attacked the Hansons
on the subject. They had formerly assured us that our cañon was
favoured, like Ireland, with an entire immunity from poisonous

reptiles; but, with the perfect inconsequence of the natural man, they were no sooner found out than they went off at score in the contrary direction, and we were told that in no part of the world did rattlesnakes attain to such a monstrous bigness as among the warm, flower-dotted rocks of Silverado. This is a contribution rather to the natural history of the Hansons than to that of snakes.

One person, however, better served by his instinct, had known the rattle from the first; and that was Chuchu, the dog. No rational creature has ever led an existence more poisoned by terror than that dog's at Silverado. Every whiz of the rattle made him bound. His eyes rolled; he trembled; he would be often wet with sweat. One of our great mysteries was his terror of the mountain. A little away above our nook, the azaleas and almost all the vegetation ceased. Dwarf pines, not big enough to be Christmas trees, grew thinly among loose stone and gravel scaurs. Here and there a big boulder sat quiescent on a knoll, having paused there till the next rain in his long slide down the mountain. There was here no ambuscade for the snakes, you could see clearly where you trod; and yet the higher I went, the more abject and appealing became Chuchu's terror. He was an excellent master of that composite language in which dogs communicate with men, and he would assure me, on his honour, that there was some peril on the mountain; appeal to me, by all that I held holy, to turn back; and at length, finding all was in vain, and that I still persisted, ignorantly foolhardy, he would suddenly whip round and make a bee-line down the slope for Silverado, the gravel showering after him. What was he afraid of? There were admittedly brown bears and California lions on the mountain; and a grizzly visited Rufe's poultry yard not long before, to the unspeakable alarm of Caliban, who dashed out to chastise the intruder, and found himself, by moonlight, face to face with such a tartar. Something at least there must have been: some hairy, dangerous brute lodged permanently among the rocks a little to the north-west of Silverado, spending his summer thereabout, with wife and family.

And there was, or there had been, another animal. Once, under the broad daylight, on that open stony hillside, where the baby pines were growing, scarcely tall enough to be a badge for a Mac-Gregor's bonnet, I came suddenly upon his innocent body, lying mummified by the dry air and sun: a pigmy kangaroo. I am ingloriously ignorant of these subjects; had never heard of such a beast; thought myself face to face with some incomparable sport of nature; and began to cherish hopes of immortality in science. Rarely have I been conscious of a stranger thrill than when I raised that singular creature from the stones, dry as a board, his innocent heart long quiet, and all warm with sunshine. His long hind legs were stiff, his tiny forepaws clutched upon his breast, as if to leap; his poor life cut short upon that mountain by some unknown accident. But the kangaroo rat, it proved, was no such unknown animal; and my discovery was nothing.

Crickets were not wanting. I thought I could make out exactly four of them, each with a corner of his own, who used to make night musical at Silverado. In the matter of voice, they far excelled the birds, and their ringing whistle sounded from rock to rock, calling and replying the same thing, as in a meaningless opera. Thus, children in full health and spirits shout together, to the dismay of neighbours; and their idle, happy, deafening vociferations rise and fall, like the song of the crickets. I used to sit at night on the platform, and wonder why these creatures were so happy; and what was wrong with man that he also did not wind up his days with an hour or two of shouting; but I suspect that all long-lived animals are solemn. The dogs alone are hardly used by nature; and it seems a manifest injustice for poor Chuchu to die in his teens, after a life so shadowed and troubled, continually shaken with alarm, and the tear of elegant sentiment permanently in his eye.

There was another neighbour of ours at Silverado, small but very active, a destructive fellow. This was a black, ugly fly—a bore, the Hansons called him—who lived by hundreds in the boarding of our house. He entered by a round hole, more neatly pierced than a man could do it with a gimlet, and he seems to have spent his life in cutting out the interior of the plank, but whether as a dwelling or a store-house, I could never find. When I used to lie in bed in the morning for a rest—we had no easy-chairs in Silverado—I would hear, hour after hour, the sharp cutting sound of his labours, and from time to time a dainty shower of sawdust would fall upon the blankets. There lives no more industrious creature than a bore.

And now that I have named to the reader all our animals and insects without exception—only I find I have forgotten the flies—

he will be able to appreciate the singular privacy and silence of our days. It was not only man who was excluded: animals, the song of birds, the lowing of cattle, the bleating of sheep, clouds even, and the variations of the weather, were here also wanting; and as, day after day, the sky was one dome of blue, and the pines below us stood motionless in the still air, so the hours themselves were marked out from each other only by the series of our own affairs, and the sun's great period as he ranged westward through the heavens. The two birds cackled awhile in the early morning; all day the water tinkled in the shaft, the bores ground sawdust in the planking of our crazy palace—infinitesimal sounds; and it was only with the return of night that any change would fall on our surroundings, or the four crickets begin to flute together in the dark.

Indeed, it would be hard to exaggerate the pleasure that we took in the approach of evening. Our day was not very long, but it was very tiring. To trip along unsteady planks or wade among shifting stones, to go to and fro for water, to clamber down the glen to the Toll House after meat and letters, to cook, to make fires and beds, were all exhausting to the body. Life out of doors, besides, under the fierce eye of day, draws largely on the animal spirits. There are certain hours in the afternoon when a man, unless he is in strong health or enjoys a vacant mind, would rather creep into a cool corner of a house and sit upon the chairs of civilization. About that time, the sharp stones, the planks, the upturned boxes of Silverado, began to grow irksome to my body; I set out on that hopeless, never-ending quest for a more comfortable posture; I would be fevered and weary of the staring sun; and just then he would begin courteously to withdraw his countenance, the shadows lengthened, the aromatic airs awoke, and an indescribable but happy change announced the coming of the night.

The hours of evening when we were once curtained in the friendly dark, sped lightly. Even as with the crickets, night brought to us a certain spirit of rejoicing. It was good to taste the air; good to mark the dawning of the stars, as they increased their glittering company; good, too, to gather stones, and send them crashing down the chute, a wave of light. It seemed, in some way, the reward and the fulfilment of the day. So it is when men dwell in the open air; it is one of the simple pleasures that we lose by living cribbed and covered in a house, that, though the coming of the day is still the most inspiriting, yet day's departure, also, and the return of night refresh, renew, and quiet us; and in the pastures of the dusk we stand, like cattle, exulting in the absence of the load.

Our nights were never cold, and they were always still, but for one remarkable exception. Regularly, about nine o'clock, a warm wind sprang up, and blew for ten minutes, or maybe a quarter of an hour, right down the cañon, fanning it well out, airing it as a mother airs the night nursery before the children sleep. As far as I could judge, in the clear darkness of the night, this wind was purely local: perhaps dependent on the configuration of the glen. At least, it was very welcome to the hot and weary squatters; and if we were not abed already, the springing up of this lilliputian valley-wind would often be our signal to retire.

I was the last to go to bed, as I was still the first to rise. Many a night I have strolled about the platform, taking a bath of darkness before I slept. The rest would be in bed, and even from the forge I could hear them talking together from bunk to bunk. A single candle in the neck of a pint bottle was their only illumination; and yet the old cracked house seemed literally bursting with the light. It shone keen as a knife through all the vertical chinks; it struck upward through the broken shingles; and through the eastern door and window, it fell in a great splash upon the thicket and the overhanging rock. You would have said a conflagration, or at the least a roaring forge; and behold, it was but a candle. Or perhaps it was yet more strange to see the procession moving bedwards round the corner of the house, and up the plank that brought us to the bedroom door; under the immense spread of the starry heavens, down in a crevice of the giant mountain, these few human shapes, with their unshielded taper, made so disproportionate a figure in the eye and mind. But the more he is alone with nature, the greater man and his doings bulk in the consideration of his fellow-men. Miles and miles away upon the opposite hilltops, if there were any hunter belated or any traveller who had lost his way, he must have stood, and watched and wondered, from the time the candle issued from the door of the assayer's office till it had mounted the plank and disappeared again into the miners' dormitory.

POEMS AND BALLADS

A Child's Garden of Verses

FOR the long nights you lay awake
And watched for my unworthy sake:
For your most comfortable hand
That led me through the uneven land:
For all the story-books you read:
For all the pains you comforted:
For all you pitied, all you bore,
In sad and happy days of yore:—
My second Mother, my first Wife,
The angel of my infant life—
From the sick child, now well and old,
Take, nurse, the little book you hold!

And grant it, Heaven, that all who read
May find as dear a nurse at need,
And every child who lists my rhyme,
In the bright, fireside, nursery clime,
May hear it in as kind a voice
As made my childish days rejoice!

R. L. S.

Contents

———

A CHILD'S GARDEN OF VERSES

———— ✳ ————

I

BED IN SUMMER

IN winter I get up at night
And dress by yellow candle-light.
In summer, quite the other way,
I have to go to bed by day.

I have to go bed and see
The birds still hopping on the tree,
Or hear the grown-up people's feet
Still going past me in the street.

And does it not seem hard to you,
When all the sky is clear and blue,
And I should like so much to play,
To have to go to bed by day?

II

A THOUGHT

IT is very nice to think
The world is full of meat and drink.
With little children saying grace
In every Christian kind of place.

III

AT THE SEA-SIDE

WHEN I was down beside the sea
A wooden spade they gave to me
   To dig the sandy shore.

My holes were empty like a cup.
In every hole the sea came up,
   Till it could come no more.

IV

YOUNG NIGHT THOUGHT

ALL night long and every night,
When my mama puts out the light,
I see the people marching by,
As plain as day, before my eye.

Armies and emperors and kings,
All carrying different kinds of things,
And marching in so grand a way,
You never saw the like by day.

So fine a show was never seen
At the great circus on the green;
For every kind of beast and man
Is marching in that caravan.

At first they move a little slow,
But still the faster on they go,
And still beside them close I keep
Until we reach the town of Sleep.

V

WHOLE DUTY OF CHILDREN

A CHILD should always say what's true
And speak when he is spoken to,
And behave mannerly at table;
At least as far as he is able.

VI

RAIN

THE rain is raining all around,
It falls on field and tree,
It rains on the umbrellas here
    And on the ships at sea.

VII

PIRATE STORY

THREE of us afloat in the meadow by the swing,
    Three of us aboard in the basket on the lea.
Winds are in the air, they are blowing in the spring,
    And waves are on the meadow like the waves there are at sea.

Where shall we adventure, to-day that we're afloat,
    Wary of the weather and steering by a star?
Shall it be to Africa, a-steering of the boat,
    To Providence, or Babylon, or off to Malabar?

Hi! but here's a squadron a-rowing on the sea—
    Cattle on the meadow a-charging with a roar!
Quick, and we'll escape them, they're as mad as they can be,
    The wicket is the harbour and the garden is the shore.

VIII

FOREIGN LANDS

UP into the cherry tree
Who should climb but little me?
I held the trunk with both my hands
And looked abroad on foreign lands.

I saw the next door garden lie,
Adorned with flowers, before my eye,
And many pleasant places more
That I had never seen before.

I saw the dimpling river pass
And be the sky's blue looking-glass;
The dusty roads go up and down
With people tramping into town.

If I could find a higher tree
Farther and farther I should see,
To where the grown-up river slips
Into the sea among the ships,

To where the roads on either hand
Lead onward into fairy land,
Where all the children dine at five,
And all the playthings come alive.

IX

WINDY NIGHTS

WHENEVER the moon and stars are set,
    Whenever the wind is high,
All night long in the dark and wet,
    A man goes riding by.
Late in the night when the fires are out,
Why does he gallop and gallop about?

Whenever the trees are crying aloud,
  And ships are tossed at sea,
By, on the highway, low and loud,
  By at the gallop goes he.
By at the gallop he goes, and then
By he comes back at the gallop again.

X

TRAVEL

I SHOULD like to rise and go
Where the golden apples grow;—
Where below another sky
Parrot islands anchored lie,
And, watched by cockatoos and goats,
Lonely Crusoes building boats;—
Where in sunshine reaching out
Eastern cities, miles about,
Are with mosque and minaret
Among sandy gardens set,
And the rich goods from near and far
Hang for sale in the bazaar;—
Where the Great Wall round China goes,
And on one side the desert blows,
And with bell and voice and drum,
Cities on the other hum;—
Where are forests, hot as fire,
Wide as England, tall as a spire,
Full of apes and cocoa-nuts
And the Negro hunters' huts;—
Where the knotty crocodile
Lies and blinks in the Nile,
And the red flamingo flies
Hunting fish before his eyes;—
Where in jungles, near and far,
Man-devouring tigers are,
Lying close and giving ear
Lest the hunt be drawing near,
Or a comer-by be seen

Swinging in a palanquin;—
Where among the desert sands
Some deserted city stands,
All its children, sweep and prince,
Grown to manhood ages since,
Not a foot in street or house,
Not a stir of child or mouse,
And when kindly falls the night,
In all the town no spark of light.
There I'll come when I'm a man
With a camel caravan;
Light a fire in the gloom
Of some dusty dining room;
See the pictures on the walls,
Heroes, fights and festivals;
And in a corner find the toys
Of the old Egyptian boys.

XI

SINGING

O F speckled eggs the birdie sings
    And nests among the trees;
The sailor sings of ropes and things
    In ships upon the seas.

The children sing in far Japan,
    The children sing in Spain;
The organ with the organ man
    Is singing in the rain.

XII

LOOKING FORWARD

W H E N I am grown to man's estate
I shall be very proud and great,
And tell the other girls and boys
Not to meddle with my toys.

XIII
A GOOD PLAY

W E built a ship upon the stairs
All made of the back-bedroom chairs,
And filled it full of sofa pillows
To go a-sailing on the billows.

We took a saw and several nails,
And water in the nursery pails;
And Tom said, "Let us also take
An apple and a slice of cake;"—
Which was enough for Tom and me
To go a-sailing on, till tea.

We sailed along for days and days,
And had the very best of plays;
But Tom fell out and hurt his knee,
So there was no one left but me.

XIV
WHERE GO THE BOATS?

D A R K brown is the river,
   Golden is the sand.
It flows along for ever,
   With trees on either hand.

Green leaves a-floating,
   Castles of the foam,
Boats of mine a-boating—
   Where will all come home?

On goes the river
   And out past the mill,
Away down the valley,
   Away down the hill.

Away down the river,
A hundred miles or more,
Other little children
Shall bring my boats ashore.

XV

AUNTIE'S SKIRTS

W H E N E V E R Auntie moves around,
Her dresses make a curious sound;
They trail behind her up the floor,
And trundle after through the door.

XVI

THE LAND OF COUNTERPANE

W H E N I was sick and lay a-bed,
I had two pillows at my head,
And all my toys beside me lay
To keep me happy all the day.

And sometimes for an hour or so
I watched my leaden soldiers go,
With different uniforms and drills,
Among the bed-clothes, through the hills;

And sometimes sent my ships in fleets
All up and down among the sheets;
Or brought my trees and houses out,
And planted cities all about.

I was the giant great and still
That sits upon the pillow-hill,
And sees before him, dale and plain,
The pleasant land of counterpane.

XVII

THE LAND OF NOD

F R O M breakfast on through all the day
At home among my friends I stay,
But every night I go abroad
Afar into the land of Nod.

All by myself I have to go,
With none to tell me what to do—
All alone beside the streams
And up the mountain-sides of dreams.

The strangest things are there for me,
Both things to eat and things to see,
And many frightening sights abroad
Till morning in the land of Nod.

Try as I like to find the way,
I never can get back by day,
Nor can remember plain and clear
The curious music that I hear.

XVIII

MY SHADOW

I H A V E a little shadow that goes in and out with me,
And what can be the use of him is more than I can see.
He is very, very like me from the heels up to the head;
And I see him jump before me, when I jump into my bed.

The funniest thing about him is the way he likes to grow—
Not at all like proper children, which is always very slow;
For he sometimes shoots up taller like an india-rubber ball,
And he sometimes gets so little that there's none of him at all.

He hasn't got a notion of how children ought to play,
And can only make a fool of me in every sort of way.
He stays so close beside me, he's a coward you can see;
I'd think shame to stick to nursie as that shadow sticks to me!

One morning, very early, before the sun was up,
I rose and found the shining dew on every buttercup;
But my lazy little shadow, like an arrant sleepy-head,
Had stayed at home behind me and was fast asleep in bed.

XIX

SYSTEM

E V E R Y night my prayers I say,
And get my dinner every day;
And every day that I've been good,
I get an orange after food.

The child that is not clean and neat,
With lots of toys and things to eat,
He is a naughty child, I'm sure—
Or else his dear papa is poor.

XX

A GOOD BOY

I W O K E before the morning, I was happy all the day
I never said an ugly word, but smiled and stuck to play.

And now at last the sun is going down behind the wood,
And I am very happy, for I know that I've been good.

My bed is waiting cool and fresh, with linen smooth and fair,
And I must off to sleepsin-by, and not forget my prayer.

I know that, till to-morrow I shall see the sun arise,
No ugly dream shall fright my mind, no ugly sight my eyes.

But slumber hold me tightly till I waken in the dawn,
And hear the thrushes singing in the lilacs round the lawn.

XXI

ESCAPE AT BEDTIME

T H E lights from the parlour and kitchen shone out
Through the blinds and the windows and bars;
And high overhead and all moving about,
There were thousands of millions of stars.
There ne'er were such thousands of leaves on a tree,
Nor of people in church or the Park,
As the crowds of the stars that looked down upon me,
And that glittered and winked in the dark.

The Dog, and the Plough, and the Hunter, and all,
And the star of the sailor, and Mars,
These shone in the sky, and the pail by the wall
Would be half full of water and stars.
They saw me at last, and they chased me with cries,
And they soon had me packed into bed;
But the glory kept shining and bright in my eyes,
And the stars going round in my head.

XXII

MARCHING SONG

B R I N G the comb and play upon it!
Marching, here we come!
Willie cocks his highland bonnet,
Johnnie beats the drum.

Mary Jane commands the party,
Peter leads the rear;
Feet in time, alert and hearty,
Each a Grenadier!

All in the most martial manner
Marching double-quick;
While the napkin like a banner
Waves upon the stick!

Here's enough of fame and pillage,
Great commander Jane!
Now that we've been round the village,
Let's go home again.

XXIII

THE COW

T H E friendly cow all red and white,
I love with all my heart:
She gives me cream with all her might,
To eat with apple-tart.

She wanders lowing here and there,
And yet she cannot stray,
All in the pleasant open air,
The pleasant light of day;

And blown by all the winds that pass
And wet with all the showers,
She walks among the meadow grass
And eats the meadow flowers.

XXIV

HAPPY THOUGHT

T H E world is so full of a number of things,
I'm sure we should all be as happy as kings.

XXV

THE WIND

I S A W you toss the kites on high
And blow the birds about the sky;
And all around I heard you pass,
Like ladies' skirts across the grass—
    O wind, a-blowing all day long,
    O wind, that sings so loud a song!

I saw the different things you did,
But always you yourself you hid.
I felt you push, I heard you call,
I could not see yourself at all—
    O wind, a-blowing all day long,
    O wind, that sings so loud a song!

O you that are so strong and cold,
O blower, are you young or old?
Are you a beast of field and tree,
Or just a stronger child than me?
    O wind, a-blowing all day long,
    O wind, that sings so loud a song!

XXVI

KEEPSAKE MILL

O V E R the borders, a sin without pardon,
    Breaking the branches and crawling below,
Out through the breach in the wall of the garden,
    Down by the banks of the river, we go.

Here is the mill with the humming of thunder,
    Here is the weir with the wonder of foam,
Here is the sluice with the race running under—
    Marvellous places, though handy to home!

Sounds of the village grow stiller and stiller,
  Stiller the note of the birds on the hill;
Dusty and dim are the eyes of the miller,
  Deaf are his ears with the moil of the mill.

Years may go by, and the wheel in the river
  Wheel as it wheels for us, children, to-day,
Wheel and keep roaring and foaming for ever
  Long after all of the boys are away.

Home from the Indies and home from the ocean,
  Heroes and soldiers we all shall come home;
Still we shall find the old mill wheel in motion,
  Turning and churning that river to foam.

You with the bean that I gave when we quarrelled,
  I with your marble of Saturday last,
Honoured and old and all gaily apparelled,
  Here we shall meet and remember the past.

XXVII

GOOD AND BAD CHILDREN

CHILDREN, you are very little,
And your bones are very brittle;
If you would grow great and stately,
You must try to walk sedately.

You must still be bright and quiet,
And content with simple diet;
And remain, through all bewild'ring,
Innocent and honest children.

Happy hearts and happy faces,
Happy play in grassy places—
That was how, in ancient ages,
Children grew to kings and sages.

But the unkind and the unruly,
And the sort who eat unduly,
They must never hope for glory—
Theirs is quite a different story!

Cruel children, crying babies,
All grow up as geese and gabies,
Hated, as their age increases,
By their nephews and their nieces.

XXVIII

FOREIGN CHILDREN

LITTLE Indian, Sioux or Crow,
Little frosty Eskimo,
Little Turk or Japanee,
O! don't you wish that you were me?

You have seen the scarlet trees
And the lions over seas;
You have eaten ostrich eggs,
And turned the turtles off their legs.

Such a life is very fine,
But it's not so nice as mine:
You must often, as you trod,
Have wearied *not* to be abroad.

You have curious things to eat,
I am fed on proper meat;
You must dwell beyond the foam,
But I am safe and live at home.
    Little Indian, Sioux or Crow,
    Little frosty Eskimo,
    Little Turk or Japanee,
    O! don't you wish that you were me?

XXIX

THE SUN'S TRAVELS

THE sun is not a-bed, when I
At night upon my pillow lie;
Still round the earth his way he takes,
And morning after morning makes.

While here at home, in shining day,
We round the sunny garden play,
Each little Indian sleepy-head
Is being kissed and put to bed.

And when at eve I rise from tea,
Day dawns beyond the Atlantic Sea;
And all the children in the West
Are getting up and being dressed.

XXX

THE LAMPLIGHTER

MY tea is nearly ready and the sun has left the sky;
It's time to take the window to see Leerie going by;
For every night at teatime and before you take your seat,
With lantern and with ladder he comes posting up the street.

Now Tom would be a driver and Maria go to sea,
And my papa's a banker and as rich as he can be;
But I, when I am stronger and can choose what I'm to do,
O Leerie, I'll go round at night and light the lamps with you!

For we are very lucky, with a lamp before the door,
And Leerie stops to light it as he lights so many more;
And O! before you hurry by with ladder and with light,
O Leerie, see a little child and nod to him to-night!

XXXI

MY BED IS A BOAT

M Y bed is like a little boat;
 Nurse helps me in when I embark;
She girds me in my sailor's coat
 And starts me in the dark

At night, I go on board and say
 Good-night to all my friends on shore;
I shut my eyes and sail away
 And see and hear no more.

And sometimes things to bed I take,
 As prudent sailors have to do;
Perhaps a slice of wedding-cake,
 Perhaps a toy or two.

All night across the dark we steer;
 But when the day returns at last,
Safe in my room, beside the pier,
 I find my vessel fast.

XXXII

THE MOON

T H E moon has a face like the clock in the hall;
She shines on thieves on the garden wall,
On streets and fields and harbour quays,
And birdies asleep in the forks of the trees.

The squalling cat and the squeaking mouse,
The howling dog by the door of the house,
The bat that lies in bed at noon,
All love to be out by the light of the moon.

But all of the things that belong to the day
Cuddle to sleep to be out of her way;
And flowers and children close their eyes
Till up in the morning the sun shall arise.

XXXIII

THE SWING

H O W do you like to go up in a swing,
   Up in the air so blue?
Oh, I do think it the pleasantest thing
   Ever a child can do!

Up in the air and over the wall,
   Till I can see so wide,
Rivers and trees and cattle and all
   Over the countryside—

Till I look down on the garden green,
   Down on the roof so brown—
Up in the air I go flying again,
   Up in the air and down!

XXXIV

TIME TO RISE

A B I R D I E with a yellow bill
Hopped upon the window sill,
Cocked his shining eye and said:
"Ain't you 'shamed, you sleepy-head!"

XXXV

LOOKING-GLASS RIVER

S M O O T H it slides upon its travel,
   Here a wimple, there a gleam—
      O the clean gravel!
      O the smooth stream!

Sailing blossoms, silver fishes,
   Paven pools as clear as air—
     How a child wishes
     To live down there!

We can see our coloured faces
   Floating on the shaken pool
     Down in cool places,
     Dim and very cool;

Till a wind or water wrinkle,
   Dipping marten, plumping trout,
     Spreads in a twinkle
     And blots all out.

See the rings pursue each other;
   All below grows black as night,
     Just as if mother
     Had blown out the light!

Patience, children, just a minute—
   See the spreading circles die;
     The stream and all in it
     Will clear by-and-by.

XXXVI

FAIRY BREAD

COME up here, O dusty feet!
   Here is fairy bread to eat.
Here in my retiring room,
   Children, you may dine
On the golden smell of broom
   And the shade of pine;
And when you have eaten well,
Fairy stories hear and tell.

XXXVII

FROM A RAILWAY CARRIAGE

FASTER than fairies, faster than witches,
Bridges and houses, hedges and ditches;
And charging along like troops in a battle,
All through the meadows the horses and cattle:
All of the sights of the hill and the plain
Fly as thick as driving rain;
And ever again, in the wink of an eye,
Painted stations whistle by.

Here is a child who clambers and scrambles,
All by himself and gathering brambles;
Here is a tramp who stands and gazes;
And there is the green for stringing the daisies!
Here is a cart run away in the road
Lumping along with man and load;
And here is a mill and there is a river:
Each a glimpse and gone for ever!

XXXVIII

WINTER-TIME

LATE lies the wintry sun a-bed,
A frosty, fiery sleepy-head;
Blinks but an hour or two; and then,
A blood-red orange, sets again.

Before the stars have left the skies,
At morning in the dark I rise;
And shivering in my nakedness,
By the cold candle, bathe and dress.

Close by the jolly fire I sit
To warm my frozen bones a bit;
Or with a reindeer-sled, explore
The colder countries round the door.

When to go out, my nurse doth wrap
Me in my comforter and cap;
The cold wind burns my face, and blows
Its frosty pepper up my nose.

Black are my steps on silver sod;
Thick blows my frosty breath abroad;
And tree and house, and hill and lake,
Are frosted like a wedding-cake.

XXXIX

THE HAYLOFT

THROUGH all the pleasant meadow-side
The grass grew shoulder-high,
Till the shining scythes went far and wide
And cut it down to dry.

These green and sweetly smelling crops
They led in waggons home;
And they piled them here in mountain tops
For mountaineers to roam.

Here is Mount Clear, Mount Rusty-Nail,
Mount Eagle and Mount High;
The mice that in these mountains dwell,
No happier are than I!

O what a joy to clamber there,
O what a place for play,
With the sweet, the dim, the dusty air,
The happy hills of hay!

XL

FAREWELL TO THE FARM

T H E coach is at the door at last;
The eager children, mounting fast
And kissing hands, in chorus sing:
Good-bye, good-bye, to everything!

To house and garden, field and lawn,
The meadow-gates we swang upon,
To pump and stable, tree and swing,
Good-bye, good-bye, to everything!

And fare you well for evermore,
O ladder at the hayloft door,
O hayloft where the cobwebs cling,
Good-bye, good-bye, to everything!

Crack goes the whip, and off we go;
The trees and houses smaller grow;
Last, round the woody turn we swing:
Good-bye, good-bye, to everything!

XLI

NORTH-WEST PASSAGE

1. Good Night

W H E N the bright lamp is carried in,
The sunless hours again begin;
O'er all without, in field and lane,
The haunted night returns again.

Now we behold the embers flee
About the firelit hearth; and see
Our faces painted as we pass,
Like pictures, on the window-glass.

Must we to bed indeed? Well then,
Let us arise and go like men,
And face with an undaunted tread
The long black passage up to bed.

Farewell, O brother, sister, sire!
O pleasant party round the fire!
The songs you sing, the tales you tell,
Till far to-morrow, fare ye well!

2. Shadow March

All round the house is the jet-black night;
    It stares through the window-pane;
It crawls in the corners, hiding from the light,
    And it moves with the moving flame.

Now my little heart goes a-beating like a drum,
    With the breath of the Bogie in my hair;
And all round the candle the crooked shadows come,
    And go marching along up the stair.

The shadow of the balusters, the shadow of the lamp,
    The shadow of the child that goes to bed—
All the wicked shadows coming tramp, tramp, tramp,
    With the black night overhead.

3. In Port

Last, to the chamber where I lie
My fearful footsteps patter nigh,
And come from out the cold and gloom
Into my warm and cheerful room.

There, safe arrived, we turn about
To keep the coming shadows out,
And close the happy door at last
On all the perils that we past.

Then, when mamma goes by to bed,
She shall come in with tip-toe tread,
And see me lying warm and fast
And in the Land of Nod at last.

The Child Alone

I

THE UNSEEN PLAYMATE

W H E N children are playing alone on the green
In comes the playmate that never was seen.
When children are happy and lonely and good,
The Friend of the Children comes out of the wood.

Nobody heard him and nobody saw,
His is a picture you never could draw,
But he's sure to be present, abroad or at home,
When children are happy and playing alone.

He lies in the laurels, he runs on the grass,
He sings when you tinkle the musical glass;
Whene'er you are happy and cannot tell why,
The Friend of the Children is sure to be by!

He loves to be little, he hates to be big,
'T is he that inhabits the caves that you dig;
'T is he when you play with your soldiers of tin
That sides with the Frenchmen and never can win.

'T is he, when at night you go off to your bed,
Bids you go to your sleep and not trouble your head;
For wherever they're lying, in cupboard or shelf,
'T is he will take care of your playthings himself!

II

MY SHIP AND I

O IT'S I that am the captain of a tidy little ship,
  Of a ship that goes a-sailing on the pond;
And my ship it keeps a-turning all around and all about;
But when I'm a little older, I shall find the secret out
  How to send my vessel sailing on beyond.

For I mean to grow as little as the dolly at the helm,
  And the dolly I intend to come alive;
And with him beside to help me, it's a-sailing I shall go,
It's a-sailing on the water, when the jolly breezes blow
  And the vessel goes a divie-divie-dive.

O it's then you'll see me sailing through the rushes and the
                                                          reeds,
  And you'll hear the water singing at the prow;
For beside the dolly sailor, I'm to voyage and explore,
To land upon the island where no dolly was before,
  And to fire the penny cannon in the bow.

III

MY KINGDOM

DOWN by a shining water well
I found a very little dell,
    No higher than my head.
The heather and the gorse about
In summer bloom were coming out,
    Some yellow and some red.

I called the little pool a sea;
The little hills were big to me;
    For I am very small.
I made a boat, I made a town,
I searched the caverns up and down,
    And named them one and all.

And all about was mine, I said,
The little sparrows overhead,
   The little minnows too.
This was the world and I was king;
For me the bees came by to sing,
   For me the swallows flew.

I played there were no deeper seas,
Nor any wider plains than these,
   Nor other kings than me.
At last I heard my mother call
Out from the house at even fall,
   To call me home to tea.

And I must rise and leave my dell,
And leave my dimpled water well,
   And leave my heather blooms.
Alas! and as my home I neared,
How very big my nurse appeared,
   How great and cool the rooms!

IV

PICTURE-BOOKS IN WINTER

SUMMER fading, winter comes—
Frosty mornings, tingling thumbs,
Window robins, winter rooks,
And the picture story-books.

Water now is turned to stone
Nurse and I can walk upon;
Still we find the flowing brooks
In the picture story-books.

All the pretty things put by,
Wait upon the children's eye,
Sheep and shepherds, trees and crooks,
In the picture story-books.

We may see how all things are,
Seas and cities, near and far,

And the flying fairies' looks,
In the picture story-books.

How am I to sing your praise,
Happy chimney-corner days,
Sitting safe in nursery nooks,
Reading picture story-books?

V

MY TREASURES

THESE nuts, that I keep in the back of the nest
Where all my lead soldiers are lying at rest,
Were gathered in autumn by nursie and me
In a wood with a well by the side of the sea.

This whistle we made (and how clearly it sounds!)
By the side of a field at the end of the grounds.
Of a branch of a plane, with a knife of my own,
It was nursie who made it, and nursie alone!

The stone, with the white and the yellow and grey,
We discovered I cannot tell *how* far away;
And I carried it back although weary and cold,
For though father denies it, I'm sure it is gold.

But of all my treasures the last is the king,
For there's very few children possess such a thing;
And that is a chisel, both handle and blade,
Which a man who was really a carpenter made.

VI

BLOCK CITY

WHAT are you able to build with your blocks?
Castles and palaces, temples and docks.
Rain may keep raining, and others go roam,
But I can be happy and building at home.

Let the sofa be mountains, the carpet be sea,
There I'll establish a city for me:
A kirk and a mill and a palace besides,
And a harbour as well where my vessels may ride.

Great is the palace with pillar and wall,
A sort of a tower on the top of it all,
And steps coming down in an orderly way
To where my toy vessels lie safe in the bay.

This one is sailing and that one is moored:
Hark to the song of the sailors on board!
And see on the steps of my palace, the kings
Coming and going with presents and things!

Now I have done with it, down let it go!
All in a moment the town is laid low.
Block upon block lying scattered and free,
What is there left of my town by the sea?

Yet as I saw it, I see it again,
The kirk and the palace, the ships and the men,
And as long as I live and where'er I may be,
I'll always remember my town by the sea.

VII

THE LAND OF STORY-BOOKS

A T evening when the lamp is lit,
Around the fire my parents sit;
They sit at home and talk and sing,
And do not play at anything.

Now, with my little gun, I crawl
All in the dark along the wall,
And follow round the forest track
Away behind the sofa back.

There, in the night, where none can spy,
All in my hunter's camp I lie,
And play at books that I have read
Till it is time to go to bed.

These are the hills, these are the woods,
These are my starry solitudes;
And there the river by whose brink
The roaring lions come to drink.

I see the others far away
As if in firelit camp they lay,
And I, like to an Indian scout,
Around their party prowled about.

So, when my nurse comes in for me,
Home I return across the sea,
And go to bed with backward looks
At my dear land of Story-books.

VIII

ARMIES IN THE FIRE

T H E lamps now glitter down the street;
Faintly sound the falling feet;
And the blue even slowly falls
About the garden trees and walls.

Now in the falling of the gloom
The red fire paints the empty room:
And warmly on the roof it looks,
And flickers on the backs of books.

Armies march by tower and spire
Of cities blazing, in the fire;—
Till as I gaze with staring eyes,
The armies fade, the lustre dies.

Then once again the glow returns;
Again the phantom city burns;
And down the red-hot valley, lo!
The phantom armies marching go!

Blinking embers, tell me true
Where are those armies marching to,
And what the burning city is
That crumbles in your furnaces!

IX

THE LITTLE LAND

WHEN at home alone I sit
And am very tired of it,
I have just to shut my eyes
To go sailing through the skies—
To go sailing far away
To the pleasant Land of Play;
To the fairy land afar
Where the Little People are;
Where the clover-tops are trees,
And the rain-pools are the seas,
And the leaves like little ships
Sail about on tiny trips;
And above the daisy tree
    Through the grasses,
High o'erhead the Bumble Bee
    Hums and passes.

In that forest to and fro
I can wander, I can go;
See the spider and the fly,
And the ants go marching by
Carrying parcels with their feet
Down the green and grassy street.
I can in the sorrel sit
Where the ladybird alit.

I can climb the jointed grass;
    And on high
See the greater swallows pass
    In the sky,
And the round sun rolling by
Heeding no such things as I.

Through that forest I can pass
Till, as in a looking-glass,
Humming fly and daisy tree
And my tiny self I see,
Painted very clear and neat
On the rain-pool at my feet.
Should a leaflet come to land
Drifting near to where I stand,
Straight I'll board that tiny boat
Round the rain-pool sea to float.

Little thoughtful creatures sit
On the grassy coats of it;
Little things with lovely eyes
See me sailing with surprise.
Some are clad in armour green—
(These have sure to battle been!)—
Some are pied with ev'ry hue,
Black and crimson, gold and blue;
Some have wings and swift are gone;—
But they all look kindly on.

When my eyes I once again
 Open, and see all things plain:
High bare walls, great bare floor;
Great big knobs on drawer and door;
Great big people perched on chairs,
Stitching tucks and mending tears,
Each a hill that I could climb,
And talking nonsense all the time—
    O dear me,
    That I could be
A sailor on the rain-pool sea,

A climber in the clover tree,
And just come back, a sleepy-head,
Late at night to go to bed.

Garden Days

I

NIGHT AND DAY

WHEN the golden day is done,
  Through the closing portal,
Child and garden, flower and sun,
  Vanish all things mortal.

As the blinding shadows fall
  As the rays diminish
Under evening's cloak, they all
  Roll away and vanish.

Garden darkened, daisy shut,
  Child in bed, they slumber—
Glow-worm in the highway rut,
  Mice among the lumber.

In the darkness houses shine,
  Parents move with candles;
Till on all, the night divine
  Turns the bedroom handles.

Till at last the day begins
In the east a-breaking,
In the hedges and the whins
  Sleeping birds a-waking.

In the darkness shapes of things,
  Houses, trees and hedges,
Clearer grow; and sparrow's wings
  Beat on window ledges.

These shall wake the yawning maid;
  She the door shall open—
Finding dew on garden glade
  And the morning broken.

There my garden grows again
  Green and rosy painted,
As at eve behind the pane
  From my eyes it fainted.

Just as it was shut away,
  Toy-like, in the even,
Here I see it glow with day
  Under glowing heaven.

Every path and every plot,
  Every bush of roses,
Every blue forget-me-not
  Where the dew reposes,

"Up!" they cry, "the day is come
  On the smiling valleys:
We have beat the morning drum;
  Playmate, join your allies!"

II

NEST EGGS

BIRDS all the sunny day
  Flutter and quarrel
Here in the arbour-like
  Tent of the laurel.

Here in the fork
  The brown nest is seated;
Four little blue eggs
  The mother keeps heated.

While we stand watching her,
    Staring like gabies,
Safe in each egg are the
    Bird's little babies.

Soon the frail eggs they shall
    Chip, and upspringing,
Make all the April woods
    Merry with singing.

Younger than we are,
    O children, and frailer,
Soon in blue air they'll be,
    Singer and sailor.

We, so much older,
    Taller and stronger,
We shall look down on the
    Birdies no longer.

They shall go flying
    With musical speeches
High overhead in the
    Tops of the beeches.

In spite of our wisdom
    And sensible talking,
We on our feet must go
    Plodding and walking.

III

THE FLOWERS

A L L the names I know from nurse:
Gardener's garters, Shepherd's purse,
Bachelor's buttons, Lady's smock,
And the Lady Hollyhock.

Fairy places, fairy things,
Fairy woods where the wild bee wings.
Tiny trees for tiny dames—
These must all be fairy names!

Tiny woods below whose boughs
Shady fairies weave a house;
Tiny tree-tops, rose or thyme,
Where the braver fairies climb!

Fair are grown-up people's trees,
But the fairest woods are these;
Where if I were not so tall,
I should live for good and all.

IV

SUMMER SUN

GREAT is the sun, and wide he goes
Through empty heaven without repose;
And in the blue and glowing days
More thick than rain he showers his rays.

Though closer still the blinds we pull
To keep the shady parlour cool,
Yet he will find a chink or two
To slip his golden fingers through.

The dusty attic spider-clad
He, through the keyhole, maketh glad;
And through the broken edge of tiles,
Into the laddered hay-loft smiles.

Meantime his golden face around
He bares to all the garden ground,
And sheds a warm and glittering look
Among the ivy's inmost nook.

Above the hills, along the blue,
Round the bright air with footing true,
To please the child, to paint the rose,
The gardener of the World, he goes.

V

THE DUMB SOLDIER

W H E N the grass was closely mown,
Walking on the lawn alone,
In the turf a hole I found
And hid a soldier underground.

Spring and daisies came apace;
Grasses hide my hiding place;
Grasses run like a green sea
O'er the lawn up to my knee.

Under grass alone he lies,
Looking up with leaden eyes,
Scarlet coat and pointed gun,
To the stars and to the sun.

When the grass is ripe like grain,
When the scythe is stoned again,
When the lawn is shaven clear,
Then my hole shall reappear.

I shall find him, never fear,
I shall find my grenadier;
But for all that's gone and come,
I shall find my soldier dumb.

He has lived, a little thing,
In the grassy woods of spring;

Done, if he could tell me true,
Just as I should like to do.

He has seen the starry hours
And the springing of the flowers;
And the fairy things that pass
In the forests of the grass.

In the silence he has heard
Talking bee and ladybird,
And the butterfly has flown
O'er him as he lay alone.

Not a word will he disclose,
Not a word of all he knows.
I must lay him on the shelf,
And make up the tale myself.

VI

AUTUMN FIRES

IN the other gardens
And all up the vale,
From the autumn bonfires
See the smoke trail!

Pleasant summer over
And all the summer flowers,
The red fire blazes,
The grey smoke towers.

Sing a song of seasons!
Something bright in all!
Flowers in the summer,
Fires in the fall!

VII

THE GARDENER

T H E gardener does not love to talk,
He makes me keep the gravel walk;
And when he puts his tools away,
He locks the door and take the key.

Away behind the currant row
Where no one else but cook may go,
Far in the plots, I see him dig,
Old and serious, brown and big.

He digs the flowers, green, red, and blue,
Nor wishes to be spoken to.
He digs the flowers and cuts the hay,
And never seems to want to play.

Silly gardener! summer goes,
And winter comes with pinching toes,
When the garden bare and brown
You must lay your barrow down.

Well now, and while the summer stays,
To profit by these garden days,
O how much wiser you would be
To play at Indian wars with me!

VIII

HISTORICAL ASSOCIATIONS

D E A R Uncle Jim, this garden ground
That now you smoke your pipe around,
Has seen immortal actions done
And valiant battles lost and won.

Here we had best on tip-toe tread,
While I for safety march ahead,
For this is that enchanted ground
Where all who loiter slumber sound.

Here is the sea, here is the sand,
Here is simple Shepherd's Land,
Here are the fairy hollyhocks,
And there are Ali Baba's rocks.

But yonder, see! apart and high,
Frozen Siberia lies; where I,
With Robert Bruce and William Tell,
Was bound by an enchanter's spell.

Envoys

I

TO WILLIE AND HENRIETTA

I F two may read aright
These rhymes of old delight
And house and garden play,
You two, my cousins, and you only, may.

You in a garden green
With me were king and queen
Were hunter, soldier, tar,
And all the thousand things that children are.

Now in the elders' seat
We rest with quiet feet,
And from the window-bay
We watch the children, our successors, play.

"Time was," the golden head
Irrevocably said;
But time which none can bind,
While flowing fast away, leaves love behind.

II

TO MY MOTHER

Y O U too, my mother, read my rhymes
For love of unforgotten times,
And you may chance to hear once more
The little feet along the floor.

III

TO AUNTIE

CHIEF of our aunts—not only I,
But all your dozen of nurselings cry—
What did the other children do?
And what were childhood, wanting you?

IV

TO MINNIE

T H E red room with the giant bed
Where none but elders laid their head;
The little room where you and I
Did for awhile together lie
And, simple, suitor, I your hand
In decent marriage did demand;
The great day nursery, best of all,
With pictures pasted on the wall
And leaves upon the blind—

A pleasant room wherein to wake
And hear the leafy garden shake
And rustle in the wind—
And pleasant there to lie in bed
And see the pictures overhead—
The wars about Sebastopol,
The grinning guns along the wall,
The daring escalade,
The plunging ships, the bleating sheep,
The happy children ankle-deep
And laughing as they wade:
All these are vanished clean away,
And the old manse is changed to-day;
It wears an altered face
And shields a stranger race.

The river, on from mill to mill,
Flows past our childhood's garden still;
But ah! we children never more
Shall watch it from the water-door!

Below the yew—it still is there—
Our phantom voices haunt the air
As we were still at play,
And I can hear them call and say:
"How far is it to Babylon?"

Ah, far enough, my dear,
Far, far enough from here—
Yet you have farther gone!
"Can I get there by candlelight?"
So goes the old refrain.
I do not know—perchance you might—
But only, children, hear it right,
Ah, never to return again!
The eternal dawn, beyond a doubt,
Shall break on hill and plain,
And put all stars and candles out
Ere we be young again.

To you in distant India, these
I send across the seas,
Nor count it far across.
For which of us forgets
The Indian cabinets,
The bones of antelope, the wings of albatross,
The pied and painted birds and beans,
The junks and bangles, beads and screens,
The gods and sacred bells,
And the loud-humming, twisted shells!
The level of the parlour floor
Was honest, homely, Scottish shore;
But when we climbed upon a chair,
Behold the gorgeous East was there!
Be this a fable; and behold
Me in the parlour as of old,
And Minnie just above me set
In the quaint Indian cabinet!
Smiling and kind, you grace a shelf
Too high for me to reach myself.
Reach down a hand, my dear, and take
These rhymes for old acquaintance' sake!

V

TO MY NAME-CHILD

I

SOME day soon this rhyming volume, if you learn with proper
                                                          speed,
Little Louis Sanchez, will be given you to read.
Then shall you discover, that your name was printed down
By the English printers, long before, in London town.

In the great and busy city where the East and West are met,
All the little letters did the English printer set;
While you thought of nothing, and were still too young to play,
Foreign people thought of you in places far away.

Ay, and while you slept, a baby, over all the English lands
Other little children took the volume in their hands;
Other children questioned, in their homes across the seas:
Who was little Louis, won't you tell us, mother, please?

Now that you have spelt your lesson, lay it down and go and play,
Seeking shells and seaweed on the sands of Monterey,
Watching all the mighty whalebones, lying buried by the breeze,
Tiny sandy-pipers, and the huge Pacific seas.

And remember in your playing, as the sea-fog rolls to you,
Long ere you could read it, how I told you what to do;
And that while you thought of no one, nearly half the world
                                                    away
Some one thought of Louis on the beach of Monterey!

VI

TO ANY READER

A S from the house your mother sees
You playing round the garden trees,
So you may see, if you will look
Through the windows of this book,
Another child, far, far away,
And in another garden, play.
But do not think you can at all,
By knocking on the window, call
That child to hear you. He intent
Is all on his play-business bent.
He does not hear; he will not look,
Nor yet be lured out of this book.
For, long ago, the truth to say,
He has grown up and gone away,
And it is but a child of air
That lingers in the garden there.

THE SONG OF RAHÉRO

A LEGEND OF TAHITI

TO ORI A ORI

Ori, my brother in the island mode,
In every tongue and meaning much my friend,
This story of your country and your clan,
In your loved house, your too much honoured
guest
I made in English. Take it, being done;
And let me sign it with the name you gave.

TERIITERA.

1. *The Slaying of Támatéa*

I T fell in the days of old, as the men of Taiárapu tell,
A youth went forth to the fishing, and fortune favoured him well.
Támatéa his name: gullible, simple, and kind,
Comely of countenance, nimble of body, empty of mind,
His mother ruled him and loved him beyond the wont of a wife,
Serving the lad for eyes and living herself in his life.

Alone from the sea and the fishing came Támatéa the fair,
Urging his boat to the beach, and the mother awaited him there,
—"Long may you live!" said she. "Your fishing has sped to a wish.
And now let us choose for the king the fairest of all your fish.
For fear inhabits the palace and grudging grows in the land,
Marked is the sluggardly foot and marked the niggardly hand,
The hours and the miles are counted, the tributes numbered and
weighed,

And woe to him that comes short, and woe to him that delayed!"
So spoke on the beach the mother, and counselled the wiser thing.
For Rahéro stirred in the country and secretly mined the king.
Nor were the signals wanting of how the leaven wrought,
In the cords of obedience loosed and the tributes grudgingly
                                                        brought.
And when last to the temple of Oro the boat with the victim sped,
And the priest uncovered the basket and looked on the face of the
                                                        dead,
Trembling fell upon all at sight of an ominous thing,
For there was the aito [1] dead, and he of the house of the king.

So spake on the beach the mother, matter worthy of note,
And wattled a basket well, and chose a fish from the boat;
And Támatéa the pliable shouldered the basket and went,
And travelled, and sang as he travelled, a lad that was well
                                                        content.
Still the way of his going was round by the roaring coast,
Where the ring of the reef is broke and the trades run riot the
                                                        most.
On his left, with smoke as of battle, the billows battered the land;
Unscalable, turretted mountains rose on the inner hand.
And cape, and village, and river, and vale, and mountain above,
Each had a name in the land for men to remember and love;
And never the name of a place, but lo! a song in its praise:
Ancient and unforgotten, songs of the earlier days,
That the elders taught to the young, and at night, in the full of
                                                        the moon,
Garlanded boys and maidens sang together in tune.
Támatéa the placable went with a lingering foot;
He sang as loud as a bird, he whistled hoarse as a flute;
He broiled in the sun, he breathed in the grateful shadow of trees,
In the icy stream of the rivers he waded over the knees;
And still in his empty mind crowded, a thousand-fold,
The deeds of the strong and the songs of the cunning heroes of
                                                        old.

And now was he come to a place Taiárapu honoured the most,
Where a silent valley of woods debouched on the noisy coast,
Spewing a level river. There was a haunt of Pai. [2]

There, in his potent youth, when his parents drove him to die,
Honoura lived like a beast, lacking the lamp and the fire,
Washed by the rains of the trade and clotting his hair in the mire;
And there, so mighty his hands, he bent the tree to his foot—
So keen the spur of his hunger, he plucked it naked of fruit.
There, as she pondered the clouds for the shadow of coming ills,
Ahupu, the woman of song, walked on high on the hills.

Of these was Rahéro sprung, a man of a godly race;
And inherited cunning of spirit and beauty of body and face.
Of yore in his youth, as an aito, Rahéro wandered the land,
Delighting maids with his tongue, smiting men with his hand.
Famous he was in his youth; but before the midst of his life
Paused, and fashioned a song of farewell to glory and strife.

House of mine (it went), house upon the sea,
Belov'd of all my fathers, more belov'd by me!
Vale of the strong Honoura, deep ravine of Pai,
Again in your woody summits I hear the trade-wind cry.

House of mine, in your walls, strong sounds the sea,
Of all sounds on earth, dearest sound to me.
I have heard the applause of men, I have heard it arise and die:
Sweeter now in my house I hear the trade-wind cry.

These were the words of his singing, other the thought of his
                                                          heart;
For secret desire of glory vexed him, dwelling apart.
Lazy and crafty he was, and loved to lie in the sun,
And loved the cackle of talk and the true word uttered in fun;
Lazy he was, his roof was ragged, his table was lean,
And the fish swam safe in his sea, and he gathered the near and
                                                          the green.
He sat in his house and laughed, but he loathed the king of the
                                                          land,
And he uttered the grudging word under the covering hand.
Treason spread from his door; and he looked for a day to come,
A day of the crowding people, a day of the summoning drum,

When the vote should be taken, the king be driven forth in dis-
grace,
And Rahéro, the laughing and lazy, sit and rule in his place.
Here Támatéa came, and beheld the house on the brook;
And Rahéro was there by the way and covered an oven to cook.[3]
Naked he was to the loins, but the tattoo covered the lack,
And the sun and the shadow of palms dappled his muscular back.
Swiftly he lifted his head at the fall of the coming feet,
And the water sprang in his mouth with a sudden desire of meat;
For he marked the basket carried, covered from flies and the sun; [4]
And Rahéro buried his fire, but the meat in his house was done.

Forth he stepped; and took, and delayed the boy, by the hand;
And vaunted the joys of meat and the ancient ways of the land:
—"Our sires of old in Taiárapu, they that created the race,
Ate ever with eager hand, nor regarded season or place,
Ate in the boat at the oar, on the way afoot; and at night
Arose in the midst of dreams to rummage the house for a bite.
It is good for the youth in his turn to follow the way of the sire;
And behold how fitting the time! for here do I cover my fire."
—"I see the fire for the cooking but never the meat to cook,"
Said Támatéa.—"Tut!" said Rahéro. "Here in the brook
And there in the tumbling sea, the fishes are thick as flies,
Hungry like healthy men, and like pigs for savour and size:
Crayfish crowding the river, sea-fish thronging the sea."
—"Well it may be," says the other, "and yet be nothing to me.
Fain would I eat, but alas! I have needful matter in hand,
Since I carry my tribute of fish to the jealous king of the land."
Now at the word a light sprang in Rahéro's eyes.
"I will gain me a dinner," thought he, "and lend the king a sur-
prise."
And he took the lad by the arm, as they stood by the side of the
track,
And smiled, and rallied, and flattered, and pushed him forward
and back.
It was "You that sing like a bird, I never have heard you sing,"
And "The lads when I was a lad were none so feared of a king.
And of what account is an hour, when the heart is empty of guile?
But come, and sit in the house and laugh with the women awhile;
And I will but drop my hook, and behold! the dinner made."

So Támatéa the pliable hung up his fish in the shade
On a tree by the side of the way; and Rahéro carried him in,
Smiling as smiles the fowler when flutters the bird to the gin,
And chose him a shining hook,[5] and viewed it with sedulous eye,
And breathed and burnished it well on the brawn of his naked
thigh,
And set a mat for the gull, and bade him be merry and bide,
Like a man concerned for his guest, and the fishing, and nothing
beside.
Now when Rahéro was forth, he paused and hearkened, and heard
The gull jest in the house and the women laugh at his word;
And stealthily crossed to the side of the way, to the shady place
Where the basket hung on a mango; and craft transfigured his
face.
Deftly he opened the basket, and took of the fat of the fish,
The cut of kings and chieftains, enough for a goodly dish.
This he wrapped in a leaf, set on the fire to cook
And buried; and next the marred remains of the tribute he took,
And doubled and packed them well, and covered the basket close
—"There is a buffet, my king," quoth he, "and a nauseous dose!"—
And hung the basket again in the shade, in a cloud of flies
—"And there is a sauce to your dinner, king of the crafty eyes!"

Soon as the oven was open, the fish smelt excellent good.
In the shade, by the house of Rahéro, down they sat to their food,
And cleared the leaves [6] in silence, or uttered a jest and laughed,
And raising the cocoanut bowls, buried their faces and quaffed.
But chiefly in silence they ate; and soon as the meal was done,
Rahéro feigned to remember and measured the hour by the sun,
And "Támatéa," quoth he, "it is time to be jogging, my lad."

So Támatéa arose, doing ever the thing he was bade,
And carelessly shouldered the basket, and kindly saluted his host:
And again the way of his going was round by the roaring coast.
Long he went; and at length was aware of a pleasant green,
And the stems and shadows of palms, and roofs of lodges between.
There sate, in the door of his palace, the king on a kingly seat,
And aitos stood armed around, and the yottowas [7] sat at his feet.

But fear was a worm in his heart: fear darted his eyes;
And he probed men's faces for treasons and pondered their speech
for lies.
To him came Támatéa, the basket slung in his hand,
And paid him the due obeisance standing as vassals stand.
In silence hearkened the king, and closed the eyes in his face,
Harbouring odious thoughts and the baseless fears of the base;
In silence accepted the gift and sent the giver away.
So Támatéa departed, turning his back on the day.
And lo! as the king sat brooding, a rumour rose in the crowd;
The yottowas nudged and whispered, the commons murmured
aloud;
Tittering fell upon all at sight of the impudent thing,
At the sight of a gift unroyal flung in the face of a king.
And the face of the king turned white and red with anger and
shame
In their midst; and the heart in his body was water and then was
flame;
Till of a sudden, turning, he gripped an aito hard,
A youth that stood with his ómare,[8] one of the daily guard,
And spat in his ear a command, and pointed and uttered a name,
And hid in the shade of the house his impotent anger and shame.
Now Támatéa the fool was far on the homeward way,
The rising night in his face, behind him the dying day.
Rahéro saw him go by, and the heart of Rahéro was glad,
Devising shame to the king and nowise harm to the lad;
And all that dwelt by the way saw and saluted him well,
For he had the face of a friend and the news of the town to tell;
And pleased with the notice of folk, and pleased that his journey
was done,
Támatéa drew homeward, turning his back to the sun.
And now was the hour of the bath in Taiárapu; far and near
The lovely laughter of bathers rose and delighted his ear.
Night massed in the valleys; the sun on the mountain coast
Struck, end-long; and above the clouds embattled their host,
And glowed and gloomed on the heights; and the heads of the
palms were gems,
And far to the rising eve extended the shade of their stems;
And the shadow of Támatéa hovered already at home.

And sudden the sound of one coming and running light as the
                                                        foam
Struck on his ear; and he turned, and lo! a man on his track,
Girded and armed with an ómare, following hard at his back.
At a bound the man was upon him;—and, or ever a word was
                                                        said,
The loaded end of the ómare fell and laid him dead.

2. *The Venging of Támatéa*

Thus was Rahéro's treason; thus and no further it sped:
The king sat safe in his place and a kindly fool was dead.

But the mother of Támatéa arose with death in her eyes.
All night long, and the next, Taiárapu rang with her cries.
As when a babe in the wood turns with a chill of doubt
And perceives nor home, nor friends, for the trees have closed her
                                                        about,
The mountain rings and her breast is torn with the voice of
                                                        despair:
So the lion-like woman idly wearied the air
For awhile, and pierced men's hearing in vain, and wounded their
                                                        hearts.
But as when the weather changes at sea, in dangerous parts,
And sudden the hurricane wrack unrolls up the front of the sky,
At once the ship lies idle, the sails hang silent on high,
The breath of the wind that blew is blown out like the flame of a
                                                        lamp,
And the silent armies of death draw near with inaudible tramp:
So sudden, the voice of her weeping ceased; in silence she rose
And passed from the house of her sorrow, a woman clothed with
                                                        repose,
Carrying death in her breast and sharpening death with her hand.

Hither she went and thither in all the coasts of the land.
They tell that she feared not to slumber alone, in the dead of
                                                        night,
In accursed places; behold, unblenched, the ribbon of light [9]
Spin from temple to temple; guided the perilous skiff,

Abhorred not the paths of the mountain and trod the verge of the
cliff;
From end to end of the island, thought not the distance long,
But forth from king to king carried the tale of her wrong.
To king after king, as they sat in the palace door, she came,
Claiming kinship, declaiming verses, naming her name
And the names of all of her fathers; and still, with a heart on the
rack,
Jested to capture a hearing and laughed when they jested back:
So would deceive them awhile, and change and return in a breath,
And on all the men of Vaiau imprecate instant death;
And tempt her kings—for Vaiau was a rich and prosperous land,
And flatter—for who would attempt it but warriors mighty of
hand?
And change in a breath again and rise in a strain of song,
Invoking the beaten drums, beholding the fall of the strong,
Calling the fowls of the air to come and feast on the dead.
And they held the chin in silence, and heard her, and shook the
head;
For they knew the men of Taiárapu famous in battle and feast,
Marvellous eaters and smiters: the men of Vaiau not least.

To the land of the Námunu-úra,[10] to Paea, at length she came,
To men who were foes to the Tevas and hated their race and
name.
There was she well received, and spoke with Hiopa the king.[11]
And Hiopa listened, and weighed, and wisely considered the thing.
"Here in the back of the isle we dwell in a sheltered place,"
Quoth he to the woman, "in quiet, a weak and peaceable race.
But far in the teeth of the wind lofty Taiárapu lies;
Strong blows the wind of the trade on its seaward face, and cries
Aloud in the top of arduous mountains, and utters its song
In green continuous forests. Strong is the wind, and strong
And fruitful and hardy the race, famous in battle and feast,
Marvellous eaters and smiters: the men of Vaiau not least.
Now hearken to me, my daughter, and hear a word of the wise:
How a strength goes linked with a weakness, two by two, like the
eyes.
They can wield the ómare well and cast the javelin far;
Yet are they greedy and weak as the swine and the children are.

Plant we, then, here at Paea, a garden of excellent fruits;
Plant we bananas and kava and taro, the king of roots;
Let the pigs in Paea be tapu [12] and no man fish for a year;
And of all the meat in Tahiti gather we threefold here.
So shall the fame of our plenty fill the island, and so,
At last, on the tongue of rumor, go where we wish it to go.
Then shall the pigs of Taiárapu raise their snouts in the air;
But we sit quiet and wait, as the fowler sits by the snare,
And tranquilly fold our hands, till the pigs come nosing the food;
But meanwhile build us a house of Trotéa, the stubborn wood,
Bind it with incombustible thongs, set a roof to the room,
Too strong for the hands of a man to dissever or fire to consume;
And there, when the pigs come trotting, there shall the feast be
                                                          spread,
There shall the eye of the morn enlighten the feasters dead.
So be it done; for I have a heart that pities your state,
And Nateva and Námunu-úra are fire and water for hate."
All was done as he said, and the gardens prospered; and now
The fame of their plenty went out, and word of it came to Vaiau.
For the men of Námunu-úra sailed, to the windward far,
Lay in the offing by south where the towns of the Tevas are,
And cast overboard of their plenty; and lo! at the Tevas' feet
The surf on all of the beaches tumbled treasures of meat.
In the salt of the sea, a harvest tossed with the refluent foam;
And the children gleaned it in playing, and ate and carried it
                                                          home;
And the elders stared and debated, and wondered and passed the
                                                          jest,
But whenever a guest came by eagerly questioned the guest;
And little by little, from one to another, the word went round:
"In all the borders of Paea the victual rots on the ground,
And swine are plenty as rats. And now, when they fare to the sea,
The men of the Námunu-úra glean from under the tree
And load the canoe to the gunwale with all that is toothsome to
                                                          eat;
And all day long on the sea the jaws are crushing the meat,
The steersman eats at the helm, the rowers munch at the oar,
And at length, when their bellies are full, overboard with the
                                                          store!"
Now was the word made true, and soon as the bait was bare,

All the pigs of Taiárapu raised their snouts in the air.
Songs were recited, and kinship was counted, and tales were told
How war had severed of late but peace had cemented of old
The clans of the island. "To war," said they, "now set we an end,
And hie to the Námunu-úra even as a friend to a friend."

So judged, and a day was named; and soon as the morning broke,
Canoes were thrust in the sea and the houses emptied of folk.
Strong blew the wind of the south, the wind that gathers the clan;
Along all the line of the reef the clamorous surges ran;
And the clouds were piled on the top of the island mountain-high,
A mountain throned on a mountain. The fleet of canoes swept by
In the midst, on the green lagoon, with a crew released from care,
Sailing an even water, breathing a summer air,
Cheered by a cloudless sun; and ever to left and right,
Bursting surge on the reef, drenching storms on the height.
So the folk of Vaiau sailed and were glad all day,
Coasting the palm-tree cape and crossing the populous bay
By all the towns of the Tevas; and still as they bowled along,
Boat would answer to boat with jest and laughter and song,
And the people of all the towns trooped to the sides of the sea
And gazed from under the hand or sprang aloft on the tree,
Hailing and cheering. Time failed them for more to do;
The holiday village careened to the wind, and was gone from
view

Swift as a passing bird; and ever as onward it bore,
Like the cry of the passing bird, bequeathed its song to the shore—
Desirable laughter of maids and the cry of delight of the child.
And the gazer, left behind, stared at the wake and smiled.

By all the towns of the Tevas they went, and Pápara last,
The home of the chief, the place of muster in war; and passed
The march of the lands of the clan, to the lands of an alien folk.
And there, from the dusk of the shoreside palms, a column of
smoke
Mounted and wavered and died in the gold of the setting sun,
"Paea!" they cried. "It is Paea." And so was the voyage done.

In the early fall of the night, Hiopa came to the shore,
And beheld and counted the comers, and lo, they were forty score:

The pelting feet of the babes that ran already and played,
The clean-lipped smile of the boy, the slender breasts of the maid,
And mighty limbs of women, stalwart mothers of men.
The sires stood forth unabashed; but a little back from his ken
Clustered the scarcely nubile, the lads and maids, in a ring,
Fain of each other, afraid of themselves, aware of the king
And aping behaviour, but clinging together with hands and eyes,
With looks that were kind like kisses, and laughter tender as sighs.
There, too, the grandsire stood, raising his silver crest,
And the impotent hands of a suckling groped in his barren breast.
The childhood of love, the pair well married, the innocent brood,
The tale of the generations repeated and ever renewed—
Hiopa beheld them together, all the ages of man,
And a moment shook in his purpose.

                              But these were the foes of his clan,
And he trod upon pity, and came, and civilly greeted the king,
And gravely entreated Rahéro; and for all that could fight or
                                        sing,
And claimed a name in the land, had fitting phrases of praise;
But with all who were well-descended he spoke of the ancient
                                        days.
And "'T is true," said he, "that in Paea the victual rots on the
                                       ground;
But, friends, your number is many; and pigs must be hunted
                                    and found,
And the lads troop to the mountains to bring the féis down,
And around the bowls of the kava cluster the maids of the town.
So, for to-night, sleep here; but king, common, and priest
To-morrow, in order due, shall sit with me in the feast."
Sleepless the live-long night, Hiopa's followers toiled.
The pigs screamed and were slaughtered; the spars of the guest-
                                    house oiled,
The leaves spread on the floor. In many a mountain glen
The moon drew shadows of trees on the naked bodies of men
Plucking and bearing fruits; and in all the bounds of the town
Red glowed the cocoanut fires, and were buried and trodden
                                      down.
Thus did seven of the yottowas toil with their tale of the clan,
But the eighth wrought with his lads, hid from the sight of man.

In the deeps of the woods they laboured, piling the fuel high
In fagots, the load of a man, fuel seasoned and dry,
Thirsty to seize upon fire and apt to blurt into flame.

And now was the day of the feast. The forests, as morning came,
Tossed in the wind, and the peaks quaked in the blaze of the day
And the cocoanuts showered on the ground, rebounding and
rolling away:
A glorious morn for a feast, a famous wind for a fire.
To the hall of feasting Hiopa led them, mother and sire
And maid and babe in a tale, the whole of the holiday throng.
Smiling they came, garlanded green, not dreaming of wrong;
And for every three, a pig, tenderly cooked in the ground,
Waited; and féi, the staff of life, heaped in a mound
For each where he sat;—for each, bananas roasted and raw
Piled with a bountiful hand, as for horses hay and straw
Are stacked in a stable; and fish, the food of desire,[13]
And plentiful vessels of sauce, and breadfruit gilt in the fire;—
And kava was common as water. Feasts have there been ere now,
And many, but never a feast like that of the folk of Vaiau.

All day long they ate with the resolute greed of brutes,
And turned from the pigs to the fish, and again from the fish to
the fruits,
And emptied the vessels of sauce, and drank of the kava deep;
Till the young lay stupid as stones, and the strongest nodded to
sleep.
Sleep that was mighty as death and blind as a moonless night
Tethered them hand and foot; and their souls were drowned, and
the light
Was cloaked from their eyes. Senseless together, the old and the
young,
The fighter deadly to smite and the prater cunning of tongue,
The woman wedded and fruitful, inured to the pangs of birth,
And the maid that knew not of kisses, blindly sprawled on the
earth.

From the hall Hiopa the king and his chiefs came stealthily forth.
Already the sun hung low and enlightened the peaks of the north;
But the wind was stubborn to die and blew as it blows at morn,

Showering the nuts in the dusk, and e'en as a banner is torn,
High on the peaks of the island, shattered the mountain cloud.
And now at once, at a signal, a silent, emulous crowd
Set hands to the work of death, hurrying to and fro,
Like ants, to furnish the fagots, building them broad and low,
And piling them high and higher around the walls of the hall.
Silence persisted within, for sleep lay heavy on all.
But the mother of Támatéa stood at Hiopa's side,
And shook for terror and joy like a girl that is a bride.
Night fell on the toilers, and first Hiopa the wise
Made the round of the house, visiting all with his eyes;
And all was piled to the eaves, and fuel blockaded the door;
And within, in the house beleaguered, slumbered the forty score.
Then was an aito dispatched and came with fire in his hand,
And Hiopa took it.—"Within," said he, "is the life of a land;
And behold! I breathe on the coal, I breathe on the dales of the
east,
And silence falls on forest and shore; the voice of the feast
Is quenched, and the smoke of cooking; the rooftree decays and
falls
On the empty lodge, and the winds subvert deserted walls."

Therewithal, to the fuel, he laid the glowing coal;
And the redness ran in the mass and burrowed within like a mole,
And copious smoke was conceived. But, as when a dam is to burst,
The water lips it and crosses in silver trickles at first,
And then, of a sudden, whelms and bears it away forthright:
So now, in a moment, the flame sprang and towered in the night,
And wrestled and roared in the wind, and high over house and
tree,
Stood, like a streaming torch, enlightening land and sea.

But the mother of Támatéa threw her arms abroad,
"Pyre of my son," she shouted, "debited vengeance of God,
Late, late, I behold you, yet I behold you at last,
And glory, beholding! For now are the days of my agony past,
The lust that famished my soul now eats and drinks its desire,
And they that encompassed my son shrivel alive in the fire.
Tenfold precious the vengeance that comes after lingering years!
Ye quenched the voice of my singer?—hark, in your dying ears,

The song of the conflagration! Ye left me a widow alone?
—Behold, the whole of your race consumes, sinew and bone
And torturing flesh together: man, mother, and maid
Heaped in a common shambles; and already, borne by the trade,
The smoke of your dissolution darkens the stars of night."

Thus she spoke, and her stature grew in the people's sight.

3. *Rahéro*

Rahéro was there in the hall asleep: beside him his wife,
Comely, a mirthful woman, one that delighted in life;
And a girl that was ripe for marriage, shy and sly as a mouse;
And a boy, a climber of trees: all the hopes of his house.
Unwary, with open hands, he slept in the midst of his folk,
And dreamed that he heard a voice crying without, and awoke,
Leaping blindly afoot like one from a dream that he fears.
A hellish glow and clouds were about him;—it roared in his ears
Like the sound of the cataract fall that plunges sudden and steep;
And Rahéro swayed as he stood, and his reason was still asleep.
Now the flame struck hard on the house, wind-wielded, a frac
        turing blow,
And the end of the roof was burst and fell on the sleepers below;
And the lofty hall, and the feast, and the prostrate bodies of folk,
Shone red in his eyes a moment, and then were swallowed of
        smoke.
In the mind of Rahéro clearness came; and he opened his throat;
And as when a squall comes sudden, the straining sail of a boat
Thunders aloud and bursts, so thundered the voice of the man.
—"The wind and the rain!" he shouted, the mustering word of
        the clan,[14]
And "up!" and "to arms, men of Vaiau!" But silence replied,
Or only the voice of the gusts of the fire, and nothing beside.

Rahéro stooped and groped. He handled his woman-kind,
But the fumes of the fire and the kava had quenched the life of
        their mind,
And they lay like pillars prone; and his hand encountered the boy,
And there sprang in the gloom of his soul a sudden lightning of
        joy.

"Him can I save!" he thought, "if I were speedy enough."
And he loosened the cloth from his loins, and swaddled the child
in the stuff;
And about the strength of his neck he knotted the burden well.

There where the roof had fallen, it roared like the mouth of hell.
Thither Rahéro went, stumbling on senseless folk,
And grappled a post of the house, and began to climb in the
smoke:
The last alive of Vaiau: and the son borne by the sire.
The post glowed in the grain with ulcers of eating fire.
And the fire bit to the blood and mangled his hands and thighs;
And the fumes sang in his head like wine and stung in his eyes;
And still he climbed, and came to the top, the place of proof,
And thrust a hand through the flame, and clambered alive on the
roof.
But even as he did so, the wind, in a garment of flames and pain,
Wrapped him from head to heel; and the waistcloth parted in
twain;
And the living fruit of his loins dropped in the fire below.
About the blazing feast-house clustered the eyes of the foe,
Watching, hand upon weapon, lest ever a soul should flee,
Shading the brow from the glare, straining the neck to see.
Only, to leeward, the flames in the wind swept far and wide,
And the forest sputtered on fire; and there might no man abide.
Thither Rahéro crept, and dropped from the burning eaves,
And crouching low to the ground, in a treble covert of leaves
And fire and volleying smoke, ran for the life of his soul
Unseen; and behind him under a furnace of ardent coal,
Cairned with a wonder of flame, and blotting the night with
smoke,
Blazed and were smelted together the bones of all his folk.

He fled unguided at first; but hearing the breakers roar,
Thitherward shaped his way, and came at length to the shore.
Sound-limbed he was: dry-eyed; but smarted in every part;
And the mighty cage of his ribs heaved on his straining heart
With sorrow and rage. And "Fools!" he cried, "fools of Vaiau,
Heads of swine—gluttons—Alas! and where are they now?

Those that I played with, those that nursed me, those that I
nursed?
God, and I outliving them! I, the least and the worst—
I, that thought myself crafty, snared by this herd of swine,
In the tortures of hell and desolate, stripped of all that was mine:
All!—my friends and my fathers—the silver heads of yore
That trooped to the council, the children that ran to the open
door
Crying with innocent voices and clasping a father's knees!
And mine, my wife—my daughter—my sturdy climber of trees,
Ah, never to climb again!"

       Thus in the dusk of the night,
(For clouds rolled in the sky and the moon was swallowed from
sight,)
Pacing and gnawing his fists, Rahéro raged by the shore.
Vengeance: that must be his. But much was to do before;
And first a single life to be snatched from a deadly place,
A life, the root of revenge, surviving plant of the race:
And next the race to be raised anew, and the lands of the clan
Repeopled. So Rahéro designed, a prudent man
Even in wrath, and turned for the means of revenge and escape:
A boat to be seized by stealth, a wife to be taken by rape.
Still was the dark lagoon; beyond on the coral wall,
He saw the breakers shine, he heard them bellow and fall.
Alone, on the top of the reef, a man with a flaming brand
Walked, gazing and pausing, a fish-spear poised in his hand.
The foam boiled to his calf when the mightier breakers came,
And the torch shed in the wind scattering tufts of flame.
Afar on the dark lagoon a canoe lay idly at wait:
A figure dimly guiding it: surely the fisherman's mate.
Rahéro saw and he smiled. He straightened his mighty thews:
Naked, with never a weapon, and covered with scorch and bruise,
He straightened his arms, he filled the void of his body with
breath,
And, strong as the wind in his manhood, doomed the fisher to
death.

Silent he entered the water, and silently swam, and came
There where the fisher walked, holding on high the flame.

Loud on the pier of the reef volleyed the breach of the sea;
And hard at the back of the man, Rahéro crept to his knee
On the coral, and suddenly sprang and seized him, the elder hand
Clutching the joint of his throat, the other snatching the brand
Ere it had time to fall, and holding it steady and high.
Strong was the fisher, brave, and swift of mind and of eye—
Strongly he threw in the clutch; but Rahéro resisted the strain,
And jerked, and the spine of life snapped with a crack in twain,
And the man came slack in his hands and tumbled a lump at his
feet.

One moment: and there, on the reef, where the breakers whitened
and beat,
Rahéro was standing alone, glowing and scorched and bare,
A victor unknown of any, raising the torch in the air.
But once he drank of his breath, and instantly set him to fish
Like a man intent upon supper at home and a savoury dish.
For what should the woman have seen? A man with a torch—
and then
A moment's blur of the eyes—and a man with a torch again.
And the torch had scarcely been shaken. "Ah, surely," Rahéro
said,
"She will deem it a trick of the eyes, a fancy born in the head;
But time must be given the fool to nourish a fool's belief."
So for a while, a sedulous fisher, he walked the reef,
Pausing at times and gazing, striking at times with the spear:
—Lastly, uttered the call; and even as the boat drew near,
Like a man that was done with its use, tossed the torch in the sea.
Lightly he leaped on the boat beside the woman; and she
Lightly addressed him, and yielded the paddle and place to sit;
For now the torch was extinguished the night was black as the pit.
Rahéro set him to row, never a word he spoke,
And the boat sang in the water urged by his vigorous stroke.
—"What ails you?" the woman asked, "and why did you drop the
brand?
We have only to kindle another as soon as we come to land."
Never a word Rahéro replied, but urged the canoe.
And a chill fell on the woman.—"Atta! speak! is it you?
Speak! Why are you silent? Why do you bend aside?
Wherefore steer to the seaward?" thus she panted and cried.

Never a word from the oarsman, toiling there in the dark;
But right for a gate of the reef he silently headed the bark,
And wielding the single paddle with passionate sweep on sweep,
Drove her, the little fitted, forth on the open deep.

And fear, there where she sat, froze the woman to stone:
Not fear of the crazy boat and the weltering deep alone;
But a keener fear of the night, the dark, and the ghostly hour,
And the thing that drove the canoe with more than a mortal's
                                                    power
And more than a mortal's boldness. For much she knew of the
                                                    dead
That haunt and fish upon reefs, toiling, like men, for bread,
And traffic with human fishers, or slay them and take their ware,
Till the hour when the star of the dead [15] goes down, and the
                                                    morning air
Blows, and the cocks are singing on shore. And surely she knew
The speechless thing at her side belonged to the grave.[16]

                                                    It blew
All night from the south; all night, Rahéro contended and kept
The prow to the cresting sea; and, silent as though she slept,
The woman huddled and quaked. And now was the peep of day.
High and long on their left the mountainous island lay;
And over the peaks of Taiárapu arrows of sunlight struck.
On shore the birds were beginning to sing: the ghostly ruck
Of the buried had long ago returned to the covered grave;
And here on the sea, the woman waxing suddenly brave,
Turned her swiftly about and looked in the face of the man.
And sure he was none that she knew, none of her country or clan:
A stranger, mother-naked, and marred with the marks of fire,
But comely and great of stature, a man to obey and admire.

And Rahéro regarded her also, fixed, with a frowning face,
Judging the woman's fitness to mother a warlike race.
Broad of shoulder, ample of girdle, long in the thigh,
Deep of bosom she was, and bravely supported his eve.

"Woman," said he, "last night the men of your folk—
Man, woman, and maid, smothered my race in smoke.

It was done like cowards; and I, a mighty man of my hands,
Escaped, a single life; and now to the empty lands
And smokeless hearths of my people, sail, with yourself, alone.
Before your mother was born, the die of to-day was thrown
And you selected:—your husband, vainly striving, to fall
Broken between these hands:—yourself to be severed from all,
The places, the people, you love—home, kindred, and clan—
And to dwell in a desert and bear the babes of a kinless man."

NOTES TO THE SONG OF RAHÉRO

INTRODUCTION.—This tale, of which I have not consciously changed a single feature, I received from tradition. It is highly popular through all the country of the eight Tevas, the clan to which Rahéro belonged; and particularly in Taiárapu, the windward peninsula of Tahiti, where he lived. I have heard from end to end two versions; and as many as five different persons have helped me with details. There seems no reason why the tale should not be true.

Note 1. *"The aito,"* quasi champion, or brave. One skilled in the use of some weapon, who wandered the country challenging distinguished rivals and taking part in local quarrels. It was in the natural course of his advancement to be at last employed by a chief, or king; and it would then be a part of his duties to purvey the victim for sacrifice. One of the doomed families was indicated; the aito took his weapon and went forth alone; a little behind him bearers followed with the sacrificial basket. Sometimes the victim showed fight, sometimes prevailed; more often, without doubt, he fell. But whatever body was found, the bearers indifferently took up.

Note 2. *"Pai," "Honoura,"* and *"Ahupu."* Legendary persons of Tahiti, all natives of Taiárapu. Of the two first, I have collected singular although imperfect legends, which I hope soon to lay before the public in another place. Of Ahupu, except in snatches of song, little memory appears to linger. She dwelt at least about Tepari—"the sea-cliffs"— the eastern fastness of the isle; walked by paths known only to herself upon the mountains; was courted by dangerous suitors who came swimming from adjacent islands, and defended and rescued (as I gather) by the loyalty of native fish. My anxiety to learn more of "Ahupu Vehine" became (during my stay in Taiárapu) a cause of some diversion to that mirthful people, the inhabitants.

Note 3. *"Covered an oven."* The cooking fire is made in a hole in the ground, and is then buried.

Note 4. *"Flies."* This is perhaps an anachronism. Even speaking of to-day in Tahiti, the phrase would have to be understood as referring mainly to mosquitoes, and these only in watered valleys with close woods, such as I suppose to form the surroundings of Rahéro's homestead. Quarter of a mile away, where the air moves freely, you shall look in vain for one.

Note 5. *"Hook"* of mother-of-pearl. Bright-hook fishing, and that with the spear, appear to the favourite native methods.

Note 6. *"Leaves,"* the plates of Tahiti.

Note 7. *"Yottowas,"* so spelt for convenience of pronunciation, *quasi* Tacksmen in the Scottish Highlands. The organisation of eight sub-districts and eight yottowas to a division which was in use (until yesterday) among the Tevas, I have attributed without authority to the next clan.

Note 8. *"Ómare,"* pronounce as a dactyl. A loaded quarter-staff, one of the two favourite weapons of the Tahitian brave: the javelin, or casting spear, was the other.

Note 9. *"The ribbon of light."* Still to be seen (and heard) spinning from one marae to another on Tahiti; or so I have it upon evidence that would rejoice the Psychical Society.

Note 10. *"Námunu-úra."* The complete name is Namunu-ura te aropa. Why it should be pronounced Námunu, dactyllically, I cannot see, but so I have always heard it. This was the clan immediately beyond the Tevas on the south coast of the island. At the date of the tale the clan organisation must have been very weak. There is no particular mention of Támatéa's mother going to Papara, to the head chief of her own clan, which would appear her natural recourse. On the other hand, she seems to have visited various lesser chiefs among the Tevas, and these to have excused themselves solely on the danger of the enterprise. The broad distinction here drawn between Nateva and Námunu-úra is therefore not impossibly anachronistic.

Note 11. *"Hiopa the king."* Hiopa was really the name of the king (chief) of Vaiau; but I could never learn that of the king of Paea—pronounce to rhyme with the Indian *ayah*—and I gave the name where it was most needed. This note must appear otiose indeed to readers who have never

heard of either of these two gentlemen; and perhaps there is only one person in the world capable at once of reading my verses and spying the inaccuracy. For him, for Mr. Tati Salmon, hereditary high chief of the Tevas, the note is solely written: a small attention from a clansman to his chief.

Note 12. *"Let the pigs be tapu."* It is impossible to explain *tapu* in a note; we have it as an English word, taboo. Suffice it, that a thing which was *tapu* must not be touched, nor a place that was *tapu* visited.

Note 13. *"Fish, the food of desire."* There is a special word in the Tahitian language to signify *hungering after fish*. I may remark that here is one of my chief difficulties about the whole story. How did king, commons, women, and all come to eat together at this feast? But it troubled none of my numerous authorities; so there must certainly be some natural explanation.

Note 14. *"The mustering word of the clan."*

> Teva te na,
> Teva te matai!
> Teva the wind,
> Teva the rain!

Note 15. Note 16. *"The star of the dead."* Venus as a morning star. I have collected much curious evidence as to this belief. The dead retain their taste for a fish diet, enter into copartnery with living fishers, and haunt the reef and the lagoon. The conclusion attributed to the nameless lady of the legend would be reached to-day, under the like circumstances, by ninety per cent of Polynesians; and here I probably understate by one-tenth.

THE FEAST OF FAMINE

MARQUESAN MANNERS

✳

1. *The Priest's Vigil*

I N all the land of the tribe was neither fish nor fruit,
And the deepest pit of popoi stood empty to the foot.[1]
The clans upon the left and the clans upon the right
Now oiled their carven maces and scoured their daggers bright;
They gat them to the thicket, to the deepest of the shade,
And lay with sleepless eyes in the deadly ambuscade.
And oft in the starry even the song of mourning rose,
What time the oven smoked in the country of their foes;
For oft to loving hearts, and waiting ears and sight,
The lads that went to forage returned not with the night.
Now first the children sickened, and then the women paled,
And the great arms of the warrior no more for war availed.
Hushed was the deep drum, discarded was the dance;
And those that met the priest now glanced at him askance.
The priest was a man of years, his eyes were ruby-red,[2]
He neither feared the dark nor the terrors of the dead,
He knew the songs of races, the names of ancient date;
And the beard upon his bosom would have bought the chief's
estate.
He dwelt in a high-built lodge, hard by the roaring shore,
Raised on a noble terrace and with tikis [3] at the door.
Within it was full of riches, for he served his nation well,
And full of the sound of breakers, like the hollow of a shell.

1162

For weeks he let them perish, gave never a helping sign,
But sat on his oiled platform to commune with the divine,
But sat on his high terrace, with the tikis by his side,
And stared on the blue ocean, like a parrot, ruby-eyed.

Dawn as yellow as sulphur leaped on the mountain height:
Out on the round of the sea the gems of the morning light,
Up from the round of the sea the streamers of the sun;—
But down in the depths of the valley the day was not begun.
In the blue of the woody twilight burned red the cocoa-husk,
And the women and men of the clan went forth to bathe in the
dusk
A word that began to go round, a word, a whisper, a start:
Hope that leaped in the bosom, fear that knocked on the heart:
"See, the priest is not risen—look, for his door is fast!
He is going to name the victims; he is going to help us at last."

Thrice rose the sun to noon; and ever, like one of the dead,
The priest lay still in his house with the roar of the sea in his
head;
There was never a foot on the floor, there was never a whisper
of speech;
Only the leering tikis stared on the blinding beach.
Again were the mountains fired, again the morning broke;
And all the houses lay still, but the house of the priest awoke.
Close in their covering roofs lay and trembled the clan,
But the agèd, red-eyed priest ran forth like a lunatic man;
And the village panted to see him in the jewels of death again,
In the silver beards of the old and the hair of women slain.
Frenzy shook in his limbs, frenzy shone in his eyes,
And still and again as he ran, the valley rang with his cries.
All day long in the land, by cliff and thicket and den,
He ran his lunatic rounds, and howled for the flesh of men;
All day long he ate not, nor ever drank of the brook;
And all day long in their houses the people listened and shook—
All day long in their houses they listened with bated breath,
And never a soul went forth, for the sight of the priest was death.

Three were the days of his running, as the gods appointed of
yore,
Two the nights of his sleeping alone in the place of gore:

The drunken slumber of frenzy twice he drank to the lees,
On the sacred stones of the High-place under the sacred trees;
With a lamp at his ashen head he lay in the place of the feast,
And the sacred leaves of the banyan rustled around the priest.
Last, when the stated even fell upon terrace and tree,
And the shade of the lofty island lay leagues away to sea,
And all the valleys of verdure were heavy with manna and
musk,
The wreck of the red-eyed priest came gasping home in the dusk.
He reeled across the village, he staggered along the shore,
And between the leering tikis crept groping through his door.

There went a stir through the lodges, the voice of speech awoke;
Once more from the builded platforms arose the evening smoke.
And those who were mighty in war, and those renowned for an art
Sat in their stated seats and talked of the morrow apart.

2. *The Lovers*

Hark! away in the woods—for the ears of love are sharp—
Stealthily, quietly touched, the note of the one-stringed harp.[4]
In the lighted house of her father, why should Taheia start?
Taheia heavy of hair, Taheia tender of heart,
Taheia the well-descended, a bountiful dealer in love,
Nimble of foot like the deer, and kind of eye like the dove?
Sly and shy as a cat, with never a change of face,
Taheia slips to the door, like one that would breathe a space;
Saunters and pauses, and looks at the stars, and lists to the seas;
Then sudden and swift as a cat, she plunges under the trees.
Swift as a cat she runs, with her garment gathered high,
Leaping, nimble of foot, running, certain of eye;
And ever to guide her way over the smooth and the sharp,
Ever nearer and nearer the note of the one-stringed harp;
Till at length, in a glade of the wood, with a naked mountain
above,
The sound of the harp thrown down, and she in the arms of her
love.
"Rua,"—"Taheia," they cry—"my heart, my soul, and my eyes,"
And clasp and sunder and kiss, with lovely laughter and sighs,

"Rua!"—"Taheia, my love,"—"Rua, star of my night,
Clasp me, hold me, and love me, single spring of delight."

And Rua folded her close, he folded her near and long,
The living knit to the living, and sang the lover's song:

> *Night, night it is, night upon the palms.*
> *Night, night it is, the land wind has blown.*
> *Starry, starry night, over deep and height;*
> *Love, love in the valley, love all alone.*

"Taheia, heavy of hair, a foolish thing have we done,
To bind what gods have sundered unkindly into one.
Why should a lowly lover have touched Taheia's skirt,
Taheia the well-descended, and Rua child of the dirt?"

"On high with the haka-ikis my father sits in state,
Ten times fifty kinsmen salute him in the gate;
Round all his martial body, and in bands across his face,
The marks of the tattooer proclaim his lofty place.
I too, in the hands of the cunning, in the sacred cabin of palm,[5]
Have shrunk like the mimosa, and bleated like the lamb;
Round half my tender body, that none shall clasp but you,
For a crest and a fair adornment go dainty lines of blue.
Love, love, beloved Rua, love levels all degrees,
And the well-tattooed Taheia clings panting to your knees."

—"Taheia, song of the morning, how long is the longest love?
A cry, a clasp of the hands, a star that falls from above!
Ever at morn in the blue, and at night when all is black,
Ever it skulks and trembles with the hunter, Death, on its track.
Hear me, Taheia, death! For to-morrow the priest shall awake,
And the names be named of the victims to bleed for the nation's
sake;
And first of the numbered many that shall be slain ere noon,
Rua the child of the dirt, Rua the kinless loon.
For him shall the drum be beat, for him be raised the song,
For him to the sacred High-place the chaunting people throng,
For him the oven smoke as for a speechless beast.

And the sire of my Taheia come greedy to the feast."
"Rua, be silent, spare me. Taheia closes her ears.
Pity my yearning heart, pity my girlish years!
Flee from the cruel hands, flee from the knife and coal,
Lie hid in the deeps of the woods, Rua, sire of my soul!"
"Whither to flee, Taheia, whither in all of the land?
The fires of the bloody kitchen are kindled on every hand;
On every hand in the isle a hungry whetting of teeth,
Eyes in the trees above, arms in the brush beneath.
Patience to lie in wait, cunning to follow the sleuth,
Abroad the foes I have fought, and at home the friends of my
                                                    youth."
"Love, love, beloved Rua, love has a clearer eye,
Hence from the arms of love you go not forth to die.
There, where the broken mountain drops sheer into the glen,
There shall you find a hold from the boldest hunter of men;
There, in the deep recess, where the sun falls only at noon,
And only once in the night enters the light of the moon,
Nor ever a sound but of birds, or the rain when it falls with a
                                                    shout;
For death and the fear of death beleaguer the valley about.
Tapu it is, but the gods will surely pardon despair;
Tapu, but what of that? If Rua can only dare.
Tapu and tapu and tapu, I know they are every one right;
But the god of every tapu is not always quick to smite.
Lie secret there, my Rua, in the arms of awful gods,
Sleep in the shade of the trees on the couch of the kindly sods,
Sleep and dream of Taheia, Taheia will wake for you;
And whenever the land wind blows and the woods are heavy with
                                                    dew,
Alone through the horror of night,[6] with food for the soul of her
                                                    love,
Taheia the undissuaded will hurry true as the dove."
"Taheia, the pit of the night crawls with treacherous things,
Spirits of ultimate air and the evil souls of things;
The souls of the dead, the stranglers, that perch in the trees of
                                                    the wood,
Waiters for all things human, haters of evil and good."
"Rua, behold me, kiss me, look in my eyes and read;
Are these the eyes of a maid that would leave her lover in need?

Brave in the eye of day, my father ruled in the fight;
The child of his loins, Taheia, will play the man in the night."

So it was spoken, and so agreed, and Taheia arose
And smiled in the stars and was gone, swift as the swallow goes;
And Rua stood on the hill, and sighed, and followed her flight,
And there were the lodges below, each with its door alight;
From folk that sat on the terrace and drew out the even long
Sudden crowings of laughter, monotonous drone of song;
The quiet passage of souls over his head in the trees; [7]
And from all around the haven the crumbling thunder of seas.
"Farewell, my home," said Rua. "Farewell, O quiet seat!
To-morrow in all your valleys the drum of death shall beat."

3. *The Feast*

Dawn as yellow as sulphur leaped on the naked peak,
And all the village was stirring, for now was the priest to speak.
Forth on his terrace he came, and sat with the chief in talk;
His lips were blackened with fever, his cheeks were whiter than
chalk;
Fever clutched at his hands, fever nodded his head,
But, quiet and steady and cruel, his eyes shone ruby-red.
In the earliest rays of the sun the chief rose up content;
Braves were summoned, and drummers; messengers came and
went;
Braves ran to their lodges, weapons were snatched from the wall;
The commons herded together, and fear was over them all.
Festival dresses they wore, but the tongue was dry in their mouth,
And the blinking eyes in their faces skirted from north to south.

Now to the sacred enclosure gathered the greatest and least,
And from under the shade of the Banyan arose the voice of the
feast.
The frenzied roll of the drum, and a swift, monotonous song.
Higher the sun swam up; the trade wind level and strong
Awoke in the tops of the palms and rattled the fans aloud,
And over the garlanded heads and shining robes of the crowd
Tossed the spiders of shadow, scattered the jewels of sun.

Forty the tale of the drums, and the forty throbbed like one;
A thousand hearts in the crowd, and the even chorus of song,
Swift as the feet of a runner, trampled a thousand strong.
And the old men leered at the ovens and licked their lips for the
food;
And the women stared at the lads, and laughed and looked to
the wood.
As when the sweltering baker, at night, when the city is dead,
Alone in the trough of labour treads and fashions the bread;
So in the heat, and the reek, and the touch of woman and man,
The naked spirit of evil kneaded the hearts of the clan.

Now cold was at many a heart, and shaking in many a seat:
For there were the empty baskets, but who was to furnish the
meat?
For here was the nation assembled, and there were the ovens
anigh,
And out of a thousand singers nine were numbered to die.
Till, of a sudden, a shock, a mace in the air, a yell,
And, struck in the edge of the crowd the first of the victims fell.[3]
Terror and horrible glee divided the shrinking clan,
Terror of what was to follow, glee for a diet of man.
Frenzy hurried the chaunt, frenzy rattled the drums;
The nobles, high on the terrace, greedily mouthed their thumbs;
And once and again and again, in the ignorant crowd below,
Once and again and again descended the murderous blow.
Now smoked the oven, and now, with the cutting lip of a shell,
A butcher of ninety winters jointed the bodies well.
Unto the carven lodge, silent, in order due,
The grandees of the nation one after one withdrew;
And a line of laden bearers brought to the terrace foot,
On poles across their shoulders, the last reserve of fruit.
The victims bled for the nobles in the old appointed way;
The fruit was spread for the commons, for all should eat to-day.

And now was the kava brewed, and now the cocoa ran,
Now was the hour of the dance for child and woman and man;
And mirth was in every heart, and a garland on every head,
And all was well with the living and well with the eight who were
dead.

Only the chiefs and the priest talked and consulted awhile:
"To-morrow," they said, and "To-morrow," and nodded and
seemed to smile:
"Rua the child of dirt, the creature of common clay,
Rua must die to-morrow, since Rua is gone to-day."

Out of the groves of the valley, where clear the blackbirds sang,
Sheer from the trees of the valley the face of the mountain
sprang;
Sheer and bare it rose, unscalable barricade,
Beaten and blown against by the generous draught of the trade.
Dawn on its fluted brow painted rainbow light,
Close on its pinnacled crown trembled the stars at night.
Here and there in a cleft clustered contorted trees,
Or the silver beard of a stream hung and swung in the breeze.
High overhead, with a cry, the torrents leaped for the main,
And silently sprinkled below in thin perennial rain.
Dark in the staring noon, dark was Rua's ravine,
Damp and cold was the air, and the face of the cliffs was green.
Here, in the rocky pit, accursed already of old,
On a stone in the midst of a river, Rua sat and was cold.

"Valley of mid-day shadows, valley of silent falls,"
Rua sang, and his voice went hollow about the walls,
"Valley of shadow and rock, a doleful prison to me,
What is the life you can give to a child of the sun and the sea?"
And Rua arose and came to the open mouth of the glen,
Whence he beheld the woods, and the sea, and houses of men.
Wide blew the riotous trade, and smelt in his nostrils good;
It bowed the boats on the bay, and tore and divided the wood;
It smote and sundered the groves as Moses smote with the rod,
And the streamers of all the trees blew like banners abroad;
And ever and on, in a lull, the trade wind brought him along
A far-off patter of drums and a far-off whisper of song.

Swift as the swallow's wings, the diligent hands on the drum
Fluttered and hurried and throbbed. "Ah, woe that I hear you
come,"
Rua cried in his grief, "A sorrowful sound to me,
Mounting far and faint from the resonant shore of the sea!

Woe in the song! for the grave breathes in the singers' breath,
And I hear in the tramp of the drums the beat of the heart of
                                                      death.
Home of my youth! no more, through all the length of the years,
No more to the place of the echoes of early laughter and tears,
No more shall Rua return; no more as the evening ends,
To crowded eyes of welcome, to the reaching hands of friends."

All day long from the High-place the drums and the singing came,
And the even fell, and the sun went down, a wheel of flame;
And night came gleaning the shadows and hushing the sounds
                                                      of the wood;
And silence slept on all, where Rua sorrowed and stood.
But still from the shore of the bay the sound of the festival rang,
And still the crowd in the High-place danced and shouted and
                                                      sang.

Now over all the isle terror was breathed abroad
Of shadowy hands from the trees and shadowy snares in the sod;
And before the nostrils of night, the shuddering hunter of men
Hurried, with beard on shoulder, back to his lighted den.
"Taheia, here to my side!"—"Rua, my Rua, you!"
And cold from the clutch of terror, cold with the damp of the dew,
Taheia, heavy of hair, leaped through the dark to his arms;
Taheia leaped to his clasp, and was folded in from alarms.

"Rua, beloved, here, see what your love has brought;
Coming—alas! returning—swift as the shuttle of thought;
Returning, alas! for to-night, with the beaten drum and the voice.
In the shine of many torches must the sleepless clan rejoice;
And Taheia the well-descended, the daughter of chief and priest,
Taheia must sit in her place in the crowded bench of the feast."
So it was spoken; and she, girding her garment high,
Fled and was swallowed of woods, swift as the sight of an eye.

Night over isle and sea rolled her curtain of stars,
Then a trouble awoke in the air, the east was banded with bars;
Dawn as yellow as sulphur leaped on the mountain height;
Dawn, in the deepest glen, fell a wonder of light;

High and clear stood the palms in the eye of the brightening
                                                        east,
And lo! from the sides of the sea the broken sound of the feast!
As, when in days of summer, through open windows, the fly
Swift as a breeze and loud as a trump goes by,
But when frosts in the field have pinched the wintering mouse,
Blindly noses and buzzes and hums in the firelit house:
So the sound of the feast gallantly trampled at night,
So it staggered and drooped, and droned in the morning light.

4. *The Raid*

It chanced that as Rua sat in the valley of silent falls,
He heard a calling of doves from high on the cliffy walls.
Fire had fashioned of yore, and time had broken, the rocks;
There were rooting crannies for trees and nesting places for flocks;
And he saw on the top of the cliffs, looking up from the pit of
                                                        the shade,
A flicker of wings and sunshine, and trees that swung in the
                                                        trade.
"The trees swing in the trade," quoth Rua, doubtful of words,
"And the sun stares from the sky, but what should trouble the
                                                        birds?"
Up from the shade he gazed, where high the parapet shone,
And he was aware of a ledge and of things that moved thereon.
"What manner of things are these? Are they spirits abroad by day?
Or the foes of my clan that are come, bringing death by a perilous
                                                        way?"

The valley was gouged like a vessel, and round like the vessel's
                                                        iip,
With a cape of the side of the hill thrust forth like the bows of a
                                                        ship.
On the top of the face of the cape a volley of sun struck fair,
And the cape overhung like a chin a gulph of sunless air.
"Silence, heart! What is that?—that, that flickered and shone,
Into the sun for an instant, and in an instant gone?
Was it a warrior's plume, a warrior's girdle of hair?
Swung in the loop of a rope, is he making a bridge of the air?"

Once and again Rua saw, in the trenchant edge of the sky,
The giddy conjuring done. And then, in the blink of an eye,
A scream caught in with the breath, a whirling packet of limbs,
A lump that dived in the gulf, more swift than a dolphin swims;
And there was the lump at his feet, and eyes were alive in the
                           lump.
Sick was the soul of Rua, ambushed close in a clump;
Sick of soul he drew near, making his courage stout;
And he looked in the face of the thing, and the life of the thing
                           went out.
And he gazed on the tattooed limbs, and, behold, he knew the
                           man:
Hoka, a chief of the Vais, the truculent foe of his clan:
Hoka a moment since that stepped in the loop of the rope,
Filled with the lust of war, and alive with courage and hope.

                         •

Again to the giddy cornice Rua lifted his eyes,
And again beheld men passing in the armpit of the skies.
"Foes of my race!" cried Rua, "the mouth of Rua is true:
Never a shark in the deep is nobler of soul than you.
There was never a nobler foray, never a bolder plan;
Never a dizzier path was trod by the children of man;
And Rua, your evil-dealer through all the days of his years,
Counts it honour to hate you, honour to fall by your spears."
And Rua straightened his back. "O Vais, a scheme for a scheme!"
Cried Rua and turned and descended the turbulent stair of the
                           stream,
Leaping from rock to rock as the water-wagtail at home
Flits through resonant valleys and skims by boulder and foam.
And Rua burst from the glen and leaped on the shore of the
                           brook,
And straight for the roofs of the clan his vigorous way he took.
Swift were the heels of flight, and loud behind as he went
Rattled the leaping stones on the line of his long descent.
And ever he thought as he ran, and caught at his gasping breath,
"O the fool of a Rua, Rua that runs to his death!
But the right is the right," thought Rua, and ran like the wind
                           on the foam,
"The right is the right for ever, and home for ever home.

For what though the oven smoke? And what though I die ere
morn?
There was I nourished and tended, and there was Taheia born."
Noon was high on the High-place, the second noon of the feast;
And heat and shameful slumber weighed on people and priest;
And the heart drudged slow in bodies heavy with monstrous
meals;
And the senseless limbs were scattered abroad like spokes of
wheels;
And crapulous women sat and stared at the stones anigh
With a bestial droop of the lip and a swinish rheum in the eye.
As about the dome of the bees in the time for the drones to fall,
The dead and the maimed are scattered, and lie, and stagger,
and crawl;
So on the grades of the terrace, in the ardent eye of the day,
The half-awake and the sleepers clustered and crawled and lay;
And loud as the dome of the bees, in the time of a swarming
horde,
A horror of many insects hung in the air and roared.
Rua looked and wondered; he said to himself in his heart:
"Poor are the pleasures of life, and death is the better part."
But lo! on the higher benches a cluster of tranquil folk
Sat by themselves, nor raised their serious eyes, nor spoke:
Women with robes unruffled and garlands duly arranged,
Gazing far from the feast with faces of people estranged;
And quiet amongst the quiet, and fairer than all the fair,
Taheia, the well-descended, Taheia, heavy of hair.
And the soul of Rua awoke, courage enlightened his eyes,
And he uttered a summoning shout and called on the clan to rise.
Over against him at once, in the spotted shade of the trees,
Owlish and blinking creatures scrambled to hands and knees;
On the grades of the sacred terrace, the driveller woke to fear,
And the hand of the ham-drooped warrior brandished a wavering
spear.
And Rua folded his arms, and scorn discovered his teeth;
Above the war-crowd gibbered, and Rua stood smiling beneath.
Thick, like leaves in the autumn, faint, like April sleet,
Missiles from tremulous hands quivered around his feet;
And Taheia leaped from her place; and the priest, the ruby-eyed,

Ran to the front of the terrace, and brandished his arms, and
cried:
"Hold, O fools, he brings tidings!" and "Hold, 'tis the love of
my heart!"
Till lo! in front of the terrace, Rua pierced with a dart.

Taheia cherished his head, and the aged priest stood by,
And gazed with eyes of ruby at Rua's darkening eye.
"Taheia, here is the end, I die a death for a man.
I have given the life of my soul to save an unsavable clan!
See them, the drooping of hams! behold me the blinking crew:
Fifty spears they cast, and one of fifty true!
And you, O priest, the foreteller, foretell for yourself if you can,
Foretell the hour of the day when the Vais shall burst on your
clan!
By the head of the tapu cleft, with death and fire in their hand.
Thick and silent like ants, the warriors swarm in the land."

And they tell that when next the sun had climbed to the noonday
skies,
It shone on the smoke of feasting in the country of the Vais.

NOTES TO THE FEAST OF FAMINE

In this ballad I have strung together some of the more striking particularities of the Marquesas. It rests upon no authority; it is in no sense, like "Rahéro," a native story; but a patchwork of details of manners and the impressions of a traveller. It may seem strange, when the scene is laid upon these profligate islands, to make the story hinge on love. But love is not less known in the Marquesas than elsewhere; nor is there any cause of suicide more common in the islands.

Note 1. *"Pit of Popoi."* Where the bread fruit was stored for preservation.

Note 2. *"Ruby-red."* The priest's eyes were probably red from the abuse of Kava. His beard (verse 18) is said to be worth an estate; for the beards of old men are the favourite head adornment of the Marquesans, as the hair of women formed their most costly girdle. The former, among this generally beardless and short-lived people, fetch to-day considerable sums.

Note 3. *"Tikis."* The tiki is an ugly image hewn out of wood or stone.

Note 4. *"The one-stringed harp."* Usually employed for serenades.

Note 5. *"The sacred cabin of palm."* Which, however, no woman could approach. I do not know where women were tattooed; probably in the common house, or in the bush, for a woman was a creature of small account. I must guard the reader against supposing Taheia was at all disfigured; the art of the Marquesan tattooer is extreme; and she would appear to be clothed in a web of lace, inimitably delicate, exquisite in pattern, and of a bluish hue that at once contrasts and harmonises with the warm pigment of the native skin. It would be hard to find a woman more becomingly adorned than "a well-tattooed" Marquesan.

Note 6. *"The horror of night."* The Polynesian fear of ghosts and of the dark has been already referred to. Their life is beleaguered by the dead.

Note 7. *"The quiet passage of souls."* So, I am told, the natives explain the sound of a little wind passing overhead unfelt.

Note 8. *"The first of the victims fell."* Without doubt, this whole scene is untrue to fact. The victims were disposed of privately and some time before. And indeed I am far from claiming the credit of any high degree of accuracy for this ballad. Even in a time of famine, it is probable that Marquesan life went far more gaily than is here represented. But the melancholy of to-day lies on the writer's mind.

TICONDEROGA

A LEGEND OF THE WEST HIGHLANDS

THIS is the tale of the man
   Who heard a word in the night
In the land of the heathery hills,
   In the days of the feud and the fight.
By the sides of the rainy sea,
   Where never a stranger came,
On the awful lips of the dead,
   He heard the outlandish name.
It sang in his sleeping ears,
   It hummed in his waking head:
The name—Ticonderoga,
   The utterance of the dead.

1. *The Saying of the Name*

On the loch-sides of Appin,
   When the mist blew from the sea,
A Stewart stood with a Cameron:
   An angry man was he.
The blood beat in his ears,
   The blood ran hot to his head,
The mist blew from the sea,
   And there was the Cameron dead.

"O, what have I done to my friend,
  O, what have I done to mysel',
That he should be cold and dead,
  And I in the danger of all?
Nothing but danger about me,
  Danger behind and before,
Death at wait in the heather
  In Appin and Mamore,
Hate at all of the ferries
  And death at each of the fords,
Camerons priming gunlocks
  And Camerons sharpening swords."

But this was a man of counsel,
  This was a man of a score,
There dwelt no pawkier Stewart
  In Appin or Mamore.
He looked on the blowing mist,
  He looked on the awful dead,
And there came a smile on his face
  And there slipped a thought in his head.

Out over cairn and moss,
  Out over scrog and scaur,
He ran as runs the clansman
  That bears the cross of war.
His heart beat in his body,
  His hair clove to his face,
When he came at last in the gloaming
  To the dead man's brother's place.
The east was white with the moon,
  The west with the sun was red,
And there, in the house-doorway,
  Stood the brother of the dead.

"I have slain a man to my danger,
  I have slain a man to my death.
I put my soul in your hands,"
  The panting Stewart saith.

"I lay it bare in your hands,
  For I know your hands are leal;
And be you my targe and bulwark
  From the bullet and the steel."

Then up and spoke the Cameron,
  And gave him his hand again:
"There shall never a man in Scotland
  Set faith in me in vain;
And whatever man you have slaughtered,
  Of whatever name or line,
By my sword and yonder mountain,
  I make you quarrel mine.[1]
I bid you in to my fireside,
  I share with you house and hall;
It stands upon my honour
  To see you safe from all."

It fell in the time of midnight,
  When the fox barked in the den
And the plaids were over the faces
  In all the houses of men,
That as the living Cameron
  Lay sleepless on his bed,
Out of the night and the other world,
  Came in to him the dead.

"My blood is on the heather,
  My bones are on the hill;
There is joy in the home of ravens
  That the young shall eat their fill.
My blood is poured in the dust,
  My soul is spilled in the air;
And the man that has undone me
  Sleeps in my brother's care."
"I'm wae for your death, my brother,
  But if all of my house were dead,
I couldnae withdraw the plighted hand,
  Nor break the word once said."

"O, what shall I say to our father,
  In the place to which I fare?
O, what shall I say to our mother,
  Who greets to see me there?
And to all the kindly Camerons
  That have lived and died long-syne—
Is this the word you send them,
  Fause-hearted brother mine?"

"It's neither fear nor duty,
  It's neither quick nor dead
Shall gar me withdraw the plighted hand,
  Or break the word once said."
Thrice in the time of midnight,
  When the fox barked in the den,
And the plaids were over the faces
  In all the house of men,
Thrice as the living Cameron
  Lay sleepless on his bed,
Out of the night and the other world
  Came in to him the dead,
And cried to him for vengeance
  On the man that laid him low;
And thrice the living Cameron
  Told the dead Cameron, no.

"Thrice have you seen me, brother,
  But now shall see me no more,
Till you meet your angry fathers
  Upon the farther shore.
Thrice have I spoken, and now,
  Before the cock be heard,
I take my leave forever
  With the naming of a word.
It shall sing in your sleeping ears,
  It shall hum in your waking head,
The name—Ticonderoga,
  And the warning of the dead."

Now when the night was over
  And the time of people's fears,

The Cameron walked abroad,
   And the word was in his ears.
"Many a name I know,
   But never a name like this;
O, where shall I find a skilly man
   Shall tell me what it is?"

With many a man he counselled
   Of high and low degree,
With the herdsmen on the mountains
   And the fishers of the sea.
And he came and went unweary,
   And read the books of yore,
And the runes that were written of old
   On stones upon the moor.
And many a name he was told,
   But never the name of his fears—
Never, in east or west,
   The name that rang in his ears:
Names of men and of clans,
   Names for the grass and the tree,
For the smallest tarn in the mountains,
   The smallest reef in the sea:
Names for the high and low,
   The names of the craig and the flat;
But in all the land of Scotland,
   Never a name like that.

2. *The Seeking of the Name*

And now there was speech in the south,
   And a man of the south that was wise,
A periwig'd lord of London,[2]
   Called on the clans to rise.
And the riders rode, and the summons
   Came to the western shore,
To the land of the sea and the heather,
   To Appin and Mamore.

It called on all to gather
From every scrog and scaur,
That loved their fathers' tartan
And the ancient game of war.
And down the watery valley
And up the windy hill,
Once more, as in the olden,
The pipes were sounding shrill;
Again in highland sunshine
The naked steel was bright;
And the lads, once more in tartan,
Went forth again to fight.

"O, why should I dwell here
With a weird upon my life,
When the clansmen shout for battle
And the war-swords clash in strife?
I cannae joy at feast,
I cannae sleep in bed,
For the wonder of the word
And the warning of the dead.
It sings in my sleeping ears,
It hums in my waking head,
The name—Ticonderoga,
The utterance of the dead.
Then up, and with the fighting men
To march away from here,
Till the cry of the great war-pipe
Shall drown it in my ear!"

Where flew King George's ensign
The plaided soldiers went:
They drew the sword in German,
In Flanders pitched the tent.
The bells of foreign cities
Rang far across the plain:
They passed the happy Rhine,
They drank the rapid Main.
Through Asiatic jungles
The Tartans filed their way,

And the neighing of the war-pipes
   Struck terror in Cathay.[3]
"Many a name have I heard," he thought,
   "In all the tongues of men,
Full many a name both here and there,
   Full many both now and then.
When I was at home in my father's house
   In the land of the naked knee,
Between the eagles that fly in the lift
   And the herrings that swim in the sea,
And now that I am a captain-man
   With a braw cockade in my hat—
Many a name have I heard," he thought,
   "But never a name like that."

3. *The Place of the Name*

There fell a war in a woody place,
   Lay far across the sea,
A war of the march in the mirk midnight
   And the shot from behind the tree,
The shaven head and the painted face,
   The silent foot in the wood,
In a land of a strange, outlandish tongue
   That was hard to be understood.

It fell about the gloaming
   The general stood with his staff,
He stood and he looked east and west
   With little mind to laugh.
"Far have I been and much have I seen,
   And kent both gain and loss,
But here we have woods on every hand
   And a kittle water to cross.
Far have I been and much have I seen,
   But never the beat of this:
And there's one must go down to that waterside
   To see how deep it is."

It fell in the dusk of the night
   When unco things betide,
The skilly captain, the Cameron,
   Went down to that waterside.
Canny and soft the captain went;
   And a man of the woody land,
With the shaven head and the painted face,
   Went down at his right hand.
It fell in the quiet night,
   There was never a sound to ken;
But all of the woods to the right and the left
   Lay filled with the painted men.

"Far have I been and much have I seen,
   Both as a man and boy,
But never have I set forth a foot
   On so perilous an employ."

It fell in the dusk of the night
   When unco things betide,
That he was aware of a captain-man
   Drew near to the waterside.
He was aware of his coming
   Down in the gloaming alone;
And he looked in the face of the man
   And lo! the face was his own.

"This is my weird," he said,
   "And now I ken the worst;
For many shall fall the morn,
   But I shall fall with the first.
O, you of the outland tongue,
   You of the painted face,
This is the place of my death;
   Can you tell me the name of the place?"

"Since the Frenchmen have been here
   They have called it Sault-Marie;
But that is a name for priests,
   And not for you and me.

It went by another word,"
　　Quoth he of the shaven head:
"It was called Ticonderoga
　　In the days of the great dead."
And it fell on the morrow's morning,
　　In the fiercest of the fight,
That the Cameron bit the dust
　　As he foretold at night;
And far from the hills of heather,
　　Far from the isles of the sea,
He sleeps in the place of the name
　　As it was doomed to be.

NOTES TO TICONDEROGA

INTRODUCTION. I first heard this legend of my own country from that friend of men of letters, Mr. Alfred Nutt, "there in roaring London's central stream;" and since the ballad first saw the light of day in *Scribner's Magazine,* Mr. Nutt and Lord Archibald Campbell have been in public controversy on the facts. Two clans, the Camerons and the Campbells, lay claim to this bracing story; and they do well: the man who preferred his plighted troth to the commands and menaces of the dead is an ancestor worth disputing. But the Campbells must rest content: they have the broad lands and the broad page of history; this appanage must be denied them; for between the name of *Cameron* and that of *Campbell,* the muse will never hesitate.

Note 1. Mr. Nutt reminds me it was "by my sword and Ben Cruachan" the Cameron swore.

Note 2. *"A periwig'd lord of London."* The first Pitt.

Note 3. *"Cathay."* There must be some omission in General Stewart's charming "History of the Highland Regiments," a book that might well be republished and continued; or it scarce appears how our friend could have got to China.

HEATHER ALE

A GALLOWAY LEGEND

FROM the bonny bells of heather
  They brewed a drink long-syne,
Was sweeter far than honey,
  Was stronger far than wine.
They brewed it and they drank it,
  And lay in a blessed swound
For days and days together
  In their dwellings underground.

There rose a king in Scotland,
  A fell man to his foes,
He smote the Picts in battle,
  He hunted them like roes.
Over miles of the red mountain
  He hunted as they fled,
And strewed the dwarfish bodies
  Of the dying and the dead.

Summer came in the country,
  Red was the heather bell;
But the manner of the brewing
  Was none alive to tell.
In graves that were like children's
  On many a mountain head,

The Brewsters of the Heather
  Lay numbered with the dead.

The king in the red moorland
  Rode on a summer's day;
And the bees hummed, and the curlews
  Cried beside the way.
The king rode, and was angry,
  Black was his brow and pale,
To rule in a land of heather
  And lack the Heather Ale.

It fortuned that his vassals,
  Riding free on the heath,
Came on a stone that was fallen
  And vermin hid beneath.
Rudely plucked from their hiding,
  Never a word they spoke:
A son and his aged father—
  Last of the dwarfish folk.

The king sat high on his charger,
  He looked on the little men;
And the dwarfish and swarthy couple
  Looked at the king again.
Down by the shore he had them;
  And there on the giddy brink—
"I will give you life, ye vermin,
  For the secret of the drink."

There stood the son and father
  And they looked high and low;
The heather was red around them,
  The sea rumbled below.
And up and spoke the father,
  Shrill was his voice to hear:
"I have a word in private,
  A word for the royal ear.

"Life is dear to the aged,
  And honour a little thing;

　　I would gladly sell the secret,"
　　　　Quoth the Pict to the king.
　　His voice was small as a sparrow's,
　　　　And shrill and wonderful clear:
　　"I would gladly sell my secret,
　　　　Only my son I fear.

　　"For life is a little matter,
　　　　And death is nought to the young;
　　And I dare not sell my honour
　　　　Under the eye of my son.
　　Take *him,* O king, and bind him,
　　　　And cast him far in the deep;
　　And it's I will tell the secret
　　　　That I have sworn to keep."

　　They took the son and bound him,
　　　　Neck and heels in a thong,
　　And a lad took him and swung him,
　　　　And flung him far and strong,
　　And the sea swallowed his body,
　　　　Like that of a child of ten;—
　　And there on the cliff stood the father,
　　　　Last of the dwarfish men.

　　"True was the word I told you:
　　　　Only my son I feared;
　　For I doubt the sapling courage
　　　　That goes without the beard.
　　But now in vain is the torture,
　　　　Fire shall never avail:
　　Here dies in my bosom
　　　　The secret of Heather Ale."

NOTE TO HEATHER ALE

　　Among the curiosities of human nature, this legend claims a high place. It is needless to remind the reader that the Picts were never ex-terminated, and form to this day a large proportion of the folk of Scotland: occupying the eastern and the central parts, from the Firth of

Forth, or perhaps the Lammermoors, upon the south, to the Ord of Caithness on the north. That the blundering guess of a dull chronicler should have inspired men with imaginary loathing for their own ancestors is already strange: that it should have begotten this wild legend seems incredible. Is it possible the chronicler's error was merely nominal? that what he told, and what the people proved themselves so ready to receive, about the Picts, was true or partly true of some anterior and perhaps Lappish savages, small of stature, black of hue, dwelling underground— possibly also the distillers of some forgotten spirit? See Mr. Campbell's *Tales of the West Highlands.*

CHRISTMAS AT SEA

THE sheets were frozen hard, and they cut the naked hand;
The decks were like a slide, where a seaman scarce could stand;
The wind was a nor'wester, blowing squally off the sea;
And cliffs and spouting breakers were the only things a lee.
They heard the surf a-roaring before the break of day;
But 'twas only with the peep of light we saw how ill we lay.
We tumbled every hand on deck instanter, with a shout,
And we gave her the maintops'l, and stood by to go about.

All day we tacked and tacked between the South Head and the
                                                      North;
All day we hauled the frozen sheets, and got no further forth;
All day as cold as charity, in bitter pain and dread,
For very life and and nature we tacked from head to head.

We gave the South a wider berth, for there the tide race roared;
But every tack we made we brought the North Head close aboard:
So's we saw the cliffs and houses, and the breakers running high,
And the coastguard in his garden, with his glass against his eye.

The frost was on the village roofs as white as ocean foam;
The good red fires were burning bright in every 'longshore home;
The windows sparkled clear, and the chimneys volleyed out;
And I vow we sniffed the victuals as the vessel went about.

The bells upon the church were rung with a mighty jovial cheer;
For it's just that I should tell you how (of all days in the year)

This day of our adversity was blessèd Christmas morn.
And the house above the coastguard's was the house where I was
born.

O well I saw the pleasant room, the pleasant faces there,
My mother's silver spectacles, my father's silver hair;
And well I saw the firelight, like a flight of homely elves,
Go dancing round the china-plates that stand upon the shelves.

And well I knew the talk they had, the talk that was of me,
Of the shadow on the household and the son that went to sea;
And O the wicked fool I seemed, in every kind of way,
To be here and hauling frozen ropes on blessèd Christmas Day.

They lit the high sea-light, and the dark began to fall.
"All hands to loose topgallant sails," I heard the captain call.
"By the Lord, she'll never stand it," our first mate, Jackson, cried.
. . . "It's the one way or the other, Mr. Jackson," he replied.

She staggered to her bearings, but the sails were new and good,
And the ship smelt up to windward just as though she understood.
As the winter's day was ending, in the entry of the night,
We cleared the weary headland, and passed below the light.

And they heaved a mighty breath, every soul on board but me,
As they saw her nose again pointing handsome out to sea;
But all that I could think of, in the darkness and the cold,
Was just that I was leaving home and my folks were growing old.

POEMS

THE VAGABOND

(To an air of Schubert)

GIVE to me the life I love,
  Let the lave go by me,
Give the jolly heaven above
  And the byway nigh me.
Bed in the bush with stars to see,
  Bread I dip in the river—
There's the life for a man like me,
  There's the life for ever.

Let the blow fall soon or late,
  Let what will be o'er me;
Give the face of earth around
  And the road before me.
Wealth I seek not, hope nor love,
  Nor a friend to know me;
All I seek the heaven above
  And the road below me.

Or let autumn fall on me
  Where afield I linger,
Silencing the bird on tree,
  Biting the blue finger:
White as meal the frosty field—
  Warm the fireside haven—

TO MY FATHER

Not to autumn will I yield,
  Not to winter even!

Let the blow fall soon or late,
  Let what will be o'er me;
Give the face of earth around,
  And the road before me.
Wealth I ask not, hope nor love,
  Nor a friend to know me.
All I ask the heaven above,
  And the road below me.

TO MY FATHER

PEACE and her huge invasion to these shores
Puts daily home; innumerable sails
Dawn on the far horizon and draw near;
Innumerable loves, uncounted hopes
To our wild coasts, not darkling now, approach:
Not now obscure, since thou and thine are there,
And bright on the lone isle, the foundered reef,
The long, resounding foreland, Pharos stands.

These are thy works, O father, these thy crown;
Whether on high the air be pure, they shine
Along the yellowing sunset, and all night
Among the unnumbered stars of God they shine;
Or whether fogs arise and far and wide
The low sea-level drown—each finds a tongue
And all night long the tolling bell resounds:
So shine, so toll, till night be overpast,
Till the stars vanish, till the sun return,
And in the haven rides the fleet secure.

In the first hour, the seaman in his skiff
Moves through the unmoving bay, to where the town
Its earliest smoke into the air upbreathes
And the rough hazels climb along the beach.
To the tugg'd oar the distant echo speaks.

The ship lies resting, where by reef and roost
Thou and thy lights have led her like a child.

This hast thou done, and I—can I be base?
I must arise, O father, and to port
Some lost, complaining seaman pilot home.

THE SICK CHILD

Child.   O MOTHER, lay your hand on my brow!
       O mother, mother, where am I now?
       Why is the room so gaunt and great?
       Why am I lying awake so late?

Mother.   Fear not at all: the night is still.
       Nothing is here that means you ill—
       Nothing but lamps the whole town through,
       And never a child awake but you.

Child.   Mother, mother, speak low in my ear,
       Some of the things are so great and near,
       Some are so small and far away,
       I have a fear that I cannot say.
       What have I done, and what do I fear,
       And why are you crying, mother dear?

Mother.   Out in the city, sounds begin;
       Thank the kind God, the carts come in!
       An hour or two more and God is so kind,
       The day shall be blue in the window-blind,
       Then shall my child go sweetly asleep,
       And dream of the birds and the hills of sheep

TO W. E. HENLEY

THE year runs through her phases; rain and sun,
Springtime and summer pass; winter succeeds;
But one pale season rules the house of death.

Cold falls the imprisoned daylight; fell disease
By each lean pallet squats, and pain and sleep
Toss gaping on the pillows.

                       But O thou!
Uprise and take thy pipe. Bid music flow,
Strains by good thoughts attended, like the spring
The swallows follow over land and sea.
Pain sleeps at once; at once, with open eyes,
Dozing despair awakes. The shepherd sees
His flock come bleating home; the seaman hears
Once more the cordage rattle. Airs of home!
Youth, love and roses blossom; the gaunt ward
Dislimns and disappears, and, opening out,
Shows brooks and forests, and the blue beyond
Of mountains.

                   Small the pipe; but O! do thou,
Peak-faced and suffering piper, blow therein
The dirge of heroes dead; and to these sick,
These dying, sound the triumph over death.
Behold! each greatly breathes; each tastes a joy
Unknown before, in dying; for each knows
A hero dies with him—though unfulfilled,
Yet conquering truly—and not dies in vain.
So is pain cheered, death comforted; the house
Of sorrow smiles to listen. Once again—
O thou, Orpheus and Heracles, the bard
And the deliverer touch the stops again!

HENRY JAMES

W H O comes to-night? We ope the doors in vain.
Who comes? My bursting walls, can you contain
The presences that now together throng
Your narrow entry, as with flowers and song,
As with the air of life, the breath of talk?
Lo. how these fair immaculate women walk

Behind their jocund maker; and we see
Slighted *De Mauves,* and that far different she,
Gressie, the trivial sphynx; and to our feast
Daisy and *Barb* and *Chancellor* (she not least!)
With all their silken, all their airy kin,
Do like unbidden angels enter in.
But he, attended by these shining names,
Comes (best of all) himself—our welcome **James.**

WANDERING WILLIE

H O M E no more home to me, whither must I wander?
  Hunger my driver, I go where I must.
Cold blows the winter wind over hill and heather;
  Thick drives the rain, and my roof is in the dust.
Loved of wise men was the shade of my roof-tree.
  The true word of welcome was spoken in the door—
Dear days of old, with the faces in the firelight,
  Kind folks of old, you come again no more.

Home was home then, my dear, full of kindly faces,
  Home was home then, my dear, happy for the child.
Fire and the windows bright glittered on the moorland;
  Song, tuneful song, built a palace in the wild.
Now, when day dawns on the brow of the moorland,
  Lone stands the house, and the chimney-stone is cold.
Lone let it stand, now the friends are all departed,
  The kind hearts, the true hearts, that loved the place of old.

Spring shall come, come again, calling up the moorfowl,
  Spring shall bring the sun and rain, bring the bees and flowers;
Red shall the heather bloom over hill and valley,
  Soft flow the stream through the even-flowing hours;
Fair the day shine as it shone on my childhood—
  Fair shine the day on the house with open door;
Birds come and cry there and twitter in the chimney—
  But I go forever and come again no more.

THE SPAEWIFE

O, I wad like to ken—to the beggar-wife says I—
Why chops are guid to brander and nane sae guia to fry.
An' siller, that's sae braw to keep, is brawer still to gi'e.
—*It's gey an' easy spierin'*, says the beggar-wife to me.

O, I wad like to ken—to the beggar-wife says I—
Hoo a' things come to be whaur we find them when we try,
The lasses in their claes an' the fishes in the sea.
—*It's gey an' easy spierin'*, says the beggar-wife to me.

O, I wad like to ken—to the beggar-wife says I—
Why lads are a' to sell an' lasses a' to buy;
An' naebody for dacency but barely twa or three.
—*It's gey an' easy spierin'*, says the beggar-wife to me.

O, I wad like to ken—to the beggar-wife says I—
Gin death's as shüre to men as killin' is to kye,
Why God has filled the yearth sae fu' o' tasty things to pree.
—*It's gey an' easy spierin'*, says the beggar-wife to me.

O, I wad like to ken—to the beggar-wife says I—
The reason o' the cause an' the wherefore o' the why,
Wi' mony anither riddle brings the tear into my e'e.
—*It's gey an' easy spierin'*, says the beggar-wife to me.

THE CELESTIAL SURGEON

IF I have faltered more or less
In my great task of happiness;
If I have moved among my race
And shown no glorious morning face;
If beams from happy human eyes
Have moved me not; if morning skies,
Books, and my food, and summer rain
Knocked on my sullen heart in vain:—
Lord, thy most pointed pleasure take

And stab my spirit broad awake;
Or, Lord, if too obdurate I,
Choose thou, before that spirit die,
A piercing pain, a killing sin,
And to my dead heart run them in!

REQUIEM

UNDER the wide and starry sky,
Dig the grave and let me lie.
Glad did I live and gladly die,
  And I laid me down with a will.

This be the verse you grave for me:
Here he lies where he longed to be;
Home is the sailor, home from sea,
  And the hunter home from the hill.